# ROSAMUNDE PILCHER

*By Rosamunde Pilcher*

Another View
The Blue Bedroom
The Day of the Storm
The Empty House
The End of Summer
Flowers in the Rain
September
The Shell Seekers
Sleeping Tiger
Wild Mountain Thyme

# THE SHELL SEEKERS

# WILD MOUNTAIN THYME

# THE DAY OF THE STORM

Rosamunde Pilcher

Hodder & Stoughton
LONDON SYDNEY AUCKLAND

*The Shell Seekers* copyright © 1987 by Rosamunde Pilcher
*Wild Mountain Thyme* copyright © 1978 by Rosamunde Pilcher
*The Day of the Storm* copyright © 1975 by Rosamunde Pilcher

*The Shell Seekers* first published in Great Britain in 1988
by New English Library Limited

*Wild Mountain Thyme* first published in Great Britain in 1980
by New English Library Limited

*The Day of the Storm* first published in Great Britain in 1975
by William Collins Sons and Co Limited

This collected volume first published in Great Britain in 1994
by Hodder and Stoughton Limited
a division of Hodder Headline PLC

The right of Rosamunde Pilcher to be identified as the Author of
the Work has been asserted by her in accordance with the
Copyright, Designs and Patents Act 1988.

10 9 8 7 6 5 4 3 2

British Library Cataloguing in Publication Data

A CIP catalogue record for this title is available from
the British Library

ISBN 0 340 62326 8

Printed and bound in Great Britain by
Mackays of Chatham PLC, Chatham, Kent

Hodder and Stoughton Ltd
A division of Hodder Headline PLC
338 Euston Road
London NW1 3BH

# THE SHELL SEEKERS

This book is for my children, and their children.

# Contents

# Prologue

# Prologue

The taxi, an old Rover smelling of old cigarette smoke, trundled along the empty, country road at an unhurried pace. It was early afternoon at the very end of February, a magic winter day of bitter cold, frost, and pale, cloudless skies. The sun shone, sending long shadows, but there was little warmth in it, and the ploughed fields lay hard as iron. From the chimneys of scattered farmhouses and small stone cottages, smoke rose, straight as columns, up into the still air, and flocks of sheep, heavy with wool and incipient pregnancy, gathered around feeding troughs, stuffed with hay.

Sitting in the back of the taxi, gazing through the dusty window, Penelope Keeling decided that she had never seen the familiar countryside look so beautiful.

The road curved steeply; ahead stood the wooden signpost marking the lane that led to Temple Pudley. The driver slowed and with a painful change of gear, turned, bumping downhill between high and blinding hedges. Moments later they were in the village, with its golden Cotswold stone houses, newsagent, butcher, the Sudeley Arms, and the church – set back from the street behind an ancient graveyard and the dark foliage of some suitably gloomy yews. There were few people about. The children were all in school, and the bitter weather kept others indoors. Only an old man, mittened and scarved, walked his ancient dog.

'Which house is it?' the taxi driver inquired over his shoulder.

She leaned forward, ridiculously excited and expectant. 'Just a little way on. Through the village. The white gates on the right. They're open. There! Here we are.'

He turned in through the gates and the car drew up at the back of the house.

She opened the door and got out, drawing her dark blue cape around her against the cold. She opened her bag and found her key, went to unlock the door. Behind her, the taxi driver manhandled open the boot of the car and lifted out her small suitcase. She turned to take it from him, but he held on to it, somewhat concerned.

'Is there nobody here to meet you?'

'No. Nobody. I live alone, and everybody thinks I'm still in the hospital.'

'Be all right, will you?'

She smiled into his kindly face. He was quite young, with fair bushy hair. 'Of course.'

He hesitated, not wishing to presume. 'If you want, I'll carry the case in. Carry it upstairs, if needs be.'

'Oh, that's kind of you. But I can easily manage . . .'

'No bother,' he told her, and followed her into the kitchen. She opened the door, and led him up the narrow, cottage stairs. Everything smelt clinically clean. Mrs Plackett, bless her heart, had not been wasting time during the few days of Penelope's absence. She quite liked it when Penelope went away, because then she could do things like wash the white paint of the bannisters, and boil dusters, and buff up the brass and silver.

Her bedroom door stood ajar. She went in, and the young man followed her, setting her case on the floor.

'Anything else I can do?' he asked.

'Not a thing. Now, how much do I owe you?'

He told her, looking shamefaced, as though it were an embarrassment to him. She paid him, and told him to keep the change. He thanked her, and they went back down the stairs.

But still he hung about, seeming reluctant to leave. He probably, she told herself, had some old granny of his own, for whom he felt the same sort of responsibility.

'You'll be all right, then?'

'I promise you. And tomorrow my friend Mrs Plackett will come. So then I won't be alone any more.'

This, for some reason, reassured him. 'I'll be off then.'

'Goodbye. And thank you.'

'No trouble.'

When he was gone, she went back indoors, and closed the door. She was alone. The relief of it. Home. Her own house, her own possessions, her own kitchen. The Aga, oil-fired, simmered peacefully to itself, and all was blissfully warm. She loosened the fastening of her cape, and dropped it across the back of a chair. A pile of mail lay on the scrubbed table, and she leafed through it, but there seemed to be nothing there either vital or interesting, so she let it lie, and crossed the kitchen, opening the glass door that led into her conservatory. The thought of her precious plants, possibly dying of cold or thirst, had bothered her somewhat during the last few days, but Mrs Plackett had taken care of them, as well as everything else. The earth in the pots was moist and loamy and the leaves were crisp and green. An early geranium wore a crown of tiny buds, and the hyacinths had grown at least three inches. Beyond the glass her garden lay winter-bound, the leafless trees black lace against the pale sky, but there were snowdrops thrusting through the mossy turf beneath the chestnut, and the first butter-gold petals of the aconites.

She left the conservatory and made her way upstairs, intending to unpack, but instead allowed herself to be diverted by the sheer delight of being home again. And so meandered about, opening doors, inspecting every bedroom, to gaze from each window, to touch furniture, to straighten a curtain. Nothing was out of place. Nothing had changed. Finally downstairs again, and in the kitchen, she picked up her letters, and went through the dining room, and then into her sitting room. Here were her most precious possessions; her desk, her flowers, her pictures. The fire was laid. She struck a match, and knelt to touch it to newspaper. The flame flickered, the dry kindling flared and crackled. She piled on logs and the flames rose high in the chimney. The house, now, was alive again, and with this pleasurable little task out of the way, there could be no further excuse for not ringing up one of her children and telling them what she had done.

But which child? She sat in her chair to consider the alternatives. It should be Nancy, of course, because she was the eldest and the one who liked to think that she was totally responsible for her mother. But Nancy would be appalled, panic-stricken, and loud with recrimination. Penelope did not think that she felt quite strong enough to cope with Nancy just yet.

Noel, then? Perhaps, as the man of the family, Noel should be spoken to. But the notion of expecting any sort of practical help or advice from Noel was so ludicrous that she found herself smiling. 'Noel, I have discharged myself from hospital and come home.' To which piece of information, his reply would, in all likelihood, be, 'Oh?'

And so Penelope did what she had known all along that she would do. She reached for the telephone and dialled the number of Olivia's London office.

'Ve-nus.' The girl on the switchboard sounded as though she were singing the name of the magazine.

'Could you put me through to Olivia Keeling, please?'

'Just a mo-ment.'

Penelope waited.

'Miss Keeling's secretary.'

Getting to speak to Olivia was a little like trying to have a chat with the President of the United States.

'Could I talk to Miss Keeling, please?'

'I'm sorry, Miss Keeling is in a meeting.'

'Does that mean she's sitting round a boardroom table, or is she in her office?'

'She is in her office . . .' The secretary sounded disconcerted, as well she might, ' . . . but she has someone with her.'

'Well, interrupt her please. This is her mother speaking, and it's very important.'

'It . . . can't wait?'

'Not for a moment,' said Penelope firmly. 'And I shan't keep her long.'

'Very well.'

Another wait. And then, at last, Olivia.

'Mumma!'

'I'm sorry to disturb you . . .'

'Mumma, is anything wrong?'

'No, nothing is wrong.'

'Thank heavens for that. Are you ringing from the hospital?'

'No, I'm ringing from home.'

'*Home?* When did you get *home?*'

'At about half past two this afternoon.'

'But I thought they were going to keep you in for at least a week.'

'That's what they intended, but I got so bored and so exhausted. I never slept a wink at night, and there was an old lady in the bed next to mine who never stopped talking. No, not talking. Raving, poor old soul. So I just told the doctor I couldn't stand another moment of it, and packed my bags and left.'

'You discharged yourself,' Olivia said, flatly, sounding resigned, but not in the least surprised.

'Exactly so. There's not a thing wrong with me. And I got a nice taxi with a dear driver and he brought me back.'

'But didn't the doctor protest?'

'Loudly. But there wasn't much he could do about it.'

'Oh, *Mumma.*' There was laughter in Olivia's voice. 'You are wicked. I was going to come down this weekend and hospital visit. You know, bring you pounds of grapes and then eat them all myself.'

'You could come here,' Penelope said, and then wished that she hadn't, in case she sounded wistful and lonely; in case it sounded as though she needed Olivia for company.

'Well . . . if you're really all right, I might put it off for a bit. I'm
actually frightfully busy this weekend. Mumma, have you spoken to
Nancy yet?'

'No. I did think about it, and then I chickened out. You know how
she fusses. I'll call tomorrow morning, when Mrs Plackett's here, and I'm
safely dug in and can't possibly be budged.'

'How are you feeling? Truthfully, now.'

'Perfectly all right. Except, as I told you, a bit short of sleep.'

'You won't do too much, will you? I mean, you won't plunge out into
the garden and start digging trenches or moving trees?'

'No, I won't. I promise. Anyway, everything's hard as iron. You
couldn't get a spade into the earth.'

'Well, thank God for small mercies. Mumma, I must go, I've got a
colleague here in the office with me . . .'

'I know. Your secretary told me. I'm sorry I disturbed you, but I wanted
you to know what was happening.'

'I'm glad you did. Keep in touch, Mumma, and cherish yourself a
little.'

'I will. Goodbye, my darling.'

'Goodbye, Mumma.'


She rang off, put the telephone back on the table, and leaned back in
her chair.

Now, there was nothing more to be done. She discovered that she was
very tired, but it was a gentle tiredness, assuaged and comforted by her
surroundings, as though her house were a kindly person, and she was
being embraced by loving arms. In the warm and firelit room and the
deep familiar armchair, she found herself surprised by, filled by, the sort
of reasonless happiness she had not experienced for years. It is because I
am alive. I am sixty-four, and I have suffered, if those idiot doctors are
to be believed, a heart attack. Whatever. I have survived it, and I shall
put it behind me, and not talk nor think about it, ever again. Because I
am alive. I can feel, touch, see, hear, smell; look after myself; discharge
myself from hospital, find a taxi and get myself home. There are snowdrops
coming out in the garden, and spring is on the way. I shall see it. Watch
the yearly miracle, and feel the sun grow warmer as the weeks slip by.
And because I am alive, I shall watch it all happen and be part of that
miracle.

She remembered the story of dear Maurice Chevalier. How does it feel
to be seventy? they had asked him. Not too bad, he had replied. When
you consider the alternative.

But for Penelope Keeling it felt a thousand times better than just not too bad. Living, now, had become not simple existence that one took for granted, but a bonus, a gift, with every day that lay ahead an experience to be savoured. Time did not last forever. I shall not waste a single moment, she promised herself. She had never felt so strong, so optimistic. As though she was young once more, starting out, and something marvellous was just about to happen.

# Nancy

She sometimes thought that for her, Nancy Chamberlain, the most straightforward or innocent occupation was doomed to become, inevitably, fraught with tedious complication.

Take this morning. A dull day in the middle of March. All she was doing . . . all she planned to do . . . was to catch the 9:15 from Cheltenham to London, have lunch with her sister Olivia, perhaps pop into Harrods, and then return home. There was nothing, after all, particularly heinous about this proposal. She was not about to indulge in a wild orgy of extravagance, nor meet a lover; in fact, it was a duty visit more than anything else, with responsibilities to be discussed and decisions made, and yet as soon as the plan was voiced to her household, circumstances seemed to close ranks, and she was faced with objections, or, worse, indifference, and left feeling as though she were fighting for her life.

Yesterday evening, having made the arrangement with Olivia over the phone, she had gone in search of her children. She found them in the small living room, which Nancy euphemistically thought of as the library, sprawled on the sofa in front of the fire, watching television. They had a playroom and a television of their own, but the playroom had no fireplace and was deathly cold, and the television was an old black and white, so it was no wonder they spent most of their time in here.

'Darlings, I have to go to London tomorrow to meet Aunt Olivia and have a talk about Granny Pen . . .'

'If you're going to be in London, then who's going to take Lightning to the blacksmith to be shod?'

That was Melanie. As she spoke, Melanie chewed the end of her pigtail and kept one baleful eye glued to the manic rock singer whose image filled the screen. She was fourteen and was going through, as her mother kept telling herself, that awkward age.

Nancy had expected this question and had her answer ready.

'I'll ask Croftway to deal with that. He ought to be able to manage on his own.'

Croftway was the surly gardener-handyman who lived with his wife in a flat over the stables. He hated the horses and constantly spooked them into a frenzy with his loud voice and uncouth ways, but part of his job was helping to cope with them, and this he grudgingly did, manhandling the poor lathered creatures into the horse-box, and then driving this unwieldy vehicle cross-country to various Pony Club events. On these occasions Nancy always referred to him as 'the groom'.

Rupert, who was eleven, caught the tail end of this exchange, and came up with his own objection. 'I've said I'll have tea with Tommy Robson tomorrow. He's got some football mags he said I could borrow. How'm I going to get home?'

This was the first that Nancy had heard of the arrangement. Refusing to lose her cool, knowing that to suggest that he change the day would instantly bring on a high-pitched flood of argument and wails of 'It's not fair,' she swallowed her irritation and said, as smoothly as she could, that perhaps he could catch the bus home.

'But that means I've got to walk from the village.'

'Oh well, it's only a quarter of a mile.' She smiled, making the best of the situation. 'Just for once it won't kill you.' She hoped that he would smile back, but he only sucked his teeth and returned his attention to the television.

She waited. For what? For some interest, perhaps, in a situation that was patently important to the whole family? Even a hopeful query about what gifts she intended to bring back for them would be better than nothing. But they had already forgotten her presence; their total concentration homed in on what they watched. She found the noise of this all at once unbearable, and went out of the room, closing the door behind her. In the hall a piercing cold enveloped her, rising from the flagged floor, seeping up the stairs to the icy voids of the landing.

It had been a bitter winter. From time to time, Nancy stoutly told herself – or any person impelled to listen – that she did not mind the cold. She was a warm-blooded creature, and it did not bother her. Besides, she enlarged, you never really felt cold in your own house. There was always so much to do.

But this evening, with the children being so disagreeable, and the prospect before her of having to go along to the kitchen and 'have a word' with the morose Mrs Croftway, she shivered and pulled her thick cardigan closely about her, as she saw the worn rug lift and shudder in the draught that poured in from beneath the ill-fitting front door.

For this was an old house that they lived in, an old Georgian vicarage in a small and picturesque Cotswold village. The Old Vicarage, Bamworth. It was a good address, and she took pleasure from giving it to people in shops. Just put it down to my account – Mrs George Chamberlain, The Old Vicarage, Bamworth, Gloucestershire. She had it embossed, at Harrods, at the head of her expensive blue writing paper. Little things like writing paper mattered to Nancy. They made a good impression.

She and George had moved here soon after they were married. Shortly before this event, the previous incumbent of Bamworth had all at once had a rush of blood to the head and rebelled, informing his superiors that no man . . . not even an unworldly man of the Church, could be expected, on his painfully meagre stipend, to live and bring up his family in a house of such monstrous size, inconvenience, and cold. The diocese, after some deliberation and an overnight visit from the Archdeacon, who caught a cold and very nearly died of pneumonia, finally agreed to build a new Vicarage. A brick bungalow was duly erected at the other end of the village, and the old Vicarage put on the market.

Which was bought by George and Nancy. 'We snapped it up,' she told her friends, as though she and George had been enormously quick off the mark and astute, and it was true that they got it for peanuts, but in time she discovered that was only because nobody else wanted it.

'There's a lot to do to it, of course, but it's the most lovely house, late Georgian, and quite a bit of land . . . paddocks and stables . . . and only half an hour to Cheltenham and George's office. Quite perfect, really.'

It was perfect. For Nancy, brought up in London, the house was the final realisation of all her adolescent dreams – fantasies nurtured by the novels that she devoured, of Barbara Cartland and Georgette Heyer. To live in the country and to be the wife of a country squire – these had long been the peak of her modest ambitions, after, of course, a traditional London Season, a white wedding with bridesmaids, and her photograph in the *Tatler*. She got it all except the London Season and, newly married, found herself mistress of a house in the Cotswolds, with a horse in the stable and a garden for church fêtes. With the right kind of friends, and the right sort of dogs; with George Chairman of the local Conservatives, and reading the lesson on Sunday mornings.

At first all had run smoothly. Then, there was no lack of money, and they had done up the old place, and Snow-cemmed the outside, and installed central heating, and Nancy had arranged the Victorian furniture that George had inherited from his parents and happily decorated her own bedroom in a riot of chintz. But as the years went by, as inflation ballooned and the price of heating oil and wages rose, it became more and more difficult to find anyone to help in the house and garden. The financial burden of simply keeping the place going grew heavier each year and she sometimes felt that they had bitten off more than they could chew.

As if that were not enough, they were also already into the horrifying expense of educating their children. Both Melanie and Rupert were at local private schools as day pupils. Melanie would probably stay at hers until she finished her A levels, but Rupert was down for Charlesworth, his father's public school; George had entered his name the day after Rupert was born, and taken out a small educational insurance at the same time, but the paltry sum that this would realise would now, in 1984, scarcely pay the first train fare.

Once, spending a night in London with Olivia, Nancy had confided in her sister, hoping perhaps for some constructive advice from that hard-headed career woman. But Olivia was unsympathetic. She thought they were fools.

'Public schools are an anachronism, anyway,' she had told Nancy. 'Send him off to the local comprehensive, let him rub shoulders with the rest of the world. It'll do him more good in the long run than all that rarefied atmosphere and old-world tradition.'

But this was unthinkable. Neither George nor Nancy had ever considered State education for their only son. In truth, from time to time Nancy had indulged in secret dreams of Rupert at Eton, trimmed with fantasies of herself at the Fourth of June in a garden-party hat; and Charlesworth, solid and reputable as it was, seemed a bit like second-best. She did not, however, admit this to Olivia.

'That's out of the question,' she said shortly.

'Well then, let him try for a bursary or a scholarship. Let him do something to help himself. What's the point of bleeding yourself white on account of one small boy?'

But Rupert was not academic. He had no hope of a bursary or a scholarship and both George and Nancy knew this.

'In that case,' said Olivia, dismissing the subject because she was bored by it, 'it seems to me that you have no alternative but to sell up the Old Vicarage and move somewhere smaller. Think of the money you'd save not having to keep the old place up.'

But the prospect of such an action filled Nancy with more horror even than the mention of State education for her son. Not simply because it would be tantamount to admitting defeat and giving up everything she had ever strived for, but also because she had an unhappy suspicion that she and George and the children, living in some convenient little house on the outskirts of Cheltenham, bereft of the horses, the Women's Institute, the Conservative Committee, the gymkhanas and the church fêtes, would become diminished, no longer of interest to their county friends and would be left to fade, like dying shadows, into a family of forgotten nonentities.

She shivered again, pulled herself together, turned from these gruesome imaginings and trod firmly down the flagged passage in the direction of the kitchen. Here the huge Aga, which never went out, rendered all comfortingly warm and cosy. Nancy sometimes thought, especially at this time of the year, that it was a pity they didn't all live in the kitchen . . . and any other family but theirs would probably have succumbed to the temptation and spent the entire winter there. But they were not any other family. Nancy's mother, Penelope Keeling, had practically lived in the old kitchen in the basement of the big house in Oakley Street, cooking and serving enormous meals at the great scrubbed table; writing letters, bringing up her children, mending clothes, and even entertaining her endless guests. And Nancy, who had both resented and felt slightly ashamed of her mother, had been reacting against this warm and informal way of life ever since. When I get married, she had sworn as a child, I shall have a drawing room and a dining room, just like other people do, and I shall go into the kitchen as seldom as I can.

George, fortunately, was of like mind. A few years before, after some serious discussion, they had agreed that the practicality of eating breakfast in the kitchen outweighed the slight lowering of standards. But further than that neither of them was prepared to go. Consequently, lunch and dinner were served in the huge, high-ceilinged dining room, with the table correctly laid, and formality taking the place of comfort. This gloomy chamber was heated by an electric fire that stood in the grate, and when they had dinner parties, Nancy turned this on a couple of hours before the meal was due to be served, and could never understand why her lady guests arrived swathed in shawls. Worse was that instance . . . never to be forgotten . . . when she had glimpsed beneath the waistcoat of a dinner-jacketed male the unmistakable traces of a thick V-necked pullover. He had not been asked again.

Mrs Croftway stood at the sink, peeling potatoes for supper. She was a very superior sort of person (far more so than her foul-tongued husband), and she wore, for her work, a white overall, as though that alone could render her cooking professional and palatable. Which it didn't, but at least Mrs Croftway's evening appearance in the kitchen meant that Nancy didn't have to cook dinner herself.

She decided to plunge straight in. 'Oh, Mrs Croftway . . . slight change of plan. I have to go to London tomorrow to have lunch with my sister. It's this problem of my mother, and impossible to talk things over on the telephone.'

'I thought your mother was out of hospital and home again.'

'Yes, she is, but I had a word with her doctor on the phone yesterday, and he says that she really shouldn't live alone any longer. It was only a slight heart attack, and she's made a marvellous recovery, but still . . . you never know . . .'

She gave these details to Mrs Croftway not because she expected much help or even sympathy, but because illness was one of the things the woman relished discussing, and Nancy hoped it might put her in a more expansive mood.

'My mother had a heart attack, she was never the same after that. Blue in the face she went and her hands so swollen we had to cut the wedding ring off her.'

'I didn't know that, Mrs Croftway.'

'She couldn't live alone any more. I had her to live with me and Croftway, she had the best front bedroom, but it crucified me, I can tell you; up and down the stairs all day long, and her with a stick banging on the floor. By the end I was a mass of nerves. Doctor said he'd never seen any woman with nerves like mine. So he put Mother in hospital and she died.'

This, apparently, was the end of the depressing saga. Mrs Croftway returned to her potatoes, and Nancy said, inadequately, 'I'm sorry . . . what a strain it must have been for you. How old was your mother?'

'Eighty-six all but a week.'

'Well . . .' Nancy made herself sound robust. 'My mother's only sixty-four, so I'm sure she'll make a good recovery.'

Mrs Croftway tossed a peeled potato into the pan and turned to look at Nancy. She rarely looked straight at people, but when she did it was unnerving because her eyes were very pale and never seemed to blink.

Mrs Croftway had her own private opinions of Nancy's mother. Mrs Keeling she was called, and Mrs Croftway had met her only once, during one of her infrequent visits to the Old Vicarage, but that had been enough for anybody. A great tall woman she was, dark-eyed as a gypsy, and dressed in garments that looked as though they should be given to a jumble sale. Pigheaded she'd been too, coming into the kitchen and insisting on washing the dishes, when Mrs Croftway had her own way of doing things and did not relish interference.

'Funny her having a heart attack,' she observed now. 'Looked strong as a bull to me.'

'Yes,' said Nancy faintly. 'Yes, it was a shock – to all of us,' she added, her voice pious as though her mother were already dead and it was safe to speak well of her.

Mrs Croftway made a grim mouth.

'Your mother only sixty-four?' She sounded incredulous. 'Looks more, doesn't she? Thought she was well into her seventies.'

'No, she's sixty-four.'

'How old are you, then?'

She was outrageous. Nancy felt herself stiffen with the sheer offensive-ness of Mrs Croftway, and was aware of the blood rushing to her cheeks. She longed to have the courage to snap at the woman; to tell her to mind her own business, but then perhaps the woman would give in her notice and she and Croftway would depart, and what would Nancy do then with the garden and the horses and the rambling house and her hungry family to feed?

'I'm . . . ' Her voice came out on a croak. She cleared her throat and tried again. 'As a matter of fact, I'm forty-three.'

'Is that all? Oh, I'd have put you down as fifty any day.'

Nancy gave a little laugh, trying to make a joke of it, for what else was there to do? 'That's not very flattering, Mrs Croftway.'

'It's your weight. That's what it is. Nothing so ageing as letting your figure go. You ought to go on a diet . . . it's bad for you, being overweight. Next thing we know' – she gave a cackle of laughter – 'it's *you* that'll be having a heart attack.'

*I hate you, Mrs Croftway. I hate you.*

'There's ever such a good diet in *Woman's Own* this week . . . You have a grapefruit one day, and a yoghurt the next. Or maybe it's the other way around . . . I could cut it out and bring it along, if you like.'

'Oh . . . how kind. Maybe. Yes.' She sounded flustered, her voice shaking. Pulling herself together, Nancy squared her shoulders and, with some effort, took charge of the deteriorating situation. 'But, Mrs Croftway, what I really wanted to talk about was tomorrow. I'm catching the nine-fifteen, so I shan't have much time to tidy up before I go, so I'm afraid you'll have to do what you can . . . and would you be *very* kind and feed the dogs for me? . . . I'll leave their dinners ready in their bowls, and then perhaps you could take them for a little run around the garden . . . and . . . ' She went on quickly before Mrs Croftway could start objecting to these suggestions. 'Perhaps you could give Croftway a message for me, and ask him to take Lightning to the blacksmith . . . he's due to be shod and I don't want to have to put it off.'

'Ooh,' said Mrs Croftway doubtfully. 'I don't know if he'll be able to manage boxing that animal on his own.'

'Oh, I'm sure he can, he's done it before . . . and then tomorrow evening, when I get back, perhaps we could have a bit of lamb for dinner.

Or a chop or something . . . and some of Croftway's delicious Brussels sprouts . . .'

It was not until after dinner that she had the opportunity to speak to George. What with getting the children to do their homework, finding Melanie's ballet shoes, eating dinner and clearing it away, ringing the vicar's wife to tell her that Nancy would not be at the Women's Guild meeting the following evening, and generally organising her life, there scarcely seemed time to exchange a word with her husband, who did not get home until seven in the evening, and then wanted to do nothing but sit in front of the fire with a glass of whisky and the newspaper.

But at last all was accomplished and Nancy was able to join George in the library. She closed the door firmly behind her, expecting him to look up, but he did not stir from behind *The Times*, so she crossed to the drinks table that stood by the window, poured herself a whisky, and then went and sat down in the armchair and faced him across the hearthrug. She knew that very soon he would reach out a hand and turn on the television in order to watch the news.

She said, 'George.'

'Um?'

'George, do listen a moment.'

He finished the sentence he was reading and then reluctantly lowered the newspaper, revealing himself as a man in his middle fifties but looking a good deal older, with thinning grey hair, rimless glasses, and the dark suit and sober tie of an elderly gentleman. George was a solicitor, and perhaps imagined that this carefully contrived appearance – as though dressed for the part in some play – would inspire confidence in potential clients, but Nancy sometimes suspected that if he would only buck himself up a bit, wear a nice tweed suit and buy a pair of hornrims, then perhaps his business would perk up a bit, too. For this part of the world, since the opening of the motorway from London, had fast become enormously fashionable. New and wealthy residents moved in, farms changed hands at staggering sums; the most decrepit of cottages were snapped up and transformed, at enormous expense, into weekend hideaways. Estate agents and building societies blossomed and prospered; exclusive shops opened in the most unlikely little towns, and it was beyond Nancy's powers of comprehension why Chamberlain, Plantwell and Richards had not climbed onto this bandwagon of prosperity and reaped some of the rewards that were surely just there for the taking. But George was old-fashioned, sticking to the traditional ways and terrified of change. He was also a cautious man, and a cagey one.

Now, 'What have I got to listen to?' he asked her.

'I'm going to London tomorrow to have lunch with Olivia. We've got to talk about Mother.'

'What's the problem now?'

'Oh, George, you know the problem. I told you, I had a word with Mother's doctor, and he says she really mustn't live alone any longer.'

'So what are you going to do about it?'

'Well . . . we'll have to find a housekeeper for her. Or a companion.'

'She won't like that,' George pointed out.

'And even if we find somebody . . . can Mother afford to pay her? A good woman would cost forty to fifty pounds a week. I know she got that enormous sum for the house in Oakley Street, and she's not spent a brass farthing on Podmore's Thatch except to build that ridiculous conservatory, but that money's capital, isn't it? Can she afford all this expense?'

George shifted in his chair, reaching for his whisky glass.

He said, 'I've no idea.'

Nancy sighed. 'She's so secretive, so damned independent. She makes herself impossible to help. If only she'd take us into her confidence, give you some power of attorney, it would make life so much easier for *me*. After all, I am the eldest child, and it's not as though Olivia or Noel ever raise a finger to help.'

George had heard all this before. 'What about her daily lady . . . Mrs What's-it?'

'Mrs Plackett. She only comes in three mornings a week to clean and she's got a house and a family of her own to look after.'

George set down his glass and sat, his face turned to the fire, his hands arranged like a little tent, fingertip to fingertip.

After a bit, he said, 'I cannot quite fathom what it is you are getting in such a state about.' He sounded as though he were speaking to some particularly dim-witted client, and Nancy was hurt.

'I am not in a state.'

He ignored this. 'Is it just the money? Or is it the possibility that you may be unable to find any woman saintly enough to agree to live with your mother?'

'Both, I suppose,' Nancy admitted.

'And what do you imagine Olivia is going to contribute to the conundrum?'

'She can at least discuss it with me. After all, she's never in her life done a single thing for Mother . . . or for any of us, for that matter,' she added bitterly, recalling past hurts. 'When Mother decided to sell Oakley Street and announced that she was going back to Cornwall to live in

Porthkerris, it was I who had the most dreadful time persuading her that it would be madness to take such a step. And she still might have gone if you hadn't found her Podmore's Thatch, where at least she's within twenty miles of us and we're able to keep an eye on her. Supposing she was in Porthkerris, now, miles away, with a groggy heart and none of us knowing what on earth was going on?'

'Let us try to keep to the point,' begged George, at his most maddening.

Nancy ignored this. The whisky had warmed her, and kindled old resentments as well.

'And as for Noel, he's practically abandoned Mother, ever since she sold Oakley Street and he had to move out. That was a blow to him. Twenty-three he was and he'd never paid a penny's worth of rent to her, ate her food and drank her gin and lived totally scot-free. It was a shock to Noel, I can tell you, when he finally had to start paying his way.'

George sighed deeply. He had no higher opinion of Noel than he had of Olivia. And his mother-in-law, Penelope Keeling, had always been a total enigma to him. The constant astonishment was that any woman as normal as Nancy should have sprung from the loins of such an extraordinary family.

He finished his drink, got up from his chair, threw another log on the fire, and went to replenish his glass. From the other side of the room he said, above the small sounds of clinking glass, 'Let us suppose that the worst happens. Let us suppose that your mother cannot afford a housekeeper.' He returned to his chair and settled himself once more opposite his wife. 'Let us suppose that you can find nobody to take on the arduous task of keeping her company. What happens then? Will you suggest that she comes to live with us?'

Nancy thought of Mrs Croftway, perpetually in a state of umbrage. The children, noisily complaining about Granny Pen's endless strictures. She thought of Mrs Croftway's mother, and her wedding ring cut off, lying in bed and banging on the floor with a stick . . .

She said, sounding desperate, 'I don't think I could bear it.'

'I don't think I could bear it either,' George admitted.

'Perhaps Olivia . . .'

'Olivia?' George's voice rose in disbelief. 'Olivia let any person intrude on that private life of hers? You have to be pulling my leg.'

'Well, Noel's out of the question.'

'It seems,' said George, 'that everything is out of the question.' He surreptitiously pushed up his cuff and looked at his watch. He did not want to miss the news. 'And I don't see that I can make any constructive suggestions until after you have had it out with Olivia.'

Nancy was offended. True, she and Olivia had never been the best of friends . . . they had, after all, nothing in common . . . but she resented the words 'had it out,' as though they never did anything but argue. She was about to point this out to George but he forestalled her by switching on the television and putting an end to the conversation. It was exactly nine o'clock, and he settled contentedly to his daily ration of strikes, bombs, murders, and financial disaster, topped off by the information that the next day was going to start very cold, and that during the course of the afternoon rain would slowly cover the entire country.

After a bit, Nancy, depressed beyond words, got up out of her chair. George, she suspected, did not even realise that she had moved. She went to the drinks table, replenished her whisky with a lavish hand, and went out of the room, closing the door quietly behind her. She climbed the stairs and went into her bedroom and through to her bathroom. She put in the bath plug, turned the taps on, and poured in scented bath oil with the same lavishness that she had employed with the whisky bottle. Five minutes later she was indulging in the most comfortable occupation she knew, which was to lie in a hot bath and drink cold whisky at the same time.

Wallowing, enveloped in bubbles and steam, she allowed herself to dissolve into an orgy of self-pity. Being a wife and mother, she told herself, was a thankless task. One devoted oneself to husband and children, was considerate to one's staff, cared for one's animals, kept the house, bought the food, washed the clothes, and what thanks did one get? What appreciation?

None.

Tears began to well in her eyes, mingling with the general moisture of bath-water and steam. She longed for appreciation, for love, for affectionate physical contact, for someone to hug her and tell her she was marvellous, that she was doing a wonderful job.

For Nancy, there was only one person who had never let her down. Daddy had been a darling, of course, while he lasted, but it was his mother, Dolly Keeling, who had consistently shored up Nancy's confidence and taken her side.

Dolly Keeling had never got on with her daughter-in-law, had no time for Olivia, and was always wary of Noel, but Nancy was her pet, spoiled and adored. It was Granny Keeling who had bought her the puff-sleeved, smocked dresses when Penelope would have sent her eldest child to the party in some antique inherited garment of threadbare lawn. It was Granny Keeling who told her she was pretty and took her on treats like tea in Harrods and visits to the pantomime.

When Nancy became engaged to George, there were terrible rows. By now her father had departed, and her mother could not be made to

understand why it was so important to Nancy that she should have a
traditional white wedding with bridesmaids and the men in morning
coats and a proper reception. Apparently it seemed to Penelope an idiotic
way to waste money. Why not a simple family service with perhaps a
lunch party afterwards, at the great scrubbed table in the basement
kitchen at Oakley Street? Or a party in the garden? The garden was huge,
masses of room for everybody, and the roses would be out . . .

Nancy wept, slammed doors, and said that nobody understood her,
nobody ever had. She finally collapsed into a sulk that might have
continued for ever had not darling Granny Keeling intervened. All
responsibility was removed from Penelope, who was delighted to be shed
of it, and everything arranged by Granny. No bride could have asked for
more. Holy Trinity, a white dress with a train, bridesmaids in pink, and
a reception afterwards at Twenty-Three Knightsbridge with a Master of
Ceremonies in a red coat and a number of enormous, top-heavy flower
arrangements. And darling Daddy, prompted by his mother, had turned
up looking divine in a morning coat, to stand by Nancy and give her
away, and even Penelope's appearance, hatless and majestic in layers of
ancient brocade and velvet, could do nothing to mar the perfection of
the day.

Oh, for Granny Keeling now. Lying in the bath, a great grown woman
of forty-three, Nancy wept for Granny Keeling. To have her there, for
sympathy and comfort and admiration. _Oh my darling, you are quite
marvellous, you do so much for your family and your mother and they all take
it quite for granted._

She could still hear the loved voice, but it was in her own imagination,
for Dolly Keeling was dead. Last year, at the age of eighty-seven, that
gallant little lady with her rouged cheeks and her painted nails and her
mauve cardigan suits had passed on in her sleep. This sad event took
place in the small Kensington private hotel where she had elected, along
with a number of other incredibly elderly people, to spend her twilight
years, and she was duly wheeled away by the undertaker with whom the
hotel management, with some foresight, had a standing arrangement.

The next morning was as bad as Nancy had feared. The whisky had left
her with a headache, it was colder than ever and pitch-dark when, at
seven thirty in the morning, she hoisted herself out of bed. She dressed,
and was mortified to discover that the waistband of her best skirt would
not meet and had to be fastened with a safety pin. She pulled on the
lamb's-wool sweater which exactly matched the skirt, and averted her
eyes from the rolls of fat that bulged over the armour of her formidable

brassière. She put on nylons, but as she usually wore thick woollen stockings, these felt dreadfully inadequate, so she decided to wear her long boots, and then could scarcely do up the zip-fastener.

Downstairs, things did not improve. One of the dogs had been sick, the Aga was lukewarm, and there were only three eggs in the larder. She put the dogs out, cleaned up the sick, and filled the Aga with its own special, enormously expensive fuel, praying meanwhile it would not go out altogether, thus providing Mrs Croftway with good cause for complaint. She shouted for the children, telling them to hurry, boiled kettles, boiled the three eggs, made toast, set the table. Rupert and Melanie appeared, more or less correctly dressed, but quarrelling because Rupert said that Melanie had lost his geography book, and Melanie said that she'd never had it in the first place and he was a stupid liar, and Mummy, she needed twenty-five pence for Mrs Leeper's leaving present.

Nancy had never heard of Mrs Leeper.

George did nothing to help. He simply appeared, sometime during all this commotion, ate his boiled egg, drank a cup of tea, and went. She heard the Rover going down the drive as she frantically stacked dishes on the draining board, ready for Mrs Croftway to deal with at her own pleasure.

'Well, if you didn't have my geography book . . .'

Outside the door, the dogs howled. She let them in, and this reminded her of their dinners, so she filled their bowls with biscuits and opened a tin of Bonzo and, in her agitation, cut her thumb on the raw edge of the lid.

'Gosh, you're clumsy,' Rupert told her.

Nancy turned her back on him and ran the cold tap over her thumb until it had stopped bleeding.

'If I don't have that twenty-five pence, Mrs Rawlings is going to be furious . . .'

She ran upstairs to put on her face. There was no time for gently blending rouge or outlining her eyebrows, and the finished result was far from satisfactory, but it couldn't be helped. There wasn't time. From her wardrobe she pulled her fur coat, the fur hat that matched it. She found gloves, her Mappin and Webb lizardskin handbag. Into this she emptied the contents of her everyday bag, and then, of course, it wouldn't close. No matter. It couldn't be helped. There wasn't time.

She rushed downstairs again, calling for the children. By some miracle, they appeared, gathering up their school-bags, Melanie jamming on her unbecoming hat. Out of the back door and around to the garage they trooped, into the car – thank God the engine started first go – and they were off.

She drove the children to their separate schools, dumping them out at the gates with scarcely time to say goodbye before she was off again, speeding for Cheltenham. It was ten minutes past nine when she parked the car in the station car park and twelve minutes past when she bought her cheap day return. At the bookstall, she jumped the queue with what she hoped was a charming smile, and bought herself a *Daily Telegraph*, and – wild extravagance – a copy of *Harpers and Queen*. After she had paid for it, she saw that it was out of date – last month's edition, in fact – but there was no time to point this out and get her money back. Besides, it didn't really matter being out of date; glossy and shiny, it would still be a marvellous treat. Telling herself this, she emerged onto the platform just as the London train drew in. She opened a door, any door, got in and found a seat. She was breathless, her heart fluttering. She closed her eyes. This, she told herself, must be how it feels when you have just escaped from fire.

After a bit, after a few deep breaths and a little reassuring chat to herself, she felt stronger. The train, mercifully, was very warm. She opened her eyes and loosened the fastenings of her fur. Arranging herself more comfortably, she looked out of the window at the iron-hard winter landscape that flew by, and allowed her frayed nerves to be lulled by the rhythm of the train. She enjoyed train journeys. The telephone could not ring, you could sit down, you didn't have to think.

The headache had gone. She took her compact from her handbag and inspected her face in its small mirror, dabbed some powder on her nose, worked her mouth to settle her lipstick. The new magazine lay on her lap, as full of delights as an unopened box of dark-coated, soft-centred chocolates. She began to turn the pages and saw advertisements for furs, for houses in the south of Spain, for time-sharing estates in the Scottish Highlands; for jewellery, and cosmetics that would not only make you look better but actually repair your skin; for cruise ships sailing to the sun; for . . .

Her desultory leafings were abruptly halted, her attention caught. A full-page spread, inserted by Boothby's, the Fine Art Dealers, announced a sale of Victorian art that was to take place in their Bond Street Galleries on Wednesday, the twenty-first of March. To illustrate this, there was reproduced a picture by Lawrence Stern, 1865–1946. The painting was entitled *The Water Carriers* (1904) and depicted a group of young women in various postures, bearing copper urns on shoulder or hip. Studying them, Nancy decided eventually that they must be slaves, for their feet were bare and their faces unsmiling (poor things, no wonder, the urns looked dreadfully heavy) and their garments minimal, flimsy draperies of grape-blue and rust-red, with an almost unnecessary revealment of rounded breast and rosy nipple.

Neither George nor Nancy were interested in art, any more than they were interested in music or the theatre. The Old Vicarage had, of course, its fair share of pictures, the sporting prints mandatory for any self-respecting country house, and some oils depicting dead stags or faithful hounds with pheasants in their mouths, which George had inherited from his father. Once, with an hour or two to spare in London, they had gone to the Tate Gallery and dutifully shuffled through an exhibition of Constables, but Nancy's only recollection of that occasion was a lot of woolly green trees and the fact that her feet had hurt.

But even Constable was preferable to this painting. She gazed at it, finding it hard to believe that any person should want such a horror hanging on the wall, let alone pay good money for it. If she had been lumbered with such an object, it would have ended its days either in some forgotten loft or on top of a bonfire.

But it was not for any aesthetic reason that Nancy's attention had been caught by *The Water Carriers*. The reason that she gazed at it with so much interest was the fact that it was by Lawrence Stern. For he had been Penelope Keeling's father, and so, Nancy's grandfather.

The strange thing was that she was almost totally unfamiliar with his work. By the time that she was born, his fame – at its peak at the turn of the century – had dwindled and died, his output long sold, dispersed and forgotten. In her mother's house in Oakley Street there had hung only three pictures by Lawrence Stern, and two of these made up a pair of panels, unfinished, depicting a couple of allegorical nymphs scattering lilies onto slopes of daisy-dotted grass.

The third picture hung on the wall of the ground-floor hall, just below the staircase, the only space in the house that could accommodate its considerable size. An oil, and product of Stern's later years, it was called *The Shell Seekers*. It had a lot of white-capped sea, and a beach, and a sky full of blowing clouds. When Penelope moved from Oakley Street to Podmore's Thatch, these three precious possessions had moved with her, the panels to end up on the landing, and *The Shell Seekers* to dwarf the sitting room, with its low, beamed ceiling. Nancy now scarcely noticed them, so familiar were they, as much part of her mother's house as the sagging sofas and armchairs, the old-fashioned flower arrangements crammed into blue and white jugs, the delicious smell of cooking.

In truth, for years Nancy had not even thought of Lawrence Stern, but now, sitting in the train, in her furs and her boots, memory caught at her coat-tails and jerked her back into the past. Not that there was much to remember. She had been born at the end of 1940, in Cornwall, in the little cottage hospital in Porthkerris, and had spent the war years at Carn Cottage, beneath the shelter of Lawrence Stern's roof. But her babyhood recollections of the old man were misty – more the awareness of a presence rather than a person. Had he ever taken her on his knee, or for a walk, or read aloud to her? If he had, then she had forgotten. It seemed that no impression was made upon her childish mind until that final day, when, with the war safely over, she and her mother had left Porthkerris for all time and caught the train back to London. For some reason, this event touched Nancy's consciousness and stayed for ever, clearly imprinted upon her memory.

He had come to the station to see them off. Very old, very tall, growing frail, leaning on a silver-handled stick, he had stood on the platform by the open window and kissed Penelope goodbye. His white hair had lain long on the tweed collar of his Inverness cape, and on his twisted, deformed hands he wore woollen mittens from which the useless fingers protruded, white and bloodless as bones.

At the very last moment, even as the train started to move, Penelope had snatched Nancy up into her arms, and the old man had reached out a hand and laid it against Nancy's rounded baby cheek. She remembered the cold of his hand, like marble against her skin. There was no time for more. The train gathered speed, the platform curved away, he stood, growing smaller, waving his great broad-brimmed black hat in a final farewell. And that was Nancy's first and last memory of him, for he died the following year.

Ancient history, she told herself. Nothing to get sentimental about. But extraordinary that any person, nowadays, should want to buy his work. *The Water Carriers.* She shook her head, uncomprehending, and then abandoned the conundrum and turned happily to the comforting unrealities of the Social Diary.

# Olivia

The new photographer was called Lyle Medwin. He was a very young man with soft brown hair that looked as though it had been cut with the aid of a soup bowl, and a gentle, kind-eyed face. He had an unworldly air about him, like some dedicated novice, and Olivia found it hard to believe that he had successfully come so far along the rat race of his chosen profession without getting his throat cut.

They stood by the table at the window of her office, where he had laid out a selection of his past work for her inspection: two dozen or so large, glossy colour prints hopefully displayed for approval. Olivia had studied them minutely and decided that she liked them. In the first place, they were lucid. Fashion photographs, she always insisted, must show the clothes, the shape of them, the drape of a skirt, the texture of a sweater, and this came across with a punchy impact that would catch any eye. But as well, the pictures breathed with life, movement, enjoyment, even tenderness.

She picked one up. A man with the build of a full-back jogging through surf, blinding white track suit against a cobalt-blue sea. Tanned skin, sweat, the very smell of salty air and physical well-being.

'Where did you take this?'

'Malibu. That was an ad I did for sports clothes.'

'And this?' She took up another, an evening shot of a girl in blowing flame-coloured chiffon, her face turned towards the glow of the setting sun.

'That was Point Reays . . . an editorial feature for American *Vogue*.'

She laid the prints down, turned to face him, leaning against the edge of the table. This brought her down to his height, and so their eyes were level.

'What's your professional experience?'

He shrugged. 'Technical college. Then a bit of free-lancing, and then

I joined Toby Stryber and worked with him for a couple of years as his assistant.'

'It was Toby who told me about you.'

'And then, when I left Toby, I went to Los Angeles. I've been living out there for the past three years.'

'And doing well.'

He smiled, deprecating. 'Okay, I guess.'

His clothes were pure Los Angeles. White sneakers, washed-out jeans, white shirt, a faded denim jacket. In deference to the bitter London weather, he had wound a coral-coloured cashmere muffler around his slender tanned neck. His appearance, though rumpled, was nevertheless deliciously clean, like fresh laundry, dried in the sunshine, but not yet ironed. She found him extremely attractive.

'Carla's told you the brief?' Carla was Olivia's Fashion Editor. 'It's for the July issue, a last feature on holiday clothes before we go into tweeds for the moors.'

'Sure . . . she mentioned location shots.'

'Any suggestions where?'

'We talked about Ibiza . . . I have contacts out there . . .'

'Ibiza.'

He was quick to accommodate her. 'But if you'd rather someplace else, it's okay by me. Morocco, maybe.'

'No.' She pushed herself away from the table and went back to her chair behind her desk. 'We haven't used Ibiza for some time . . . but I think not beach shots. Rural backgrounds would be a bit different, with goats and sheep and hardy peasants tilling fields. You could rope some of the locals in to add a bit of authenticity. They have wonderful faces and they love having their pictures taken . . .'

'Great . . .'

'Talk to Carla about it then . . .'

He hesitated. 'So, I've got the job?'

'Of course you've got the job. Just do it well . . .'

'Sure. Thanks . . .' He began to gather up his prints and stack them into a pile. The buzzer on Olivia's intercom rang, and she pressed the button and spoke to her secretary.

'Yes?'

'An outside call, Miss Keeling.'

She looked at her watch. It was twelve fifteen.

'Who is it? I'm just going out for lunch.'

'A Mr Henry Spotswood.'

Henry Spotswood. Who the hell was Henry Spotswood? And then the name came back to her, and she remembered the man she had met two

evenings before at the Ridgeways' cocktail party. Greying hair and as tall
as she was. But he had called himself Hank.

'Put him through, Jane, would you?'

As she reached for the telephone, Lyle Medwin, the folder of photographs under his arm, made his soft-footed way across the room and
opened the door.

''Bye,' he mouthed as he let himself out and she raised her hand and
smiled, but he had already gone.

'Miss Keeling?'

'Yes.'

'Olivia, Hank Spotswood here, we met at the Ridgeways'.'

'Of course.'

'I have a free hour or two. Any chance of lunch?'

'What, today?'

'Yeah, right now.'

'Oh, I am sorry, I can't make it. My sister's coming up from the country
and I'm having lunch with her. I'm already late, I should be on my way.'

'Oh, that's too bad. Well, what about dinner this evening?'

His voice, remembered, filled in the details. Blue eyes. A pleasant,
strong-featured, wholly American face. Dark suit, Brooks Brothers shirt
with a button-down collar.

'I'd like that.'

'Great. Where would you like to eat?'

For perhaps an instant she debated, and then made up her mind.

'Wouldn't you like, just for once, not to have to eat in a restaurant or
an hotel?'

'What does that mean?'

'Come to my house, and I'll give *you* dinner.'

'That would be great.' He sounded surprised but by no means unenthusiastic. 'But isn't that a chore for you?'

'No chore,' she told him, smiling over the homely word. 'Come about
eight o'clock.' She gave him the address and a simple direction or two
in case he found himself a moronic taxi driver, and they said goodbye
and she rang off.

Hank Spotswood. That was good. She smiled to herself, then looked
at her watch, put Hank out of her mind, sprang to her feet, collected
hat, coat, bag and gloves, and stalked from the office to keep her lunch
date with Nancy.

Their venue was Kettners in Soho, where Olivia had booked a table.
This was where she always came for business lunches, and she saw no
reason to make any other arrangement, although she knew that Nancy
would have been much more at home in Harvey Nichols, or some place

full of exhausted women resting their feet after a morning's shopping.

But Kettners it was, and Olivia was late, and Nancy was waiting for her, fatter than ever, in her heather wool sweater and skirt and a fur hat roughly the same colour as her faded fair curls, which made her look as though she had grown another head of hair. There she sat, a single female in a sea of business men, with her handbag on her lap and a large gin and tonic on the small table in front of her, and she appeared so ridiculously out of place that Olivia knew a pang of guilt, and as a result sounded more effusive than she felt.

'Oh, Nancy, I'm sorry, I'm terribly sorry, I got held up. Have you been waiting long?'

They did not kiss. They never kissed.

'It's all right.'

'You've had a drink, anyway . . . you don't want another, do you? I booked a table for a quarter to one, and we don't want to lose it.'

'Good afternoon, Miss Keeling.'

'Oh, hello, Gerard. No, not a drink, thank you, we're a bit pushed for time.'

'You have a table ordered?'

'Yes. A quarter to one. I'm afraid I'm a bit late.'

'No matter – if you'd like to come through.'

He led the way, but Olivia waited for Nancy to heave herself to her feet, gather up her bag and her magazine, and pull her sweater down over her considerable rump before she followed him. The restaurant was warm and packed and loud with masculine conversation. They were led to Olivia's usual table, in a far corner of the room, where after the customary obsequious ceremony, they were finally seated on a curved banquette, the table pushed back over their knees and the massive menus produced.

'A glass of sherry while you decide?'

'Perrier for me, please, Gerard . . . and for my sister . . .' She turned to Nancy. 'You'd like some wine?'

'Yes, that would be very nice.'

Olivia, ignoring the wine list, ordered a half bottle of the house white.

'Now, what do you want to eat?'

Nancy did not really know. The menu was terrifyingly large and all in French. Olivia knew that she could sit there all day, debating over it, so she made a few suggestions, and in the end Nancy agreed to consommé and then escalope of veal with mushrooms. Olivia ordered an omelette and a green salad and, with this settled and the waiter gone, 'What sort of journey did you have up this morning?' she asked.

'Oh, very comfortable, really. I caught the nine-fifteen. It was a bit of a rush getting the children off to school, but I made it.'

'How are the children?'

She tried to sound as though she was really interested, but Nancy knew that she was not and so did not, thankfully, expound on the subject.

'All right.'

'And George?'

'He's well, I think.'

'And the dogs?' Olivia persevered.

'Fine . . .' Nancy started to say and then remembered. 'One of them was sick this morning.'

Olivia screwed up her face. 'Don't tell me. Not until we've eaten.'

The wine waiter appeared, with Olivia's Perrier and Nancy's half bottle. These were deftly opened and the wine poured. The man waited. Nancy remembered that she was meant to taste it, so she took a sip, pursed her lips professionally, and pronounced it delicious. The bottle was placed on the table and the wine waiter, expressionless, withdrew.

Olivia poured her own Perrier. 'Don't you ever drink wine?' Nancy asked her.

'Not during business lunches.'

Nancy raised her eyebrows, appearing almost arch. 'Is this a business lunch?'

'Well, isn't it? Isn't that what we're here to do? Talk business about Mumma.' The baby name as usual irritated Nancy. All three of Penelope's children called her by a different name. Noel addressed her as Ma. Nancy, for some years, had called her Mother, which she considered suitable to their ages and to Nancy's own station in life. Only Olivia – so hard-hearted and sophisticated in every other way – persisted with 'Mumma'. Nancy sometimes wondered if Olivia realised how ridiculous she sounded. 'We'd better get on with it. I haven't got all day.'

Her cool tones were the last straw. Nancy, who had travelled up from Gloucestershire for this meeting, who had wiped up dog's sick and cut her thumb on the Bonzo tin, somehow got her children to school and caught the train by the skin of her teeth, experienced a great surge of resentment.

*I haven't got all day.*

Why did Olivia have to be so brusque, so heartless, so unfeeling? Was there never to be an occasion when, cosily, they could talk as sisters without Olivia flaunting her busy career, as though Nancy's life, with its solid priorities of home, husband, and children, counted for nothing?

When they were small, it was Nancy who was the pretty one. Fair-haired, blue-eyed, with sweet ways, and (thanks to Granny Keeling) pretty clothes. It was Nancy who had attracted eyes, admiration, men. Olivia was brainy and ambitious, obsessed by books, exams, and academic achievement; but plain, Nancy reminded herself, so plain. Painfully tall and thin, flat-chested and bespectacled, she displayed an almost arrogant lack of interest in the opposite sex, relapsing into a disdainful silence whenever one of Nancy's boyfriends turned up, or disappearing up to her bedroom for a book.

And yet, she had her redeeming features. She would not have been her parents' daughter had she not been blessed with these. Her hair, which was very thick, was the colour and sheen of polished mahogany, and the dark eyes, inherited from their mother, glittered, like those of some bird's, with a sort of sardonic intelligence.

So what had happened? The gangling, brilliant University student, the sister no man would dance with, had somehow, sometime, somewhere, transformed herself into this phenomenon, of Olivia at thirty-eight. This formidable career woman, this Editor of *Venus*.

Her appearance today was as uncompromising as ever. Ugly, even, but almost frighteningly chic. Deep-crowned black velour hat, voluminous black coat, cream silk shirt, gold chains and gold earrings, knuckle-duster rings on her hands. Her face was pale, her mouth very red; even her enormous black-rimmed spectacles she had somehow turned into an enviable accessory. Nancy was no fool. As she followed Olivia across the crowded restaurant to their table, she had sensed the frisson of masculine interest, seen the covert glances and the turned heads and known that they had not been turned for pretty her, but for Olivia.

Nancy had never guessed at the dark secrets of Olivia's life. Right up to that extraordinary happening, five years ago, she had honestly believed that her sister was either a virgin or totally sexless. (There was, of course, another and more sinister possibility, which occurred to Nancy after ploughing her way dutifully through a biography of Vita Sackville-West, but this, she told herself, really didn't bear thinking about.)

The classic example of an ambitious and clever woman, Olivia had apparently been absorbed by her career, which had steadily advanced until she was finally made Features Editor of *Venus*, the intelligent, up-market magazine for women, on which she had worked for seven years. Her name figured on the flagstaff page; from time to time her photograph appeared in its pages, illustrating some article, and once, answering questions in a family show, she had been on television.

And then, with everything going for her, in mid-stream of life, as it were, Olivia took that unexpected and uncharacteristic step. She went on holiday to Ibiza, met a man called Cosmo Hamilton, and never came home. At least, she did finally come back, but not until after she had spent a year out there living with him. The first her editor knew of it was a formal letter, sent from Ibiza, handing in her resignation. When the mind-boggling news filtered through, via their mother, Nancy had at first refused to believe it. She told herself that it was all too shocking; but it was, in fact, because in some obscure way, she felt that Olivia had stolen a march on her.

She could not wait to tell George, to have him as dumbfounded as she had been, but his reaction took her quite unawares.

'Interesting,' was all he said.

'You don't seem very surprised.'

'I'm not.'

She frowned. 'George, it's Olivia we're talking about.'

'Certainly it's Olivia.' He looked at his wife's bewildered face and almost laughed. 'Nancy, you surely don't imagine that Olivia has lived like a good little nun all her life? That secretive girl with her flat in London and her evasive ways. If you believed that, you're a bigger fool than I thought.'

Nancy felt tears sting the back of her eyes. 'But . . . but, I thought . . .'

'What did you think?'

'Oh, George, she's so *unattractive*.'

'No,' George told her. 'No, Nancy, she is not unattractive.'

'But I thought you didn't like her.'

'I don't,' said George, and opened his newspaper, thus putting an end to the discussion.

It was unlike George to expound so forcefully on any subject. It was also unlike him to be so perceptive but, with hindsight and a good deal of mulling over this new turn of events, Nancy finally decided that he was probably right about Olivia. Once she had come to terms with the situation, she did not find it hard to turn it to her own advantage. Being able to boast of such a dashing relation seemed to Nancy both glamorous and sophisticated – like an old Noel Coward play – and provided one glossed over the living-in-sin bit, Olivia and Cosmo Hamilton provided quite a good conversation stopper at dinner parties. 'Olivia, you know, my clever sister, it's too romantic. She's thrown everything up for love. Living in Ibiza now . . . the most beautiful house.' Her imagination raced ahead to other delightful, and hopefully free, possibilities. 'Perhaps next summer George and I and the children will join her for a few weeks. It depends on the Pony Club events, though, doesn't it? We mothers are slaves to the Pony Club.'

But although Olivia asked their mother to go and stay and Penelope accepted with delight and spent more than a month with her and Cosmo, no such invitation ever came the way of the Chamberlains, and for this Nancy had never forgiven her sister.

·     ·     ·

The restaurant was very warm. Nancy felt, all at once, far too hot. She wished she had worn a blouse instead of a sweater, but she couldn't take the sweater off, so instead she took another cool mouthful of wine. Despite the warmth she realised that her hands were trembling.

Beside her, Olivia said, 'Have you *seen* Mumma?'

'Oh, yes.' She set down her glass. 'I went to see her in hospital.'

'How was she?'

'Very well, considering.'

'Are they certain it was a heart attack?'

'Oh, yes. They had her in intensive care for a day or two. And then they put her in a ward and then she discharged herself and went home.'

'The doctor can't have liked that very much.'

'No, he was annoyed. That's why he rang me, and that's when he told me that she shouldn't live alone.'

'Have you considered a second opinion?'

Nancy bridled. 'Olivia, he's a very good doctor.'

'A country GP.'

'He would be very offended . . .'

'Rubbish. I consider there is no point in doing anything about a companion or a housekeeper until she's seen a consultant.'

'You know she'd never see a consultant.'

'Then let her be. Why should she have some dim woman foisted on her if she wants to live on her own? She's got nice Mrs Plackett coming in three mornings a week, and I'm sure the people in the village will all rally round and keep an eye on her. After all, she's lived there for five years now, and everyone knows her.'

'But suppose she has another attack, and dies, just because there's nobody to help her. Or falls down the stairs. Or has a car crash and kills somebody.'

Olivia, unforgivably, laughed. 'I never knew you had such a vivid imagination. And let's face it, if she's going to have a car crash, she'll have one whether there's a housekeeper there or not. I honestly don't think we should worry.'

'But we have to worry.'

'Why?'

'It's not just the housekeeper . . . there are other things to be considered. The garden, for instance. Two acres of it, and she's always done it all herself. Digging the vegetables and mowing the lawn. Everything. She can't be expected to go on coping with that sort of physical work.'

'She isn't going to,' Olivia told her, and Nancy frowned, 'I had a long gas with her on the telephone the other evening –'

'You didn't tell me that.'

'You've scarcely given me the chance. She sounded splendid, robust and cheerful. She told me that she thought the doctor was a fool, and that if she had another woman living with her, she'd probably murder her. The house is too small and they'd do nothing but trip over each other, with which I wholeheartedly agreed. As for the garden, even before she had the so-called heart attack, she'd decided it was getting a bit too much for her, so she got in touch with the local garden contractors and has arranged for a man to come and work two or three days a week. I think he's starting next Monday.'

All this did nothing to put Nancy in a better frame of mind. It was as though Olivia and Mother had been conspiring behind her back.

'I'm not sure I think that's a very good idea. How do we know what sort of a person they'll send? It could be anybody. Surely she could have found some nice man from the village.'

'All the nice men from the village are already employed at the electronics factory at Pudley . . .'

Nancy would have argued on, but was forestalled by the arrival of her soup. It came in a round brown earthenware pot and smelled delicious. She suddenly realised how hungry she was, took up her spoon, and reached for a warm brown croissant.

After a bit, she said stiffly, 'You never considered discussing the matter with George and me.'

'For heaven's sake, what is there to discuss? It has nothing to do with any person but Mumma. Honestly, Nancy, you and George treat her as though she were senile; she's sixty-four, in the prime of life, strong as an ox and as independent as she's ever been. Stop interfering.'

Nancy was enraged. 'Interfering! Perhaps if you and Noel interfered, as you term it, a little more often, it would take some of the load from my shoulders.'

Olivia became icy. 'Firstly, don't you ever bracket me with Noel. And secondly, if you have a load on your shoulders, you dreamt it up and put it there yourself.'

'I don't know why George and I bother. We certainly get no thanks.'

'What is there to thank you for?'

'A lot. If I hadn't convinced Mother it was madness, she'd have taken herself back to Cornwall and be living in some fisherman's hut by now.'

'I could never understand why you thought that was such a bad idea.'

'Olivia. Miles away from all of us, at the other end of the country . . . it was ridiculous. I told her so. You can never go back, that's what I said. That was all she was trying to do, recapture her youth. It would have been a disaster. And besides, it was George who found Podmore's Thatch for her. And even you can't say that it isn't the most charming, perfect house in every way. And all thanks to George. Don't forget that, Olivia. All thanks to George.'

'Three cheers for George.'

There came at this point another interruption, while Nancy's soup bowl was removed and the escalope of veal and the omelette were served. The last of the wine was emptied into Nancy's glass, and Olivia began to help herself to salad. When the waiter had left them once more, Nancy demanded, 'And what is this gardener going to cost? Contract gardeners are notoriously expensive.'

'Oh, Nancy, does it matter?'

'Of course it matters. Can Mother afford it? It's very worrying. She's always been so secretive about money, and at the same time so dreadfully extravagant.'

'Mother? Extravagant? She never spends a brass farthing on herself.'

'But she never stops entertaining. Her food and drink bills must be astronomical. And that ridiculous conservatory she built at the cottage. George tried to dissuade her. She'd have been much better off spending the money on double glazing.'

'Perhaps she didn't want double glazing.'

'You refuse to be concerned, don't you?' Nancy's voice shook with indignation. 'To consider the possibilities?'

'And what are the possibilities, Nancy? Enlighten me.'

'She could live to be ninety.'

'I hope she does.'

'Her capital won't last for ever.'

Olivia's eyes glittered with amusement. 'Are you and George afraid of being left with a destitute, dependent parent on your hands? Yet another drain on your finances after you've paid the upkeep of that barn of a house, and wheeled your children off to the most expensive schools?'

'How we choose to spend our money is none of your affair.'

'And how Mumma chooses to spend hers is none of *your* business.'

This retort silenced Nancy. Turning from Olivia, she concentrated her attention on her veal. Olivia, watching her, saw the colour rise in her sister's cheeks, the slight tremor of mouth and jowl. For God's sake, she thought, she's only forty-three, and she looks a fat, pathetic, old woman. She was filled suddenly with pity for Nancy and a certain guilt, and found herself saying, in a more kindly and encouraging tone, 'I shouldn't worry too much if I were you. She got a socking price for Oakley Street, and there's a good chunk of that still to go, even after buying Podmore's Thatch. I don't suppose old Lawrence Stern realised it, but with one thing and another, he really left her quite comfortably off. Which was just as well for you and me and Noel, because, let's face it, our father was never anything, financially, but a dead loss . . .'

Nancy, all at once, realised that she had come to the end of her rope. She was exhausted with argument, and she hated it when Olivia spoke of darling Daddy in that way. Under normal circumstances she would have sprung to the defence of that dear, dead man. But now, she hadn't the energy. The meeting with Olivia had been a total waste of time. Nothing had been decided – about Mother, or money, or housekeepers, or anything; Olivia, as always, had talked rings around her, and now had left Nancy feeling as though she had been run over by a steam-roller.

Lawrence Stern.

The delicious meal was over. Olivia glanced at her watch, and asked Nancy if she'd like coffee. Nancy asked if there was time, and Olivia said yes, she'd got another five minutes, so Nancy said she would, and Olivia ordered coffee; and Nancy, reluctantly putting out of her mind images of the delicious puddings she had spied on the sweet trolley, reached out for the *Harpers and Queen* she had bought for the train and which lay now on the padded velvet seat beside her.

'Have you seen this?'

She leafed through the pages until she came to the Boothby's advertisement, and handed the magazine to her sister. Olivia glanced at it and nodded. 'Yes, I did see it. It's coming up for sale next Wednesday.'

'Isn't it extraordinary?' Nancy took the magazine back. 'To think any person should want to buy a horror like that?'

'Nancy, I can assure you, a lot of people want to buy a horror like that.'

'You have to be joking.'

'Certainly not.' Seeing her sister's genuine bewilderment, Olivia laughed. 'Oh, Nancy, where have you and George been these last few years? There's been an enormous resurgence of interest in Victorian painting. Lawrence Stern, Alma-Tadema, John William Waterhouse . . . they're commanding enormous sums in the art dealers' sales.'

Nancy studied the gloomy *Water Carriers* with what she hoped was a new eye. It didn't make any difference. 'But *why*?' she persisted.

Olivia shrugged. 'A new appreciation of their technique. Rarity value.'

'When you say enormous sums, what do you mean, exactly? I mean, how much will this go for?'

'I've no idea.'

'A guess.'

'Well . . .' Olivia turned down her mouth, considering. 'Maybe . . . two hundred thousand.'

'Two hundred *thousand*? For that?'

'Give or take the odd twenty pence.'

'But why?' Nancy wailed again.

'I've told you. Rarity value. Nothing's worth anything unless somebody wants it. Lawrence Stern was never a prolific painter. If you look at the minute detail in that picture, you'll see why. It must have taken months to complete.'

'But what's happened to all his work?'

'Gone. Sold. Probably sold straight off the easel, with the paint still wet. Every self-respecting private collection or public art gallery in the world will have a Lawrence Stern somewhere around the place. It's only every now and then that one of his pictures comes on the market nowadays. And don't forget, he stopped painting long before the war, when his hands became too crippled even to hold a brush. I imagine he sold everything he could and was glad to, just to keep himself and his family alive. He was never a rich man, and it was fortunate for us that he inherited a huge London house from his father, and then was able, later on, to buy the freehold of Carn Cottage. The sale of Carn Cottage went a long way towards educating the three of us, and the proceeds from Oakley Street are what Mumma's living on now.'

Nancy listened to all this, but not with her fullest attention. Her concentration wavered, as her mind went off at a tangent, exploring possibilities, speculating.

She said, sounding as casual as she could, 'What about Mother's pictures?'

'*The Shell Seekers*, you mean?'

'Yes. And the two panels on the landing.'

'What about them?'

'If they were sold now, would they be worth a lot of money?'

'I imagine, yes.'

Nancy swallowed. Her mouth was dry. 'How much?'

'Nancy, I'm not in the business.'

'Roughly.'

'I suppose . . . close on five hundred thousand.'

'Five hundred thousand.' The words made scarcely any sound. Nancy leaned back in her chair seat, utterly stunned. Half a million. She could see the sum written out, with a pound sign and lots of lovely noughts. At that moment, the waiter brought their coffee, black and steaming and fragrant. Nancy cleared her throat and tried again. 'Half a million.'

'Roughly.' Olivia, with one of her rare smiles, shunted the sugar bowl in Nancy's direction. 'So you see why you and George need have no fears on Mumma's behalf.'

That was the end of the conversation. They drank their coffee in silence, Olivia settled the bill, and they got up to go. Outside the restaurant, as they were travelling in different directions, they ordered two taxis and, as Olivia was pushed for time, she took the first one. They said goodbye on the pavement and Nancy watched her go. While they lunched, it had started to rain, quite heavily, but Nancy, standing in the downpour, scarcely noticed it.

Half a million.

Her own taxi drew up. She told the driver to take her to Harrods, remembered to tip the doorman, and clambered aboard. The taxi moved forward. She sat back in her seat and looked through the streaming windows at passing London, her eyes unseeing. She had achieved nothing with Olivia, but the day had not been wasted. She could feel her heart thumping with stealthy excitement.

Half a million pounds.


One of the reasons that Olivia Keeling had made such a success of her career was that she had developed the ability to clear her mind, and so beam in her considerable intelligence on one set of problems at a time. She ran her life like a submarine, divided into watertight compartments, each impregnably sealed from the others. Thus, this morning, she had put Hank Spotswood out of her mind, and so been able to give her entire attention to sorting out Nancy. On returning to the office, even as she walked through the door of that prestigious building, Nancy and all her trivial anxieties of home and family were blanked out, and Olivia was once more the Editor of *Venus*, with thought of nothing but the successful advancement of her paper. During the afternoon, she dictated letters, organised a session with her Advertising Manager, arranged a promotion luncheon to be held at the Dorchester, and had a long-overdue row with the Fiction Editor, informing the poor female that, if she could not find better stories than the efforts which she thought fit to submit to Olivia for approval, then *Venus* would cease altogether to publish fiction, and the Fiction Editor would find herself out of a job. The Fiction Editor, a single parent endeavouring to bring up two children, duly burst into tears, but Olivia was adamant; the magazine had priority over all else, and she simply handed the woman a Kleenex and gave her two weeks' grace in which to produce some magic rabbit out of her hat.

But it was all fairly draining. She realised that it was Friday and the end of the week, and was grateful for this. She worked on until six o'clock, clearing her desk, before finally gathering up her belongings, taking the lift down to the basement garage, collecting her car, and setting off for home.

The traffic was appalling, but she was used to rush-hour traffic and accepted it. *Venus*, with a mental slam of the watertight door, ceased to exist; it was as though the afternoon had never happened, and she was back in Kettners again, with Nancy.

She had been brusque with Nancy, accused her of over-reacting, made little of her mother's illness, dismissed the country doctor's prognosis. This was because Nancy invariably turned mole-hills into mountains . . . poor girl, what else did she have to do with her boring life . . . but also because Olivia, as though she were still a child, did not want to think of Penelope as anything but well. Immortal even. She did not want her to be ill. She did not want her to die.

A heart attack. That it could happen to her mother, of all people, who had never been sick in all her life. Tall, strong, vital, interested in everything, but most important, always *there*. Olivia remembered the basement kitchen at Oakley Street, the heart of that great rambling London house, where soup simmered, and people sat around the scrubbed table and talked for hours over brandy and coffee, while her mother did the ironing or mended sheets. When anyone mentioned the word 'security', Olivia thought of that comforting place.

And now. She sighed. Perhaps the doctor was right. Perhaps Penelope should have some person living with her. The best thing would be for Olivia to go and see her, talk things over, and, if necessary, see if they could come to some sort of an arrangement. Tomorrow was Saturday. I shall go and see her tomorrow, she told herself and felt at once much better. Drive down to Podmore's Thatch in the morning and spend the day. With the decision made, she put it all out of her mind and allowed the resultant void to fill slowly with pleasurable anticipation of the evening that lay ahead.

By now, she was nearly home. But first she turned in at her local supermarket, parked the car, and did some shopping. Crusty brown bread, butter, and a pot of pâté de foie gras; chicken Kiev, and the makings of a salad. Olive oil, fresh peaches, cheeses; a bottle of Scotch, a couple of bottles of wine. She bought flowers, an armful of daffodils, loaded all this loot into the boot of her car, and drove the short distance that took her to Ranfurly Road.

Hers was one of a terrace of small red brick Edwardian houses, each with its bulging bay window and front garden and tiled path. From the outside it looked almost painfully ordinary, which only increased the impact of its unexpected and sophisticated interior. The cramped rooms of the ground floor had been transformed into a single spacious area, with the kitchen divided from the dining room only by a counter, like a little bar, and an open staircase leading to the upper floor. At the far end of the room, French windows led out into the garden, and these gave a strangely rural view, for beyond the garden fence was a church with its own half acre or so of land, where Sunday-school picnics were held in the summer-time, and a huge oak tree spread its branches.

Because of this it would have seemed natural had Olivia decorated her house in country style, with sprigged cottons and pine furniture, but the impact she had contrived was cool and modern as a penthouse flat. The basic colour was white. Olivia loved white. The colour of luxury, the colour of light. White tiled floor, white walls, white curtains. Knobbly white cotton on the deep, sinfully comfortable sofas and chairs, white lamps and shades. And the result was not cold, for this pristine canvas she had splashed with touches of primary brightness. Cushions of scarlet and Indian pink, Spanish rugs, startling abstracts framed in silver. The dining-room table was glass, the chairs black, and one wall of her dining room she had painted cobalt blue and hung with a gallery of photographs of family and friends.

It was, as well, warm, immaculate, and shiningly clean. This was because Olivia's neighbour, with whom she had had a long-standing arrangement, came in each day to wash and polish. Now, she could smell the polish, mingled with the scent from a bowl of blue hyacinths, bulbs she had planted last autumn and which had finally reached their peak of scented perfection.

Unhurried, consciously unwinding, she set about her preparations for the coming evening. Drew the curtains, lit the fire (which was gas with sham logs, but as comforting and genuine as a proper fire), put a tape on the stereo, .poured herself a Scotch. In the kitchen, she concocted a salad, made a dressing for this, laid the table, put the wine to cool.

It was now nearly seven-thirty, and she went upstairs. Her bedroom was at the back of the house, looking out over the garden and the oak tree, and this too was white, with a thick fitted carpet and an enormous double divan bed. She looked at the bed, and thought about Hank Spotswood, deliberated for a moment or two, and then stripped and remade it, replacing the sheets with clean ones of shining, icy, freshly ironed linen. When she had done this, and only then, she undressed and ran herself a bath.

For Olivia, the ritual of her evening bath was her one indulgence in total relaxation. Here, soaking in scented steam, she allowed her mind to drift, her thoughts to wander. It was an interlude conducive to pleasant reflections – holidays to be considered, clothes for the coming months, vague fantasies concerning her current man. But somehow this evening, she found herself back with Nancy, wondering if she was home by now in that dreadful house with her graceless family. True, she had problems, but they all seemed to be self-induced. She and George, with all their pretensions, lived far beyond their means, and yet managed to convince themselves that they had the right to so much more. It was hard not to smile at the recollection of Nancy's face, jaw sagging and eyes goggling, when Olivia had told her the probable worth of the Lawrence Stern paintings. Nancy had never been any good at hiding her thoughts, especially if you caught her unawares, and the blank astonishment had been, almost at once, replaced with an expression of calculating avarice, as Nancy doubtless envisaged school bills paid, the Old Vicarage double-glazed, and security ensured for the entire Chamberlain clan.

This did not worry Olivia. She had no fears for *The Shell Seekers*. Lawrence Stern had given the painting to his daughter as a wedding present and it was more precious to her than all the money in the world. She would never sell it. Nancy – and for that matter Noel – would simply have to bide their time until nature took its course and Penelope turned up her toes and died. Which, Olivia devoutly hoped, would not be for years.

She mentally abandoned Nancy and let her mind move on to other, more attractive concerns. That clever young photographer, Lyle Medwin. Brilliant. A real find. And perceptive, too.

'Ibiza,' he had said, and she had, involuntarily, repeated the word, and perhaps he had caught some question in her voice or expression, for he had at once made an alternative suggestion. Ibiza. Now, she realised, squeezing her sponge so that hot water trickled like balm over her nakedness, that memories had stirred and stayed, hovering around at the back of her consciousness, ever since that small and apparently insignificant exchange.

She had not thought of Ibiza for months. But, 'Rural backgrounds . . .' she had suggested. 'With goats and sheep and hardy peasants tilling fields.' She saw the house, long and low, red-tiled, hung with bougainvillaea and trellises of vines. Heard cowbells and cocks crowing. Smelt the warm resin of pine and juniper, blown in from the sea on a warm wind. Felt again the nailing heat of the Mediterranean sun.

# Cosmo

On holiday with friends during the early summer of 1979, Olivia met Cosmo Hamilton at a party on a boat.

She disliked boats. She disliked the close quarters, the claustrophobia caused by too many people crowded into too small a space, the constant banging of shin and head on davit and boom. This particular boat was a thirty-foot cruiser, moored out in the harbour and reached by means of a power dinghy. Olivia went because the rest of her party were going, but she did so reluctantly, and it was just as bad as she had feared, with too many people, no place to sit, and everybody being dreadfully jolly and bluff, drinking Bloody Marys, and discussing with much noisy laughter the momentous party they had all been to the previous evening, and which Olivia and her friends had not.

She found herself standing, hand clamped around her glass, in the cockpit of the yacht, along with about fourteen other people. It was like trying to be sociable in a very crowded lift. And another awful thing about being on a boat was that there was no way you could leave. You couldn't simply walk out of the door and into the street and find a taxi and go home. You were stuck. Jammed, moreover, face to face with a chinless man, who seemed to think that you would find it fascinating to be told that one was in the Guards, and how long it took one to drive, in one's fairly fast car, from one's place in Hampshire to Windsor.

Olivia's face ached with boredom. When he turned for a moment to get his glass refilled, she instantly made her escape, stepping up out of the cockpit and making her way forward, passing en route an almost totally naked girl sunbathing on top of the cabin roof. On the foredeck, she found a corner of empty deck and there sat, her back propped against the mast. Here, the babble of voices continued to assault her ears, but at least she was alone. It was very hot. She stared despondently at the sea.

A shadow fell across her legs. She looked up, fearing the Guardsman from Windsor, and saw that it was the man with the beard. She had noticed him as soon as she stepped on board, but they had not spoken. His beard was grey, but his hair was thick and white, and he was very tall and spare and muscular, dressed in a white shirt and faded, salt-bleached jeans.

He said, 'Do you need another drink?'

'I don't think so.'

'Do you want to be alone?'

He had a charming voice. She did not think he looked the sort of man who would refer to himself as 'one'. She said, 'Not necessarily.'

He squatted beside her. Their eyes came level and she saw that his were the same pale, soft blue as his jeans. His face was lined and deeply tanned, and he looked as though he might be a writer.

'Can I join you then?'

She hesitated, and then smiled. 'Why not?'

His name was Cosmo Hamilton. He lived on the island, had lived here for twenty-five years. No, he was not a writer. To begin with he had run a yacht charter business and then had a job as agent for a firm in London which ran package holidays, but now he was a gentleman of leisure.

Olivia, despite herself, became interested.

'Don't you get bored?'

'Why should I get bored?'

'With nothing to do.'

'I have a thousand things to do.'

'Name two.'

His eyes gleamed with amusement. 'That's almost insulting.'

And, indeed, he looked so fit and active that it probably was. Olivia smiled. 'I didn't mean it literally.'

His own smile warmed his face, like a light, and caused his eyes to crinkle up at the corners. Olivia felt as though her heart, very stealthily, was stirring and turning over.

'I have a boat,' he told her, 'and a house and a garden. Shelves of books, two goats, and three dozen bantams. At the last count. Bantams are notoriously prolific.'

'Do you look after the bantams, or does your wife do that?'

'My wife lives in Weybridge. We're divorced.'

'So you're alone.'

'Not entirely. I have a daughter. She's at day school in England, so she lives with her mother during the term and then comes out here for the holidays.'

'How old?'

'Thirteen. She's called Antonia.'

'She must love being here for holidays.'

'Yes. We have a good time. What are you called?'

'Olivia Keeling.'

'Where are you staying?'

'At Los Pinos.'

'Are you alone?'

'No, with friends. That's why I'm here. One of our party was given the invitation and we all tagged along.'

'I saw you come on board.'

She said, 'I hate boats,' and he began to laugh.

The next morning he turned up at the hotel in search of her. He found her alone, by the pool. It was early and her friends were presumably still in their bedrooms, but Olivia had already swum, and had ordered her breakfast to be served on the poolside terrace.

'Good morning.'

She looked up, into the sun, and saw him standing there in a dazzle of light.

'Hello.'

Her hair was wet and sleek from her swim and she was wrapped in a white towelling robe.

'May I join you?'

'If you want.' She put out a foot and pushed a chair in his direction. 'Have you had breakfast?'

'Yes.' He sat down. 'A couple of hours ago.'

'Some coffee?'

'No, not even coffee.'

'What can I do for you then?'

'I came to see if you'd like to spend the day with me.'

'Does that invitation include my friends?'

'No. Just you.'

He was looking straight at her, his eyes steady and quite unblinking. She felt as though she had been thrown a challenge, and for some reason this disconcerted her. Not for years had Olivia been disconcerted. To cover this unfamiliar nervousness and give herself something to do, she took up an orange from the basket of fruit on the table and began to try to peel it.

She said, 'What am I going to say to the others?'

'Just tell them you're going to spend the day with me.'

The peel of the orange was tough and hurt her thumbnail. 'What are we going to do?'

'I thought we'd take my boat out . . . take a picnic . . . Here.' He sounded impatient, leaned forward and took the orange away from her. 'You'll never peel it that way.' He reached into his back pocket, produced a knife and began to score the orange into four sections.

Watching his hands, she said, 'I hate boats.'

'I know. You told me yesterday.' He returned the knife to his pocket, deftly peeled the fruit, and handed it back to Olivia. 'Now,' he said, as she silently took it, 'what are you going to say? Yes or No?'

Olivia leaned back in her chair and smiled. She broke the orange into segments and began to eat them, one by one. In silence, Cosmo watched her. Now the heat of the morning was intensifying, and, with the delicious taste of fresh citrus on her tongue, she felt warm and content as a cat in the sun. Slowly, she finished the orange. When it was done, she licked her fingers and looked across the table at the man who waited. She said, 'Yes.'

Olivia discovered that day that she didn't hate boats after all. Cosmo's was not nearly as big as the one on which the party had been held, but infinitely nicer. For one thing, there were just the two of them, and for another they didn't just bob pointlessly about at the mooring, but cast off and hauled up the sail and slipped away, past the harbour wall and out into the open sea and around the coast to a blue deserted inlet that the tourists had never taken the trouble to find. There they dropped anchor and swam, diving from the deck, and clambering aboard again by means of a maddeningly contrary rope ladder.

The sun was now high in the sky and it was so hot that he rigged an awning over the cockpit and they ate their picnic in the shade of this. Bread and tomatoes, slices of salami, fruit and cheese, and wine that was sweet and cool because he had tied lengths of twine to the necks of the bottles and lowered them into the sea.

And later, there was space to stretch out on the deck and peacefully sunbathe; and later still, when the wind had dropped, and the sun was sliding down out of the sky, and the reflected light from the water shimmered on the white-painted bulkhead of the cabin, room to make love.

The next day he turned up again, in his battered tough little open-top, a Citroën 2 CV that looked more like a mobile dustbin than anything else, and drove her away from the coast, inland, to where he had his house. By now, not unnaturally, the rest of her party were becoming a little peeved by Olivia. The man who had been included for her delight had taxed her with this, and they had had words, whereupon he had relapsed into a fetid sulk. Which made him all the easier to leave.

It was another beautiful morning. The road led up into the mild hills, through sleepy golden villages and past small white churches, farms where goats grazed in the thin fields, and patient mules harnessed to grinding wheels trod in circles.

Here it was as it had been for centuries, untouched by commerce and tourism. The surface of the road deteriorated, modern tarmac was left behind, and the Citroën finally ground and bumped its way down a narrow, unmade track, dark and cool in the shade of a grove of umbrella pines, and came to rest beneath a massive olive tree.

Cosmo switched off the engine and they got out of the car. Olivia felt the cool breeze on her face, and caught a glimpse of the distant sea. A path led on, downhill, through an orchard of almonds, and beyond this lay his house. Long and white, red-roofed, stained purple with bougainvillaea blossom, it commanded an uninterrupted view of the wide valley, sloping down towards the coast. Along the front of the house was a terrace, trellised with vines, and below the terrace a small tangled garden spilled down to a little swimming pool, glinting clear and turquoise in the sunshine.

'What a place,' was all she could find to say.

'Come indoors and I'll show you around.'

It was a confusion of a house. Random stairways led up and down, and no two rooms seemed to be on the same level. Once it had been a farmhouse, and upstairs still were living room and kitchen, while the rooms on the ground floor, which once had been byre and stable and sty, were the bedrooms.

Inside, it was austere and cool, whitewashed throughout and furnished in the simplest of styles. A few coloured rugs on the rough wooden floors, locally made furniture, cane-seated chairs, scrubbed wooden tables. Only in the sitting room were there curtains, elsewhere the deeply embrasured windows had to make do with shutters.

But also there were delights. Deep-cushioned sofas and chairs, draped in colourful cotton blankets; jugs of flowers; rough baskets by the open fireplace, filled with logs. In the kitchen, copper saucepans hung from a beam, and there was the smell of spices and herbs. And everywhere were evidences of the obviously cultured man who had occupied this place for twenty-five years. Hundreds of books, not just on shelves, but spilling over onto tables, window-ledges, and the cupboard beside his bed. And there were good pictures and many photographs, and racks of long-playing records neatly stacked by the record player.

At last, the tour of inspection finished, he led the way through a low door and down yet another flight of stairs, and so out again, by way of a red-tiled lobby, and onto the terrace.

She stood, with her back to the view, and gazed up at the face of the house. She said, 'It's more perfect than I could have imagined.'

'Go and sit down and look at the view and I'll bring you a glass of wine.'

There were a table and some basket chairs set about on the flags, but Olivia did not want to sit. Instead, she went to lean against the white-washed wall, where earthenware tubs spilled lemon-scented ivy-leaved geraniums, and an army of ants, endlessly occupied, marched to and fro in well-regulated troops. The quiet was immeasurable. Listening, she caught the tiny muted sounds that were part of this quiet. A distant cowbell. The soft cackling murmur of contented hens, hidden away somewhere in the garden but clearly audible. The stirring of the breeze.

A whole new world. They had driven only a few kilometres, but she could have been a thousand miles from the hotel, her friends, the cocktails, the crowded swimming pool, the bustling streets and shops of the town, the bright lights and the blaring discos. Farther away still were London, *Venus*, her flat, her job – fading into unreality; forgotten dreams of a life that had never been real. Like a vessel that has been empty for too long, she felt herself filled with peace. I could stay here. A small voice, a hand tugging at her sleeve. This is a place where I could stay.

She heard him behind her, descending the stone stairway, the heels of his loose sandals slapping against the treads. She turned and watched him emerge through the dark aperture of the door (he was so tall that he automatically ducked his head). He was carrying a bottle of wine and two tumblers, and the sun was high and his shadow was very black. He set down the glasses and the frosty, beaded bottle and reached into the pocket of his jeans and produced a cigar, which he lit with a match.

When this was going, she said, 'I didn't know you smoked.'

'Only these. Every now and again. I used to be a fifty-a-day man, but I finally kicked the habit. Today, however, seems to be a suitable occasion for self-indulgence.' He had already uncorked the bottle and now poured the wine into the tumblers; he picked one up and handed it to Olivia. It was icily cold.

'What shall we drink to?' he asked her.

'Your house, whatever it's called.'

'Ca'n D'alt.'

'To Ca'n D'alt, then. And its owner.'

They drank. He said, 'I watched you from the kitchen window. You were so very still. I wondered what you were thinking.'

'Just that . . . up here . . . reality fades.'

'Is that a good thing?'

'I think so. I'm . . .' She hesitated, searching for the right words, because all at once it became enormously important to use exactly the right words. 'I'm not a domesticated creature. I'm thirty-three, the Features Editor of a magazine called *Venus*. It's taken me a long time to get there. I've worked for my living and my independence ever since I left Oxford, but I'm not telling you this because I want you to be sorry for me. I've never wanted anything else. Never wanted to be married or have children. Not that sort of permanence.'

'So?'

'It's just that . . . this is the sort of place that I think I could stay. I wouldn't feel trapped or rooted here. I don't know why.' She smiled at him. 'I don't know why.'

'Then stay,' he said.

'For today? For tonight?'

'No. Just stay.'

'My mother always told me never to accept an open-ended invitation. There must always be a date of arrival, she said, and a date of departure.'

'She was quite right. Let's say the date of arrival is today and the date of departure you can decide for yourself.'

She gazed at him, assessing motives, implications. Finally, 'You're asking me to move in with you?'

'Yes.'

'What about my job? It's a good job, Cosmo. Well paid and responsible. It's taken me all my life to get as far as I have.'

'In that case, it's time you took a sabbatical. No man, or woman, for that matter, can work for ever.'

A sabbatical. A year. Twelve months could be called a sabbatical. Longer was running away.

'I have a house as well. And a car.'

'Lend them to your best friend.'

'And my family?'

'You can invite them out here to stay with you.'

Her family, here. She imagined Nancy broiling by the swimming pool while George sat indoors, wearing a hat for fear of getting sunburnt. She imagined Noel taking himself off to prowl the topless beaches and returning for dinner with the spoils of the day, probably some blonde and nubile girl speaking no known language. She imagined her mother . . . but that was different, not ridiculous at all. This was exactly her mother's environment; this enchanting, meandering house, this tangled garden. The almond groves, the sun-baked terrace, even the bantams – especially the bantams – would fill her with delight. It occurred to Olivia that perhaps, in some obscure way, this was why she, instantly, had taken such a liking to Ca'n D'alt and felt so at ease and totally at home.

She said, 'I am not the only one with a family. You too have commitments to be considered.'

'Only Antonia.'

'Isn't that enough? You wouldn't want to upset her.'

He scratched the back of his neck and looked, for an instant, slightly embarrassed. He said, 'Perhaps this isn't exactly the right moment to mention it, but there have been other ladies.'

Olivia laughed at his discomfiture. 'And Antonia didn't mind?'

'She understood. She's philosophical. She made friends. She's very self-contained.'

A silence fell between them. He seemed to be waiting for her reply. Olivia looked down into her glass of wine. 'It's a big decision, Cosmo,' she said at last.

'I know. You must think about it. How would it be if we got ourselves something to eat and talked the matter over?'

Which they did, returning to the house where he said that he would make pasta, with a mushroom and ham sauce, and as he was obviously a much better cook than she, Olivia took herself off and back into the garden. She found her way to his vegetable patch, picked a lettuce and some tomatoes, and discovered, deep in shady leaves, a cluster of baby courgettes. These spoils she bore back to the kitchen, where she stood at the sink and made a simple salad. They ate their meal at the kitchen table, and afterwards Cosmo said it was time for a siesta, so they went to bed together and it was even better than it had been the time before.

And at four o'clock, when the heat of the day had eased a little, they went down to the pool and swam, naked, and then lay in the sun to dry.

He talked. He was fifty-five. He had been called up the day he left school, and had been on Active Service for most of the war. He found that he enjoyed the life, and so, when the war was over and he could think of nothing else that he wanted to do, he signed on as an officer in the Regular Army. When he was thirty, his grandfather died and left him a little money. Financially independent for the first time in his life, he resigned his commission, and without ties or responsibilities of any sort, set out to see the world. He travelled as far as Ibiza, unspoiled in those days and still amazingly cheap, fell in love with the island, decided that this was where he would put down his roots, and travelled no farther.

'What about your wife?' Olivia asked.

'What about her?'

'When did she happen?'

'My father died, and I went home for his funeral. I stayed for a bit, helping my mother to sort out his affairs. I was forty-one by then, not a young man any longer. I met Jane at a party in London. She was just about your age. She ran a flower shop. I was lonely – I don't know why. Perhaps it was something to do with losing my father. I'd never felt lonely in my life before, but I did then, and for some reason, I didn't want to come back here by myself. She was very sweet, and very ready to get married, and she thought Ibiza sounded madly romantic. That was my biggest mistake. I should have brought her out here first, rather like taking your girl-friend to meet your family. But I didn't. We were married in London, and the first time she set eyes on this place it was as my wife.'

'Was she happy here?'

'For a bit. But she missed London. She missed her friends and the theatre and concerts at the Albert Hall and shopping and meeting people and going away for weekends. She got bored.'

'What about Antonia?'

'Antonia was born out here. A proper little Ibecenco. I thought having a baby would calm her mother down a bit, but it only seemed to make matters worse. So we agreed, quite amicably, to part. There wasn't any acrimony, but then there wasn't anything much to be acrimonious about. She took Antonia with her and kept her until she was eight, and then, once she'd started proper school, she started coming out here, in the summer and at Easter time, to spend her holidays with me.'

'Didn't you find that something of a tie?'

'No. She was no trouble at all. There's a nice couple, Tomeu and Maria, who have a little farm down the lane. Tomeu helps me in the garden and Maria comes in to clean the house and keep an eye on my daughter. They're all the best of friends. Antonia's bilingual as a result of this.'

Now, it was much cooler. Olivia sat up and reached for her shirt, put her arms into the sleeves and did up the buttons. Cosmo also stirred, announcing that all this conversation had made him thirsty and he needed something to drink. Olivia said that she felt like a nice cup of tea. Cosmo told her that she didn't look like one, but he got to his feet and ambled off, disappearing up through the garden towards the house in order to put the kettle on. Olivia stayed by the pool, revelling in being alone, because she knew that in a little while he would be back. The water of the swimming pool was motionless. At the far end of this stood a statue of a boy playing a pipe, his image reflected in the water as though in a mirror.

A sea-gull flew overhead. She tipped back her head to watch its graceful passage, wings painted pink by the light of the setting sun, and she knew, in that instant, that she would stay with Cosmo. She would give herself, like some wonderful gift, a single year.

.    .    .

Burning your boats, Olivia discovered, was more traumatic than it sounded. There was much to do. First they made the journey back to the hotel, Los Pinos, to pack up her belongings, pay the bill, and check out. They did all this in the most clandestine fashion, terrified of being spotted, and instead of seeking out her friends and explaining the situation, Olivia took the coward's way and left an inadequate letter at the reception desk.

Then there were cables to be sent, letters to be written, telephone calls made to England on crackling incoherent lines. When all was accomplished, she thought that she would feel elated and free, but instead found herself trembling with panic and sick with fatigue. She was sick. She kept this fact from Cosmo, but when later he found her prone on the sofa weeping tears of exhaustion that she could not stop, all was revealed.

He was very understanding. He put her to bed in Antonia's little room where she could be alone and quiet, and left her to sleep for three nights and two days. She only stirred to drink the hot milk he brought her, and to eat a slice of bread and butter or a piece of fruit.

On the third morning, she awoke and knew it was over. She was recovered, refreshed, filled with a wonderful sense of well-being and vitality. She stretched, got out of bed and opened the shutters to the early morning, pearly and sweet, and smelt the dew-damp earth and heard the crowing cocks. She put on her robe and went upstairs to the kitchen. She boiled a kettle and made a pot of tea. With the teapot and two cups on a tray, she went through the kitchen and down the other flight of stairs to Cosmo's room.

It was still shuttered and dark, but he was awake.

As she came through the door, he said, 'Well, hello.'

'Good morning. I've brought you early-morning tea.' She set down the tray beside him and went to fling wide the shutters. Slanted rays of early sun filled the room with light. Cosmo stretched out an arm for his watch.

'Half past seven. You're an early bird.'

'I came to tell you that I am better.' She sat on his bed. 'And to say I'm sorry that I've been so feeble, and to say thank you for being so understanding and kind.'

'How are you going to thank me?' he asked her.

'Well, one way had occurred to me, but perhaps it's too early in the morning.'

Cosmo smiled and shunted himself sideways to make space for her.

'Never too early,' he said.

Afterwards, 'You are very accomplished,' he told her.

She lay, content in the curve of his arm. 'Like you, Cosmo, I have had some experience.'

'Tell me, Miss Keeling,' he said, in the voice of someone doing a bad imitation of Noel Coward, 'when did you first lose your virginity? I know our listeners would love to be told.'

'My first year at University.'

'What college?'

'Is it relevant?'

'It could be.'

'Lady Margaret Hall.'

He kissed her. He said, 'I love you,' and he didn't sound like Noel Coward any longer.

The days slipped by, cloudless, hot, long and idle, filled with only the most aimless of occupations. Swimming, sleeping, strolling down to the garden to feed the bantams or collect the eggs, or to do a little harmless weeding. She met Tomeu and Maria, who appeared quite unruffled by her arrival and greeted her each morning with broad smiles and much handshaking. And she learned a little kitchen Spanish and watched Maria make her massive paellas. Clothes ceased to matter. She spent her days with no make-up, slopping around, barefoot, in old jeans or a bikini. Sometimes they ambled up to the village with a basket to do a little shopping, but by tacit agreement they did not go near the town or the coast.

With time to consider her life, she realised that this was the first time she had not been working, striving, hauling her way up the ladder of her chosen profession. From the earliest age, her ambition had been to be, quite simply, the best. Top of her class, top in the list of examination results. Studying for scholarships, for O levels, for A levels, revising into the small hours in order to achieve the sort of grades that would ensure her a place at University. And then Oxford, with the whole process starting all over again, a gradual build-up to the final nerve-racking peak of Finals. With First Class Honours in English and Philosophy, she could reasonably have taken a bit of time off, but her built-in driving force was too strong; she was terrified of losing momentum, of missing chances, and went straight to work. That was eleven years ago, and she had never let up.

All over. Now, there were no regrets. She was suddenly wise, realising that this meeting with Cosmo, this dropping out, had happened just in time. Like a person with a psychosomatic illness, she had found the cure before diagnosing the complaint. She was deeply grateful. Her hair shone, her dark eyes, thick-lashed, were lustrous with contentment, and even the bones of her face seemed to lose their stressful angles and become rounded and smooth. Tall, rake-thin, tanned brown as a chestnut, she looked in the mirror and saw herself, for the first time ever, as truly beautiful.

One day, she was alone. Cosmo had gone down to the town to collect the papers and his mail and to check up on his boat. Olivia lay on the terrace and watched two small, unknown birds flirting together in the branches of an olive tree.

As she idly observed their capers, she became aware of a strange sense of vacuum. Analysing this, pinning it down, she discovered that she was bored. Not bored with Ca'n D'alt, nor with Cosmo, but bored with herself and her own emptied mind, standing bare and cheerless as an empty room. She considered this new set of circumstances at some length, and then got up out of the chair and went indoors to find something to read.

When Cosmo returned she was so deep in her book that she did not even hear him, and was quite startled when he suddenly appeared beside her. 'I'm hot and thirsty,' he was telling her, but then stopped short to stare. 'Olivia, I didn't know you wore spectacles.'

She laid down the book. 'Only for reading and working and having business lunches with hard-headed men I'm trying to impress. Otherwise I wear contact lenses.'

'I never guessed.'

'Do you mind them? Are they going to change our relationship?'

'Not at all. They make you look enormously intelligent.'

'I am enormously intelligent.'

'What are you reading?'

'George Eliot. *The Mill on the Floss.*'

'Don't start identifying with poor Maggie Tulliver.'

'I never identify with anyone. You have a marvellous library. Everything I want to read, or reread, or have never had time to read. I shall probably spend the whole of the year with my nose in a book.'

'That's all right by me, provided you emerge every now and then to satisfy my carnal lusts.'

'I'll do that.' He bent and kissed her, spectacles and all, and went indoors to fetch himself a can of beer.

She finished *The Mill on the Floss* and started in on *Wuthering Heights* and then Jane Austen. She read Sartre, *A la Recherche du Temps Perdu*, and, for the first time in her life, *War and Peace*. She read classics, biographies, novels by authors she had never even heard of. She read John Cheever and Joseph Conrad, and a battered copy of *The Treasure*

*Seekers*, which took her straight back over the years to the house in Oakley Street where she had been a child.

And as these books were all familiar old friends to Cosmo, they were able to spend their evenings deep in long literary discussions, usually to the background accompaniment of music; the 'New World,' and Elgar's 'Enigma Variations,' and symphonies or operas in their entirety.

To keep in touch, he had *The Times* sent out from London each week. One evening, after reading an article on the treasures of the Tate Gallery, she told him about Lawrence Stern.

'He was my grandfather, my mother's father.'

Cosmo was gratifyingly impressed. 'But how enormously exciting. Why did you never tell me before?'

'I don't know. I don't usually talk about him. Anyway, nowadays most people have never even heard of him. He went out of date and became forgotten.'

'What a painter he was.' He frowned, deep in calculations. 'But he was born . . . when was it . . . in the 1860s. He must have been a very old man when you came into the world.'

'More than that, he was dead. He died in 1946, in his own bed, in his own house, in Porthkerris.'

'Did you used to go to Cornwall for holidays and things?'

'No. The house was always let to other people, and finally my mother sold it. She had to, because she was perpetually strapped for cash and that was another reason we never went away for holidays.'

'Did you mind?'

'Nancy minded most dreadfully. And Noel would have minded too, except that he was particularly good at looking after himself. He always made friends with the right boys, and managed to wangle invitations to go sailing and skiing, and join jolly parties in villas in the south of France.'

'And you?' Cosmo's voice was loving.

'I didn't mind. I didn't want to go away. We lived in a huge house in Oakley Street with an equally huge garden at the back, and I had all the museums and the libraries and the art galleries right there, just for the taking.' She smiled, remembering those full and satisfying days. 'Oakley Street belonged to my mother. At the end of the war Lawrence Stern made it over to her. My father was a fairly –' she sought for the right word – 'lightweight sort of person. Not a man with drive or many resources. I think my grandfather must have known this, and was anxious that she should be independent and at least have a home in which to bring up her family. Besides, he was eighty then, and crippled with arthritis. He knew that he would never live there again.'

'Does your mother live there still?'

'No. It became too unwieldy and expensive to run, so this year she finally decided to sell, and move out of London. She had dreams of going back to Porthkerris, but my sister Nancy talked her out of that and instead found her a cottage in a village called Temple Pudley in Gloucestershire. To give Nancy her due, it's perfectly charming, and Mother is very happy there. The only gruesome thing about it is its name. Podmore's Thatch.' She screwed up her nose in distaste and Cosmo laughed. 'Admit it, Cosmo, it is a bit twee.'

'You could rename it. Mon Repos. Is it filled with beautiful paintings by Lawrence Stern?'

'No. Unfortunately. Only three. I wish she had more. I think, the way the market's going, they could be very valuable in a year or two.'

The conversation turned to other Victorian artists, and finally to Augustus John, and Cosmo went off to find the two volumes of his biography, which she had read but wished to read again. They discussed him at length and agreed that, for all his wicked ways, they had nothing but admiration for that randy old lion, and yet both considered his sister Gwen to be the better artist.

And after that they showered and put on reasonably respectable clothes and walked up to the village, to Pedro's bar, where you could sit out under the stars and have a drink. And a young man with a guitar materialised and sat on a wooden chair and quite simply, with no ceremony, began to play the second movement of the Rodrigo *Guitar Concerto*, filling the warm darkness with that plangent and stately music, the very essence of Spain.


Antonia was due to arrive in a week's time. Already Maria had started spring cleaning her bedroom, hauling all the furniture out onto the terrace, whitewashing the walls, laundering blankets and covers, and beating rugs with much venom and a cane switch.

Such urgent activity brought the appearance of Antonia that much nearer and Olivia was filled with apprehension. This was not entirely selfish, although the prospect of sharing Cosmo with another woman, even if she was only thirteen and his daughter, was dismaying, to say the least of it. The true anxiety lay within herself, because she was frightened of failing Cosmo, of saying the wrong thing, or doing something tactless. According to Cosmo, Antonia was both charming and uncomplicated, but this did nothing to reassure Olivia, because she had never had anything to do with children. Noel had been born when she was almost ten, and by the time he was out of babyhood, Olivia had virtually left home and gone out into the world. There were Nancy's offspring, of course, but they were so unattractive and unbearably bad-mannered that Olivia made a point of having as little to do with them as possible. So what did one say? What did one talk about? What were they all going to do with themselves?

One late afternoon, when they had had their swim and were stretched out in long chairs by the pool, she confided in Cosmo.

'It's just that I don't want to spoil things for you both. You obviously feel very close to each other, and I can't believe she won't think I'm alienating your affections. After all, she's only thirteen. It's a difficult sort of age, and a little jealousy would be the most understandable and natural reaction.'

He sighed. 'How can I convince you that it won't be like that?'

'Three's a bad number at the best of times. Sometimes, she's bound to want you to herself, and I may not be perceptive enough to get out of the way. Admit it, Cosmo, I do have a case.'

Considering this, he did not reply at once. At last, with a sigh, he said, 'There is obviously no way I can persuade you that none of what you fear is going to happen. So let's indulge in a little sideways thinking. How would it be if, while Antonia is with us, we ask another person to come and stay? Make it a sort of house party. Would that ease your mind?'

This suggestion put an entirely different aspect to the situation. 'Yes. Yes, it would. You're brilliant. Who shall we ask?'

'Anyone you like, provided it's not a young, handsome, and virile man.'

'What about my mother?'

'Would she come?'

'Like a shot.'

'She won't expect us to occupy separate bedrooms, will she? I'm too old to go corridor-creeping, I'd probably fall down the stairs.'

'My mother has illusions about nobody, least of all me.' She sat up, suddenly excited. 'Oh, Cosmo, you'll adore her. I can't wait for you to meet her.'

'In that case, we have no time to waste.' He heaved himself out of his chair and reached for his jeans. 'Come on, girl, move your backside. If we can get your mother lined up and Antonia organised, then they can meet up at Heathrow and come out together on the same flight. Antonia's always a bit windy about flying alone, and your mother would probably enjoy the company.'

'But where are we going?' Olivia asked, buttoning her shirt.

'We'll walk up to the village and use the telephone in Pedro's. Have you got her number at Podmore's Thatch?'

He said the name with relish, causing it to sound more embarrassing than usual, and looked at his watch. 'It's about six thirty in England. Will she be at home? What will she be doing at six thirty in the evening?'

'She'll be gardening. Or cooking dinner for ten people. Or pouring someone a drink.'

'Can't wait to get her here.'


The flight from London via Valencia was due at nine fifteen. Maria, who could not wait to see Antonia again, volunteered to come in and cook the dinner. Leaving her to prepare this mammoth feast, they drove to the airport. They were both, though neither would admit it, in a state of some nervous excitement and because of this arrived far too early, and so had to hang about the soulless Arrivals lounge for half an hour or more before the girl on the Tannoy announced in crackling Spanish that the plane had touched down. Then there was more delay, while passengers disembarked, went through Immigration, claimed their luggage; but finally the doors opened, and a flood of humanity surged to freedom. Tourists, pale-faced and travel-weary; families of locals with strings of children; sinister dark-spectacled gentlemen in sharp suits; a priest and a pair of nuns; . . . and then at last, just as Olivia was beginning to fear that they had missed the flight, Penelope Keeling and Antonia Hamilton.

They had found a trolley on which to pile their luggage, but had chosen one with balky wheels that kept shooting off in the wrong direction, and for some reason this had them both in giggles, and so engrossed were they in talking and laughing and trying to keep the wretched thing on a straight course, that they did not instantly catch sight of Cosmo and Olivia.

Part of Olivia's nervous apprehension sprang from the fact that she was always afraid, after a period of separation from Penelope, that her mother might have changed. Not aged, exactly, but perhaps appear tired, or diminished in some dreaded, subtle way. But the moment she caught sight of her, anxiety faded. It was all right. Penelope looked vital as ever and marvellously distinguished. Tall and straight-backed, with her thick greying hair twisted up into a knot at the back of her head and her dark eyes bright with amusement, even the struggles with the trolley did nothing to detract from her dignity. She was, inevitably, slung about with bags and baskets, and was dressed in her old blue cape, an officer's boat cloak that she had bought second-hand from an impoverished Naval widow at the end of the war and worn ever since, on all occasions from weddings to funerals.

And Antonia . . . Olivia saw a tall and slender child, looking older than her thirteen years. She had long, straight, strawberry-blonde hair, and wore jeans, a T-shirt and a red cotton jacket.

There was no time for more. Cosmo raised his arms and called his daughter's name, and they were seen. Antonia abandoned Penelope and the trolley and came running towards them, hair flying, a pair of rubber swimming flippers in one hand and a canvas satchel in the other, dodging through the throng of baggage-laden humanity to throw herself into Cosmo's arms. He caught her up and swung her round, long spindly legs flying, kissed her soundly, and set her down on her feet again.

'You've grown,' he told her accusingly.

'I know, a whole inch.'

She turned to Olivia. She had freckles across her nose and a full, sweet mouth, too big for her heart-shaped face, and her eyes were greeny-grey and fringed with long, thick, very fair eyelashes. Their expression was open and smiling, full of interest.

'Hello. I'm Olivia.'

Antonia disentangled herself from her father's arms, tucked the rubber flippers under her arm, and held out a hand. 'How do you do?'

And Olivia, looking down at the young, bright face, knew that Cosmo had been right, and all her fears unfounded. Charmed and disarmed by Antonia's mannerly grace, she shook the outstretched hand. 'I'm glad you're here,' she told her, and then, with that safely over, abandoned father and daughter and went to claim her own relation, still patiently guarding the luggage. Penelope, with soundless delight, flung wide her arms in one of her typical expansive gestures, and Olivia happily cast herself into them, to hug enormously, to press her face against her mother's cool firm cheek, to smell the long-familiar scent of patchouli.

'Oh, my darling pet,' said Penelope, 'I can't believe I'm really here.'

Joined by Cosmo and Antonia, they all started talking at once.

'Cosmo, this is my mother, Penelope Keeling . . .'

'You met up all right at Heathrow?'

'No trouble at all; I carried a newspaper and wore a rose between my teeth.'

'Daddy, we had a hilarious flight. Someone was sick . . .'

'Is this all your luggage?'

'How long did you have to wait at Valencia?'

'. . . and the air hostess spilt a whole glass of orange juice over a *nun*.'

Finally, Cosmo got matters under control, took charge of the trolley, and led the way out of the terminal, into the warm, dusky blue starlit darkness, filled with the smell of petrol and the sound of cicadas. Somehow, they all crammed into the Citroën, Penelope in the front and

Antonia and Olivia jammed together in the back. The luggage was piled on top of the passengers and at last they were off.

'How's Maria and Tomeu?' Antonia wanted to know. 'And the bantams? And Daddy, do you know something, I got top marks in French. Oh, look, there's a new disco. And a roller-skating rink. Oh, we must go roller-skating, Daddy, can we? And I really want to learn to wind-surf these holidays . . . is it frightfully expensive to have lessons?'

The now familiar road climbed up and away from the town and into the countryside, where the hills were pricked with the lights of random farmhouses, and the air was heavy with the scent of pine. When they turned into the track that led down to Ca'n D'alt, Olivia saw that Maria had turned on all the outside lights and these shone out like a celebration through the branches of the almond trees. And even as Cosmo stopped the car, and they were commencing to unload themselves, Maria and Tomeu were there, coming towards them through all this brightness; Maria stocky and sun-browned in her black dress and apron, and Tomeu shaven for the occasion and wearing a clean shirt.

'*Hola, señor*,' called Tomeu, but Maria had no thoughts for any person but her darling child.

'Antonia.'

'Oh, Maria.' She was out of the car and away, running down the path and into Maria's embrace.

'*Antonia. Mi niña. Favorita. Cómo está usted?*'

They were home.

Penelope's bedroom, which had once been a donkey's stable, led directly off the terrace. It was so small that there was room only for the bed and a chest of drawers, and a row of wooden pegs had to do duty as a wardrobe. But Maria had given it the same ruthless treatment as Antonia's room, and it shone clean and white and smelled of soap and freshly ironed cotton, and Olivia had filled a blue and white jug with yellow roses and stood this, with some carefully chosen books, on the wooden bedside table. Two tiled steps led up to a second door, and she opened this and explained to her mother the whereabouts of the only bathroom.

'The plumbing's a bit erratic; it depends on the state of the well, so if the loo doesn't work the first time, you just have to go on trying.'

'I think it's all quite perfect. What an enchanting place.' She divested herself of her cape, hung it on a peg, and turned to stoop over the bed and open her suitcase. 'And what a dear man Cosmo seems. And how well you're looking. I've never seen you look so well.'

Olivia sat on the bed and watched her mother unpack.

'You're an angel to come at such short notice. It's just that I thought it might be easier, having Antonia, if you were here as well. Not that that's the only reason I asked you. Ever since I set eyes on this place, I've been wanting to show it to you.'

'You know I love doing things on the spur of the moment. I phoned Nancy and told her I was coming and she was mad with envy. And a bit cross, too, because she hadn't been invited, but I didn't take the slightest bit of notice of that. And as for Antonia, what a darling pet of a child. Not in the least shy, laughing and chatting the whole day. I do wish Nancy's children could be half as companionable and well-mannered. Heaven only knows what sin I committed to be landed with such a pair of grandchildren . . .'

'And Noel? Have you seen Noel lately?'

'No, haven't set eyes on him for months. I rang him up the other day to make sure he was still alive. He was.'

'What's he doing with himself?'

'Well, he's found himself a new flat, somewhere off the King's Road. What it's going to cost him I didn't dare to ask, but that's his problem. And he's thinking of leaving the publishing world and going into advertising – he says he's got some very good contacts. And he was just off to Cowes for the weekend. The usual.'

'And you? How are things with you? How's Podmore's Thatch?'

'Dear little house,' said Penelope fondly. 'The conservatory's finished at last, I can't tell you how pretty it is. I've planted a white jasmine and a vine, and bought rather a smart basket chair.'

'About time you had some new garden furniture.'

'And the magnolia flowered for the first time and I've had the wistaria pruned. And the Atkinsons came for a weekend, and it was so warm we were able to have dinner in the garden. They were asking after you and send their dearest love.' She smiled, becoming motherly, her expression one of satisfied affection. 'And when I get home, I shall be able to tell them that I have never seen you look so well. Blooming. Beautiful.'

'Was it an awful bombshell for you, my staying with Cosmo and throwing up my job and generally behaving like a lunatic?'

'Perhaps. But after all, why not? You've worked all your life; sometimes, when I saw you so tired and strained, I worried for your health.'

'You never said.'

'Olivia, your life and what you do with it is none of my business. But that doesn't mean I have no concern for you.'

'Well, you were right. I was ill. After I'd done it, cut the cords and burnt my boats, I sort of went to pieces. I slept for three days. Cosmo was angelic. And after that I was all right. I hadn't realised I was so tired.

I think if I hadn't done this thing, I might well have ended up in some nut-house, having a tiny *crise de nerfs*.'

'Don't even suggest such a thing.'

As they spoke, Penelope moved to and fro, laying her clothes away in the chest of drawers, reaching up to hang the shabby and familiar dresses that she had brought with her. It was typical of Penelope that there should be nothing new or fashionable, bought especially for the holiday, and yet Olivia knew that her mother would imbue even these timeless garments with her own brand of distinction.

But, surprisingly, there was something new. From the bottom of the suitcase was taken a gown of emerald-green wild silk, which, held up and shaken free of its creases, revealed itself as a gold-embroidered caftan, rich and voluptuous as something from the *Arabian Nights*.

Olivia was suitably impressed. 'Wherever did you get that heavenly thing?'

'Isn't it delicious? I think it's Moroccan. I bought it off Rose Pilkington. Her mother had brought it home from some Edwardian jaunt to Marrakesh and she found it in the bottom of an old trunk.'

'You'll look like an Empress in it.'

'Ah, but that is not all.' The caftan, fitted onto a hanger, joined the ranks of faded cottons, and Penelope reached for her capacious leather satchel and began to rummage about in its depths. 'You know I wrote and told you that dear old Aunt Ethel had died? Well, she left me a little legacy. It arrived a couple of days ago, just in time for me to bring out here.'

'Aunt Ethel left you something? I didn't think she had anything to leave.'

'Nor I. But somehow typical of her, surprising us all right up to the very end.'

And, indeed, Aunt Ethel had always been surprising.

Lawrence Stern's only and very much younger sister, she had decided, at the end of the first world war, that at thirty-three, and with the flower of British manhood cruelly depleted by the slaughter of the French battlefields, she had little option but to accept inevitable spinsterhood. Undepressed by this, she had set about enjoying her single state as much as was humanly possible. She had lived in a tiny house in Putney, long before that area became fashionable, where, to make ends meet, she took in the odd lodger (or lover? her family were never quite sure) and gave piano lessons. Not a potentially exciting existence, but Aunt Ethel made it exciting, living, penurious as she was, every day to the full. When Olivia, Nancy, and Noel were children, a visit from Aunt Ethel was always keenly awaited, not because she brought them presents, but because she was such fun, and not like an ordinary grown-up at all. And going to her house was the greatest of treats, simply because you could never be sure what was going to happen next. Once, as they sat down to the lopsided cake she had baked for their tea, the bedroom ceiling had collapsed. Another time, they had lit a bonfire at the end of her tiny garden, and the fence caught fire and the fire brigade, bells clanging, had to be summoned. As well, she taught them the Can-Can and vulgar music-hall songs loaded with *double entendres* which caused Olivia to shake with guilty laughter, although Nancy had always pursed her lips and pretended not to understand.

She had looked, Olivia remembered, like a little stick insect, with child-sized feet and dyed red hair, a smoking cigarette never far from her hand. But despite her raffish appearance and life-style (or perhaps because of it), her circle of friends was legion, and there was scarcely a town in the country where Aunt Ethel did not have a dear old school chum or an erstwhile beau. A good deal of her time was spent visiting these friends – who were always begging her to come and stay and give them a good laugh – but between these forays to provincial England, she homed back to London, to the art exhibitions and concerts that were the breath of life to her; to her copious letter-writing, her current lodger, her piano students, and her telephone. She was always ringing up her stockbroker, who must have been a patient man, and if her meagre shares went up a point in the course of the day, she would allow herself two pink gins instead of one as the sun went over the yard-arm. She called them her little drinky-poos.

In her seventies, when the pace and expense of London finally became too much even for her, Aunt Ethel moved to Bath, to be near her dearest friends, Milly and Bobby Rodway. But then Bobby Rodway passed on, to be followed shortly by Milly, and Aunt Ethel was left alone. She managed for a bit, indestructible and cheerful as ever, but age was creeping up on her, and she ended up tripping over the milk bottle and breaking her hip on her own front doorstep. After that, she went downhill like a rocket, and eventually became so frail and incapable that she was placed, by the authorities, in an old folks' home. Here, shawled, forgetful, and tremulous, she was regularly visited by Penelope, who drove down to Bath from London and, more recently, Gloucestershire, in her old Volvo. Once or twice Olivia accompanied her mother on these occasions, but they left her feeling so depressed and sad that she always tried to find some excuse not to go.

'The dear old thing,' Penelope now said fondly. 'Do you know, she was nearly ninety-five? Far too old . . . ah, here it is.'

She found at last what she was searching for, and withdrew, from the satchel, an old and worn leather jewel box. She pressed the catch, and the lid sprang open, and there, cushioned in faded velvet, lay a pair of earrings.

'Oh.' The small sign of wonder was quite involuntary, but the sight of them filled Olivia with such delight. They were beautiful. Jewelled gold and enamel, fashioned in the form of a cross, with ruby and pearl pendants, and a circle of smaller pearls joining the arms of the cross to the gold stud. They were trinkets from another age, with all the intricate splendour of the Renaissance.

'These belonged to Aunt *Ethel?*' was all she could think of to say.

'Amazing, aren't they?'

'But where did the old girl get these?'

'I've no idea. They've been languishing in the bank for the past fifty years.'

'They look antique.'

'No. Victorian, I think. Probably Italian.'

'Perhaps they belonged to her mother?'

'Yes, perhaps. Perhaps she won them in a card game. Or was given them by a rich and adoring lover. With Aunt Ethel, it's anybody's guess.'

'Have you had them valued?'

'I haven't had time. And, although they're very pretty, I don't suppose they're worth much. Anyway, they're exactly right with my caftan. Don't you think they're made for each other?'

'Yes, I do.' Olivia returned the box to her mother. 'But when you get home, promise me to have them valued and get them insured.'

'I suppose I should. I'm so stupid about things like that.' And she dropped the box back into her bag.

The unpacking was now completed. Penelope closed the empty suitcase, stowed it under the bed, and turned to the mirror that hung on the wall. She took the tortoiseshell pins from her coil of hair and shook it loose, so that it lay, grey-streaked but thick and strong as ever, down her back. Swinging it forward over one shoulder, she took up her hairbrush. With satisfaction, Olivia watched the remembered ritual, the raised arm, the long, sweeping strokes.

'And you, my darling? What is your future?'

'I shall stay here for the year. A sabbatical.'

'Does your Editor know you intend returning?'

'No.'

'Will you go back to *Venus?*'

'Maybe. Maybe I'll move on.'

Penelope laid down her brush, took the long tassel of hair in her hand, twisted it, folded it, and pinned it back into place. She said, 'Now I must go and wash myself and then I'm ready for anything.'

'Don't fall over the steps.'

She took herself off in the direction of the bathroom. Olivia, waiting for her, stayed where she was, sitting on the bed, feeling herself filled with gratitude for Penelope's calm and practical acceptance of the situation. She thought about having another sort of mother, avid with curiosity and romantic images, linking Olivia with Cosmo, imagining her daughter standing at some altar in a white dress designed to look well from the back. The very idea made her laugh and shudder all at the same time.

When Penelope returned, she got to her feet.

'Now, how about something to eat?'

'I am rather hungry.' She looked at her watch. 'Dear heavens, it's nearly half past eleven.'

'Half past eleven is nothing. You're in Spain now. Come on, let's go and see what Maria's concocted for us.'

So together they went out onto the terrace. Beyond the lights, the darkness was thick and warm as blue velvet, and Olivia led the way up the stone stairs to the kitchen, where they found Cosmo and Antonia and Maria and Tomeu sitting around the candle-lit table, carousing with a bottle of wine, and all talking at once, in a castanet clatter of Spanish.


'She is splendid,' Cosmo said.

They were alone together again and it was like coming home. They had made love and now lay in the darkness, Olivia cradled in the curve of his arm. They talked quietly, so as not to disturb the other sleeping occupants of the house.

'Mumma? I knew you would love her.'

'I see now where you got your looks.'

'She's a hundred times better looking than I am.'

'We must show her off. No one would forgive me if I let her go back to England and they'd never even met her.'

'What does that mean?'

'We'll throw a party. As soon as possible. Start the social ball rolling.'

A party. This was a whole new idea. Since that first abortive party on the boat, Cosmo and Olivia had spent all their time alone together, talking to nobody but Tomeu and Maria and the few local men who patronised Pedro's bar.

She said, 'But who will we invite?'

She felt rather than heard his laughter. His arm tightened around her shoulders. 'My darling, surprise, surprise, I've friends all over the island. I have, after all, lived here for twenty-five years. Did you imagine that I was a social outcast?'

'I never thought about it,' she told him truthfully. 'I haven't wanted anybody but you.'

'And I have wanted nobody but you. Anyway, I thought you needed a rest from people. I was frightened for you, those days when you did nothing but sleep. I decided then that it would be better to take things quietly for a bit.'

'Yes.' She had not realised any of this, had taken their solitude entirely for granted. Now, with hindsight, she wondered why she had not questioned their self-imposed period of retreat. 'I never thought about that, either.'

'Time to think about it now. How does the idea of a party appeal to you?'

She discovered that it did. 'Enormously.'

'Informal or terribly grand?'

'Oh, terribly grand. My mother has brought her party frock.'

The next day, over breakfast, he made a list of names, both aided and impeded by his daughter.

'Oh, Daddy, you must ask Madame Sangé.'

'I can't, she's dead.'

'Well, Antoine, then. Surely he can come.'

'I thought you didn't like that randy old goat.'

'I don't much, but I'd like to see him. And the Hardback boys, they're terribly nice; they might ask me wind-surfing and then we wouldn't have to pay for lessons.'

The list was finally completed, and Cosmo departed for Pedro's bar to spend the morning telephoning. The proposed guests who were not on the telephone were contacted by means of written invitations that were delivered by Tomeu driving, at some danger to himself and anyone else he happened to meet on the road, Cosmo's Citroën. Replies flooded back, and the final count was seventy. Olivia was impressed, but Cosmo modest. He told her that he had always been one to hide his light under a bushel.

An electrician was summoned to fix strings of coloured lights around the area of the swimming pool. Tomeu swept and tidied, set up trestle-tables, manhandled cushions and chairs. Antonia was put to polishing glasses, washing china seldom used, sent to search on some forgotten shelf for tablecloths and napkins. Olivia and Cosmo, with a list as long as her arm, made an exhausting trip to the town and came back laden with groceries, olive oil, roasted almonds, bags of ice cubes, oranges, lemons, and crates of wine. And all the time, Maria and Penelope worked in the kitchen, where, in total accord and without a word of a common language, they boiled hams, roasted birds, concocted paellas, whipped eggs, stirred sauces, kneaded bread, and sliced tomatoes.

Finally, all was ready. The guests were due at nine, and at eight o'clock Olivia went to have a shower and change. She found Cosmo, shaved and smelling delicious, sitting on the bed trying to fit his gold links into the cuffs of his best shirt.

'Maria's put so much starch on this bloody thing, I can't get the holes open.'

She sat beside him and took the shirt and the cuff-links from him. He watched her. 'What are you going to wear?' he asked.

'I have two beautiful new dresses that I bought to stun the hotel guests at Los Pinos and I never wore either of them. Never had time. You came into my life, and since then I've been forced to walk around in rags.'

'Which will you wear?'

'They're in the cupboard. You can choose.'

He got up and opened the cupboard door and rattled around with the hangers, and finally found the dresses. One short, a brilliant pink chiffon, with layers of cloudlike skirts. The other long, sapphire-blue, waistless, flowing from a deep cuff and shoe-string shoulder-straps. He chose the blue one, as she had known he would, and she kissed him and gave him back his shirt, and went to shower. When she returned from the bathroom, he had gone. She dressed slowly, with immense care, making up her face, dressing her hair, fixing earrings, spraying scent. Finally she buckled the delicate sandals and then lifted the dress up and over her head. It settled over her body cool and light as a breath of air. As she moved, it moved with her. It was like being dressed in a breeze.

A knock came at her door. She said, 'Come in' and it was Antonia. 'Olivia, do you think this is all right? . . .' She stopped and gazed. 'Oh. You look so lovely. What a scrumptious dress.'

'Thank you. Now let's look at you.'

'My mother bought it for me in Weybridge, and it looked all right in the shop, but I'm not sure about it now. Maria says it's not grand enough.' It was a white sailor dress with a pleated skirt and a square collar braided in navy blue. Her brown legs, white-sandalled, were bare, and she had braided two thin plaits of her red-gold hair and tied them back with a navy-blue bow.

'I think it's perfect. You look clean and crisp as . . . I don't know. A brand-new paper bag?'

Antonia giggled. 'Daddy says you must come. People have started to arrive.'

'Is my mother there?'

'Yes, she's out on the terrace, looking fantastic. Oh, do come . . .'
She grabbed Olivia's hand and tugged her out through the door, and
hand in hand, under the lights, they made their way down the terrace.
Olivia saw Penelope already deep in conversation with some man and
knew that she had been right, for in her silken caftan and her inherited
jewels, her mother looked, indeed, like an Empress.

After that evening, the whole pattern of their lives at Ca'n D'alt changed.
After weeks of aimless solitude, it seemed that now they never had a
day to themselves. Invitations flooded in, for dinner parties, picnics,
barbecues, boat trips. Cars came and went, there never seemed to be
fewer than a dozen people around the swimming pool, and many of them
were youngsters of Antonia's age. Cosmo finally got around to fixing the
wind-surfing lessons, and they would all drive down to the beach where
these were held, and Olivia and Penelope would lie on the sand, ostensibly
watching Antonia's efforts to master the maddeningly difficult sport,
but actually engaged in Penelope's favourite occupation, which was
people-watching. As the people they watched on this particular beach,
both young and old, were almost totally naked, her comments were
hilarious and the two of them spent most of the time in hopeless,
goggle-eyed giggles.

Sometimes, every now and then, came the gift of a lazy day. Then
they never stirred from the house and the garden, and Penelope, wearing
an old straw hat and looking, with her newly acquired tan and her shabby
cotton dress, like a native Ibecenco, found a pair of secateurs and
attacked Cosmo's straggling roses. They swam constantly, for exercise and
refreshment, and when the evenings grew cooler, went for little rural
strolls, through cornfields and past small houses and farmyards where
naked-bottomed babies played happily in the dust along with the goats
and the hens, while their mothers unpegged washing, or drew water from
the well.

When it was time, at last, for Penelope to leave, none of them wanted
her to go. Cosmo, goaded by Olivia and his daughter, formally invited
her to stay for longer but, though touched, she refused.

'After three days, fish and guests stink, and I've been with you for a
month.'

'But you're not a fish nor a guest, and you don't stink a bit,' Antonia
assured her.

'You're very sweet, but I must get home. I've been away too long already. My garden will never forgive me.'

'You'll come again, though, won't you?' Antonia insisted.

Penelope did not reply. Across the silence, Cosmo looked up and into Olivia's eyes.

'Oh, do say you'll come.'

Penelope smiled and patted the child's hand. 'Maybe,' she told her. 'One day.'

They all went to the airport to see her off. Even after they had said goodbye to her, they lingered on, waiting to watch her plane take off. When it had gone, the sound of engines fading, dying into the immensity of the sky, and there was no longer any reason to stay, they turned and went back to the car and drove home in silence.

'It doesn't seem the same without her, does it?' Antonia said sadly as they made their way down the terrace.

'Nothing ever does,' Olivia told her.

Podmore's Thatch,
Temple Pudley,
Glos.

Aug 17th

My dear Olivia and Cosmo,

How can I thank you for being so endlessly kind and for giving me such an unforgettable holiday? No day passed when I did not feel welcome and cherished, and I have returned home with as many memories as a crowded photograph album. Ca'n D'alt is a truly magic place, your friends charming and so hospitable, and the island – even, or perhaps I should say especially, the topless beaches – quite fascinating. I miss you all so much, in particular Antonia. It is a long time since I have spent so much rewarding time with such an enchanting young person. I could go on drivelling for ever, but I think you both know how grateful I am. I am sorry I have not written before, but there hasn't been a moment. The garden is a riot of weeds and the rose beds are nothing but dead heads. Perhaps I should find a gardener.

Talking of gardeners, I stopped off in London for a couple of days on my way home, stayed with the Friedmanns and went to a delicious concert at the Festival Hall. Also took the earrings to Collingwood's to be valued, as you said I must, and you won't believe it, but the man said they were worth at least £4,000. When I'd finished fainting I inquired about insuring them, but the premium quoted was so enormous, I simply took them to the bank as soon as I got home, and left them there. Poor things, they seem doomed to spend their lives in the bank. I could sell them, I suppose, but they are so pretty. Still, nice to know that they're there, and the money realisable if I suddenly decide to do something mad, like buy myself a motor tractor for cutting the grass. (This explains reference to gardeners.)

Nancy and George and the children came for lunch last Sunday, ostensibly to hear about Ibiza, but really to tell me the iniquities of the Croftways, and how they had been invited to luncheon by the Lord Lieutenant. I gave them pheasant and fresh cauliflower from the garden, and apple crumble laced with mincemeat and brandy, but Melanie and Rupert grizzled and argued, and made no effort to disguise their boredom. Nancy is useless with them, and George doesn't seem even to notice their appalling manners. I became so irritated with Nancy that, to tease, I told her about the earrings. She showed no particular interest – she never once went to see poor Aunt Ethel – until I came to the magic words, four thousand pounds, whereupon she sprang to attention, for all the world like a gun dog scenting game. Her mind has always been easy to read, and I knew that her imagination was racing ahead, perhaps to Melanie's coming-out dance, with a paragraph or two in the social page of *Harpers and Queen*. 'Melanie Chamberlain, one of the prettiest debutantes this year, wore white lace and her grandmother's famous gold and ruby earrings.' Perhaps I was mistaken.

How cruel I am, and disloyal to my daughter, but I cannot resist sharing the little joke with you.

My thanks again. So inadequate, but what other words are there for gratitude?

With love, Penelope.

The months passed. Christmas came and went. Now it was February. There had been rain and some storms, and they spent much of their time indoors with a blazing fire, but all at once came a breath of spring to the air, blossom on the almond trees, and enough warmth at midday to sit for a while out of doors.

February. By now Olivia believed that she knew everything there was to know about Cosmo. But she was wrong. One afternoon, walking up from the garden with a basket of little bantams' eggs in her hand, she heard a car approaching, and stopping beneath the olive tree. As she climbed the steps to the terrace, she saw a strange man coming towards her. Obviously a local, but dressed more formally than was the usual, in a brown suit and collar and tie. On his head was a straw hat, and he carried a folder of papers.

She smiled inquiringly and he doffed the hat. '*Buenos días.*'

'*Buenos días.*'

'Señor Hamilton?'

Cosmo was indoors, writing letters.

'Yes?'

He spoke in English. 'If I could see him. Tell him Carlos Barcello. I will wait.'

Olivia went in search of Cosmo and found him at his desk in the living room.

'You have a visitor,' she told him. 'By the name of Carlos Barcello.'

'Carlos? Oh, God, I forgot he was coming.' He laid down his pen and got to his feet. 'Better go and have a word.' He left her, running down the stairs. She heard his greeting. '*Hombre!*'

She took the eggs into the kitchen and laid them, one by one, into a yellow china bowl. Then, filled with curiosity, she went to the window and watched Cosmo and Mr Barcello, whoever he was, making their way down to the swimming pool, deep in conversation. They stayed there for a bit and then returned to the terrace, where they spent some time inspecting the well. After that she heard them come indoors, but they appeared to get no farther than the bedroom. The lavatory was flushed. She wondered if Mr Barcello was a plumber.

They went out onto the terrace again. There was a bit more chat, and then they said goodbye and she heard Mr Barcello's car start up and drive away. Presently Cosmo's footsteps sounded on the stairs, and she heard him going into the living room, throw a log on the fire and, presumably, settle down once more to his letter-writing.

It was nearly five o'clock. She boiled a kettle and made a pot of tea, and carried this through to him.

'Who was that?' she asked, setting down the tray.

He was still writing, 'Um?'

'Who was your visitor? Mr Barcello.'

He turned in his chair to smile at her in some amusement.

'Why do you sound so curious?'

'Well, of course I'm curious. I've never seen him before. And he's pretty smartly turned out for a plumber.'

'Who said he was a plumber?'

'Isn't he?'

'Good God, no,' said Cosmo. 'He's my landlord.'

'Your *landlord*?'

'Yes, my landlord.'

She felt, all at once, shivery with cold. She folded her arms across her chest, gazing at him; willing him, in some way, to explain to her that she had misunderstood, was mistaken.

'You mean you don't own this house?'

'No.'

'You've lived here for twenty-five years and you don't own it.'

'I told you. No.'

It seemed to Olivia almost obscene. The house, so lived-in, full of their shared memories; the tended garden, the little swimming pool; the view. It wasn't Cosmo's. Never had been. It all belonged to Carlos Barcello.

'Why did you never buy it?'

'He would never sell.'

'You never thought of looking for another?'

'I didn't want another house.' He got to his feet, slowly, as though the letter-writing had wearied him. He pushed the chair aside and went to take a cigar from the box on the shelf over the fireplace. With his back to her, he went on, 'And anyway, once Antonia started school, I was committed to paying her fees. After that, I couldn't afford to buy anything.' There was a jar of spills on the hearth and he stooped to take one and held it to the flames for a light.

*I couldn't afford to buy anything.* They had never talked about money. The subject was one that had never come up between them. During the months that they had been together, Olivia had, without question, chipped in with her share of the ordinary day-to-day expenses of living. Paying for a carton of groceries at the market checkout, or a tankful of petrol. Sometimes, as naturally happens, he would find himself short of ready cash, and then Olivia picked up the bill for drinks in a bar or one of their occasional evenings out. She was, after all, not penniless, and just because she was living with Cosmo did not mean that she expected to be kept by him. Questions stirred at the back of her mind, but she felt afraid to ask them, because she was afraid of what the answers might be.

She watched him in silence. The cigar lighted, he threw the spill into the flames and turned to face her, his shoulders supported by the mantelshelf.

He said, 'You look very shocked.'

'I am shocked, Cosmo. I find it almost impossible to believe. It goes against the grain of something I feel most strongly about. To own your own house has always seemed to me the most important of priorities. It gives you security in every sense of the word. Oakley Street belonged to my mother, and because of that, as children, we always felt safe. Nobody could take it away from us. One of the best feelings in the world was coming home, indoors, off the street, and closing the door and knowing you were home.'

He made no comment on this, only asked her, 'Do you own your house in London?'

'Not yet. But I shall in two years' time, when I finally pay off the building society.'

'What a business woman you are.'

'You don't have to be a business woman to work out that it's uneconomic to pay rent for twenty-five years and at the end of the day have nothing to show for it.'

'You think I'm a fool.'

'Cosmo, no. I don't think that. I suppose I can see how it all came about, but that doesn't stop me being concerned.'

'For me.'

'Yes, for you. I've just realised that I've been living with you all this time, and never given a thought to what we've been living on.'

'Do you want to know?'

'Not unless you want to tell me.'

'The income from a few investments that my grandfather left me, and my Army Pension.'

'And that's all?'

'That's the sum of it.'

'And if anything should happen to you, your Army Pension will die with you.'

'Naturally.' He grinned at her, trying to coax a smile into her intent and frowning face. 'But let's not bury me just yet. I am, after all, only fifty-five.'

'But Antonia?'

'I can't leave her what I haven't got. I simply hope that by the time I drop off the hook, she'll have found herself a rich husband.'

They had been arguing, but without heat. When he came out with this, however, all Olivia's instincts rose to the boil and she lost her temper.

'Cosmo, don't say things like that, don't talk in that ghastly archaic Victorian way, condemning Antonia to dependence on some man for the rest of her life. She should have money of her own. Every woman should have something of her own.'

'I didn't realise that money was so important to you.'

'It's not important to me. It never has been. It's only important if you haven't got any. And because it buys lovely things; not fast cars or fur coats or cruises to Hawaii or any of that rubbish, but real, lovely things, like independence and freedom and dignity. And learning. And time.'

'Is this why you've worked all your life? So that you could cock a snook at the arrogant male, the Victorian paterfamilias?'

'That's not fair! You make me sound like the worst sort of Women's Libber, an aggressive great lesbian with a foul placard.'

He did not reply to this outburst, and she felt instantly ashamed, wishing the angry words unsaid. They had never really quarrelled before. Her quick rage died and reason took its place. She answered his question, her voice deliberately calm. 'Yes. It is one of the reasons. I told you my father was a lightweight sort of man. He never influenced me in any way. But I am always determined to emulate my mother, to be strong and independent of everybody. And, as well, I have a creative need to write, and the sort of journalism which is my profession fulfils that need. So, I'm lucky. I do what I love to do, and I get paid for it. But that isn't all. There's a compulsion somewhere, a driving force that's too strong to fight. I need the conflict of a demanding job, decisions, deadlines. I need the pressures, the flow of adrenalin. It turns me on.'

'And does it make you happy?'

'Oh, Cosmo. Happiness. There's not a Blue-bird, an End to the Rainbow. I suppose what it boils down to is that if I'm working, I'm never totally unhappy. And if I'm not working, I'm never totally happy. Does that make sense?'

'So you haven't been totally happy here?'

'These months with you are different, like nothing that's ever happened before. It's been like a dream, stolen out of time. And I'll never cease to be endlessly grateful to you for giving me something that no person can ever take away. A good time. Not a good *time*, but a *good* time. But you can't dream for ever. You have to wake up. Soon, I shall start getting restless and probably irritable. And you will wonder what is wrong with me and so shall I. And I shall make a small private analysis of the problem and discover that it's time I went back to London, picked up the threads, and got on with my life.'

'When will that be?'

'Next month maybe. March.'

'You said a year. That's only ten months.'

'I know. But Antonia comes out again in April. I think I should be gone by then.'

'I thought you enjoyed each other's company.'

'We did. That's why I'm going. She mustn't expect me to be here; I mustn't become important to her. Besides, I have a lot of problems waiting for me, not least sorting out a job for myself.'

'Will you get your old job back?'

'If I don't I'll get a better one.'

'You're very confident.'

'I have to be.'

He sighed deeply, and then, with a gesture of impatience, flung the half-smoked cigar into the fire. He said, 'If I asked you to marry me, would you stay?

She said hopelessly, 'Oh, Cosmo.'

'You see, I find it hard to contemplate a future without you.'

'If I married any man,' she told him, 'it would be you. But I told you, that first day I came to Ca'n D'alt. I've never wanted to be married, have children. I love people. I'm fascinated by them, but I need my privacy too. To be myself. To live alone.'

He said, 'I love you.'

She crossed the small space that lay between them and put her arms around his waist and laid her head against his shoulder. Through his sweater, his shirt, she could hear the beat of his heart.

She said, 'I made tea, and we never drank it and now it will be cold.'

'I know.' She felt his hand touch her hair. 'Will you come back to Ibiza?'

'I don't think so.'

'Will you write to me? Keep in touch.'

'I'll send you Christmas cards with robins on them.'

He put his hands on either side of her head and turned her face up to his. The expression in his pale eyes was immeasurably sad.

'Now I know,' he told her.

'Know what?'

'That I'm going to lose you for ever.'

# Noel

At half past four on that cold, dark, wet March Friday, while Olivia threatened her Fiction Editor with dismissal and Nancy wandered bemusedly around Harrods, their brother Noel cleared his desk in the futuristic offices of Wenborn & Weinburg, Advertising Agents, and took himself home.

The office did not close until five thirty, but he had worked there for five years and reckoned that the occasional early departure was no more than his due. His colleagues, used to his ways, raised not so much as an eyebrow, and if he chanced to encounter one of the senior partners on his way to the lift, he had his cover story ready: he was feeling lousy, probably getting flu, and was going home to bed.

He did not meet one of the senior partners and he was not going home to bed, but to drive to Wiltshire for the weekend, to stay with some people called Early, whom he had never met. Camilla Early was an old school friend of Amabel's and Amabel was Noel's current woman.

'They're having a house party for the local point-to-point on Saturday,' Amabel had told him. 'It might be all right.'

'Have they got central heating?' Noel asked cautiously. At this time of the year, he had no intention of spending so much as an hour shivering over an inadequate log fire.

'Oh, heavens yes. Actually, they're loaded. They used to fetch Camilla from school in an enormous Bentley.'

It sounded hopeful. The sort of place where one might meet useful people. Going down in the lift, he put the problems of the day behind him and let his mind go nosing ahead. If Amabel was on time, they should be out of London before the Friday-evening exodus of traffic. He hoped that she would bring her car, so that they could make the journey in that. His Jag was making strange knocking sounds, and if they went in her car, there was always the possibility that he wouldn't be expected to pay for the petrol.

Outside the office, Knightsbridge streamed with rain, and stood solid with traffic. Usually Noel made the journey back to Chelsea by bus, or even, on summer evenings, walked down Sloane Street, but now, gripped by the bitter cold, he damned expense and flagged down a taxi. Halfway down the King's Road, he stopped the driver and got out, paid him off and turned into his own street to walk the short distance to Vernon Mansions.

His car stood parked at the pavement – an E-type Jaguar, marvellously macho, but ten years old. He had bought it from a chap who had gone bankrupt, and so had got it for peanuts, but it was only after he got it home that he discovered the copious rust on the underside of its chassis, and dicey brakes, and the fact that it absorbed petrol like a thirsty man drinks beer. And now that knocking sound had started. He paused to glance at the tyres and give one of them a kick. Soft. If by some unhappy chance he was compelled to use it this evening, he must stop at a garage and put in some air.

He left the car, crossed the pavement, and let himself in through the main door of the building. Inside it smelt stale and stuffy. There was a small lift, but since he lived on the first floor, he went up the stairs. These were carpeted and so was the narrow passage that led to his own door. He unlocked this and went in and closed it behind him, and was home. Home.

It was a joke, really.

The flats had been designed as pieds-à-terre for business men finally defeated by the sheer exhaustion of commuting daily from the depths of Surrey or Sussex or Buckinghamshire. Each had a tiny hallway, with a cupboard where you were meant to keep all your City clothes. Then there were a minuscule bathroom, a kitchen the size of a galley in a small yacht, and a sitting room. Here, a pair of louvred doors folded back to reveal a sort of kennel totally taken up by a double bed. This was not only impossible to make, but, in summer-time, hideously airless, so much so that in the warm weather Noel usually ended up sleeping on the sofa.

The décor and the furniture had come with the place and were included in the hugely inflated rent. All was beige or brown and incredibly dull. The living-room window faced out over the blank brick wall of a newly erected supermarket, a narrow alley, and a row of lock-up garages. The sunlight never penetrated, and the walls, which had once been cream, had darkened to the colour of old margarine.

But it was a good address. To Noel, that mattered more than anything else. Part of his image, like the showy car, the Harvie & Hudson shirts, the Gucci shoes. All these details were intensely important, because in his youth, due to family circumstances and financial pressures, he had not been sent to a public school, but educated at a day school in London, and so had been deprived of the easy friendships and useful connections of attending Eton or Harrow or Wellington. This was a resentment that continued, even at the age of almost thirty, to rankle.

Leaving school and finding a job had posed no problem. A post was ready and waiting for him in his father's family firm, Keeling & Philips, an old-established and traditional publishing company in St James's, and for five years he had worked there before moving on to the infinitely more interesting and lucrative business of advertising. But his social life was a different matter altogether, and here he was thrown back on his own resources. Which were, fortunately, legion. He was tall, good-looking, clever at games, and even as a boy had learned to cultivate a sincere and open manner that swiftly disarmed. He knew how to be charming to older women, to be discreetly respectful of older men, and, with the patience and cunning of a well-trained spy, infiltrated with little difficulty the upper circles of London society. For years he had been on the dowagers' lists of suitable young men for debutante dances, and during the Season he scarcely slept, returning from some ball in the early sunlight of a summer dawn, stripping off his tails and his starched shirt, taking a shower, and going to work. Weekends saw him at Henley, or Cowes, or Ascot. He was invited to ski in Davos, fish in Sutherland, and every now and then his handsome face appeared in the glossy pages of *Harpers and Queen*, 'enjoying a joke with his hostess'.

It was, in its way, an achievement. But all at once, it was not enough. He was fed up. He seemed to be getting nowhere. He wanted more.

The flat crouched around him, watching like a depressed relation, waiting for him to take some action. He drew the curtains and switched on the lamp and things looked marginally better. He took *The Times* from his coat pocket and tossed it on the table. Pulled off his coat and flung it across a chair. He went into the kitchen and poured a strong whisky and filled the glass with ice from the fridge. He went back to the sitting room and sat down on the sofa and opened the paper.

He turned first to the stock-market prices and saw that Consolidated Cables had gone up a point. He turned next to the racing page. Scarlet Flower had come in fourth, which meant that was fifty quid down the drain. He read a review of a new play, and then the sale-room news. He saw that a Millais had gone, at Christie's, for nearly eight hundred thousand pounds.

Eight hundred thousand.

The very words made him feel almost physically sick with frustration and envy. He laid down the paper and took a mouthful of whisky, and thought about the Lawrence Stern, *The Water Carriers*, which was coming

up for sale at Boothby's next week. Like his sister Nancy, he had never
had any opinion of his grandfather's work, but unlike Nancy, he had not
missed out on this extraordinary resurgence in the art world of interest
in those old Victorian painters. Over the last few years he had watched
the prices in the sale rooms slowly rising until now they had reached
these mammoth sums that seemed to him out of all proportion.

The top of the market, and he had nothing to sell. Lawrence Stern
was his grandfather, and yet he had nothing. None of them did. At
Oakley Street there had only been the three Sterns, and these his
mother had taken with her to Gloucestershire, where they dwarfed the
low-ceilinged rooms of Podmore's Thatch.

What were they worth? Five hundred, six hundred thousand? Perhaps,
against all odds, he should make some effort at talking her into selling.
If he did manage to persuade her, the profits would, of course, have to
be divided. Nancy, for one, would insist on her share, but even so, there
should be a good chunk for Noel. His imagination nosed cautiously
ahead, filled with brilliant schemes. He would chuck his nine-to-five job
with Wenborn & Weinburg, and set up on his own. Not advertising,
but commodity broking, gambling on a super-scale.

All that was needed was a prestigious address in the West End, a
telephone, a computer, and a lot of nerve. He had plenty of that. Milking
the punters, buttering up the big investors, moving into the big time.
He knew an almost sexual stirring of excitement. It could happen. All
that was missing was the capital to set the exercise into motion.

*The Shell Seekers.* Perhaps, next weekend, he would go down and visit
his mother. He hadn't seen her for months, but she had lately been
unwell – Nancy, in doomlike tones, had given him this news over the
telephone – so this would give him a good excuse for calling in at
Podmore's Thatch, and then he could ease the conversation gently
around to the subject of the pictures. If she started making excuses, or
bringing up such objections as Capital Gains Tax, he would mention his
friend Edwin Mundy, who was an antique dealer and an expert in flogging
stuff in Europe and stashing cash away in Swiss banks where it would be
safe from the insatiable maw of the Inland Revenue. It was Edwin who
had first alerted Noel to the enormous prices being paid in New York
and London for the old allegorical works so fashionable at the turn of
the century, and once even had suggested that Noel come into partnership
with him. But Noel, after some thought, had demurred. Edwin, he knew,
sailed dangerously close to the wind, and Noel had no intention of
spending even so much as a week in Wormwood Scrubs Prison.

It was all almost insuperably difficult. He sighed deeply, finished his
whisky, looked at his watch. A quarter past five. Amabel was coming to

pick him up at half past. He heaved himself out of the sofa, collected his suitcase from the cupboard in the hall and swiftly packed for the weekend. He was an expert at this – having had years of practice – and it took no more than five minutes. After that, he stripped off his clothes and went into the bathroom to shave and shower. The water was boiling, which was one of the good things about living in this benighted rabbit hutch, and after his shower, warm and scented, he felt better. He dressed again in clean casual clothes – cotton shirt, cashmere sweater, tweed jacket; he put his washbag on top of his suitcase, zipped it up and bundled his dirty linen into a corner of the kitchen for his daily lady to find and, hopefully, deal with.

Sometimes she didn't. Sometimes she didn't even come. He recalled, with the deepest nostalgia, the old way of life, before his mother had decided, with thought for no person but herself, to sell Oakley Street. For there he had enjoyed the best of everything. The independence of a latch key and his own suite of rooms at the top of the house, along with the endless advantages of living at home. Constant hot water, open fires, food in the larder, drink in the wine cellar, a great garden for the summer weather, the pub across the road, the river at his doorstep, his washing done, his bed made, his shirts ironed, and for all this he had not been expected to pay for so much as a roll of lavatory paper. As well, his mother was as independent as her son, and if she was not deaf to creaking stairs and the light tread of feminine feet going past her bedroom door, then she acted as though she were and never commented. He had imagined that this idyllic way of life was permanent, that, if any changes were to be made, he would be the one to make them, and when she first told him of her intention to sell out and move to the country, he felt as though his feet had been knocked from beneath him.

'But what about me? What the hell am I going to do?'

'Noel, my darling, you are twenty-three now, and you've lived in this house for the whole of your life. Perhaps it's time you flew the nest. I'm sure you'll be able to make other arrangements.'

Other arrangements. Paying rent, buying food, buying Scotch, spending money on horrible things like Vim for the bath and laundry bills. Right up to the very last moment he had clung on at Oakley Street, hoping against hope that she would change her mind, and he hadn't actually moved out until the furniture van arrived to load her possessions for transport to Gloucestershire. In the end most of his things went too, because there was no space in the ratty little flat he had found himself for the accumulated clobber of a lifetime, and these were now stacked in the small and cluttered room at Podmore's Thatch which was known, euphemistically, as Noel's.

He went there as little as possible, resentful not only of his mother's extraordinary behaviour, but also because it irked him to see her so contentedly settled in the country, and without him. He felt that she should at least have the decency to show a little nostalgia for the good old days when they had lived together, but she didn't seem to miss him in the least.

He found this hard to understand because he missed her very much.

These poignant musings were brought to a halt by the arrival of Amabel, only fifteen minutes late. The buzzer sounded and when he went to open the door she stood outside bearing her luggage, two bulging tote bags, one of which sprouted a pair of muddy green wellingtons.

'Hi.'

He said, 'You're late.'

'I know. Sorry.' She came in and dumped the tote bags and he closed the door and gave her a kiss.

'What held you up?'

'I couldn't get a taxi, and the traffic's hell.'

A taxi. His heart sank. 'Didn't you bring your car?'

'It's got a puncture. And I haven't got a spare tyre, and anyway, I don't know how to change the wheel.'

This was to be expected. At anything practical, she was totally useless, and probably one of the most disorganised women he had ever met. She was twenty, and tiny as a child, small-boned and thin to the point of emaciation. Her skin was so pale as to be almost transparent, her eyes, grape-green, were large and thickly lashed, her hair long and fine and straight, worn loose and usually falling over her face. She wore, on this cold, wet evening, clothes remarkable for their meagre inadequacy. Skinny jeans and a T-shirt, and a skimpy denim jacket. Her shoes were flimsy, and her ankles bare. All in all, she looked like an anorexic from Bermondsey, but she was in fact the Honourable Amabel Remington-Luard, and her father was Lord Stockwood, with large estates in Leicestershire. Which was what had attracted Noel to Amabel in the first place, coupled with the fact that he, for some obscure reason, found her waif-like appearance enormously sexy.

So now they would have to drive to Wiltshire in the Jag. Swallowing his annoyance, he said, 'Well, we'd better get moving. We'll have to stop at a garage to get some air in the tyres and fill up with petrol.'

'Gosh, I'm sorry.'

'You know the way?'

'Where? To the garage?'

'No. To where we're going in Wiltshire.'

'Yes, of course I do.'

'What's the house called?'

'Charbourne. I've been there heaps of times.'

He stood looking down at her, and then at her so-called luggage. 'Are these all the clothes you've got?'

'I've brought my wellingtons.'

'Amabel, it's still winter, and we're meant to be going to a point-to-point tomorrow. Have you got a coat?'

'No, I left it in the country last weekend.' She shrugged her bony shoulders. 'But I can borrow something. Camilla's bound to have stacks of suitable garments.'

'That's not the point. We've got to *get* there first, and the heater in the Jag's not always very reliable. The last thing I want is to have to nurse you through pneumonia.'

'Sorry.'

But she did not sound particularly sorry. Stifling his irritation, Noel turned and pulled open the sliding door of his cupboard, felt around in its overcrowded interior, and finally found what he was looking for, which was a gentleman's overcoat of incredible age; thick dark tweed, with a faded velvet collar and a lining of tattered rabbit fur.

'Here,' he said. 'You can borrow this.'

'Gosh.' She seemed inordinately delighted; not, he knew, by his concern, but by the faded grandeur of the ancient garment. She adored old clothes and spent much of her time and money scouting round the stalls of Portobello Road, buying droopy evening dresses from the 1930s, or beaded bags. Now she took the dignified old wreck of a coat from him and put it on. It engulfed her, but at least the hem did not drag on the floor.

'Oh, what a scrumptious coat. Where on earth did you get it?'

'It was my grandfather's. I nicked it out of my mother's cupboard when she sold her London house.'

'I couldn't keep it, could I?'

'No, you couldn't. But you can wear it this weekend. The point-to-pointers will wonder what's hit them, but it'll give them something to talk about.'

She hugged the coat about her and laughed, not so much at his mild joke but with the sheer animal pleasure of wearing a fur-lined coat, and she looked so much like a wicked, greedy child that he found himself filled with a sudden physical desire for her. In normal circumstances he would, then and there, have taken her straight to bed, but right now there was not time. That would have to wait until later.

The journey to Wiltshire was no worse than he had expected. The rain never ceased, and the traffic out of London was three lanes deep and snail-slow. But at last they were on the motorway and able to get up some speed, and the knocking sound in the engine obligingly did not make itself evident, and the heater, faintly, worked.

For a little they talked, and then Amabel fell silent. He thought that she had probably gone to sleep, which was what she usually did on such occasions, but then he became aware of various shiftings and gropings going on in the seat beside him, and knew that she was not asleep.

He said, 'What's up?'

She said, 'There's something crackling.'

'Crackling?' He was filled with alarm, imagining the Jag about to burst into flame. He even slowed down slightly.

'Yes. Crackling. You know. Like a bit of paper.'

'Where?'

'Inside the coat.' She groped again. 'There's a hole in the pocket. I think it's something inside the lining.'

Much relieved, Noel accelerated back to eighty. 'I thought we were in for a conflagration,' he told her.

'Once I found an old half-crown down the lining of a coat of my mother's. Perhaps this is a five-pound note.'

'More likely an old letter, or a bit of chocolate wrapping. We'll investigate when we get there.'

An hour later they reached their destination. Amabel, somewhat to Noel's surprise, managed not to lose the way, directing him off the motorway, through various small country towns, and finally down a narrow winding road that led through darkened farm land to the village of Charbourne. Even in the rain and the darkness this seemed picturesque, with a main street flanked by deep cobbled pavements and thatched cottages fronted by small gardens. They passed a pub and a church, drove through an avenue of oak trees, and then came to an imposing pair of gates.

'This is it.'

He turned in through the gates, past a small lodge, and up a driveway leading through parkland. In the beam of his headlights he saw the house, square, white and Georgian, with the pleasing proportions and symmetry of that period. Lights shone from behind drawn curtains, and Noel circled the wide gravelled sweep and drew up at the front door.

He stopped the engine and they got out of the car and collected their luggage from the boot and went up the steps to the closed front door. Amabel found a wrought-iron bell-pull and gave it a tug but then said, 'We don't have to wait,' and opened the door herself.

They stepped into a stone-flagged lobby, with another glassed door that led into the hall. The lights were on, and Noel saw that this was large and panelled, with an impressive stairway rising to the upper floor. As they hesitated, a door at the far end of the hall was opened and a woman appeared, bustling forward to let them in. She was stout and white-haired, wearing a flowered pinafore over her good turquoise-blue Courtelle dress. The gardener's wife, Noel decided, come in to give a hand over the weekend.

She opened the door. 'Good evening. Come along in. Mr Keeling and Miss Remington-Luard? That's right. Mrs Early's just gone up for her bath and Camilla and the Colonel are down at the stables, but Mrs Early said I was to watch out for you and show you up to your rooms. This all your luggage, is it? What a dreadful night. Did you have a bad drive? The rain's something awful, isn't it?' By now they were inside. There was an open fire in the marble fireplace, and the house felt splendidly warm. The gardener's wife closed the door. 'If you'd just like to follow me. Can you manage your luggage?'

They could. Amabel, still bundled in the old coat, carried her tote bag with the wellingtons, and Noel carried the other tote bag and his own suitcase. Thus burdened, they followed the stout lady as she led them up the stairs.

'Camilla's other guests arrived at tea-time, but they're up in their rooms now, changing. And Mrs Early asked me to tell you that dinner's at eight, but if you'd like to be down by a quarter to, there'll be drinks in the library, and you can meet everyone else then . . .'

At the turn of the stairs an archway gave onto a passage that led towards the back of the house. There was a scarlet carpet on the floor, sporting prints adorned the walls, and Noel noticed the pleasant smell inherent in well-kept country houses, compounded of freshly ironed linen, polish, and lavender.

'Now this is your room, dear.' She opened a door and stood aside for Amabel to go through. 'And you, Mr Keeling, are along here . . . and there's the bathroom in between. I think you've got everything, but if you do need something, just let us know.'

'Thank you so much.'

'And I'll tell Mrs Early you'll be down about a quarter to eight.'

With a delightful smile she went, closing the door behind her. Noel, left alone, set down his suitcase and stood looking around him. His years of weekending in strange houses had sharpened his perceptions to such a degree that he was able, almost from the moment he walked through a new front door, to gauge the possibilities of the days that lay ahead and accord them his own private system of grading.

One Star was the bottom, usually a dank country cottage complete with draughts, lumpy beds, unappetising food, and nothing but beer offered to slake a man's thirst. Fellow guests were inclined to be unengaging relations with badly behaved children. If caught in such a situation, Noel very often remembered a sudden and pressing engagement and took himself back to London first thing on the Sunday morning. Two Star applied in the main to houses in the Army belt of Surrey, with a party consisting of a lot of athletic girls and young cadets from Sandhurst. Tennis was normally the accepted entertainment, played on a mossy court and topped off by an evening visit to the local pub. Three Star were rambling, unpretentious country estates, with lots of dogs around, and horses in the stables, smouldering log fires, lavish nursery food, and, almost always, splendid wine. Four Star was the top, the homes of the immensely rich. A butler, your unpacking done for you, and a fire in your bedroom. The raison d'être for Four Star weekends was usually some coming-out dance, taking place in the neighbourhood. There would be a vast chandelier-lit marquee, set up in the garden; a band, imported at hideous expense from London to play the night away, and champagne still flowing at six o'clock in the morning.

Charbourne, he had instantly decided, was Three Star, and he was well content. He had, obviously, not been given the best guest-room, but this was, nevertheless, totally adequate. Old-fashioned, comforting, with solid Victorian furniture and heavy chintz curtains, and containing everything an overnight visitor could possibly need. He took off his coat and slung it across the bed, and went to open a second door that led into a spacious carpeted bathroom with an enormous bath encased in mahogany. There was another door on the other side of this room, and he crossed the floor and tried the handle, half expecting to find it locked; but it opened, and he was in Amabel's room. He found her, still draped in the fur-lined coat, taking random garments from her tote bag, which she dropped, like fallen leaves, on the floor at her feet.

She looked up and saw the grin on his face.

'What's that for?' she asked him.

'Our hostess is obviously a woman of good sense and broad-mindedness.'

'How do you mean?' She could be very obtuse.

'I mean that under no circumstances would she ever put us in a double room, but what we choose to do with ourselves in the privacy of the night is absolutely none of her business.'

'Oh well,' said Amabel, 'I expect she's had plenty of practice.' She rummaged deep in the tote bag and pulled out a long black stringy garment.

'What's that?' he asked.

'It's what I'm going to wear tonight.'

'Isn't it a bit crumpled?'

She gave it a shake. 'It's jersey. It's not meant to crumple. Do you think the water's hot?'

'Bound to be.'

'Oh, goody. I'm going to have a bath. Run it for me, would you?'

He returned to the bathroom, put in the plug, and turned on the taps. Then he went back to his own room and unpacked, hanging his suits in the spacious wardrobe and laying his clean shirts in the drawers. At the bottom of his suitcase was a silver hunting flask. By now he could hear Amabel splashing about in the water, and scented steam wreathed, like smoke, through the open door. With the flask in his hand he went through to the bathroom, collected two tooth-tumblers, half filled them with whisky and then topped them up with water from the cold tap. Amabel had decided to wash her hair. She was always washing her hair, but it never looked any different. He gave her one of the tumblers, putting it on a stool by the bath where she could reach it when she'd got the soap out of her eyes. Then he went into her room, collected his grandfather's coat off the floor and took it back to the bathroom, where he settled himself on the lid of the lavatory, placed his own drink carefully on the soap tray of the wash-basin, and began to investigate.

The steam was clearing. Amabel sat up, pushed her long sodden locks away from her face and opened her eyes. She saw the drink and reached for it.

'What are you doing?' she asked.

'Looking for the five-pound note.'

Feeling through the heavy material, he located the crackling, deep in the hem. He put his hand on the relevant pocket and found the hole, but it was too small for his hand to get through, so he tore it a bit more and tried again. Groping down between the tweed and the dry backs of rabbit skins, his fingertips encountered fluff and scraps of fur. He set his teeth, imagining a dead mouse or something unspeakably disgusting, but quashed such horrors and persevered. At last, in the very corner of the hem, his fingers encountered what they were looking for. Cautiously he withdrew and freed his hand. The coat slipped from his knee and onto the floor and he was left holding a piece of flimsy folded paper, old and browned as some precious parchment.

'What is it?' Amabel wanted to know.

'Not a five-pound note. A letter, I think.'

'Gosh, how disappointing.'

Delicately, so as not to tear it, he opened it out. Saw the sloping, old-fashioned writing, the letters formed with a finely nibbed pen.

Dufton Hall.
Lincolnshire.

8th May, 1898.

Dear Stern,

I thank you for your letter from Rapallo and note that by now you will
have returned to Paris. I hope to be able to travel to France next
month when, D. V., I will call upon you at your studio and inspect
the oil sketch of *The Terrazzo Garden*. When the necessary travel
arrangements have been made, I shall send you a telegram informing
you of the date and time of my visit.
Yours truly,

Ernest Wollaston.

He read this in silence. When he had finished, he sat for a moment deep
in thought, and then raised his head and looked at Amabel.
 He said, 'Amazing.'
 'What does it say?'
 'What an amazing thing to find.'
 'Oh, Noel, for God's sake, read it to me.'
 He did so. When he had finished, Amabel was none the wiser. 'What's
so amazing about that?'
 'It's a letter to my grandfather.'
 'So what?'
 'Have you never heard of Lawrence Stern?'
 'No.'
 'He was a painter. A very successful Victorian painter.'
 'I never knew that. No wonder he had such a super coat.'
 Noel ignored this irrelevance. 'A letter from Ernest Wollaston.'
 'Was he a painter, too?'
 'No, you ignoramus, he was not a painter. He was a Victorian industrial-
ist. A self-made millionaire. He was eventually elevated to the peerage
and called himself Lord Dufton.'
 'And what about the picture . . . what's it called?'
 '*The Terrazzo Garden*. It was a commission. He commissioned Lawrence
Stern to paint it for him.'
 'Never heard of that, either.'
 'You should have done. It's very famous. For the last ten years it's been
hanging in the Metropolitan Museum in New York.'

'What does it look like?'

Noel was silent for a moment, frowning with the effort of recalling a painting that he had only seen reproduced in the pages of some aesthetic periodical. 'A terrace. Italy, obviously, that was why he'd been in Rapallo. A group of women, leaning on a balustrade; roses growing all over the place. Cypress trees and blue sea, and a boy playing a harp. It's very beautiful, of its kind.' He looked at the letter again, and it all fell into place and he knew exactly how it had happened. 'Ernest Wollaston had made a packet and moved up in society, probably built himself this impressive great house in Lincolnshire. And he would buy furniture for it, and have carpets specially woven in France, and because he had no inherited portraits or Gainsboroughs or Zoffanys to hang on his walls, he would commission the most prestigious artist of the day to paint a picture for him. In those days, it was a little like asking some guy to make a film. Locations, costumes, models would all have to be considered. Then, when this had been decided and researched, the artist would make a rough oil sketch for his client to see. He had months of work ahead of him, and he had to be pretty sure that at the end of the day it was going to be exactly what the man wanted and that he got paid his money for it.'

'I see.' She lay back in the water, with her hair floating around her, like Ophelia, and considered all this. 'But I still don't see why you're looking so excited.'

'It's just that . . . I'd never thought about those first oil sketches. Or if I had, I'd forgotten about them.'

'Are they that important?'

'I don't know. They might be.'

'Clever little me, then, finding the letter crackling away in the coat.'

'Yes. Clever little you.'

After a bit, he folded the letter, put it in his pocket, finished his drink and stood up. He looked at his watch. 'It's half past seven,' he told her. 'You'd better get your skates on.'

'Where are you going?'

'To change.'

He left her, still wallowing, and went back into his room, closing the door behind him. Then, very quietly, he opened the other door and stepped out into the passage, and made his way back to the staircase and down into the hall. On the thick carpeting his footsteps made no sound. At the bottom of the stairs he paused, hesitating. There was nobody around, although voices and pleasant domestic clatterings came from the direction of the back quarters of the house, along with fragrant smells of delicious cooking. These, however, did not divert him, because for the moment he had no thoughts for anything except where there might be a telephone.

He found one almost at once, right there in the hall, in a glassed-in cubby-hole beneath the stairs. He went in and closed the door, lifted the receiver and dialled a London number. Almost immediately the call was answered.

'Edwin Mundy here.'

'Edwin, it's Noel Keeling.'

'Noel. Long time no see.' His voice was husky and expensive, with faint undertones of the cockney accent that he had never succeeded in losing. 'How are things with you?'

'Fine, but look, I haven't much time. I'm down in the country. I just wanted to ask you something.'

'Anything, old boy.'

'I'm talking about Lawrence Stern. Are you with me?'

'Yes.'

'Would you know if ever any of his rough oil sketches for major paintings have come on the market?'

There was a pause. Then Edwin said cagily, 'That's an interesting question. Why? Have you got any?'

'No. And I don't know if any exist. That's why I'm calling you.'

'I've never heard of any coming up in any of the important sale rooms. But, of course, there are small dealers all over the country.'

'What would . . .' Noel cleared his throat and tried again. 'At the present state of the market, what would such a thing fetch?'

'Depends on the painting. If it was one of his important works, I suppose about four or five thousand . . . but don't take my word for it, old boy, that's just a rough guess. I can't say for sure until I've seen it.'

'I told you. I have nothing.'

'Then why the call?'

'I've just realised that such sketches might still be around, without any of us knowing about them.'

'You mean, in your mother's house?'

'Well, they'd have to be somewhere.'

'If you could find them,' Edwin continued, at his most urbane, 'I imagine you'll let me handle them for you.'

But Noel was not going to commit himself as easily as that. 'I'd have to get my hands on them first.' And then, before Edwin could say any more, 'I've got to go, Edwin. Dinner's in five minutes and I haven't even changed. Thanks for your help, and sorry to trouble you.'

'No trouble, dear boy. Glad to be of help. An interesting possibility. Good hunting.'

He rang off. Slowly, Noel replaced the receiver. Four to five thousand pounds. More than he had dared to imagine. He took a deep breath, opened the door and stepped out into the hall. There was still nobody about, and as no one had witnessed his action, there was no necessity to leave any money to pay for the call.

# Hank

At the very last moment, when all was ready and waiting for her dinner à deux with Hank Spotswood, Olivia remembered that she had not called her mother with the suggestion that she drive to Gloucestershire the following day and spend a leisurely Saturday with her. The white telephone stood by the sofa, and she was actually sitting there, and dialling the number, when she heard a taxi come crawling down the street. She knew instinctively that it was Hank. She hesitated. Her mother, once on the telephone, liked to talk, giving and being given news, and there would be no question of simply making the arrangement and hanging up. She heard the taxi halt at her gate, stopped dialling and replaced the receiver. She would call later on. Her mother never went to bed until midnight.

She got to her feet, straightened the dented cushion, and glanced around, checking that all was perfection. It was. Low lights, drinks waiting, ice in the ice bucket, soft music, scarcely audible, on the stereo. She turned to the looking-glass over the mantelpiece and touched her hair, rearranged the collar of her cream satin Chanel shirt. There were pearls in her ear lobes and her makeup was pearly too, soft and very feminine, unlike the startling maquillage she affected during the day. Waiting, she heard the gate open and shut. Footsteps. The doorbell rang.

She went, without hurry, to let him in.

'Good evening.'

He stood on the doorstep in the rain. A rugged, handsome man in his late forties, bearing, predictably, a sheaf of long-stemmed red roses.

'Hi.'

'Come along in. What a horrible evening. But you found the way.'

'Sure. No problem.' He stepped indoors and she closed the door, and he handed her the flowers.

'A small offering,' he told her and smiled, and she had forgotten his attractive smile and his even, very white American teeth.

'Oh, they're lovely.' She took them and automatically bent her head to smell them, but they had been cruelly forced in some hot-house, and so had no scent. 'How very kind of you. Take off your coat and help yourself to a drink, and I'll go and put them in water right away.'

She bore them off to her little kitchen, found a jug, filled it with water, and put the roses in just as they were, without taking time to arrange them in any way. They fell, as roses do, gracefully into shape. Carrying the jug, she returned to the sitting room, and put it, with some ceremony, in the place of honour on top of her walnut bureau. The red of the flowers against the white walls was bright as drops of blood.

She turned to him. 'That was very thoughtful. Now, have you got a drink?'

He had. 'I took a Scotch. I hope that's in order.' He set down his glass. 'Now what can I fix for you?'

'The same. With water and ice.'

She sank down in the corner of the sofa, curled her feet up beside her, and watched him as he dealt with bottles and glasses. When he brought the drink over to her, she put up her hand to take it, and then he collected his own and let himself down in the armchair that stood across the hearth. He raised his glass. 'Cheers.'

'Good health,' said Olivia.

They drank. They began to talk. It was all very easy and relaxed. He admired her house, was interested in her pictures, asked about her job, wanted to know how she had become acquainted with the Ridgeways, at whose party, a couple of nights ago, they had met. And then, tactfully prompted, he began to tell her about himself. He was in the carpet business, and over in this country for the International Textile Conference. He was staying at the Ritz. He was a New Yorker, but had moved south to work in Dalton, Georgia.

'That must be quite a change of life-style. New York to Georgia.'

'Yes.' He looked down, turning his glass in his hands. 'But the move came at an opportune time. My wife and I had recently separated, and it made the domestic arrangements a good deal easier.'

'I'm sorry.'

'Nothing to be sorry about. Just one of those things.'

'Do you have children?'

'Yes. Two teenagers. A boy and a girl.'

'Do you get to see them?'

'Sure. They spend their summer vacation with me. The South is great for kids. They can play tennis all the year round, ride, swim. We belong to the local country club, and they met up with a lot of youngsters their own age.'

'Sounds fun.'

There came a pause, during which Olivia tactfully waited, giving him the chance to produce a wallet of photographs of his children, which, blessedly, he did not. She began to like him more and more. She said, 'Your glass is empty. Would you like another drink?'

They talked on. The conversation switched to more serious subjects: American politics, the economic balance between their two countries. His opinions were both liberal and practical, and though he told her that he voted Republican, he seemed deeply concerned with the problems of the Third World. After a little, she glanced at her watch and realised, with some surprise, that it was already nine o'clock.

She said, 'I think perhaps it's time we ate.'

He got to his feet, collected their empty glasses, and followed her into the little dining room. She switched on the low lights, and the charmingly ordered table was revealed, laid with crystal and shining silver and a centrepiece of early lilies. The lights, though soft, were bright enough for him to spy instantly her single cobalt-blue wall, covered from floor to ceiling with framed photographs, and he was at once diverted.

'Hey, look at all this. What a great idea.'

'Family photographs always seem to me such a problem. I never know where to put them, so I solved the puzzle by simply papering the wall with them.'

She went behind the counter of the small kitchen, collecting pâté and brown bread, while he stood with his back to her and inspected the photographs with the interest and attention of a man at an art gallery.

'Who's this pretty girl here?'

'That's my sister Nancy.'

'She's lovely.'

'She was,' Olivia agreed. 'But she's let herself go, as they say. You know, put on weight and generally become very middle-aged. But she *was* lovely when she was a girl. That was taken just before she was married.'

'Where does she live?'

'In Gloucestershire. She's got two horrible children and a boring husband and her idea of heaven is to trail round a point-to-point with two Labradors on leads, hooting greetings at all her friends.' He turned to frown in a perplexed fashion and Olivia laughed. 'You don't even know what I'm talking about, do you?'

'No. But I get the gist.' He went back to the photographs. 'And who's this handsome lady?'

'That's my mother.'

'Have you got one of your father?'

'No, my father's dead. But that's my brother Noel. The good-looking man with the blue eyes.'

'He certainly is good-looking. Is he married?'

'No. He's almost thirty now and he still isn't married.'

'Has he got a girlfriend?'

'Not a resident one. He never has a resident girlfriend. He spends his whole life being terrified of committing himself. You know, the sort of man who never accepts an invitation to a party in case a better one turns up.'

Hank's shoulders shook with amusement. 'You're not very kindly about your family.'

'I know. But what's the point in clinging to sentimental illusions, especially when you've reached my age?'

She came out from behind the counter and laid the pâté and the butter and the crusty brown bread out on the table. She found matches and lit the candles.

'And who's this?'

'Which one are you looking at?'

'This guy, with the young girl.'

'Oh.' She moved to stand beside him. 'That's a man called Cosmo Hamilton. And the girl is his daughter Antonia.'

'What a pretty kid.'

'I took that five years ago. She must be eighteen now.'

'Are they related to you?'

'No. He's a friend. He was a friend. A lover, actually. He has a house in Ibiza, and five years ago I took a year off work . . . a sabbatical; and spent it there, living with him.'

Hank raised his eyebrows. 'A year. That's a long time to live with a man.'

'It passed very quickly.'

She felt his eyes upon her face. 'Were you fond of him?'

'Yes. Fonder than I've ever been of any person.'

'Why didn't you marry him . . . or perhaps he already had a wife?'

'No, he didn't have a wife. But I didn't want to marry him because I didn't want to marry anybody. I still don't.'

'Do you still see him?'

'No. I said goodbye to him, and that was the end of the affair.'

'And the daughter, Antonia?'

'I don't know what's happened to her.'

'Do you write?'

Olivia shrugged. 'I send him Christmas cards. That was what we agreed. A Christmas card every year, with a robin on it.'

'That doesn't sound very generous.'

'No, it doesn't, does it? And it's probably impossible for you to understand. But the important thing is that Cosmo *does*.' She smiled. 'Now, if you've finished with my friends and relations, how about pouring the wine and we'll have something to eat?'

He said, 'Tomorrow's Saturday. What do you usually do with your Saturdays?'

'Sometimes I go away for the weekend. Sometimes I just stay here. Unwind, relax, ask a few friends round for a drink.'

'Have you got anything planned for tomorrow?'

'Why?'

'I have no meetings fixed. I thought we might take a car and go off somewhere together . . . you could show me some of this famous countryside I'm always hearing about but never have time to go and inspect.'

Dinner was finished, the dishes abandoned, the dining-room lights switched off. With brandy and coffee, they had returned to the fireside, only now they were both on the sofa, sitting at either end, half turned towards each other. Olivia's dark head rested on an Indian pink cushion, her legs curled beneath her. One of her patent-leather slippers had dropped off and lay on the carpet at her feet.

She said, 'Tomorrow, I'd planned to go and see my mother in Gloucestershire.'

'Is she expecting you?'

'No. But I was going to call her before I went to bed.'

'Do you have to go?'

Olivia considered this. She had meant to go, had decided to go, and had felt better for making the decision. But now . . .

'No, I don't *have* to go,' she told him. 'But she's been unwell and I haven't seen her for too long, and I ought to.'

'How much persuading would it take to make you change your mind?'

Olivia smiled. She took another mouthful of the strong dark coffee and replaced the little cup, with much care, exactly in the centre of its saucer.

'How would you persuade me?'

'I could tempt you with the promise of a four-star meal. Or a ride on the river. Or a country walk. Whatever pleases you most.'

Olivia considered this lure.

'I suppose I could put her off for a week. It's not as though she were expecting me, and so she won't be disappointed.'

'You'll come, then.'

She made up her mind. 'Yes, I'll come.'

'Shall I hire a car?'

'I have a perfectly good car of my own.'

'Where shall we go?'

Olivia shrugged and laid down her coffee cup. 'Wherever you want. The New Forest; up the river to Henley. We could go to Kent and look at the gardens at Sissinghurst.'

'Shall we decide tomorrow?'

'If you want.'

'What time shall we start?'

'Early, I think. Then we'll get out of London before the worst of the traffic.'

'In that case, perhaps I should start making tracks back to my hotel.'

'Yes,' said Olivia. 'Perhaps you should.'

But neither of them moved. Down the length of the huge white sofa, their eyes met and held. It was very quiet. The stereo was silent, the tapes long finished, and outside the rain streamed against the window panes. A car went down the road, and the little carriage clock on Olivia's mantelpiece ticked away the passing moments. It was nearly one o'clock.

He moved towards her, as she had known he would, and put an arm around her shoulders and drew her towards him so that her head no longer rested on the pink cushion but lay against the warm bulk of his chest. With his other hand, he smoothed her hair from her cheek, then, placing his fingers beneath her chin to turn up her face, bent and kissed her mouth. His hand moved from her chin to her throat, and down to the curve of her tiny breasts. He said, at last, 'I've been wanting to do that all evening.'

'I think I've been wanting you to do it.'

'If we're starting off so early in the morning, isn't it pretty silly, my going all the way to the Ritz just to get four hours' sleep and then come back for you?'

'Dreadfully silly.'

'May I stay?'

'Why not?'

He drew back, gazing down at her upturned face, and his eyes were filled with a curious mixture of desire and amusement.

'There is only one snag,' he told her. 'I have no razor nor toothbrush.'

'I have both. Brand new. For emergencies.'

He began to laugh. 'You are an amazing woman,' he told her.
'So I've been told.'

Olivia awoke, as she always did, early. Seven thirty in the morning. The
curtains were drawn, but not completely, and through the gap between
them the air flowed in, fresh and cold. It was just light and the sky was
clear. Perhaps it was going to be a fine day.

For a little she lay, drowsy and relaxed, smiling with contentment,
remembering last night and anticipating with pleasure the day that lay
ahead. She turned her head on the pillow and gazed with deep satisfaction
at the sleeping man who occupied the other side of her vast bed. One
arm was tucked beneath his head, the other lay across the thick white
blanket. This was deeply tanned, as was the whole of his healthy, youthful
body, and softly furred with tiny golden hairs. She put out her hand and
touched his forearm, as she would have touched some piece of porcelain
or sculpture, just for the sheer animal pleasure of feeling its shape and
curve beneath her fingertips. The light touch did not disturb him, and
when she drew her hand away, he still slept.

Her drowsiness had gone, to be replaced by the usual restless energy.
She was fully awake now and raring to go. Cautiously she sat up, turned
back the covers, got out of the bed. She pushed her bare feet into slippers
and reached for her pale pink woollen gown, pulled it on, and tied the
sash around her narrow waist. She went out of the room, closing the
door behind her, and down the stairs.

She drew back the curtains and saw that, indeed, it promised to be a
perfect day. There had been a light frost in the night, but the pale sky
was cloudless and the first low rays of winter sun were already penetrating
the deserted street. She opened the front door and took in the milk,
carried this to the kitchen, and stowed the bottles away in the fridge.
She cleared the dinner dishes from the previous evening and stacked
them in the dish washer, and then laid the table for breakfast. She put
coffee on to perk, found bacon and eggs, a packet of cereal. She returned
to the sitting room to straighten cushions, remove glasses and coffee
cups, light the fire. The roses he had brought her had started to open,
the petals curling back from the tight inner buds, like hands opening in
supplication. She paused to smell them, but, poor things, they still had
no scent. Never mind, she told them, you're beautiful. You'll just have
to be content with your good looks.

The post, with a rattle of the letter-box, fell upon the mat inside the
front door. She was just about to go and collect this, and was already
halfway across the room, when the telephone rang, and she made a dive

for the receiver, not wishing the shrill bell to disturb the man who still slept upstairs.

'Hello.'

In the mirror over the mantelpiece she was face to face with her own reflection, morning-bare, her dark hair falling across one cheek. She pushed it back, and then, because there had been no response, said, 'Hello?' again.

There was a click and a buzz and then a feminine voice spoke. 'Olivia?'

'Yes.'

'Olivia, it's Antonia.'

'Antonia?'

'Antonia Hamilton. Cosmo's Antonia.'

'Antonia!' Olivia sank into the corner of the sofa, tucking up her feet, cradling the receiver to her ear. 'Where are you speaking from?'

'Ibiza.'

'You sound as though you're just next door.'

'I know. It's a good line, thank God.' Something in the young voice caught at Olivia's attention. She felt the smile on her face fade, her fingers tightened around the smooth white surface of the receiver.

'Why are you calling?'

'Olivia. I had to let you know. I'm afraid it's rather sad. My father's dead.'

Dead. Cosmo dead. 'Dead.' She said the word, whispered it, but did not know that she was saying it.

'He died late on Thursday night. In hospital . . . the funeral was yesterday.'

'But . . .' Cosmo, dead. It was not believable. 'But . . . how? Why?'

'I . . . I can't tell you – not over the telephone.'

Antonia, without Cosmo in Ibiza. 'Where are you ringing from?'

'From Pedro's.'

'Where are you living?'

'At Ca'n D'alt.'

'Are you alone there?'

'No. Tomeu and Maria moved in to keep me company. They've been marvellous.'

'But . . .'

'Olivia, I have to come to London. I can't stay here, because the house doesn't belong to me and . . . oh, a thousand other reasons. Anyway, I'll have to get some sort of a job. If I came . . . could I stay with you for a few days, just until I get myself settled? I wouldn't ask you such a favour, only there isn't anyone else.'

Olivia hesitated, hating herself for hesitating, but only too aware that every instinct in her being was reacting violently against the thought of any person, even Antonia, invading the precious privacy of her house and her life.

'What . . . what about your mother?'

'She's married again. She lives in the North now, near Huddersfield. And I don't want to go there . . . I'll explain that later, too. It's only for a few days, like I said, just until I get myself organised.'

'When do you want to come?'

'Next week. Maybe Tuesday, if I can get a flight. Olivia, it would only be for a few days, just until I get myself organised.'

Her pleading voice, over the miles of telephone cable, sounded young and vulnerable, as it had when she was a child. Suddenly, Olivia remembered Antonia as she had first seen her, running across the polished floor of the Ibiza airport, to fling herself into Cosmo's arms. And she was filled with disgust at herself. This is Antonia, you selfish cow, appealing for help. This is Cosmo's Antonia and Cosmo is dead, and the fact that she's turning to you is the greatest compliment she could pay you. For once in your life, stop thinking of yourself.

As though Antonia could see her, she smiled, comforting, reassuring. She said, making her voice warm and strong, 'Of course you can come. Let me know when your flight is due, and I'll meet you at Heathrow. You can tell me everything then.'

'Oh, you are a saint. I won't be any trouble.'

'Of course you won't.' Her practical, well-trained mind moved on to other possible difficulties. 'Are you all right for money?'

'Oh.' Antonia sounded surprised, as though she had not even considered such details, which she probably hadn't. 'Yes. I think so.'

'You've got enough to pay for the air ticket?'

'Yes, I think so. Just.'

'Be in touch, then, and I'll expect you.'

'Thank you so much. And . . . I'm sorry to tell you about Daddy . . .'

'I'm sorry too.' It was the understatement of her life. She closed her eyes, shutting away the pain of a loss that she had not yet fully absorbed. 'He was a very special person.'

'Yes.' Antonia was crying. She could hear, see, almost feel the tears. 'Yes . . . goodbye, Olivia.'

'Goodbye.'

Antonia rang off.

After a little, clumsily, Olivia replaced her own receiver. She felt, all at once, immensely cold. Curled in the corner of the sofa, she wrapped her arms around herself, staring at her neat and shining sitting room where nothing had changed, nothing had moved, and yet everything was different. For Cosmo had gone. Cosmo was dead. For the rest of her life Olivia would have to live in a world in which there was no Cosmo. She thought of that warm evening outside Pedro's where they had sat and listened to the boy playing the Rodrigo concerto on his guitar, and filling the night with the music of Spain. Why that occasion in particular, when there was a whole cornucopia of memories from her months with Cosmo?

A step on the stair made her look up. She saw Hank Spotswood coming down towards her. He wore her white towelling bathrobe, and he did not look ridiculous in this because it was a man's one anyway and fitted him easily. She was pleased that he did not look ridiculous. She could not have borne him, at that moment, to have appeared looking ridiculous. And this was crazy, too, for what did it matter how he looked, when Cosmo was dead?

She watched him, saying nothing. He said, 'I heard the telephone.'

'I hoped it wouldn't wake you.'

She did not know that her face was ashen, her dark eyes like two holes in her face.

He said, 'What's wrong?'

He had a stubble of beard and his hair was tousled. She thought of last night and was glad it was him.

'Cosmo has died. The man I told you about last night. The man in Ibiza.'

'Oh, dear God.'

He was down the stairs, across the floor, sitting beside her; gathering her wordlessly into his arms as though she were a hurt child in need of comfort. With her face pressed against the rough white towelling of her own bathrobe, she wished, violently, that she were able to cry. Longed for tears to come, for grief to spill over in some physical way that would ease the tight pain of misery that held her in its grip. But this did not happen. She had never been much good at crying.

'Who was that on the telephone?' he asked.

'Cosmo's daughter, Antonia. Poor child. He died on Thursday night. The funeral was yesterday. I don't know any more.'

'What age a man was he?'

'I suppose . . . about sixty. But so young.'

'What happened?'

'I don't know. She didn't want to talk about it over the telephone. She just said he died in hospital. She . . . she wants to come to London. She's coming next week. She's going to stay with me for a few days.'

He said nothing to this, but his arms tightened about her, his hand gently patting her shoulder, as though he soothed a highly strung animal.

After a bit, she felt comforted. She had stopped feeling cold. She freed her hands and laid them against his chest and drew away from him, composed now, and herself again.

'I'm sorry,' she apologised. 'I'm not usually so emotional.'

'Is there anything I can do?'

'There's nothing anybody can do. It's all over.'

'What about today? Would you rather we called it all off? I'll just disappear, get out of your way, if you'd like me to. You'd maybe like to be alone.'

'No, I don't want to be alone. The last thing I want is to be alone.' She marshalled her flying thoughts, set them into order, and knew that her first priority was to let her mother know that Cosmo had died. She said, 'But I'm afraid Sissinghurst or Henley are out. I'll have to go to Gloucestershire after all, and see my mother. I told you she'd been unwell, but I didn't tell you that she had a slight heart attack. And she was so fond of Cosmo. When I was living in Ibiza, she came and stayed with us. It was such a happy time. One of the happiest times of my life. So I have to tell her that he's died, and I want to be there when I do it.' She looked at Hank. 'Would you mind coming with me? I'm afraid it's a dreadfully long drive, but she'll give us lunch and we can spend a peaceful afternoon with her.'

'I'd be pleased to come. And I'll drive you.'

He was like a rock. She managed a smile, filled with affectionate gratitude. 'I'll ring her now.' She reached for the telephone receiver. 'Tell her to expect us for lunch.'

'Couldn't we take her out for a meal?'

Olivia dialled the number. 'You don't know my mother.'

He accepted this, and got to his feet. 'I smell coffee perking,' he observed. 'How would it be if I cooked the breakfast?'

They were out of the house and away by nine o'clock in the morning, Olivia in the passenger seat of her own dark green Alfasud, and Hank at the wheel. He drove, at first, with the greatest care, anxious not to forget that he was on the wrong side of the road, but after they had stopped to fill up with petrol, he became more confident, picked up speed, and they headed down the motorway towards Oxford at a steady seventy.

They did not talk. His concentration was all for the other traffic and the great road that curved ahead of them. Olivia was content to be silent, her chin sunk deep in the fur collar of her coat, her eyes watching but not seeing the dull countryside that flew past the windows.

But after Oxford, it got better. It was a sparkling winter day, and as the low sun rose in the winter sky, the frost on plough and grass melted, and lacy black trees threw long shadows across road and field. Farmers had started ploughing, and hosts of gulls followed the tractors and the furrows of newly turned black earth. They passed through small towns bustling with Saturday-morning busyness. Narrow streets were lined with the cars of country families, in from outlying districts to do the weekend shopping, and pavements teemed with mothers and children and peram-bulators, and market stalls piled with garish garments, plastic toys and balloons, flowers, and fresh fruit and vegetables. Farther on still, outside a village pub, they came upon a meet, the cobbled yard a-clatter with horses' hooves, the air loud with the bay and whimper of hounds, the cry of hunting horns, and the raised voices of the huntsmen resplendent in their pink coats. Hank could scarcely believe his good fortune. 'Will you look at that?' he kept saying, and he would have stopped the car to watch, but a young policeman firmly moved him on. He drove off, but reluctantly, glancing back over his shoulder for a last glimpse of the traditional English scene.

'It was like something out of a movie, with that old inn and the cobbled yard. I wish I'd had my camera.'

Olivia was pleased for him. 'You can't say I'm not giving you your money's worth. We could have driven all over the country and never found anything as good as that.'

'This is obviously my lucky day.'

Now the Cotswolds lay ahead. The roads narrowed, winding through watery meadows and over small stone bridges. Houses and farmsteads, built of honey-coloured Cotswold stone, stood golden in the sunshine, with cottage gardens that, in summer, would be a riot of colour, and orchards of plum and apple trees.

'I can understand why your mother chose to live here. I've never seen such countryside. And everything's so green.'

'Funnily enough, she didn't come here for the lovely countryside. When she sold up the London house, she had every intention of going to live in Cornwall. She'd lived there as a girl, you see, and I think she yearned to go back. But my sister Nancy thought it was too far away, too far from all her children. So she found this house for her. As things have turned out, perhaps it's all been for the best, but at the time I was angry with Nancy for interfering.'

'Does your mother live alone?'

'Yes. But that's another aggravation. The doctors now say she ought to have a companion, a housekeeper, but I know she'll resent this most dreadfully. She's enormously independent and not even very old. Only sixty-four. I feel it's an insult to her intelligence to start treating her as though she's already senile. As it is, she never stops. Cooks and gardens and entertains and reads everything she can lay her hands on, and listens to music, and rings people up and has long, satisfying conversations. Sometimes she takes herself off abroad to stay with old friends. France, usually. Her father was a painter, and she spent much of her girlhood in Paris.' She turned her head to smile at Hank. 'But why am I telling you about my mother? Before very long, you'll be able to see it all for yourself.'

'Did she like Ibiza?'

'Adored it. Cosmo's place was an old Ibecenco farmhouse, inland, up in the hills. Very rural. Just my mother's cup of tea. Whenever she found herself with a spare moment, she disappeared into the garden with a pair of secateurs, just as though she were at home.'

'Does she know Antonia?'

'Yes. She and Antonia were out with us at the same time. They made great friends. No age barrier. My mother's marvellous with young people. Much better than I could ever be.' She was silent for a moment, and then added, in an impulsive rush of honesty, 'I'm not very sure of myself even now. I mean, I want to help Cosmo's child, but I don't relish the thought of having anyone to live with me, for however short a time. Isn't that a shameful thing to have to admit?'

'Not shameful. Quite natural. How long will she stay?'

'I suppose until she finds herself a job and somewhere to live.'

'Has she got any qualifications for a job?'

'I've no idea.'

Probably not. Olivia sighed deeply. The morning's events had left her drained of emotion and physically exhausted. It was not just that she had yet to come to terms with the shock and grief of Cosmo's death, but on top of this she felt surrounded, besieged by other people's problems. Antonia would arrive, would come and stay, would have to be comforted, encouraged, supported, and, in all likelihood, at the end of the day, be helped to find some sort of a job. Nancy would continue to telephone Olivia and badger her with the question of a housekeeper for their mother, while Mother was going to fight, tooth and nail, any suggestion that she should have anyone to live with her. And on top of all this . . .

Her thoughts abruptly stopped dead. And then carefully backtracked. Nancy. Mother. Antonia. But of course. The solution was there. The problems, arranged together, could be made to cancel each other out, like those fraction sums one used to be given at school, with the answer one of beautiful simplicity.

She said, 'I've just had the most wonderful idea.'

'What's that?'

'Antonia can come and live with my mother.'

If she expected instant enthusiasm from him, she did not get it. Hank considered this at some length before asking cautiously, 'Will she want to?'

'Of course. I told you, she loved Mumma. When she left Ibiza, Antonia didn't want her to go. And how much better, when she's only just lost her father, to have a few weeks of quiet and recovery with somebody like my mother before she starts hiking the streets of London trying to find herself a job.'

'You've got a point there.'

'And on Mumma's side, it wouldn't be like having a housekeeper, it would be like having a friend to stay. I'll suggest it today. See what she thinks. But I'm certain she won't say no. I'm almost certain she won't say no.'

Solving problems and making decisions invariably revitalised Olivia, and all at once she felt better. She sat up, pulled down the sun screen, and inspected herself in the mirror set in its back. She saw her face, still deathly pale, and there were smudges, like bruises, beneath her eyes. The dark fur of her coat collar emphasised this pallor, and she hoped that her mother would not remark upon it. She put on a bit of lipstick and combed her hair, then folded back the sun screen and turned her attention to the road ahead.

By now they had come through Burford, there were only three miles or so to go, and the way was familiar. 'We turn right, here,' she told Hank, and he swung the car into the narrow lane, signposted 'Temple Pudley,' and slowed down to a cautious crawl. The road climbed, twisting up the side of a hill, and at its summit the village came into view, nestled like a child's toy in the dip of the valley, and the silver waters of the Windrush, like a ribbon, winding by. The first houses came to meet them; golden stone cottages of great antiquity and beauty. They saw the old wool church, sheltered by yews. A man was driving a flock of sheep, and outside the pub, which was called the Sudeley Arms, cars were parked. Here, Hank drew up and turned off the engine.

Slightly surprised by this, Olivia turned to look at him. 'Are you by any chance feeling in need of a drink?' she asked him politely.

He smiled and shook his head. 'No. But I think you would prefer to have a little time with your mother alone. I'll get out here and join you later, if you'll tell me how to find her house.'

'It's the third one down the road. On the right, with a pair of white gates. But you don't have to do this.'

'I know.' He patted her hand. 'But I think it would make things easier for both of you.'

'You're very sweet,' she told him, and meant it.

'I'd like to bring something for your mother. If I suggested to the landlord that he sell me a couple of bottles of wine, would he oblige?'

'I'm sure, particularly if you tell him they're for Mrs Keeling. He'll probably flog you his most expensive claret.'

He grinned, opened the door, and got out of the car. She watched him cross the cobbled yard and disappear through the entrance of the pub, cautiously ducking his tall head beneath the lintel. When he had gone, she undid her safety belt, slid behind the driving wheel, and started up the engine. It was nearly twelve o'clock.

Penelope Keeling stood in the middle of her warm and cluttered kitchen and tried to think what she had to do next, and then decided there was nothing, because all that could be was already accomplished. She had even found time to go upstairs and change out of her working clothes and into others suitable for an unexpected luncheon party. Olivia was always so elegant, and the least one could do was to tidy oneself up a bit. With this in mind, she had put on a thick cotton brocade skirt (much loved and very old; the material had started its life as a curtain), a man's striped woollen shirt, and a sleeveless cardigan the colour of crimson peonies. Her stockings were dark and thick, her shoes heavy lace-ups. Gold chains were slung about her neck, and with her hair newly dressed and a bit of scent sprayed about her person, she felt quite festive and filled with pleasant anticipation. Olivia's visits were few and far between, which only made them all the more precious, and ever since the early-morning telephone call from London, she had been in a flurry of preparation.

But now all was ready. Fires lit in the sitting room and the dining room, drinks set out, wine opened to chambré. Here, in the kitchen, the air was filled with the scent of slowly roasting sirloin, baking onions, and crisping potatoes. She had made pastry, peeled apples, sliced beans (from the deep freeze), scraped carrots. Later, she would arrange cheeses on a board, grind the coffee, decant the thick cream she had fetched from the village dairy. Tying on an apron to protect her skirt, she washed up the few pieces of kitchen equipment that stood about, and set them in the rack on the draining board. She stowed away a saucepan or two, wiped down the table with a damp cloth, filled a jug and watered her geraniums. Then she took off her apron and hung it on its peg.

Her washing machine had stopped churning. She never did a wash unless the day was good for drying, because she had no spin dryer. She liked laundry to be hung in the open air, giving it a delicious fresh smell, and making it infinitely easier to iron. Olivia and her friend would be arriving at any moment, but she collected the big wicker basket and emptied the tangle of damp linen into this, and, with it hitched up onto her hip, she went out of the kitchen, through the conservatory, and into the garden. She crossed the lawn, went between the gap in the privet hedge and so on to the orchard. Half of this was no longer an orchard. She had created a marvellously prolific vegetable garden, but the other half stayed as it had always been, with gnarled old apple trees, and the Windrush flowing silently beyond the hawthorn hedge.

A long rope was strung between three of these trees, and here Penelope pegged out her washing. Doing this, on a bright fresh morning, was one of her deepest delights. A thrush was singing, and at her feet, thrusting through the tufty damp grass, bulbs were already beginning to shoot. She had planted these herself, thousands of them; daffodils and crocus and scylla and snowdrops. When these faded and the summer grass grew deep and green, other wild flowers raised their heads. Cowslips and cornflowers and scarlet poppies, all grown from seed that she had scattered herself.

Sheets, shirts, pillow-cases, stockings, and night-dresses flapped and danced in the thin breeze. When the basket was empty, she picked it up and made her way back to the house, but slowly, in no hurry, visiting first her vegetable garden to check that the rabbits had not been feasting on the young spring cabbage, and then back to pause by her little tree of Viburnum Fragrans, its twiggy stems smothered in deep pink blossom that smelled, miraculously, of summer. She would fetch her secateurs and clip a sprig or two, to scent the sitting room. She moved on, with every intention of going back indoors, but was diverted once more. This time by the delightful prospect of her house, set back beyond the wide, green lawn. There it stood, washed in sunshine, against a backdrop of bare-branched oak trees and a sky of the most pristine blue. Long and low it lay, whitewashed and half-timbered, with its netted thatch jutting out over the upstairs windows like thick, beetling eyebrows.

Podmore's Thatch. Olivia thought it a ridiculous name, and she felt embarrassed every time she had to say it; she had even suggested that Penelope think up some other name for the old place. But Penelope knew that you couldn't change the name of a house any more than you could change the name of a person. Besides, she had found out from the vicar that William Podmore had been the village thatcher more than two hundred years ago, and the cottage was named for him. Which settled the matter then and there.

Once, it had been two cottages, but it had been converted into one by some previous owner by the simple expedient of knocking doorways in the dividing wall. This meant that the house had two entrances, two rickety stairways, and two bathrooms. It also meant that all the rooms led into each other, which was inconvenient if you happened to crave a bit of privacy. So, downstairs were kitchen, dining room, sitting room, and then the old kitchen of the second house, which Penelope used as a garden room, and where she kept her straw hats, her rubber boots, her canvas apron, flower pots, trugs, and trowels. Over this was a cramped cell filled with all Noel's belongings, and then, in a row, three larger bedrooms. The one over the kitchen was her own.

Also, dark and fusty beneath the thatch, a loft ran the length of the roof, and this was filled with everything that Penelope could not bear to throw away when she finally departed from Oakley Street, and for which there was no space anywhere else. For five years she had promised herself that *this* winter, she would clear and sort it all out, but each time she climbed the wobbly steps and had a look around, she became disheartened by the enormity of the task and feebly put it off for a little longer.

The garden, when she came here, was a wilderness, but that had been part of the fun. She was a manic gardener and spent every spare moment of her days out of doors, clearing weeds, digging beds, barrowing great loads of manure, cutting out dead wood, planting, taking cuttings, raising seeds. Now, after five years, she was able to stand there and gloat over the fruits of her labour. And did so, forgetting Olivia, forgetting the time. She often did this. Time had lost its importance. That was one of the good things about getting old: you weren't perpetually in a hurry. All her life, Penelope had looked after other people, but now she had no one to think about but herself. There was time to stop and look, and, looking, to remember. Visions widened, like views seen from the slopes of a painfully climbed mountain, and having come so far, it seemed ridiculous not to pause and enjoy them.

Of course, age brought its other horrors. Loneliness and sickness. People were always talking about the loneliness of old age, but at sixty-four, which admittedly was not very old, Penelope relished her solitude. She had never lived alone before, and at first had found it strange, but gradually had learned to accept it as a blessing and to indulge herself in all sorts of reprehensible ways, like getting up when she felt like it, scratching herself if she itched, sitting up until two in the morning to listen to a concert. And food was another thing. All her life she had cooked for her family and friends and she was an excellent cook, but she discovered, as time went by, an underlying penchant for the most disgusting snacks. Baked beans eaten cold, with a teaspoon, out of the tin. Bottled salad cream spread over her lettuce, and a certain sort of pickle which she would have been ashamed to set on her table in the old days of Oakley Street.

Even sickness brought its own compensations. Ever since that small hiccup of a month ago, which the stupid doctors insisted on calling a heart attack, she had become, for the first time in her life, aware of her own mortality. This was not frightening, for she had never been afraid of death, but it had honed her perceptions, and reminded her sharply of what the Church calls the sins of omission. She was not a religious woman, and she did not brood on her sins, which had probably, from the Church's point of view, been legion, but she did start counting up the things that she had never done. Along with fairly impractical fantasies like trekking the mountains of Bhutan, or crossing the Syrian desert to visit the ruins of Palmyra, which she accepted now that she would never do, was the yearning desire, almost a compulsion, to go back to Porthkerris.

Forty years was too long. That long ago, at the end of the war, she had got into the train with Nancy, said goodbye to her father, and left for London. The following year the old man had died, and she had left Nancy in the care of her mother-in-law to travel to Cornwall for his funeral. After the funeral, she and Doris had spent a couple of days clearing Carn Cottage of his possessions, and then she had had to return to London and the pressing responsibilities of being a wife and mother. Since then she had never been back. She had meant to. I'll take the children for holidays, she had told herself. Take them to play on the beaches where I played, to climb the moors and look for wild flowers. But it had never happened. Why had she not gone? What had happened to the years, speeding away as they had, like swiftly flowing water pouring under a bridge? Opportunities had come and gone, but she had never grasped them, mostly because there was no time, or no money to pay for the train fares; she was too busy running the big house, coping with the lodgers, bringing up the children, coping with Ambrose.

For years she had kept Carn Cottage, refusing to sell the house, refusing to admit to herself that she would never go back. For years, through an agent, it had been let to a variety of tenants, and all this time she'd told herself that one day, sometime, she would return. She would take the children and show them the square white house on the hill with its secret high-hedged garden and the view of the bay and the lighthouse.

This went on until finally, at a time when she found herself at her lowest ebb, she heard from the agent that an elderly couple had been to see the house, and wished to buy it for their retirement. They were, as well as elderly, enormously wealthy. Penelope, struggling to keep her head above water, with three children to educate and a feckless husband to support, found herself with no alternative but to accept their massive offer, and Carn Cottage, finally, was sold.

After that, she didn't think any more about going back to Cornwall. When she sold Oakley Street, she made a few noises about going to live there, fancying herself in a granite cottage with a palm tree in the garden, but Nancy had overridden this suggestion, and perhaps, after all, it was just as well. Besides, to give Nancy her due, as soon as Penelope had set eyes on Podmore's Thatch, she knew that she didn't want to live anywhere else.

But still . . . it would be nice, just once, before she finally turned up her toes and died . . . to go back to Porthkerris again. She could stay with Doris. Perhaps Olivia would come with her.


Olivia turned the Alfasud in through the open gates, drove across the scrunching gravel, past the sagging wooden shed which did duty as garage and tool store, and drew up at the back of Podmore's Thatch. The half-glassed front door led into a tiled porch. Here hung coats and mackintoshes; a selection of hats decorated the pointed antlers of a moth-eaten stag's head, and a blue and white china umbrella stand sprouted parasols, walking-sticks, and an old golf-club or two. From the porch, she stepped straight into the kitchen, which simmered with warmth and smelt, mouth-wateringly, of roasting beef.

'Mumma?'

There was no reply. Olivia crossed the kitchen and went out into the conservatory, and at once spied Penelope at the far end of the lawn, standing as though in a trance, with an empty washing basket balanced on one hip and the fresh breeze blowing her hair into disorder.

She opened the garden door and stepped out into the chill, bright sunshine.

'Hello!'

Penelope started slightly, saw her daughter, and came at once across the grass to greet her.

'Darling.'

Olivia had not seen her since she had been ill, and now searched intently for some sign of change, fearful of finding it. But apart from the fact that her mother seemed a little thinner, she appeared to be in her normal good health, with colour in her cheeks and the usual youthful, long-legged spring in her step. She wished that she did not have to wipe the happiness from her mother's face by telling her that Cosmo was dead. It occurred to her then that people went on living until somebody told you they were dead. Perhaps it was a pity that anybody ever told anybody anything.

'Olivia, how lovely to see you.'

'What are you doing, standing there with an empty washing basket?'

'Just that. Standing and staring. What a heavenly day. Did you have a good drive?' She glanced over Olivia's shoulder. 'Where's your friend?'

'He stopped off at the pub to buy you a present.'

'He didn't need to do that.'

She stepped past Olivia and went inside, giving her shoes a cursory wipe on the mat. Olivia followed, and closed the door behind them. The conservatory was stone-floored, furnished with basket chairs and stools and a lot of faded cretonne cushions. It was very warm, leafy with greenery and pot plants, and heavy with the scent of freesias, which grew in abundance and were Penelope's favourite flower.

'He was being tactful.' She dropped her bag on the stripped-pine table. 'I've got something to tell you.'

Penelope set the washing basket down beside Olivia's bag and turned to face her daughter. Slowly, her smile faded; her beautiful dark eyes turned wary, but when she said, 'Olivia, you are as white as a ghost,' her voice was firm and strong as always.

Olivia took courage from this. She said, 'I know. I only heard this morning. It's sad news, I'm afraid. Cosmo's dead.'

'Cosmo. Cosmo Hamilton? Dead?'

'Antonia called me from Ibiza.'

'Cosmo,' she said again, her face filled with the utmost of grief and distress. 'I can scarcely believe it . . . that dear man.' She did not weep, as Olivia had known she would not. She never cried. In all her life Olivia had never seen her mother cry. But the colour had drained from her cheeks, and instinctively, as though to still a racing heart, she laid a hand on her breast. 'That dear, dear man. Oh, my darling, I am so sorry. You were so much to each other. Are you all right?'

'Are *you* all right? I've been dreading telling you.'

'Just shocked. So sudden.' Her hand went out to grope for a chair, found one. Slowly, she lowered herself into it. Olivia was alarmed. 'Mumma?'

'So silly. I feel a little odd.'

'How about a brandy?'

Penelope smiled faintly, closed her eyes. 'What a brilliant idea.'

'I'll get it.'

'It's in the –'

'I know where it is.' She dropped her bag on the table, pushed forward a stool. 'Put your feet up . . . just stay there . . . I won't be a moment.'

The brandy bottle lived in the sideboard in the dining room. She found it and carried it into the kitchen, took glasses from the cupboard, poured two large, medicinal tots. Her hand was shaking, and the bottle knocked against the glass. She spilt a little on the table top, but it didn't matter. Nothing mattered except Mumma and her dicey heart. Don't let

her have another attack. Oh, dear God, don't let her have another
attack. She picked up the two glasses and carried them back to the
conservatory.

'Here.'

She put the drink into her mother's hand. In silence, they sipped.
The neat brandy warmed and comforted. After a couple of mouthfuls,
Penelope managed a faint smile.

'Do you imagine it's one of the frailties of old age when you need a
drink as badly as that?'

'Not at all. I needed one too.'

'My poor darling.' She drank a little more. The colour was returning
to her cheeks. 'Now,' she said. 'Tell me all over again.'

Olivia did so. But there wasn't very much to tell. When she fell silent,
'You loved him, didn't you,' Penelope said, and she was not asking a
question, but stating a fact.

'Yes, I did. In that year, he became part of me. He changed me, as no
other person ever has.'

'You should have married him.'

'That's what he wanted. But I couldn't, Mumma. I couldn't.'

'I wish you had.'

'Don't wish that. I'm better as I am.'

Penelope nodded. Understanding. Accepting. 'But Antonia? What
about her? That poor child. Was she there when it happened?'

'Yes.'

'What will become of her? Will she stay in Ibiza?'

'No. She can't. The house never belonged to Cosmo. She has nowhere
to live. And her mother has remarried and lives in the North. And I
don't suppose there's much money.'

'But what will she do?'

'She's coming back to England. Next week. To London. She's going
to stay with me for a day or two. She says she'll have to get a job.'

'But she's so young. What age is she now?'

'Eighteen. Not a child any longer.'

'She was such a dear child.'

'Would you like to see her again?'

'More than anything.'

'Would you . . .' Olivia took another mouthful of the brandy. It
burned in her throat, warmed her stomach, filled her with strength and
courage. 'Would you have her here to stay with you? To live with you
for a couple of months?'

'Why do you ask that?'

'For a number of reasons. Because I think Antonia will need time to get herself pulled together and decide what she's going to do with her life. And because I have Nancy on the back of my neck telling me that the doctors say you shouldn't live alone after your heart attack.'

It was said with no prevarication, the way she had always said things to her mother, honestly, with no devious beatings about the bush. It was one of the characteristics that had rendered their relationship so satisfactory, and one of the reasons why, even in the most strained of circumstances, they never quarrelled.

'The doctors are talking rubbish,' Penelope told her robustly. The brandy had warmed her, too.

'I think they are, but Nancy doesn't, and until you do have someone here with you, then she's never going to be off the telephone. So you see, if you agreed to having Antonia to stay, you'd be doing me a good turn too. And you'd like it. Wouldn't you? That month in Ibiza, you never stopped giggling together. She'd be company for you, and you'd be able to help her through a bad time.'

But still Penelope was doubtful.

'Won't it be dreadfully dull for her? I don't lead a very exciting life, and at eighteen she may have turned into a sophisticated young lady.'

'She didn't sound sophisticated. She sounded just the way she used to. And if she craves bright lights and discos and chaps, we can always introduce her to Noel.'

Heaven forbid. But Penelope did not say this.

'When would she come?'

'She plans to arrive in London on Tuesday. I could bring her down next weekend.'

Anxiously she watched her mother, willing her to agree to the plan. Penelope, however, had fallen silent and appeared to be thinking of something quite different, for an expression of amusement came over her face, and her eyes were suddenly filled with laughter.

'What's the joke?'

'I suddenly remembered that beach where Antonia learned to windsurf. And all those bodies lying around, brown as kippered herrings, and elderly ladies with their sagging, leathery breasts. What a sight! Do you remember how we laughed?'

'I'll never forget.'

'What a happy time that was.'

'Yes. The best. Can she come?'

'Come? If she wants to, of course she can come. For as long as she likes. It will be good for me. It will make me young again.'

So, by the time Hank arrived, the crisis was over, Olivia's suggestion agreed upon, and grief and shock and sadness – for the moment – put aside. Life went on, and stimulated and comforted both by the brandy and her mother's company, Olivia felt once more able to cope. When the doorbell rang, she sprang to her feet and went through the kitchen to let Hank in. He brought with him a brown paper carrier bag, which, on being introduced to Penelope, he duly handed over. She set it on the table, and being one of those people to whom it is really worthwhile giving presents, instantly opened it. The two bottles were unwrapped from their tissue paper, and her delight was gratifying.

'Château Latour, Gran Cru! You kind man. Don't tell me you persuaded Mr Hodgkins at the Sudeley Arms to part with these?'

'Like Olivia told me, as soon as he knew who they were for, he couldn't wait to produce them.'

'I never knew he kept such a thing in his cellar. Wonders will never cease. Thank you very much indeed. We'd drink them for lunch; only I've already opened some wine . . .'

'You keep them for a celebration,' he told her.

'I'll do that.' She put them on the dresser, and Hank took off his coat. Olivia hung it with the other ratty ones in the porch, and then they all trooped through to the living room.

This was not large, and it was a constant wonder to Olivia how many of Penelope's most precious and personal possessions she had managed to cram into it. Favourite old sofas and chairs, loose-covered in mattress ticking, draped in bright Indian bed covers, and scattered with tapestry cushions. Her bureau, open as always, was stuffed with old bills and letters. Her sewing table, her lamps, her priceless rugs, laid on top of the hair-cord carpet. Books and pictures were everywhere, patterned china ewers filled with dried flowers. Photographs, ornaments, small items of silver covered every horizontal surface, and as well, strewn about were magazines, newspapers, seed catalogues, and a bundle of unfinished knitting. All the enthusiasms of her busy life were encompassed within its four walls, but, as always happened when a person first saw it, Hank's attention was immediately caught by the picture that hung over the immense open fireplace.

It measured perhaps five feet by three and dominated the room. *The Shell Seekers*. Olivia knew that she would never tire of the painting, even if she lived with it for most of her life. Its impact hit you like a gust of cold, salty air. The windy sky, racing with clouds; the sea, scudding with white caps, breaking waves hissing up onto the shore. The subtle pinks and greys of the sand; shallow pools left by the ebbing tide and shimmering with translucent reflected sunlight. And the figures of the three children, grouped to the side of the picture; two girls with straw hats and dresses bundled up, and a boy. All brown-limbed, barefoot, and intent on the contents of a small scarlet bucket.

'Hey.' He seemed, for once, lost for words. 'What a great picture.'

'Isn't it.' Penelope beamed at him, with her usual proud delight. 'My most precious possession.'

'For God's sake . . .' He searched for the signature. 'Who's it by?'

'My father. Lawrence Stern.'

'Your father was Lawrence Stern? Olivia, you never told me that.'

'I left it for my mother to tell you. She's far more knowledgeable than I am.'

'I thought he was . . . you know . . . a pre-Raphaelite.'

Penelope nodded. 'Yes, he was.'

'This is more like the work of an Impressionist.'

'I know. It's interesting, isn't it?'

'When was it done?'

'About 1927. He had a studio on the North Beach at Porthkerris, and he painted that from his studio window. It's called *The Shell Seekers* and I am the little girl on the left.'

'But why is his style so different?'

Penelope shrugged. 'A number of reasons. Any painter has to move, to change. Otherwise he wouldn't be worth his salt. Also, by then, he had started to get arthritis in his hands, and he wasn't physically able to do that very fine, detailed, meticulous work any longer.'

'What age was he then?'

'In 1927? I suppose about sixty-two. He was a very old father. He didn't marry until he was fifty-five.'

'Have you any other of his paintings?' He glanced around him, at walls crammed with pictures as though for an exhibition.

But, 'Not in here,' Penelope told him. 'Most of these were done by his colleagues. There is a pair of unfinished panels, but they're up on the landing. They were the very last work he did, and by then his arthritis was so bad he could scarcely hold the brush. Which was why he never finished them.'

'Arthritis? How cruel.'

'Yes. It was very sad. But he was enormously good about it, very philosophical. He used to say, "I've had a good run for my money," and left it at that. But it must have been dreadfully frustrating for him. Long after he had stopped painting, he still kept his studio, and when he was depressed or had what he called a Black Dog on his shoulder, he used to take himself off and go back to the studio and just sit there in the window, looking at the beach and the sea.'

'Do you remember him?' Hank asked Olivia.

She shook her head. 'No. I was born after he died. But my sister Nancy was born in his house in Porthkerris.'

'Do you still have the house down there?'

'No,' Penelope told him sadly. 'Finally, it had to be sold.'

'Do you ever go back?'

'I haven't been for forty years. But, oddly enough, just this morning, I was thinking that I really must go and see it all again.' She looked at Olivia. 'Why don't you come with me? Just for a week. We could stay with Doris.'

'Oh . . .' Taken unawares, Olivia hesitated. 'I . . . I don't know . . .'

'We could go any time . . .' Penelope bit her lip. ' . . . but how silly of me. Of course you can't make sudden snap decisions.'

'Oh, Mumma, I'm sorry, but it is a bit difficult. I'm not due for a break until the summer, and I'm meant to be going to Greece with some friends. They've got a villa and a yacht.' This was not strictly true, as the tentative plan had not yet been finalised, but holidays were so precious, and Olivia longed for the sun. As soon as the words were out, however, she was filled with guilt, because she saw the momentary disappointment cloud Penelope's face, to be instantly replaced with an understanding smile.

'Of course. I should have thought. It was just an idea. And I don't have to have company.'

'It's a long drive on your own.'

'I can perfectly easily go by train.'

'Take Lalla Friedmann. She'd love a trip to Cornwall.'

'Lalla. I never thought of her. Well, we'll see . . .' And abandoning the topic, Penelope turned to Hank. 'Now, here we are chattering away, and this poor man hasn't even got a drink. What would you like?'

Lunch was slow, leisurely, and delicious. As they consumed the delicate pink sirloin, which Hank had kindly carved, the crisp and nutty vegetables, the horseradish sauce, the Yorkshire pudding, and rich brown gravy, Penelope bombarded him with questions. About America; about his home and his wife and his children. Not, Olivia knew, as she went around the table pouring wine, because she felt she had to be polite and make conversation, but because she was genuinely interested. People were her passion, particularly if they were strangers from a foreign shore, and even more specially if they happened to be both personable and charming.

'You live in Dalton, Georgia? I can't imagine Dalton, Georgia. Do you live in an apartment, or do you have a house with a garden?'

'I have a house, and I have a garden, too, but we call it a yard.'

'I suppose, in such a climate, you can grow practically everything.'

'I'm afraid I don't know that much about it. I employ a landscaper to keep the place neat. I have to admit that I don't even cut my own grass.'

'That's good sense. Nothing to be ashamed of.'

'And you, Mrs Keeling?'

'Mumma's never had any help,' Olivia told him. 'All you see beyond the window is entirely her own creation.'

Hank was incredulous. 'I can't believe it. For one thing, there's so much of it.'

Penelope laughed. 'You mustn't look so horrified. To me it's not a tedious task, but a tremendous pleasure. However, one can't go on indefinitely, so, on Monday morning, rattle of drums, fanfare of trumpets, I am starting to employ a gardener.'

Olivia's jaw dropped. 'You are? You really are?'

'I told you I was going to look around for someone.'

'Yes, but I scarcely believed you would.'

'There's a very good firm in Pudley. Called Autogarden, which doesn't seem to me to be a very imaginative name, but that's beside the point. And they're going to send a young man out three days a week. That should get the worst of the digging done, and if he's amenable I'll get him to do other things for me as well, like sawing logs and humping coal. Anyway, we'll see how it goes. If they send a lazy lout or it costs too much, I can quite easily cancel the arrangement. Now, Hank, have another helping of beef.'

The mammoth luncheon took up most of the afternoon. When finally they rose from the table, it was nearly four o'clock. Olivia offered to do the dishes, but her mother refused to let her, and instead they all put on coats and went out into the garden for a bit of fresh air. They wandered around, inspecting things, and Hank helped Penelope to tie up a straying branch of clematis, and Olivia found a cluster of aconites beneath one of the apple trees and picked herself a tiny bunch to take back to London.

When it was time to say goodbye, Hank kissed Penelope.

'I can't thank you enough. It's been great.'

'You must come back.'

'Maybe. One day.'

'When do you return to America?'

'Tomorrow morning.'

'What a short visit. How sad. But I have so enjoyed meeting you.'

'Me too.'

He went to the car and stood holding the door open for Olivia to get in.

'Goodbye, Mumma.'

'Oh, my darling.' They embraced. 'And I'm sorry about Cosmo. But you mustn't be sad. Just be grateful that you had that time with him. No looking back over your shoulder. No regrets.'

Olivia put on a brave smile. 'No. No regrets.'

'And unless I hear to the contrary, I'll expect you next weekend. With Antonia.'

'I'll be in touch.'

'Goodbye, my darling.'

They had gone. She had gone. Olivia, in her beautiful chestnut-brown coat, with the mink collar turned up around her ears, and the little bunch of aconites clutched in her hand. Like a child. Penelope was filled with sadness for her. Your children never stopped being children. Even when they were thirty-eight and successful career women. You could bear anything for yourself, but seeing your children hurt was unendurable. Her heart went with Olivia, heading back to London; but her body, tired now and weary from the day's activities, took her slowly back indoors.

The next morning the tiredness, the lassitude were still with her. She awoke feeling depressed and could not think why, and then remembered Cosmo. It was raining, and for once she expected no guests for Sunday lunch, and so she stayed in bed until half past ten, when she got up and dressed and walked down to the village to collect her Sunday newspapers. The church bells were tolling, and a handful of people made their way beneath the lychgate for Morning Service. Not for the first time Penelope wished that she were truly religious. She believed, of course, and went to church at Christmas and Easter, because without something to believe in, life would be intolerable. But now, seeing the little procession of villagers filing up the gravel path between the ancient leaning gravestones, she thought it would be good to join them with the certainty of finding comfort. But she did not. It had never worked before and it was unlikely to work now. It was not God's fault; just something to do with her own attitude of mind.

Home again, she lit the fire and read *The Observer*, and then assembled herself a small meal of cold roast beef, an apple, and a glass of wine. She ate this at the kitchen table and then went back into the sitting room and took a little nap. Awakening, she saw that the rain had stopped, so she pulled herself off the sofa, put on her boots and her old jacket, and went out into the garden. She had pruned her roses in the autumn and fed them well with compost, but there was still some dead wood around, and she plunged into the thicket of thorns and set to work.

As always when thus employed, she lost all sense of time, and her mind was full of nothing but her roses when, straightening to ease her aching back, she was startled to see two figures coming across the grass towards her; for she had not heard a car arrive and was not expecting visitors. A girl and a man. A tall and exceptionally handsome young man, with dark hair and blue eyes, his hands in his pockets. Ambrose. Her heart missed a beat, and she told herself not to be a fool, because it wasn't Ambrose, coming at her out of the past, but her son Noel, who resembled his dead father so exactly that his unexpected appearances often gave her this uncanny turn.

Noel. With, naturally enough, a girl.

She pulled herself together, put a smile on her face, dropped her secateurs into her pocket, drew off her gloves, and edged herself out of the rose bed.

'Hello, Ma.' Reaching her side, still with his hands in his pockets, he leaned forward to give her a peck on the cheek.

'What a surprise. Where have you sprung from?'

'We've been staying in Wiltshire. Thought we'd come by to see how you're doing.' Wiltshire? Drop by from Wiltshire? They had come miles out of their way. 'This is Amabel.'

'How do you do.'

'Hello,' said Amabel, making no move to shake hands. She was tiny as a child, with seaweedy hair and round, pale green eyes like two gooseberries. She wore an enormous ankle-length tweed coat that seemed familiar, and which, after a second look, Penelope recognised as an old one of Lawrence Stern's, which had mysteriously disappeared during the move from Oakley Street.

She turned back to Noel.

'Staying in Wiltshire? Who have you been staying with?'

'Some people called Early, friends of Amabel's. But we left after lunch, and I thought that as I hadn't seen you since you were in hospital, I'd drop by and find out how you're getting on.' He beamed upon her with his most delightful smile. 'I must say, you're looking fantastic. I thought I'd find you all pale and ailing with your feet up on the sofa.'

Mention of the hospital irritated Penelope.

'Just a stupid scare. There's not a thing wrong with me. As usual, Nancy's blown a mountain out of a mole-hill, and I hate being fussed over.' And then she felt remorseful, for really it was very kind of him to come all this way just to see her. 'You're sweet to be so concerned, and I'm splendidly well. And it's lovely to see you both. What time is it? Heavens, nearly half past four. Would you like a cup of tea? Let's go in and have one. You take Amabel in, Noel. There's a good fire in the sitting room. I'll join you in a moment, when I've dealt with my boots.'

He did this, ambling away from her across the grass towards the conservatory door. She watched them go and then went indoors herself by way of the garden room, where she changed into her shoes and hung up her coat, and then went upstairs, through the empty bedrooms, to her own room, where she washed her hands and tidied her hair. Down the other stairs, and in the kitchen, she put on the kettle and laid a tray. She found some fruit cake in a tin. Noel loved fruit cake, and the girl, Amabel, looked as though she could do with a bit of feeding up. Penelope wondered if she was anorexic. It would not be surprising. Noel found himself the most extraordinary girlfriends.

She made the tea and carried the tray through to the sitting room where Amabel, who had taken off Lawrence's coat, crouched like a thin cat in the corner of the sofa, while Noel piled logs on the dying ashes in the grate. Penelope set down the tray, and Amabel said, 'What a smashing house.'

Penelope tried to warm to her. 'Yes. It's friendly, isn't it?'

The gooseberry eyes were turned on *The Shell Seekers*.

'That's a smashing picture.'

'Everybody remarks on it.'

'Is it Cornwall?'

'Yes, Porthkerris.'

'I thought so. I went there once for a holiday, but it rained all the time.'

'Oh dear.' She could think of nothing else to say and filled in the ensuing pause with the business of pouring the tea. When this was done, cups handed round, and the fruit cake cut, she started the conversation up again.

'Now. Tell me about your weekend. Was it fun?'

Yes, they told her, it had been fun. A house party of ten, and a point-to-point on the Saturday, and then dinner at someone else's house, and then a dance, and they hadn't got to bed until four o'clock.

It sounded, to Penelope, inexpressibly awful, but she said, 'How nice.'

That seemed to exhaust their news, so she started in on her own, and told them about Olivia's visit with her American friend. Amabel stifled a yawn, and Noel, perched on a low stool by the fire, with his teacup on the floor by his side and his long legs folded like jack-knives, listened politely but, Penelope felt, without too much attention. She debated telling him about Cosmo, and then decided against it. She thought about telling him that Antonia was going to come and stay at Podmore's Thatch, but decided against that, too. He had never known Cosmo, and was not much interested in the affairs of his family. He was, in truth, not much interested in anything but himself, for he resembled his father not only in looks but in character as well.

She was about to ask him about his work and how it was going, and had opened her mouth to do this, when he forestalled her by saying, 'Ma, talking of Cornwall . . .' (had they been?) ' . . . did you know that one of your father's pictures is coming under the hammer at Boothby's this week? *The Water Carriers.* Rumour has it that it'll go for something like two hundred thousand. Be interesting to see if it does.'

'Yes, I did know. Olivia mentioned it during lunch yesterday.'

'You should make a trip to London. Be in at the kill. Ought to be amusing.'

'Are you going to go?'

'If I can get away from the office.'

'It's extraordinary how fashionable those old works have become. And the prices people pay. Poor Papa would turn in his grave if he knew what they were going for.'

'Boothby's must have made a fortune out of them. Did you see their advertisement in *The Sunday Times?*'

'I haven't read *The Times* yet.'

It lay, folded, on the seat of her armchair. Noel reached for it, opened it, and finding what he looked for, turned back the pages, and handed it across. She saw, in the bottom corner, one of the regular advertisements inserted by Boothby's, the Fine Art Dealers.

'Minor Work or Major Discovery?'

Her eyes moved to the small print. Apparently two small oil paintings had come on the market, in appearance and subject matter very similar. One had fetched three hundred and forty pounds, the other over sixteen thousand.

Aware of Noel's eyes upon her, she read on.

Boothby's sales have done much to inspire the recent reappraisal of this neglected Victorian period. Our experience and advice are at the disposal of potential clients. If you have a work of this period which you would like appraised, why not telephone our expert, Mr Roy Brookner, who will be pleased to travel and offer advice, entirely free of charge.

There was the address and the telephone number and that was all.

Penelope folded the paper and laid it down. Noel waited. She raised her head and looked at him.

'Why did you want me to read this?'

'Just thought you'd be interested.'

'In having my pictures appraised?'

'Not all of them. Just the Lawrence Sterns.'

'For insurance purposes?' asked Penelope evenly.

'If you like. I don't know how much you've got them insured for now. But don't forget, the market's at its peak just now. A Millais fetched eight hundred thousand the other day.'

'I don't own a Millais.'

'You . . . wouldn't consider selling?'

'*Selling?* My father's pictures?'

'Not *The Shell Seekers*, of course. But maybe the panels?'

'They're unfinished. They're probably worth nothing.'

'That's what you think. That's why you should have them valued. Now. When you know what they're worth, you might even change your mind. After all, hanging up there on the landing, nobody sees them, and you probably never even look at them. You'd never miss them.'

'How could you possibly know whether I would miss them or not?'

He shrugged. 'Just taking a guess. It's not as though they're very good, and the subject matter is nauseous.'

'If that is how you feel about them, what a very good thing it is that you no longer have to live with them.' She turned from him. 'Amabel, my dear, I wonder if you would like another cup of tea.'

Noel knew that when his mother became frosty and dignified, she was on the verge of losing her temper, and to continue to press his point would do more harm than good and simply reinforce her stubbornness. At least he had brought the subject up, and sown the seeds of his idea. Left alone, she might well come around to his way of thinking. And so, with his most delightful smile, and one of his disconcerting about-turns, he conceded defeat.

'All right. You win. I won't talk about it any more.' He set down his cup, turned back his cuff, and looked at his watch.

'Are you pressed for time?' his mother asked him.

'We oughtn't to stay too long. We've got a long drive back to London and the traffic'll be gruesome. Ma, do you know if my squash racket's up in my room? I've got a game fixed up, and it doesn't seem to be anywhere in the flat.'

Much relieved at the change of subject, 'I don't know,' Penelope said. His small room here at Podmore's Thatch was stacked with his boxes and trunks and various pieces of sporting equipment, but as he went into it as little as possible, for he rarely spent a night in the place, she had no idea what lay amongst the muddle. 'Why don't you go and look?'

'I'll do that.' He unfolded his long legs and stood up, said, 'Shan't be a moment,' and took himself off. They heard his footsteps go up the stairs. Amabel sat there, stifling another yawn, and looking like a disconsolate mermaid.

'Have you known Noel for long?' Penelope asked, despising herself for sounding both stilted and formal.

'About three months.'

'Do you live in London?'

'My parents live in Leicestershire, but I've got a flat in London.'

'Do you have a job?'

'Only when I have to.'

'Would you like another cup of tea?'

'No, but I'd love another slice of cake.'

Penelope gave her one. Amabel ate it. Penelope wondered if she would notice if Penelope picked up a newspaper and read it. She thought how charming the young could be, and how grossly uncharming, for Amabel, it seemed, had never been taught to eat with her mouth shut.

In the end, defeated, she stopped trying, picked up the tea things, and carried them out to the kitchen, leaving Amabel looking as though she were about to fall asleep. By the time she had washed up the cups and saucers, Noel had not reappeared. Presumably he was still hunting for the elusive squash racket. Thinking that she would help him, she went up the kitchen stairs and along, through the bedrooms, to his end of the house. The door to his room stood open, but he was not inside. Puzzled, she hesitated, and then heard cautious footsteps creaking above her. The loft? What was he doing in the loft?

She looked up. The old wooden ladder led to the square aperture in the ceiling.

'Noel?'

A moment later he appeared, first long legs and then the rest of him, easing himself out of the loft and down the ladder.

'What on earth are you doing up there?'

He reached her side. There was fluff on his jacket and a bit of cobweb in his hair.

'Couldn't find the squash racket,' he told her. 'Thought it might be in the loft.'

'Of course it's not in the loft. There's nothing in the loft but a lot of old rubbish from Oakley Street.'

He laughed, dusting himself down. 'You can say that again.'

'You can't have looked properly.' She went into the cramped little bedroom, shifted some coats and a pair of cricket pads, and instantly found the squash racket hidden beneath them. 'It's here, you idiot. You were always hopeless at finding things.'

'Oh, hell. Sorry. Thanks anyway.' He took it from her. She watched him, but there was nothing devious in his expression.

She said, 'Amabel is wearing my father's coat. When did you lay your hands on that?'

Even this did not throw him. 'I nicked it during the big move. You never wore it, and it's so splendidly grand.'

'You should have asked me.'

'I know. Do you want it back?'

'Of course I don't. You keep it.' She thought of Amabel, draped in its shabby luxury. Amabel and, doubtless, countless other girls. 'I am sure you will put it to better use than I ever could.'

They found Amabel fast asleep. Noel woke her, and she struggled to her feet, yawning and bug-eyed, and he helped her into the coat, and kissed his mother goodbye, and drove Amabel away. When they had gone, she went back indoors. She closed the door and stood in the kitchen, filled with unease. What had he hoped to find in the loft? He had known perfectly well that the squash racket was not there, so what had he been looking for?

She went back to the sitting room, put a log on the fire. The *Sunday Times* lay where she had dropped it on the floor. She stooped and picked it up and read once more the Boothby's advertisement. Then she went to her desk, found scissors, carefully clipped it out, and stowed it away in one of the small drawers of her bureau.


In the middle of the night, she awoke with a dreadful start. A wind had risen; it was very dark, and it was raining again. Her windows rattled and raindrops dashed against the glass. 'I went to Cornwall, but it rained all the time,' Amabel had said. Porthkerris. She remembered the rain, driven in from the Atlantic on clouts of wind. She remembered her bedroom at Carn Cottage, lying in the darkness as she lay now, with the sound of waves breaking on the beach far below and the curtains stirring at the open windows and the beams of the lighthouse swinging their way across the white-painted walls. She remembered the garden, scented with escallonia, and the lane that led up onto the moor, and the view from the top, the spread of the bay, the brilliant blue of the sea. The sea was one of the reasons she wanted so much to go back. Gloucestershire was beautiful, but it had no sea, and she had a hunger for the sea. The past is another country, but the journey could be made. There was nothing to stop her going. Alone or in company, it didn't matter. Before it was too late, she would take the road west to that rugged claw of England where, once, she had lived, and loved and been young.

# Lawrence

She was nineteen. Between news bulletins, anxiously listened to, the radio played tunes like 'Deep Purple' and 'These Foolish Things,' and music from the last Fred Astaire and Ginger Rogers film. All summer the town had been packed with holidaymakers. Shops sprouted buckets and spades and beach balls, smelling rubbery in the hot sun, and smart ladies on holiday staying at the Castle Hotel shocked the locals by walking the streets in beach pyjamas, and sunbathing in daring two-piece bathing costumes. Most of the holidaymakers had gone now, but on the sands there were still a few about, and the tents and bathing boxes had not yet been dismantled and put away. Penelope, walking at the edge of the sea, saw the children, cared for by uniformed nannies who sat in deck-chairs and knitted, the while keeping an eye on small charges who dug sand-castles, or ran shrieking into the shallow waves.

It was a warm and sunny Sunday morning, too good to be indoors. She had asked Sophie to come with her, but Sophie had chosen to stay in the kitchen to cook the lunch, and Penelope left her slicing vegetables for a chicken casserole. And Papa, after breakfast, had put on his old wide-brimmed hat and taken himself off to his studio. From there, Penelope would collect him. Together they would walk back up the hill, to Carn Cottage and the traditional midday meal that awaited them.

'Don't let him go into the pub, my darling. Not today. Bring him straight home.'

She had promised. By the time they sat down to Sophie's cassoulet, it would all be over. By then they would know.

She had come to the end of the beach – to the rocks, and the diving board. She climbed the flight of concrete steps and came out in a narrow cobbled lane, winding downhill between the irregular, whitewashed houses. There were a lot of cats about, scavenging for fish scraps in the gutters, and seagulls soared overhead, or settled on roof-tops and chimneys to survey the world with cold yellow eyes and scream defiance at nothing in particular.

At the bottom of the hill stood the church. The bells were ringing for Morning Service, and a great many more people than usual were congregating to tread heavily up the gravel pathway and disappear into the darkness beyond the great oaken doors. Dark-suited, piously hatted, with serious faces and a solemn gait, they came from all over the town. There weren't many smiles, and nobody said good morning.

It was five to eleven. In the harbour the tide was at half ebb, and fishing boats, tied up to the wall, leaned, propped on wooden stanchions. It was all strangely deserted. Only a group of children playing with an old pilchard box, and, on the other side of the harbour, a man working on his boat. The sound of hammer blows rang across the deserted sands.

The church clock began to strike the hour, and the gulls, perched on the tower top, rose in a cloud of white wings, their voices raised in a clamour of fury at being disturbed by the reverberant bell. She went on, walking slowly, her hands in the pockets of her cardigan; sudden small gusts of breeze blowing her long dark hair in strands across her cheeks. All at once, she became aware of her solitude. No other person was about, and as she turned from the harbour and began to climb a steep street, she heard, through open windows, the final chimes of Big Ben. She heard the voice begin to speak. Imagined families indoors, gathered around their wirelesses, staying close, getting comfort from one another.

Now, she was truly in Downalong, in the old part of the town, making her way through the baffling maze of cobbled lanes and unexpected squares towards the open shores of the North Beach. She could hear the sound of breakers crashing on the shore, and felt the wind. It plucked at the skirt of her cotton dress and blew her hair into disorder. She turned the corner and saw the beach. She saw Mrs Thomas' little shop, open for an hour for the sale of newspapers. The racks outside its door were stacked with these, headlines tall and grave as tombstones. She had a few coppers in her pocket, and her stomach, knocking with apprehension, felt empty, so she went inside and bought herself, for twopence, a bar of Cadbury's peppermint chocolate.

'Out for a walk, are you, my love?' Mrs Thomas asked her.

'Yes. I'm going to fetch Papa. He's at the studio.'

'Best place to be on such a morning. Out of doors.'

'Yes.'

'Balloon's gone up, then.' She handed the bar of chocolate across the counter. 'We're at war with those dratted Germans Mr Chamberlain says.' Mrs Thomas was sixty. She had already lived through one devastating war, as had Penelope's father and millions of other innocent people all over

Europe. Mrs Thomas' husband had been killed in 1916, and her son
Stephen had already been called up as a private soldier in the Duke of
Cornwall's Light Infantry. 'Had to happen, I suppose. Couldn't go on
doing nothing. Not with those poor Poles dying like flies.'

'No.' Penelope took her chocolate.

'Love to your father then, my dear. Keeping well, is he?'

'Yes, he's well.'

'Goodbye, then.'

'Goodbye.'

Out in the street again, she felt cold. The wind was stronger now and
her thin dress and cardigan felt inadequate. She unwrapped the chocolate
and began to eat it. War. She looked up at the sky, half expecting hordes
of bombers to appear then and there, like the formations she had seen
on the newsreels, wave after wave of them, devastating Poland. But there
were only clouds, blown before the wind.

War. It was a strange word. Like Dead. The more you said it, the more
you thought about it, the more incomprehensible it became. Munching
chocolate, she went on, down the narrow cobbled lane that led to
Lawrence Stern's studio, to find him and tell him that it was time for
lunch, and that he wasn't to drop in at the pub for a beer, and that the
war, finally, had started.

His studio was an old net loft, high-ceilinged and draughty, with a
great north window facing out over the beach and the sea. Long ago, he
had put in a large pot-bellied stove, with a pipe chimney that rose to the
roof-top, but even when this was roaring, the place was never warm.

It was not warm now.

Lawrence Stern had not worked for more than ten years, but the tools
of his trade were all about, as though, at any moment, he might take
them up and start to paint again. The easels and canvases, the half-used
tubes of colour, the palettes encrusted with dried paint. The model's
chair stood on the draped dais, and a rickety table held the plaster cast
of a man's head and a pile of back numbers of *The Studio*. The smell was
deeply nostalgic, of oil paint and turpentine mingled up with the salty
wind that poured in through the open window.

She saw the wooden summer surf-boards, stacked in a corner, and a
striped bathing towel, tossed, forgotten, across a chair. She wondered if
there would be another summer; if they would ever be used again.

The door, caught by the draught, slammed shut behind her. He turned
his head. He sat sideways on the window-seat, long legs crossed, an elbow
propped on the sill. He had been watching the seabirds, the clouds, the
turquoise and azure sea, the endlessly breaking rollers.

'Papa.'

He was seventy-four. Tall and distinguished, with a deeply lined, deeply tanned face and a pair of brilliant, unfaded blue eyes. His clothes were both dashing and youthful. Faded sail-red canvas trousers, an old green corduroy jacket, and, in lieu of a necktie, a spotted handkerchief knotted at his throat. Only his hair betrayed his age, snow-white and worn unfashionably long. His hair and his hands, twisted and crippled by the arthritis which, so tragically, had put an end to his career.

'Papa.'

His gaze was sombre, as though he did not recognise her, as though she were a stranger, a messenger bearing dreaded news, which, in fact, she was. Then, abruptly, he smiled, and raised an arm in a familiar gesture of loving welcome.

'My darling.'

She went to his side. Beneath her feet the uneven wooden floor scrunched with blown sand, as though someone had spilled a bag of sugar. He drew her close.

'What are you eating?'

'Chocolate peppermint.'

'You'll ruin your appetite.'

'You always say that.' She drew away from him. 'Do you want a piece?'

He shook his head. 'No.'

She put the remains of the bar in her cardigan pocket. She said, 'The war's started.'

He nodded.

'Mrs Thomas told me.'

'I know. I knew.'

'Sophie's making a casserole. She said I wasn't to let you go to the Sliding Tackle for a drink. She said I was to bring you straight home.'

'In that case, we'd better go.'

But he did not move. She closed the windows and latched them shut. When this was done the sound of the breakers was not nearly so loud. His hat was lying on the floor. She picked it up and gave it to him, and he put it on and got to his feet. She took his arm and they started out on the long walk home.

Carn Cottage stood high on the hill above the town, a small, square white house set in a garden surrounded by high walls. Going in through the gate in the wall and shutting it behind you was like going into a secret place where nothing could reach you – not even the wind. Now, at the end of the summer, the grass was still very green, and Sophie's borders ablaze with Michaelmas daisies and snapdragons and dahlias. Up the face of the house climbed pink ivy-leaved geraniums and a clematis which each May produced a riot of pale lilac-coloured flowers. There were, in addition, a vegetable plot, hidden away behind an escallonia hedge, and, at the back of the house, a small field, with a puddle of a pond, where Sophie kept her hens and ducks.

She was in the garden, watching for them, while she picked an armful of dahlias. When she heard the gate shut, she straightened up and came to meet them, looking like a little boy in her trousers and espadrilles and her blue and white striped pullover. Her dark hair was cut very short, accentuating the slender tanned neck and the neat shape of her head. Her eyes were dark, large, and lustrous. Everyone said they were her best feature until she smiled, and after that they weren't too sure.

She was Lawrence's wife and Penelope's mother. She was French. Her father, Philippe Charlroux, and Lawrence had been contemporaries, sharing a Paris studio in the old carefree days before the 1914 war, and Lawrence had first known Sophie as a very small child, playing in the gardens of the Tuileries and sometimes accompanying her father and his friends to the cafés where they gathered to drink and harmlessly roister with the pretty girls of the city. They had all been very close, not imagining that this pleasant existence need ever cease, but the war had come, tearing not only them and their families apart, but their countries, the whole of Europe, their world.

They lost each other. By 1918 Lawrence was over fifty. Too old to be a soldier, he had spent the four terrible years driving an ambulance in France. Finally he had been wounded in the leg and invalided home. But he was alive. Others were not so lucky. Philippe, he knew, was dead. But he did not know what had become of his wife and child. When it was all over, he returned to Paris to look for them, but it was hopeless. And Paris was sad, cold, and hungry. Every other person, it seemed, wore the black of mourning, and the streets of the city, which had never failed to fill him with delight, seemed to have lost their spell. He returned to London, to the old family house in Oakley Street. By now his parents were dead and the house was his, but far too large and rambling for a single man. He solved this by occupying only the basement and the ground floor, and letting the upper rooms to any soul who needed a home and was able to pay him some rent. In the big garden at the back of his house was his studio. He opened it up, cleared out some of the accumulated rubbish, and, putting memories of war resolutely behind him, he picked up his brushes, and with them, the threads of his life.

He found it hard going. One day, as he struggled with a devilishly difficult composition, one of his lodgers came to tell him that he had a visitor. Lawrence was furious, for not only was he in a rage of frustration but he hated to be disturbed in his work. With an expression of disgust

he flung down his brushes, wiped his hands on a bit of rag, and went to
see who it could be, marching into his kitchen through the garden door.
A young girl stood there, by the stove, with her hands outstretched to
its warmth as though she were bone-cold. He did not recognise her.

'What do you want?'

She was intensely thin, with dark hair bundled into a homely knot at
the back of her head, and wearing an old threadbare coat, beneath which
the hem of her skirt hung uneven. Her shoes were broken and she
resembled nothing so much as a little waif, a down-and-out.

She said, 'Lawrence.'

Something in her voice tugged at his memory. He went to her side,
took her chin in his hand, and turned her face towards the window and
the light.

'Sophie.'

He could scarcely believe it, but, 'Yes, it's me,' she said.

She had come to England to find him. She was alone. He had been
her father's best friend. 'If anything happens to me,' Philippe had told
her, 'find Lawrence Stern and go to him. He'll help you.' And now
Philippe was dead, and her mother was dead, too, swept away in the
influenza epidemic that had raged through Europe in the aftermath of
war.

'I came to Paris to look for you,' Lawrence told her. 'Where were
you?'

'In Lyons, living with my mother's sister.'

'Why didn't you stay with her?'

'Because I wanted to find you.'

She stayed. She had arrived, he had to admit, at a fortuitous time,
when he was between mistresses, for he was a sensuous and very attractive
man, and ever since his first student days in Paris, a series of beautiful
women had passed into and through and out of his life like a well-ordered
bread queue. But Sophie was different. A child. As well, she kept house
with the efficiency of any well-brought-up French girl, cooking and
shopping and mending and washing curtains and scrubbing floors. He
had never been so well cared for. For her part, she soon lost her waif-like
appearance, and although she never put on an ounce of weight, a colour
bloomed in her cheeks, her hair took on a chestnut shine, and soon he
was using her as his model. She brought him luck. He was painting well,
and selling too. He gave her some money to buy herself something to
wear, and she came back preening and proud in the cheap little dress.
She was beautiful, and it was then that he stopped thinking of her as a
child. She was a woman, and it was as a woman that she came to him
one night, and climbed composedly into the bed beside him. She had a

charming body and he did not turn her away, for he was, perhaps for the
first time in his life, in love. She became his mistress. Within weeks, she
was pregnant. In high delight, Lawrence married her.

It was during her pregnancy that they first travelled to Cornwall. They
ended up in Porthkerris, which had already been discovered by painters
from all over the country, and where many of Lawrence's contemporaries
had settled. The first thing they did was to rent the net loft that was to
become his studio, and here, for two long winter months, they lived,
camping in fearful discomfort and total happiness. Then Carn Cottage
came on the market, and Lawrence, with a good commission under his
belt, put in an offer and bought the place. Penelope was born at Carn
Cottage and they spent every summer there, but when the gales of the
autumn equinox began to blow, they either closed Carn Cottage, or
rented it to winter tenants, and returned to London, to the basement of
the warm, friendly, crowded old house in Oakley Street. These journeys
were always made by car, for by now Lawrence was the proud possessor
of a massive 4½-litre Bentley tourer, with a canvas hood that folded down
and huge Lucas headlamps. It had a running board, which was good for
picnics, and great leather straps to buckle down the bonnet. Some years,
in the spring, they would gather up Lawrence's sister Ethel, along with
a number of bags and boxes, and take the ferry to France, and then drive
down to the mimosa trees and red rocks and blue seas of the Mediterranean
to stay with Charles and Chantal Rainier, old friends from the pre-war
days in Paris, who owned a faded, shuttered villa with a garden full of
cicadas and lizards. On these occasions, they spoke only French, including
Aunt Ethel, who always became immensely Gallic the moment they hit
Calais, sporting a Basque beret, worn at a rakish angle, and smoking
innumerable Gauloise cigarettes. Everywhere the grown-ups went, Penelope went too, the child of a mother young as a sister, and a father old
enough to be her grandparent.

She thought they were perfect. Sometimes, invited to other children's
homes, sitting through prim and formal meals with grim nannies making
sure of your table manners, or being forced to play team games by some
beefy father, she wondered how they could endure their restricted,
disciplined lives, and could not wait to get home.

Now, Sophie did not say anything about the new war that had started.
She simply came to kiss her husband, put her arm around her daughter,
and showed them the flowers she had picked. Dahlias. A great explosion
of them, in orange and purple and scarlet and yellow.

'I think,' she told them, 'they make me think of the Russian Ballet.'
She had never lost her charming accent. 'But they have no scent.'
She smiled. 'No matter. I thought you might be late. I'm glad you're

not. Let's go and open a bottle of wine, and then have something to eat.'

Two days later, on the Tuesday, their war started in earnest. The front-door bell rang, and Penelope, going to answer it, found Miss Pawson on the doorstep. Miss Pawson was one of those very masculine ladies who turned up in Porthkerris from time to time. The misfits of the thirties, Lawrence called them, who, undesirous of the normal joys of husband, home, and children, earned their livings in a number of ways, usually associated with animals, and taught riding, or ran kennels, or photographed other people's dogs. Miss Pawson bred King Charles spaniels and was a well-known sight, exercising these creatures on the beach, or being dragged through the town by them on their multiple leash.

Miss Pawson lived with Miss Preedy, a demure lady who taught dancing. Not folk-dancing, nor ballet, but some strange new conception of the art, based on Greek friezes, deep breathing, and eurhythmics. Every now and again, she held a Display in the Town Hall, and once Sophie had bought tickets, and they had all dutifully gone. It was an eye-opener. Miss Preedy and five of her students (some very young, others old enough to know better) walked onto the stage barefoot, and wearing orange knee-length tunics and head bands, low on their foreheads. They arranged themselves in a semicircle, and Miss Preedy stepped forward. Speaking in a high, clear voice to reach those at the back of the hall, she told them that perhaps a little explanation was necessary, and went on to give them this. It seemed that her method was not *dancing* in the accepted sense of the word, but a series of exercises and movements that were in themselves an extenuation of the body's natural functions.

Lawrence muttered, 'Dear God,' and Penelope had to dig him in the ribs with her elbow to keep him quiet.

Miss Preedy burbled on for a bit and then stepped back into her place and the fun began. She clapped her hands, gave the order 'One,' and she and her students all lay down on their backs as though stunned or dead. The mesmerised audience had to crane its neck in order to see them. Then, 'Two,' and they all very slowly raised their legs in the air, toes pointing to the ceiling. The orange tunics fell away, revealing six pairs of voluminous matching bloomers, caught at the knee with elastic. Lawrence began to cough, sprang to his feet and disappeared, like a dose of salts, up the aisle and out through the doors at the back. He did not return, and Sophie and Penelope were left to sit through the next two hours, convulsed with suppressed laughter, their seats shaking, their hands clamped to their mouths.

When she was sixteen, Penelope had read *The Well of Loneliness*. After that she looked at Miss Pawson and Miss Preedy with new eyes, but still remained innocently baffled by their relationship.

And now here was Miss Pawson at the door, in her stout shoes, her trousers, her zip-up jacket, her collar and tie, and a beret on her cropped grey head, pulled down sideways at a cocky angle. She carried a clipboard with papers, and her gas mask was slung over one shoulder. She was obviously dressed for battle and, given a rifle and a belt of bullets, would have been an asset to any self-respecting band of guerrillas.

'Good morning, Miss Pawson.'

'Is your mother in, dear? I've come to see about billeting evacuees.'

Sophie appeared and they led Miss Pawson into the sitting room. As this was so obviously an official occasion, the three of them sat at the table in the middle of the room, and Miss Pawson unscrewed her fountain pen.

'Now.' No beating about the bush; it was urgent as a Conference of War. 'How many rooms have you got?'

Sophie looked a little surprised. Miss Pawson and Miss Preedy had been several times to Carn Cottage, and knew perfectly well how many rooms there were. But she was so enjoying herself that it would have been churlish to spoil the fun, and Sophie told her, 'Four. This room and the dining room, and Lawrence's study and the kitchen.'

Miss Pawson wrote 'four' in the relevant box of her form.

'And upstairs?'

'Our bedroom, and Penelope's bedroom, and the guest room and the bathroom.'

'Guest room?'

'I don't want anybody living in the guest room, because Lawrence's sister Ethel is quite elderly and alone in London, and if the bombs start, then she may want to come and live with us.'

'I see. Now, lavatories.'

'Oh yes,' Sophie assured her, 'we've got a lavatory. In the bathroom.'

'Only one lavatory?'

'There's an outside one, in the yard at the back of the kitchen, but we use it as a log store.'

Miss Pawson wrote, 'One lavatory, one privy.'

'Now, how about the attics?'

'Attics?'

'How many bods could you sleep up there?'

Sophie was horrified. 'I wouldn't put anybody in the attics. They're dark and full of spiders.' And then added, doubtfully, 'I suppose in the old days, the maids *did* use to sleep there. Poor things.'

This was enough for Miss Pawson.

'In that case, I'll put you down for three in the attic. Can't be too choosy these days, you know. Mustn't forget there's a war on.'

'Have we got to have evacuees?'

'Oh yes, everybody has to. All got to do our bit.'

'Who will they be?'

'Probably East Enders from London. I'll try to get you a mother and a couple of kids. Well . . .' She gathered her papers up and got to her feet. 'I must be on my way. I've got a dozen or more visits to make.'

She took herself off, still grim and tight-lipped. When she said goodbye, Penelope half expected her to salute — but she didn't, just strode away down the garden. Sophie closed the door and turned to face her daughter, torn between laughter and dismay. Three people living in the attic. They went upstairs to inspect this gloomy loft, and it was even worse than they remembered. Dark, dirty, and dusty, full of cobwebs and smelling of mice and sweaty shoes. Sophie screwed up her nose and tried to open one of the dormer windows, but it was stuck fast. Old wall paper, in a hideous pattern, peeled from the ceiling. Penelope reached up and took the dangling corner and tore it loose. It fell to the floor in coils, bringing with it a cloud of plaster dust.

She said, 'If we painted it all white, it mightn't be so bad.' She went to the other window, rubbed a bit of glass clean, and looked out. 'And there's the most marvellous view . . .'

'Evacuees won't want to look at the view.'

'How do you know? Oh, come on, Sophie, don't be so despondent. If they come, they've got to have a bedroom. It's this or nothing.'

It was her first bit of War Work. She stripped the wallpaper and whitewashed walls and ceiling, washed the windows, painted the woodwork, and scrubbed the floor. Sophie, meanwhile, took herself off to an auction sale where she bought a carpet, three divan beds, a mahogany wardrobe and chest of drawers, four pairs of curtains, an etching entitled *Off Valparaiso* and a statuette of a girl with a beach-ball. For all this she paid eight pounds, fourteen shillings, and ninepence. The furniture was delivered and humped up the stairs by a kindly man in a cloth cap and a long white apron. Sophie gave him a tankard of beer and half a crown and he went away happy, and then she and Penelope made up the beds and hung the curtains, and after that there was nothing to do but wait — hoping against hope that they would not come — for the evacuees.

They came. A young mother and two small boys. Doris Potter, Ronald and Clark. Doris was a blonde, with a Ginger Rogers hair-style and a tight black skirt. Her husband was called Bert, and had already been called up and was in France with the Expeditionary Force. Her sons, aged

seven and six, were called Ronald and Clark after Ronald Colman and
Clark Gable. They were under-sized and skinny and pale, with knobbly
knees and rough dry hair that stuck up on end like the bristles of a brush.
They had all come, in a train, from Hackney. They had never been
farther than Southend before, and the children wore luggage labels tied
to their skimpy jackets, in case they got lost on the journey.

The peaceful pattern of life at Carn Cottage was shattered by the
arrival of the Potters. Within two days, Ronald and Clark had broken a
window, wet their beds, picked all the flowers in Sophie's border, eaten
unripe apples and been sick, and set fire to the tool shed, which burned
to the ground.

Lawrence was philosophical about this last, merely remarking that it
was a pity they hadn't been inside it.

At the same time, they proved pathetically timid. They didn't like the
country, and the sea was too big, and they were frightened of cows and
hens and ducks and wood-lice. They were frightened, too, of sleeping in
the attic bedroom, but this was only because they took turns scaring each
other to death with ghost stories.

Meal times became a nightmare, not because there was any lull in
conversation, but because Ronald and Clark had never been taught the
simplest of manners. They ate with their mouths open, drank with their
mouths full, grabbed for the butter dish and knocked over the water jug,
quarrelled and hit each other, and flatly refused to eat Sophie's wholesome
vegetables and puddings.

On top of this, there was the constant noise. The simplest action was
accompanied by shrieks of joy, fury, indignation, and insult. Doris was
no better. She never addressed her children in anything but a yell.

'What do you think you're doing, you dirty little tyke? You do
that again, and I'll belt you one over the ear'ole. Look at your 'ands and
your knees. They're filthy. When did you last wash them? Dirty little
scrubber.'

Penelope, reeling from the din, realised two things. One was that
Doris, in her rough, slap-happy way, was a good mother, and fond of her
stringy little boys. The other was that she yelled at them because she had
been yelling at them all their lives, up and down the length of the
Hackney street where they had been born and bred, just as, in all
probability, Doris' mother had yelled at her. She simply didn't realise
there was any other way of doing things. And so, not surprisingly, when
Doris called for Ronald and Clark, they never answered her. Whereupon,
instead of going to search for them, she simply raised her voice another
octave and shrieked again.

At last Lawrence could bear it no longer, and told Sophie that unless the Potters quietened down a bit, he would be forced to pack a bag, leave home, and go and live in his studio. He meant it, too, and Sophie, enraged at being put in such a position, stormed into the kitchen and had it out with Doris.

'Why do you scream at zem all ze time?' When she was upset, her accent became more pronounced than usual, but now she was so angry that she sounded like a Marseilles fishwife. 'Your cheeldren are only just around ze corner. You don't have to *scream. Mon Dieu*, this is a little house, and you are driving us all *mad*.'

Doris was taken aback, but had the good sense not to be offended. She was an easy-going girl, and astute as well. She knew that, with the Sterns, she and the two boys had found a good billet. She'd heard a few nasty tales from other evacuated families, and she didn't want to be moved in with some toffee-nosed old cow who'd treat her like a servant and expect her to live in the kitchen.

'Sorry,' she said, in her careless fashion. She grinned. 'I s'pose it's just my way.'

'And your cheeldren . . .' Sophie was simmering down, but still decided to strike while the iron was hot. ' . . . must learn ze table manners. If you cannot teach them, then I will. And they must learn to do as zey are told. They will, if you speak quietly. They aren't deaf, but you will make them so if you scream.'

Doris shrugged. 'Okay,' she agreed good-naturedly. 'We'll 'ave a try. And now, 'ow about those potatoes for dinner? Want me to peel them for you?'

After that, things got better. The noise lessened, the children, badgered by Sophie and Penelope in turn, learned to say please and thank you, eat with their mouths shut, and ask for the salt and pepper. Some of this even rubbed off on Doris, who became quite dainty, crooking her little finger, and dabbing at the corner of her mouth with her napkin. Penelope took the boys to the beach and taught them to make a sandcastle, and they became so intrepid, they actually paddled. Then school started, and they were out of the house most of the day. Doris, who had thought that all soup came out of a can, began to learn a little rudimentary cooking, and helped with the housework. Things settled down. They would never be the same, but at least now they were bearable.

The rooms on the second floor of the house in Oakley Street were occupied by Peter and Elizabeth Clifford. Other tenants came and went, but they had lived there for fifteen years, during which they had become the Sterns' closest friends. Peter was now seventy. A Doctor of

Psychoanalysis, he had studied in Vienna under Freud, and ended a prestigious career as Professor in one of the big London teaching hospitals. Retired, however, he did not cease to work, but returned each year to Vienna to lecture at the University.

They had no children, and on these occasions, he had been invariably accompanied by his wife. Elizabeth, a few years younger than Peter, was, in her own way, just as brilliant. Before her marriage, she had travelled widely, studied in Germany and France, and produced a series of thoughtful, semi-political novels, articles, and essays, gems of precise and scholarly construction that had earned her a much-respected international reputation.

It was the Cliffords who first made Lawrence and Sophie aware of the sinister things going on in Germany. To them they talked long into the night, sitting over coffee and brandy, curtains drawn, their troubled voices conveying their anxiety and apprehension. But only to them. As far as the outside world was concerned, they remained intensely discreet, and kept their views to themselves. This was because many of their friends in Austria and Germany were Jewish, and their official visits to Vienna provided good cover for their own personal undercover operations.

Under the eye of the authorities, and at great personal risk to themselves, they made contacts, obtained passports, saw to travel arrangements, and lent money. Their enterprise and fortitude resulted in a number of Jewish families' getting out of the country, escaping across the guarded borders to reach the safety of England, or to travel on and settle in the United States. All arrived penniless, having been forced to abandon property, possessions, and wealth, but all, at least, were free. This dangerous work continued right up to the start of 1938, when it was made clear by the new regime that their presence was no longer welcome. Somebody had talked. They were suspect and blacklisted.

In January, at the beginning of the New Year, 1940, Lawrence and Sophie and Penelope held a family conference. With Carn Cottage now bulging, and Doris and her children established, presumably, for the duration of the war, it was agreed that there could be no question of them returning to Oakley Street. But Sophie did not want to simply abandon her London home. She had not seen it for six months, and she needed to check on the tenants, make black-out curtains for the basement, list inventories, find some person willing to dig the garden. She wanted to collect their winter clothes, for the weather had turned bitterly cold and Carn Cottage had no central heating; and she wanted to see the Cliffords.

Lawrence thought this a splendid idea. Apart from anything else, he was worried about *The Shell Seekers*, which hung over the fireplace in their bedroom. When the bombing started, as it undoubtedly would, he feared for the picture.

Sophie told him that she would take care of *The Shell Seekers*, arranging for it to be crated and duly transported to the relative safety of Porthkerris. She rang Elizabeth Clifford to tell her that they were coming. Three days later they all walked down to the station, and Penelope and Sophie got on the train. Lawrence did not. He had chosen to stay behind, to keep an eye on the little household, and to be left in the tender care of Doris, who seemed quite happy to take on this responsibility. It was the first time he and Sophie had been separated since their marriage, and Sophie was in tears as the train drew out, as though fearful that she would never see him again.

The journey seemed to take for ever. The train was icy cold, there was no restaurant car, and at Plymouth they were joined by a draft of sailors, who piled in until the carriages were packed tight, and the corridors filled with kitbags and smoking seamen and card games. Penelope found herself jammed into her corner seat by a young boy, stiff and uncomfortable in his brand-new uniform, and when the train started up again, he promptly fell asleep with his head on her shoulder. Darkness fell early, and after that you couldn't even read by the meagre, dimmed lights. To make everything worse, they were held up at Reading and finally drew into Paddington three hours late.

London, blacked out, was a mystery city. They managed, by great good chance, to find a taxi, which they shared with a couple of strangers heading in the same direction. The taxi chuntered down the dark, semi-deserted streets, and the rain poured down and it was still piercingly cold. Penelope's heart sank. Home-coming had never been like this.

But Elizabeth, warned, was ready for them, and listening for the arrival of the taxi. As they paid this off, and felt their way down the ink-dark area steps to their own basement front door, it was flung open and they were bustled inside before any illegal gleam of light could penetrate the black-out.

'Oh, my poor things, I thought you were never coming. You're so dreadfully late.'

It was a great reunion, with hugs and kisses, and explanations, and descriptions of the dreadful journey, and finally much laughter, because it was such a relief to be at last out of the cold and the darkness and the train, and home.

The big, familiar room stretched the depth of the house. The street end was the kitchen-dining room, the garden end the sitting room. Now, it was bright with light, for Elizabeth had tacked blankets at the windows in lieu of black-out curtains, and she had lit the stove; a pot of chicken soup simmered, and the kettle sang. Sophie and Penelope took off their coats and warmed their hands, and Elizabeth made a pot of tea and a stack of hot cinnamon toast. Before long, they were sitting at the table, just as they always had, eating the impromptu snack (Penelope was starving) and all talking at once, exchanging months' worth of news. Depression lifted and the tedious train journey became a thing of the past and was forgotten.

'And how is my darling Lawrence?'

'Marvellously well, but worried about his *Shell Seekers*, in case the house gets bombed and the picture destroyed. That's one of the reasons we're here, to have it crated up and take it back to Cornwall with us.' Sophie laughed. 'He doesn't seem to be bothered about the rest of his possessions.'

'And who is taking care of him?' She was told about Doris. 'Evacuees! Oh, my poor things. What an invasion for you.' She chattered on, telling them all that had happened in the last few weeks. 'I have a confession to make. The young man in the attic was called up, and moved out, and I have allowed another young couple to take his place. They are refugees from Munich. They have been in this country for a year, but had to leave their lodgings in St John's Wood, and could find nowhere else to live. They were desperate, so I suggested they come here. You must forgive my high-handedness, but their plight was desperate, and I know they will be good tenants.'

'But of course. I am so glad. How sensible of you.' Sophie smiled lovingly. Elizabeth would never falter in her brave work. 'What are they called?'

'Friedmann. Willi and Lalla. I want you to meet them. They are coming down for coffee tonight, so why don't you bring Penelope up after supper and join us? When you've settled yourselves in. Peter longs to see you both. And it will be good to talk. It will be like the old days.'

As she spoke, she radiated enthusiasm, her most endearing and infectious characteristic. She never changed. Her handsome, wrinkled face was as bright-eyed and intensely intelligent as ever; her thick, wiry grey hair bundled up into a knot at the back of her head, where it teetered uncertainly, skewered by a few black hairpins. Her clothes were unfashionable and yet dateless, her swollen-knuckled hands adorned with many rings.

'Of course we will come,' Sophie told her.

'About nine o'clock? What a treat.'

They went, and found the Friedmanns there before them, sitting around the glowing gas stove in the Cliffords' old-fashioned parlour. They

were very young, and very mannerly, springing to their feet in order to
be introduced. But, Penelope thought, they were old, too. They had
about them a sort of poverty-stricken dignity that was beyond age, and
when they smiled and said hello, their smiles did not reach their eyes.

At first all was well. A little small talk took place. They learned that
Willi Friedmann, in Munich, had studied for the law, but now earned a
living doing translations for a London publisher. Lalla taught music,
giving piano lessons. Lalla, in her strange, pale way, was beautiful, and
sat composedly, but Willi's hands were nervous; he chain smoked, and
seemed to find it hard to be still.

He had been in England for a year, but, covertly observing him,
Penelope thought that he had the appearance of a man who had only
just made it. She was filled with compassion for him, trying to imagine
his life, coping as he must with the daunting prospect of making a future
for himself in an alien country, bereft of his friends and colleagues, and
having to earn some sort of a living in an undemanding and unfulfilling
way. Also, it was likely that he was constantly bedevilled by the almost
unbearable anxiety for a family still living in Germany. She imagined a
father, a mother, brothers and sisters whose fate, even now, might well
have been sealed by a midnight summons. A ring at the bell, a knocking
at the door tearing the night apart, confirming the most horrible of fears.

Presently, Elizabeth went out to her little kitchen and fetched in a
tray with cups and hot coffee and a dish of biscuits. Peter brought out a
bottle of Cordon Bleu cognac and tiny coloured glasses. These were
dispensed. Sophie turned to Willi with her charming smile and said, 'I
am so pleased you have come to live here. I hope you will be very happy.
I am only sorry that we shan't be here too, but we must go back to
Cornwall and look after everybody there. And we will not let the
basement. If we want to come to London and see you all, it is better that
we have our own rooms to stay in. But if the bombing starts, you must
all be sure to use them as an air-raid shelter.'

It was a sensible and timely suggestion. So far, there had been no more
than the odd air-raid warning, to be followed, almost at once, by the
all-clear. But everybody was ready. London sandbagged to the hilt, the
parks dug with trenches and air-raid shelters, water tanks erected and
filled with emergency supplies. Barrage balloons floated overhead, and
all across the city the anti-aircraft guns crouched, camouflaged with
netting, and manned by troops who waited, minute by minute, hour by
hour, week by week, for the attacks to start.

A sensible and timely suggestion, but it had a shocking effect on Willi
Friedmann.

He said, 'Yes.' He abruptly tossed his brandy down and did not demur when Peter, without saying anything, refilled his glass. Willi began to talk. He was grateful to Sophie. He was grateful to Elizabeth for all her kindness. Without Elizabeth he would be homeless. Without people like Elizabeth and Peter, he and Lalla would probably be dead. Or worse . . .

Peter said, 'Oh, come now, Willi,' but Willi had started and did not seem to know how to stop. He had finished his second brandy and was far enough gone to reach for the bottle and help himself to a third. Lalla sat without moving, staring at her husband with round dark eyes that were filled with horror, but she did not try to halt him.

He talked. The flow of words became a torrent, pouring over the heads of the five mesmerised people who sat and listened to him. Penelope looked at Peter, but Peter, watchful and grave, had eyes only for the poor demented young man. Perhaps Peter knew that he needed to talk. That, sometime, it all had to spill out, and why not now, when he and his wife were warm and safe in the thickly curtained room, and with friends.

It went on and on and he told them more – things that he had seen, things that he had heard, things that had happened to his friends. After a bit Penelope did not want to listen, and longed to cover her ears with her hands and close her eyes and blot the blackened images away. But she listened just the same, and slowly was consumed by a horror and repugnance that had nothing to do with watching newsreels or listening to wireless bulletins or reading the paper. Suddenly, it became personal, and terror breathed down the back of her own neck. Man's inhumanity to man, unleashed, was an obscenity, and that obscenity was each person's own private responsibility. This, then, was the meaning of the word WAR. It wasn't just having to carry your gas mask, and do the black-out, and giggle at Miss Pawson, and paint the attic for the evacuees; but a nightmare infinitely more terrible, from which there could be no grateful awakening. It had to be endured, and this could only be done, not by running away, or putting your head under the blankets, but by picking up a sword and going to meet it.

She didn't have a sword, but the next morning, early, she walked out of the house, having told Sophie that she was going shopping. When she returned, just before lunch, and patently empty-handed, Sophie was puzzled.

'But I thought you were going shopping.'

Penelope pulled out a chair and sat in it and faced her mother over the kitchen table and told her that she had walked until she found a recruiting office, had gone inside, and signed on, for the duration of the war, with the Women's Royal Naval Service.

# Antonia

The dawn came stealthily, reluctantly. Finally, she had slept again, but awoke to a darkness growing opaque, and knew that morning was on its way. It was very quiet. Cold air flowed through the open window, and, framed by the casement, the chestnut tree raised bare branches to the grey and starless sky.

Cornwall, as it had been, still filled her mind, like a brilliant dream, but even as she lay there, the dream folded its wings and slipped away, back into the past, where, perhaps, it belonged. Ronald and Clark were little boys no longer, but grown men, gone out into the world. Their mother was not Doris Potter, but Doris Penberth, nearly seventy now, and still living in the little white house deep in the old cobbled streets of Porthkerris. Lawrence and Sophie were long gone, and the Cliffords too; and Carn Cottage was gone, and finally Oakley Street as well, which left her here, in Gloucestershire, in her own bed, in her own house, Podmore's Thatch. She was – and this was one of the occasions when the fact took her by surprise, as though the years had encapsulated themselves and played a cruel trick upon her – not nineteen, but sixty-four. Not even middle-aged, but elderly. An elderly woman with a stupid little heart flutter that had landed her in hospital. An elderly woman with three grown-up children, and a whole new cast of characters, with their attendant problems, who now inhabited her life. Nancy, Olivia, and Noel. And, of course, Antonia Hamilton, who was arriving to stay . . . when was she arriving? At the end of next week? No, at the end of this week. For this was Monday. Monday morning. Mrs Plackett came on Monday mornings, cycling from Pudley, steady as a rock on her sit-up-and-beg bicycle. And the gardener. The new gardener was starting work today, at half past eight.

This, as nothing else could do, stirred Penelope to action. She turned on her bedside light and looked at her watch. Half past seven. It was important to be up, dressed, and about before the gardener arrived, otherwise he would imagine that he had come to labour for a lazy old woman. *A lazy master makes a lazy servant.* Who had come out with that archaic proverb? Her mother-in-law, of course. Dolly Keeling. Who else? She could hear her saying it, while she ran her fingers along the edge of the mantelpiece to check for dust, or stripped the sheets off her bed, in order to be sure that the long-suffering daily made it properly. Poor Dolly. She, too, had gone, keeping up appearances until the very last moment, but leaving no sense of loss behind her. Which was sad.

Half past seven. No time to waste on memories of Dolly Keeling, whom she had never liked. Penelope got out of bed.

An hour later, she had bathed and dressed, stoked the boiler, unlocked all the doors, and eaten her breakfast. Strong coffee, a boiled egg, toast and honey. Sitting over her second cup of coffee, she listened for the sound of an approaching car. She had not before had dealings with the horticultural contractors, but she knew that they sent their men out to work in smart little green vans with AUTOGARDEN written in white capitals on their sides. She had seen them buzzing about, and very smart and efficient they looked, too. She felt a little apprehensive. She had never employed a gardener in her life, and hoped that he would be neither surly nor opinionated. She must tell him very firmly, right away, to prune nothing, to cut nothing back without her permission. She would start him off on something simple and down to earth. The hawthorn hedge at the bottom of the orchard. He could trim that down. She supposed that he was capable of using her little chain-saw. Was there enough petrol for the motor in the garage? Should she go and look, while there was still time to go and get some more?

There was not time, for at that moment these anxious speculations were abruptly interrupted by the unexpected sound of footsteps on gravel, approaching the house. Penelope set down her coffee cup and got to her feet, peering across the room and out of the window. She saw him, in the quiet, chill morning light, coming towards her. A tall young man in a khaki oilskin jacket and jeans tucked into black rubber boots. He was bareheaded, brown-haired. As she watched him, he stopped for an instant, looking about him, uncertain, perhaps, of his surroundings. She saw the set of his shoulders, the lift of his chin, the angle of his jaw. Yesterday, seeing her son Noel approach across the lawn, Penelope's heart had missed a beat, and now the same scary thing happened. She laid a hand on the table, closed her eyes. She breathed deeply. Her galloping heart settled down. She opened her eyes again. The doorbell rang.

She went through the porch to open the door. He stood there. Tall. Taller than herself. He said, 'Good morning.'

'Good morning.'

'Mrs Keeling?'

'Yes.

'I'm from Autogarden.'

He did not smile. His eyes were unblinking, blue as chips of glass, his face thin and brown, rough with the early-morning cold, the skin drawn tight across high cheek bones. A red woollen scarf was knotted at his throat, but his hands were bare.

She looked beyond him, over his shoulder. 'I was listening for a car.'

'I came on my bike. Left it at the gate. I wasn't sure if this was the house.'

'I thought Autogarden always sent their men to work in those green vans.'

'No. I bicycled.' Penelope frowned. He put a hand into his pocket. 'I've a letter from my boss.' He took it out, unfolded it. She saw the letter heading, the authentication of his identity. She was instantly embarrassed. 'I never thought for a moment you weren't genuine. I just imagined . . .'

'This is Podmore's Thatch?' He put the letter back in his pocket.

'Yes, of course it is. You'd . . . you'd better come in.'

'No. I won't disturb you. If you could just show me what you want me to do . . . show me where you keep the garden tools. Coming on the bike, I wasn't able to bring any with me.'

'Oh, never mind, I have everything.' She knew she sounded flustered, but that was because she was flustered. 'If . . . you'll just wait a moment. I'll get a coat . . .'

'That's all right.'

She went and found her coat, and her boots, and took the garage key from its hook. Outside again, she saw that he had collected his bike from the gate, and was leaning it up against the wall of the house.

'It won't be in the way there, will it?'

'No, of course not.'

She led the way across the gravel, unlocked the garage doors. He helped her open them and she turned on the light, and there was the usual confusion; her old Volvo, the three children's bicycles which she hadn't the heart to throw away, a mouldering pram, the motor mowers, a selection of rakes and hoes and spades and forks.

She edged her way through this collection, making for a decrepit chest of drawers, relic of Oakley Street, where she kept hammers and screwdrivers, rusty tins of nails, and odds and ends of garden twine. On top of this was the chain-saw.

'Can you use one of these?'

'Sure.'

'Well, we'd better see if there's some petrol.' There was, mercifully. Not much, but enough.

'What I'd really like you to do is trim up my hawthorn hedge.'

'Fine.' He shouldered the chain-saw, and took up the petrol can in his other hand. 'Just point me in the right direction.'

But she took him there, to be sure that he made no mistake, leading him around the house, across the frosty lawn, through the gap in the privet hedge, and across the orchard. The thicket of hawthorn, a tangle of thorny boughs, reared up before them. Beyond it, quietly, coldly, flowed the little river Windrush.

'You've got a lovely place here,' he observed.

'Yes. Yes, it is lovely. Now I want you to cut it down to *this* height. No lower.'

'Do you want to keep any of the trimmings for firewood?'

Penelope had not thought of this. 'Is it worth keeping?'

'Burns beautifully.'

'All right. Keep the bits you think will be of use. And make a bonfire of the rest.'

'Right.' He set down the saw and the petrol can. 'That's it, then.'

His tone was dismissive, but she refused to be dismissed. 'Are you here for the day?'

'Till four thirty, if that's all right by you. Summertime, I start at eight and finish at four.'

'What about your lunch break?'

'I take an hour. Twelve to one.'

'Well . . .' She was talking to the back of his head. 'If you want anything, I shall be in the house.'

He was squatting on his haunches, unscrewing the cap of the chain-saw with a long-fingered, capable hand. He made no reply to her remark, simply nodded. She was made to feel intrusive, in the way. She turned and made her way back up the garden, a little annoyed, and yet amused at herself for being so outfaced. In the kitchen her coffee cup, half empty, waited on the table. She took a mouthful, but it had gone cold, so she threw it down the sink.

By the time Mrs Plackett arrived, the chain-saw had been whining for half an hour, and from the bottom of the orchard, bonfire smoke spiralled into the still morning air, filling the garden with the delicious scent of burning wood.

'He's come, then,' said Mrs Plackett as she appeared through the door, for all the world like a ship in full sail. She wore, as it was wintry, her fur pixie hood, and carried her plastic bag containing working shoes and pinafore. She knew all about Penelope's decision to employ a gardener, just as she knew almost everything that went on in her employer's life. They were very good friends and kept nothing from each other. When Mrs Plackett's daughter Linda was 'caught' by the boy who worked in the Pudley garage, Mrs Keeling was the first person Mrs Plackett told. And Mrs Keeling had been a tower of strength, fiercely opposed to the notion that Linda should marry the feckless fellow, and knitting the baby a lovely white matinée coat. And in the end she had been right, because soon after the baby was born, Linda met Charlie Wheelwright, as nice a chap as Mrs Plackett had ever known, and he had married Linda and taken the little bastard on as well, and now there was another baby on the way. Things had a way of working out for the best. There was no denying that. But still, Mrs Plackett remained grateful to Mrs Keeling for her kind and practical counsel at a time of real stress.

'The gardener, you mean? Yes, he's come.'

'Saw the bonfire smoke as I cycled through the village.' She took off her fur pixie hood, unbuttoned her coat. 'But where's the van?'

'He came on his bike.'

'What's his name?'

'I didn't ask.'

'What's he like?'

'He's young, and well-spoken and very good-looking.'

'Hope they haven't sent you one of those fly-by-nights.'

'He doesn't look like a fly-by-night.'

'Oh, well.' Mrs Plackett tied on her pinafore. 'We'll just have to see.' She rubbed her swollen red hands together. 'Bitter morning, it is. Not so much cold as damp.'

'Have a cup of tea,' suggested Penelope, as she always did.

'Well, I wouldn't mind,' said Mrs Plackett, as she always did.

The morning was on its way.

Mrs Plackett, having chased the Hoover round the house, polished the brass stair rods, scrubbed the kitchen floor, dealt with a pile of ironing, and used at least half a tin of furniture polish, took herself off at a quarter to twelve, in order to be home again, in Pudley, in time to give her husband his dinner. She left behind her a house shining cleanly and smelling sweetly. Penelope glanced at the clock, and set about preparing lunch for two. A pot of home-made vegetable soup was put to heat. From the larder she fetched half a cold chicken, a crusty loaf of brown bread. There were some stewed apples in a dish, a jug of cream.

She laid the kitchen table with a checked cotton cloth. If it had been sunny, she would have laid the table in the conservatory, but the clouds hung dark and low and the day had never come to anything. She put a tumbler and a can of beer by his place. Afterwards, perhaps he would like a cup of tea. The fragrant broth began to simmer. Soon, he would come. She waited.

At ten past twelve, when he had still not appeared, she went in search of him. She found a neatly cut hedge, a smouldering bonfire, and a stack of little logs, but no sign of the gardener. She would have called him, but as she did not know his name, this was impossible. She went back to the house, beginning to wonder if, after a single morning's work, he had decided to chuck his hand in and go home, never to return. But, at the back of the house, she found his bicycle, so knew that he was still around. She walked across the gravel to the garage, and there came upon him, just inside the door, sitting on an upturned bucket, eating a dull-looking sandwich made of white bread, and apparently engrossed in what could only be *The Times* crossword.

Discovering him at last in such cramped, cold, and uncomfortable surroundings filled her with indignation.

'What on *earth* are you doing?'

He sprang to his feet, startled out of his skin by her unexpected appearance and the tone of her voice, dropping his paper and knocking over the bucket, which made a hideous clatter. His mouth was still full of sandwich, which he had to chew and swallow before he could say anything. He turned red and was obviously enormously embarrassed.

'I'm . . . having my lunch.'

'Having your *lunch*?'

'Twelve to one. You said it would be all right.'

'But not out *here*. Not sitting on a bucket in the garage. You must come into the house, and have it with me. I thought you understood that.'

'Have it with *you*?'

'What else? Don't your other employers give you your midday meal?'

'No.'

'I've never heard of anything so dreadful. How can you possibly do a day's work on a sandwich?'

'I manage.'

'Well, you don't manage with me. Throw that horrible bit of bread away, and come indoors.'

He looked nonplussed, but did as he was told, not throwing the sandwich away, to be sure, but wrapping it up in a bit of paper and stowing it in the bag of his bicycle. Then he picked up the newspaper

and stowed that away as well, retrieved the bucket and set it in its
accustomed corner. With all this done, she led him indoors. He shed his
jacket, revealing a much-mended navy-blue guernsey sweater. Then he
washed his hands, and dried them, and took his place at the table. She
set before him a big bowl of steaming soup, told him to cut bread and
help himself to butter. She took a smaller bowl for herself and settled
down beside him.

He said, 'This is really very kind of you.'

'Not kind at all. Simply the way I've always done things. No. That's
not right. Because I've never had a gardener before. But when my parents
had any person to work for them out of doors, they always joined us for
the midday meal. I think I never realised things were done differently.
I'm sorry. Perhaps the little mix-up was all my fault. I should have made
myself more clear.'

'I didn't realise.'

'No, of course you didn't. Now, tell me about yourself. What's your
name?'

'Danus Muirfield.'

'What a perfect name.'

'I thought it was quite ordinary.'

'Perfect for a gardener, I mean. Some people have names that are
exactly right for their professions. I mean, what could Charles de Gaulle
have been but the saviour of France? And poor Alger Hiss. Born with a
name like that, he simply *had* to be a spy.'

He said, 'When I was a boy, we had a rector in our church and he was
called Mr Paternoster.'

'There you are . . . that just proves my point. Where were you a boy?
Where were you brought up?'

'Edinburgh.'

'Edinburgh. You're Scottish.'

'Yes, I suppose I am.'

'What does your father do?'

'He's a lawyer. A Writer to the Signet.'

'What a lovely title. So romantic. Didn't you want to be a lawyer too?'

'For a bit I thought I might, but then . . .' He shrugged. 'I changed
my mind. Went to Horticultural College instead.'

'How old are you?'

'Twenty-four.'

She was surprised. He looked older. 'Do you like working for Autogarden?'

'It's all right. It makes for variety.'

'How long have you worked for them?'

'About six months.'

'Are you married?'

'No.'

'Where do you live?'

'In a cottage on Sawcombe's farm. Just outside Pudley.'

'Oh, I know the Sawcombes. Is it a nice house?'

'It's all right.'

'Who looks after you?'

'I look after myself.'

She thought of the horrible white bread sandwich. Imagined the cheerless cottage, with an unmade bed and washing hung around the stove to dry. She wondered if he ever made himself a proper meal.

'Were you at school in Edinburgh?' she asked him, suddenly intrigued by this young man, wanting to know what had happened to him, the circumstances and motivation that had brought him to such a humble life.

'Yes.'

'Did you go straight to Horticultural College from school?'

'No. I went out to America for a couple of years. I worked on a cattle range in Arkansas.'

'I've never been to America.'

'It's a great place.'

'Did you never think of staying there . . . for good, I mean?'

'I thought of it, but I didn't.'

'Were you in Arkansas all the time?'

'No. I travelled around. I saw a lot of the country. I spent six months in the Virgin Islands.'

'What an experience!'

He had finished his soup. She asked him if he would like more, and he said that he would, so she filled his bowl again. As he picked up his spoon, he said, 'You said you'd never had a gardener before. Have you looked after this place all by yourself?'

'Yes,' she told him with some pride. 'It was a wilderness when I came here.'

'You're obviously very knowledgeable.'

'I don't know about that.'

'Have you always lived here?'

'No. I've lived most of my life in London. But I had a big garden there, too, and before that, when I was a girl, I lived in Cornwall, and there was a garden there. I'm lucky. I've always had gardens. I can't imagine being without one.'

'Do you have a family?'

'Yes. Three children. All grown up. One married. I've two grand-children as well.'

He said, 'My sister has two children. She's married to a farmer in Perthshire.'

'Do you go back to Scotland?'

'Yes. Two or three times a year.'

'It must be very beautiful.'

'Yes,' he said. 'It is.'

After the soup, he ate most of the chicken, and all the stewed apple. He would not drink the beer, but accepted gratefully her offer of a cup of tea. When he had drunk the tea, he glanced at the clock and got to his feet. It was five minutes to one.

He said, 'I've finished the hedge. I'll bring the logs up to the house, if you'll show me where to store them. And perhaps you'd like to tell me what you want done next. And also how many days a week you need me to come.'

'I suggested three days to Autogarden, but if you work at this speed, I may only take two.'

'That's all right. It's up to you.'

'How do I pay you?'

'You pay Autogarden, and they pay me.'

'I hope they pay you well.'

'It's all right.'

He reached for his jacket and put it on. She said, 'Why didn't they give you a van to come to work in?'

'I don't drive.'

'But all young people drive nowadays. You could easily learn.'

'I didn't say I couldn't drive,' said Danus Muirfield. 'I said I didn't.'

When she had shown him where to put the logs and had set him to work again, double-trenching her vegetable plot, Penelope returned to her kitchen to wash up the lunch dishes. *I didn't say I couldn't drive. I said I didn't.* He had not accepted the can of beer. She wondered if he had been caught for drunk driving and had had his licence taken away from him. Perhaps he had killed some person, had taken the pledge, and sworn that alcohol, no more, should cross his lips. The very idea of such horror filled her with chill. And yet, a tragedy of such massive proportions was not beyond the bounds of possibility. And it would explain a lot about him . . . the tenseness in his face, the unsmiling mouth, the bright, unblinking eyes. There was something there, veneered by wariness. Some mystery. But she liked him. Oh yes, she liked him very much.

•    •    •

At nine o'clock the next evening, which was a Tuesday, Noel Keeling turned his Jaguar into Ranfurly Road, and drove down the dark, rainy street to stop outside his sister Olivia's house. He was not expected, and had prepared himself to find her out, which she usually was. She was the most social woman he knew. But, surprisingly, the lights burnt behind the drawn curtains of her sitting-room window, so he got out of the car, locked it, and went up the little path to ring the bell. A moment later, it was opened, and Olivia stood there, wearing a flame-red woollen housecoat, no make up, and her spectacles. Obviously not dressed for company. He said, 'Hello.'

'Noel.' She sounded astonished, as well she might, for he was not in the habit of dropping in on her, despite the fact that he lived only a couple of miles away. 'What are you doing?'

'Just calling. Are you busy?'

'Yes, I am. Trying to do some reading for a meeting tomorrow morning. But that doesn't matter. Come on in.'

'I've been having a drink with some friends in Putney.' He smoothed down his hair, followed her into her sitting room. As usual, it was marvellously warm, firelit, filled with flowers . . . he envied her. He had always envied her. Not just her success, but the competence with which she seemed to handle every facet of her busy life. On the low table by the fire was her brief-case, sheaves of papers, pages of proof, but she stooped to bundle these into some sort of order and remove them to her desk. He went to the fireside, ostensibly to warm his hands at the flames, but actually to cast his eye over the invitations that she had propped on the mantelpiece, and generally check on her social engagements. He saw that she had been asked to a wedding to which he had not, and also a private view at a new gallery in Walton Street.

She said, 'Have you had anything to eat?'

He turned to face her. 'A few canapes.' He pronounced it the way it was spelt, which was one of the few old family jokes that they still shared.

'Do you want something?'

'What are you offering?'

'There's the remains of a bit of quiche I had for supper. You can eat that up if you want. And biscuits and cheese.'

'That'd be great.'

'I'll get it then. Help yourself to a drink.'

He accepted this kind offer, pouring himself a stiff whisky and soda, while she disappeared through to her little kitchen beyond the dining room, turning on lights as she went. There, in a companionable fashion, he joined her, pulling a tall stool to the little counter that separated the two rooms, for all the world like a man in a pub chatting up the barmaid.

He said, 'I went and saw Ma on Sunday.'

'Did you? I saw her on Saturday.'

'She told me you'd been. With a fancy American in tow. How do you think she's looking?'

'Marvellous, considering.'

'Do you think it really was a heart attack?'

'Well, a warning anyway.' She looked at him, her mouth wry. 'Nancy's already got her buried ten feet under the daisies.' Noel laughed, shook his head. Nancy was one of the few things he and Olivia had always agreed about. 'Of course, she does too much. She's always done too much. But at least she's agreed to getting some help in the garden. That's a beginning.'

'I tried to get her to say she'd come up to London tomorrow.'

'For what reason?'

'Go to Boothby's. Watch the Lawrence Stern come under the hammer. See what it fetches.'

'Oh yes, *The Water Carriers*. I'd forgotten it was tomorrow. Did she say she would?'

'No.'

'Well, why should she? It's not as though she was going to make any money out of it.'

'No.' Noel looked down into his glass. 'But she would if she sold her own.'

'If you mean *The Shell Seekers*, think again. She'd die before letting that picture go.'

'How about the panels?'

Olivia's expression was deeply suspicious. 'Did you talk to Mumma about this?'

'Why not? They're dreadful pictures, admit it. They simply moulder away at the top of the stairs. She'd never even notice their going.'

'They're unfinished.'

'I wish everybody would stop telling me they're unfinished. My bet is that they have a rarity value that is beyond price.'

After a little, she said, 'Supposing she did agree to sell them.' Olivia took out a tray, set plates and a fork and knife upon it, a dish of butter, a wooden platter of cheese. 'Are you going to suggest what she does with the resultant loot, or are you going to leave that to her discretion?'

'The money you give away while you're alive is worth twice what you leave when you die.'

'Which means that you want to get your greedy little paws on it.'

'Not just me. All three of us. Oh, don't look so po-faced, Olivia, it's nothing to be ashamed of. These days everybody's short of capital, and don't tell me Nancy isn't mad to get her hand on a bit of extra cash. She's always drooling on about how expensive everything is.'

'You and Nancy, maybe. But you can count me out.'

Noel turned his glass. 'You wouldn't say no, though?'

'I don't want anything from Mumma. She's given us enough. I just want her to be there, well, and secure, with no money worries, and able to enjoy herself.'

'She's comfortably off. We all know that.'

'Do we? What about the future? She may live to be a very old lady.'

'All the more reason to sell those dismal nymphs. Invest the capital for her twilight years.'

'I don't want to discuss it.'

'So you don't think it's a good idea?'

Olivia did not reply to this, simply picked up the tray and bore it back to the fireside. Following her, he decided that no woman could look so straight-backed and formidable as Olivia when you were trying to do something of which she did not approve.

She set down the tray with something of a thump on the low table. Then she straightened, facing him across the room. She said, 'No.'

'Why not?'

'I think that you should leave Mumma alone.'

'All right.' With easy grace he gave in, knowing that, in the long term, this was the best way to get what he wanted. He settled himself in one of her deep armchairs, perched forward so that he could deal with his impromptu meal. Olivia moved to stand with her shoulders against the mantelpiece, her hands deep in the pockets of her gown. He felt her eyes upon him as he picked up the fork, sliced into the quiche. 'We'll forget about selling the panels. Talk about something else.'

'Like what?'

'Like, have you ever seen, or heard Ma mention, or even suspected the existence of, any rough oil sketches that Lawrence Stern would have done for all his major works?'

He had spent the day debating as to whether or not he should take Olivia into his confidence about his discovery of the old letter and its subsequent possibilities. In the end, he had decided to take the risk. Olivia was an important ally to win. Only she, of all three of them, had any influence on their mother. As he asked the question, he kept his eyes on her face, saw her expression stiffen into wariness, alert with suspicion. This was to be expected.

After a bit, she said, 'No.' This, too, was to be expected, but he knew that she was telling the truth, because she always did. 'Never.'

'You see, there must have been some.'

'What started you on this wild-goose chase?'

He told her about finding the letter.

'*The Terrazzo Garden*? That's in the Metropolitan in New York.'

'Exactly so. And if a rough oil sketch was done for *The Terrazzo Garden*, then why not for *The Water Carriers* and *The Fisherman's Courtship* and all the other old classics that are now incarcerated in boring museums in every self-respecting capital in the world.'

Olivia thought about this. Then she said, 'They were probably destroyed.'

'Oh, rubbish. The old boy never destroyed anything. You know that as well as I do. No house was ever so full of the junk of ages as Oakley Street. Unless it's Podmore's Thatch. You know, that loft of Ma's is a positive fire risk. If any insurance man saw what's been crammed up there, under the thatch, he'd have a fit.'

'Have you been up there lately?'

'Went on Sunday, to search for my squash racket.'

'Was that all you were searching for?'

'Well, I did have a look around.'

'For a folio of rough oil sketches.'

'Something like that.'

'But you didn't find them.'

'Of course not. You couldn't find an elephant in all that clutter.'

'Did Mumma know what you were looking for?'

'No.'

'You are a despicable creep, Noel. Why do you always have to do everything the back-handed way?'

'Because she's no more idea what's in that loft than she knew what was up in the attics of Oakley Street.'

'What is up there?'

'Everything. Old boxes; chests of clothes and bundles of letters. Dressmaker's dummies, toy perambulators, footstools, bags of tapestry wool, weighing machines, boxes of wooden blocks, piles of magazines tied together with string, knitting patterns, old picture frames . . . you name it, it's there. And like I said, it's all a hideous fire risk. The thatch does nothing to help. One spark on a windy day and the whole house would go up like a furnace. One simply hopes Ma will have time to fling herself from some window before she's incinerated. I say, this is a delicious quiche. Did you make it?'

'I never make anything. I buy it all from the supermarket.' She pushed herself away from the mantelpiece and crossed the room to the table behind him. He heard her pour a drink, and allowed himself a smile, because he knew that he had aroused her anxieties, and so caught her attention, and, hopefully, her sympathy. She came back to the fireside and sat on the sofa facing him, with the glass cradled in her hands.

'Noel, do you *really* think it's dangerous?'

'Yes. Honestly. Truthfully. I do.'

'What do you think we should do?'

'Clear the whole place out.'

'Mumma would never agree to that.'

'All right, then, *sort* it out. But half of the junk up there is only fit for a bonfire, like the bundles of magazines and the knitting patterns and tapestry wool . . .'

'Why the tapestry wool?'

'It's alive with moth.'

She said nothing to this. He had finished the quiche and now started in on the cheese, a particularly delicious wedge of Brie.

'Noel. You're not just blowing this all up just so that you've got a good excuse to go snooping? If you do find those rough sketches or anything else of value, remember that everything in that house belongs to Mumma.'

He met her eye, assuming an expression of blameless innocence. 'You surely don't think I'd *steal* them.'

'I wouldn't put it past you.'

He chose to ignore this. 'If we found those rough sketches, have you any idea what they're worth? At least five thousand each.'

'Why do you talk about them as if you *know* they're there?'

'I *don't* know they're there! I just suspect that they might be. But more important is that the loft is a potential fire risk and I think something should be done about it.'

'Do you think we should get the whole house reassessed for insurance while we're about it?'

'George Chamberlain looked after all that when he bought the place for Ma. Perhaps you should have a word with him. And I'm not doing anything this weekend. I'll go down on Friday evening and tackle the Herculean task. I'll give Ma a ring, tell her I'm coming.'

'Will you ask her about the sketches?'

'Do you think I should?'

Olivia did not answer at once. And then she said, 'No, don't.' He looked at her in some surprise. 'I think it might fuss her, and I don't want her fussed. If they turn up, we can tell her, and if they aren't there, it makes no difference anyway. But, Noel, you're not to say another word to her about selling her pictures. They really are nothing to do with you.'

He put his hand to his heart. 'Scout's honour.' He smiled. 'You've come around to my way of thinking.'

'You're a devious villain, and I shall never come round to your way of thinking.'

He accepted this with equanimity, finished his supper in silence, and then got to his feet and went to replenish his glass.

From behind him, she said, 'Are you really going? To Podmore's Thatch, I mean.'

'No reason not to.' He returned to his chair. 'Why?'

'You could do something for me.'

'I could?'

'Do you know who I mean by Cosmo Hamilton?'

'Cosmo Hamilton? But of course. Lover boy from sunny Spain. Don't say he's come into your life again?'

'No, he hasn't come into my life. He's gone out of it. He's dead.'

For once, Noel was truly startled and shocked. 'Dead!' Olivia's face was calm, but very pale and still, and he regretted his facetiousness. 'Oh, I am sorry. But what happened?'

'I don't know. He died in hospital.'

'When did you hear?'

'On Friday.'

'But he was a young man.'

'He was sixty.'

'What a bloody thing to happen.'

'Yes. I know. But the thing is, he has this young daughter, Antonia. She's arriving tomorrow at Heathrow from Ibiza, and she's going to stay here for a few days, and then go down to Podmore's Thatch and keep Mumma company for a bit.'

'Does Ma know?'

'Of course. We fixed it on Saturday.'

'She never said anything to me.'

'I don't suppose she did.'

'How old is this girl . . . Antonia?'

'Eighteen. I'd intended taking her myself and staying the weekend, but I've got tied up with a man . . .'

Noel, himself again, raised an eyebrow. 'Business or pleasure?'

'Purely business. A French designer, queer as a coot, staying at the Ritz, and I really want to spend some time with him.'

'So?'

'So if you are going to Gloucestershire on Friday night, you'd do me a favour if you'd drive her down with you.'

'Is she pretty?'

'Does your answer depend on it?'

'No, but I'd like to be told.'

'At thirteen, she was charming.'

'Not fat and spotty?'

'Not in the least. When Mumma came out to stay with us in Ibiza, Antonia was there at the same time. They became tremendous friends. And since Mumma was ill, Nancy drones on about the fact that she shouldn't live alone. But if Antonia's with her, she won't be alone. I thought it was rather a good idea.'

'You've got it all worked out, haven't you?'

Olivia ignored this gibe. 'Will you take her?'

'Sure, I don't mind.'

'When will you pick her up?'

Friday evening . . . he considered . . . 'Six o'clock.'

'I'll make a point of being back from the office. And, Noel . . .' Suddenly she smiled. She had not smiled all evening, but she smiled now, and for an instant there was a fondness between them, a companionship. They might have been any affectionate brother and sister who had just spent a pleasant hour together. ' . . . I'm grateful.'


The next morning, from the office, Olivia rang Penelope.

'Mumma.'

'Olivia.'

'Mumma, look, I've had to change my plans. I can't come down this weekend after all, I've got to do some business with a poncy Frenchman, and Saturday and Sunday are the only days he seems to be able to give me. I'm terribly sorry.'

'But what about Antonia?'

'Noel's bringing her down. He hasn't phoned you yet?'

'Not a word.'

'He will. He's coming down on Friday, and staying for a couple of days. We had a long family conference last night and decided you simply must have that loft of yours cleared out before the whole place goes up in smoke; I hadn't realised it was such a squirrel hoard. You are a naughty old thing.'

'A family conference?' Penelope sounded surprised, as indeed she was. 'You and Noel?'

'Yes, he dropped in yesterday evening and I gave him supper. He told me he'd been up to the loft to look for something, and that there's so much junk up there, it's a real fire risk. So we agreed that he should come down and clear it out. Don't worry, we're not really being overbearing, just concerned, and he's promised he won't throw anything away or burn it without your consent. I think it's rather kind of him. And he actually volunteered to do the job, so don't go all stuffy and say we're treating you like an idiot.'

'I'm not being stuffy at all, and I think it's rather kind of Noel, too. I've been meaning to tidy it up myself, every winter for the past five years, but it's such a task, it was never difficult to find an excuse not to do it. Do you think Noel can manage on his own?'

'Antonia'll be there. She'd probably rather enjoy it. But don't *you* go humping anything.'

Penelope was struck by a bright idea. 'I could ask Danus to come for the day. Another pair of strong arms wouldn't come amiss, and he could be in charge of the bonfire.'

'Who's Danus?'

'My new gardener.'

'I forgot about him. What's he like?'

'A dear man. Has Antonia arrived yet?'

'No. I meet her off the plane this evening.'

'Send her my love and say I can't wait to see her.'

'I'll do that. And she and Noel will be with you on Friday evening, in time for dinner. I'm just sorry I'm not going to be there too.'

'I shall miss you. But another time.'

''Bye then, Mumma.'

'Goodbye, my darling.'


In the evening, Noel rang.

'Ma.'

'Noel.'

'How are you?'

'I'm splendid. I hear you're coming down for the weekend.'

'Olivia's spoken to you?'

'This morning.'

'She says I've got to come and empty the loft. She says she's having nightmares about you going up in smoke.'

'I know, she told me. I think it's a good idea, and very kind of you.'

'Well, that's a turn-up for the books; we thought you'd be livid.'

'Then you thought wrong,' Penelope retorted, a little weary of this new image of herself as a pigheaded, unco-operative old lady. 'And I shall get Danus in for the day to help you. He's my new gardener, and I'm sure he won't mind. And he's terribly good at lighting bonfires.'

Noel hesitated and then said, 'Great.'

'And you're bringing Antonia with you. I'll expect you then, on Friday evening. And don't drive too fast.'

She was about to put the receiver down and cut him off, but he sensed this, and yelled 'Ma!' and she put it to her ear again.

'I thought we'd finished.'

'I wanted to tell you about the sale. I went along to Boothby's this afternoon. How much do you think *The Water Carriers* went for?'

'I've no idea.'

'Two hundred and forty-five thousand, eight hundred pounds.'

'Dear heaven. Who bought it?'

'An American art gallery. Denver, Colorado, I think.'

She shook her head in wonder, as though he could see her.

'What a sum of money.'

'Makes you sick, doesn't it?'

'It certainly,' she told him, 'makes you think.'

Thursday. By the time Penelope had got herself out of bed and downstairs, the gardener was already at work. She had given him a key to the garage, so that he could gain access to the garden tools, and from her bedroom window he could be observed toiling in the vegetable garden. She did not disturb him, because, during that first day, she had been made to realise that he was not only hard-working, but a private sort of person, and would not relish her constantly appearing to give him the time of day, check on his activities, and generally make a nuisance of herself. If he needed anything, then he would come and ask her. If not, then he would simply get on with his task.

But still, at a quarter to twelve, with the sketchy housework accomplished, and a batch of bread proving on the Aga, she untied her apron and went down the garden to have a word, and remind him that she was expecting him, indoors, for lunch. It was warmer today, and there was quite a lot of blue sky. Not much heat in the sun, but still, she would lay the table in the conservatory, and they would eat their meal out there.

'Good morning.'

He looked up and saw her, and straightened his back, leaning on the spade. The still morning air was filled with robust and heartening smells; freshly turned earth and the rotted compost mixed with a quantity of horse manure, which he had borrowed from her carefully nurtured heap.

'Good morning, Mrs Keeling.'

He had shed his jacket and sweater and worked in his shirt sleeves. His forearms were brown and knotted with lean muscle. As she watched him, he put up a hand and wiped a smear of mud from his chin with his wrist. The gesture caused a piercing sensation of déjà vu, but now she was prepared for this, and it did not cause her heart to hiccup, but simply filled her with pleasure.

'You look warm,' she told him.

He nodded. 'It's warm work.'

'Lunch will be ready at twelve.'

'Thank you. I'll be in.'

He went back to his digging. A robin was hovering around, as much, Penelope guessed, for company as for worms. Robins were delightfully gregarious. She turned and left him to his labours, and made her way back to the house, picking a bunch of early polyanthus on the way. The flowers were velvety and richly scented, and brought to mind the pale primroses of Cornwall, studding the sheltered hedgerows at a time when the rest of the country was in the grip of winter.

I must go soon, she told herself. Spring in Cornwall is such a magical time. I must go soon, otherwise it will be too late.


She said, 'Danus, what do you do on weekends?'

Today she was giving him cold ham and baked potatoes and cauliflower cheese. For pudding, there were jam tarts and a baked egg custard. Not a snack, but a proper meal, and she sat and ate it with him, and wondered if, at this rate, she would become enormously stout.

'Nothing much.'

'I mean, do you work for anybody at weekends?'

'I sometimes give a Saturday morning to the Pudley Bank Manager. He'd rather play golf than garden and his wife complains about the weeds.'

Penelope smiled. 'Poor man. What about Sunday?'

'My Sundays are free.'

'Would you come here for the day . . . as a job, I mean. I'll pay you, I won't pay Autogarden, and that's quite fair, because it isn't gardening I want you to do.'

He looked a little surprised, as well he might.

'What is it you want me to do?'

She told him about Noel and the attic. 'There is such a lot of rubbish up there, I know, and it'll all have to be humped downstairs and sorted out. He can't possibly do it all by himself. I thought if you could be here to give him a hand, it really would be a help.'

'Of course I'll come. But as a favour. You don't need to pay me.'

'But –'

'No,' he said firmly. 'I don't want to be paid. What time shall I be here?'

'About nine in the morning.'

'Fine.'

'Quite a little party for lunch. I have a young girl coming to stay for a few weeks. Noel's bringing her with him tomorrow evening. She's called Antonia.'

'That'll be nice for you,' said Danus.

'Yes.'

'A bit of company.'


Nancy was not a great one for reading newspapers. If she had to go to the village to shop, which she did most mornings, because there was a singular lack of communication between herself and Mrs Croftway, and they always seemed to be running out of butter or instant coffee, or gravy browning, then she usually dropped in at the newsagents and bought herself a *Daily Mail* or a copy of *Woman's Own* to peruse over the sandwich and chocolate biscuit that comprised her lunch, but *The Times* did not enter the house until the evening, brought home by George in his brief-case.

Thursday was Mrs Croftway's day off, which meant that Nancy was in the kitchen when George returned from work. They were having fish cakes for dinner, which Mrs Croftway had already concocted, but Croftway had brought in a basket of his horrible, overgrown, bitter Brussels sprouts, and Nancy stood at the sink, preparing these, hating the task and fairly sure that the children would refuse to eat them, as the sound of the car came up the drive. After a moment or two the back door opened and shut and her husband joined her, looking worn and insubstantial in his sober clothes. She hoped that he had not had a tiresome day. When he had a tiresome day, he was inclined to take it out on her.

She looked up, and smiled firmly. George so seldom looked cheerful that it was important not to be depressed by his gloom, and to keep up the illusion – even if only she was taken in by it – of an affectionate and companionable relationship.

'Hello, darling. Had a good day?'

'All right.'

He dumped his brief-case on the table, and from it withdrew *The Times*. 'Have a look at this.'

Nancy was amazed by such forthcoming-ness. Most evenings he simply grunted and took himself off to the library for a quiet hour or so before dinner. Something riveting must have happened. She hoped it was not an atomic bomb. She abandoned the sprouts, dried her hands, and went to stand beside him. He spread the paper out on the table, turned to the Arts page, and pointed, with a long pale forefinger, to a specific column.

She peered hopelessly at the blur of print. She said, 'I haven't got my glasses.'

He sighed, resigned to her incompetence. 'The sale-room news, Nancy. Your grandfather's picture was sold yesterday at Boothby's.'

'Was it yesterday?' She had not forgotten about *The Water Carriers*. On the contrary, the conversation she had had with Olivia over lunch at Kettners had occupied her thoughts ever since, but so obsessed had she been with the probable value of the painting that still hung at Podmore's Thatch, that she had lost track of the days. She had never been very good at remembering dates.

'Do you know what it fetched?' Nancy, open-mouthed, shook her head. 'Two hundred and forty-five thousand, eight hundred pounds.'

He spoke the magic words in measured tones, so that there was no possible chance of her mishearing him. Nancy felt quite faint. She laid her hand on the kitchen table in order to steady herself and continued to goggle at him.

'Bought by some American. Sickening the way anything of value always has to go out of the country.'

She found her voice at last. 'And it was a terrible picture,' she told him.

George smiled chillily, and without a touch of humour. 'Fortunately, for Boothby's and for the previous owner, not everybody is of your opinion.'

But Nancy scarcely registered this dig. She said, 'So Olivia wasn't far wrong.'

'What does that mean?'

'We talked about it, that day we had lunch at Kettners. She guessed it would bring in something like that.' She looked at George. 'And she guessed that *The Shell Seekers*, and the other two pictures Mother still has, are probably worth half a million. Perhaps she was right about that as well.'

George said, 'No doubt. Our Olivia is scarcely ever wrong about anything. The sort of circles she moves in, she can keep that long nose of hers very close to the ground.'

Nancy reached for a chair and took the weight off her legs. She said, 'George, do you suppose Mother realises what they're worth?'

'I shouldn't suppose so.' He pursed his lips. 'I'd better have a word. We should get the insurance premiums bumped up. Any person could walk into that house and simply lift them off the walls. As far as I can see, she's never locked a door in her life.'

Nancy began to feel excited. She had not previously told George of her conversation with Olivia because George did not like her sister, and was patently disinterested in anything that she might have to say. But now that George had brought the subject up himself, it made everything much simpler.

She said, striking while the iron was hot, 'Perhaps we should go and see Mother. Talk things over.'

'The insurance, you mean?'

'If the premiums go up too much, she may . . .' Nancy's voice went rough. She cleared her throat. ' . . . she may decide that it's simpler to sell them. Olivia said the market's at its peak just now for these old Victorian works . . .' (that sounded marvellously sophisticated and knowledgeable, and Nancy felt quite proud of herself) ' . . . and it would be a pity to miss the opportunity.'

For once George seemed to be considering her point of view. He pursed his lips, read the paragraph once more, and then neatly, precisely, folded up the paper.

He said, 'It's up to you.'

'Oh, George. Half a million. I can hardly imagine so much money.'

'There'd be taxes, of course, to pay.'

'But even so! We must go. Anyway, I haven't been to see her for far too long. It's time I checked up on how things are going with her. And then I can bring up the subject. Tactfully.' George looked doubtful. They both knew that tact was not Nancy's strongest point. 'I'll go right away and give her a ring.'


'Mother.'

'Nancy.'

'How are you?'

'Very well. And you?'

'Not doing too much?'

'Are you referring to me or you?'

'You, of course. Has the gardener started work?'

'Yes, he came on Monday, and again today.'

'I hope he's satisfactory.'

'Well, he satisfies me.'

'And have you thought any more about having someone to live with you? I put an advertisement in our local paper, but I haven't had any replies, I'm afraid. Not so much as a phone call.'

'Oh, you don't need to worry about that any more. Antonia's coming tomorrow evening, she's going to stay with me for a bit.'

'Antonia? Who's Antonia?'

'Antonia Hamilton. Oh dear, I suppose we've all forgotten to tell you. I thought Olivia might have given you the news.'

'No,' Nancy told her frostily. 'Nobody's told me anything.'

'Well, that nice friend of Olivia's, the one she lived with when she was in Ibiza, it was so dreadfully sad; he died. And so his daughter's going to come here for a bit just to pull herself together and give herself time to decide what she's going to do next.'

Nancy was enraged. 'Well, I must say, I do think somebody might have let me know. I wouldn't have taken the trouble to put the advertisement in, if I'd known.'

'I'm so sorry, darling, but somehow with one thing and another, I've been so busy and I forgot. But anyway, it means that you don't need to worry about me any longer.'

'But Mother, what sort of a girl is she?'

'I think, probably, very sweet.'

'How old?'

'Only eighteen. She'll be splendid company for me.'

'When is she arriving?'

'I told you. Tomorrow evening. Noel's bringing her down from London. He's going to spend the weekend and clear out the attic. He and Olivia have decided that it's a fire risk.' There was a pause in the conversation, and then she went on, 'Why don't you all come over and join us for lunch on Sunday? Bring the children. And then you can see Noel and meet Antonia.'

And bring up the subject of the pictures.

'Oh . . .' Nancy hesitated. ' . . . I think that would be all right. Just wait a moment, till I have a word with George . . .'

She left the receiver dangling and went in search of her husband. She did not have to search far. She found him, as she knew she would, deep in his armchair, concealed by *The Times*.

'George.' He lowered the paper. 'She's asked us all for lunch on Sunday.' She hissed this in a whisper, as though her mother could overhear, although the telephone was far out of earshot.

'I can't go,' said George instantly. 'I have a Diocesan luncheon and meeting I have to attend.'

'In that case, I'll take the children.'

'I thought the children were spending the day with the Wainwrights . . .'

'So they are. I'd forgotten. Well, I'd better just go by myself.'

'It seems,' said George, 'that you had.'

Nancy returned to the telephone.

'Mother?'

'Yes, I'm still here.'

'George and the children seem to be otherwise engaged on Sunday, but I'd love to come over if it's all right by you.'

'On your own?' (Did Mother sound a little relieved? Nancy put the notion from her head.) 'What a treat. Come about twelve and we can have a chat. I'll see you then.'

Nancy replaced the receiver and went to tell George of the arrangement. She also told him, at some length, of the thoughtlessness and high-handedness of Olivia, who had found, with no difficulty at all, a companion for their mother, and had not even bothered to let Nancy know of the arrangement.

' . . . and she's only eighteen. Probably some little flibbertigibbet who'll lie in bed all day and expect to be waited on. Making more work for Mother. You would think, wouldn't you, George, that Olivia *might* have let me know. At least talked it over. After all, I have taken on the responsibility of keeping an eye on Mother, and yet none of them ever even considers me. It does seem incredibly thoughtless . . . George?'

But George had switched off; stopped listening. Nancy sighed and left him, returning to the kitchen to work off her resentments on what remained of the Brussels sprouts.


Noel and Antonia did not arrive from London until nearly a quarter past nine in the evening, by which time Penelope had them both dead in a twisted mass of metal (the Jaguar) by the side of the motorway. It was a night of black rain, and she kept going to the kitchen window to peer hopefully through it in the general direction of the gate, and was just beginning to contemplate ringing the police, when she heard the sound of the car engine racing down the road from the village, slowing up, changing gear, and turning – thank you, God – through the gates to draw up at the back door.

She took a second to compose herself. Nothing put Noel in a worse mood than to be fussed over, and after all, if they had not left London until six or after, it had been stupid to allow herself to get into such a state. She shed her anxieties, put a calm and smiling expression on her face, and went to turn on the outside light and open the door.

She saw the long, racy, slightly battered shape of Noel's car. He was already climbing out of it, and going to open the other door. Out of this emerged Antonia, lugging some sort of haversack behind her. She heard Noel say, 'You'd better run for cover,' and Antonia did just that, with her head down against the rain, scuttling for the shelter of the porch and straight into Penelope's waiting arms.

She dropped the haversack on the doormat and they hugged, holding each other very tight, Penelope filled with relief and affection, and Antonia simply thankful to be here at last, safe and in the arms of just about the only person whom, at the moment, she wanted to be with.

'Antonia.' They drew apart, but Penelope still held her arm, drawing her through the inner door, away from the dark, cold, wet night, and into the warmth of the kitchen. 'Oh, I thought you were never going to get here.'

'So did I.'

She looked the same, much as she had looked at thirteen. Taller, of course, but just as slender . . . she had a beautiful long-legged figure . . . and her face had grown to her mouth, but otherwise nothing much seemed to have changed. Still the freckles on her nose, the slanting, greenish eyes, the long, thick, fair eyelashes. Still the red-gold hair, shoulder-length, heavy and straight. Still, even, the same sort of clothes; blue jeans, and a white sweat shirt with a man's thick V-necked sweater pulled over it.

'It is so lovely to have you here. Did you have a good drive down? Was it dreadfully rainy?'

'Pretty bad.'

Antonia turned as Noel came through the door to join them, bearing not only Antonia's suitcase and his own bag, but the abandoned haversack as well.

'Oh, Noel.' He set down the cases. 'What a perfectly dreadful night.'

'Let's hope we don't have rain the entire weekend, otherwise we won't get a thing done.' He sniffed. 'Something smells good.'

'Shepherd's pie.'

'I'm ravenous.'

'No wonder. I'll take Antonia up and show her her room, and then we'll have dinner. Give yourself a drink. I'm sure you need one. We'll be down in a moment. Come along, Antonia . . .'

She picked up the haversack and Antonia carried her case, and Penelope led the way upstairs, across a tiny landing, through the first bedroom and into the second.

'What a marvellous house,' said Antonia from behind her.

'It's not for privacy. All the rooms lead into each other.'

'Like Ca'n D'alt.'

'It used to be two cottages. There are still two staircases and two doors. Now here we are.' She set down the haversack and glanced around the carefully prepared room, checking that she had forgotten nothing. It looked very nice. The white, closely fitted carpet was new, but all else dated back to Oakley Street. The twin beds, with their polished, wheel-back heads; the rose-flowered curtains that did not match the bedspreads. The little mahogany dressing table, and the balloon-backed chairs. She had filled a lustre jug with polyanthus and turned down one of the beds to reveal crisp white linen and pink blankets. 'This cupboard

is the wardrobe, and through the other door is the bathroom. Noel's
room is just beyond and you'll have to share the bathroom with him, but
if he's using it, you can come to the other end of the house and use mine.
Now . . .' With all explained, she turned to Antonia. 'What would you
like to do? Have a bath? There's plenty of time.'

'No. I'll just wash my hands if I may. And then I'll come down.'

There were shadows like smudges beneath her eyes. Penelope said,
'You must be tired.'

'I am, rather. I think it's a sort of jet lag. I haven't quite caught up
with myself yet.'

'Never mind, you're here now. You don't have to go anywhere else,
not until you want to. Come down when you're ready and Noel will give
you a drink.'

She returned to the kitchen, where she found Noel, with a large, dark
whisky and soda, sitting at the table and reading the paper. She closed
the door behind her, and he looked up. 'Everything okay?'

'Poor child, she looks drained.'

'Yes. She didn't talk much on the way down. I thought she was
sleeping, but she wasn't.'

'She hasn't changed in the very least. I think she was the most
attractive child I ever knew.'

'You mustn't put ideas into my head.'

She gave him a cautionary glance. 'You behave yourself this weekend,
Noel.'

He looked the picture of innocence. 'Now what could you mean by
that?'

'You know perfectly well what I mean.'

He grinned, still good-humoured, unabashed. 'By the time I've finished
barrowing all that rubbish out of your attic, I'll be too shagged to do
anything except pass out in my own little bunk.'

'I certainly hope so.'

'Oh, come off it, Ma, you must realise she's not at all my type . . .
white eyelashes have no appeal. Makes me think of rabbits. I'm starving.
When are we going to eat?'

'When Antonia comes down.' She went to open the oven door and
check on the shepherd's pie to make certain that it was neither overcooked
nor inedible. Which it wasn't. She closed the door. Noel said, 'What did
you think about Wednesday's sale? *The Water Carriers.*'

'I told you. Quite unbelievable.'

'Have you decided what you're going to do?'

'Have I got to do anything?'

'You're being obtuse. It went for almost a quarter of a million! You own three Lawrence Sterns, and the financial responsibility, if nothing else, completely alters the situation. Do what I suggested the last time I was here. Get them professionally valued. If you still don't want to sell them, then for God's sake have them reinsured. Any cunning joker could walk into the house one day when you're out in the rose beds and simply walk off with them. Don't be too stupid about it all.'

Across the table, she eyed him, torn between a sort of motherly gratitude for his concern and a nasty suspicion that her son – so like his father – was up to something. He met her eyes with a clear and open blue gaze, but she remained undecided.

She said at last, 'All right, I'll think about it. But I shall never sell my darling *Shell Seekers*, and I shall continue to get the utmost satisfaction and comfort from looking at it. It's all I've got left of the old days, and being a child, and Cornwall and Porthkerris.'

He looked slightly alarmed. 'Hey. Just listen to those sobbing violins. It's not like you to start getting maudlin.'

'I'm not being maudlin. It's just that, lately, I've developed this yearning to be there again. It's something to do with the sea. I want to look at the sea again. And why not? There's nothing to stop me going. Just for a few days.'

'Are you sure that's wise? Isn't it better to remember it as it was? Everything changes, and never for the better.'

'The sea doesn't change,' Penelope told him stubbornly.

'You'd know nobody.'

'I know Doris. I could stay with her.'

'Doris?'

'She was our evacuee at the beginning of the war. Lived with us at Carn Cottage. She never went back to Hackney. She just stayed at Porthkerris. And we still correspond and she's always asking me to go and visit her . . .' She hesitated, and then, 'Would you come with me?' she asked her son.

'Come *with* you?' He was so taken aback by her suggestion that he made no attempt to conceal his astonishment.

'It would be company.' That sounded pathetic, as though she were lonely. She tried another tack. 'And it might be fun for us both. I don't regret many things in my life, but I do regret never taking you all to Porthkerris when you were children. But I don't know; things just never worked out that way.'

A faint embarrassment lay between them. Noel decided to turn it all into a joke. 'I'm a bit long in the tooth for sand-castles on the beach.'

His mother was not particularly amused. 'There are other diversions.'

'Such as what?'

'I could show you Carn Cottage, where we used to live. Your grand-father's studio. The Art Gallery that he helped to start. You seem so interested, all of a sudden, in his pictures, I should have thought you would be interested in seeing where it all began.'

She did this sometimes; delivered a glancing blow, right beneath the belt. Noel took a mouthful of whisky, composing himself. 'When would you go?'

'Oh. Soon. Before the spring is over. Before summer comes.'

He knew relief at having a watertight excuse. 'I couldn't get away then.'

'Not even for a long weekend?'

'Ma. We're up to our eyes in the office, and I'm not due for leave until July at the earliest.'

'Oh well, in that case it's impossible.' To his relief she abandoned the subject. 'Noel, would you be kind and open a bottle of wine?'

He got to his feet. He felt a bit guilty. 'I'm sorry. I would have come with you.'

'I know,' she told him. 'I know.'

By the time Antonia reappeared it was a quarter to ten. Noel poured the wine, and they all sat down to eat the shepherd's pie, and the fresh fruit salad, and biscuits and cheese. Then Noel made coffee for himself, and, announcing that he was going up to the loft to give it a preliminary once-over before starting work the next day, took himself off upstairs, bearing his coffee with him.

When he had gone, Antonia, as well, rose to her feet, and began to stack the plates and glasses, but Penelope stopped her.

'There's no need. I'll put it all in the dish washer. It's nearly eleven, and you must long for your bed. Perhaps you'd like a bath now?'

'Yes, I would. I don't know why, but I feel frightfully dirty. I think it's something to do with being in London.'

'I always feel that way, too. Take lots of hot water and have a good soak.'

'That was a lovely dinner. Thank you.'

'Oh, my dear . . .' Penelope was touched, and all at once found herself at a loss for words. And yet there was so much to be said. 'Perhaps, when you're in bed, I'll come up and say good night to you.'

'Oh, will you?'

'Of course.'

When she had gone, Penelope slowly cleared the table, stacked the dish washer, put out the milk bottles, laid the breakfast. Upstairs, in this house where sounds echoed through open doors and wooden ceilings, she heard Antonia run the bath; heard, high above, Noel's muffled footsteps as he edged his way around the cluttered loft. Poor man, he had taken on himself a gargantuan task. She hoped that he would not lose heart halfway through and that she would not be left with an even bigger muddle than before. The bath water, gurgling, ran away down the waste-pipe. She hung up the tea towel, turned off the lights, and went upstairs.

She found Antonia in bed, awake, and turning the pages of a magazine Penelope had left on the bedside table. Her bare arms were brown and slender, and her silky hair spread itself out over the white linen pillow-slip.

She closed the door behind her.

'Did you have a good bath?'

'Blissful.' Antonia smiled. 'I put in some of those delicious bath salts I found. I hope that was all right.'

'That was what you were meant to do.' She sat on the edge of the bed. 'It's done you good. You don't look so weary.'

'No. It's woken me up. I feel all alert and chatty. I couldn't possibly go to sleep.'

From overhead, beyond the beamed ceiling, came the sound of something being dragged across a floor.

Penelope said, 'Perhaps that's just as well, with the din that Noel's creating.'

At that moment, there was a thud, as though some heavy article had been inadvertently dropped, and then Noel's voice. 'Oh, bloody hell.'

Penelope began to laugh, and Antonia laughed too, and then quite suddenly was not laughing any longer, for her eyes were filling with tears.

'Oh, my dear child.'

'So silly . . .' She sniffed and groped for a handkerchief and blew her nose. 'It's just that it's so wonderful to be here, with you, and be able to laugh about silly things again. Do you remember how we used to laugh? When you were staying with us, funny things happened all the time. It was never quite the same after you left.'

She was all right. She was not going to weep. The tears had receded, scarcely shed, and Penelope said gently, 'Do you want to talk?'

'Yes, I think I do.'

'Do you want to tell me about Cosmo?'

'Yes.'

'I was so sorry. When Olivia told me . . . I was so shocked . . . so sorry.'

'He died of cancer.'

'I didn't know.'

'Lung cancer.'

'But he didn't smoke.'

'He used to. Before you knew him. Before Olivia knew him. Fifty a day or more. He kicked the habit, but it killed him just the same.'

'You were with him?'

'Yes. I've been living with him for the past two years. Ever since my mother remarried.'

'Did that upset you?'

'No. I was very happy for her. I don't much like the man she chose, but that's beside the point. She does. And she's left Weybridge and gone to live in the North, because that's where he comes from.'

'What does he do?'

'He has some sort of woollen business . . . worsteds, weaving, that sort of thing.'

'Have you been there?'

'Yes, I went the first Christmas they were married. But it was dreadful. He has two of the most ghastly sons, and I couldn't wait to get out of the house before one of them actually raped me. Well, maybe that's a bit of an exaggeration, but that's the reason I couldn't have gone to my mother after Daddy died. I just couldn't. And the only person I could think of who would help me was Olivia.'

'Yes, I see; but tell me more about Cosmo.'

'Well, he was all right. I mean, there didn't seem to be anything wrong with him. And then, about six months ago, he started this horrible coughing. It used to keep him awake at nights, and I'd lie and listen and try to tell myself that it was nothing very serious. But finally I persuaded him to go and see his doctor, and he went into the local hospital for an X-ray and a check-up. He never, actually, came out. They opened him and removed half of one of his lungs and then closed him up again, and said that he'd soon be able to come home, but then he had a post-operative collapse, and that was it. He died in hospital. He never recovered consciousness.'

'And you were alone?'

'Yes. I was alone, but Maria and Tomeu were always around, and I never imagined such a thing was going to happen, so I wasn't actually all that worried or frightened. And it all happened so quickly. One day, it seemed, we were together, at Ca'n D'alt, just the way we'd always been, and the next day he was dead. Of course it wasn't the next day. It just seemed that way.'

'What did you do?'

'Well . . . it sounds dreadful, but we had to have a funeral. You see, in Ibiza only the shortest time can elapse between death and the burial.

It has to happen the very next day. You wouldn't think that in a day, on an island where practically nobody has a telephone, the news would get around, but it did. Like bush telegraph. He had so many friends. Not just people like us, but all the local people as well, men he'd drunk with in Pedro's bar, and the fishermen down in the harbour, and the farmers who lived around us. They were all there.'

'Where was he buried?'

'In the graveyard of the little church in the village.'

'But . . . it's a Catholic church.'

'Of course. But that was all right. Daddy wasn't a church-goer, but as a child he'd been baptised and received into the Catholic Church. Also, he'd always been very friendly with the village priest. Such a kind man . . . enormously comforting. He conducted the service for us, not in the church, but by the graveside, in the sunlight. By the time we left, you couldn't see the grave for flowers. It looked so beautiful. And then everybody came back to Ca'n D'alt, and Maria had made some things to eat, and they all had some wine, and then they all went away again. And that was what happened.'

'I see. It all sounds very sad, but quite perfect. Tell me, have you told Olivia all this?'

'Bits of it. She didn't really want to hear too much.'

'That's in character. When Olivia is deeply touched or distressed, she hides her feelings away, almost as though she were pretending to herself that nothing had happened.'

'Yes. I know. I realised that. And it didn't matter.'

'What did you do when you were with her in London?'

'Not much. I went to Marks and Spencers and got myself some warm clothes. And I went and saw Daddy's solicitor. That was a pretty depressing interview.'

Penelope's heart sank for the girl. 'Did he leave you nothing?'

'Virtually nothing. He had nothing to leave, poor darling.'

'What about the house in Ibiza?'

'That never belonged to us. It belongs to a man called Carlos Barcello. And I wouldn't want to stay there. Even if I did, I couldn't pay the rent.'

'His boat. What happened to that?'

'He sold that soon after Olivia left. He never bought another.'

'But the other things. His books, and furniture and pictures?'

'Tomeu has arranged with a friend to store them for me until such time as I need them, or can bear to go back and get them.'

'It's hard to believe, Antonia, I know, but that time will come.'

Antonia put her arms behind her head and gazed at the ceiling. She said, 'I'm all right now. I'm sad, but I'm not sad that he didn't go on living. He would have been ill and frail, and he wouldn't have lasted for more than another twelve months. The doctor told me that. So it was better that he went the way he did. My only real sadness is the years that were wasted after Olivia went. He never had another woman. He loved Olivia very much. I think, probably, she was the love of his life.'

It was quiet now. The thumpings and footsteps from the loft had ceased, and Penelope guessed that Noel had decided to chuck his hand in and had taken himself back downstairs.

After a little, she said, choosing her words with some care, 'Olivia loved him too. As much as she has ever been able to give her heart to any man.'

'He wanted to marry her. But she wouldn't.'

'Do you blame her for that?'

'No. I admire her. It was honest, and very strong.'

'She's a special person.'

'I know.'

'She just has never wanted to marry. She has this horror of dependence, and committal, and putting down roots.'

'She has her career.'

'Yes. Her career. That matters to her more than anything else in the world.'

Antonia considered this. She said, 'It's funny. You could understand it better if she'd had a miserable childhood, or suffered some dreadful trauma. But with you for a mother, I can't imagine anything like that ever happening to her. Is she so different from your other children?'

'Totally.' Penelope smiled. 'Nancy is the very opposite. All she ever dreamed about was being a married woman with a house of her own. A little bit the Lady of the Manor, perhaps, but what of it? She does no harm. She's happy. At least, I imagine she's happy. She's got exactly what she always wanted.'

'How about you?' Antonia asked. 'Did you want to be married?'

'Me? Heavens, it's so long ago, I can scarcely remember. I don't think I thought very much about it. I was only nineteen and it was wartime. In wartime, one didn't think very far into the future. Just lived from day to day.'

'What happened to your husband?'

'Ambrose? Oh, he died, some years after Nancy was married.'

'Were you lonely?'

'I was alone. But that's not the same as being lonely.'

'I never knew anyone who died before. Not before Cosmo.'

'The first experience of losing someone close to you is always the most shattering. But time passes, and you come to terms with it.'

'I suppose so. He used to say, "all life is a compromise".'

'That was wise. For some, it has to be. For you, I should like to think that there was something better in store.'

Antonia smiled. The magazine had long since fallen to the floor, and her eyes had lost their feverish brightness. She was, like a child, becoming drowsy.

'You're tired,' Penelope told her.

'Yes. I'll sleep now.'

'Don't wake too early.' She got up off the bed, and went to draw back the curtains. The rain had ceased, and out of the darkness came the hoot of an owl. 'Good night.' She went to the door, opened it, turned off the light.

'Penelope.'

'What is it?'

'It's just so lovely to be here. With you.'

'Sleep well.' She closed the door.

The house was silent. Downstairs, all the lights were out. Noel had obviously decided to call it a day, and gone to bed. There was nothing more to be done.

In her room, she pottered about, taking her time, cleaning her teeth, brushing her hair, putting night-cream on her face. In her night-dress she went to draw back the heavy curtains. Through the open window a breeze stirred, cold and damp, but smelling earthily sweet, as though her garden, with spring nearly upon them, was stirring, woken from the long winter sleep. The owl hooted again, and it was so quiet that she could hear the soft whisper of the Windrush flowing on its way beyond the orchard.

She turned from the window and climbed into bed and turned off the light. Her body felt heavy and tired, grateful for the comfort of cool sheets and soft pillows, but her mind stayed wide awake, because Antonia's innocent curiosity had stirred up the past in a disconcerting and not wholly welcome fashion, and Penelope had answered her questions with some caution, neither lying nor telling the whole truth. The truth was too confused to tell, devious and long ago. Too long ago to start unravelling the strands of motivation and reason and the sequence of events. She had not talked of Ambrose, nor mentioned his name, nor thought about him, for longer than she could remember. But now, she lay open-eyed, gazing into the gloomy darkness that was not truly dark, and knew that she had no option but to go back. And it was an extraordinary experience; like watching an old film, or discovering a dog-eared photograph album, turning the pages, and being amazed to find that the sepia snapshots had not faded at all, but had stayed evocative, clear, and sharp-edged as ever.

# Ambrose

The Wren Officer squared her papers and unscrewed her fountain pen.

'Now then, Stern, what we have to decide is which Category to put you in.'

Penelope sat on the other side of the desk and looked at her. The Wren Officer had two blue stripes on her sleeve and a neat crop of hair. Her collar and tie were so stiff and tight that they looked as though they might choke her; her watch was a man's, and beside her, on the desk-top, lay her leather cigarette case and a hefty gold lighter. Penelope recognised another Miss Pawson and felt quite kindly towards her.

'Have you any qualifications?'

'No. I don't think so.'

'Shorthand? Typing?'

'No.'

'University degree?'

'No.'

'You must call me "Ma'am".'

'Ma'am.'

The Wren Officer cleared her throat, finding herself disconcerted by the guileless expression and dreamy brown eyes of the new Wren Rating. She wore uniform, but somehow it didn't look right on her; she was too tall, and her legs were too long, and her hair was a disaster, soft and dark and bundled up into a loose coil that looked neither neat nor secure.

'You went to school, I presume?' She half expected to be told that Wren Stern had been educated at home, by a genteel governess. She looked that sort of girl. Taught a little French, and water-colour painting and not much else. But Wren Stern said, 'Yes.'

'Boarding school?'

'No. Day schools. Miss Pritchett's when we were living in London, and the local Grammar School when we were living in Porthkerris. That's in Cornwall,' she added kindly.

The Wren Officer found herself longing for a cigarette.

'This is the first time you've been away from home?'

'Yes.'

'You must call me "Ma'am".'

'Ma'am.'

The Wren Officer sighed. Wren Stern was going to be one of those problems. Cultured, half-educated, and totally useless. 'Can you cook?' she asked without much hope.

'Not very well.'

There was no alternative. 'In that case, I'm afraid we'll have to make you a Steward.'

Wren Stern smiled agreeably, seeming pleased that they had at last come to some decision.

'All right.'

The Wren Officer made a few notes on the form, and then screwed the top back on her pen. Penelope waited for the next thing to happen. 'I think that's it.' Penelope got to her feet, but the Wren Officer was not finished. 'Stern. Your hair. You must do something about it.'

'What?' asked Penelope.

'It mustn't touch your collar, you know. Naval regulations. Why don't you get the hairdresser to cut it off?'

'I don't want it cut off.'

'Well . . . make some sort of effort. Try to get the hang of a neat little bun.'

'Oh. Yes. All right.'

'Off you go then.'

She went. 'Goodbye.' The door half closed behind her and then opened again. 'Ma'am.'

She was drafted to the Royal Naval Gunnery School, HMS *Excellent*, at Whale Island. She was a Steward, but, perhaps because she 'spoke proper', was made an Officer's Steward, which meant that she worked in the wardroom; laying up tables, serving drinks, telling people they were wanted on the telephone, polishing silver and waiting at meals. Also, before darkness fell, she had to go around all the cabins and do the black-out, knocking on doors, and, if there was someone inside, saying 'Permission to darken ship, sir.' She was, in fact, a glorified parlour maid, and was paid a parlour maid's wages, thirty shillings a fortnight. Every two weeks, she had to attend pay parade, lining up until it was time to salute the sour-faced Pay Commander – who looked as though he hated women and probably did – say her name, and be handed the meagre buff envelope.

Asking permission to darken ship was just part of a whole new language she had had to learn, and she had spent a week at a training depot doing this. A bedroom was a cabin; the floor, the deck; when she went to work, she was going on board; a Make and Mend was a half day; and if you had a row with your friend it was called Parting Brass Rags, but as she didn't have a friend to have a row with, the occasion to use this seamanlike expression never arose.

Whale Island really *was* an island, and you had to cross a bridge to get there, which was quite exciting and made it seem like going on board a ship even if you weren't. A very long time ago it had started life as a mudbank in the middle of Portsmouth Harbour, but by now was a large and important Naval Training Establishment, with a parade ground and a drill shed and a church, and jetties, and huge batteries where the men did their training. Administrative offices and accommodation were housed in a lot of neat red-brick blocks and buildings. The lower deck quarters were square and plain, like council houses, but the wardroom was quite grand, a country manor with the football field as its estate.

The noise was incessant. Bugles blew and pipes sounded and daily orders came crackling out over the Tannoy system. Men in training went everywhere at the double, their boots going thump-thump-thump on the tarmac. On the parade ground, Chief Petty Officers screamed themselves into apoplexy at squads of terrified young seamen doing their best to master the complexities of Close Order Drill. Each morning, the ceremony of Captain's Divisions and Colours took place, with the Royal Marine Band blasting out 'Braganza' and 'Hearts of Oak'. If you were caught out of doors while the White Ensign climbed the flagpole, you had to face the quarterdeck and stand to attention, saluting, until it was all over.

The Wrens' quarters, where Penelope was sent to live, were in a requisitioned hotel at the north end of the town. Here, she shared a cabin with five other girls, all sleeping in double-decker bunks. One of the girls had dreadful BO, but as she never washed, this was hardly surprising. The quarters were two miles from Whale Island, and as no naval transport was provided and there were no buses, Penelope put through a telephone call to Sophie to ask her to send her old school bicycle. Sophie promised to do this. She would put it on a train, and Penelope would duly collect it from Portsmouth Station.

'And how are you, my darling?'

'All right.' It was horrible to hear Sophie's voice and not be with her. 'How are you? How's Papa?'

'Miss Pawson has taught him to use a stirrup-pump.'

'And Doris, and the boys?'

'Ronald has got into the football team. And we think that Clark has measles. And I have snowdrops in the garden.'

'Already?' She wanted to see them. She wanted to be there. It was horrible to think of them all at Carn Cottage and not to be with them. To think of her own darling private bedroom, with the curtains stirring in the sea breeze and the beams of the lighthouse crossing the walls.

'Are you happy, my darling?'

But before Penelope could answer, pip-pip-pip went the telephone and they were cut off. She put the receiver back on the hook and was glad that they had been cut off before she had time to answer, because she wasn't happy. She was lonely and homesick and bored. She didn't fit in to this strange new world and feared she never would. She should have become a nurse, or a land-girl, or gone to make munitions – anything, rather than take that dramatic, impulsive decision which had landed her in this dismal, apparently permanent plight.

The next day was a Thursday. It was February now, still cold, but the sun had shone all day, and at five o'clock Penelope, off duty at last, left the island, saluted the Officer of the Watch, and made her way across the narrow bridge. The tide was high, and Portsdown Hill, in the dying light, looked tantalisingly rural. When her bicycle arrived, she would perhaps be able to go for solitary rides, and find a bit of grass to sit on. As it was, the empty hours of evening stretched ahead, and she wondered if she had enough money to take herself to the cinema.

A car was coming down the bridge behind her. She went on walking. It slowed down and stopped alongside, a racy little MG with the hood folded down.

'Where are you headed for?'

For a moment, she could hardly believe he was talking to her. It was the first time any man had, except to say he wanted peas and carrots, or to order a pink gin. But there wasn't anybody else around, so he had to be. Penelope recognised him. The tall, dark, blue-eyed Sub Lieutenant whose name was Keeling. She knew that he was on his Gunnery course, because in the wardroom he wore the gaiters, white flannels and white muffler that were regulation dress for Officers under instruction. But now he was in everyday uniform and looked cheerful and carefree, a man setting out to enjoy himself.

She said, 'The Wrennery.'

He leaned over and opened the door. 'Hop in, then, and I'll give you a lift.'

'Are you going that way?'

'No. But I can do.'

She got in beside him and slammed the door shut. The little car shot forward, and she had to hold on to her hat.

'I've seen you around, haven't I? You work in the wardroom.'

'That's right.'

'Enjoying it?'

'Not much.'

'Why did you take the job, then?'

'I couldn't do anything else.'

'Is this your first posting?'

'Yes. I only joined up a month ago.'

'How do you like the Navy?'

He seemed so keen and enthusiastic that she didn't like to tell him that she hated it. 'It's all right. I'm getting used to it.'

'Bit like boarding school?'

'I didn't go to boarding school, so I wouldn't know.'

'What's your name?'

'Penelope Stern.'

'I'm Ambrose Keeling.'

There wasn't time for very much more. In five minutes they were there, turning through the gates of the Wrens' quarters, and stopping with a scrunch of gravel at the doors, which caused the Regulating Petty Officer to glance out of her window with a disapproving frown.

He switched off the engine, and Penelope said, 'Thank you very much,' and reached out to open the door.

'What are you doing for the rest of the evening?'

'Nothing, really.'

'Neither am I. Let's go and have a drink at the Junior Officers' Club.'

'What . . . now?'

'Yes. Now.' His blue eyes danced with amusement. 'Is that such a disastrous suggestion?'

'No . . . not a bit. It's just that . . .' Ratings in uniform were not allowed into Officers' clubs. ' . . . I'll have to go and change into plain clothes.' That was another thing she had learned at the Training Depot – to call civilian clothes 'plain clothes'. She felt quite proud of herself for remembering all these rules and regulations.

'That's all right. I'll wait for you.'

She left him there, in his little car, reaching for a cigarette to while away the time. She went indoors and bolted up the stairs, two at a time, not wanting to waste a moment, terrified that if she took too long, he would lose patience and drive away and never speak to her again.

In her cabin, she tore off her uniform and slung it across her bunk; washed her face and hands, took the pins from her hair and shook it loose. Brushing it, she revelled in the comforting, familiar weight about her shoulders. It was like being free again, herself again, and she felt her confidence returning. She opened the communal wardrobe and pulled out the dress that Sophie had given her for Christmas, and the ratty old musquash jacket that Aunt Ethel had wanted to give to a jumble sale, but which Penelope had rescued and kept for herself. She found a pair of stockings that was not laddered and her best shoes. She didn't need a handbag, because she hadn't any money and she never wore make up. She ran downstairs again, signed in the Regulating Book, and went out through the door.

It was nearly dark now, but he was still there, sitting in his little car, and still smoking the same cigarette.

'I'm sorry I've been so long.' Breathlessly, she got back in beside him.

'Long?' He laughed, stubbed out his cigarette, and tossed it away. 'I've never known a woman so speedy. I was quite prepared to wait half an hour at least.'

The fact that he had prepared himself to wait so long for her was both surprising and gratifying. She smiled at him. She had forgotten to put on any scent and hoped that he would not notice the moth-ball smell of Aunt Ethel's coat.

'It's the first time I've been out of uniform since I joined up.'

He started the engine.

'How does it feel?' he asked.

'Heavenly.'

They went to the Junior Officers' Club in Southsea, and he led her upstairs and they sat at the bar, and he asked her what she wanted to drink. She wasn't quite sure what to ask for, so he ordered two gin and oranges, and she didn't tell him that she had never drunk gin in her life.

And when the drinks came, they talked, and it was all very easy, and she told him that she lived in Porthkerris and that her father had gone there because he was an artist, but now he didn't paint any longer; she told him that her mother was French.

'That explains it,' he said.

'Explains what?'

'I don't know, exactly. Something about you. I noticed you at once. Dark eyes, Dark hair. You look different to all the other Wrens.'

'I'm about ten feet taller.'

'It's not that, though I like tall women. A sort of . . .' He shrugged, becoming quite Gallic himself. ' . . . *je ne sais quoi*. Have you lived in France?'

'No. I've stayed there. One winter we took a flat in Paris.'

'Do you speak French?'

'Of course.'

'Have you got brothers and sisters?'

'No.'

'Me neither.' He told her about himself. He was twenty-one. His father, who had run the family business, which was something to do with publishing, had died when Ambrose was ten. When he left public school, he could have gone into the same publishing firm, but he did not want to spend his life in an office . . . besides, a war was obviously looming . . . and so he joined the Royal Navy. His widowed mother lived in a flat in Knightsbridge, in Wilbraham Place, but at the outbreak of war she had abandoned this and gone to stay in a country hotel in a remote corner of Devon.

'She's better there, out of London. She's not very strong, and if the bombing does start, she'd be more of a hindrance than a help.'

'How long have you been at Whale Island?'

'A month. Hopefully, I've only got another two weeks. Depends on the exams. Gunnery's my last course. I've already got Navigation, Torpedoes, and Signals tucked under my belt, thank God.'

'Where will you go then?'

'Divisional School for a final week, and then to sea.'

They finished their drinks, and he ordered a second round. Then they went into the dining room and had dinner. After dinner, they drove round Southsea for a bit, and then, because she had to report back to quarters at half past ten, he took her home.

She said, 'Thank you so much,' but the formal words didn't begin to express the gratitude she felt, not just for the evening they had spent together, but because he had come along just when she needed him most, and now she had a friend and wouldn't have to feel lonely any longer.

He said, 'You free on Saturday?'

'Yes.'

'I've got tickets for a concert. Would you like to come?'

'Oh . . .' She could feel the smile, unstoppable, spreading across her face. 'I'd love it.'

'I'll pick you up then. About seven. Oh, and Penelope . . . get a Late Pass.'

The concert was in Southsea. Anne Zeigler and Webster Booth singing songs like 'Only a Rose' and 'If You Were the Only Girl in the World'.

> What e'er befall
> I'll still recall
> That sunlit mountain side.

Ambrose held her hand. That night, when he took her back, he parked the car a little way from quarters, down a quiet lane, and took her in his arms, moth-bally coat and all, and kissed her. It was the first time any man had kissed her, and it took some getting used to, but after a bit she got the hang of it and did not find it unpleasant in the very least. Indeed, his closeness, his clean-cut masculinity, the fresh smell of his skin aroused within her a physical response that came as a totally new experience. A stirring, deep inside. A pain that was not a pain.

'Darling Penelope, you are the most delicious creature.'

But, over his shoulder, she caught sight of the clock on the dashboard, and saw that it was twenty-five past ten. Reluctantly, she drew back, disentangling herself from his embrace, automatically putting up a hand to tidy her disordered hair.

She said, 'I have to go. I mustn't be late.'

He sighed, reluctantly letting her go. 'Bloody clock. Bloody time.'

'I'm sorry.'

'Not your fault. We'll just have to make other plans.'

'What sort of plans?'

'I've got a short weekend coming up. How about you? Could you get one?'

'This weekend?'

'Yes.'

'I could try.'

'We could drive up to town. Take in a show. Stay the night.'

'Oh, what a wonderful idea. I haven't had any leave yet. I'm sure I could fix it.'

'The only thing is . . .' He looked worried. 'My mother's let her flat to some boring Army pongo, so we can't go there. I suppose I could go to my club, but . . .'

It was lovely to be able to solve his problems. 'We'll go to my house.'

'*Your* house?'

Penelope began to laugh. 'Not my house in Porthkerris, stupid. My house in London.'

'You've got a house in London?'

'Yes. In Oakley Street. It's so easy. I've got a key and everything.'

It was too easy. 'Is it your *own* house?'

She was still laughing. 'Not my very own. It's Papa's.'

'But won't they mind? Your parents, I mean.'

'*Mind?* Why on earth should they mind?'

He thought of telling her why and then decided against it. A French mother and a father who was an artist. Bohemians. He had never known a bohemian, but he began to realise that he had met one now.

'No reason,' he assured her hastily. He could scarcely believe his luck.

'But you looked so surprised.'

'Perhaps I was,' he admitted, and then smiled, at his most charming. 'But perhaps I must stop being surprised by you. Perhaps I should just accept the fact that nothing you could do would surprise me.'

'Is that a good thing?'

'It can't be bad.'

He took her back to quarters then, and they kissed good night and she left him and went in, and so bemused and incapable was she that she forgot to sign the book and had to be called back by the Wren on Regulating Duty, who was in a filthy temper because the young Leading Seaman whom she fancied had taken another girl to the cinema.

She got the pass and Ambrose laid his plans. A friend . . . a Lieutenant in the RNVR with enviable connections with the world of theatre . . . managed to get hold of two tickets for *The Dancing Years* at the Drury Lane Theatre. He wangled a bit of petrol and borrowed a fiver from another gullible chum. Midday on the following Saturday saw him driving in through the gates of the Wrennery, to draw up before the doorway in a flourish of flying gravel. A Wren happened to be passing, so he told her to be a love and find Wren Stern and tell her that Sub Lieutenant Keeling was ready and waiting. Her eyes goggled a bit at the racy little car and the handsome young officer, but Ambrose was used to being goggled at and dismissed her patent envy and admiration as no more than his due.

'Nothing you could do would surprise me,' he had told Penelope glibly, but nevertheless, when she finally appeared, it was hard not to be a little astonished, for she wore uniform, carried her old fur jacket and a leather satchel slung over a shoulder, and that was all.

'Where's your luggage?' he asked, as she got into the car, bundling the fur down into the space between her feet.

'Here.' She held up the handbag.

'*That's* your luggage? But we're going away for the weekend. We're going to the theatre. You don't intend wearing that flaming uniform the whole time, do you?'

'No, of course I don't. But I'm going home. There are clothes there. I'll find something to wear.'

Ambrose thought of his mother, who liked to buy an outfit for every occasion, and then spent two hours getting herself into it.

'What about a toothbrush?'

'My toothbrush and my hair-brush are in my bag. That's all I need. Now, are we going to London, or aren't we?'

It was a fine bright day; a day for escaping, for being on holiday, for going off for the weekend with a person you were really fond of. Ambrose took the road that led over Portsdown Hill, and at the top Penelope looked back at Portsmouth and cheerfully said goodbye to it. They went through Purbrook and across the Downs to Petersfield, and at Petersfield they decided that they were hungry, so stopped and went into a pub. Ambrose ordered beer, and a kind woman made them Spam sandwiches, which she served daintily garnished with a sprig of bright yellow cauliflower out of a piccalilli jar.

They went on, through Haslemere and Farnham and Guildford, and they came into London by way of Hammersmith and down the King's Road and turned into Oakley Street, blissfully familiar, with the Albert Bridge at the end of it, and the gulls, and the salty, muddy smell of the river, and the sound of tugs hooting.

'It's here.'

He parked the MG and turned off the engine, and sat regarding, with some awe, the tall face of the dignified old terrace house.

'Is this it?'

'Yes. I know the railings need painting, but we haven't had time. And of course it's miles too big, but we don't live in it all. Come on, I'll show you.'

She gathered up her bag and her coat, and she helped him put up the hood in case it should rain. With this accomplished, he collected his grip, and stood there, filled with pleasant anticipation, waiting for Penelope to go up the impressive pillared steps to the great front door, take out a key and let him in, and felt slightly let down when, instead, she led the way down the pavement, opened the wrought-iron gate, and ran down the area steps to the basement. He followed, closing the gate behind them, and saw that it was not a depressing area, but rather a cheerful one, with whitewashed walls and a scarlet dustbin, and a number of earthenware tubs which, in summer, no doubt, would burgeon with geraniums and honeysuckle and pelargoniums.

The door, like the dustbin, was scarlet. He waited while she unlocked this and then, cautiously, followed her indoors, to find himself in a light and airy kitchen unlike any he had ever seen before. Not that he had seen many. His mother never went into her kitchen except to tell Lily, the cook-general, how many people were coming to lunch the next day. Because she had to spend no time in her kitchen, and certainly never worked there, its décor was of no importance to her, and Ambrose remembered it as an uninviting, inconvenient place of much gloom, painted bottle-green and smelling of the sodden wooden draining board. When she wasn't carrying coal, preparing meals, dusting furniture, or waiting at table, Lily occupied a bedroom off this kitchen, which was furnished with an iron bedstead and a yellow varnished chest of drawers. She had to hang her clothes on a hook at the back of the door, and when she wanted to have a bath she had to have it in the middle of the afternoon when nobody else needed the bathroom, and before she changed into her best uniform of black dress and muslin apron. At the outbreak of war, Lily had shaken the life out of Mrs Keeling by giving in her notice and going off to make munitions. Mrs Keeling could find no one to take her place, and Lily's defection was one of the reasons she had chucked in the sponge and retired to sit the war out in darkest Devon.

But this kitchen. He put down his grip and gazed about him. Saw the long, scrubbed table, the motley variety of chairs, the pine dresser laden with painted pottery plates and jugs and bowls. Copper saucepans, beautifully arranged by size, hung from a beam over the stove, along with bunches of herbs and dried garden flowers. There were a basket chair, a shining white refrigerator, and a deep white china sink beneath the window, so that any person impelled to do the washing-up could amuse himself at the same time by watching people's feet go by on the pavement. The floor was flagged and scattered with rush-mats, and the smell was of garlic and herbs, like a French country *épicerie*.

He could hardly believe his eyes. 'Is this your *kitchen*?'

'It's our everything room. We live down here.'

He realised then that the basement took up the entire depth of the house, for at the far end, French windows gave out onto the green of a garden. It was divided, however, into two separate areas by means of a wide curved archway, hung with heavy curtains in a design that Ambrose did not recognise as the work of William Morris. 'Of course,' Penelope went on, dumping her coat and her bag on the kitchen table, 'when the house was built, all this space was simply a warren of pantries and store rooms, but Papa's father opened them all up and made what he called a garden room. But we use it as a sitting room. Come and see.' He set down his grip, took off his hat, and followed her.

Passing beneath the archway, he saw the open fireplace, set with bright Italian tiles, the upright piano, the old-fashioned gramophone. Large, well-worn sofas and chairs stood about, loose-covered in a variety of faded cretonnes, draped in silken shawls, scattered with handsome tapestry cushions. The walls were whitewashed, a backcloth for books, ornaments, photographs . . . the memorabilia, he guessed, of years. The space left over by these was filled by pictures, so vibrant with sun-drenched colour that Ambrose could almost feel the heat beating back from those flag-stoned terraces, those simmering, black-shadowed gardens.

'Are those pictures by your father?'

'No. We've only got three of his paintings, and those are all in Cornwall. He has arthritis in his hands, you see. Hasn't worked for years. These ones were all done by his great friend, Charles Rainier. They worked together in Paris, before the last war, and they've been friends ever since. The Rainiers live in the most heavenly house, right down in the South of France. We used to go and stay with them, quite often . . . we used to drive there, in the car . . . look . . .' She took a photograph from the shelf and held it out for him to see. 'Here we all are, en route . . .'

He saw the usual little family group, carefully posed, Penelope with pigtails and a skimpy cotton dress. And her parents, he supposed, and some female relation. But what really caught his attention was the car.

'That's an old four-and-a-half litre Bentley!' And he could not keep the awe from his voice.

'I know. Papa adores it. Just like Mr Toad in _The Wind in the Willows_. When he drives it, he takes off his black hat and puts on a leather motoring helmet, and he refuses to put up the hood, and if it rains we all get drenched.'

'Do you still have it?'

'Heavens, yes. He'd never get rid of it.'

She went to replace the photograph, and Ambrose's eyes, instinctively, were drawn back to Charles Rainier's seductive pictures. He could not think of anything more glamorous than driving, in carefree, pre-war days, to the South of France in a 4½-litre Bentley, headed for a world of nailing sunshine, resin-scented pines, al fresco meals, and swimming in the Mediterranean. He thought of wine, drunk beneath a trellis of vines. Of long, lazy siestas, with shutters closed for coolness, and love in the afternoon and grape-sweet kisses.

'Ambrose.'

Jarred from his daydream, he looked at her. In innocence, she smiled, pulled off her uniform hat, threw it down on a chair, and, still lost in and bemused by his own fantasy, he imagined her taking everything else off as well – then he could make love to her, right here and now, on one of those large and inviting sofas.

He took a step towards her, but it was already too late, for she had turned from him and gone to struggle with the latch of the French windows. The spell was broken. Cold air flooded into the room, and he sighed, dutifully following her on into the frosty London day, in order to be shown the garden.

'You must come and look . . . it's huge, because ages ago, the people who lived next door sold Papa's father their bit of garden. I'm sorry for the people who live there now, they've only got a horrid little yard. And the wall at the bottom of the garden is very old, Tudor, I think; I suppose this must once have been a Royal orchard or a pleasure garden or something.'

It was indeed an extremely large garden, with grass and borders and flower beds and a sagging pergola.

'What's the shed?' he asked.

'It's not a shed. It's my father's London studio. But I can't show it to you because I haven't got the key. Anyway, it's just full of canvases and paint, garden furniture and camp-beds. He's a terrible hoarder. We all are. We none of us throw anything away. Every time we come to London, Papa says he's going to clear out the studio, but he never does. It's a sort of nostalgia, I suppose. Or sheer laziness.' She shivered. 'Cold, isn't it? Let's go back in, and I'll show you the rest.'

Wordlessly, he followed her, his expression of polite interest giving no hint of his racing mind, which was working busily as an adding machine, calculating assets. For, despite the well-worn shabbiness and unconventional arrangement of this old London house, he found himself deeply impressed by its size and grandeur, and decided that it was infinitely preferable to his mother's perfectly appointed flat.

As well, he was mulling over the other scraps of information which Penelope had dropped, so lightly, as though they were of no importance, about her family and their marvellously romantic and bohemian life-style. His own, by comparison, seemed inordinately dull and stereotyped. Brought up in London, yearly holidays at Torquay or Frinton, school, and then the Navy. Which, up to now, had simply been an extension of school, with a bit of drill thrown in. He hadn't even been to sea yet, and wouldn't be sent until he'd finished his courses.

But Penelope was cosmopolitan. She had lived in Paris; her family owned not only this London house, but one in Cornwall. He considered the place in Cornwall. He had lately read Daphne du Maurier's *Rebecca*, and imagined just such a house as Manderley; something vaguely Elizabethan, perhaps, with a driveway a mile long, lined with hydrangeas. And her father was a famous artist, and her mother was French, and she appeared to think nothing of driving to the South of France, to stay with friends, in a 4½-litre Bentley. The 4½-litre Bentley filled him with envy as nothing else could do. He had always longed for just such a car, a status symbol that would turn heads, proclaiming wealth and masculinity, with just a touch of eccentricity thrown in for added flavour.

Now, reflecting on all this, and anxious to find out more, he went behind her, indoors, across the basement, and up a dark and narrow stairway. Through another door, and they were in the main hall of the house, spacious and elegant, with a beautiful fanlight over the front door, and a wide, shallow-stepped stairway curving to the next floor. Stunned by such unexpected grandeur, he gazed about him.

'I'm afraid it's very shabby,' she admitted, sounding apologetic. Ambrose did not think it was shabby in the least. 'And that horrible great faded patch on the wallpaper is where *The Shell Seekers* used to hang. It's Papa's favourite picture, and he didn't want it bombed, so Sophie and I had it crated and carted away to Cornwall. The house doesn't seem quite the same without it.'

Ambrose moved towards the stair, anxious to ascend and see more, but 'This is as far as we go,' Penelope told him. She opened a door. 'This is my parents' bedroom. It used to be the dining room, I think, and it looks over the garden. It's lovely in the mornings, because it gets all the sun. And this is my room, facing out over the street. And the bathroom. And this is where my mother keeps her Hoover. And that's it.'

The tour of inspection was over. Ambrose returned to the foot of the staircase, and stood there, looking upwards.

'Who lives in the rest of the house?'

'Lots of people. The Hardcastles, and then the Cliffords, and then the Friedmanns in the attics.'

'Lodgers,' said Ambrose. The word stuck in his throat, because it was a word that his mother had always uttered with the greatest disdain.

'Yes, I suppose they are. It's lovely. It's like having friends around all the time. And that reminds me, because I must go and tell Elizabeth Clifford we're here. I tried to ring her, but the number was engaged, and then I forgot to try again.'

'Are you going to tell her I'm here too?'

'Of course. Coming with me? She's a darling, you'll love her.'

'No. I think not.'

'In that case, why don't you go back to the kitchen and put a kettle on the stove and we can have a cup of tea or something. I'll see if I can borrow a bit of cake or something off Elizabeth, and then after tea we'll have to go out and buy ourselves eggs and bread and stuff; otherwise we shan't have anything to eat for breakfast.'

She sounded like a little girl playing Wendy Houses.

'All right.'

'Shan't be a moment.'

She left him, running up the staircase on her long legs, and Ambrose stood there in the hall and watched her go. He chewed his lip. Usually so sure of himself, he was filled by unfamiliar uncertainty, and the uneasy suspicion that, by coming here, to Penelope's house, he had somehow lost control of the situation. This was disturbing, because it had never happened before, and he had a horrid premonition that her extraordinary mixture of naïvety and sophistication could well have the same effect on him as a tremendously strong dry martini, leaving him both legless and incapable.

The big stove in the kitchen was unlit, but there was an electric kettle, so he filled that and switched it on. The darkness of the February afternoon had closed in, and the big shadowy room felt cold, but the fireplace in the sitting room was laid with sticks and paper, so he lit it with his lighter and watched the sticks catch, and then added some coal from a copper bucket and a log or two. By the time Penelope came running down the stairs it was burning well and the kettle sang.

'Oh, clever man, you've lit the fire. That always makes everything much more cheerful. There wasn't any cake, but I borrowed a bit of bread and some margarine. Something's missing, though.' She stood frowning, trying to puzzle this out, and then realised what it was. 'The clock. Of course, it hasn't been wound. Wind the clock, Ambrose. It's got such a comforting tick-tock.'

The clock was an old-fashioned one, high on the wall. He pulled up a chair and stood on it, opened the glass, set the hands, and wound the big key. While he was thus occupied, Penelope opened cupboards, took out cups and saucers, found a teapot.

'Did you see your friend?' With the clock going, he climbed down from the chair.

'No, she wasn't in, but I went on up and found Lalla Friedmann. I'm quite glad I saw her, because I was a bit worried about them. They're refugees, you see, a young Jewish couple from Munich, and they've had the most ghastly time. The last time I saw Willi, I thought perhaps he was going to have a breakdown.' She thought of telling Ambrose that it was because of Willi that she joined the Wrens, and then decided against it. She wasn't sure that he would understand. 'Anyway, she says he's much better, and he's got a new job and she's going to have a baby. She's such a nice person. She teaches music, so she must be frightfully clever. Do you mind having your tea without milk?'

After tea, they walked up to the King's Road, found a grocer's and did a little shopping, and then they returned to Oakley Street. It was nearly dark, so they pulled all the black-out curtains, and she made up the beds with clean sheets while he sat and watched her.

'You can sleep in my room, and I'll sleep in my parents' bed. Would you like to have a bath before you change? There's always heaps of hot water. Or would you like a drink?'

Ambrose said yes on both counts, so they went back downstairs and she opened a cupboard and brought out a bottle of Gordon's and a bottle of Dewar's and a bottle of something strange and unlabelled that smelt of almonds.

'Who does all this belong to?' he asked.

'Papa.'

'Won't he mind if I drink it?'

She gazed at him in astonishment. 'But that's what it's there for. To give to friends.'

This was new ground once more. His mother doled out sherry in tiny glasses, but if he wanted gin, he had to produce it for himself. He did not, however, make any remark, but simply poured himself a hefty Scotch and, carrying this in one hand and his grip in the other, made his way upstairs, to the bedroom allocated to him. It felt strange, taking off his clothes in such alien, feminine surroundings, and as he undressed he prowled a bit, like a cat making itself at home: looking at pictures, sitting on the bed, inspecting the titles of the books on the bookshelf. He expected Georgette Heyer and Ethel M. Dell, but found instead Virginia Woolf and Rebecca West. Not only a bohemian but an intellectual as well. This made him feel sophisticated. Wearing his Noel Coward dressing gown and carrying his bath towel, his wash bag, and the whisky, he made his way down the hall. In the cramped bathroom he shaved, and then ran a bath and soaked for a bit. The bath was far too short for his long legs, but the water was boiling. Back in the bedroom, he dressed again, embellishing his uniform with a starched shirt, a black satin tie from Gieves, and his best black half-Wellington boots, polished up with a handkerchief. He brushed his hair, turning his head this way and that in order to admire his profile, and then, content, picked up the empty tumbler and went down the stairs.

Penelope had disappeared, presumably to hunt through her mother's wardrobe for something to wear. He hoped that she would not shame him. By firelight, the sitting room looked satisfactorily romantic. He poured himself another Scotch and looked through the piles of gramophone records. Most of them were classics, but he found Cole Porter sandwiched between Beethoven and Mahler. He put the record on the old gramophone, wound up the handle.

> You're the top,
> You're the Coliseum,
> You're the top,
> You're the Louvre Museum.

He began to dance, eyes half closed, holding an imaginary girl in his arms. Perhaps after the theatre and a spot of supper, they would go on to a night-club. The Embassy or the Bag of Nails. If he ran out of money, they'd probably take a cheque. With a bit of luck, it wouldn't bounce.

'Ambrose.'

He hadn't heard her coming. Slightly embarrassed at being caught out in his little pantomime, he turned. She came across the room towards him, shy of her appearance, anxious for his approval, waiting for him to make some comment. But Ambrose found himself, for once, without words, for, in the soft light of lamp and fire, she was very beautiful. The dress she had finally unearthed had perhaps been fashionable five years ago. It was made of creamy chiffon, splashed with crimson and scarlet flowers, and the flowing skirt fitted over her slender hips and then flared out into folds. The bodice had little buttons down the front, and there was a sort of cape, in layers, which moved as she moved, fluttering like butterfly wings. Her hair she had swept up, revealing the long and perfect line of neck and shoulder, and as well a remarkable pair of dangling silver-and-coral earrings. She had put on some coral lipstick and smelt delicious.

He said, 'You smell delicious.'

'Chanel Number 5. I found some in the bottom of a bottle. I thought it might have gone a bit stale . . .'

'Not stale.'

'No . . . do I look all right? I tried on about six dresses, but I thought this was the best. It's dreadfully old and a bit short, because I'm taller than Sophie, but . . .'

Ambrose set down his drink and reached out his hand. 'Come here.'

She came, and placed her hand on his. He pulled her into his arms and kissed her, very gently and tenderly, because he did not want to do anything that might disarrange her elegant hair or her modest make up. Her lipstick tasted sweet. He drew away from her, smiling down into her warm, dark eyes.

'I almost wish,' he told her, 'that we didn't have to go out.'

'We'll come back,' she told him, and his heart leaped in anticipation.


*The Dancing Years* was very romantic and sad and quite unreal. There were a lot of dirndls and lederhosen, and pretty songs, and the characters all fell in love with each other, and then bravely renounced each other and said goodbye, and every other tune was a waltz. When it was over, they went out into the pitch-black streets, drove up Piccadilly, and went to Quaglino's for dinner. A band was playing and couples danced on the stamp-sized floor, all the men in uniform and a good many of the girls as well.

Boum.
Why does my heart go boum,
Me and my heart go boum-boumpety-boum,
All the time.

Between courses, Ambrose and Penelope danced too, but it wasn't really dancing because there was space only to stand in one spot and shift from foot to foot. But that was all right, because they had their arms around each other and their cheeks touched and every now and then Ambrose would kiss her ear or murmur something outrageous.

It was nearly two o'clock before they returned to Oakley Street. Holding hands, stifling laughter, they made their way in the inky darkness through the wrought-iron gate and down the steep stone steps.

'Who bothers about bombs?' Ambrose said. 'We can just as easily kill ourselves stumbling around in the black-out.'

Penelope detached herself from him, found the key and the lock and finally got the door open. He walked past her into the warm, velvety blackness. He heard her close the door behind them, and then, when it was safe to do so, she turned on the light.

It was very quiet. Above them, the other occupants of the house slumbered in silence. Only the ticking of the clock disturbed the stillness, or the passing of a car in the street outside. The fire that he had lighted was nearly out, but Penelope went through to the far end of the room to stir the embers and turn on a lamp. Beyond the archway the living room was suffused with light, like a stage set after the curtain has just gone up. Act One, Scene One. All that was needed were the actors.

He did not immediately join her. He felt pleasantly tipsy, but had reached the point when he knew that he wanted another drink. He went to the whisky bottle and poured himself a tot, filling the tumbler with soda from the siphon. Then he turned off the kitchen light and went through to the flickering flamelight and the huge cushioned sofa and the girl he had desired all evening.

She knelt on the hearthrug, close to the warmth of the fire. She had taken off her shoes. As he appeared, she turned her head and smiled. It was late, and she might have been tired, but her dark eyes were bright, her face glowing.

She said, 'Why is a fire such a companionable thing? Like having another person in the room.'

'I'm glad it's not. Another person, I mean.'

She was relaxed, peaceful. 'It was a good evening. It was fun.'

'It's not over yet.'

He sat, lowering himself onto a low, wide-lapped chair. He set down his drink. He said, 'Your hair is all wrong.'

'Why wrong?'

'Too tidy for love.'

She laughed, and then put up her hands, and began slowly to unpin the elegant knot. He watched her in silence, the classic feminine gesture of raised arms, the flimsy cape of her dress falling against her long neck like a little scarf. The last pin was removed, and she shook her head and the long dark mass of hair, like a tassel of silk, fell down over her shoulders.

She said, 'Now I'm me again.'

From the kitchen, the old clock struck two gentle resounding notes.

She said, 'Two o'clock in the morning.'

'A good time. The right time.'

She laughed again, as though nothing he could say could give her anything but delight. So close to the blazing fire, it was immensely warm. He set down his glass and pulled off his jacket, unknotted the tie and stripped it loose, unbuttoned the restricting collar of his starched shirt. Then he stood up, and stooping, pulled her to her feet. Kissing her, burying his face in the clean, scented profusion of her hair, his hands felt, beneath the flimsy silk of her dress, the slenderness of her young body, her rib cage, the steady beat of her heart. He picked her up in his arms – and for a girl so tall, she was amazingly weightless – took a couple of strides and set her down on the sofa, and she was still laughing, lying there with that magical hair spread all over the threadbare cushions. Now, his own heart thumped like a drum, and every nerve in his body jangled with need of her. At times, during his short relationship with her, he had found himself wondering whether or not she was a virgin, but he no longer wondered, for it had ceased to matter. Sitting beside her, he began, very gently, to undo the tiny buttons down the front of her dress. She lay there, complaisant, not trying to stop him, and when he began to kiss her again, her mouth, her neck, her round and creamy breasts, her response was both sweet and accepting.

'You're so beautiful.' After he said this, he realised, somewhat to his own surprise, that he had spoken instinctively, from his heart. 'You're beautiful too,' Penelope told him, and put her strong young arms around his neck, and drew him down. Her mouth was open and ready for him, and he knew then that all of her was simply waiting for him.

The firelight flamed, warming them, lighting their love. Memories stirred, deep in his subconscious, of a night nursery, drawn curtains – long-lost images of babyhood. Nothing to harm, nothing to disturb. Security. And as well, this flying sense of elation. But, too, somewhere at the very edge of this exultation, a small voice of common sense.

'Darling.'

'Yes.' A whisper. 'Yes.'

'Are you all right?'

'All right? Oh, yes, all right.'

'I love you.'

'Oh.' No more than a breath. 'Love.'


In the middle of April, somewhat to her surprise, for she was hopelessly impractical about such matters, Penelope was informed by the authorities that she was due for a week's leave. She accordingly presented herself, with a queue of other Wrens, at the office of the Regulating Petty Officer and, when her turn came, requested a rail pass to Porthkerris.

The Petty Officer was a cheerful lady from Northern Ireland. She had a freckled face and frizzy red hair, and looked quite interested when Penelope told her where she wanted to go.

'That's in Cornwall, isn't it, Stern?'

'Yes.'

'Is that where you live?'

'Yes.'

'Lucky girl.' She handed over the pass, and Penelope thanked her and went out of the room clutching her ticket to freedom.

The train journey was endless. Portsmouth to Bath. Bath to Bristol. Bristol to Exeter. At Exeter she had to wait an hour and then get onto the slow, stopping train that would take her on to Cornwall. She did not mind. She sat, in the dirty train, in a corner seat and stared through the soot-smeared window. Dawlish, and her first glimpse of the sea; only the English Channel, but still, better than nothing. Plymouth, and the Saltash Bridge, and what looked like half of the British Navy at mooring in the Sound. And then Cornwall, and all the small halts with their saintly and romantic names. After Redruth, she let down the window by its leather strap and hung out, not wanting to miss the first glimpse of the Atlantic, the dunes and the distant breaking rollers. Then the train trundled over the Hayle Viaduct, and she saw the estuary, filled with the flood tide. She pulled her suitcase off the luggage rack and went to stand in the corridor as they rounded the last curve and drew into the junction.

It was by now half past eight in the evening. She opened the heavy door and stepped thankfully down, lugging her case behind her, and with her uniform hat stuffed into the pocket of her jacket. The air felt warm and sweet and fresh, and the low sun cast long beams down the platform and out of its dazzle walked Papa and Sophie, come to meet her.

It was unbelievably wonderful to be home. The first thing she did was to race upstairs, tear off her uniform, and put on some proper clothes – an old cotton skirt, an Aertex shirt left over from school, a darned cardigan. Nothing had changed; the room was just the way she had left it, only tidier and shiningly clean. When, bare-legged, she ran downstairs again, it was to go from room to room, a thorough inspection, just to make sure that there, as well, everything was exactly the same. Which it was.

To all intents and purposes. Charles Rainier's portrait of Sophie, which had once held pride of place over the sitting-room mantelpiece, had been moved to a less important position and its place taken by *The Shell Seekers*, which had, after a number of inevitable delays, arrived from London. It was too large for the room, and the light was insufficient to do justice to its depth of colour, but still, it looked very handsome.

And the Potters had changed for the better. Doris had lost her pudgy curves and become quite slender, and she was letting her dyed hair grow out, so that now, half peroxide and half mousy brown, it resembled nothing so much as the coat of a piebald pony. And Ronald and Clark had grown, and were losing their spindliness and city-bred pallor. Their hair had grown as well, and their cockney voices had a distinct overtone of pure Cornish. And the ducks and hens had doubled in number, and one old hen had gone all broody and had, when nobody was looking, hatched out a brood of chicks in a broken wheelbarrow hidden deep in a thicket of brambles.

All Penelope wanted was to catch up on everything that had happened since the day – which now seemed immeasurably distant – when she had climbed on the train and set off for Portsmouth. Lawrence and Sophie did not let her down. Colonel Trubshot was running the ARP (Air-Raid Precautions) and being a nuisance to everybody. The Sands Hotel had been requisitioned and was full of soldiers. Old Mrs Treganton – the town's dowager, and a terrifying lady with dangling earrings – had tied an apron around her waist and was in charge of the Services canteen. There was barbed wire on the beach and they were building concrete pill-boxes, spiked with sinister guns, all along the coast. Miss Preedy had given up her dancing class and was now teaching physical training in a girls' school that had been evacuated from Kent, and Miss Pawson, in the black-out, had tripped over her stirrup-pump and bucket and broken her leg.

When at last they ran out of things to tell her, they hoped, naturally enough, to hear their daughter's tidings; every detail of her new – and, to them, unimaginable – life. But she didn't want to tell them. She didn't want to talk about it. She didn't want to think about Whale Island and

Portsmouth. She didn't even want to think about Ambrose. Sooner or later, of course, she would have to. But not now. Not this evening. She had a week. It could wait.

From the top of the hill, the land lay exposed, drowsing in the sunlight of a warm spring afternoon. The great bay to the north glittered blue, dazzled with sun pennies. Trevose Head was hazy, a sure sign of continuing good weather. To the south curved the other bay, with the Mount and its Castle, and in between lay farmland, winding high-hedged lanes, emerald fields where cattle grazed amongst the outcrops of granite. The wind was light, scented with thyme, and the only sounds the occasional bark of a dog, or the pleasant chuntering of a distant tractor.

They had walked, she and Sophie, the five miles from Carn Cottage. They took the narrow lanes that led up onto the moor, where the grassy hedges were studded with wild primroses, and ragged robin and celandine burst from the ditches in a profusion of pink and yellow. Finally they had climbed the stile and made their way up the turfy path, winding through thickets of bramble and bracken, which led to the summit of the hill; to the carns of lichened rock, piled tall as cliffs, where once, thousands of years ago, the small men who inhabited this ancient land had stood to watch the square-sailed ships of the Phoenicians sail into the bay, to drop anchor and trade their eastern treasures for the precious tin.

Now, weary from the long hike, they rested, Sophie supine on a patch of turf, with an arm across her eyes against the glare of the sun. Penelope sat beside her, elbows resting on her knees, her chin in her hand.

Far up in the sky a plane, a tiny silver toy, flew over. They both looked up and watched it go. Sophie said, 'I don't like planes. They remind me of the war.'

'Do you ever forget it?'

'Sometimes, I let myself. I pretend it hasn't happened. It's easy to pretend on a day like this.'

Penelope put out her hand and tugged at a tuft of grass.

'Nothing much has happened yet, has it?'

'No.'

'Do you suppose it will?'

'Of course.'

'Do you worry about it?'

'I worry for your father. He worries. He has been through it all before.'

'So have you . . .'

'Not as he did. Never as he did.'

Penelope threw away the grass and reached out to pull at another tuft.

'Sophie.'

'Yes.'

'I'm going to have a baby.'

The sound of the aircraft engine died, absorbed into the summery immensity of the sky. Sophie stirred, slowly sat up. Penelope turned her head and met her mother's eyes, and saw on that youthful, sunburned face an expression that could only be described as one of the deepest relief.

'Is this what you have not been telling us?'

'You knew?'

'Of course we knew. So reticent, so silent. Something had to be wrong. Why did you not tell us before?'

'Nothing to do with being ashamed or apprehensive. I just wanted it to be the right time. I wanted to have time to talk about it.'

'I have been so worried. I felt you were unhappy and regretted what you had done, or that you were in some sort of trouble.'

Penelope wanted to laugh. 'Aren't I?'

'But of course you aren't in trouble!'

'You know, you never fail to amaze me.'

Sophie ignored this. She became practical. 'You are certain you are having a child?'

'Certain.'

'Have you seen a doctor?'

'I don't need to. Anyway, the only doctor I could go to in Portsmouth was the Naval Surgeon, and I didn't want to go to him.'

'When is the baby due?'

'In November.'

'And who is the father?'

'He's a Sub Lieutenant. At Whale Island. Doing his Gunnery course. He's called Ambrose Keeling.'

'Where is he now?'

'Still there. He failed his exams, and he had to stay on and do the whole course again. It's called a re-scrub.'

'What age is he?'

'Twenty-one.'

'Does he know you're pregnant?'

'No. I wanted to tell you and Papa before anyone else.'

'Are you going to tell him?'

'Of course. When I get back.'

'What will he say?'

'I've no idea.'

'It doesn't sound as though you know him very well.'

'I know him well enough.' Far below, in the valley a man with a dog at his heels came through a farmyard, opened a gate and began to climb the hill to where his milk cows grazed. Penelope lay back on her elbows and watched him go. He wore a red shirt and the dog ran circles around him. 'You see, you were right about my being unhappy. At the beginning, when I was sent to Whale Island, I don't suppose I've ever been so miserable in my life. I was such a fish out of water. And I was homesick and I was lonely. That day I joined up, I thought I was picking up a sword and going out to fight, along with everybody else, and I found myself doing nothing but handing round vegetables, drawing black-out curtains, and living with a lot of females with whom I had nothing in common. And there was nothing I could do about it. No escape. Then I met Ambrose, and after that everything started to get better.'

'I didn't realise that it was as bad as that.'

'I didn't tell you. What good would it have done?'

'If you have a baby, you will have to leave the Wrens?'

'Yes. I'll be discharged. Probably dishonourably.'

'Will you mind?'

'Mind? I can't wait to get out.'

'Penelope . . . you didn't get pregnant on purpose?'

'Heavens no. Even I couldn't be as desperate as that. No. It just happened. One of those things.'

'You know . . . you surely know . . . that you can take precautions.'

'Of course, but I thought the man always did that.'

'Oh, my darling, I had no idea you were so naïve. What a rotten mother I have been.'

'I've never thought of you as a mother. I've always thought of you as a sister.'

'Well, I've been a rotten sister.' She sighed. 'What are we going to do now?'

'Go back and tell Papa, I suppose. And then go back to Portsmouth and tell Ambrose.'

'Will you marry him?'

'If he asks me.'

Sophie thought about this. Then she said, 'I know you must feel very strongly about this young man, otherwise you would not be carrying his child. I know you well enough to know that. But you mustn't marry him just because of the baby.'

'You married Papa when I was on the way.'

'But I loved him. I loved him always. I couldn't imagine an existence without him. Whether he had married me or not, I would never have left him.'

'If I do marry Ambrose, will you come to my wedding?'

'Nothing would keep us away.'

'I'd want you to be there. And then, afterwards . . . when he finishes at Whale Island, he'll be sent to sea. Can I come home and live with you and Papa? Have the baby at Carn Cottage?'

'What a question to ask! What else would you do?'

'I suppose I could become a professional fallen woman, but I'd much rather not.'

'You'd be useless at it, anyway.'

Penelope was filled with grateful love. 'I knew you'd be like this. How awful it would be to have a mother like other people's mothers.'

'Perhaps if I was, I should be a better person. But I am not good. I am selfish. I think about nobody but myself. This terrible war has started and things are going to get very bad before it is all over. Sons will be killed, and daughters too, and fathers and brothers, and all I can feel is thankful because you are coming home. I've missed you so much. But now we can be together again. How ever bad things get, at least we'll be together.'


Ambrose, with a stiff drink in his hand, telephoned his mother.

'Coombe Hotel.' The voice was feminine and intensely genteel.

'Is Mrs Keeling there?'

'If you just wait a moment, I'll go and look for her. I believe she's in the lounge.'

'Thank you.'

'Who shall I say is calling?'

'Her son. Sub Lieutenant Keeling.'

'*Thenk* you.'

He waited.

'Hello?'

'Mummy.'

'Darling boy. How lovely to hear you. Where are you calling from?'

'Whaley. Mummy. Look. I've got something to tell you.'

'Good news, I hope.'

'Yes. Splendid news.' He cleared his throat. 'I'm engaged to be married.'

Total silence.

'Mummy?'

'Yes, I'm still here.'

'You all right?'

'Yes. Yes, of course. Did you say you were going to be married?'

'Yes. The first Saturday in May. At the Chelsea Registry Office. Can you come?'

It sounded as though he were inviting her to a little party.

'But . . . when? . . . who? . . . Oh dear, you have flustered me.'

'Don't get flustered. She's called Penelope Stern. You'll like her,' he added without much hope.

'But . . . when did all this happen?'

'It's just happened. That's why I'm ringing. To let you know at once.'

'But . . . who is she?'

'She's a Wren.' He tried to think of something to tell his mother that would reassure her. 'Her father's an artist. In Cornwall.' Silence again. 'They've got a house in Oakley Street.' He thought of mentioning the 4½-litre Bentley, but his mother had never been much of a one for cars.

'Darling. I'm sorry to sound so unenthusiastic, but you are very young . . . your career . . .'

'There's a war on, Mummy . . .'

'I do know. I of all people should know that.'

'You'll come to our wedding?'

'Yes. Yes, of course . . . I'll come up to town for the weekend. I'll stay at the Basil Street.'

'That's great. You can meet her then.'

'Oh, Ambrose . . .'

She sounded quite tearful.

'Sorry about taking you unawares. But don't worry.' Pip-pip-pip went the phone. 'You'll love her,' he repeated, and hastily rang off before she had time to implore him to put more money in the box.

Left with the buzzing receiver in her hand, Dolly Keeling slowly replaced it on the hook.

From behind her little desk under the stairs, where she had been pretending to add an account, but was in fact listening in to every word, Mrs Musspratt looked up and smiled inquiringly, her head cocked to one side like a beady-eyed bird.

'Good news, I hope, Mrs Keeling.'

Dolly pulled herself together, gave a little toss of her head, assumed an expression of cheerful enthusiasm.

'So exciting. My son is to be married.'

'Oh, splendid. How romantic. These brave young people. When?'

'I beg your pardon?'

'When is the happy event to take place?'

'In two weeks. The first Saturday in May. In London.'

'And who is the lucky girl?'

She was becoming a little too inquisitive. Forgetting herself. Dolly put the woman in her place. 'I haven't yet had the pleasure of meeting her,' she said with dignity. 'Thank you for coming to find me, Mrs Musspratt.' And with that she left the woman to her sums and returned to the residents' lounge.

The Coombe Hotel had years before been a private house, and the lounge had once been its drawing room. It had a high white marble mantelpiece enclosing a tiny grate, and a number of bulging sofas and armchairs upholstered in white linen smothered with pink roses. A few water-colours, hung too high, were dotted about the walls, and there was a bow-window looking out onto the garden. The garden had gone to seed since the outbreak of war. Mr Musspratt did what he could with the grass cutter, but the gardener had gone to war and the borders were full of weeds.

There were eight permanent residents living in the hotel, but four of them had closed ranks and set themselves up as the élite, the hard core of the little community. Dolly was one of them. The others were Colonel and Mrs Fawcett Smythe and Lady Beamish. They played bridge together in the evenings, and had laid claim to the best chairs, around the fire, in the lounge, and the best tables, by the window, in the dining room. The others had to make do with chilly corners where the light was scarcely sufficient to read, and the tables in the way of the pantry door. But they were so sad and down-trodden anyway that nobody thought to pity them. Colonel and Mrs Fawcett Smythe had moved to Devon from Kent. They were both in their seventies. The Colonel had spent most of his life in the Army, and so was very good at telling everybody what that feller Hitler was going to do next, and putting his own interpretation on snippets of news that appeared in the daily papers relating to secret weapons and the movement of warships. He was a small, nut-brown man with a bristling moustache, but he made up for his lack of inches by a barking, parade-ground manner and a military bearing. His wife was fluffy-haired and quite colourless. She knitted a lot, and said 'Yes dear,' and agreed with everything her husband said, which was just as well for everybody, because Colonel Fawcett Smythe, contradicted, went red in the face and looked as though he were about to have a seizure.

Lady Beamish was even better. Of all of them, she was the only one unafraid of bombs or tanks or anything that the Nazis might unleash upon her. She was over eighty, tall and stout, with grey hair screwed into a knot at the back of her head and a pair of relentlessly cold grey eyes. She was very lame (the result, she had told an impressed audience, of a hunting accident) and had to walk with a hefty stick. When she was not actually on the move, she propped this article by the side of her chair, where it invariably got in the way of passers-by, either tripping them up or painfully clouting them across the shins. She had come reluctantly to the Coombe Hotel to sit out the war, but her home in Hampshire had been requisitioned by the Army, and her hard-pressed family had finally bullied and persuaded her to retire to Devon. 'Put out to grass,' she grumbled constantly, 'like some old war-horse.'

Lady Beamish's husband had been a senior official in the Indian Civil Service, and she had lived much of her life in that great subcontinent, the jewel in the crown of the British Empire, which she always referred to as 'Inja'. She must, Dolly often thought, have been a tower of strength to her spouse, queening it at garden parties, and, in times of trouble, coming up trumps. It was not hard to imagine her, armed only with solar-topi and silken sunshade, quelling a riotous mob of natives with those steely eyes, or, should the rioters decline to be quelled, rallying the ladies and making them tear up their petticoats for bandages.

They were waiting for Dolly where she had left them, gathered around the tiny fire. Mrs Fawcett Smythe with her knitting, Lady Beamish slapping patience cards onto her portable table, the Colonel standing with his back to the flames, warming his bottom, and bending and stretching his rheumatic knees like a stage policeman.

'Well.' Dolly sat down in her chair.

'What was all that about?' Lady Beamish asked, putting a black knave on a red queen.

'That was Ambrose. He's going to be married.'

This announcement caught the Colonel unawares, with his legs bent. It seemed to take some concentration to get them straight again.

'Well, I'll be jiggered,' he said.

'Oh, how exciting,' quavered Mrs Fawcett Smythe.

'Who's the girl?' asked Lady Beamish.

'She's . . . she's an artist's daughter.'

Lady Beamish turned down the corners of her mouth.

'An artist's daughter?' Her voice was deep with disapproval.

'I'm sure he's very famous,' said Mrs Fawcett Smythe consolingly.

'What's she called?'

'Er . . . Penelope Stern.'

'Penelope *Stein*?' The Colonel's hearing was not always very reliable.

'Oh, heavens, no.' They were all very sorry for the poor Jews, of course, but it was unimaginable that one's son should *marry* one. 'Stern.'

'I've never heard of an artist called Stern,' said the Colonel, as though Dolly were pulling a fast one on him.

'And they have a house in Oakley Street. And Ambrose says I will love her.'

'When are they getting married?'

'The beginning of May.'

'Are you going?'

'Of course I must be there. I shall have to ring the Basil Street, book a room. Perhaps I should go a little earlier, go round the shops, find something to wear.'

'Is it going to be a very large affair?' asked Mrs Fawcett Smythe.

'No. The Chelsea Registry Office.'

'Oh dear.'

Dolly felt moved to assert herself, take up cudgels on behalf of her son. She could not abide the thought of any of them becoming sorry for her. 'Well, wartime, you know, and with Ambrose going to sea at any moment . . . perhaps it's the most practical . . . though, I must say, I had always had dreams of a really pretty wedding in a church with an arch of swords. But there it is.' She shrugged bravely. 'C'est la guerre.'

Lady Beamish went on with her patience. 'Where'd he meet her?'

'He didn't say. But she's a Wren.'

'Well, that's something anyway,' Lady Beamish remarked. She sent Dolly a sharp, meaningful glance as she said this, which Dolly was careful not to intercept. Lady Beamish knew that Dolly was only forty-four. Dolly had told her at some length of her own frailties; the horrid headaches (she called them migraines) that were apt to strike her low at the most opportune moments; and there was her back trouble, which could be brought on by any simple domestic task such as bed-making or a session at the ironing board. Working stirrup-pumps or driving ambulances was simply out of the question. But still Lady Beamish remained unsympathetic, and from time to time made unkind remarks about Bomb-Dodgers and people who Didn't Pull Their Weight. Now, 'If Ambrose has chosen her, she'll be a darling,' Dolly told them all firmly. 'And,' she added, 'I've always wanted a daughter.'

It wasn't true. Upstairs in her bedroom, alone and unobserved, she could be herself, let all pretences drop. Awash with self-pity and loneliness, pierced by the jealousy of spurned love, she turned for comfort to her treasure box, her wardrobe, stuffed with feminine, expensive clothes. Inspected this little outfit, and then that. The soft chiffons and fine wools slid past beneath her hands. She took down a filmy dress and went to the long mirror, holding it up in front of her. One of her favourites. She had always felt so pretty in it. So pretty. In the looking-glass, she met her own eyes. They filled with tears. Ambrose. Loving a woman other than herself. Marrying her. She dropped the dress on the padded stool, and threw herself upon the bed and wept.

.     .     .

Summer had come. London was sweet with blossom and lilac. Sunlight lay, a warm benediction, on pavement and roof-top, reflected from the silvery curves of high-floating barrage balloons. It was May; a Friday; noon. Dolly Keeling, ensconced in the Basil Street Hotel, sat on the sofa by the open window of the upstairs lounge and waited for the arrival of her son and his fiancée.

When he came, running up the stairs two at a time, carrying his hat, looking marvellously handsome in his uniform, she was filled with delight, not simply at the sight of him, but, as well, because he appeared to be on his own. Perhaps he had come to tell her that he had decided to call the whole thing off, and that he wasn't going to be married after all. Eagerly, she got to her feet and went to greet him.

'Hello, Mummy . . .' He stooped to kiss her. His height was one of her pleasures, because it made her feel vulnerable and helpless.

'My darling . . . where's Penelope? I thought you were coming together.'

'We did. Drove up from Pompey this morning. But she wanted to get out of uniform, so I dropped her at Oakley Street and came on here. She won't be long.'

The tiny hope died, almost at birth, but still, she could have Ambrose to herself for a little time more. And it was easier to talk, just the two of them.

'Well, we'll just have to wait for her. Come along and sit down and you can tell me everything that's going to happen.' She caught the eye of the waiter, ordered a sherry for herself and a pink gin for Ambrose. 'Oakley Street. Are her parents there?'

'No. That's the bad news. Her father's got bronchitis. She only heard last night. They're not going to be able to make the wedding.'

'But surely her mother could come?'

'She says she has to stay in Cornwall and look after the old boy. And he is really old. Seventy-five. I suppose they don't want to take any risks.'

'But it does seem a shame . . . only little me at the wedding.'

'Penelope's got an aunt who lives in Putney. And some friends called Clifford. They're going to come. That's enough.'

Their drinks arrived, and were put down on Dolly's account. They raised their glasses. Ambrose said, 'I look towards you,' and Dolly smiled complacently, certain that the other occupants of the hotel lounge were watching them, their eyes caught by the handsome young Naval Officer and the pretty woman who looked far too young to be his mother.

'And your own plans?'

He told her. He had finally passed his Gunnery exams, had a week coming up at Divisional School, and would then be sent to sea.

'But your honeymoon?'

'No honeymoon. Married tomorrow, a night at Oakley Street, and then back on Sunday to Portsmouth.'

'And Penelope?'

'I'm putting her on the train for Porthkerris on Sunday morning.'

'Porthkerris? Is she not coming back to Portsmouth with you?'

'No. Actually.' Biting his thumb-nail, he gazed from the window as though something riveting were about to happen in the street below. Which it wasn't. 'She's got a bit of leave.'

'Oh dear. What a little time you'll have together.'

'Can't be helped.'

'No. I suppose not.'

She turned to set down her sherry glass and saw the girl reach the top of the stairs, standing there, hesitating, looking around her, looking for somebody. A very tall girl, with long dark hair caught back from her forehead – a schoolgirl's hair, plain and undressed. Her face, with its creamy complexion and deep-set dark eyes, was remarkable for its sheer unadornment; the gleam of unpowdered skin, the pale mouth, the dark brows, natural and unplucked and strongly shaped. She wore, on that hot day, clothes more suitable for a country holiday than a formal luncheon in a London hotel. A dark-red cotton dress with white spots and a white belt around its slender waist. White sandals on her feet, and . . . Dolly had to take a second look, just to be sure . . . yes, bare legs. Who on earth could she be? And why was she looking this way? And coming towards them? And smiling . . .

Oh, dear God.

Ambrose was getting to his feet. 'Mummy,' he was saying, 'this is Penelope.'

'Hello,' said Penelope.

Dolly just managed not to gape. She could feel her jaw dropping, but jerked it back into place and transformed the grimace into a brilliant smile. Bare legs. No gloves. No handbag. No hat. Bare legs. She hoped that the head waiter would allow them into the restaurant.

'My dear.'

They shook hands. Ambrose busied himself drawing up another chair, and signalling the waiter. Penelope sat in the full light of the window and faced Dolly with a gaze disconcerting in its unblinking directness. She is eyeing me, Dolly told herself, and knew the stirrings of resentment. She had no right to eye her future mother-in-law, and start up this tiresome fluttering of her heart. Dolly had expected youth, shyness, diffidence, even. Certainly not this.

'So nice to meet you . . . and you had a good drive up from Portsmouth. Yes, Ambrose has been telling me . . .'

'Penelope, what do you want to drink?'

'An orange or something. With ice, if there is any.'

'Not a sherry? Not a glass of wine?' Dolly tried tempting her, smiling still to cover her discomfiture.

'No. I'm hot and thirsty. Just orange.'

'Well, I've ordered a bottle of wine for luncheon. We can have our little toast then.'

'Thank you.'

'I'm sorry about your parents' not being able to be there tomorrow.'

'Yes. I know. But Papa caught flu, and then he didn't go to bed and he started wheezing. The doctor's put him to bed for a week.'

'Is there nobody else who could look after him?'

'Except Sophie, you mean?'

'Sophie?'

'My mother. I call her Sophie.'

'Oh, I see. Yes. Is there nobody else who could take care of your father?'

'Only Doris, our evacuee. And she's got her own two boys to keep an eye on. Besides, Papa's a rotten patient; Doris wouldn't stand a chance with him.'

Dolly made a little gesture with her hands.

'I suppose, like the rest of us, you're servantless now.'

'We always have been,' Penelope told her. 'Oh, thank you, Ambrose, that's perfect.' She took the glass from his hand, drank half of it in what looked like a single mouthful, and then set it down on the table.

'You always have been? Have you never had any help in the house?'

'No. Not servants. People staying who lent a hand, but never servants.'

'But who does the cooking?'

'Sophie. She loves it. She's French. She's a marvellous cook.'

'And the housework?'

Penelope looked slightly nonplussed, as though she had never considered housework. 'I don't know. It seems to get done. Sooner or later.'

'Well.' Dolly allowed herself a little laugh, worldly, *mondaine*. 'It all sounds very charming. And bohemian. And very soon, I hope, I shall have the pleasure of meeting your parents. Now, let's talk about tomorrow. What are you going to wear for your wedding?'

'I don't know.'

'You don't *know*?'

'I haven't thought about it. Something, I suppose.'

'But you must go shopping!'

'Oh, heavens no, I won't go shopping. There are masses of things at Oakley Street. I'll find something.'

'You'll *find* something . . .'

Penelope laughed. 'I'm afraid I'm not a clothes person. We none of us are. And we none of us ever throw anything away. Sophie's got some pretty things stashed away at Oakley Street. This afternoon Elizabeth Clifford and I are going to have a good old rootle-round.' She looked at Ambrose. 'Don't look so worried, Ambrose, I won't let you down.'

He smiled bleakly. Dolly told herself that she felt heart-sorry for the poor boy. Not a loving glance, not a tender touch, not a quick kiss had passed between him and this extraordinary girl he had found and decided to marry. Were they in love? Could they possibly be in love and continue to behave in such a careless fashion? Why was he marrying her if he was not besotted by her? Why was he marrying . . .?

Her thoughts, probing, came upon a possibility so appalling that they did a swift about-turn and scuttled for home.

And then, timidly, emerged again.

'On Sunday you're going home, Ambrose tells me.'

'Yes.'

'On leave.'

Ambrose was staring at Penelope, trying to catch her eye. Dolly was aware of this, but Penelope, apparently, was not. She simply sat there, continuing to look calm and unruffled.

'Yes. For a month.'

'Will you stay at Whale Island?'

Ambrose started waving his hand about, and finally, as though he could think of nothing else to do with it, clamped it over his mouth.

'No, I'm being discharged.'

Ambrose let out a great noisy sigh.

'For good?'

'Yes.'

'Is that usual?' She felt proud of herself, still smiling, but icy-voiced.

Penelope, too, smiled. 'No,' she told Dolly.

Ambrose, perhaps deciding that the situation could get no worse, now sprang to his feet. 'Let's go and get something to eat. I'm starving.'

Composedly, slowly, Dolly collected herself, her handbag, her white gloves. Standing, she looked down at Ambrose's future wife, with her dark eyes and her tassel of hair, and her careless grace. She said, 'I am not sure whether they will allow Penelope into the restaurant. She doesn't seem to be wearing any stockings.'

'Oh, for God's sake . . . they won't even notice.' He sounded angry and impatient, but Dolly smiled to herself, because she knew that his anger was directed, not at herself, but Penelope, because she had let the cat out of the bag.

She is pregnant, she told herself, leading the way across the lounge towards the dining room. She has trapped him, caught him. He does not love her. She is forcing him to marry her.

After luncheon, Dolly excused herself. She was going upstairs for a little lie down. A silly headache, she explained to Penelope, with just a hint of accusation in her voice. I have to be so careful. The slightest excitement . . . Penelope looked a little taken aback, because the luncheon had scarcely been exciting, but said that she quite understood; that she would see Dolly at the Registry Office tomorrow; that it had been a delicious lunch, and thank you very much. Dolly got into the archaic lift and rose upwards like a caged bird.

They watched her go. When he guessed that she was out of earshot, Ambrose turned to Penelope.

'Why the hell did you have to tell her?'

'What? That I'm pregnant? I didn't tell her. She guessed.'

'She didn't have to guess.'

'She'll know sooner or later. Why not now?'

'Because . . . well, that sort of thing upsets her.'

'Is that why she's got a headache?'

'Yes, of course it is . . .' They made their way downstairs. 'It's started everything off on the wrong foot.'

'Then I'm sorry. But I honestly can't see that it makes any difference. Why should it matter to her? We're getting married. And what business is it of anybody but ours?'

He could come up with no reply to this. If she could be so obtuse, then there was no explaining. In silence they emerged into the warm sunshine and walked down the street to where he had parked his car. She laid a hand on his arm. She was smiling. 'Oh, Ambrose, you're not really bothered? She'll get over it. Water under the bridge, Papa always says. Nine-day wonder. And then it'll be forgotten. Besides, once the baby arrives, she'll be delighted. Every woman looks forward to her first grandchild and dotes on it.'

But Ambrose was not so sure. They drove at some speed down Pavilion Road, down the King's Road, turning into Oakley Street. When he drew up outside the house, 'Are you coming in?' she asked him. 'Come and meet Elizabeth. You'll love her.'

But he declined. He had other things to do. He would see her tomorrow. 'All right.' Penelope was tranquil and did not argue. She gave him a kiss, got out of the car, and slammed the door shut. 'I shall now go and dig myself up a wedding dress.'

He grinned reluctantly. Watched her run up the steps and let herself in through the front door. She waved, and was gone.

He put the car into gear, did a U-turn and sped back the way they had come. He crossed Knightsbridge and drove through the gates into the park. It was very warm, but cool beneath the trees, and he parked the car and walked a little way, and found a seat and sat upon it. The trees rustled in the breeze and the park was full of pleasant summer sounds . . . children's voices and bird-song, with the continuous rumble of London traffic as background music.

He felt morose and gloomy. It was all very well, Penelope saying that it didn't matter, and that his mother would get used to the idea of a shotgun marriage – for indeed, what else was it? – but he knew perfectly well that she would never forget and probably never forgive. It was just very unfortunate that the Sterns were not going to be at the wedding tomorrow. They, with their liberal views and bohemian attitudes, might possibly have been able to swing the balance, and even if Dolly refused to come round to their way of thinking, at least she might be made to realise that there was another point of view.

For, according to Penelope, they were not a bit bothered about the forthcoming baby; quite the opposite – they were thrilled, and had made it clear, through their daughter, that Ambrose was in no way expected to make an honest woman of her.

Being told that he was a prospective father had knocked the ground from beneath his feet as nothing else could possibly do. He was shaken, appalled, and furiously angry – with himself for letting himself be caught in the classic, dreaded trap, and with Penelope for having taken him in. 'Are you all right?' he had asked her, and 'Oh, yes, all right,' she had replied, and, in the heat of the moment, and with one thing and another, there simply hadn't been time to double-check.

And yet, she had been very sweet. 'We don't need to get married, Ambrose,' she had assured him. 'Please don't think you have to.' And she had looked so calm and untroubled about the whole sorry affair that he had found himself doing a swift about-face and considering the possibilities on the other side of the coin.

Perhaps he was not, after all, in such a fix. Things could be very much worse. She was, in her strange way, beautiful. And well-bred. Not any common little girl, picked up in some Portsmouth pub, but the daughter of well-to-do, if unconventional, parents. Parents, moreover, of property. That enviable house in Oakley Street was not to be sneezed at, and a place in Cornwall was definitely an added bonus. He saw himself sailing in the Helford Passage. And there was always, at the end of the road, the possibility of inheriting a 4½-litre Bentley.

No. He had done the right thing. Once his mother had got over the little hiccup of discovering that Penelope was pregnant, then things should be all right. Besides, there was a war on. It was going to blow up at any moment and it would last for a long time, and they wouldn't be able to see much of each other, or even live together, until it was over. Ambrose had no doubt that he would survive. His imagination was not vivid, and he was not troubled by nightmares of engine-room explosions, or being drowned, or freezing to death in the winter seas of the Atlantic. And by the time it was finished, he would probably feel more like settling down and taking on the role of family man than he did at the moment.

He shifted in his chair, which was hard-backed and hideously uncomfortable. He noticed, for the first time, the lovers who lay only a few yards away, entwined on the bruised grass. Which gave him a splendid idea. He got off the chair and walked back to his car, drove out of the Park, around Marble Arch and into the quiet streets of Bayswater. He was whistling under his breath.

> I get no kick from champagne,
> Mere alcohol doesn't thrill me at all,
> So tell me, why should it be true . . .

Outside a tall, self-respecting house, he parked by the pavement's edge and made his way down basement steps to a flower-filled area. He rang the bell of the yellow front door. He was taking a chance, of course, but at four o'clock in the afternoon, she was usually around, taking a nap, or pottering in her tiny kitchen, or otherwise unoccupied. The chance paid off. She came to the door with her blonde hair tousled and a lacy negligee held modestly across her rounded, lavish breasts. Angie. Who had, when Ambrose was seventeen, gently relieved him of his virginity, and to whom he had fled, in times of trouble, ever since.

'Oh.' Her face lit up, filled with delight. 'Ambrose!'

No man could have had a better welcome.

'Hello, Angie.'

'It's ages since I've seen you. Thought you must be bobbing about in the ocean by now.' She held out a plump and motherly arm. 'Don't stand there on the doorstep. Come along in.'

Which he did.

As Penelope opened the front door of Oakley Street, Elizabeth Clifford leaned over the bannister and called her name. Penelope went upstairs.

'How did it go?'

'Not very well.' Penelope grinned. 'She's the worst. All hatted and gloved and furious because I wasn't wearing stockings. She said we wouldn't be allowed into the restaurant because I wasn't, but of course we were.'

'Does she realise you're having a child?'

'Yes. I didn't actually tell her, but the dawning of knowledge suddenly broke. You could tell. Much better, really. Ambrose was furious, but she might just as well know.'

'I suppose so,' said Elizabeth, but had it in her heart to feel sorry for the poor woman. Young people, even Penelope, could be dreadfully unperceptive and unfeeling. 'Do you want a cup of tea, or something?'

'Later, I'd love one. Look, I've got to find something to wear tomorrow. Do help me.'

'I've been nosing around in an old trunk . . .' Elizabeth led the way into her bedroom, where a variety of crushed and shredded garments were piled upon the enormous double bed she shared with Peter. 'Isn't this one rather nice? I bought it to go to Hurlingham . . . I think it was 1921. When Peter was in his cricket-playing period.' She took a dress from the top of the pile; creamy linen, very fine; long-waisted, shapeless, hem-stitched. 'It looks a bit grubby, but I could wash and iron it and have it ready for tomorrow. And look, there are even shoes to match – don't you adore the *diamanté* buckles? . . . and cream silk stockings.'

Penelope took the dress and went to the mirror, holding it up in front of her, gazing with half-closed eyes, turning her head this way and that to gauge the effect.

'It's a lovely colour, Elizabeth. All wheatey. Could I really borrow it?'

'Of course.'

'What about a hat? I suppose I ought to wear a hat. Or put my hair up, or something.'

'And we'll have to find a petticoat. It's so fine it's transparent, and your legs will show.'

'Can't have my legs showing. Dolly Keeling would have a fit . . .'

They began to laugh. Laughing, tearing off the red cotton dress, pulling the pale linen over her head, Penelope began to feel quite light-hearted. Dolly Keeling was a pain in the neck, but she was marrying Ambrose, not his mother, so what did it matter what that lady thought of her?


The sun shone. The sky was blue. Dolly Keeling, having breakfasted in bed, rose at eleven. Her headache, though it had not actually disappeared, had subsided. She bathed, dressed her hair, and put on her face. This took a long time, for it was important that she should look both youthful and impeccable, and hopefully put everyone else, including the bride, into the shade. With the final eyelash tweaked into place, she stood up, shed her filmy gown and donned her finery. A lilac silk dress, with a loose, floating coat of the same material. A fine straw halo hat, worn off the face, and bound with lilac grosgrain ribbon. Her totter-heeled, peep-toe shoes, her long white gloves, her white kid handbag. The ultimate reflection in the mirror reassured and bolstered her morale. Ambrose would be proud of her. She took a final couple of aspirin, doused herself in Houbigant, and went downstairs to the lounge.

Ambrose was waiting for her, looking devastating in his best uniform, and smelling as though he had just come straight from an expensive barber, which he had. There was an empty glass on the table at his side, and when she kissed him she smelt the brandy on his breath, and her heart went out to her dear boy, because he was, after all, only twenty-one, and bound to be nervous.

They went downstairs and took a taxi to the King's Road. Driving along, Dolly held Ambrose's hand, tightly, in her own little white-gloved fingers. They did not talk. It was no good talking. She had been a good mother to him . . . no woman could have done more. And as for Penelope . . . well, some things were better left unsaid.

The cab drew up outside the imposing edifice of the Chelsea Town Hall. They stepped out onto the warm, breezy pavement, and Ambrose paid the driver. While he was doing this, Dolly rearranged herself, smoothed her skirts, touched her hat to make certain that it was safely anchored, and then glanced about her. A few yards away, another person waited. It was a bizarre little figure, even tinier than herself, and with the thinnest black silk legs that Dolly had ever seen. Their eyes met. Dolly, flustered, hastily looked away, but it was too late, for already the other woman had moved forward, her face alight with eager anticipation, to pounce upon Dolly, grasping her wrist with a grip like a vice, and proclaiming, 'You have to be the Keelings. I knew it. Knew it in my bones the moment I set eyes on you.'

Dolly gaped, convinced that she was being attacked by a lunatic, and Ambrose, turning from the cab as it drove away, was as taken aback as his mother.

'I'm sorry, I – '

'I'm Ethel Stern. Lawrence Stern's sister.' She was buttoned into a child-size scarlet jacket with much frogging and embellishment, and wore on her head a vast, billowing black velvet tam o' shanter. 'Aunt Ethel to you, young man.' She released Dolly's arm and thrust her hand in Ambrose's direction. When he did not instantly take it, a dreadful uncertainty crossed Aunt Ethel's wrinkled features.

'Don't say I've got the wrong family?'

'No. No, of course not.' He had reddened slightly, embarrassed by the encounter and her outlandish appearance. 'How do you do? I am Ambrose, and this is my mother, Dolly Keeling.'

'Thought I couldn't be mistaken. I've been waiting for hours,' she went on chattily. Her hair was dyed dark red, and her hectic make up haphazard, as though she had applied it with her eyes shut. Her blackened eyebrows did not quite match, and the dark lipstick was already beginning to seep up into the wrinkles of skin around her mouth. 'I'm usually late for everything, so I made a big effort today, and of course was far too early.' All at once her expression altered to one of deepest tragedy. She was like a little clown; an organ-grinder's monkey. 'My dear, isn't it absolutely bloody about poor Lawrence? Poor devil, he'll be so disappointed.'

'Yes,' said Dolly faintly. 'We were so looking forward to meeting him.'

'Always enjoys a trip to London. Any old excuse will do . . .' At this point, she let out a screech, causing Dolly to jump out of her skin, and began waving her arms in the air. Dolly saw the taxi come trundling up from the other direction, and from this emerged Penelope and presumably the Cliffords. They were all laughing, and Penelope looked totally relaxed and not in the least nervous.

'Hello! Here we all are. What perfect timing. Aunt Ethel. Gorgeous to see you . . . Ambrose, hello.' She gave him a quick peck. 'You've never met the Cliffords, have you? Professor and Mrs Clifford. Peter and Elizabeth. And this is Ambrose's mother . . .' Everybody looked pleasant and shook hands and said 'How do you do.' Dolly smiled and nodded and was charming, the while her eyes busy, darting from one face to another, missing nothing, making their usual instant assessment.

Penelope looked as though she were wearing fancy dress, and yet, maddeningly, beautiful too – stunning and distinctive. She was so tall and slender, and the long, loose creamy dress, an heirloom, Dolly guessed, only served to accentuate this enviable elegance. Her hair she had knotted up into a loose coil at the nape of her neck, and she wore an enormous straw hat of acid green, wreathed with daisies.

Mrs Clifford, on the other hand, resembled a retired governess, probably very clever and brainy, but dowdily attired. The Professor was slightly smarter (but then it was always easier for a man to be well dressed) in a dark grey flannel pin-striped suit and a blue shirt. He was tall and thin, hollow-cheeked, ascetic. Quite attractive in a scholarly way. Dolly was not the only one who thought him attractive. From the corner of her eye she had spied Aunt Ethel greet him with an embrace, hanging from his neck and kicking up her little old legs behind her like the soubrette in a musical comedy. She wondered if perhaps Aunt Ethel was slightly mad, and hoped this did not run in the family.

Finally, they were all organised by Ambrose, who told them that if they did not get going soon, then he and Penelope would miss their slot. Aunt Ethel settled her hat, and they trooped indoors for the ceremony. Which took no time at all, and was over before Dolly had found a moment to dab at her eyes with her lace-trimmed handkerchief. Then they all trooped out again and moved on to the Ritz, where Peter Clifford, acting on instructions from Cornwall, had booked a table for lunch.

There is nothing like delicious food and a quantity of champagne, all dispensed by an urbane host, for improving any situation. Everybody, even Dolly, began to relax, despite the fact that Aunt Ethel chain-smoked throughout the meal and told countless questionable anecdotes, screaming with laughter long before the punch line was even reached. The Professor was charming and attentive, and told Dolly that he liked her hat, and Mrs Clifford seemed really interested in life at the Coombe Hotel and wanted to hear all about the people who lived there. Dolly told her, dropping the name of Lady Beamish more than once. And Penelope took off her acid-green hat and hung it on her chair, and darling Ambrose got to his feet and made a dear speech, referring to Penelope as his wife, whereupon everybody gave a little cheer. All in all it was a good party, and by the time it was over, Dolly felt that she had made friends for life.

But the best of everything has to come to an end, and at last, reluctantly, it was time to gather their belongings, push back their little gilt chairs, get to their feet and head for their various destinations – Dolly to the Basil Street, the Cliffords to an early evening concert at the Albert Hall. Aunt Ethel went on to Putney, and the young couple to Oakley Street.

It was while they stood, mildly tipsy, in the foyer, waiting for the taxis that would finally disperse them, that the event occurred which doomed for ever Penelope's relationship with her mother-in-law. For Dolly, woozy with champagne, and feeling sentimental and magnanimous, took Penelope's hands in her own and, gazing up at her, said, 'My dear, now that you are Ambrose's wife, I should like you to call me Marjorie.'

Penelope blinked in some astonishment. It seemed a funny thing to call your mother-in-law Marjorie, when you knew perfectly well that her name was Dolly. However, if that was what she wanted . . .

'Thank you. Of course I will.' She stooped and kissed the soft and scented cheek offered so graciously.

And for a year, she did call her Marjorie. Writing to thank for a birthday present, 'Dear Marjorie . . .' she began the letter. Phoning the

Coombe Hotel to give news of Ambrose, 'Oh, Marjorie, it's Penelope speaking,' she was to say.

It was not until many months had passed, by which time it was too late to rectify the situation, that she realised that Dolly had really said, in the foyer of the Ritz, 'My dear, I should like you to call me Madre.'


On the Sunday morning, Ambrose drove Penelope to Paddington to put her on the *Riviera* for Cornwall. The train, as usual, was stuffed to the gunwales with troops, seamen, and soldiers, kitbags and gas masks and tin hats. It had been impossible to book a seat, but Ambrose found an empty corner that he piled with her luggage, so that no other person could claim it.

They returned to the platform to say goodbye. It was hard to find the words, because all at once everything was alien and new; they were husband and wife, and neither knew what was expected of them. Ambrose lit a cigarette and stood smoking it, gazing up and down the platform, glancing at his watch. Penelope longed for the guard to blow his whistle, for the train to start to move, for it all to be over.

She said, with some violence, 'I hate goodbyes.'

'You'll have to get used to them.'

'I don't know when I'll see you again. In a month, when I come back to Portsmouth for my discharge, will you be gone?'

'Most likely.'

'Where will they send you?'

'It's anybody's guess. The Atlantic. The Med.'

'The Med would be nice. Anyway, sunny.'

'Yes.'

Another pause.

'I wish Papa and Sophie could have been there yesterday. I so wish you could have met them.'

'When I get some decent leave, I'll maybe get down to Cornwall for a few days.'

'Oh, do.'

'I hope everything goes all right. The baby, I mean.'

She blushed a little. 'I'm sure it will be all right.'

He looked at his watch again. She said, in some desperation, 'I'll write to you. You must – '

But at that moment the guard's whistle pierced the air. At once the usual small panic ensued. Doors were banged, voices raised, a man came sprinting, catching the train at the last possible second. Ambrose dropped his cigarette, ground it out with his heel, stooped and kissed his wife, bundled her aboard, and slammed the door behind her. She let down the window and hung out. The train began to move.

'Will you write and let me know your new address, Ambrose?'

An extraordinary thought occurred to him. 'I don't know *your* address.'

She began to laugh. He was running now, keeping alongside. 'It's Carn Cottage,' she shouted, above the din of clanking wheels. 'Carn Cottage, Porthkerris.'

Now the train was going too fast for him, and he slowed to a halt, stood there, waving her away. The train took the curve of the platform, and belching steam, rolled out of sight. She was gone. He turned and began the long walk back up the deserted platform.

Carn Cottage. The Elizabethan manor that he had dreamt up for himself, the sailboat on the Helford River – faded and dissolved, gone for ever. Carn Cottage. It sounded disappointingly ordinary, and he could not help feeling that he had, in some way, been cheated.

But still. She had gone. And his mother had returned to Devon and it was all safely over. Now, all he had to do was drive himself to Portsmouth and report for duty. In a funny way, he realised, as he ambled in the direction of the car park, he was looking forward to getting back to routine, and Service life and his shipmates. Men, on the whole, were easier to live with than women.

A few days later, on 10th of May, the Germans invaded France, and the war started in earnest.

# Sophie

It was the beginning of November before they saw each other again. After the long months of separation, there came a telephone call out of the blue. Ambrose, from Liverpool. He had a few days' leave, was catching the first available train and coming to Carn Cottage for the weekend.

He came, stayed, and departed again. Due to a number of adverse circumstances, the visit was an unqualified disaster. One was the fact that it rained, a steady downpour, for the entire three days. Another was that Aunt Ethel, never the most tactful nor conventional of guests, was also there at the time. The other reasons were too numerous, and too disheartening, to be either analysed or counted.

When it was over, and he had returned to his destroyer, Penelope decided that it had all been too depressing even to think about, and so, with the single-mindedness of youth, coupled with advanced pregnancy, firmly put the unhappy episode out of her mind. There were other, more important things, to think about.


The baby arrived, bang on cue, at the end of November. She was not born, as her mother had been, in Carn Cottage, but at the little cottage hospital in Porthkerris. She made her appearance so swiftly that the doctor did not arrive until it was all over, and Penelope and Sister Rogers were left to cope on their own. Which they did, efficiently and neatly. Once Penelope had been set, more or less, in order, Sister Rogers, as was the custom, bore the baby away, to wash it and tidy it up generally and dress it in the tiny vest and gown and the Shetland shawl which Sophie – it went without saying – had unearthed from some drawer, smelling strongly of moth-balls.

Penelope had always held her own private theories about babies. She had never had anything to do with them; had never even held one, but she believed implicitly that once you actually saw your own child for the first time, you would recognise it instantly. Why, of course, you would say, moving aside the swaddling shawl with a gentle forefinger and gazing down at the new little face, why, of course. It's you.

But this did not happen. When Sister Rogers finally returned, bearing the infant with as much pride as if she had just given birth herself, and laid her tenderly into Penelope's waiting arms, Penelope stared at the child with sinking disbelief. Fat, fair, with cornflower-blue, rather closely set eyes, huge chubby cheeks, and the general aspect of a cabbage rose, she resembled no person that Penelope had ever known. Certainly neither of her parents; nor Dolly Keeling; and as for the Sterns, she might not have had a drop of their blood coursing through her hour-old veins.

'Isn't she a beauty?' cooed Sister Rogers, leaning over the bed to gloat.

'Yes,' Penelope admitted faintly. If there had been any other mothers in the hospital, she would have insisted that there had been a mix-up and she had been presented with another woman's baby, but as she was the only maternity case in the place, this was hardly likely.

'Look at those blue eyes! Like a little flower, she is. I'll leave you with her for a moment, while I go and ring your mother.'

But Penelope did not want to be left with the baby. She couldn't think of anything to say to it. 'No, take her, Sister, please. I might drop her or do something awful.'

Sister, tactfully, did not question this. Some young mothers were funny, and heaven knew, she'd seen a few. 'Right then,' she scooped the woolly bundle back into her arms. 'Who's a little love, then?' she asked it. 'Who's Sister's little pet?' And, with her apron crackling, she went out of the room.

Penelope, thankful to be rid of the pair of them, lay back upon the pillows. Lay, gazing at the ceiling. She had a baby. She was a mother. She was the mother of Ambrose Keeling's child.

Ambrose.

She discovered, to her dismay, that it was no longer possible to ignore and put out of her mind all that had happened during that dreadful weekend, which had been doomed before it even started, because Ambrose's projected visit had been the cause of the only real row she had had with her mother. Penelope and Aunt Ethel had gone off for the afternoon together, to have tea with some decrepit old acquaintance of Aunt Ethel's, who lived in Penzance. Returning to Carn Cottage, a delighted Sophie informed Penelope that she had a lovely surprise waiting for her upstairs. Dutifully she had followed her mother up to her room, and there saw, instead of her own much-loved bed, a new and monstrous double bed, which took up all the space. They had never quarrelled before, but in a gust of uncharacteristic rage, Penelope lost her temper and told Sophie that she had no right, it was *her* bedroom, and it was *her* bed. And it wasn't a lovely surprise at all, it was a hateful surprise. She didn't want a double bed, it was hideous, she wouldn't sleep in it.

And Sophie's quick Gallic temperament flared to match her own. No man who had been bravely fighting a war could be expected to make love to his wife in a single bed. What did Penelope expect? She was a married woman now, a little girl no longer. This was no longer *her* bedroom, it was *their* bedroom. How could she be so childish? And Penelope had burst into furious tears and shouted that she was *pregnant*, and she didn't want to be made love to, and by the end of it they were both screaming at each other like a couple of fish-wives.

There had never been such a fight before. It upset everybody. Papa was furious with the pair of them, and others in the house crept around on tiptoe as though an explosion had taken place. Eventually, of course, they made it up, apologised and kissed, and the matter was not mentioned again. But it did not augur well for Ambrose's visit. Indeed, looking back, it did much to contribute to the resultant disaster.

Ambrose. She was Ambrose's wife.

Her lips trembled. She felt the lump swelling in her throat. Tears gathered, welled into her eyes, fell, unchecked, sliding down her cheeks, soaking the pillow-case. Once started, it was impossible to stop. It was as though all the unshed tears of years had decided to come at once. She was still crying when her mother arrived, bursting joyously through the door. Sophie was dressed in the rust-red canvas trousers and fisherman's guernsey which she had been wearing when Sister Rogers telephoned, and as well, bore in her arms a huge bunch of Michaelmas daisies, hastily gathered from her border as she made her way through the garden.

'Oh, my darling, you clever girl, and in no time at all . . .' She dropped the flowers onto a chair and came to embrace her child. 'Sister Rogers says . . .' She stopped. The joy faded from her face and was replaced by an expression of acute concern. 'Penelope.' She sat on the edge of the bed and reached for Penelope's hand. 'My darling, what is it? Why do you cry? Was it so difficult, so bad?'

Incoherent with weeping, Penelope shook her head. Her nose was running, her face blotched and swollen.

'Here,' ever practical, Sophie produced a clean handkerchief scented and fresh. 'Blow your nose, mop up your tears.'

Penelope took the handkerchief and did as she was told. Already, she felt marginally better. Just having Sophie there, sitting beside her, improved the situation. When she had blown, and mopped, and sniffed for a bit, she felt strong enough to pull herself into a sitting position, and Sophie pummelled the pillows and turned them over, so that the wet, tear-soaked sides were on the bottom.

'Now. Tell me, what is it? There is nothing wrong with the baby?'

'No. No, it isn't the baby.'

'Then what?'

'Oh, Sophie, it's Ambrose. I don't love Ambrose. I should never have married him.'

It was out. It was said. The relief of having actually admitted it, out loud, was enormous. She met her mother's eyes, and saw them grave, but Sophie, as always, was neither surprised nor shocked. She simply sat, silent, for an instant, and then said his name, 'Ambrose', as though it were the answer to some unsolved conundrum.

'Yes. I know now. It's all been the most ghastly mistake.'

'When did you know?'

'That weekend. Even as he got off the train and came walking up the platform towards me, I was filled with misgiving. It was like seeing a stranger coming and one that I didn't particularly want to see. I didn't think it was going to be like that. I felt a bit shy about seeing him again after all these months, but I never imagined it would be like that. Driving back to Carn Cottage with him beside me, and the rain bucketing down, I tried to pretend that it was nothing – just an awkwardness between us. But as soon as he walked into Carn Cottage I knew that it was hopeless. He was wrong. Everything was wrong. The house rejected him and he didn't fit. And after that, it just went on getting steadily worse.'

Sophie said, 'I hope that had nothing to do with Papa and me.'

'Oh, nothing, nothing,' Penelope hastened to assure her. 'You were angels to him, both of you. It was me that was so vile to him. But I couldn't help it. I was bored by him. It felt like having the most impossible stranger to stay. You know, how people say, so-and-so will be in your neighbourhood, so nice, I know you will be kind to him. And you are kind, and you ask them for the weekend and it's all a nightmare of suffocating boredom. And I know it rained all the time, but that shouldn't have mattered. It was him. He was so uninteresting, so useless. Do you know, he couldn't even clean his own shoes? He'd never cleaned his own shoes. And he was rude to Doris and Ernie and he thought the boys no better than a pair of urchins. He's a snob. He couldn't understand why we all sat down to meals together. He couldn't think why Doris and Clark and Ronald weren't all banished to live in the kitchen. I think that was what upset me more than anything else. I never realised that he – that *anybody* for that matter – could think such things; could *say* them; could be so hateful.'

'In fairness, my darling, I don't think you can blame him for his views. That is the way he has been brought up. It is perhaps we who are out of line. We have always conducted our domestic lives quite differently from other people.'

But Penelope was not to be comforted. 'It wasn't just *him*. Like I told you, it was me as well. I was horrible to him. I didn't know I could be so horrible. I didn't want him there. I didn't want him to touch me. I wouldn't let him make love to me.'

'In the condition you were in at the time, that is hardly surprising.'

'He didn't think it was surprising. He was just angry and resentful.' She gazed at Sophie in some despair. 'It's all my fault. You said that I shouldn't marry him unless I truly loved him and I didn't listen to you. But I *do* know that if I had been able to bring him to Carn Cottage, to meet you both, before we even got engaged, then I would never, in a thousand years, have married him.'

Sophie sighed. 'Yes. It is unfortunate that there was no time for that. And as well, it was unfortunate that Papa and I were not able to be at your wedding. Even at that last moment, it might have been possible to change your mind and back away. But it's no good looking back. It's too late.'

'You didn't like him, did you, Sophie? You and Papa? Did you think I must have gone out of my mind?'

'No, we didn't think that.'

'What am I to do?'

'My darling, at the moment, there is nothing that you can do. Except, I think, grow up a little. You're not a child any longer. You have responsibilities now, a child of your own. We are in the middle of this dreadful war, and your husband is at sea with the Atlantic Convoys. There is nothing for it, but to accept the situation and carry on. Besides,' she smiled, remembering, 'he came to see us at a bad time. All that rain, and Aunt Ethel there as well, smoking her cigarettes, and nipping back her gin, and coming out with her usual outrageous and hideously outspoken remarks. And as for you, no pregnant woman is ever quite herself. Perhaps, next time you see Ambrose, things will be different. You might feel differently.'

'But, Sophie, I've made such a fool of myself.'

'No. You were just very young and caught up in circumstances that were totally beyond you. Now, please, for my sake, cheer up. Smile and ring the bell, and Sister Rogers will bring my first grandchild into the room for me to see. And we will forget that this conversation ever took place.'

'Will you tell Papa?'

'No. It would trouble him. I don't like him worried.'

'But you never have secrets from him.'

'This one I shall keep.'


It was not only Penelope who found herself nonplussed by the baby's appearance. Lawrence, coming, the next day, to view for the first time, was equally puzzled.

'My darling, who *does* she look like?'

'I've no idea.'

'She is very sweet, but she doesn't appear to have anything to do with either you or her father. Perhaps she is like Ambrose's mother?'

'Not in the very least. I've decided she's a throw-back, come from generations away. Probably the spitting image of some long-dead ancestor. Whatever, to me it's all a mystery.'

'No matter. She seems to have come fully equipped. Which is all that really counts.'

'Have the Keelings been told?'

'Yes, I sent a cable to Ambrose's ship, and Sophie telephoned his mother at her hotel.'

Penelope made a face. 'Brave old Sophie. And what did Dolly Keeling have to say?'

'Apparently she sounded delighted. Always hoped it would be a little girl.'

'Bet she's telling all her cronies and Lady Beamish that it's a seven-month baby.'

'Oh, well, if appearances matter so much to her, what harm does it do?' Lawrence hesitated for a moment and then continued. 'She also said that it would be very nice if the baby could be called Nancy.'

'*Nancy?* Where on earth did she get that from?'

'That was her mother's name. It might be a good idea. You know,' he made a small expressive gesture with his hand, 'help to smooth things over a little bit.'

'All right, we'll call her Nancy.' Penelope sat up to peer at the baby's face. 'Nancy. Actually, it suits her quite well.'

Lawrence, however, was less concerned about the baby's name than he was about her behaviour.

'Not going to yell all the time, is she? Can't stand yelling babies.'

'Oh, Papa, of course not. She is very placid. She just eats her mother, and then sleeps, and then wakes up and eats her mother again.'

'Little cannibal.'

'Do you think she'll be pretty, Papa? You've always had a discerning eye for a pretty face.'

'She'll be all right. She'll be a Renoir. Fair and bloomy as a rose.'


And then, Doris. Most of the evacuees, unable to bear their exile another moment, had returned, in dribs and drabs, to London, but Doris, Ronald and Clark stayed on and were now permanent residents of Carn Cottage and part of the family. In June, during the retreat of the British Expeditionary Force from France, Doris' husband Bert had been killed. The tidings were brought to them by the telegraph boy, cycling up the hill from the Porthkerris Post Office. He had opened the gate in the wall and come whistling through the garden, where Sophie and Penelope were hard at work grubbing weeds from the border.

'Telegram for Mrs Potter.'

Sophie knelt up, her hands covered in earth, her hair awry, and an expression on her face that Penelope had never seen before. 'Oh, *mon Dieu.*'

She took the orange envelope and the boy went away. The door in the wall banged shut behind him.

'Sophie?'

'It must be her husband.'

After a little, 'What are we to do?' Penelope whispered.

Sophie did not reply. She simply wiped her hand on the seat of her cotton trousers and slit the envelope open with a black-nailed thumb. She took out the message and read it, and then folded it and put it back into the envelope.

'Yes,' she said. 'He is dead.' She got to her feet. 'Where is Doris?'

'Up in the paddock, hanging out washing.'

'And the boys?'

'They'll be back from school any moment now.'

'I must tell her before they come. If I am not back, keep them busy. She must have time. Before she tells them, she must have time.'

'Poor Doris.' It sounded painfully inadequate, banal to the point of idiocy, but what else could one say?

'Yes. Poor Doris.'

'What will she do?'

What Doris did was to be immensely brave. She wept, of course, unleashing her grief and rage in a sort of tirade against her young husband, who had been such a bloody fool as to go and get himself killed. But once that was over and she had pulled herself together, and she and Sophie were drinking a comforting hot strong cup of tea together, sitting over the kitchen table, her thoughts were all for her sons.

'Poor little buggers, what's life going to be like for them without a dad?'

'Children are resilient.'

'How the hell am I going to manage?'

'You will.'

'Suppose I ought to go back to Hackney. Bert's mum . . . well, she'll need me, maybe. She'll want to see the boys.'

'I think that you should go. Make certain that she is all right. And if she is, I think you should come back to us. The boys are happy here, they have made their friends, it would be cruel to uproot them now. Let them keep what security they have.'

Doris stared at Sophie. She sniffed a bit. She had only just stopped crying and her face was swollen and blotchy. 'But I can't just stay here, indefinite-like.'

'Why not? You are happy with us.'

'You're not just being kind?'

'Oh, my dear Doris, I don't know now what we would do without you. And the boys are like our own children. We would miss you so much if you left us.'

Doris thought about this. 'I'd rather stay than anything. I've never been so happy as what I've been here. And now, with Bert gone . . .' Her eyes filled with tears again.

'Don't cry, Doris. The boys mustn't see you crying. You must show them how to be brave. Tell them to be proud of their father, dying for such a cause, to free all those poor people in Europe. Teach them to be good men, just as he was.'

'He wasn't all that good. He was a bloody nuisance sometimes.' The tears receded, and the ghost of a smile showed on Doris's face. 'Coming home drunk from the football; falling into bed with his boots on.'

'Don't forget those things,' Sophie told her. 'They are all part of the person that he was. It is good to remember the bad times as well as the good. After all, that is what life is all about.'

And so Doris stayed. And when Penelope's baby was born, she could not wait to see it. A little girl. Doris had always longed for a daughter, and now, with Bert dead, it did not look as though she would ever have one. But this baby . . . She was the only one of them instantly besotted by the infant.

'Ooh, she's *lovely*.'

'Do you think so?'

'Penelope, she's beautiful. Can I pick her up?'

'Of course.'

Doris stooped and gathered the child into her practised and capable arms, stood gazing down at her with an expression on her face of adoring motherhood that made Penelope feel slightly ashamed, because she knew that she was incapable of such transparent devotion.

'We none of us know who she looks like.'

But Doris did. Doris knew exactly whom she resembled. 'She's the spitting image of Betty Grable.'

And no sooner had mother and child returned to Carn Cottage than Doris took Nancy over, and Penelope, assuaging a certain guilt by telling herself that she was doing Doris a good turn, was happy to let her. It was Doris who bathed Nancy and washed her nappies, and, when Penelope grew bored with breast-feeding, made up the bottles and nursed the infant herself, sitting on a low chair in the warm kitchen, or by the sitting-room fire. Ronald and Clark were equally devoted, bringing their school friends home to admire the new arrival. As the winter slowly passed, Nancy thrived, grew hair, teeth, grew fatter than ever. From the tool-shed Sophie produced Penelope's old high-wheeled, strap-slung perambulator, and this was polished up by Doris, and pushed, with some pride, up and down the hills of Porthkerris, with many stops to show Nancy off to any passer-by who happened to be interested, and many who were not.

Nancy's temperament remained sweet and placid. She lay in her pram in the garden, either sleeping, or tranquilly observing passing clouds or the fluttering branches of the white cherry tree. When the spring came and the blossoms fell, her blankets were scattered with white petals. Soon she was lying on a rug, reaching for a tinkling rattle. Then she was sitting up, hitting two clothes-pegs together.

She was a source of much amusement to Sophie and Lawrence and a source of much comfort and joy to Doris. But Penelope, dutifully playing with the child, building bricks, turning the pages of battered picture books, privately decided that she was dreadfully dull.

Meanwhile, beyond the frontiers of this tiny domestic world, the storm of the war, reverberating, dark-clouded, gathered momentum. Europe was occupied, Lawrence's beloved France overrun, and no day passed that he did not anguish for that country, and fear for old friends. In the Atlantic the U-boats prowled, hunting the slow convoys of naval destroyers and helpless merchant ships. The Battle of Britain had been won, but at terrible cost of planes, pilots, and airfields, and the Army, re-formed after France and Dunkirk, were taking up positions in Gibraltar and Alexandria, in anticipation of the next onslaught of German military might.

And, of course, the bombing had started. The endless raids on London.

Night after night, the warning sirens sounded, and night after night, the massive formations of Heinkels, black-crossed and sinister, throbbed in, across the Channel, out of the darkness of France.

At Carn Cottage, they listened each morning to the news, and their hearts bled for London. On a more personal level, Sophie's concern was for Oakley Street, and the people who lived there. The Friedmanns, on her instructions, had moved from the attics to the basement, but the Cliffords stayed where they had always been, on the second floor, and every time there was news of a raid (which was most mornings), Sophie imagined them dead, wounded, blown up, or buried in rubble.

'They are too old to be enduring this dreadful experience,' she told her husband. 'Why don't we ask them to come and live here, with us?'

'My darling girl, we have no space. And even if we had, they wouldn't come. You know that. They are Londoners. They would never leave.'

'I would be happier if I could see them. Talk to them. Make certain that they are all right . . .'

Covertly, Lawrence watched his young wife, sensing her restlessness. For two years, she had been stuck here, at Porthkerris, his Sophie who had never lived more than three months in any place during the whole of their married life. And Porthkerris in wartime was grey and dull and empty, very different from the lively town to which they had thankfully escaped every summer before the war. She was not bored, for she was never bored, but day-to-day life became, steadily, increasingly difficult, as food grew short, rations grew smaller, and a new and more tiresome shortage cropped up every day – shampoo, cigarettes, matches, camera films, whisky, gin – any tiny luxury that helped to oil the drudge of existence. Housekeeping also became more difficult. Everything had to be queued for, and then lugged back up the hill from the town, because none of the tradespeople had petrol to deliver any longer. Petrol was perhaps the greatest deprivation of all. They still had the old Bentley, but it spent most of its life in the recesses of Grabney's Garage, simply because they were not allowed enough fuel to drive it more than a few miles.

And so, he understood the restlessness. Wise in the ways of women, he understood and sympathised. She needed, he knew, to get away from them all for a few days. He bided his time, waiting for an opportunity to bring the subject up, but it seemed now that they were never alone; the little house buzzed with activity and voices. Doris and the boys, Penelope and now the baby filled every room, every waking hour, and when they finally fell into bed each night, Sophie was so exhausted that she was usually asleep by the time that Lawrence climbed in beside her.

Finally, one day, he caught her on her own. He had been digging potatoes, painfully, for his crippled hands had difficulty in wielding the spade and groping for the earthy roots, but he finally had filled a basket and carried it indoors, through the back door, where he found his wife sitting at the kitchen table disconsolately shredding a cabbage.

'Potatoes.' He dumped them on the floor by the stove.

She smiled. Even when she was down in the dumps, she could always provide that smile for him. He pulled up a chair and sat and looked at her. She was too thin. There were lines around her mouth, around her beautiful dark eyes.

He said, 'Alone at last. Where is everybody?'

'Penelope and Doris have taken the children down to the beach. They will be back presently, for lunch.' She took another chop or two at the cabbage. 'And I am giving them this to eat, and the boys will say that they hate it.'

'Just cabbage. Nothing else?'

'Macaroni cheese.'

'You make the best.'

'It is boring. Boring to cook and boring to eat. I don't blame them for complaining.'

He said, 'You have too much to do.'

'No.'

'Yes. You are tired and fed up.'

She looked up and met his eyes. After a little, 'Does it show so much?' she asked him.

'Only to me, who knows you so well.'

'I am ashamed. I hate myself. Why should I be discontented? But I feel so useless. What am I doing? Making nets and cooking meals. I think of women all over Europe, and I hate myself, but I can't help it. And if I have to go and queue for another hour for an oxtail that some other person has just bought, I think I shall start to have hysterics.'

'You should go away for a day or two.'

'Go away?'

'Go to London. See your house. Stay with the Cliffords. Reassure yourself.' He reached out and put his hand over hers, covering it with earth from the potato patch. 'We listen to the news of the bombing, and we're horrified, but disaster relayed is often more frightening than the horror itself. The imagination bolts, the heart sinks in dread. But, in truth, nothing is ever so bad as we think it is going to be. Why don't you go to London and find that out for yourself?'

Looking, already, more cheerful, Sophie considered this. 'Will you come too?'

He shook his head. 'No, my dear. I am too old for junketings, and junketings are exactly what you need. Stay with the Cliffords, giggle with Elizabeth. Go shopping with her. Get Peter to take you out to lunch at the Berkeley or L'Ecu de France. I believe the food there is still excellent, despite all the shortages. Call up your friends. Go to a concert, the theatre. Life goes on. Even in London in wartime. Especially, perhaps, in London, in wartime.'

'But will you not mind if I go without you?'

'I shall mind more than I can say. Not a moment will pass when I shall not miss you.'

'For three days? Could you bear it for three days?'

'I can bear it. And when you come back you can spend three weeks telling me everything you have done.'

'Lawrence, I love you so much.'

He shook his head, not refuting this, but simply letting her know that she had no need to tell him. He leaned forward and kissed her mouth, and then got to his feet and went to the sink to wash the mud from his hands.

The night before she was due to catch the train to London, Sophie went to bed early. Doris was out, gone to some hop in the town hall, and the children already asleep. Penelope and Lawrence sat up for a little, listening to a concert on the radio, but then Penelope began to yawn, put away her knitting, kissed her father good night, and made her way upstairs.

The door to Sophie's bedroom stood open, the light still shone. Penelope put her head around the door. Sophie was in bed, and reading.

'I thought you came up early to get your beauty sleep.'

'I am too excited to sleep.' She laid down her book on the eiderdown. Penelope went to sit beside her. 'I wish you were coming with me.'

'No. Papa's right. You'll have much more fun on your own.'

'What shall I bring back for you?'

'I can't think of anything.'

'I shall find something special. Something that you never dreamed you wanted.'

'That'll be nice. What are you reading?' She picked up the book. '*Elizabeth and her German Garden*. Sophie, you must have read that a hundred times.'

'At least. But I always go back to it. It comforts me. Soothes me. It reminds me of a world that once existed and will exist again when the war is finished.'

Penelope opened it at random and read aloud. 'What a happy woman I am, living in a garden, with books, babies, birds and flowers and plenty of leisure to enjoy them.' She laughed and laid the book down again.

'You've got all those things. It's just the leisure you're missing out on. Good night.' They kissed.

'Good night, my darling.'


She telephoned from London, her voice joyous over the crackling line.

'Lawrence. It's me. Sophie. How are you, my darling? Yes, I am having a wonderful time. You were quite right, nothing is as bad as I thought it would be. Yes, of course, there is bomb damage, great holes in terraces of houses, like teeth knocked out, but everybody is brave and cheerful and carrying on as though nothing had happened. And there is *so* much going on. We have been to two concerts, we heard Myra Hess at lunch-time, so perfect, you would have loved her. And I have seen the Ellingtons and that nice boy, Ralph, who was studying at the Slade; he is in the RAF now. And the house is fine, standing up to all the bangs and thumps, and it is so lovely to be back, and Willi Friedmann is growing vegetables in the garden . . .'

When he could get a word in edgeways, 'What are you doing this evening?' Lawrence asked.

'We are going out for dinner with the Dickinses; Peter and Elizabeth and I. You remember them, he is a doctor, he used to work with Peter . . . they live out near Hurlingham?'

'How will you get there?'

'Oh, by taxi, or tube. The tubes are extraordinary, the stations full of sleeping people. They sing and have lovely parties and then they all go to sleep. Oh, my darling, there are the pips. I must hang up. Love to everybody, and I'll be home the day after tomorrow.'


That night, Penelope awoke with a terrifying start. Something – some sound, some alarm. The baby, perhaps. Had Nancy cried out? She lay listening, but all she could hear was the frightened thudding of her own heart. This gradually subsided. Then she heard the footsteps crossing the landing, the creaking boards of the staircase, the click as a light was switched on. She got out of bed and went out of her room and leaned over the bannisters. The hall light burned.

'Papa?'

There was no reply. She crossed the landing and looked into his bedroom. The bed was disturbed, but empty. She returned to the landing, hesitated. What was he doing? Was he ill? Listening, she heard him moving about in the sitting room. Presently all was still. He was wakeful, that was all. Sometimes when he was wakeful, he did this: took himself downstairs, built up the fire, found himself a book to read.

She returned to bed. But sleep eluded her. She lay in the darkness and watched the dusky sky beyond the open window. Down on the beach, a flood tide murmured, rollers shushing in on the sand. Listening to the ocean's stirring, she waited, wide-eyed, for the dawn.

At seven, she got up and went downstairs. He had switched on the radio. There was music. He was waiting for the early-morning news.

'Papa.'

He put up a hand, motioning her to be silent. The music faded. The time signal sounded. 'This is London. The seven-o'clock news.' Alvar Liddell reading it. The calm voice, dispassionate, objective, told them what had happened. Told them of last night's bombing raid on London . . . incendiaries, land-mines, high explosives had all been showered upon the city. Fires still burned, but were under control . . . the docks had been hit . . .

Penelope put out her hand and switched the radio off. Lawrence looked up at her. He wore his old Jaeger dressing-gown, the stubble on his chin glinted white.

He said, 'I couldn't sleep.'

'I know. I heard you come down.'

'I have been sitting here, waiting for the morning.'

'There have been other raids. It will be all right. I'll make tea. Don't worry. We'll have a cup of tea, and then we'll ring Oakley Street. It'll be all right, Papa.'

They tried to put a call through, but the operator told them that, after last night's raid, there were no lines to London. All morning, hour by hour, they tried to get through. Without success.

'Sophie will be trying to ring us, Papa, just as we are trying to ring her. She'll be just as frustrated as we are, and just as anxious, because she knows that we are worried.'

But it was midday before the telephone finally rang. Penelope, chopping vegetables for soup at the kitchen sink, heard the bell, dropped the knife and ran for the sitting room, wiping her hands on her apron as she went. But Lawrence, sitting beside the instrument, had already picked up the receiver. She went to kneel beside him, leaning close, so as not to miss a word.

'Hello? Carn Cottage here. Hello?'

A buzz, a squeak, a strange burring sound, and then, at last, 'Hello.' But it was not Sophie's voice.

'Lawrence Stern speaking.'

'Oh, Lawrence, this is Lalla Friedmann. Yes, Lalla from Oakley Street.

I couldn't get through before. I have been trying for over two hours. I – ' Her voice suddenly broke and stopped.

'What is it, Lalla?'

'You aren't alone?'

'Penelope is with me. It's . . . Sophie, isn't it?'

'Yes. Oh, Lawrence, yes. And the Cliffords. All of them. They have all been killed. A land-mine fell directly on the Dickinses' house. There is nothing left. We went to see, Willi and I. This morning, when they had not returned, Willi tried to ring the Dickinses, but of course it was impossible. So we went ourselves to find out what had happened. We had been before, one Christmas, so we knew the way. We took a taxi, but then we had to walk . . .'

Nothing left.

' . . . and when we reached the end of the street, it was cordoned off; nobody was allowed there, and the firemen were still working. But we could see. The house had disappeared. Nothing there but a great crater. And there was a policeman and I spoke to him. And he was very kind, but he said there is no hope. No hope, Lawrence.' She began to weep. 'All of them. Dead. I am so sorry. I am so sorry to tell you.'

Nothing left.

Lawrence said, 'It was good of you to go and look for them. And good of you to ring me up . . .'

'It is the *worst thing I have ever had to do.*'

'Yes,' said Lawrence. 'Yes.' He sat there. After a little, he hung up, his twisted fingers fumbling as he tried to replace the receiver. Penelope turned her head and laid it against the thick wool of his sweater. The silence that ensued was empty of everything. A vacuum.

'Papa.'

He put up a hand, stroked her hair.

'Papa.'

She looked up at him, and he shook his head. She knew that he wanted only to be left alone. She saw then that he was old. He had never seemed so to her before, but now she knew that he would never be anything else. She got to her feet and went out of the room and closed the door.

Nothing left.

She went upstairs and into her parents' bedroom. The bed, on this ghastly morning, had never been made. The sheets were still awry, the pillow dented from her father's sleepless head. He had known. They both had. Hoping, keeping up their courage, but filled with deadly certainty. They had both known.

Nothing left.

On the table at Sophie's side of the bed lay the book that she had been reading the night before she went to London. Penelope went and sat there and picked up the book. It fell open in her hands at that well-worn page.

'What a happy woman I am, living in a garden, with books, babies, birds and flowers and plenty of leisure to enjoy them. Sometimes I feel as if I were blest above all my fellows in being able to find happiness so easily.'

The words dissolved and were lost, like figures seen through a rainwashed window. To find happiness so easily. Sophie had not only found happiness, but radiated it. And now, there was nothing left. The book slipped from her fingers. She lay down, burying her streaming face in Sophie's pillow, the linen cool as her mother's skin, and smelling sweetly of her scent, as though she had, just a moment before, gone from the room.

# Roy Brookner

Although a competent games player and a wizard of keen-eyed speed on the squash courts, Noel Keeling was not a man addicted to physical labour. At weekends, if dragooned by his hostess into an afternoon of tree-cutting, or communal gardening, he invariably took on to himself the least arduous of tasks, gathering small branches for a bonfire, or cutting the dead heads off the roses. He would volunteer to mow the lawn, but only if the machine was one he could ride, and made a point of seeing that another person – usually some besotted girl – trundled the wheelbarrow of grass cuttings to the compost heap. If things grew really tough, with fence posts having to be sledge-hammered into rocky ground, or an enormous hole excavated for a newly acquired shrub, he had perfected the art of slinking indoors, where he would eventually be discovered, by exhausted and indignant fellow-guests, at ease in front of the television, watching cricket or golf, with the Sunday newspapers strewn, like leaves, all about him.

Accordingly, he laid his plans. The whole of Saturday would be spent, quite simply, nosing around, sifting through the contents of every trunk, every box, every battered lop-sided chest of drawers. (The actual heavy work, the pushing and heaving, and humping of rubbish down the two narrow flights of stairs, could be safely left until the next day, with the new gardener to act as labourer, and Noel having to do nothing more strenuous than give the orders.) If he was successful in his search and came upon what he was looking for . . . one, two, or even more of Lawrence Stern's rough oil sketches . . . then he was going to play it very cool. *These might be interesting*, he would say to his mother, and depending on her reaction would carry on from there. *Might be worth having some expert to cast his eye; I've got this chum, Edwin Mundy . . .*

The next morning he was up early, to cook himself a vast breakfast of bacon, egg, and sausage, four slices of toast, and a pot of black coffee.

Eating this at the kitchen table, he watched the rain pour down the window-pane and was glad of it, because there could be no chance of his being seduced out into the garden and asked to perform some task for his mother. When he was onto his second cup of coffee and fully awake, she appeared in her dressing-gown, looking mildly surprised at his appearance, so early on a Saturday morning, and so spry.

'You won't make too much noise, will you, darling? I'd like Antonia to sleep as long as she can. Poor child, she must have been exhausted.'

'I heard you gassing away into the small hours. What were you talking about?'

'Oh, just things.' She poured herself some coffee. 'Noel, you won't throw anything away, will you, without asking me first?'

'I'm not going to do anything except find out what you've got stashed away up there. The burning and destruction can wait until tomorrow. But you must be sensible. Old knitting patterns and wedding photographs circa 1910 are definitely for the chop.'

'I dread to think what you're going to turn up.'

'You never know,' Noel told her, smiling wide-eyed into her face. 'You simply never know.'

He left her drinking coffee, and went upstairs. But before he could start work, one or two practical difficulties had to be ironed out. The loft had only one tiny window, set deep in the east gable, and the single light bulb, suspended from the centre beam of the thatched roof, was so weak and dim, it did little to supplement the small gleam of grey daylight. Noel went back downstairs and demanded of his mother a good strong bulb. She unearthed one from a box under the stairs, and he took this back to the loft and, balancing on a rickety chair, unscrewed the old bulb and screwed in the new. But, turning on the switch, he realised that even this did not give enough light to perform the careful investigation he had in mind. A lamp, that was what he needed. There was one right there, an old standard lamp with a crooked broken shade and a long, trailing flex, but no plug. This entailed a further journey downstairs. He took another strong bulb out of the cardboard box and asked his mother if she had a spare plug. She said that she hadn't. Noel said that he had to have one. She said, in that case, take one from some other appliance. He said that he would need a screwdriver. She told him that there was one in her useful drawer, and, beginning to look a little exasperated, she pointed it out to him.

'That one, Noel, in the dresser.'

He opened the drawer to a tangle of picture wire, fuses, hammers, boxes of tacks, and flattened tubes of glue. Stirring around, he came upon a small screwdriver, and with this removed the plug from her iron.

Upstairs again, he rewired, with some difficulty, the plug to the flex of the old lamp and, praying that it would be long enough, eased it down the stairs and plugged it into the socket on the landing. For what felt like the hundredth time, he went back up the stairs, pressed the switch of the lamp, and breathed a sigh of relief as the light went on. Easily discouraged by the smallest difficulty, he felt quite drained, but now all was illuminated, and he could, at last, begin.

By midday he had worked his way half down the length of the cluttered and dusty attic. Had gone through three trunks, a worm-eaten desk, a tea-chest, and two suitcases. He had found curtains and cushions, a number of wine-glasses wrapped in newspaper, photo albums, massive in their sepia dullness, a doll's tea-set, and a pile of age-yellowed pillowcases, worn beyond repair. He had found leather-bound account books, the entries meticulous in faded copperplate handwriting; bundles of letters, tied in ribbon; half-finished tapestries stuck with rusty needles, and some instructions for operating the very latest invention, a knife-cleaning machine. Once, coming upon a large cardboard folder tied with tapes, hope had risen. With hands trembling with excitement, he had untied the tapes, only to be faced with a number of governessy water-colours depicting the Dolomites, and executed by God knows whom. The disappointment was tremendous, but he gathered up his energy and continued with his task. There were ostrich feathers, and silken shawls with long tangled fringes; embroidered table-cloths, yellowed at their folds; jigsaws, and some half-finished knitting. He found a chessboard, but no chess men; playing cards, a 1912 edition of *Burke's Landed Gentry*.

He did not find anything remotely resembling a work of Lawrence Stern.

Footsteps sounded on the stair. He was perched, dusty, and grimy, on a footstool, disconsolately reading a Household Hint on how to launder black woollen stockings, and, looking up, saw Antonia at the open door. She wore jeans and sneakers and a white sweater, and it crossed his mind that it was a pity about the pale eyelashes, because she had a quite sensational figure.

'Hello,' she said; sounding shy and tentative, as though reluctant to disturb him.

'Hello there.' He closed the battered book with a bang and dropped it on the floor at his feet. 'When did you surface?'

'About eleven o'clock.'

'I didn't wake you?'

'No. I didn't hear a thing.' She moved towards him, edging through and stepping over the painfully sorted lumber. 'How are you getting on?'

'Slowly. The general idea is to sort the wheat from the chaff. Try to get rid of anything that's a possible fire risk.'

'I hadn't any idea it would be as bad as this.' She stopped to look about her. 'Where's it all come from?'

'You may well ask. The attics at Oakley Street. And other attics of other houses, going back through the centuries, by the look of things. It must be an inherited failing, this total inability ever to throw anything away.'

Antonia stooped and picked up a scarlet silk shawl. 'This is pretty.' She draped it around her shoulders, arranging the tangled fringe. 'How does it look?'

'Bizarre.'

She removed the shawl, folding it with care. 'Penelope sent me up to find out if you wanted something to eat.'

Noel glanced at his watch and saw, with some surprise, that it was half past twelve. The day had not lightened, and so intent had he been on his task that he had lost all sense of time. He realised that he was not only hungry, but thirsty as well. He pulled himself off the footstool and onto his feet. 'What I need more than anything else is a gin and tonic.'

'Are you coming back this afternoon?'

'Have to. Otherwise it'll never get done.'

'If you like, I'll come and help.'

But he did not want her around . . . did not want anybody watching. 'That's sweet of you, but I'm better on my own, working at my own pace. Come on . . .' He shooed her in front of him, towards the door. 'Let's go and see what Ma's got for lunch.'

By half past six that evening, the long search was over, and Noel knew that he had drawn a blank. The attics of Podmore's Thatch were empty of treasure. Not so much as a single Lawrence Stern sketch had turned up, and the entire project had been a total waste of time. Coming to terms with this bitter truth, he stood, with his hands in his pockets, and surveyed the trail of confusion which was all that he had achieved. Tired and dirty, with hopes dashed, his gloom burnt to resentment. This was mostly directed against his mother, whose fault everything was. She had probably, at some time or other, destroyed the sketches, or sold them for a song, or even given them away. Her mindless generosity, along with her squirrel-like obsession with hoarding rubbish, had always maddened him, and now he let that fury flare, silently raging. His time was precious to him, and he had wasted a day going through the flotsam of God knew how many generations, simply because she had never got around to doing it for herself.

By now in a filthy temper, for a moment he actually contemplated abandoning ship and taking the escape route normally earmarked for One Star weekends, which was to remember suddenly a pressing engagement in London, make his goodbyes, and head for home.

But this was not possible, because he had gone too far and said too much. It was he who had initiated the exercise (house unsafe, fire risk, inadequate insurance, et cetera) and also told Olivia about the possible existence of the sketches. Now, although he was pretty sure that they didn't exist, he could imagine Olivia's caustic remarks should he duck out, leaving the job unfinished, and, thick-skinned as he was, he did not relish the prospect of a tongue-lashing from his clever sister.

There was nothing for it. He would have to stay. With some venom he kicked aside a broken doll's cot and, switching off the lights, took himself downstairs.


During the night, the rain ceased, the low clouds blown away and dispersed by a soft south-east wind. Sunday morning dawned clear-skied and tranquil, the stillness pierced only by a chorus of bird-song. It was this which awoke Antonia. The first rays of sunlight were slanting into her bedroom through the open window; these lay warm on the carpet, picked out the deep pink of the roses that patterned the curtains. She got out of bed and went to inspect the day, leaning bare forearms on the sill, smelling the damp and mossy-scented air. The thatch was so low that it tickled the top of her head, and she saw the dew glittering on the grass, and the two thrushes carolling away in the chestnut tree – the sweet mistiness of a perfect spring morning.

It was half past seven. All yesterday it had rained, and they had not emerged outdoors. Antonia, still unrecovered from traumas and travels, could have asked for nothing better than a house-bound day. She was left alone, snugged by the fire, with the raindrops streaming down the window-panes and the lights on because it was so grey and dark. She had found a book, an Elizabeth Jane Howard she had never read, and after lunch curled up on the sofa to lose herself in it. From time to time Penelope would appear to put a log on the fire, or search for her spectacles, and later she joined Antonia, not to chat, but to read the papers, and later still, bring tea. Up in the attic, Noel, on his own, had spent the long day, finally appearing in what was, obviously, a very bad temper.

This made Antonia a little uncomfortable. She and Penelope were now in the kitchen, companionably preparing dinner, and one look at Noel's expression was enough to bring on a feeling of doom, and a certainty that his disgruntlement was about to destroy the peaceful mood of the day.

To be honest, everything about Noel made her feel a little uncomfortable. He had all Olivia's dark, quick-tongued vitality, but none of his sister's warmth. He made Antonia feel plain and gauche, and she found it difficult to think of things to say to him that were neither banal nor boring. When he came through the kitchen door, with a face black as thunder and a streak of dust down one side of his cheek, to pour himself a strong whisky and demand of his mother why the hell she'd brought all that clobber down to Gloucestershire from Oakley Street, Antonia's legs had quaked at the prospect of a scene, or, worse, an evening of silent sulks, but Penelope took it all in her stride, was unprovoked by his attack, and was obviously not about to be browbeaten by her son.

'Laziness, I suppose,' she told Noel airily. 'It was easier to pack it all into the removal van than to start deciding what to do with it. I'd enough on my plate without going through all those old books and letters.'

'But who collected them all in the first place?'

'I've no idea.'

Defeated, silenced by her good humour, he tossed the whisky down the back of his throat, and at once became a little more relaxed. He even managed a wry smile. 'You are,' he told his mother, 'the most impossible woman.'

She accepted this, as well. 'Yes, I know, but we can't all be perfect. And just think how good I am at other things. Like cooking meals for you and always having the right sort of drink in the cupboard. Your father's mother, if you recall, never kept anything in her sideboard except bottles of sherry that tasted like raisins.'

He screwed up his face in remembered distaste. 'What *is* for dinner?'

'Baked trout with almonds, new potatoes, and raspberries and cream. No less than you deserve. And you can choose a suitable bottle of wine and then take your drink upstairs and have a bath.' She smiled at her son, but her dark eyes were sharp. 'I'm certain you need one, after all that hard labour.'

And so, after all, it had been an easy evening. Tired, they had all gone to bed early and Antonia had slept through the night. Now, with the resilience of youth, and for the first time for days and days, she felt herself again. She wanted to be out of doors, running through grass, filling her lungs with cool fresh air. The spring morning waited for her and she knew that she must be part of it.

She dressed, went downstairs, took an apple from the bowl on the kitchen dresser, and let herself out through the conservatory and into the garden. Eating the apple, she crossed the lawn. The dew soaked through her canvas sneakers and they left a trail of footprints on the damp grass. Under the chestnut tree and through the gap in the privet hedge, she found herself in the orchard. A rough path wound down through the unkept grass, already spiked by the daffodil shoots, past the remains of a bonfire, and around a newly trimmed hawthorn hedge. Beyond, she came upon the river, flowing deep and narrow between high banks. She followed this downstream, beneath an arch of willows, and then the willows thinned out and the river wound onwards through wide water meadows filled with grazing cattle; beyond these the gentle hills climbed to the sky. There were sheep on the upland pastures, and in the distance a man, with a dog at his heels, climbed the slope towards them.

Now, she was close upon the village. The old church with its square tower, the golden stone-slated cottages, lay in the curve of the road. Smoke rose straight into the motionless air, from chimneys, from newly kindled fires. The sun was climbing in the crystal sky, and its thin warmth made the bridge smell of creosote. It was a good smell. She sat on the bridge, with her damp legs dangling, and finished the apple. She flung the core into the clear, streaming water, and watched it go, swept away for ever.

Gloucestershire, she decided, was all quite poetically beautiful, and exceeded anything that she might have imagined. And Podmore's Thatch was perfect, and most particularly of all, so was Penelope. Just being with Penelope made you feel calm and safe and secure, and as though life – lately so unbearably dreadful and sad – was still something exciting and filled with future joys. 'You can stay,' she had told Antonia, 'as long as you like,' and this was a temptation in itself, but she knew that she couldn't. On the other hand, what was she going to do?

She was eighteen. She had no family, no home, no money, and was qualified to do nothing. During those few days she had spent in London, she had confided in Olivia.

'I don't even know what I *want* to do. I mean I've never had a great sense of vocation about anything. It would be much easier if I had. And even if I did suddenly decide to be a secretary or a doctor or a chartered accountant, to learn how to do anything costs so much money.'

'I could help you,' Olivia had said.

Antonia at once became agitated. 'No, you mustn't even think of it. I'm not your responsibility.'

'In a way, you are. You're Cosmo's child. And I wasn't thinking so much of writing enormous cheques. I was thinking that I could help you in other ways. Introduce you to people. Have you ever thought of modelling?'

Modelling. Antonia's mouth dropped in astonishment. 'Me? I couldn't be a model. I'm not a bit beautiful.'

'You don't have to be beautiful. You just have to have the right shape and you've got it.'

'I couldn't be a model. I get self-conscious if someone points a camera in my direction.'

Olivia laughed. 'You'd get over that. All you'd need is a good photographer, someone who'd give you confidence. I've seen it happen before. Ugly ducklings blossom into swans.'

'Not me.'

'Don't be so timid. There's nothing wrong with your face unless it's those white eyelashes. And yet they're wondrously long and thick. I can't think why you don't wear mascara.'

Her eyelashes were the greatest source of shame to Antonia, and mention of them made her blush with embarrassment.

'I've tried, Olivia, but I can't. I'm allergic to it, or something. My eyelids swell up, and then my cheeks, and I look like a turnip lantern, and my eyes start streaming and all the black runs down my face. A disaster, but I can't do anything about it.'

'Why don't you have them dyed?'

'*Dyed?*'

'Yes. Dyed black. In a beauty parlour. And then all your troubles would be over.'

'But wouldn't I be allergic to dye?'

'I shouldn't think so. You'd have to find out. Anyway, this is all beside the point. We're talking about you getting a job as a photographic model. Just for a year or two. You'd earn good money and you could save a bit, and then when you've decided what you do want to do, you'd have a little capital behind you; be independent. Think about it, anyway, while you're down at Podmore's Thatch. Let me know what you've decided and I'll arrange a sitting.'

'You are kind.'

'Not at all. Just practical.'

Considered objectively, it wasn't a bad idea. The thought of actually doing such a job filled Antonia with alarm, but if she could earn some money that way, surely it was worth a bit of agonising and embarrassment and having one's face caked in make up. And anyway, however hard she thought, she couldn't come up with anything else that she really did want to do. She quite liked cooking and gardening and planting things and picking fruit – during the two years she had spent with Cosmo in Ibiza, she had done little else – but it wasn't possible to make much of a career out of picking fruit. And she didn't want to work in an office, and she didn't want to work in a shop, nor a bank, nor a hospital, so what was the alternative?

Across the valley, from the church tower, a single bell began to toll, bringing a sort of melancholy tranquillity to the peaceful scene. Antonia thought of other bells; goat bells in Ibiza, discordant, clanging away in the early mornings across the rocky arid fields that surrounded Cosmo's house. That and the crowing of cocks, and the crickets of the darkness . . . all sounds of Ibiza, gone for ever, swept away into the past. She thought about Cosmo, and for the first time was able to do this without having her eyes fill with tears. Grief was like a terrible burden, but at least you could lay it down by the side of the road and walk away from it. Antonia had come only a few paces, but already she could turn and look back and not weep. It wasn't anything to do with forgetting. It was just accepting. Nothing was ever so bad once you had accepted it.

The church bell clanged on for ten minutes or so, and then abruptly ceased. The silence that followed it slowly filled with the small sounds of the morning. The flowing water, the lowing of cattle, the distant baa-ing of sheep. A dog barked. A car started up. Antonia realised that she was ravenously hungry. She got to her feet and walked back off the bridge and began to retrace her steps, heading for Podmore's Thatch and breakfast. Boiled eggs, perhaps, and brown bread and butter and strong tea. The very idea of such delicious food filled her with satisfaction. Mindlessly happy for the first time in weeks, she began to run, ducking her head beneath the trailing branches of the willows, light-hearted and free as a girl to whom something wonderful was just about to happen.

By the time she came to the hawthorn hedge and the gate that led into Penelope's orchard, she was out of breath and warm with exertion. Panting, she leaned on the gate for a moment, and then opened it and went through. As she did this, a movement caught her eye, and she looked up and saw a man wheeling a barrow down the twisting path that led from the garden, making his way beneath Penelope's washing line and between the gnarled apple and pear trees. A young man, tall and long-legged. Not Noel. Somebody new.

She closed the gate. Its click caught his attention and he glanced up and saw her.

'Good morning,' he called, and came on, the barrow trundling over the tussocky grass, its wheel squeaking, in need of oil. Antonia stayed where she was, watching his progress. By the burnt-out bonfire he stopped, set down the barrow, and straightened his back to stand, observing her. He wore patched and faded jeans, tucked into rubber boots, and a frayed and baggy sweater over a bright blue shirt. The collar of this was turned up around his neck, and his eyes were the same bright blue; deep-set and unblinking in his weather-tanned face.

He said, 'Lovely day.'

'Yes.'

'Been for a walk?'

'Just down to the bridge.'

'You must be Antonia.'

'Yes, I am.'

'Mrs Keeling told me you'd be coming.'

'I don't know who you are.'

'The gardener. Danus Muirfield. I've come to help for the day. Help clear the attic. Burn all the rubbish.'

The wheelbarrow contained a few cardboard boxes, old newspapers, a long pitchfork. He took hold of the pitchfork and with it began stirring up the sodden ashes of the previous fire, scraping them aside to clear a dry patch of ground.

'There's a mountain of stuff that'll have to be burnt,' Antonia told him. 'I went up to the attic yesterday and saw it all.'

'That's all right; we've got the whole day to do it.'

She liked his saying 'we'. It seemed to include her, unlike Noel's cool rejection of her tentative offer to help him. It made her feel not only part of the whole project, but welcome as well.

'I haven't had my breadfast yet, but as soon as I have I'll come and give you a hand.'

'Mrs Keeling's in the kitchen, boiling eggs.'

Antonia smiled. 'I hoped it would be boiled eggs.'

But he did not smile back. 'You go and eat them,' he told her. He drove the prongs of the pitchfork into the black earth and turned to collect a wad of newspaper. 'You can't do a hard day's work on an empty stomach.'


Nancy Chamberlain, with pigskin-gloved hands firmly clenched on the wheel of her car, drove through the smiling sunlit Cotswolds towards Podmore's Thatch, and Sunday lunch with her mother. She was in a good mood, her high spirits attributable to a number of factors. The unexpectedly bright day was one of them, the blue skies affecting not only herself but her household as well, so that the children had not quarrelled at breakfast, George had come out with a dry joke or two over his Sunday-morning sausages, and Mrs Croftway had actually offered to take the dogs for their afternoon walk.

Without the chore of a huge Sunday lunch to be prepared, there had, for once, been time for everything. Time for Nancy to take trouble with her appearance (she was wearing her best coat and skirt, and the crêpe de Chine blouse with the bow at the neck); time to deliver Melanie and

Rupert to the Wainwrights; time to wave George off to his Diocesan meeting; time, even, to go to church. Going to church always made Nancy feel pious and good, just as attending committee meetings made her feel important. So, for once, her own image of herself matched up to her ambitions. She was a well-organised country lady, with children invited to spend the day with suitable friends, a husband involved in worthwhile duties, and servants devoted.

All this filled her with a sleek and unaccustomed confidence, and as she drove, she planned exactly what she was going to do and say during the course of the afternoon. At a suitable moment, alone with her mother, perhaps over coffee, she would bring up the subject of Lawrence Stern's pictures. Mention the enormous price that *The Water Carriers* had fetched, and point out the short-sightedness of not taking advantage of the market while it was at its peak. She saw herself doing this, reasoning quietly, making it clear that she was thinking only of her mother's good.

Sell. Just the panels, of course, which hung, unobserved and unappreciated, on the landing outside Penelope's bedroom. Not *The Shell Seekers*. There could be no question of disposing of that painting, so loved and so much part of her mother's life, but still, Nancy would quote George and become very business-like. Suggest reassessment and possibly reinsurance. Surely Penelope, touchy as she was about her possessions, could raise no objection to such sensible and daughterly concern?

The winding road crested the hill and below, in the valley, the village of Temple Pudley was revealed, glittering like a flint in the sunlight. There was little sign of activity save the plume of dark bonfire smoke that poured from her mother's garden. So absorbed had Nancy been in her plans for selling the panels and releasing hundreds of thousands of lovely pounds that she had forgotten the real purpose of the weekend, which was to clear out the loft at Podmore's Thatch and dispose of all the rubbish. She hoped that she would not be roped in for any of the dirty work. She was not dressed for bonfires.

Moments later, as the church clock struck the half hour, she turned in through the gate of her mother's house and drew up by the open door. She saw Noel's old Jaguar parked by the garage, an unfamiliar bicycle leaning against the wall of the house, and a forlorn group of unburnable objects that had obviously been dumped, pending disposal. Some scales designed for weighing infants, a doll's perambulator missing a wheel, an iron bedstead or two, and a couple of chipped chamberpots. She picked her way past these and went indoors.

'Mother.'

The kitchen, as always, was redolent with delicious smells, roasting lamb, chopped mint, a newly sliced lemon. Nancy was reminded of childhood and the massive meals that had been concocted then, in the huge basement kitchen at Oakley Street. Breakfast seemed a long time away, and her mouth began to water.

'Mother!'

'I'm here.'

Nancy found her in the conservatory, not doing anything, just standing deep in thought. She saw that her mother was dressed, not for an occasion, as Nancy was, but in her oldest clothes. A worn and faded denim skirt, a cotton shirt with a frayed collar, and a darned cardigan with sleeves pushed up to her elbows. Nancy put down her lizard handbag, drew off her gloves, and went to give her parent a kiss.

'What are you doing?' she asked her.

'I'm trying to decide where we should eat lunch. I was just going to lay the table in the dining room, and then I thought, it's such a beautiful day, why not have it here. And it's marvellously warm, even with the door open to the garden. Do admire my freesias! Aren't they precious? How nice to see you and how smart you look. Now, what do you think? Shall we eat out here? Noel can carve in the kitchen and we can all carry our plates through. I think it would be fun. The first picnic of the year, and everybody's so dirty anyway, it might be easier.'

Nancy peered in the direction of the orchard and the billowing smoke that poured above the privet hedge and up into the pristine sky.

'How's it all going?'

'Like a bomb. Everybody's hard at work.'

'Not you, I hope.'

'Me? I've done nothing except cook the lunch.'

'And the girl . . . Antonia?' Nancy pronounced the name coolly. She still had not forgiven Olivia and Penelope for the presence of Antonia, and could not help hoping that the arrangement would prove to be a total failure.

But her hopes were dashed.

'She's been up since dawn, and pitched in with the others as soon as she'd eaten her breakfast. Noel's up in the attic, giving orders right, left, and centre, and Danus and Antonia are carting the rubbish and stoking the bonfire.'

'I hope she's not going to be a nuisance to you, Mother.'

'Oh, heavens no, she's a darling.'

'What does Noel think of her?'

'To begin with, he said she wasn't his type because she's got pale eyelashes. Can you imagine it? He's never going to find himself a wife if he refuses to look further than her eyelashes.'

'To begin with? Has he changed his mind?'

'Only because there's another young man around, and Antonia seems to have made friends with him. Noel was always the most dreadful dog in the manger, and I think his nose has been quite put out of joint.'

'Another young man? Are you talking about your gardener?'

'Danus. Yes. Such a dear boy.'

Nancy was shocked. 'You mean Antonia's taken up with the *gardener*?'

Her mother only laughed. 'Oh, Nancy, if you could just see your own face. You mustn't be such a snob, and you mustn't make a single judgment until you've met the young man.'

But Nancy remained unconvinced. What could be going on? 'I hope they're not burning anything you want to keep.'

'No. Noel's really being very good. Every now and then, Antonia is sent to fetch me, and I have to go and give my opinion about something or other. There was one small argument concerning a worm-eaten desk. Noel said it was to go on the fire, but Danus said it was too good to burn and that the worm could be treated. So I said that if he wanted to treat the worm . . . lucky old worm . . . he could keep the desk for himself. Noel was none too pleased. Stumped upstairs in a sulk, but that's neither here nor there. Now come along, we must make up our minds. Let's have lunch here. You can help me lay the table.'

Which they did, companionably together. The leaves of the old pine table were opened up and the table spread with a dark-blue linen cloth. Nancy fetched silver and glasses from the dining room, her mother folded white linen napkins into mitres. The final touch was a pink potted geranium set into a flowered cache pot, placed in the middle of the table. The result was delightful, both pretty and informal, and Nancy, standing back, marvelled, as she always did, at her mother's natural talent for creating not only an ambience, but a real visual pleasure out of the most mundane of objects. Nancy supposed it was something to do with having an artist for a father, and thought in a dissatisfied way of her own dining room, which, however hard she tried, never looked anything except dark and dull.

'Now,' said Penelope, 'there's nothing for us to do except wait for the workers to come and eat. Sit here in the sun while I go and tidy myself up, and then I'll bring you a drink. What would you like? A glass of wine? A gin and tonic?'

Nancy said she would like a gin and tonic, and, left alone, removed her jacket and took stock of her surroundings. When her mother had first announced the intention of building a conservatory, she and George had come out strongly against the notion. It was a foolish luxury, was their opinion, a wild extravagance that Penelope could not possibly afford. But their advice had been ignored, and the delicate airy addition duly erected. Now, warm, scented, leafy and flower-filled, it was, Nancy had to admit, an enviable place, but she had never managed to find out how much it had cost. Which brought her, inevitably, back to the vexing question of money. When her mother returned, with her hair dressed, her face powdered, and smelling of her best scent, Nancy, settled in the most comfortable of the basket chairs, was wondering if this was the right moment to bring up the subject of selling the panels, and was even trying out a few tactful opening sentences; but she was forestalled by Penelope's steering the conversation into a quite different and totally unexpected tack.

'Here you are. Gin and tonic . . . I hope it's strong enough.' For herself she had poured a glass of wine. She pulled forward another chair and sank into it, her long legs outstretched and her face turned up to the warmth of the sun. 'Oh, isn't this blissful? What are your family doing today?'

Nancy told her.

'Poor George. Fancy being stuck indoors all day, with a lot of moose-faced bishops. And who are the Wainwrights? Have I ever met them? So good for the children to get off on their own. For that matter, so good for all of us to get off on our own. Would you like to come to Cornwall with me?'

Nancy, startled, turned a face of astonishment and disbelief upon her mother.

'Cornwall?'

'Yes. I want to go back to Porthkerris. Quite soon. I've suddenly become possessed by this tremendous urge. And it would be so much more fun if I had somebody with me.'

'But . . .'

'I know. I haven't been there for forty years, and it will all be changed and I shan't know anybody. But I still want to go. To see it all again. Why not come too? We could stay with Doris.'

'With *Doris*?'

'Yes, with Doris. Oh, Nancy, you haven't forgotten Doris. You couldn't have. She practically brought you up until you were four years old and we left Porthkerris for good.'

Of course Nancy remembered Doris. She had no clear recollection of her grandfather, but she remembered Doris, with her sweet talcum-powdery smell, and her strong arms and the soft comfort of her bosom. The first clear memory of Nancy's life included Doris. She had been sitting in some sort of push-chair in the little field behind Carn Cottage, surrounded by foraging ducks and hens, while Doris pegged out a line of washing in the strong sea-breeze. The image was imprinted on her mind for ever, bright and colourful as an illustration in a picture book. She was Doris, with her hair blowing and her arms upstretched; saw the flapping sheets and pillow-cases; saw the starch-blue sky.

'Doris still lives in Porthkerris,' Penelope went on. 'She's got a little house, Downalong, we used to call it; the old bit of the town, around the harbour. And now that the boys have gone, she's got a spare bedroom. She's always asking me to go and stay. And she'd love to see you. You were her baby. She cried when we left. And you cried too, though I don't suppose you realised what it was all about.'

Nancy bit her lip. Staying with an old servant in a pokey cottage in a Cornish town was not her idea of a holiday. Besides . . .

'What about the children?' she asked. 'There wouldn't be space for the children.'

'What children?'

'Melanie and Rupert, of course. I couldn't go on holiday without them.'

'For heaven's sake, Nancy, I'm not asking the children. I'm asking you. And why can't you go on holiday without them? They're old enough to be left with their father and Mrs Croftway. Indulge yourself. Get away on your own. It wouldn't be for long. Just a few days, no more than a week.'

'When do you plan to go?'

'Soon. As soon as I can.'

'Oh, Mother, it's so difficult. I've got so much on my plate . . . the church fête to be planned, and the Conservative Conference . . . I have to have a lunch party that day. And then Melanie's Pony Club camp . . .'

Her voice trailed away as she ran out of excuses. Penelope said nothing. Nancy took another sustaining mouthful of the icy gin and tonic and stole a sideways glance at her mother. She saw the clear-cut profile, the closed eyes.

'Mother?'

'Um?'

'Perhaps later on . . . when I haven't so much on my plate. September, maybe.'

'No.' She was adamant. 'It has to be soon.' She raised a hand. 'Don't worry about it. I know you're busy. It was just an idea.'

A silence fell between them, which Nancy found uncomfortable, loaded with unspoken reproach. But why should she feel guilty? She couldn't possibly take off, with so little notice, so little time to set things in order, to Cornwall.

Nancy was not good at sitting in silence. She liked to keep up a constant flow of chat. Trying to drum up some other lively source of conversation, she found her mind a blank. Really, Mother could be dreadfully irritating at times. It wasn't Nancy's fault. It was just that she was so busy, so involved in house, husband, and children. It wasn't fair suddenly to be made to feel so guilty.

It was thus that Noel found them. If Nancy had had a good morning, then Noel had had a gruesome one. Going through all that stuff in the attic yesterday had been one thing because there had always stayed, at the back of his mind, the conviction that he was about to turn up something immensely valuable. The fact that he hadn't had made this morning's toil no easier. Also, he had been slightly thrown by the appearance of Danus. Expecting some thick-headed, muscle-bound country boy, he had instead been confronted by a cool and silent young man, and had found himself disconcerted by his straight and unblinking blue gaze. The fact that Antonia had taken so instantly to Danus did nothing to improve Noel's disposition, and the sound of their companionable chatter as they journeyed up and down the narrow stairs with armfuls of cardboard boxes and broken furniture became, during the course of the morning, an increasing irritation. The altercation over the worm-eaten desk was almost the last straw, and by a quarter to one, with everything more or less cleared, and what remained pushed to the side of the wall, he had had more than enough. Also he was dirty. He needed a shower, but more, he needed a drink, so he compromised by washing his face and hands, came downstairs, and poured himself a dry martini of mind-boggling strength. With this in his hand he took himself through the kitchen to the sun-baked conservatory, and his mood was not improved by the sight of his mother and his sister, relaxed in basket chairs and looking as though neither of them had done a stroke of work all day.

At the sound of his footstep, Nancy glanced up. She smiled brightly, as though for once she was actually pleased to see him.

'Hello, Noel.'

He did not return the smile, simply leaned a shoulder against the jamb of the open door, and surveyed the pair of them. His mother appeared to have fallen asleep.

'What do you two think you're doing, lounging there in the sunshine, while others work their fingers to the bone?'

Penelope never moved. Nancy's smile lost a little of its spontaneity, but remained there, stuck on her face. Noel eventually acknowledged it with a nod of his head. 'Hi,' he said, and went to pull a chair away from the carefully laid lunch table, and take, at last, the weight from his legs.

His mother opened her eyes. She had not been asleep.

'Are you finished?'

'Yes, I'm finished. Done for. A physical wreck.'

'I didn't mean you, I meant the attic.'

'Just about. All we need is some busy housewife to go up and sweep the floor, and then the job's done.'

'Noel, you are a wonder. What would I have done without you?'

But her grateful smile was wasted on him. 'I'm ravenous,' he told her. 'When's lunch?'

'Whenever you want it.' She set down her glass of wine and sat up to gaze out beyond the pot plants and into the garden. Smoke continued to billow up into the sky, but there was no sign of the others. 'Perhaps someone should fetch Danus and Antonia, and then I'll go and make the gravy.'

There was a pause. Noel waited for Nancy to volunteer for this not very arduous task, but she was intent on picking a small piece of fluff from her skirt and generally acting as though she hadn't heard. Noel said, 'I haven't the energy.' He leaned back, tipping his chair. 'You go, Nancy, the exercise will do you good.'

Nancy, recognising this as a dig at her ample figure, instantly took umbrage, as he had known she would do.

'Thank you very much.'

'You don't look as if you'd raised a finger all morning.'

'Just because I happen to tidy myself up before I come out for lunch.' She glanced pointedly in his direction. 'Which is more than I can say for you.'

'What does George wear for Sunday lunch? A frock-coat?'

Nancy, belligerent, sat up. 'If that's meant to be funny . . .'

They snacked on, niggling at each other, sounding much as they always had. In rising exasperation and impatience, Penelope knew that she could not listen for another moment. She got abruptly to her feet. 'I shall fetch them,' she announced, and her offspring let her go, across the sunlit lawn, across the rough, uncut winter grass, while they stayed where they were, unappreciative of the sweet-scented warmth of the conservatory, not speaking, not looking at each other. They nursed their drinks and their mutual animosity.

She was upset. She had allowed them to upset her. She could feel the blood coursing to her cheeks, her heart begin its uneven jigging dance. She went slowly, taking her time, breathing deeply, telling herself not to be a fool. They did not matter, those grown-up children of hers, who still behaved like the children they no longer were. It did not matter that Noel thought of no person but himself, or that Nancy had become so smug and self-righteous and middle-aged. It did not matter that none of them, not even Olivia, wanted to come to Cornwall with her.

What had gone wrong? What had become of the babies she had borne and loved and brought up and educated and generally cared for? The answer was, perhaps, that she had not expected enough of them. But she had learned the hard way, in the London years after the war, not to expect anything of any person except herself. Without parents or old friends to support her, she was left with only Ambrose and his mother to turn to, and within months she had realised the futility of doing any such thing. Alone, she was – in more ways than one – thrown back on her own resources.

Self-reliance. This was the key word, the one thing that could pull you through any crisis fate chose to hurl at you. To be yourself. Independent. Not witless. Still able to make your own decisions and plot the course of what remains of your life. I do not need my children. Knowing their faults, recognising their shortcomings, I love them all, but I do not *need* them.

She prayed that she never would.

She was calmer now, able, even, to smile at herself. She went through the gap in the privet hedge and saw the orchard sloping away, dappled in sunlight and shadow. At the end of it the enormous bonfire still crackled and flamed, belching forth smoke. Danus and Antonia were there, Danus raking in the red-hot ashes, Antonia sitting on the edge of the wheelbarrow watching him. They had shed sweaters and were in their shirt-sleeves and talking nineteen to the dozen, their voices clear in the still air.

So absorbed and companionable did they appear, it seemed a pity to disturb them, even to announce that it was time to come indoors and eat roast spring lamb, lemon soufflé, and strawberry shortcake. So she stayed where she was, allowing herself the pleasure of simply watching the charming pastoral scene. Then Danus paused to lean on his pitchfork, and make some unheard remark, and Antonia laughed. And the sound of her laughter brought back, with a piercing clarity, ringing across the years, the memory of other laughter, and the unexpected ecstasies and physical joys that happen, perhaps, only once in any person's life-time.

*It was good. And nothing good is ever lost. It stays part of a person, becomes part of one's character.*

Other voices, other worlds. Recalling that ecstasy, she was filled, not with a sense of loss, but of renewal and rediscovery. Nancy and Noel and the tedious irritations they had unleashed were forgotten. They did not matter. Nothing mattered but this instant, this moment of truth.

She might have stood there, daydreaming, at the top of the orchard for the rest of the day, but Danus all at once spied her and waved, and she made a trumpet of her hands to call and tell them that it was lunch-time. He acknowledged this with a gesture of his hand, then drove his pitchfork into the earth and stooped to collect their abandoned sweaters. Antonia got off the wheelbarrow, and he put her sweater around her shoulders and tied the sleeves in a knot beneath her chin. Then they started up the orchard path, up between the trees, walking side by side; both tall and slender and tanned and young, and, to Penelope's eyes, quite beautiful.

She found herself filled with gratitude. Not simply to them for all the hard work they had accomplished during the course of the morning, but *for* them as well. They had, without saying a word, restored her tranquillity of mind, her sense of values, and she sent up a swift and heartfelt thank you to the twist of fate (or was it the hand of God? – she wished that she could be certain . . .) that had introduced them, like a second chance, into her life.


One thing that could be fairly said in Noel's favour was that his evil moods were short-lived. By the time the little party finally assembled, he was on to his second dry martini (having refreshed, as well, his sister's glass), and Penelope was much relieved to find them actually chatting quite amicably.

'Here we all are. Now, Nancy, you haven't met Danus, and you haven't met Antonia. This is my daughter, Nancy Chamberlain. Noel, you be in charge of the bar . . . give them both something to drink, then perhaps you'd come and carve the lamb for me . . .'

Noel set down his glass and rose with exaggerated effort to his feet.

'What would you like, Antonia?'

'A lager would be delicious.' She leaned against the table, her legs endless in their faded jeans. When Nancy's daughter, Melanie, wore jeans, she looked appalling in them, because her bottom was so big. But jeans on Antonia looked fantastic. Nancy decided that life was really very unfair. She wondered if she should put Melanie on a diet, and at once put the idea out of her head, because Melanie automatically always did the very opposite of anything that her mother suggested.

'How about you, Danus?'

The tall young man shook his head. 'Something soft would be great. A juice. Glass of water would do.'

Noel bucked slightly, but Danus was adamant, so he shrugged and disappeared indoors. Nancy turned to Danus.

'Don't you drink at all?'

'Not alcohol.' He was very good-looking. Well-spoken. A gentleman. Extraordinary. What on earth was he doing, being her mother's gardener?

'Have you never?'

'Not really.' He sounded quite untroubled about it all.

'Perhaps,' Nancy pursued the subject, because it was so extraordinary to meet a man who would not even down a half-pint of lager, 'you don't like the taste?'

He seemed to be considering this, then said, 'Yes, perhaps that is why.' His face was very serious, but even so Nancy could not be sure whether or not he was laughing at her.

The tender lamb, the roast potatoes, the peas and the broccoli had been gratefully consumed, the wine-glasses refilled, and the puddings served. With everybody relaxed and cheerful once more, the conversation turned to how they were all to spend the rest of the day.

'I,' Noel announced, pouring cream from a pink and white pitcher over his strawberry shortcake, 'am calling it a day, drawing stumps, and pulling out. I'll drive back to London, and that way, with a bit of luck, I'll miss the worst of the weekend traffic.'

'Yes, I think you should,' his mother agreed. 'You've done quite enough. You must be exhausted.'

'What else is there to be done?' Nancy wanted to know.

'The last of the clobber to be carted and burnt and the floor of the attic swept.'

'I'll do that,' said Antonia promptly.

Nancy thought of something else. 'What about all those things that have been piled up outside Mother's front door? The bedsteads and the broken perambulator. You can't leave them there indefinitely. They make Podmore's Thatch look like a tinker's camp.'

There was a pause while everybody waited for someone else to make a suggestion. Then Danus spoke. 'We could take them to the dump at Pudley.'

'How?' asked Noel.

'If Mrs Keeling doesn't mind, we could put them in the back of her car.'

'No, of course I don't mind.'

Noel said, 'When?'

'This afternoon.'

'Is the dump open on a Sunday?'

'Oh, heavens yes,' Penelope assured him. 'It's always open. There's a dear little man who lives there, in a sort of shed. The gates are never locked.'

Nancy was horrified. 'You mean he lives there all the time? In a shed by the dump? What is the local Council thinking of? It must be dreadfully unhygienic.'

Penelope laughed. 'I don't think he's the sort of person who's fussy about hygiene. Frightfully dirty and unshaven, but quite charming. Once we had a dustmen's strike and we had to hump all our own rubbish, and he couldn't have been more helpful.'

'But . . .'

She was interrupted, however, by Danus, which was in itself surprising, because he had scarcely spoken all through the meal.

'In Scotland, there's a dump outside the little town where my grandmother lives, and an old tramp has lived there for thirty years.' He enlarged on this. 'In a wardrobe.'

'He lives in a *wardrobe*?' Nancy sounded more horrified than ever.

'Yes. It's quite a big one. Victorian.'

'But how dreadfully uncomfortable.'

'You'd think so, wouldn't you? But he seems quite happy. He's a very well-known figure, much respected. Walks all over the countryside in rubber boots and an old raincoat. People give him cups of tea and jam sandwiches.'

'But what does he do in the evening?'

Danus shook his head. 'I've no idea.'

'Why are you so worried about his evenings?' Noel wanted to know. 'I should have thought his entire existence so awful that how he spends his evenings is a small thing to bother about.'

'Well, it must be dreadfully dull. I mean, he obviously hasn't got a television, or a telephone . . .' Nancy's voice trailed away as she struggled to imagine such deprivations.

Noel shook his head, wearing the exasperated expression that Nancy remembered from the past, when he was a clever little boy trying to make Nancy understand the rules of some simple card game.

'You're hopeless,' he told her, and she relapsed into a hurt silence. Noel turned to Danus.

'Do you come from Scotland?'

'My parents live in Edinburgh.'

'What does your father do?'

'He's a lawyer.'

Nancy, filled with curiosity, forgot her little umbrage. 'Did you never want to be a lawyer too?'

'When I was at school, I thought I might have followed in his footsteps. But then I changed my mind.'

Noel leaned back in his chair. 'I always visualise Scotsmen as being tremendously sporty. Stalking stags and killing grouse and fishing. Does your father do those things?'

'He fishes and plays golf.'

'Is he also an Elder of the Kirk?' Noel came out with this in a fake Scottish accent that set his mother's teeth on edge. 'Isn't that what you call it in the frozen North?'

Danus, impassive, did not rise.

'Yes, he is an Elder. He's also an Archer.'

'I'm not with you. Enlighten me.'

'A member of the Honourable Company of Archers. The Queen's Bodyguard when she comes to Holyrood House. On such occasions, he puts on an archaic uniform and looks resplendent.'

'What does he guard the Queen's body with? Bows and arrows?'

'Right.'

For a moment, the two men eyed each other. Then, 'Fascinating,' said Noel, and took another helping of strawberry shortcake.

The gargantuan meal, at last, was finished, rounded off by freshly made coffee and dark dessert chocolate. Noel pushed back his chair, yawned with enormous satisfaction, and said that he was going up to pack his bag and depart before he fell into a coma. Nancy began, in a desultory way, to stack the empty cups and saucers.

'What are you going to do?' Penelope asked Danus. 'Go back to your bonfire?'

'It's burning all right. Why don't we get rid of the stuff that's got to go to the dump first. I'll load it into your car.'

There was a momentary pause. Then Penelope said, 'If you can wait till I've cleared up the dishes, I'll drive you.'

Noel stopped, mid-yawn, his arms above his head. 'Oh, come off it, Ma, he doesn't need a chauffeur.'

'Actually,' said Danus, 'I do. I don't drive.'

There was another, longer pause, during which time both Noel and Nancy gazed at him in open-mouthed disbelief.

'You don't drive? You mean, you can't? How the hell do you get about?'

'I bicycle.'

'What an extraordinary chap you are . . . Have you got high principles about air pollution, or something?'

'No.'

'But . . .'

Antonia broke into the conversation. She said very quickly, 'I can drive. If you'll let me, Penelope. I'll drive, and Danus can show me the way.'

She looked at Penelope across the table, and simultaneously they smiled, like two women sharing a secret. Penelope said, 'How kind that would be. Why don't you go now, while Nancy and I see to all this, and then when you get back, we can all go down to the orchard and finish the bonfire together.'

'Actually,' said Nancy, 'I have to get home. I can't stay all afternoon.'

'Oh, stay, just for a little. I've hardly talked to you. You can't have anything important to do . . .'

She got to her feet, reached for a tray. Antonia and Danus, as well, stood up, said goodbye to Noel, and took themselves off, out through the kitchen. As their mother began to pile the coffee cups onto the tray, Noel and Nancy sat in silence, but as soon as they heard the front door safely slam, and knew that the others were out of earshot, they both began to speak at once.

'What an extraordinary chap he is.'

'So solemn. He never smiles . . .'

'How did you get hold of him, Ma?'

'Do you know anything about his background? He's obviously well-bred. It seems very fishy that he should be a gardener . . .'

'And all this carry-on about not drinking and not driving. Why the hell doesn't he drive?'

'I think,' Nancy pronounced importantly, 'that he probably killed somebody while he was drunk, and he's had his licence taken away.'

This was so uncomfortably close to Penelope's own anxious speculations that all at once she knew that she could not listen to another word, and sprang to Danus' defence.

'For goodness' sake, at least give the poor man time to get out through the front gate before you start tearing his character to shreds.'

'Oh, come off it, Ma, he's an odd fellow and you know it as well as we do. If he's telling the truth, he comes from an eminently respectable and probably well-to-do family. What's he doing slaving away for an agricultural worker's wage?'

'I've no idea.'

'Have you asked him?'

'I most certainly haven't. His private life is his own concern.'

'But, Mother, did he arrive with any sort of credentials?'

'Of course he did. I engaged him through a garden contractor.'

'Do they know if he's honest?'

'*Honest?* Why shouldn't he be honest?'

'You're so naïve, Mother, you'd trust any person who looked vaguely presentable. After all, he is working around the house and the garden, and you're on your own.'

'I am not on my own. I have Antonia.'

'Antonia, by the looks of it, is as besotted by him as you are . . .'

'Nancy, what gives you the right to say such things?'

'If I wasn't concerned about you, I wouldn't have the need to say them.'

'And what do you imagine that Danus might do? Rape Antonia and Mrs Plackett, I suppose. Murder me, strip my house of its possessions, and head for Europe. That wouldn't do him much good. There's nothing of value here anyway.'

She spoke in thoughtless heat, and as soon as the words were out instantly regretted them, for Noel pounced with the speed of a cat upon a mouse.

'Nothing of value! What about your father's pictures? Will nothing I say persuade you to understand that you are vulnerable here; you have no sort of an alarm system, you never lock a door, and without a doubt you are under-insured. Nancy's right. We know nothing about this oddball you've employed as a gardener, and even if we did, it's crazy – under any circumstances – not to take some sort of positive action. Sell, or reinsure, or do bloody *something*.'

'I have a funny feeling that you would like me to sell.'

'Now, don't start getting het up. Think rationally. Not *The Shell Seekers*, of course, but certainly the panels. Now, while the market's high. Find out what the wretched things are worth, and then put them up for sale.'

Penelope, who all this time had been standing, now sat down again. She put an elbow on the table and rested her forehead in the palm of her hand. With her other hand, she reached for the butter knife, and with it began to score a deep pattern of marks on the coarse weave of the dark-blue table-cloth.

After a bit, 'What do you think, Nancy?' she asked.

'Me?'

'Yes, you. What do you have to say about my pictures and my insurance and my private life in general?'

Nancy bit her lip, took a deep breath, and then spoke, her voice coming out clear and high-pitched, making her sound as though she were making a speech at the Women's Institute. 'I think . . . I think Noel is right. George believes that you should reinsure. He told me so, after he read about the sale of *The Water Carriers*. But the premiums would, naturally, be very high. And the insurance company may insist on tighter security. After all, they have to consider their client's investment.'

'You sound to me,' said her mother, 'as though you are quoting George word for word, or else reading from some incomprehensible manual. Have you no ideas of your own?'

'Yes,' said Nancy, sounding normal again. 'I do. I think you should sell the panels.'

'And raise, maybe, a quarter of a million?'

She spoke the words casually. The discussion was going better than Nancy had dared to hope, and she felt herself grow warm with excitement. 'Why not?'

'And once I've done that, what am I expected to do with the money?'

She looked at Noel. He shrugged elaborately. He said, 'The money you give away when you're alive is worth twice the money you give away when you're dead.'

'In other words, you want it now.'

'Ma, I didn't say that. I'm simply generalising. But face it; to go to bed with a nest-egg like that would be tantamount to simply handing it over to the Government.'

'So you think I should hand it over to you.'

'Well, you've got three children. You could unload a certain amount of it onto them, split into three. Keep a bit for yourself, to enjoy life. You've never been able to do that. Always had your nose to the grindstone. You used to travel all over the place with your parents. You could travel again. Go to Florence. Back to the south of France.'

'And what would you two do with all that lovely money?'

'I suppose Nancy would spend it on her children. As for me, I'd move on.'

'Into what?'

'New fields, pastures green. Set up on my own . . . commodity broking, perhaps . . .'

He was his father all over again. Perpetually dissatisfied with his lot, envious of others, materialistic and ambitious, and unshakeable in his belief that the world owed him a living. It could have been Ambrose who spoke to her, and this, as nothing else could have done, finally caused Penelope to lose her patience.

'Commodity broking.' She made no effort to keep the scorn from her voice. 'You must be out of your mind. You'd be as well to put your entire capital on a single horse, or a turn of the roulette wheel. You are quite shameless and sometimes you fill me with despair and disgust.' Noel opened his mouth to defend himself, but she talked him down, raising her voice. 'Do you know what I think? I don't think you give a hoot what happens to me, or to my house or my father's pictures. You care only what happens to yourself, and how swiftly and easily you can get your hands on yet more money.' Noel closed his mouth, his face tightening in anger and the colour draining from his thin cheeks. 'I haven't sold the panels and I may never sell them, but if I do I shall keep everything for myself, because it is mine, and mine to do as I like with, and the greatest gift a parent can leave a child is that parent's own independence. As for you, Nancy, and your children, it was you and George who made the decision to send them to those ridiculously expensive schools. Perhaps if you'd been a little less ambitious for them, and had spent more time on teaching them mannners, they'd have turned out a great deal more appealing than they are at the moment.'

Nancy, with an immediacy that surprised even herself, sprang to the defence of her offspring. 'I'll thank you not to criticise my children.'

'It's about time somebody did.'

'And what right have you to say a word against them? You take no interest in them. You show more interest in your endless eccentric friends and your wretched garden. You never even come and see them. Never come to see us, however often we invite you . . .'

It was Noel who lost his patience. 'Oh, for God's sake, Nancy, shut up. Your bloody children are neither here nor there. We're not talking about your children. We're trying to have an intelligent discussion . . .'

'They have everything to do with it. They're the future generation . . .'

'God help us . . .'

' . . . and a great deal more worthy of financial support than some hare-brained scheme of yours for making yet more money. Mother's right. You'd squander the lot of it, gamble it away . . .'

'Coming from you, that's laughable. You haven't a single opinion of your own, and you know bloody nothing about bloody anything . . .'

Nancy sprang to her feet. 'I've had enough. I'm not staying here to be insulted. I'm going home.'

'Yes,' said her mother. 'I think it's time you both went. And I think, as well, that it's a very good thing Olivia isn't here. Listening to this appalling conversation, she would destroy you both. For that reason alone, if she were with us, I am perfectly certain that neither of you would have had the courage to even start such a disgraceful discussion. And now . . .' She, too, got to her feet, and picked up the tray. 'You are both, as you never cease to tell me, busy people. There can be no point in wasting the rest of the afternoon in fruitless argument. I, meantime, shall go and start the washing-up.'

As she headed towards the kitchen, Noel fired his final malicious shot. 'I'm sure Nancy would love to help you. Nothing she likes better than getting down to a sinkful of dishes.'

'I've already said, I've had enough. I'm going home. And as for the washing-up, there's no need for Mother to martyr herself. Antonia can do it when she gets back. After all, isn't she meant to be the housekeeper?'

Penelope, at the open door, stopped dead. She turned her head and looked at Nancy, and there was an expression of disgust in her dark eyes that caused Nancy to suspect that she had actually gone too far.

But her mother did not throw the tray of coffee cups at her. She simply said very quietly, 'No, Nancy. She is not meant to be a housekeeper. She is my friend. My guest.'

She went. Presently they heard the sound of taps running, the clatter of china and cutlery. A silence fell between them, disturbed only by a large bluebottle, which, under the mistaken delusion that it was suddenly high summer, decided that this was the moment to break cover and emerge from its winter hiding. Nancy reached for her jacket, put it on. Buttoning it, she raised her head and looked at Noel. Across the table, their eyes met. He pulled himself to his feet.

'Well,' he said quietly. 'You made a right bloody mess of that.'

'Speak for yourself,' Nancy snapped.

He left her, disappearing upstairs to collect his things. Nancy stayed where she was, waiting for him to return, determined to retain her dignity, to nurse her hurt feelings, to suffer no loss of face. She filled in the time checking on her appearance, combing her hair, powdering her flushed and mottled face, applying a layer of lipstick. She was deeply upset and longed to escape, but hadn't the nerve to do it on her own; Mother had always had a way with her, and Nancy was determined that she was going to leave this house without making any sort of an apology. After all, what had she got to apologise for? It was Mother who had been so impossible, Mother who had said all those unforgivable things.

When she heard Noel return, she snapped shut her compact, slipped it into her bag, and went through to the kitchen. The dish washer whirred, and Penelope, her back to them, scoured saucepans at the sink.

'Well, we're on our way,' said Noel.

Their mother abandoned the saucepans, shook her hands dry, and turned to face them. Her apron and her reddened face did nothing to detract from her dignity, and Nancy remembered that her rare outbursts had never lasted more than a few moments. She had never, in her life, borne a grudge, never sulked. Now, she even smiled, but it was a funny sort of smile. As though she was sorry for them, had, in some way, defeated them.

She said, 'It was good of you to come,' and sounded as though she meant it. 'And thank you, Noel, for all your hard work.'

'No problem.'

She reached for a towel and dried her hands. They all trooped out of the kitchen, through the front door, to where the two cars waited on the gravel sweep. Noel slung his grip into the back of the Jaguar, got in behind the wheel, and, with a cursory wave of the hand, shot out through

the gate to disappear in the direction of London. He had not said goodbye to either of them, but neither mother nor daughter commented on
this.

Instead, in silence, Nancy too got into her car, fastened her safety-belt,
drew on her pigskin gloves. Penelope stood watching these preparations
for departure. Nancy could feel her mother's dark gaze upon her face,
could feel the blush start, creep up her neck into her cheeks.

Penelope said, 'Be careful, Nancy. Drive safely.'

'I always do.'

'But, just now, you're upset.'

Nancy, staring at the driving wheel, felt tears rush to her eyes. She
bit her lip. 'Of course I'm upset. Nothing is so upsetting as family rows.'

'Family rows are like car accidents. Every family thinks, "It couldn't
happen to us," but it can happen to everybody. The only way to avoid
them is to drive with the greatest care and have much consideration for
others.'

'It isn't that we don't consider you. We're simply thinking of your own
good.'

'No, Nancy, that is not so. You just want me to do what *you* want me
to do, which is to sell my father's pictures and hand over the loot before
I die. But I'll sell my father's pictures when I choose to. And I'm not
going to die. Not for a long time.' She stepped back. 'Now, off you go.'
Nancy wiped the stupid tears from her eyes, switched on the ignition,
put the car into gear, let off the hand-brake. 'And remember to give my
love to George.'

She was gone. Penelope stood there, on the gravel outside her open
door, long after the sound of Nancy's car had been swallowed into the
still warmth of the miraculous spring afternoon. Glancing down, she saw
a groundsel thrusting its way between the stone chips. She stooped and
pulled it out, tossed it away, and then turned and went indoors.

She was alone. Blessed solitude. The saucepans could wait. She went
through the kitchen and into the sitting room. The evening would turn
chilly, so she lit a match and kindled the fire. When the flames were
licking to her satisfaction, she got up off her knees and went to her desk
and found the torn scrap of newspaper with the advertisement for
Boothby's, which Noel, a week ago, had drawn to her attention. *Ring
Mr Roy Brookner.* She laid it in the centre of her blotter, secured it with
her paperweight, and then returned to the kitchen. Opening a drawer,
she took from it her small, sharp vegetable knife, and then made her way
upstairs to her bedroom. This was now filled with golden afternoon
sunlight pouring through the west window, winking on silver and reflected
in mirrors and glass. She put the knife on her dressing-table and went to

open the doors of the huge Victorian wardrobe, which only just fitted beneath the sloping ceiling. The wardrobe was filled with her clothes. She took them all out and laid them, in armfuls, on her bed. This involved a certain amount of to-ing and fro-ing, but gradually the big bed, with its cotton crochet cover, was piled with every sort of garment, resembling the jumble stall at the church fête, or possibly the ladies' cloakroom at some manic party.

But the wardrobe stood empty, its back wall revealed. Years ago, this had been papered in a dark and heavily embossed design, but beneath these variations could be discerned other irregularities: the panels and strappings that made up the fabric of the solid old piece of furniture. Penelope took up the knife and reaching into its capacious interior, ran her fingers over the bumpy surface of the wallpaper, feeling her way by her sense of touch. Finding what she sought, she inserted the blade of the knife low down, in the angle of back and floor, and drew it upwards, slitting the paper as though she were opening an envelope. She judged the measurements with concentrated care. Two feet on the vertical, three feet across, and then two feet down again. Unsupported, the flap of wallpaper sagged, curled, and finally collapsed, to reveal the object that had been hidden behind it for the past twenty-five years. A battered cardboard folder, tied with string and secured to the mahogany panels by straps of sticky tape.

That evening, in London, Olivia rang Noel.

'How did you get on?'

'All done.'

'Did you find anything exciting?'

'Not a bloody thing.'

'Oh, dear.' He could hear the amusement in her voice, and silently cursed her. 'All that hard work for nothing. Never mind. Better luck next time. How's Antonia?'

'She's okay. I think she's taken a fancy to the gardener.'

He had hoped to shock her. 'Well, that's very nice,' said Olivia. 'What's he like?'

'Odd.'

'Odd? Do you mean queer?'

'No. I mean he's odd. Fish out of water. Square peg in a round hole. Upper-class, public school, so what's he doing being a gardener? Another thing – he doesn't drive a car and he doesn't drink. And he never smiles. Nancy's convinced he's hiding a dark secret, and for once I'm inclined to agree with her.'

'How does Mumma like him?'

'Oh, she likes him all right. Treats him like a long-lost nephew.'

'In that case, I shouldn't worry. Mumma's no fool. How is she?'

'The usual.'

'Not too tired?'

'Fine, as far as I could see.'

'You didn't say anything about the sketches? Mention them? Ask her about them?'

'Not a word. If they ever existed, she's probably forgotten about them. You know how vague she is.' He hesitated, and then went on casually. 'Nancy was there for lunch. Started quoting George on re-insurance. There was a bit of a row.'

'Oh, Noel.'

'You know what Nancy's like. Tactless as hell, stupid bitch.'

'Was Mumma upset?'

'A bit. I smoothed things over. But now she's even more stubborn than ever about things.'

'Well, I suppose it's her affair. Anyway, thank you for taking Antonia down.'

'My pleasure.'


Monday morning again. By the time Penelope came downstairs, Danus had arrived and was already hard at work in the vegetable garden. The next caller was the postman in his little red van, and then Mrs Plackett, stately on her bicycle, with her apron in her bag and the news that the Pudley ironmonger was having a sale and why didn't Mrs Keeling buy herself a new coal shovel. They were discussing this important project when Antonia appeared, and was duly introduced to Mrs Plackett. Pleasantries were exchanged, and their various weekend activities relayed. Then Mrs Plackett collected Hoover and dusters and climbed the stairs. Monday was her day for the bedrooms. Antonia began to fry bacon for her breakfast, and Penelope took herself into her sitting room, shut the door, and sat down at her desk to telephone.

It was ten o'clock. She dialled the number.

'Boothby's, Fine Art Dealers. Can I help you?'

'Would it be possible to speak to Mr Roy Brookner?'

'Just hold on for a moment.'

Penelope held on. She felt nervous.

'Roy Brookner.' A deep voice, cultured, very pleasant.

'Mr Brookner, good morning. My name is Mrs Keeling, Penelope Keeling, and I'm calling from my home in Gloucestershire. In *The Sunday*

*Times* last week you had an advertisement regarding Victorian paintings.
It gave your name and the number to ring.'

'Yes?'

'I wondered if you would be in this neighbourhood sometime in the
near future?'

'You have something you want me to look at?'

'Yes. Some works by Lawrence Stern.'

There was the very smallest hesitation. 'Lawrence Stern?' he repeated.
'Yes.'

'You're sure they are Lawrence Sterns?'

She smiled. 'Yes, quite sure. Lawrence Stern was my father.'

Another slight pause. She imagined him reaching for a note pad,
unscrewing the cap of his fountain pen.

'Could you give me your address?' Penelope did so. 'And your telephone
number?' She did this as well. 'I'm just consulting my engagement diary.
Would this week be too soon?'

'The sooner the better.'

'Wednesday? Or Thursday?'

Penelope calculated, laid swift plans. 'Thursday would be best.'

'What time on Thursday?'

'The afternoon? About two o'clock?'

'Splendid. I have another call to make in Oxford; I can deal with that
in the morning and then come on to you.'

'If you make for Pudley, that's the easiest. The village is signposted.'

'I shall find the way,' he assured her. 'Two o'clock on Thursday. And
thank you, Mrs Keeling, for calling me.'


Waiting for him to arrive, Penelope pottered about her conservatory,
watering a cyclamen, snipping off dead geranium heads and browned
leaves. The weather had turned gusty, the east wind bringing with it
enormous sailing clouds and blinking sunshine. But the early warmth was
doing its work, for already there were yellow daffodil heads bobbing in
the orchard, the first primroses were showing their pale faces, and the
sticky buds of the chestnut were splitting open, to reveal the frilly,
delicate green of the baby leaves.

She was dressed in her tidiest clothes, as befitted the importance and
formality of the occasion, and occupied her mind by trying to decide how
Mr Brookner would look. With the only clues his name, and his voice
over the telephone, there was little to go on, and every time she thought
about it, she came up with a different image. He would be very young,
a brainy student, with a bulging forehead and a pink bow-tie. He

would be elderly, academic, immensely knowledgeable. He would be business-like and bouncy, with jargon at his fingertips and a mind like an adding machine.

He was, of course, none of these things. When, a little after two o'clock, she heard the slam of a car door, shortly followed by the ring of the front-door bell, she set down the watering can and went through the kitchen to let him in. Opening the door, she was faced with his back view, standing there on the gravel gazing about him, as though appreciative of country quiet and rural surroundings. He turned at once. A very tall and distinguished gentleman, with dark hair sliding back from a high tanned forehead and deep-brown eyes observing her politely from behind heavy horn-rims. He wore a quietly patterned and well-cut tweed suit, a checked shirt, and a discreetly striped tie. Given a bowler hat and a pair of field-glasses, he could have graced the smartest of race meetings.

'Mrs Keeling.'

'Yes. Mr Brookner. Good afternoon.' They shook hands.

'I was just admiring the view. What a beautiful spot, and a charming house.'

'I'm afraid you have to come into it through the kitchen. I haven't got a front hall . . .' She led the way indoors, and he was immediately diverted by the beguiling prospect of the far door leading into the conservatory, at that moment filled with sunshine, and bosky with greenery.

'I wouldn't bother about a front hall if I had a kitchen as pretty as this . . . and a conservatory as well.'

'I built the conservatory, but the rest of the house is very much as I found it.'

'Have you lived here long?'

'Six years.'

'Do you live alone?'

'Most of the time. At the moment I have a young friend staying, but she's gone off for the afternoon. She's driving my gardener to Oxford . . . They've taken the motor mower in the back of my car and they're going to get it sharpened.'

Mr Brookner looked a little surprised.

'You have to go all the way to Oxford to get it sharpened?'

'No, but I wanted them out of the way while you were here,' Penelope told him bluntly. 'And they're buying seed potatoes as well, and some stuff for the garden, so the trip won't be wasted. Now, would you like a cup of coffee? . . .'

'No, thank you.'

'Right.' He stood there, unimpatient, and looking as though he might be prepared to hang about for ever. 'Well, in that case, I suppose we'd better not waste any more time. Shall we go up and look at the panels first?'

'Whatever you say,' said Mr Brookner.

She led him out of the kitchen and up the narrow stairs to the tiny landing.

'. . . here they are, hanging on either side of my bedroom door. These were the very last paintings my father ever did. I don't know if you knew, but he suffered most dreadfully from arthritis. By the time these were done, he could scarcely hold his brushes, and so, you see, they were never finished.' She stood aside, making room for Mr Brookner to move forward, inspect, stand back – (only a foot or two, otherwise he'd have gone backwards down the stairs) – move in again. He said nothing. Perhaps he didn't like them. To cover her sudden nervousness, she began to speak again. 'They've always been a bit of a joke. We had this little house in Porthkerris, you see, up at the top of the hill, and never any money to spend on it, so it became dreadfully shabby. The hall there was decorated in an old Morris paper, but it grew worn and torn and my mother couldn't afford to replace it, so she suggested that Papa should paint two long decorative panels that would hide the worst of the worn bits. And she wanted something in his old style, allegorical, fabulous, that she could keep for ever and call her own. So he did, and these were the result. But he couldn't finish them. However, Sophie . . . my mother . . . didn't mind. She said she loved them even better just the way they were.'

Still he made no comment. She wondered if he was plucking up his courage to tell her that they were worth nothing, when, all at once, he turned and smiled.

'You call them unfinished, Mrs Keeling, and yet they are marvellously complete. Not so finely detailed, of course, or meticulous as those great works he executed at the turn of the century, but still, perfect in their own way. And what a colourist he was. Look at the blue of that sky.'

She was filled with gratitude towards him. 'I am so pleased you like them. My children have always either ignored them, or been particularly scathing about them, but they've always given me enormous pleasure.'

'And so they should.' He turned from his absorbed inspection. 'Is there anything else you want me to see, or is that all?'

'No. I have more downstairs.'

'May we go and look?'

'Of course.'

Downstairs again, and into the sitting room. His eyes at once fell upon *The Shell Seekers*. Before his arrival, she had switched on the small strip light that illuminated the picture, and now it waited for his consideration. At this moment, on this particular day, it seemed to Penelope more dear than ever, fresh and bright and cool as the day it had been painted.

After a long time, 'I didn't know,' said Mr Brookner, 'that such a work existed.'

'It's never been exhibited.'

'When was it done?'

'1927. His last big picture. The North Beach at Porthkerris, painted from his studio window. One of the children is myself. It's called *The Shell Seekers*. When I was married, he gave it to me as a wedding present. That was forty-four years ago.'

'What a present. What a possession, for that matter. You're surely not having to contemplate selling this?'

'No. I'm not selling this. But I wanted you to see it.'

'I'm glad I have.'

His eyes went back to the picture. After a bit, she realised that he was simply occupying himself until she should choose to make her next move.

'That's all, I'm afraid, Mr Brookner. Except for some sketches.'

He turned from *The Shell Seekers*, his features impassive. 'Some sketches?'

'By my father.'

He waited for her to enlarge on this, and when she did not, 'Am I going to be allowed to see them?' he asked.

'I don't know if they're worth anything, or even if they would interest you.'

'I can't say until I've had a look at them.'

'Of course not.' She reached behind the sofa and produced the battered cardboard folder tied with string. 'They're in here.' Mr Brookner, taking it from her, lowered himself into the seat of a wide-lapped Victorian chair. He laid the folder on the carpet at his feet, and with long, sensitive fingers, untied the knotted string.


Roy Brookner was a man of considerable experience in his job, and over the years had become immune to both shock and disappointment. He had even learned to deal with the worst nightmare of all, which was the classic one of the little old lady, finding herself, probably for the first time in her life, short of money, and deciding to have appraised, and then to sell, her most treasured possession. Boothby's would be informed of this intention, and Roy Brookner would duly make the appointment, and the – probably long – journey to see her. And at the end of the day his would be the heart-breaking task of informing her that the painting was not a Landseer; the Chinese jar, thought to be Ming, was nothing of the sort; and the ivory seal of Catherine de Médici did not, in fact, date from that lady's period, but the late nineteenth century; and so, they were worthless.

Mrs Keeling was not a little old lady, and she was the daughter of Lawrence Stern, but even so, he opened the covers of the folder without much hope. What he expected to discover he really did not know. What he found was of such heart-stopping importance that, for a moment, he could scarcely believe his eyes.

Sketches, Penelope Keeling had said, but she had not told what sketches. They were painted in oil, on canvas, the canvases ragged-edged and still showing the rusty impression of tack marks where once they had been nailed to their stretchers. One by one, taking his time, he took them up, gazed in incredulous wonder, laid them aside. The colours were unfaded, the subject matters instantly recognisable. In mounting excitement, he started a mental catalogue. *The Spirit of Spring. The Lover's Approach. The Water Carriers. The Sea-God. The Terrazzo Garden . . .*

It was almost too much. Like a man half-way through an enormous gourmet meal, he found himself sated, incapable of continuing. He paused, his hands stilled, hanging loosely between his knees. Penelope Keeling, standing by the empty fireplace, awaited his judgement. He looked up and across the short distance that separated them. For a long moment neither of them spoke. But the expression on his face told her everything she wanted to know. She smiled, and the smile lit up her dark eyes, and it was as though all the years that she had lived had never happened, and for an instant he saw her as the beautiful young woman she must once have been. And the thought occurred to him that if he had been young when she was young, he would probably have fallen in love with her.

He said, 'Where have these come from?'

'I've had them for twenty-five years, hidden in the back of my wardrobe.'

He frowned. 'But where did you come upon them?'

'They were in my father's studio, in the garden of our house in Oakley Street.'

'Does anyone else know of their existence?'

'I don't think so. But I have a feeling that Noel, my son, had begun to suspect – though why, I have no idea – that they did exist. But I can't be sure of this.'

'What makes you think so?'

'He's been searching around, going through the attic. And became extremely bad-tempered when he found nothing. I'm certain he was looking for something specific, and I'm fairly sure it was the sketches.'

'It sounds a little as though he knows what they would be worth.' He reached down to turn over another canvas. '*Amoretta's Garden*. How many are there altogether?'

'Fourteen.'

'Are they insured?'

'No.'

'Is that why you hid them?'

'No. I hid them because I didn't want Ambrose to find them.'

'Ambrose.'

'My husband.' She sighed. Her smile died, taking with it that vibrant flash of youth. She was her age again, a handsome, grey-haired woman in her sixties and tired of standing. She left the fireplace and went to sit in the corner of the sofa, resting one arm along its back. 'You see, we never had any money. That was the crux of the matter, the root of all the trouble.'

'Did you live with your husband at Oakley Street?'

'Yes. After the war. I'd spent all the war in Cornwall because I had a child to look after. And then my mother was killed in the Blitz, so I stayed on to care for Papa as well. And he handed Oakley Street over . . . and a . . .' Suddenly she laughed, hopeless, shaking her head. 'So garbled. It makes no sense. How can you possibly understand?'

'You could try starting at the beginning and going right through to the end.'

'That would take all day.'

'I have all day.'

'Oh, Mr Brookner, I would bore you to death.'

'You are Lawrence Stern's daughter,' he told her. 'You could read me the telephone directory from cover to cover and I should remain fascinated.'

'What a nice man you are. In that case . . .'

'In 1945 my father was eighty. I was twenty-five, married to a Lieutenant in the Navy, and the mother of a four-year-old child. For a little while I had been in the Wrens – that's when I met Ambrose – but when I knew I was having a baby, I got my discharge and went home to Porthkerris. I stayed there for the rest of the war. I scarcely saw Ambrose during those years. He was at sea most of the time, in the Atlantic, and then the Mediterranean, and finally in the Far East. I'm afraid it didn't bother me very much. Ours was a thoughtless wartime affair, a relationship that never would have got off the ground in peacetime.

'Then, there was Papa. He'd always been an enormously youthful and energetic man, but after Sophie was killed, he grew suddenly old before my very eyes, and there could be no question of my leaving him. But then the war ended, and everything changed. All the men came home, and Papa said that it was time for me to go back to my husband. I'm ashamed to say that I didn't want to, and it was then that he told me that he'd made over the title deeds of his house in Oakley Street, so that I would always have a base, security for my children, and financial independence. After that, I had no excuse to stay. Nancy and I left Porthkerris for the last time. Papa came to see us off at the station, and say goodbye to us, and that was a last time as well, because he died the following year, and I never saw him again.

'The house in Oakley Street was enormous. So big that Papa and Sophie and I had always lived in the basement, and let out the upper floors to lodgers. That way, we could make the establishment, more or less, wash its face. I carried on with that arrangement. A couple called Willi and Lalla Friedmann had lived there all through the war, and they stayed on. They had a little girl, and she was company for Nancy, and they were my permanant tenants. For the rest of the house, it was a fairly floating population, coming and going. Artists, mostly, and writers, and young men trying to get a toe in the door of television. My sort of people. Not Ambrose's.

'Then Ambrose came home. Not only did he come home, but he left the Navy and accepted a job in his father's old family firm, the publishers Keeling and Philips, in St James's. I was rather surprised when Ambrose told me this, but I think on the whole he did the right thing. I found out later that he'd blotted his copy-book when he was out in the Far East – antagonised his Captain and got a bad personal report. So, if he had stayed in the Navy, I don't suppose he'd have got very far.

'So there we were. We didn't have much, but we had more than most young couples. We were young, we were healthy, Ambrose had a job, and we had a house to live in. But apart from that, we had nothing, no common ground on which to build any sort of a relationship. Ambrose was intensely conventional and something of a social snob . . . he had great ideas about always making friends with the right people. And I was eccentric and careless and, I suppose, impossibly unreliable. But the things that were important to Ambrose seemed trivial to me, and I couldn't share his enthusiasms. And then, there was the vexing question of money. Ambrose never gave me anything. I suppose he reckoned I had my own private means, which in a way I had, but I was perpetually strapped for cash. As well, in my family, money was something that one, hopefully, had, but never spoke about. During the war, I'd managed on my Naval Allowance, and Papa used to put a little each month into my account to pay the housekeeping bills, but as there were no luxuries to spend money on, and everybody was bone-shabby anyway, it didn't seem to matter very much.

'But, married to Ambrose, living in London, put a very different complexion on things. By now my second daughter Olivia had been born, so that was another mouth to feed. Also, the old house was in a dreadful state of repair. Not bombed, thankfully, but cracked and dilapidated and generally falling to bits. It had to be rewired, and the roof had to be repaired. Then the plumbing went wrong, and of course everything needed painting. When I spoke to Ambrose about this, he told me it was my house and so my responsibility, so in the end I sold four precious paintings by Charles Rainier that had belonged to Papa, and those raised enough cash to do the most rudimentary of repairs, but at least the roof stopped leaking, and I could stop agonising as to whether or not the children were going to electrocute themselves by stuffing their fingers into the old-fashioned wall sockets.

'And then, the final straw. Ambrose's mother, Dolly Keeling – she'd spent the entire war bomb-dodging in Devon – came back to live in London. She took a little house in Lincoln Street, and from the moment she arrived, she began to make trouble. She'd never liked me. I don't really blame her. She never forgave me for starting the baby, for 'trapping' Ambrose into marriage. He was her only child and she was intensely possessive. So, she re-possessed him. All at once, being married to Ambrose was rather like looking after another person's dog. Every time you open the door, it bolts for home. Ambrose bolted for his mother. He used to drop in for a little drink on his way home from the office . . . the tea-and-sympathy syndrome, I suppose. He used to take her shopping on Saturday mornings, drive her to church on Sundays. It was enough to put anyone off going to church for life.

'Poor man. Divided loyalties are not easy companions to live with. And he deeply needed the adulation and attention that he got from Dolly and which I was incapable of giving him. Also, Oakley Street was never the most peaceful place in the world. I liked my friends around me; Lalla Friedmann and I had always been very close. And I liked children. Lots of children. Not just Nancy, but all her little school friends as well. In fine weather, the garden swarmed with them, hanging upside-down from ropes, or sitting in cardboard grocery cartons. And the little school friends all had mothers, who drifted in and out, and sat in the kitchen, drinking coffee and gossiping. There was a constant activity – jam being made, or somebody cutting out a dress or making scones for tea, and always toys all over the floor.

'Ambrose couldn't bear it. He said that it got on his nerves, returning from work to such bedlam. He began to resent the close quarters we lived in, especially as we owned the whole of the spacious house. He began to talk about chucking the tenants out, giving us room to spread. He talked about a dining room for dinner parties, and a drawing room for cocktail parties, and a bedroom and dressing room and bathroom, en suite, for ourselves. And I lost my temper and asked him what we were going to live on if we didn't have the rents coming in. And he went into a three-week sulk, and spent more time than ever with his mother.

'Just existing became an uphill struggle. Money was something that we argued about all the time. I didn't even know what he earned, so I had no sort of hold on him that way. But I knew he must earn something, so what did he do with it? Buy drinks for his friends? Buy petrol for the little car his mother had given him? Buy clothes? He was always a very natty dresser. I became intensely curious. I began nosing around. I found and read his bank statement, and saw that he was over a thousand pounds overdrawn. I was so naïve, so simple, I finally decided that he'd found himself a mistress and was spending his entire salary on keeping her in mink coats and a Mayfair flat.

'Finally, he told me himself. He had to. He owed five hundred pounds to a bookmaker, and he had to pay the debt within a week. I was making soup, I remember, stirring the big pot so that the dried peas wouldn't stick to the bottom. And I asked him how long he'd been backing horses, and he said for three or four years. And I asked about other things, and then it all came out. I think he was what nowadays would be called a compulsive gambler. He used to play at private gaming clubs. He had taken one or two big risks on the stock exchange and they hadn't come off. And all the time, I'd never had the slightest suspicion. But now he confessed, was even slightly shamefaced, but desperate. He had to get the money.

'I told him I hadn't got it. I told him to go to his mother, but he said' that he'd been to her before and she'd helped him, but he hadn't the nerve to go to her again. And then he said, why not sell the pictures, the three Lawrence Sterns, which was all I had of my father's work. And when he said that I became almost as frightened as he was, because I knew that he was quite capable of simply waiting until he had the house to himself, removing the pictures and carting them off to a sale room. *The Shell Seekers*, as well as being my most treasured possession, was also my comfort and solace. I couldn't live without it, and he knew this, so I told him I'd raise the five hundred pounds, and I did, by selling my engagement ring, and my mother's engagement ring as well. And after that, he became quite cheerful again, and his old perky, self-satisfied self. For a little he stopped gambling. He'd had a bad fright. But before long, it started again, and we were back to the old hand-to-mouth existence.

'Then, in 1955, Noel was born, and at the same time we were faced with the first of the big school bills. I still had the little house in Cornwall, Carn Cottage. After Papa died, it belonged to me, and I clung on to it for years, letting it out to any person who would rent it, and telling myself that one day I should be able to take my children there, to spend a summer. But I never did. And then I got a marvellous offer for the house, too good to refuse, and I sold it. When I did that, I knew that Porthkerris had gone for ever and the last link broken. When I sold Oakley Street, I had plans to return to Cornwall. To buy a little granite cottage with a palm tree in the garden. But my children intervened and talked me out of it and finally my son-in-law found Podmore's Thatch, and so, after all, I shall spend the twilight of my years in Gloucestershire, and not within sight and sound of the sea.'


'I've told you all this, and I still haven't got to the point, have I? I still haven't told you about finding the sketches.'

'They were in your father's studio?'

'Yes, hidden away behind an artist's accumulation of years.'

'When did it happen? When did you find them?'


'Noel was about four. And, to accommodate our growing family, we had taken in another couple of rooms. But the tenants filled the rest of the house. Then, one day, a young man appeared at the door. He was an art student, very tall and thin and poor-looking and quite charming. Someone had told him that I might be able to help him, because he had won a place at the Slade, but could find nowhere to live. I hadn't a corner to put him, but I liked the look of him, and I asked him in and gave him a meal and a glass of lager, and we talked. By the time he was ready to go, I was so taken with him, I couldn't bear the fact that I was unable to help him. And then I thought of the studio. A wooden shed in the garden, but stoutly built and watertight. He could sleep there, and work there; I could give him his breakfast, and he could come into the house to use the bathroom and do his washing. I suggested this, and he jumped at it. So then and there, I found the key, and we went out and inspected the studio. It was dirty and dusty and stacked with old divan beds and chests of drawers, as well as my father's easels and palettes and canvases, but it was sound and rainproof and it had a northern skylight, which made it all the more desirable to the young man.

'We agreed on a rent and a day of entry. He went, and I started work.

It took days, and I had to get my friend the rag-and-bone man to help me, and bit by bit, he loaded all the old rubbish into his little cart and drove it away. It took a number of journeys, but at last we were down to the final load. And it was then, at the very back of the studio, lost behind an old chest, that I found the folder of sketches. I recognised them immediately for what they were, but had no idea of their worth. At that time Lawrence Stern was unfashionable, and if a painting of his came up, it went, maybe, for five or six hundred pounds. But finding those sketches was like being given a present from the past. I had so little of his work. And I thought that if Ambrose knew about them, he was immediately going to demand that they be sold. So I took them indoors, and up to my bedroom. I taped them to the back of my wardrobe, and then I found a roll of wallpaper and papered them in. And that's where they've been ever since. Until last Sunday evening. Then, I knew, all at once, that it was time to let them see again the light of day, and to show them to you.'

'So now you know.' She glanced at her watch. 'What hours it's taken to tell you. I'm sorry. Would you like a cup of tea? Have you time for a cup of tea?'

'Yes, I have time. But I'm still greedy for more.' She raised her brows in question. 'Please don't think me curious or impertinent, but what became of your marriage? What became of Ambrose?'

'My husband? Oh, he left me . . .'

'Left you?'

'Yes.' To his astonishment he saw her face light up with amusement. 'For his secretary.'

'Soon after I found the sketches and had hidden them, Ambrose's old secretary, Miss Wilson, who'd been with Keeling and Philips for ever, retired, and a new girl came to take her place. She was young, and I suppose she must have been quite pretty. She was called Delphine Hardacre. Miss Wilson had always been called Miss Wilson, but Delphine was never referred to as anything but Delphine. One day Ambrose told me he was going up to Glasgow on business; the printing side of the firm was based there, and he stayed away for a week. Afterwards, I found out that he hadn't been to Glasgow at all, but up to Huddersfield with Delphine, to be presented to her parents. The father was immensely rich, something to do with heavy engineering, and if he thought Ambrose was a bit old for his daughter, this was obviously balanced out by the fact that she'd found a nice class of man for herself, and was besotted by him. Soon after this, Ambrose came home from the office and told me that he was leaving. We were in our bedroom. I'd washed my hair and was brushing it dry, sitting at my dressing-table, and Ambrose sat on the bed behind me, and the entire conversation took place through the medium of my mirror. He said he was in love with her. That she gave him everything I never had. That he wanted a divorce. Once divorced, he would marry her, and meantime, he was leaving Keeling and Philips, as was Delphine, and they were moving north to make a home for themselves in Yorkshire, where her father had offered him a position in his company.

'I must say for Ambrose, once he got around to organising himself, he made a good job of it. It was all so neat, so cut and dried, such a perfect _fait accompli_ that there really wasn't anything for me to say. There wasn't anything I wanted to say. I knew that I didn't mind his going. I would be better on my own. I would keep my children, and I would have my house. I agreed to everything, and he got off the bed and went downstairs, and I went on brushing my hair, and felt very peaceful.

'A few days later his mother came to see me; not to commiserate, nor, to give her her due, to blame, but simply to make quite certain that because of Ambrose's defection, I would not keep the children, either from him or from her. And I told her that my children were not my possessions, to give or withhold, but people in their own right. They must do what they wanted, see who they wanted to see, and I would never stop them. Dolly was much relieved, because although she'd never had much time for Olivia and Noel, she worshipped Nancy, and Nancy loved her. They were of like mind, those two, with everything in common. When Nancy married, it was Dolly who arranged her big London wedding, and, because of this, Ambrose made the journey from Huddersfield to give her away. That was the only occasion we ever saw each other after the divorce. He had changed, become very prosperous-looking. He'd put on a lot of weight, his hair had gone grey, and his complexion was very red. I remember, that day, that he wore, for some reason, a gold watch-chain, and he looked the very picture of a man who had lived in the North for the whole of his life and done nothing but make money.

'After the wedding, he went back to Huddersfield, and I never saw him again. He died about five years later. He was still a comparatively young man, and it was a dreadful shock. Poor Dolly Keeling, she outlived him by years, but she never got over losing her son. And I was sorry, too. I think with Delphine he at last found the life he was looking for. I wrote to her, but she never answered my letter. Perhaps she thought that

I was presumptuous to write. Or perhaps she simply didn't know what to say in reply.'

'And now I really *am* going to make some tea.' She rose to her feet, her hand raised to secure the tortoiseshell hairpin that pierced her knot of hair. 'Will you be all right on your own for a moment or two? Are you warm enough? Would you like me to light the fire?'

He assured her that he would be, he was, he did not need a fire, so she left him, absorbed once more in the sketches, and went out to the kitchen and filled the kettle and put it on to boil. She felt very peaceful, just as she had felt that summer evening, brushing her hair and listening to Ambrose telling her that he was leaving her for good. This, she told herself, was how Catholics must feel when they have been to confession – cleansed, freed, and finally exonerated. And she was grateful to Roy Brookner for having listened; and grateful as well, that Boothby's had sent her a man not simply professional, but human and understanding as well.

Over tea and gingerbread, they became, once more, business-like. The panels would be sold. The sketches catalogued and taken to London for appraisal. And *The Shell Seekers*? That, for the moment, would stay where it was, over the fireplace of the sitting room at Podmore's Thatch.

'The only hitch about selling the panels,' Roy Brookner told her, 'is the time factor. As you know, Boothby's have just mounted a big sale of Victorian paintings, and there won't be another for at least six months. Not in London. Maybe our New York sale room would be able to handle them, but I'd have to find out when they are scheduling their next sale.'

'Six months? I don't want to wait six months. I want to sell them *now*.'

He smiled at her impatience. 'Would you consider a private buyer? Without the competition of an auction, you mightn't get such a good price, but perhaps you'd be prepared to take the risk.'

'Could you find me a private buyer?'

'There is an American collector, from Philadelphia. He came over to London with the express intention of bidding for *The Water Carriers*, but he lost the sale to the representative of the Denver Museum of Fine Arts. He was very disappointed. He has no Lawrence Sterns, and they come on the market so seldom.'

'Is he still in London?'

'I'm not sure. I could find out. He was staying at the Connaught.'

'You think he might want the panels?'

'I'm certain he would. But of course the sale would depend on how much he was prepared to offer.'

'Will you get in touch with him?'

'Of course.'

'And the sketches?'

'It's up to you. It would be worth waiting a few months before we sold them . . . give us time to advertise and arouse interest.'

'Yes, I see. Perhaps in their case it would be better to wait.'

So it was agreed. Roy Brookner, then and there, commenced to catalogue the sketches. This took some time, but when he had finished, and presented her with a signed receipt, he returned them to their folder and neatly bound and tied the string. After that was done, she led him out of the room and back up the stairs to the landing, and he gently lifted the panels from the wall, leaving only a few cobwebs behind and two long strips of unfaded wallpaper.

Outside, all was loaded into the back of his impressive car, the sketches in the boot, and the panels, carefully wrapped in a tartan rug, laid on the back seat. With these stowed to his satisfaction, he stepped back and slammed the car door shut. He turned to Penelope.

'It's been a pleasure, Mrs Keeling. And thank you.'

They shook hands. 'I've so enjoyed meeting you, Mr Brookner. I hope I didn't bore you.'

'I've never been less bored in my life. And as soon as I have any news, I'll be in touch.'

'Thank you. And goodbye. Safe journey.'

'Goodbye, Mrs Keeling.'


He telephoned the next day.

'Mrs Keeling. Roy Brookner here.'

'Yes, Mr Brookner.'

'The American gentleman I mentioned to you, Mr Lowell Ardway, is no longer in London. I rang the Connaught, and they told me that he's gone to Geneva. His intention is to return direct to the United States from Switzerland. But I have his address in Geneva, and I'll write today to tell him about the panels. I'm certain when he knows they are available, he'll return to London to look at them, but we may have to wait a week or two.'

'I can wait for a week or two. I just couldn't bear to wait for six months.'

'I can assure you, you won't have to do that. And as for the sketches, I showed them to Mr Boothby and he was immensely interested. Nothing so important has come on the market for years.'

'Have you . . .' It seemed almost indelicate to inquire. 'Have you any idea what they might be worth?'

'In my estimation, no less than five thousand pounds each.'

Five thousand pounds. Each. Replacing the receiver, she stood there, in her kitchen, trying to comprehend the enormity of the figure. Five thousand pounds multiplied by fourteen was . . . impossible to do it in her head. She found a pencil and worked out the sum on her shopping list. It came to seventy thousand pounds. She reached for a chair and sat down, because her knees had, quite suddenly, gone weak.

Thinking about it, it was not so much the idea of riches that astonished her, but her own reaction to it. Her decision to summon Mr Brookner, to show him the sketches, to sell the panels was going to change her life. It was as simple as that, but still took a little getting used to. Lawrence Stern's two insignificant, unfinished paintings, which she had always loved but never thought of any value, were now with Boothby's, awaiting an offer by an American millionaire. And the bundle of sketches, hidden, and out of mind for years, had all at once become worth seventy thousand pounds. A fortune. It was like winning the pools. Considering her altered status, she remembered the young woman who had done just this thing, and whom Penelope had watched, in disbelief, on television, pouring champagne over her head and shrieking, 'Spend, spend, spend!'

An astonishing scene, like something from a manic fairy-tale. And yet now she found herself in more or less the same situation, and realised – and this was the astonishment – that it neither appalled nor overwhelmed her. Instead, she was filled with the gratitude of a person lavished with unexpected largesse. *The greatest gift a parent can leave a child is that parent's own independence.* That was what she had said to Noel and Nancy, and she knew that it was true and the freedom of security was priceless. Also, there were the possibilities of self-indulgent pleasures.

But what pleasures? She was inexperienced in extravagance, having saved and contrived and penny-pinched for the whole of her married life. She had felt no resentment or envy of other people's luxuries, but simply had been grateful to be able to raise and educate her children and still keep her head above water. It was not until she had sold the house in Oakley Street that she was able to lay claim to any sort of capital, and this had at once been prudently invested – to produce a modest income and be spent the way she most enjoyed spending money. On food, wine, entertaining her friends. Then there were presents – in these she was immensely generous – and, of course, her garden.

Now, if she wanted, she could do up the house from floor to ceiling. Everything she owned was worn and shabby beyond belief, but she liked things that way. The battered Volvo was eight years old, and had been second-hand when she bought it. Perhaps she should splash out on a Rolls-Royce, but there was nothing wrong with the Volvo – yet – and it would be something of a sacrilege to load up the boot of a Rolls with bags of peat and earthy pots of plants for the garden.

Clothes, then. She had, however, never been interested in clothes, an attitude of mind set for ever by the long years of war and the deprivation of the years that followed it. Many of her favourite garments had been purchased at the Temple Pudley Church Jumble Sale, and her naval officer's boat cloak had kept her warm for forty winters. She could always give herself a mink coat, but she had never relished the idea of wearing a garment made out of a lot of dear little furry dead animals, and she'd look a fool wandering down the village street on a Sunday morning to pick up the papers dressed up to the nines in mink. People would think she'd gone mad.

She could travel. But somehow, at sixty-four and not, it had to be faced, in the best of health, she knew that she was too old to start out across the world on her own. The days of leisurely car journeys, the Train Bleu and the mail-boats, were over. And the thought of foreign airports and ripping through space in supersonic jets she had never found particularly appealing.

No. None of these things. For the moment, she would do nothing, say nothing, tell nobody. Mr Brookner had come and gone and no one knew of his visit. Until he got in touch with her again, it was better to carry on as if nothing had happened. She told herself that she would put him out of her mind, but found this impossible. Each day, she waited to hear from him. Every time the telephone rang, she dashed for it, like an eager girl awaiting a call from her lover. But, unlike that eager girl, as the days went by and nothing happened, she stayed unanxious, unperturbed. There was always tomorrow. There was no hurry. Sooner or later he would have news for her.

Meantime, life went on and spring, in more ways than one, was in the air. The orchard was bright with drifts of daffodils, their yellow trumpets dancing in the breeze. Trees were misted in the tender green of new foliage, and in the sheltered beds close to the house the wallflowers and polyanthus opened their velvety faces, filling the air with nostalgic scent. Danus Muirfield, with the vegetable garden neatly planted, had given the lawn its first cut of the season and was now engaged in hoeing, raking, and mulching all the borders. Mrs Plackett came and went, started in on an orgy of spring-cleaning and washed all the bedroom curtains. Antonia pegged them out, like banners, on the line. Her energy was enormous, and she gladly took on any task that Penelope could not be bothered to do for herself, like driving to Pudley to do the huge weekly shopping, or clearing out the store cupboard and scrubbing all the shelves. When she was not occupied indoors, she could usually be found in the garden, erecting a trellis for the sweet-pea seedlings, or clearing the terrace tubs of their early narcissus and filling them with geraniums and fuchsias and nasturtiums. If Danus was there, she was never far from his side, and their voices floated across the garden as they laboured together. Seeing them, pausing to watch from an upstairs window, Penelope was filled with satisfaction. Antonia was a different person from that strained and exhausted girl that Noel had driven down from London; she had lost the pale sadness that she had brought from Ibiza, lost the dark rings beneath her eyes. Her hair shone, her skin bloomed, and as well there was an aura about her, undefinable, but still, to Penelope's experienced eye, unmistakable.

Antonia, she suspected, had fallen in love.


'I think the nicest thing in the world is doing something constructive in a garden on a fine morning. It's a combination of the best of everything. In Ibiza, the sun was always so hot and you got dreadfully sweaty and sticky, and then you'd have to go and jump into the pool.'

'We haven't got a pool here,' Danus pointed out. 'I suppose we could always go and jump into the Windrush.'

'It would be icy. I put my feet in the other day and it was terrible. Danus, will you always be a gardener?'

'Why do you suddenly ask that?'

'I don't know. I was just thinking. You seem to have so much behind you. School and going to America and then your Horticultural degree. It seems a bit of a waste if you're never going to do anything but plant other people's cabbages and pull up other people's weeds.'

'But I'm not always going to do that, am I?'

'Aren't you? Then what are you going to do?'

'Save up until I've got enough to buy a bit of land, have my own place, grow vegetables, sell plants, bulbs, roses, gnomes, anything anybody wants to buy.'

'A garden centre?'

'I'd specialise in something . . . roses or fuchsias, just to be a bit different from all the others.'

'Would it cost an awful lot? To start up, I mean?'

'Yes. The cost of land's high, and it would need to be large enough to make it a viable proposition.'

'Couldn't your father help you? Just to get started.'

'Yes, he could if I asked him. But I'd prefer to do it on my own. I'm twenty-four now. Perhaps by the time I'm thirty I'll be able to establish myself.'

'Six years to wait seems for ever. I'd want it now.'

'I've learned to be patient.'

'Whereabouts? I mean, where would you have this garden centre?'

'I'm not bothered. Wherever it was needed. I'd prefer to stay this end of the country, though. Gloucestershire, Somerset.'

'I think Gloucestershire's the best. It's so beautiful. And think of the market. All those rich commuters from London, buying gorgeous golden stone houses and wanting their gardens filled with goodies. You'd make a fortune. If I were you, I'd stay right here. Find yourself a little house, and a couple of acres. That's what I'd do.'

'But you're not going to open a garden centre. You're going to be a model.'

'Only if I can't think of anything else to do.'

'You're a funny creature. Most girls would give their eyes for a chance like that.'

'Wouldn't that rather defeat the purpose?'

'Besides, you wouldn't want to spend your life hoeing turnips.'

'I wouldn't grow turnips. I'd grow delicious things like corn on the cob and asparagus and peas. And don't look so sceptical. I'm very proficient. In Ibiza we never bought a single vegetable. We grew them all, and fruit as well. We had orange trees and lemons, too. Daddy used to say there was nothing more splendid than a gin and tonic with a slice of freshly picked lemon. They taste quite different to horrid, bought, shop ones.'

'I suppose you could grow lemons in a glasshouse.'

'The nice thing about lemon trees is that they fruit and flower at the same time. That way they always look pretty. Danus, did you never want to be a lawyer like your father?'

'Yes, I did at one time. Thought I'd follow in the old man's footsteps. But then I went to America, and after that, things sort of changed. And I decided to spend my life using my hands rather than my head.'

'But you do use your head. Gardening takes a lot of thought, a lot of knowledge and planning. And if you get your garden centre, you'll have to do all the accounts and the ordering and the taxes . . . I don't call that not using your head. Was your father disappointed that you stopped wanting to be a lawyer?'

'To begin with. But we talked it over and he came round to seeing my point of view.'

'Wouldn't it be utterly awful to have a father you couldn't talk to? Mine was perfect. You could tell him anything. I wish you could have met him. And I can't even show you my darling Ca'n D'alt, because some other family are living in it now. Danus, was it anything special that made you switch careers? Was it something that happened in America?'

'Perhaps.'

'Was what happened something to do with why you don't drive a car and never take a drink?'

'Why do you ask that?'

'I just think about it sometimes. I just wondered.'

'Does it bother you? Would you like me to be like Noel Keeling, racing up and down the motorway in an E-type, and reaching for a drink every time things get rough?'

'No, I wouldn't want you to be like Noel. If you were like Noel, I shouldn't be here, helping you. I'd be lying in a deck-chair, leafing over the pages of a magazine.'

'Then why don't you just leave well alone? Here, you're planting a seedling, not hammering in a nail. Do it gently, like you were putting a baby to bed. Tuck it in, no more. It has to have room to grow. It has to have space to breathe.'

She was bicycling. Free-wheeling downhill between fuchsia hedges hung with pink and purple ballerinas. The road ahead curved white and dusty, and in the distance was a sea blue as sapphire. There was a Saturday morning feeling. She wore sand-shoes. She came to a house, and it was Carn Cottage, but it wasn't Carn Cottage because it had a flat roof. Papa was there, wearing his wide-brimmed hat, sitting on a camp-stool, with his easel set up before him. He didn't have arthritis, and he was painting long strokes of colour on the canvas, and when she stood by him to watch, he did not look up, but said, 'One day they will come, to paint the warmth of the sun and the colour of the wind.' She looked over the edge of the roof, and it was a garden like Ibiza, with a pool. Sophie was swimming in the pool, to and fro. She was naked; her hair wet and sleek as a seal's fur. There was a view from the roof, but it wasn't the bay, it was the North Beach, with the tide out, and she was herself, searching, with a scarlet bucket filled with huge shells. Scallops and mussels and shining cowries. But she wasn't searching for shells, she was searching for something, somebody else; he was somewhere around. The sky became dark. She made her way across the deep sand, struggling against the wind. The bucket grew impossibly heavy, so she set it down and left it. The wind brought a sea mist with it, curling in over the beach like smoke, and she saw him walking out of the smoke towards her. He was in uniform but his head was bare. He said, 'I've been looking for you,' and took her hand, and together, they came to a house. They went in through the door, but it wasn't a house, it was the Art Gallery in the back streets of Porthkerris. And Papa was there again, sitting on a battered couch in the middle of the empty floor. He turned his head. 'I would like to be young again,' he told them. 'To be able to watch it all happening.'

She was filled with happiness. She opened her eyes and the happiness stayed, the dream more real than reality. She could feel the smile on her face, as though someone had set it there. The dream faded, but the sense of tranquil contentment remained. Her eyes took in, contentedly, the shadowy details of her own bedroom. The gleam of the brass bedrail, the looming shape of the huge wardrobe, the open windows with curtains moving lightly in the flow of sweet night air.

*I would like to be young again. To be able to watch it all happening.*

She was all at once very wide awake and knew that she would not sleep again. She pushed back the blankets and got out of bed, felt for her slippers, reached for her dressing-gown. In the darkness, she opened her door and went downstairs to the kitchen. She switched on the light. All was warm and orderly. She filled a saucepan with milk and put it on to heat. Then she took a mug down from the dresser, put in a spoonful of honey, filled it to the brim with hot milk, stirred. Carrying the mug, she went across the dining room, into the sitting room. She switched on the light that illuminated *The Shell Seekers*, and in its gentle glow, stirred the fire to life. As it blazed, she carried the mug to the sofa, arranged cushions, curled up in a corner with her feet tucked beneath her. Above her the picture shone out into the half-light, brilliant as a stained-glass window with the sun behind it. It was her own personal mantra, pervasive as a hypnotist's charm. She gazed, concentration intent, unblinking, waiting for the spell to work, the magic to happen. She filled her eyes with the blue of sea and sky, then felt the salty wind; smelt seaweed and damp sand; heard the scream of gulls, the drumming of the breeze in her ears.

Safely there, she could allow herself to recall the various and many occasions in her life when she had done just this thing – shut herself away, alone, closeted with *The Shell Seekers*. Thus she had sat, from time to time, during those bleak London years just after the war, bedevilled, sometimes near defeated, by shortages, by lack of money and a paucity of affection; by Ambrose's hopelessness and a frightening loneliness that, for some reason, could not be filled by the company of her children. Thus she had sat the night Ambrose packed his bags, abandoned his family, and headed for Yorkshire, prosperity, and the warm young body of Delphine Hardacre; and, again, when Olivia, most precious of Penelope's offspring, left Oakley Street for good, to set up her own establishment and embark upon her brilliant career.

*You must never go back*, they all told her. *Everything will be changed.* But she knew that they were wrong because those things that she most craved were elemental, and blessedly, unless the world blew itself up, remained unchanging.

*The Shell Seekers.* Like an old and trusted friend, the picture's constancy filled her with gratitude. And, as one becomes possessive of friends, she had clung to it, lived with it, refused even to speak of letting it go. But now, all at once, things were different. There was not simply a past, but a future as well. Plans to be made, delights in store, a whole new prospect ahead. Besides, she was sixty-four. There weren't that number of years left to be wasted, gazing nostalgically back over her shoulder. She said aloud, 'Perhaps I don't need you any more.' The picture made no comment. 'Perhaps it is time to let you go.'

She finished her drink. Laid down the empty mug, reached for the rug that lay folded over the back of the sofa, settled down on the soft pillows with the blanket for warmth, spread over the length of her body. *The Shell Seekers* would keep company, keep watch, smile down upon her sleeping form. She thought of the dream, and Papa saying, *They will come, to paint the warmth of the sun and the colour of the sky.* She closed her eyes. I would like to be young again.

# Richard

By the summer of 1943, Penelope Keeling, along with most other people, felt as though the war had been going on for ever, and moreover, would continue for ever. It was a treadmill of boredom – shortages and black-out, relieved by occasional flashes of horror, terror, or resolution, as British battleships were blown out of the sea, disaster befell Allied troops, or Mr Churchill came on the wireless to tell everybody how splendidly they were doing.

It was like the last two weeks before you had a baby, when you knew for certain that the baby was never going to come, and you were going to look like the Albert Hall for the rest of your life. Or being in the middle of a very long, curving railway tunnel, the brightness of day long left behind, and the tiny spark of light at the end of the tunnel not yet in evidence. It would be there one day. Of that no person had the slightest doubt. But meantime all was darkness. You just trod on, one foot at a time, dealing with the day-to-day problems of feeding people, keeping them warm, seeing the children had shoes, and trying to stop the fabric of Carn Cottage from falling into neglect and disrepair.

She was twenty-three, and sometimes thought that except for next week's film at the little cinema down in the town, there didn't seem to be anything to look forward to. Going to the cinema had become quite a cult with her and Doris. Doris called it going to the pictures, and they never missed a single show. Totally unselective, they sat through anything that came their way, simply to escape, if only for an hour or two, from the tedium of their existence. At the end of the show, having dutifully stood to attention for the cracked record of 'God Save The King,' they would stumble out into the pitch-dark street, either incapable with excitement, or awash with sentiment, and make their way home, walking arm in arm, giggling feebly, tripping over kerbstones, and climbing, by the light of the stars, the steep streets that led to home.

As Doris invariably remarked, it made a nice change.

Which it did. One day, Penelope supposed, this grey limbo of war would end, but it was hard to believe and difficult to imagine. Being able to buy steaks and marmalade oranges; not being frightened to listen to the news bulletins; letting the lights from the windows stream out into the darkness without danger of a random bomber or a stream of abuse from Colonel Trubshot. She thought about returning to France, driving down to the south, to the mimosa and the hot sun. And bells, ringing from silenced church towers, not to warn of invasion but to celebrate Victory.

Victory. The Nazis defeated, Europe freed. Prisoners of war, herded into camps all over Germany, would come home. Servicemen would be demobilised, families reunited. This last was Penelope's own private stumbling-block. Other wives prayed for and lived for their husbands' safe return, but Penelope knew that she did not very much mind if she never saw Ambrose again. This was not heartless, it was just that as the months passed, her memories of him had faded and become, somehow, less and less likely. She wanted the war to finish – only a lunatic would wish for anything else – but she did not relish the prospect of starting all over again with Ambrose – her scarcely known and almost forgotten husband – and trying to come to terms with her thoughtless marriage.

At times, when she was feeling low, a shameful hope would seep up out of her subconscious and skulk around at the back of her mind. A hope that something would happen to Ambrose. Not that he should be killed, of course. That was unthinkable. She wished no person dead, and certainly not a man as young, handsome, and life-loving as he. But if only, between Mediterranean battles and night patrols and U-boat hunts, he could sail into harbour and there come upon some young lady – a nurse, perhaps, or a Wren Officer – infinitely more attractive than his wife, with whom he would fall violently in love, and who, in the fullness of time, would take Penelope's place by his side and fulfil all Ambrose's wildest dreams of happiness.

He would, of course, write to tell her of this amorous entanglement.

Dear Penelope,

I hate to do this, but there is only one way to tell you. I have met Another. What has happened between us is too big for either of us to fight. Our love for each other . . . et cetera, et cetera . . .

Every time she received one of his infrequent missives – usually impersonal aerogrammes, one page reduced to the size and shape of a snapshot – her heart lifted in the faint hope that here at last was just such a letter, but she was invariably doomed to disappointment. Reading the few scrawled lines giving her news of wardroom friends whom she had never met, or describing a party in some other nameless ship, she knew that nothing had changed. She was still married to him. He was still her husband. And she would slip the aerogramme back into its envelope, and later – perhaps days later – sit down to try to answer it, writing an even duller letter to Ambrose than he had written to her. 'We had tea with Mrs Penberth. Ronald has joined the Sea Scouts. Nancy can draw a house.'

Nancy. Nancy was no longer a baby, and as she grew and developed, Penelope became fascinated by the child, and unexpectedly maternal. Seeing her turn from infant to toddler was like watching a bud open into a flower – a slow process, but delightful. She was, as Papa had promised, a Renoir, rose and gold, with sweeping dark lashes and small pearly teeth, and she remained the precious pet of Doris and most of Doris' friends. Sometimes Doris would wheel the perambulator home from some gathering, bearing in triumph an outgrown smock or party dress bequeathed by another young mother. This would be washed and immaculately ironed and Nancy tricked out in her new finery. Nancy loved being tricked out. 'Isn't she a beauty,' Doris would coo, as much to Nancy as anyone else, and Nancy would smile, much satisfied, and smooth the skirts of her new dress with fat and appreciative fingers.

At such moments, she was Dolly Keeling all over again, but even this did not spoil Penelope's pleasure and amusement. 'You're a little madam,' she told Nancy and hoisted the child up into her arms to hug her. 'A real little hoot.'

Keeping Nancy and the boys clothed and the household fed took up almost every moment of her and Doris' time. Rations had shrunk to laughable proportions. Every week, she walked down the steep streets to the town and Mr Ridley's grocer's shop. She was 'registered' with Mr Ridley. There, she handed over the family ration books and was sold, in return, minute quantities of sugar, butter, margarine, lard, cheese, and bacon. The meat ration was even worse, because you had to queue down the pavement for hours, without any idea of what you were queueing for, and when you bought vegetables or fruit at the greengrocer's they were all tipped into your string bag, just the way they were, earth and all, because there was no paper for paper bags and it was considered unpatriotic to ask for one.

Strange receipes, dreamed up by the Ministry of Food, appeared in the papers, purporting to be not only economical but nourishing and delicious as well. Mr Woolton's sausage pie, made with nigh-fatless pastry and a chunk of corned beef. A certain cake, rendered moist with the help of grated carrot, and a casserole dish that consisted almost entirely of potato.

GO EASY ON BREAD, EAT POTATOES INSTEAD, they were exhorted by poster, just as they were exhorted to DIG FOR VICTORY, and warned that CARELESS TALK COSTS LIVES. Bread was wheat, which had to be imported, at immense peril to ships and lives, from the other side of the Atlantic. White bread had long since disappeared from the shelves of the bakers' shops, and its place taken by something called a National Loaf, which was greyish-brown and had husky shreds in it. Tweed bread, Penelope called it, and pretended to like it, but Papa pointed out that it was exactly the same colour and texture as the new utility lavatory paper, and decided that the Minister of Food and the Minister of Supply – the two gentlemen presumably responsible for such necessities of life – had somehow got their lines crossed.

It was all very difficult, and yet, at Carn Cottage, they were better off than most. They still had Sophie's ducks and hens, and made full use of the copious eggs that these obliging creatures produced, and they had Ernie Penberth.

Ernie was a Porthkerris man, had lived Downalong all his life. His father was the town greengrocer, making his collections and deliveries in a horse-drawn cart; his mother, Mrs Penberth, a redoubtable character, was a pillar of the Women's Guild and regular chapel-goer. As a boy, Ernie had contracted tuberculosis and spent two years in the sanatorium at Tehidy, but once recovered, had been employed by Sophie on the most casual of terms, turning up when needed to do odd jobs about the place or to help with the heavy digging in the garden. His appearance was not impressive, for he was short of stature and sallow-skinned, and because of his illness had failed his medical for the Army. So, instead of going to the war as a soldier, Ernie worked on the land, helping a local hard-pressed farmer whose own sons had been called up. Any spare time, however, that could be gleaned from this arduous labour, was dedicated to helping out the little household at Carn Cottage, and, over the years, Ernie made himself increasingly indispensable, for he proved to be a man who could turn his hand to anything; not only growing magnificent vegetables, but mending fences and lawn-mowers, unfreezing pipes and fixing fuses. He could even wring a chicken's neck, when none of the rest of them could contemplate putting to death some faithful old bird, who'd kept them in eggs for years, but was now fit only for the pot.

When food grew really short, and the meat ration shrank to a joint of oxtail for six people, Ernie, by some magic, always came to the rescue, turning up at the back door bearing a rabbit, or a couple of mackerel, or a brace of wood pigeon he had shot himself.

Meantime, Penelope and Doris did what they could to help inject a little variety into meal times. It was at this period that Penelope initiated the habit of a lifetime, which was to carry, whenever she went out for a walk, a haversack, bucket, or basket. Nothing was too humble to be spied, collected, and carted home. A turnip or cabbage, fallen from a cart, was borne back to Carn Cottage in triumph to form the basis of some nourishing vegetarian dish or broth. Hedgerows were gleaned for blackberries, rose hips, elderberries; and early dew-spangled meadows searched for mushrooms. They lugged home twigs and fir cones for kindling fires, fallen branches, driftwood from the beach to be sawn into logs – anything burnable that would keep the hot-water boiler going and the sitting-room fire alight. Hot water was especially precious. Baths were not allowed to be more than three inches deep – Papa painted a sort of Plimsoll line, and above this no person was allowed to go – and they had fallen into the economical habit of queueing up for the same bath water; children first and then the grown-ups, the final occupant soaping furiously before the water turned chill.

Clothes were another vexing problem. Most of everybody's clothes ration went on keeping the children shod and replacing old and worn sheets and blankets, and there was nothing left over for personal needs. Doris, who was dressy, found this a great frustration, and was for ever fashioning herself some new garment out of an old one, letting down a hem, or cutting up a cotton dress to make a blouse. Once she turned a blue laundry bag into a dirndl skirt.

'It's got LINEN embroidered on the front,' Penelope pointed out when Doris modelled it for her approval.

'Perhaps people will think that's what I'm called.'

Penelope was unbothered by the way she looked. She wore her old clothes, and when they fell to bits, raided Sophie's cupboards and purloined anything that still hung there. 'How can you bear to?' Doris asked her, feeling that Sophie's clothes were sacred, and perhaps she was right. But Penelope was cold. She buttoned herself into a Shetland cardigan that had belonged to her mother, and would not allow herself a twinge of sentiment.

Most of the time she went bare-legged, but when the cold east winds of January blew, she reverted to the thick black stockings left over from her days in the WRNS, and when her threadbare overcoat finally disintegrated, she cut a hole in the middle of an old car rug (Black Watch tartan with a woollen fringe) and wore it as a poncho.

Papa said she looked like a Mexican gypsy in it, but he smiled as he said it, delighted by her enterprise. He did not smile, these days, very often. He had grown, since Sophie's death, immensely old and frail. His old leg wound from the First World War had started, for some reason, to play up. The cold, damp wintry weather caused him considerable pain,

and he had taken to walking with a stick. He was bowed, he had grown
very thin, his crippled hands curiously waxy and lifeless, like the hands
of a man already dead. Incapable now of doing very much around the
house and garden, he spent most of his time, mittened and shawled in
rugs, by the sitting-room fire, reading the newspapers or well-loved books,
listening to the wireless, or writing letters in his painful, uncertain hand,
to old friends who lived in other parts of the country. Sometimes, when
the sun shone and the sea was blue and dancing with white caps,
he would announce that he felt like a little fresh air, whereupon Penelope
would fetch his caped overcoat and his big hat and his stick, and they
would set out together, arm in arm, to make their way down the steep
streets and alleyways and into the heart of the little town, strolling along
the harbour wall, watching the fishing boats and the gulls, perhaps calling
in at the Sliding Tackle for a drink of anything that the landlord could
produce from beneath his counter; and if he had nothing to produce,
then downing tumblers of watery, lukewarm beer. Other times, if he was
feeling strong enough, they went on as far as the North Beach and the
old studio, locked now and seldom entered; or took the sloping lane that
led to the Art Gallery, where he was happy to sit, contemplating the
collection of paintings that he and his colleagues had somehow gathered
together, and lost in an old man's silent and lonely memories.

And then in August, by which time Penelope had resigned herself to the
fact that nothing exciting was ever going to happen again, it did.

It was the boys, Ronald and Clark, who started the ball of speculation
rolling. They returned from school in high dudgeon, having missed their
afternoon game of football because they were, it seemed, no longer
allowed to use the town rugger field at the top of the hill. It, along with
two of Willie Pendervis' best pasture fields, had been requisitioned,
surrounded by miles of barbed-wire fencing, and forbidden to all. The
reason for this was the cause of much discussion. Some said it was to
be an armoury depot in readiness for the Second Front. Others, a
prisoner-of-war camp; or, yet again, a powerful wireless station for sending
secret coded messages to Mr Roosevelt.

Porthkerris, in short, was rife with rumour.

Doris was the bearer of the next mysterious manifestation of war-like
activity. Out for a walk with Nancy, she came home by way of the main
road, and returned to Carn Cottage bursting with news.

'That old White Caps Hotel – the one that's stood empty for months
. . . Well, it's all been done up. Painted and scrubbed, bright as a penny,
and the car park's full of trucks and those American Jeep things, and

there's a smashing Royal Marine Commando on guard at the gate. That's right. Royal Marines. I saw his cap badge. Fancy that. Bit of fun having a few soldiers round the place . . .'

'Royal Marines? What on earth are they doing here?'

'Perhaps they're going to invade Europe. Do you suppose it's the start of the Second Front?'

Penelope considered this unlikely. 'Invade Europe from Porthkerris? Oh, Doris, they'd all drown themselves trying to get round Land's End.'

'Well, it's got to be something.'

And then, overnight, it seemed, Porthkerris lost its North Pier. More barbed-wire entanglements appeared, clear across the harbour road just past the Sliding Tackle, and all beyond, including the Fish Market and the Salvation Army hut, were declared Admiralty property. The deep water moorings at the end of the pier were cleared of fishing boats, and their place taken by a dozen or so small landing craft. All of this was discreetly guarded by a handful of Royal Marine Commandos, wearing battledress and green berets. Their presence in the town caused a mild stir, but still nobody could come up with a reasonable explanation of what it was all about.

It was not until the middle of the month that they were finally enlightened. There had come a spell of perfect weather, warm and breezy, and this particular morning Penelope and Lawrence had taken themselves out of doors, she to sit on the front-door step and shell peas for lunch, and he to recline in a deck-chair set up on the grass, with his hat tipped over his eyes to shade them from the glare. As they sat there, in companionable silence, a sound reached their ears – the bottom gate being opened and shut. Both looked up, and presently observed General Watson-Grant making his way up the stone steps between the fuchsia hedges.

While Colonel Trubshot was in charge of the ARP in Porthkerris, General Watson-Grant commanded the local Home Guard. Lawrence detested Colonel Trubshot, but he had a lot of time for the General who, although he had spent most of his Army life stationed in Quetta and skirmishing with the Afghans, had, on retirement, put these war-like activities behind him and, instead, absorbed himself in peaceful pursuits and accomplishments, for he was a keen gardener and the possessor of a considerable collection of stamps. Today he did not wear his Home Guard uniform but a cream drill suit, probably fashioned in Delhi, and a battered panama hat with a faded black silk ribbon. He carried a stick, and glancing up to see Penelope and Lawrence waiting for him, raised this in greeting.

'Good morning. Another lovely day.'

He was a small man, spare as a whip, with a stubbly moustache and a leather-coloured skin, legacy of years on the North-West Frontier. Lawrence watched his approach with pleasure. The General called only from time to time, but his visits were always welcome. 'Not interrupting you, am I?'

'Not at all. We're doing nothing but enjoy the sun. Forgive me if I don't get up. Penelope, get the General a chair.'

Penelope, who wore her cooking apron and no shoes, set aside the colander of pea pods and stood up.

'Good morning, General Watson-Grant.'

'Ah, Penelope. Nice to see you, my dear. Busy with the cookhouse? Left Dorothy slicing beans.'

'Would you like a cup of coffee?'

The General considered her offer. He had walked a long way, and was not a coffee man, preferring gin. Lawrence knew this, and made the token gesture of looking at his watch. 'Twelve o'clock. Surely something a little stronger. What have we got, Penelope?'

She laughed. 'I don't think very much, but I'll look.'

She went into the house, dark after the brightness of outdoors. Found, in the dining-room sideboard, a couple of bottles of Guinness, tumblers and a bottle opener. She put these on a tray, carried them out and set them down on the front-door step, and then went back to fetch the General his chair. This she set up for him, and he settled himself gratefully, perched forward, with his bony knees sticking up and his narrow trousers riding high, revealing knobbly ankles in yellow socks and leather brogues shiny as chestnuts.

'This is the life,' he remarked.

Penelope took the cap off a bottle and poured his drink. 'It's Guinness, I'm afraid. We've had no gin for months.'

'Just the ticket. As for the gin, we finished our ration a month ago. Mr Ridley's promised me a bottle when his next allocation comes through, but heaven knows when that's going to be. Well. Cheers.'

He downed half the long drink in what appeared to be a single swallow. Penelope returned to her pea-podding and listened while the two elderly men inquired after each other's health and exchanged a few scraps of gossip and comments on the weather and the general state of the war. She was, however, pretty certain that this was not the reason for the General's visit and, when there came a pause in the conversation, she chipped in.

'General Watson-Grant, I'm sure you're the very person to tell us what's going on in Porthkerris. The camp on the rugger pitch, and the harbour closed, and the Royal Marines moving in. Everybody's guessing, but nobody knows. Ernie Penberth is our usual source of information, but he's harvesting, and we haven't seen him for three weeks.'

'As a matter of fact,' said the General, 'I do know.'

Lawrence said quickly, 'Don't tell us if it's secret.'

'I've known for some weeks but it's all been kept under wraps. However, now I can tell you. It's a training exercise. Cliff-climbing. The Royal Marines are instructing.'

'And who are they going to instruct?'

'A company of United States Rangers.'

'United States Rangers? You mean we are about to be invaded by _Americans?_'

The General looked amused. 'Better Americans than Germans.'

'Is the camp for the Americans?' Penelope asked.

'Exactly so.'

'Have the Rangers arrived yet?'

'No, not yet. I imagine we'll know when they do. Poor devils. They've probably spent their lives on the prairie or the flat plains of Kansas, never seen the sea in their lives. Imagine being dumped down at Porthkerris and then invited to climb Boscarben Cliffs.'

'Boscarben Cliffs?' Penelope felt quite faint. 'I can't think of anything worse than being taught to climb at Boscarben. The cliffs there are perpendicular and about a thousand feet high.'

'I suppose that's the whole idea,' said the General. 'Though, I must say I agree with you, Penelope. The very prospect gives me vertigo. Rather them than me, poor bloody Yanks.' Penelope grinned. The General had never minced his words, and this was one of the things she most liked about him.

'And the landing craft?' Lawrence asked.

'Transport. They'll take them round to the cliffs by sea. Should think they'll be dead with mal de mer before they've even landed the craft on the shingle at the foot of the cliffs.'

Penelope felt even sorrier for the poor young Americans. 'They'll wonder what's hit them. And what will they do with their spare time? Porthkerris isn't exactly a hotbed of wild social activity, and the Sliding Tackle's not the most lively pub in the world. Besides, there's nobody here. All the young people have gone. Nobody left but grass widows and little children and old people. Like us.'

'Doris will be thrilled,' Lawrence observed. 'American soldiers, all talking like film stars, will make a nice change.'

The General laughed. 'It's always a problem to know what to do with a lot of randy soldiery. But by the time they've been up and down the

Boscarben Cliffs a couple of times, I don't suppose they'll have much energy left for . . .' He paused, searching for an acceptable word. 'Gallivanting' was all he could come up with.

It was Lawrence's turn to laugh. 'I think it's all very exciting.' He was struck by a bright idea. 'Let's go and gawp, Penelope. Now that we know what it's all about, let's go and see for ourselves. We'll go this afternoon.'

'Oh, Papa. There's nothing to see.'

'Plenty to see. Bit of new blood around the place. We could do with something happening, provided it's not a stray bomb. Now, General, your drink is finished . . . have the other half.'

The General consider this proposal. Penelope said quickly, 'There isn't any more. Those were the last two bottles.'

'In that case' – the General laid his empty tumbler on the grass by his feet – 'I should be on my way. See how Dorothy's getting on with tiffin.' He pulled himself, with some difficulty, out of the sagging deck-chair, and they all followed suit. 'That was splendid. Most refreshing.'

'Thank you for coming. And putting us in the picture.'

'I thought you might like to know. Thought you were probably wondering what it was all about. It makes everything feel a bit more hopeful, doesn't it? As though we might be staggering towards the conclusion of this flaming war.' He tipped his hat. 'Goodbye, Penelope.'

'Goodbye. And my regards to your wife.'

'I'll convey them.'

'I'll see you to the gate,' said Lawrence, and they moved off together. Penelope, watching them make their way down the garden, was reminded of two old dogs. A dignified St Bernard and a wiry little Jack Russell. They reached the steps and began, with some care, to descend them. She stooped to pick up the pan of shellèd peas and the colander of pods and carried them indoors, to find Doris and relay everything that General Watson-Grant had told her and Lawrence.

'Americans.' Doris could scarcely believe their good fortune. 'Americans in Porthkerris. Oh, thank God for that, a bit of life at last. Americans.' She repeated the magic word. 'Well, we thought of a lot of funny things, didn't we, but we never came up with *Americans*.'


General Watson-Grant's visit had the effect on Lawrence of a shot in the arm. Over lunch they all talked of nothing else, and when Penelope emerged from the kitchen, after clearing the meal away and washing up the dishes, she found him waiting for her, already dressed for outdoor activity, with a worn corduroy jacket to protect his old bones from the nippy breeze, and a scarlet muffler wound round his neck. He wore his hat and his mittens, and sat patiently, leaning against the hall chest, with his hands resting on the horn handle of his stick.

'Papa.'

'Let's be off then.'

She had a thousand things to do. Vegetables to be thinned and weeded, the grass to be cut, and a pile of ironing to be dealt with.

'You really want to go?'

'Said I did, didn't I? Said I wanted to go and gawp.'

'Well, you'll have to wait a moment or two, till I find a pair of shoes.'

'Get a move on then. We haven't all day.'

Which was exactly what they had, but she didn't say this. She went back into the kitchen, to tell Doris the plan, and to give Nancy a quick kiss, and then ran upstairs to put on sand shoes, wash her face, brush her hair and tie it back with an old silk scarf. She took a cardigan out of a drawer, tied it round her shoulders, ran downstairs again.

He waited just as she had left him, but when she appeared, heaved himself to his feet.

'You look beautiful, my darling.'

'Oh, Papa, thank you.'

'On our way then, to inspect the Military.'

As soon as they were out of doors, she was glad that he had made her come, for it was a perfect afternoon, bright and blue with the tide in and the bay capped with scuds of white foam. Trevose Head was drowned in haze, but the breeze was cool and smelt salty. Reaching the main road, they crossed it and stood for a moment gazing out over the buttress-like wall that formed part of the cliff. They looked down onto roof-tops and steep gardens and crooked lanes which led to a small railway station and so down onto the beach. Before the war, in August the beach would have been crowded, but now it was almost deserted. The barbed-wire entanglements, which had been erected in 1940, still stood between the putting green and the sand, but there was an open gap in the middle, and through this a handful of families had made their way, with children running, screaming to paddle, and dogs chasing the gulls along the edge of the waves. Far below, out of the wind, a tiny walled garden revealed itself, where pink roses smothered an old apple tree and a palm rattled its dry leaves in the wind.

After a little, they sauntered on, down the slope of the hill. The road curved, and the White Caps Hotel was revealed, a detached stone house in a row of similar houses, with heavy sash windows facing out over the bay. It had stood empty and dilapidated for some time, but now they saw that it had been freshened up with white paint and looked startlingly trim. The tall iron railings which fronted the car park had been painted too, and the car park was full of khaki trucks and Jeeps. At the open gateway, a young Marine stood guard.

'Well, I never did,' Lawrence remarked. 'Doris got it right for once.'

They drew closer. Saw the white flagstaff, the flag snapping in the wind. Newly scrubbed granite steps led up to the front door sparkling in the sunshine. They paused to stare. The young Marine, on guard at the pavement's edge, stared back at them, impassive.

After a bit, 'We'd better get moving,' Lawrence said. 'Otherwise, we'll be shunted on, like a couple of street-walkers.'

But before they could do this, there came a flurry of activity from inside the building. The inner glassed door was opened, and two uniformed figures appeared. A Major and a Sergeant. They ran down the steps with a fine military clatter of booted feet, crossed the gravel and got into one of the Jeeps. The Sergeant drove. He started the engine, backed, and turned. As they came through the gate, the young Marine on guard saluted and the Officer returned his salute. Emerging onto the main road, they paused for a second, but there was no traffic, and at once the Jeep turned out and down the hill in the direction of the town, at some speed and creating a good deal of din.

Penelope and her father watched it disappear beyond the curved terrace of quiet houses. When the sound of the Jeep engine had died away, 'Come,' said Lawrence, 'let's get on.'

'Where are we going?'

'To see the landing craft, of course. And then the Gallery. We haven't been for weeks.'

The Gallery. That meant goodbye to any plans for the rest of the afternoon. Ready with objections, Penelope turned towards him, but saw his dark eyes bright with the prospect of pleasure, and hadn't the heart to spoil his fun.

She smiled, assenting, and slipped her hand beneath his arm.

'All right. The landing craft, and then the Gallery. But let's take our time. No point in getting exhausted.'


The Gallery, even in August, was always chill. The thick granite walls kept out the warmth of the sun, and the tall windows let in all the draughts. Also the floor was slate-flagged, and there was no form of heating, and today the wind, gusting up from the North Beach, delivered from time to time great clouts upon the building, causing the framework of the northern skylight to shudder and rattle. Mrs Trewey, who was on duty by the door, sat at an old card table piled with catalogues and picture postcards, with a rug around her shoulders and a small electric fire scorching her shins.

Penelope and Lawrence were the only visitors. They sat side by side on the long, aged leather couch that stood in the middle of the floor. They sat in silence. This was the tradition. Lawrence did not wish to talk. He liked to be left alone, perched forward, his chin resting upon his hands, supported by his stick, intent upon the familiar works, remembering, communing contentedly with his old friends, many of whom were now dead.

Penelope, accepting this, sat back, huddled into her cardigan, with her long bare brown legs stretched out in front of her. Her sneakers had holes in the toes. She thought about shoes. Nancy needed shoes, but she needed a new thick sweater as well, with the winter coming on, and there were insufficient clothes coupons for both. It would have to be shoes. As for a sweater, perhaps Penelope could unearth some old hand-knitted garment, unravel the wool, and re-knit it for Nancy. This had been done before, but it was a tedious and fiddly job, and she did not relish the prospect. How wonderful it would be to go and buy new wool, rose pink or primrose yellow, thick and soft, and knit Nancy something really pretty.

Behind them the door opened and shut. A draught of cold air stirred and died. Another visitor. Neither Penelope nor her father shifted. Footsteps. A man. A few words were exchanged with Mrs Trewey. And then came the slow, halting tread of booted feet as the newcomer made his way around the room. After ten minutes or so, he moved into the edge of Penelope's vision. Still thinking about Nancy's sweater, she turned her head and looked at him, and saw the back view of what could only be the Royal Marine Major who had been driven away, so dashingly, in the Jeep. Khaki battledress, green beret, a crown on his shoulder-straps. Unmistakable. She watched his progress as he moved slowly towards them, his hands clasped behind his back. Then, when he was only a few yards away, he turned, aware of their presence, perhaps diffident of disturbing them. He was tall and wiry, his face unremarkable save for a pair of astonishingly light and clear blue eyes.

Penelope met his glance, and felt embarrassed to be caught staring. She turned away. It was left to Lawrence to break the ensuing silence. All at once he became aware of the newcomer, and raised his head to see who it could be.

There came another gust of wind, another shudder and rattle of glass. When this had died, Lawrence said, 'Good afternoon.'

'Good afternoon, sir.'

Beneath the brim of his great black hat, Lawrence's eyes narrowed in puzzlement. 'Aren't you the man we watched set off in the Jeep?'

'That's right sir, You were on the other side of the road. I thought I recognised you.' His voice was cool, lightly pitched.

'Where's your Sergeant?'

'Down at the harbour.'

'It hasn't taken you long to find this place.'

'I've been here three days, and this is the first opportunity I've had to pay a visit.'

'You mean, you knew about the Gallery?'

'But of course. Who doesn't?'

'Far too many people.' Another pause while Lawrence's eyes travelled over the stranger. On such occasions, he had a sharp and brilliant regard, which many people, subjected to it, found unnerving. The Royal Marine Major, however, did not appear to be unnerved. He simply waited, and Lawrence, liking his coolness, visibly relaxed. He said abruptly, 'I'm Lawrence Stern.'

'I thought you might be. I hoped you would be. I'm honoured to meet you.'

'And this is my daughter, Penelope Keeling.'

He said, 'How do you do,' but made no move to come forward and shake her hand.

Penelope said, 'Hi.'

'You'd better tell us your name.'

'It's Lomax, sir. Richard Lomax.'

'Well, Major Lomax.' Lawrence patted the worn leather beside him. 'Come and sit down. You make me feel uncomfortable, standing there. Never was much of a one for standing.'

Major Lomax, still looking unperturbed, complied with this suggestion, coming to settle himself on Lawrence's other side. He leaned forward, relaxed, his hands between his knees.

'It was you who started up the Gallery, wasn't it, sir?'

'Me and a lot of other people. Early 1920s, it was. This used to be a chapel. Stood empty for years. We got it for a song, but then had the problem of filling it with only the best of paintings. To form a nucleus of a rare collection, we all donated a favourite work. See.' He leaned back, and used his stick as a pointer. 'Stanhope Forbes. Laura Knight. What a particular beauty that is.'

'And unusual. I always associate her with circuses.'

'That was done at Porthcurno.' His stick moved on. 'Lamorna Birch. Munnings. Montague Dawson. Thomas Millie Dow. Russell Flint . . .'

'I must tell you, sir, that my father had one of your paintings. Unfortunately, when he died, his house was sold and the picture went as well . . .'

'Which one was that?'

They talked on. Penelope stopped listening. She stopped brooding about Nancy's wardrobe, and started thinking about food instead. Supper this evening. What could she give them? Macaroni cheese? There was a rind of Cheddar left over from the week's ration, which could be grated into a sauce. Or cauliflower cheese. But they'd had cauliflower cheese two nights ago, and the children would complain.

'. . . you have no modern works here?'

'As you can see. Does that bother you?'

'No.'

'You like them, though?'

'Miró and Picasso I love. Chagall and Braque fill me with joy. Dali I hate.'

Lawrence chuckled. 'Surrealism. A cult. But soon, after this war, something splendid is going to happen. I and my generation, and the generation which followed it, have gone as far as we can go. The prospect of the revolution which will come to the world of art is something which fills me with enormous excitement. For that reason only, I should like to be a young man again. To be able to watch it all happening. Because, one day, they will come. As we came. Young men with bright visions and deep perceptions and tremendous talent. They will come, not to paint the bay and the sea and the boats and the moors, but the warmth of the sun and the colour of the wind. A whole new concept. Such stimulation. Such vitality. Marvellous.' He sighed. 'And I shall be dead before it even begins. Do you wonder I feel regretful? To miss all that.'

'There is only so much each man can do in his lifetime.'

'True. But it is hard not to be greedy. It is human nature always to want more.'

Another silence fell. Penelope, thinking of supper, glanced at her watch. It was a quarter to four. By the time they reached Carn Cottage it would be nearly five.

She said, 'Papa, we should go.'

He scarcely heard her. 'Hm?'

'I said, it's time we started for home.'

'Yes. Yes, of course.' He collected himself, gathered himself up, but before he could struggle to his feet, Major Lomax was upright and ready to help him. 'Thank you . . . very kind. Age is a terrible thing.' He was finally erect. 'Arthritis is worse. I haven't painted for years.'

'I'm sorry.'

When they were finally ready to make their way, Major Lomax walked to the door with them. Outside, in the windy cobbled square, his Jeep was parked. He was apologetic. 'I'd like to be able to drive you home, but it's against regulations to take civilians in Service vehicles.'

'We prefer to walk,' Lawrence assured him. 'We take our time. Nice to talk to you.'

'I hope I'll see you again.'

'But of course. You must come and have a meal with us.' He stood considering this brilliant idea. Penelope, with a sinking heart, knew exactly what he was going to say next. She dug him in the ribs with her elbow but he ignored her warning, and it was too late. 'Come and have supper this evening.'

She hissed at him furiously. 'Papa, there isn't anything *for* supper. I don't even know what we're going to eat.'

'Oh.' He looked hurt, let down, but Major Lomax made it all right. 'So very kind of you, but I'm afraid this evening is no good for me.'

'Another time, maybe.'

'Yes, sir. Thank you. Another time I should like that very much.'

'We're always around.'

'Come on, Papa.'

'*Au revoir* then, Captain Lomax.' He raised his stick in farewell, took heed at last of Penelope's urging, and moved forward. But still, he was put out.

'That was rude,' he reproached her. 'Sophie never refused a guest, even if there was nothing more to offer him than bread and cheese.'

'Well, he couldn't have come anyway.'

Arm in arm, they made their way down the sloping cobbles towards the harbour road, and the first stage of the long walk home. She did not look back but still had the feeling that Major Lomax stayed where he was, standing by his Jeep, watching their progress until they finally turned the corner by the Sliding Tackle and were lost from his view.

The excitement and stimulation of the afternoon, added to the long walk and copious intakes of fresh air, rendered the old man very tired. It was with some relief that Penelope finally steered him up the garden and through the open front door of Carn Cottage, where he at once collapsed into a chair and sat, slowly getting his breath. She removed his hat and hung it up, unwound the muffler from his neck. She took one of his mittened hands between her own and rubbed it gently, as though this small attention might bring the life back to his waxy twisted fingers.

'Next time we go to the Gallery, Papa, we'll get a taxi to take us back.'

'We should have taken the Bentley. Why didn't we take the Bentley?'

'Because we can't get any petrol for it.'

'Not much use without petrol.'

After a little, he was sufficiently recovered to make his way into the sitting room, where she settled him into the familiar sagging cushions of his chair.

'I'll make you a cup of tea.'

'Don't bother. I'll have a little sleep.'

He leaned back and closed his eyes. She knelt at the fire and put a match to paper, waited until sticks and coal had kindled. He opened his eyes. 'A fire in August?'

'I don't want you getting cold.' She stood up. 'You're all right?'

'Of course.' He smiled at her, a smile of grateful love. 'Thank you for coming with me. It was a good afternoon.'

'I'm happy you enjoyed it.'

'Enjoyed meeting that young man. Enjoyed talking to him. Haven't talked like that for a long time. A long time. We will have him here for a meal, won't we? I'd like to see him again.'

'Yes, of course.'

'We'll get Ernie to shoot some pigeon. He'd like pigeon . . .' His eyes closed again. She left him.


By the end of August, the harvest had been gathered in, the United States Rangers had taken possession of the new camp at the top of the hill, and the weather had broken.

The harvest was a good one, and the farmers were well satisfied. Doubtless, in the fullness of time, they would be given a pat on the head by the Ministry of Agriculture. As for the American troops, they made less impact on Porthkerris than had been feared. Gloomy forebodings by staunch chapel-goers proved unfounded, and there were no drunks, brawls, or rapes. On the contrary, they seemed exceptionally well-behaved and well-mannered. Young, rangy, and crew-cut, wearing camouflage jackets and red berets, they padded the streets in their rubber-soled boots and, apart from a few statutory wolf whistles and friendly overtures to the children, whose pockets soon bulged with chocolate and chewing-gum, their presence made little difference to the day-to-day life of the little town. Under orders, perhaps for security reasons, they kept a low profile, and made the journey between the camp and the harbour sardined into the backs of trucks or driving Jeeps with trailers piled with ropes, crampons, and grappling irons. On these occasions, they would whistle dutifully at any lady who happened to pass, as though anxious to live up to the wild reputation that had preceded them. But as the days went by and their exhaustive training proceeded, it became clear that General Watson-Grant had been right, and men who spent their waking hours enduring wild sea journeys and the chilling face of the Boscarben Cliffs had no thought in mind, at the end of the day, but a hot shower, food and sleep.

To add to their discomfort, the weather, after weeks of sunshine, had become appalling. The wind swung around to the north-west, the barometer dropped, and the rain came in squalls, low grey clouds of it, pouring in from the ocean. Down in the town, the wet cobbles of the narrow streets shone like fish scales, and gutters ran with rogue water and sodden scraps of rubbish. At Carn Cottage, the flower borders were blown to wet ribbons, an old tree lost a branch, and the kitchen was festooned with wet washing, because there was no other place to dry it.

It was enough, as Lawrence remarked, gazing from the window, to damp anybody's ardour.

The sea was grey and angry. Stormy rollers thundered in onto the North Beach, depositing a fresh scouring of flotsam far beyond the usual high-water line. But, as well as flotsam, other and more interesting objects were washed up. The sad remains of a merchant ship, torpedoed and sunk out in the Atlantic months or weeks before, and finally carried ashore by the tides and the prevailing wind: a lifebelt or two, some shattered decking, and a number of wooden crates.

Ernie Penberth's father, out in the early morning with his horse and vegetable cart, was the first to spy them. At eleven o'clock on the same day, Ernie appeared at the back door of Carn Cottage. Penelope was peeling apples, and looked up from this task to see him there, his black oilskin dripping with water and a saturated cap pulled down over his nose. But he was grinning.

'Like some tinned peaches, would you?'

'Tinned peaches? You're pulling my leg.'

'My dad's got two crates of them down at the shop. Picked them up off the North Beach. Got them back and opened them up. Californian tinned peaches. Good as fresh.'

'What a windfall! Can I really have some?'

'He's put aside six for you. Thought the children would like them. Says if you like, to go down; you can get them any time.'

'He is a *saint*! Oh, Ernie, thank you. I'll go this afternoon, before he changes his mind.'

'He won't do that.'

'Do you want to eat with us?'

'No, better get back. Thanks all the same.'

As soon as lunch was over, Penelope duly set out, booted, buttoned into an old yellow oilskin, and with a woollen hat pulled down over her ears. She carried two sturdy shopping baskets, and once she had become accustomed to the force of the wind – which threatened, from time to time, to hurl her off her feet – and gusts of rain, driving needle-sharp into her face, the wild weather became exhilarating and she began to enjoy herself. Dropping down into the town, she found it strangely deserted. The storm had driven everyone indoors, but the feeling of isolation, of having the place to herself, served only to increase her satisfaction. She was made to feel intrepid, like an explorer.

Mr Penberth's greengrocery store was Downalong, half-way along the harbour road. It was possible to reach by a maze of back lanes, but instead she chose the way that led by the sea and, turning the corner by the Lifeboat House, stepped out into the teeth of the gale. The tide was high, the harbour a-brim with raging grey water. Screaming gulls were blown in all directions, fishing boats rocked and swayed at anchor, and at the far end of the North Pier, she saw the landing craft bobbing and dancing at their moorings. The weather was obviously too wild even for the Commandos to venture out.

It was with some relief that she came at last to the greengrocer's, a tiny triangular building at the junction of two narrow lanes. As she opened the door and stepped inside, a bell jangled overhead. The shop was empty, smelling pleasantly of parsnips and apples and earth, but when she shut the door, a curtain in the back wall was raised and Mr Penberth appeared, wearing his usual garb of navy-blue guernsey and mushroom-shaped cap.

'It's me,' she said unnecessarily, dripping water all over his floor.

'Thought it might be.' He had his son's dark eyes and the same grin, though fewer teeth. 'Walk down, did you? That's some bugger of a day. But the gale's blown itself out, it'll be fair by evening. Just heard the shipping forecast on the wireless. Get my message, did you? Ernie tell you about the tinned peaches?'

'Why else do you think I'm here? Nancy hasn't tasted a peach in her life.'

'Better come through to the back. Keeping them *hidden*, I am. People find out I've got tinned peaches, and my life won't be worth living.' He held aside the curtain and she carried her baskets through into the cramped and cluttered space at the back of the shop, which did duty as store-room and office. Here simmered a black stove, which was never allowed to go out, and here Mr Penberth did his telephoning, and made himself cups of tea when business was quiet. Today it smelt strongly of fish, but Penelope scarcely noticed this, her attention being wholly taken up by the piles of cans that were stacked on every available horizontal surface . . . Mr Penberth's loot of the morning.

'What a find! Ernie said they were on the North Beach. How did you get the crates back here?'

'Fetched my neighbour. He gave me a hand. Humped them home in the cart. Six be enough for you, will it?'

'More than enough.'

He loaded three into each of her baskets. 'How are you off for fish?' he asked.

'Why?'

Mr Penberth disappeared beneath the knee-hole of his desk and emerged with the source of the fishy smell. Penelope, looking into the bucket, saw it was nearly filled with blue-and-silver mackerel. 'One of the boys was out this morning, swapped me these for some of the peaches. Mrs Penberth won't eat mackerel, says they're dirty fish. Thought you could use them. Fresh, they are.'

'If I could have half a dozen, they'd do us for supper.'

'Lovely,' said Mr Penberth. Rummaging, he unearthed an old news-paper, bundled the fish into clumsy parcels, and laid them on top of the peach tins. 'There.' Penelope picked up the baskets. They were extremely heavy. Mr Penberth frowned. 'Going to manage, are you? Not too weighty for you? I could bring them up, mind, next time I'm your way in the cart, but the mackerel won't stay fresh for another day.'

'I'll manage.'

'Well, I hope you'll all enjoy them . . .' He saw her to the door. 'How's Nancy?'

'Blooming.'

'Tell her and Doris to come and see us soon. Haven't set eyes on them for a month or more.'

'I'll tell them. And thank you, Mr Penberth, so much.'

He opened the door to the tinkle of the bell. 'It's a pleasure, my dear.'

Weighed down with peaches and fish, Penelope set off for home. Now, well into the afternoon, there were a few more people around, emerging to shop or go about their business. And Mr Penberth had been right about the weather forecast. The tide had turned, the wind already was beginning to drop, the rain to ease off. She looked up and saw, high in the sky beyond the racing black clouds, a ragged scrap of blue. Enough to make a cat a pair of trousers. She walked briskly, feeling relatively cheerful, for once not having to worry over what she was going to give everyone for supper. But after a bit the laden baskets began to take their toll, her hands ached and her arms felt as though they were being tugged out of their sockets. It crossed her mind that perhaps she had been wrong in refusing Mr Penberth's offer of delivery, but almost at once this thought was chased from her mind by the sound of a fast-approaching vehicle, coming from behind her, from the direction of the North Pier.

The road was narrow and the puddles deep. Not wishing to be drenched in a wave of dirty water, she stepped aside to wait until the oncoming car was safely past. It shot by, and then, a few yards on and with a screech of brakes, almost immediately halted. She saw the open Jeep, the two familiar uniformed occupants. Major Lomax and his Sergeant. The Jeep stayed where it was, its engine running, but from it Major Lomax, unfolding his long legs, stepped out into the road and walked back to where she stood.

Without preliminaries, he said, 'You look overburdened.'

Grateful for an excuse to be shed of her baskets, Penelope set them down on the pavement and straightened to face him. 'I am.'

'We met the other day.'

'I remember.'

'Have you been shopping?'

'No. Collecting a present. Six tins of peaches. They were blown up this morning on the North Beach. And some mackerel.'

'How far have you got to carry them?'

'Home.'

'Where's that?'

'At the top of the hill.'

'Can't they be delivered?'

'No.'

'Why not?'

'Because I want to eat them tonight.'

Amused, he smiled. The smile did something extraordinary to his face and caused her to look at, and really see him, for the first time. 'Unremarkable' had been her own private verdict, that day he had ambled in on them at the Gallery, but now she saw that, on the contrary, he was not unremarkable in the very least, for his well-ordered features, his strangely brilliant blue eyes, and that unexpected smile assembled themselves into a pattern of quite extraordinary charm.

He said, 'Perhaps we can help.'

'How?'

'We can't give you a ride, but I can see no reason why Sergeant Burton shouldn't drive your peaches home.'

'He'd never find the way.'

'You underestimate him.' With that, he stooped and picked up the baskets. He said, quite crossly, 'You shouldn't be carrying these. You'll hurt yourself.'

'I carry shopping all the time. Everybody has to . . .'

She was ignored. Major Lomax was already on his way back to the Jeep. Penelope, still feebly protesting, went after him. 'I can manage . . .'

'Sergeant Burton.'

The Sergeant switched off the engine. 'Sir?'

'These are to be delivered.' He stowed the baskets firmly on the back seat of the Jeep. 'The young lady will give you directions.'

The Sergeant turned to her, waiting politely. With no apparent alternative, Penelope did as she was told. ' . . . up the hill, and then right at Grabney's Garage, and then follow the road till you get to the top. There's a high wall and it's called Carn Cottage. You'll have to leave the Jeep on the road and walk through the garden.'

'Anyone at home, miss?'

'Yes. My father.'

'What's his name, miss?'

'Mr Stern. If he doesn't hear you . . . if nobody answers the bell, just leave the baskets on the doorstep.'

'Right, miss.' He waited.

Major Lomax said, 'That's settled, then. Carry on, Sergeant. I'll walk the rest of the way. See you back at HQ.'

'Sir.'

He saluted, started up his engine, and was off, with his cargo looking strangely domestic on the back seat of the Jeep. It rounded the corner by the Lifeboat House and was gone. Penelope was left with the Major. She felt ill at ease, disconcerted by this unexpected turn of events. She also felt unsatisfied with her appearance, which normally troubled her not in the very least. There was, however, nothing to be done about it, except pull off the unbecoming woollen hat and shake loose her hair. She did this, stuffing the hat into the pocket of her oil-skin.

He said, 'Shall we go?'

Her hands were cold, so she put them into her pockets as well.

'Do you really want to walk?' she asked him doubtfully.

'I wouldn't be here if I didn't.'

'Haven't you anything else you should be doing?'

'Like what?'

'An exercise to plan, or a report to be written?'

'No. The rest of the day is my own.'

They began to walk. A thought struck Penelope. She said, 'I hope your Sergeant doesn't get into trouble. I'm sure he's not allowed to carry people's shopping in his Jeep.'

'If anybody gives him a rocket, it's me. And how are you so sure?'

'I was in the Wrens for about two months, so I know all about rules and regulations. I wasn't allowed to carry a handbag or an umbrella. It made life very difficult.'

He appeared interested. 'When were you in the Wrens?'

'Oh, ages ago. In 1940. I was in Portsmouth.'

'Why did you leave?'

'I had a baby. I got married and I had a baby.'

'I see.'

'She's nearly three. She's called Nancy.'

'Is your husband in the Navy?'

'Yes. He's in the Mediterranean, I think. I'm never very sure.'

'How long is it since you've seen him?'

'Oh . . . ' She could not remember and did not want to. 'Ages.' As she said this, high above, the clouds parted for an instant, and a watery gleam of sunshine broke through. The wet streets threw back the reflection of this light, and stone and slate were washed in gold. Amazed, Penelope turned up her face to this momentary brilliance. 'It really is clearing. Mr Penberth said it would. He listened to the weather forecast and he said the storm would blow over. Perhaps it will be a beautiful evening.'

'Yes, perhaps it will.'

The sunlight disappeared as swiftly as it had come, and all was grey again. But the rain had finally stopped.

She said, 'Don't let's go up through the town. Let's go by the sea and up by the railway station. There's a flight of steps that comes out exactly opposite the White Caps Hotel.'

'I'd like that. I haven't really found my way around yet, but I suppose you know it like the back of your hand. Have you lived here always?'

'In the summertime. In winter we lived in London. And in between we went to France. My mother was French. We had friends there. But we've been in Porthkerris ever since the outbreak of war. I suppose we'll all stay here till it ends.'

'How about your husband? Doesn't he want you around when he comes ashore?'

They had turned into a narrow lane that ran alongside the beach. Pebbles had been flung up onto this by the high tide, and scraps of seaweed and a ravelled end of tarry rope. She stooped and picked up a pebble and flung it out into the sea. She said, 'I told you. He's in the Mediterranean. And even if I could be with him, I couldn't, because I have to take care of Papa. My mother was killed in the Blitz in 1941. So I have to stay with him.'

He did not say, I'm sorry. He said again, 'I see,' and sounded as though he really did.

'It's not just him and me and Nancy. We've got Doris living with us

and her two boys. They were evacuees. She's a war widow. She never
went back to London.' She looked at him. 'Papa liked talking to you that
day in the Gallery. He was cross with me because I couldn't ask you for
supper . . . he said I was very rude. I didn't mean to be. It's just that
there wasn't anything I could think of to eat.'

'I much enjoyed meeting him. When I knew I was being sent here, it
crossed my mind that perhaps I might see the famous Lawrence Stern,
but I never really imagined it would happen. I thought he'd be too old
and frail to go out and about. When I saw you first, up on the road
outside HQ, I knew at once that it had to be him. And then, when I
walked into the Gallery and you were actually there, I could scarcely
believe my luck. Such a painter, he was.' He looked down at her. 'Have
you inherited his talent?'

'No. It's very frustrating. Often I see something that is so beautiful it
hurts, like an old farm building, or foxgloves growing in a hedge, blowing
in the wind against a blue sky. And I wish so much that I could capture
them, put them on paper, keep them for ever. And, of course, I can't.'

'It's not easy to live with one's own inadequacies.'

It occurred to her then that he did not look a man who knew what
the word 'inadequate' meant. 'Do you paint?'

'No. Why do you ask?'

'Talking to Papa, you sounded so knowledgeable.'

'If I did, it was because I was brought up by an immensely artistic and
creative mother. As soon as I could walk, I was marched around every
gallery and museum in London, *and* made to go to concerts.'

'It sounds as though you might have been put off culture for life.'

'No. She did it quite tactfully and made it all immensely interesting.
Made it fun.'

'And your father?'

'My father was a stockbroker, in the City.'

She thought about this. Other people's lives were always fascinating.
'Where did you live?'

'Cadogan Gardens. But after he died, my mother sold the house because
it was too big, and moved into a smaller one in Pembroke Square. She's
there now. She stayed there all through the bombing. She said she'd
rather be dead than live anywhere but London.'

Penelope thought of Dolly Keeling, snug in her little bolt-hole at the
Coombe Hotel, playing bridge with Lady Bloody Beamish and writing
long loving letters to Ambrose. She sighed, because thinking about Dolly
always made her feel a bit depressed. There was always this guilty feeling
that Dolly should be asked to stay at Carn Cottage for a few days, if only
to see her granddaughter. Or that Penelope should suggest visiting the

Coombe Hotel, taking Nancy with her. But both prospects were so appalling that she never found it too difficult to put them hastily out of her mind, and start thinking about something else instead.

The narrow road leaned uphill. They had left the sea behind them and now walked up between rows of whitewashed, terraced fishermen's cottages. A door opened and a cat emerged, followed by a woman with a basket of washing, which she proceeded to peg out on a line slung across the face of her house. As she did this, the sun came out again, quite strongly now, and she turned a smiling face upon them.

'That's a bit better, isn't it? Never seen such rain as we had this morning. Be lovely before long.'

The cat wound itself around Penelope's ankles. She stooped to stroke it. They went on. She took her hands out of her pockets and unbuttoned her oilskin. She said, 'Did you join the Royal Marines because you didn't want to be a stockbroker, or because of the war?'

'Because of the war. I'm known as an Hostilities Only Officer. I always think it sounds a bit derogatory. But neither did I want to be a stockbroker. I went to University and read Classics and English Literature, and then I got a job teaching little boys in a prep school.'

'Did the Royal Marines teach you how to climb?'

He smiled. 'No. I was climbing long before that. I was sent to a boarding school in Lancashire, and there was a Master there who used to take a gang of us climbing in the Lake District. I got completely bitten at fourteen years old, and I just went on doing it.'

'Have you climbed abroad?'

'Yes. Switzerland. Austria. I wanted to go to Nepal, but it would have meant months of preparation and travelling and I never could spare the time.'

'After the Matterhorn, the Boscarben Cliffs must look easy.'

'No,' he assured her drily, 'no, they are not easy.'

They continued on their way, ascending, taking the hidden, twisting lanes that the visitors never found, and mounting flights of granite steps so steep that Penelope was left with no breath for conversation. The last flight zigzagged up the face of the cliff between the railway station and the main road, finally to emerge directly opposite the old White Caps Hotel.

Warm with exertion, Penelope rested, leaning against the wall, waiting to catch her breath and for her heart to stop pounding. Major Lomax, coming behind her, appeared to be unaffected. She saw the Marine on guard eyeing them dispassionately across the road, but his expression gave nothing away.

When she could speak, she said, 'I feel like a bit of chewed string.'

'Small wonder.'

'I haven't come that way for years. When I was small, I used to run up all the way from the beach. It was a sort of self-imposed endurance test.'

She turned, leaning her arms on the top of the wall, and looked down the way they had come. The sea, ebbing, was calmer now, reflecting the blue of the clearing sky. Far below, on the beach, a man walked his dog. The wind had dropped to a fresh breeze, scented by the damp mossy smell of gardens soaked by rain. It was a smell loaded with nostalgia, and for once Penelope found herself caught off-guard, and was suffused with a mindless ecstasy that she had not known since she was a child.

She thought of the last couple of years, the boredom, the narrowness of existence, the dearth of anything to look forward to. Yet now, in a single instant, the curtains had been whipped aside, and the windows beyond thrown open onto a brilliant view that had been there, waiting for her, all the time. A view, moreover, laden with the most marvellous possibilities and opportunities.

Happiness – remembered from the days before the war, before Ambrose, before Sophie's shocking death. It was like being young again. But I am young. I am only twenty-three. She turned from the wall to face the man who stood beside her and was filled with gratitude, because in some way it was he who had wrought this miracle of déja`vu.

She found him watching her, and wondered how much he perceived, how much he knew. But his stillness, his silence gave nothing away.

She said, 'I must go home. Papa will be wondering what's happened to me.'

He nodded, accepting this. They would say goodbye, part. She would go on her way. He would cross the road, return the salute of the man on guard duty, run up the steps, disappear through the glassed door and perhaps never be seen again.

She said, 'Would you like to come to supper?'

He did not instantly reply to this suggestion, and for a dreadful moment she thought he was going to refuse. Then he smiled. 'That's very kind.'

Relief. 'This evening?'

'You're sure?'

'Perfectly. Papa would so like to see you again. You can continue your conversation.'

'Thank you. That would be delightful.'

'About seven thirty, then.' She sounded horribly formal. 'I'm . . . I'm able to ask you because for once we've got something to eat.'

'Let me guess. Mackerel and tinned peaches?'

Formality, restraint melted. They dissolved into laughter, and she knew that she would never forget the sound of it, because it was their first shared joke.

She found Doris agog with curiosity. 'Here, what's going on? There was I, minding my own business, and this smashing Sergeant turns up at the door with your baskets. Asked him in for a cup of tea, but he said he couldn't stay. How did you pick him up?'

Penelope sat at the kitchen table and told the whole story of the unexpected encounter. Doris listened with eyes growing round as marbles. When Penelope finished, she let out a screech of coy delight. 'Ask me, and it looks like you've got an admirer . . .'

'Oh, Doris, I've asked him for supper.'

'When?'

'This evening.'

'Is he coming?'

'Yes, he is.'

Doris' face fell. 'Oh, hell.' She sat back in her chair, the very picture of despondency.

'Why hell?'

'I won't be here. Going out. Taking Clark and Ronald over to Penzance to see the Operatic Society do *The Mikado*.'

'Oh, Doris. I was counting on you being here. I need someone to help me. Can't you put it off?'

'No, I can't. There's a bus organised, and anyway it's only on for two nights. And the boys have been looking forward to it for weeks, poor little blighters.' Her expression became resigned. 'Never mind, can't be helped. I'll give you a hand with the cooking before I go, and get Nancy to bed. But I'm not half vexed that I'm missing all the fun. Hasn't been a proper man in the house for years.'

Penelope did not mention Ambrose. Instead she said, 'What about Ernie? He's a proper man.'

'Yes. He's all right.' But poor Ernie was dismissed. 'He doesn't count, though.'

Like a couple of young girls kindled with innocent excitement, they set to work; they peeled vegetables, made a salad, buffed up the old dining-room table, gave little-used silver a cursory clean, polished the crystal wine-glasses. Lawrence, alerted, heaved himself out of his chair and made his way cautiously down to the cellar where, in happier days, he had stored his considerable stock of French wine. Now there was little remaining, but he returned bearing a bottle of what he termed Algerian plonk and also a dusty bottle of port, which he proceeded, with the utmost care, to decant. Penelope knew that no greater tribute could be paid to a guest.

At twenty-five past seven, with Nancy asleep in her bed, Doris and the boys departed, and all as ready as it would ever be, she fled upstairs to her room to do something about her own appearance. She changed into a clean shirt, pushed her bare feet into a pair of scarlet court shoes, brushed her hair, plaited it, wound it up into a coil, pinned it in place. She had no powder, no lipstick, and had used the last of her scent. A long and critical gaze in the mirror afforded small satisfaction. She looked like a governess. She found a string of scarlet beads and fastened them around her neck and, as she did this, heard the gate at the bottom of the garden open and click shut. She went to the window and saw Richard Lomax making his way up the fragrant garden, up the stepped path towards the house. She saw that he, too, had changed, from battledress to the semi-formality of khaki drill and a chestnut shining Sam Browne. He carried, discreetly, a wrapped parcel that could only contain a bottle.

Since saying goodbye, she had been a-brim with the anticipation of seeing him again. But now, watching his approach, knowing that he would in an instant be ringing the front-door bell, she was assailed by panic. Cold feet, Sophie had always called this dropping of the heart, caused by an impetuous action suddenly regretted. Supposing the evening wasn't all right, but turned out to be all wrong, and with no Doris to help her jolly it along? It was perfectly possible that she had been mistaken about Richard Lomax. That the flash of ecstasy, the unexplained happiness, the extraordinary sensation of closeness and familiarity could simply have been part of an illusion, springing from her own rising spirits and the fact that the sun, after days of rain, had decided to shine.

She moved from the window, took a last glance at her reflection, settled the red necklace, and went out of the room and down the stairs. As she did this, the doorbell rang. She crossed the hall and opened the door, and he smiled and said, 'I hope I'm not too late, or too early.'

'Neither. You found the way?'

'It wasn't difficult. What a beautiful garden.'

'The storm hasn't done it any good.' She stepped back. 'Come in.'

He did so, removing his green beret with its scarlet flash and silver badge. She closed the door. He laid his beret on the chest and turned to face her. He held up the wrapped parcel and said, 'This is for your father.'

'How kind.'

'Does he drink Scotch?'

'Yes . . .'

It was going to be all right and she hadn't been wrong about him. He wasn't ordinary. He was immensely special because he had brought with him, into Carn Cottage, not only a certain glamour but ease as well. She remembered the spiky misery of having Ambrose there. The tensions and the silences and the way everybody, affected by the prickly atmosphere, became irritable and crotchety. But with this tall stranger came only the most comfortable of presences. He might have been an old friend of many years, calling to renew acquaintance, to catch up on mutual news. The sense of déjà vu returned, more strongly than ever. So strong was it, that she half expected the sitting-room door to be flung open and Sophie to emerge, laughing and talking nineteen to the dozen, and throwing her arms around the young man's neck, and kissing him on both cheeks. *Oh, my darling, I have so been looking forward to seeing you again.*

' . . . but we haven't had a bottle in the house for months. He'll be delighted. He's in the sitting room, waiting for you . . .' She went to open the door. 'Papa. Our guest has come . . . and he's brought you a present . . .'


'This posting of yours,' said Lawrence. 'How long is it for?'

'I've no idea, sir.'

'And you wouldn't tell me even if you knew. Do you suppose next year we'll be ready to invade Europe?'

Richard Lomax smiled, but was giving nothing away. 'I should hope so.'

'These Americans . . . They seem to be keeping themselves very much to themselves. We'd imagined every sort of high jinks.'

'They haven't exactly come here for a holiday. Also, they're highly professional soldiers and a totally self-contained unit. They have their own officers, their own canteen, their own recreations.'

'How do you get on with them?'

'Very well, on the whole. They're fairly wild . . . perhaps not as disciplined as our own troops but, individually, very courageous.'

'And you're in overall charge of the whole operation?'

'No. Colonel Mellaby is the Officer Commanding. I'm simply the Training Officer.'

'Like working with them?'

Richard Lomax shrugged. 'It's certainly different.'

'And Porthkerris. Had you ever been here before?'

'No. Never. My holidays were usually spent in the North, climbing mountains. But I'd always known about Porthkerris, because of the artists who'd come here. I'd seen paintings of the harbour, in the various galleries my mother insisted I visit, and it's extraordinary how unique, how instantly recognisable it was. Unchanged. And the light. The glaring light off the sea. I could scarcely believe it, until I experienced it for myself.'

'Yes. It has a magic. You never get used to it, however long you live here.'

'You've been in Porthkerris for some years now?'

'Since the early 1920s. I brought my wife here just after we were married. We had no house, so we camped out in my studio. Like a couple of gypsies.'

'Is that your wife's portrait in the sitting room?'

'Yes. That was Sophie. She must have been about nineteen when that was painted. Charles Rainier did it. We all took a house near Varengeville one spring. It was meant to be a holiday, but he became restless if he wasn't working, so Sophie agreed to sit for him. It took less than a day, but it was one of the best things he'd ever done. But, of course, he had known her all her life, as I had. Known her since she was a child. You can work fast when you are so close to your model.'

The dining room was shadowy in the dying light. Only the candles provided illumination and the last shafts of the sinking sun, piercing through the windows in beams that struck back a reflected lustre from crystal and silver and the polished surface of the circular mahogany table. The dark wallpaper contained the room like the lining of a jewel box, and beyond the swags of heavy, faded velvet, caught back with frayed silken ropes and tassels, airy lace curtains stirred in the draught from the open casement.

It was growing late. Soon the window would have to be closed, the black-out curtains drawn. Their meal was over. The soup, the grilled fish, the delicious treat of peaches had been consumed and the plates cleared away. From the sideboard, Penelope had fetched a dish of Cox's orange pippins, windfalls from the tree at the top of the orchard, and set it in the middle of the table. Richard Lomax had taken one, was peeling it with a pearl-handled fruit knife. His hands were long, with square-tipped fingers. She watched them dealing so neatly with the knife, the unbroken coil of peel dropping onto the plate. He sliced the apple into four neat quarters.

'Do you still have the studio?'

'Yes, but it's deserted now. I seldom go there. I cannot work and the walk is too far for me.'

'I'd like to see it.'

'Any time. I have the key.' Across the table, he smiled at his daughter. 'Penelope will take you.'

Richard Lomax sliced the apple quarters again.

'Charles Rainier . . . is he still alive?'

'As far as I know. Provided he hasn't opened his mouth too wide and been murdered by the Gestapo. Hopefully not. His home is in the south of France. If he behaves himself, he should survive . . .'

She thought of the Rainiers' house, the roof smothered in bougainvillaea, the red rocks dropping down to the gentian sea, the feathery yellow mimosa. She thought of Sophie, calling down from the terrace to say that it was time to stop swimming because lunch was ready. In the face of such dazzling images, it was hard to realise that Sophie was dead. This evening – ever since Richard Lomax's arrival – she had been with them; not dead, but alive; even now, sitting in the empty chair at the head of the table. It was not easy to find good reason for this persistent illusion; that everything was as it had been. That nothing had changed. Whereas, in truth, everything had changed. Fate had been cruel; flung the war at them, torn their family life apart; seen Sophie and the Cliffords killed in the Blitz. Fate, perhaps, had thrown Penelope at Ambrose. But it was she who had let him make love to her, started Nancy, and finally married him. Looking back, she did not regret the making love, which she had enjoyed just as much as he had; even less did she regret the arrival of Nancy, and indeed now, could not imagine life without her deliciously pretty and engaging child. What she did regret, most bitterly, was that idiotic marriage. *You mustn't marry him unless you love him*, Sophie had said, but for once in her life Penelope had not heeded Sophie's advice. Ambrose was her first relationship, and she had no one to compare him with. Her parents' blissful marriage did not help. She imagined that all marriages were just as blissful, so getting married was a good idea. Faced with the situation, Ambrose, when he had got over his initial dismay, seemed to think it was a good idea too. So they had gone ahead and done it.

A dreadful, ghastly mistake. She didn't love him. Had never loved him. She had nothing in common with him, and not the least wish ever to see him again. She looked across at Richard Lomax, his quiet face turned towards Lawrence. Her eyes dropped to his hands, now clasped on the table before him. She thought of taking his hands in hers, and lifting them and pressing them to her cheek.

She wondered if he was married too.

'I never met the man,' Lawrence was saying, 'but it seemed to me that he must have been a very dull fellow.' They were still on the subject of portrait painters. 'One might have expected unimagined misdemeanours and indiscretions . . . he certainly had ample opportunity . . . but as it was, it doesn't appear that he ever put a foot wrong. Beerbohm did a cartoon of him, you know, gazing from his window at a long queue of society ladies all waiting to have themselves immortalised by him.'

Richard Lomax said, 'I liked his sketches better than his portraits.'

'I agree. All those elongated ladies and gentlemen in hunting gear. Ten feet tall and impossibly arrogant.' He reached for the port decanter, filled his glass, and handed the decanter on to his guest. 'Tell me, do you play backgammon?'

'Yes, I do.'

'Fancy a game?'

'I'd be delighted.'

It was nearly dark. Penelope got up from the table and closed the windows and pulled all the curtains, the horrible black ones and the lovely velvet ones. Saying something about coffee, she went out of the room and down the passage to the kitchen. She did the kitchen black-out and then turned on the light, to the expected disorder of saucepans, dirty plates and cutlery. She put the kettle on. She heard the men move through to the sitting room, heard coal being shovelled onto the fire, all to the continuous and companionable murmur of conversation.

Papa was in his element, having the time of his life. If he enjoyed the backgammon, it was likely that he would invite Richard Lomax back for another session. Finding a clean tray, taking coffee cups from the cupboard, she smiled.

The game finished just as the clock struck eleven. Lawrence had won. Richard Lomax, conceding defeat with a smile, got to his feet. 'I think it's time I went.'

'I'd no idea it was as late as that. I've enjoyed myself. We must do it again.' Lawrence thought about this, and added, 'If you'd like to.'

'Very much, sir. I'm afraid I can't make any specific plans, because my time isn't my own . . .'

'That's all right. Any evening. Just drop in. We're always here.' He began to struggle out of his chair, but Richard Lomax stopped him with a hand on his shoulder. 'Don't get up . . .'

'Well . . .' Gratefully the old man sank back against the cushions. 'Maybe I won't. Penelope will see you out.'

While they played, she had sat knitting by the fire. Now she drove her needles into the ball of wool and stood up. He turned to smile at her. She went to open the door, heard him say, 'Good night, sir, and thank you again . . .'

'Not at all.'

She led the way through the dark hall and opened the front door. Outside, the garden was drowned in a blue light, heavy with the scent of stock. An eyelash of a moon hung in the sky. Far below, on the beach, the sea whispered. He emerged to stand beside her on the doorstep, his beret in his hand. They both gazed upwards, at threads of cloud and the faint gleam of the moon. There was no wind, but a damp chill emanated from the lawn, and Penelope, hugging herself, shivered.

He said, 'I've hardly talked to you all evening. I hope you don't think I was being very ill-mannered.'

'You came to talk to Papa.'

'Not entirely, but I'm afraid that's how it worked out.'

'There'll be another time.'

'I hope so. Like I said, my time is scarcely my own . . . I can't make plans or dates . . .'

'I know.'

'But I'll come when I can.'

'Do that.'

He pulled on his beret, settled it on his head. The moonlight flashed on the silver badge. 'It was a delicious dinner. Mackerel has never tasted so good.' She laughed. 'Good night, Penelope.'

'Good night, Richard.'

He turned and walked away, swallowed into the bloomy dusk of the garden, and was gone. She waited to hear the gate click shut behind him. Standing there in her thin shirt, she found her arms rough with goose bumps. She shivered again and went back into the house, closing the door behind her.


Two weeks passed before they saw him again. For some extraordinary reason this did not fret Penelope. He had said that he would come when he could, and she knew that he would. She could wait. She thought about him a great deal. During the busy days, he was never completely out of her mind, and at night he invaded her dreams, causing her to wake with drowsy contentment, smiling, clinging to the memory of the dream before it should fade and die.

Lawrence was more concerned than she. 'Haven't heard from that nice chap Lomax,' he would grumble from time to time. 'I was looking forward to another session of backgammon.'

'Oh, he'll come, Papa,' she reassured him, tranquil because she knew it was true.

Now it was September. Indian Summer. Chilly evenings and nights, and days of cloudless skies and glowing, golden sun. Leaves were starting to change colour, to drop, drifting in the still air, onto the grass of the lawn. The border in front of the house was bright with dahlias, and the last roses of the summer opened their velvety faces and filled the air with a fragrance which, because it was so precious, seemed twice as strong as the scents of June.

A Saturday. Over lunch, Clark and Ronald announced that they were going down to the beach, to meet a gang of their school friends and swim. Doris, Penelope, and Nancy were not invited to join them. Accordingly, they took themselves off, scampering down the garden path as though there was not a moment to be lost, laden with towels and spades, a packet of jam sandwiches, and a bottle of lemonade.

With the boys out of the way, the warm afternoon fell silent and empty. Lawrence retired to the sitting room for a little snooze by the open window. Doris took Nancy out into the garden. Penelope, with the dishes done and the kitchen straight, walked up to the paddock and unpegged the day's massive wash. Back in the kitchen, she folded the piles of sweet-scented linen, sheets, and towels; set shirts and pillow-cases aside for ironing. Later. That could be done later. The outdoors beckoned. She went out of the kitchen and across the hall, where only the grandfather clock ticked, and a drowsy bee buzzed at a window-pane. The front door stood open, golden light streaming across the worn carpet. Across the lawn, Doris sat in an old garden chair with a basket of mending on her lap, and Nancy played contentedly in her sand-pit. The sand-pit had been built by Ernie and the sand brought up from the beach in Mr Penberth's vegetable cart. In fine weather, it kept Nancy endlessly amused. She sat there now, wearing a pair of patched overalls and nothing else, and built sand-pies with an old tin bucket and a wooden spoon. Penelope joined them. Doris had spread an old blanket on the ground and she lay on this and watched Nancy, amused by the concentration on the child's face, entranced by the sweep of dark lashes on rounded cheek, the dimpled hands patting the sand.

'You haven't been ironing, have you?' Doris asked.

'No. Too hot.'

Doris held up a shrunken shirt, its ragged collar split like a grin. 'Suppose there's any point in mending this?'

'No. Turn it into a polishing rag.'

'We've got more polishing rags in this house than clothes. You know, when this bleeding war ends, the best thing for me is going to be able to go out and buy clothes. New clothes. Dozens of them. I'm sick and tired of making do. Look at this jersey of Clark's. I mended it last week and there's another great hole in the elbow. How the hell do they do it?'

'They're growing lads.' Idle, Penelope rolled onto her back, unbuttoning her shirt, pulling her skirt above her bare knees. 'They can't help bursting out of their clothes.' She closed her eyes against the glare of the sun. 'Remember how skinny and pale they were when you first came here? You'd scarcely recognise them now, so brawny and brown, and Cornish as they could be.'

'I'm glad they're not older.' Doris broke off a length of darning wool and threaded her needle. 'Wouldn't want them to be soldiers. Couldn't bear to . . .'

She stopped. Penelope waited. 'What couldn't you bear?' she prompted.

Doris' reply came in an agitated whisper. 'We've got a visitor.'

The sun blanked out. A shadow lay across her supine body. She opened her eyes and saw, standing at her feet, the dark outline of a man's form. In some panic, she sat up, rearranging her sprawled legs, reaching to re-button her shirt . . .

'I'm sorry,' said Richard. 'I didn't mean to startle you.'

'Where did you spring from?' She scrambled to her feet, dealt with the final button, and pushed her hair out of her face.

'I came in by the top gate, across the garden.'

Her heart was racing. She hoped she was not blushing. 'I never heard you.'

'Is this a bad time to call?'

'Not a bit. We're not doing anything.'

'I've been stuck in an office all day, and suddenly I could bear it no longer. I thought, with a bit of luck, I'd find you here.' His eyes moved from Penelope to Doris, who sat in her chair as though mesmerised, the mending basket still in her lap, the threaded needle held aloft, like some sort of symbol. 'I don't think we've ever met. I'm Richard Lomax. You must be Doris.'

'That's right.' They shook hands. Doris, mildly flustered, added, 'Pleased to meet you. I'm sure.'

'Penelope told me about you, and your two sons. Are they not around?'

'No, they've gone swimming with their chums.'

'Sensible fellows. You were out the other night when I came for dinner.'

'Yes. I took the boys to *The Mikado*.'

'Did they enjoy it?'

'Oh, loved it. Ever such good tunes. And funny too. They didn't half laugh.'

'I'm glad.' He turned his attention to Nancy, who sat staring up at him, nonplussed by the arrival of this tall stranger into her life. 'Is this your little girl?'

Penelope nodded. 'Yes. This is Nancy.'

He squatted to her height. 'Hello.' Nancy stared. 'How old is she?'

'Nearly three.'

There was sand on Nancy's face and the seat of her overalls was damp. 'What are you doing?' Richard asked her. 'Making sand-pies? Here, let me have a go.' He took up the little bucket and removed the wooden spoon from Nancy's unresisting hand. He filled the bucket, pressed down the sand, and turned it out into a perfect sand-pie. Nancy instantly demolished it. He laughed and gave her back her toys. 'She has all the right instincts,' he remarked, and settled himself on the grass, removing his beret and unbuttoning the tight collar of his khaki battle-dress.

Penelope said, 'You look hot.'

'I am. It's too warm to be dressed like this.' He undid the rest of the buttons and removed the offending garment, rolling up the sleeves of his cotton shirt and at once becoming quite human-looking and comfortable. Perhaps encouraged by this, Nancy clambered out of the sand-pit and came to sit on Penelope's knee, where she had a good view of the new arrival and could stare, unblinking, at his face.

'I never can guess how old other people's children are,' he said.

'Do you have children of your own?' Doris asked innocently.

'Not that I know of.'

'Come again?'

'I'm not married.'

Penelope bent her head, laid her cheek against the silky fronds of Nancy's hair. Richard leaned back on his elbows, turned his face up to the sun. 'It's as hot as midsummer, isn't it? Where else should one be but sitting in a garden? Where's your father?'

'Having a sleep. He's probably awake by now. In a moment, I'll go and tell him you're here. He's longing to see you and have another game of backgammon.'

Doris looked at her watch, stowed her needle, and set down the mending basket on the grass. She said, 'It's nearly four o'clock. Why don't I go and make us all a cup of tea? You'd like one, wouldn't you, Richard?'

'I can't think of anything I'd like more.'

'I'll tell your father, Penelope. He likes having tea in the garden.'

She left them. They watched her go. Richard said, 'What a nice girl . . .'

'Yes.'

Penelope began to pick daisies, to fashion them into a chain for Nancy. 'What have you been doing all this time?'

'Scrambling on the cliffs. Bouncing around in the surf in those God-forsaken landing craft. Getting wet. Drafting orders, planning exercises, and writing long reports.'

They fell silent. She added another daisy to the chain. After a bit, he said abruptly, 'Do you know General Watson-Grant?'

'Yes, of course. Why do you ask that?'

'Colonel Mellaby and I have been asked to have a drink with him on Monday.'

She smiled. 'So have Papa and I. Mrs Watson-Grant rang up this morning to invite us. Mr Ridley, the grocer, came up with a couple of bottles of gin and they decided it was a good excuse to throw a little party.'

'Where do they live?'

'About a mile away; up the hill, out of the town.'

'How will you get there?'

'The General's going to send his car for us. His old gardener can drive. He gets petrol, you see, because of being in the Home Guard. I'm sure it's all dreadfully illegal, but it's very kind of him, because otherwise we couldn't go.'

'I hoped you'd be there.'

'Why?'

'So that I'll know somebody. And because I thought, afterwards, I could take you out for dinner.'

The daisy chain had grown quite long. She held it out like a garland between her hands. She said, 'Are you inviting Papa and me, or just me?'

'Just you. But if your father wants to come . . .'

'He won't. He doesn't like being out late.'

'Will you?'

'Yes.'

'Where shall we go?'

'I don't know.'

'There's the Sands Hotel . . .'

'That's been requisitioned since the beginning of the war. Now, it's full of convalescent wounded.'

'Or the Castle?'

The Castle. Her spirits sank at the very thought of the place. During Ambrose's first unfortunate visit to Carn Cottage, Penelope, in desperation, and casting about for some way to amuse her husband, suggested that they go to the Castle for the Saturday night dinner-dance. The evening had been no more successful than the rest of the weekend. The chill and formal dining-room had been half empty, the food dull, and the other residents aged. From time to time a dispirited band had played a selection of out-of-date tunes, but they couldn't even dance, because Penelope by then was so enormous that Ambrose could not get his arms around her.

She said quickly, 'No, don't let's go there. There are old waiters like tortoises, and most of the people staying are in wheelchairs. It's dreadfully depressing.' She considered the question, and came up with a far more cheerful suggestion. 'We could go to Gaston's Bistro.'

'Where's that?'

'Just above the North Beach. It's tiny, but the food's not bad. Sometimes, on birthdays and things, Papa takes me and Doris there.'

'Gaston's Bistro. It sounds highly unexpected. Are they on the phone?'
'Yes.'

'I'll ring and book a table.'


'Doris, he's asked me out for dinner.'

'Get away! When?'

'On Monday. After the Watson-Grants' party.'

'Did you say you'd go?'

'Yes. Why? Do you think I should have refused?'

'Refused? You'd have needed your head examined. I think he's lovely. I dunno, reminds me of Gregory Peck in a funny way.'

'Oh, Doris, he's not a bit like Gregory Peck.'

'Not to look at, but he's got that quiet way. You know what I mean. What are you going to wear?'

'I haven't thought. I'll find something.'

Doris became exasperated. 'You know, you drive me nuts sometimes. Go and get something new. You never spend a brass farthing on yourself. Go down the town to Madame Jolie and see what she's got.'

'I haven't got any clothing coupons. I spent my last on horrible tea-towels and a warm dressing-gown for Nancy.'

'For goodness' sake, you only need seven. Surely between the six of us we can rustle up seven clothing coupons. And if we can't, I know where I can buy Black Market ones.'

'That's against the law.'

'Oh, to hell with the law. This is an occasion. Your first date for years. Live dangerously. On Monday morning, go down the town and buy yourself something pretty.'


She could not remember when she had last been inside a dress shop, but as Madame Jolie was really Mrs Coles, the Coastguard's wife, and fat and homely as anybody's grandmother, there was no reason to feel intimidated.

'My dear life, I haven't seen you in here for years,' she remarked as Penelope came through the door.

'I want a new dress,' Penelope told her, wasting no time.

'I haven't anything very special in stock, dear, most of it's that Utility stuff. Can't get anything else. But there is one pretty red that would fit you. Red was always your colour. Patterned in daisies this one is. It's rayon, of course, but it's got a nice silky feel.'

She fetched it. Penelope, closeted into a minute curtained cubicle, pulled off her clothes and slipped the red dress over her head. It felt soft, and smelt excitingly new. Emerging from behind the modest curtain, she did up the buttons and buckled the red patent belt.

'Oh, it's perfect,' said Madame Jolie.

She went to the long mirror and gazed at her reflection, trying to see herself with Richard's eyes. The dress had a square neck and padded shoulders, and a skirt of flaring pleats. The wide belt made her waist appear tiny, and when she turned to inspect the back view, the skirt fanned out as she moved, and the effect was so feminine, so becoming, that she found herself filled with delight at her own appearance. No garment had ever given her such confidence. It was a bit like falling in love, and she knew that she had to possess it.

'How much is it?'

Madame Jolie groped down the back of her neck for the price ticket. 'Seven pounds ten shillings. And seven coupons, I'm afraid.'

'I'll have it.'

'You've made the right decision. Fancy that, the first dress you tried on. Thought of it the moment you walked in. Might have been made for you. What a stroke of luck.'


'Papa, do you like my new dress?' She took it out of the paper bag, shook it out of its folds, held it in front of her. In his chair, he took off his spectacles and leaned back on the cushions with half-closed eyes, the better to get the effect.

'That's a good colour for you . . . yes, I like that. But why have you suddenly bought yourself a new dress?'

'Because we're going for a drink with the Watson-Grants this evening. Had you forgotten?'

'No, but I've forgotten how we're getting there.'

'The General's sending his car for us.'

'How kind.'

'And someone will bring you back. Because I'm going out for dinner.'

He put his spectacles on again and, for a long moment, surveyed his daughter over the top of them. Then he said, 'With Richard Lomax,' and it wasn't a question.

'Yes.'

He reached for his newspaper. 'Good.'

'Papa, listen. You think I should go?'

'Why shouldn't you?'

'I'm a married lady.'

'But not a bourgeois nitwit.'

She hesitated. 'Suppose I get involved?'

'Is that likely?'

'It might be.'

'So. Get involved.'

'You know something, Papa? I really like you.'

'I am gratified. Why?'

'A thousand reasons. But mostly because we've always been able to talk.'

'It would be a disaster if we couldn't. As for Richard Lomax, you are no longer a child. I don't wish to see you hurt, but your mind is your own. You make your own decisions.'

'I know,' she said. She did not say 'I have.'


They were the last to arrive at the Watson-Grants' party. This was because, by the time John Tonkins, the General's old gardener, called to collect them, Penelope was still at her dressing-table, agonising as to how to do her hair. She had finally decided to wear it up and then, at the last moment and in some exasperation, torn out all the pins and shaken it loose. After that, she had to find some sort of coat, for warmth, for the new dress was flimsy and the September evening chill. She had no coat, only her tartan poncho, and that looked so terrible that more moments had to be wasted searching for an old cashmere shawl of Sophie's. Clutching this, running downstairs in search of her father, she found him in the kitchen, having decided on the spur of the moment that he had to clean his shoes.

'Papa. The car's there. John's waiting.'

'I can't help that. These are my good shoes and they haven't been cleaned for four months.'

'How do you know it's four months?'

'Because that was the last occasion we went to the Watson-Grants'.'

'Oh, Papa.' His crippled hands struggled with the tin of boot polish. 'Here. I'll do them.'

She accomplished this as swiftly as she could, wielding brushes and getting brown polish all over her hands. She washed her hands while he was putting on his shoes, and then knelt to tie the laces for him. At last, at Lawrence's pace, they made their way out of the house and across the garden to the top gate, where John Tonkins and the old Rover awaited them.

'I'm sorry we've kept you, John.'

'Doesn't matter to me, Mr Stern.' He held the door open and Lawrence painfully inserted himself into the front seat. Penelope got into the back. John took his place at the wheel and they were off. But not very fast, for John Tonkins was wary of his employer's car and drove as though it were a time bomb that might explode if he went faster than thirty miles an hour. Finally, at seven o'clock, they trundled up the drive of the General's enviable garden, which burgeoned with rhododendrons, azaleas, camellias, and fuchsias, and drew to a crunching halt at the front door of the house. Three or four other cars were already parked on the gravel. Penelope recognised the Trubshots' old Morris, but not the khaki staff car with its Royal Marine insignia. A young Marine driver sat behind the wheel, whiling away the time by reading *Picture Post*. Getting out of the Rover, she found herself secretly smiling.

They went indoors. Before the war, a uniformed parlour maid would have been waiting to let them in, but now, there was nobody. The hall was empty and a buzz of conversation led them across the sitting room to where, in the General's conservatory, the party was already in full swing.

It was a very large and elaborate conservatory, built by the Watson-Grants when the General had finally retired from the Army and they left India for good, and which they had furnished with potted palms, long rattan chairs, camel stools, tiger-skin rugs, and a brass gong slung between the ivory tusks of some long-defunct elephant.

'Oh, there you are at last!' Mrs Watson-Grant had spied them and came to greet them. She was a small, spare woman with shingled hair, tanned to leather by the cruel suns of India, a chain-smoker and an inveterate bridge player. In Quetta, if rumours were to be believed, she had spent most of her life on the back of a horse, and had once stood her ground in the face of a charging tiger and coolly shot it dead. Now, she was reduced to running the local Red Cross and Digging for Victory in her vegetable garden, but she missed the social whirl of the old days, and it was typical that, having laid her hands on a couple of bottles of gin, she instantly threw a party. 'Late as usual,' she added, for she had never been one for calling a spade anything but a spade. 'What'll you drink? Gin and orange, or gin and lime? And, of course, you know everybody. Except perhaps Colonel Mellaby and Major Lomax . . .'

Penelope looked about her. Saw the Springburns from St Enedoc and Mrs Trubshot, tall and wraith-like, veiled in lilac chiffon and wearing an enormous hat with a velvet bow and a buckle. With Mrs Trubshot was Miss Pawson, standing there four-square in a pair of lace-up shoes with rubber soles thick as tank-treads. She saw Colonel Trubshot, who had button-holed the unknown Colonel Mellaby and was holding forth as usual, doubtless airing his opinions on the conduct of the war. The Royal Marine Colonel was a great deal taller than Colonel Trubshot, a handsome man with a bristling moustache and thinning hair, and he had to stoop slightly in order to hear what was being said. From the expression on his face of polite, attentive boredom, Penelope guessed that it was not fascinating. She saw Richard standing at the far side of the room, with his back to the garden. Miss Preedy was with him. Miss Preedy, wearing an embroidered Hungarian blouse and a folk-weave skirt and looking as though she were about to spring into a Gopak. He said something to her, and she burst into a gale of giggles, tucking her head demurely to one side, and he looked up, caught Penelope's eye, and sent her just the ghost of a wink.

'Penelope.' General Watson-Grant materialised at her elbow. 'You've got a drink? Thank God you're here. I was afraid you wouldn't come.'

'I know. We're late. We kept poor John Tonkins waiting.'

'No matter. I just felt a bit anxious for these Royal Marines. Poor chaps, invited to a party and then find themselves in a roomful of washed-up old odds and sods. I'd have asked more cheerful company for them, but I couldn't think of any. Only you.'

'I shouldn't worry. They look quite happy.'

'I'll introduce you.'

'We already know Major Lomax.'

'Do you? When did you meet him?'

'Papa got talking to him in the Gallery.'

'They seem nice fellers.' The General's eyes, hostly, strayed. 'I'm going to rescue Mellaby. He's had ten minutes of undiluted Trubshot, and that's enough for any man.'

He left her as abruptly as he had appeared, and, abandoned, Penelope went to talk to Miss Pawson and hear about her stirrup-pumps. The party progressed. For some time Richard neither sought her out nor claimed her, but this did not matter, for it simply extended the anticipation of finally finding herself at his side and being with him again. As though performing some ritual dance, they circled, never within earshot; smiling into other faces, listening to other conversations. Eventually, finding herself by the open door that led out into the garden, Penelope turned to set down her empty glass, but was diverted by the prospect of the General's garden. The sloping lawn streamed with golden light, clouds of midges danced in the dark shade of the trees. The still air was alive with the cooing of wood-pigeons and sweet with the scents of a warm September evening.

'Hello.' He had come to stand beside her.

'Hello.'

He took the empty glass out of her hand. 'Do you want another drink?'

She shook her head. 'No.'

He found space on a table bearing a potted palm and set the glass down. 'I spent half an hour feeling anxious because I thought perhaps you weren't going to arrive.'

'We're always late for everything.'

He glanced about him. 'I am entranced by this marvellous ambience. We could be in Poona.'

'I should have warned you.'

'Why should you? It's delightful.'

'I think a conservatory is the most enviable of rooms. One day, if I ever have a proper house of my own, I shall build one. Just as big and spacious and sunny as this.'

'And will you fill it with tiger skins and brass gongs?'

She smiled. 'Papa says all that's missing is the punkah wallah.'

'Or perhaps a horde of dervishes, erupting from the shrubbery, bent on death and destruction. Do you suppose our host shot the rug?'

'More likely Mrs Watson-Grant. The drawing room is set about with photographs of her in a pith helmet, with the spoils of the chase laid out at her feet.'

'Have you met Colonel Mellaby?'

'Not yet. He's been lionised. I couldn't get near him.'

'Come and I'll introduce you. And then, I think, he'll say it's time for us to leave. He'll take us as far as the HQ in the staff car, and then we'll have to walk. Do you mind?'

'Not at all.'

'And your father . . .?'

'John Tonkins will take him home.'

He put a hand beneath her elbow. 'Come, then . . .'

It happened as he said it would. Introduced to Penelope Colonel Mellaby made a little polite small talk, and then glanced at his watch and announced that it was time to depart. Farewells were said. Penelope confirmed that Lawrence would be taken home to Carn Cottage, and kissed him goodnight. The General saw the three of them to the door, and Penelope gathered up her shawl from the chair where she had left it. Outside, the Royal Marine driver, hastily stowing his *Picture Post*, sprang from the car and held open the door. The Colonel got into the front and Penelope and Richard took the back seats. In a stately fashion they drove away, but the Royal Marine driver was not nearly so timid as poor John Tonkins had been, so that in no time they had reached the old White Caps Hotel and were piling out again.

'You two are going out for dinner? Take the car and my driver if you want.'

'Thank you, sir, but we'll walk. It's a lovely evening.'

'Certainly is. Oh well, have a good time.' He gave them an avuncular nod, dismissed his driver, turned on his heel, and made his way up the steps to disappear through the door.

Richard said, 'Shall we go?'

It was indeed a beautiful evening, pearly and still; the calm sea translucent, gleaming like the inside of a shell. The sun had set, but the huge sky stayed streaked with the pink of its afterglow. They walked, dropping down into the town, by empty pavements and past shuttered shops.

There were few people about, but, mingling with these locals, strayed aimless groups of American Rangers, with a leave pass under their belts and no apparent way of diverting themselves. One or two had found girls, giggling sixteen-year-olds who hung on to their elbows. Others queued up outside the cinema, waiting for it to open, or trod the streets in their soft-soled boots, searching for likely pubs. When they spied Richard approaching, these groups were apt to melt mysteriously out of sight.

Penelope said, 'I'm sorry for them.'

'They're all right.'

'It would be nice if people could ask them to parties, too.'

'I don't think they'd have very much in common with General Watson-Grant's guests.'

'He was a bit embarrassed at having asked you to meet a washed-up lot of odds and sods.'

'Did he say that? He was quite wrong. I found them all fascinating.'

This seemed a bit of an overstatement. 'I like the Springburns. He farms over at St Enedoc. And I love the Watson-Grants.'

'How about Miss Pawson and Miss Preedy?'

'Oh, they're lesbians.'

'I suspected. And the Trubshots?'

'The Trubshots are a cross we all mutually bear. She's not so bad, but he's a pain in the neck; he's head of the ARP, and he's always running people in for showing chinks of light, and they have to go to court and be fined.'

'Not the best way, I admit, to win friends and influence people but I suppose he's just doing his job.'

'You're much nicer than Papa and I are about him. And the other thing we can never understand is why such a shrimp of a man married such a tall lady. He scarcely comes up to her waist.'

Richard thought about this. He said, 'My father had a small friend who did exactly the same thing. And when my father asked him why he hadn't chosen a female of his own size, he replied that if he had, they would always have been known as that funny little couple. Perhaps that's why Colonel Trubshot proposed to Mrs Trubshot.'

'Yes, perhaps it is. I never thought of that.'

She led him towards the North Beach by the shortest route, through back lanes and cobbled squares, up an enormously steep hill, and then down a twisting, stepped alley-way. Emerging from this, they stepped out onto the curved, cobbled road that skirted the north shore. A row of long, whitewashed cottages faced out over the bay, the flood tide, and the long breakers.

He said, 'I've seen this bay often enough from the sea, but I've never actually been here . . .'

'I like it better than the other beach. It's always empty and wild, and somehow much more beautiful. Now, we're nearly there. It's that little cottage with the sign hanging out and the window-boxes.'

'Who is Gaston?'

'A genuine Frenchman, from Brittany. He used to fish out of Newlyn, in a crabber. He married a Cornish girl, and then he lost his leg in a dreadful accident at sea. After that he couldn't go fishing any longer, so he and Grace, that's his wife, opened this place. They've been running it now for nearly five years.' She hoped he was not thinking it all looked a bit humble. 'Like I said, it's not very grand.'

He smiled, reaching out to open the door. 'I don't like grand places.'

Overhead, a bell tinkled. They went inside to a flagged passageway, and were at once assailed by the smell of mouth-watering food, spiced with garlic and herbs, and the sound of muted music. A jinky accordion. Paris, and nostalgia. An open archway led into the little dining room, beamed and whitewashed, the tables set with red gingham cloths and folded white napkins. There were candles and mugs of fresh flowers on each table, and in a mammoth fireplace, drift-wood sparked and flickered.

Two of the tables were already occupied. A white-faced young Flight Lieutenant and his girl-friend . . . or perhaps his wife . . . and an elderly couple who looked as though they might well have strayed to Gaston's as a change from the tedium of the Castle Hotel. However, the best table, the one in the window, stood empty.

As they hesitated, Grace, who had heard the bell ring, appeared, with something of a flourish, through the swing-door at the back of the room.

'Good evening. Major Lomax, is it? You booked a table. I've put you in the window. Thought you'd like the view, and . . .' Over his shoulder, she spied Penelope. Her freckled, sun-browned face, under its thatch of bleached hair, split into an astonished grin. 'Hello. What are you doing here? I didn't know you were coming.'

'No, I don't suppose you did. How are you, Grace?'

'Lovely. Hard-worked as ever, of course, but we don't talk about that. Brought your father, have you?'

'No, not this evening.'

'Oh well, nice to get out on your own for a change.' Her eyes strayed, with some interest, to Richard.

'You don't know Major Lomax.'

'It's nice to meet you. Now, where do you want to sit? Facing the view? You might as well make the most of it, because we'll have to draw the dratted black-out in a moment. Want something to drink, do you, and then I'll get the menu and you can order.'

'What can we have to drink?'

'Not much . . .' She wrinkled her nose. 'There's some sherry, but it's South African and tastes of raisins.' She leaned across Richard, making a play of rearranging his cutlery. 'Like some wine?' she breathed into his ear. 'We always keep a bottle or two for Mr Stern when he comes. I'm sure he wouldn't object if you was to have one.'

'But how splendid.'

'Don't make too much of a song and dance about it, though. There are others present. I'll get Gaston to decant it, and then they won't see the label.' She dropped a mammoth wink, produced a menu, and left them to it.

When she had gone, Richard sat back in his chair and looked amazed. 'What treatment. Does this always happen?'

'Usually. Gaston and Papa are tremendous friends. He doesn't ever come out of the kitchen, but when Papa's here and the other customers have all gone, he'll emerge with a bottle of brandy, and he and Papa'll sit into the small hours, putting the world to rights. And the music is Grace's idea. She says the room is so small, it stops people listening to other people's conversations. I know just what she means. In the dining room at the Castle, all you can hear is whispering and knives and forks scratching on plates. I'd rather have music. It makes it feel a bit like being in a film.'

'Does that appeal to you?'

'It creates an illusion.'

'Do you like the cinema?'

'Love it. Doris and I go twice a week, sometimes, in the winter-time.

Never miss a show. There's not much else to do in Porthkerris these days.'

'But it was different before the war?'

'Oh, of course, everything was different. And we were never here during the winter because we always spent it in London. We had a house in Oakley Street. We still do, but we don't go there.' She sighed. 'You know, one of the things I most hate about this war is being stuck in one place. It's difficult enough getting out of Porthkerris with only one bus a day and no petrol for the car. I suppose that's the price you pay for having been brought up to a nomad's existence. Papa and Sophie never stayed long in any one place. On any excuse, without any warning, we used to pack up and head for France or Italy. It made life marvellously exciting.'

'You were an only child?'

'Yes. And very spoiled.'

'I don't believe that.'

'It's true. I was always with grown-ups, and treated like an adult. My best friends were my parents' friends. But that doesn't sound so odd when you remember how young my mother was. More like a sister, really.'

'And beautiful.'

'You're thinking of her portrait. Yes, she was lovely. But more than that, she was warm and funny and loving. Hot-tempered one moment, and laughing the next. And she could make a home anywhere. She carried a sort of security about with her. I can't think of a single person who didn't love her. I still think about her every day of my life. Sometimes, she seems very dead. And other times, I can't believe that she isn't somewhere in the house and that a door won't open and she'll be there. We were dreadfully self-sufficient – selfish, I suppose. We never wanted, nor needed, other people. And yet, when I think about it, our houses constantly bulged with visitors, quite often stray acquaintances who simply didn't have anywhere else to go. But friends, too. And family. Aunt Ethel and the Cliffords used to come every summer.'

'Aunt Ethel?'

'Papa's sister. She's a great character, mad as a hatter. But she hasn't been to Carn Cottage for ages, partly because Doris and Nancy have taken over her room, and partly because she's left London and gone to live in wild Wales with some potty friends who breed goats and do hand weaving. You can laugh but it's true. She always had the oddest chums.'

'And the Cliffords?' he prompted, longing to hear more.

'That's not so funny. The Cliffords don't come because they're dead. They were killed by the same bomb that killed Sophie . . .'

'I'm sorry. I didn't realise.'

'Why should you? They were Papa's dearest friends. They shared

Oakley Street with us. When it happened, when he heard over the telephone, he changed. He became very old. Quite suddenly. In front of my eyes.'

'He's a fantastic man.'

'He is very strong.'

'Is he lonely?'

'Yes. But then most old people are.'

'He is fortunate to have you.'

'I could never leave him, Richard.'

They were interrupted by the arrival of Grace, bursting through the swing-doors with two carafes of white wine in her hands.

'There we are.' She set them on the table, with another meaningful wink carefully concealed from the eyes of the other diners. 'And now, I'm sorry but it's getting dark, and I'm going to have to do the black-out.' She dealt deftly with the layers of curtains, tucking them in at the sides so that no gleam of light should penetrate. 'Have you decided what you're going to eat?'

'We haven't even looked at the menu. What would you recommend?'

'I'd have the mussel soup and then the fish pie. The meat's rotten this week. Tough as old bones and nothing but gristle.'

'All right, we'll go for fish.'

'And nice fresh broccoli and green beans? Lovely. Won't be a moment.'

She took herself off, whisking empty plates from other tables as she went. Richard poured the wine. He raised his glass. 'Good health.'

'*Santé.*'

The wine was light and cool and fresh. It tasted of France, and other summers, other times. Penelope set down her glass. 'Papa would approve of that.'

'Now, tell me more.'

'What, about Aunt Ethel and her goats?'

'No, about you.'

'That's boring.'

'I don't find it so. Tell me about being in the Wrens.'

'That's the last thing I want to talk about.'

'Didn't you enjoy it?'

'I hated every moment.'

'Then why did you join?'

'Oh, a stupid impulse. We were in London and . . . something happened . . .'

He waited. 'What happened?'

She looked at him. She said, 'You'll think I'm a fool.'

'I doubt it.'

'It's a long story.'

'We have time.'

And so she took a deep breath and began to tell him; starting with Peter and Elizabeth Clifford, and carrying on to that evening when she and Sophie had gone up to their flat for coffee and met, for the first time, the Friedmanns. 'The Friedmanns were young. They were refugees from Munich. They were Jewish.' Across the table, Richard listened, his eyes upon her, his face quiet. She realised that she was saying things that she had never been able to bring herself to tell to Ambrose. 'And Willi Friedmann started to talk about what was happening to the Jews in Nazi Germany. What people like the Cliffords had been trying to tell the world for years, but nobody wanted to listen. And for me, it made the war a personal thing. Horrifying; frightening; but personal. So the next day, I went out and walked into the first recruiting office I came to, and joined the Wrens. End of story. Pathetic, really.'

'Not pathetic in the very least.'

'It wouldn't have been if I hadn't almost instantly regretted it. I was homesick, and I didn't make any friends, and I hated having to live with a lot of strangers.'

Richard was sympathetic. 'You're not the only person to feel that way. Where did they send you?'

'Whale Island. The Royal Naval Gunnery School.'

'Is that where you met your husband?'

'Yes.' She looked down, picked up her fork, drew, with its prongs, a criss-cross pattern on the checked table-cloth. 'He was a Sub Lieutenant, doing his courses.'

'What's he called?'

'Ambrose Keeling. Why do you ask?'

'I thought I might have come across him, but I never have.'

'I don't suppose you would,' she told him coolly. 'He's much younger than you are. Oh, good . . .' Her voice rose in relief. 'Here's Grace with our soup.' She added swiftly, 'I've just realised how hungry I am,' so that Richard would think that she was relieved because the soup had arrived, and not because there was now good reason to stop talking about Ambrose.

It was eleven o'clock before they finally set out for home, making their way through the lightless lanes of shuttered houses, climbing the hill. It had become much colder, and Penelope bundled herself in Sophie's shawl and was grateful for its scented comfort. High above, clouds sailed across a sky flung with stars, and as they ascended, leaving the crooked streets of Downalong far below them, the wind made itself felt, fresh and strong, blowing from the Atlantic.

They came at last to Grabney's Garage, and the last hill. Penelope paused, to push her hair out of her face, and gather the shawl more securely about her shoulders.

He said, 'I'm sorry.'

'Why?'

'Such a walk. I should have got a taxi.'

'I'm not tired. I'm used to it. I do it two or three times a day.'

He took her arm, lacing his fingers with hers, and they set off once more. He said, 'I'm going to be fairly occupied during the next ten days, but when the opportunity presents itself, perhaps I can drop in and see you all. Have another game of backgammon.'

'Any time,' she told him. 'Just appear. Papa would love to see you. And there's always some sort of meal on the table, even if it's only soup and bread.'

'That's kind.'

'Not kind at all. You're the kind one. I haven't had such a lovely evening for years . . . I'd forgotten how it felt, being taken out for dinner.'

'And after four years of Service life, I'd forgotten what it felt to be anywhere except a Mess, with a lot of other men who do nothing but talk shop. So perhaps we're doing each other a good turn.'

They came to the wall, the tall gate. She stopped and turned to him.

'Do you want to come in for a cup of coffee or anything?'

'No. I'll get back. I've got an early start.'

'As I said, Richard. Come any time.'

'I will,' he said. He put his hands on her shoulders and stooped to kiss her cheek. 'Good night.'

She went in through the gate, through the garden, into the sleeping house. In her bedroom, at her dressing-table, she halted, gazing at the dark-eyed girl who stood there, framed in the long mirror. She loosened the knot of the shawl, let it fall to the floor at her feet. Slowly, one by one, she began to undo the buttons of the daisy-patterned red dress, but then abandoned the buttons and, instead, leaned forward to inspect her face, to put up a hand and touch, with tentative fingers, the cheek he had kissed. She found herself blushing, saw the rosy glow suffuse her face. Laughing at herself, she undressed, turned off the lights, drew back the curtains, and got into bed; to lie wide-eyed, watching the dark sky beyond the open window, hearing the murmur of the sea, feeling the beat of her own heart; to go over, in her mind, every single word that he had spoken during the course of the evening.

•    •    •

Richard Lomax was true to his promise. Over the next few weeks he came and went, and his random appearances, unexpected and unannounced, soon became totally taken for granted by the occupants of Carn Cottage. Lawrence, inclined to be despondent at the start of another long, house-bound winter, cheered up the moment he heard Richard's voice. Doris had already made up her mind that he was lovely, and the fact that he was always willing to play football with her sons, or help them mend their bicycles, did nothing to quench her enthusiasm. Ronald and Clark, at first a little in awe of such a splendid figure, soon lost all inhibitions, called him by his Christian name, and asked endless questions as to how many battles he had been in, if he had ever parachuted from an aeroplane, and how many Germans he had slain. Ernie liked him because he was unpretentious, prepared to get his hands dirty and, unasked, sawed, split, and stacked a monumental pile of logs. Even Nancy finally thawed, and one evening, when Doris was out and Penelope occupied in the kitchen, allowed Richard to take her upstairs and give her a bath.

For Penelope, it was an extraordinary time – a time of reawakening, as though, for longer than she cared to remember, she had been only half alive. Now, day by day, her inner vision cleared, and her perceptions were sharpened by a new awareness. One manifestation of this was the sudden significance of popular songs. There was a wireless in the kitchen at Carn Cottage which, because Doris enjoyed its company, was seldom turned off. Sitting on a corner of the dresser, it relayed *Workers' Playtime*, read news bulletins, talked and sang to itself, for all the world like some lunatic relation, heard but not heeded. But one morning, as Penelope scraped carrots at the sink, Judy Garland came on.

> It seems that we have stood and talked like this before
> We looked at each other in the same way then,
> But I can't remember where or when.
> The clothes you are wearing are the clothes you wore,
> The smile you are smiling you were smiling then . . .

Doris burst in. 'What's wrong with you?'

'Um?'

'Standing there at the sink with a knife in one hand and a carrot in the other; gazing out the window. Feeling all right, are you?'

There were other, less banal, instances of this sharpening sensitivity. The most ordinary of prospects caused her to stop and stare. The last of the leaves dropped from the trees, and the bare branches made lace against pale skies. Sun after rain turned cobbled streets blue as fish scales, dazzling to the eye. Autumn winds, whipping the bay to a scud of white caps, brought with them, not cold, but a surging sense of vitality. She was filled with physical energy, tackling tasks she had put off for months, cleaning silver, labouring in the garden, and at weekends rounding up the children and taking them for massive walks, up onto the moor, down to the cliffs beyond the North Beach. Best of all, perhaps strangest of all, when days passed and Richard did not come, she suffered no anxious speculation. She knew that, sooner or later, he would be there, bringing with him that same aura of ease and familiarity that had struck her so instantly on the occasion of his first visit. And when he did appear, it was like a marvellous bonus, a gift of joy.

Trying to analyse, to find a reason, for her own tranquil acceptance of the situation, she discovered that there was nothing ephemeral about either her relationship with Richard Lomax, nor the rare new quality of her days. On the contrary, she was aware only of a sort of timelessness, as though it was all part of a plan, a predestined design, conceived the day she was born. What was happening to her had been meant to happen, was going to go on happening. Without any recognisable beginning, it did not seem possible that it could ever have an end.


'. . . there was a day, in the middle of every summer, called Open Day. All the artists buffed up their studios . . . and some of them needed a good deal of buffing . . . and set out their work and their finished canvases, and the general public went around, from one studio to another, inspecting, and sometimes buying. Of course, some of the visitors simply did the rounds out of curiosity . . . rather like nosing around other people's houses . . . but a lot of bona fide buyers came as well. Like I said, some of the studios were fairly grubby and basic, even in those days, but Sophie always gave Papa's a tremendous spring-clean, and filled it with flowers, and gave the visitors shortbread biscuits and glasses of wine. She said a little refreshment helped the sales along . . .'

It was now the end of October, a Sunday, and early in the afternoon. During his sporadic visits to Carn Cottage, Richard had reiterated, more than once, his desire to see Lawrence Stern's studio, but somehow a suitable opportunity had never arisen. Today, however, he was, for once, free, and Penelope, impulsively abandoning other plans, had offered to take him. Now, they were on their way, walking as usual, the big old key heavy in the pocket of her cardigan.

The weather was cool and fresh, a west wind blowing gusts of sunshine and shadow across the sea, the low clouds forming and dispersing to reveal glimpses of an eggshell-blue sky. The harbour road was almost deserted, the few summer tourists having long departed. All shops were shut, and the locals, being Sabbath-observing Methodists, were keeping themselves to themselves, sleeping off Sunday dinners, or perhaps pottering in hidden gardens.

'Are there any of your father's pictures still in the studio?'

'Heavens no. Well, maybe the odd half-finished sketch or canvas. Nothing more. When he was working he was grateful to be able to sell everything he produced, sometimes letting them go scarcely before the paint was dry. It was our living, you see. All except *The Shell Seekers.* That was never even exhibited. For some reason it was a very personal picture. He would never consider selling it.' They had turned off the harbour road and were now climbing up into the baffling warren of narrow streets and alleys that lay beyond. 'I came this way the day war was declared to fetch Papa and take him home for lunch. When the church clock struck eleven, all the gulls, perched on the tower, took off, and flew up into the sky.' They rounded the last corner and the North Beach was revealed, and, as always, the force of the wind came as a shock, causing them to hesitate for a second, catching their breath, before continuing down the twisting lane that led to the studio.

Penelope fitted the key in the heavy door and turned it. The door swung open and she led the way inside and was at once assailed by shame, for it was months since she had been down here, and the huge airy room presented an instant impression of disarray and neglect. The air felt cold and yet stuffy, all smelled of turpentine, wood-smoke, tar, and damp. The cold clear northern light, which flooded in through the tall windows, picked out in cruel detail the general dilapidation and muddle.

Behind her, Richard closed the door. She said bluntly, 'It looks dreadful. And it's damp.' She crossed the floor, unlatched the window and, with some difficulty, forced it open. Like a flood of icy water, the wind poured in. She saw the deserted beach, the tide far out, the line of white rollers misted in spume.

He came to join her. He said, with some satisfaction, '*The Shell Seekers.*'

'Of course. It was painted from this window.' She turned back to survey the scene. 'Sophie would have a fit if she could see Papa's studio looking like this.'

The floor, and indeed every horizontal surface, was coated with a film of sand. A table was stacked with a pile of dog-eared magazines, an unemptied ashtray, a forgotten bathing towel. The velvet curtain which draped the model's chair was faded and dusty, and a pile of cinders lay on the hearth in front of the old pot-bellied stove. Beyond this, two divans were set in the angle of the wall, spread with striped blankets and scattered with cushions, but the cushions sagged and a marauding mouse had been at one of them, eaten a hole in the corner and left a trail of stuffing.

Scarcely knowing where to start, Penelope set about trying to improve the situation. She found an old paper sack and into this emptied the leaking cushion and the contents of the ashtray, and set all aside to be later dumped into the nearest dustbin. She snatched the other cushions from the divans, flung them to the floor, stripped off the blankets and took them to the open window, to be shaken vigorously out into the cold fresh air. Mouse-droppings and bits of fluff were whisked away by the wind. Once the blankets and the cushions, plumped up, had been replaced things immediately began to look marginally better.

Meanwhile Richard, apparently unbothered by the disorder, was prowling, taking all in, fascinated by the clues and clutter of another man's lifetime, the memorabilia and *objets trouvés* which stood all about. Shells and sea pebbles and scraps of drift-wood, collected and preserved for their colour and form; photographs drawing-pinned to the walls; the plaster cast of a hand; a pottery jug filled with sea-birds' feathers and dried grasses, fragile as dust. Lawrence's easels and stacks of old canvases and sketch-books; the trays of dried-out paint-tubes; the old palettes and jars of brushes, stained with the vermilion and ochre and cobalt and burnt sienna that he had loved to use.

'How long is it since your father worked?'

'Oh, years.'

'And yet this is all still here.'

'He would never throw anything away, and I haven't the heart to.'

In front of the pot-bellied stove, he paused.

'Why don't we light the fire? Wouldn't that help to dry the place up?'

'It might. But I haven't any matches.'

'I have.' He squatted, gingerly, to open the doors of the stove and stir the ashes with the stub end of a poker. 'And there's some newspaper here, and a bit of kindling and some drift-wood.'

'What if a jackdaw's made a nest in the chimney?'

'If he has, we'll soon know.' Straightening, he took off his green beret, tossed it aside, unbuttoned his battledress jacket. Rolling up the sleeves of his shirt, he set to work.

While Richard cleared out dead ashes and twisted scraps of newspaper into spills, Penelope unearthed, from behind a stack of surf-boards, a broom and began to sweep the sand from tables and floor. She found a sheet of cardboard, collected the sand onto this, and emptied it out of the window. The beach was no longer deserted. In the distance, out of nowhere, a pair of tiny figures had appeared. A man and a woman with a dog. The man threw a stick for the dog and it ran into the surf to retrieve it. She shivered. The air was cold. She half-shut the window and latched it and, with no more to be accomplished, went to curl up in the corner of the divan, just as, when she was a child, at the sleepy end of a long sunlit day of swimming and play, she had snuggled next to Sophie to be read a book or told a story.

Now she watched Richard, and there was the same safe and peaceful feeling. Somehow he had coaxed and cajoled the beginnings of a fire. Twigs snapped and crackled. A flame flickered. He fed in, cautiously, a bit of wood. She smiled, for he seemed to her as intent as a schoolboy building a camp-fire. He looked up and caught the smile.

'Were you ever a Boy Scout?' she asked him.

'Yes. I even learned to tie knots and make a stretcher out of two poles and a raincoat.'

He stacked on a log or two and the tarry wood spluttered and flared. He closed the doors of the stove, adjusted the draught, and stood up, wiping his hands on the seat of his trousers.

'That's it.'

'If we had some tea and some milk, we could boil a kettle and have a hot cup of tea.'

'That's about as good as saying if we had some bacon, we could have bacon and eggs, if we had some eggs.' He pulled up a stool and sat facing her. There was a streak of soot on his right cheek but she didn't tell him about it. 'Is that what you used to do? Make tea down here?'

'Yes, after surfing. The very thing, when you were all cold and shivery. And there were always gingerbread biscuits to dunk in the tea. Some years, if there'd been bad storms during the winter, the sand came up to the window, in great banks. But other years, it was like it is today, with a twenty-foot drop, and we had to climb down to the beach by a rope ladder.' She rearranged her legs, settled more comfortably into the cushions. 'Nothing like nostalgia. I'm like an old person, aren't I? I seem to talk all the time about the way things used to be. You must find it very boring.'

'I don't find it boring at all. But sometimes I get the impression that your life ended the day war broke out. And that's wrong, because you're very young.'

'I'm twenty-four. Just,' she amended.

He smiled. 'When was your birthday?'

'Last month. You weren't there.'

'September.' For a moment he considered this and then nodded, in a satisfied way. 'Yes. That's right. That fits.'

'How do you mean?'

'Do you ever read Louis MacNeice?'

'I never heard of him.'

'An Irish poet. The best. I shall now introduce you to him, reciting from memory, and probably embarrassing you most dreadfully.'

'I don't embarrass easily.'

He laughed. Without preamble, he began:

'September has come, it is hers
Whose vitality leaps in the autumn,
Whose nature prefers
Trees without leaves and a fire in the fireplace.
So I give her this month and the next
Though the whole of my year should be hers who has rendered
    already
So many of its days intolerable or perplexed
But so many more so happy.
Who has left a scent on my life, and left my walls
Dancing over and over with her shadow
Whose hair is twined in all my waterfalls
And all of London littered with remembered kisses.'

A love poem. Unexpectedly, a love poem. She was not embarrassed but found herself deeply moved. The words, spoken in Richard's quiet voice, aroused a flurry of emotions, but sadness too. *All of London littered with remembered kisses.* She thought back to Ambrose and the night they had gone to the theatre, and out to dine and then back to Oakley Street, but the memories were flat and colourless and did nothing to stir her senses as the words of the poem had done. All of which was, to say the least of it, depressing.

'Penelope.'

'Um . . .?'

'Why do you never talk about your husband?'

She looked up sharply, for a dreadful instant wondering if she had been actually thinking aloud.

'Do you *want* me to talk about him?'

'Not particularly. But it would be natural. I've known you all . . . what is it . . . nearly two months now, and in all that time you've never voluntarily spoken of him nor mentioned his name. Your father's the same. Each time we get remotely near the subject, the conversation is changed.'

'The reason for that is simple. Ambrose bores him. Ambrose bored Sophie too. They had nothing in common. Nothing to say to each other.'

'And you?'

She knew that she had to be honest, not only with Richard but with herself. 'I don't talk about him because it's something I'm not very proud of. I don't come out of it very well.'

'Whatever that means, you don't imagine I would think any the less of you?'

'Oh, Richard, I have no idea what you would think.'

'Try me.'

She shrugged, at a loss for words. 'I married him.'

'Did you love him?'

Once more she strove for truth. 'I don't know. But he was good-looking and kind, and the first real friend I made after joining up and was sent to Whale Island. I'd never had a . . .' She hesitated, searching for the right word, but what was there to say except boyfriend? 'I'd never had a boyfriend before, never had any sort of a relationship with a man of my own age. He was good company, and he liked me, and it was new and it was different.'

'Was that _all_?' He appeared totally nonplussed, as well he might, after this garbled explanation.

'No. There was another reason. I was pregnant with Nancy.' She arranged her face into a bright smile. 'Does that shock you?'

'For God's sake, of course it doesn't shock me.'

'You look shocked.'

'Only because you actually married the man.'

'I didn't have to marry him.' It was important to reassure him, lest he was picturing Lawrence with a shotgun and Sophie in tears of recrimination. 'Papa and Sophie were never like that. They were the original free souls. Ordinary social conventions meant nothing to them. I was on leave when I told them about the baby coming. Under normal circumstances, I might just have stayed at home and had Nancy, and Ambrose would have been none the wiser. But I was still in the Wrens. My leave finished and I had to go back to Portsmouth, and so of course I had to see Ambrose again. And I had to let him know about the baby. It was only fair. I told him that he didn't have to marry me . . . but . . .' She hesitated, actually finding it impossible to remember exactly what had happened. ' . . . once he'd got used to the idea, he seemed to think that we ought to get married. And I was rather touched because I hadn't really expected him to do anything of the sort. Once we'd made up our minds, there was no time to be lost because Ambrose had finished his courses and was about to be sent to sea. So it was fixed, and that was it. Chelsea Registry Office on a fine May morning.'

'Had your parents met him?'

'No. And they couldn't come to the wedding because Papa was ill with bronchitis. So they didn't meet until months later, when he came down to Carn Cottage on a weekend leave. And the moment he walked into the house, I knew that it was all wrong. It was the most terrible, horrible mistake. He didn't belong to us. He didn't belong to me. And I was horrible to him. Enormously pregnant and bored and irritable. I didn't even try to make it fun for him. That's one of the things I'm ashamed of. And I'm ashamed because I always thought of myself as mature and intelligent, and at the end of the day all I did was to make the silliest decision any woman can.'

'You mean getting married.'

'Yes. Admit it, Richard, you would never have done anything so foolish.'

'Don't be too sure. I came very close to it three or four times, but at the last moment common sense always caused me to draw back.'

'You mean that you knew you weren't in love, that it wasn't right for you?'

'Partly that. And partly the fact that, for the past ten years, I've known that this war was coming. I'm thirty-two now. I was twenty-two when Hitler and the Nazi party first came on the scene. At University, I had a great friend. Claus von Reindorp. A Rhodes scholar and a brilliant student. He wasn't a Jew, but a member of one of the old German families. We talked a lot about what was happening in his homeland. Even then, he was filled with foreboding. One summer, I went to Austria to climb in the Tyrol. I was able to feel the temperature for myself, see the writing on the wall. Your friends, the Cliffords, were not the only people to realise that there were terrible times ahead.'

'What happened to your friend?'

'I don't know. He went back to Germany. For a little, he wrote to me and then the letters stopped. He simply disappeared out of my life. I can only hope that, by now, he is safely dead.'

She said, 'I hate this war. I hate it as much as anybody. I want it to end, for the killing and the bombing and the battles to stop. And yet I dread its ending, too. Papa is growing old. He can't have much longer to live, and without him to take care of, and without a war, I shall have no reason not to go back to my husband. I see myself and Nancy living in some horrible little villa in Alverstoke or Keyham, and the prospect fills me with dread.'

The admission was out. The words hung in a silence between them. She suspected disapproval and needed, more than anything, reassurance. In some distress she turned to him. 'Do you hate me for being so selfish?'

'No.' He leaned forward and laid his hand over her own where it lay, palm up, upon the striped blanket. 'The very opposite.' Her hand was freezing cold but his touch was warm, and she closed her fingers around his wrist, needing his warmth, willing it to spread, to reach every part of her being. Instinctively, she lifted his hand and pressed it to her cheek. At precisely the same moment, they both spoke. 'I love you.'

She looked up and into his eyes. It was said. It was done. It could never be unsaid.

'Oh, Richard.'

'I love you,' he repeated. 'I think I've been in love with you since the first moment I set eyes on you, standing with your father on the other side of the road, with your hair blowing in the wind, and you looking like some ravishing gypsy.'

'I didn't know . . . I really didn't know . . .'

'And from the very beginning, I knew that you were married, and yet that made no difference at all. I couldn't get you out of my mind. And looking back, I don't think I even tried. And when you asked me to Carn Cottage, I told myself it was because of your father, because he enjoyed my company and his games of backgammon. So I came, and I came back . . . to see him, of course, but as well, because if I was with him, I knew that you would never be far away. Surrounded by children and endlessly occupied, but still there. That was all that mattered.'

'That was all that mattered to me, too. I didn't try to analyse it. I only knew that everything changed colour when you walked through the door. It felt as though I'd known you always. Like the best of everything, in the past and the future, all happening at once. But I didn't dare to call it love . . .'

He was beside her now, no longer sitting a yard away, but beside her, his arms around her, holding her so close that she could feel the vital drum-beat of his heart. Her face was pressed to his shoulder, his fingers twined and tangled in her hair. 'Oh, my darling, darling girl.' She drew away, her face turned up to his, and they kissed like lovers who have been parted for years. And it was like coming home, and hearing a door being shut, and knowing that you were safe; with the intrusive world shut out, and nothing and nobody to come between you and the only person in the world you wanted to be with.

She lay on her back, her dark hair spilling out over the old faded cushions.

'Oh, Richard . . .' It was a whisper, but she was not capable of more. 'I never knew. I never even guessed that I could feel like this . . . that it could be like this.'

He smiled. 'It can be better than this.'

She looked up into his face and knew what he was saying, and knew that she wanted nothing more. She began to laugh, and his mouth came down on her open, laughing mouth, and words, sweet as they had been, became all at once unnecessary and no longer enough.

The old studio was no stranger to love. The pot-bellied stove, bravely burning, comforted with its warmth; the wind, streaming in through the half-open windows, had seen it all before. The blanketed divans, where once Lawrence and Sophie had shared their mutual joy, received this new love like kindly accomplices. And afterwards, in the deep peace of passion spent, all was tranquillity, and they lay quiet, entwined in each other's arms, watching the clouds tumbling across the sky and listening to the timeless thunder of breakers pounding up onto the empty beach.

She said, 'What will happen?'

'How do you mean?'

'What will we do?'

'Continue to love each other.'

'I don't want to go back. To things as they were before.'

'We can never do that.'

'But we have to. We can't escape reality. And yet I want there to be tomorrow and tomorrow and tomorrow and to know that on all those tomorrows I can spend every waking hour with you.'

'I want that too.' He sounded sad. 'But it's not to be.'

'This war. I hate it so much.'

'Perhaps we should be grateful. That it brought us together.'

'Oh, no. We would have met. Somehow. Somewhere. It was written in the stars. The day I was born, some celestial Civil Servant put a rubber stamp on you, with my name on it, in great big capital letters. This man is reserved for Penelope Stern.'

'Except I wasn't a man the day you were born. I was a prep-school boy, struggling with the inky miseries of my Latin grammar.'

'It makes no difference. We still belong together. You were always there.'

'Yes. I was always there.' He kissed her then, reluctantly, raised his wrist to look at his watch. 'It's nearly five o'clock . . .'

'I hate the war, and I hate clocks, too.'

'Unfortunately, my darling, we can't stay here for ever.'

'When shall I see you again?'

'Not for a bit. I've got to go away.'

'For how long?'

'Three weeks. I shouldn't be telling you, so you mustn't breathe a word.'

She was filled with alarm. 'But where are you going?'

'I can't say . . .'

'What are you going to do? Is it dangerous?'

He laughed. 'No, you ninny, of course it's not dangerous. A training exercise . . . part of my job. So no more questions.'

'I'm frightened that something will happen to you.'

'Nothing will happen to me.'

'When will you be back?'

'The middle of November?'

'Nancy has a birthday at the end of November. She'll be three.'

'I'll be back then.'

She thought about it. 'Three weeks,' she sighed. 'It seems for ever . . .

'Absence is the wind that blows out the little candle, but fans the embers of a fire to a great blaze.

'Still, I could do without it.'

'Will it help to remember how much I love you?'

'Yes. A bit.'

The winter was upon them. Bitter east winds assaulted the countryside, and moaned down across the moor. The sea, turbulent and angry, turned the colour of lead. Houses, streets, the very sky appeared bleached with cold. At Carn Cottage, fires were lit first thing in the morning and kept going all day, fuelled with small rations of coal and anything else that would burn. The days grew short, and with the black-out curtains drawn at tea-time, the nights very long. Penelope reverted to her poncho and her thick black stockings, and taking Nancy out for her afternoon walks involved much bundling of the child into woollen sweaters, leggings, bonnets, and gloves.

Lawrence, his old bones chilled, warmed his hands at the fire and became restless and morose. He was bored.

'Where's Richard Lomax got to? Hasn't been here for three weeks or more.'

'Three weeks and four days, Papa.' She had started counting them.

'Never stayed away so long before.'

'He'll be back for his backgammon.'

'What's he doing with himself?'

'I've no idea.'

Another week passed, and still there was no sign of him. Despite herself, Penelope began to worry. Perhaps he was never coming back. Perhaps some Admiral or General, sitting in state at Whitehall, had decided that Richard was destined for other things, and had posted him off to the North of Scotland, and she would never see him again. He hadn't written, but perhaps he was forbidden to. Or perhaps . . . and this was almost unthinkable . . . with the Second Front looming in the future, he had been parachuted into Norway or Holland; an advance scout sent to pave the way for Allied troops . . . her anxious, over-worked imagination turned and fled from the prospect.

Nancy's birthday was imminent, and this was a good thing, for it gave Penelope something else to think about. She and Doris were planning a small party. Invitations to tea were sent out to ten little female friends. Ration points were squandered on chocolate biscuits, and Penelope, with hoarded ounces of butter and margarine, made a cake.

Nancy was now old enough to look forward to her special day, and for the first time in her short life realised what it was all about. It was about presents. After breakfast, she sat on the hearthrug by the sitting-room fire and opened her parcels, watched, in some amusement, by her mother and her grandfather, and, adoringly, by Doris. She was not disappointed. Penelope gave her a new doll and Doris clothes for the doll, lovingly contrived from scraps of material and odds and ends of knitting wool. There was a sturdy wooden wheelbarrow from Ernie Penberth, and a jigsaw puzzle from Ronald and Clark. Lawrence, always on the lookout for signs of inherited talent, had bought his grandchild a box of coloured pencils; but Nancy's best present of all came from her grandmother, Dolly Keeling. A large box to be opened, layers of tissue paper torn away; and finally, a new dress. A party dress. Layers of white organdie, trimmed with lace and smocked in pink silk. Nothing could have given Nancy more delight.

Kicking aside her other gifts, 'I want to put it on *now*,' she announced, and started then and there to struggle out of her dungarees.

'No, it's a party dress. You can put it on this afternoon, for your party. Look, here's your doll, dress her up in her new clothes. Look at the party dress Doris has made for her. And it's got a petticoat as well, with lace . . .'

Later in the morning, 'You'll have to move out of the sitting room, Papa,' Penelope told him. 'We've got to have the party in here, and space to play games.' She heaved the table to the edge of the floor.

'And where am I meant to take myself? The coal shed?'

'No. Doris has lit the fire in the study. You can be quiet and peaceful in there. Nancy doesn't want any males about the place. She's made that very clear. Even Ronald and Clark have to stay out of the way. They're going to have tea with Mrs Penberth.'

'Aren't I allowed to come and eat birthday cake?'

'Yes, of course you are. We mustn't allow Nancy to become too dictatorial.'

The little guests arrived at four o'clock, urged through the front door by mothers or grannies, and for a gruelling hour and a half Doris and Penelope were in sole charge. The party followed the usual pattern. All had brought small gifts for Nancy, which had to be opened. One child wept and said she wanted to go home, and another, a bossy little madam with ringlets, asked if there was going to be a conjuror. Penelope told her briskly that there wasn't.

Games were played. 'I sent a letter to my love and on the way I dropped it,' they all piped in unison, sitting cross-legged in a circle on the sitting-room floor. One little guest, perhaps over-excited, wet her knickers and had to be taken upstairs and lent a dry pair.

> The farmer's in his den
> The farmer's in his den
> Heigh-ho, my daddy-o,
> The farmer's in his den.

Penelope, already exhausted, looked at the clock and could scarcely believe that it was only half past four. There was still an hour to be survived before mothers and grannies would reappear to claim their little darlings and take them away.

They played 'Pass the Parcel'. All went well until the bossy child in ringlets said that Nancy had *snatched* the parcel and it was *her* turn to undo the paper. Nancy objected and got a clout over the ear from the ringleted one, whereupon she promptly hit back. Penelope made soothing noises and tactfully separated them. Doris appeared at the door and said that tea was ready. No announcement had ever been more welcome.

Games were thankfully abandoned and they all trooped into the dining room, where Lawrence was already seated in his carver chair at the head of the table. The curtains were drawn, the fire alight, and all was festive. For a moment, the children were silenced, either by the awe-inspiring sight of the old man, sitting there like a patriarch, or else by the prospect of food. They gazed at the starched white cloth, the bright mugs and plates, the straws for sucking lemonade and the crackers. The feast included jellies and sandwiches, iced biscuits and jam tarts, and, of course, the cake. They took their places at the table, and for a little while all was silent, save for the sound of munching. There were accidents, of course: sandwiches dropped on the carpet and a mug of lemonade upset, soaking the table-cloth, but this was all routine and speedily dealt with. Then crackers were pulled, paper hats unfolded and placed on heads, and garish brooches and trinkets pinned to dresses. Finally, Penelope lit the three candles on the cake, and Doris turned off the overhead light. The dark room became a stage set, a magic place, the candle flames reflected in the wide eyes of the children who sat around the table.

Nancy, in the place of honour beside her grandfather, stood up on her chair and he helped her to cut the cake.

> 'Happy birthday to you . . .
> Happy birthday to you.
> Happy birthday, dear Nancy . . .'

The door opened and Richard walked in.


'I couldn't believe it. When you appeared, I thought I was seeing things. I couldn't believe it was true.' He seemed thinner, older, grey with fatigue. He needed a shave, and his battledress was creased and soiled. 'Where have you been?'

'The back of beyond.'

'When did you get back?'

'About an hour ago.'

'You look exhausted.'

'I am,' he admitted. 'But I said I'd be here for Nancy's party.'

'You stupid man, that didn't matter. You should be in bed.'

They were alone. Nancy's little visitors had all departed, each one with a balloon and a lollipop. Doris had taken Nancy upstairs to give her a bath. Lawrence had suggested a glass of whisky, and had gone in search of a bottle. The sitting room was still in disorder, with all the furniture out of place, but they sat, unconcerned, in the midst of it all, Richard supine in an armchair, and Penelope on the hearthrug at his feet.

He said, 'The whole exercise took longer . . . was more complicated . . . than we'd anticipated. I couldn't even write you a letter.'

'I guessed that.'

A silence fell. In the warmth of the fire, his eyelids drooped. Fighting sleep, he sat up, rubbed his eyes, ran a hand over his stubbly chin. 'I must look a total wreck. I haven't shaved, and I haven't slept for three nights. Now I'm incapable. Which is sad, because I'd planned to take you out and have you to myself for the rest of the evening, and hopefully the rest of the night as well; but somehow I don't think I can make it. I'd be no use. Fall asleep in the soup. Do you mind? Can you wait?'

'Of course. I don't mind anything now that you're safely back again. I
had terrifying visions of you being intrepid and getting killed or captured.'

'You overestimate me.'

'When you were away, it felt like for ever, but now you're here again
and I can actually look at you and touch you, it's as though you'd never
been away at all. And it wasn't just me that missed you. It was Papa,
too, pining for his backgammon.'

'I'll come up one evening and we'll have a game.' He leaned forward
and took her face in his hands. He said, 'You are just as ravishingly
beautiful as I remembered you.' His tired eyes crinkled up in amusement.
'Perhaps more so.'

'What's so funny?'

'You. Had you forgotten that you are wearing a most unbecoming paper
hat?'

He stayed only for a little while, long enough to drink the whisky
Lawrence had brought him. After that, exhaustion took over and,
swallowing yawns, he pulled himself to his feet, apologised for being such
dull company, and said good night. Penelope saw him out. In the darkness
beyond the open door, they kissed. Then he left her, making his way
down the garden, headed for a hot shower, his bunk, and sleep.

She came indoors and closed the door. She hesitated for a moment,
needing time to collect her flying thoughts, and finally went into the
dining room, found a tray, and started on the tedious business of
clearing up the remains of Nancy's party.

She was in the kitchen, washing up at the sink, when Doris joined
her.

'Nancy's asleep already. Wanted to go to bed in her new dress.' She
sighed. 'I'm bushed. I thought that party was never going to end.' She
flicked a towel from the rack, and came to dry. 'Has Richard gone?'

'Yes.'

'Thought he'd be taking you out for supper tonight.'

'No. He's gone back to catch up on his sleep.'

Doris wiped and stacked a pile of plates. 'Still, it was nice, him turning
up like that. Expecting him, were you?'

'No.'

'Thought not.'

'Why do you say that?'

'I was watching you. You went all white in the face. All bright-eyed.
Like you was going to faint.'

'I was just surprised.'

'Oh, come off it, Penelope. I'm not a fool. It's like forked lightning
when you two are together. I could see the way he looked at you. He's

potty about you. And by the looks of you, since he walked into your life, it's mutual.'

Penelope was washing a Peter Rabbit mug. She turned it over in her hands, in the soapy water. 'I didn't realise it showed so much.'

'Well, don't sound so miserable about it. Nothing to be ashamed of, having a fling with a handsome chap like Richard Lomax.'

'I don't think I'm just having a fling. I know I'm not. I'm in love with him.'

'Get away.'

'And I don't exactly know what I'm going to do . . .'

'It's as serious as *that?*'

Penelope turned her head and looked at Doris. Their eyes met, and it occurred to her, at that moment, that they had become, over the years, very close. Sharing responsibilities, sorrows, frustrations, secrets, jokes, and laughter, they had built themselves a relationship that went beyond the bounds of mere friendship. In fact, as much as any person could, Doris . . . worldly, practical, and infinitely kind . . . had filled the aching void left by Sophie's death. And so it was easy to confide.

'Yes.'

There was a pause. 'Sleeping with him, are you?' asked Doris, marvellously casual.

'Yes.'

'How the hell did you manage that?'

'Oh, Doris, it wasn't very difficult.'

'No . . . I mean . . . well, *where?*'

'The studio.'

'I'll be buggered,' said Doris, who only swore when she found herself at a total loss for words.

'Are you shocked?'

'Why should I be shocked? It's nothing to do with me.'

'I'm married.'

'Yes, you're married, worse luck.'

'Don't you like Ambrose?'

'You know I don't. Never said as much, but a straight question deserves a straight answer. I think he's a rotten husband and a rotten father. He scarcely ever comes to see you, and don't tell me he doesn't get leave. He hardly ever writes. And he doesn't even send Nancy a birthday present. Honest, Penelope, he's not worthy of you. Why you ever married the man is a mystery to me.'

Penelope said hopelessly, 'I was having Nancy.'

'That's a bloody reason if ever I heard one.'

'I never thought you'd say that.'

'What do you think I am? Some sort of a saint?'

'Then you don't disapprove of what I'm doing?'

'No, I don't. Richard Lomax is a _real_ gentleman, head and shoulders over a twerp like Ambrose Keeling. And why shouldn't you have some fun? You're only twenty-four and, God knows, life's been dull enough for you these past few years. I'm just surprised you haven't gone off the rails before, the sort of woman you are. Except, let's face it, before Richard came, we were a bit short of local talent.'

Despite herself, despite everything, Penelope started to laugh. 'Doris, I don't know what I'd do without you.'

'Lots of things, I expect. At least now I know which way the wind's blowing. And I think it's great.'

'But how will it end?'

'There's a war on. We don't know how anything's going to end. We just have to grasp each fleeting moment of joy as it whizzes by. If he loves you and you love him, then you just go ahead. I'm right behind you both and I'll do everything I can to help. Now, for God's sake, let's get these dishes out of the way before the boys get home and it's time to start cooking the supper.'


It was December. Before they knew it, Christmas was upon them, with all its attendant trimmings. It was hard, in the denuded shops of Porthkerris, to buy anything suitable for anybody, but presents were somehow assembled and wrapped and hidden, just like any other year. Doris made a War Time Christmas Pudding from a Ministry of Food recipe, and Ernie promised to wring the neck of a likely fowl, in lieu of a turkey. General Watson-Grant provided, from his garden, a little spruce, and Penelope dug out the box of Christmas-tree decorations — the baubles and trinkets left over from her own childhood, the gilded fir-cones and paper stars and chains of tarnished tinsel.

Richard had Christmas leave, but was going to London to spend a few days with his mother. Before he left, however, he came to Carn Cottage to deliver his gifts for them all. They were wrapped in brown paper and tied with red ribbon, and labelled with stickers bright with holly and robins. Penelope was deeply touched. She imagined him shopping, buying the ribbon; sitting, perhaps on his bed, in his austere cabin at the Royal Marine HQ, painstakingly wrapping, and tying bows. She tried to imagine Ambrose doing anything so personal and time-consuming but failed.

She had bought, for Richard, a scarlet lamb's-wool muffler. It had cost not only money but precious clothing coupons as well, and probably he would think it hopelessly impractical, for it could not be worn with uniform and he was never in plain clothes. But so luxurious was it, so cheerful and Christmassy, that Penelope had been unable to resist. She wrapped it in tissue paper, and found a box for it, and, when Richard had piled his gifts beneath their tree, she gave him the package to take with him to London.

He turned it over in his hands. 'Why don't I open it now?'

She was horrified. 'Oh, no, you mustn't. You must keep it till Christmas morning.'

'All right. If you say so.'

She did not want to say goodbye. But, 'Have a happy time,' she told him, smiling.

He kissed her. 'You too, my darling.' It was like being torn apart. 'Happy Christmas.'

Christmas morning started early as ever, and was the usual riot of excitement, with all six of them gathered in Lawrence's bedroom, the grown-ups drinking mugs of tea, and the children bundled on his big bed to open their stockings. Trumpets tootled, and tricks were played and apples eaten, and Lawrence put on a false nose with a Hitler moustache, and everybody fell about with laughter. Breakfast came next, and then, traditionally, they all trooped into the sitting room and started on the presents piled under the tree. Excitement rose. Soon the floor was piled with paper and tinselled string, the air filled with shrieks of glee and satisfaction. 'Oh, thanks, Mum, it was just what I wanted. Look, Clark *a hooter* for my *bike*.'

Penelope had set Richard's present aside, and left it to open last of all. The others were not so strong-minded. Doris tore the paper off hers and produced from the wrappings a silk scarf, of extravagant size and richness, and patterned in all the colours of the rainbow.

'I've never had such a thing before!' she crowed, and proceeded to fold it into a triangle, toss it over her head, and knot it beneath her chin. 'How do I look?'

Ronald told her. 'Like Princess Elizabeth on her pony.'

'Ooh,' she was delighted. 'Very la-di-da.'

For Lawrence, there was a bottle of whisky; for the boys, proper lethal, professional catapults. For Nancy, a doll's tea-set, white china, gold-rimmed, and painted with tiny flowers.

'What's he given you, Penelope?'

'I haven't opened it yet.'

'Open it now.'

She did so, with all their eyes upon her. Untied the bow and folded back the crisp brown paper. Inside was a white box, edged in black. Chanel No 5. She took the lid off the box and saw the square bottle set in folds of satin, the crystal stopper, the precious golden liquid contents.

Doris was open-mouthed. 'I've never seen such a size of a bottle. Not outside a shop, I haven't. And Chanel No 5! You aren't half going to smell good.'

Inside the lid of the box was a tightly folded blue envelope. Surreptitiously, Penelope removed this and put it into the pocket of her cardigan. Later, when the others were clearing up the littered paper, she went upstairs to her room and opened the letter.

My darling girl.

Happy Christmas. This has come to you from across the Atlantic. A good friend of mine was in New York, where his cruiser was re-fitting, and he brought it back when they returned to England. To me, the scent of Chanel No 5 evokes everything that is glamorous and sexy and light-hearted and fun. Lunch at the Berkeley; London in May with the lilac blossom out; with laughter, and love; and you. You are never out of my thoughts. You are never out of my heart.

Richard

It was the same dream. She thought of it as Richard's country. Always the same. The long, wooded land, the house at the end of it, flat-roofed, a Mediterranean house. The swimming pool, and Sophie swimming there, and Papa at his easel, his face blanked out by the shadow cast by the brim of his hat. And then the empty beach, and the knowledge that she was seeking not for shells but for a person. He came, and she saw him coming, from far off, and was filled with joy. But before she could reach his side, the mist rolled in from the sea, a dark fog rising like a tide, so that at first he appeared to be wading in it, and then drowning.

'Richard.'

She awoke, reaching for him. But the dream dissolved and he was gone. Her hands felt only the cold sheets on the other side of the bed. She could hear the sea murmuring on the beach, but there was no wind. All was quiet and still. So what had disturbed her, what lay at the edge of consciousness? She opened her eyes. Darkness was fading and, beyond the open window, the sky pale with the coming dawn, the half-light making clear the details of her own familiar room. The brass rail at the end of the bed, her dressing table, the tilted mirror reflecting the sky. She saw the little armchair, the open suitcase on the floor beside it, already half-packed . . .

That was it. The suitcase. Today. I am going away today. On holiday; for seven days; and with Richard.

She lay and thought about him for a bit, and then remembered that puzzling dream. Never altering. Always the same sequence. Nostalgic images of lost contentment; then the searching. The whole fading to uncertainty and that final sense of loss. But, on analysis, perhaps after all it was not so puzzling, for the dream had first invaded her sleep soon after Richard returned from London at the beginning of January, and had recurred at irregular intervals during the past two and a half months.

Which had proved a time of the most painful frustration because, so occupied and involved had he become in his job, that she had scarcely seen him. The training exercise, in proportion to the bitter weather, had visibly intensified. This was made evident by the increasing number of troops and Army vehicles to be seen about the place. Convoys now frequently choked the narrow streets of the town and the harbour, and the Commando establishment on the North Pier seethed with military activity.

Things, quite obviously, were hotting up. This was confirmed, when, soon after the New Year, a company of sappers arrived overnight, made their way out to the deserted moorland beyond the Boscarben Cliffs, and there set up a firing range. It looked sinister with barbed wire, red warning flags, and huge War Department signs warning the civilian population to keep out, and threatening death and destruction if they didn't. When the wind was in the right direction, the sporadic sounds of gun-fire, day and night, could be clearly heard in Porthkerris. At night-time, it was particularly disquieting because, woken with a start and a pounding heart, you could never be quite sure exactly what was taking place.

From time to time, Richard did appear, unheralded as always. His step in the hall, his raised voice never failed to fill her with joy. Usually these visits came after supper, when he would sit with herself and Papa, drink coffee, and later, play backgammon into the small hours. Once, telephoning and making the arrangement at the very last moment, he had taken her down to Gaston's for dinner, where they drank a bottle of Gaston's excellent wine and talked their way through weeks of absence from each other.

'Tell me about Christmas, Richard. How was your Christmas?'

'Quiet.'

'What did you do?'

'Took in concerts. Went to the Midnight Service at Westminster Abbey. Talked.'

'Just you and your mother?'

'A few friends dropped in. But most of the time just the two of us.'

It sounded companionable. She was curious. 'What did you talk about?'

'Lots of things. You.'

'Did you tell her about me?'

'Yes.'

'What did you tell her?'

He reached across the table and took her hand. 'That I'd found the only person in the world with whom I wanted to spend the rest of my life.'

'Did you tell her that I'm married, and that I have a child?'

'Yes.'

'What was her reaction to that piece of news?'

'Surprise. Then sympathy and understanding.'

'She sounds nice.'

He smiled. 'I like her.'

Then, before they realised what was happening, the long winter was nearly over. In Cornwall, spring comes early. A scent in the air, a warmth in the sun makes itself evident, whilst the rest of the country continues to shiver. This year was no different. In the midst of warlike preparations, gun-fire, and hovering helicopters, migrating birds made their appearance in sheltered valleys. Despite the tall headlines in the newspapers, the speculation and rumours of the imminent invasion of Europe, the first of the balmy days stole up upon them, blue-skied, sweet-smelling, halcyon. Buds swelled on trees, the moor was misted green with young bracken, and the roadside banks starred with the creamy faces of wild primroses.

On just such a day, Richard found himself free, without any pressing demands upon his time, and they were able, at last, to return to the studio. To light the fire and let it light their love; to inhabit once more their own private and secret world; to assuage their separate needs and allow them to become a single, shining entity.

Afterwards, 'How long until we come here again?' she wanted to know.

'I wish I knew.'

'I am greedy. I always want more. I always want a tomorrow.'

They sat by the window. Beyond, all was sunlit, the sands a dazzling white, the deep-blue sea dancing with sunpennies. Gulls, drifting on the wind, wheeled and screamed, and just below them, by a rock pool, two small boys searched for shrimps.

'Right now, tomorrows are at a premium.'

'You mean the war?'

'Like birth and death, it is part of life.'

She sighed. 'I do try not to be selfish. I remind myself of the millions of women in the world who would give all they had to be in my shoes, safe and warm and fed and with all my family about me. But it isn't any good. I just feel resentful because I can't be with you all the time. And somehow what makes it worse is that you're actually *here*. You're not guarding Gibraltar, or fighting in the jungles of Burma, or on some destroyer in the Atlantic. You're *here*. And yet the war comes between us, and keeps us apart. It's just that, with everything boiling up, and endless talk of the invasion, I have this terrible feeling that time is slipping by. And all we can grab is a few stolen hours.'

He said, 'I have a week's leave at the end of the month. Will you come away with me?'

While she spoke, she had been watching the two boys and their shrimping nets. One of them had found something, deep in the green weed. He squatted to inspect it, soaking the seat of his trousers. A week's leave. A week. She turned her head and looked at Richard, convinced that she had either misheard him, or that he was teasing her out of her dissatisfaction.

He read the expression on her face, and smiled. 'I really mean it,' he assured her.'

'A whole week?'

'Yes.'

'Why didn't you tell me before?'

'I was saving it. The best for the end.'

A week. Away from everything, everybody. Just the two of them. 'Where would we go?' she asked cautiously.

'Anywhere you want. We could go to London. Stay at the Ritz and do the round of theatres and night-clubs.'

She considered this. London. She thought of Oakley Street. But London was Ambrose, and Oakley Street a house haunted by the ghosts of Sophie and Peter and Elizabeth Clifford. She said, 'I don't want to go to London. Is there an alternative?'

'Yes. An old house called Tresillick, over on the south coast, on the Roseland Peninsula. It's neither large nor grand, but it has gardens sloping down to the water, and an enormous purple wistaria smothered all over its face.'

'You know this house?'

'Yes. I stayed there one summer when I was still at University.'

'Who lives there?'

'A friend of my mother's. Helena Bradbury. She's married to a man called Harry Bradbury, a Captain in the Royal Navy commanding a Cruiser with the Home Fleet. After Christmas, my mother wrote to her, and a couple of days ago I got a letter from her, inviting us to stay.'

'Us?'

'You and me.'

'She knows about me?'

'Obviously.'

'But if we stay with her, won't we have to sleep in different bedrooms and be dreadfully discreet?'

Richard laughed. 'I've never known such a woman as you for raising difficulties.'

'I'm not raising difficulties. I'm being practical.'

'I don't imagine those sort of problems will arise. Helena is renowned for her broad-mindedness. She was brought up in Kenya, and for some reason ladies who were brought up in Kenya are seldom bound by prissy conventions.'

'Have you accepted her invitation?'

'Not yet. I wanted to talk to you first. There are other considerations. Your father is one of them.'

'Papa?'

'Will he raise objections to my taking you off on my own?'

'Richard, you surely know him better than that.'

'Have you told him about us?'

'No. Not in so many words.' She smiled. 'But he knows.'

'And Doris?'

'I did tell Doris. She thinks it's all splendid. She thinks you're lovely, just like Gregory Peck.'

'In that case, there's nothing to stop us. So . . .' He got to his feet. '. . . come on. Get your skates on and get moving. We have business to attend to.'

There was a telephone-box on the corner by Mrs Thomas' shop, and they crowded into it together and closed the door, and Richard put through a call to Tresillick. Penelope, standing so close, could hear the phone ringing at the other end.

'Hello.' The female voice, ringing loud and clear, was easily audible to Penelope, and nearly deafened Richard. 'Helena Bradbury here.'

'Helena. It's Richard Lomax.'

'Richard, you devil! Why haven't you been in touch with me before?'

'I'm sorry, but there's really been no opportunity – '

'Get my letter?'

'Yes. I – '

'Coming to stay?'

'If we may.'

'Wonderful! I'm just livid to think you've been in this neck of the woods all this time, and I didn't know until I heard from your mother. When are you both coming?'

'Well, I've got a week's leave coming up at the end of March. Would that be okay by you?'

'End of March? Oh hell. I shan't be here. Going up to Chatham to spend a bit of time with the old man. Can't you make it another time? No, of course you can't. Silly bloody question. Well, no matter. Come anyway. The house is yours, you can just take it over. There's a Mrs Brick, she lives in the cottage. She has a key. Comes and goes. I'll leave some food in the larder. Just make yourselves at home . . .'

'But that's too kind – '

'No skin off my nose. If you feel like paying your way, you can cut the grass for me. Just too sickening that I shan't be here. Never mind, another time. Drop me a line and let me know when Mrs Brick should expect you. Must fly now. Nice to talk. Goodbye.'

She rang off. Richard, left with the humming receiver in his hand, slowly replaced it.

He said, 'A lady of few words but swift action,' putting his arms around Penelope and kissing her. For the first time, standing there in the smelly, stuffy telephone-box, she allowed herself to believe that it really was going to happen. They were going away together, not on leave, that horrible Service word, but on holiday.

'Nothing can stop it, can it, Richard? Nothing can go wrong?'

'No.'

'How shall we get there?'

'We shall have to work it out. A train to Truro, perhaps. A taxi.'

'But wouldn't it be more fun to drive?' She was struck by a brilliant idea. 'We'll take the Bentley. Papa will lend us the Bentley.'

'Haven't you forgotten something?'

'What's that?'

'The small matter of petrol.'

She had indeed forgotten. But, 'I shall speak to Mr Grabney,' she told him.

'And what will he do?'

'He will get us petrol. Somewhere. Somehow. Black market, if necessary.'

'Why should he do that?'

'Because he is my friend and I have known him all my life. You wouldn't object to driving me to Roseland in a borrowed Bentley fuelled with black market petrol?'

'No. Provided that I have a written affidavit to the effect that we're not going to end up in jail.'

She smiled. Her imagination flew ahead. She saw them setting off, bowling down the high-hedged lanes of the south, with Richard at the wheel and their luggage piled on the back seat. She said, 'You know something? By the time we go, it will be spring again. It really will be spring.'

It was a secret house, tricky to locate, buried deep in a remote and inaccessible corner of the country that had not changed, either its ways or its appearance, for centuries. From the road it was invisible, protected from all eyes by woods and a rutted driveway, bordered by high banks of hydrangea. Finally discovered, it revealed itself as a house that had stood, four-square, for centuries, gathering about it outbuildings, stables, and protective walls, all verdant with flowering creepers, ivy, mosses, and ferns.

In front of the house, the garden, half-wild and half-cultivated, sloped in a series of lawns and terraces down to the shores of a winding, wooded tidal creek. Narrow paths beckoned seductively, leading the way through clumps of camellia, azalea, and Pink Pearl rhododendron. At the water's edge, the unkempt grass was yellow with drifts of wild daffodils, and there was a rickety wooden jetty, where a small dinghy dipped at its mooring.

The wistaria which covered the face of the house had not yet bloomed, but there was blossom everywhere, and alongside the terrace stood a wild white cherry. When the wind touched it, the petals drifted like blown snow.

As promised, Mrs Brick had been there to meet them, emerging from the front door as the old Bentley drew up at the back of the house and came to a thankful halt. Mrs Brick had wild white hair and a wall-eye, sturdy stockings, and a pinafore which tied at the waist.

'You Major and Mrs Lomax, are you?'

Penelope was silenced by this mode of address, but Richard took it coolly in his stride. 'Yes, that's right.' He climbed down from the car. 'And you must be Mrs Brick.' He approached her, holding out his hand.

It was Mrs Brick's turn to be disconcerted. She wiped her reddened hand on the back of her pinafore before putting it in his.

'That's right.' It was difficult to decide exactly where the wall-eye was looking. 'Just stayed to see you in. Mrs Bradbury said. Shan't be here tomorrow. Got your bags, have you?'

They followed her indoors, into a slate-flagged hallway with a stone staircase curving to the upper floor. The treads of this staircase were worn down with the usage of years, and there was a damp, musty smell, not unpleasant and vaguely reminiscent of antique shops.

'Just show you round. Dining room and drawing room . . . under dust-sheets. Mrs Bradbury hasn't used them since the war. Uses the library, in here. Need to keep the fire going, keep you warm. And if the sun shines, you can open the French windows, go out on the terrace. Now come and I'll show you the kitchen . . .' They trailed obediently after her. 'Have to riddle the range and fill it every evening, otherwise there won't be no hot water . . .' Demonstrating this, she took hold of a brass knob and plunged it in and out once or twice, causing sinister disturbance in the bowels of the old stove. 'There's a cold ham in the larder and I got in milk and eggs and bread. Mrs Bradbury said.'

'You've been very kind.'

But she had no time to waste on pleasantries. 'Now. Upstairs.' They gathered up suitcases and bags and followed her. 'Bathroom and lavvy here, down the passage.' The bath stood on legs and the taps were copper and the lavatory cistern had a chain and a handle with PULL written on it. 'Pesky old lavvy this one is. If it doesn't work the first time, you have to wait a bit and then try again.'

'Thank you for telling us.'

There was no time, however, to dwell upon the complexities of the plumbing, for already she was bustling away and ahead of them, to open another door at the head of the stairs, thus releasing onto the landing a gust of airy sunshine from the room beyond. 'Here we are. Put you in the best guest, got a view from here, you have. Hope the bed's all right. Put a hot-water bottle in to dry out the damp. And mind how you step out onto the balcony. The wood's rotten. Might fall through. That's it, then.' She had done her duty. 'I'll be off.'

Penelope, for the first time, managed to get a word in. 'Shall we see you again, Mrs Brick?'

'Oh, I'll be in and out. Odd hours. Keep an eye on you. Mrs Bradbury said.'

And with that, she was gone.

Penelope could not look at Richard. She stood, with her hand clenched over her mouth, somehow managing to control her mirth, until she heard the slam of a door and knew that Mrs Brick was out of earshot. After that it didn't matter. She lay on her back on the huge downy bed, and finally wiped the tears of laughter from her cheeks. Richard came to sit beside her.

He said, 'We'll have to make up our minds which one is her good eye, otherwise it might lead to insurmountable complications.'

'Pesky old lavvy this one is. She was just like the White Rabbit, saying "Faster, faster".'

'How does it feel to be Mrs Lomax?'

'Unbelievable.'

'I expect Mrs Bradbury said.'

'I see now what you meant about ladies who were brought up in Kenya.'

'Will you be happy here?'

'I think I might manage it.'

'How can I help to make you happy?'

She began to laugh again. He stretched out beside her and took her, thoughtfully and without haste, into his arms. Beyond the open window, small sounds made themselves evident. The cry of distant gulls. Closer to hand, the soft murmur of a wood-pigeon. A breeze moved, rustling the branches of the white cherry tree. Slowly, the waters of a flood tide crept up, to fill the empty mudbanks of the creek.

Later, they unpacked and settled in. Richard put on old corduroys, a white polo-necked sweater, worn suede brogues. Penelope hung his uniform at the very back of the wardrobe, and they kicked the suitcases out of sight, beneath the bed. 'It feels,' said Richard, 'like the beginning of the school holidays. Let's go and explore.'

They inspected the house first, opening doors, discovering unexpected stairways and passages, getting their bearings. Downstairs, in the library, they opened the French windows, glanced at the titles of some of the books, found an old wind-up gramophone and a pile of delectable records. Delius, Brahms, Charles Trenet, Ella Fitzgerald.

'We can have musical evenings.'

A fire smouldered in the huge fireplace. Richard stooped to pile on more logs from the basket by the hearth and, straightening, came face to face with an envelope addressed to himself, and propped against the clock that stood in the middle of the mantelpiece. He took it down and slit it open, and inside found a message from their absent hostess.

Richard. The lawn-mower is in the garage, tin of petrol alongside. Key of the wine cellar hanging over the cellar door. Help yourself to contents. Have a good time. Helena.

They took themselves out of doors, by way of the kitchen and the warren of stone-flagged larders, sculleries, store-rooms, and laundries that lay beyond, opening a final door and emerging onto a cobbled stable-yard strung with washing lines. The old stables were now put to use as garages, tool-sheds, and wood-stores. They found the mower and, also, a pair of oars and a furled sail.

'These will be for the dinghy,' Richard observed in a satisfied way. 'When the tide comes up, we can go for a sail.'

Farther on, they came to an ancient wooden door set in a lichened granite wall. Richard put his shoulder to it and shoved it open, and they found themselves in what had once been the vegetable garden. They saw the sagging glasshouses and a broken cucumber frame, but the weeds of years had taken over, and all that could be discerned of the garden's former glory was a clump of overgrown rhubarb, a carpet of mint, and one or two very old apple trees, gnarled as ancient men but, yet, misted with pale-pink blossom. The warm air was filled with the scent of this.

It was sad to see such a wilderness. Penelope sighed. 'A shame. It must have been lovely once. All box hedges and neat beds.'

'It was like that when I stayed before the war. But then there were two gardeners. Impossible, on your own, to keep a place like this going.'

They emerged by a second door, found a path leading down to the creek. Penelope picked a bunch of daffodils, and they sat on the jetty and watched the tide seeping in. When they felt hungry, they went back to the house and ate bread and ham and some wrinkled apples that they found in the larder. Late in the afternoon, when the tide was high, they borrowed oilskins from the Bradburys' cloakroom, collected the oars and the sail, and took out the little dinghy. In the shelter of the creek, they made slow progress, but once out into open water, the breeze caught them. Richard slammed down the centre-board and hauled in the main sheet. The little dinghy listed alarmingly, but held its own, and they sped, close-hauled and spray-drenched, across the deep and choppy waters of the Passage.

It was a secret house. A house that seemed to slumber in the past. Life here, it was clear, had never been anything but quiet and leisurely, lived at a snail's pace: and like a very old and erratic clock, or perhaps a very old and erratic person, it had lost all sense of time. This gentle influence was very strong. By the end of the first day, sleepy and stunned by the soft air of the south coast, Richard and Penelope, unresisting, were seduced by Tresillick's drowsy spell, and after that, time ceased to have importance or even to exist. They saw no newspapers, never turned on the wireless and, if the telephone rang, they left it to ring, knowing that the call was not for them.

The days and nights flowed slowly into each other, unbroken by the necessity for regular meals, or urgent appointments, or the tyranny of clocks. Their only contact with the outside world was Mrs Brick who, true to her word, came and went. Her visits were irregular, to say the least of it, and they never had any idea when she would turn up. Sometimes they would come upon her at three o'clock in the afternoon, polishing, scrubbing, or wielding an old-fashioned sweeper over the worn carpets. One morning, very early, when they were still in bed, she burst in upon them, bearing a tray of tea, but before they had collected their wits and found words to thank her, she had drawn back the curtains, commented on the weather, and gone.

As Richard remarked, it could have been very embarrassing.

Also, like some benevolent hobgoblin, she kept them provided with food. Going into the kitchen to forage for a meal, they would find, on the slate shelf in the larder, a dish of ducks' eggs, a trussed fowl, a pat of farm butter, or a freshly baked loaf of bread. Potatoes were peeled and carrots scraped, and once she had left them a couple of Cornish pasties so enormous that even Richard was unable to finish his.

'We haven't even given her our ration cards,' Penelope pointed out in some wonder. She had lived with ration cards for so long that this abundance seemed to her nothing short of a miracle. 'Where on earth does it all come from?'

They were never to find out.

The weather, that early spring, was fitful. When it rained, which it did with drowning intensity, they either put on waterproofs and went for long wet walks, or stayed by the fireside, with books to be read, or a game of piquet to be played. Some days were blue and warm as summer. They spent them out of doors, picnicking on the grass, or supine on battered old garden chairs. One morning, feeling energetic, they took the Bentley and drove the short distance to St Mawes, to wander around the village, inspect the sailing boats, and end up having a drink on the terrace of the Idle Rocks Hotel.

It was a day of cloud and sunshine, the sun blinking in and out, the soft, sweet air spiced by the freshness of the salt breeze. Penelope leaned back in her chair, her eyes on a brown-sailed fishing boat chugging its way out to the open sea.

'Richard, do you ever think about luxury?' she asked him.

'I don't crave it, if that's what you mean.'

'Luxury, I think, is the total fulfilment of all five senses at once. Luxury is now. I feel warm; and, if I wish, I can reach out and touch your hand. I smell the sea and, as well, somebody inside the hotel is frying onions. Delicious. I am tasting cold beer, and I can hear gulls, and water lapping, and the fishing boat's engine going chug-chug-chug in the most satisfactory sort of way.'

'And what do you see?'

She turned her head to look at him, sitting there with his hair ruffled, and wearing his old sweater, and the leather-patched Harris tweed jacket that smelt of peat. 'I see you.' He smiled. 'Now it's your turn. Tell me your luxury.'

He fell silent, entering the spirit of the game, considering. At last, 'I think, perhaps, contrast,' he told her. 'Mountains, and the bitter cold of snow, all glittering beneath a blue sky and a savage sun. Or lying, baking, on a hot rock, and knowing that, when you can't bear the heat another moment, the cold, deep sea is only a yard away, waiting for you to dive.'

'How about being out on a freezing wet day, and coming home, chilled to the bone, and being able to wallow in an immensely hot, deep bath?'

'That's a good one. Or spending a day at Silverstone, deafened by racing cars, and then, on the way home, stopping off at some vast, incredibly beautiful cathedral, and going in, and just listening to the silence.'

'How awful it would be to crave for sables and Rolls-Royces and huge, vulgar emeralds. Because I'm certain that, once you got them, they would become diminished, simply because they were yours. And you wouldn't want them any more, and you wouldn't know what to do with them.'

'Would it be the wrong sort of luxury to suggest that we have lunch here?'

'No, it would be a lovely one. I was wondering when you were going to suggest it. We can eat fried onions. My mouth's been watering for the past half hour.'


But their evenings, perhaps, were the best of all. With the curtains drawn and the fire blazing, they listened to music, working their way through Helena Bradbury's collection of records, and taking turns to get up and change the needle and wind the handle of the old wooden gramophone. Bathed and changed, they dined by the fireside, drawing up a low table, setting it with crystal and silver, eating whatever Mrs Brick had left for them, and drinking the bottle of wine which Richard, acting on instructions, had fetched up from the cellar. Outside, the night wind, blowing off-shore, nudged and rattled against the windows, but this only served to underline their own seclusion, their snugness and their undisturbed solitude.

One night, very late, they listened to the whole of the *New World*

*Symphony*. Richard lay on the sofa, and Penelope sat on a pile of cushions on the floor, her head leaning against his thigh. The fire had collapsed to a pile of ashes, but as the last notes finally died away, they did not move, simply staying as they were, with Richard's hand on her shoulder, and Penelope lost in dreams.

He stirred at last, and broke the spell.

'Penelope.'

'Yes.'

'We have to talk.'

She smiled. 'We've done nothing else.'

'About the future.'

'What future?'

'Our future.'

'Oh, Richard . . .'

'No. Don't look so worried. Just listen. Because it's important. You see, one day, I want to be able to marry you. I find it impossible to contemplate a future without you, and this means, I think, that we should get married.'

'I already have a husband.'

'I know, my darling. I know only too well, but still, I have to ask you. Will you marry me?'

She turned, and took his hand, and laid it against her cheek. She said, 'We mustn't tempt Providence.'

'You don't love Ambrose.'

'I don't want to talk about it. I don't want to talk about Ambrose. He doesn't belong here. I don't want even to say his name aloud.'

'I love you more than words can say.'

'I too, Richard. I love you. You know that. And I can think of nothing more perfect than to be your wife, and to know that nothing can ever separate us again. But not now. Don't let's talk about it now.'

For a long time he was silent. Then he sighed. 'All right,' he said. He bent and kissed her. 'Let's go to bed.'


Their last day was bright and fair, and Richard, doing his duty and paying his rent, trundled the motor mower from the garage, and cut the grass. It took a long time, and Penelope helped by barrowing the grass cuttings to the compost heap at the back of the stable, and clipping all the edges with a pair of long-handled shears. They did not finish until four o'clock in the afternoon, but the sight of the sloping lawns, smooth as velvet and striped in two different shades of green, was worth all the effort and eminently satisfactory. When they had cleaned and oiled the mower and put it back in its place, Richard announced that he was parched and was about to make them both a cup of tea, so Penelope went back to the front of the house and sat in the middle of the newly mown lawn and waited for him to bring it to her.

The fresh-cut grass smelt delicious. She leaned back on her elbows and watched a pair of kittiwakes, come to perch on the end of the jetty, and marvelled at them, so small and pretty compared to the wild great herring-gulls of the north. Her hands moved over the grass, stroking it as one might stroke the fur of a cat. Her fingers came upon a dandelion which the mower had missed. She pulled at it, tugging the leaves and the shoot, trying to dislodge the root. But the root was stubborn, as dandelions always are, and broke, and she was left with only the plant and half the root in her hand. She looked at it, and smelt its bitter smell and the fresh smell of the damp earth adhering to and dirtying her hands.

A footstep on the terrace. 'Richard?' He had come with their tea, two mugs on a tray. He lowered himself beside her. She said, 'I have found a new luxury.'

'And what is that?'

'It's sitting on a newly mown lawn, all by yourself and without the one you love. You're alone but you know that you're not going to be alone for very long, because he's only gone for a little while, and in a moment or two he's going to come back to you.' She smiled. 'I think that's the best one yet.'

Their last day. Tomorrow, early in the morning, they would be leaving; returning to Porthkerris. She closed her mind to the prospect, refusing to envisage it. Their last evening. They sat as usual, close to the fire, Richard on the sofa, and Penelope curled up on the floor beside him. They did not listen to music. Instead, he read aloud to her MacNeice's *Autumn Journal*; not just the love poem, which he had quoted that far-off day in Papa's studio, but the whole of the book, from beginning to end. It was very late when he came to the last words.

> Sleep to the noise of running water
> Tomorrow will be crossed, however deep;
> There is no river of the dead or Lethe
> Tonight we sleep
> On the banks of the Rubicon – the die is cast
> There will be time to audit
> The accounts later, there will be sunlight later
> And the equation will come out at last.

He slowly closed the book. She sighed, not wanting it to be finished. She said, 'So little time. He knew the war was inevitable.'

'I think, by the autumn of 1938, most of us did.' The book slipped from his hand onto the floor. He said, 'I am going away.'

The fire had died. She turned her head and looked up into Richard's face and found it filled with sadness.

'Why do you look like that?'

'Because I feel I am betraying you.'

'Where are you going?'

'I don't know. I can't say.'

'When?'

'As soon as we get back to Porthkerris.'

Her heart sank. 'Tomorrow.'

'Or the next day.'

'Will you be coming back?'

'Not immediately.'

'Have they given you another job?'

'Yes.'

'Who's going to take your place?'

'Nobody. The operation's over. Finished. Tom Mellaby and his administrative staff will be staying on at the RMHQ to wind everything down, but the Commandos and the Rangers will be moving out in a couple of weeks. So Porthkerris will get back its North Pier, and as soon as the rugger pitch has been de-requisitioned, Doris' boys will be able to play football again.'

'So it's all over?'

'That part of it is, yes.'

'What happens next?'

'We'll have to wait and see.'

'How long have you known about this?'

'Two, three weeks.'

'Why didn't you tell me before?'

'Two reasons. One is that it's still secret, classified information, although it won't be for very much longer. The other is that I didn't want anything to spoil this little time we've had together.'

She was filled with love for him. 'Nothing could have spoiled it.' She said the words, and realised that they were true. 'You shouldn't have kept it to yourself. Not from me. You must never keep anything from me.'

'Leaving you will be the hardest thing I've ever had to do.'

She thought about his going and the emptiness beyond. Tried to imagine life without him and, dismally, failed. Only one thing was certain. 'The worst will be saying goodbye.'

'Then don't let's say it.'

'I don't want it to be over.'

'It's not over, my darling girl.' He smiled. 'It hasn't even begun.'


'He has gone?'

She knitted. 'Yes, Papa.'

'He never said goodbye.'

'But he came to see you; to bring you a bottle of whisky. He didn't want to say goodbye.'

'Did he say goodbye to you?'

'No. He just walked away, down the garden. That was the way we planned it.'

'When will he be back?'

She came to the end of her row, changed needles, started another. 'I don't know.'

'Are you being secretive?'

'No.'

He fell silent. Sighed. 'I shall miss him.' Across the room, his dark, wise eyes rested upon his daughter. 'But not, I think, as much as you will.'

'I'm in love with him, Papa. We love each other.'

'I know that. I've known it for months.'

'We are lovers.'

'I know that too. I've watched you bloom, become radiant. A shine on your hair. I've longed to be able to hold a brush, to paint that radiance and capture it for ever. Also . . .' He became prosaic. '. . . You don't go away for a week with a man and spend the time talking about the weather.' She smiled at him, but said nothing. 'What will become of you both?'

'I don't know.'

'And Ambrose?'

She shrugged. 'I don't know that either.'

'You have problems.'

'A marvellous understatement.'

'I am sorry for you. I am sorry for you both. You deserve a better fortune than to find each other in the middle of a war.'

'You . . . you like him, don't you, Papa?'

'I never liked a man so well. I should like him as a son. I think of him as a son.'

Penelope, who never wept, all at once felt tears prick at the back of her eyes. But this was no time for sentiment. 'You are a villain,' she told her father. 'I've said so many times before.' The tears, mercifully, receded. 'You shouldn't be condoning this. You should be cracking your horsewhip

and grinding your teeth, and daring Richard Lomax to darken your
doorstep ever again.'

She was rewarded by a gleam of amusement. 'You insult me,' he told
her.

Richard was gone, the vanguard of a general exodus. By the middle of
April, it was clear to the inhabitants of Porthkerris that the Royal Marine
Training Scheme, their own small involvement in the war, was over.
The American Rangers and the Commandos – as quietly and inconspicu-
ously as they had come – departed, and the narrow streets of the town
were empty and strangely quiet, no longer ringing with the tramp of
booted feet, or the din of military vehicles. The landing craft disappeared
from the harbour, towed away one night under cover of darkness;
barbed-wire barriers were removed from the North Pier; and the Commando Headquarters were de-requisitioned and handed back to the
Salvation Army. Up on the hill, the temporary Nissen huts of the
American Base stood forlorn and empty, and from the deserted ranges
out at Boscarben no longer came the sound of gun-fire.

Finally, all that remained as evidence of the long winter's military
activity was the Royal Marine Headquarters at the old White Caps Hotel.
Here, the Globe and Laurel still snapped at the mast-head, the Jeeps
stayed, parked in the forecourt, the sentry stood on duty by the gate, and
Colonel Mellaby and his staff came and went. Their continued presence
was a reminder, and gave credence, to everything that had taken place.

Richard was gone. Penelope learned to live without him, because there
was no alternative. You couldn't say 'I can't bear it' because if you didn't
bear, the only other thing to do was to stop the world and get off, and
there did not seem any practical way to do this. To fill the void and
occupy her hands and mind, she did what women, under stress and in
times of anxiety, have been doing for centuries: immersed herself in
domesticity and family life. Physical activity proved a mundane but
comforting therapy. She cleaned the house from attic to cellar, washed
blankets, dug the garden. It did not stop her from wanting Richard, but
at least, at the end of it, she had a shining, sweet-smelling house and
two rows of freshly planted young cabbages.

Also, she spent much time with the children. Theirs was a simpler
world, their conversation basic and uncomplicated, and she was
comforted by their company. Nancy, at three, had become a little person;
engaging, single-minded, and determined; her remarks and pointed obser-
vations a source of constant wonder and amusement. But Clark and
Ronald were growing up, and their arguments and opinions she found

astonishingly mature. She gave them her full attention, helped them with their shell collections, listened to their problems, and answered their questions. For the first time she saw them, not simply as a pair of noisy little boys, with two hungry mouths that had to be fed, but equals. People in their own right. The future generation.

One Saturday, she took the three children to the beach. Returning to Carn Cottage, she found General Watson-Grant there, on the point of departure. He had come to see Lawrence. They had had a pleasant chat. Doris had given them tea. He was now on his way home.

Penelope walked with him to the gate. He paused, to touch with his stick, and admire, a clump of hostas, thick with quilted leaves and tall white spiky flowers. 'Handsome things,' he remarked. 'Wonderful ground cover.'

'I love them, too. They're so exotic.' They moved on, by the escallonia hedge, which was already bursting with dark-pink buds. 'I can't believe summer's here. Today, when the children and I were on the beach, we saw the old man with a face like a turnip, raking all the flotsam from the sands. And there are tents going up already, and the ice-cream parlour has opened. I suppose, before long, the first of the visitors will be arriving. Like swallows.'

'Have you had news of your husband?'

'. . . Ambrose? He's well, I think. I haven't heard from him for some time.'

'Do you know where he is?'

'The Med.'

'He'll miss this show, then.'

Penelope frowned. 'Sorry?'

'I said, he'll miss this show. Going into Europe. The invasion.'

She said faintly, 'Yes.'

'Bloody bad luck on him. I tell you something, Penelope. I would give my right arm to be young again, and to be able to be in the thick of it. It's taken a long time to get this far. Too long. But now the whole country's ready and waiting to pounce.'

'Yes. I know. The war has suddenly become terribly important again. Walking down a street in Porthkerris, you can listen to an entire news bulletin, from one house to the next. And people buy newspapers, and read them, then and there, on the pavement outside the paper shop. It's like it was at the time of Dunkirk, or the Battle of Britain, or El Alamein.'

They had reached the gate. Once more they stopped, the General leaning on his stick.

'Good to see your father. Came on an impulse. Felt like a bit of a chin-wag.'

'He needs company these days.' She smiled. 'He misses Richard Lomax and his backgammon.'

'Yes. He told me.' Their eyes met. His regard was kindly, and she found time to wonder just how much Lawrence had thought fit to tell his old friend. 'To be honest, I hadn't realised young Lomax had gone. Have you heard from him?'

'Yes.'

'How's he getting on?'

'He didn't really say.'

'That follows. I don't suppose security's ever been so tight.'

'I don't even know where he is. The address he gave me is nothing but initials and numbers. And the telephone might never have been invented.'

'Oh, well. No doubt you'll hear from him soon.' He opened the gate. 'Now I must be on my way. Goodbye, my dear. Take care of your father.'

'Thank you for coming.'

'A pleasure.' Suddenly he raised his hat and leaned forward to give her a peck on the cheek. She was left wordless, for he had never in his life done such a thing before. She watched him go, stepping out briskly with his walking-stick.

The whole country's waiting. Waiting was the worst. Waiting for war; waiting for news; waiting for death. She shivered, closed the gate, and made her way slowly back up the garden.

Richard's letter arrived two days later. The first downstairs in the early morning, Penelope saw it lying where the postman had left it, on the hall chest. She saw the black italic writing, the bulky envelope. She took it into the sitting room, curled up in Papa's big chair, and opened it. There were four sheets of thin yellow paper, folded tight.

Somewhere in England

May 20th, 1944.

My darling Penelope,

Over the last few weeks I have settled down a dozen times to write to you. On each occasion I have got no further than the first four lines, only to be interrupted by some telephone call, loud hailer, knock on the door, or urgent summons of one sort or another.

But at last has come a moment in this benighted place when I can be fairly certain of an hour of quiet. Your letters have all safely come, and are a source of joy. I carry them around like a lovesick schoolboy and read and reread them, time without number. If I cannot be with you, then I can listen to your voice.

Now, I have so much to say. In truth, it is difficult to know where to start, to remember what we spoke about and when we stayed silent. The unsaid is what this letter is about.

You never wanted to talk about Ambrose, and while we were at Tresillick, and inhabiting our own private world, there seemed little point. But, just lately, he has seldom been out of my mind, and it is clear that he is the only stumbling-block between us, and our eventual happiness. This sounds appallingly selfish, but one cannot take another man's wife away from him and remain a saint. And so my mind, apparently of its own volition, plots ahead. To confrontation, admission, blame, lawyers, courts, and an eventual divorce.

There is always the possibility that Ambrose will be gentlemanly and allow you to divorce him. To be honest, I see no earthly reason why he should do this, and I am perfectly prepared to stand up in court as the guilty co-respondent and let him divorce you. If this happens, he must have access to Nancy, but that is a bridge we must cross when we reach it.

All that matters is that we should be together, and eventually – hopefully sooner than later – married. The war will, one day, be over. I shall be demobilised and returned, with thanks and a small gratuity, to civilian life. Can you deal with the prospect of being the wife of a school-teacher? Because this is all I want to do. Where we shall go, where we shall live, and how it will be, I cannot tell, but if I have any choice, I should like to go back to the North, to be near the Lakes and the mountains of the Peak district.

I know it all seems a long way off. A difficult road lies ahead, strewn with obstacles which, one by one, will have to be overcome. But thousand-mile journeys begin with the first step, and no expedition is the worse for a little thought.

On reading this through, it strikes me as the letter of a happy man who expects to live for ever. For some reason, I have no fears that I will not survive the war. Death, the last enemy, still seems a long way off, beyond old age and infirmity. And I cannot bring myself to believe that fate, having brought us together, did not mean us to stay that way.

I think of you all at Carn Cottage, imagine what you are doing, and wish I were with you, sharing the laughter and domestic doings of what I have come to think of as my second home. All of it was good, in every sense of the word. And in this life, nothing good is truly lost. It stays part of a person, becomes part of their character. So part of you goes everywhere with me. And part of me is yours, for ever. My love, my darling,

Richard

On Tuesday, the sixth of June, the Allied Forces invaded Normandy. The Second Front had started, and the last long battle begun. The waiting was over.

The eleventh of June was a Sunday.

Doris, visited by a fit of religious zeal, had carted her boys off to church, and Nancy to Sunday school, leaving Penelope to cook the lunch. For once the butcher had turned up trumps and produced, from under his counter, a small leg of spring lamb. This was now in the oven, roasting and smelling delicious, and surrounded by crisping potatoes. The carrots simmered, the cabbage was shredded. For pudding, they would eat rhubarb and custard.

It was nearly twelve o'clock. She thought of mint sauce. Still wearing her cooking apron, she went out of the back door and made her way up the slope of the paddock. It was breezy. Doris had done a big wash and pegged it out on the line, and sheets and towels flapped and snapped in the wind like ill-set sails. The ducks and hens, penned into their run, saw Penelope coming and set up a great cackling, expecting food.

She found the mint, picked a sharply scented bunch of springs; but as she walked back through the long grass towards the house, she heard the sound of the bottom gate open and shut. It was too early for the church-goers' return, and so she went by way of the stone steps that led down onto the front lawn and stood there, waiting to see who was coming to call.

The visitor appeared, taking his time. A tall man, in uniform. A green beret. For the fraction of an instant, long enough for her heart to leap, she thought it was Richard, but at once saw that it was not. Colonel Mellaby reached the top of the path and paused. He raised his head and saw her watching him.

Everything, suddenly, was very still. Like a film caught in a single frame because the projector has broken down. Even the breeze dropped. No bird sang. The green lawn lay between them like a battlefield. She was motionless, waiting for him to make the first move.

Which he did. With a click and a whirr, the film started up again.

She went to meet him. He looked changed. She had not realised that he was so pale and gaunt.

It was she who spoke first. 'Colonel Mellaby.'

'My dear . . .' He sounded like General Watson-Grant, being at his very nicest, and from that second she knew, without doubt, what he had come to tell her.

She said, 'Is it Richard?'

'Yes. I'm so sorry.'

'What's happened?'

'It's bad news.'

'Tell me.'

'Richard's . . . been killed. He's dead.'

She waited to feel something. Felt nothing. Only the bunch of mint clutched tight in her fist, a strand of hair across her cheek. She put up a hand and pushed this aside. Her continued silence lay between them like a great uncrossable chasm. She knew this, and was sorry for him, but could do nothing to help.

At last, with an enormous and visible effort, he continued. 'I heard this morning. Before he went, he asked me . . . he said if anything happened to him, I was to come at once and let you know.'

She found her voice at last. 'It was good of you.' It didn't sound like her own voice. 'When did it happen?'

'On D-Day. He went over with the men he'd trained here. The Second United States Rangers.'

'He didn't have to go?'

'No. But he wanted to be with them. And they were proud to have him.'

'What happened?'

'They landed on the flank of Omaha Beach with the United States First Division, at a place called Pointe de Hué, near the bottom of the Cherbourg peninsula.' His voice was more confident now, he spoke unemotionally, of matters which he understood. 'From what I can gather, they had some difficulty with their equipment. The rocket-propelled grapnels became wet during the crossing, and failed to work properly. But they did climb the cliff, and they took the German gun battery at the top. They achieved their objective.'

She thought of the young Americans who had spent their winter here in Porthkerris; an ocean away from their own homes, their own families.

'Were there many casualties?'

'Yes. In the course of the assault, at least half of them died.'

And Richard with them. She said, 'He didn't think he was going to be killed. He said that death, the last enemy, still seemed a long way off. It's good that he thought that, isn't it?'

'Yes.' He chewed his lip. 'You know, my dear, you don't have to be brave. If you want to cry, don't try to stop it. I'm a married man, with children of my own. I would understand.'

'I'm married, too, and I have a child.'

'I know.'

'And I haven't cried for years.'

He was reaching for his breast pocket, unbuttoning the flap. From the pocket he produced a photograph. 'One of my sergeants gave me this. He was in charge of the camera, and he took this one day when they were all out at Boscarben. He thought . . . I thought . . . that you might like to have it.'

He handed it to her. Penelope looked down at the photograph. Saw Richard, turning as though to glance over his shoulder, to be caught unawares and smile at the cameraman. In uniform, but bareheaded, and with a coil of climbing rope slung over his shoulder. It must have been a breezy day, just like today, for his hair was ruffled. In the background lay the long horizon of the sea.

She said, 'That was very kind. Thank you. I didn't have a photograph of him.'

He fell silent. They both stood there, unable to think of anything more to say.

Finally, 'You'll be all right?' he asked her.

'Yes, of course.'

'I'll leave you then. Unless there is anything else I can do.'

She thought about this. 'Yes. Yes, there is something. My father is in the house. In the sitting room. You'll find him quite easily. Will you go, now, and tell him about Richard?'

'You really want me to do that?'

'Somebody has to. And I'm not sure that I'm strong enough.'

'Very well.'

'I'll be there in a moment. I'll give you time to break the news, and then I'll come.'

He went. Up the path, up the front-door steps, through the door. Not only a kindly man, but a courageous one. She stood where he had left her, with her bunch of mint in one hand, and the photograph of Richard in the other. She remembered the ghastly morning of the day that Sophie died, and how she had railed and wept, and longed now for just such a flood of emotion. But there was nothing. She felt simply numb, and cold as ice.

She looked at Richard's face. Nevermore. Never again. Nothing left. She saw his smile. Remembered his voice reading aloud to her.

She remembered the words. Quite suddenly, they were there, filling her mind like a once-forgotten song.

> . . . the die is cast,
> There will be time to audit
> The accounts later, there will be sunlight later
> And the equation will come out at last.

There will be sunlight later. She thought, I must tell Papa that. And it seemed as good a way as any to start out on the left-over life that lay ahead.

# Doris

Podmore's Thatch. A bird sang, its voice piercing the silence of the grey dawn. The fire had died, but the light over *The Shell Seekers* burnt on, as it had burnt throughout the night. Penelope had not slept, but now she stirred, like a sleeper awakening from a deep and untroubled dream. She stretched her legs beneath the thick woollen blanket, spread her arms and rubbed at her eyes. She looked about; saw, in the soft light, her own sitting room, the reassurance of possessions, flowers, plants, desk, pictures; the window open onto her own garden. She saw the lower branches of the chestnut tree, the buds not yet sprung into leaf. She had not slept, but wakefulness had not left her fatigued. On the contrary, she was steeped in a sort of calm contentment, a tranquillity that sprang, perhaps, from the rare self-indulgence of total recall.

Now she had come to the end. The play was over. The illusion of theatre was strong. Footlights dimmed, and in the dying light the actors turned to make their way from the stage. Doris and Ernie, young as they would never be young again. And the old Penberths and the Trubshots, and the Watson-Grants. And Papa. All dead. Long dead. Last of all went Richard. She remembered him smiling, and realised that time, that great old healer, had finally accomplished its work, and now, across the years, the face of love no longer stirred up agonies of grief and bitterness. Rather, one was left feeling simply grateful. For how unimaginably empty the past would be without him to remember. Better to have loved and lost, she told herself, than never to have loved at all. And knew that it was true.

From the mantelpiece her golden carriage clock struck six. The night was gone. It was tomorrow. Another Thursday. What had happened to the days? Trying to puzzle out this conundrum, she discovered that two weeks had flown by since Roy Brookner's visit, when he had taken away the panels and the sketches. And still she had had no word from him.

Also, she had heard nothing from either Noel or Nancy. With that last quarrel lying sour between them all, they had simply taken themselves off and remained apart from their mother and resolutely incommunicado. This bothered her a good deal less than her children probably imagined. In time, no doubt, they would be in touch again, not apologising, but acting as though nothing untoward had ever taken place. Until such time, she had too much on her mind, and no energy to waste fretting over infantile umbrages and hurt feelings. There were better things to think about and far too much to do. As usual, house and garden had claimed most of her attention. The April days, in typical fashion, altered continuously. Grey skies, livid green leaves, drenching showers, and then sunshine again. The forsythias flamed, butter-yellow; the orchard became a carpet of daffodils and violets and primroses.

Thursday. Danus would come this morning. And perhaps, today, Roy Brookner would ring up from London. Considering this possibility, she found herself convinced that today he would ring. It was more than a feeling. Stronger than that. A premonition.

By now the single bird had been joined in song by a dozen others and the air was filled with their chorus. Impossible now to consider sleep. She got off the sofa, turned off the light, and went upstairs to draw herself an enormously hot and very deep bath.

Her premonition was right, and the call came through in the middle of lunch.

The sweet dawn had collapsed into a grey day, overcast and drizzly and offering no inducement to picnic out of doors, or in the conservatory. So they sat, she and Antonia and Danus, around the kitchen table, to consume an enormous spaghetti bolognaise and a platter of crudités. Because of the weather, Danus had spent the morning clearing out the garage. Penelope, going to her desk to find a telephone number, had become waylaid, diverted by its clutter, and stayed there, paying overdue bills, rereading old letters, and throwing out a number of company reports which she had never even bothered to take out of their envelopes. Antonia had cooked the lunch.

'You are not only an excellent gardener's boy, but a first-class cook,' Danus told her, grating Parmesan cheese over his spaghetti.

The telephone rang.

Antonia said, 'Shall I get it?'

'No.' Penelope set down her fork and got to her feet. 'It's probably for me anyway.' She did not answer the call in the kitchen, but went through to the sitting room, closing doors behind her.

'Hello.'

'Mrs Keeling?'

'Speaking.'

'It's Roy Brookner here.'

'Yes, Mr Brookner.'

'I'm sorry I've been so long in getting in touch with you. Mr Ardway was visiting friends in Gstaad, and didn't return to Geneva until a couple of days ago, when he found my letter waiting for him at his hotel. He flew into Heathrow this morning, and I have him here in my office. I've shown him the panels, and told him that you're prepared to sell them privately, and he's very grateful for the opportunity. He has offered fifty thousand for each of them. That's a hundred thousand for the pair. Pounds sterling, of course not dollars. Would that be acceptable to you, or would you prefer to have a little time to think about it? He'd like to return to New York tomorrow but is perfectly prepared, if necessary, to postpone his flight, if you feel you need more time to come to an agreement. Personally, I feel it is a very fair offer, but if . . . Mrs Keeling? Are you still there?'

'Yes, I'm still here.'

'I'm sorry. I thought perhaps we'd been cut off.'

'No. I'm still here.'

'Have you any comment to make?'

'No.'

'Would the sum I've mentioned be acceptable to you?'

'Yes. Perfectly acceptable.'

'So you'd like me just to go ahead and finalise the sale?'

'Yes. Please.'

'Mr Ardway, I need hardly tell you, is delighted.'

'I'm so glad.'

'I'll be in touch. And, of course, payment will be made as soon as the transaction has gone through.'

'Thank you, Mr Brookner.'

'It's perhaps not the appropriate time to mention it, but there will, of course, he considerable taxes to be paid. You realise that?'

'Yes, of course.'

'Have you an accountant, or some person who looks after your affairs?'

'I've got Mr Enderby, of Enderby, Looseby and Thring. They're solicitors in the Gray's Inn Road. Mr Enderby took care of everything when I sold Oakley Street and bought this house.'

'In that case, perhaps you should get in touch with him and let him know the situation.'

'Yes. Yes, I'll do that . . .'

A pause. She wondered if he was going to ring off.

'Mrs Keeling?'

'Yes, Mr Brookner.'

'Are you all right?'

'Why?'
'You sound a little . . . faint?'
'That's because I'm finding it difficult to sound anything else.'
'You're quite happy with the arrangement?'
'Yes. Quite happy.'
'In that case, goodbye, Mrs Keeling . . .'
'No, Mr Brookner, wait. There's something else.'
'Yes.'
'It's about *The Shell Seekers*.'
'Yes?'
She told him what she wanted him to do.

She replaced, very slowly, the receiver. She was sitting at her newly ordered desk, and went on sitting there for some moments. It was very quiet. From the kitchen, she could hear the murmur of voices. Antonia and Danus, who never seemed to run out of things to say to each other. She went back and found them, still sitting at the table, having finished their spaghetti and now moved on to fruit and cheese and coffee. Her own plate had disappeared.

'I put yours in the oven to keep warm,' Antonia told her, and rose as if to fetch it, but Penelope stopped her.

'No. Don't bother. I don't want any more.'
'A cup of coffee then?'
'No. Not even that.' She sat in her chair, her arms folded on the table. She smiled because she could not help smiling, because she loved them both, and was about to offer them what she considered the most precious gift in the entire world. A gift which she had offered to each of her three children and which they had, one by one, turned down.

'I have a proposition to make,' she said. 'Will you both come to Cornwall with me? Come to Cornwall and we'll spend Easter there? Together. Just the three of us.'

Podmore's Thatch,
Temple Pudley,
Gloucestershire.

April 17th, 1984

My darling Olivia,

I am writing to tell you a number of things which have happened and which are about to happen.

That last weekend, when Noel brought Antonia down, and cleared out the attic and Nancy came for Sunday lunch, we had, and I am sure you have not been told about this, a real blazer of a row. It was, inevitably, about money, and the fact that they considered I should sell my father's pictures right now, while the market is high. Their concern, they assured me, was all for myself, but I know them both too well. It is they who need the money.

When they had finally departed, I had time to think it all over, and the next morning telephoned Mr Roy Brookner of Boothby's. He came down and saw the panels, and took them away with him. He has found me a private buyer, an American, who has offered me a hundred thousand pounds for the pair. This offer I have accepted.

There are many ways I could spend this sudden windfall but, right now, I am going to do what I have been wanting to do for a long time, and that is go back to Cornwall. As neither you nor Noel nor Nancy felt that you had the time or the desire to come with me, I have invited Antonia and Danus. Danus was at first hesitant about accepting my invitation. It did come rather out of the blue, and I think he was embarrassed, and perhaps felt I was being, in some way, sorry for him and a little patronising. I think he is a very proud young man. But I finally persuaded him that he would be doing us a kindness; we need a strong male to deal with luggage, porters, and head waiters. In the end, he agreed to speak to his employer and see if he could get the week off. This he has done, and we leave tomorrow morning, Antonia and myself sharing the driving. We shall not stay with Doris as there is not space in her little house for three visitors, so I have booked in at the Sands Hotel, and we shall be there over Easter.

I chose the Sands because I remember it as being unpretentious and homely. When I was a child, whole families used to come from London for the summer holidays. They came year after year, and brought their children and their chauffeurs and their nannies and their dogs, and every summer the management organised a little tennis tournament, and there was a party in the evening, when the grown-ups fox-trotted in dinner jackets and the children danced Sir Roger de Coverley and were given balloons. During the war, it was turned into a hospital and filled with poor wounded boys tucked up in scarlet blankets; where they were taught how to make baskets by pretty VADs in white caps.

But when I told Danus where we were going, he looked a little astonished. Apparently, the Sands is now very up-market and grand, and I think he was concerned, in the nicest possible sort of way, about the expense. But, of course, it doesn't matter what it costs. This is the first time in my life I have actually written that sentence. It gives me the most extraordinary sensation, and I feel as though I had suddenly become a totally different person. I do not object to this in the very least, and feel as excited as a child.

Yesterday, Antonia and I drove to Cheltenham and shopped. This new Penelope took over, and you would not have recognised your frugal mother, but I think would have approved. We went quite mad. Bought dresses for Antonia, and a delicious cream satin shirt, and jeans and cotton pullovers and a yellow oilskin and four pairs of shoes. Then she disappeared into a beauty shop to have her fringe trimmed, and I went off on my own and spent money on delightful, unnecessary necessities for my holiday. A new pair of canvas lace-ups, some talcum powder, a huge bottle of scent. Camera films and face cream, and a cashmere pullover the colour of violets. I bought a thermos flask, and a tartan rug (for picnics), and a pile of paperbacks to keep myself amused (including *The Sun Also Rises* – it's years since I read Hemingway). I bought a book on British birds, and another lovely one full of maps.

When I had completed this orgy of extravagance, I called in at the bank, then treated myself to a cup of coffee, and went to collect Antonia. I found her looking quite unfamiliar and very beautiful. Not only had she had her hair trimmed, but her eyelashes dyed. It totally changes her appearance. At first she was a bit embarrassed about it, but by now has got used to the idea and can be observed, only every now and then, taking admiring glances at herself in the mirror. I have not been so happy for a long time.

Mrs Plackett comes in tomorrow and will clean and lock up the house after we have left. We return on Wednesday, 25th.

There is just one more thing. *The Shell Seekers* has gone. I have given it, as a memorial to my father, to the Art Gallery in Porthkerris which Papa helped to found. In a strange way, I need it no longer, and I like to think that others – ordinary people – will be able to share the pleasure and delight that it has always given me. Mr Brookner arranged for its transport to the West Country, and a van duly arrived and carted it away. The gap over the fireplace is very apparent, but one day I shall fill it with something else. Meantime, I look forward to seeing it hanging, for all the world to see, in its new home.

I have not written to Noel nor Nancy. They will find out about everything sooner or later, and will probably be extremely resentful and annoyed, but I can't help that. I have given them all I can, and

they always want more. Perhaps now they will stop pestering me, and
get on with their own lives.

But you, I believe, will understand.

My love, as always,
Mumma

Nancy was feeling a little uncomfortable with herself. The reason for this
was because she had not been in touch with her mother since that
abortive Sunday when the terrible row over the paintings had blown up,
and Penelope had rounded on the pair of them and given her and Noel
such a distasteful and distressing piece of her mind.

It wasn't that Nancy felt guilty. On the contrary, she had been deeply
hurt. Mother had come out with accusations that could never be unsaid,
and Nancy had allowed the days to pass in frigid non-communication
because she expected Penelope to make the first move. To telephone, if
not to apologise, then to chat, to ask after the children, perhaps to
suggest a meeting. To prove to Nancy that all was forgotten and relations
between them once more on a normal footing.

Nothing, however, happened. No such call came through. At first
Nancy remained resolutely offended, nursing her umbrage. She resented
the sensation that she had been put in the doghouse. She had, after all,
done nothing wrong. Simply spoken up, concerned for the good of them
all.

But gradually, she became worried. It was not like Mother to sulk.
Was it possible that she was unwell? She had worked herself up into a
terrible state, and that surely could not be good for an elderly woman
who had suffered a heart attack. Had this had its repercussions? She
quailed at the thought, pushed the niggle of anxiety out of her mind.
Surely not. Surely, if so, Antonia would have been in touch. She
was young and probably irresponsible, but even she could not be as
irresponsible as that.

Concern became an obsession that Nancy could not get out of her
mind. During the last day or so, she had actually gone to the telephone
more than once and picked it up, intending to dial the Podmore's Thatch
number, only to replace the receiver because she couldn't think what she
was going to say, and could dream up no reason for saying it. And then
inspiration struck. Easter loomed. She would invite Mother and Antonia
over to the Old Vicarage for Easter lunch. This would involve no loss
of face, and over roast lamb and new potatoes, they would all become
reconciled.

She was engaged in the not very arduous task of dusting the dining

room when this brilliant plan occurred to her. She set down the duster
and the tin of polish and went straight to the kitchen and the telephone.
She dialled the number and waited, smiling socially, all ready to put that
smile into her voice. She heard the ringing sound. It was not answered.
Her smile faded. She waited for a long time. Finally, feeling totally let
down, she replaced the receiver.

She rang again at three in the afternoon and again at six. She rang
Faults, and asked the man to check the line. 'It's ringing out,' he told
her.

'I know it's ringing out. I've been listening to it ringing out all day.
There must be something wrong.'

'Are you certain the person you are calling is at home?'

'Of course she's at home. She's my mother. She's always at home.'

'If you leave it with me, I'll check and ring you back.'

'Thank you.'

She waited. He rang back. There was nothing wrong with the line.
Mother, it seemed, was simply not there.

By now Nancy was not so much worried as thoroughly annoyed. She
rang Olivia in London.

'Olivia.'

'Hello.'

'Nancy here . . .'

'Yes. I guessed.'

'Olivia, I've been trying to get hold of Mother, and there's no reply
from Podmore's Thatch. Have you any idea what can have happened?'

'Of course there's no reply. She's gone to Cornwall.'

'To *Cornwall*!'

'Yes. She's gone off for Easter. Taken the car, along with Antonia and
Danus.'

'Antonia and *Danus*?'

'Don't sound so horrified.' Olivia's voice was filled with amusement.
'Why shouldn't she? She's been wanting to go for months, and none of
us would go with her, so she's taken them for company.'

'But surely they're not all staying with Doris Penberth? There wouldn't
be room.'

'Oh, no, not with Doris. They're staying at the Sands.'

'*The Sands*?'

'Oh, Nancy, do stop repeating everything I say.'

'But the Sands is the best. One of the best hotels in the country. It's
written up everywhere. It costs the *earth*.'

'But haven't you heard? Mother's got the earth. She's sold the panels
to a millionaire American for a hundred thousand pounds.'

Nancy wondered if she was going to be sick, or faint. Probably faint. She could feel the blood pour from her cheeks. Her knees trembled. She reached for a chair.

'A hundred thousand pounds. It's not possible. They couldn't be worth that. Nothing's worth a hundred thousand pounds.'

'Nothing's worth anything unless somebody wants it. There's the rarity value as well. I tried to explain all this to you that day we lunched at Kettners. Lawrence Sterns seldom come on the market, and this American, whoever he is, probably wants those panels more than anything else in the world. And doesn't care what he pays for them. Luckily for Mumma. I couldn't be more pleased for her.'

But Nancy's mind still raced. A hundred thousand pounds. 'When did all this happen?' she managed at last.

'Oh, I don't know. Sometime quite recently.'

'How do *you* know about it?'

'She wrote me a long letter and told me everything. Told me about the row she'd had with you and Noel. You are dreadful. I've told you over and over to leave her alone, but you wouldn't. Just nagged incessantly until she couldn't stand it another moment. I guess that's why she finally decided to sell the panels. Probably realised that that was the only way to stop your endless needling.'

'That's totally unfair.'

'Oh, Nancy, stop pretending to me and stop pretending to yourself.'

'They've got a terrible hold on her.'

'Who have?'

'Danus and Antonia. You should never have sent the girl to live with Mother. And I don't trust Danus further than I could throw him.'

'Neither does Noel.'

'Doesn't that worry you?'

'Not in the least. I have great faith in Mumma's judgement.'

'And what about the money she's squandering on them? Right now. Living in luxury at the Sands Hotel. With her gardener.'

'Why shouldn't she squander the money? It's hers. And why shouldn't she squander it on herself and two young people she happens to be fond of? Like I said, she asked us all to go with her and none of us would. We had our chance and we turned it down. We have no one to blame but ourselves.'

'When I was invited, the Sands Hotel was never mentioned. It was going to be bed-and-breakfast in Doris Penberth's spare bedroom.'

'Is that what stopped you from accepting? The thought of pigging it with Doris? Would you have gone if the Sands Hotel had been dangled in front of your nose, like a carrot before a donkey?'

'You have no right to say that.'

'I have every right. I'm your sister, God help me. And there's another thing you should know. Mumma's gone to Porthkerris because she's been yearning to for ages; but also, she's gone to see *The Shell Seekers*. She's donated it to the Art Gallery there, in memory of her father, and she wants to look at it, hanging in its new home.'

'Donated it?' For a moment, Nancy thought she had misheard, or certainly misunderstood her sister. 'You mean, she's *given* it away?'

'Just that.'

'But it's probably worth thousands. Hundreds of thousands.'

'I'm sure everybody concerned appreciates that.'

*The Shell Seekers*. Gone. The sense of injustice perpetrated upon her and her family left Nancy cold with rage. 'She always told us,' she said bitterly, 'that she couldn't live without that picture. That it was part of her life.'

'It was. For years, it was. But I think now that she feels she can do without it. She wants to share it. She wants other people to enjoy it.'

Olivia, it was quite obvious, was on Mother's side.

'And what about us? What about her family? Her grandchildren. Noel. Does Noel know about this?'

'I've no idea. I don't suppose so. I haven't seen nor heard of him since he took Antonia down to Podmore's Thatch.'

'I shall tell him.' It was a threat.

'Do that,' said Olivia, and rang off.

Nancy slammed down the receiver. Damn Olivia. Damn her. She lifted the instrument once more and with shaking hands dialled Noel's number. She could not remember when she had been so upset.

'Noel Keeling.'

'Nancy here.' She spoke grimly, feeling important, calling a family conference.

'Hi.' He did not sound enthusiastic.

'I've just been speaking to Olivia. I tried to ring Mother, but there was no reply, so I called Olivia to see if she knew what was going on. She did know, because Mother had written her a letter. She wrote to Olivia, but she never bothered to get in touch with either you or me.'

'I don't know what you're talking about.'

'Mother's gone to Cornwall, and she's taken Danus and Antonia with her.'

'Good God.'

'And they're staying at the Sands Hotel.'

That caught his attention.

ᐧ ᔩ

'The Sands? I thought she was going to stay with Doris. And how can she afford the Sands? It's one of the most bloody expensive hotels in the country.'

'I can tell you how. Mother's sold the panels. For a hundred thousand pounds. Without, I may say, discussing it with any of us. A hundred thousand pounds, Noel. Which, by the looks of it, she intends to squander. And that's not all. She's given *The Shell Seekers* away. Gifted the picture to the Art Gallery in Porthkerris, if you please. Simply handed it over, and heaven knows what it must be worth. I think she must be mad. I don't believe she knows what she's doing. I told Olivia what I believe. That those two young people, Antonia and Danus, have got a sinister hold on her. It happens, you know. You read about such things in the papers. It's criminal. It shouldn't be allowed. There must be something we can do to stop it. Noel. Noel? Are you still there?'

'Yes.'

'What do you say?'

Noel said 'Shit' and rang off.

The Sands Hotel,
Porthkerris,
Cornwall.

Thursday, 19th April.

Darling Olivia,

Well, here we all are, and we've been here for a whole day. I cannot tell you how beautiful it all is. The weather is like high summer and there are flowers everywhere. And palm trees, and little cobbled streets, and the sea is the most wonderful blue. A greener blue than the Mediterranean, and then a very dark blue out on the horizon. It is like Ibiza, only better, because everything is green and lush, and in the evenings, when the sun has gone down, it's all damp and smells leafy.

We had a wonderful trip down. I drove most of the way and then Penelope a bit, but Danus didn't because he doesn't drive. Once we'd got onto the motorway it didn't take any time at all, and your mother couldn't believe how fast we were going. When we got to Devon, we took the old road over Dartmoor, and ate our picnic on the top of a rock, with views in all directions, and there were small shaggy ponies who were pleased to consume the crusts of our sandwiches.

The hotel is out of this world. I've never stayed in an hotel before and I don't think Penelope has either, so it's all new experience. She kept telling us how comfortable and cosy it was all going to be, but when we finally came up the drive (between banks of hydrangeas) it was instantly obvious that we'd let ourselves in for a life of luxury. A Rolls and three Mercedes parked in the forecourt, and a uniformed porter to deal with our luggage. Danus calls it our matched luggage, because each of our suitcases is just as battered and disreputable as the others.

Penelope, however, has taken everything in her stride. By everything, I mean enormously thick carpets, swimming pools, Jacuzzis, private bathrooms, televisions by our beds, huge bowls of fresh fruit, and flowers everywhere. We have clean sheets and towels every day. Our rooms are all in the same corridor, and have adjoining balconies, looking out over the gardens and the sea. From time to time, we step out onto them and converse with each other. Just like Noel Coward's *Private Lives*.

As for the dining room, it is like being taken out for dinner in the most expensive restaurant in London. I am sure I shall become quite blasé about oysters, lobsters, fresh strawberries, thick Cornish cream, and fillet steaks. It is splendid having Danus with us, because he gives much thought as to what we are to drink with this delicious food. He seems to know an awful lot about wines, but he never drinks himself. I don't know why, any more than I don't know why he doesn't drive a car.

There is so much to do. This morning we went down into the town, and our first port of call was Carn Cottage, where your mother used to live. But it was sad because, like so many houses down here, it has been turned into an hotel, the lovely stone wall demolished, and most of the garden bulldozed into a car park. But we went into what remains of the garden and the hotel lady brought us out a cup of coffee. And Penelope told us about how it used to be, and how her mother had planted all the old roses, and the wistaria, and then she told us about her being killed in London during the Blitz. I never knew about this. When she told us, I wanted to cry, but I didn't, I just hugged her, because her eyes went all bright with tears, and somehow I couldn't think of anything else to do.

After Carn Cottage we went on, deep into the heart of the little town, to find the Art Gallery and to see *The Shell Seekers*. The Gallery is not large, but a particularly attractive one, with whitewashed walls and a huge northern skylight. They have hung *The Shell Seekers* in quite the most important position and it looks utterly at home, bathed in the cold brilliant light of Porthkerris, where it was originally conceived. The Art Gallery lady was elderly, and I don't think she remembered Penelope, but she certainly knew who she was and made a great fuss of her. Apart from this, there don't seem to be a great many people still alive whom she knew and remembers from the old days. Except Doris, of course. She is going to see Doris tomorrow afternoon, and have tea with her. She is much looking forward to this, and seems excited at the prospect. And on Saturday, we are going out on the Land's End road, and taking a picnic to the cliffs at Penjizal. The hotel provides picnics in fancy cardboard boxes, with real knives and forks, but Penelope does not consider these proper picnics, so we shall stop off on the way and buy fresh bread and butter and pâté and tomatoes and fresh fruit and a bottle of wine. If it goes on being as warm as this, I expect that Danus and I shall swim.

And then on Monday, Danus and I are going to go over to the south coast, to Manaccan, where a man called Everard Ashley is running a nursery garden. Danus was at Horticultural College with this man, and he wants to go and look at the nursery, and maybe get a few tips. Because, in the fullness of time, this is what he wants to do, but it's difficult because you need a lot of capital for such a venture, and he hasn't got any. Never mind, it's always worth picking other people's brains, and it'll be fun to go over and see the other side of this magical county.

From all this, you will gather that I am very happy. I couldn't have believed that, so soon after Cosmo's death, I could be happy again. I hope it's not wrong. I don't think it is, because it feels nothing but right.

Thank you for everything. For being so endlessly kind and patient and for fixing for me to stay at Podmore's Thatch. Because if you hadn't done that, I wouldn't be here, living the life of Riley with the two people I like absolutely most in the whole world. Except, of course, yourself.

My love,
Antonia

Her children, Nancy, Olivia and Noel, had . . . Penelope was forced to admit . . . been maddeningly right. Porthkerris, to all intents and purposes, was changed. Carn Cottage was not the only house with a bulldozed garden, an hotel sign over the gate, and striped umbrellas set up on the newly constructed terrace. The old White Caps Hotel had been hideously enlarged and converted into holiday flats, and the harbour road, where once the artists had lived and worked, had become a fairground of amusement arcades, discos, fast-food restaurants, and souvenir shops. In the harbour itself, most of the fishing boats were gone. Now only one or two remained, and the empty moorings were filled by pleasure craft offering, for enormously inflated sums of money, day trips to see the seals, with a few queasy hours of mackerel fishing thrown in as an added inducement.

And yet, astonishingly enough, it was not so changed. Now, in the spring, the town was still comparatively empty, for the first flood of tourists would not arrive until Whitsun. There was time to dawdle, space to stand and look. And nothing could ever alter that marvellous blue, silken sweep of the bay, nor the curve of the headland, nor the baffling muddle of streets and slate-roofed houses tumbling down the hill to the water's edge. The gulls still filled the sky with their screams, the air still smelled of salty wind and privet and escallonia, and the narrow lanes of the old town, maze-like, were as confusing as they had ever been.

Penelope walked to visit Doris. It was pleasant to be alone. The company of Danus and Antonia had proved nothing but delight, but still, for a little while, solitude was welcome. In the sunlight of the warm afternoon, she made her way down through the aromatic gardens of the hotel, onto the road above the beach, past terraces of Victorian houses, and descended into the town.

She searched for a florist's. The one she remembered was now a dress shop, filled with the sort of clothes that tourists, mad to spend their money, mistakenly buy. Elasticated sun tops in Day-glo pink, enormous T-shirts emblazoned with the features of pop stars, and crotch-hugging jeans that caused one pain just to look at them. She found a flower shop at last, in a crooked corner where, a long time ago, an old cobbler in a leather apron had put new soles on their shoes, and charged them one and threepence for his work. She went in and bought a huge bouquet for Doris. Not anemones or daffodils, but more exotic blooms. Carnations and iris and tulips and freesias, an armful of them, wrapped in crisp, pale-blue tissue paper. A little farther on down the street, she turned into an off-licence and bought, for Ernie, a bottle of the Famous Grouse whisky. Laden with these purchases, she continued on her way, deep into Downalong, where the lanes were so narrow that there was no space for pavements, and the whitewashed houses crowded in on either side, with steep granite steps climbing to brightly painted front doors.

The Penberth house was tucked into the very heart of this labyrinth. Here Ernie had lived with his mother and father, and down these alleys Doris and Penelope and Nancy had come on wartime winter afternoons, to call on old Mrs Penberth, and be given saffron cakes and strong tea out of a pink teapot.

Now, remembering, it seemed extraordinary to Penelope how long it had taken her to realise that Ernie, in his shy and silent way, was courting Doris. And yet, perhaps, not so extraordinary. He was a man of few words, and his presence at Carn Cottage, saying little, and working like ten men, became, quite naturally, something that they all took for granted. Oh, *Ernie will do it* was the cry when something really horrible had to be accomplished, like a hen slaughtered, or the gutters cleaned out. And he always did. Nobody ever thought of him as an eligible man; he was just one of the family, undemanding, uncomplaining, and perpetually good-natured.

It was not until the autumn of 1944 that the penny finally dropped. Penelope walked into the kitchen at Carn Cottage one morning to find Doris and Ernie having a cup of tea together. They sat at the kitchen table, and in the middle of the table stood a blue and white jug crammed with dahlias.

She surveyed the scene. 'Ernie, I didn't know you were here . . .'

He was embarrassed. 'Just dropped in.' He pushed his cup and saucer away and got to his feet.

She looked at the flowers. Dahlias, with all the work they entailed, were no longer grown at Carn Cottage. 'Where did these come from?'

Ernie pushed back his cap and scratched his head. 'My dad grew them in his allotment. Brought a few up for . . . for you.'

'I've never seen such gorgeous ones. They're enormous.'

'Yes.' Ernie put his cap back on, and shifted his feet. 'Got a bit of kindling to chop.'

He moved towards the door.

Doris said, 'Thanks for the flowers.'

He turned, nodded. 'Nice cup of tea,' he told her.

He went. Moments later, from the backyard, could be heard sounds of chopping.

Penelope sat down at the table. She looked at the flowers. She looked at Doris, though Doris would not meet her eye. Penelope said, 'I have a funny feeling that I have disturbed something.'

'Like what?'

'I don't know. You tell me.'

'Nothing to tell.'

'He didn't bring these flowers for *us*, did he? He brought them for you.'

Doris tossed her head. 'What's it matter who he brought them for?'

It was then that realisation dawned and Penelope could not imagine why she had not latched on before. 'Doris, I think Ernie fancies you.'

Doris was instantly scathing. 'Ernie Penberth? Tell us another.'

But Penelope refused to be put off. 'Has he ever said anything to you?'

'Never says much to anyone, does he?'

'You like him, though?'

'Nothing there to dislike.'

Her manner was too offhand to be convincing. Something was up. 'He's courting you.'

'Courting?' Doris sprang to her feet, collecting cups and saucers with the maximum of clatter. 'He wouldn't know how to court a fly.' She dumped the china onto the draining board and turned on the taps. 'Besides,' she added, over the rush of water, 'he's such a funny-looking chap.'

'You'd never find a nicer – '

'And I've no intention of ending my days with a man who's not even as tall as me.'

'Just because he's not another Gary Cooper, that's no reason to turn up your nose. And I think he's nice-looking. I like his black hair and his dark eyes.'

Doris turned off the taps and swung round, leaning against the sink and folding her arms. 'But he never *says* anything, does he?'

'With you talking non-stop most of the time, he can scarcely get a word in edgeways. Anyway, actions speak louder than words. Look at him, bringing you flowers.' She thought back. 'And he never stops doing things for you. Mending the washing line, bringing you little treats from under his father's greengrocery counter.'

'So what?' Doris frowned suspiciously. 'You trying to get me married off to Ernie Penberth? Trying to get rid of me or something?'

'I am simply,' said Penelope in a sanctimonious fashion, 'thinking of your future happiness.'

'In a pig's eye. Well, you can think again. The day we heard Sophie'd been killed, I promised myself I wasn't moving from here until this bloody war is over. And when Richard went . . . well, it just made me more determined than ever. I don't know what you're going to do . . . go back to that Ambrose or never go back, but the war's ending soon, and you're going to have to make up your mind, and I'm going to be around to see you through it, whatever you decide. And if you go back to him, then who's going to look after your dad? I'll tell you right now. I am. So we'll have no more talk about Ernie Penberth, thank you very much.'

She kept her word. She wouldn't marry Ernie, because she wouldn't leave Papa. It wasn't until after the old man died that she found herself free at last to think about herself and her sons and her own future. She made her decision. Within two months, she had become Mrs Ernie Penberth, and she left Carn Cottage for good. Ernie's father had recently died, and old Mrs Penberth moved out of the house and went to live with her sister, so that Doris and Ernie would have a place to themselves. Ernie took over the family greengrocery business, and he took over Doris' sons as well, but he and Doris never had any children of their own.

And now . . . Penelope paused, looking about her and getting her bearings. She was nearly at her destination. The North Beach was close. She could feel the tug of the wind, and smell its salty tang. Rounding a final corner, she started down a steep hill, at the bottom of which stood the white cottage, set back from the street and fronted by a cobbled yard. Here a string of washing flapped in the breeze, and pots and containers, set all about, were bright with daffodils and crocus and blue grape hyacinths and trailing greenery. The front door was painted blue, and she went across the cobbles, ducking beneath the washing line, and raised her fist to knock upon it. But before she could do this, it was flung open and there stood Doris.

Doris. Dashing and dressy; pretty and bright-eyed as ever, no fatter, no thinner. Her hair was silver-white, short and curly; there were lines on her face, of course, but her smile hadn't altered and neither had her voice.

'I've been waiting for you. Watching from the kitchen window.' She might have arrived that very day, straight from Hackney. 'What took you so long? Forty years, I've been waiting for this.' Doris. With lipstick and earrings, and a scarlet cardigan over a frilled white blouse. 'Oh for God's sake, don't just stand there on the doorstep, come along in.'

Penelope went, stepping straight into the tiny kitchen. She put the flowers and the bag containing the whisky bottle down on the kitchen table, and Doris shut the door behind them. She turned. They faced each other, smiling like idiots, lost for words. And then the smiles turned to laughter, and they fell into each other's arms, hugging and holding like a pair of reunited schoolgirls.

Still laughing, still wordless, they drew apart. It was Doris who spoke first. 'Penelope, I can't believe it. I thought perhaps I wouldn't know you. But you're just as tall and long-legged and lovely as ever. I was so afraid you'd be different, but you're not . . .'

'Of course I'm different. I'm grey-haired and elderly.'

'If you're grey-haired and elderly, then I've got one foot in the grave. Pushing seventy, I am. Least, that's what Ernie's always telling me when I get a bit above myself.'

'Where is Ernie?'

'Thought we'd like to be on our own for a bit. Said he couldn't stand it. Taken himself off to his allotment. It's his life-saver since he retired from the greengrocery business. I said to him, take you away from carrots

and turnips and you're like a man suffering from withdrawal symptoms.'
She screamed with the old noisy familiar mirth.

Penelope said, 'I've brought you some flowers.'

'Oh, they're beautiful. You shouldn't have . . . Look, I'll put them in
a jug, you go through to the sitting room and make yourself comfortable.
I've got the kettle on, too, thought you'd be ready for a cup of tea . . .'

The sitting room lay beyond the kitchen, through an open door. Going
through was a little like stepping back into the past, for all was cosy and
cluttered, much as Penelope remembered it from old Mrs Penberth's day,
and the old lady's treasures were yet in evidence. She saw the lustre china
in the glass-fronted cabinet, the Staffordshire dogs on either side of the
fireplace, the lumpy sofas and armchairs with lace-edged antimacassars.
But there were changes too. The huge television set was shiningly new,
as were the brilliantly patterned chintz curtains; and over the mantelpiece,
where once a much-enlarged sepia photograph of old Mrs Penberth's
soldier brother, killed in the First World War, had held pride of place,
now hung the portrait of Sophie, painted by Charles Rainier, which
Penelope had given to Doris after Lawrence Stern's funeral.

'You can't give me this,' Doris had said.

'Why not?'

'Your mother's picture?'

'I want you to have it.'

'But why me?'

'Because you loved Sophie as much as any of us. And you loved Papa
too, and took care of him for me. No daughter could have done more.'

'It's too good of you. It's too much.'

'It's not enough! But it's all I've got to give you.'

She stood now, in the middle of the room, and looked at the portrait,
and thought that after forty years, it had lost none of its appeal and
charm and gaiety. Sophie at twenty-five, with her slanted eyes and her
enchanting smile and her gamine crop of hair, and a scarlet silk-fringed
scarf knotted casually about her sun-browned shoulders.

'Pleased to see it again?' asked Doris.

Penelope turned as she came through the door, bearing the jug of
loosely arranged flowers, which she placed, with some care, in the middle
of a table.

'Yes. I'd forgotten how charming it was.'

'Bet you wish you'd never parted with it.'

'No. It's just nice to see it again.'

'Gives this place a touch of class, doesn't it? It's been ever so admired.
I've even been offered a fortune for it, but I wouldn't sell. I wouldn't let
that picture go for all the tea in China. Now come on, let's sit down and

make ourselves comfortable and get chatting before that old Ernie comes back. I wish you were here with me, I've asked you often enough. Are you really staying at the Sands? With all those millionaires! What's happened? Have you won the pools or something?'

Penelope explained her changed circumstances. She told Doris about the gradual, miraculous re-appreciation of Lawrence Stern's work on the world art market; told her about Roy Brookner, and the offer for the panels.

Doris was dumbfounded. 'A hundred thousand for those two little pictures! It's like nothing I've ever heard. Oh, Penelope, I am pleased for you.'

'And I've given *The Shell Seekers* to the Porthkerris gallery.'

'I know. I read all about it in the local paper, and then Ernie and I went along and had a look for ourselves. Seemed funny seeing that picture there. Brought back ever such a lot of memories. But won't you miss it?'

'A bit, I suppose. But life has to go on. We're all getting older. Time to put our houses in order.'

'You can say that again. And talking of life going on, what do you think of Porthkerris! Bet you didn't recognise the old place. We never know what the folk are going to do next, though heaven knows the developers had their way for a year or two after the war. The old cinema's a supermarket now . . . I expect you noticed. And your father's studio was demolished and a block of holiday flats built right there, looking out over the North Beach. And we had a few years of hippies – that was unsavoury, I can tell you. Sleeping on the beach, and peeing any place they fancied. It was disgusting.'

Penelope laughed. 'And the old White Caps is a block of flats, too. And as for Carn Cottage . . .'

'Didn't it make you *weep*? Your mother's lovely garden. I should have written to warn you how things were.'

'I'm glad you didn't. Anyway, it doesn't matter. Somehow, it doesn't matter any more.'

'I should think not, living in luxury up at the Sands! Remember when it was a hospital? You wouldn't have gone near the place unless you had two broken legs.'

'Doris, it's not just because I'm feeling rich I'm staying at the Sands and not with you. It's because I've brought a couple of young friends down here with me, and I knew you wouldn't have had space for all of us.'

'Of course. Who are they, these friends?'

'The girl's called Antonia. Her father's just died, and she's living with me just now. And the young man is called Danus. He helps me in the garden in Gloucestershire. You'll meet them. They think it's too much for an old lady to walk back up the hill, so they said they would come and fetch me in the car.'

'That'll be nice. But I wish you'd brought Nancy. I'd love to see my Nancy again. And why didn't you come back to Porthkerris before? We can't be expected to fill in forty years in just a couple of hours . . .'

However, they made a fairly good stab at it, scarcely drawing breath, asking questions, answering them, catching up on children and grandchildren.

'Clark married a girl in Bristol and he's got two kiddies . . . here they are on the mantelpiece; that's Sandra and that's Kevin. She's ever such a bright little girl. And these are Ronald's youngsters . . . he lives in Plymouth. His father-in-law runs a furniture factory and he's taken Ron into the business . . . they come down for summer holidays, but they have to put up in a bed-and-breakfast up the road, because there's not space for them here. Now tell me about Nancy. What a little love she was.'

And then it was Penelope's turn, but of course she'd forgotten to bring any photographs. She told Doris about Melanie and Rupert and, with some effort, managed to make them sound attractive.

'Live near you, do they? Are you able to see them?'

'They're about twenty miles away.'

'Oh, that's too far, isn't it? But you like living in the country? Better than London? I wasn't half horrified when you wrote and told me about Ambrose walking out on you like that. What a thing to do. But then, he was always a useless sort of a chap. Nice-looking, of course, but I never felt he really fitted in. Even so, walking out on you! Selfish bugger. Men never think of anyone but themselves. That's what I say to Ernie when he leaves his dirty socks on the bathroom floor.'

And then, with husbands and families safely disposed of, they began to remember, recalling the long years of war through which they had lived together, sharing not only the sorrows and the fears and the tedious boredom but, as well, the bizarre and ludicrous happenings which, in retrospect, could be nothing but hysterically funny.

Colonel Trubshot, stalking the town in his tin hat and his ARP armband, missing his way in the black-out and falling over the harbour wall and into the sea. Miss Preedy giving a Red Cross lecture to a lot of uninterested ladies and getting herself tangled up in her own bandages. General Watson-Grant drilling the Home Guard on the school playground, and old Willie Chirgwin spearing his big toe with a bayonet and having to be carted off to hospital in an ambulance.

'And going to the cinema,' Doris reminded Penelope, wiping tears of laughter from her cheeks. 'Remember going to the cinema? Twice a week we used to go and never miss a single show. Remember Charles Boyer in *Hold Back the Dawn*? There wasn't a dry eye in the house. I went through three handkerchiefs and I was still howling when I came out.'

'It was lovely, wasn't it? And I suppose there wasn't much else to do. Except listen to *Workers' Playtime* on the wireless and Mr Churchill injecting us with doses of moral courage from time to time.'

'The best was Carmen Miranda. I never missed a Carmen Miranda film.' Doris sprang to her feet and placed a hand, fingers spread, upon her hip. 'Ay-ay-ay-ay-aye, I love you verry much. Ay-ay-ay-ay-aye, I think you're grrrand . . .'

The door slammed and Ernie walked in. Doris, finding this interruption even funnier than her own act, collapsed backwards onto the sofa and lay there, weeping and incapable with mirth.

Ernie, embarrassed, looked from one face to the other. 'What's up with you two?' he asked, and Penelope, realising that his wife was beyond answering his question, pulled herself together, got up out of her chair and went to greet him.

'Oh, Ernie . . .' She wiped her eyes, subdued her hopeless giggles. 'I am sorry. What a stupid pair we are. We've been remembering things and laughing so much. Please forgive us.' Ernie seemed even smaller than ever, and older too, and his black hair had turned frosty white. He wore an old guernsey and he had taken off his working boots and put on his carpet slippers. His hand in hers felt rough and horny as it always had, and she was so pleased to see him, she wanted to embrace him but refrained from doing so, knowing that it would only cause him even more embarrassment. 'How are you? How splendid it is to see you again.'

'Good to see you too.' They shook hands solemnly. His eyes went back to his wife, by now sitting up, blowing her nose and more or less in charge of herself again. 'Heard that noise going on, I thought someone was killing the cat. Had tea, have you?'

'No, we haven't had tea. We haven't had time to have tea. We've been talking too much.'

'The kettle just about boiled itself dry. I filled it up when I came in.'

'Oh, God, I'm sorry. I forgot.' Doris got to her feet. 'I'll go and make a pot of tea now. Penelope's brought you a bottle of whisky, Ernie.'

'Lovely. Thank you very much.' He pushed back the cuff of his guernsey and looked at his large workman-like watch. 'Half past five.' He glanced up, a rare twinkle in his eye. 'Why don't we skip tea and go straight onto the whisky?'

'Ernie Penberth! You old toper! What a suggestion.'

'I think,' said Penelope firmly, 'that it's an extremely good one. After all, we haven't been together for forty years. If we don't celebrate now, then when are we going to?'

Thus the reunion turned into something of a party. The whisky loosened even Ernie's tongue, and the three of them might have continued to carouse into the evening had it not been for the eventual arrival of Danus and Antonia. Penelope had lost all sense of time, and the ring at the doorbell surprised her just as much as it did Ernie and Doris.

'Now who can that be?' asked Doris, resenting the interruption.

Penelope looked at her watch. 'Good heavens, it's six o'clock. I'd no idea it was so late. It'll be Danus and Antonia, come to fetch me . . .'

'Time goes fast when you're enjoying yourself,' Doris remarked and pulled herself out of her chair to go and answer the door. They heard her say, 'Come along in, she's all ready for you. A bit tipsy, like we all are, but none the worse for wear.' And Penelope hastily finished her drink and put the empty glass down on the table, so that they would not think that they had interrupted anything. Then they all streamed into the little room, and Ernie hauled himself to his feet, and everybody was introduced. Ernie took himself off to the kitchen and came back with another couple of glasses.

Danus scratched the back of his head and glanced about him, his eyes filled with amusement. 'I thought you were meant to be having a tea-party.'

'Oh, tea.' Doris' voice dismissed the idea of anything so tame. 'We forgot about tea. We've been talking and laughing so much, we forgot all about having tea.'

Antonia said, 'What a lovely room. This is just the sort of house I most love. And all your flowers in the little courtyard.'

'That's what I call my garden. Be nice to have a proper garden, but then, like I always say, you can't have everything.'

Antonia's eyes fell upon Sophie's portrait. 'Who's the girl in the painting?'

'That? Why, that's Penelope's mum. Can't you see the likeness?'

'She's beautiful!'

'Oh, she was lovely. There was never anyone like her. French she was . . . wasn't she, Penelope? Sounded ever so sexy the way she talked, just like Maurice Chevalier. And when she was vexed, ooh, you should have heard her. Like a little fishwife, she was.'

'She looks so young.'

'Oh, yes, she was. Years younger than Penelope's dad. Like sisters you were, weren't you, Penelope?'

Ernie, to draw attention, noisily cleared his throat. 'Like a drink, would you?' he asked Danus.

Danus grinned and shook his head. 'It's more than kind of you, and I hope you don't think I'm being unfriendly, but I don't drink.'

Ernie, for once in his life, looked totally nonplussed.

'Ill, are you?'

'No. Not ill. It just doesn't agree with me.'

Ernie was obviously much shaken. He turned, without much hope, to Antonia. 'Suppose you don't want one neither?'

She smiled. 'No. Thank you. And I'm not being unfriendly either, but I have to drive the car back up the hill and navigate all those steep corners. I'd better not.'

Ernie shook his head sadly and screwed the cap back on the bottle. The party was over. It was time to go. Penelope stood up, shook the creases out of her skirt, checked on her hairpins.

'Not off, are you?' Doris was reluctant to finish it all.

'We must go, Doris, though I don't want to in the very least. I've been here long enough.'

'Where did you leave the car?' Ernie asked Danus.

'Up at the top of the hill,' Danus told him. 'We couldn't find anywhere nearer without a double yellow line.'

'Right bugger, isn't it? Rules and regulations everywhere. I'd better walk up with you and help you get it turned. Not much room there, and you don't want to start no argument with a granite wall.'

Danus, gratefully, accepted his offer. Ernie put on his cap and changed back into his boots. Danus and Antonia said goodbye to Doris, and she said 'Pleased to have met you,' and the three of them departed together to go and collect the Volvo. Doris and Penelope were, once more, left together. But now, for some reason, the laughter had gone. A silence fell between them, as though having talked so much, they had all at once run out of things to say. Penelope felt Doris' eyes upon her, and turned her head to meet that steady regard.

Doris said, 'Where did you find him, then?'

'Danus?' She made her voice light. 'I told you. He works for me. He's my gardener.'

'Upper-class sort of gardener.'

'Yes.'

'He looks like Richard.'

'Yes.' His name was out. Spoken. She said, 'You realise he's the only person neither of us has mentioned all afternoon. We remembered everybody else, but never him.'

'Didn't seem much point. I only said his name then, because that young man's got such a look of him.'

'I know. It struck me, too, the first time I ever set eyes on him. It . . . took a little getting used to.'

'Is he anything to do with Richard?'

'No. I don't think so. He comes from Scotland. The likeness is just an extraordinary coincidence.'

'Is that why you've taken such a fancy to him?'

'Oh, Doris. You make me sound like a sad old lady with a gigolo in tow.'

'Charmed you, has he?'

'I like him very much. I like him for the way he looks and I like him for the way he is. He's gentle. Good company. He makes me laugh.'

'Bringing him here . . . to Porthkerris . . .' Doris looked anxious for her friend. ' . . . not trying to revive old memories, are you?'

'No. I asked my children to come with me. I asked each one in turn, but none of them was able or willing. Not even Nancy. I wasn't going to tell you that, but now I have. So Danus and Antonia came in their place.'

Doris did not comment on this. For a little they were silent, each occupied with her own thoughts. Then Doris said, 'I dunno. Richard being killed like that . . . it was cruel. I always found it hard to forgive God for letting that man be killed. If ever there was a man who should have lived . . . It stays with me, that day we heard. It was one of the worst things that happened during the war. And I could never get it out of my head that, when he died, he took part of you with him, and left no part of himself behind.'

'He did leave part of himself.'

'But nothing you could touch, or feel, or hold. It would have been better if you'd had a baby by him. That way, you'd have had a good excuse never to go back to Ambrose. You and Nancy and the baby could have made a good life for yourselves.'

'I often thought about that. I never did anything to stop having a baby by Richard; I just never conceived one. And Olivia was my consolation. She was the first child I had after the war, and she was Ambrose's child, but for some reason she was always special. Not different, just special.' She went on, carefully choosing her words, admitting to Doris something that she had scarcely admitted to herself, and certainly to no other living person. 'It was as though some physical part of Richard had stayed within me. Preserved, like delicious food in an icebox. And when Olivia was born, some atom, some corpuscle, some cell of Richard's became, through me, part of her.'

'But she wasn't his.'

Penelope smiled, shook her head. 'No.'

'But she felt like his.'

'Yes.'

'I can understand.'

'I knew you would. That's why I told you. And you'll understand when I tell you that I'm glad Papa's studio was demolished to make way for a block of flats, and has gone for ever. I know, now, that I'm strong enough to cope with almost anything, but I don't think I would ever have been strong enough to go back there.'

'No. I can understand that, too.'

'There's another thing. When I went back to live in London, I got in touch with his mother.'

'I wondered about that.'

'It took me a long time to pluck up the courage, but finally I did, and telephoned her. We had lunch together. It was an ordeal for both of us. She was charming, and friendly, but we had nothing to talk about except Richard, and in the end I realised it was too much for her. After that, I left her alone; never saw her again. If I had been married to Richard, I could have comforted and consoled her. As it was, I think I simply added to her personal sense of tragedy.'

Doris said nothing. From outside, from beyond the open door, they heard the sound of the Volvo, trundling cautiously down the steep and narrow street. Penelope stooped and picked up her handbag. 'That's the car. It's time for me to go.'

They went together, through the kitchen and into the sunshine of the little courtyard. They put their arms about each other, and kissed, with much affection. There were tears in Doris' eyes. 'Goodbye, Doris darling. And thank you for everything.'

Doris dashed the stupid tears away. 'Come again soon,' she told her. 'Don't wait another forty years, or we'll all be pushing up the daisies.'

'Next year. I'll come next year, on my own, and stay with you and Ernie.'

'What a time we'll have.'

The car appeared, stopped at the side of the road. Ernie clambered out of it and stood, like a footman, holding the door open, waiting for Penelope to step inside.

'Goodbye, Doris.' She turned to go, but Doris was not finished with her.

'Penelope.'

She turned back. 'Yes?'

'If he's Richard, then who's Antonia supposed to be?'

Doris was no fool. Penelope smiled. 'Myself?'

'The first time I ever came here was when I was seven years old. It was a great occasion, because Papa had bought a *car*. We'd never had one before, and this was our first expedition. It was the first of many, but I always remember that one, because I simply couldn't get over the astonishing fact that Papa actually knew how to get the engine started, and then *drive* it.'

They sat, the three of them, on the Penjizal cliffs, high above the blue Atlantic, in a grassy hollow sheltered from the breeze by a towering boulder of lichened granite. All about, studding the turfy grass, were clumps and cushions of wild primroses and the pale-blue, feathery heads of scabious. The sky was cloudless, the air filled with the thunder of rollers and the screams of the wheeling seabirds. Midday, and in April, warm as midsummer – so warm that they had spread the new tartan rug to loll upon, and found cool shade for the luncheon basket.

'What kind of a car was it?' Danus lay on the sloping turf, propped up on an elbow. He had pulled off his sweater and rolled up the sleeves of his shirt. His muscular forearms were sun-browned, his face, turned towards her, filled with amusement and interest.

'A 4½–litre Bentley,' she told him. 'It was rather old, but he couldn't afford a new car, and it became the pride of his heart.'

'How splendid. Did it have leather straps to hold down the bonnet, like a cabin trunk?'

'Exactly. And a running board, and a hood we could never get the hang of, so we never put it up even if it poured with rain.'

'A car like that would be worth a fortune nowadays. What became of it?'

'When Papa died, I gave it to Mr Grabney. I couldn't think what else to do with it. And he'd always been so kind, keeping it for us in his garage all through the war and never charging us a penny of rent. And another time . . . a really important time . . . he laid his hands on some black market petrol for me. I could never thank him enough for that.'

'Why didn't you keep it?'

'I couldn't afford to keep a car in London, and I didn't really need one. I just used to walk everywhere, pushing perambulators filled with babies and shopping. Ambrose was furious when he heard I'd given the Bentley away. It was the first thing he asked about after I got back from Papa's funeral. When I told him what I'd done, he sulked for a week.'

Danus was sympathetic. 'I'm not sure I blame him.'

'No. Poor man. He must have been dreadfully disappointed.'

Penelope sat up, to gaze out over the edge of the cliff and inspect the state of the tide. It was on the ebb, but still not fully out. When this happened, the great rock pool, which she had promised Danus and Antonia, would at last be revealed, like a huge blue jewel, glinting in the sunlight and perfect for diving and swimming. 'Another half hour,' she judged, 'and you should be able to bathe.'

She leaned back once more, propped against the bank, and rearranged her legs. She wore her old denim skirt, a cotton shirt, her new sneakers, and a battered straw gardening hat. The sun was so brilliant that she felt grateful for its speckled shade. Beside her, Antonia, who had been lying with eyes closed, apparently asleep, now shifted, rolling over onto her stomach and resting her cheek on her crossed arms. 'Tell us more, Penelope. Did you come here often?'

'Not often. It was a long way to drive, and then such a long walk from the farmhouse where we left the car. And in those days there was no cliff path. So we used to have to fight our way through gorse and brambles and bracken before we finally reached this spot. And then we always had to be certain that it was low tide so that Sophie and I could swim.'

'Didn't your father swim?'

'No. He said he was too old. He used to sit up here with his broad-brimmed hat, and his easel, and his little folding stool, and paint or draw. Having, of course, opened a bottle of wine, poured himself a glass, lighted up a cigar, and generally made himself comfortable.'

'What about winter? Did you ever come in wintertime?'

'Never. We were in London. Or Paris, or Florence. Porthkerris and Carn Cottage belonged to the summer.'

'How perfect.'

'No less perfect than your father's divine house in Ibiza.'

'I suppose so. Everything's relative, isn't it?' Antonia rolled sideways, propping her chin in her hand. 'How about you, Danus? Where did you go for your summers?'

'I hoped nobody would ask that.'

'Oh, come on. Tell us.'

'North Berwick. My parents took a house every summer there; they played golf while my brother and sister and I sat on the frigid beach with our nannie and built sand-castles in the howling wind.'

Penelope frowned. 'Your brother? I didn't know you had a brother. I thought it was just your sister and yourself.'

'Yes, I had a brother, Ian. He was the eldest of the three of us. He died of meningitis when he was fourteen.'

'Oh, my dear, what a tragedy.'

'Yes. Yes, it was. My mother and father never really got over it. He was the golden boy, bright and good-looking, and a natural games player – the son that every parent dreams of having. To me, he was a sort of god, because he knew how to do everything. When he was old enough, he played golf, too, and so, eventually, did my sister, but I was always hopeless and not even particularly interested. I used to go off on my own, on my bike, and look for birds. I found that infinitely more entertaining than struggling with the complexities of golf.'

'North Berwick doesn't sound a very nice place to go,' Antonia remarked. 'Didn't you ever go anywhere else?'

Danus laughed. 'Yes, of course. My great friend at school was called Roddy McCrae. His parents owned a croft, right up in the north of Sutherland, near Tongue. Also they had fishing rights on the Naver, and Roddy's father taught me how to cast. When I outgrew North Berwick, I spent most of my holidays with them.'

'What's a croft?' Antonia asked.

'A but and ben. A two-roomed stone farmhouse. Dead basic. No plumbing, no electricity, no telephone. The end of the world, the back of beyond, out of touch with the world. It was great.'

A silence fell. It occurred to Penelope that this was perhaps only the second time she had heard Danus talk about himself. She felt sad for him. To lose a much-loved older brother at such a tender age must have been a traumatic experience. To feel, perhaps, that he could never quite match up to that brother was worse. She waited, thinking that maybe, having broken the ice of his reserve and actually confided, he might wish to continue. But he did not. Instead, he stirred himself, stretched, and then pulled himself to his feet. 'The tide is out,' he told Antonia. 'The rock pool is waiting for us. Do you feel brave enough to swim?'


They had gone, scrambling over the cliff's rim to take the precipitous path that led down to the rocks. The pool waited still as glass, glittering and brilliantly blue. Penelope, waiting to watch them reappear, thought of her father. Remembered him with his wide-brimmed hat and his easel and his wine and his contented, concentrated solitude. One of the frustrations of her life had been the fact that she had not inherited his talent. She was not a painter, she could not even draw, but his influence had been enormously strong, and she had lived with this so long that, quite naturally, she was able to observe any prospect with his acute, all-seeing artist's eye. All was exactly as it had always been, except for the winding green ribbon of the cliff path, trodden by walkers, which dipped and climbed through the green young bracken, following the convolutions of the coast.

She gazed at the sea, trying to decide how, if she were Papa, she would endeavour to paint it. For, although it was blue, it was a blue made up of a thousand different hues. Over sand, shallow and translucent, it was jade-green, streaked with aquamarine. Over rocks and seaweed, it darkened to indigo. Far out, where a small fishing boat bucketed its way across the waves, it became a deep Prussian blue. There was little wind, but the ocean lived and breathed; swelled in from distant depths, formed waves. The sunlight, shining through these as they curved to break, transformed them to moving sculptures of green glass. And, finally, all was drowned in light, that unique suffused brilliance that had first brought the painters to Cornwall, and had driven the French Impressionists into a passion of creativity.

A perfect composition. All that was needed were human figures to provide proportion and vitality. They appeared. Far below and minimised by distance, Antonia and Danus made their slow way across the rocks towards the pool. She watched their progress. Danus carried the bathing towels. When at last they reached the flat rock that overhung the pool, he dropped them and walked to the edge of the rock. He flexed and dived, making scarcely a splash as he cleaved the water. Antonia followed. Swimming, they broke the surface of the pool into sunlit splinters. She heard their raised voices, their laughter. Other voices, other worlds. *It was good and nothing good is truly lost.* Richard's voice. *He looks like Richard.*

She had never swum with Richard, for theirs had been a wartime, winter love affair, but now, watching Danus and Antonia, she felt again, with a physical intensity that was beyond mere recall, that numbing shock of cold water. Remembered the exhilaration, the sense of wellbeing, as clearly as if her own body were still young, untouched by sickness or the passing years. And there were other pleasures, other delights. The sweet contact of hands, arms, lips, bodies. The peace of passion spent, the joy of waking to sleepy kisses and reasonless laughter . . .

Long ago, when she was very small, Papa had introduced her to the fascinating delights of a geometrical compass and a sharp pencil. She had taught herself to draw patterns, flower heads, petals and curves, but nothing had given her so much pleasure as simply describing, on a sheet of clean white paper, a circle. So fine, so precise. The pencil moving, drawing the line behind it, and finishing up, with marvellous finality, exactly where it had begun.

A ring was the accepted sign of infinity, eternity. If her own life was that carefully described pencil line, she knew all at once that the two ends were drawing close together. I have come full circle, she told herself, and wondered what had happened to all the years. It was a question which, from time to time, caused her some anxiety and left her fretting with a dreadful sense of waste. But now, it seemed, the question had become irrelevant, and so the answer, whatever it was, was no longer of any importance.

.    .    .

'Olivia.'

'Mumma! What a lovely surprise.'

'I realised I'd never wished you a happy Easter. I am sorry, but perhaps it's not too late. And I wasn't sure if I would catch you; I thought you might still be away.'

'No. I just got back this evening. I've been in the Isle of Wight.'

'Who were you staying with?'

'The Blakisons. Do you remember Charlotte? She used to be Food Editor on *Venus*, and then she left to start a family.'

'Was it fun?'

'Divine. It always is staying with them. A huge house-party. And all done with no visible effort whatsoever.'

'Was that nice American there with you?'

'Nice American? Oh, you mean Hank. No, he's back in the States.'

'I thought he was such a specially dear person.'

'Yes he was. He is. He's going to get in touch again the next time he comes over to London. But, Mumma, tell me all about you. How are things going?'

'We're having a wonderful time. Living in the lap of luxury.'

'About time too, after all these years. I had a long letter from Antonia. She sounded ecstatically happy.'

'She and Danus have been out all day. They took the car over to the south coast to see some young man with a nursery garden. They're probably back by now.'

'How's Danus behaving himself?'

'He's been an enormous success.'

'Do you still like him as much?'

'Just as much. If anything, more. But I've never known a man so reserved. Perhaps it's something to do with being Scottish.'

'Has he told you why he doesn't drink or drive?'

'No.'

'He's probably a reformed alcoholic.'

'If he is, it's his own business.'

'Tell me what you've been doing. Have you seen Doris?'

'Of course. And she's blooming. Lively as ever. And on Saturday, we spent the day out on the cliffs at Penjizal. And yesterday morning, we were all very dutiful and went to church.'

'Nice service?'

'Lovely. The Porthkerris church is particularly beautiful, and of course it was stuffed with flowers, and the pews filled with people in astonishing hats, and the music and the singing quite exceptional. We had a rather boring visiting Bishop preaching to us, but the music made up for even the tedium of his sermon. And then at the end, a full procession, and we all surged to our feet and sang "For All the Saints Who From Their Labours Rest". Coming home, Antonia and I decided it was quite one of our favourite hymns.'

Olivia laughed. 'Oh, Mumma. That, coming from you! I didn't even know you had a favourite hymn.'

'Darling, I'm not quite an atheist. I just can't help being slightly sceptical. And Easter is always particularly disturbing, with the Resurrection and the promise of after-life. I can never quite bring myself to believe it. And although I would adore to see Sophie and Papa, there are dozens of other people I can very well do without ever seeing again. And just imagine the crush! Just like being invited to the most enormous, boring cocktail party, where you spend your whole time looking for the amusing people you really want to see.'

'How about *The Shell Seekers*? Have you seen it?'

'It looks wonderful. Utterly at home. As though it had been there all its life.'

'You don't regret giving it away?'

'Not for a moment.'

'And what are you doing right now?'

'I've had a bath, and I'm lying on my bed, reading *The Sun Also Rises*, and ringing you up. After that I shall call Noel and Nancy, and then I shall dress for dinner. It's always so dreadfully grand, and there's a man in the restaurant tinkling away at a grand piano. Just like the Savoy.'

'How terribly smart. What are you wearing?'

'My caftan. It's fairly threadbare, but if you half-close your eyes, the holes don't show.'

'You'll look fantastic. When are you coming home?'

'Wednesday. We'll be back at Podmore's Thatch on Wednesday evening.'

'I'll call you there.'

'Do that, my darling. God bless you.'

''Bye, Mumma.'

She dialled Noel's number and waited for a moment or two, listening to the phone ringing out, but there was no reply. She put down the receiver. He was probably still off somewhere, in the country, on one of his long and social weekends. She picked up the instrument once more and called Nancy.

'The Old Vicarage.'

'George?'

'Yes.'

'Penelope here. Happy Easter!'

'Thank you,' said George, but he did not return her greeting.

'Is Nancy around?'

'Yes, she's somewhere. Do you want to speak to her?'

(Why else should I be ringing, you silly man?) 'If I could.'

'Hold on, and I'll fetch her.'

She waited. It was pleasant to lie there, relaxed and warm, propped by massive pillows, but Nancy took so long to come to the phone that she became impatient. What could the girl be doing? To pass the time, she picked up her book, and had even read a paragraph or two before, at last: 'Hello.'

She laid down the book. 'Nancy. Where were you? At the bottom of the garden?'

'No.'

'Did you have a good Easter?'

'Yes, thank you.'

'What did you do?'

'Nothing in particular.'

'Did you have visitors?'

'No.'

Her voice was frigid. This was Nancy at her most disagreeable, her most offended. What could have happened now? 'Nancy, what's wrong?'

'Why should anything be wrong?'

'I have no idea, but it obviously is.' Silence. 'Nancy, I think you'd better tell me.'

'I just feel . . . a little hurt and upset. That's all.'

'What about?'

'What about? You ask me, as if you don't know perfectly well what about.'

'I wouldn't ask you, if I knew.'

'Wouldn't you be hurt if you were me? I hear nothing from you for weeks. Nothing. And then when I ring Podmore's Thatch to ask you and Antonia to come and spend Easter with us, I find that you've gone. Gone to Cornwall, taking her and that gardener with you, and all without a word to either George or myself.'

So that was it. 'To be honest, Nancy, I didn't think you'd be interested.'

'It's not a question of being interested. It's a question of concern. Just taking off like that, without a word to anyone; anything could happen, and we wouldn't know where you were.'

'Olivia knew.'

'Oh, *Olivia*. Yes, of course *she* knew, and great satisfaction it gave her as well, being able to put me in the picture. I find it astonishing that you find it necessary to tell her what you're up to, and yet not a word to me.' She was now in full flood. 'Everything that happens, I seem to hear about second-hand, through Olivia. Everything you do. Everything you decide. Getting that gardener to work for you. Having Antonia to live with you, when I'd spent weeks of time and a good deal of hard cash putting advertisements into the newspaper for a housekeeper. Then selling the panels, and *giving away The Shell Seekers*. Without a word of consultation with George and myself. It's impossible to understand. I am, after all, your eldest child. If you owe me nothing else, you could consider my feelings. And then disappearing off to Cornwall like that, with Antonia and the gardener in tow. A pair of strangers. And yet when I suggested Melanie and Rupert should come, you refused to countenance the idea. Your own grandchildren! But you take a pair of strangers. About whom none of us know anything at all. They're taking advantage of you, Mother. You surely can see that. Think you're a soft touch, no doubt, though I couldn't have believed that you could be so blind. It's all so hurtful . . . so thoughtless . . .'

'Nancy . . .'

' . . . if this is how you behaved towards poor Daddy, it's no wonder he left you. It's enough to make anyone feel rejected and unwanted. Granny Keeling always said that you were the most unfeeling woman she'd ever known. We've tried to be responsible for you, George and I, but you don't make it easy for us. Going off, without a word . . . spending all that money. We all know what staying at the Sands will cost you . . . and *giving The Shell Seekers* away . . . when you know how much we all need . . . so hurtful . . .'

Stored resentments boiled over. Nancy, by now almost incoherent, at last ran out of steam. For the first time, Penelope was able to get a word in edgeways.

'Have you finished?' she asked politely. Nancy made no answer. 'May I speak now?'

'If you wish.'

'I rang you up to wish you all a Happy Easter. Not to have a row. But if you want one, you can have one. In selling the panels, I simply did what you and Noel have been urging me to do for months. I got a hundred thousand pounds for them, as Olivia probably told you, and for the first time in my life, I decided to spend a little of it on myself. You know I'd been planning to come back to Porthkerris, because I asked you to come with me. I asked Noel, and I asked Olivia too. You all had excuses. You none of you wanted to come.'

'Mother, I gave you my reasons . . .'

'Excuses,' Penelope repeated. 'I had no intention of coming on my own. I wanted cheerful company, to share my pleasure. So Antonia and Danus have come with me. I am not yet so senile that I cannot choose my own friends. And as for *The Shell Seekers*, that picture was mine. Don't ever forget that. Papa gave it to me as a wedding present, and now, with it hanging in the Art Gallery at Porthkerris, I feel I've simply handed it back to him. To him, and the thousands of ordinary people who will now be able to go and look at it, and perhaps know some of the comfort and pleasure that it's always given me.'

'You can have no idea of its worth.'

'I have a great deal more idea than you have ever had. You've lived with *The Shell Seekers* all your life, and scarcely looked at it.'

'I didn't mean that.'

'No, I know you didn't.'

'It's . . .' Nancy groped for words. 'It's as though you actually wanted to hurt us . . . as though you disliked us . . .'

'Oh, Nancy.'

' . . . and why is it always Olivia you tell things too, and never me?'

'Perhaps because you seem to find it so hard to understand anything I ever do.'

'How can I understand when you behave in such an extraordinary way, never taking me into your confidence . . . treating me like a fool . . . It was always Olivia. You always loved Olivia. When we were children, it was always Olivia, so clever and so funny. You never tried to understand me . . . if it hadn't been for Granny Keeling . . .'

She had reached the point where, awash with self-pity, she was ready to recall every long-ago wrong she imagined had been inflicted upon her. Penelope, exhausted by the conversation, suddenly realised that she could take no more. She had already taken too much, and to have to listen to the adolescent blubs of a forty-three-year-old woman was more than she could bear.

She said, 'Nancy, I think we should finish this conversation.'

' . . . I don't know what I would have done without Granny Keeling. Having her there, just made my life possible . . .'

'Goodbye, Nancy.'

' . . . because you never had any time for me . . . never gave me anything . . .' Carefully replacing the receiver, Penelope hung up on her daughter. The angry, raised voice was, mercifully, silenced. At the open windows, filmy curtains stirred in the breeze. Her heart, as always after these distressing occasions, was going jiggety-jig. She reached for her pills, took two, washed them down with water, and lay back on the downy pillows, closing her eyes. She thought about simply giving in. She felt quite drained, and for a moment more than ready to succumb to exhaustion, even tears. But she would not be upset by Nancy. She would not weep.

After a little, when her heart had settled down again, she put back the covers and got out of bed. She wore a cool and airy dressing-gown, and her long hair was loose. She went to the dressing-table and sat, eyeing, without much satisfaction, her own reflection. Then she reached for her hairbrush and began, with long, slow, and soothing strokes, to brush her hair.

*It was always Olivia. You always loved Olivia.*

That was true. From the moment she was born, and Penelope had first set eyes upon her, a tiny dark infant, with a nose too big for its plain little face, she had experienced this indescribable nearness to her. Because of Richard, Olivia was special. But that was all. She had never loved her more than Nancy and Noel. She had loved them all, her children. Loved each one the best, but for different reasons. Love, she had found, had a strange way of multiplying. Doubling, trebling itself, so that, as each child arrived, there was always more than enough to go round. And Nancy, the first-born, had had more than her share of love and attention. She thought of the small Nancy, so sturdy and engaging, staggering around the garden at Carn Cottage on her short fat legs. Chasing the hens, pushing the wheelbarrow Ernie had made for her, petted and spoiled by Doris, perpetually surrounded by loving arms and smiling faces. What had happened to that little girl? Was it really possible that Nancy had no recall whatsoever of those early days?

Sadly, it appeared that this was so.

*You never gave me anything.*

That was not true. She knew that it was not true. She had given Nancy what she had given all her children. A home, security, comfort, interest, a place to bring their friends, a stout front door to keep them safe from the outside world. She thought of the big basement in Oakley Street, smelling of garlic and herbs, and warm from the big stove and the open fire. She remembered them all, chattering like sparrows and hungry as hunters, pouring in on dark winter evenings from school; to drop their satchels, tear off their coats, and settle down to consume vast quantities of sausages, pasta, fish cakes, hot buttered toast, plum cake, and cocoa. She remembered that marvellous room at Christmas time, with the sprucy smell of the tree and Christmas cards strung everywhere, like washing, on lines of red ribbon. She thought of the summers, the French windows open to the garden beyond, the shade of the trees, the scent of tobacco plants and the wallflowers. She thought of the children who had played, screaming aimlessly, in that garden. Nancy had been one of them.

She had given Nancy all this, but she had not been able to give Nancy what she wanted (Nancy never said 'wanted,' she said 'needed'), because there had never been money enough to pay for the material possessions and lavish treats the girl craved. Party frocks, doll's perambulators, a pony, boarding school, a coming-out dance, and a London Season. A large and pretentious wedding had been the peak of her ambitions, but she had achieved this heart's desire only through the timely intervention of Dolly Keeling, who had arranged (and footed the bill for) the entire extravagant, embarrassing affair.

She laid down her brush at last. She was still enraged with Nancy, but the simple task had calmed her. Once more orderly, she felt better, stronger, in charge of herself, able to make decisions. She coiled, twisted the tail of hair, reached for her tortoiseshell pins, and drove them neatly, and with some force, into place.

Half an hour later, when Antonia came in search of her, she was back in bed. Sitting up, with pillows plumped, possessions to hand, and her book in her lap.

A tap at the door, and Antonia's voice. 'Penelope?'

'Come in.' The door opened, and Antonia's head appeared around the edge of it. 'I just came to . . .' She entered the room, closing the door behind her. 'You're in bed!' Her expression was one of the gravest concern. 'What's wrong? Are you ill?'

Penelope closed the book. 'No, not ill. Just a little tired. And I don't feel like coming down for dinner. I'm sorry. Were you waiting for me?'

'Not for long.' Antonia lowered herself onto the edge of the bed. 'We went down to the bar, but when you didn't come, Danus sent me up to see if anything was the matter.'

Antonia, she saw, was dressed for the evening. She wore a narrow black skirt over which she had belted the oversized cream satin shirt that they had, together, bought in Cheltenham. Her copper-gold hair hung, shining and clean, to her shoulders, and her face, clear-skinned as a sweet apple, was innocent of artifice. Save of course those amazingly long, black eyelashes.

'Don't you want anything to eat? Would you like me to call room service and have a tray sent up for you?'

'Perhaps. Later. But I can do that for myself.'

'I expect,' said Antonia accusingly, 'that you've been doing too much, walking too far, without Danus and me to make sure that you didn't.'

'I haven't overdone anything. I just got cross.'

'But what was there to get cross about?'

'I rang Nancy to wish her a happy Easter and received a flood of abuse in return.'

'How horrid of her. What on earth was it all about?'

'Oh, everything. She seems to think I'm senile. That I neglected her as a child and am extravagant in my old age. That I'm secretive and irresponsible and I don't know how to choose my friends. I think it's all been festering for some time, but my bringing you and Danus with me to Porthkerris proved the last straw. It all boiled over and came out on top of me.' She smiled. 'Oh well. Better out than in, as my darling Papa used to say.'

Antonia, however, remained indignant. 'How *could* she upset you so much?'

'I didn't let her upset me. I got cross instead. Much more healthy. And let's face it, there is always a funny side to every situation. I hung up on her, and imagined her storming back to George in floods of unbecoming tears, unleashing onto him all the iniquities of her feckless mother. And George, taking refuge behind *The Times*, saying nothing. He's always been the most uncommunicative of men. Why Nancy chose to marry him in the first place is beyond all comprehension. No wonder their children are so miserably unattractive. Rupert with his mannerless ways, and Melanie with her baleful glare, always chewing the ends of her pigtails.'

'I don't think you're being very kind.'

'No, I'm not. I'm being malicious. But I'm glad it's happened, because it's helped me make up my mind. I'm going to give you a present.' Her huge leather handbag stood on the bedside table. She reached for it, rummaged deep into its capacious interior. Her fingers found what they were looking for. She withdrew the worn leather jewel case. 'Here,' she said, and handed it to Antonia. 'These are for you.'

'For me?'

'Yes. I want you to have them. Take it. Open it.'

Almost reluctantly, Antonia took the jewel case. Pressed the little catch and snapped it open. Penelope watched her face. Watched her eyes widen in disbelief, her mouth drop open with amazement.

'But . . . these aren't for me.'

'They are. I am giving them to you. I want you to have them. Aunt Ethel's earrings. She left them to me when she died, and I brought them out to Ibiza that time I stayed with you all, and wore them to Cosmo and Olivia's party. Do you remember?'

'But of course I do. And you can't give them to me. I'm sure they're far too valuable.'

'No more so than our friendship. No more so than the pleasure you have brought me.'

'But they must be worth thousands.'

'I think four thousand. I could never afford the insurance for them, so I had to keep them in the bank. I picked them up that day we went to Cheltenham. And I don't suppose you'll be able to afford the insurance either, so they'll probably have to go back to the bank. Poor things, they don't have much of a life, do they? But you can wear them now, this evening. Your ears are pierced, they won't drop out. Put them on, and let's see how they look.'

But Antonia still hesitated. 'Penelope, if they're worth so much, shouldn't you keep them for Olivia or Nancy? Or your granddaughter. Perhaps Melanie should have them.'

'Olivia will want you to have the earrings, I know. They will remind her of Ibiza and Cosmo and she will agree with me that it's entirely appropriate that they should be yours. And Nancy has become so tediously greedy and materialistic that she doesn't deserve anything. And as for Melanie, I doubt that she would ever learn to appreciate their beauty. Now, put them on.'

Antonia, still looking doubtful, did so, removing them one by one from the worn velvet and slipping the fine golden wires into the lobes of her ears. She pushed back her hair.

'How do they look?'

'Perfect. Exactly what you needed to finish off that pretty outfit. Go to the mirror and see for yourself.'

Antonia did so, slipping off the bed and crossing the room to stand in front of the dressing-table. Penelope watched her reflection in the mirror, and thought she had never seen any girl look quite so sensational.

'They are totally right for you. You need to be tall to wear such lavish jewellery. And if ever you find yourself strapped for cash, you can always flog them or hock them to a pawnbroker. A nice little nest-egg for you to fall back on.'

But Antonia remained silent, struck wordless by the magnificence of the gift. Then, after a little, she turned from the mirror and came back to Penelope's bedside. She shook her head, and said, 'I'm bewildered. I can't think why you should be so kind to me.'

'One day, when you're as old as I am, I think you'll find the answer to that.'

'I'll make a deal with you. I'll wear them this evening, but tomorrow morning you may have had second thoughts, and if you have, I'll give them back.'

'I shan't have second thoughts. Now that I've seen you wear them, I

am more certain than ever that they should belong to you. Now, let's
not talk about them any more. Sit down again and tell me about your
day. Danus won't mind. He can wait another ten minutes. And I want
to hear everything. Don't you love that south coast? So different from
here, all woods and water. I spent a week there once, during the war. In
a house with a garden that sloped down to a creek. There were wild
daffodils everywhere, and kittiwakes sitting on the end of the jetty. I
sometimes wonder what's happened to that old house, and who lives
there now.' But this was all beside the point. 'Now. Where did you go?
And who did you see? And was it fun?'

'Yes, it was lovely. A lovely drive. And interesting too. We saw this
huge market garden; with glasshouses and propagating sheds and a shop
where people can come and buy plants and watering cans and things.
They grow tomatoes and early potatoes and all sorts of exotic vegetables
like mange-tout peas.'

'Who owns it?'

'Some people called Ashley. Everard Ashley was at Horticultural
College with Danus. That's why we went.'

She stopped, as though this were all there was to be said. Penelope
waited for more, but Antonia fell silent. Such reticence was unexpected.
She glanced sharply at Antonia, but she had dropped her eyes and her
hands fiddled with the empty jewel case, opening the lid and snapping
it shut again. Penelope felt the stirrings of unease. Something was awry.
Gently, she prompted. 'Where did you have lunch?'

'We had it with the Ashleys in the kitchen of their house.'

Pleasant visions of an intimate pub lunch in some delectable inn faded
and died.

'Is Everard married?'

'No. He lives with his parents. It's his father's farm. They run the
place together.'

'And Danus wants to do something on the same lines?'

'He says so.'

'Have you discussed it with him?'

'Yes. Up to a point.'

'Antonia. What is wrong?'

'I don't know.'

'Have you had a quarrel?'

'No.'

'But something has happened.'

'Nothing has happened. That's what's wrong. I get so far, and then I
get no further. I think I know him. I think I'm close to him, and then
he puts up this reserve. It's like having a gate slammed shut in your face.'

'You're fond of him, aren't you?'

'Oh, yes.' A tear seeped from beneath the lowered lashes, began to slide down Antonia's cheek.

'In love with him, I think.'

A long silence. Antonia nodded.

'But you think that he is not in love with you?'

The tears were falling fast now. Antonia put up a hand and wiped them away. 'I don't know. He couldn't be. We've been together so much over these last few weeks . . . surely by now, he has to know, one way or another . . . there comes a sort of point of no return, and I think we've passed it.'

Penelope said, 'It's my fault. Here . . .' She reached out to the bedside table and handed Antonia a wad of tissues. Antonia lustily blew her nose. When she had done this, she asked, 'Why should it be your fault?'

'Because I've been thinking only of myself. I wanted company, selfish old woman that I am. And so I asked you and Danus to come here with me. Perhaps, too, I was interfering a little. Matchmaking. It's always fatal. I thought I was being so clever. But perhaps it was all the most dreadful mistake.'

Antonia looked despairing. 'What is it about him, Penelope?'

'He's reserved.'

'It's more than reserve.'

'Pride, perhaps.'

'Too proud to love?'

'Not that, exactly. But I think he has no money. He knows what he wants, but hasn't the cash to lay his hands on it. Any sort of a business needs massive capital these days. And so he has no prospects. Perhaps he feels he's in no position to become involved.'

'Involvement wouldn't necessarily mean the responsibility of marriage.'

'I think with a man like Danus, it probably would.'

'I could just be with him. We would work something out together. We work well together. In every sort of way.'

'Have you told him this?'

'I can't. I've tried, but I can't.'

'Then I think you must try again. For both your sakes. Tell him how you feel. Lay your cards on the table. You're good friends, if nothing else. Surely you can be truthful with him?'

'You mean, tell him that I love him, and that I want to spend the rest of my life with him, and that I don't care if he hasn't a penny to his name, and I don't even care if he doesn't want to marry me?'

'Put like that, I admit it does sound a little crude. But . . . yes. I suppose that is what I mean.'

'And if he tells me to go on my way?'

'You'll be hurt and bruised, but at least you'll know where you stand. And for some reason, I don't think he will tell you to go on your way. I think he'll be honest with you, and you'll find that the explanation for his attitude is something quite apart and separate from his relationship with you.'

'How could it be?'

'I don't know. I wish I did. I would like to know why he neither drinks nor drives a car. It's none of my business, but I should like to be told. He's holding something back, of that I'm certain. But knowing him, I cannot believe it's anything shameful.'

'I wouldn't really mind if it was.' Antonia's tears had ceased. She blew her nose once more and said, 'I'm sorry. I didn't mean to bawl like that.'

'Sometimes it's better. Better out than in.'

'It's just that he's the first man I've ever been really attracted to or close to. If there had been strings of others, I suppose I'd be better at coping. But I can't help the way I feel, and I don't think I can bear the thought of losing him. When I saw him first, at Podmore's Thatch, I knew he was special, knew he was going to be somebody very important in my life. And somehow, when we were there, it was all right. It was easy and natural, and we could talk together, and work together, and plant things, and there wasn't any tension. But here, it's different. It's turned into an unreal situation, something I don't seem to have any control over . . .'

'Oh, my darling, it is my fault. I am sorry. I thought it would be romantic for you and special. Now you mustn't cry again. You'll ruin your pretty face and spoil the entire evening . . .'

'I wish I wasn't me . . .' Antonia blurted. 'I wish I was Olivia. Olivia would never get into a mess like this.'

'You're not Olivia. You're yourself. You're beautiful and you're young. You have everything before you. Never wish to be another person, not even Olivia.'

'She's so strong. So wise.'

'And you will be too. You'll wash your face and comb your hair, and go downstairs and tell Danus that I'm having a quiet evening by myself, and then you'll have a drink with him, and go in to dinner, and over dinner you'll tell him everything that you've told me. You're not a child. You're neither of you children. This situation cannot continue, and I won't allow you to make yourself miserable. Danus is a kind man. Whatever happens, whatever he says, he would never deliberately hurt you.'

'No. I know that.' They kissed. Antonia got off the bed and went through to the bathroom to wash her face. Emerging, she stood at the dressing-table and used Penelope's comb to tidy her hair.

'The earrings will bring you luck,' Penelope told her. 'And give you confidence. Now, quick, it's time you went. Danus will be wondering what has become of the pair of us. And remember, speak out and don't be afraid. Don't ever be afraid of being honest and truthful.'

'I'll try not to.'

'Good night, my darling.'

'Good night.'

# Danus

Penelope awoke to yet another clear-skied and pristine morning and to pleasant and recognised sounds – the sea, washing gently onto the beach far below; gulls calling, and a thrush, just below her window, making a great din about something or other; a car coming up the drive, changing gear, drawing to a halt on the gravel; a man whistling.

It was ten past eight. She had slept for twelve hours, right around the clock. She felt rested, filled with energy, enormously hungry. It was Tuesday. The last day of the holiday. This realisation filled her with some dismay. Tomorrow morning, they must pack up and set off on the long drive back to Gloucestershire. She felt impelled by a sense of selfish urgency, because there were a number of things that she still hadn't done and which she wished to do. She lay making a mental list, for once putting her own priorities first. Danus and Antonia, and the dilemma in which they found themselves, must for the moment take second place. Later, she would think about their problems. Later, she would talk to them. For the moment, her time must be her own.

She got up, took a bath, did her hair, put on her clothes. Then, fresh and scented, cleanly dressed, she sat at the writing table in her room and wrote, on the thick, expensively embossed paper provided by the hotel, a letter to Olivia. It was not a very long letter, more of a note, to let Olivia know that she had given Aunt Ethel's earrings to Antonia. For some reason, it was important that Olivia knew about this. She put the letter into an envelope, addressed, stamped, and sealed it down. Then she picked up her bag and her keys and went downstairs.

She found the foyer deserted, revolving doors standing open to the cool air and fresh scents of morning. Only the hall porter stood behind his desk, and a woman in a blue overall vacuumed the carpet. She said good morning to both of them, posted her letter, and went into the empty dining room to order breakfast. Orange juice, two boiled eggs,

toast and marmalade, black coffee. By the time she had come to the end
of this, one or two other guests had filtered down, to take their places,
open newspapers, discuss the coming day. Golf games were planned, and
sightseeing trips. Penelope listened, and was glad that she did not have
to consider any other person. There was still no sign of either Danus or
Antonia, and for this she was shamefully grateful.

She left the dining room. It was now nearly half past nine. Crossing
the foyer, she paused by the hall porter's desk.

'I'm going down to the Art Gallery. At what time does it open, do
you know?'

'About ten o'clock, I think, Mrs Keeling. Driving down, are you?'

'No. I'm going to walk. It's such a beautiful morning. But perhaps, if
I called you when I'm ready, you could arrange for a taxi to come and
fetch me.'

'Of course.'

'Thank you.' She left him, stepping out with conscious pleasure into
the sunshine and sweet gusts of cool and breezy air, which heightened
her sense of freedom and irresponsibility. As a child, Saturday mornings
had felt just so, aimless and empty, ready to be filled with unexpected
delights. She walked slowly, savouring scent and sound, pausing to gaze
at gardens, the glittering expanse of the bay, to watch a man walk his
dog across the sands. Thus, by the time she eventually turned off the
harbour road and set off up the steep cobbled street that led to the
Gallery, she saw that its door stood open, but at such an hour and so
early in the year, she found it, understandably, deserted, save for the
young man who sat behind the desk at the entrance. He was a cadaverous
individual, with long locks of hair, wearing patchworked jeans and an
enormous speckled sweater. He yawned as though he had had no sleep,
but when Penelope appeared he swallowed his yawn, sat up in his chair,
and offered to sell her a catalogue.

'No, I don't need a catalogue, thank you. Later, perhaps, I might buy
some postcards.'

Dreadfully fatigued, he sank back in his chair. She wondered who had
thought fit to employ him as a curator, and then decided that he probably
did the job for love.

*The Shell Seekers* waited for her, impressive in its new home, hung in
the centre of the long, windowless wall. She walked across the echoing
floor and made herself comfortable on the ancient leather couch where,
years ago, she used to sit with Papa.

He had been right. They had come, those young artists, as he had said
they would. *The Shell Seekers* was flanked, framed, by abstracts and
primitives, all bursting with colour and light and life. Gone were the

lesser paintings (*Fishing Boats at Night; Flowers in my Window*) which in the old days had filled in the soaring spaces. Now she recognised the works of other painters, the new artists who had come to take their place. Ben Nicholson, Peter Lanyon, Brian Winter, Patrick Heron. But in no way did they overwhelm *The Shell Seekers*. Rather, they enhanced the blues and greys and shimmering reflections of Papa's favourite picture, and she decided it was a little like going into a room filled with beautiful furniture both traditional and starkly modern, where no piece clashed nor fought with its neighbour, simply because each was the creation of a craftsman, and the very best of its period.

She settled, content and peaceful, to feast and fill her eyes.

When the interruption occurred, and another visitor came through the door behind her, she was scarcely aware of it. A murmured conversation took place. Then footsteps, slowly pacing. And all at once it was as it had been before, on that gusty August day during the war, and she was twenty-three years old again, with holes in her sneakers, and Papa sitting beside her. And Richard walked in; into the gallery, and into their lives. And Papa told him, 'They will come . . . to paint the warmth of the sun and the colour of the wind.' And that was how it had all begun.

The footsteps approached. He was there, awaiting her attention. She turned her head. Thinking of Richard, she saw Danus. Disorientated, lost in time, she looked at him; a stranger.

He said, 'I'm disturbing you.'

His familiar voice broke the weird spell. She pulled herself together, shook off the past, arranged her features into a smile.

'Of course not. I was in a dream.'

'Shall I leave you in peace?'

'No, no.' He was alone. He wore a navy-blue guernsey. His eyes, watching her, seemed strangely brilliant, intensely blue, unblinking. 'I'm saying goodbye to *The Shell Seekers*.' She shifted her position, patted the worn leather beside her. 'Come and join me in my lonely communion.'

He did this, sitting half-turned to face her, one arm along the back of the couch, his long legs crossed.

'Are you better this morning?'

She could not remember having been ill. 'Better?'

'Last night. Antonia said that you were feeling unwell.'

'Oh, that.' She dismissed it. 'I was just a little tired. I'm perfectly all right this morning. How did you know where to find me?'

'The hall porter told me.'

'Where is Antonia?'

'Packing.'

'Packing? Already? But we don't leave until tomorrow morning.'

'She's packing for me. This is what I've come to tell you. This, and a lot of other things. I have to leave today. I'm catching the train to London and then, this evening, the night train back to Edinburgh. I have to go home.'

She could think of only one reason for such precipitous and urgent action. 'Your family. Something's wrong. Is someone ill?'

'No. Nothing like that.'

'But why?' Her thoughts flew back to last night and Antonia. Antonia sitting in tears upon her bed. *You must be truthful and honest*, she had told Antonia, certain, with all the arrogance of experience, that she was giving only the most sound of advice. Instead, it appeared, she had simply meddled, interfered, and destroyed. The plan had misfired. Antonia's brave gesture, her laying of cards upon the table, had in no way cleared the air; frankness had provoked a confrontation – possibly an irredeemable quarrel – and now she and Danus had decided that the only course to take was to part.

There could be no other explanation. She felt herself near tears. 'I am to blame,' she reproached herself. 'It is all my fault.'

'There is no blame. What has happened has nothing to do with you.'

'But it was I who *told* Antonia . . .'

He interrupted. 'And you were right. And if, last night, she had said nothing, then I would have spoken. Because yesterday, that day we spent together, was a sort of catalyst. Everything changed. It was like crossing a watershed. Everything became very simple and very clear.'

'She loves you, Danus. You've surely realised that.'

'That's why I have to go.'

'Does she mean so little to you?'

'No. The opposite. The very opposite. More than love. She has become part of me. Saying goodbye will be like tearing up my own roots. But I have to.'

'I am bewildered.'

'I don't blame you.'

'What *happened* yesterday?'

'I think we both suddenly grew up. Or perhaps this thing that's been happening between us grew up. Up to yesterday, everything we'd done together had been unimportant, quite trivial, harmless. Messing about in the garden at Podmore's Thatch, swimming off the rocks at Penjizal. Nothing important. Nothing serious. I think this was probably my fault. I wasn't looking for a significant relationship. It was the last thing I wanted. And then yesterday we went to Manaccan. I'd talked before to Antonia about my dreams of one day having a place of my own, and she'd discussed it all with me, but in the most casual and light-hearted of ways, and I never realised how deeply she'd taken those discussions to heart. Then Everard Ashley began to show us around, and as we went, an extraordinary thing happened. We became a couple. It was as though, whatever we did, we were going to do it together. And Antonia was as enthusiastic and interested as I was, bubbling over with questions and ideas and plans, and all at once, bang in the middle of a glasshouse full of tomatoes, I knew that she was part of my future. Part of me now. I can't imagine life without her. Whatever I do, I want to do with her, and whatever happens to me, I want it to happen to both of us.'

'And why shouldn't that be allowed to happen?'

'There are two reasons. The first is strictly practical. I have nothing to offer Antonia. I am twenty-four and I have no money, no house, no private means, and my weekly wage is that of a labouring gardener. A market garden, a place of my own, is simply a pipe-dream. Everard Ashley has gone in with his father, but I should have to buy and I have no capital.'

'There are banks who lend money. Or perhaps a government grant?' She thought of his parents. From the scraps of information that Danus had dropped from time to time, the impression given had been one of a family, if not rolling in riches, then certainly not without their fair share of worldly goods. 'Couldn't your parents possibly help you?'

'Not, I think, to that extent.'

'Have you asked them?'

'No.'

'Have you discussed your plans with them?'

'Not yet.'

Such defeatism was unexpected and so irritating. Disappointed in him, she found herself losing patience. 'I'm sorry, but I cannot see what all the fuss is about. You and Antonia have found each other, you love each other, and you want to spend the rest of your lives together. You must snatch at happiness, hold it tight and never let it go. To do anything else is morally wrong. Such chances never come again. What does it matter if you have to manage on a shoe-string? Antonia can get a job; most young wives do. Other young couples keep their heads above water, simply because they've got their priorities right.' He said nothing to this, and she frowned. 'I suppose it's your pride. Stupid, stubborn Scottish pride. And if so, you're being extremely selfish. How can you go away and leave her, and make her so unhappy? What's wrong with you, Danus, that you can turn your back on love?'

'I said there were two reasons. And I've told you one of them.'

'And what is the other?'

He said, 'I am an epileptic.'

She found herself frozen to stillness, without words, incapable. She looked at his face, into his eyes, and his gaze was untroubled and his eyes did not drop. She longed to embrace him, to hold him, comfort him, but did not do any of these things. Random thoughts took shape, flew about aimlessly in all directions, like startled birds. The answer to all those unasked questions. This man is Danus.

She took a deep breath. She said, 'Have you told Antonia?'

'Yes.'

'Do you want to tell me?'

'That's why I'm here. Antonia sent me. She said you, of all people, had to know. Before I go and leave you, I have to give my reasons.'

She laid a hand on his knee.

'I am listening.'

'I suppose it all starts with my mother and father. And with Ian. I told you, I think, that my father's a lawyer. His family have been lawyers for three generations, and my mother's father was a Law Lord in the Scottish courts. Ian was destined to follow in my father's footsteps, join the family firm, and generally conform to tradition. And he would have been a good lawyer, because anything he set his hand to was always a success. But at fourteen Ian died. And, inevitably, it fell to me to take his place. I'd never even thought about what I wanted to do. I just knew that that was what I had to do. I suppose you could say I was programmed, like a computer. Well, I got through school and, although I was never as bright as Ian, I managed to pass the necessary exams and won a place at Edinburgh University. But I was still very young, so, before I went to University, I took a couple of years off to travel and see a bit of the world. I went to America. I bummed around from coast to coast, did any job that came my way, and then ended up in Arkansas, working on a cattle ranch for a man called Jack Rogers. He had a hell of a spread, it stretched for miles, and I was one of the hands, helping to round up cattle and mend fences, and living in a bunk house with three other guys.

'The ranch was incredibly remote. The nearest town was called Sleeping Creek, and that was forty miles away, and no great shakes when you got there. I used to drive down sometimes, to take Sally Rogers shopping for stores, or to pick up supplies and equipment for Jack. It was a whole day's journey, bumping the truck down a dirt road and ending up coated in brown dust.

'Then one day, towards the end of my time there, I became ill. Felt lousy, started vomiting and shivering and then ran a raging temperature. I must have become delirious because I don't remember being moved out of the bunk house and into the ranch house, but that's where I found myself, with Sally Rogers nursing me. She did a good job, and, after a week or so, I'd recovered and was back on my legs again. We decided it had been some virus I'd picked up, and when I could walk three paces without keeling over, I went back to work again.

'And then, soon after, with no warning . . . nothing . . . I blacked out. Went over like a felled tree, flat on my back and stayed unconscious for about half an hour. There seemed to be no reason, but a week later it happened again, and I felt so appallingly ill that Sally piled me into the truck and drove me to the doctor in Sleeping Creek. He listened to my tale of woe and made some tests. A week later, I went back to see him and he told me that I had epilepsy. He gave me drugs to take, four times a day. He said I'd be okay if I took them. He said there wasn't anything else he could do for me.'

He fell silent. Penelope felt that some comment was expected of her but could think of nothing to say that was neither trite nor banal. There was a long pause and then, painfully, Danus continued.

'I'd never been ill in my life. I'd never had anything worse than measles. I asked the doctor, *why*? And he asked me a few questions, and we finally ran it down to a kick I'd got on the head at school when I'd been playing rugger. I'd suffered concussion, but nothing worse. Until now. I had epilepsy. I was nearly twenty-one, and I was an epileptic.'

'Did you tell those kind people you were working for?'

'No. And I made the doctor promise that he would honour his medical confidence. I didn't want anybody to know. If I couldn't deal with it on my own, then I wasn't going to be able to deal with it at all. Eventually, I came back to this country. I flew to London and caught the night sleeper back to Edinburgh. By then I had made up my mind that I wasn't going to take up that place at Edinburgh University. With time to think about it, I'd discovered the truth. That I could never take Ian's place. And I was afraid of failing, and letting my father down. Also, there was something else I'd found out during those last months. That I needed to be out of doors. I needed to work with my hands. I wanted no one standing at my shoulder, with expectations of me that I could never fulfil. Telling my parents all this was one of the worst things I've ever had to do. At first, they were disbelieving. And then hurt, and desperately disappointed. I didn't blame them. I was destroying every plan they'd ever made. Finally, they became resigned and made the best of it. But, after all that, I couldn't bring myself to tell them about my epilepsy.'

'You never *told* them? But how could you not?'

'My brother died of meningitis. I felt that, with one thing and another, they'd had enough to cope with. And what good would it have done to load them with yet more worry and anguish. And I was all right. I was taking the drugs and I wasn't blacking out. To all intents and purposes, I was perfectly normal. All I had to do was register with a new young doctor . . . a man who knew nothing of me or my medical history. And he gave me a permanent prescription for my drugs. After that, I enrolled for three years at a Horticultural College in Worcestershire. That was all right, too. I was just another ordinary guy. Did everything the other students did. Got drunk, drove a car, played football. But still, I was epileptic. I knew that, if I stopped taking the drugs, it would all start happening again. I pretended not to think about it, but you can't stop what goes on inside your head. It was always there. A great weight, like a loaded haversack that you can never put down.'

'If only you'd shared your problem, it mightn't have felt so heavy.'

'I did eventually. I was forced into it. When I finished college, I managed to get the job with Autogarden in Pudley. I saw an advertisement in the paper, and applied and was accepted. I worked till Christmas and then I went home for a couple of weeks. Over New Year, I got flu. I was in bed for five days, and I ran out of drugs. I couldn't go and get them for myself, so finally I had to ask my mother to go and pick them up, and then of course it all came out.'

'So she knows. Oh, thank heavens for that. She must have wanted to strangle you for being so secretive.'

'In an extraordinary way, I think she was relieved. She'd suspected something was up, and had imagined the very worst but had kept her fears to herself. That's the trouble with my family, we've always kept things to ourselves. It's something to do with being Scottish and independent, and not wanting to be thought a nuisance. That's the way we were brought up. My mother was never demonstrative, never what you might call particularly cosy; but that day, after she'd shot off and got my pills from the chemist, she sat on my bed and we talked for hours. She even talked about Ian, which she'd never done before. And we remembered good times and we laughed. And then I told her that I'd always realised that I was second-best, and that I could never take Ian's place, and, with that, she became her old brisk and business-like self and told me not to be a blithering idiot; I was my own self and she didn't want me any other way; all she wanted was to see me well again. Which meant another diagnosis and a second opinion. No sooner was I on my feet after the flu than I was sitting in an eminent neurosurgeon's consulting room, being asked a thousand questions. There were more tests and an EEG . . . a brain-scan . . . but at the end of the day I was told that no accurate diagnosis could be made while I was taking drugs. So I was to go off them for three months and then go back for a second consultation. If I was careful, I should come to no harm, but under no circumstances was I to drink alcohol or drive a car.'

'And when is the three months up?'

'It's overdue now. Two weeks overdue.'

'But that's foolish. You must waste no more time.'

'That's what Antonia told me.'

Antonia. Penelope had almost forgotten about Antonia. 'Danus, what happened yesterday evening?'

'You know most of it. We met in the bar, and waited for you, and when you didn't come, Antonia went upstairs to find you. And while I was on my own, I sat and made mental lists of every single thing I was going to tell her. And I imagined that it was going to be hideously difficult, and found myself searching for the right words, and composing ridiculously formal sentences. But then she came back, wearing the earrings that you had given her, and looking so sensationally adult and beautiful that all those carefully prepared phrases flew out of the window, and I just told her what was in my heart. And as I spoke, she started speaking too, and then we began to laugh, because we both realised that we were saying the same thing.'

'Oh, my dear boy.'

'What I'd been afraid of was hurting or distressing her. She'd always seemed to me so very young and so very vulnerable. But she was amazing. Immensely practical. And, like you, horrified to know that I'd let the weeks slide by without making that second appointment.'

'But now it's made?'

'Yes. I called at nine o'clock this morning. I'm to see the neurosurgeon on Thursday, and have another EEG then. I should have the results almost at once.'

'You'll ring us up at Podmore's Thatch and let us know?'

'Of course.'

'If you've been three months without drugs and without a black-out, surely the prognosis is hopeful.'

'I can't let myself think about it. I daren't hope.'

'But you'll come back to us?'

For the first time, Danus seemed uncertain of himself; he hesitated. '. . . I don't know. The thing is, I may have to have some form of treatment. It may take months. I may have to stay in Edinburgh . . .'

'And Antonia? What will happen to Antonia?'

'I don't know. I don't know what's going to happen to me. Right now, I can see no prospect of being able ever to give her the good life she deserves. She's eighteen. She could do anything with her life, have anybody. She only has to ring Olivia, and within months she'll be on the front page of every glossy magazine in the country. I can't allow her to commit herself to me until I can see some sort of future for the both of us. There really is no alternative.'

Penelope sighed. But, against her better judgement, she respected his reasoning. 'If you have to be parted for a while, it might be best for Antonia to go back to London and Olivia. She can't simply hang around at Podmore's Thatch with me. She'd die of boredom. She'll be better with a job. New friends. New interests . . .'

'Will you be all right without her there with you?'

'Oh, of course.' She smiled. 'Poor Danus, I am sorry for you. Illness is hateful, whatever form it takes. I am ill. I had a heart attack but would admit it to nobody. I walked out of the hospital and told my children that the doctors were idiots. I insisted that there was nothing wrong with me. But, of course, there is. If I get upset, my heart jumps up and down like a yo-yo, and I have to take a pill. At any moment, it might conk out altogether and I shall be left lying with my toes turned up. But until such time, I am really very much happier pretending that nothing at all has happened. And you and Antonia mustn't worry about me being on my own. I have my dear Mrs Plackett. But it's no good pretending that I shan't miss you both. We've had a good time. And this last week, I could have asked for no better companions. I do thank you for coming to this so special place.'

He shook his head in smiling bewilderment. 'I'll never know why you've always been so exceptionally kind to me.'

'That's easily explained. I took to you right away because of the way you look. Quite uncannily like a man I knew during the war. It was as though, from the very first, I recognised you. Doris Penberth, too, remarked on the resemblance, that evening you and Antonia came to fetch me from her house. Doris and Ernie and I are the only people left who remember him. He was called Richard Lomax, and he was killed on D-Day at Omaha Beach. Saying that someone was the love of your life sounds the most banal cliché, but that's what he was to me. When he died, something in me died as well. There was never anybody else.'

'But your husband?'

Penelope sighed, shrugged her shoulders. 'I'm afraid ours was never a very satisfactory marriage. If Richard had survived the war, I should have left Ambrose, and taken Nancy and gone to live with Richard. As it was, I went back to Ambrose. It seemed the only thing to do. And I felt a little guilty about him. I was young and selfish when we married, and we were parted almost at once. The marriage had never had a chance. I felt I owed Ambrose that chance, if nothing else. Also, he was Nancy's father. And I wanted more children. Finally, I knew that I would never, wholly, love again. There could never be another Richard. And it seemed the sensible thing, just to make the best of what I had. I have to admit that Ambrose and I didn't make much of a success of our life together, but I had Nancy, and then I had Olivia, and then Noel. Little children, for all their tedious ways, can be a great comfort.'

'Have you ever spoken to your children about this other man?'

'No. I never told them, never spoke his name. For forty years I never spoke of him. Until the other day when I was with Doris, and she talked of Richard as though he'd just that moment walked out of the room. It was lovely. Not sad any longer. I lived with sadness for so long. And a loneliness that nothing and nobody could assuage. But, over the years, I came to terms with what had happened. I learned to live within myself, to grow flowers, to watch my children grow; to look at paintings and listen to music. The gentle powers. They are quite amazingly sustaining.'

'You'll miss *The Shell Seekers*.'

She was touched by his perception.

'No, Danus. Not any more. *The Shell Seekers* has gone, as Richard has gone. I shall probably never say his name again. And you will keep what I have told you to yourself, for ever.'

'I promise.'

'Good. Now, as we seem to have talked ourselves to a standstill, isn't it time we thought about moving? Antonia will be thinking that we have disappeared for good.' Danus stood up and held out a hand to help her to her feet. These, she discovered, ached. 'I am too tired to walk up the hill. We'll ask that long-haired young man to phone for a taxi to take us back to the hotel. And I shall leave *The Shell Seekers* and all the memories of my past behind me. Right here; in this funny little Gallery, where they all started, and where it is entirely appropriate that they should end their days.'

# Penelope

The hall porter of the Sands Hotel, resplendent in his dark green uniform, slammed the car door shut and wished them a safe journey. Antonia drove. The old Volvo moved forward, down the curve of the drive, between the banks of hydrangeas, and turned out into the road. Penelope did not look back.

It was a good day for leaving. The spell of perfect weather seemed, for the time being, to have broken. During the night a mist had rolled in from the sea and all was veiled in moisture, dispersing to gather again, like smoke. Only once, just before they reached the motorway, did the fog clear, admitting a diffused gleam of sunlight, and the estuary was revealed. It was ebb-tide. The mud-flats lay empty of life, save for the eternal, scavenging seabirds, and in the distance could be glimpsed the white rollers of the Atlantic breaking in over the sand-bar. Then the steep embankment of the new road reared skywards, and all was gone.

So the leaving, the parting, was over. Penelope settled to the long drive. She thought about Podmore's Thatch, and discovered that she longed to be home. With satisfaction, she anticipated arrival, entering her own house, inspecting her garden, unpacking, opening windows, reading her mail . . .

Beside her, Antonia asked, 'Are you all right?'

'Did you think I should be in tears?'

'No. But leaving somewhere you love is always painful. You waited so long to come back. And now we're going away again.'

'I am fortunate. I have my heart in two places, so wherever I am, I am content.'

'Next year, you must come again. Stay with Doris and Ernie. That'll give you something to look forward to. Cosmo always said that life wasn't worth living unless you had something to look forward to.'

'Dear man, how right he was.' She thought about this. 'I'm afraid, for the moment, your future looks a little bleak and lonely.'

'Only for the moment.'

'It's better to be realistic, Antonia. If you steel yourself for the worst news of Danus, then anything better comes as a wonderful bonus.'

'I know that. And I don't have any illusions about him. I realise that it may take a long time and, for him, I hate the prospect. But for me, selfishly, knowing about his being ill makes everything so much easier. We really do love each other and nothing else matters . . . that's the most important thing of all, and that's what I'm going to hang on to.'

'You've been very brave. Sensible and brave. Not that I expected anything else of you. I'm really very proud of you.'

'I'm not really brave. But nothing's so bad if you can *do* something. On Monday, driving home from Manaccan, and neither of us saying a word, and knowing something was wrong, and with no idea of what it was . . . that was the worst. I felt that he was tired of me, that he wished I wasn't there, that he'd gone to see his friend on his own. It was really horrible. Isn't misunderstanding the most horrible thing in the world? I'll never let it happen to me again. And I know it won't ever happen again between Danus and me.'

'It was as much his fault as yours. But I think that painful reserve is inbred in him, inherited from his parents and very much part of the way he was brought up.'

'He told me that was what he loved so much about you. The way you were always more than ready to discuss *anything*. And, more important, to listen. He told me that, as a child, he never really talked to his parents, and never felt truly close to them. So sad, isn't it? They probably adored him, but just never got around to telling him.'

'Antonia, if Danus has to stay in Edinburgh and undergo treatment, or even has to go to hospital for a while . . . have you thought what you want to do?'

'Yes. If I may, I'll stay with you for another week or two. By then we should know which way the wind is going to blow. And if it's a long-term thing, then I'll ring Olivia and accept that offer of help. Not that I want to be a photographer's model. There's really no job I'd dislike more, but if I could earn some decent money doing it, I could put it by and save it up, and then when Danus is well again, at least we'd have the smallest beginnings of a start in life. And that'll give me something to work for. I won't feel I'm totally wasting my time.'

As they travelled up the backbone of the county and the coastline receded, the fog had melted and rolled away. On the high ground, sunshine washed over fields and farms and moorland, and the old engine houses of disused tin mines pointed to the cloudless spring sky, jagged as broken teeth.

Penelope sighed. She said, 'So strange.'

'What's so strange?'

'First it was my life. And then Olivia's. And then Cosmo came. And then you. And now it's your future we talk about. A strange progression.'

'Yes.' Antonia hesitated, and then went on. 'One thing you don't have to worry about. There's not all that much wrong with Danus. I mean, he's not impotent or anything.'

The significance of this observation took an instant to sink in. Penelope turned her head and looked at Antonia. Antonia's charming profile was intent on the road ahead, but a faint blush warmed her cheeks.

She turned back to look out of the window, smiling secretly to herself. She said, 'I *am* glad.'


The church clock of Temple Pudley struck five o'clock as they turned into the gate of Podmore's Thatch and drew to a halt. The front door stood open, and smoke curled from a chimney. Mrs Plackett was there, waiting for them. The kettle sang, and she had made a batch of scones. No home-coming could have been more welcome.

Mrs Plackett was vociferous, torn between wanting to hear their news and to give them hers.

'Look at you, how brown you are! Must have had the same good weather as we have. Mr Plackett's had to water our vegetables, ground is so dry. And thanks for the postcard, Antonia. Was that your hotel with all the flags flying? Looked like a palace to me. Had vandals in the churchyard, broke all the flower vases and wrote disgusting words on the tombstones with spray paint. Got a few bits in for you; bread and butter and milk and a couple of chops for your supper. Have a good drive, did you?'

They were finally able to tell her that, yes, they had had a good drive, the roads had been clear, and they were dying for a cup of tea.

It was only then that it dawned on Mrs Plackett that three people had set off for Cornwall and only two had returned.

'Where's Danus? Drop him off at Sawcombe's, did you?'

'No, he didn't come with us. He had to go back to Scotland. He caught the train yesterday.'

'To Scotland? That was a bit unexpected, wasn't it?'

'Yes. But it couldn't be helped. And we had five wonderful days together.'

'That's all that matters. Did you see your old friend?'

'Doris Penberth? Yes, of course. And I may tell you, Mrs Plackett, that we talked ourselves dry.' Mrs Plackett was making the tea. Penelope sat at the table and helped herself to a scone. 'You are the dearest thing to be here to meet us.'

'Well, I said to Linda, thought I'd best come along. Get the house aired. Pick a few flowers. Know you don't like the house without flowers. And that's another bit of news. Linda's Darren's started walking. Toddled clear across the kitchen the other day.' She poured tea. 'It's his birthday on Monday. Said I'd give Linda a hand, ask you if you'd mind if I came Tuesday instead. And I cleaned the windows, and put your mail on your desk . . .' She drew out a chair and seated herself, her large competent arms crossed on the table before her. ' . . . a great pile there was, lying on the mat inside the door . . .'

She went at last, pedalling homewards on her stately bicycle to give Mr Plackett his tea. While they gossiped, Antonia had unloaded the car and carried their cases upstairs. She was, presumably, unpacking, for she had not reappeared, and so, as soon as Mrs Plackett was gone, Penelope did what she had been wanting to do ever since she came through the door. The conservatory first. She filled a can and watered all the pot plants. Then picked up a pair of secateurs and went out into the garden. The grass needed cutting, the iris were out, and the far end of the border was a mass of red and yellow tulips. The first of the early rhododendrons had flowered, and she picked a single bloom and marvelled at its pale-pink perfection, collared in stiff dark-green leaves, and decided that no human hand could achieve such satisfying arrangement of petal and stamen. After a little, holding the flower, she wandered on down through the orchard, awash with fruit blossom, and through the gate to the river bank. The Windrush flowed quietly by, slipping away beneath the overhanging branches of willow. There were cowslips out, and clumps of pale-mauve mallow, and, as she walked, a mallard emerged from a reedy thicket and proceeded to swim downstream, followed, to Penelope's enchantment, by half a dozen fluffy ducklings. She walked as far as the wooden bridge, and then, having for the moment had her fill, made her way slowly back to the house. As she crossed the lawn, Antonia called from the upstairs window of her bedroom.

'Penelope.' Penelope stopped, looked upwards. Antonia's head and shoulders were framed in a tangle of honeysuckle 'It's after six o'clock. Would you mind if I telephoned Danus? I promised I would, just to let him know we're safely back.'

'Of course. Use the phone in my bedroom. And send my love.'

'I will.'

In the kitchen, she found a lustre jug and filled it with water, and into it placed the rhododendron flower. She carried this through to the living room, already lavishly decorated by Mrs Plackett's unprofessional but loving hands. She put the jug on her desk, picked up her mail, and settled herself in her armchair. The dull buff-coloured letters, most likely containing bills, were dropped to the floor. The others . . . she leafed them through. A thick white envelope looked interesting. She recognised Rose Pilkington's spidery handwriting. She slit the envelope with her thumb. She heard a car turning in at the gate, to draw up and stop at the front door.

She did not move from her chair. A stranger would ring the bell, a friend would simply walk indoors. This visitor did just that thing. Footsteps crossed the kitchen, the hall. The door of the living room opened and her son Noel walked into the room.

She could scarcely have been more surprised. 'Noel!'

'Hello.' He wore a pair of fawn twill trousers, a sky-blue sweater, a red-spotted cotton handkerchief knotted at his neck. He was very tanned and looked quite amazingly handsome. Rose Pilkington's letter was forgotten.

'Where have you sprung from?'

'Wales.' He shut the door behind him. She raised her face, expecting one of his perfunctory kisses, but he did not stoop to embrace her. Instead, with some grace, he arranged himself in front of the fireplace, his shoulders propped against the mantelpiece, his hands in his trouser pockets. Behind his head, the wall where once *The Shell Seekers* had hung looked bare and empty. 'I was there for Easter weekend. Now I'm on my way back to London. Thought I'd drop in.'

'Easter weekend? But it's *Wednesday*.'

'It was a long weekend.'

'How very convenient for you. Did you enjoy yourself?'

'Very much, thank you. And how was Cornwall?'

'Magic. We got back about five o'clock. I haven't even unpacked yet.'

'And where are your travelling companions?' His voice had an edge to it. She looked at him sharply, but his eyes veered away and he would not meet her gaze.

'Danus is in Scotland. He went back yesterday, by train. And Antonia is upstairs, in my bedroom, ringing him up to let him know that we have arrived safely.'

Noel raised his eyebrows. 'From that bit of information, it's hard to guess exactly what has happened. Returning to Scotland seems to indicate that relations became strained while you all lived it up at the Sands Hotel. And yet, at this moment, Antonia is talking to him on the telephone. You'll have to explain.'

'There's nothing to explain. Danus had an appointment in Edinburgh which he had to keep. As simple as that.' Noel's expression implied that he did not believe her. She decided to change the subject. 'Do you want to stay for supper?'

'No, I must get back to London.' But he did not shift himself.

'A drink then . . . would you like a drink?'

'No, I'm all right.'

She thought, *I will not let him bully me.* She said, 'But I would like one. I would like a whisky and soda. Perhaps you'd be kind enough to get it for me.'

He hesitated, and then went through to the dining room. She heard cupboards being opened, the clink of glass. She stacked the letters that lay on her lap, and laid them neatly on the table beside her chair. When he returned, she saw that he had changed his mind about that drink, and carried two glasses. He gave her one, and returned to his former position.

He said, 'And *The Shell Seekers?*'

So that was it. She smiled. 'Was it Olivia who told you about *The Shell Seekers*, or was it Nancy?'

'Nancy.'

'Nancy was deeply hurt that I'd done such a thing. Personally offended. Is that how you feel? Is that what you've come to tell me?'

'No. I just want to know what in God's name induced you to do such a thing.'

'My father gave it to me. In giving it to the Gallery, I feel that I've simply given it back to him.'

'Have you any idea what that picture is worth?'

'I know what it's worth to me. As for a financial appraisal, it's never been exhibited before and so it has never been valued.'

'I rang my friend, Edwin Mundy, and told him what you'd done. He'd never seen the picture, of course, but he had a very clear idea of what it would fetch in a sale room. Do you know the price he put on it . . .?'

'No, and I don't wish to be told.' Noel opened his mouth to tell her but found himself on the receiving end of a warning glance so formidable that he shut it again, and said nothing. 'You are angry,' his mother told him. 'Because, for some reason, both you and Nancy feel that I have given away something which, by rights, belongs to you. It doesn't, Noel. It never did. As for the panels, you should be gratified that I took your advice. You urged me to sell them, and it was you who put me on to Boothby's and Mr Roy Brookner. Mr Brookner found me a private buyer and I was offered a hundred thousand for them. I accepted this. The money is there, to be included in my estate when I die. Doesn't that satisfy you, or do you want more?'

'You should have discussed it with me. I am, after all, your son.'

'We had discussed it. Over and over. And each time the discussion came to nothing, or ended in a row. I know what you want, Noel. You want money *now*. In your hand. To squander as you wish on some wild-goose idea that will in all probability come to nothing. You've got a perfectly good job but you want a better one. Commodity broking. And once you've got that out of your system, and probably lost every penny you possess in the process, then it'll be something else . . . some other pot of gold at the end of a non-existent rainbow. Happiness is making the most of what you have, and riches is making the most of what you've got. You have so much going for you. Why can't you see that? Why do you always want more?'

'You talk as though I think only of myself. I don't. I'm thinking of my sisters as well, and your grandchildren. One hundred thousand sounds a lot, but there'll be taxes to pay, and if you continue to squander it on any lame dog that comes your way and takes your fancy – '

'Noel, don't talk to me as though I were senile. I am perfectly in charge of my senses; I shall choose my own friends and make my own decisions. Going to Porthkerris, staying at the Sands, taking Danus and Antonia to keep me company was the first time in my life, the very first time, that I have experienced the joys of extravagance and generosity. For the first time in my life, I didn't have to weigh the worth of every penny. For the first time, I was able to give with no worry about the cost. It was an experience that I shall never forget, and made all the more heart-warming by the grace and gratitude with which it was received.'

'Is that what you want? Endless gratitude?'

'No, but I think you should try to understand. If I'm wary of you and your needs and your schemes, it's because I've lived through it all before with your father, and I'm not about to start again.'

'You can scarcely blame me for my father.'

'I don't. You were just a little boy when he walked out on us all. But in you he left a lot of himself behind. Good things. His looks, his charm, and his undoubted abilities. But other characteristics as well, which are not so commendable – grand ideas; lavish tastes; and no respect for other people's property. I am sorry. I hate to say such things. But it seems the time has come for you and me to be quite open with each other.'

He said, 'I had no idea you disliked me so much.'

'Noel, you are my son. Can't you see that if I didn't love you beyond all else, I would never trouble to say these things?'

'You have an odd way of showing love. Giving all you possess to strangers . . . nothing to your children.'

'You talk like Nancy. Nancy told me that I never gave her anything. What is wrong with you both? You and Nancy and Olivia were my life. For years you were everything I lived for. And yet now, hearing you say such things, I am filled with despair. I feel that somewhere and somehow I have totally and utterly failed you.'

'I think,' said Noel slowly, 'that you have.'

After that, there seemed to be nothing more to say. He finished his drink, turned and set the glass on the mantelpiece. He was, it was obvious, about to take his leave, and the thought of his going with the bitterness of their quarrel still between them was more than Penelope could bear. 'Stay for supper with us, Noel. We won't be late. You'll be back in London by eleven.'

'No. I must go.' He moved away.

She pulled herself out of her chair and followed him through the kitchen and out of the door. Without looking at her, or meeting her eyes, he got into his car, slammed the door shut, fastened his seat-belt, switched on the ignition.

'Noel.' He faced his mother, his handsome features unsmiling, antagonistic, without love. She said, 'I am sorry.' He nodded briefly, acknowledging her apology. She tried to smile. 'Come back again soon.' But the car was already moving, and her words drowned in the roar of its supercharged engine.

When he had gone, she went back indoors. She stood at the kitchen table and thought about supper, and could not think what she meant to do. With an enormous effort she gathered her wits; she made her way to the larder, fetched potatoes, carried the basket to the sink. She turned on the cold tap and watched it run. She thought of tears but was beyond weeping.

She stood there, incapable, for some minutes. Then the kitchen telephone rang sharply once and jerked her back to reality. She opened the drawer, took out her small, sharp knife. When Antonia came running down the stairs to find her, she was peacefully peeling potatoes.

'I'm sorry, we talked for ages. Danus says he'll pay you for the call. It must have cost pounds.' Antonia sat on the table and swung her legs. She was smiling and looked sleek and satisfied as a little cat. 'He sent you his dearest love, and says he's writing you a long letter. Not a bread-and-butter letter, a toast-and-marmalade one. And he's seeing the doctor tomorrow morning, and he's going to ring us the moment he knows what the verdict is. He sounded terrific, not worried in the very least. And he says the sun's shining, even in Edinburgh. I'm sure that's a good sign, aren't you? A hopeful one. If it had been raining, it wouldn't be nearly so cheerful for him. Did I hear voices? Did you have a caller?'

'Yes. Yes, I did. It was Noel, on his way back to London from a weekend in Wales. A very *long* weekend, he assured me.' It was all right, her voice was fine, just right, casual and quite steady. 'I asked him to stay for supper, but he wanted to get back. So he had a drink and took himself off.'

'I'm sorry I missed him. But there was so much to say to Danus. I couldn't stop chattering. Would you like me to do those potatoes? Or shall I go and find a cabbage or something? Or lay the table? Isn't it lovely to be home? I know it's not my home but it feels like it, and it's somehow so perfect to be back again. You feel like that too, don't you? You're not regretting anything?'

'No,' Penelope told her. 'I regret nothing.'


The next morning at nine o'clock, she made two telephone calls to London, and two appointments. One of them was with Lalla Friedmann.


Danus' appointment was at ten o'clock and they had worked out the previous evening that it would be at least half past eleven before he could get himself to a telephone, to let them know the doctor's verdict. But the call came just before eleven and it was Penelope who answered it because Antonia was down in the orchard, hanging out a line of washing in the breezy wind.

'Podmore's Thatch.'

'It's Danus.'

'*Danus!* Oh dear, Antonia's out in the garden. What news? Tell me at once. What news have you for us?'

'I haven't any news.'

Penelope's heart dropped with disappointment. 'Didn't you see the doctor?'

'Yes, I did, and then I went up to the hospital for my EEG, but . . . and you're never going to believe this . . . the computer there is on the blink and they couldn't give me the results.'

'I *don't* believe it. How utterly exasperating! How long have you got to wait?'

'I don't know. They couldn't say.'

'So what are you going to do?'

'Do you remember me telling you about my friend Roddy McCrae? I had a drink with him last night in the Tilted Wig, and he's off tomorrow

morning for a week's fishing in Sutherland. He asked me to go with him,
to stay in the croft, and I've decided to accept his invitation, and just
take off. If I have to wait two days to hear the results of the brain-scan,
I might as well wait a week. And at least I won't be kicking my heels
at home, biting the ends off my fingernails and driving my mother
insane.'

'So when will you return to Edinburgh?'

'Thursday, probably.'

'Is there no way that your mother can get in touch with you at the
croft, and let you have some news?'

'No. I told you, it's at the back of beyond. And, to be truthful, I've
lived so long with this thing, I can wait another seven days.'

'In that case, perhaps it's better to go. And, in the meantime, we'll
keep our fingers crossed. We won't stop thinking about you for a single
moment. You promise to call us the moment you get back?'

'Of course. Is Antonia around . . .?'

'I'll fetch her. Hold on.'

She left the receiver hanging by its cable and went out through the
conservatory. Antonia was ambling back across the grass with the empty
washing basket under her arm. She wore a pink shirt, the sleeves rolled
up to her elbows, and a navy-blue cotton skirt, blowing in the wind.

'Antonia. Quick, it's Danus . . .'

'Already?' The colour flowed from her cheeks. 'Oh, what did he say?
What's happened?'

'No news yet because the computer's broken down . . . but let him
tell you for himself. He's waiting on the telephone. Here . . . I'll take
the basket.'

Antonia thrust it at her and fled indoors. Penelope carried the basket
to the garden seat which stood outside the sitting-room window. Really,
life was too cruel. If it wasn't one thing, then it was another. But better,
perhaps, under the circumstances, that Danus should take himself off
with his friend. The company of an old colleague was sometimes the
answer on such occasions. She imagined the two young men in that
world of endless moors and towering hills, bitter-cold northern seas, and
deep, brown, fast-flowing rivers. They would fish together. Yes, it was a
good decision that Danus had made. Fishing was said to be immensely
therapeutic.

A movement caught the corner of her eye. She looked, and watched
Antonia emerge from the conservatory and come across the grass towards
her. The girl looked despondent, dragging her feet like a child. She
thumped herself down beside Penelope and said, 'Damn.'

'I know. It's very frustrating. For all of us.'

'Beastly bloody old computer. Why can't they make these things *work*? And why does it have to happen to *Danus*?'

'I must say, it is the cruellest of luck. But there's nothing to be done, so we must just make the best of it.'

'It's all very well for *him*; he's going off fishing for a week.'

Penelope had to smile. 'You sound,' she told Antonia, 'like a neglected wife.'

'Do I really?' Antonia became remorseful. 'I don't mean to. It's just that another week to wait seems *endless*.'

'I know. But it's much better that he shouldn't just sit around and wait for the telephone to ring. Nothing in this world is more demoralising. He's much better to be happily occupied. I'm sure you don't grudge him that. And the week will pass. You and I will occupy ourselves happily. I'm going to London on Monday. Would you like to come with me?'

'To London? Why?'

'Just to see some old friends. I haven't been for long enough. If you'd like to come with me, we could take the car. But if you'd rather stay here, perhaps you'd drive me to Cheltenham and I'll catch the train.'

Antonia thought about this suggestion. Then she said, 'No. I think I'll stay. I might have to go back to London soon enough, and it's a waste to miss a single day in the country. And Mrs Plackett isn't coming on Monday because of Darren's birthday, so I'll do the housework and cook a delicious dinner for you to come home to. Besides' – she smiled, looking more like her old self again – 'there's always the faintest possibility that Danus might find himself within ten miles of a telephone and decide to ring me up. It would be a tragedy if I wasn't here.'

And so Penelope went to London alone. As they had planned, Antonia drove her to Cheltenham and she caught the 9.15. In London, she visited the Royal Academy and lunched with Lalla Friedmann. Afterwards, she took a taxi and drove to the Gray's Inn Road, and the offices of Enderby, Looseby & Thring, Solicitors. She gave her name to the girl who sat behind the reception desk and was led up two flights of narrow stairs to Mr Enderby's private office. The girl knocked and opened the door.

'Mrs Keeling to see you, Mr Enderby.'

She stood back. As Penelope went through the door, Mr Enderby rose to his feet and came from behind his desk to greet her.

In the old and penniless days, Penelope would have got herself from the Gray's Inn Road to Paddington Station either by bus or by tube. In her mind, she had actually planned to do this thing, but when she eventually emerged onto the pavement outside the premises of Enderby, Looseby & Thring, she discovered that the prospect of battling her way across London by public transport was, all at once, quite untenable. A cruising taxi approached; she stepped forward and flagged it down.

In the taxi, she sat back, grateful to be alone, absorbed in her thoughts, recollecting her conversation with Mr Enderby. Much had been discussed, decided, and accomplished. There was nothing more to be done. Achievement had been reached, but it had all been exhausting, and she found herself at the end of her rope, both physically and mentally. Her head ached; her feet seemed too large for their shoes. In addition, she felt both grubby and hot, for the afternoon, although overcast and sunless, was warm; the air heavy, stale and used. Gazing from the taxi window, waiting for the traffic lights to change from red to green, she was suddenly overwhelmed and depressed by all she saw. The size of the city; the millions of human beings who thronged the streets, their faces anxious and worried, all hurrying as though fearful of being late for some life-or-death appointment. Once she had lived in London. It had been her home. Here she had brought up her family. Now, she could not imagine how she had endured those years.

She had intended catching the 4.15, but the traffic in the Marylebone Road had reached proportions so appalling that, by the time the taxi passed Madame Tussaud's, she was resigned to missing this and catching a later train. At Paddington, she peeled off notes to pay the enormous, inflated fare, checked on train times, and then found a phone booth and rang Antonia to tell her that she would be arriving in Cheltenham at a quarter to eight. Having done that, she bought herself a magazine, went into the Station Hotel, ordered a pot of tea, and sat down to wait.

The train journey, hot, crowded, and uncomfortable, took for ever, and the relief of finally arriving, alighting, knowing it was over, was enormous. Antonia was there on the platform as she stepped from the train, and it was bliss to be met, kissed, taken in hand, responsible for herself no longer. They went through the barrier and out into the station-yard, and Penelope looked up at the clear evening sky, smelled trees and grass and gratefully breathed, filling her lungs with the sweet fresh air.

'I feel,' she told Antonia, 'that I have been away for weeks.'

Settled into her old Volvo, they headed for home.

'Did you have a good day?' Antonia asked.

'Yes, but I'm totally drained. I feel unwashed and exhausted, just like an old refugee. And I'd forgotten what a hassle London can be. Just getting from one place to another uses up most of the day. That's why I missed my train. And the one I caught was packed with commuters, and a man with the hugest bottom in the world chose to come and sit beside me.'

'There's chicken fricassee for supper, but perhaps you don't feel like eating so late in the day.'

'What I really want is a hot bath, and then my bed . . .'

'In that case, as soon as we get back, that's what you shall have. And when you're in bed, I shall come and see if you'd like a little supper and, if you do, I shall bring it up on a tray, and you can eat it there.'

'You are the dearest child.'

'I'll tell you something. Podmore's Thatch feels funny without you.'

'How did you spend your lonely day?'

'I cut the grass. I got the motor mower started and it looks terribly professional.'

'Did Danus ring?'

'No. But then, I didn't really expect him to.'

'Tomorrow's Tuesday. Another two days and we should be hearing from him.'

Antonia said, 'Yes.' They fell silent. The road ahead wound its way up into the Costwold countryside.


She thought that she would sleep, but she did not. True sleep eluded her; she dozed, and woke. Tossed, turned, dozed again. Half-dreams were bedevilled by voices, by words and scraps of conversation that made no sense. Ambrose was there, and Dolly Keeling, rabbiting on about some room she was going to decorate in magnolia. And then Doris, chatting nineteen to the dozen, and cackling with her high-pitched laughter. Lalla Friedmann, young again. Young and frightened, because her husband Willi was going out of his mind. *You never gave me anything. You never gave us anything. You must be insane. They are taking advantage of you.* Antonia was getting into a train and going away for ever. She was trying to tell Penelope something, but the train whistle screamed and Penelope could only see her mouth opening and shutting, and became agitated because she knew that what Antonia was saying was of immense importance. And then the old dream; the empty beach and the blanketing fog and the desolation because there was no other person in the world except her.

The darkness was never-ending. From time to time, arousing herself, she turned on the light to look at her watch. Two o'clock. Half past three. A quarter past four. The sheets of her bed were twisted and rumpled, and there was no solace there for limbs heavy with uneasy fatigue. She longed for the light.

It came at last. She watched it come and was calmed. She dozed once more, then opened her eyes. Saw the first low shafts of sunlight, a pale sky clear of cloud; she heard the birds, calling and answering. And then the thrush from the chestnut tree.

The night was, thankfully, over. At seven, unrested, more strangely tired than ever, she climbed slowly from her bed, found her slippers and dressing-gown. Everything seemed the most enormous effort, so that even these simple actions took conscious thought and concentration. She went to the bathroom, washed her face and cleaned her teeth, moving with care, so as to make no sound and possibly disturb Antonia. Back in her room, she dressed, sat at her mirror, brushed and coiled and pinned her hair. She saw the smudges, like bruises, under her dark eyes, the pallor of her skin.

She went downstairs. She thought about making a cup of tea, and then decided against it. Instead, she went out, through the conservatory, unlocking the glass door and stepping into her garden. The air was cool and diamond-sharp. Its impact caused her to shiver and pull her cardigan around her, but it was refreshing too, as cold spring water is refreshing, or a plunge into an icy pool. The newly cut lawn glittered with dew, but the first warm rays of sunshine had touched one corner, and here the dew was melting and the grass showed a different shade of green.

Her spirits rose, comforted as always by the sight of grass, trees, borders . . . her own sanctuary, which she had created herself by five years of hard and satisfying labour. All of today she would spend here. There was much to be done.

She reached the terrace, where stood the old wooden seat. In crannies between the slate flags were planted clumps of thyme and aubrietia (which, later in the year, would become fat cushions of white and purple flowers) – but also, inevitably, grew weeds. A brazen dandelion caught her eye and she stooped to tug it out, jerking at the stubborn, sturdy root. But it seemed that even this small physical effort was too much, for, as she straightened, she felt so strange, light-headed, and disorientated, that it occurred to her that she was about to faint. Instinctively, she reached for the back of the seat and, with this to steady her, managed to lower herself into a sitting position. Uncertain, she waited for what was going to happen next. It happened almost instantly. A pain, like a red-hot current, shot up her left arm, encircled her chest, and clamped shut, an ever-tightening band of steel. She could not breathe and she had never known such agony. She closed her eyes and opened her mouth to scream the pain away, but no sound came from her lips. Existence shrank to pain. To pain, and the fingers of her right hand, which were still clenched around the remains of the dandelion. For some reason, it was enormously important to keep holding on to it. She could feel the cold, damp earth that clung to its roots; smell the strong and pungent fragrance of that earth. Far away, and faintly, she heard the thrush singing.

And then, stealing up, came other scents and other sounds. The freshly cut grass of a long-ago lawn; a lawn that sloped to the water's edge, where grew the wild daffodils. The salt smell of a flood tide, rising to fill the creek. The kittiwakes calling. A man's footstep.

The ultimate luxury. She opened her eyes. The pain was gone. The sun was gone. Perhaps behind a cloud. It didn't matter. Nothing mattered.

He was coming.

'Richard.'

He was there.


At Ranfurly Road, at a quarter past nine on Tuesday morning, May 1st, Olivia stood in her little kitchen, perking coffee, boiling an egg for her breakfast, and leafing through the morning's mail. She had done her hair and her face, as was her custom, but was not yet dressed for the day's work. Amongst her mail, she found a highly coloured picture of Assisi, where one of the Art editors had gone for his holiday. She turned it over to read his facetious greeting, and as she did this, the telephone rang.

Still holding the postcard, she went across the living room to answer the call.

'Olivia Keeling.'

'Miss Keeling?' A woman's voice, a country voice.

'Yes.'

'Oh, I've caught you! I was so afraid you'd have left for your office . . .'

'No, I don't leave till half past nine. Who is this?'

'Mrs Plackett. From Podmore's Thatch.'

Mrs Plackett. With painful care, as though its disposal were of the utmost importance, Olivia placed the gaudy postcard on the mantelpiece, propped against the gilt frame of the mirror. Her mouth was dry. 'Is Mumma all right?' she somehow asked.

'Miss Keeling, I'm afraid . . . well, it's sad news. I am sorry. Your mother's died, Miss Keeling. This morning. Quite early, before any of us was here.'

Assisi; under a sky quite impossibly blue. She had never been to Assisi. Mumma was dead. 'How did it happen?'

'A heart attack. Quite sudden it must have been. In the garden.

Antonia found her, just sitting there on the garden seat. She'd been weeding. There was an old dandelion in her hand. She must have had a bit of a warning to get to the seat. She . . . she didn't looked distressed, Miss Keeling.'

'Has she been unwell?'

'Not unwell at all. Came back from Cornwall brown as a berry and just her usual self. But yesterday she was in London for the day . . .'

'Mumma was in London? Why didn't she let me know?'

'I don't know, Miss Keeling. I don't know why she went. She took the train from Cheltenham, and when Antonia met her at the station in the evening, she said Mrs Keeling was really tired. Had a bath and went to bed, soon as she got home, and Antonia gave her a little supper on a tray. But perhaps she'd overdone things.'

Mumma, dead. The dreaded, the unimaginable had happened. Mumma was gone for ever, and Olivia, who had loved her almost more than any other human being, could feel nothing except terribly cold. Her arms, in the loose sleeves of her dressing-gown, were covered with goose bumps. Mumma was dead. The tears and anguish and agonising sense of loss were there, and yet not there, and she was grateful for this. Later, she told herself, I shall grieve. For the present, grief would be set aside, like a package to be opened at a more convenient time. It was the old ruse that she had learned from hard experience. The closing of the watertight compartment, the beaming in of all one's concentration onto the practical problem, the highest priority. First things first.

She said, 'Tell me about it, Mrs Plackett.'

'Well. I got in this morning, eight o'clock. Don't usually come on Tuesdays, but yesterday was my grandson's birthday, so I changed my day. And came early, because I've got Mrs Kitson to clean out as well on Tuesdays. Let myself in with my own key, and nobody around. Was just dealing with the boiler when Antonia came downstairs. Said where was Mrs Keeling, because her bedroom door was open and her bed was empty. Well, we couldn't think. Then I saw the conservatory door was open, so I said to Antonia, "She'll be out in the garden." Antonia went to look. Then I heard her calling my name. And I went running. And I saw.'

Olivia gratefully recognised in Mrs Plackett's voice the tones of a countrywoman who had experienced such crises before. She was a lady of mature years. She had probably faced up to, and coped with, death many times over, and it held no fears or horrors for her.

'First thing I had to do was calm Antonia down. She was really shocked, weeping and crying and shivering like a kitten. But I gave her a cuddle, and set her down with a cup of tea, and she came out of it like a brave girl, and she's sitting here now, in the kitchen with me. Soon as she was all right, I rang the doctor in Pudley, and he came within ten minutes, and I took the liberty of calling Mr Plackett as well. He's on the last shift just now at the electronics factory, so he was able to come over on his bicycle. He and the doctor, they carried Mrs Keeling indoors and up the stairs to her room. She's there now, on her bed, decent and peaceful. You don't have to worry yourself about that.'

'What did the doctor say?'

'He said a heart attack, Miss Keeling. Probably instant. And he signed the death certificate. Left it here with me. And then I said to Antonia, "Better ring Mrs Chamberlain", but she said to ring you first. I should maybe have got in touch earlier, but I didn't want you to think of your poor mother dead, and still out in the garden.'

'That was very thoughtful of you, Mrs Plackett. So nobody else has been told?'

'No, Miss Keeling. Just you.'

'Right.' Olivia looked at her watch. 'I'll let Mrs Chamberlain know, and my brother as well. Then I'll drive down to Podmore's Thatch, just as soon as I've organised myself. I should be with you around lunch-time. Will you still be there?'

'Don't think about it, Miss Keeling. I'll be here as long as you want me to.'

'I shall have to stay a few days. Perhaps you could make up a bed for me in the other spare bedroom. And make sure there's enough food in the house. If necessary, Antonia can take the car, and do some shopping in Pudley. It'll be good for her to have something to do.' A thought occurred to her. 'What about the young gardener – Danus? Is he around?'

'No, Miss Keeling. He's in Scotland. Went straight there from Cornwall. Had an appointment to keep.'

'That's unfortunate. Never mind, it can't be helped. Give my love to Antonia.'

'Do you want to speak to her?'

'No,' said Olivia. 'No. Not just now. It can wait.'

'I'm sorry, Miss Keeling. I'm sorry to be the one to tell you.'

'Somebody had to. And, Mrs Plackett . . . thank you.'

She rang off. She looked out of the window and saw, for the first time, that it was a beautiful day. It was a perfect May morning, and Mumma was dead.


Afterwards, when it was all over, Olivia was to wonder what on earth they would have done without Mrs Plackett. For all her own experience of life, she had never before had to cope with a funeral. There was, she discovered, much to be done. And the initial hurdle, on arrival at Podmore's Thatch, was the task of dealing with Nancy.

George Chamberlain had answered the telephone at the Old Vicarage when Olivia rang from London, and, for the first time in her life, she had been deeply thankful to hear the lugubrious tones of her brother-in-law. She had told him what had happened as simply and as quickly as she could, explained that she was, herself, going straight to Podmore's Thatch, and then rang off, leaving him to break the sad news to Nancy. She had hoped, for the moment, that that would be the end of it but, as she turned the Alfasud into the gates of Podmore's Thatch, she saw Nancy's car and realised that she was not going to get off as lightly as she had hoped.

She was no sooner out of her own car, than Nancy was there, bursting out of the open door and bearing down with arms outstretched, her blue eyes starting, her face swollen with weeping. Before Olivia could take evasive action, Nancy had flung her arms around her sister, pressing her hot cheek against Olivia's own pale, cool one, and dissolving once more into noisy sobs.

'Oh, my dear . . . I came straight over. When George told me, I just came. I had to be with you all. I . . . I had to be *here* . . .'

Olivia stood still as stone, enduring for as long as was acceptably polite the messy, distasteful embrace. Then, gently, she detached herself. 'That was good of you, Nancy. But there was no need – '

'That's what George said. He said I'd just be a nuisance.' Nancy felt up the sleeve of her cardigan for a sodden handkerchief, endeavoured to blow her nose and generally pull herself together. 'But of course I couldn't stay at home. I had to be here.' She gave herself a little shake, drew her shoulders back. She was being plucky. 'I knew I had to come. The drive was a nightmare; I felt quite shaky when I got here, but Mrs Plackett made me a cup of tea and I'm better now.'

The prospect of supporting Nancy in her grief and getting her through the next few hours was almost more than Olivia could bear. 'You mustn't stay,' she told her sister, casting about for some watertight reason for getting Nancy out of the house. Inspiration struck. 'You have your children and George to consider. You mustn't neglect them. I have no one but myself to think about, so I am the obvious person to be here.'

'But your job?'

Olivia turned back to her car and retrieved her small suitcase from the back seat.

'It's all fixed. I'm not going back to the office until Monday morning.

Come on, let's go inside. We'll have a drink and then you can go home.
If you don't need a gin and tonic, I do.'

She led the way, and Nancy followed. The familiar kitchen was neat,
scrubbed; felt warm, but dreadfully empty.

'What about Noel?' Nancy asked.

'What about him?'

'You told him?'

'Of course. As soon as I'd rung George. I spoke to him at his office.'

'Was he very, very shocked?'

'Yes, I think he was. He didn't say very much.'

'Is he coming down here?'

'Not at the moment. I told him if I needed him, I'd be in touch.'

Nancy, as though incapable of standing for more than two minutes,
pulled out a chair and sat at the table. Her dramatic flight from the Old
Vicarage to Podmore's Thatch had apparently left her no time either to
comb her hair, powder her nose, or find herself a blouse that matched
her skirt.

She looked not only distraught but a mess, and Olivia knew a surge of
the old, irritated impatience. Whatever happened, good or bad, Nancy
always made a drama of it and, moreover, cast herself in the leading role.

'She went to London yesterday,' Nancy was saying. 'We don't know
why. Just went off on the train, on her own, for the whole day. Mrs
Plackett said she returned home quite exhausted.' She sounded offended,
as though, yet again, Penelope had pulled a fast one on her. Olivia half
expected her to add, *And she never even told us she was planning to die.* To
change the subject, she asked, 'Where is Antonia?'

'She's gone to Pudley to do some shopping.'

'Have you seen her?'

'Not yet.'

'And Mrs Plackett?'

'Upstairs, I think, getting your room ready.'

'In that case, I'll take my bag up and have a word with her. You stay
here. When I come back, we'll have that drink, and then you can get
back to George and the children . . .'

'But I can't simply leave you on your own . . .'

'Of course you can,' Olivia told her coolly. 'We can keep in touch by
telephone. And I'm better on my own.'

Nancy finally departed. With her gone, Olivia and Mrs Plackett were at
last able to get down to business.

'We'll have to get in touch with an undertaker, Mrs Plackett.'

'Joshua Bedway. He's the best man for the job.'

'Where is he?'

'Right here, in Temple Pudley. He's the village carpenter, does under-taking as a sideline. He's a good man, very tactful and discreet. Does a lovely job.' Mrs Plackett glanced at the clock. It was nearly a quarter to one. 'He'll be home now, having his dinner. Like me to give him a ring?'

'Oh, would you? And ask him to come as soon as possible.'

Mrs Plackett did this, with no histrionics, no pious lowering of the voice. A simple explanation was given and a simple request made. She might have been asking him to come and mend a gate. When she rang off, her expression was satisfied, as though with a job well done.

'That's it, then. He'll be here at three. I'll come with him. Be easier for you to have me here.'

'Yes,' said Olivia. 'Yes, it would be much easier.'

They then sat at the kitchen table and made lists. By now, Olivia was onto her second gin and tonic, and Mrs Plackett had accepted a small glass of port. A real treat, she told Olivia. She was very partial to port.

'Next person to get hold of, Miss Keeling, is the vicar. You'll want a church service, of course, and a Christian burial. Need to fix on a plot in the graveyard, and then a day and a time for the funeral. And then speak about hymns and such-like. You'll have hymns, I hope. Mrs Keeling loved her concerts, and a bit of music's nice at a funeral.'

Discussing practical details made Olivia feel marginally better. She unscrewed her fountain pen. 'What's the vicar's name?'

'The Reverend Thomas Tillingham. Mr Tillingham, he's known as. Lives in the Vicarage, next to the church. Best would be to give him a tinkle, and maybe ask him over tomorrow morning. Give him a cup of coffee.'

'Did he know my mother?'

'Oh, yes. Everybody in the village knew Mrs Keeling.'

'She was never exactly a regular church-goer.'

'No. Maybe not. But always ready to help with the organ fund, or the Christmas jumble. And every now and then, she'd ask the Tillinghams for dinner. Best lace-mats on the table, and a bottle of her best claret.'

It was not hard to imagine. Olivia, for the first time that day, found herself smiling. 'Entertaining her friends; that was what she really loved.'

'She was a lovely lady in every way. You could talk to her about anything.' Mrs Plackett took a ladylike sip of her port. 'And another thing, Miss Keeling. You should let Mrs Keeling's solicitor know that she's with us no more. Bank accounts, that sort of thing. That will all have to be attended to.'

'Yes, I'd thought of that.' Olivia wrote: Enderby, Looseby & Thring.

'And we'll have to put notices in the papers. *The Times* and the *Telegraph*, perhaps . . .'

'And then, flowers in the church. It's nice to have flowers, and you may not find time to do them yourself. There's a nice girl in Pudley. She's got a little van. When Mrs Kitson's old mother-in-law died, she did lovely flowers.'

'Well, we'll see. But first, we'll have to decide when the funeral is to be.'

'And after the funeral . . .' Mrs Plackett hesitated. 'Nowadays a lot of people don't think it's necessary, but I believe it's nice for folk to come back to the house and have a cup of tea and a bit of something to eat. Fruit cake's nice. 'Course, it depends on the time of the service, but when friends come a long way – and I've no doubt there'll be many from far afield – it seems pretty thankless to send them away without so much as a cup of tea. And somehow, it makes things easier. You can have a bit of a talk, and talking takes the edge off sadness. Makes you feel you're not alone.'

The old-fashioned country custom of a wake had not occurred to Olivia, but she saw the common sense of Mrs Plackett's suggestion. 'Yes, you're perfectly right. We'll organise something. But I should warn you, I'm a useless cook. You'll have to help me.'

'You leave it to me. Fruit cake's my speciality.'

'In that case, that seems to be everything.' Olivia laid down her pen and leaned back in her chair. Across the table, she and Mrs Plackett surveyed each other. For a moment, neither spoke. Then Olivia said, 'I think, Mrs Plackett, you were probably my mother's best friend. And right now, I know perfectly well that you're mine.'

Mrs Plackett became embarrassed. 'I've done no more than I should, Miss Keeling.'

'Is Antonia all right?'

'I think so. She was shocked, but she's a sensible girl. Good idea, sending her to do the shopping. I gave her a list as long as my arm. Keep her busy. Make her feel useful.' With that, Mrs Plackett downed the last of her port, set the empty wineglass on the table, and heaved herself to her feet. 'Well, if it's all right with you, I'll take myself home and give Mr Plackett a bite to eat. But I'll be back at three, to let Joshua Bedway into the house. And I'll stay till he's finished and gone.'

Olivia went to the door with her and saw her away, stately as ever on her bicycle. Standing there, she heard the sound of an approaching car, and the next moment the Volvo turned in at the gate. Olivia stayed where she was. Fond as her affections were for Cosmo's daughter, and sorry for the girl as she felt, she knew that she, herself, was incapable of dealing with yet another flood of emotion, another damp and teary embrace. The carapace of reserve, strong as an armour, was, for the time being, her sole defence. She watched as the Volvo drew to a halt, watched Antonia unbuckle her seat-belt and climb out from behind the steering wheel. As she did this, Olivia folded her arms, the body language gesture of physical rejection. Over the roof of the car, across the few feet of gravel that separated them, their eyes met. There was a pause, and then Antonia closed the door of the car with a soft clunk and came, walking, towards her.

'You're here,' was all she said.

Olivia unfolded her arms and laid her hands on Antonia's shoulders. 'Yes. I'm here.' She leaned forward and they kissed, formally, touching cheeks. It was going to be all right. There were to be no histrionics. For this deliverance Olivia was deeply grateful, but she felt sad too, because it is always sad when someone you have known as a child finally grows up, and you know that they will never be truly young again.


At exactly three o'clock, Joshua Bedway was there, driving up in his little van, with Mrs Plackett beside him. Olivia had harboured fears that he would be attired in inky black, with an expression of gloom to match, but all he had done was to change from his overalls into a decent suit and a black tie, and his sunburnt countryman's face did not look to her as though it could stay sombre for very long.

For the moment, however, he was both saddened and sympathetic. He told Olivia that her mother would be very much missed in the village. In the six years that she had lived in Temple Pudley, she had made herself, he said, very much part of the little community.

Olivia thanked him for his kind words, and with formalities over, Mr Bedway produced, from some pocket, his notebook. There were one or two details, he told her, and proceeded to list them. Listening to him, it dawned upon her that, at his job, he was a true professional, and for this she was deeply grateful. He spoke of The Plot and The Sexton and The Registrar. He asked questions and Olivia answered them. When he finally closed his notebook, returned it to its pocket, and said, 'I think that's all, Miss Keeling; you can safely leave the rest to me,' she did just that, gathered up Antonia, and walked out of the house.

They did not go down to the river, but made their way out of the gate and across the road, to climb a stile and follow the old bridle track that climbed the hill behind the village. It led through fields filled with grazing sheep and their lambs; the hawthorn hedges were coming into flower, and mossy ditches were cushioned in wild primroses. At the top of the hill stood a stand of ancient beeches, their roots exposed, eroded by centuries of wind and weather. Reaching these, hot and breathless from the climb, they sat, with a feeling of some accomplishment, and surveyed the view.

It stretched for miles, a great chunk of unspoiled English countryside, basking in the warm sunshine of an exceptional spring afternoon. Farms, fields, tractors, houses, all were minimised by distance to toy size. Steeply below them, Temple Pudley slumbered, a random cluster of gold stone houses. The church was half hidden by yews, but Podmore's Thatch and the whitewashed walls of the Sudeley Arms were clearly visible. Smoke, like tall plumes of grey feather, rose from chimneys, and in one garden a man had lit a bonfire.

It was marvellously quiet. The only sounds were the baa-ing of the sheep and the rustle of the breeze in the beech branches overhead. Then, high in the blue, an aeroplane, like a sleepy bee, hummed drowsily across the sky, but did nothing to disturb the peace.

For some time, they did not speak. Since their reunion, Olivia had spent all her time either making or receiving telephone calls (two of these, both quite pointless, were from Nancy), and there had been no chance to talk. Now she looked at Antonia, sitting there on the tussocky grass just a few feet away, in her faded jeans and her pink cotton shirt. Her sweater, discarded during the long hot climb up the hill, lay beside her, and her hair fell forward, hiding her face. Cosmo's Antonia. Despite her own battened-down misery, Olivia's heart went out to her. Eighteen was too young for so many awful things to be happening. But nothing could be changed, and Olivia knew that, with Penelope gone, Antonia had become, once more, her responsibility.

She said, breaking the silence, 'What will you do?'

Antonia turned and looked at her. 'How do you mean?'

'I mean, what will you do now? Now that Mumma's gone, you no longer have reason to stay at Podmore's Thatch. You'll have to start making decisions. Think about your future.'

Antonia turned away again, drew up her knees, and rested her chin on them. 'I have thought.'

'Do you want to come to London? Take up that offer of mine?'

'Yes, if I may. I'd like to do that. But eventually. Not just now.'

'I don't understand.'

'I thought that perhaps . . . it would be a good idea, if I just stayed here for a bit. I mean . . . what's going to happen to the house? Will it be sold?'

'I imagine so. I can't live here, and neither can Noel. And I don't suppose Nancy would want to move to Temple Pudley. It's not nearly grand enough for her and George.'

'In that case, people will want to come and look around, won't they? And you're far more likely to get a good price for it if it's furnished, and there are flowers around the place, and the garden's looking nice. I thought perhaps I could stay and see to everything, and show prospective buyers around, and keep the grass cut. And then, when it is sold, and it's all over, perhaps then I could come back to London.'

Olivia was surprised. 'But, Antonia, you'd be all alone. By yourself, in the house. Wouldn't you mind that?'

'No. No, I wouldn't mind. It's not that sort of house. I don't think I'd ever really feel alone there.'

Olivia considered this idea, and realised that it was, in fact, a sound one. 'Well, if you're sure, I think we'd all be enormously grateful to you. Because none of the family are going to be able to hang around, and Mrs Plackett has other commitments. Of course, nothing has been decided yet, but I am certain that the house will be sold.' She thought of something else. 'However, I don't see why you should have to do the garden as well. Surely Danus Muirfield will be coming back to work.'

Antonia said, 'I don't know.'

Olivia frowned. 'I thought he'd simply gone to Edinburgh to keep an appointment.'

'Yes. With a doctor.'

'Is he ill?'

'He has epilepsy. He's an epileptic.'

Olivia was filled with horror. 'An epileptic? But how perfectly ghastly. Did Mumma know?'

'No, neither of us knew. He didn't tell us until the very end of our holiday in Cornwall.'

Olivia found herself intrigued. She had never set eyes on the young man, and yet all she had heard about him, from both her sister, her mother, and Antonia, only served to whet her interest. 'What a very secretive person he must be.' Antonia made no comment to this. Olivia thought some more. 'Mumma told me he didn't drink or drive, and you mentioned that, too, in your letter. I suppose this is why.'

'Yes.'

'And what happened in Edinburgh?'

'He saw the doctor and he had another brain-scan, but the computer in the hospital had broken down, so that he couldn't get the results of his tests. He rang us up to tell us this. Last Thursday, it was. And then he went off with a friend to fish for a week. He said that it was better than hanging around at home, kicking his heels.'

'And when is he returning from his fishing trip?'

'On Thursday. The day after tomorrow.'

'Will he know the result of the brain-scan then?'

'Yes.'

'And after that, what happens? Is he coming back to Gloucestershire to work?'

'I don't know. I suppose it depends on how ill he is.'

It all sounded rather sad and hopeless. And yet, on consideration, not totally surprising. As long as Olivia could remember, a succession of oddballs and lame ducks – like bees to honey – had found their way into Mumma's life. She had never failed to support and sustain them, and this generosity of energy – and sometimes hard cash – was one of the things about his mother that drove Noel up the wall. And was, perhaps, why he had taken such an instant dislike to Danus Muirfield.

She said, 'Mumma liked him, didn't she?'

'Yes, I think she was very fond of him. And he was sweet with her. He looked after her.'

'Was she very upset when he told her about his illness?'

'Yes. Not for herself, but for him. And it was a shock to be told. Something unimaginable. Cornwall was magic, and we were having such fun . . . it was as though nothing bad could ever happen again. Just a week ago. When Cosmo died, I thought that was the worst. But I don't think any week's ever been so dreadful, or so long as this one.'

'Oh, Antonia, I am sorry.'

She feared that Antonia was about to succumb to tears, but now Antonia turned and looked at her, and Olivia saw with relief that her eyes were dry and her face, though serious, quite composed.

She said, 'You mustn't be sorry. You've got to be glad that there was just time enough for her to go back to Cornwall before she died. She loved every moment of it. I think, for her, it was like being young again. She never ran out of energy or enthusiasm. Every day was filled. She didn't waste a single moment.'

'She was very fond of you, Antonia. Having you with her must have doubled her pleasures.'

Antonia said painfully, 'That's another thing I have to tell you. She gave me the earrings. The earrings Aunt Ethel left her. I didn't want to take them, but she insisted. I've got them now, in my room at Podmore's Thatch. If you think I should give them back . . .?'

'Why should you give them back?'

'Because they've very valuable. They're worth four thousand pounds. I feel they should go to you, or to Nancy, or to Nancy's daughter.'

'If Mumma hadn't wanted you to have them, she wouldn't have given them to you.' Olivia smiled. 'And you didn't have to tell me about the earrings, because I already knew. She wrote me a letter to tell me what she'd done.'

Antonia was puzzled. 'Why did she do that, I wonder?'

'I suppose she was thinking of you and your good name. She wanted nobody accusing you of pinching them out of her jewel box.'

'But that's weird! She could have told you any time.'

'These things are better in writing.'

'You don't think she had some sort of premonition? That she knew that she was going to die?'

'We all know that we are going to die.'

The Reverend Thomas Tillingham, vicar of Temple Pudley, called at Podmore's Thatch at eleven o'clock the next morning. Olivia did not look forward to the interview. Her acquaintance of vicars was slim and she was uncertain as to how they would deal with each other. Before his arrival, she endeavoured to prepare herself for all exigencies, but this was difficult to do because she had no idea what sort of a man he was going to be. Perhaps elderly and cadaverous, with a fluting voice and archaic views. Or young and trendy, favouring outlandish schemes for bringing religion up to date, inviting his congregation to shake hands with each other, and expecting them to sing new-fangled and jolly hymns to the accompaniment of the local pop group. Either prospect was daunting. Her greatest dread, however, was that the vicar might suggest that, together, he and Olivia should kneel in prayer. She decided that, should such an horrific eventuality arise, she would cook up a little headache, plead ill health, and dash from the room.

But all her fears were, mercifully, unrealised. Mr Tillingham was neither young nor old; simply a nice, ordinary, middle-aged man in a tweed jacket and a dog-collar. She could perfectly understand why Penelope had liked to ask him for dinner. She met him at the door and led him into the conservatory, which was the most cheerful place she could think of. This proved something of a brainwave for they discussed Penelope's pot plants, and then her garden, and the conversation thus naturally led itself to the matter in hand.

'We shall all miss Miss Keeling most dreadfully,' Mr Tillingham said. He sounded truly sincere, and Olivia found it easy to believe that he wasn't referring wistfully to the delicious dinners that he would enjoy no longer. 'She was immensely kind, and she added a great flavour to our village life.'

'That's what Mr Bedway said. He's such a nice man. And especially nice for me, because you see I've never had anything to do with a funeral before. I mean, I've never had to arrange one. But Mrs Plackett and Mr Bedway, between them, have kept me straight.'

As though on cue, Mrs Plackett now made her appearance, bearing a tray with two mugs of coffee and a plate of biscuits. Mr Tillingham spooned a great deal of sugar into his mug and got down to churchly business. It did not take very long. Penelope's funeral would take place on Saturday, at three o'clock in the afternoon. They decided on the form of service and then came to the question of music.

'My wife is the organist,' Mr Tillingham told Olivia. 'She would be very happy to play, if you would like her to.'

'How kind, and I would like her to. But no mournful music. Something beautiful that people know. I'll leave it to her.'

'And hymns?'

They decided on a hymn.

'And a lesson?'

Olivia hesitated. 'Like I said, Mr Tillingham, I'm a total novice at this sort of thing. Perhaps I could leave it all to you.'

'But wouldn't your brother like to read the lesson?'

Olivia said, no, she didn't think that that was something that Noel would want to do.

Mr Tillingham came up with one or two more details, which were swiftly dealt with. He then finished his coffee and rose to his feet. Olivia went with him, through the kitchen and out of the front door, to where his shabby Renault was parked on the gravel.

'Goodbye, Miss Keeling.'

'Goodbye, Mr Tillingham.' They shook hands. She said, 'You've been so kind.' He smiled, a smile of unexpected charm and warmth. He hadn't really smiled before, but now his homely features were so transformed that all at once Olivia stopped thinking about him as a vicar and consequently found it quite easy to come out with something that had been lurking about at the back of her mind ever since he walked into the house. 'I don't really understand why you should be so kind and accommodating. After all, we both know that my mother wasn't a regular church-goer. She wasn't even very religious. And the idea of Resurrection and after-life she found very hard to swallow.'

'I know that. Once we discussed it, but we came to no agreement.'

'I'm not even certain that she believed in God.'

Mr Tillingham, still smiling, shook his head, reached out his hand for the door handle of his car. 'I wouldn't worry too much about that. She may not have believed in God, but I'm pretty certain God believed in her.'

•     •     •

The house, bereft of its owner, was a dead house, the shell of a body, its heartbeat stopped. Desolate, strangely silent, it seemed to wait. The quiet was a physical thing, inescapable, pressing like a weight. No footstep, no voice, no rattling saucepans from the kitchen; no Vivaldi, no Brahms burbling in comforting fashion from the tape player on the kitchen dresser. Doors closed, stayed closed. Each time she climbed the narrow stairs, Antonia came face to face with the closed door of Penelope's bedroom. Before, it had always stood open, allowing glimpses of garments flung across a chair, gusts of air blowing from the open window, the sweet smell that was Penelope's own. Now, just a door.

Downstairs was no better. Her chair, empty by the sitting-room fireplace. The fire unlit, the desk folded shut. No friendly clutter, no laughter, no more warm and spontaneous embraces. In the world where Penelope had lived, existed, breathed, listened, remembered, it had been possible to believe that nothing too dreadful could ever go wrong. Or if it did . . . and to Penelope it had . . . then there were ways of coping, of accepting, of refusing to admit defeat.

She was dead. On that ghastly morning, stepping from the conservatory out into the garden, seeing Penelope slumped there on the old wooden garden seat, with her long legs outstretched and her eyes closed, Antonia had told herself sharply that Penelope was simply resting for a moment; savouring the sharp, early air, the pale warmth of the early sun. The obvious was, for an insane instant, too horrifyingly final to contemplate. Existence without that source of constant delight, that rock-like security was unthinkable. But the unthinkable had happened. She was gone.

The worst was getting through each day. Days, which previously had never been long enough to contain their various activities, now stretched to eternity; an age ticked by between sunrise and darkness. Even the garden afforded no comfort, because Penelope was not there to bring it to life, and it took a real effort to go out of doors and find something there to do, like pulling weeds or picking an armful of daffodils, to be arranged in a jug and placed somewhere. Anywhere. It didn't matter. Nothing mattered any more.

Being so alone was a terrifying experience. She had never known what it was to feel so alone. Before, there had always been *someone*. At first, Cosmo; and then, when Cosmo died, the comforting knowledge that Olivia was there. In London, maybe, and miles from Ibiza, but still *there*. At the end of a telephone call saying, 'It's all right, come to me, I will take care of you.' But Olivia, for the time being, was unapproachable. Practical, organised, making lists, speaking on the telephone – it seemed that she was never off the telephone. She had made it perfectly clear to

Antonia, without actually saying so, that this was no time for long, intimate conversations, no time for confidences. Antonia had the wit to realise that, for the first time, she was seeing the other side of Olivia: the cool and competent business woman who had fought her way up the ladder of her career to become Editor of *Venus*, and, in the process, had schooled herself to be ruthless with human frailties and intolerant of sentimentality. The other Olivia, the Olivia that Antonia had first known in what she already thought of as the old days, was in all likelihood too vulnerable for exposure, and for the time being had shut herself away. Antonia understood and respected this, but it made nothing easier for herself.

Because of this barrier that stood between them, and also because it was obvious that Olivia already had more than enough on her plate, Antonia had told her little about Danus. They had spoken of him casually, up on the windy hilltop while Mr Bedway was doing the unimaginable things that he had to do at Podmore's Thatch, but nothing important had been said. At least, nothing truly important. He *has epilepsy*, Antonia had told Olivia. He *is an epileptic.* But she had not said, I love him. He is the first man I have ever loved and he feels the same way about me. He loves me, and we have been to bed together, and it wasn't frightening, the way I always thought it would be, it was just utterly right, and it was magic, all at the same time. I don't care what the future holds for us, I don't care about him not having any money. I want him to come back to me just as soon as he can, and if he is ill, I shall wait until he is well again, and I shall take care of him and we will live in the country and grow cabbages together.

She had not said this because she knew that Olivia's mind was on other things . . . there was, indeed, the likelihood that she might not even be interested and would not want to hear. Living together in the same house as Olivia was like sitting next to a stranger on a train. There was no real point of contact, and Antonia found herself isolated in her own unhappiness.

Before, there had always been someone. Now there was not even Danus. He was away, far in the north of Sutherland, unreachable by telephone or telegram or any normal form of communication. She told herself that he could not have cut himself away from her more completely if he had decided to take a dug-out canoe up the Amazon, or drive a team of huskies across the polar ice-cap. Not being able to get in touch with him was almost unbearable. Penelope was dead, and Antonia needed him. As though telepathy were some sort of a reliable radar system, she spent most of her waking hours sending him positive thought messages, urging him to receive them, to feel impelled to get in touch. To drive, if necessary, twenty miles to the nearest call-box, to dial the number of Podmore's Thatch and so find out what was wrong.

However, this did not happen, and Antonia was scarcely surprised. For comfort, he will ring on Thursday, she told herself. He gets back to Edinburgh on Thursday, and he will ring then, at the very first opportunity. He promised. He will ring to tell me . . . us? . . . the results of the brain-scan and the doctor's prognosis. (How extraordinary that this now seemed of the lesser urgency.) And then I shall tell him that Penelope is dead, and he will come, by some means or other, and he will be here, and I shall be able to be strong again. Antonia needed that strength in order to endure the ordeal of Penelope's funeral. Without Danus beside her, she was not certain that she was going to be able to cope.

Slowly, slowly, the hours passed. Wednesday dragged by, and it was Thursday. Today he will ring. Thursday morning. Thursday midday. Thursday afternoon.

No call came.

At half past three, Olivia went out, to walk to the church and there meet the girl from Pudley who was going to do the flowers for the funeral service. Left alone, Antonia pottered aimlessly around the garden, achieving nothing, and then wandered down to the orchard to unpeg a line of tea-towels and pillowcases from the washing line. The church clock struck four o'clock, and all at once, like a revelation, she knew that she could not wait another moment. The time had come to take some positive action, and if she did not act immediately, she would either have hysterics, or bolt down the slope to the banks of the Windrush and there drown herself. She abandoned the washing basket, walked up the garden, through the conservatory and into the kitchen, picked up the telephone and dialled the Edinburgh number.

It was a warm, slumbrous afternoon. The palms of her hands were clammy, her mouth felt dry. The kitchen clock ticked away the seconds at a faster speed than the beating of her own heart. Waiting for someone to answer the call, she found herself undecided as to exactly what she was going to say. If Danus was not there, and his mother came to the telephone, then a message would have to be left for him. *Mrs Keeling has died. Please, can you tell Danus. And will you ask him to call me. Antonia Hamilton. He has the number.* So far, so good. But would she have the nerve to go on and ask Mrs Muirfield if there was news from the hospital, or would that be intrusive and enormously unfeeling? Supposing the diagnosis had come through and was unhopeful. Danus' mother would scarcely relish sharing her natural distress with a total stranger, a disembodied voice calling from the depths of Gloucestershire. On the other hand . . .

'Hello?'

With thoughts flying in all directions, Antonia was taken unawares and almost dropped the receiver.

'I . . . oh . . . is that Mrs Muirfield?'

'No. I'm sorry, but Mrs Muirfield is not here at the moment.' The voice was female, very Scottish, and immensely refined.

'Well . . . when will she be back?'

'I'm sorry, but I have no idea. She went to a meeting of the Save the Children Fund, and then I think she's going to tea with a friend.'

'And Mr Muirfield?'

'Mr Muirfield's at his office.' The reply was brisk, as though Antonia's query was a stupid one – and it was – and the answer obvious. 'He'll not be home until half past six.'

'Who is that speaking?'

'I'm Mrs Muirfield's help.' Antonia hesitated. The voice, whose owner perhaps wanted to get on with her dusting, became impatient. 'Do you want me to take a message?'

In some desperation, 'Danus isn't there, is he?' Antonia asked.

'Danus is away fishing.'

'I know. But he was meant to be coming back today and I thought he might have arrived.'

'No. He's not come and I've no idea when he's expected.'

'Well, perhaps . . .' There was no alternative. ' . . . could you take a message?'

'You'll have to wait till I get the paper and pencil.' Antonia waited. Some time passed. 'Ready now.'

'Just say Antonia called. Antonia Hamilton.'

'Give me a moment till I write it down. An-Ton-Ia Ham-Il-Ton.'

'Yes, that's right. Just say . . . tell him . . . Mrs Keeling died on Tuesday morning. And the funeral is at Temple Pudley, at three o'clock on Saturday afternoon. He'll understand. He'll maybe,' she said, praying that he would be able to make it, that he would be there, 'he'll maybe want to come.'


At Podmore's Thatch, on Friday morning at ten o'clock, the telephone rang. It was the fourth telephone call since breakfast, and all of them had been answered by Antonia, flying from wherever she was in order to be the first person to pick up the receiver. But right now Antonia was out, gone to the village to pick up the daily newspapers and the milk, and so it was Olivia, sitting at the kitchen table, who rose to her feet and took the call.

'Podmore's Thatch.'

'Miss Keeling?'

'Speaking.'

'Charles Enderby here, of Enderby, Looseby and Thring.'

'Good morning, Mr Enderby.'

He did not offer the usual condolences, because he had already done this when Olivia had spoken to him to tell him formally, as Penelope's solicitor, that her mother had died.

'Miss Keeling, I am of course making the journey to Gloucestershire on Saturday in order to attend Mrs Keeling's funeral, but it's occurred to me that perhaps, if it is convenient to you all, that I might, when it is over, have a meeting with yourself and your brother and sister; just to go over the points of your mother's will that might need explaining, and to put you all in the picture. It seems, perhaps, a little precipitous, and of course you are at perfect liberty to suggest an alternative date, but it does seem a good opportunity when all the family will be under one roof. It shouldn't take more than half an hour.'

Olivia considered the suggestion. 'I can't think why we shouldn't. The sooner the better, and it's not often that the three of us are together.'

'Would you suggest a time?'

'Well, the service starts at three, and there'll be a cup of tea here afterwards for anybody who wants to come back to the house. I suppose by five o'clock it should all be over. How about five o'clock?'

'Splendid. I'll make a note of that. And will you let Mrs Chamberlain and your brother know?'

'Yes, of course.'


She rang the Old Vicarage.

'Nancy. Olivia here.'

'Oh, Olivia, I was just about to ring you. How are you? How is everything going? Do you need me at Podmore's Thatch? I can easily come over. I can't tell you how useless I feel, and . . .'

Olivia interrupted, cutting her sister short. 'Nancy, Mr Enderby's been on the phone. He wants a family meeting after Mumma's funeral, to get her will sorted out. Five o'clock. Can you be here?'

'Five o'clock?' Nancy's voice was shrill with alarm. Olivia might have suggested some clandestine and suspicious assignment. 'Oh, no, not five o'clock. I can't.'

'For heaven's sake, why not?'

'George has a meeting with the vicar and the archdeacon. It's about the curate's stipend. Terribly important. We'll have to come straight home after the funeral . . .'

'This is important too. Tell him to put the meeting off.'

'Olivia, I couldn't do that.'

'In that case, you'll have to come to the funeral in two cars, and you'll have to drive yourself home. You've got to be there . . .'

'Can't we meet Mr Enderby another time?'

'Yes, of course we can, but it won't be nearly so convenient. And I've already told Mr Enderby that we *will* be here, so you really have no alternative.' Olivia's voice, even to herself, sounded dictatorial and sharp. She added in kinder tones, 'If you don't want to drive yourself home that evening, then you can stay the night, and go back the next morning. But you must be here.'

'Oh, all right.' Nancy gave in, but grudgingly. 'But I won't stay the night, thank you all the same. It's Mrs Croftway's day off and I'll have to cook the children their supper.'

Bugger Mrs Croftway. Olivia stopped trying to be kind. 'In that case, will you ring Noel and tell him he's got to be here too. It will be one less thing for me to do, and hopefully will stop you from feeling so useless.'

After a long spell of dry weather, during which the level of the river had dropped disastrously and the salmon pools lay shallow and still, the rains came to Sutherland. These were blown in on fat grey clouds, rolling from the west, blotting out sky and sunshine, settling on the tops of the hills, sinking into the glens, turning to mist, to the light patter of falling raindrops. The heather, burned dry as tinder, drank in the moisture, absorbed it, spilled the excess off into peaty crannies that dribbled into tiny burns, and so into larger burns, and so on down the hillsides into the river itself. A solid day of rain was enough to revitalise the flow of water. It swelled, gathered force, spewed whitely over into deep pools, plunged on, down the gentle slope of the glen, headed for the open sea. By Thursday morning, the prospect of fishing, which up to now had proved totally unproductive, was all at once rife with exciting possibilities.

Thursday was the day that the two young men had planned to return to Edinburgh. Now they stood in the open doorway of the desolate croft, watching the rain, and discussing the situation. After a week of indifferent sport, the temptation to postpone their return was one that was hard to resist. But there were, of course, obstacles to this course of action.

Eventually, 'I don't have to be in the office until Monday,' Roddy said. 'So far as I'm concerned, it's neither here nor there. The decision's up to you, old chum. You're the one who wants to get home and find out what the bloody doctors have decided. If you can't wait another day to hear their verdict, then we'll pack up and leave now. But it seems to me that you've waited so long, you might as well wait another day and enjoy yourself in the process. And I don't suppose your mother will get her knickers in a twist if you don't show up this evening. You're a big boy now, and if she listens to the weather forecasts, she'll guess what's happened.'

Danus smiled. The casual fashion in which Roddy came straight to the nub of his dilemma filled him with gratitude. They had been friends for years, but over the last few days, with only each other for company, had become immensely close. Here, in this remote and inaccessible part of the world, there were few diversions, and in the evenings, once they had cooked their supper and built up the peat fire, there was nothing to do but talk. It was good for Danus to talk, good to come out with everything that he had miserably, ashamedly kept to himself for far too long. He told Roddy about America, and the sudden onset of his illness, and, brought out into the open, his experiences lost much of their terror. With all this out of the way, he was able to confide further. To explain his decision to switch careers; and to outline his plans for the future. He told Roddy about going to work for Penelope Keeling at Podmore's Thatch. He described the idyllic week in Cornwall. Finally, he told him about Antonia.

'Marry the girl,' had been Roddy's advice.

'I want to. One day. But I have to get myself sorted out first.'

'What is there to sort out?'

'If we married, we'd have children. I don't know if epilepsy is hereditary.'

'Oh, balls, of course it isn't.'

'And my work isn't exactly lucrative. In fact, I haven't got two brass farthings to rub together.'

'Get a loan from your old man. He can't be strapped for cash.'

'I could, of course, but I'd rather not.'

'Pride will get you nowhere, chum.'

'I suppose not.' He thought about it, but would not commit himself. 'I'll see,' was all he would promise.

Now, he turned up his face to the dripping skies and thought about getting home, and the vital verdict, lying in wait for his arrival. He thought about Antonia, filling in the days at Podmore's Thatch, listening for the telephone, waiting for his call.

He said, 'I promised Antonia I'd ring today, as soon as I got back to Edinburgh.'

'You can do that tomorrow. If she's the girl I think she is, she'll understand.' The river, by now, would be in spate. In his imagination, Danus felt the weight and pleasing balance of his salmon rod, as yet unused. Heard the spin of the reel, felt the tug of a bite. There was a certain pool where the big fish lurked. Roddy grew impatient. 'Come on, make up your mind. Let's live dangerously and give ourselves another day. So far, we've caught nothing but trout and we've eaten those. The salmon are down there waiting for us. We owe it to them to give them a sporting chance.'

He was, quite obviously, itching to go. Danus turned his head and looked at his friend. Roddy's ruddy features held the expression of a small boy yearning for the treat of a lifetime, and Danus knew that he hadn't the heart to deny him.

He grinned, gave in. 'Okay. We'll stay.'

The next day, early, they set off to drive south. The back of Roddy's car was laden with bags, rods, gaffs, waders, creels, and, also, the two hefty salmon they had landed during the course of the previous afternoon, for the decision to stay on had proved more than worthwhile. The little croft, cleaned, cleared, and safely shuttered, disappeared into the hills behind them. Ahead lay the long narrow road, winding and dipping across the desolate moor of Sutherland. The rain had ceased, but the sky was still smudged by watery clouds, and the shadows of these drifted across the endless miles of bog and heather. With the moor finally traversed, they dropped down into Lairg, crossed the river at Bonar Bridge, and rounded the blue waters of the Dornoch Firth. Then up and over the winding, precipitous slopes of Struie and so to the Black Isle. Now the road was wide and fast and they were able to pick up speed. Old landmarks raced in upon each other, were reached and passed at an alarming rate. Inverness, Culloden, Carrbridge, Aviemore, and then the road curved south from Dalwhinnie, to climb the Cairngorms by the bleak hills of Glengarrie. By eleven o'clock, they had bypassed Perth, and were onto the motorway, slicing through Fife like a surgeon's knife, and the two great bridges that span the Forth revealed themselves, glittering in the bright morning light and looking as though they had been constructed of wire. Across the river, and they were on the approach road to Edinburgh. Observed from a distance, the spires and towers of the ancient city, the crag and bulk of the Castle with its flag snapping at the masthead presented, as always, a silhouette timeless and unchanging as an old print.

The motorway ended. The car slowed down to forty, then thirty miles an hour. The traffic thickened. They came to houses, shops, hotels, traffic lights. They had scarcely spoken during the entire journey. Now Roddy broke the silence.

'It's been great,' he said. 'We'll do it again sometime.'

'Yes. Sometime. I can't thank you enough.'

Roddy tapped out a tattoo on the steering wheel with his fingernails. 'How do you feel?'

'Okay.'

'Apprehensive?'

'Not really. Just realistic. If I have to live with this thing for the rest of my life, then that's what I'll have to do.'

'You never know.' The lights turned green. The car moved forward. 'It might be good news.'

'I'm not thinking about it. I'd rather expect the worst and be ready to cope with it.'

'Whatever it is . . . whatever they've found out . . . you won't let it get you down, will you? I mean, if things look pretty black, don't keep it to yourself. If there's no one else you feel you can talk to, there's always me, ready and available.'

'How do you feel about hospital visiting?'

'A cinch, old boy. Always had an eye for a pretty nurse. I'll bring you grapes and eat them all myself.'

Queensferry Road; the Dean Bridge. Now they were into the wide streets and perfectly proportioned terraces of the New Town. Freshly cleaned, washed in sunshine, their stonework was the colour of honey; in Moray Place the trees were misty with fresh green foliage, and flowering cherries hung heavy with blossom.

Heriot Row. The tall, narrow house that was home. Roddy drew up at the pavement's edge and switched off the engine. They got out and unloaded Danus' belongings, including the creel which contained his precious fish, and piled it all on the doorstep.

With this accomplished, 'That's it then,' said Roddy, but still hesitated, as though reluctant to abandon his old friend. 'Want me to come in with you?'

'No,' Danus told him. 'I'll be fine.'

'Ring me at the flat this evening.'

'I'll do that.'

Roddy delivered an affectionate thump on Danus' shoulder. 'Adiós, then, old chap.'

'It's been great, Roddy.'

'And good luck.'

He got back into his car and drove away. Danus watched him go, then reached into the pocket of his jeans for the latch key and opened the massive black-painted door. It swung inwards. He saw the long-familiar hallway, the graceful curved staircase. All was immaculate and orderly, the silence broken only by the ticking of the tall clock which had once belonged to Danus' great-grandfather. Furniture gleamed with polish and years of care, and a bowl of hyacinths stood on the chest by the telephone, filling the air with their heavy and sensuous scent.

He hesitated. Upstairs a door opened and shut. Footsteps. He looked up as his mother appeared at the head of the stair.

'Danus.'

He said, 'The fishing turned good. I stayed an extra day.'

'Oh, Danus . . .'

She looked just as she usually did, neat and elegant, wearing a smooth tweed skirt and a lamb's-wool sweater, and without a hair of her grey head out of place. And yet she looked different. She was coming down the stairs towards him . . . running down the stairs, which in itself was extraordinary. He stared at her. On the bottom step she stopped, her eyes on a level with his, her hand closed over the polished newel post at the foot of the bannister.

She said, 'You're all right.' She wasn't crying, but her blue eyes were brilliant as though with unshed tears. He had never before seen her in such a state of emotional excitement. 'Oh, Danus, it's all right. There's nothing wrong with you. There never has been. They rang yesterday evening, and I had a long chat with the specialist. That diagnosis you had in America was totally wrong. All these years . . . and you've never had epilepsy at all. You've never been an epileptic.'

He could not say anything. His brain had stopped working, had turned to cotton wool, and he could think no coherent thought. And then, only one thought. 'But . . .' It took effort even to speak, and the sound of his voice came out in a croak. He swallowed and started again. 'But the black-outs?'

'Caused by the virus you contracted and your very, very high temperature. Apparently that can happen. And it happened to you. But it's not epilepsy. It never was. And if only you hadn't been such a stupid clunk and kept it all to yourself, you would have saved yourself all these years of anguish.'

'I didn't want you to be worried. I was thinking of Ian. I didn't want you to go through it all a second time.'

'I'd go through hell-fire and brimstone rather than have you make yourself miserable. And it was all for nothing. For no reason. You're *all right*.'

All right. Never epilepsy. It had never happened. Like a bad dream, and as terrifying, but it had never really happened. He was all right. No more pills, no more uncertainty. Relief rendered him weightless, as though at any moment he might take off and float to the ceiling. Now, he could do anything. Everything. He could marry Antonia. *Oh, dear God, I can marry Antonia and we can have children, and I simply can't thank you enough. Thank you for this miracle. I'm so grateful, I shall never stop being grateful. I shall never forget. I promise you that I shall never forget. I . . .*

'Oh, Danus, don't stand there looking like a pudding. Don't you understand?'

He said, 'Yes.' And then he said, 'I love you.' Although it was true, and had always been true, he could not remember ever before having said such a thing to her. His mother promptly burst into tears, which was another new experience, and Danus put his arms around her and held her so tightly that after a bit she stopped crying and started sniffing instead, and feeling around for her handkerchief. Finally, they drew apart and she blew her nose and wiped her eyes, and touched her hair, settling it back into place.

'So stupid,' she told him. 'The last thing I meant to do was weep. But it was such wonderful news to have, and your father and I have been sick with frustration, not being able to get hold of you and share it with you, and put your mind at rest. But now I have told you, there's something else I think you should know. A phone message came through for you yesterday afternoon. I was out, but Mrs Cooper took it down and left it for me to find. I'm afraid it might be rather distressing news, but I hope you won't be too upset . . .'

Already, before his eyes, she was reverting once more to her usual practical manner. Demonstrations of emotion and affection were, for the time being, over. Tucking her handkerchief up her sleeve, she pushed Danus gently out of the way and went to the chest where stood the telephone, to pick up the message pad that lived by the instrument. She leafed over the pages.

'Here it is. From somebody called Antonia Hamilton. You'd better read it for yourself.'

Antonia.

He took the pad, saw Mrs Cooper's pencilled, loopy handwriting.

Antonia Hamilton rang 4 o'clock Thurs says Mrs Keeling died Tues funeral 3 o'clock Temple Pudley Sat afternoon thinks you might like to be there hope I've got it right. L Cooper.

The family gathered for their mother's funeral. The Chamberlains were the first to arrive. Nancy in her own car, and George driving his stodgy and elderly Rover. Nancy wore a navy-blue coat and skirt and a felt hat of quite startling unbecomingness. Her features, beneath its jutting brim, were sternly set and brave.

Olivia, dressed, for courage and composure, in her favourite dark grey Jean Muir, greeted and kissed them both. Kissing George felt like kissing a knuckle-bone, and he smelt of moth-balls and faintly antiseptic, like a dentist. As though they were guests and strangers, she led them through to the warm and flowery sitting room. And, as though they were guests, she found herself making conversation, apologising.

'I am sorry I couldn't ask you both to lunch. But as you probably saw, Mrs Plackett's laid the dining-room table for tea, and pushed back all the chairs, and Antonia and I have spent the morning making sandwiches. We lunched off the crusts.'

'Don't worry. We had a bite in a pub on the way.' Nancy settled herself, with a sigh of relief, in Mumma's chair. 'Mrs Croftway's out for the day, so we had to dump the children with friends in the village. We left Melanie in tears. She's dreadfully cut up about her Granny Pen. Poor child, the first time she's experienced death. Face to face, as it were.' Olivia could think of nothing to say to this. Nancy drew off her black gloves. 'Where's Antonia?'

'Upstairs. Changing.'

George looked at his watch. 'She'd better get a move on. It's twenty-five to three already.'

'George, it takes exactly five minutes to walk from here to the church.'

'Maybe. But we don't want to be rushing in at the last moment. Most unseemly.'

'And Mother?' Nancy's voice was hushed. 'Where is Mother?'

'She's there, in the church, ready and waiting for us,' Olivia told her briskly. 'Mr Bedway suggested a family procession from the house, but somehow I jibbed at the prospect. I do hope you both agree.'

'And when does Noel arrive?'

'Any moment now, I hope. He's driving from London.'

'The traffic on a Saturday is always heavy,' George pronounced. 'He'll probably be late.'

But his gloomy prophecy proved unfounded, for five minutes later, the country quiet was shattered by the familiar sounds of their brother's arrival: the roar of the Jaguar's engine, the grinding of tyres on gravel as he braked to a halt, the slam of a car door. A moment or so later he had joined them, looking immensely tall and dark and elegant in a grey suit which had no doubt been tailored for him with expensive business lunches in mind, and was somehow too ostentatious for a small country funeral.

No matter, he was here. Nancy and George sat and looked at him, but Olivia rose to her feet and went to give him a kiss. He smelt of Eau Sauvage, and not disinfectant, and for this small mercy she was grateful.

'What sort of a drive did you have?'

'Not too bad, but the traffic was hellish. Hello, Nancy. Hi, George. Olivia, who's the old boy in the blue suit hovering around the garage?'

'Oh, that'll be Mr Plackett. He's going to come and house-sit while we're all in the church.'

Noel raised his eyebrows. 'Are we expecting bandits?'

'No, but it's the local custom. Mrs Plackett insisted. It's either bad luck or not *comme il faut* to leave the house empty during a funeral service. So she fixed for Mr Plackett to stay, and he's been told to keep the fires going, and put kettles on to boil, and such.'

'How very well organised.'

George once more looked at his watch. He was getting restive. 'I really think we should leave. Come along, Nancy.'

Nancy stood, and went to the mirror that hung over Mumma's desk, in order to check the angle of her dreadful hat. This done, she drew on her gloves. 'What about Antonia?'

'I'll call her,' said Olivia, but Antonia was already downstairs, waiting for them in the kitchen, sitting on the scrubbed wooden table and talking to Mr Plackett, who had made his way indoors and taken up his post as caretaker. As they came through the kitchen door, she got off the table and smiled politely. She wore a navy-and-white-striped cotton skirt and a white shirt with a frilled collar, over which she had pulled a navy-blue cardigan. Her bright and shining hair was drawn back into a pony-tail and tied with a navy-blue ribbon. She looked young as a schoolgirl, and as diffident, and quite dreadfully pale.

'Are you all right?' Olivia asked her.

'Yes, of course.'

'George says it's time we went . . .'

'I'm ready.'

Olivia led the way, out through the porch, stepping into the pale, clear sunshine. The others followed, a small and sombre party. As they set out across the gravel, a new sound began. The church bell, tolling gravely. Measured peals rang out over the tranquil countryside, and rooks, disturbed, scattered, cawing from the tree-tops. They're ringing the bell for Mumma, Olivia told herself, and all at once, everything was coldly real. She paused, waiting for Nancy to catch up with her, to walk by her side. And doing this, turning back, she caught sight of Antonia suddenly stopping dead in her tracks. She had been pale before, but now she was white as a sheet.

'Antonia, what is it?'

Antonia looked panic-stricken, 'I . . . I've forgotten something.'

'What have you forgotten?'

'I . . . a . . . handkerchief. I haven't got a handkerchief. I must have one . . . I won't be a moment. Don't wait. You go on . . . I'll catch you up . . .'

And she bolted back into the house.

Nancy said, 'How extraordinary. Is she all right?'

'I think so. She's upset. Perhaps I should wait for her . . .'

'You can't wait,' George told her firmly. 'There's no time to wait. We'll be late. Antonia will be all right. We'll keep a seat for her. Now, come along, Olivia . . .'

But even as they stood there, hesitating, there occurred yet another interruption: the sound of a car being driven far too fast down the road that ran through the village. It appeared around the corner by the pub, slowed down, and drew up only a few feet away, by the open gate of Podmore's Thatch. A dark green Ford Escort, and unfamiliar. Silenced by surprise, they watched while its driver got out from behind the wheel and slammed the door shut behind him. A young man, unrecognised as his car. A man whom Olivia had never before seen in her life.

He stood there. They all stared, and nobody said a word, and in the end it was he who broke the silence. He said, 'I'm sorry. For arriving so precipitously and so late. I had rather a long way to drive.' He looked at Olivia and saw the total bewilderment written all over her face. He smiled. 'I don't think we've ever met. You must be Olivia. I'm Danus Muirfield.'

But of course. Tall as Noel, but heavier in build, with wide shoulders and a deeply sun-tanned face. A most personable young man, and Olivia found an instant to realise exactly why Mumma had become so fond of him. Danus Muirfield. Who else?

'I thought you were in Scotland' was all she could think of to say.

'I was. Yesterday. It wasn't until yesterday that I heard about Mrs Keeling. I am most dreadfully sorry . . .'

'We're just going to the church now. If you . . .'

He interrupted her. 'Where's Antonia?'

'She went back into the house. Something she'd forgotten. I don't think she'll be long. If you want to wait, Mr Plackett's in the kitchen . . .'

George, by now at the end of his patience, could bear to listen no longer. 'Olivia, we have no time to stand and chat. And there can be no question of waiting. We must go. Now. And this young man can hurry Antonia along and make certain that she isn't late. Now, let's stand here no longer . . .' He began to herd them all forward, as though they were sheep.

'Where will I find Antonia?' Danus asked.

'In her room, I expect,' Olivia called back over her shoulder. 'We'll keep seats for you both.'

He found Mr Plackett sitting at the kitchen table peacefully reading his *Racing News*.

'Where's Antonia, Mr Plackett?'

'Went upstairs. Looked in tears to me.'

'Do you mind if I go and find her?'

'No skin off my nose,' said Mr Plackett.

Danus left him and ran, two at a time, up the narrow stairway. 'Antonia!' Unfamiliar with the upstairs geography of the house, he opened doors, found a bathroom and a broom cupboard. 'Antonia!' Down the small landing and a third door opened into a bedroom, obviously occupied but at the moment empty. At the other side of this stood yet another door, leading into the far end of the house. Without knocking, he burst through it and there found her at last, sitting forlornly on the edge of her bed, and in floods of tears.

Relief made him feel quite light-headed. 'Antonia.' He was beside her in two strides, sitting, taking her into his arms, pressing her head onto his shoulder, kissing the top of her head, her forehead, her streaming, swollen eyes. Her tears tasted salty, and her cheeks were wet, but nothing mattered except that he had found her, and was holding her, and loved her more than any human being on earth, and was never, never going to be separated from her again.

At last, 'Didn't you hear me call?' he asked.

'Yes, but I didn't think it was true. I couldn't really hear anything except that terrible bell. I was all right until the bell started and then . . . all at once I knew I was going to fall to bits. I couldn't go on with the others. I miss her so much. Everything's dreadful without her. Oh, Danus, she's dead, and I loved her so much. And I want her. I want her all the time . . .'

'I know,' he told her. 'I know.'

She continued to sob onto his shoulder. 'Everything's been so awful. Since you went. So awful. There wasn't anybody . . .'

'I'm sorry . . .'

'And I've been thinking about you so much. All the time. I did hear you calling but I couldn't believe it . . . it was really you. It was just that awful bell, and me, making it up. I wanted you to be here so much.'

He said nothing. She continued to weep, but the sobs were subsiding, the worst of her storm of grief just about over. After a little, he loosened his grip of her and she drew away, turning her face up to his. A lock of hair fell across her forehead, and he smoothed this back, and then reached for his clean handkerchief and gave it to her. He watched tenderly while she wiped her eyes, and lustily, like a child, blew her nose.

'But, Danus, where have you been? What happened? Why didn't you telephone?'

'We didn't get back to Edinburgh until yesterday at noon. The fishing was too good to leave, and I hadn't the heart to deny Roddy his fun. When I got home, my mother gave me your message. But every time I tried to call, the telephone here was engaged.'

'It never stops ringing.'

'In the end, I just said, to hell with it, and got into my mother's car and drove.'

'You drove,' she repeated. The significance of this took a second or two to sink in. 'You *drove*? Yourself?'

'Yes. I can drive again. And I can drink myself silly if I so choose. Everything's all right. I'm not an epileptic and I never was one. It all started with a mistaken diagnosis by that doctor in Arkansas. I was ill. For a time I was very ill. But it was never epilepsy.'

For a terrible moment, he thought she was about to burst into tears again. But all she did was to fling her arms about his neck and hug him so tightly that he wondered if he was about to choke to death. 'Oh, Danus, my darling, it's a miracle.'

Gently he disentangled himself, but kept a hold on both her hands. 'But that's not the end of it. It's just the beginning. A whole new start. For both of us. Because, whatever I do, I want us to do it together. I don't know what the hell it will be, and I still have nothing to offer you, but please, if you love me, don't let's ever be apart again.'

'Oh, no. Don't let's. Ever.' She had stopped crying, tears were forgotten, she was his own dear Antonia again. 'We'll get that market garden. Somehow. Someday. And we'll find the money somewhere . . .'

'I really don't want you to go to London and be a model.'

'I wouldn't if you made me. There must be other ways.' All at once, she was struck by a brilliant idea. 'I know. I can sell the earrings. Aunt Ethel's earrings. They're worth at least four thousand pounds . . . I know it's not very much, but it would be a beginning, wouldn't it? It would give us something to start with. And Penelope wouldn't mind. When she gave them to me, she said I could sell them if I wanted.'

'Don't you want to keep them? To remember her by?'

'Oh, Danus, I don't need the earrings for remembrance. I have a thousand things to remember her by.'

All the time they had been talking, the bell from the church tower had continued its tolling. Bong, Bong, Bong, out across the countryside. Now, abruptly, it stopped.

They looked at each other. He said, 'We must go. We have to be there. We mustn't be late.'

'Yes, of course.'

They stood up. Swiftly, composedly, she tidied her hair, smoothed her fingers across her cheeks. 'Does it show that I've been crying?'

'Only a little. No one will remark upon it.'

She turned away from the mirror. 'I'm ready,' she told him, and he took her hand, and together they went from the room.


As the family walked to church, the toll of the bell grew louder, clanging above them, silencing all other sounds from the village. Olivia saw the cars parked along the pavement's edge, the little stream of mourners making their way beneath the lychgate and up the path that wound between the ancient, leaning gravestones.

Bong. Bong. Bong.

She paused for a moment to exchange a word with Mr Bedway, and then followed the others into the church. After the warm sunshine out of doors, the cold struck chill, from flagged floors and unheated stone. It was a little like walking into a cave, and there was a strong musty smell, suggestive of death-watch beetle and organ mould. But all was not gloom, for the girl from Pudley had done her work, and everywhere one looked stood profusions of spring flowers. Also, the church, being so small, was filled. This comforted Olivia, who had always found the sight of empty pews intensely depressing.

As they made their way down the aisle, the tolling abruptly stopped. In the ensuing silence, their footsteps clattered on the bare flags. The two front pews stood empty, and they took their places, filing in. Olivia, Nancy, George, and then Noel. This was the moment that Olivia had dreaded, for, at the altar steps, the coffin waited. In cowardly fashion, she averted her eyes and looked about her. Dotted amongst the sea of unfamiliar country faces . . . the inhabitants, she supposed, of Temple Pudley, come to pay their last respects . . . she found others, known for years, and converged from far afield. The Atkinsons from Devon; Mr Enderby of Enderby, Looseby & Thring; Roger Wimbush, the portraitist, who years ago, when he was an art student, had made his home in Lawrence Stern's old studio in the garden of Oakley Street. She saw Lalla and Willi Friedmann, distinguished as ever, with their pale, cultured refugee faces. She saw Louise Duchamp, immensely chic in inky black; Louise, the daughter of Charles and Chantal Rainier, and one of Penelope's oldest friends, who had made the long journey from Paris to England in order to be here. Louise looked up and caught Olivia's eye, and smiled. Olivia smiled back, touched that she had felt impelled to come so far, and grateful for her presence.

With the bell stilled, music now began, seeping into the dusty silence of the church. Mrs Tillingham, as promised, was playing the organ. The Temple Pudley organ was not a fine instrument, being both breathless and aged, like an old man, but even these defects could not mar the cool perfection of the *Eine Kleine Nachtmusik*. Mozart. Mumma's favourite. Had Mrs Tillingham known, or had she simply made an inspired guess?

She saw old Rose Pilkington, nearing ninety but gallant as ever, wearing a black velvet cape and a violet straw hat so battered that it looked as though it had travelled around the world twice. Which it probably had. Rose's wrinkled nut of a face was tranquil; from it her faded eyes gazed out in peaceful acceptance of what had happened and what was about to happen. Simply to look at Rose made Olivia feel ashamed of her own cowardice. She faced forward, listened to the music, looked at last at Mumma's coffin. But could scarcely see it, because it was awash with flowers.

From the back of the church, from the open doorway, came the sounds of a small disturbance, and hushed voices. Then footsteps made their way swiftly down the aisle, and Olivia turned to see Antonia and Danus slip into the empty pew behind them.

'You made it.'

Antonia leaned forward. She was, apparently, recovered, with colour back in her cheeks. 'I'm sorry we're so late,' she whispered.

'Just in time.'

'Olivia . . . this is Danus.'

Olivia smiled. 'I know,' she said.

Overhead, far above, the tower clock struck three.

With the service almost over, and a short tribute spoken, Mr Tillingham announced the hymn. Mrs Tillingham played the first few bars, and the congregation, with hymn-books at the ready, rose to their feet.

For all the Saints who from their labours rest
Who thee by faith before the world confessed
Their name, O *Jesu*, be forever blest

Alleluia

The villagers of Temple Pudley were familiar with the tune, and their voices, raised, caused the old worm-eaten rafters to ring. It wasn't perhaps the most suitable hymn for a funeral, but Olivia had chosen it because it was the only one she knew that Mumma really liked. She mustn't forget any of the things that Mumma really liked; not just lovely music, and having people to stay, and growing flowers, and ringing up for long chats just when you most hoped she would. But other things – like laughter, and fortitude and tolerance, and love. Olivia knew she must not let these qualities go from her life, just because Mumma had gone. Because, if she did, then the nicer side of her complex personality would shrivel and die, and she would be left with nothing but her inborn intelligence, and her relentless, driving ambition. She had never contemplated the security of marriage, but she needed men – if not as lovers, then as friends. To receive love, she must remain a woman prepared to give it, otherwise she would end up as a bitter and lonely old lady, with a cutting tongue and probably not a friend in the world.

But the next few months would not be easy. As long as Mumma was alive, she knew that some small part of herself had remained a child, cherished and adored. Perhaps you never completely grew up until your mother died.

Thou was their Rock, their Fortress and their Might,
Thou, Lord, their Captain in the well-fought fight.

She sang. Loudly. Not because she had a particularly strong voice, but because, like that child whistling in the dark, it helped to boost her courage.

Thou, in the darkness drear, their one true Light,

Alleluia

Nancy had succumbed to tears. All the way through the service she had kept them resolutely at bay, but all at once she was beyond caring, and let them flow. Her sobs were noisy, and doubtless embarrassing to others, but there was nothing she could do about them except, from time to time, noisily blow her nose. Soon she would have used up all the Kleenex she had stuffed, with some forethought, into her bag.

She wished, beyond all else, that she could have seen Mother again . . . or even just spoken to her . . . after that last, dreadful telephone conversation when Mother had called from Cornwall, to wish them all gaily a happy Easter. But Mother had behaved in the most extraordinary fashion, and some things, there was no doubt, were better said, aired and out in the open. But finally, Mother had hung up on Nancy, and before Nancy had either the time or the opportunity to put things straight between them, Mother had died.

Nancy did not blame herself. But lately waking in the middle of the night, she had found herself strangely alone in the darkness, and weeping. She wept now, not minding if people saw, not caring if they listened to her grief. That grief was evident, and she was not ashamed. The tears flowed and she made no effort to stop them, and they flowed like water, damping down the hard, hot embers of her own unacknowledged guilt.

> O may Thy soldiers, faithful, true and bold
> Fight as the Saints who nobly fought of old
> And win, with them, the victor's crown of gold

> Alleluia

Noel did not join in the singing, did not even go through the motions of holding an open hymnal. He stood, at the end of the pew, motionless, with one hand in his jacket pocket and the other resting on the wooden rail in front of him. His handsome face showed no expression, and it was impossible for any person to imagine what he was thinking.

> Oh, blest communion! Fellowship Divine!
> We feebly struggle, they in glory shine.

Mrs Plackett, near the back of the church, raised her voice in joyful praise. Her hymnal was held high, her considerable chest outflung. It was a lovely service. Music, flowers, and now a rousing hymn . . . just what Mrs Keeling would have enjoyed. And a good turn-out too. All the village had come. The Sawcombes, and Mr and Mrs Hodgkins from the Sudeley Arms. Mr Kitson, the Bank Manager from Pudley, and Tom Hadley, who ran the newsagents, and a dozen or so others. And the family were holding up well, all except for that Mrs Chamberlain, sobbing away for all the world to hear. Mrs Plackett did not believe in letting emotion show. Keep yourself to yourself had always been her motto. Which was one of the reasons she and Mrs Keeling had always been such friends. A true friend, Mrs Keeling had been. She was going to leave a real hole in Mrs Plackett's life. Now she glanced around the crowded church, made a few mental calculations. How many of them would be coming back to the house for tea? Forty? Forty-five, perhaps.

With a bit of luck, Mr Plackett would have remembered to put the kettles on to boil.

Yet all are one in Thee, for all are Thine.

Alleluia.

She hoped there would be enough fruit cake.

# Mr Enderby

By a quarter past five the funeral tea was over, the rearguard of the stragglers had said goodbye and taken themselves home. Olivia, seeing them off, watched the last car turn the corner by the gate and then, in some relief, turned and went back into the house. The kitchen hummed with activity. Mr Plackett and Danus, who had spent the last half-hour directing traffic and endeavouring to untangle a number of ineptly parked cars, had now moved indoors and were helping Mrs Plackett and Antonia collect and wash up all the tea-things. Mrs Plackett was at the sink, elbow-deep in suds. Mr Plackett, obliging as ever, stood at her side and dried the silver teapot. The dishwasher whirred, Danus came through the door with another trayful of cups and saucers, and Antonia was getting the vacuum cleaner out of its cupboard.

Olivia felt unnecessary and at a loss. 'What am I supposed to do?' she asked Mrs Plackett.

'Not a thing.' Mrs Plackett did not turn from the sink; her reddened hands set saucers in the rack with the speed and accuracy of a conveyor belt. 'Many hands make light work, I always say.'

'It was a fantastic tea. And not a crumb of your fruit cake left.'

But Mrs Plackett had neither the time nor the inclination to chat. 'Why don't you go into the sitting room and take the weight off your feet? Mrs Chamberlain and your brother and the other gentleman are there now. Another ten minutes and the dining room will be straight, and ready for your little meeting.'

It was an excellent suggestion, and Olivia did not argue with it. She was very tired and her back ached from standing. Going through the hall, she thought about nipping up the stairs, soaking in a boiling bath, and then getting into bed, with cool sheets, soft pillows, and an absorbing book. Later, she promised herself. The day was not yet over. Later.

In the sitting room, already cleared of all traces of the tea-party, she found Noel, Nancy and Mr Enderby, all disposed in comfortable fashion, and making polite small talk. Nancy and Mr Enderby sat in the armchairs on either side of the hearth, but Noel had taken up his usual position, with his back to the fire, his shoulders propped against the mantelshelf. As Olivia appeared, Mr Enderby rose to his feet. He was a man in his early forties, but with his bald head, rimless spectacles, and sober clothes, he appeared much older. Despite this, his manner was easy and relaxed, and during the course of the afternoon Olivia had observed him making himself known to the other guests, replenishing teacups and handing around sandwiches and cake. As well, he had spent some time talking to Danus, which was nice, because Nancy and Noel had chosen to ignore him. The holiday in Cornwall at Mumma's expense and the wild extravagance of the Sands Hotel were obviously still rankling.

'I am sorry, Mr Enderby, I'm afraid we're running a little late.' She sank thankfully into the corner of the sofa, and Mr Enderby once more sat down.

'No matter. I am in no hurry.'

From the dining room came sounds of the vacuum cleaner being wielded. 'They've just got to clean up the crumbs and then we can start. How about you, Noel? Have you got some pressing date in London?'

'Not this evening.'

'And Nancy? You're not pushed for time?'

'Not really. But I have to collect the children, and I promised that I wouldn't be late.' Nancy, having blubbed her way through most of the service, was now recovered and looked quite cheerful again. Perhaps because she had removed her hat. George was already gone, having taken his leave in the churchyard, sent on his way by Nancy with loud admonitions to drive carefully and to give her regards to the Archdeacon, both of which he had promised to do. 'And I'd like to be back before dark. I hate driving, by myself, in the dark.'

The sound of the vacuum cleaner ceased. The next moment, the door opened and Mrs Plackett's head, still wearing her funeral hat, came around the edge of it.

'That's it then, Miss Keeling.'

'Thank you so much, Mrs Plackett.'

'If it's all right by you, Mr Plackett and me are on our way home.'

'Of course. And I can't thank you enough.'

'It's been a pleasure. See you tomorrow.'

She went. Nancy frowned. 'Tomorrow's Sunday. Why is she coming tomorrow?'

'She's going to help me clear out Mumma's room.' Olivia stood up. 'Shall we go?'

She led the way into the dining room. All was orderly, and a green baize cloth had been draped over the table.

Noel raised his eyebrows. 'Looks like a board meeting.' Nobody remarked on his observation. They sat down, Mr Enderby taking his place at the head of the table, with Noel and Olivia on either side of him. Nancy sat by Noel. Mr Enderby opened his brief-case and took out various papers, which he laid before him. It was all very formal, and he was in charge. They waited for him to begin.

He cleared his throat. 'To begin with, I am very grateful that you all agreed to stay on after your mother's funeral. I hope it hasn't inconvenienced any of you. A formal will-reading is, of course, not strictly necessary, but it did seem to me a fortuitous opportunity, while you are all together under one roof, to let you know how your mother wished to dispose of her estate and, if necessary, to explain any points that you might not fully understand. Now . . .' From the papers before him, Mr Enderby took up a long envelope and drew out the heavy, folded document. Unfolding it, he spread it on the table. Olivia saw Noel avert his eyes, inspect his fingernails, as though anxious not to be seen glancing out of the corner of his eye, like a schoolboy cheating in examinations.

Mr Enderby adjusted his spectacles. 'This is the last will and testament of Penelope Sophia Keeling née Stern, dated the eighth of July, 1980.' He glanced up. 'If you don't mind, I shan't read verbatim, but will simply outline your mother's wishes as we come to them.' They all nodded agreement to this. He continued. 'To begin with, there are two bequests outside the family. To Mrs Florence Plackett, 43 Hodges Road, Pudley, Gloucestershire, the sum of two thousand pounds. And to Mrs Doris Penberth, 7 Wharf Lane, Porthkerris, Cornwall, five thousand pounds.'

'How splendid,' said Nancy, for once approving of her mother's generosity. 'Mrs Plackett's been such a treasure. What Mother would have done without her, I really can't imagine.'

'And Doris, too. Doris was Mumma's dearest friend. They went through the war together; they became very close.'

'I believe,' said Mr Enderby, 'that I have met Mrs Plackett, but I don't think Mrs Penberth was with us today.'

'No. She couldn't come. She telephoned to explain. Her husband was unwell and she didn't feel that she could leave him. But she was dreadfully upset.'

'In that case, I shall write to both these ladies and let them know of the bequests.' He made a note. 'Now. With that disposed of, we come to family matters.' Noel leaned back in his chair, felt in his breast pocket, and took out his silver pen. He began to play with this, loosening the cap with his thumb, and then snapping it shut again. 'To begin with, there are specific items of furniture which she wanted each of you to have. For Nancy, the Regency sofa table in the bedroom. I believe your mother used it as a dressing table. For Olivia, the desk in the sitting room, once the property of Mrs Keeling's father, the late Lawrence Stern. And for Noel, the dining-room table and set of eight dining-room chairs. Which, I imagine, we are sitting on now.'

Nancy turned to her brother. 'Where will you put them in that rabbit-warren of a flat? There's not room to swing a cat in it.'

'Perhaps I shall buy another flat.'

'It will have to have a dining room.'

'It will,' he told her shortly. 'Please go on, Mr Enderby.'

But Nancy was not finished. 'Is that *all*?'

'I don't understand, Mrs Chamberlain.'

'I mean . . . what about her jewellery?'

Here we go, thought Olivia. 'Mumma didn't have any jewellery, Nancy. She sold her rings years ago to pay our father's debts.'

Nancy bridled as she always did when Olivia spoke in that hard voice about dear, dead Daddy. There was no reason to be so blunt, to say such things in front of Mr Enderby.

'What about Aunt Ethel's earrings? The ones Aunt Ethel left her? They must be worth at least four or five thousand pounds. Is there no mention of them?'

'She's already given them away,' Olivia told her. 'To Antonia.'

A silence followed this pronouncement. It was broken by Noel, who put his elbow on the table and ran his fingers, in despairing fashion, through his hair. He said, 'Oh, dear God.' Across the green baize Olivia met her sister's eyes. Very blue, staring, bright with outrage. A flush crept into Nancy's cheeks. She spoke at last. 'That cannot be true?'

'I'm afraid' – Mr Enderby's tones were measured – 'that it is true. Mrs Keeling gave the earrings to Antonia while they were on holiday together in Cornwall. She told me about the gift the day she came to see me in London, the day before she died. She was adamant that there should be no argument about these, nor question of rightful possession.'

'How did *you* know,' Nancy asked Olivia, 'that Mother had done such a thing?'

'Because she wrote and told me.'

'They should have gone to Melanie.'

'Nancy, Antonia was very good to Mumma, and Mumma was very fond of her. Antonia made the last few weeks of her life intensely happy. And she went to Cornwall with her, and kept her company, which none of us could be bothered to do.'

'You mean, we should be grateful for *that*? If you ask me, the boot's on the other foot . . .'

'Antonia *is* grateful . . .'

The argument, which might have gone on for ever, was brought to an end by Mr Enderby, once more discreetly clearing his throat. Nancy subsided into outraged silence, and Olivia breathed a sigh of relief. For the moment it was over, but she was fairly certain that the matter would never rest, and the fate of Aunt Ethel's earrings would be brought up and worried over far into the future.

'I'm sorry, Mr Enderby. We're holding you up. Please carry on.'

He sent her a grateful look, and resumed business. 'Now, we come to the residue of the estate. When Mrs Keeling drew up this will, she made it very clear to me that she wished there to be no disagreement among the three of you as to the disposal of her property. Accordingly, we decided that everything should be sold, and the sum realised divided among you all. In order to do this, it was necessary to appoint trustees of her estate, and it was agreed that the executors, Enderby, Looseby and Thring, should take this on. Is that quite clear, and quite acceptable? Good. In that case . . .' He began to read. 'I devise and bequeath all my estate, both real and personal, unto my trustees upon trust to sell, call in, and convert the same into money. Yes, Mrs Chamberlain?'

'I don't know what that means.'

'It means the residue of Mrs Keeling's estate, which includes this house and its contents, her portfolio of stocks and shares, and her current bank account.'

'All sold, and then added together, and then divided into three?'

'Exactly so. After, of course, outstanding debts, taxes and stamp duties, and funeral expenses have been paid.'

'It sounds dreadfully complicated.'

Noel reached into a pocket and produced his diary. He pressed it open at a blank page, removed the cap from his pen. 'Perhaps, Mr Enderby, you could elucidate, and we can make some sort of a rough calculation.'

'Very well. We'll start with the house. Podmore's Thatch, with its outbuildings and mature garden, is worth, I imagine, no less than two hundred and fifty thousand. Your mother paid a hundred and twenty thousand for it, but that was five years ago, and the value of property has risen considerably since then. Also, it is a highly desirable piece of real estate, and within easy commuting reach of London. The contents of the house I cannot be so certain of. Maybe ten thousand pounds? Then, at the moment, Mrs Keeling's share portfolio stands at roughly twenty thousand.'

Noel whistled. 'As much as that? I had no idea.'

'Nor me,' said Nancy. 'Where did all that money come from?'

'It was the residue from the sale of the house in Oakley Street. Carefully invested, after your mother had bought Podmore's Thatch.'

'I see.'

'And her current account?' Noel had listed all these figures in his diary, and was obviously itching to add them up and get a final grand total.

'Her current account, at the moment, stands high, with the injection of the hundred thousand pounds she received from the sale of the two panels painted by her father, Lawrence Stern, and which were sold to a private buyer by Boothby's. All of this, of course, will be subject to duties and tax.'

'Even so . . .' Noel did his swift calculation. 'That works out at over three hundred and fifty thousand.' Nobody remarked upon this staggering sum. In silence, he screwed the cap back onto his pen, placed it on the table, and leaned back in his chair. 'All things considered, girls, not a bad score.'

'I am pleased,' said Mr Enderby drily, 'that you are satisfied.'

'So that's it.' Noel stretched hugely, and made as if to rise from his chair. 'What do you say that I go and get us all a drink? You'd like a whisky, Mr Enderby?'

'Very much. But not at this moment. I'm afraid our business is not quite finished.'

Noel frowned. 'But what else is there to discuss?'

'There is a codicil to your mother's will, dated the thirtieth of April, 1984. This, of course, re-dates the former will, but as it changes nothing which has already been stated, this is irrelevant.'

Olivia thought back. 'The thirtieth of April. That was the day she came to London. The day before she died.'

'Exactly so.'

'She came expressly to see you, Mr Enderby?'

'I believe so.'

'To draw up this codicil?'

'Yes.'

'Perhaps you had better read it to us.'

'I am about to, Miss Keeling. But before I do so I think I should mention that it is written in Mrs Keeling's handwriting, and signed by her in the presence of my secretary and my clerk.' He commenced to read aloud. 'To Danus Muirfield, Tractorman's Cottage, Sawcombe's Farm, Pudley, Gloucestershire, I leave fourteen rough oil sketches of major works painted by my father, Lawrence Stern, between the years 1890 and 1910. These are titled as follows— *The Terrazzo Garden, The Lover's Approach, Boatman's Courtship, Pandora* . . .'

The oil sketches. Noel had suspected their existence, confided these suspicions to Olivia; had searched his mother's house for them, but drawn a blank. Now, she turned her head and looked, across the table, at her brother. He sat there, frozen to stillness, and intensely pale. A nervous tic jerked the angle of his jaw-bone. She wondered how long he would remain silent before exploding into furious protest.

'. . . *The Water Carriers, A Market in Tunis, The Love Letter* . . .'

Where had they been, all these years? Who had possessed them? Where had they come from?

'. . . *The Spirit of Spring, Shepherd's Morning, Amoretta's Garden* . . .'

Noel could last out no longer. 'Where were they?' His voice was harsh with outrage. Mr Enderby, so rudely interrupted, remained admirably calm. He had probably anticipated just such an outburst. He glanced up at Noel over the top of his spectacles. 'Perhaps you will allow me to finish, Mr Keeling, and then I will explain.'

There was an uncomfortable pause. 'Go on, then.'

Mr Enderby, without hurry, continued. '*The Sea-God, The Souvenir, The White Roses,* and *The Hiding Place.* These works are at present in the possession of Mr Roy Brookner, of Boothby's, Fine Art Dealers, New Bond Street, London WI, but are scheduled for sale in New York at the first possible opportunity. If I should die before this sale takes place, then they are for Danus Muirfield either to keep or to sell, according to his personal wishes.' Mr Enderby sat back in his chair and waited for comment.

'Where were they?'

Nobody said anything. The atmosphere had become uncomfortably tense. And then Noel repeated his question. 'Where were they?'

'For a number of years, your mother kept them hidden at the back of the wardrobe in her bedroom. She placed them there herself, and wallpapered them into position, so that they should not be found.'

'She didn't want us to know about them?'

'I don't think her children really came into it. She was hiding them from her husband. She found the sketches in her father's old studio at Oakley Street. At that time, there were certain financial difficulties, and she didn't want the sketches to be sold in order, simply, to raise some cash.'

'When did they finally come to light?'

'She asked Mr Brookner to come to Podmore's Thatch, to appraise and possibly buy two other works painted by your grandfather. It was then that she showed him the portfolio of sketches.'

'And when did you first hear of their existence?'

'Mrs Keeling told me the whole story the day that she drew up the codicil. The day before she died. Mrs Chamberlain, did you want to say something . . .'

'Yes. I haven't understood a word of what you're saying. I don't know what you're talking about. Nobody's ever mentioned these sketches to me, and this is the very first I've ever heard of them. And what is all the fuss about? Why does Noel seem to think they're so important?'

'They're important,' Noel told her with weary patience, 'because they're valuable.'

'Rough sketches? I thought those would be things you threw away.'

'Not if you had any sense.'

'Well, how much are they worth?'

'Four, five thousand each. And there are fourteen of them. *Fourteen!*' he repeated, shouting the word at Nancy as though she were deaf. 'So work that sum out, if you're capable of such advanced arithmetic, which I doubt.'

Olivia, in her head, had already worked it out. Seventy thousand. Despite Noel's appalling behaviour, she knew a pang of sympathy for him. He had been so certain that they were there, somewhere, at Podmore's Thatch. Had even spent one long, dismally wet Saturday incarcerated in the loft, on the pretence of clearing out his mother's rubbish, but, actually, searching for them. She wondered if Penelope had known the true reason for his industry and, if so, what had prompted her to keep silent. The answer was probably that Noel was his father all over again, and Penelope did not completely trust him. And so she had said nothing, but given them into the custody of Mr Brookner, and finally, the day before she died, decided to leave them to Danus.

But *why*? For what reason?

'Mr Enderby . . .' It was the first time she had spoken out since the subject of the codicil was raised, and Mr Enderby appeared relieved to hear her quiet voice, and gave her his full attention. ' . . . did she give any reason for leaving the sketches to Danus Muirfield? I mean' – she chose her words carefully, not wishing to appear resentful or greedy – 'they were obviously very special and personal possessions . . . and she's only known him for a short time.'

'I can't, of course, answer that question because I don't know what the answer is. But she was obviously very fond of the young man, and I think wished to help him. I believe he wants to start some small business, and will be grateful for the capital.'

'Can we contest it?' Noel asked.

Olivia turned to him. 'We're not contesting anything,' she told him flatly. 'Even if it were legally possible, I would have nothing to do with it.'

Nancy, who had been struggling with mental arithmetic, now reentered the discussion. 'But five fourteens are seventy. Do you mean that young man gets seventy thousand pounds?'

'If he sells the sketches, Mrs Chamberlain, yes.'

'But surely, that's dreadfully wrong. She hardly knew him. He was her *gardener*.' It took Nancy only moments to work herself up into a state of high agitation. 'It's outrageous. I was right about him all along. I always said he had some sinister hold over Mother. I said that to you, didn't I, Noel, over the telephone, when I told you about her giving *The Shell Seekers* away? And Aunt Ethel's earrings . . . given away. And now this. It's the last straw. Everything. Just given away. She can't have been in her right mind. She'd been ill, and her judgement was affected. There's no other possible explanation. There must be some action we can take.'

Noel, for once, was on Nancy's side. 'I, for one, am not about to sit back and let this all wash over me . . .'

' . . . she obviously wasn't in her right mind . . .'

' . . . there's too much at stake . . .'

' . . . just taking advantage . . .'

Olivia could bear it no longer. 'Stop it. Be quiet.' She spoke quietly, but with a controlled fury which the editorial staff of *Venus* had learned, over the years, both to fear and respect. Noel and Nancy, however, had never heard this voice before. They stared at her in some astonishment but, taken off their guard, were startled to silence. In the ensuing quiet, Olivia began to speak.

'I don't want to hear any more. It's all over. Mumma's dead. We buried her today. Hearing you both wrangling away like a couple of mangy dogs, one would think you'd forgotten that. You can't think, or speak, of anything but what you're going to get out of her. And now we know, because Mr Enderby's just told us. And Mumma was never out of her mind . . . on the contrary, she was the most intelligent woman I ever knew. All right, so she was generous to a fault, but never unthinkingly so. She was practical. She planned ahead. How else do you think she managed, all those years we were growing up, with scarcely two pennies to rub together, and a husband who gambled away every brass farthing he could lay his hands on? As far as I'm concerned, I'm more than content, and I think you should be too. She gave us all a magical childhood, and a terrific start in life, and now that she's dead, it's evident that each of us is comfortably provided for. As for the earrings' – she looked at Nancy in cold accusation – 'if she wanted Antonia to have them, and not you or Melanie, then I am certain she had good reason.' Nancy's eyes dropped. She picked at a scrap of fluff on the sleeve of her jacket. 'And if Danus gets the sketches, and not Noel, then I'm certain there was good reason for that as well.' Noel opened his mouth, and then changed his mind and shut it again, without saying a word. 'She made her own will. She did what she wanted to do. And that is all that matters, and nobody is to say one more word.'

Without once raising her voice, she had said it all. In the uncomfortable pause that followed, she sat waiting for Noel or Nancy to offer objections to the tongue-lashing she had delivered to them. After a little, across the table, Noel shifted in his chair. Olivia sent a dagger-glance in his direction, tensed for further infighting, but it seemed that he had nothing to say. In a gesture that admitted defeat more clearly than any spoken word, he put up a hand to rub his eyes, and then to smooth back his dark hair. He straightened his shoulders, adjusted the knot of his black silk tie. Self-possession returned to him. He even managed a wry smile. 'After that little outburst,' he said to the company in general, 'I think we all deserve that drink.' He rose to his feet. 'A whisky for you. Mr Enderby?'

And so, smoothly, he brought the meeting to a close, and also broke the tension. Mr Enderby, obviously much relieved, accepted Noel's offer, and began collecting his papers together and stowing them away in his brief-case. Nancy, murmuring something about powdering her nose, gathered her tattered dignity about her, picked up her handbag, and left the room. Noel, in search of ice, went after her. Olivia and the lawyer were left alone.

She said, 'I'm sorry.'

'Don't be sorry. It was a splendid speech.'

'You don't think Mumma was out of her mind, do you?'

'Not for an instant.'

'You spoke to Danus this afternoon. Did he strike you as a devious character?'

'The very opposite. I would say a young man of integrity.'

'But still, I would really like to know what prompted her to leave him such an enormous legacy.'

'I don't suppose, Miss Keeling, that we shall ever know.'

She accepted this. 'When will you tell him?'

'Whenever is a suitable time.'

'Do you think now is a suitable time?'

'Yes, if it would be possible to speak to him privately.'

Olivia smiled. 'You mean, after Noel and Nancy have gone.'

'It might be better to wait till then.'

'Won't that make you rather late getting home?'

'Perhaps I could phone my wife.'

'Of course. I want Danus to know as soon as possible because he'll

probably be around tomorrow, and it might make things a little con-
strained between us, if I know and he doesn't.'

'I perfectly understand.'

Noel returned, carrying the ice bucket. He said, 'Olivia, there's a
message for you on the kitchen table. Danus and Antonia have gone to
have a drink at the Sudeley Arms. They'll be back at half past six.'

He came out with this quite naturally, saying their names, for the first
time, without resentment or venom. Which was, under the circumstances, reassuring. Olivia turned to Mr Enderby. 'Can you wait till
then?'

'Of course.'

'I am grateful. You've been endlessly patient with us.'

'Part of my job, Miss Keeling. Just part of my job.'

Having spent some time upstairs, combing her hair, powdering her
nose, and generally pulling herself together, Nancy rejoined them in the
dining room and announced that she was on her way home.

Olivia was surprised. 'Aren't you going to stay for a drink with us?'

'No. Better not. I've a long way to go. Don't want any accidents.
Goodbye, Mr Enderby, and thank you for your help. Please don't get up.
Goodbye, Noel. Safe journey back to London. You stay where you are,
Olivia, I'll see myself out.'

But Olivia put down her glass and went with her sister. Out of doors,
they found the flawless spring day sinking into cool and scented evening.
The sky was high and clear, stained pink towards the west. A breeze
rustled the topmost branches of trees, and from the hill behind the village
came, clearly, the voices of sheep and their lambs.

Nancy looked about her. 'How lucky we were with the weather. It just
made everything possible. It went well, Olivia. You arranged everything
perfectly.'

She was, it was apparent, doing her very best to be agreeable.

Olivia said, 'Thank you.'

'A lot of work. I realise that.'

'Yes. It took some organising. And there are still one or two details to
be seen to. A headstone for Mumma's grave. But we can talk about that
some other time.'

Nancy got into her car. 'When do you go back to London?'

'Tomorrow evening. I have to be in the office on Monday morning.'

'I'll be in touch then.'

'Do.' Olivia hesitated, and then remembered her good resolutions of
the afternoon. Mumma had never let any of her children go without a
goodbye kiss. She leaned through the open window of the car and kissed
Nancy on the cheek. 'Drive safely,' she told her sister, and then, feeling

reckless (in for a penny, in for a pound), added, 'My love to George and the children.'

Going back indoors, she found that the two men had left the dining room and returned to the comfort of the sitting room. Noel had drawn the curtains and made up the fire, but once he had finished his whisky and soda, he looked at his watch, got to his feet, and said that it was time he took his leave. Mr Enderby suggested that this might be a good moment to telephone his wife, so Olivia left him doing this and accompanied Noel to the front door.

She said, 'I feel as though I've done nothing but see people off all day.'

'You'll be tired. Better have an early night.'

'I think probably we're all tired. It's been a long day.' It was getting cooler. She folded her arms against a shiver of chill. 'I'm sorry about the way things worked out, Noel. It would have been nice for you to have the sketches. God knows you worked hard enough looking for them. But as it is, there's not a mortal thing you can do about it. And, admit it, we've none of us done so badly. This house will go for a bomb. So don't brood on imagined injustices. Otherwise you'll end up with the worst sort of spiritual indigestion, all twisted and bitter.'

He smiled. Without much joy, but still a smile.

'It's a hell of a pill to have to swallow, but it seems I have no alternative. And yet I should like to know why she never told us about those sketches, never mentioned their existence. And why did she leave them to that young man?'

Olivia shrugged. 'She was fond of him? Sorry for him? Wanted to help him?'

'There's something more to it than that.'

'Maybe,' she admitted. She gave him his goodbye kiss. 'But I don't suppose we'll ever find out.'

He got into the Jaguar and drove away, and Olivia stayed where she stood, listening to the receding din of his car, waiting until the roar of the faulty exhaust died away into the still of the evening and could be heard no longer. Country sounds once more took over – the sheep from the sloping fields across the road, the rising wind, stirring high branches, a dog barking. She heard brisk footsteps approaching from the village, and young voices. Danus and Antonia, returning from the Sudeley Arms. Their heads appeared over the top of the wall, and as they came through the open gateway, she saw that Danus had his arm around Antonia's shoulders, and Antonia had wound a scarlet muffler around her neck, and her cheeks were pink. She looked up and saw Olivia waiting for them.

'Olivia. What are you doing, standing out here on your own?'

'Noel's just left. I heard you coming. Have you had a good time?'

'We just went for a drink. I hope you didn't mind. I've never been inside the pub before. It's lovely. Really old-fashioned, and Danus played darts with the postman.'

'Did you win?' Olivia asked him.

'No. I was hopeless. I had to stand him a pint of Guinness.'

Together they made their way back into the house. In the warm kitchen, Antonia unwound her muffler. 'Is the family meeting over?'

'Yes. And Nancy's gone too. But Mr Enderby's still here.' She turned to Danus. 'He wants a word with you.'

Danus appeared to find this hard to believe. 'With *me?*'

'Yes. He's in the sitting room. Perhaps you'd better not keep him waiting because the poor man wants to get home to his wife.'

'But what's he got to say to *me?*'

'I've no idea,' Olivia fibbed. 'Why don't you go and find out?'

Looking bemused, he went. The door closed behind him.

'Why on earth does he want to talk to Danus?' Antonia's expression was one of deep apprehension. 'You don't suppose it's something dreadful?'

Olivia leaned against the edge of the kitchen table. 'No, I don't suppose so for a moment.' Antonia, however, did not look convinced. Not wishing to continue the conversation, Olivia firmly changed the subject. 'Now, what are we going to eat for supper? Is Danus staying?'

'If you don't mind.'

'Of course I don't mind. He'd better stay the night as well. We'll find a bed for him somewhere.'

'That would make everything much easier. He hasn't lived in his cottage for two weeks, and it'll be all damp and cheerless.'

'Tell me what happened in Edinburgh. Did he get a clean bill of health?'

'Yes, he did. He's all right, Olivia. He's well. He's not an epileptic and he never was one.'

'That's wonderful news.'

'Yes. Like a miracle.'

'He means a lot to you, doesn't he?'

'Yes.'

'And you, I think, to him.'

Antonia, radiant, nodded.

'So what plans have you made?'

'He wants to start a nursery garden . . . go into business on his own. And I'm going to help him. We're going to do it together.'

'How about his job with Autogarden?'

'He's going back to work on Monday, and giving them a month's notice. They've been so good to him, about all this time he's had to take off, he feels that working out his notice is the very least he can do.'

'And after that?'

'We'll take off and go and look for some place we can afford to rent or buy. Somerset, maybe. Or Devon. But I meant what I said about staying here, and we won't go until Podmore's Thatch has been sold and the furniture taken away. Like I said, I can show people round, and Danus can take care of the garden.'

'What a frightfully good idea. But he mustn't go back to his cottage, he must stay here with you. I'll be much happier knowing that he's around and you aren't on your own. And he can have the use of Mumma's car, and you can keep me in touch as to how many prospective clients come rolling in. And I'll keep Mrs Plackett on, if she's willing, until such time as the house is sold. She can give the place a good spring-clean, and she'll be company for you while Danus is rotavating other people's gardens.' She smiled as though she had planned it all herself. 'How neatly it's all worked out.'

'There's just one thing. I shan't be coming back to London.'

'I gathered that.'

'You were so sweet to say you'd help me, and I was really grateful, but I wouldn't have been any good as a model. I'm far too self-conscious.'

'You're probably right. You'll be much happier in a pair of wellies with your fingernails full of mud.' They laughed. 'You are happy, aren't you, Antonia?'

'Yes. Happier than I ever thought I'd be again. It's been a funny sort of day. Tremendously happy and dreadfully sad all at the same time. But somehow I think Penelope would have understood. I dreaded the funeral. Cosmo's was the only other I'd ever been to, and that was so shatteringly awful that I dreaded going to another. But this afternoon was quite different. More of a celebration, really.'

'That's the way I wanted it to be. That's the way I planned it. And now . . .' Olivia yawned. ' . . . it's all safely over. Finished.'

'You look tired.'

'You're the second person who's told me that this evening. It usually means I'm looking old.'

'You don't look old. Go upstairs and have a bath. Don't worry about supper. I'll cook supper. There's some soup in the larder and lamb chops in the refrigerator. If you like, I'll bring up a little tray and you can have it in bed.'

'I'm not as old and tired as that.' Olivia pushed herself away from the table and arched her aching back. 'But I will go and get into a bath. If Mr Enderby leaves before I appear again, will you give him my apologies?'

'Of course.'

'And say goodbye to him for me. Tell him I'll be in touch.'

Five minutes later, when Danus and Mr Enderby, their business over, came into the kitchen, Antonia was at the sink scraping carrots. She turned from the sink to smile at them, waiting for something to be said; for one of them to explain what it was they had been talking about. But neither did, and in the face of such masculine solidarity she hadn't the nerve to ask. Instead she gave Mr Enderby Olivia's message.

'She's rather tired, and went up to have a bath. But she told me to say goodbye to you, and to apologise, and she hopes you'll understand.'

'But of course.'

'She says she'll be in touch.'

'Thank you for telling me. And now I must be on my way. My wife is expecting me home for dinner.' He shifted his brief-case to his left hand. 'Goodbye, Antonia.'

'Oh . . .' Caught unawares, Antonia hastily wiped her hand on her apron. 'Goodbye, Mr Enderby.'

'And the best of luck.'

'Thank you.'

He took himself off, striding out through the door, with Danus behind him. Antonia, left on her own, returned to her carrot scraping, but her mind was not on her work. Why had he wished her the best of luck, and what on earth was happening? Danus had not appeared particularly crestfallen, so perhaps it was something nice. Perhaps – happy thought – Mr Enderby had taken a liking to Danus, as they chatted over the teacups, and was offering to help them raise a bit of cash to help buy their nursery garden. It seemed unlikely, but for what other reason had he wished to speak to him . . .?

She heard Mr Enderby's car drive away. She stopped scraping and leaned against the sink, waiting, with the knife in one hand and the carrot in the other, for Danus to return.

'What did he say to you?' she asked, before he had even got through the door. 'Why did he want to talk to you?'

Danus removed the knife and the carrot, set them on the draining board, and took her in his arms.

'I have something to tell you.'

'What?'

'You're not going to have to sell Aunt Ethel's earrings.'


'Yoo-hoo!'

'Mrs Plackett?'

'Where are you?'

'Up here, in Mumma's bedroom.'

Mrs Plackett climbed the stairs.

'Made a start, have you?'

'Not really. I'm just trying to decide how we're going to do it. I don't think there's going to be anything worth keeping. All Mumma's clothes were so old and so unconventional I can't imagine anyone would want them. I've got these rubbish bags. We'll just fill them and leave them all out for the dustbin men.'

'Mrs Tillingham's having a jumble sale next month. In aid of the Organ Fund.'

'Well. We'll see. I'll let you decide. Now, perhaps you could empty the wardrobe, and I'll start on the chest of drawers.'

Mrs Plackett set to work, flinging wide the doors of the wardrobe, and commencing to unload armfuls of shabby and dearly familiar garments. As she laid them across the bed . . . some so well-worn as to be threadbare, Olivia averted her eyes. It seemed indecent even to look. She had dreaded this sad task, and it seemed that it was going to be even more heart-rending than she had anticipated. Encouraged by Mrs Plackett's down-to-earth presence, she went on her knees and opened the bottom drawer. Sweaters and cardigans, much darned at the elbow. A white Shetland baby shawl; a navy-blue guernsey which Mumma used to wear for gardening.

As they laboured, 'What's going to happen to the house then?' Mrs Plackett inquired.

'It's going to be put on the market and sold. It's what Mumma wished, and none of us would want to live here anyway. But Antonia and Danus are going to live here, and show people round, and generally keep things going until such time as it is sold. When that happens, we'll get rid of the furniture.'

'Antonia and Danus?' Mrs Plackett, nodding sagely to herself, considered the implications of this. 'That's very nice.'

'And afterwards, they're going to go off and look for some bit of land they can rent or buy. They want to start a nursery garden together.'

'Sounds to me,' said Mrs Plackett, 'as though they're gathering twigs. Where are they, by the way? Didn't see either of them when I came into the house.'

'They went to church.'

'They did?'

'You sound approving, Mrs Plackett.'

'It's nice when young people go to church. Doesn't often happen these days. And I'm pleased that they're going to be together. Do lovely for

each other, I've always thought. Mind, they're young enough. But for
all that, they seem to have their heads screwed on. What about this?'

Olivia looked. Mumma's old boat cape. She had a sudden flash of
piercing memory. Mumma and the young Antonia arriving at Ibiza
Airport; Mumma wearing the cape, and Antonia running to throw herself
into Cosmo's arms. It all seemed dreadfully long ago.

She said, 'That's too good to throw away. Put it by for the church
jumble.'

But Mrs Plackett appeared reluctant to do this. 'Thick and warm as
anything it is. Years of wear in it yet.'

'Then you have it. It'll keep you cosy on your bicycle.'

'That's very kind of you, Miss Keeling. I'd be grateful.' She laid it over
a chair. 'I'll think of your mother every time I wear it.'

Another drawer. Underclothes, night-dresses, woollen tights, belts,
scarves; a Chinese silk shawl, lavishly fringed and embroidered with
scarlet peonies. A black lace mantilla.

The wardrobe was nearly empty. Mrs Plackett reached into its depths.
'Just look at this!' She held it out, still on its padded hanger. A dress,
youthful and skimpy, made of some cheap material that hung limply. A
red dress, patterned with white daisies, with a square neckline and bulky
pads in the shoulders. 'I've never seen this before.'

'Neither have I. I wonder why Mumma kept *that*. Looks like something
she might have worn during the war. Throw it out, Mrs Plackett.'

The top drawer. Creams and lotions, emery boards, old scent bottles,
a box of powder, a swansdown puff. A string of glass beads the colour of
amber. Earrings. Worthless scraps of junk jewellery.

And then the shoes. All her shoes. Shoes were the worst of all,
more intensely personal then anything else. Olivia became increasingly
ruthless. The rubbish bags bulged.

Finally, painfully, all was done. Mrs Plackett knotted tight the plastic
bags, and between them they thumped them down the stairs and out of
doors to where the dustbins stood.

'They'll be collected tomorrow morning. And that'll be the end of it
for you.'

Back in the kitchen, Mrs Plackett put on her coat.

'I can't thank you enough, Mrs Plackett.' Olivia watched as Mrs
Plackett carefully folded her boat cape, packed it into a carrier-bag. 'I
couldn't have faced it on my own.'

'Very pleased to be able to help, I'm sure. Well, I must be off. See to
Mr Plackett's dinner. Have a safe journey back to London, Miss Keeling,
and you take care of yourself. Try and have a bit of a rest. It's been a
busy weekend.'

'I'll keep in touch, Mrs Plackett.'

'That's right. And come back and see us. I wouldn't like to think I wasn't going to see you again.'

She mounted her bicycle and rode away, a sturdy upright figure, with the carrier-bag dangling from her handlebars.

Olivia went back upstairs into Mumma's room. Stripped of all personal possessions, it stood unbelievably empty. Before long, Podmore's Thatch would be sold, and this room would belong to another person. There would be other furniture, other clothes, other scents, other voices, other laughter. She sat on the bed, and saw, beyond the window, the fresh green leaves of the flowering chestnut. Hidden somewhere in its branches, the thrush was singing.

She looked about her. Saw the bedside table, with its white china lamp and pleated parchment shade. The table had a little drawer. They had overlooked this drawer and never got around to clearing it. She opened it now and found a bottle of aspirins, a single button, the stub of a pencil, an out-of-date diary. And, at the back, a book.

She reached into the drawer and took it out. A thin book, bound in blue. *Autumn Journal* by Louis MacNeice. It bulged with some bulky marker, and, where this had been inserted, fell open of its own accord. There she found the wad of thin yellow paper, tightly folded . . . a letter perhaps? And a photograph.

The photograph was of a man. She glanced at it and then laid it aside, and started to unfold the letter, but was diverted by a passage of poetry that leaped to her eye from the pages of the book, much as a remembered name will leap from a sheet of newsprint . . .

September has come, it is hers
Whose vitality leaps in the autumn
Whose nature prefers
Trees without leaves and a fire in the fireplace.
So I gave her this month and the next
Though the whole of my year should be hers who has rendered already
So many of its days intolerable or perplexed
But so many more so happy.
Who has left a scent on my life, and left my walls
Dancing over and over with her shadow
Whose hair is twined in all my waterfalls
And all of London littered with remembered kisses.

The words were not new to her. As a student at Oxford, Olivia had discovered MacNeice, become hooked, and voraciously devoured everything that he had ever written. And yet now, after the passage of many years, she found herself as freshly touched and moved as at her first encounter with the poem. She read it again, and then set the book down. What had been its significance to Mumma? She took up the photograph once more.

A man. In some sort of uniform but bareheaded. He turned, smiling at the photographer, as though caught unawares, and a coil of climbing rope was looped across his shoulder. His hair was ruffled, and in the far distance lay the long line of the sea's horizon. A man. Unknown to Olivia, and yet, in some odd way, familiar. She frowned. A resemblance? Not so much a resemblance as a reminder. But of whom? Someone . . .?

But of course. And once recognised, obvious. Danus Muirfield. Not his features, nor his eyes, but other, more subtle likenesses. The shape of the head, the lift of his chin. The unexpected warmth of his smile.

Danus.

Was this man, then, the answer to the question to which neither Mr Enderby, nor Noel, nor Olivia had been able to find an answer?

By now deeply intrigued, she took up the letter and unfolded the fragile pages. The paper was lined, and the writing scholarly, with letters neatly formed by a broad-nibbed pen.

Somewhere in England

May 20th, 1944.

My darling Penelope,

Over the last few weeks I have settled down a dozen times to write to you. On each occasion, I have got no further than the first four lines, only to be interrupted by some telephone call, loud hailer, knock on the door, or urgent summons of one sort or another.

But at last has come a moment in this benighted place when I can be fairly certain of an hour of quiet. Your letters have all safely come and are a source of joy. I carry them around like a lovesick schoolboy and read and reread them, time without number. If I cannot be with you, then I can listen to your voice . . .

She was very aware of being alone. The house, around her, lay empty and silent. Mumma's room was silent, the quiet disturbed only by the whisper of pages, read and then set aside. The world, the present were forgotten. This was the past Olivia uncovered, and it was Mumma's past, unsuspected until now, and unimagined.

> There is always the possibility that Ambrose will be gentlemanly and allow you to divorce him . . . All that matters is that we should be together, and eventually – hopefully sooner than later – married. The war will, one day, be over . . . But thousand-mile journeys begin with the first step, and no expedition is the worse for a little thought.

She laid the page aside, and went on to the next one.

> . . . For some reason, I have no fears that I will not survive the war. Death, the last enemy, still seems a long way off, beyond old age and infirmity. And I cannot bring myself to believe that fate, having brought us together, did not mean us to stay that way.

But he had been killed. Only death could have ended such a love. He had been killed and he had never come back to Mumma, and all his hopes and plans for the future had come to nothing, ended for eternity by some bullet or shell. He had been killed and she had simply carried on. Gone back to Ambrose, and battled through the rest of her life without remorse or bitterness, or a trace of self-pity. And her children had never known. Nor guessed. Nobody had ever known. Somehow, this seemed saddest of all. *You should have talked about him, Mumma. Told me. I would have understood. I would have wanted to listen.* She discovered, to her surprise, that her eyes had filled with tears. These now spilled over and ran down her cheeks, and the sensation was strange and unfamiliar, as though it were happening to another person and not herself. And yet she wept for her mother. *I want you to be here. Now. I want to talk to you. I need you.*

Perhaps it was good to cry. She had not cried for Mumma when she died but she wept now. Privately, with no one to jeer at her weakness, she allowed the tears to fall unchecked. The tough and intimidating Miss Keeling, Editor-in-Chief of *Venus*, might never have existed. She was a schoolgirl again, bursting in through the door of that huge basement room in Oakley Street, calling 'Mumma!' and knowing that, from somewhere, Mumma would answer. And as she wept, that armour which she had gathered about herself – that hard shell of self-control – broke up and disintegrated. Without that armour she could not have got through the first few days of living in a cold world where Mumma no longer existed. Now, released by grief, she was human again and once more herself.

After a little, more or less recovered, she took up the final page of the letter, and read to its conclusion.

. . . and wish I were with you, sharing the laughter and domestic doings of what I have come to think of as my second home. All of it was good, in every sense of the word. And in this life, nothing good is truly lost. It stays part of a person, becomes part of their character. So part of you goes everywhere with me. And part of me is yours for ever. My love, my darling,

Richard

Richard. She said the name aloud. *Part of me is yours for ever.* She folded the letter and put it back, with the photograph, between the pages of *Autumn Journal.* She closed the book, and lay back on the pillows, and gazed at the ceiling, and thought, now I know it all. But knew that she did no such thing; just knew that she needed above all to learn every tiny detail of what had happened. How they had met; how he had come into her life, how they had fallen so inevitably and deeply in love; how he had been killed.

But who knew? Only one person. Doris Penberth. Doris and Mumma had lived all through the war together. There would have been no secrets between them. Excitedly, Olivia laid plans. Sometime . . . maybe in September when things at the office were usually quiet . . . Olivia would take a few days off from work and drive to Cornwall. First, she would write to Doris and suggest a visit. In all likelihood, Doris would invite Olivia to stay. And Doris would talk, and remember Penelope, and little by little she would bring Richard's name into the conversation, and eventually Olivia would know it all. But they wouldn't just talk. Doris would show Olivia Porthkerris, and all the places that had been so much part of Mumma's life, and which Olivia had never known. And she would take her to see the house where Mumma had once lived, and they would visit the little Art Gallery which Lawrence Stern had helped to start, and Olivia would see *The Shell Seekers* once more.

She thought of the fourteen sketches, executed by Lawrence Stern at the turn of the century and now the property of Danus. She remembered Noel, yesterday evening, saying goodbye.

*Why did she leave them to that young man?*

*She was fond of him? Sorry for him? Wanted to help him?*

*There's something more to it than that.*

*Maybe. But I don't suppose we'll ever find out.*

She had supposed wrong. Mumma had left the sketches to Danus for a number of reasons. Noel, with his endless needling, had driven her beyond the limits of patience, but in Danus she had found a person worth helping. While they were at Porthkerris, she had watched his love for

Antonia grow and flower, guessed that, in the fullness of time, he would probably marry the girl. They were special to her, and she was anxious to give them some sort of start in life. But, most important reason of all, Danus had reminded her of Richard. She must have noticed – the first time she laid eyes on him – the strong physical resemblance, and so felt an immediate and close affinity with the young man. Perhaps, through Danus and Antonia, she had felt she was being offered some sort of a second chance of happiness . . . a vicarious identification with them. Whatever – they had rendered her last few weeks of life extremely happy, and for this she had thanked them, in her usual spectacular fashion.

Now, Olivia looked at her watch. It was nearly midday. In moments, Danus and Antonia would return from church. She got off the bed and went to close and latch the window for the last time. At the mirror she paused to check on her reflection and make certain that her face betrayed no trace of tears. Then she picked up the book, the letter and the photograph safe within its pages, and went out of the room, closing the door behind her. Downstairs in the deserted kitchen, she took up the heavy iron poker and used it to lift the lid from the boiler. A furnace heat flowed up, scorching her cheeks, and she dropped Mumma's secret into the heart of the glowing red coals and watched it burn.

It took only seconds, and then was gone for ever.

# Miss Keeling

The middle of June, and the summer was at its height. The warm and early spring had kept its promise, and the whole country basked in a heat wave. Olivia revelled in this. She relished the warmth and the sun-baked streets of London; the sight of crowds of tourists strolling, lightly clad; of striped umbrellas set up on the pavements outside pubs; of lovers lying supine, entwined, beneath the shade of the trees in the park. All conspired to create the sensation of living perpetually abroad, and where others wilted, her own vitality leaped. She was Miss Keeling once more, at her most dynamic, and *Venus* claimed all her attention.

She was grateful for the therapy of absorbing satisfying work, and content, for the time being, to put the family, and all that had happened, out of her mind. Since Penelope's funeral, she had seen neither Nancy nor Noel, although, from time to time, she had spoken to them on the telephone. Podmore's Thatch, put on the market, had been snapped up almost immediately, and for an inflated sum far beyond even Noel's wildest dreams. With this business concluded, and the contents of the house sold at auction, Danus and Antonia had departed. Danus had bought Mumma's old Volvo, and into this, they had packed their few possessions and taken off in the direction of the west country to look for some place to set up a little nursery garden that they could call their own. They had telephoned Olivia to say goodbye, but that had been a month ago, and since then she had had no word of them.

Now, a Tuesday morning, and she sat at her desk. A new young Fashion Editor had joined her staff, and Olivia was reading the proofs of her first attempt at editorial copy. *Your Best Accessory Is You.* That was good. Instantly intriguing. *Forget about scarves, earrings, hats. Concentrate on eyes, glowing skin, the shine of sparkling health . . .*

The intercom buzzed. Without raising her eyes Olivia flipped the switch. 'Yes?'

'Miss Keeling,' her secretary said, 'I have an outside call for you. Antonia's on the line. Will you speak to her?'

Antonia. Olivia hesitated, taking this in. Antonia was gone from her life, incarcerated somewhere in the west country. Why should she telephone, out of the blue? What did she want to talk about? Olivia resented interruption. And what a time to ring. She sighed, removed her spectacles, and sat back in her chair. 'All right, you'd better put her through.' She reached for the telephone.

'Olivia?' The youthful, familiar voice.

'Where are you?'

'In London. Olivia, I know you're dreadfully busy, but you wouldn't be able to have lunch today, would you?'

'Today?' Olivia could not keep the dismay from her voice. Today, she knew, was packed with appointments, and she had planned a working lunch-hour, with a sandwich at her desk. 'It's rather short notice.'

'I know and I'm sorry but it's really important. Please say you will, if you possibly can.'

Her voice rang with urgency. What on earth had happened now? Reluctantly, Olivia reached for her appointment diary. A session with the Chairman at half past eleven, and then a meeting with the Advertising Manager at two. She did a few swift calculations. The Chairman would probably not claim more than an hour of her time, but that did not leave . . .

'Oh, Olivia, *please*.'

Reluctantly, she gave in. 'All right. But it will have to be a fairly speedy lunch. I must be back here at two.'

'You're a saint.'

'Where shall we meet?'

'You say.'

'Kettners, then.'

'I'll book a table.'

'No, I'll take care of that.' Olivia had no intention of sitting at some undistinguished table next to the kitchen door. 'I'll get my secretary to do it. One o'clock, and don't be late.'

'I won't be . . .'

'Antonia. Where is Danus?'

But Antonia had already rung off.


The taxi jerked its slow way through the midday traffic and the crowded, summery streets. In it Olivia sat, vaguely apprehensive. Antonia's voice over the telephone had betrayed a state of some agitation, and Olivia was not perfectly certain of what sort of reception she was about to receive. She imagined their reunion. Saw herself walking into Kettners and finding Antonia waiting for her. Antonia would be wearing her usual worn jeans and cotton shirt, and would look, in that costly venue of expense-account business men, totally out of place. *It's really important.* What could be so important that she had claimed an hour of Olivia's precious day, and would not take No for an answer? It was hard to believe that anything could possibly have gone wrong for Danus and Antonia, but it was always better to prepare oneself for the worst. Various eventualities presented themselves. They had been unable to find any suitable plot in which to raise their cabbages, and Antonia now wanted to discuss some alternative plan. They had found a plot but felt unenthusiastic about the house that went with it, and wished Olivia to travel to Devon, view it, and give her opinion. Antonia had started a baby. Or perhaps they had discovered that after all they had little in common, and so no future to share, and had decided to part.

Quailing at the prospect, Olivia prayed that this was not the case.

The taxi drew up outside the restaurant. She got out, paid off the driver, crossed the pavement, and went in through the door. Inside, as always, it was crowded and warm, bustling with activity. As always, it smelled of mouth-watering food, fresh coffee, and expensive cigars. The prosperous business men were there, lining the bar, and there, too, sitting at a small table, was Antonia. But she was not alone because Danus was at her side, and Olivia scarcely recognised them. For they were not wearing their usual casual, comfortable gear, but were dressed up to the nines. Antonia's shining hair was coiled up at the back of her head, and she wore Aunt Ethel's earrings and a delectable dress of Wedgwood blue, splashed with huge white flowers. And Danus was sleek and groomed as a racehorse, in a dark grey suit so smoothly cut as to fill Noel Keeling's heart with envy. They looked sensational; young, rich, and happy. They looked beautiful.

They spied Olivia at once, rose to their feet, and came to greet her.

'Oh, Olivia . . .'

Olivia, gawping, pulled herself together. She kissed Antonia, turned to Danus. 'This is unexpected. For some reason I didn't think you were going to be here.'

Antonia laughed. 'That's what I wanted you to think. I wanted it to be a surprise.'

'Wanted what to be a surprise?'

'This is our wedding lunch. That's why it was so important that you came. We got married this morning.'

The party was on Danus. He had ordered champagne, and the bottle waited in a bucket of ice by their table. For once, Olivia, made reckless by celebration, broke her rule about not drinking at lunch-time, and it was she who raised her glass and toasted their happiness.

They talked. There was much to be told and much to hear. 'When did you come to London?'

'Yesterday morning. We stayed last night at the Mayfair, and it's almost as grand as the Sands. And when we get back this afternoon, we're going to get into the car and drive to Edinburgh and have a couple of days with Danus' mother and father.'

'How about the sketches?' Olivia asked Danus.

'We spent yesterday afternoon with Mr Brookner at Boothby's. It was the first time we'd actually seen them.'

'Are you selling them?'

'Yes. They're going to be shipped to New York next month and auctioned there at the beginning of August. At least, thirteen of them are going. We're keeping one. *The Terrazzo Garden*. We felt we had to keep just one.'

'Of course. And what about the nursery garden? Did you have any luck?'

They told her. After much searching, they had found, in Devon, what they were looking for. Three acres of land, once the walled garden of a large old house. The property included a small garden and sizeable glasshouses in good repair, and Danus had put in an offer, which had been accepted.

'That's wonderful! But where are you going to live?'

'Oh, there was a cottage as well, not very large and very dilapidated. But because of it being so grotty, well, that brought the price down and we were able to afford it.'

'So what are you using for money until such time as the sketches are sold?'

'We got a bridging loan from the bank. And to save money, we'll do as much of the renovation work on the cottage as we can.'

'Where will you live meantime?'

'We've hired a caravan.' Antonia could scarcely contain her excitement. 'And Danus has bought a cultivator, and we're going to plant an enormous crop of potatoes, just to clean the ground. And after that we'll really be able to start. And I'm going to keep hens and ducks, and sell the eggs . . .'

'How far are you from civilisation?'

'Only three miles to a little market town . . . that's where we'll sell our produce. And flowers and plants too. The greenhouse will be crammed with early blooms. And pot plants, and . . . oh, Olivia, I can't wait to show it to you. When the house is finished, will you come and stay?'

Olivia considered the invitation. She had already drunk three glasses of champagne and had no intention of making rash commitments that she might later regret.

'Will your cottage be warm?'

'We're going to put in central heating.'

'And it will have plumbing? I won't have to go down the garden every time I need the loo?'

'No, we promise you won't have to do that.'

'And there will be boiling-hot bath water at all hours of the day?'

'Boiling.'

'And you will have a guest room? Which I will not have to share with human being, cat, dog, or hen?'

'You shall have it all to yourself.'

'And the guest room will have a wardrobe filled, not with some other person's fusty evening dresses and moth-eaten fur coats, but with twenty-four brand-new coat-hangers?'

'All padded.'

'In that case' – Olivia sat back in her chair – 'you'd better get busy. Because I shall come.'

Later, on the pavement, they stood in the warm sunshine, waiting for the taxi that would take Olivia back to her office.

'What fun it's been. Goodbye Antonia.' They hugged enormously and kissed with much affection.

'Oh, Olivia . . . thank you for everything. But mostly, thank you for coming today.'

'It's I who should thank you both for inviting me. I haven't had such a lovely surprise, nor such a delicious boozy lunch, in years. After all that champagne, I doubt if I shall be able to make any sense for the rest of the afternoon.'

The taxi trundled up. Olivia turned to Danus. 'Goodbye, dear boy.' He kissed her on both cheeks. 'Take care of Antonia. And lots of luck.'

He opened the taxi door for her, and she got in and he slammed the door shut behind her. '*Venus*,' she told the driver briskly, and as the taxi moved forward, she waved furiously out of the back window. Antonia and Danus waved back and Antonia blew kisses, and then they turned and began to walk in the opposite direction, away from Olivia, hand in hand.

She settled back in her seat with a sigh of satisfaction. All, for Antonia and Danus, had ended well. And Mumma had been right in her judgement, because they were the sort of young people who deserved encouragement, and to be given, if necessary, a helping hand. Which she had done. Now, it was up to them, with their tumbledown cottage and their cultivator and their hens and plans for the future, and their marvellous, unshakeable optimism.

And what of Penelope's children? How would they handle their good fortune, and how would they fare? Nancy, she decided, would indulge herself in some way. Perhaps buy a Range Rover, in which to lord it over her cronies at the local point-to-points, but that would be all. All else would go on funding the status symbol of the most expensive private education for Melanie and Rupert. At the end of which they would emerge ungrateful and probably unimproved.

She thought of Noel. Noel, as yet, still worked at the same job, but as soon as he was able to lay hands on his inheritance, Olivia had a fairly shrewd idea that he would chuck advertising and cook up some brilliant scheme for going it alone. Commodity broking, or perhaps some sky-high property dealings. As likely as not, he would run through his capital, and at the end of the day end up married to some rich, well-connected, and hideous girl, who would worship and adore him, and to whom he would be consistently unfaithful. Olivia found herself smiling. He was an impossible man but, after all, her brother, and in her heart she wished him well.

Which left only herself, and there were no question marks there. Olivia would invest Mumma's money prudently, with old age and retirement in mind. She imagined herself in twenty years' time – alone, unmarried, and still living in the little house in Ranfurly Road. But independent, even quite comfortably off. Able to afford the small pleasures and luxuries she had always enjoyed. Going to the theatre and concerts, entertaining her friends, taking holidays abroad. Perhaps, for company, she would have a little dog. And she would go to Devon and stay with Danus and Antonia Muirfield. And when they came to London, bringing with them the brood of children which they would doubtless have, they would visit Olivia, and she would show those children her favourite museums and galleries, and take them to the ballet and the pantomime at Christmas. She would be like a nice aunt. No, not an aunt, a nice grandmother. It would be like having grandchildren. And it occurred to her then, that these grandchildren would be Cosmo's grandchildren too. Which was strange. Like watching a tangle of loose threads unravel and plait themselves into a single braided cord, stretching ahead into the future.

The taxi halted. She looked, and saw, in some surprise, that they had arrived, were parked alongside the prestigious building that housed the offices of _Venus_. Cream stone and plate glass glittered with reflected sunlight, and the topmost floors pierced the starch-blue sky.

She got out and paid the driver. 'Keep the change.'

'Oh. Thanks very much, love.'

She went up the broad white steps that led to the massive entrance, and as she did so, the commissionaire stepped forward to hold open the door for her.

'It's a lovely day, Miss Keeling.'

She paused, to turn upon him a smile the brilliance of which he had never seen before.

'Yes,' she said. 'It's a particularly lovely day.'

She went through the door. Into her kingdom, her world.

# WILD MOUNTAIN THYME

For Robin and Kirsty and Oliver

# CONTENTS

# CHAPTER 1

## FRIDAY

Once, before the bypass had been built, the main road ran through the heart of the village, a constant stream of heavy traffic that threatened to rattle the heart out of the gracious Queen Anne houses and the small shops with their bulging windows. Woodbridge had been, not such a long time ago, simply a place you drove through in order to reach some other place.

But since the opening of the bypass, things had changed. For the better, said the residents. For the worse, said the shopkeepers and the garage proprietors and the man who had run the lorry-drivers' restaurant.

Now, the people of Woodbridge could go shopping and cross the road without taking their lives into their hands or having their pet dogs securely leashed. At weekends, children with brown velvet caps jammed down over their eyebrows, and mounted on a variety of shaggy steeds, trotted off to their local pony club meets, and already there had been a positive flowering of open-air events, garden parties and charity fêtes. The lorry-drivers' café became an expensive delicatessen, a ramshackle tobacconist sold out to a precious young man who dabbled in antiques, and the vicar had begun to plan a festival for next summer, in order to celebrate the tricentenary of his small, perpendicular church.

Woodbridge had come into its own again.

The clock on the church tower was pointing to ten minutes to twelve on a chill February morning when a big shabby Volvo turned the corner by the saddlers, and came slowly down the main street between the wide cobbled pavements.

The young man at the wheel saw the whole long empty curve of it, his eye undeflected by thundering streams of traffic. He saw the charming irregularity of houses and bow-fronted shops, the beckoning perspective, and a distant glimpse of willow-fringed meadows. Far above, in a wintry sky full of sailing clouds, a plane droned in towards Heathrow. Otherwise it was very quiet, and there seemed to be scarcely anybody about.

He passed a pub, newly painted and with tubs of bay trees at either side of the door; a hairdresser, Carole Coiffures. The wine merchant with his bow-fronted bottle-glass window, and an antique shop stuffed with overpriced relics of better days.

He came to the house. He drew the car into the pavement's edge and switched off the engine. The sound of the plane died, thrumming, into the morning quiet. A dog barked, a bird sang hopefully from a tree, as though deluded that the thin sunshine meant that spring had come. He got out of the car, slammed the door shut, and stood looking up at the flat, symmetric face of the house, with its fanlighted door and pleasing proportions. Flush on the pavement it stood, a flight of stone steps leading up to the front door and tall sash windows discreetly veiled in filmy curtains.

It was, he thought, a house that had never given anything away.

He went up the steps and rang the doorbell. The surround of the bell was brass and brightly polished, as was the lion's head knocker. The door was painted yellow, new and bright looking, without a sunblister or a scratch upon it. In the lea of the house, out of the sun, it was cold. He shivered inside his thick donkey jacket and rang the bell again. Almost at once there were footsteps, and the next instant the yellow front door opened for him.

A girl stood there, looking rather cross, as though she had been interrupted, disturbed by the bell, and wanted to waste as little time as possible. She had long, milk-fair hair, and she wore a tee shirt bulging with puppy fat, an apron, knee stockings and a pair of scarlet leather clogs.

'Yes?'

He smiled and said, 'Good morning,' and her impatience instantly melted into quite a different expression. She had realised that it wasn't the man about the coal, or someone collecting for the Red Cross, but a tall and personable young man, long-legged in his well scrubbed jeans, and bearded like a Viking. 'I wondered if Mrs Archer was in?'

'I'm so sorry.' She looked quite sorry, too. 'But I'm afraid not. She is gone to London today. To shop.'

She was, he reckoned, about eighteen, and from her accent, some sort of Scandinavian. Swedish, probably.

He said, with what he hoped was engaging ruefulness, 'Isn't that just my luck? I should have phoned or something, but I thought I'd take the chance of catching her at home.'

'Are you a friend of Mrs Archer's?'

'Well, I used to know the family, some years ago. But we've been . . . well, sort of out of touch. I was passing, on my way up to London from the West Country. I thought it would be nice to come and say hello. Just an idea I had. It doesn't matter.'

He began, diffidently, to back away. As he had hoped, the girl delayed him.

'When she comes back, I could tell her that you have been here. She will be back in time for tea.'

At that moment, with splendid timing, the church clock began to chime for midday.

He said, 'It's only twelve o'clock now. I can scarcely hang around till then. Never mind, I'll maybe be down this way again some time.' He looked up and down the street. 'There used to be a little café here . . .'

'Not any more. It is a delicatessen now.'

'Well, perhaps I can get a sandwich in the pub. It seems a long time since breakfast.' He smiled down at her from his great height. 'Goodbye, then. It's been nice meeting you.' He turned as though to leave. He could feel her hesitation, her decision, as though he had directed them himself. She said, 'I could . . .'

With one foot already on the upper step, he turned back.

'What could you do?'

'Are you really an old friend of the family?' She longed to be put out of her doubt.

'Yes, I really am. But I have no way of proving it to you.'

'I mean, I was just going to get the lunch for myself and the baby. I could get it for you, too.'

He looked reproachful, and she began to blush. 'Now, that's very foolhardy of you. I'm sure you've been warned, time and time again, about strange men coming to the door.'

She looked distressed. She obviously had. 'It is just that, if you are a friend of Mrs Archer's. Mrs Archer would want me to ask you in.' She was lonely and probably bored. All au pair girls seemed to be lonely and bored. It was an occupational hazard.

He said, 'You mustn't get yourself into trouble.'

Despite herself, she began to smile. 'I don't think I will.'

'Supposing I steal the silver? Or start trying to make violent love to you?'

For some strange reason this possibility did not alarm her in the least. Rather, she seemed to regard it as a joke, and so to be reassured. She even gave a small, conspiratorial giggle. 'If you do, I shall scream and the whole village will come to my rescue. Everybody knows what everybody does in Woodbridge. Everybody talks all the time. Chat, chat. Nobody has a secret.' She stepped back, opening the yellow door wide. The long, pretty hallway was invitingly revealed.

He hesitated for just long enough to make it seem genuine and then shrugged, said, 'All right,' and followed her over the threshold, wearing the expression of a man who has been finally, reluctantly, persuaded. She closed the door. He looked down into her face. 'But you may have to take the consequences.'

She laughed again, excited by the little adventure. She said, in hostess-like tones, 'Would you like to take off your coat?'

He did so, and she hung it up for him.

'If you would like to come to the kitchen, perhaps you would like a glass of beer?'

'Well, thank you.'

She led the way, down the passage that led to the back of the house, to the modern kitchen, built out into the south-facing garden and flooded now with pale sunlight. Everything shone with cleanliness and order; bright surfaces, a gleaming cooker, stainless steel and polished teak. The floor was blue and white tiles, which looked Portuguese. There were plants along the windowsill, and a table at the window was laid for lunch. He saw the high chair, the bright plastic table mat, the small spoons, the Beatrix Potter mug.

He said, 'You've got a baby to look after.'

She was at the fridge, getting him a can of beer. 'Yes.' She closed the fridge door and went to take a pewter mug from a hook on the scrubbed pine dresser. 'He's Mrs Archer's grandchild.'

'What's he called?'

'Thomas. He's called Tom.'

'Where's he now?'

'In his cot, having his morning rest. In a moment, I'll go up and get him, because he'll be ready for his lunch.'

'How old is he?'

'Two.' She handed him the can and the mug, and he opened the can and poured it carefully, without a head.

'I suppose he's staying here, is he? I mean, his parents are away, or something.'

'No, he lives here.' Her smiling, dimpled face took on an expression of woe. 'It's very sad. His mother is dead.' She frowned. 'It is funny that you do not know that.'

'I told you. I've been out of touch since I last saw the Archers. I had no idea. I *am* sorry.'

'She was killed in a plane crash. She was coming home from a holiday in Yugoslavia. She was their only child.'

'So they look after the grandchild?'

'Yes.'

He took a mouthful of beer, cool and delicious. 'What about the father?'

The girl had turned her rounded back on him, was stooping to investigate something in an oven. A fragrant smell filled the kitchen, and his mouth watered. He had not realised how hungry he was.

She said, 'They were separated. I don't know anything about him.' She closed the oven and straightened up. She gave him another searching look. 'I thought you would have known about that, too.'

'No. I don't know about anything. I was out of this country for a bit. I was in Spain and I was in America.'

'Yes. I see.' She looked at the clock. 'If I leave you, will you be all right? I have to go up and get Thomas.'

'If you're sure you can trust me not to help myself to the spoons.' He was teasing her, and she cheered up and smiled again. 'I don't think you'll do that.' She was wholesome, creamy as a tumbler of milk.

He said, 'What's your name?'

'Helga.'

'Are you Swedish?'

'Yes.'

'They're lucky, the Archers. I mean, having someone like you.'

'I'm lucky, too. It is a good job, and they are very kind. Some girls get terrible places. I could tell you some stories.'

'Do you go to classes in the afternoons?'

'Yes. English and history.'

'Your English sounds perfect to me.'

'I am doing literature. Jane Austen.'

She looked so pleased with herself that he laughed. He said, 'Run along, Helga, and get that baby. I'm starving, even if he isn't.' For some reason she blushed again, and then went away and left him alone in the shining, sunny kitchen.

He waited. Heard her go upstairs, her footsteps cross the floor of the room above. He heard her voice, speaking quietly; curtains being drawn back. He laid down his beer and went, soft-footed, rubber-soled, back down the hall and opened the door at the bottom of the staircase. He went in. There were the chintzes, the grand piano, the orderly bookshelves, the unassuming water colours. A fire had been laid in the Adam grate, but was, as yet, unlit. Even so, the room was warm with central heating and heavy with the scent of hyacinths.

Its neatness, its order, its air of well-bred, well-moneyed smugness, enraged him, as it always had. He longed for muddled knitting, strewn newspapers, a dog or a cat on some familiar cushion. But there was nothing. Only the slow ticking of the clock on the mantelpiece bore witness to any sort of activity.

He began to prowl around. The grand piano was a repository of photographs. Mr Archer in a top hat, proudly displaying some minor order bestowed upon him by the queen at Buckingham Palace; his moustache like a toothbrush, his morning coat strained across his spreading stomach. Mrs Archer as a misty girl, dressed for her wedding. The baby, propped up on a fur rug. And Jeannette.

He picked up the stylised portrait and stood, looking down at it. Pretty, as she had always been pretty. Sexy even, in her extraordinary, fastidious way. He remembered her legs, which were sensational, and the shape of her well-manicured hands. But nothing much else. Not her voice, not her smile.

He had married her because the Archers hadn't wanted their daughter to be the mother of an illegitimate baby. When the disastrous news had been broken to them that their precious only child had been having an affair with, actually living with, that dreadful Oliver Dobbs, their tidy little world had fallen apart. Mrs Archer had taken to her bed with a *crise de nerfs,* but Mr Archer, harking back to his brief years as a soldier, had straightened his tie and his back and taken Oliver out to lunch at his London club.

Oliver, unimpressed and not a little amused, had recorded
the subsequent discussion with the detachment of a totally
impartial observer. Even at the time it had seemed as unreal as
a scene from an old-fashioned play.

Only daughter, Mr Archer had said, plunging in at the deep
end. Always had great plans for her. No question or recriminations, hindsight never did a man any good, but the question
was, what was Oliver going to do about this baby?

Oliver said that he didn't think he could do anything. He
was working in a fish-and-chips shop, and he couldn't afford
to marry anyone, let alone Jeannette.

Mr Archer cleared his throat, and said that he didn't want
to tread on toes, or to appear curious, but it was obvious to
him that Oliver came from a good family, and he knew for a
fact that Oliver had been to a well-known school, so was there
any reason that he had to work in a fish-and-chips shop?

Oliver said that yes, there was a reason. The reason was that
he was a writer, and the fish-and-chips shop job was the sort
of undemanding occupation he needed to keep himself alive
in order to be able to write.

Mr Archer cleared his throat again and began to talk about
Oliver's parents, and Oliver told Mr Archer that his parents,
who lived in Dorset, were not only penniless, but unforgiving.
Living on an army pension, they had denied themselves everything in order to be able to scrape up enough money to send
Oliver to that exclusive school. When he had finally walked
out of it at the age of seventeen, they had tried, in a broken-
hearted sort of way, to persuade him to follow some sensible,
conventional course. To join the army, the navy, perhaps. To
become a chartered accountant, a banker, a lawyer. But he
could only be a writer, because by then he already was a
writer. Defeated at last, they washed their hands of their son,
cutting him off without the proverbial shilling, and remaining
sulkily and stubbornly incommunicado.

This obviously disposed of Oliver's parents. Mr Archer tried
another tack. Did Oliver love Jeannette? Would he make her
a good husband?

Oliver said that he didn't think he would make her a good
husband, because he was so terribly poor.

Mr Archer then cleared his throat for the third and last time
and came to the point. If Oliver agreed to marry Jeannette and
provide the baby with a legitimate father, then he, Mr Archer,

would see to it that ... er ... financially, the young couple would be all right.

Oliver asked, how all right? And Mr Archer elucidated, his eyes steadily holding Oliver's across the table, but his anxious hands shifting his wineglass, straightening a fork, crumbling a roll. By the time he was done, his place setting was in chaos, but Oliver realised that he was on to a good thing.

Living in Jeannette's flat in London, with a steady income coming in each month to his bank account, he could give up the job in the fish-and-chips shop and get down to finishing his play. He already had a book under his belt, but that was still with an agent, and the play was something else, something that he had to get down, before it ate his soul out like some ghastly cancer. That was how it was with writing. He was never happy unless he was living two lives. A real life with women and food and drinking in pubs with friends; and the other life. teeming with his own people, who were more vital and sympathetic than anyone he ever met in the normal course of events. And certainly, he thought, more interesting than the Archers.

Over the lunch table, the two men had come to an agreement. Later, it was consolidated by lawyers' letters and drafts and signatures. Oliver and Jeanette were duly married in a registry office, and this seemed to be all that mattered to the Archers. The alliance lasted no more than a few months. Even before the child was born, Jeannette had gone back to her parents. Boredom she could stand, she said, and loneliness too, but abuse and physical violence were more than she was prepared to endure.

Oliver scarcely noticed her going. He stayed in her flat and peacefully, without any sort of interruption, finished the play. When it was done, he left the flat, locked the door and posted Jeannette the key. He took himself off to Spain. He was in Spain when the baby was born, and still there when he read, in some week-old paper, of his wife's death in the Yugoslavian air disaster. By then Jeannette had become a person who had happened to Oliver a long time ago, and he discovered that the tragedy aroused little emotion in him. She belonged to the past.

Besides, by then he was well into his second novel. So he thought about Jeannette for perhaps five minutes and then plunged thankfully back into the company of the infinitely more compelling characters who were now going about their business within the confines of his own head.

When Helga came downstairs again, he was back in the kitchen sitting on the window seat, with his back to the sun, and enjoying his beer. The door opened, and she appeared, carrying the child in her arms. He was larger than Oliver had imagined, dressed in red overalls with a bib and a white sweater. His hair was a sort of reddish gold, like new pennies, but Oliver couldn't see his face, which was buried in Helga's delectable neck.

Helga smiled at Oliver over Thomas's shoulder.

'He's shy. I have told him that there is a visitor, and he doesn't want to look at you.' She bent her head to say to the little boy, 'Look, you silly. He is a nice man. He has come to have lunch with us.'

The child made a mooing, negative sound and buried his face still deeper. Helga laughed and brought him over to his high chair and inserted him into it, so that at last he had to let go of her. He and Oliver looked at each other. The child had blue eyes and seemed sturdy. Oliver didn't know much about children. Nothing, in fact. He said, 'Hi.'

'Say hello, Thomas,' Helga prompted. She added, 'He does not like to talk.'

Thomas stared at the stranger. One-half of his face was red from being pressed into a pillow. He smelled of soap. Helga clipped a plastic bib around his neck, but he didn't take his eyes off Oliver.

Helga went to the stove to collect their meal. From the oven she took a shepherd's pie, a dish of brussells sprouts. She put a little into a round dish, mashed it up with a fork and set it down on the tray of Thomas's high chair. 'Now, eat it up,' and she put his spoon into his hand.

'Does he feed himself?' asked Oliver.

'Of course. He's two now, not a baby anymore. Are you, Thomas? Show the man how you can eat up your dinner.' Thomas responded by laying down his spoon. His blue eyes fixed, unwinking, on Oliver, and Oliver began to feel self-conscious.

'Here,' he said. He set down his glass of beer, and reaching over, took up the spoon, filled it with squashed meat and potato, and steered it towards Thomas's mouth. Thomas's mouth opened, and it all disappeared. Thomas, munching, continued to stare. Oliver gave him back the spoon. Thomas finished his mouthful and then smiled. A good deal of the smile was shepherd's pie, but there was, as well, the glimpse of an engaging double row of small pearly teeth.

Helga, putting down Oliver's plate in front of him, caught sight of the smile.

'There now, he has made a friend.' She brought another plate and sat herself at the head of the table, so that she could help Thomas. 'He's a very friendly little boy.'

'What does he do all day?'

'He plays, and he sleeps, and in the afternoons he goes for a walk in his push-chair. Usually Mrs Archer takes him, but today I will take him.'

'Does he look at books and things?'

'Yes, he likes picture books, but sometimes he tears them.'

'Does he have toys?'

'He likes little cars and blocks. He doesn't like teddies or rabbits or things like that. I don't think he likes the feel of fur. You know what I mean?'

Oliver began to eat the shepherd's pie, which was very hot and delicious. He said, 'Do you know a lot about babies?'

'At home in Sweden I have younger brothers and sisters.'

'Are you fond of Thomas?'

'Yes, he is nice,' She made a face at the child. 'You are nice, aren't you Thomas? And he doesn't cry all the time like some children do.'

'It must be rather. . . dull for him, being brought up by his grandparents.'

'He is too little to know whether it is dull or not.'

'But it'll be dull when he's older.'

'A child on his own is always sad. But there are other children in the village. He will make friends.'

'And you? Have you made friends?'

'There is another au pair girl. We go to classes together.'

'Haven't you got a boyfriend?'

She dimpled. 'My boyfriend is at home in Sweden.'

'He must miss you.'

'We write to each other. And it is only for six months. At the end of six months, I shall go back to Sweden.'

'What will happen to Thomas then?'

'I expect Mrs Archer will get another au pair girl. Would you like some more shepherd's pie?'

The meal progressed. For dessert there was fruit or yoghurt or cheese. Thomas ate yoghurt. Oliver peeled an orange. Helga, at the stove, made coffee.

She said to Oliver, 'Do you live in London?'

'Yes, I've got a basement flat just off the Fulham Road.'

'Is that where you are going now?'
'Yes. I've been in Bristol for a week.'
'On holiday?'
'Who'd go to Bristol for a holiday in February? No, I have a play being put on at the Fortune Theatre there. I went down to do a small rewrite. The actors complained they couldn't get their tongues round some of my lines.'
'A writer?' She turned wide-eyed. 'You write *plays*? And get them *performed*? You must be very good.'
'I like to think so.' He filled his mouth with sections of orange. Their taste, and the bitter tang of the peel, reminded him of Spain. 'But it's what other people think that really matters. The critics, and the people who pay to come to the theatre.'
'What is the play called?'
'*Bent Penny.* And don't ask me what it's about, because I haven't got time to tell you.'
'My boyfriend writes. He writes articles on psychology for the university journal.'
'I'm sure they're fascinating.'
'But it isn't the same as writing plays.'
'No. Not quite the same.'
Thomas had finished his yoghurt. Helga wiped his face and took off his bib and lifted him out of his high chair. He came to stand by Oliver, balancing himself by placing his hands on Oliver's knee. Through the worn denim, Oliver could feel their warmth, the grip of the little fingers. Thomas gazed up at Oliver and smiled again, a grin with dimples and that row of little teeth. He put up a hand to touch Oliver's beard, and Oliver stooped so that he could reach it. Thomas laughed. Oliver picked him up and held him on his knee. He felt solid and warm.
Helga seemed gratified by all these friendly advances. 'Now he has made friends. If I got a book, you could show him the pictures while I put the plates in the dishwasher. Then I have to take him for a walk.'
Oliver had already decided that it was time to leave, but he said, 'All right' so Helga went to find a book, and he and Thomas were left alone.
Thomas was fascinated by his beard. Oliver hoisted him up so that he stood on Oliver's knee and their eyes were on a level. Thomas tugged his beard. Oliver yelped. Thomas laughed. He tried to tug it again, but Oliver caught his hand and held

it in his own. 'That hurt, you brute.' Thomas stared into his eyes. Oliver said softly, 'Do you know who I am?' and Thomas laughed again, as though the question were a great joke.

Helga came back with the book and laid it on the table, a large and brightly coloured book with farm animals on the shiny cover. Oliver opened it at random and Thomas sat down again on his knee, leaning forward on the table, to peer at the pictures. As Helga went about her work putting plates away and scrubbing out the dish that had contained the shepherd's pie, Oliver turned the pages, and said the names of the animals, and pointed to the farmhouse and the gate and the tree and the haystack. And they came to a picture of a dog, and Thomas barked. And then to a picture of a cow, and he made mooing sounds. It was all very companionable.

Then Helga said it was time for Thomas to come upstairs and be dressed in his outdoor clothes, so she gathered him up and bore him away. Oliver sat and waited for them to come down again. He looked at the immaculate kitchen, and out into the immaculate garden, and he thought of Helga leaving and the next au pair girl coming, and the pattern repeating itself until Thomas was eight years old, and of an age to be sent to some well-established and probably useless prep school. He thought of his son, slotted, labelled, trapped on the conveyor belt of a conventional education, expected to make the right friends, play the accepted games, and never question the tyranny of meaningless tradition.

Oliver had escaped. At seventeen he had cut and run, but only because he had had the twin weapons of his writing and his own single-minded, rebellious determination to go his own way.

But how would Thomas fare?

The question made him feel uncomfortable, and he rejected it as being hypothetical. It was none of Oliver's business what school Thomas went to, and it didn't matter anyway. He lit another cigarette, and idly opened Thomas's picture book again, lifting the front cover. He saw on the white fly sheet, written in Mrs Archer's neat black-inked script,

> Thomas Archer
> For his Second Birthday
> From Granny.

And all at once it did matter. A sort of rage rose within

Oliver, so that if Jeannette's mother had been standing nearby, he would have attacked her; with words that only he knew how to use; with his fists if necessary.

*He is not Thomas Archer, you sanctimonious bitch. He is Thomas Dodds. He is my son.*

When Helga came downstairs, carrying Thomas dressed in a sort of ski suit and a woollen hat with a bobble on it, Oliver was already waiting for her in the hall. He had put on his coat, and he said, 'I have to go now. I have to get back to London.'

'Yes, of course.'

'It was very kind of you to give me lunch.'

'I will tell Mrs Archer that you were here.'

He began to grin. 'Yes. Do that.'

'But . . . I don't know your name. To tell her, I mean.'

'Just say Oliver Dobbs.'

'All right, Mr Dobbs.' She hesitated, standing at the bottom of the stairs, and then said, 'I have to get the pram and my coat from the cloakroom. Will you hold Thomas for a moment?'

'Of course.'

He lifted the child out of her arms, hoisting him up against one shoulder.

'I won't be long, Thomas.' Helga assured him, and she turned and went down the passage beneath the staircase, and disappeared through a half-glassed door.

A pretty, trusting, stupid little girl. He hoped they would not be too hard on her. *You can be as long as you like, my darling.* Carrying his son he went down the hall, let himself out through the yellow front door, went down the steps and got into his waiting car.

Helga heard the car go down the street, but she did not realise it was Oliver's. When she returned with the push-chair, there was no sign of either the man or the child.

'Mr Dobbs?'

He had left the front door open, and the house was invaded by the bitter cold of the afternoon.

'Thomas?'

But outside was only the empty pavement, the silent street.

## CHAPTER 2

## FRIDAY

The most exhausting thing in the world, Victoria Bradshaw decided, was not having enough to do. It was infinitely more exhausting than having far too much to do, and today was a classic example.

February was a bad time for selling clothes. She supposed it was a bad time, really, for selling anything. Christmas was forgotten, and the January sales just a gruesome memory. The morning had started hopefully, with thin sunshine and a light icing of frost, but by early afternoon it had clouded over, and now it was so cold and wet that people with any sense at all were staying at home by fires or in centrally heated flats, doing crosswords or baking cakes or watching television. The weather gave them no encouragement to plan wardrobes for the spring.

The clock edged around to five o'clock. Outside, the bleak afternoon was darkening swiftly into night. The curved shop window had SALLY SHARMAN written across it. From the inside of the shop this presented itself backwards, like writing seen in a mirror, and beyond these hieroglyphics Beauchamp Place was curtained in rain. Passersby, umbrellaed and gusted by wind, struggled with parcels. A stream of traffic waited for the Brompton Road lights to change. A figure, camouflaged by rainproof clothing, ran up the steps from the street and burst through the glass-panelled door like a person escaping, letting in a gust of cold air before the door was hastily slammed shut again.

It was Sally, in her black raincoat and her huge red fox hat. She said, 'God, what a day,' furled her umbrella, took off her gloves and began to unbutton her coat.

'How did it go?' Victoria asked.

Sally had spent the afternoon in the company of a young designer who had decided to go into the wholesale trade.

'Not bad,' she said, draping her coat over the umbrella stand to drip. 'Not bad at all. Lots of new ideas, good colours. Rather mature clothes. I was surprised. I thought his being so young, it would have been all jeans and workmen's shirts, but not at all.'

She pulled off her hat, shook it free of raindrops, and finally emerged as her usual, lanky, elegant self. Narrow trousers tucked into tall boots, and a string-like sweater that on anyone else would have looked like an old floor-cloth, but on Sally was sensational.

She had started life as a model and had never lost her beanpole shape or the ugly, jutting, photogenic bones of her face. From being a model, she had gravitated to the editorial pages of a fashion magazine, and from there, using her accumulated know-how, her many connections, and a natural flair for business, had opened her own shop. She was nearly forty, divorced, hard-headed, but far more tender-hearted than she liked anybody to suspect. Victoria had worked for her for nearly two years and was very fond of her.

Now, she yawned. 'I really hate business lunches. I always feel hung over by the middle of the afternoon, and somehow that throws me for the rest of the day.'

She reached into her immense handbag and took out cigarettes and an evening paper, which she tossed down on to the glass counter. 'What's been happening here?'

'Practically nothing. I sold the beige overdress, and some female came in and dithered for half an hour over the paisley coat, and then she went out again and said she'd think about it. She was put off by the mink collar. She says she's a wild-life supporter.'

'Tell her we'll take it off and put on plastic fur instead.' Sally went through the curtained doorway into the small office at the back of the shop, sat at her desk and began to open the mail.

She said, 'You know, Victoria, I've been thinking, this would be a terribly good time for you to take a couple of weeks off. Things'll start livening up soon, and then I shan't be able to let you go. Besides, you haven't had a holiday since goodness knows when. The only thing is, February isn't very exciting anywhere. Perhaps you could go and ski, or stay with your mother in Sotogrande. What's Sotogrande like in February?'

'Windy and wet, I should think.'

Sally looked up. 'You don't want to take two weeks off in February,' she announced resignedly. 'I can tell by your voice.' Victoria did not contradict her. Sally sighed. 'If I had a mother who had a gorgeous house in Sotogrande, I'd stay with her every month of the year if I could. Besides, you look as though you need a holiday. All skinny and pale. It makes me feel guilty having you around, as though I worked you too hard.' She opened another envelope. 'I thought we'd paid that electricity bill. I'm sure we paid it. It must be the computer's fault. It must have gone mad. Computers do, you know.'

To Victoria's relief the question of her suddenly taking a holiday at the end of February was, for the moment, forgotten. She picked up the newspaper that Sally had tossed down, and for lack of anything better to do, leafed idly through it, her eye skimming the usual disasters, both great and small. There were floods in Essex, a new conflagration threatened in Africa. A middle-aged earl was marrying his third wife, and in Bristol rehearsals were under way at the Fortune Theatre for Oliver Dobbs' new play, *Bent Penny*.

There was no reason why she should have noticed this little scrap of news. It was tucked in at the end of the last column on the entertainments page. There was no headline. No photograph. Just Oliver's name, which leapt out at her, like a shout of recognition, from the small print.

' . . . it's a final demand. What a nerve, sending a final demand. I know I wrote a cheque last month.' Victoria said nothing, and Sally looked at her. 'Victoria . . . ? What are you staring at?'

'Nothing. Just this bit in the paper about a man I used to know.'

'I hope he's not being sent to jail.'

'No, he writes plays. Have you ever heard of Oliver Dobbs?'

'Yes, of course. He writes for television. I saw one of his short plays the other night. And he did the script for that marvellous documentary on Seville. What's he been doing to get himself in the news?'

'He's got a new production coming off in Bristol.'

'What's he like?' Sally asked idly, half her mind still on the iniquities of the London Electricity Board.

'Attractive.'

This caught Sally's attention. She was all in favour of attractive men. 'Did he attract you?'

'I was eighteen and impressionable.'

'Weren't we all, darling, in the dim days of our youth. Not that that applies to you. You're still a blooming child, you fortunate creature.' Suddenly she lost interest in Oliver Dobbs, in the final demand, in the day, which had already gone on far too long. She leaned back and yawned. 'To hell with it. Let's shut up shop and go home. Thank the Lord for weekends. All at once the prospect of nothing to do for two days is total paradise. I shall spend this evening sitting in a hot bath and watching television.'

'I thought you'd be going out.'

Sally's private life was both complicated and lively. She had a string of men friends, none of whom seemed to be aware of the others' existence. Like an adroit juggler, Sally kept them all on the go, and avoided the embarrassment of inadvertently muddling their names by calling them all 'darling'.

'No, thank God. How about you?'

'I'm meant to be going out to have a drink with some friends of my mother's. I don't suppose it will be very thrilling.'

'Oh, well,' said Sally, 'You never know. Life is full of surprises.'

One of the good things about working in Beauchamp Place was that it was within walking distance of Pendleton Mews. The flat in Pendleton Mews belonged to Victoria's mother, but it was Victoria who lived there. Most of the time she enjoyed the walk. Down shortcuts and narrow back roads, it only took half an hour and provided a little pleasant exercise and fresh air at the beginning and the end of the day.

But this evening it was so cold and wet that the prospect of a trudge through icy wind and rain was almost more than she could bear; so, breaking her own rule about never taking taxis, she succumbed, without much resistance, to temptation, walked up to the Brompton Road and finally flagged down a cab.

Because of one-way streets and snarled-up traffic, it took perhaps ten minutes longer to reach the Mews than if she had made the journey on foot, and cost so much that she simply handed the driver a pound note and let him count out the meagre change. He had set her down at the arch that divided the Mews from the road, so there was still a little way to go, across the puddles and the shining wet cobbles before she reached at last the haven of her own blue front door. She

opened the door with her latch key, reached inside and switched
on the light; climbed the steep, narrow stairs, carpeted in worn
beige Wilton, and emerged at the top directly into the small
sitting room.

She shed umbrella and basket and went to draw the chintz
curtains against the night. The room at once became enclosed
and safe. She lit the gas fire and went through to the tiny
kitchen to put on a kettle for a cup of coffee; switched on the
television and then switched it off again, put a Rossini overture
on the record player, went into her bedroom to take off raincoat and boots.

The kettle, competing with Rossini, whistled for attention.
She made a mug of instant coffee, went back to the fireside,
pulled her basket towards her and took out Sally's evening
paper. She turned to the item about Oliver Dobbs and the new
play in Bristol.

*I was eighteen and impressionable,* she had said to Sally, but
she knew now that she had also been lonely and vulnerable,
a ripe fruit, trembling on its stalk, waiting to fall.

And Oliver, of all men, had been standing at the foot of the
tree, waiting to catch her.


Eighteen, and in her first year at art school. Knowing nobody,
intensely shy and unsure of herself, she had been both flattered
and apprehensive when an older girl, perhaps taking pity on
Victoria, had flung a vague invitation to a party in her direction.

'Goodness knows what it'll be like, but I was told I could
ask anybody I wanted. You're meant to bring a bottle of
something, but I don't suppose it matters if you come empty
handed. Anyway, it's a good way to meet people. Look, I'll
write down the address. The man's called Sebastian, but that
doesn't matter. Just turn up if you feel like it. Any time; that
doesn't matter either.'

Victoria had never had such an invitation in her life. She
decided that she wouldn't go. And then decided that she would.
And then got cold feet. And finally put on a pair of clean jeans,
stole a bottle of her mother's best claret, and went.

She ended up in a top floor flat in West Kensington, clutching her bottle of claret and knowing nobody. Before she had
been there two minutes somebody said 'How immensely kind,'
and removed the bottle of claret, but nobody else said a single

word to her. The room was filled with smoke, intense men in beads, and girls with grey faces and long seaweed-like hair. There was even a grubby baby or two. There was nothing to eat and – once she had parted with the claret – nothing recognisable to drink. She could not find the girl who suggested that she come and was too shy to join any of the tight, conversational groups gathered on floor, cushions or the single sagging sofa that had curly wire springs protruding from between arm and seat. She was, as well, too diffident to go and get her coat and leave. The air was filled with the sweet and insidious smell of marijuana, and she was standing in the bay window, lost in nerve-wracking fantasies of a possible police raid, when suddenly somebody said, 'I don't know you, do I?'

Startled, Victoria swung round, so clumsily that she almost knocked the drink out of his hand.

'Oh, I am sorry . . . '

'It doesn't matter. It hasn't spilled. At least,' he added, generously, 'not very much.'

He smiled as though this were a joke, and she smiled back, grateful for any friendly overture. Grateful too that out of such woebegone company the only man who had spoken to her was neither dirty, sweaty, nor drunk. On the contrary, he was perfectly presentable. Even attractive. Very tall, very slender with reddish hair that reached to the collar of his sweater, and an immensely distinguished beard.

He said, 'You haven't got a drink.'

'No.'

'Don't you want one?'

She said no again, because she didn't and also because if she said that she did, he might go away to get her one and never come back again.

He seemed amused. 'Don't you like it?'

Victoria looked at his glass. 'I don't exactly know what it is.'

'I don't suppose anybody does. But this tastes like . . . ' He took a mouthful, thoughtfully, like a professional taster, rolling it round his mouth, finally swallowing it. ' . . . red ink and aniseed balls.'

'What's it going to do to the inside of your stomach?'

'We'll worry about that in the morning.' He looked down at her, a frown of concentration furrowing his brow. 'I *don't* know you, do I?'

'No. I don't suppose you do. I'm Victoria Bradshaw.' Even saying her own name made her feel embarrassed, but he did not seem to think that there was anything embarrassing about it.

'And what do you do with yourself?'

'I've just started at art college.'

'That explains how you got to this little do. Are you enjoying it?'

She looked around. 'Not very much.'

'I actually meant art college, but if you're not enjoying this very much, why don't you go home?'

'I thought it wouldn't be very polite.'

He laughed at that. 'You know, in this sort of company, politeness doesn't count all that much.'

'I've only been here for ten minutes.'

'And I've only been here for five.' He finished his drink, tipping back his remarkable head and pouring the remains of the noxious tumbler down the back of his throat as easily as if it had been a cold and tasty beer. Then he set the glass down on the window ledge and said, 'Come on. We're leaving.' And he put a hand under her elbow and steered her expertly towards the door, and without making the vaguest of excuses or even saying goodbye, they left.

At the top of the dingy staircase, she turned to face him.

'I didn't mean that.'

'What didn't you mean?'

'I mean that I didn't want *you* to leave. I wanted *me* to leave.'

'How do you know I didn't want to leave?'

'But it was a party!'

'I left those sort of parties behind light years ago. Come on, hurry up, let's get out into the fresh air.'

On the pavement, in the soft dusk of a late summer's night, she stopped again. She said, 'I'm all right now.'

'And what is that supposed to mean?'

'I can get a taxi, and go home.'

He began to smile. 'Are you frightened?'

Victoria became embarrassed all over again. 'No, of course not.'

'Then what are you running away from?'

'I'm not running away from anything. I simply ...'

'Want to go home?'

'Yes.'

'Well you can't.'

'Why not?'

'Because we're going to go and find a spaghetti house or something, and we're going to buy a proper bottle of wine, and you are going to tell me the story of your life.'

An empty taxi hove into view, and he hailed it. It stopped and he bundled her in. After he gave the taxi driver directions, they drove in silence for about five minutes, and then the taxi stopped and he bundled her out again. He paid off the taxi and led her across the pavement into a small and unpretentious restaurant, with a few tables crowded around the walls and the air thick with cigarette smoke and the good smells of cooking food. They were given a table in the corner without enough room for his long legs, but somehow he arranged them so that his feet didn't trip the passing waiters, and he ordered a bottle of wine and asked for a menu, and then he lit a cigarette and turned to her and said, 'Now.'

'Now what?'

'Now tell me. The story of your life.'

She found herself smiling. 'I don't even know who you are. I don't know what your name is.'

'It's Oliver Dobbs.' He went on, quite kindly, 'You have to tell me everything, because I'm a writer. A real honest-to-God published writer, with an agent and an enormous overdraft, and a compulsion for listening. Do you know, nobody listens enough. People fall over themselves trying to tell other people things, and nobody ever listens. Did you know that?'

Victoria thought of her parents. 'Yes, I suppose I do.'

'You see? You suppose. You're not sure. Nobody's ever sure of anything. They should listen more. How old are you?'

'Eighteen.'

'I thought you were less when I saw you. You looked about fifteen standing there in the window of that crumby joint. I was about to ring the welfare and tell them that a tiny junior minor was out on the streets at night.'

The wine came, uncorked, a litre bottle dumped on to the table. He picked it up and filled their glasses. He said, 'Where do you live?'

'Pendleton Mews.'

'Where's that?'

She told him and he whistled. 'How very smart. A real Knightsbridge girl. I didn't realise they went to art college. You must be immensely rich.'

'Of course I'm not rich.'

'Then why do you live in Pendleton Mews?'

'Because it's my mother's house, only she's living in Spain just now, so I use it.'

'Curiouser and curiouser. Why is Mrs Bradshaw living in Spain?'

'She's not Mrs Bradshaw, she's Mrs Paley. My parents divorced six months ago. My mother married again, to this man called Henry Paley, and he has a house in Sotogrande because he likes playing golf all the time.' She decided to get it all over in a single burst. 'And my father has gone to live with some cousin who owns a mouldering estate in Southern Ireland. He's threatening to breed polo ponies, but he's always been a man of great ideas but little action, so I don't suppose he will.'

'And little Victoria is left to live in London.'

'Victoria is eighteen.'

'Yes, I know, old and experienced. Do you live alone?'

'Yes.'

'Aren't you lonely?'

'I'd rather be alone than live with people who dislike each other.'

He made a face. 'Parents are hell, aren't they? My parents are hell, too, but they've never done anything so definite as divorcing each other. They just moulder on in darkest Dorset, and everything – their reduced circumstances, the cost of a bottle of gin, the fact that the hens aren't laying – is blamed on either me or the government.'

Victoria said, 'I like my parents. It was just that they'd stopped liking each other.'

'Have you got brothers or sisters?'

'No. Just me.'

'No one to take care of you?'

'I take very good care of myself.'

He looked disbelieving. '*I* shall take care of you,' he announced, magnificently.

After that evening Victoria did not see Oliver Dobbs again for two weeks, and by that time she knew that she was never going to see him again. And then it was a Friday evening, and she was so miserable that she compulsively spring-cleaned the flat, which did not need it, and then decided to wash her hair.

It was while she was kneeling by the bath with her head under the shower that she heard the bell ring. She wrapped herself up in a towel and went to open the door, and it was

Oliver. Victoria was so pleased to see him that she burst into tears, and he came in and shut the door and took her in his arms, then and there, at the foot of the stairs, and dried her face with the end of the towel. After this they went upstairs, and he produced a bottle of wine out of his jacket pocket, and she found some glasses, and they sat by the gas fire and drank wine together. And when they had finished the wine, she went into her bedroom to get dressed, and to comb out her long, fair, damp tresses, and Oliver sat on the end of the bed and watched her. And then he took her out for dinner. There were no apologies, no excuses for his two weeks silence. He had been in Birmingham, he told her, and that was all. It never occurred to Victoria to ask him what he had been doing there.

And this proved to be the pattern of their relationship. He came and went, in and out of her life, unpredictable, and yet strangely constant. Each time he came back, she never knew where he had been. Perhaps Ibiza, or perhaps he had met some man who owned a cottage in Wales. He was not only unpredictable, he was strangely secretive. He never spoke about his work, and she did not even know where he lived, except that it was a basement flat in some street off the Fulham Road. He was moody, too, and once or twice she had seen a terrifying flash of uncontrollable temper, but this all seemed to be an acceptable part of the fact that he was a writer and a true artist. And there was another side to the coin. He was funny and loving and immensely good company. It was like having the kindest sort of older brother who was, at the same time, irresistibly attractive.

When they were not together, she told herself that he was working. She imagined him at his typewriter, writing and rewriting, destroying, starting again, never achieving his own goals of perfection. Sometimes, he had a little money to spend on her. At others, none at all, and then Victoria would provide the food and cook it for him in the mews flat, and she would buy him a bottle of wine and the small cigars that she knew he loved.

There came a bad period when he went through a slough of despondency. Nothing would go right and nothing seemed to be selling, and it was then that he took the night job in a little café, piling dirty dishes into the automatic washer. After that things began to get better again, and he sold a play to Independent Television, but he still went on washing dishes in order to be able to earn enough money to pay his rent.

Victoria had no other men friends, and did not want them. For some reason, she never imagined Oliver with other women. There was no occasion for jealousy. What she had of Oliver was not much, but it was enough.

The first she heard of Jeannette Archer was when Oliver told her that he was going to be married.

It was early summer, and the windows of Victoria's flat were open to the mews. Below, Mrs Tingley from number fourteen was bedding out geraniums in her decorative tubs, and the man who lived two doors down was cleaning his car. Pigeons cooed from rooftops, and the distant hum of traffic was deadened by trees in full leaf. They sat on the window seat, and Victoria was sewing a button on to Oliver's jacket. It hadn't fallen off, but it was going to, and she had offered to sew it on before it did. She found a needle and thread and put a knot in the thread and had pushed the needle into the worn corduroy when Oliver said, 'What would you say if I told you I was going to be married?'

Victoria pushed the needle right into her thumb. The pain was minute but excruciating. She pulled the needle carefully out and watched the red bead of blood swell and grow. Oliver said, 'Suck it, quickly, or it'll drip all over my coat,' and when she didn't, he took her wrist and thrust her thumb into his mouth. Their eyes met. He said, 'Don't look at me like that.'

Victoria looked at her thumb. It throbbed as though some person had hit it with a hammer. She said, 'I don't know any other way to look.'

'Well say something then. Don't just stare at me like a lunatic.'

'I don't know what I'm meant to say.'

'You could wish me luck.'

'I didn't know . . . that you . . . I mean, I didn't know that you were . . . ' She was trying, even at this ghastly juncture, to be rational, polite, tactful. But Oliver scorned such euphemisms and interrupted brutally.

'You mean, you never realised that there was anybody else? And that, if you like it, is a line straight from an out-of-date novel. The kind my mother reads.'

'Who is she?'

'She's called Jeannette Archer. She's twenty-four, a nicely brought-up girl with a nice flat and a nice little car, and a good job, and we've been living together for the past four months.'

'I thought you lived in Fulham.'

'I do sometimes, but I haven't just lately.'

She said, 'Do you love her?' because she simply had to know.

'Victoria, she's going to have a child. Her parents want me to marry her so that the baby will have a father. It seems to matter to them very much.'

'I thought you didn't pay regard to parents.'

'I don't if they're like mine, complaining and unsuccessful. But these particular parents happen to have a lot of money. I need money. I need money to buy the time to write.'

She knew that she would cry. Her thumb still ached. Her eyes were filling with tears, and so that he shouldn't see them, she dropped her head and started to try to sew on the button, but the tears brimmed over and rolled down her cheeks and fell, great drops on the corduroy of his coat. He saw them and said, 'Don't cry.' And he put a hand under her chin and lifted her streaming face.

Victoria said, 'I love you.'

He leaned forward and kissed her cheek. 'But you,' he told her, 'don't happen to be having a baby.'

The clock on the mantelpiece astonished her by chiming, with silvery notes, seven o'clock. Victoria looked at it, disbelieving, and then at her wrist watch. Seven o'clock. The Rossini had finished long ago, the dregs in her coffee mug were stone cold, outside it was still raining, and in half an hour she was due at a party in Campden Hill.

She was assailed by the usual small panic of one who has lost all trace of time, and all thoughts of Oliver Dobbs were, for the moment, forgotten. Victoria sprang to her feet and did a number of things in quick succession. Took the coffee mug back into the kitchen, turned on a bath, went into her room to open her wardrobe and take out various garments, none of which seemed suitable. She took off some clothes and searched for stockings. She thought about ringing up for a taxi. She thought about calling Mrs Fairburn and pleading a headache, and then thought better of it, because the Fairburns were friends of her mother's, the invitation was a long-standing one, and Victoria had a horror of causing offence. She went into the steaming bathroom and turned off the taps and splashed in some bath oil. The steam became scented. She disposed of her long hair in a bathcap, slathered cold cream on her face and wiped it all off again with a tissue. She climbed into the scalding water.

Fifteen minutes later she was out once more and dressed. A black silk turtleneck with a peasant-embroidered smock on top of it. Black stockings, black shoes with very high heels. She blackened her thick lashes with mascara, clipped in earrings, sprayed on some scent.

Now, a coat. She drew back the curtains and opened the window and leaned out to gauge the weather. It was very dark and still windy, but the rain, for the moment, seemed to have ceased. Below, the mews was quiet. Cobbles shone like fish scales, black puddles reflected the light from the old-fashioned street lamps. A car was turning in from the street, under the archway. It nosed down the mews like a prowling cat. Victoria withdrew her head, closed the windows and the curtains. She took an old fur coat from the back of the door, bundled herself into its familiar comfort, checked for her keys and wallet, turned off the gas fire and all the upstairs lights, and started downstairs.

She had taken one step when the doorbell rang.

She said, 'Damn.' It was probably Mrs Tingley come to borrow milk. She was always running out of milk. And she would want to stand and talk. Victoria ran to the foot of the stairs and flung open the door.

On the far side of the mews, beneath a lamp, the prowling car was parked. A big old Volvo estate car. But of its driver there was no sign. Puzzled, she hesitated, and was about to go and investigate, when, from the dark shadows at the side of the door, a figure moved soundlessly forward, causing Victoria nearly to jump out of her skin. He said her name, and it was as though she had been taken, very swiftly, down twenty-three storeys in a very fast lift. The wind blew a scrap of newspaper the length of the mews. She could hear the beating of her own heart.

'I didn't know if you'd still be living here.'

She thought, these things don't happen. Not to ordinary people. They only happen in books.

'I thought you might have moved. I was sure you'd have moved.'

She shook her head.

He said, 'It's been a long time.'

Victoria's mouth was dry. She said, 'Yes.'

Oliver Dobbs. She searched for some change in him but

could find none. His hair was the same, his beard, his light eyes, his deep and gentle voice. He even wore the same sort of clothes, shabby and casual garments that on his tall, lean frame did not look shabby at all but somehow contrived and distinctive.

He said, 'You look as though you're just going out.'

'Yes, I am. I'm late as it is. But . . . ' She stepped back ' . . . you'd better come in, out of the cold.'

'Is that all right?'

'Yes.' But she said again, 'I have to go out,' as if her going out were some sort of an escape hatch from a possibly impossible situation. She turned to lead the way back upstairs. He began to follow her and then hesitated. He said, 'I've left my cigarettes in the car.'

He plunged back into the outdoors. Halfway up the stairs Victoria waited. He returned in a moment, closed the door behind him. She went up, turning on the light at the head of the stairs, and going to stand with her back to the unlit gas fire.

Oliver followed her, his eyes alert, instantly scanning the pretty room, the pale walls, the chintzes, patterned with spring flowers. The pine corner-cupboard that Victoria had found in a junk shop and stripped herself, her pictures, her books.

He smiled, satisfied. 'You haven't changed anything. It's exactly the way I remembered. How marvellous to find something that hasn't changed.' His eyes came back to her face. 'I thought you'd have gone. I thought you'd have married some guy and moved. I was so certain that the door would be opened by a complete stranger. And there you were. Like a miracle.'

Victoria found that she could think of absolutely nothing to say. She thought, I have been struck speechless. Searching for words, she found herself looking around the room. Beneath the bookcase was the cupboard where she kept a meagre collection of bottles. She said, 'Would you like a drink?'

'Yes, I'd like one very much.'

She laid down her bag and went to crouch by the cupboard. There was sherry, half a bottle of wine, a nearly empty bottle of whisky. She took out the whisky bottle. 'There isn't much, I'm afraid.'

'That's marvellous,' He came to take the bottle from her. 'I'll do it.' He disappeared into the kitchen, at home in her flat as if he had walked out only yesterday. She heard the chink of glass, the running of the tap.

'Do you want one?' he called.

'No thank you.'

He emerged from the kitchen with the drink in his hand. 'Where's this party you're going to?'

'Campden Hill. Some friends of my mother's.'

'Is it going on for long?'

'I don't suppose so.'

'Will you come back for dinner?'

Victoria almost laughed at this, because this was Oliver Dobbs, apparently inviting her to have dinner with him in her own flat.

'I imagine I will.'

'Then you go to your party, and I'll wait here.' He saw the expression on her face and added quickly, 'It's important. I want to talk to you. And I want to have time to talk to you.'

It sounded sinister, as though someone was after him, like the police, or some Soho heavy with a switch knife.

'There's nothing wrong, is there?'

'How anxious you look! No, there's nothing wrong.' He added, in a practical fashion, 'Have you got any food in the house?'

'There's some soup. Some bacon and eggs. I could make a salad. Or, if you wanted, we could go out. There's a Greek restaurant around the corner, it's just started up . . .'

'No, we can't go out.' He sounded so definite that Victoria began to be apprehensive all over again. He went on, 'I didn't want to tell you right away until I knew what the form was with you. The thing is, there's someone else in the car. There are two of us.'

'Two of you?' She imagined a girlfriend, a drunken crony, even a dog.

In answer Oliver laid down his glass and disappeared once more down the stairs. She heard the door open and his footsteps crossing the mews. She went to the head of the stairs and waited for him to return. He had left the door open, and when he reappeared he closed this behind him, carefully with his foot. The reason that he did this was that his arms were otherwise occupied with the weight of a large, mercifully sleeping, baby boy.

# CHAPTER 3

## FRIDAY

It was a quarter past seven, at the end of a gruelling day, before John Dunbeath finally turned his car into the relative quiet of Cadogan Place, down the narrow lane between tightly parked cars, and edged it into a meagre gap not too far from his own front door. He killed the engine, turned off the lights, and reached into the back seat for his bulging briefcase and his raincoat. He got out of the car and locked up.

He had left his office, and commenced the daily ordeal of the journey home, in lashing rain, but now, half an hour or so later, it seemed to be easing up a little. Dark and still windy, the sky, bronzed with the reflected glow of the city lights, seemed to be full of ominous, racing clouds. After ten hours spent in an overheated atmosphere, the night air smelled fresh and invigorating. Walking slowly down the pavement, his briefcase slapping against his leg, he took one or two deep and conscious lungfuls, and was refreshed by the cold wind.

With his key ring in his hand, he went up the steps to the front door. It was black, with a brass handle and a letter box that the porter polished every morning. The tall old London house had been turned, some time ago, into flats, and the lobby and staircase, although carpeted and neatly kept, always smelled stale and stuffy, unaired and claustrophobic with central heating. This odour greeted him now, as it greeted him every evening. He shut the door with the seat of his pants, collected his mail from its pigeon hole and began to climb the stairs.

He lived on the second floor, in an apartment that had been cunningly contrived from the main bedrooms of the original house. It was a furnished flat, found for him by a colleague

when John had left New York and come to work in London
at the European headquarters of the Warburg Investment
Corporation, and he had arrived at Heathrow off the plane
from Kennedy and taken instant possession. Now, six months
later, it had become familiar. Not a home, but familiar. A
place for a man alone to live.

He let himself in, turned on the lights and saw on the hall
table his message from Mrs Robbins the daily lady whom
the porter had recommended should come in each morning
and clean the flat. John had only seen her once, at the very
beginning, when he had given her a key and told her more or
less what he wanted her to do. Mrs Robbins had made it clear
that this was quite unnecessary. She was a stately person,
portentously hatted and wearing her respectability like armour.
At the end of the encounter he was fully aware that he had not
been interviewing her, but that Mrs Robbins had been judging
him. However, it seemed that he had passed muster, and she
duly took him on, along with one or two other privileged
persons who also lived in the house. Since then, he had never
set eyes on her, but they corresponded by means of notes that
they left for each other, and he paid her, weekly, in the same
fashion.

He dropped his briefcase, slung his raincoat on to a chair,
picked up Mrs Robbins' letter, and along with the rest of his
mail took it into the sitting room. Here all was beige and
brown and totally impersonal. Another person's pictures hung
upon the wall, another person's books filled the shelves which
flanked the fireplace, and he had no wish for it to be any
different.

Sometimes, for no particular reason, the emptiness of his
personal life, the need for welcome, for love, would overwhelm
him, breaking down the careful barriers which he had painfully
built. On these occasions, he could not stop the memories flood-
ing back. Like coming home to the shining brilliance of the New
York apartment, with its white floors and its white rugs, and
a sort of perfection which Lisa had achieved with her eye for
colour, her passion for detail and her total disregard for her
husband's bank balance. And, inevitably, Lisa would be there,
waiting for him – for these memories belonged to the beginning
of their marriage – so beautiful that she took your breath
away, wearing something gauzy by de la Renta, and smelling
unbearably exotic. And she would kiss him, and put a martini
into his hand, and be glad to see him.

But most times, like this evening, he was grateful for quiet, for peace; for time to read his mail, to have a drink, to re-assemble himself after the day's work. He went around the room turning on lights; he switched on the electric fire which instantly became a pile of rustic logs, flickering in the pseudo firebasket. He drew the brown velvet curtains and poured himself a Scotch, and then read the message from Mrs Robbins.

Her notes were always brief and abbreviated, rendering them as important sounding as cables.

> Laundry missing pair sox and 2 hankchfs.
> Miss Mansell called says will you ring her this evng.

He leafed through the rest of his mail. A bank statement, a company report, a couple of invitations, an airmail letter from his mother. Putting these aside for later perusal, he sat on the arm of the sofa, reached for the telephone and dialled a number.

She came on almost at once, sounding breathless as she always did, as though perpetually in a tearing hurry.

'Hello?'

'Tania.'

'Darling. I thought you'd never call.'

'Sorry, I'm only just back. Just picked up your message now.'

'Oh, poor sweet, you must be exhausted. Listen, something maddening's cropped up, but I can't make this evening. The thing is, I'm going down to the country *now*. Mary Colville rang up this morning, and there's some dance going on, and some girl's got flu, and she's desperate about her numbers, and I simply had to say I'd go. I tried to say no, and explain about this evening, but then she said would *you* come down tomorrow, for the weekend.'

She stopped, not because she hadn't got plenty more to say, but because she had run out of breath. John found himself smiling. Her spates of words, her breathlessness, her confused social arrangements were all part of the charm that she held for him, mostly because she was so diametrically different from his ex-wife. Tania had, perpetually, to be organised, and was so scatty that the thought of organising John never entered her pretty feather-head.

He looked at his watch. He said, 'If you're going to be at some dinner party in the country this evening, aren't you running things a little fine?'

'Oh, darling, yes, I'm going to be desperately late, but that's not what you're meant to say at all. You're meant to be desperately disappointed.'

'Of course I'm disappointed.'

'And you will come down to the country tomorrow?'

'Tania, I can't. I just heard today. I have to go to the Middle East. I'm flying out tomorrow morning.'

'Oh, I can't bear it. How long are you going for?'

'Just a few days. A week at the outside. It depends on how things go.'

'Will you call me when you get back?'

'Yes, sure.'

'I rang Imogen Fairburn and told her I couldn't make it this evening, so she understands, and she says she's looking forward to seeing you even if I can't be there too. Oh, darling, isn't everything grim? Are you furious?'

'Furious,' he assured her, mildly.

'But you do understand, don't you?'

'I understand completely, and you thank Mary for her invitation and explain why I can't make it.'

'Yes, I will, of course I will, and . . . '

Another of her characteristics was that she could never finish a phone call. He interrupted firmly.

'Look, Tania, you have an appointment this evening. Get off the line and finish your packing and get moving. With luck, you'll arrive at the Colvilles no more than two hours late.'

'Oh, darling I do adore you.'

'I'll call you.'

'You do that.' She made kissing sounds. 'Bye.' She hung up. He put the receiver back on the hook and sat looking at it, wondering why he couldn't feel disappointed when a charming and engaging female stood him up for a more exciting invitation. He mulled over this problem for a moment or two, and finally decided that it didn't matter anyway. So he dialled Annabel's and cancelled the table he had ordered for this evening and then he finished his drink and went to have a shower.

Just as he was on the point of leaving for the Fairburns' a call came through from his vice-president, who had had, on his journey home in the company Cadillac, one or two important thoughts about John's projected trip to Bahrein.

Discussing these, getting them collated and noted, had taken a good fifteen minutes, so that by the time John finally arrived at the house in Campden Hill, he was nearly three quarters of an hour late.

The party was obviously in full swing. The street outside was jammed with cars – it took him another frustrating five minutes to find a scrap of space in which to park his own – and light and a steady hum of conversation emanated from beyond the tall, curtained first-floor windows. When he rang the bell the door was opened almost immediately by a man (hired for the occasion?) in a white coat, who said, 'Good evening,' and directed John up the stairs.

It was a pleasant and familiar house, expensively decorated, thickly carpeted, smelling like an extravagant hothouse. As John ascended, the sound of voices swelled to a massive volume. Through the open door that led into Imogen's drawing room, he could discern an anonymous crush of people, some drinking, some smoking, some munching canapés, and all intent on talking their heads off. A couple were sitting at the head of the stairs. John smiled and excused himself as he stepped around them, and the girl said, 'We're just having a tiny breath of air,' as though she felt she must apologise for being there.

By the open door was a table set up as a bar, with another hired waiter in attendance.

'Good evening, sir. What'll it be?'

'Scotch and soda, please.'

'With ice, sir, naturally.'

John grinned. The 'naturally' meant that the barman had recognised him for the American that he was. He said, 'Naturally,' and took the drink. 'How am I going to find Mrs Fairburn?'

'I'm afraid you'll just have to go and look for her, sir. Like a needle in a ruddy haystack, I'd say.'

John agreed with him, took a spine-stiffening slug of whisky and plunged.

It wasn't as bad as it might have been. He was recognised, greeted, almost at once, drawn into a group, offered a smoked salmon roll, a cigar, a racing tip. 'Absolute certainty, old boy, three-thirty at Doncaster tomorrow.' A girl he knew slightly came and kissed him and, he suspected, left lipstick on his cheek. A tall young man with an old man's balding head swam forward and said, 'You're John Dunbeath, aren't you? Name's

Crumleigh. Used to know your predecessor. And how are things in the banking world?'

He was nursing his drink, but a waiter nipped up and refilled his glass when he wasn't looking. Somebody trod on his shoe. A very young man wearing a brigade tie materialised at his elbow, trailing a protesting female by the arm. She was perhaps seventeen years old, and her hair looked like dandelion floss. '...this girl wants to meet you. Been eyeing you across the room.'

'Oh, Nigel, you are *awful*.'

Mercifully, he spied his hostess. He excused himself, and edged, with some difficulty, across the room to her side. 'Imogen'.

'John! Darling!'

She was immensely pretty. Grey-haired, blue-eyed, her skin smooth as a young girl's, her manner unashamedly provocative.

He kissed her politely, because she was obviously expecting to be kissed, with that flower-like face turned up to his.

'This certainly is a party.'

'So gorgeous to see you. But Tania couldn't come. She telephoned, something about having to go down to the country. So terribly disappointing. I was so looking forward to seeing you *both*. Never mind, you came and that's all that matters. Have you had a word with Reggie? He's longing to have a long, boring chat with you about the stock market or something.' A couple hovered, waiting to say goodbye. 'Don't go away,' Imogen told John out of the corner of her mouth, and then turned from him, all smiles. 'Darling. Do you really have to go? Such a sadness. Heavenly to see you. So glad you enjoyed it ...' She came back to John. 'Look, as Tania hasn't come, and you're on your own, there's a girl that perhaps you could go and chat up. She's pretty as paint, so I'm not letting you in for anything gruesome, but I don't think she knows many people. I mean, I asked her, because her mother's one of our greatest friends, but somehow she seems a little out of her depth. Be an angel, and be sweet to her.'

John, whose party manners had been rigorously drilled into him by his American mother (Imogen knew this, otherwise she would never have appealed to him for help) said that he would be delighted. But where was the girl?

Imogen, who was not tall, stood on tiptoe, and searched with her eyes. 'There. Over in the corner.' Her little feminine hand closed over his wrist like a vice. 'I'll take you over and introduce you.'

Which she proceeded to do, shouldering her way across the stifling room without once releasing her grip of him. John tagged along, willy-nilly, feeling like a bulky liner in the tow of a tug. They emerged at last, and it seemed to be a quiet corner of the room, perhaps because it was furthest from the door and the bar, but all at once there was room to stand, or move your elbows or even sit.

'Victoria.'

She was perched on the arm of a chair, talking to an elderly man who was obviously going on to some other party, for he was wearing a dinner suit and a black tie. When Imogen said her name, she stood up, but whether this was out of politeness to Imogen, or to escape from her companion, it was impossible to say.

'Victoria, I do hope I'm not interrupting something absolutely riveting, but I do want you to meet John, because his girlfriend hasn't been able to come tonight, and I want you to be terribly kind to him.' John, embarrassed both for himself and the girl, continued to smile politely. 'He's an American, and he's one of my most favourite people . . .'

With a clearing of the throat, and a small, imperceptible gesture of farewell, the elderly man in the dinner suit also stood up and eased himself away.

' . . . and John' – the grip on his wrist had not lessened. Perhaps the blood stream to his hand had already seized up and in a moment his fingers would start falling off, – 'this is Victoria. And her mother is one of my best friends, and when Reggie and I were in Spain last year, we went and stayed with her. At Sotogrande. In the most heavenly house you've ever seen. So now you've got *lots* to talk about.'

She let go of his wrist at last. It was like being freed from handcuffs.

He said, 'Hello, Victoria.'

She said, 'Hello.'

Imogen had chosen the wrong words. She was not pretty as paint. But she had a scrubbed, immaculate look to her that reminded him, with some nostalgia, of the American girls he had known in his youth. Her hair was pale and silky, straight and long, cut cunningly to frame her face. Her eyes were blue, her face neatly boned, her head supported by a long neck and narrow shoulders. She had an unremarkable nose, disarmingly freckled, and a remarkable mouth. A sweet and expressive mouth with a dimple at one corner.

It was an out-of-doors sort of face. The sort of face one expected to encounter at the tiller of a sailboat or at the top of some hair-raising ski-slope; not at a London cocktail party.

'Did Imogen say Sotogrande?'

'Yes.'

'How long has your mother lived out there?'

'About three years. Have you ever been to Sotogrande?'

'No, but I have friends who golf, and they get out there whenever they can.'

'My stepfather plays golf every day. That's why he chose to go and live there. Their house is right on the fairway. He steps out of the garden gate and he's playing the tenth hole. It's as easy as that.'

'Do you play golf?'

'No. But there are other things to do. You can swim. Play tennis. Ride, if you want to.'

'What do you do?'

'Well, I don't very often go out, but when I do I play tennis mostly.'

'Does your mother come back to this country?'

'Yes. Two or three times a year. She dashes round from one art gallery to another, sees about six plays, buys some clothes, and then goes back again.'

He smiled at this, and she smiled back. There came a small pause. The subject of Sotogrande seemed to have exhausted itself. Her eyes moved over his shoulder, and then quickly, as though she did not wish to appear ill-mannered, back to his face again. He wondered if she was expecting somebody.

He said, 'Do you know many people here?'

'No, not really. Not anybody really.' She added. 'I'm sorry your girlfriend couldn't come.'

'Like Imogen said, she had to go down to the country.'

'Yes.' She stooped to take a handful of nuts out of a dish that had been placed on a low coffee-table. She began to eat them, putting them into her mouth one at a time. 'Did Imogen say you were an American?'

'Yes, I think she did.'

'You don't sound like an American.'

'How do I sound?'

'Sort of halfway between. Mid-Atlantic. Alistair Cooke type American.'

He was impressed. 'You have a sharp ear. I have an American mother and British father. I'm sorry . . . a Scottish father.'

'So you're really British?'

'I have a dual passport. I was born in the States.'

'Whereabouts?'

'Colorado.'

'Was your mother skiing at the time, or do your parents live there?'

'No, they live there. They have a ranch in Southwest Colorado.'

'I can't imagine where that is.'

'North of New Mexico. West of the Rockies. East of the San Juans.'

'I'd have to have an atlas. But it sounds very spectacular.'

'It is spectacular.'

'Were you riding a horse before you could walk?'

'Just about.'

She said, 'I can imagine it,' and he had a strange feeling that she probably could. 'When did you leave Colorado?'

He told her. 'At eleven years old I was sent East to school. And then I came over to this country and I went to Wellington, because that's where my father had been. And after that I went to Cambridge.'

'You really do have a dual nationality, don't you? What happened after Cambridge?'

'I went back to New York for a spell, and now I'm back in London. I've been here since the summer.'

'Do you work for an American firm?'

'An investment bank.'

'Do you get back to Colodaro?'

'Sure, whenever I can. Only I haven't been for some time, because things have been pretty busy over here.'

'Do you like being in London?'

'Yes, I like it very much.' Her expression was very thoughtful. He smiled. 'Why, don't you?'

'Yes. But just because I know it so well. I mean I can't imagine, really, living anywhere else.'

There came, for some reason, another lull. Once more her eyes strayed, only this time it was to the gold watch strapped to her slender wrist. Having a pretty girl look at her watch while he was chatting her up was an unfamiliar experience for John Dunbeath. He expected to be irritated, but instead found himself mildly amused, although the joke was against himself.

'Are you expecting someone?' he asked her.

'No.'

He thought that her face had a private look about it; composed, polite, but private. He wondered if she was always like this, or if their lines of communication were being cut by the murderous impossibility of cocktail party conversation. In order to keep this going, she had asked him a number of friendly questions, but there was no knowing whether she had listened to half of his polite replies. They had talked banalities and found out nothing about each other. Perhaps she wanted it this way. He could not decide whether she was totally uninterested or simply shy. Now, she had started glancing around the crowded room once more as though desperate for a means of escape, and he began to wonder why she had come in the first place. Suddenly exasperated, and ready to cast formalities aside, he was about to ask her this, but she forestalled him by announcing, without preamble, that she ought to be going. '. . . it's getting late, and I seem to have been here for ages.' At once she seemed to realise that this remark was perhaps not much of a compliment to him. 'I am sorry, I didn't mean it that way. I didn't mean that I seem to have been *here* for ages, I meant that I seem to have been at the party for ages. I . . . I've very much enjoyed meeting you, but I shouldn't be too late.' John said nothing. She smiled brightly, hopefully. 'I ought to get home.'

'Where's home?'

'Pendleton Mews.'

'That's very close to where I live. I'm Cadogan Place.'

'Oh, how nice.' Now, she was beginning to sound desperate. 'It's so quiet, isn't it?'

'Yes, it's very quiet.'

Stealthily, she set down her glass, and hitched the strap of her bag up on to her shoulder. 'Well, then, I'll say goodbye . . . '

But all at once he was consumed with an unfamiliar and healthy annoyance, and told himself that he was damned if he was going to be palmed off like this. Anyway, with his Scotch finished and no Tania to attend to, the party had gone sour for him. Tomorrow, and the long flight to Bahrein loomed on the edge of his mind. He still had to pack, check his papers, leave messages for Mrs Robbins.

He said, 'I'm going too.'

'But you've only just arrived.'

He finished his drink and laid down the empty tumbler. 'I'll take you home.'

'You don't need to take me home.'

'I know I don't need to, but I may as well.'

'I can get a taxi.'

'Why get a taxi, when we're going in the same direction?'

'There's really no need . . .'

He was becoming bored by the tedious argument. 'No problem. I don't want to be late either. I have a plane to catch in the early morning.'

'To America?'

'No, to the Middle East.'

'What are you going to do there?'

He put a hand under her elbow in order to propel her in the direction of the door. 'Talk,' he told her.

Imogen was torn between astonishment that he had hit it off so swiftly with her dearest friend's daughter, and a certain peevishness that he had stayed at her party for such a short time.

'But, John darling, you've only just come.'

'It's a great party, but I'm headed for the Middle East tomorrow; an early flight, and . . .'

'But tomorrow's *Saturday*. It's too cruel having to fly off on a Saturday. I suppose that's what happens if you're a budding tycoon. But I wish you could stay a little longer.'

'I wish I could too, but I really must go.'

'Well, it's been divine, and sweet of you to come. Have you talked to Reggie? No, I don't suppose you have, but I'll tell him what's happening, and you must come for dinner when you get home again. Goodbye, Victoria. Heaven to see you. I'll write and tell your mother you're looking fabulously well.'

On the landing he said, 'Have you got a coat?'

'Yes. It's downstairs.'

They went down. On a chair in the hall was a mound of coats. She dug from this an unfashionable fur, probably inherited and much worn. John helped her into it. The man in the starched white coat opened the door for them, and they emerged into the windy darkness and walked together up the pavement to where he had parked his car.

Waiting at the end of Church Street for the lights to change, John became aware of pangs of hunger. He had eaten a sandwich for lunch and nothing since. The clock on his dashboard told him that it was nearly nine o'clock. The lights changed, and they moved out and into the stream of traffic that poured east towards Kensington Gore.

He thought about eating dinner. He glanced at the girl beside him. Her closeness, her reserve, was a challenge. It intrigued him, and against all reason he found himself wanting to break it down, to find out what went on behind that private face. It was like being confronted by a high wall, a notice saying No Trespassers, and imagining that beyond lay the promise of enchanting gardens and inviting tree-shaded walks. He saw her profile, outlined against the lights, her chin deep in the fur collar of the coat. He thought, well, why not?

He said, 'Do you want to come and have dinner with me someplace?'

'Oh . . . ' She turned towards him. 'How kind.'

'I have to eat, and if you'd like to join me . . . '

'I do appreciate it, but if you don't mind, I really should get back. I mean, I'm having dinner at home. I arranged to have dinner at home.'

It was the second time she had used the word 'home', and it disconcerted him, with its implication of close relatives. He wondered who waited for her. A sister, a lover, or even a husband. Anything was possible.

'That's all right. I just thought if you weren't doing anything.'

'Really so kind of you, but I can't . . . '

A long silence fell between them, broken only by her giving him directions as to how to get most easily to Pendleton Mews. When they reached the archway that separated the mews from the street, she said, 'You can put me down here. I can walk the rest.'

But by now he was feeling stubborn. If she would not have dinner with him, at least he would drive her to her door. He turned the car into the narrow angle beneath the arch and let it idle its way down between the garages and the painted front doors and the tubs that would soon be bright with spring flowers. The rain had stopped, but the cobbles were still damp and shone, like some country street, in the lamplight.

'Which number?' he asked.

'It's right at the .very end. I'm afraid there's scarcely room to turn. You'll have to back out.'

'That's all right.'

'It's this one.'

The lights were on. They shone from upstairs windows and

through the small pane of glass at the top of the blue front door. She peered anxiously upwards as though expecting a window to be flung open and a face to appear, announcing bad news.

But nothing happened. She got out of the car, and John got out too, not because he wanted to be invited in, but because he had been meticulously brought up, and good manners insisted that a girl should not be simply dumped on her doorstep, but that her latchkey should be located, her door politely opened, her safety and well-being assured.

She had found her key. She had opened her door. She was, obviously, anxious to get away and up the stairs.

'Thank you so much for bringing me back. Really kind of you, and you didn't need to bother . . . '

She stopped. From upstairs there came the unmistakable wail of a furious child. The sound rooted them to where they stood. They stared at each other, the girl looking as astonished as John felt. The wails continued, rising in volume and fury. He expected some sort of an explanation, but none came. In the hard light from the staircase, her face was, all at once, very pale. She said in a strained sort of way, 'Good night.'

It was a dismissal. He thought, damn you. He said, 'Good night, Victoria.'

'Have a good time in Bahrein.'

To hell with Bahrein. 'I will.'

'And thank you for bringing me home.'

The blue front door was closed in his face. The light beyond was turned off. He looked up at the windows, secret behind the drawn curtains. He thought, and to hell with you too.

Getting back into his car he reversed at top speed down the length of the mews and out into the street, missing the side of the archway by inches. There he sat for a moment or two endeavouring to recover his natural good humour.

A baby. Whose baby? Probably her baby. There was no reason why she shouldn't have a baby. Just because she looked such a child herself, there was no reason why she shouldn't have a husband or a lover. A girl with a baby.

He thought, *I must tell Tania that. It'll make her laugh. You couldn't come to Imogen's party, so I went by myself and got hooked up with a girl who had to go home to her baby.*

As his annoyance abated, so did his hunger, and their going left him feeling flat. He decided to skip dinner and instead go back to his flat and make a sandwich. His car moved forward, and deliberately his thoughts moved with it, ahead to the following day, to the early start, the drive to Heathrow, the long flight to Bahrein.

## CHAPTER 4

## FRIDAY

Oliver was on the sofa, holding the child standing up on his knees. As Victoria came up the stairs the first thing she saw was the back of Oliver's head and the round, red, tear-drenched face of his son. He, surprised by her sudden appearance, stopped crying for an instant, and then, realising that it was no person he knew, at once started up again.

Oliver jigged him hopefully up and down, but it did no good. Victoria dropped her bag and came around to stand in front of them, unbuttoning her coat.

'How long has he been awake?'

'About ten minutes.' The child roared furiously, and Oliver had to raise his voice in order to make himself heard.

'What's wrong with him?'

'I imagine he's hungry.' He got to his feet, heaving his burden with him. The little boy wore dungarees and a wrinkled white sweater. His hair was copper-gold, the curls at the nape of his neck tangled and damp. The only information Victoria had managed to elicit from Oliver before she had left for the Fairburns' was that the child was his son, and with that she had had to be content. She had left them together, the baby sound asleep on the sofa and Oliver peacefully downing his whisky and water.

But now . . . She gazed with sinking apprehension. She knew nothing about babies. She had scarcely held a baby in her life. What did they eat? What did they want when they wept so heartbreakingly?

She said, 'What's he called?'

'Tom.' Oliver jigged him again, tried to turn him around in

his arms. 'Hey, Tom. Say hello to Victoria.'

Tom took another look at Victoria and then let them know, lustily, what he thought of her. She took off her coat and dropped it on to a chair. 'How old is he?'

'Two.'

'If he's hungry, we should give him something to eat.'

'That makes sense.'

He was being no use at all. Victoria left him and went into the kitchen to search for suitable food for a baby. She stared into the cupboard at racks of spices, Marmite, flour, mustard, lentils, stock cubes.

What was he doing, back in her flat, back in her life, after three years of silence? What was he doing with the child? Where was its mother?

Jam, sugar, porridge oats. A packet brought, the last time she had been in London, by Victoria's mother, for the purpose of making some special sort of biscuit.

'Will he eat porridge?' she called.

Oliver did not reply, because over the yells of his son he did not hear the question; so Victoria went to the open door and repeated it.

'Yes, I suppose so. I suppose he'll eat anything, really.'

Feeling near exasperation, she went back to the kitchen, put on a pan of water, poured in some oats, found a bowl, a spoon, a jug of milk. When it had started to cook, she turned down the heat and went back into the sitting room and saw that already it had been taken over by Oliver, it was no longer hers. It was filled with Oliver, with his possessions, his empty glass, his cigarette stubs, his child. The child's coat lay on the floor, the sofa cushions were crushed and flattened, the air rang with the little boy's misery and frustration.

She could bear it no longer. 'Here,' she said and took Thomas firmly in her arms. Tears poured down his cheeks. She said to Oliver, 'You make sure the porridge doesn't burn,' and she bore Tom into the bathroom and set him down on the floor.

Steeling herself to cope with steaming nappies, she un-buttoned his dungarees and found that he wasn't wearing nappies at all, and was, miraculously, dry. There was, ob-viously, no pot in this childless establishment, but with a certain amount of contriving she persuaded him to use the grown-up lavatory. For some reason this mild accomplishment stopped his tears. She said, 'What a good boy,' and he looked up at her, still tear-drenched, and disarmed her with a sudden grin. Then he found her sponge and began to chew it, and she was so thankful that he had stopped crying that she let him. She buttoned up his clothes and washed his face and hands. Then she led him back into the kitchen.

'He's been to the loo,' she told Oliver.

Oliver had poured himself another whisky, thus finishing Victoria's bottle. He had his glass in one hand and a wooden spoon in the other, with which he stirred the porridge. He said, 'I think this sort of looks ready.'

It was. Victoria put some into a bowl, poured milk over it, sat at the kitchen table with Tom on her knee, and let him get on with it, which he did. After the first mouthful, she hastily reached for a tea towel and wrapped it around his neck. In a moment the bowl was empty and Thomas apparently ready for more.

Oliver eased himself away from the cooker. 'I'm going out for a moment.'

Victoria was filled with alarm, and suspicions that if he went he would never come back and she would be left with the child. She said, 'You can't.'

'Why not?'

'You can't leave me alone with him. He doesn't know who I am.'

'He doesn't know who I am either, but he seems quite happy. Eating himself to a standstill.' He laid the palms of his hands flat on the table and stooped to kiss her. It was three years since this had happened, but the after-effects were alarmingly familiar. A melting sensation, a sudden sinking of the stomach. Sitting there with his child heavy on her knee, she thought, oh, no. 'I shall be gone about five minutes. I want to buy cigarettes and a bottle of wine.'

'You'll come back?'

'How suspicious you are. Yes, I'll come back. You're not going to get rid of me as easily as that.'

He was, in fact, away for fifteen minutes. By the time he returned, the sitting room was once more neat, cushions plumped up, coats put away, the ashtrays emptied. He found Victoria at the kitchen sink, wearing an apron and washing a lettuce. 'Where's Thomas?'

She did not turn round. 'I put him into my bed. He isn't crying. I think he'll go to sleep again.'

Oliver decided that the back of her head looked implacable. He put down the brown grocery bag containing the bottles and went to turn her to face him.

'Are you angry?' he asked.

'No. Just wary.'

'I can explain.'

'You'll have to.' She turned back to the sink and the lettuce.

He said, 'I'm not explaining if you won't listen properly. Leave that and come and sit down.'

'I thought you wanted to eat. It's getting terribly late.'

'It doesn't matter what time it is. We've all the time in the world. Come on. Come and sit down.'

He had brought wine and another bottle of whisky. While Victoria untied her apron and hung it up, he found ice cubes and poured two drinks. She had gone back to the sitting room, and he joined her there and found her settled on a low stool with her back to the fire. She did not smile at him. He handed her the glass and raised his own.

'Reunions?' he suggested as a toast.

'All right.' Reunions sounded harmless enough. The glass was cold to her fingers. She took a mouthful and felt better. More able to deal with what he was about to tell her.

Oliver sat on the edge of the sofa and faced her. There were artistic patches in the knees of his jeans, and his suede boots were worn and stained. Victoria found herself wondering on what he chose to spend the fruits of his considerable success. Whisky, perhaps. Or a house in a more salubrious part of London than the Fulham back street where he had lived before. She thought of the big Volvo parked in the mews outside. She saw the gold watch on his long, narrow wrist.

He said again, 'We have to talk.'

'You talk.'

'I thought you'd be married.'

'You said that before. When I opened the door.'

'But you're not.'

'No.'

'Why not?'

'I never met anybody I wanted to marry. Or perhaps I never met anybody who wanted to marry me.'

'Did you go on with your painting?'

'No. I threw that up after a year. I wasn't good enough. I had a little talent, but not enough. There's nothing more discouraging than having just a little talent.'

'So what do you do now?'

'I have a job. In a dress shop in Beauchamp Place.'

'That doesn't sound very demanding.'

She shrugged, 'It's all right.' They were not meant to be talking about Victoria, they were meant to be talking about Oliver. 'Oliver . . . '

But he did not want her questions, perhaps because he had not yet made up his mind what the answers would be. He quickly interrupted her. 'How was the party?'

She knew that this was a red herring. She looked at him, and he met her gaze with watchful innocence. She thought, what does it matter? Like he says, we have all the time in the world. Sooner or later he's going to have to tell me. She said, 'The usual. Lots of people. Lots of drink. Everybody talking and nobody saying anything.'

'Who brought you home?'

She was surprised that he was sufficiently interested to want to know this, and then remembered that Oliver had always been interested in people, whether he knew them or not; whether he even liked them. He would sit in buses and listen to other people's conversations. He would talk to strangers in bars, to waiters in restaurants. Everything that happened to him was filed away in the retentive storehouse of his memory, mulled over and digested, only to reappear at some later date in something he was writing, a scrap of dialogue or a situation.

She said, 'An American.'

He was instantly intrigued. 'What sort of an American?'

'Just an American.'

'I mean bald-headed, middle-aged, hung about with cameras? Earnest? Sincere? Come along now, you must have noticed.'

Of course Victoria had noticed. He had been tall, not as tall as Oliver, but more heavily built, with wide shoulders and a flat stomach. He looked as though he played furious squash in his spare time, or jogged round the park in the early mornings, wearing sneakers and a track suit. She remembered dark eyes, and hair almost black. Crisp, wiry hair, the sort that has to be closely cut or it gets out of hand. His had been expertly barbered, probably by Mr Trumper or one of the more exclusive London establishments, so that it lay on his well-shaped head like a smooth pelt.

She remembered the strong features, the tan, and the marvellous white American teeth. Why did Americans all seem to have such beautiful teeth?

She said, 'No, he wasn't any of those things.'

'What was his name?'

'John. John something. I don't think Mrs Fairburn's very good at introductions.'

'You mean he didn't tell you himself? He can't have been a true-blooded American. Americans always tell you who they are and what they do, before you've even decided whether you want to meet them or not. "Hi! " ' He put on a perfect New York accent. ' "John Hackenbacker, Consolidated Aloo-minum. Glad to have you know me." '

Victoria found herself smiling, and this made her feel ashamed, and as though she must stand up for the young man who had brought her home in his sleek Alfa-Romeo. 'He wasn't a bit like that. And he's flying to Bahrein tomorrow,' she added, as though this were a point in the American's favour.

'Ah! An oil man.'

She was becoming tired of his teasing: 'Oliver, I have no idea.'

'You seem to have made remarkably little contact. What the hell did you talk about?' An idea occurred to him, and he grinned. 'I know, you talked about me.'

'I most certainly didn't talk about you. But I think it's about time you started talking about you. And about Thomas.'

'What about Tom?'

'Oh, Oliver, don't fence.'

He laughed at her exasperation. 'I'm not being kind, am I? And you're simply bursting to know. All right, here it is. I've stolen him.'

It was so much worse than she had imagined that Victoria had to take a long, deep breath. When that was safely over, she was calm enough to ask, 'Who did you steal him from?'

'Mrs Archer. Jeannette's mother. My erstwhile mother-in-law. You probably didn't know, but Jeannette was killed in an air crash in Yugoslavia, just a little while after Tom was born. Her parents have looked after him ever since.'

'Did you go and see him?'

'No. Never went near him. Never set eyes on him. Today was the first time I ever saw him.'

'And what happened today?'

He had finished his drink. He got up and went into the kitchen to pour himself another. She heard the clink of the bottle, the ice going into the glass, the tap being turned on and off. Then he returned and resumed his seat, leaning back on the deep cushions of the sofa, with his long legs stretched out in front of him.

'I've been in Bristol all week. I've got a play coming off at the Fortune Theatre, it's in rehearsal now, but I had to do some work with the producer, rewrite some of the third act. Driving back to London this morning, I was thinking about the play. I wasn't really paying attention to the road, and suddenly I realised I was on the A.30, and there was a signpost to Woodbridge, and that's where the Archers live. And I thought, why not? And I turned the car and went to call. As simple as that. A whim, you might say. The hand of fate stretching out its grubby paw.'

'Did you see Mrs Archer?'

'No. Mrs Archer was in London, buying sheets at Harrods or something. But there was a choice au pair girl called Helga who needed little encouragement to invite me in for lunch.'

'Did she know you were Tom's father?'

'No.'

'So what happened?'

'She sat me down at the kitchen table and went upstairs to fetch Tom. And then we had lunch. Good healthy fare. Everything was good and healthy, and so clean it looked as though it had been through a steriliser. The whole house is one enormous steriliser. There isn't a dog or a cat or a readable book in the place. The chairs look as though no one ever sat in them. The garden's full of horrible flower beds, like a cemetery, and the paths look as if they've been drawn with a ruler. I'd forgotten its utter soullessness.'

'But it's Tom's home.'

'It stifled me. It's going to stifle him. He had a picture book with his name written in the front. "Thomas Archer. From Granny." And somehow that finished me, because he's not Thomas Archer, he's Thomas Dodds. So then the went to get his beastly perambulator, to take him out for a walk, and I picked him up and carried him out of the house and put him in the car and drove him away.'

'But didn't Thomas *mind?*'

'He didn't seem to. Seemed quite pleased, in fact. We stopped off somewhere and spent the afternoon in a little park. He played on the swings and in the sandpit, and a dog came up and talked to him. And then it began to rain, so I bought him some biscuits and we got back into the car again and came back to London. I took him to my flat.'

' I don't know where your flat is.'

'Still in Fulham. Same place. You've never been there I know, but you see, it isn't really a living place, it's a working place. It's a basement and grotty as hell, and I have an arrangement with a large West Indian lady who lives on the first floor, and she's meant to come and clean it up once a week, but it never seems to look any better. Anyway, I took Tom there, and he obligingly fell asleep on my bed, and then I rang the Archers.'

He came out quite casually with this. Moral cowardice was something from which Oliver had never suffered, but Victoria felt quite weak at the thought.

'Oh, *Oliver*.'

'No reason why I shouldn't. After all, he's my child.'

'But she must have been out of her mind with worry.'

'I told the au pair girl my name. Mrs Archer knew he was with me.'

'But . . .'

'You know something? You sound the way Jeannette's mother sounded. As though I had nothing but evil intentions. As though I were going to harm the child, bash his brains out on a brick wall, or something.'

'I don't think that at all. It's just that I can't help but be sorry for her.'

'Well don't be.'

'She'll want him back.'

'Yes, of course she wants him back, but I've told her that for the time being I'm keeping him myself.'

'Can you do that? Legally, I mean? Won't she get the police, or lawyers, or even high court judges?'

'She's threatened all those things. Litigation, ward of court, in the space of ten minutes she threw everything at my head. But you see, she can't do anything. Nobody can do anything. He's my child. I'm his father. I'm neither a criminal nor otherwise unfit to take care of him.'

'But that's just the point. You can't take care of him.'

'All that's required of me is to provide a home for Tom with resources and facilities for taking care of him.'

'In a basement in Fulham?'

There was a long silence while Oliver, with slow deliberation, stubbed out his cigarette. 'That,' he told her at last, 'is why I am here.'

So, it was out. The cards were on the table This was why he had come to her.

She said, 'At least you're being honest.'

Oliver looked indignant. 'I'm always honest.'

'You want me to look after Tom?'

'We can look after him together. You wouldn't want me to take him back to that mouldy flat, would you?'

'I can't look after him.'

'Why not?'

'I'm working. I have a job. There isn't any room for a child here.'

He said, in a false voice, 'And what would the neighbours say?'

'It's nothing to do with the neighbours.'

'You can tell them I'm your cousin from Australia. You can say that Tom is my aborigine offspring.'

'Oh, Oliver, stop joking. This is nothing to joke about. You've stolen that child of yours. Why he isn't howling his head off with misery and fright is beyond my comprehension. Mrs Archer is obviously distraught, we're going to have the police on the doorstep at any moment, and all you do is make what you think are funny remarks.'

His face closed up. 'If you feel like that about it, I'll take the child and go.'

'Oh, Oliver, it's not that. It's just that you have to be sensible.'

'All right, I'll be sensible. Look, I've got on my most sensible expression.' Victoria refused even to smile at him. 'Oh, come along. Don't be angry. I wouldn't have come if I'd thought it would make you angry.'

'I don't know why you did come.'

'Because I thought of you as being exactly the right sort of person who'd help me. I thought of you, and I thought of telephoning first, but then I imagined some stranger – or worse, some stiff-necked husband – answering the call. And then what was I going to say? This is Oliver Dobbs, the well-known author and playwright, speaking. I have a baby I'd like your wife to look after. Wouldn't that have gone down a treat?'

'What would you have done if I hadn't been here?'

'I don't know. I'd have thought of something. But I wouldn't have taken Tom back to the Archers.'

'You may have to. You can't take care of him . . . '

Oliver interrupted her, as though she had never started to speak. 'Look, I have a plan. Like I said, the Archers haven't got a leg to stand on, but still there's the chance that they'll try to make trouble. I think we should get out·of London. Go away for a little. There's this play of mine coming off in Bristol, but as far as that's concerned I've done all I can do. The first night's on Monday, and after that it's at the mercy of the critics and the general public. So let's go away. You and me and Tom. Let's just take off. We'll go to Wales or the north of Scotland, or down to Cornwall and watch the spring coming. We'll ... '

Victoria gazed at him in total disbelief. She was shocked, outraged, indignant. Did he imagine – did he really imagine – that she had so little pride? Had he never truly known how much he had hurt her? Three years ago Oliver Dobbs had walked out of her life, shattering everything, and leaving her alone to put the pieces together as best she might. But now he decided that he needed her once more, simply to look after his child. And so here he sat, already making plans, trying to seduce her with words, believing that it was only a matter of time before he wore down her resistance.

' ... no tourists, empty roads. We won't even have to book in at hotels, they'll all be longing for business, desperate to have us ... ' He went on, hatching plans, leading Victoria on to images of blue seas and fields of yellow daffodils; of carefree escape, and winding country lanes. And she listened, marvelling at his selfishness. He had helped himself to his son. He wanted, for the time being, to keep his son. He needed someone to take care of his son. And so, Victoria. It was as simple as an elementary mathematical formula.

He stopped at last. His face was alight with enthusiasm, as though he could not envisage any objection to this delightful project. After a little, Victoria said, because she really wanted to know, 'Out of interest, what made you think of me?'

'I suppose because you're the sort of person that you are.'

'You mean, stupid?'

'No, not stupid.'

'Forgiving, then?'

'You could never be unforgiving. You wouldn't know how. Besides, it was a good time we had together. It wasn't a bad time. And you're pleased to see me again. You have to be otherwise you'd never have let me into your house.'

'Oliver, some bruises don't necessarily show.'

'What's that supposed to mean?'

'For my sins, I loved you. You knew that.'

'But you see,' he reminded her carefully, 'I didn't love anybody. And you knew that.'

'Except yourself.'

'Perhaps. And what I was trying to do.'

'I don't want to be hurt again. I'm not going to be hurt again.'

A smile touched his mouth. 'You sound very determined.'

'I'm not coming with you.'

He did not reply, but his eyes, pale and unblinking, never left her face. Outside, the wind rattled a window pane. A car started up. A girl's voice called some person's name. Perhaps she was going to a party. From far off came the distant hum of London traffic.

He said, 'You can't spend the rest of your life avoiding being hurt. If you do that, then you turn your back on any sort of relationship.'

'Just say that I don't want to be hurt by you. You're too good at it.'

'Is that the only reason that you won't come with us?'

'I think it's enough of a reason, but there are other things as well. Practical considerations. For one thing, I have a job . . .'

'Selling clothes to idiotic females. Ring up and make some excuse. Say your grandmother's died. Say you've suddenly had a baby . . . now that would be nearly true! Send in your resignation. I'm a rich man now. I'll take care of you.'

'You've said that before. A long time ago. But you didn't.'

'What a prodigious memory you have.'

'Some things really can't be forgotten.' From the mantelpiece her little clock chimed. It was eleven o'clock. Victoria stood up and put her empty glass beside the clock, and as she did so, she saw his reflection, watching her through the looking glass which hung on the wall behind it.

He said, 'Are you afraid? Is that what it is?'

'Yes.'

'Of me, or of yourself?'

'Both of us.' She turned from the mirror. 'Let's go and have some supper.'

It was nearly midnight by the time they finished the make-shift meal, and Victoria was suddenly so tired that she had not even the energy to collect the plates and the empty glasses and wash them up. Oliver was pouring the last of the wine into his glass and reaching for another cigarette, apparently settled for the night, but Victoria stood up, pushing back her chair, and said 'I'm going to bed.'

He looked mildly surprised. 'That's very unsocial of you.'

'I can't help it if it's unsocial. If I don't go to bed I'll fall asleep on my feet.'

'What do you want me to do?'

'I don't want you to do anything.'

'I mean,' he spoke patiently, as though she were being immensely unreasonable, 'Do you want me to go back to Fulham? Do you want me to spend the night in my car? Do you want me to wake Thomas up and bear him off into the night, never to darken your door again? You only have to say.'

'You can't take Thomas. He's sleeping.'

'Then I'll go back to Fulham and leave him here with you.'

'You can't do that either. He might wake up in the middle of the night and be frightened.'

'In that case I'll stay here.' He assumed the expression of a man prepared to be accommodating, at whatever cost to himself. 'Where would you like me to sleep? On the sofa? On top of some chest of drawers? On the floor outside your bedroom door, like an old dog, or a faithful slave?'

She refused to rise to his teasing. 'There's a divan in the dressing room,' she told him. 'The room's full of suitcases and my mother's London clothes, but the bed's longer than the sofa. I'll go and make it up . . . '

She left him, with his cigarette and his glass of wine and the chaos of unwashed dishes. In the tiny slip of a dressing room, she found blankets and a pillow. She removed dress boxes and a pile of clothes from the divan and made it up with clean sheets. The room smelled stuffy and rather mothbally (her mother's fur coat?) so she opened the window wide, and the curtains stirred in the cold damp air which blew in from the darkness beyond.

From the kitchen now came sounds as if Oliver had decided to stack the supper plates, or possibly wash them. Victoria was surprised, because domesticity had never been his strong suite, but she was touched as well, and tired as she was, knew an impulse to go and help him. But if she went to help him, they would only start talking again. And if they started talking, then Oliver would start, all over again, trying to persuade her to go away with him and Thomas. So she left him to it, and went into her bedroom. Here, only a small lamp burned on the dressing table. On one side of the double bed, Thomas slumbered, one arm outflung, his mouth plugged by his thumb. She had taken off everything except his vest and pants, and folded clothes lay on a chair, his small shoes and socks on the floor beneath it. She stooped to lift him out of the bed. His weight was warm and soft in her arms. She carried him to the bathroom and somehow persuaded him to use the lavatory again. He scarcely woke: his head lolled, his thumb stayed determinedly in his mouth. She put him back into the bed, and he sighed contentedly and slept once more. She prayed that he would sleep until morning.

She straightened up, and listened. It seemed that Oliver had decided that he had had enough of the supper dishes, and he had returned to the living room, where he had started telephoning. Only Oliver would start telephoning at midnight. Victoria undressed, brushed her hair, put on her nightdress and cautiously slipped into the other side of the bed. Tom never stirred. She lay on her back and stared at the ceiling, and then closed her eyes, waiting for sleep. But sleep would not come. Her brain whirled with images of Oliver, with memories, with a sort of throbbing excitement which maddened her because it was the last thing in the world that she wanted to feel. Finally, in desperation, she opened her eyes again, and reached for a book, intending to read herself to calmness and so to unconsciousness.

From the next room, the telephoning stopped, and the television was switched on. But most of the programmes had finished by now anyway, and eventually Oliver apparently decided to call it a day. She heard him moving about, switching off lights. She heard him go to the bathroom. She lay down her book. His footsteps crossed the little landing, and stopped outside her door. The handle turned. The door opened. His tall figure appeared, silhouetted against the bright light beyond.

He said, 'Not asleep?'

'Not yet,' said Victoria.

They spoke softly, so as not to disturb the sleeping child. Oliver, leaving the door open, crossed the floor and came to sit on the edge of the bed.

'Who were you calling?' she asked.

'Just a guy. Nothing important.'

'I made up the bed for you.'

'I know. I saw.'

But he made no move to go. 'What will you do tomorrow?'

she asked him. 'With Thomas?'

He smiled. He said 'I'll decide tomorrow.' He touched her book. 'What are you reading?'

It was a paperback. Victoria held it up for him to see the front cover. She said, 'It's one of those books that you read over and over again. About once a year, I take it out, and it's like being with an old friend.'

Oliver read the title aloud. *'The Eagle Years.'*

'Have you read it?'

'Perhaps.'

'It's by this man called Roddy Dunbeath and it's all about being a little boy in Scotland between the wars. I mean, it's a sort of autobiography. And he and his brothers were brought up in this beautiful house called Benchoile.'

Oliver had laid his hand over her wrist. His palm was warm, his fingers strong, but the caress very gentle.

'It was in Sutherland, somewhere. With mountains all around and their own private loch. And he had a falcon that used to come and take food out of his mouth . . . '

His hand began to move up her bare arm, pressing the flesh beneath his touch, as though he were massaging life back into some limb which had been paralysed for years.

' . . . and a pet duck and a dog called Bertie that liked eating apples.'

'I like eating apples,' said Oliver. He lifted a long strand of hair away from her neck and laid it on the pillow. She could feel the solid, throbbing beat of her own heart. Her skin, where he had touched her, felt as though it were standing on tip toe. She went on talking, desperately, trying to control these alarming physical manifestations with the sound of her own voice.

' . . . and there was a place with a waterfall, where they used to go for picnics. And there was a stream running across the beach, and the hills were filled with deer. He says that the waterfall was the heart of Benchoile . . . '

Oliver leaned down and kissed her mouth and the flow of words was mercifully stopped. She knew that he hadn't been listening anyway. Now, he drew aside the blankets which covered her, and slid his arms beneath her back, and his lips moved away from her mouth and across her cheek and into the warm hollow of her neck.

'Oliver,' She said his name, but her voice made no sound. His going had left her frozen, but now the weight and the warmth of his body warmed her own, melting resolution, and stirring to life long-forgotten instincts. She thought, *oh, no,* and laid her hands against his shoulders and tried to push him away, but he was a thousand times stronger than Victoria and the puny resistance was pathetic, pointless as trying to topple some immense tree.

'Oliver. No.'

She might not have spoken aloud. He simply continued his gentle love-making, and after a little, her hands, as though of their own volition, slid away from his shoulders, under his jacket, around his back. He smelled clean, of clothes dried in the open air. She felt the thin cotton of his shirt, the rib cage, the hard muscles beneath his skin. She heard him say, 'You've stopped pretending.'

The last shred of common sense made her say, 'But Oliver, Thomas . . .'

She sensed his amusement, his silent laughter. He drew away from her and stood up, towering over her. 'That can easily be arranged,' he told her, and he stooped and lifted her up into his arms as easily and lightly as he had carried his son. She felt weightless, dizzy, as the walls of her bedroom spun and slid away and he bore her through the open door, across the bright landing, and into the airy darkness of the little dressing room. It still smelled of camphor, and the bed on which he placed her was hard and narrow, but the curtains stirred in the soft wind, and the starched linen of the pillow lay cool beneath her neck.

She said, looking up into the shadowed blur that was his face, 'I never meant this to happen.'

'I did,' said Oliver, and she knew that she should be angry, but by then it was too late. Because by then she wanted it to happen anyway.

Much later – she knew it was much later, because she had heard the clock in the sitting room strike two with its silvery chimes – Oliver hoisted himself up on to one elbow and leaned over Victoria in order to grope for his jacket and take his cigarettes and lighter from the pocket. The flame illuminated the tiny room for a second, and there came the gentle darkness again and the glow of the cigarette tip.

She lay in the curve of his arm, her head pillowed on his naked shoulder.

He said, 'Do you want to make plans?'

'What sort of plans?'

'Plans for what we're going to do. You and me and Thomas.'
'Am I coming with you?'
'Yes.'
'Have I said I'm coming with you?'
He laughed. He kissed her. 'Yes,' he said.
'I don't want to be hurt again.'
'You mustn't be so afraid. There's nothing to be afraid of.
Just the prospect of a holiday, an escape. Lots of laughter.
Lots of love.'

Victoria did not reply. There was nothing to say, and her
thoughts were so confused that there was nothing much to
think, either. She only knew that for the first time since he
had left her, she felt safe again, and at peace. And she only
knew that tomorrow, or perhaps the next day, she was going
away with Oliver. Once more, she was committed. For better
or for worse, but maybe it would work this time. Maybe he
had changed. Things would be different. And perhaps, if he
felt so strongly about Thomas, he would feel strongly about
other things. Permanent things. Like loving one person and
staying with her forever. But whatever happened, the die had
been cast. Victoria had passed the point of no return.

She sighed deeply, but the sigh was prompted by confusion
rather than unhappiness. 'Where shall we go?' she asked
Oliver.

'Anywhere you like. Is there an ashtray in this benighted
cupboard of a room?'

Victoria reached out and groped for the one she knew lay
on the bedside table, and handed it to him.

He went on, 'What was the name of that place you were
babbling about, when you were so patently anxious not to be
made love to? The place in the book, *The Eagle Years?*'

'Benchoile.'
'Would you like to go there?'
'We can't.'
'Why not?'
'It's not a hotel. We don't know the people who live there.'
'I do, my darling innocent.'
'What do you mean?'
'I know Roddy Dunbeath. I met him about two years ago.
Sat next to him at one of those dismal television award
dinners. He was there on account of his last book, and I was
there because I was given some piddling little statue for a
television script I wrote about Seville. Anyway, there we were,

surrounded by moronic starlets and shark-like agents, and thankful for each other's company. By the end of the evening we were friends for life, and he gave me a standing invitation to visit him at Benchoile whenever the spirit moved me. So far I haven't taken it up, but if you want to go there, there's no reason on earth why we shouldn't.'

'Do you really mean that?'

'Of course I do.'

'Are you certain it wasn't just one of those things people say at the end of a good evening and then forget about, or even regret for the rest of their lives?'

'Not at all. He meant it. Even gave me his card in a rather old-fashioned way. I can find out the telephone number and ring him up.'

'Will he remember you?'

'Of course he'll remember me. And I shall tell him that I and my wife and my child want to come and spend a few days with him.'

'It sounds like an awful lot of people. And I'm *not* your wife.'

'Then I shall say my mistress and my child. He'll jump at that. He's rather Rabelaisian. You'll love him. He's very fat, and extremely, politely drunk. At least, he was by the end of that dinner. But Roddy Dunbeath, drunk, is ten times more charming than most men are stone cold sober.'

'It'll take us a long time to drive to Sutherland.'

'We'll take it in stages. Anyway, we have a long time.'

He stubbed out his cigarette, and leaned over Victoria once more, in order to put the ashtray on the floor. She found that she was smiling into the darkness. She said, 'You know, I think I'd rather go to Benchoile than anywhere else in the world.'

'It's better than that. You're going to Benchoile with me.'

'And Thomas.'

'You're going to Benchoile with me and Thomas.'

'I can't think of anything more perfect.'

Oliver gently placed his hand on her stomach; slowly, he slid it up her body, over her rib cage, to cup one small, naked breast. 'I can,' he told her.

## CHAPTER 5

## SUNDAY

In the middle of February, the cold weather arrived. Christmas had been sunny and the New Year mild and still, and the weeks of winter crept past, with some rain and a little frost and nothing much else. 'We're going to be lucky,' said people who knew no better, but the shepherds and the hill-farmers were wiser. They eyed the skies and smelled the wind and knew that the worst was still to come. The winter was simply waiting. Biding its time.

The real frosts started at the beginning of the month. Then came the sleet, swiftly turning to snow, and then the storms. 'Straight from the Urals,' said Roddy Dunbeath, as the bitter wind whined in over the sea. The sea turned grey and angry, sullen as the colour of wet slate, and creaming breakers flooded in over the Creagan sands, depositing a long tidemark of undigested rubbish. Old fish boxes, ragged nets, knotted twine, plastic detergent bottles, rubber tyres, even a disfigured shoe or two.

Inland, the hills were cloaked in white, their summits lost in the dark, racing sky. Snow blew from the open fields and piled in steep drifts, choking the narrow roads. Sheep, heavy in their winter wool, could survive, but the cattle searched for shelter in the angles of the drystone dikes, and the farmers tractored fodder to them twice a day.

Accustomed to, and expecting, cruel winters, the local people accepted all this hardship with stoic calm. The smaller hill crofts and isolated cottages were cut off entirely, but walls were thick and peat stacks high, and there was always plenty of oatmeal, and feedstuff for the stock. Life continued. The scarlet post-van made its daily round of the glens, and sturdy housewives, wearing rubber boots and three cardigans, emerged from doorways to feed hens and hang out lines of washing in the freezing wind.

Now, it was Sunday.

> The Lord's my Shepherd, I'll not want
> He makes me down to lie
> In pastures green . . .

The pipes in the church were faintly warm, but the draughts excruciating. The congregation, thinned to a mere handful by the weather, bravely raised their voices in the last hymn of the morning service, but their efforts were almost drowned by the fury of the wind outside.

Jock Dunbeath, standing alone in the Benchoile pew, held his hymnbook in mittened hands but did not look at it, partly because he had sung this hymn all his life and knew the words by heart and partly because, by some oversight, he had left his reading spectacles at home.

Ellen had fussed him. 'You must indeed be mad thinking you'll get to the kirk today. The roads are blocked. Would you not stop off at Davey's and get him to drive you?'

'Davey has enough to do.'

'Then why not sit by the fire and listen to the nice man on the wireless? Would that not do as well for once?'

But he was stubborn, immovable, and she finally sighed and tossed her eyes to heaven and gave in. 'But don't be blaming me if you die in a drift on your way.'

She sounded quite excited at the thought of such a happening. Disaster was the spice of life to Ellen, and she was always the first to say 'I told you so'. Irritated by her, in a hurry to get away, he forgot his spectacles, and was then too pigheaded to go back for them. However, his determination was vindicated, and, in the old Landrover, grinding in bottom gear down the four miles of the glen, he had managed to make it safely and had come to church. Chilled as he was, and blind as a bat without his glasses, he was glad that he had made the effort.

All his life, unless prevented by illness, war, or some other act of God, he had come to church on Sunday mornings. As a child because he had had to; as a soldier because he needed to;

as a grown man because he was the Laird of Benchoile and it was important to be involved, to uphold the established traditions, to set a good example. And now, in his age, he came for comfort and reassurance. The old church, the words of the service, the tunes of the hymns, were some of the very few things in his life that hadn't changed. Perhaps, at the end of the day, the only thing.

> Goodness and mercy all my days,
> Shall surely follow me,
> And in God's house for ever more
> My dwelling place shall be.

He closed his hymnbook, bowed his head for the blessing, collected his driving gloves and his old tweed cap from the seat beside him, buttoned up his overcoat, wound himself up in his scarf, started up the aisle.

'Morning, sir.' It was a friendly sort of church. People came out with conversation in their ordinary voices – none of those pious whispers as though there were a body dying in the next room. 'Terrible weather. Good morning, Colonel Dunbeath, and how are the roads up with you...? Well, Jock, and you're a fine one, making the trip to the kirk on a day like this.'

That was the minister himself, coming up at Jock from behind. Jock turned. The minister, the Reverend Christie, was a well-set-up man with a pair of shoulders like a rugby player, but still Jock topped him by half a head.

He said, 'I thought you'd be a bit thin on the ground this morning. Glad I made the effort.'

'I imagined you all cut off up at Benchoile.'

'The telephone's dead. There must be a line down somewhere. But I managed the road in the Landrover.'

'It's a bitter day. Why don't you come into the Manse for a glass of sherry before you start back?'

His eyes were kind. He was a good man, with a homely and hospitable wife. For a moment Jock let himself imagine the living room at the Manse. The chair, which would be drawn up for him by an enormous fire, the air fragrant with the smell of roasting Sunday mutton. The Christies had always done themselves very well. He thought of the dark, sweet, warming sherry, the comfortable presence of Mrs Christie, and for a small instant was tempted.

But, 'No,' he said. 'I think I'd better get back before the weather worsens. Ellen will be expecting me. And I would not want the constable to find me frozen in a snowdrift with the smell of alcohol on my breath.'

'Ah, well, that's understandable.' The minister's kindly countenance and robust manner masked his concern. He had been shocked this morning to see Jock sitting solitary in his pew. Most of the congregation, for some reason, gathered themselves at the back of his church, and the laird, isolated like some outcast, had stuck out like a sore thumb.

He looked old. It was the first time that Mr Christie had seen him looking really old. Too thin, too tall, his tweed hanging loose on the lanky frame, the fingers of his hands swollen and red with the cold. The collar of his shirt was loose on his neck, and there had been a hesitancy in his actions, fumbling for his hymnbook, for the pound note that was his weekly contribution to the offertory plate.

Jock Dunbeath of Benchoile. How old was he? Sixty-eight, sixty-nine? Not old for nowadays. Not old for hereabouts, where the menfolk seemed to go on well into their eighties, sprightly and active, digging their gardens and keeping a few hens, and making small tottery excursions to the village inn for their evening dram. But last September Jock had suffered a slight heart-attack, and since then, thought Mr Christie, he seemed to have gone visibly downhill. And yet, what could one do to help? If he had been one of the country folk, Mr Christie would have gone visiting, taken a batch of his wife's scones, perhaps offered to cut a stack of kindling; but Jock was not country folk. He was Lieutenant Colonel John Rathbone Dunbeath, late of the Cameron Highlanders, the Laird of Benchoile and a Justice of the Peace. He was proud, but he was not poor. He was old and lonely, but he was not poor. On the contrary, he was a well-respected landowner with a large house and a farm in hand, twelve thousand or so acres of hill, a thousand or more sheep, some arable land, some stalking, some fishing. In all respects, an enviable property. If the big house was rambling and shabby, and the laird's shirt had a frayed collar, it was not because he was poor. It was because his wife was dead, he was childless, and old Ellen Tarbat, housekeeper to Jock and his brother Roddy, was getting beyond it.

And somewhere, sometime, before the eyes of them all, the old man seemed to have given up.

Mr Christie searched for some remark that would keep their conversation going. 'And how is the family?' was a useful starter on most occasions, but not this one, because Jock didn't have a family. Only Roddy. Oh well, thought the minister, any port in a storm.

'And how is your brother keeping?'

Jock responded with a gleam of humour. 'You make him sound like a box of herring. I think he's all right. We don't see that much of each other. Keep to ourselves, you know, Roddy in his house and me in mine.' He cleared his throat. 'Sunday lunch. We have Sunday lunch together. It's companionable.'

Mr Christie wondered what they talked about. He had never known two brothers so different, one so reserved and the other so outgoing. Roddy was a writer, an artist, a raconteur. The books that he had written, some almost twenty years or so ago, were all still in print, and the paperback editions could always be found on station bookstalls and in the racks of the most unlikely country shops. *A classic* said the blurb on the back covers, under the photograph of Roddy that had been taken thirty years ago. *A breath of the outdoors. Roddy Dunbeath knows his Scotland and presents it, with native perception, within the pages of this book.*

Roddy did not come to church unless it was Christmas or Easter or somebody's funeral, but whether this was due to his inner convictions or his inherent idleness, the minister did not know. Roddy did not even appear very often in the village. Jess Guthrie, the shepherd's wife, did his shopping for him. 'And how is Mr Roddy, Jess?' the grocer would inquire, fitting the two bottles of Dewars down the side of the carton of groceries, and Jess would avert her eyes from the bottles and reply, 'Oh, he's no so bad,' which could have meant anything.

'Is he working on anything just now?'

'He mentioned something about an article for the *Scottish Field*. I . . . I never really know.' Jock ran a diffident hand down the back of his head, smoothing down the thinning grey hair. 'He never talks much about his work.'

A lesser man might have been discouraged, but Mr Christie pressed on, and asked after the third Dunbeath brother.

'And what news of Charlie?'

'I had a letter at Christmas. He and Susan were skiing. At Aspen. That's in Colorado, you know,' he added in his mannerly way, as though Mr Christie mightn't.

'Was John with them?'

There was a small pause. Jock put back his head. His eyes, pale and watering a little in the cold, fixed on some distant, unfocused spot beyond the minister's head.

'John doesn't work in New York any longer. Got sent to the London branch of his bank. Works there now. Been working there for six months or more.'

'But that's splendid.'

The church was nearly empty now. They began to tread, side by side, up the aisle towards the main door.

'Yes. Good thing for John. Step up the ladder. Clever boy. Suppose he'll be president before we know where we are. I mean president of the bank, not president of the United States of America . . .'

But Mr Christie was not to be diverted by this mild joke. 'I didn't mean that, Jock. I meant that if he's living in London, it shouldn't be too hard for him to get up to Sutherland and spend a few days with you and Roddy.'

Jock stopped dead and turned. His eyes narrowed. He was suddenly alert, fierce as an old eagle.

Mr Christie was a little taken aback by that piercing glance. 'Just an idea. It seems to me that you need a bit of young company.' And someone to keep an eye on you, as well, he thought, but he did not say this aloud. 'It must be ten years since John was last here.'

'Yes. Ten years.' They moved on, slow-paced. 'He was eighteen.' The old man appeared to be debating with himself. The minister waited tactfully, and was rewarded. 'Wrote to him the other day. Suggested he come up in the summer. He was never interested in the grouse, but I could give him a bit of fishing.'

'I'm sure he needs no such bait to lure him north.'

'Haven't had an answer yet.'

'Give him time. He'll be a busy man.'

'Yes. The only thing is, these days I'm not quite sure how much time I have to give.' Jock smiled, that rare wry smile that warmed the chill from his features and never failed to disarm. 'But then, it comes to all of us. You of all men know that.'

They let themselves out of the church, and the wind caught the minister's robes and sent the black skirts ballooning. From the porch, he watched Jock Dunbeath clamber painfully up into the old Landrover and set off on his uncertain journey home. Despite himself he sighed, heavy-hearted. He had tried. But, at the end of the day, what could anybody do?

No more snow had fallen and Jock was glad of this. He trundled through the quiet, shuttered village and over the bridge and turned inland where the road sign pointed to Benchoile and Loch Muie. The road was narrow and single-tracked, with passing places marked by black and white painted posts, but there was no other traffic of any sort. The Sabbath, even in weather like this, cast its gloom over the countryside. Beset by icy draughts, hunched over the wheel, with his scarf up to his ears and his tweed cap pulled down over his beak of a nose, Jock Dunbeath let the Landrover take its own way home, like a reliable horse, up the tracks in the snow that they had made themselves that morning.

He thought about what the minister had said. He was right, of course. A good man. Concerned and trying not to show it. But he was right.

*You need a bit of young company.*

He remembered Benchoile in the old days when he, and his friends, and his brothers' friends, had all filled the house. He remembered the hall overflowing with fishing boots and creels, tea on the lawn beneath the silver birches, and in August the sunlit purple hills echoing to the crack of guns. He remembered house parties for the Northern Meetings Hunt Ball in Inverness, and girls coming downstairs in long, pretty dresses, and the old station wagon driving off to collect guests off the train at Creagan Halt.

But those days, like everything else, were gone. For the brothers, youth had gone. Roddy had never married; Charlie had found himself a wife, and a sweet one too, but she was an American girl, and he had gone back with her to the States, and made a life for himself as a cattleman, ranching his father-in-law's spread in Southwest Colorado. And although Jock had married, he and Lucy had never had the children they so ardently wanted. They had been so happy together that even this cruel trick of fate could not mar their content. But when she had died, five years ago, he had realised that he had never before known the true meaning of loneliness.

*You need a bit of young company.*

Funny, the minister bringing John's name up like that, just days after Jock had written him the letter. Almost as though he had known about it. As a child, John had visited Benchoile regularly, in the company of his parents, and then, as he grew older, alone with his father. He had been a quiet, serious little boy, intelligent beyond his years, and with a searching curiosity that manifested itself in a long stream of endless questions. But even in those days, Roddy had been his favourite uncle, and the two of them would go off for hours on end, to search for shells, or watch the birds, or stand, on still summer evenings, casting their trout rods over the deep brown pools of the river. In all respects, a likeable and satisfactory boy, but still, Jock had never been able to get close to him. The main reason for this was that John did not share with Jock his abiding passion for shooting. John would blissfully lure and catch and slay a fish, and very soon became accomplished at the sport, but he refused to go up the hill with a gun, and if he stalked a deer, would carry nothing more deadly than his camera.

And so the letter had not been an easy one to write. For John had not been to Benchoile for ten years, and this gap of time had left a yawning void that Jock had found almost impossible to bridge with words. Not, he assured himself quickly, that he didn't like the boy. He remembered John Dunbeath at eighteen as a composed, reserved young man with disturbingly mature attitudes and opinions. Jock respected these, but he found his coolness and his polite self-confidence a little disconcerting. And since then they had somehow lost touch. So much had happened. Lucy had died and the empty years had slipped away. Charlie had written, of course, giving news. John had gone to Cambridge, played squash and rackets for the University, and left with an honours degree in economics. He had then returned to New York and there joined the Warburg Investment Corporation, a position that he achieved entirely on his own merits and without any assistance from his influential American connections. For some time he had been at the Harvard Business School, and after some time, inevitably, he had married. Charlie was too loyal a father to spell out the details of this misalliance to Jock, but gradually, reading between the lines of his brother's letters, Jock realised that all was not well with the young couple. So he was distressed, but not surprised, when the news came through that the marriage had broken up, divorce proceedings were being taken, and legal settlements made. The only good thing about it was that there were no children.

The divorce, painfully, was finally accomplished, and John's career, apparently untouched by the traumas of his personal life, continued to go from strength to strength. The appointment in London was the latest in a succession of steady promotions. Banking was a world about which Jock Dunbeath knew nothing, and this was another reason why he felt so totally out of touch with his American nephew.

*Dear John,*
*You father tells me that you are now back in this*
*country and working in London.*

It wouldn't have been so hard if he had felt that he had anything in common with the young man. Some shared interest that would have provided him with a starting point.

*If you are able to get a little time off, perhaps you*
*would think about making the journey north and*
*spending a few days in Benchoile.*

He had never been much of a letter writer and it had taken him nearly half a day to finally compose this one, and even then the finished result did not satisfy him. But he signed it, and wrote the address on the envelope and stuck down the flap. It would have been so much easier, he thought wistfully, if only John had shown some interest in the grouse.

These reflections had brought him halfway home. The narrow, rutted, snow-filled road took a turn and the length of Loch Muie slid into view, grey as iron beneath the lowering sky. There was a light on in Davey Guthrie's farmhouse, and away at the end of the loch stood Benchoile itself, sheltered by the stand of pines which stood silhouetted, black as ink, against the snow-covered slopes of the hill.

Built of grey stone, long and low, turreted and gabled, it faced south, across a wide sloping lawn, to the loch. Too big, draughty and unheatable, shabby and constantly in need of repair, it was, nevertheless, his home, and the only place, in all his life, that he had ever really wanted to be.

Ten minutes later, he was there. Up the slope and through

the gates, over the rattle of the cattle grid, and down the short tunnel of wild rhododendrons. In front of the house the drive opened up into a wide gravel sweep. At the far end of this was an ornate stone arch which attached the house, by one corner, to the old stable block where Jock's brother Roddy lived. Beyond the arch was a spacious cobbled yard, and at the far end of this were the garages, which were originally built to house carriages and shooting brakes but now contained Jock's old Daimler and the aged green MG into which Roddy squeezed his bulk when the spirit moved him to make some excursion into the outside world.

Alongside these two ill-assorted vehicles, in a thick gloom occasioned by the dreariness of the day, Jock Dunbeath finally homed the Landrover, pulled on the brake, and killed the engine. He took the folded wad of Sunday newspapers off the seat beside him, got out of the car, slammed the door shut, and went out into the yard. Snow lay thick on the cobbles. The light was on in Roddy's sitting room. Cautiously, anxious not to slip or fall, he made his way across the yard to Roddy's front door, and let himself in.

Although it was often referred to as a flat, Roddy's house was, in fact, a two-storey dwelling, converted out of the old stables at the end of the war, when Roddy had come back to Benchoile to live. Roddy, fired by enthusiasm, had architected the conversion himself. The bedrooms and bathrooms were downstairs, the kitchen and the living room upstairs, and access to these rooms was by an open teak stair, like a ship's ladder.

Jock stood at the foot of these and called, 'Roddy!'

Roddy's footsteps creaked across the floorboards over Jock's head. In a moment his brother's bulk appeared, and Roddy peered down at him over the rail of the stairhead.

'Oh, it's you,' said Roddy, as though it might be anybody else.

'Brought the papers.'

'Come on up. What a bloody awful day.'

Jock mounted the stairs, and came out at the top in the living room where Roddy spent his days. It was a marvellous room, light and large, the ceiling gabled to the shape of the roof, and one wall taken up by an enormous picture window. This had been designed to frame a view over the loch to the mountains, which, in fine weather, took the breath away. But this morning what could be seen was enough to chill the soul. Snow and grey water, running before the wind and capped in white; the hills on the far shore were lost in murk.

It was a man's room, and yet a room of taste and even beauty; lined with books and cluttered with a number of objects which, though worth little, were visually pleasing. A carved overmantel; a blue and white jar filled with pampas grasses; a dangling mobile of paper fishes, probably Japanese. The floorboards had been sanded and polished and sparsely scattered with rugs. Elderly armchairs and a sofa sagged invitingly. In the cavern of a fireplace (which had had to be specially constructed at the time of the conversion, and had proved to be the most costly item of all) a couple of birch logs sizzled on a bed of peat. The room had an extraordinary and quite unique smell about it. Compounded of cigar smoke, and peat smoke too, and the sharp aroma of linseed oil.

Roddy's old Labrador, Barney, lay supine on the heathrug. At Jock's appearance, he raised his grizzled nose, and then yawned and went back to sleep again.

Roddy said, 'Have you been to the kirk?'

'Yes.' Jock began to unbutton his overcoat with frozen fingers.

'Did you know the telephone's dead? There must be a line down somewhere.' He gave his brother a long, measuring look. 'You appear to be blue with cold. Have a drink.' He moved ponderously towards the table where he kept his bottles and glasses. He had already, Jock noticed, provided himself with a large, dark whisky. Jock did not ever drink in the middle of the day. It was one of his rules. But somehow today, ever since the minister had mentioned that glass of sherry, he had been thinking about it.

'Have you got some sherry?'

'Only the pale kind. Dry as a bone.'

'That'll do very nicely.'

He took off his coat and went to stand in front of the fire. Roddy's mantelpiece was always littered with undusted bits and pieces. Curling photographs, old pipes, a mug of pheasant quills, and out-of-date invitations, probably unanswered. There was today, however, a sparkling new card propped against the clock, impressively copper-plated, gold-edged and marvellously pretentious.

'What's this? Looks like a royal command.'

'Nothing so splendid. A dinner at the Dorchester. Television awards. Best documentary of the year. God knows why I've been invited. I thought I'd been crossed off all the lists. Actually, apart from the tedium of the after-dinner speeches,

I used to quite enjoy those occasions. Met a lot of new young
writers, new faces. Interesting to talk to.'

'Are you going to this one?'

'I'm getting too elderly to travel the length of the country
for a free hangover.' He had laid down his whisky, located
the sherry, found a suitable glass, poured his brother's drink.
Now he retrieved a smouldering, half-smoked cigar from an
ashtray, picked up the two glasses and came back to the
fireside. 'If it were to take place somewhere civilised, like
Inverness, I might deign to add tone to what will otherwise
be a vulgar brawl. As it is . . . ' He raised his glass. 'Slainthe,
old boy.'

Jock grinned. 'Slainthe.'


Roddy was nine years Jock's junior. When they were young,
Roddy had been the handsome one of the three brothers, the
dallying charmer who had broken more hearts than could be
decently counted, and who never lost his own. Women adored
him. Men were never quite so sure. He was too good-looking,
too clever, too talented at all the sorts of things that it was
not considered manly to be talented at. He drew and he wrote
and he played the piano. He could even sing.

On shoots he always seemed to get the prettiest girl of the
party into his butt, and quite often forgot that the object of
the exercise was to slay grouse. No sound, no blast would
come from his butt, while the grouse sailed serenely over him
in coveys, and at the end of the drive he would be found deep
in conversation with his companion, his gun unfired, and his
dog wheeking and frustrated at his feet.

Naturally brilliant, he had skimmed through his school-
days without apparently doing a stroke of work, and had gone
on to Oxford in a blaze of glory. Trends were started by
Roddy Dunbeath and fashions set. Where others sported
tweed, he favoured corduroy, and soon everybody was wearing
corduroy. He was president of the OUDS and a renowned
debater. Nobody was safe from his wit, which was usually
gentle, but could be barbed.

When the war broke out, Jock was already a regular soldier
with the Camerons. Roddy, impelled by a deep patriotism
which he had always kept to himself, joined up the day that
war was declared. He signed on, to everybody's surprise, with
the Royal Marines, on account of, he said, they had such a

pretty uniform; but in no time at all, he was training to be a Commando, struggling up precipitous cliffs on the end of a rope and hurling himself from training planes with tightly closed eyes and his hand clenched around the rip cord of his parachute.

When it was all over and the country was at peace again, it seemed to Jock Dunbeath that everyone who wasn't married, rushed to rectify the situation. There was a veritable epidemic of matrimony, and Jock himself had fallen prey to it. But not Roddy. Roddy picked up his life where he had left it in 1939 and went on from there. He made himself a home at Benchoile and started to write. *The Eagle Years* came out first, and then *The Wind In The Pines,* and then *Red Fox.* Fame embraced him. He went on lecture tours, he made after-dinner speeches, he appeared on television.

By now he was putting on weight. While Jock stayed thin and spare, Roddy became stout. Gradually his girth spread, his chin doubled, his handsome features were lost in heavy jowls. And yet, he was as attractive as ever, and when the gossip columns in the daily papers ran out of tidbits about the nobility, they would print blurred photographs of Roddy Dunbeath (*The Eagle Years*) dining with Mrs So-and-So, who was, as everybody knew, a champion of wild life.

But youth had gone, lost somewhere over the years, and at last even his mild fame began to slip away. No longer fêted in London, he returned, as he had always returned, to Benchoile. He occupied himself in writing short articles, the scripts for television nature films, even small items for the local newspapers. Nothing changed him. He was still the same Roddy, charming and witty, the engaging raconteur. Still willing to squeeze his bulk into his velvet jacket and drive himself for miles down dark country roads to make up the numbers at some remote dinner party. And – even more astonishing – somehow getting himself home again in the small hours of the morning, half-asleep and awash with whisky.

For he was drinking too much. Not uncontrollably nor offensively, but still he seldom seemed to have a glass out of his hand. He began to slow down. He, who had always been physically indolent, was now becoming chronically idle. He could scarcely make the effort to get himself into Creagan. His life had become encapsulated at Benchoile.

'What are the roads like?' he asked now.

'Passable. You wouldn't have got far in the MG.'

'No intention of going anywhere.' He took the cigar from his mouth and aimed it at the fireplace. It made a tiny flame. He stooped to lift more logs from the great basket that stood by the hearth, and toss them into the grey ashes of the peat. Dust rose in a cloud. The fresh logs flickered and caught fire. There was a small explosion, and one or two sparks flew out on to the aged hearthrug. The smell of burning wool filled Jock's nostrils, and Roddy trod them out with the sole of his brogue.

'You should have a fireguard,' said Jock.

'Can't stand the look of the things. Besides, they keep all the heat in.' He gazed thoughtfully down at his fireplace. 'Thought I might get one of those chain curtains. Saw one advertised the other day, but now I can't remember where I saw it.' He had finished his drink. He began to drift back towards the bottles on the table. Jock said, 'You've hardly time for another. It's past one o'clock already.'

Roddy looked at his watch. 'Well, bless my soul, so it is. It's a wonder Ellen hasn't yet given us her weekly screech. I suppose you couldn't persuade her to use the old gong. She could bring it out into the stable yard and ring it there. It would be so much more in keeping if I could be summoned to Sunday lunch in the big house by the dignified rumble of a gong. Gracious living and all that. We mustn't let ourselves go, Jock. We must keep up appearances even if there is no person to appreciate our efforts. Think of those old empire builders, dining in the jungle in their starched shirts and black ties. There's backbone for you.'

The glass of sherry had freed Jock's inhibitions a little. 'This morning the minister told me that we need some young company at Benchoile,' he told Roddy.

'Well, what a pretty thought.' Roddy hesitated over the whisky bottle, thought better of it and poured himself a small sherry instead. 'Handsome lads and pretty lasses. What happened to all those young relations of Lucy's? The house used to be running with her nephews and nieces. They were all over the place. Like mice.'

'They've grown up. Married. That's what happened to them.'

'Let's stage a grand reunion and get them all back again. We'll put a notice in the personal column of the *Times*. "The Dunbeaths of Benchoile require young company. All applications will be given consideration." We might get some rather amusing replies.'

Jock thought of the letter that he had written to John. He had not told Roddy about that letter. Cautiously, he had made up his mind that when a reply came from John, and not before, he would take Roddy into his confidence.

But now, he found that resolution wavering. He and Roddy saw so little of each other, and it was seldom that they found themselves on such easy and companionable terms as they were at this moment. If he brought the business of John up now, then they could discuss it over Sunday lunch. After all, sometime, it all had to be thrashed out. He finished his sherry. He squared his shoulders. He said, 'Roddy . . .'

But was interrupted by a banging on the door downstairs, and then a blast of icy air as it was opened. A voice, shrill and cracked, rose from the foot of the stairs.

'It's past one o'clock. Did you know that?'

Roddy looked resigned. 'Yes, Ellen, we did.'

'Have you got the colonel with you?'

'Yes, he's here.'

'I saw the Landrover in the garage, but he's not been near the big house. You'd better both come over now, or the bird'll be ruined.' Ellen had never been one for much formality.

Jock laid down his empty glass and went to collect his coat. 'Were coming now, Ellen, he told her. 'Wer'e coming right away.'

## CHAPTER 6

## MONDAY

The fact that the telephone lines were down and the phone not working was of small concern to Roddy Dunbeath. Where others tried six or seven times in a morning to make outside calls, jigged the receiver in empty exasperation, and finally trod out into the snow to the nearest functioning call box, Roddy remained unperturbed. There was no person with whom he wished to get in touch, and he actively enjoyed the sensation of being undisturbed and unreachable.

And so, when the phone on his desk suddenly began to ring at half past eleven on Monday morning, he was at first startled out of his skin and then irritated.

During the night the wind had died, having first blown all the clouds out of the sky, and the morning had dawned, late and clear and still. The sky was a pale, arctic blue. The sun, rising over the foot of the loch, turned the snowclad country-side first pink, and then a dazzling white. The lawn in front of the house was patterned with the random tracks of rabbits and hares. A deer had been there, too, feeding off the young shrubs that Jock had planted at the back end of the year and tree shadows lay like long, smokey blue bruises. As the sun climbed over the rim of the hills, the sky deepened in blue, and this was reflected in the waters of the loch. Frost glittered, and the icy air was so still that when Roddy opened his window to throw out a handful of crusts for his birds, he could hear the baa-ing of the sheep which grazed on the slopes at the far side of the water.

It was not a day for much activity. But, with a certain resolution, and a deadline hanging over his head, Roddy had managed to finish the first draft of his article for the *Scottish Field*. With this behind him, he succumbed once more to idleness and was sitting at his window with a cigar and his binoculars at the ready. He had seen greylags feeding on the worn stubble of the arable fields beyond the pines. Sometimes, in hard weather like this, they would settle in their thousands.

The telephone rang. He said, aloud, 'Oh, bloody hell,' and at the sound of his voice Barney raised his head from the hearthrug. Thump thump went his tail. 'It's all right, old boy, it's not your fault.' He laid down his binoculars, got up, and went reluctantly to answer it.

'Roddy Dunbeath.'

There came strange peeping sounds. For a moment Roddy felt hopeful that the tiresome instrument was still out of order, but then the peeping sounds stopped and a voice came on, and hope died.

'Is that Benchoile?'

'The Stable House, yes. Roddy Dunbeath here.'

'Roddy. This is Oliver Dobbs.'

After a little, Roddy said, 'Who?'

'Oliver Dobbs.' It was a pleasant voice, young, deep, vaguely familiar. Roddy dug about, without noticeable success, in his unreliable memory.

'I'm not with you, old boy.'

'We met at a dinner in London a couple of years ago. Sat next to each other . . . '

Recollection dawned. Of course, Oliver Dobbs. Clever young man. A writer. Won some prize. They'd had a great crack together. 'But of course.' He reached behind him for a chair, settled himself for conversation. 'My dear boy, how splendid to hear you. Where are you calling from?'

'The Lake District.'

'What are you doing in the Lake District?'

'I'm taking a few days off. I'm driving up to Scotland.'

'You're going to come here, of course.'

'Well, that's what I'm calling about. I tried to ring you yesterday, but they said the phone lines were down. When we met, you issued an invitation to come and see you at Benchoile, and I'm afraid I'm taking it up.'

'Nothing to be afraid of. I couldn't be more pleased.'

'We thought perhaps we might be able to come and stay for a couple of days.'

'Of course you must come.' The prospect of a couple of

days in the company of that lively and intelligent young man was quite stimulating. But, 'Who's we?' asked Roddy.

'Well, there's the rub,' said Oliver Dobbs. 'We're a sort of family. Victoria and me and Thomas. He's only two, but he's quite undemanding and very well-behaved. Would there be room for us all, because if not Victoria says we can go to a pub if there's such a thing nearby.'

'Never heard such rubbish.' Roddy was quite indignant. Benchoile hospitality had always been legendary. True, during the last five years, since Lucy died, the entries in the battered leather-bound visitors' book, which lived on the hall table in the big house, were few and far between, but that didn't mean that there wasn't still the warmest of welcomes for any person who wished to come and stay. 'Of course you must come here. When will you arrive?'

'Perhaps about Thursday? We thought we'd drive up the West Coast. Victoria's never been to the Highlands.'

'Come by Strome Ferry and Achnasheen.' Roddy knew the Scottish highways like the back of his hand. 'And then down Strath Oykel to Lairg. You've never seen such country in your life.'

'Have you got snow up there?'

'We've had a lot, but the good weather's back again. By the time you get here, the road should be clear.'

'And you're sure you don't mind us coming?'

'Absolutely delighted. We'll expect you Thursday about lunchtime. And stay,' he added with the expansiveness of a potential host who has no intention of being involved in the tedious necessities of airing sheets or dusting bedrooms or cooking meals, 'stay as long as you like.'

The telephone call, coming out of the blue as it had, left Roddy in a pleasurable state of mild excitement. After he had replaced the receiver, he sat for a little, finishing his cigar, and anticipating, with the satisfaction of a boy, the forthcoming visit.

He loved young people. Trapped in the spreading bulk and the balding head of approaching old age, he still thought of himself as young. Inside, he still felt young. He remembered with pleasure the instant rapport that had sprung up between himself and Oliver Dobbs. How they had sat through that dinner, serious-faced and boiling with suppressed laughter at the endless, cliché-ridden speeches.

At one point, Oliver had made some remark, thrown from

the corner of his mouth, about the chest measurements of the lady across the table from them, and Roddy had thought, 'You remind me of me.' Perhaps that was it. Oliver was his alter ego, the young man Roddy had once been. Or perhaps the young man he would like to have been, if circumstances had been different, if he had been born to a different way of life, if there had been no war.

The pleasure had to be shared. Not only that, Ellen Tarbat had to be told. She would put on a face, shake her head, accept the tidings in martyred resignation. This was customary and meant nothing. Ellen always put on a face, shook her head and looked martyred, even if one happened to be the bearer of delightful news.

Roddy stubbed out his cigar, and without bothering to put on a coat, got up out of his chair and started down the stairs. His dog followed him. They went out into the cold morning air together, crossed the icy cobbles of the stableyard, and let themselves in through the back door of the big house.

The passages that lay beyond were stone-floored, cold, and seemingly endless. Doors gave off to coal sheds, woodsheds, laundries, store rooms, cellars, pantries. He came at last through a green-baize-covered door, and emerged into the big hall of the old house. Here, the temperature rose by a few degrees. Sun poured in through long windows and the glassed inner front door. It sent long beams, dancing with dust motes, down the turkey-rugged staircase and quenched the fire, which smouldered in the immense grate, to a bed of dusty ashes. Roddy stopped to replenish this from the basket of peats which stood alongside and then went in search of his brother.

He found Jock, inevitably, in the library, sitting at the unfashionable roll-top desk, which had belonged to their father, and dealing with the endless accounts and paper work related to the management of the farm.

Since Lucy had died, the drawing room had, by wordless consent, been closed and shut away, and this was now the apartment in which Jock spent his days. It was one of Roddy's favourite rooms, shabby and worn, the walls lined with books, the old leather-covered chairs sagging and comfortable as old friends. Today this room too was filled with the pale sunlight of the winter's day. Another fire burned in the hearth, and Jock's two golden Labradors lay, drugged in the warmth.

As Roddy opened the door, Jock looked up, over the spectacles which habitually slid to the end of his long beak of a nose. Roddy said, 'Good morning.'

'Hello,' He took off the spectacles, leaning back in his chair. 'And what might you be wanting?'

Roddy came in and shut the door. He said, 'I am the bearer of pleasing news.' Jock sat politely, waiting to be pleased. 'You might even say, I was some sort of a fairy godmother, granting all your wishes.'

Jock still waited. Roddy smiled and let his weight cautiously down into the armchair nearest the fire. After his trek across the yard and down the arctic passages of Benchoile, his feet felt cold, so he toed off his slippers and wriggled his stockinged feet in the warmth. There was a hole in one of his socks. He would have to get Ellen to mend it.

He said, 'You know, yesterday, you said that the minister at Creagan said that what we needed at Benchoile was some young company. Well, we're going to get it.'

'Who are we going to get?'

'A delightful and bright young man called Oliver Dobbs and what he pleases to call his "sort of family".'

'And who is Oliver Dobbs?'

'If you weren't such an old reactionary, you'd have heard of him. A very clever young man with a string of literary successes to his name.'

'Oh,' said Jock. 'One of those.'

'You'll like him.' That was the extraordinary thing, Jock probably would. Roddy had called his brother a reactionary, but Jock was nothing of the kind. Jock was a liberal, through and through. Beneath his chilling, eagle-proud appearance lay concealed the real man, gentle, tolerant, well-mannered. Jock had never disliked a man on sight. Jock had always been willing and ready, in his reserved and diffident way, to see the other man's point of view.

'And what,' asked Jock mildly, 'does the "sort of family" consist of?'

'I'm not quite sure, but whatever it is, we may well have to keep it from Ellen.'

'When are they coming?'

'Thursday. Lunchtime.'

'Where are they going to sleep?'

'I thought over here, in the big house. They've a small child and there's more space.'

'You'll have to tell Ellen.'

'I am steeling myself to do that very thing.'

Jock sent him a long amused look, and Roddy grinned. Jock leaned back in his chair and rubbed his eyes with the gesture of a man who had been up all night. He said, 'What time is it?' and looked at his watch. Roddy, who was longing for a drink, said it was twelve o'clock, but Jock didn't notice the hint, or if he did he took no account of it, but said, instead, 'I'm going out for a walk.'

Roddy suppressed his disappointment. He would go back to his own house and pour himself a drink there. He said 'It's a beautiful morning.'

'Yes,' said Jock. He looked out of the window. 'Beautiful. Benchoile at its most beautiful.'

They talked for a little and then Roddy departed, with conscious courage, kitchenwards, in search of Ellen. Jock got up from his desk, and with the dogs at his heel, went out of the room and across the hall to the gunroom. He took down a shooting jacket, shucked off his slippers, climbed into a pair of green rubber boots. He took down his cap, pulled it down over his nose. A muffler to wind round his neck. He found knitted mittens in the pocket of the jacket and pulled them on. His fingers protruded from the open ends, swollen and purple as beef sausages.

He found his stick, a long shepherd's crook. He let himself thankfully out of the house. The cold air hit him, the piercing chill of it biting deep into his lungs. For days he had been feeling unwell. He put it down to tiredness and the bitter weather, but all at once, in the meagre warmth of the February sun, he felt a little better. Perhaps he should get out and about more, but one needed good reason to make the required effort.

Tramping over the creaking snow towards the loch, he thought of the young people whom Roddy had invited to stay, and he was not dismayed, as many men of his age would have been, by the prospect. He loved young people as much as his brother, but somehow he had always been shy with them, had never been much good with them. He knew that his manner, and his upright, soldierly appearance, were off-putting, but what could you do about the way you looked? Perhaps, if he had had children of his own, it would have been different. With children of your own, there would be no necessity to break down the barriers of shyness.

People to stay. They would have to get the rooms ready, light fires, perhaps open the old nursery. He had forgotten to ask Roddy the age of the child who was coming to stay. A pity there would be no fishing, but the boat was laid up anyway, and the boathouse locked for the winter.

His mind strayed back to other house-parties, other children. He and his brothers when they were small. Their friends, and then Lucy's numerous young nephews and nieces. Rabbit's friends and relations he had called them. He smiled to himself. Rabbit's friends and relations.

He had reached the edge of the loch. It stretched before him, edged with ice from which the winter-pale rushes grew in straggling clumps. A pair of peewits flew overhead, and he raised his head to watch their passing. The sun in his eyes was blinding, and he put up a hand as shade from the dazzle. His dogs nuzzled into the snow, scenting exciting smells. They inspected the ice, in small nervous darts, but were not brave, or perhaps foolhardy, enough to venture out onto the shining surface.

It was indeed a beautiful day. He turned back to look at the house. It lay, a little above him, across the snow-covered slope; familiar, loved, secure. Sunlight glinted on windows, smoke issued from chimneys, rising straight up in the still air. There was a smell of moss, of peat, and the resin of the spruces. Behind the house, the hills rose to meet the blue sky. His hills. Benchoile hills. He felt immensely content.

Well, the young company were coming. They would be here on Thursday. There would be laughter, voices, footsteps on the stairs. Benchoile was waiting for them.

He turned away from the house and set out once more upon his walk, his stick in his hand, his dogs at his heel, his spirit untroubled.

When he did not put in an appearance for his midday meal, Ellen became worried. She went to the front door to look for him, but saw only the single line of footprints that led to the edge of the loch. He had been late many times before, but now her Highland instincts were dark with foreboding. She went to find Roddy. He rang Davey Guthrie and in a moment Davey appeared in his van and the two men set out together to look for Jock.

It was not a difficult search, for the prints of him and his dogs lay clear in the snow. They found the three of them in the lea of a dry-stone dike. Jock lay quietly, his face serene and turned up to the sun. The dogs were wheeking and anxious, but it was instantly clear that their master would never know anxiety again.

## CHAPTER 7

## TUESDAY

Thomas Dodds, wearing new red rubber boots, squatted at the water's edge, fascinated by this strange new phenomenon that had suddenly come into his life, and staring at it with the mesmerised, unblinking gaze of some old seafarer. It was all bigger and brighter and wetter than anything he had ever before encountered in his short life, and there were, as well, the added diversions of the little choppy waves, so sunlit and cheerful, the screaming of the sea birds which wheeled in the cold air over his head, and the occasional passing boat. Every now and then he dug up a handful of gritty sand and threw it into the sea.

Behind him, a few yards off, Victoria sat on the shingly beach and watched him. She wore thick, corduroy trousers and three sweaters, two of them her own and one borrowed from Oliver, and she sat huddled, with her knees pulled up and her arms wrapped around them for warmth. It was, indeed extremely cold. But then, at ten o'clock on a February morning in the north of Scotland – well, nearly the north of Scotland – it would have been surprising if it had been anything else.

It wasn't even a proper beach, just a narrow strip of shingle between the wall of the hotel garden and the water. It smelt fishy and tarry, and was littered with scraps of debris from the boats that plied up and down the long sea loch on their way to and from the fishing grounds. There were bits of string, an old fish-head or two, and a damp furry object, which on investigation proved to be a rotting doormat.

'The back of beyond,' Oliver had said yesterday evening as the Volvo topped the pass and began the long gradual descent to the sea, but Victoria thought that the isolation was beautiful. They were now much further north than they had intended to come, and so far west that if you took another step, you fell into the sea; but the views, the sheer size and grandeur of the country, the colours, and the brilliance of the sparkling air had made the long drive more than worthwhile.

Yesterday morning they had woken to a Lake District streaming in rain, but as they drove up into Scotland a wind had sprung up from the west, and the clouds had been blown away. All yesterday afternoon, and this morning again, the sky was clear, the air piercingly cold. Snow-covered peaks of distant hills glittered like glass, and the waters of the sea loch were a dark indigo blue.

The loch, Victoria had discovered, was called Loch Morag. The little village, with its tiny shops and fleet of fishing boats tied up at the sea wall, was also called Loch Morag, and the hotel was the Loch Morag Hotel. (Oliver said that he expected the manager was called Mr Lochmorag and his wife, Mrs Lochmorag.) Built for the sole purpose of catering to fishermen – both freshwater and sea fishing, the brochure boasted, was on their doorstep – it was large and ugly, constructed of some strange stone the colour of liver, and much crenellated, towered and turreted. Indoors, it was furnished with worn turkey carpets and uninspired wallpaper the colour of porridge, but there were peat fires burning in the public rooms and the people were very kind.

'Would the wee boy like high tea?' had asked the comfortable lady in the mauve dress who appeared, in this quiet season, to have taken on the duties not only of head waitress and barmaid, but receptionist as well. 'Maybe a boiled egg, or a wee bit oatcake?' Thomas stared at her, unhelpfully. 'Or a jeely. Would you like a jeely, pet?'

In the end they had settled for a boiled egg and an apple, and the kind lady (Mrs Lochmorag?) brought it up to his bedroom on a tray, and sat with Thomas while Victoria had a bath. When she emerged from the bathroom, she found Mrs Lochmorag playing with Thomas and the pink and white calico pig that they had bought him in London before they left, along with a wardrobe of clothes, a toothbrush and a pot. Victoria had wanted to buy an endearing teddy bear, but Oliver informed her that Thomas did not like fur, and chose the pig himself.

The pig was called Piglet. He wore blue trousers and red

braces. His eyes were black and beady and Thomas approved
of him.

'You've got a lovely wee boy, Mrs Dobbs. And what age is
he?'

'He's two.'

'We've made friends, but, mind, he hasn't said a word to
me.'

'He . . . he doesn't talk very much.'

'Oh, he should be talking by now.' She heaved Thomas onto
her knee. 'What a lazy wee boy, not saying a word. You can
say Mummy, now, can't you? Are you not going to say
Mummy? Are you not going to tell me the name of your pig?'
She took piglet and jigged him up and down, making him
dance. Thomas smiled.

'He's called Piglet,' Victoria told her.

'That's a bonny name. Why does Thomas not say Piglet?'

But he did not say Piglet. He did not indeed say anything
very much. But this in no way detracted from his charm. In
fact, it added to it, because he was such a cheerful and
undemanding child that four days of his company had been
nothing but pleasure. In the car, during the long drive north,
he sat on Victoria's knee, hugging his new toy, and gazing out
of the window at passing lorries, fields, towns; obviously
enjoying all the new and strange sights, but seeing no reason
to comment upon them. When they stopped for meals or to
stretch their legs, Thomas joined them, eating bacon and eggs
or drinking milk or munching the slices of apple that Oliver
peeled and cut up for him. When he became tired or bored,
he plugged his mouth with his thumb, settled himself with
endearing confidence in Victoria's arms, and either slept or
sang to himself, with eyes drooping and dark lashes silky
against his round red cheeks.

'I wonder why he doesn't talk more?' she had said to Oliver
once, when Thomas was safely asleep on her lap and could
not overhear the discussion.

'Probably because nobody's ever talked to him. Probably
they were all too busy sterilising the house and manicuring the
garden, and boiling his toys.'

Victoria did not agree with Oliver. No child, so well-adjusted
and content, could have been neglected in the smallest way. Indeed, his behaviour and his sunny disposition gave every indi-
cation that he had spent his short life enveloped in affection.

She said as much and instantly aroused Oliver's ire. 'If they were so marvellous with him, then how come he doesn't seem to be missing them? He can't have been particularly fond of them if he hasn't asked for them once.'

'He hasn't asked for anything,' Victoria pointed out. 'And most likely his being so confident and unafraid is all to do with the way he's been brought up. Nobody's ever been unkind to him, so he doesn't expect unkindness. That's why he's being so good with us.'

'Balls,' said Oliver shortly. He could not stand a single good word being said on the Archers' behalf.

Victoria knew he was being unreasonable. 'If Thomas howled for his grandparents all the time, and complained, and wet his pants and generally behaved like most children would under the same circumstances, I suppose you'd have blamed that on the Archers, too.'

'You're talking in hypothetical circles.'

'I'm not.' But she didn't know what a hypothetical circle was, and so couldn't argue further. Instead, she lapsed into silence. *But we must ring up Mrs Archer,* she thought. Or write to her or something. Oliver must let her know that Thomas is all right. Some time.

It was, perhaps, their only quarrel. Otherwise, the entire undertaking, which could have been, and even deserved to be, disastrous, was proving an unqualified success. Nothing had gone wrong. Everything had proved simple, easy, delightful. The winter roads were fast and empty; the scenery, the open skies, the stunning countryside, all contributed to their pleasure.

In the Lake District it had rained, but they had put on waterproofs and walked for miles, with Thomas, cheerful as ever, atop his father's shoulders. There had been fires burning pleasantly in their bedrooms at the little lakeside hotel, and boats moored at the jetty that lay at the end of the garden, and in the evening a kindly chambermaid had watched over Thomas while Oliver and Victoria dined by candlelight, on grilled trout and rare beefsteaks that had never seen the inside of a deep freeze.

That night, lying in the soft darkness, in feather-bedded warmth, in Oliver's arms, she had watched the curtains stirring at the open window and felt the cool damp air on her cheeks. From the quiet darkness beyond the window came the sounds of water and the creak of the boats tied up at the jetty, and there had come a distrust of such perfect content. Surely, she told herself, it could not go on. Surely something would happen that would spoil it all.

But her apprehension was unfounded. Nothing happened. The next day was even better, with the road pouring north to Scotland and the sun coming out as they crossed the border. By the afternoon, the great peaks of the Western Highlands lay ahead of them, iced in snow, and at the foot of Glencoe they stopped at a pub for tea and ate homemade scones dripping with butter. And after that the countryside grew more and more magnificent, and Oliver told Victoria that it was called Lochaber, and he began to sing 'The Road to the Isles.'

'Sure by *Tummel* and Loch *Rannoch* and Loch*aber* we will go . . .'

Today Loch Morag. Tomorrow, or perhaps the next day, Benchoile. Victoria had lost all sense of time. She had lost all sense of anything. Watching Thomas, she hugged herself more tightly and rested her chin on her knees. Happiness, she decided, should be tangible. A thing you could take hold of and put somewhere safe, like a box with a lid or a bottle with a stopper. And then, later, sometime when you were miserable, you could take it out and look at it and feel it and smell it, and you would be happy again.

Thomas was tiring of throwing sand into the sea. He straightened up on his small legs and looked about him. He spied Victoria, sitting there, where he had left her. He grinned, and began to stump unsteadily towards her up the littered little beach.

Watching him filled her heart with an almost unbearable tenderness. She thought, if I can feel like this about Thomas, after only four days, how does Mrs Archer feel, not even knowing where he is?

It didn't bear thinking about. Basely, cowardly, she pushed the idea to the back of her mind and opened her arms to Thomas. He reached her and she hugged him. The wind blew her long hair across his cheek, and tickled. He began to laugh.

While Victoria and Thomas sat on the beach and waited for him, Oliver was telephoning. The previous night had been the first performance of *Bent Penny* at Bristol, and he couldn't wait to hear what the critics had said in the morning papers.

He was not exactly on tenterhooks, because he knew that the play was good – his best, in fact. But there were always elements and reactions that were apt to take one unawares. He wanted to know how the show had gone, how the audience had responded, and whether Jennifer Clay, the new little actress getting her first big chance, had justified the faith that the producer and Oliver had put in her.

He was on the telephone to Bristol for nearly an hour, listening while the ecstatic reviews were read aloud to him along six hundred miles of humming wires. The critics from the *Sunday Times* and the *Observer,* he was told, were coming down to see the play at the end of the week. Jennifer Clay was on the brink of being swept to stardom, and there had already come interested noises from a couple of important West End managements.

'In fact, Oliver, I think we've got a hit on our hands.'

Oliver was gratified, but he had watched the show in rehearsal, and he was not particularly surprised. The Bristol call finally finished, he rang his agent, and all the good news was confirmed. As well, there had been feelers from New York about his play *A Man In The Dark,* which had done so well in Edinburgh a summer ago.

'Would you be interested?' the agent asked.

'What do you mean, "interested"?'

'Would you be prepared to go to New York if you have to?'

Oliver loved New York. It was one of his favourite places. 'I'd be prepared to go even if I didn't have to.'

'How long are you going to be away?'

'Couple of weeks.'

'Can I get in touch with you?'

'After Thursday, I'll be at Benchoile, in Sutherland. Staying with a guy called Roddy Dunbeath.'

'*Eagle Years* Dunbeath?'

'The very man.'

'What's the phone number?'

Oliver reached for his leather diary, thumbed through it. 'Creagan two three seven.'

'OK, I've got it. If I have any fresh news I'll call you.'

'You do that.'

'Good luck, then, Oliver. And congratulations.'

His agent rang off. After a little, as though reluctant to put an end to such a momentous conversation, Oliver replaced his own receiver, and sat looking at it for a moment or two, while slowly, relief flooded through him. It was over. *Bent Penny* was launched, like a child sent out into the world. A child conceived with passion, brought to life in the most agonising birth pains, nursed and coaxed to maturity, and bludgeoned into shape, it was, at last, no longer Oliver's responsibility.

All over. He thought of the production, the rehearsals, the personality problems, the temperaments, the tears. The chaos, the panics, the rewriting, the total despair.

*I think we've got a hit on our hands.*

It would make him, probably, a lot of money. It might even make him rich. But this was of small account compared to the easement of his spirit, and the sense of freedom that existed now that it was all behind him.

And ahead . . . ? He reached for a cigarette. There was something waiting for him, but he wasn't sure what. He only knew that the subconscious edge of his imagination, the part that did all the work, was already filling with people. People living in a certain place, a certain style. Voices had conversations. The dialogues had a form and a balance all their own, and the words, and the faces of the individuals who spoke them, swam up, as they always did, out of his prodigious memory.

These first stirrings of life made everyday existence, for Oliver, as intense and dramatic as it is for most men when they fall in love. This, for him, was the best part of writing. It was the same as the anticipation of waiting in a darkened theatre for the curtain to go up on the first act. You didn't know what was going to happen, but you knew that it would be marvellous and tremendously exciting and better – much better – than anything you had ever seen before.

He got up off the bed and went to the window and flung it open to the icy morning air. Gulls wheeled and screamed over the funnel of a weather-beaten fishing boat as she butted her way, against the western wind, out to the open sea.

On the far side of the dark blue water the hills were frosted in white, and below him was the hotel garden and the scrap of a beach. He looked down upon Victoria and his son Thomas. They did not know he was watching. As he observed them, Tom grew tired of his game of throwing sand into the water, and turned and made his way up the beach to Victoria's side. She opened her arms to him and drew him close, and her long fair hair blew all over his red chubby face.

The combination of this delightful scene and his own euphoric frame of mind filled Oliver with an unfamiliar content. He knew that it was ephemeral; it might last a day or even an hour or two. But all at once it seemed that the world was a brighter and a more hopeful place; that the smallest incident could take on immense significance; that affection would turn to love, and love – that humdrum word – to passion.

He closed the window and went downstairs to tell them his good news.

## CHAPTER 8

## THURSDAY

Miss Ridgeway, that impeccable private secretary of undetermined years, was already at her desk when, at a quarter to nine in the morning, John Dunbeath emerged from the lift onto the ninth floor of the new Regency House Building and the opulent, elegant offices of the Warburg Investment Corporation.

She looked up as he came through the door, her expression, as always, polite, pleasant and impassive.

'Good morning, Mr Dunbeath.'

'Hi.'

He had never before had a secretary whom he did not call by her Christian name, but sometimes the formality of 'Miss Ridgeway' stuck in his throat. They had, after all, worked together for some months. It would have been so much easier to call her Mary or Daphne or whatever her name was, but the truth of the matter was that he hadn't even found this out, and there was something so strictly formal about her manner that he had never plucked up the courage to ask.

Sometimes, watching her as she sat there, with one shapely leg crossed over the other, taking down his letters in her faultless shorthand, he pondered on her private life. Did she care for an aged mother and take an interest in good works? Did she go to concerts at the Albert Hall and spend her holidays in Florence? Or did she, like a secretary in some film, remove her spectacles and shake loose her mouse pale hair, receive lovers and indulge in scenes of unbridled passion?

He knew that he would never know.

She said, 'How was the trip?'

'OK. But the plane was late getting in yesterday evening. We got held up in Rome.'

Her eyes moved over his dark suit, his black tie. She said, 'You got the cable all right? The one from your father?'

'Yes. Thanks for that.'

'It came on Tuesday morning. I thought you'd want to know. I sent a copy through to Bahrein right away. The original is on your desk with some personal mail...' John moved through to his own office, and Miss Ridgeway rose from her chair and followed him. '... and yesterday's *Times* that the announcement was in. I thought you'd like to see it.'

She thought of everything. He said, 'Thank you,' again and opened his briefcase and took out the report, the twelve pages of foolscap, covered with his own neat writing, that he had composed in the aeroplane during the flight back to London.

'You'd better get one of the typists on to this right away. The vice-president will want to see it as soon as possible. And when Mr Rogerson gets in, tell him to give me a buzz.' He glanced at his desk. 'And this morning's *Wall Street Journal?*'

'I have it, Mr Dunbeath.'

'And the *Financial Times* as well. I didn't have time to pick one up.' She started out of the office, but he called her back. 'Hang on a moment.' She returned and he dealt out more papers. 'I want the file on this. And if you can, find me some information on a Texas company called Albright; they've been drilling in Libya. And this has to be telexed through to Sheikh Mustapha Said, and this... and this...'

After a little, 'Is that all?' asked Miss Ridgeway.

'For the moment.' He grinned. 'Except that I'd appreciate a large cup of black coffee.'

Miss Ridgeway smiled understandingly, becoming quite human. He wished that she would smile more. 'I'll get it,' she said, and left him, closing the door, without a sound, behind her.

He sat at his gleaming desk and debated for a moment as to what he should do first. His In tray was piled high, letters neatly clipped to their relevant files, and, he knew, arranged in their order of priority, with the most urgent documents on the top. The three personal letters had been placed in the middle of his blotter. The blotting paper was, as it was every day, new and pristine white. There was also the copy of yesterday's *Times*.

He reached for the green telephone to make an internal call.

'Mr Gardner please.'

He tucked the receiver under his chin and opened the newspaper to the back page.

'John Dunbeath here. Is he in yet?'

'Yes, he's in, Mr Dunbeath, but he's not in the office right now. Shall I get him to call you?'

'Yes, do that.' He replaced the receiver.

DUNBEATH. Suddenly, on 16 February at Benchoile in Sutherland, Lt. Col. John Rathbone Dunbeath, D.S.O., J.P., late Cameron Highlanders, in his 68th year. Funeral Service in the Parish Church, Creagan, 10.30am, Thursday 19 February.

He remembered the old boy, tall and lean, every inch a retired soldier; his pale glare and his prow of a nose; his long legs striding easily up the hill through knee-high heather; his passion for fishing, for shooting grouse, for his land. They had never been close, but there was still an empty sense of loss, as there must be when a man, bound close by family and blood, dies.

He laid down the paper and took his father's cable from the envelope in which Miss Ridgeway had protectively placed it. He read what he had already read, in Bahrein, two days previously.

YOUR UNCLE JOCK DIED RESULT OF A HEART ATTACK BENCHOILE MONDAY 16 FEBRUARY STOP FUNERAL CREAGAN 10:30 THURSDAY MORNING 19 FEBRUARY STOP WOULD BE GRATEFUL IF YOU COULD REPRESENT YOUR MOTHER AND MYSELF STOP FATHER

He had sent cables from Bahrein. To his parents in Colorado, explaining why he would not be able to comply with his father's request. To Benchoile, to Roddy, he had sent sympathy and more explanations, and before he left Bahrein, he had found time to write Roddy a letter of condolence, which he had posted by first-class mail on his arrival at Heathrow.

The other two letters waited for his attention, one envelope hand-written, the other typed. He picked up the first and began to open it, and then stopped, his attention caught by the writing. An old-fashioned pen nib, black ink, the capitals strongly defined. He looked at the postmark and saw 'CREAGAN'. The date was the tenth of February.

He felt his stomach contract. *A ghost going over your grave* his father used to say when John was a small boy and scared by the unknown. *That's what it is. A ghost going over your grave.*

He slit the envelope and took out the letter. His suspicions were confirmed. It was from Jock Dunbeath.

> Benchoile,
> Creagan,
> Sutherland.
> Wednesday,
> 11 February.

Dear John,

Your Father tells me that you are now back in this country and working in London. I do not know your address, so I am sending this to your office.

It seems a long time since you stayed with us. I looked it up in the visitors' book and it seems to be ten years. I realise that you are a very busy man, but if you are able to get a little time off, perhaps you would think about making the joursey north and spending a few days at Benchoile. It is possible to fly to Inverness or to catch a train from Euston in which case either I or Roddy would come to Inverness to meet you. There are trains to Creagan, but they are few and far between and involve several hours delay.

We have had a mild winter, but I think cold weather is on the way. Better now than in the Spring when late frosts play havoc with the young grouse.

Let me know what you think and when it might be convenient for you to visit us. We look forward to seeing you again.

With best wishes,

Affectionately,

*Jock*

The arrival, out of the blue, of this extraordinary invitation; the coincidence of timing, the fact that it had been written only days before Jock's fatal heart attack, were intensely disturbing. John sat back in his chair and read the letter through again, consciously searching for some inner meaning between the carefully penned and characteristically stilted lines. He could find none.

*It seems to be ten years.*

It was ten years. He remembered himself at eighteen with Wellington behind him and all the joys of Cambridge ahead, spending part of the summer holidays with his father at Benchoile. But he had never gone back.

Now, it struck him that perhaps he should feel guilty about this lapse. But too much had happened to him. Too much had been going on. He had been at Cambridge, then New York, and then Harvard, spending all his vacations in Colorado, either at his father's ranch, or else skiing at Aspen. And then Lisa had come into his life, and after that all his spare energy had been spent in simply keeping up with her. Keeping her happy, keeping her amused, keeping her in the high style which she was convinced was her due. Being married to Lisa meant the end of vacations in Colorado. She was bored by the ranch and too fragile to ski. But she adored the sun, so they went to the West Indies, to Antigua, the Bahamas, where John missed the mountains and tried to work off his physical needs in scuba diving or sailing.

And after the divorce, he had buried himself so deeply in his work that somehow there didn't even seem to be time to get out of the city. It was his president in New York who had finally read the riot act, and had him posted to London. Not only was it a promotion, he told John, but it would make a vital and necessary change of pace. London was quieter than New York, the rat race not so frantic, the ambience generally more easy-going.

'You'll be able to get North and see Jock and Roddy,' his father had said over the telephone when John had called to give him the news, but somehow with one thing and another John had never got around to doing this. Now, it struck him that he should feel guilty about this lapse. But the truth was that Benchoile, though undoubtedly beautiful, held no irresistible lure for John. Having been brought up in the heart of the Rockies, he had found the hills and glens of Sutherland peaceful, but somehow tame. There was fishing, of course, but fishing in Colorado, in the tributaries of the mighty Uncompahgre, which ran through his father's spread, was unsurpassable. Benchoile had a farm, but again, that seemed small compared to the endless ranges of the ranch, and the grouse shooting, with its rules and shibboleths, its traditions of butt and beat, had left the young John totally cold.

Even as a boy, he had rebelled against slaughtering wildlife, and had never gone hunting, for mule deer or elk, with the other men, and there seemed no reason, just because he was staying in Scotland and it was expected of him, to give up the habits and convictions of a lifetime.

Finally, and this was the most important reason of all, he had never thought that his Uncle Jock liked him very much. 'He's just reserved. He's shy,' John's father had assured him, but still, try as he could, John had never been able to work up a rapport with his father's eldest brother. Conversations between the two of them, he remembered, had never done more than creak painfully along, like wagon wheels in need of a good greasing.

He sighed, and laid the letter down, and picked up the last envelope. This time he slit it open without inspecting it first, and with his mind still brooding over the letter from Jock, he unfolded the single sheet of paper. He saw the old-fashioned letter head, the date.

> McKenzie, Leith & Dudgeon,
> Solicitors, Writers to
> The Signet.
> 18 Trade Lane,
> Inverness.
> Tuesday, 17th February.

John Dunbeath, Esq.,
Warburg Investment Corporation,
Regency House,
London.

*John Rathbone Dunbeath Deceased*

Dear Mr Dunbeath,

I have to inform you that under the terms of the Will of your Uncle, John Rathbone Dunbeath, you have been bequeathed the Benchoile Estate in Sutherland.

I suggest that you take an early opportunity to come north and see me in order to make practical arrangements for the management and future of the property.

I shall be happy to see you at any time.

Yours sincerely,

*Robert McKenzie.*

When Miss Ridgeway came back into the room, bearing his black coffee in a fine white Wedgwood cup, she found John sitting, motionless at his desk, an elbow on his blotter, the bottom half of his face covered by his hand.

She said, 'Here's your coffee,' and he looked up at her, and the expression in his dark eyes was so sombre that she was moved to ask if he was all right, if anything had happened.

He did not reply at once. And then he sat back in his chair, letting his hand fall to his lap, and said that yes, something had happened. But after a long pause, during which he showed no signs of wishing to elucidate on this remark, she laid the cup and saucer beside him, and left him alone, closing the door between them with her usual tactful care.

# CHAPTER 9

## THURSDAY

As they drove east, up and away from the mild-mannered sea lochs of the West of Scotland, leaving the farms and villages and the smell of sea wrack behind them, the countryside changed character with dizzying abruptness, and the empty road wound upwards into a wilderness of desolate moorland, apparently uninhabited except for a few stray sheep and the occasional hovering bird of prey.

The day was cold and overcast, the wind from the east. Grey billows of cloud moved slowly across the sky, but every now and then there came a break in the gloom, a ragged scrap of pale blue appeared, and a gleam of thin wintry sunshine, but this only seemed to accentuate the loneliness rather than do anything to alleviate it.

The undulating land stretched in all directions, as far as the eye could see, patchworked in winter-pale grasses and great tracts of dark heather. Sometimes this was broken by a gaping peat-pit or the sombre black of bog. Then scraps of snow began to appear, like the white spots on a piebald horse, and lay where it had been trapped in corries and ditches and in the lea of low drystone dikes. As the gradient steepened, the snow grew thicker, and at the head of the moor – the roof-ridge, as it were, of the country – it was all about them, a blanket of white six inches deep or more, and the road was ice-rutted and treacherous beneath the wheels of the Volvo.

It was like finding oneself in the Arctic, or on the moon. Certainly in some place that one had never even remotely imagined visiting. But then, just as abruptly, the wild and desolate moor was behind them. They had crossed the watershed, and, imperceptibly, the road began to slope downhill once more. There were rivers and waterfalls and stands of larch and fir. First appeared isolated cottages, and then hill farms and then villages. Presently they were running alongside an immense inland loch, and there was the great rampart of a hydroelectric dam and beyond this a little town. The main street ran by the water's edge, and there was a hotel and a number of small boats pulled up on the shingle. A signpost pointed to Creagan.

Victoria became excited. 'We're nearly there.' She leaned forward and took from the cubbyhole on the dashboard the Ordnance Survey map that Oliver had bought. With Thomas's dubious help, she opened it out. One corner spread out over the driving wheel, and Oliver flipped it back. 'Whatch it, you'll blind me.'

'It's only about another six miles to Creagan.'

Thomas, using Piglet as a weapon, struck the map a blow and knocked it from Victoria's hands and on to the floor.

Oliver said, 'Put it away before he tears it to pieces.' He yawned and shifted in his seat. It had been a hard morning's drive.

Victoria rescued the map and folded it up and replaced it. The road ahead of them wound steadily downhill, between steep banks of bracken and copses of silver birch. A small river kept them company, chuckling and sparkling on its way in a series of little pools and waterfalls. The sun, obligingly, came out from behind a cloud; they turned a final corner, and ahead, glinting and silvery, lay the sea.

She said, 'It's really amazing. You leave one coast behind you, and you drive up and over the moor and through the snow, and then you come to another sea. Look, Thomas, there's the sea.'

Thomas looked, but was unimpressed. He was getting tired of driving. He was getting tired of sitting on Victoria's knee. He put his thumb in his mouth and flung himself backwards, striking her a resounding blow on the chest with the back of his bullet-hard head.

His father snapped, 'Oh, for God's sake, sit still.'

'He has sat still,' Victoria was moved to point out in Thomas's defence. 'He's been a very good boy. He's just getting bored. Do you suppose there's a beach at Creagan? I mean a proper sandy one. We haven't found a proper sandy beach yet. All the ones on the West seemed to be covered in stones. If there was one I could take him.'

'We'll ask Roddy.'

Victoria thought about this. Then she said, 'I *do* hope he isn't going to mind us all turning up like this. I hope it isn't going to be difficult.' She had never quite got rid of this apprehension.

'You've already said that a dozen times, at regular intervals. Stop being so anxious.'

'I can't help feeling that you cornered Roddy. Perhaps he didn't have time to think up an excuse.'

'He was delighted. Jumped at the chance of a little lively company.'

'He knows you, but he doesn't know Tom and me.'

'In that case, you'll both have to be on your best behaviour. If I know Roddy, he won't care if you've got two heads and a tail. He'll just say how do you do, very nicely, and then, I hope and believe, will hand me an enormous gin and tonic.'

Creagan, when they reached it, proved a surprise. Victoria had expected the usual small Highland township with its single narrow main street, flanked by rows of plain stone houses built flush on the pavement. But Creagan had a wide, tree-lined street, with deep cobbled sidewalks on either side. The houses, which stood back from the road and were separated from it by quite large gardens, were all detached and remarkably attractive, with the simple proportions and elegant embellishments associated with the best period of Scottish domestic architecture.

In the middle of the town the main street opened up into a wide square, and in the centre of this, sitting on a sward of grass, rather as though it had been set carefully down in the middle of a green carpet, rose the granite walls and slate-capped tower of a large and beautiful church.

Victoria said, 'But it's lovely! It's like a French town.'

Oliver, however, had noticed something else. 'It's empty.'

She looked again, and saw that this was true. A stillness brooded over Creagan, like the pious gloom of a Sabbath. Worse, for there was not even the cheerful clangour of bells. As well, there seemed to be scarcely anybody about, and only a few other cars. And ... 'All the shops are shuttered,' said Victoria. 'They're closed and all the blinds have been pulled down. Perhaps it's early closing.'

She rolled down the window on her side of the car to let the icy air blow in on her face. Thomas tried to put his head out, and she pulled him back onto her knee. She smelled the salt of the sea and the tang of sea wrack. Overhead a gull began to scream from a rooftop.

'There's a shop open,' said Oliver.

It was a small newsagent, with plastic toys in the window and a rack of coloured postcards at the door. Victoria rolled up the window again, for the blast of cold air was bitter. 'We can go and buy postcards there.'

'What do you want postcards for?'

'To send to people.' She hesitated. Ever since that morning by Loch Morag, her conscience had been constantly troubled by the nagging awareness of Mrs Archer's anxiety and distress for Thomas. The opportunity to confide in Oliver had not, so far, presented itself, but now . . . She took a deep breath and went on with the bold determination of one intent upon striking while the iron is hot. 'We can send one to Thomas's grandmother.'

Oliver said nothing.

Victoria took no notice of this lack of response. 'Just a line. To let her know he's safe and sound.'

Oliver still said nothing. This was not a good sign. 'Surely it couldn't do any harm.' She could hear the pleading note in her own voice, and despised herself for it. 'A postcard, or a letter or *something*.'

'How you do bang on.'

'I'd like to send her a postcard.'

'We're not sending her a bloody thing.'

She could not believe that he could be so blinkered. 'But why be like that? I've been thinking . . .'

'Well, stop thinking. If you can come to no conclusion more intelligent than that one, then simply make your mind a blank.'

'But . . .'

'The whole point of coming away was to get away from the Archers. If I'd wanted them on my doorstep, hounding me with lawyer's letters and private detectives, I'd have stayed in London.'

'But if she *knew* where he was . . .'

'Oh, shut up.'

It was not so much what he said as the tone of voice that he used to say it. A silence grew between them. After a little,

Victoria turned her head and looked at him. His profile was stony, his lower lip jutted, his eyes narrowed, and staring straight at the road ahead. They had left the town behind them, and the car was picking up speed when they turned a corner and came, all at once, upon the signpost, pointing inland, to Benchoile and Loch Muie. Oliver was caught unawares. He braked abruptly, and swung the car around with a screech of tyres. They started up the single-track road, heading for the hills.

Unseeing, Victoria gazed ahead. She knew that Oliver was wrong, which was perhaps one of the reasons that he was being so stubborn. But Victoria could be stubborn, too. She said, 'You've already told me that she hasn't got a leg to stand on, legally. That she can't do anything to get Thomas back. He's your child, and your responsibility.'

Again, Oliver said nothing.

'So if you're so certain of yourself, there can be no reason not to let her know that he's all right.'

He still was silent, and Victoria played her final card. 'Well, you may not intend telling Mrs Archer that Thomas is safe and well, but there's nothing to stop me writing to her.'

Oliver spoke at last. 'If you do,' he said quietly. 'If you so much as pick up a telephone, I promise you, I'll batter you black and blue.'

He sounded as though he actually meant it. Victoria looked at him in astonishment, searching for some sign to put her mind at rest, to convince herself that this was simply Oliver, using words as his strongest weapon. But she found no reassurance. The coldness of his anger was devastating, and she found herself trembling as though he had already struck her. His stony features blurred as her eyes filled with sudden, ridiculous tears. She looked away, quickly, so that he should not notice them, and later, surreptitiously, wiped them away.

So it was that, with the sourness of the quarrel between them, and Victoria struggling not to cry, that they came to Benchoile.

Jock Dunbeath's funeral had been a big and important affair, as befitted a man of his position. The church was full and later the graveyard, crowded with sombrely clad men, from all walks of life, who had come – some many miles and from all directions – to pay their respects to an old and much-liked friend.

But the wake that followed was small. Only a few close colleagues made the journey to Benchoile, there to gather about the blazing fire in the library and to partake of Ellen's homemade shortbread, washed down with a dram or two of the best malt whisky.

One of these was Robert McKenzie, not only the family lawyer, but as well a lifetime friend of Jock Dunbeath. Robert had been Jock's best man when Jock married Lucy, and Jock was godfather to Robert's eldest boy. Robert had driven up that morning from Inverness, appeared in the church wearing his long black overcoat that made him look like one of the undertakers, and afterwards had acted as pallbearer.

Now, with his duties behind him, and a drink in his hand, he had become once more his usual brisk and businesslike self. In the middle of the proceedings, he drew Roddy aside.

'Roddy, if it's possible, I'd like a word with you sometime.'

Roddy sent him a keen glance, but the other man's long face was set in its usual professional lines, and gave nothing away. Roddy sighed. He had been expecting something like this, but scarcely so soon.

'Anytime, old boy. What do you want me to do, nip down to Inverness? Beginning of next week, maybe?'

'Later, perhaps that would be a good idea. But I'd rather have a moment or two now. I mean, when this is over. It won't take more than five minutes.'

'But of course. Stay and have a bit of lunch. It won't be more than soup and cheese, but you're more than welcome.'

'No, I won't do that. I have to get back. I've a meeting at three o'clock. But if I could just stay on after the others have gone?'

'Absolutely. No trouble at all . . . ' Roddy's eyes wandered away from the lawyer. He spied an empty glass in somebody's hand. 'My dear fellow, another dram for the road . . . '

It was not a gloomy gathering. Indeed, there were nothing but happy memories to recall, and soon there were smiles and even laughter. When the guests finally took themselves off, driving away in Range Rovers, or estate cars, or battered farm vans, Roddy stood outside the open front door of Benchoile and saw them on their way, feeling a little as though he were saying goodbye to the guns at the end of an enjoyable day's shoot.

The simile pleased him, because it was so exactly the way
that Jock would have liked it. The last car made its way down
through the rhododendrons, over the cattle grid, and out of
sight around the corner. Only Robert McKenzie's old Rover
remained.

Roddy went back indoors. Robert waited for him, standing
in front of the mantelpiece, with his back to the fire.

'That went very well, Roddy.'

'Thank God it didn't rain. Nothing worse than a funeral
in a downpour.' He had had only two whiskies. Robert still
had a bit in his glass, so Roddy poured himself another small
one. 'What was it you wanted to talk to me about?'

'Benchoile,' said Robert.

'Yes, I imagined it was that.'

'I don't know if Jock told you what he intended doing with
the place?'

'No. We never discussed it. There never seemed to be any
pressing need to discuss it.' Roddy considered this. 'As things
have turned out, perhaps we should have.'

'He never said anything about young John?'

'You mean Charlie's boy? Never a word. Why?'

'He's left Benchoile to John.'

Roddy was in the act of pouring water into his tumbler. A
little of it spilled on to the tray. He looked up. Across the
room his eyes met Robert's. Slowly he laid down the water
jug. He said, 'Good God.'

'You had no idea?'

'No idea at all.'

'I know Jock meant to talk it over with you. Had every
intention of doing so, in fact. Perhaps the opportunity never
came up.'

'We didn't see all that much of each other, you know. More
or less lived in the same house, but didn't see that much of
each other. Didn't really talk . . . ' Roddy's voice trailed off.
He was confused, confounded.

Robert said gently, 'Do you mind?'

'Mind?' Roddy's blue eyes widened in astonishment. 'Mind?
Of course I don't mind. Benchoile was never mine, the way
it was Jock's. I know nothing about the farm; I have nothing
to do with the house or the garden; I was never particularly
interested in the stalking or the grouse. I simply roost in her.
I'm the lodger.'

'Then you didn't expect you'd be taking over?' Robert

was considerably relieved. One could never imagine Roddy
Dunbeath being disagreeable about anything, but he might
well have been disappointed. Now, it appeared, he was not
even that.

'To tell you the truth, old boy, I never even thought of it.
Never thought of Jock dying. He always seemed such a tough
old thing, walking the hill, and bringing the sheep down with
Davey Guthrie, and even working in the garden.'

'But,' Robert reminded him, 'he had had a heart attack.'

'A very mild one. Nothing to worry about, the doctor said.
He seemed to be all right. Never complained. But then, of
course, Jock was never a man to complain . . . ' Once more
the sentence drifted to silence. Even for Roddy Dunbeath,
thought the lawyer, his thought processes seemed more than
usually vague.

'But Roddy, since Jock died, surely you must have wondered
what was going to happen to Benchoile?'

'To tell you the truth, old boy, I haven't had much time
for wondering. Hell of a lot to organise, you know, when
something like this happens. I've been waking up in a cold
sweat in the middle of the night, trying to remember what it
is I've forgotten to do.'

'But . . . '

Roddy began to smile. 'And of course, half the time I
haven't forgotten it at all.'

It was impossible. Robert abandoned Roddy's future, and
brought the discussion sharply back into line.

'About John, then. I've written to him, but I haven't yet
had a reply to my letter.'

'He's been in Bahrein. I had a cable from him. That's why
he wasn't here this morning.'

'I've invited him to come up and see me. The future of the
property will have to be discussed.'

'Yes, I suppose it will.' Roddy thought about this. He said,
with some conviction, 'He won't want to live here.'

'What makes you so certain?'

'Just that I can't imagine he would have the smallest interest
in the place.'

'Jock didn't seem to think that.'

'It was hard to know, sometimes, exactly what Jock was
thinking. I never thought he particularly liked Charlie's boy.
They were always so intensely polite to each other. It's not a
good sign, you know, when people are too polite. Besides,

John Dunbeath has a career of his own. He's a clever, cool, successful young man, wheeling and dealing and making a lot of money. Not that he needs to make a lot of money, because he's always had it through his mother. And that's another thing, he's an American.'

'Half American,' Robert permitted himself a smile. 'And I'd have thought you'd be the last man in the world to hold that against him.'

'I don't hold it against him. I have nothing against John Dunbeath. I mean that. He was an exceptional boy and extremely intelligent. But I don't see him as the laird of Benchoile. What would he do with himself? He's only twenty-eight.' The more Roddy thought about it, the more preposterous the idea became. 'I shouldn't think he knows one end of a sheep from the other.'

'It doesn't take much intelligence to learn.'

'But why *John*?' The two men looked at each other glumly. Roddy sighed. 'I know why of course. Because Jock had no children and I had no children and there wasn't anybody else.'

'What do you think will happen?'

'I suppose he'll sell it. It seems a pity, but for the life of me, I can't think what else he'd do with the place.'

'Let it? Come here for holidays?'

'A weekend cottage with fourteen bedrooms?'

'Well then, keep the farm in hand and sell the house?'

'He'd never get rid of the house unless he let the shooting and the stalking rights go with it, and Davey Guthrie needs that land for his sheep.'

'If he does sell Benchoile, what will you do?'

'That's the sixty-four thousand dollar question, isn't it? But I've lived here, on and off, all my life, and perhaps that's too long for any man to stay in one place. I shall move away. I shall move abroad. Somewhere distant.' Robert had visions of Roddy in Ibiza, wearing a panama hat. 'Like Creagan,' he finished, and Robert laughed.

'Well, I'm glad you know,' he said, and finished his drink and set down the empty glass. 'And I hope, between us all, we'll be able to sort it all out. I . . . I expect John will want to come here sooner or later. To Benchoile, I mean. Will that be all right?'

'Right as rain, old boy. Anytime. Tell him to give me a ring.'

They moved towards the door.

'I'll be in touch.'

'You do that. And Robert, thank you for today. And for everything.'

'I'll miss Jock.'

'We all will.'

He drove away, headed for Inverness and his three o'clock meeting, a busy man with much to think about. Roddy watched the Rover disappear, and then he was all alone, and he knew that now it was really over. And successfully over, which was so surprising. No small mishaps had occurred, and the funeral had passed in an orderly and soldierly fashion, just as if Jock had organised it himself, and not his singularly disorganised brother. Roddy drew a long sigh, part relief and part sadness. He looked up at the sky, hearing the chatter of greylags high above the clouds, but they stayed out of sight. A thin wind moved up the glen from the sea, and the slate grey surface of the water shivered beneath its touch.

Jock was dead and Benchoile now belonged to young John. So perhaps this day was not only the end of the beginning, but also, if John decided to sell it all, the beginning of the end. The idea would take some getting used to, but in Roddy's book, there was only one way to tackle such gargantuan problems, and that was as slowly as possible, a single step at a time. This meant no anticipation and no precipitant action. Life would move quietly on.

He looked at his watch. It was now half past twelve. His thoughts moved ahead to the remainder of the day, and he suddenly remembered the approaching car, and the young family coming to spend a few days at Benchoile. Oliver Dobbs and some female or other and their child. It occurred to Roddy that Oliver was the sort of man who would always have some female or other in tow.

They would be arriving at any moment, and the prospect lifted his spirits. The day was a sad one, but, thought Roddy, where God closes a window, he opens a door. What this old saying had to do with Oliver Dobbs, he couldn't be sure, but it helped one to realise that there could be no time for useless grieving, and Roddy found this comforting.

Thinking of comfort brought him sharply back to an awareness of the physical agony that he had endured all morning.

It was to do with his kilt. He had not worn this garment for two years or more, but for the laird's funeral, it had seemed appropriate to put it on. Accordingly, this morning he had taken it, reeking of camphor, from the cupboard, only to discover that he had put on so much weight that the kilt would scarcely go round him, and after struggling with it for five minutes or more, he had been forced to take himself over to the big house and enroll the aid of Ellen Tarbat.

He found her in the kitchen, dressed in the inky black that she kept for funerals, and with her gloomiest hat – and none of Ellen's hats were very cheerful – already skewered to her head by an immense jet-headed hat pin. Ellen's tears for Jock had been shed privately, decently, behind the closed door of her bedroom at the top of the house. Now, dry-eyed and tight-lipped, she was engaged in polishing the best tumblers before setting them out on the damask-covered table in the library. When Roddy appeared, clutching his kilt about him like a bathtowel, she said, 'I told you so,' as he had known she would, but she laid down the tea towel and came manfully to his aid, heaving her puny weight on the leather straps of the kilt, like a tiny groom trying to tighten the girth of some enormous, overfed horse.

Finally, by brute force, the pin of the buckle went into the last hole of the leather strap.

'There,' said Ellen triumphantly. She was quite red in the face, and a few stray white hairs had escaped from her bun.

Roddy held his breath. Now, he let it out cautiously. The kilt tightened across his belly like a pair of tightly laced stays, but the straps, miraculously, held.

'You've done it,' he told her.

Ellen tidied her hair. 'If you were to ask me, I'd say it was about time you went on a diet. Or else you'll need to take your kilt into Inverness and get the man to let it out. Otherwise you'll be giving yourself a seizure, and it's yourself we'll be burying next.'

Infuriated, Roddy strode from the kitchen. The kilt straps had held, somehow, all morning, but now, gratefully, he realised he need suffer no longer, and accordingly he made his way back to the Stable House, took off his finery and climbed into the most comfortable clothes he owned.

He was just shrugging himself into his old tweed jacket when he heard the approaching car. From his bedroom window, he saw the dark blue Volvo approaching up the drive between the rhododendrons and come to a halt at the edge of the grass in front of the house. Roddy gave a cursory glance in the mirror, smoothed down his ruffled hair with his hand,

and went out of the room. His old dog Barney hauled himself to his feet and followed. He had spent the morning shut up and alone, and was not going to risk being left behind again. The two of them emerged from the stable yard just as Oliver climbed out from behind the driving wheel of the car. He saw Roddy and slammed the car door shut behind him. Roddy went towards him, feet crunching over the gravel, his hand outstretched in welcome.

'Oliver!'

Oliver smiled. He looked just the same, Roddy thought, with some satisfaction. He did not like people to change. At the television dinner Oliver had worn a velvet jacket and a flamboyant tie. He was now in faded corduroys and a huge Norwegian sweater, but otherwise he seemed just the same. Same coppery hair, same beard, same smile.

Oliver came towards him, and they met in the middle of the gravel. The very sight of him, tall and young and handsome, gave Roddy new heart.

'Hello, Roddy.'

They shook hands, Roddy taking Oliver's hand in both his own, so pleased was he to see him.

'My dear fellow, how are you? How splendid you were able to make it. And right up to time, too. Did you have trouble finding us?'

'No trouble at all. We bought an Ordnance Survey map in Fort William and simply followed the red lines.' He looked about him, at the house, the slope of the lawn, the grey waters of the loch, the hills beyond. 'What a fantastic place.'

'Yes, it's lovely, isn't it?' Side by side they regarded the view. 'Not much of a day to see it on, though. I'll have to arrange some better weather for you.'

'We don't mind about the weather. However cold it is, all Victoria seems to want to do is sit on beaches.' This reminded Oliver of the other occupants of his car. He seemed to be about to do something about them, but Roddy stopped him.

'Look . . . just a minute, old boy. I think we should have a word first.' Oliver looked at him. Roddy scratched the back of his neck, searching for the right words. 'The thing is . . . ' But there seemed no way of getting around it, so he brought it straight out. 'My brother died at the beginning of the week. Jock Dunbeath. His funeral was this morning. In Creagan.'

Oliver was horrified. He stared at Roddy, taking this in, and then he said, 'Oh, God,' and there was everything in his voice; distress and sympathy and a sort of agonised embarrassment.

'My dear fellow, please don't feel badly about it. I wanted to tell you right away, so that you'd understand the situation.'

'We came through Creagan. We saw all the shutters down, but we didn't know the reason.'

'Well, you know how it is. People like to pay their respects in this part of the world, 'specially when it's a man like Jock.'

'I'm so dreadfully sorry. But, when did this happen?'

'Monday. About midday. Just about this time. He was out with the dogs and he had a heart attack. We found him in the lea of one of the dikes.'

'And you couldn't get in touch with me and tell us not to come, because you didn't know where I was. What a ghastly situation for you.'

'No, I didn't know where you were, but even if I had, I wouldn't have got in touch with you. I've been looking forward to seeing you, and I should have been most disappointed if you hadn't come.'

'We can't possibly stay.'

'Of course you can stay. My brother is dead, but the funeral is over, and life must go on. The only thing is, I'd originally planned that you should sleep in the big house. But it struck me that without Jock there, it might be a little depressing for you, so if you don't mind rather close quarters, you'll be staying in the Stable House with me. Ellen, Jock's housekeeper, and Jess Guthrie from the farm have made up the beds and lit the fires, so everything's ready for you.'

'Are you sure you wouldn't rather we just took ourselves off again?'

'My dear boy, it would make me miserable. I've been looking forward to a little young company. Don't get nearly enough of it these days . . .'

He glanced across at the car, and saw that the girl, perhaps tiring of sitting there while the two men talked, had got out of it, and now she and the little boy were making their way, hand in hand, down the slope of the grass towards the water's edge. She was dressed more or less as Oliver was dressed, in trousers and a thick sweater. She had tied a red and white cotton scarf around her head, and the red of the scarf was the same as the little boy's dungarees. In such a setting, they made a charming picture, investing the grey, brooding scene with colour and a certain innocence.

'Come and meet them,' said Oliver, and they began to walk slowly back towards the car.

'Just one thing more,' said Roddy. 'I'm taking it for granted that you're not married to this girl?'

'No, I'm not.' Oliver's expression was amused. 'Do you mind?'

The inference that Roddy Dunbeath's attitudes might well be out of date and out of touch made Roddy feel mildly indignant. 'Heavens, no. I don't mind in the very least. Anyway, it's nothing to do with me, it's your affair entirely. There is just one point, though. It would be much better if the people who work at Benchoile believe you to be married. It sounds old-fashioned, I know, but people are old-fashioned up here, and I wouldn't want to offend them. I'm sure you understand.'

'Yes, of course.'

'Ellen, the housekeeper, would probably have a heart attack and pass out on me if she knew the wicked truth, and God knows what would happen to Benchoile if that happened. She's been here forever, longer than most people can remember. She arrived in the first instance, fresh from some remote Highland croft, to look after my younger brother, and she's remained, immovable as a rock, ever since. You'll meet her, but don't expect a devoted, smiling, gentle old dear. Ellen is as tough as old boots and can be twice as unpleasant! So you see, it's quite important not to offend her.'

'Yes, of course.'

'Mr and Mrs Dobbs, then?'

'Mr and Mrs Dobbs,' Oliver agreed.

Victoria, with Thomas's fat hand held firmly in her own, stood by the reedy margins of Loch Muie and struggled with a terrible conviction that she had come to a place where she had no business to be.

It is better to travel hopefully than to arrive. Arrival, it seemed, had brought nothing but a sense of desolation and disappointment. This was Benchoile. But the Benchoile that Victoria had imagined was the Benchoile seen through the eyes of the ten-year-old boy that Roddy Dunbeath had been. *The Eagle Years* was a saga of summertime, of blue skies and long golden evenings and hills purple with heather. An idyll that bore no relation to this windswept and foreboding scene. It seemed to Victoria unrecognisable. Where was the little rowing boat? Where was the waterfall where Roddy and his brothers had picnicked? Where the children, running barefoot?

The answer was simple. Gone forever. Shut away between the covers of a book.

This now, was Benchoile. So much sky, so much space, so quiet. Only the sough of the wind in pine branches and the lap of grey water on the shingle. The size and the silence of the hills was unnerving. They enclosed the glen, rose sheer from the opposite shore of the loch. Victoria's eyes followed their slope, upwards, past great bastions of rock and scree, over swelling shoulders dark with heather, to distant summits veiled in the scudding grey sky. Their very size, their watchfulness, had an obliterating effect. She felt shrunk, dwarfed, insignificant as an ant. Incapable of dealing with anything, least of all the sudden deterioration of her relationship with Oliver.

She tried to call it a silly quarrel, but knew that it was more than that, a breach both bitter and unexpected. That it had blown up at all was Victoria's own fault. She should have kept quiet about sending the stupid postcard to Mrs Archer. But at the time it had seemed important, an issue worth fighting for. And now everything was spoiled, and not a word had either of them spoken since Oliver's last violent outburst. And perhaps that was Victoria's fault too. She should have stood up for herself, given threat for threat, and, if necessary, threatened blow for blow. Proved to Oliver that she had a will of her own instead of sitting mesmerised like a rabbit, and with her eyes so full of tears she couldn't even see the road ahead.

She felt overwhelmed. By the quarrel, by Benchoile, by a physical tiredness that made her ache, by the uncomfortable feeling that she had mislaid her own identity. Who am I? What am I doing in this outlandish place? How did I ever get here?

'Victoria.' She had not heard them approaching across the grass, and Oliver's voice startled her. 'Victoria, this is Roddy Dunbeath.'

She turned to face a man huge and shabby as a much-loved teddy bear. His clothes looked as though they had been thrown at him, his sparse grey hair blew in the wind, his features were lost in fat. But he was smiling at her. His blue eyes were warm with friendliness. Before them, Victoria's depression, her first fearful impressions of Benchoile, abated a little.

She said, 'Hello.' They shook hands. He looked down at Thomas. 'And who's this?'

'This is Tom.' She stooped and lifted him up to her shoulder. Tom's cheeks were intensely red, and he had mud on his mouth where he had been tasting pebbles.

'Hello, Tom. How old are you?'

'He's two,' Oliver told him, 'and you'll be delighted to hear that he scarcely ever utters a word.'

Roddy considered this. 'Well, he appears to be quite healthy, so I don't suppose you've got anything to worry about.' He looked back at Victoria. 'I'm afraid Benchoile isn't at its best today. There's too much cloud about.'

There was an old black Labrador at his heels. Thomas caught sight of him, and wriggled, wanting to be put down so that he could go and pat the dog. Victoria set him back on his feet, and he and the dog looked at each other. Then Thomas touched the soft, grizzled muzzle.

'What is he called?' asked Victoria.

'Barney. He's very old. Almost as old as I am.'

'I thought you'd probably have a dog.'

'Victoria,' Oliver explained, 'is one of your fans, Roddy.' He sounded quite cheerful and ordinary again, and Victoria wondered if the quarrel that had blown up that morning was, for the time being, forgotten.

'How splendid,' said Roddy. 'Nothing I like better than having a fan about the place.'

Victoria smiled. 'I was looking for the waterfall.'

'Even on a fine day you can't see it from here. It's hidden behind an outcrop. There's a little bay. Perhaps if the weather clears and I can find the key to the boathouse, we'll get over one day and you can see it for yourself.' A gust of wind, with a cutting edge like a knife, keened down upon them. Victoria shivered and Roddy was galvanised into hostly action. 'Now, come along, we'll all get pneumonia standing here. Let's get your cases out of the car and get you all settled in.'

Again, it was like nothing that Victoria had imagined. For Roddy led them, not into the big house, but through the archway into the stableyard, and so on to what was obviously his own little house. The bedrooms were on the ground floor. 'This is for you and Oliver,' said Roddy, going ahead of them like a well-trained hotel porter. 'And there's a dressing room off it, where I thought you could put the child; and here's the

bathroom. It's all pretty cramped I'm afraid, but I hope you'll
be comfortable.'

'I think it's perfect.' She set Tom down on the bed, and
looked about her. There was a window facing out over the
water, and a deep windowsill, upon which stood a little jug of
snowdrops. She wondered if it was Roddy who had put them
there.

'It's a funny sort of house,' he told her. 'The living room and
the kitchen are upstairs, but I like it that way. Now, when
you've unpacked and made yourselves comfortable, come up
and we'll have a drink and something to eat. Does Thomas
like soup?'

'He likes anything.'

Roddy looked suitably amazed. 'What an accommodating
child,' he remarked, and went off and left her.

Victoria sat on the edge of the bed, and lifted Thomas on to
her knee and began to divest him of his little jacket. And all
the time her eyes went around the room, loving it because it
was so right, whitewashed and simply furnished, and yet
containing all that any person could possibly need. It even
had a fireplace, built across one corner of the room, in which
a stack of peats was smouldering, and there was a basket containing more peat alongside the hearth, so that one could replenish it oneself, keep it going all night if need be. She thought
of going to sleep by firelight, and it seemed, all at once, the most
romantic thing in the world. Perhaps, she told herself cautiously, perhaps after all, everything was going to be all right.

Oliver appeared behind her, bearing the last of the suitcases.
He put this down and shut the door behind him.

'Oliver ...'

But, abruptly, he interrupted her. 'Something ghastly's
happened. Roddy's brother died at the beginning of the week.
That was his funeral in Creagan this morning. I mean, that's
why all the blinds were down.'

Victoria stared at him, over the top of Thomas's head, in
horrified disbelief. 'But why didn't he let us know?'

'He couldn't. He didn't know where we were. And anyway,
he swears he wanted us to come.'

'He's just saying that.'

'No, I don't think he is. In a way, I think we're probably
the best thing that could happen to him. You know, give him
something to think about. Anyway, we're here now. We can't
go away again.'

'But . . .'

'And there's another thing. We're Mr and Mrs Dobbs like in the hotel register. Apparently, there's a string of old retainers who'll all give notice if they know the terrible truth.' He began nosing around, opening cupboards and doors, like a great, long cat making itself at home. 'What a fantastic setup. Is this where Thomas is sleeping?'

'Yes. Oliver, perhaps we should only stay one night.'

'What do you mean? Don't you like it here?'

'I love it, but . . .'

He came to drop a kiss on her open, protesting mouth, and Victoria was silenced. The quarrel still lay between them. She wondered if the kiss was meant as an apology, or whether she was going to have to be the first to say she was sorry. But before she was able to make up her mind about this, one way or the other, he had kissed her again, patted Thomas on the head, and left them. She heard him running upstairs, heard his voice mingling with Roddy's. She sighed, and lifted Thomas off the bed and took him to the bathroom.

It was midnight and very dark. Roddy Dunbeath, steeped in brandy, had taken a torch and whistled up his dog, and gone the rounds of the big house, to make sure, he explained to Oliver, that the doors and windows were all securely closed, and that old Ellen, up in her attic bedroom, was safe for the night.

Oliver wondered, safe from what? They had been introduced, formally, to Ellen during the course of the evening, and she had seemed to him not only older than God but just as formidable. Victoria had long since gone to bed. Thomas was sleeping. Oliver lit the cigar that Roddy had given him and took it out of doors.

The silence that greeted him was immense. The wind had dropped and there was scarcely a sound. His footsteps crunched as he went across the gravel, and then fell silent when he reached the grass. He could feel its cold dampness through the soles of his shoes. He reached the loch and began to walk along the edge of the water. The air was icy. His light clothes – the velvet jacket and the silk shirt – were no protection, and the cold washed over his body like a freezing shower. He revelled in the shock of it and felt refreshed and stimulated.

His eyes grew accustomed to the darkness. Slowly, the

massive presence of the surrounding hills began to take shape. He saw the translucent shimmer of the loch. From the trees behind the house, an owl hooted. He came to the little jetty. Now, his footsteps sounded hollow on the wooden planking. At the end, he stopped, and threw the butt of the cigar into the water. It sizzled and then was dark.

The voices were there. The old woman. *It's not the way your father would have done it.* She had been living in his head for months, but she was Ellen Tarbat. And yet she was not Ellen from Sutherland. She was called Kate and she came from Yorkshire. *Your father didn't do things that way, not that way at all.* She was embittered, she was worn, she was indestructible. *He was always a man to pay his way. And proud. When I buried him, I did it with ham. Mrs Hackworth buried her man, but she's that mean, she did it with nobbut buns.*

She was Kate, but she was Ellen too. This was the way it happened. Past and present, fantasy and reality, all spun together like a steel rope, so that he did not know where one ended and the other began. And this thing inside him would begin to grow, like some tumour, until it took over altogether, and he would become possessed by it, and by the people who fought to get out of the inside of his head; to get down on paper.

And for weeks, perhaps months, he would exist in a shambling vacuum, incapable of anything except the most basic and essential of bodily functions; like sleeping, and ambling around the corner to the pub, and buying cigarettes.

The anticipation of this state filled him with trembling excitement. Despite the cold, he found that the palms of his hands were sweaty. He turned and looked back at the dim bulk of the house. A light burned in the attic, and he imagined old Ellen pottering about, putting her teeth into a tumbler, saying her prayers, getting into bed. He saw her, lying, staring at the ceiling, her nose sticking up over the edge of the sheet, waiting for the fitful sleep of old age.

There were other lights. From Roddy's sitting room, from behind drawn curtains. But the bedroom below it, where Victoria slept, was in darkness.

He made his way, slowly, back to the house.

She was asleep, but she woke when he came in and turned on the light by their bed. He sat beside her, and she turned over on the pillow and yawned, and saw who it was and said his name. She wore a nightdress of thin white lawn, edged with lace, and her pale hair spread on the pillow like strands of primrose-coloured silk.

He pulled off his tie and undid the top button of his shirt, and she said, 'Where have you been?'

'Out.'

'What time is it?'

He kicked off his shoes. 'Late.' He leaned across and took her head between his hands. Slowly, he began to kiss her.


He slept at last, but Victoria lay awake in his arms for an hour or more. The curtains were drawn back and the cold night air flowed in through the open window. In the hearth the peat fire burned steadily, and its flicker and glow were reflected in patterns of light on the low, white ceiling. The quarrel of the morning had been dissolved in love. Victoria was reassured. She lay there in the tranquil knowledge − as calming as a sedative − that nothing this perfect could possibly go wrong.

# CHAPTER 10

## FRIDAY

She was suddenly, intensely, wide awake, disoriented, with no idea where she was meant to be. She saw the wide window, and beyond it, the sky – pale, pristine, cloudless. The outline of the hills was sharp as glass, the topmost peaks touched by the first rays of the rising sun. Benchoile. Benchoile, possibly at its best. It looked as if it were going to be a beautiful day. Perhaps she could take Thomas to the beach.

Thomas. Thomas's grandmother. Mrs Archer. Today she was going to write to Mrs Archer.

Just like that, while she slept, her mind, perhaps realising that Victoria was capable of dithering about this problem, indefinitely, had apparently made itself up. The letter would be written this morning, posted at the earliest opportunity. She would find out the address by going to the post office in Creagan and asking for the relevant telephone directory. Woodbridge was in Hampshire. It was only a small place. There would not be many Archers living in such a small place.

The form of the letter began to frame itself. *I am writing to let you know that Thomas is well and very happy.*

And Thomas's father? Beside her Oliver slumbered soundlessly, his head turned away from her, his long arm stretched outside the covers, the palm of his hand turned up, the fingers curled and relaxed. Victoria raised herself on her elbow and looked down at his untroubled face. He seemed, in that moment, defenceless and vulnerable. He loved her. Love and fear could not share the same bed. She was not afraid of Oliver.

And anyway – cautiously she lay back on her pillows – Oliver
need never know. *Oliver did not want me to write to you,* she
would put, *so perhaps it would be better if you do not acknowledge this letter or try to get in touch.*

She could not think why this harmless deception had not
occurred to her before. Mrs Archer would understand. All
she would want was reassurance about her missing grandson.
And Victoria would promise, at the end of the letter, to write
again, to keep in touch. It would seem that it was going to be
quite a correspondence.

From the next room, from beyond the closed door, came
sounds of Thomas stirring. A strange sound, 'Meh, meh, meh,'
disturbed the morning quiet. Thomas, singing. She imagined
him sucking his thumb, thumping Piglet against the wall by
his bed. After a little the singing stopped, there were scuffling
sounds, the door opened and Thomas appeared.

Victoria pretended to be asleep, lay with her eyes closed.
Thomas climbed up on to the bed and lay on top of her,
forcing her eyelids open with a stubby thumb. She saw his
face, only inches from her own, the blue eyes alarmingly close,
his nose nearly touching her own.

She had not yet written to his grandmother, but today she
was going to, and the knowledge freed Victoria of guilt and
filled her with tenderness towards Thomas. She put her arms
around him and hugged him, and he laid his cheek on hers
and thoughtfully kicked her in the stomach. After a little,
when it became obvious that he was not going to be still for a
moment longer, she got out of bed. Oliver still slept, undisturbed. She took Thomas into his room and dressed him,
and then dressed herself. They left Oliver sleeping, and hand-
in-hand climbed the stairs to forage for breakfast.

The domestic arrangements at Benchoile appeared to be
fluid – the two establishments, the big house and the Stable
House, running, as it were, in harness. Yesterday they had
lunched on soup and cheese in Roddy's cheerful, littered living
room, eating off a table drawn up to the window, the meal as
informal as a picnic. Dinner, on the other hand, was a quite
different affair, served in the immense dining room of the big
house. By some unspoken agreement, they had all changed for
this occasion. Oliver had put on his velvet jacket, and Roddy
wore a straining doublet made of tartan, with a cummerbund
filling the gap between his shirt and the dark trousers, which
would no longer do up around his waist. A fire had burned in

the grate, there were candles in the silver candlesticks, and tall, dim portraits of varied Dunbeaths looked down upon them from the panelled walls. Victoria had wondered which was Jock, but didn't like to ask. There was something vaguely unnerving about the empty chair at the head of the table. She felt as though they were all intruding, as though they had walked into another man's house, without permission, and at any moment the owner was going to walk in and find them there.

But she, apparently, was the only one of them troubled by this uneasy guilt. Oliver and Roddy talked incessantly, of their world of writers, publishers, producers, about which Victoria knew nothing. The conversation flowed, well-oiled by an abundance of wine. And even the old woman, Ellen, had seemed to see nothing amiss in such good spirits on the very night of the laird's funeral. To and fro she trod in her worn-down shoes, her best apron over her black dress, handing the heavy ashets through the hatch that led to the kitchen, and taking away the used plates. Victoria had made signs that she would like to help, but Roddy had stopped her. 'Jess Guthrie's in the kitchen, giving Ellen a hand. She'll be mortally offended if you so much as rise from your chair,' he had told Victoria when Ellen was out of earshot, and so she had sat, against all her better instincts, and let herself be waited on with the others.

At one point during the course of the meal Ellen had taken herself off for ten minutes or more. When she returned with the coffee tray, she had announced, without preamble, that the wee boy was sleeping like an angel, and Victoria realised that she had made the journey down the long stone passages and across the stableyard, to check on Thomas, and was touched.

'I was just going to look at him myself,' she told Ellen, but Ellen's mouth had bunched up, as though Victoria had said something indecent. 'And why should you be getting up from your dinner, when there's me here to see to the child?' Victoria felt reprimanded.

Now, the following morning, she struggled with the inconsistencies of another person's kitchen, but, by the lengthy expedient of opening one door after another, she ran to earth eggs, bread, a jug of milk. Thomas was no help at all, and always seemed to be under her feet. She found suitable plates and mugs, knives and forks. Some butter and a jar of instant coffee. She laid the small plastic-topped table, set Thomas up on a chair, tied a tea towel around his neck, took the top off his egg. He settled down, silently, to demolish it.

Victoria made herself a cup of coffee and pulled up a chair to face him. She said, 'Would you like to go to the beach today?'

Thomas stopped eating and looked at her, the egg yolk running down his chin. She wiped it away. As she did this the door that led into the house from the stableyard opened and shut. Footsteps came slowly up the stairs. The next moment Ellen appeared at the open kitchen door.

'Good morning,' said Victoria.

'Yes, and you're up and about already. You're an early starter, Mrs Dobbs.'

'Thomas woke me.'

'I came over to see if you'd like me to give him his breakfast, but I see you've already seen to that yourself.'

Her manner was disconcerting, because you could never tell by her voice whether you were doing the right thing or not. And it was no help looking at her face, because her expression was one of constant disapproval, the faded eyes cold and beady and her mouth pursed as though someone had run a string around it and then pulled it tight. Her hair was thin and white, dragged back from her temples and screwed into a tight little bun. Beneath it her scalp gleamed pinkly. Her figure seemed to have shrunk with age, so that all her clothes – her ageless and seemly clothes – appeared to be a size too big. Only her hands were large and capable, red with scrubbing, the joints swollen and twisted like old tree roots. She stood with these folded across her stomach, over the flowered apron, and looked as though, in her long life, she had never once stopped working. Victoria wondered how old she was.

She said, tentatively, 'Perhaps you'd like a cup of coffee?'

'I never touch the stuff. It doesn't agree with me at all.'

'A cup of tea, then?'

'No, no. I've had my tea.'

'Well, why don't you sit down? Take the weight off your feet?'

For a moment, she thought that even this mild overture of friendliness was going to be rejected, but Ellen, perhaps seduced by Tom's unblinking stare, reached for a chair, and settled herself at the head of the table.

'Eat up your egg, then,' she said to Thomas, and then to Victoria, 'He's a beautiful child.' Her Highland voice turned this into, 'He's a peautiful chilt.'

'Are you fond of children?'

'Oh, yes, and there used to be so many of them at Benchoile, all over the place.' She had come, it was obvious, to see Thomas and have a gossip. Victoria waited, and inevitably the old voice rambled on. 'I came here to look after Charlie when he was a baby. Charlie was the youngest of the boys. I looked after the others as well, but I had Charlie all to myself. Charlie's in America now, you know. He married an American lady.' Casually, as though they could not help themselves, her hands went out to spread Thomas's toast with butter, to cut the toast into fingers for him.

Victoria said, 'I feel so badly, us arriving to stay so soon after . . . I mean, we didn't know, you see . . .'

She stopped, lost in confusion and wishing that she had never started, but Ellen was quite unperturbed.

'You mean, the laird dying so suddenly like that, and the funeral only yesterday?'

'Well, yes.'

'It was a beautiful funeral. All the grand people were there.'

'I'm sure.'

'Mind, he was a lonely man. He had no children of his own, you see. It was a great sorrow to Mrs Jock that she was never able to have any babies. "There you are Ellen," she used to say, "and there's the empty nursery upstairs, waiting for the babies, and it doesn't look as though there's going to be a single one." And, indeed, there wasn't.'

She put another finger of toast into Thomas's hand.

'What happened to her?'

'She died. Five years ago or more. She died. She was a beautiful lady. Always laughing.' She told Thomas, 'Yes, yes, you are eating a splendid breakfast.'

'Didn't your baby . . . didn't Charlie ever have any children?'

'Oh, yes, Charlie had a boy, and what a bright little lad he was. They used to come over for the summers, all three of them, and what good times those were. Picnics up the hill or on the beach at Creagan. "I've too much to do in the house to come for picnics." I used to tell him, but John would say, "But Ellen, you must come too, it'll not be a proper picnic without you." '

'He was called John?'

'Yes, he was named for the Colonel.'

'You must have missed him when he had to go back to America.'

'Oh, the place seemed empty after they had gone. Like a tomb.'

Victoria, watching Ellen, suddenly liked her very much. She stopped, feeling intimidated or even shy. She said, 'I knew a little bit about Benchoile before I got here yesterday, because I'd read all Roddy's books.'

'Those were the best times of all, when the boys were young. Before that war.'

'He must have been a funny little boy with all his strange pets.'

Ellen clicked her tongue and held up her hands in horror at the memory. 'I sometimes thought he'd be the death of me. Just a wee devil. He looked like an angel, mind, but you never knew what Roddy would be up to next. And when it came to washing his clothes, as likely as not the pockets would be filled with mealy worms.'

Victoria laughed. 'That reminds me,' she said, 'I wonder if there's somewhere I could do some washing. We've been travelling for four days and I haven't been able to wash anything, and soon we're all going to run out of clothes.'

'You can put them in the washing machine.'

'If I brought it all over to the big house after breakfast, perhaps you could show me where the washing machine is, and how to use it.'

'Now, you don't worry about that. I'll see to the washing. You don't want to spend your holiday doing washing. And ...' she added, with cunning innocence ' ... if you should want to be away on a wee outing with your husband, I could keep an eye on the child for you.'

She was obviously longing to get her hands on Thomas, to get him to herself. Victoria thought of the letter she was going to write. 'I ought to do some shopping, in that case. We seem to have run out of toothpaste, and Oliver's bound to want cigarettes. If I took our car to Creagan this morning, would you really look after Thomas for me? He doesn't like shopping very much.'

'And why should he like shopping? It's a dull occupation for a little man.' She leaned forward, nodding her head at Thomas as though already they had some sort of a conspiracy going between them. 'You'll stay with Ellen, won't you pet?

You'll help Ellen with the washing?'

Thomas stared at the small brown wrinkled face bobbing up and down so close to his own. Victoria watched for his reaction to this in some anxiety. It would be embarrassing if he screamed and hurt Ellen's feeling. But Thomas and Ellen recognised each other. They were years apart in age, but they both belonged to the same world. Thomas had finished his breakfast. He got off his chair and rescued Piglet from the floor by the refrigerator and took him to show Ellen.

She took the pig and bounced him up and down on the table as though he were dancing.

> Kitty Birdy had a pig
> She could do an Irish jig

sang Ellen in her cracked old voice. Thomas smiled. He laid his hand on her knee, and her own gnarled hand came down to close on the fat fingers.


It was amazing how simple, how straightforward, things became as soon as you had reached a decision. Problems ironed themselves out, difficulties dissolved. Ellen bore Thomas and the washing away, thus relieving Victoria, in a single stroke, of two of her most pressing commitments. Roddy and Oliver, probably sleeping off the brandy they had consumed the evening before, had still not appeared. Victoria, in search of writing paper, went into Roddy's living room and found the curtains still undrawn and the atmosphere thick with stale cigar smoke. She drew the curtains and opened the windows and emptied the ashtrays into the remains of last night's fire.

In the letter rack on Roddy's littered desk, she found writing paper both plain and headed. She hesitated for a moment, debating which to use. If she used the plain paper, and wrote no address, then Mrs Archer would still not know where to find them. But surely this smacked a little of secrecy, as though she and Oliver really had something to hide.

Besides, the headed paper, thickly embossed, had a certain opulence about it, which would in itself be reassuring. 'BENCHOILE, CREAGAN, SUTHERLAND.' She imagined Mrs Archer being impressed by the very simplicity of this. So she took a sheet of the headed paper, and found an envelope lined with dark blue tissue. She found, in a tarnished silver mug, a ball-point pen. It was as though some person had arranged it all, ready for her, making it even easier.

Dear Mrs Archer,

I am writing to let you know that Thomas is well and very
happy. Ever since we left London, he has been very good,
hardly cried at all, and has never woken up at nights. He is
eating well, too.

She paused, chewing the pen, debating whether she should
tell Mrs Archer that not once had Thomas asked for his
grandmother. She finally decided that this would not be tactful.

As you can see we are now in Scotland and the sun is
shining, so maybe we will be able to take Thomas to the
beach.

She paused again, and then went on to the final and most
tricky bit of all.

Oliver does not know I am writing to you. We did discuss it,
but he was very against the idea. So perhaps it would be
better if you do not acknowledge this letter or try to get in
touch. I will write later again and let you know how
Thomas is.

With best wishes,

Yours sincerely,

Victoria ... Victoria what? She was not Victoria Dobbs
and she no longer felt like Victoria Bradshaw. In the end she
wrote just her Christian name and left it at that. She put the
letter in its envelope and put the envelope into her cardigan
pocket. Downstairs, she crept into the bedroom and collected
her handbag with her money in the wallet. Oliver hadn't moved.
She let herself out again, and got into the Volvo, and drove
herself to Creagan.


Roddy Dunbeath, wearing a large blue-and-white striped
apron which made him look like a successful pork butcher,
stood at the counter in his little kitchen, chopped vegetables

for the lunchtime pot of soup, and tried, at the same time, to
disregard the fact that he was suffering from a hangover. At
twelve o'clock he was going to pour himself a sustaining,
medical horse's neck, but it was only now a quarter to twelve,
and so he was filling in the time – and so managing to resist
jumping the gun – with a little soothing culinary activity. He
liked cooking. Was, in fact, an excellent chef, and it made it
all the more enjoyable having a little house party to cook for
besides himself.

The house party in question, whether by private arrangement, or by chance, was happily living up to Benchoile traditions, and had taken itself off. By the time Roddy had prised
himself out of bed this morning, the girl Victoria and the child
had disappeared. Roddy was thankful for this. He had a horror
of visitors hanging about and looking bored, and he needed
peace and quiet in which to attend to his small domestic
duties.

But he went through to the big house to make a few polite
inquiries, and was told by Ellen that Victoria had taken the
Volvo and gone to Creagan. The little boy was with Ellen,
helping her to hang washing on the line, and playing with
the basket full of pegs.

Oliver, when he finally put in an appearance, seemed unperturbed by all this independent activity on the part of his
family. In fact, thought Roddy, if anything he appeared
relieved to be shed of them for an hour or two. Together, he
and Roddy had eaten an enormous breakfast, and together
had hatched a plan to drive, that afternoon, up to Wick.
There, a friend of Roddy's, tiring of the rat race in the south,
and the endless commuting, had started a small printing
business, specialising in limited editions of beautifully hand-
bound books. Roddy, interested in anything that smacked of
genuine craftsmanship, had been meaning for some time to go
and see the presses working, and to be shown around the
bindery, and Oliver, when the idea was put to him, was equally
enthusiastic.

'What about Victoria?' Roddy asked.

'Oh, she'll probably want to do something with Thomas.'

The telephone call to Wick was made, and the visit arranged.
Whereupon Oliver, after a bit of restless prowling, admitted
that he wanted to do some work, so Roddy lent him a scribbling
pad and sent him off to the library in the big house, where,
with a bit of luck, Oliver had spent the morning, undisturbed.

In the meantime Roddy, left to himself, had lit a roaring fire, written a couple of letters, and was now making soup. The air was filled with the crisp, sharp smell of celery, sunlight streamed through the window, Vivaldi burbled from his transistor. The telephone started to ring.

Roddy swore, and went on cutting celery, as though the telephone would somehow answer itself. But of course it didn't, so he laid down the knife and wiped his hands on a tea towel and went through to the living room.

'Roddy Dunbeath.'

'Roddy. It's John Dunbeath.'

Roddy sat down. Luckily there was a chair behind him. He could not have been more astonished. 'I thought you were in Bahrein.'

'No, I got back yesterday morning. Roddy I'm so dreadfully sorry about Jock. And that I couldn't make the funeral.'

'My dear boy, we quite understood. Good of you to send the cable. Where are you calling from? London? You sound as though you're in the next room.'

'No, I'm not in London. I'm in Inverness.'

'*Inverness?*' Roddy's thought processes, blunted by last night's cognac, were not working in what you would call top gear. 'How you do get around. When did you get to Inverness?'

'I caught the Highlander last night, I was here this morning. I've spent the morning with Robert McKenzie. He said it would be OK if I rang you ... if I came to Benchoile.'

'But of course. How *splendid*. Stay for a few days. Stay for the weekend. When can we expect you?'

'Well, this afternoon sometime. I'm hiring a car. Would it be all right if I came this afternoon?'

'Marvellous ... ' Roddy started to say, and then remembered the complications. He struck his forehead with the heel of his hand, a theatrical gesture of recall, totally wasted when there was no person to observe it. 'Oh, damn, except that I won't be here. I've arranged to go up to Wick. I've got a chap staying and we're going to go there and look at a printing press. But that doesn't matter. We'll be back sometime, and Ellen'll be here.'

'How is Ellen?'

'Indestructible. Puts us all in the shade. I'll tell her you're coming. I'll tell her to expect you.'

'I hope I'm not putting you out.'

Roddy remembered that he had always been an intensely

well-mannered person. 'Not putting us out at all.' He added, because there seemed no point in not doing so, 'Besides, it's your house now. You don't have to ask yourself to stay.'

There was a tiny silence. Then, 'Yes,' said John and he sounded thoughtful. 'Yes. That's one of the things I want to talk to you about. There's an awful lot to discuss.'

'We'll have a good old chin-wag after dinner,' Roddy promised him. 'Anyway, see you later. I'm really looking forward to it. It's been too long, John.'

'Yeah,' said John, suddenly sounding very American. 'I guess it's been too long.'


Victoria returned ten minutes or so later, just as Roddy had finished the soup, tidied the kitchen, and poured himself the longed-for brandy and ginger ale. He was sitting by the window, watching a flock of black-and-white shelduck which had settled down to feed by the edge of the loch, when he heard the sound of the returning car. A moment or so later the downstairs front door opened and shut.

He called, 'Victoria!'

'Hello,'

'I'm up here. All on my own. Come and join me.'

Obediently, she came running up the stairs, and saw him at the far end of the room, sitting in solitary state, with only Barney for company.

'Where is everybody?' she asked, coming over to join him.

'Oliver's in the big house, closeted in the library and working. And Thomas is still with Ellen.'

'Perhaps I should go and get him.'

'Don't be ridiculous. He's perfectly all right. Sit down. Have a drink.'

'No, I don't want a drink.' But she sat beside him, pulling off her scarf. He thought, all at once, how pretty she was. Yesterday, when he had first seen her, he had not thought her pretty at all. She had seemed to him both shy and colourless; dull, even. At dinner she had scarcely said a word, and Roddy had been hard put to understand what Oliver saw in her. But this morning, she was a different person. Shining eyes, pink cheeks, a mouth all smiles. Now, Roddy found himself wondering why Oliver didn't marry the girl. Perhaps it had something to do with her background. How old was she? Where had he met her? How long had they been together?

She looked ridiculously youthful to be the mother of a two-year-old boy, but then young people these days seemed to plunge into relationships when they were scarcely out of school, committing themselves to domesticity in a manner that the young Roddy would have found intensely frustrating. She had, he noticed, beautiful teeth.

He said, 'You're looking very bright eyed and bushy tailed. Something good must have happened in Creagan.'

'It's just that it's such a beautiful morning. You can see for miles, and everything's all sparkly and bright. I didn't mean to be so long. I only went to buy some toothpaste and cigarettes and things, but Ellen said she didn't mind looking after Thomas, and Creagan is so pretty, I just stayed there and looked around, and I went into the church, and into that house they call The Deanery, but it's a craft shop now.'

Her enthusiasm was endearing. 'Did you buy anything?'

'No, but I might go back and buy something. They've got beautiful Shetland sweaters. And then I went and looked at the beach. I can't wait to take Thomas. You'd have thought it would be cold, but it wasn't. The sun was quite warm.'

'I'm glad you had a good morning.'

'Yes.' She met his eyes, and some of the brightness went out of her face. 'I somehow didn't get the chance to say anything last night, but... Well, Oliver told me about your brother, and I was so sorry. I just feel so awful about us all being here.'

'You mustn't feel awful. You're good for me.'

'It's just something else for you to worry about. I've been feeling guilty all morning because I should have been helping you or Ellen, instead of simply abandoning Thomas.'

'Do you good to get away from Thomas for an hour or so.'

'Well, as a matter of fact, it was rather nice.' They smiled, in complete understanding. 'Did you say that Oliver was working?'

'That's what he said.'

Victoria made a little face. 'I didn't realise that he wanted to work.'

'Probably wants to get some idea down on paper before it goes out of his head.' He remembered the projected trip to Wick that afternoon and told her about it. 'We'll take you with us if you like, but Oliver thought you'd want to do something with Tom.'

'I'd rather stay here.'

'In that case, you can do something for me. There's a young man arriving some time during the afternoon. He's going to stay for a day or two. So if we're not back, perhaps you could look after him, pour the tea, generally make him welcome.'

'Yes of course. But where's he going to sleep? We seem to have filled your house.'

'He's going into the big house. I've already had a word with Ellen and she's alight with excitement; linen sheets on the bed, everything scoured and polished.'

'I'd have thought she already had enough to do without more visitors arriving.'

'Ah, but you see, this young man is Ellen's precious baby. In fact, he's my nephew John Dunbeath.'

Victoria stared at Roddy in astonishment. 'John Dunbeath. You mean your brother Charlie's boy? Ellen told me about him this morning at breakfast. But I thought he was in America.'

'No, he's not. In fact, he's just telephoned me from Inverness.'

'Ellen must be over the moon.'

'She is. Not just because he's coming to stay, but because John is the new laird of Benchoile. My brother Jock has left Benchoile to John.'

Victoria was confused. 'But I thought you were the new laird.'

'Heaven forbid.'

She smiled. 'But you'd be such a wonderful laird.'

'You're very kind, but I'd be a useless one. I'm too old, too set in my evil ways. Better a new young broom to sweep us all clean. When I told Ellen the news a gleam came into her beady eye, but whether it was a tear or a glitter of triumph I wouldn't be able to say.'

'Don't be horrid about her. I like her.'

'I like her too, but one day she'll drive me into a nuthouse.' He sighed and looked down at his empty glass. 'Are you *sure* you wouldn't like a drink?'

'Quite sure.'

'In that case, be a good girl and go and run Oliver and that little boy of yours to earth, and tell them lunch will be ready in about ten minutes.' He heaved himself off the window seat and went to throw more logs on to his dying fire. As usual they sparked violently, and as usual Roddy tramped the glowing embers to death on his long-suffering hearthrug.

Victoria went to do as he had asked. At the top of the stairs, she paused.

'Where did you say I'd find Oliver?'

'In the library.'

She left him, clattering down the open treads like an eager child. Alone, Roddy sighed again. He debated, and finally succumbed. He poured himself another drink, and took it through to the kitchen where he inspected his fragrant soup.


Victoria put her head around the door. 'Oliver.'

He was not writing. He sat at the desk in the window, with his arms hanging loose and his legs outstretched, but he was not actually writing.

'Oliver.'

He turned his head. It took a second or two for him to recognise her. Then his blank eyes came to life. He smiled, as though she had just woken him up. He put up a hand to rub the back of his neck.

'Hi.'

'It's lunchtime.'

She closed the door behind her. He held out a long arm and she went over to him, and he drew her close, burying his face in her thick sweater; nuzzling, like a child, into its warmth. Memories of last night filled her with sweetness. She laid her chin on the top of his head, and looked down at the desk and sheets of paper, covered with scribbles and doodles and Oliver's narrow, tight writing.

She said again, 'It's time for lunch.'

'It can't be. I've only been here five minutes.'

'Roddy says you've been here since breakfast.'

'Where did you get to?'

'Creagan.'

'What were you doing there?'

'Shopping.' He put her away from him, and looked up into her face. Coolly, Victoria met his eyes, and repeated herself. 'Shopping. I bought you cigarettes. I thought you'd soon be running out.'

'Marvellous girl.'

'And there's someone else coming to stay; arriving this afternoon.'

'Who's that?'

'John Dunbeath. Roddy's nephew.' She put on a spurious

Highland accent. 'The new young laird of Benchoile.'

'Good God,' said Oliver. 'It's like living in a novel by Walter Scott.'

She laughed. 'Do you want some lunch?'

'Yes.' He pushed the scribbling pad away from him, and stiffly, stood up. He stretched and yawned. 'But I want a drink first.'

'Roddy's longing for someone to have a drink with him.'

'Are you coming too?'

'I'll find Thomas first.' They moved towards the door. 'Ellen's had him all morning.'

'Bully for Ellen,' said Oliver.


John Dunbeath, driving the hired Ford, came through Eventon, and the road swung east. To his right lay the Cromarty Firth beneath the cloudless winter sky; blue as the Mediterranean and in all the extravagance of a flood tide. Beyond it, the peaceful hills of the Black Isle drew a skyline sharp as a razor in the clear, glittering light. Rich farmland swept down to the edge of the water, sheep grazed on the upper slopes, and scarlet tractors, minimised to toys by the distance, were out ploughing the rich dark earth.

The dazzling brightness of the day came as an unexpected bonus. John had left London cloaked in grey rain, and boarded the Highlander in a state of unrelieved exhaustion. Weary from forty-eight hours of ceaseless activity, suffering from jet lag, and still in a mild state of shock occasioned by Jock Dunbeath's unthought-of bequest, he had drunk two enormous whiskies, and fallen into a sleep so deep that the sleeping car attendant had had to come and shake him awake, and inform him that the train had actually arrived at Inverness Station five minutes before.

Now, on his way to Benchoile, and with nothing but necessarily unhappy news to impart to all who lived there, he could not get rid of the feeling that he was going on holiday.

Part of this was due to association of ideas. The further he got from London and the closer to Benchoile, the clearer and more vivid became the memories. He knew this road. The fact that he had not driven it for ten years did not seem to matter at all. He felt that it could have been yesterday, and the only thing amiss was the fact that his father was not beside him, cheerful with anticipation, and anxious for John not to miss a single familiar landmark.

The road forked. He left the Cromarty Firth behind him and climbed up and over Struie and down to the further magnificence of the Dornoch Firth. He saw the wooded slopes on the distant shore, and behind these the snow-capped ramparts of the hills of Sutherland. Far to the east lay the open sea, still and blue as a day in summer. He rolled down the window of the car and caught the smells, damp and evocative, of moss and peat, and the sharp tang of the sea wrack washed up on the shoreline far below him. The road sloped away, and the Ford idled its way down the smoothly cambered curves.

Forty minutes later, he was through Creagan. He began to slow down in anticipation of the turning to Benchoile. He came upon it and left the main road, and now all was familiar in quite a different way. For he was back on Benchoile land. Here was the path that he had taken one grey day with his father and Davey Guthrie, that led over the distant summit of the hill and down into the desolate glen of Loch Feosaig. There they had fished, and late in the evening, Jock had driven around by the road to collect them and bring them home.

Below him purled the river, and he passed the spot where he had once stood for two hours or more, fighting a salmon. The first line of grouse butts swung into view; the Guthries' farmhouse. The trodden garden was cheerfully bannered with washing, and the tethered sheepdogs raged at the passing car.

He rounded the final bend of the road. Before him lay the long sweep of Loch Muie, and at the end of it, slumbering, solitary in the late afternoon sunshine, the old grey house.

This was the worst of all, but his heart was hardened and his mind made up. *I shall sell it,* he had told Robert McKenzie this morning, because, from the moment he had read the lawyer's letter, he had known that there was nothing else that he could possibly do.

Whether she had been watching for the car or not, John had no idea, but Ellen Tarbat appeared almost instantly. He had only time to open the boot of the Ford and take out his suitcase before she was there, coming out of the front door, down the steps towards him. A little tottery about the legs, smaller than he remembered her, strands of white hair escaping from her bun, her red, knotted old hands flung wide in welcome.

'Well, well, and you are here. And what a delight to see you again after all these years.'

He laid down his suitcase and went to embrace her. He had to bend almost double to receive her kiss and her frailness, her lack of substance, were unnerving. He felt that he should urge her indoors before she was caught up by a breath of wind and blown away. And yet she had pounced on his suitcase and had started to try to lug it indoors before he could stop her, and he had to forcibly wrest it from her grasp before she would let it go.

'What do you think you're doing? I'll carry that.'

'Well, let's get in, away from the cold.'

She led the way back up the steps and into the house, and he followed her and she closed the big doors carefully behind her. He walked into the big hall and was assailed by a smell made up of peat smoke and pipe smoke and floor polish and leather. Blindfolded, or drunk, or dying, he would have known by that smell that he was back at Benchoile.

'And did you have a good journey? What a surprise when Roddy told me this morning that you were coming. I thought you were away with all those Arabs.'

'Where's Roddy?'

'He and Mr Dobbs have gone to Wick. But he'll be back this evening.'

'Is he all right?'

'He seems to be bearing up very well. It was a terrible thing your uncle dying, and such a shock to us all . . . ' She had begun to lead the way upstairs, very slowly, one hand on the bannister. ' . . . but I had a premonition. When he did not come in for his lunch, I was certain that something had happened. As, indeed, it had.'

'Perhaps it was a good way for him to go.'

'Yes, yes, you are right. Out on a walk, with his dogs. Enjoying himself. But it is a terrible thing for the folk who are left behind.'

She had reached the turn of the stair. She paused, to sigh, to draw fresh breath for the next flight. John shifted his suitcase from one hand to the other. They went on up.

'And now you have come to Benchoile. We wondered, Jess and I, what would happen with the colonel dying so suddenly, but it didn't seem very fitting to start inquiring. So when Roddy came to tell me this morning, you can imagine my delight. "Why," I said to him, "that is the right person for

Benchoile. Charlie's boy! There was never anybody like Charlie." '

He did not want to continue this line of conversation. He changed the subject firmly. 'And how about yourself, Ellen? How have you been keeping?'

'I am not getting any younger, but I manage to keep busy.'

Knowing the size of the house, he wondered how she would manage to do anything else. They had now, at last, reached the landing. John wondered where he was sleeping. He had a ghastly suspicion that Ellen might have put him in his uncle's bedroom; it was just the sort of horror she would be capable of springing on him, and he was thankful when she led him towards the best spare bedroom where, before, his father had stayed. She opened the door to a flood of sunlight and a gust of cold, fresh air. 'Oh,' said Ellen, and went to close the windows, and John, following her into the room, saw the high, wide beds with their white starched cotton covers, the dressing table with the curly framed mirror, the velvet-covered chaise-longue. Even the blast of fresh air could not dispel the smell of polish and carbolic. Ellen, it was obvious, had been busy.

'You won't find anything changed.' Having closed the windows Ellen pottered about, straightening a starched linen mat, opening the immense wardrobe to check on coat hangers, and letting out a wave of camphor. John laid down his suitcase on the luggage rack at the foot of one of the beds, and went to the window. The sun was beginning to slip out of the sky and a rosy flush stained the hilltops. The mown grass of the lawn spread as far as a shrubbery, and beyond this to a copse of silver birch, and as he stood there, two figures appeared through these trees, making their way slowly towards the house. A girl, and a little boy. Behind them, looking more exhausted than they, an old black Labrador. 'And the bathroom's just through that door, I've put clean towels out, and . . .'

'Ellen. Who's that?'

Ellen joined him at the window, peering with her old eyes.

'That is Mrs Dobbs and her little boy Thomas. The family is staying with Roddy.'

They had emerged from the trees and were now out in the open. The child, tagging behind his mother, suddenly spied the water, and began to make for the loch's edge. The girl hesitated, and then resignedly, followed him.

'I thought that you and she could have tea together in the library, and Thomas can have his tea with me.' She went on, tempting him, 'There's a batch of scones in the oven and heather honey on the tray.' When John neither spoke, nor turned from the window, Ellen was a little put-out. After all, she had opened the heather honey specially for him. 'I've put towels on the rail, so that you can wash your hands,' she reminded him, with some asperity.

'Yes. Sure.' He sounded abstracted. Ellen left him. He heard her slow descent of the staircase. The girl and the child seemed to be having a small argument. Finally, she stopped and picked him up and started to carry him up towards the house.

John left the window and went out of the room and downstairs, and out of the front door. They saw him at once, and the girl, perhaps startled by his sudden appearance, stood still. He crossed the gravel and started down the slope of the lawn. He could not tell the exact moment of her recognition. He only knew that he had recognised her instantly, as soon as she appeared through the trees.

She wore jeans and a brilliant green sweater with suede patches on the shoulders. Her face, and the child's face, so close, observed his approach. The two pairs of wide blue eyes were ridiculously alike. There were freckles on her nose that had not been there before.

Mrs Dobbs. With, doubtless, the child who had been making such a hullaballoo the night John drove her home. Mrs Dobbs.

He said, 'Hello, Victoria.'

She said, 'Hello.'


Now, there were four of them around the dinner table, and the empty chair at its head was no longer empty.

Victoria wore a caftan of soft blue wool, the neck and the edges of the sleeves threaded with gold. She had, for the evening, put up her hair, but the arrangement seemed to John Dunbeath to have been ineptly contrived. It trailed one or two pale strands of hair, and served, instead of making her look sophisticated, only to enhance her air of extreme youth. The exposed back of her long neck seemed, all at once, as vulnerable as a child's. Her eyes were darkened, her beautiful mouth very pale. The shut-away, secret expression was still there. For some reason, this pleased John. It came with some satisfaction to realise that if he had not been able to break down the barrier, then neither had Oliver Dobbs.

'They're not married,' Roddy had told him over a drink

before dinner, when they were waiting for the Dobbses to appear. 'Don't ask me why. She seems a charming little thing.'

'Charming, and reserved. Perhaps in bed, in love, those defences came down. His eyes moved from Victoria to Oliver, and he was annoyed to discover that from these pretty images his instincts shied like a nervous horse. Firmly, he brought his attention back to what Roddy was saying.

'... the great thing is to keep investing capital in the land. Not only money, but resources and time. The aim is to make one good blade of grass grow where nothing grew before; to keep up employment for the local people; to stop the endless drift of the country population to the big cities.'

This was Roddy Dunbeath, revealing a totally unexpected side to his character. Victoria, helping herself to an orange from the bowl in the middle of the table, wondered how many people had heard him expound thus on a subject that was obviously close to his heart. For he spoke with the authority of a man who had lived in Scotland all his life, who recognised its problems, and was prepared to argue to the hilt against any easy solution that he believed to be inadequate or impractical. People seemed to lie at the root of it all. Everything came back to people. Without people there could be no sort of community. Without communities there could be no sort of future, no sort of life.

'How about forestry?' asked John Dunbeath.

'It depends how you go about it. James Dochart, who farms Glen Tolsta, planted a stretch of hill with woodland, maybe four hundred acres ...'

She began to peel the orange. He had been at Benchoile for about five hours. She had had five hours in which to get over the shock of his sudden appearance, but she still felt bewildered. That the young American she had met in London, and John Dunbeath, nephew to Roddy and only son of Ellen's beloved Charlie, should be one and the same person, still seemed impossible, unacceptable.

He sat now, at the end of the softly candle-lit table, relaxed and attentive, his eyes on Roddy, his expression sombre. He wore a dark suit and a very white shirt. His hand, on the table, slowly turned his glass of port. The candlelight gleamed on the heavy gold of his signet ring.

'... but he did it in a way that meant those four hundred acres still support some cows and four hundred sheep, and his lambing has improved. But forestry, the way the state goes about it, is no answer to the hill-farmer's problem. A solid mass of sitka spruce, and you're left with a three per cent return on capital and another shepherd out of a job.'

Mrs Dobbs. She wondered if Roddy had told him that she wasn't married to Oliver, or whether he had guessed this for himself. Either way, he seemed to take it for granted that Thomas was her child. She told herself that this was a good thing. She and Oliver had come beyond justifications and explanations. This was the way she wanted it to be. She had wanted to belong to somebody, to be needed, and now she belonged to Oliver and she was needed by Tom. She began to break the orange into segments. Juice dripped over her fingers, and on to the delicately trellised Meissen plate.

'How about the tourist industry?' John was asking. 'Highlands and Islands.'

'Tourism is very tempting, very nice, but it's also dangerous. There is nothing more dismal than a community depending on tourists. You can convert holiday cottages, you can build log-cabin chalets, you can even open your house to summer visitors, but given one bad summer and the wet and the cold frighten the ordinary family man away. All right, if he's a fisherman or a hill walker or a bird watcher, he probably won't object to a bit of rain. But a woman with three children, trapped in a small cottage for a long, wet fortnight, is going to insist on being taken to Torremolinos next summer. No, any population must have jobs for men, and it's their jobs that are being lost.'

Oliver sighed. He had had two glasses of port and he was becoming sleepy. He listened to the conversation, not because it was of much interest to him, but because he found himself fascinated by John Dunbeath. The epitome, one would have thought, of the quiet, well-bred, Down-Easter, with his Brooks Brothers shirt, and elusive mid-Atlantic accent. As he talked, Oliver observed him covertly. What made him tick? What were the motivations behind that polite, reserved facade? And what – most intriguing of all – did he think about Victoria?

That they had already met in London, he knew. Victoria herself had told him this evening, while Oliver soaked in a bath, and she brushed her hair, and they talked through the open door.

'So extraordinary,' she had said, in her lightest and most casual of voices. He knew that voice. It was Victoria's keep-out sign, and always aroused his avid curiosity. 'He was the

man who brought me home from the party that evening. Do
you remember? When Tom was crying.'

'You mean John Hackenbacker of Consolidated Aloomi-
num? Well, I never did. How extraordinary.' This was
fascinating. He mulled it over, squeezing spongefuls of peat-
brown water over his chest. 'What did he say when he saw
you again?'

'Nothing really. We had tea together.'

'I thought he was flying off to Bahrein.'

'He was. He's flown back again.'

'What a little bird of passage he is. What does he do when
he's not flying hither and yon?'

'I think he's in banking.'

'Well, why isn't he in London, where he should be, cashing
people's cheques?'

'Oliver, he's not that sort of a banker. And he's got a few
days leave to try and sort out his uncle's estate.'

'And how does he feel about being the new young laird of
Benchoile?'

'I didn't ask him.' She sounded cool. He knew he was
annoying her, and went on with his teasing.

'Perhaps he fancies himself in a kilt. Americans always
adore dressing themselves up.'

'That's a stupid generalisation.'

There was now a definite edge to her voice. She was, Oliver,
realised, sticking up for the new arrival. He got out of the bath
and wrapped a towel around himself and came through to the
bedroom. Victoria's anxious blue eyes met his through her
mirror.

'That's a very long word for you to use.'

'Well, he's not that sort of an American at all.'

'What sort of an American is he?'

'Oh, I don't know.' She laid down her comb and picked up
her mascara brush. 'I don't know anything about him.'

'I do.' Oliver told her. 'I went and talked to Ellen while
she was bathing Tom. Get on the right side of her, and she's a
mine of the most delicious morsels of gossip. It seems that
John Dunbeath's father married a veritable heiress. And now
he's been landed with Benchoile. To him who has shall be
given. He's obviously been walking about with a silver spoon
sticking out of his mouth since the day he was born.' Still
wrapped in the bath towel, he began to prowl around the
bedroom, leaving wet footmarks on the carpet.

She said, 'What are you looking for?'
'Cigarettes.'

To he who has shall be given. Roddy had given Oliver a cigar.
He leaned back in his chair, and through its smoke, through
narrowed eyes, he watched John Dunbeath. He saw the dark
eyes, the heavy, tanned features, the closely cut pelt of black
hair. He looked, Oliver decided, like a tremendously wealthy
young Arab, who had just climbed out of his djellabah and
into a Western suit. The malice of the simile pleased him.
He smiled. John looked up at that moment and saw Oliver
smiling at him, but although there was no antagonism in his
face, he did not smile back.
'What about the oil?' he said.
'The oil, the oil.' Roddy sounded like Henry Irving intoning
'The bells, the bells!'
'Do you reckon it belongs to Scotland?'
'The nationalists think so.'
'How about the private millions that British and American
companies have invested before the oil could be discovered?
If it hadn't been for that, the oil would still be under the
North Sea, and nobody would know about it.'
'They say this is what happened in the Middle East . . .'
Their voices faded to a soft murmur. Their words became
indistinguishable. The other voices moved in, the real voices.
Now the girl was there, sullen and pushy.
*And where do you think you're going?*
*I'm going to London. I'm going to get a job.*
*What's wrong with Penistone? What's wrong with getting a
job in Huddersfield?*
*Oh, Mum, not that sort of job. I'm going to be a model.*
*A model. Tarting up and down some street with no knickers
on, more like.*
*It's my life.*
*And where are you going to live?*
*I'll find somewhere. I've got friends.*
*You move in with that Ben Lowry, and I'm finished with
you. I tell you straight, I'm finished . . .*
' . . . soon there won't be any real craftsmen left. And I mean
real ones, not the wierdos who come from God knows where
and set themselves up in windswept sheds to print silk scarves
that no one in their right minds would ever buy. Or to weave

tweed that looks like dishcloths. I'm talking about the traditional craftsmen. Kiltmakers and silversmiths, being seduced away by the big money to be earned in the rigs and the refineries. Now, take this man we went to see today. He's got a good business going. He started with two men, and now he's employing ten, and half of them are under twenty.'

'What about his markets?'

'This is it. He'd already contacted his market outlets before he came north.' Roddy turned to Oliver. 'Who was that publisher he worked for before – when he was in London? He told us the name, but I can't remember it.'

'Umm?' Oliver was dragged back into the conversation. 'Sorry, I wasn't really paying attention. The publisher? Hackett and Hansom, wasn't it?'

'Yes, that's it, Hackett and Hansom. You see . . .'

But then Roddy stopped, suddenly aware that he had been holding forth for far too long. He turned to Victoria to apologise, but at this instant, to her obvious horror, she lost herself in an enormous yawn. Everybody laughed, and she was covered in confusion.

'I'm not really bored, I'm just sleepy.'

'And no wonder. We're behaving abominably. I am sorry. We should have saved it for later.'

'It's all right.'

But the damage was done. Victoria's yawn had broken up and ended the discussion. The candles were burning down and the fire was nearly out, and Roddy looked at his watch and realised that it was half past ten. 'Good heavens, is that the time?' He put on an impeccable Edinburgh accent. 'How it flies, Mrs Wishart, when you're enjoying yourself.'

Victoria smiled. 'It's the fresh air,' she said, 'that makes you sleepy. Not the lateness of the hour.'

Oliver said, 'We're not used to it.' He leaned back in his chair and stretched.

'What are you going to do tomorrow?' Roddy asked. 'What are we all going to do tomorrow? You can choose, Victoria. What would you like to do? It's going to be a good day, if we can rely on the weather forecast. How about the waterfall. Shall we take a picnic over to the waterfall? Or has anybody got a better suggestion?'

Nobody had. Pleased with his notion, Roddy enlarged on the plan. 'We'll take the boat across if I can find the key to the boathouse. Thomas would like a boat trip, wouldn't he?

And Ellen will pack us a nose-bag. And when we get over there we'll light a fire to keep us warm.'

This seemed to meet with everybody's approval, and on this note, the evening began to come to an end. Oliver finished his port, stubbed out his cigar, and stood up.

'Perhaps,' he said, mildly, 'I should take Victoria off to bed.'

This suggestion was made to the company in general, but as he said it, he looked at John. John's face remained impassive. Victoria pushed back her chair, and he got to his feet and came around the table to hold it for her.

She said, 'Good night, Roddy' and came to kiss him.

'Good night.'

'Good night John.' She did not kiss John. Oliver went to open the door for her. As she went through it he turned back to the dusky room, and said with his most charming smile, 'See you in the morning.'

'See you,' said John.

The door closed. Roddy threw more peat on the fire, stirred it to life. Then he and John drew chairs up to its warmth and resumed their discussion.

## CHAPTER 11

## SATURDAY

The weather forecasters had been only partially correct. The sun indeed was shining, but intermittent clouds blew across its face, driven by a western wind, and the very air had a liquidity about it, so that hills, water, sky, all looked as though they had been painted by a huge sodden brush.

The house and the garden were sheltered by the curve of the hills, and only the smallest breeze had shaken the trees as they waited to embark themselves and an immense amount of equipment into the old fishing boat, but they had no sooner moved forty yards or so from the shore, when the true force of the wind made itself felt. The surface of the beer-brown water was flurried and driven with quite large waves, foam-crested and splashing over the gunwales. The occupants of the boat huddled into the various waterproof garments that had been gleaned from the Benchoile gunroom and handed around at the start of the voyage. Victoria wore an olive drab oilskin with enormous toggle-fastened poacher's pockets, and Thomas had been wrapped in a shooting jacket of immense antiquity, lavishly stained with the blood of some long-defunct bird or hare. This garment restricted him considerably, and Victoria was thankful for this, because it made the task of holding him still less difficult, his one idea apparently being to cast himself bodily overboard.

John Dunbeath, without any spoken agreement, had taken the oars. They were long and heavy, and the sound of creaking rowlocks, the faint piping of the wind, and the splash of break-ing waves against the side of the boat were the only sounds. He wore a black oilskin that had once belonged to his uncle

Jock, and a pair of green shooting boots, but his head was bare, and his face wet with spray. He rowed expertly, powerfully, the swing of his body driving the prow of the balky old boat through the water. Once or twice he slipped his oars in order to look over his shoulder and judge how far the wind and the run of the water were carrying them off course, and to get his bearings. He looked very much at home, at ease. But then he had done this thing, and come this way, many times before.

Amidships, on the centre thwart, sat Roddy and Oliver. Roddy with his back to Victoria, and with his dog Barney secure between his knees; Oliver astride the thwart, leaning back with his elbows propped on the gunwale. Both men had their eyes on the approaching shore, Roddy scanning the hillside through his binoculars. From where she sat, Victoria could see only the outline of Oliver's forehead and chin. He had turned up the collar of his jacket, and his long legs, straddled in their faded jeans, ended in a pair of aged sneakers. The wind caught his hair and blew it back from his face, and the skin, fine-drawn over his cheekbones, was burned russet with the wind.

In the bottom of the boat, pools of water, inevitably, slopped. Every now and then, when he thought about it, Roddy would lower his binoculars on their leather strap and bail absent-mindedly, dipping the water up with an old tin bowl and emptying it overboard. It didn't seem to make much difference. Anyway, the picnic baskets, the box of kindling, the bundles of tarpaulins and rugs had all been stowed with care, out of reach of the puddles. There seemed to be enough food to feed an army, and various vacuum flasks and bottles had a special basket to themselves, with divisions, so that they did not bang together and break.

Roddy, having finished with a little bit of bailing, took up his binoculars again, and began to cover the hill.

'What are you looking for?' Oliver asked.

'Deer. It's amazing how hard they are to see on a hill face. Last week when we had the snow you could pick them out from the house, but there don't seem to be any about today.'

'Where will they be?'

'Over the hill, probably.'

'Do you get a lot here?'

'Sometimes as many as five hundred. Deer and does. In cold weather they come down and eat the fodder we put out for the cattle. In the summer they bring their young down, after dark, to graze in the pastures and drink from the loch. You can drive up the old cattle road from the foot of the loch. Keep the headlights of the car turned off, and you take them unawares. Then turn the lights on to them, and it's a beautiful sight.'

'Do you shoot them?' Oliver asked.

'No. Our neighbour over the hill has the stalking rights. Jock let them to him. However, the deep freeze at Benchoile is full of haunches of venison. You should get Ellen busy on it before you take yourselves off again. It can be dry and tough, but Ellen's a way with venison. It's delicious.' He lifted the leather strap over his head and handed the binoculars to Oliver. 'Here, you have a look, see if you can spot anything with your young eyes.'

Now, in the magical way that such things come about, the other shore, their destination, drew nearer and began to reveal its secrets. No longer was it a landscape blurred by distance, but a place of rocky outcrops, emerald green swards, white pebble beaches. Bracken, dense as fur, coated the lower slopes of the hill. Higher up, this gave way to heather and the occasional lonely Scots pine. The distant skyline was edged by the uneven outline of a drystone dike, the march wall between Benchoile land and the neighbouring property. In places this dike had broken, leaving a gap like a missing tooth.

But there was still no sign of the waterfall. Holding Thomas in the circle of her arms, Victoria leaned forward, meaning to ask Roddy about this, but at that moment the boat swept past a great promontory of rock, and the little bay was revealed before them.

She saw the white shingle beach, and purling down the hillside, the burn, tumbling and twisting through heather and bracken, until, twenty feet or so above the beach, it leaped out over a ledge of granite and spouted down into the pool at its base. White as a mare's tail, dancing in the sunlight, fringed with rushes and moss and fern, it lived up to all Victoria's expectations.

Roddy turned to smile at her face of open-mouthed delight.

'There you are,' he told her. 'Isn't that what you came all this way to see?'

Thomas, as excited as she was, lurched forward and escaped from her hold. Before she could catch him, he had stumbled, lost his balance, and fallen forward against his father's knee.

'Look!' It was one of his few words. He banged Oliver's leg with his fist. 'Look!'

But Oliver was still engrossed with Roddy's binoculars, and either did not notice Thomas, or else paid no attention. Thomas said, 'Look,' again, but in the throes of trying to get his father to listen to him, he slipped and fell, bumping his head on the thwart and finishing up in the bottom of the boat, sitting in three inches of icy water.

He began, not unnaturally, to cry, and the first wail was out before Victoria, scrambling forward, could rescue him. As she picked him up, and lifted him back into her arms, she looked up and saw the expression on John Dunbeath's face. He was not looking at her, he was looking at Oliver. He was looking as though, quite happily, he could have punched Oliver in the nose.


The keel ground up on to the shingle: John shipped his oars and climbed overboard, and heaved the prow of the boat up on to the dry beach. One by one they alighted. Thomas was carried to safety by Roddy. Oliver took the forward painter and tied it up to a large, concrete-embedded spike, which was, perhaps, for this very purpose. Victoria handed out picnic baskets and the rugs to John, and finally, herself jumped ashore. The shingle of the beach crunched beneath the soles of her shoes. The sound of the waterfall filled her ears.

There seemed to be a strict protocol for Benchoile picnics. Roddy and Barney led the way up the beach, and the others followed, a straggling, laden procession. Between the waterfall pool and the tumbledown walls of the ruined croft was a sward of grass, and here they set up camp. There was a traditional fireplace, a ring of blackened stones and charred wood bearing witness to previous picnics, and it was very sheltered, although high above, the clouds still raced. The midday sun blinked in and out, but when it shone, it shed a real warmth, and the dark waters of the loch took on the blue of the sky and danced with sun pennies.

The group shed their bulky waterproofs. Thomas set off by himself to explore the beach. John Dunbeath took up a stick and began to scrape together the ashes in the fireplace. From the drink basket Roddy took two bottles of wine, and stood them at the edge of the pool, to cool. Oliver lit a cigarette. Roddy, his wine safely dealt with, stopped to watch a pair of

birds, twittering and anxious, circling a rock ledge at the edge
of the waterfall.

'What are they?' asked Victoria.

'Dippers. Water ouzels. It's early for them to be nesting.' He
began to climb the steep bank in order to investigate this.
Oliver, with the binoculars still dangling around his neck,
watched for a moment, and then followed him. John was
already searching for kindling for the fire, gathering handfuls
of dry grass and charred heather stalks. Victoria was about
to offer her help, when she spied Thomas, heading for the loch
and the pretty waves. She ran after him, jumping down on to
the beach, and catching him up, just in time, into her arms.

'Thomas!' She held him close and laughed into his neck.
'You can't go into the water.'

She tickled him and he chuckled, and then arched his back
protesting and frustrated. 'Wet!' he shouted into her face.

'You're wet already. Come along, we'll find something else
to do.'

She turned and carried him back up the beach, to where the
pool overflowed to a shallow stream that ran over the pebbles
to the loch. Beside this she set Thomas, and stooping, picked
up a handful of stones, and began to throw them, one by one,
into the water. Thomas was diverted by the little splashes they
made. After a little he squatted down on his haunches and began to throw pebbles for himself. Victoria left him and went
back to the picnic place, and removed the plastic mug from the
top of a vacuum flask. She took this back to Thomas.

'Look.' She sat beside him and filled the mug with stones.
When it was full, she poured them out into a heap. 'Look, it's
a castle.' She gave him the mug. 'You do it.'

Carefully, one at a time, with starfish hands, Thomas filled
the mug. The occupation absorbed him. His fingers, red with
cold, were clumsy, his perseverance touching.

Watching him, filled with the tenderness that was by now
becoming familiar, Victoria wondered about maternal instincts.
Was one meant to have them, if one didn't have a child of
one's own? Perhaps, if Thomas had not been such an engaging
person, she would never have experienced this basic, unreasonable surge of protective affection. But there it was. Like a
child in some sentimental old film, he seemed to have found
his way into her heart, made himself snug and was there to
stay.

The whole situation was odd to say the least of it. When he

had first told Victoria about stealing Thomas from the Archers, Victoria, although shocked at Oliver, had also been moved. That Oliver Dobbs, of all people, should be so aware of his own parenthood as to take this extraordinary step was somehow a marvellous thing.

And to begin with, he had seemed both amused and involved; buying Thomas a toy, carrying him around on his shoulders, even playing with him in the evenings before Victoria put him to bed. But, like a child quickly bored by a new diversion, his interest seemed to have waned, and now he took little notice of Thomas.

The incident in the boat was typical of his attitude. Against all Victoria's better instincts, it was becoming impossible not to suspect that Oliver's impulsive removal of his son had not been prompted by fatherly pride and a real sense of responsibility, but that in his own oblique way he was simply getting back at his parents-in-law. The taking of Thomas from them sprang more from reasons of spite than reasons of love.

It really didn't bear thinking about. Not just because of the slur this cast upon Oliver's motivations and so upon his character, but because it rendered Thomas's future – and indirectly her own – miserably precarious.

Thomas banged her with his fist and said, 'Look.' Victoria looked, and saw the tumbled pile of pebbles and his beaming, grubby face, and she pulled him up on to her knee and hugged him.

She said, 'I love you. Do you know that?' and he laughed as though she had made some tremendous joke. His laughter eased everything. It would all be all right. She loved Thomas and she loved Oliver, and Oliver loved Victoria, and obviously – in his own undemonstrative way – loved Thomas as well. With so much loving around the place, surely nothing could destroy the family that they had become.

Behind her, she heard the crunch of footsteps coming down the beach towards them. She turned and saw John Dunbeath. Beyond him, the fire now blazed, plumed with blue smoke. The other two men had disappeared. She searched for them, and saw their distant figures, more than halfway up towards the march wall, and still climbing.

John said, 'I guess we won't get our lunch for another hour. They've gone up to search for the deer.'

He reached her side, and stood a moment, looking out across the water, to the distant sunlit blur of the house, half hidden in the trees. From here it looked infinitely desirable, like a house in a dream. Smoke rose from a chimney, a white curtain blew, like a flag, from an open window.

Victoria said, 'It doesn't matter. About lunch, I mean. If Thomas gets hungry we can always feed him something to stave off his pangs till the others get back.'

He sat beside them, leaning back with his elbows in the shingle. 'You're not hungry, are you?' he asked Thomas.

Thomas said nothing. After a bit, he clambered off Victoria's knee and went back to his game with the plastic cup.

Victoria said, 'Don't you want to go and look for deer too?'

'Not today. Anyway I've seen them before. And that's quite a climb. I didn't realise Oliver would be so energetic and interested in wildlife.'

There was no hint of criticism in his voice, but even so Victoria sprang to Oliver's defence. 'He's interested in everything. New experiences, new sights, new people.'

'I know it. Last night after you'd gone to bed, Roddy finally got round to telling me that he's another writer. It was funny, because when I was introduced to him, I thought "Oliver Dobbs, I know that name", but the associations eluded me. And then when Roddy told me, the penny dropped. I've read a couple of his books, and I saw one of his plays on television. He's a very clever man.'

Victoria's heart warmed towards him. 'Yes, he is clever. He's just had a new play put on in Bristol. Its called *Bent Penny*. The first night was on Monday, and his agent says he's got a hit on his hands. It's probably going to the West End, just as soon as they can find a theatre.'

'That's great.'

She went on extolling Oliver, as though praise of him could in some way obliterate the memory of the fleeting expression she had caught on John Dunbeath's face when Thomas fell in the boat. 'He hasn't always been successful. I mean, it's a notoriously difficult business to get started in, but he never wanted to do anything else, and I don't think he ever got discouraged or lost faith in himself. His parents practically disowned him because he didn't want to go into the army, or be a lawyer, or do anything like that. So, at the beginning, he really didn't have any security at all.'

'How long ago was that?'

'I suppose from the moment he left school.'

'How long have you known him?'

Victoria leaned forward and picked up a handful of pebbles. So close to the water's edge they were wet and shining and cold to touch. 'About three years.'

'Was he successful then?'

'No. He used to take dreadful, undemanding jobs, just to earn enough money to buy the groceries and pay the rent. You know, like barrowing bricks and mending roads and washing dishes in a fish-and-chips shop. And then a publisher began to take interest in him, and he got a play on television. And since then things have just snowballed, and he's never looked back. He and Roddy met through television, I expect Roddy told you. That's why we came to Benchoile. I read *The Eagle Years* when I was at school, and I've reread it at regular intervals ever since. When Oliver told me he knew Roddy and we were coming here to stay, I could hardly believe it was true.'

'Has it lived up to its expectations?'

'Yes. Once you get used to it not being summer all the time.'

John laughed. 'It certainly isn't that.' She thought he looked much younger when he laughed.

The sun had, for the last moment or so, been hidden behind a cloud, but now it came racing out again, and its brightness and warmth were so welcome, that Victoria lay back on the beach, and turned her face up to the sky.

She said, 'The only thing that spoiled coming here was being told about your uncle dying. I felt we should have turned right round and gone away again, but Roddy wouldn't hear of it.'

'It's probably the best thing in the world that could have happened. A bit of company for him.'

'Ellen told me you used to come here when you were a little boy. I mean, when you weren't in Colorado.'

'Yes. I used to come with my father.'

'Did you love it?'

'Yes. But it was never home. Colorado and the ranch were my real home.'

'What did you do when you used to come here? Did you slay deer and grouse and do manly things like that?'

'I used to fish. But I don't like shooting. I never have. It made life a little difficult.'

'Why?' It was hard to imagine life for John Dunbeath ever being difficult.

'I suppose because I was the odd man out. Everybody else did it. Even my father. My uncle Jock didn't understand it at all.' He grinned. 'Sometimes I thought he didn't even like me very much.'

'Oh, I'm sure he liked you. He wouldn't have left Benchoile to you if he hadn't liked you.'

'He left it to me,' John told her flatly, 'because there wasn't anybody else.'

'Did you guess he was going to leave it to you?'

'It never entered my head. That probably sounds crazy to you, but its true. I got back from Bahrein and found this lawyer's letter waiting for me on my desk.' He leaned forward to pick up a handful of pebbles and started to pitch them, with deadly accuracy, at a lichened rock which jutted from the edge of the loch. He said, 'There was another letter as well, from Jock. I guess he wrote it just a couple of days before he died. It's a funny feeling getting a letter from a person who's already dead.'

'Ar . . . are you going to come and live here?'

'I couldn't, even if I wanted to.'

'Because of your job?'

'Yes. That and other reasons. I'm based in London just now, but I may be sent back to New York at the drop of a hat. I have commitments. I have my family.'

'Your family?' She was taken by surprise. But, on consideration, why should she be so surprised? She had met John in London, at a party, as a single man, but that did not mean that he had not left a wife and children behind him in the States. Businessmen all over the world were forced to lead such lives. There was nothing unusual about such a situation. She imagined his wife; pretty and chic as all young American women seemed to be, with a space-age kitchen and a station wagon in which to fetch the children from school.

He said, 'By family, I mean my mother and father.'

'Oh,' Victoria laughed, feeling foolish. 'I thought you meant you were married.'

With immense care, he pitched the last stone. It hit the rock and fell into the water with a miniature splash. He turned to look at her. He said, 'I was married. Not any more.'

'I'm sorry.' There didn't seem to be anything else to say.

'That's all right.' He smiled reassuringly and she said 'I didn't know.'

'Why should you know?'

'No reason. It's just that people have been talking about you, telling me about you. Roddy and Ellen I mean. But nobody said anything about your being married.'

'It only lasted a couple of years, and they never met her anyway.' He leaned back on his elbows and looked out across the loch towards the hills and the old house. He said, 'I wanted to bring her to Benchoile. Before we were married I used to tell her about it, and she seemed quite enthusiastic. She'd never been to Scotland and she had all sorts of romantic imaginings about it. You know, skirling pipes and swirling mists and Bonnie Prince Charlie draped in tartan. But after we were married . . . I don't know. There never seemed to be time to do anything.'

'Was . . . the divorce why you came to live in London?'

'One of the reasons. You know, a clean break, all the rest of it.'

'Did you have children?'

'No. Just as well, the way things turned out.'

She knew then that she had been wrong about John. Meeting him for the first time, he had impressed her as being self-contained, self-reliant, and totally cool. Now she realised that beneath that smooth veneer was a person just like anybody else; vulnerable, capable of being hurt, probably lonely. She remembered that he had been meant to have a girlfriend with him that evening, but for some reason she had let him down. And so he had asked Victoria to have dinner with him, and Victoria had refused. Thinking of this, she now felt, in some obscure way, as though she had let him down.

She said, 'My parents got divorced. When I was eighteen. You'd have thought I'd have been old enough by then to cope with the situation. But it does something to your life. Nothing's ever quite the same again. Security is lost forever.' She smiled. 'Now, that's something that Benchoile has got and to spare. Security oozes out of the walls. I suppose it's something to do with the people who've lived in the house, and the way people live there now, as though nothing has changed in a hundred years.'

'That's right. It certainly hasn't altered in my lifetime. It even smells the same.'

She said 'What will happen to it now?'

He did not answer at once. And then he told her. 'I shall sell it.'

Victoria stared at him. His dark eyes, unblinking, met hers, and beneath their steady regard, she slowly realised that he meant what he said.

'But, John, you *can't.*'

'What else can I do?'

'Keep it on.'

'I'm not a farmer. I'm not a sportsman. I'm not even a true-blooded Scot. I'm an American banker. What could I do with a place like Benchoile?'

'Couldn't you run it . . . ?'

'From Wall Street?'

'Put a manager in.'

'Who?'

She cast about for some person, and came up, inevitably, with, 'Roddy?'

'If I'm a banker, then Roddy is a writer, a dilettante. He's never been anything else. Jock, on the other hand, was the strong pillar of the family and an exceptional man. He didn't just stride around Benchoile with a dog at his heels and a string of instructions. He worked. He went up the hill with Davey Guthrie and brought the sheep down. He helped with the lambing and the dipping. He went to the market in Lairg. As well, it was Jock who kept an eye on the forestry, took care of the garden, mowed the grass.'

'Isn't there a gardener?'

'There's a pensioner who cycles up from Creagan three days a week, but keeping the kitchen garden in vegetables and the house in logs seems to take up most of his time.'

But Victoria was still unconvinced. 'Roddy seems to know so *much* about everything. Last night . . .'

'He knows a lot, because he's lived here all his life, but what he can actually *do* is another matter altogether. I'm afraid that without Jock, supporting him and giving him a shove every now and then, Roddy is in mortal danger of simply sinking into the ground.'

'You could give him a chance.'

John looked regretful, but he shook his head. 'This is a big property. There's 12,000 acres of hill to be farmed, fences to be kept up, a thousand or more sheep to be reared. There's cattle involved, and crops, and expensive machinery. All that adds up to a lot of money.'

'You mean you don't want to risk losing money?'

He grinned. 'No banker wants to risk that. But in fact, it isn't that. I could probably afford to lose a bit, but no property is worth holding on to, unless it's a viable proposition and capable, at least, of washing its own face.'

Victoria turned away from him, sitting up with her arms wrapped around her knees, looking back across the water to the old house. She thought of the warmth of that house, of its hospitality, of the people who lived there. She did not think of it as a viable proposition.

She said, 'What about Ellen?'

'Ellen is one of the problems. Ellen and the Guthries.'

'Do they know you're going to sell Benchoile?'

'Not yet.'

'Does Roddy?'

'I told him last night.'

'What did he say?'

'He wasn't surprised. He said he hadn't expected me to do anything else. And then he poured himself the biggest cognac you've ever seen and changed the subject.'

'And what do you suppose will happen to Roddy?'

'I don't know,' said John, and for the first time he sounded miserable. She turned her head over her shoulder, and once more their eyes met. His own were bleak and sombre, and she was moved to sympathy for him in his dilemma.

She said, impulsively, 'He drinks too much. Roddy, I mean.'

'I know it.'

'I love him.'

'I love him, too. I love them all. That's why it's so ghastly.'

She felt impelled to try to cheer him. 'Perhaps something will turn up.'

'Who are you, Mr Micawber? No, I'm going to sell it. Because I have to. Robert McKenzie, he's the lawyer in Inverness, he's fixing an advertisement for me. It'll go into all the big national newspapers around the middle of the week. Desirable Highland Sporting Property For Sale. So you see, I can't go back now. I can't change my mind.'

'I wish I could make you.'

'You can't, so don't let's talk about it anymore.'

Thomas was getting bored with his game. He was also getting hungry. He had dropped his plastic mug, and now he came to climb on to Victoria's knee. John looked at his watch. He said, 'It's nearly one o'clock. I think you and I and Thomas should go and find something to eat . . .'

They got slowly to their feet. Victoria brushed shingle from the seat of her jeans. She said, 'What about the others?' and turned to look up the hill, and saw Oliver and Roddy already on their way down, moving a great deal faster than they had on the way up.

'They're feeling hungry, too, and thirsty as well, no doubt,' said John. 'Come along . . .' he stooped and hoisted Thomas up into his arms, and led the way back to where his fire smouldered '. . . let's see what Ellen's put in the picnic baskets.'

Perhaps because of the picnic – which had been so successful – and the memories of former happy parties that this had evoked, the conversation that night at dinner did not concern the literary world of London, nor the problems of the future of Scotland, but became instead, a feast of reminiscence.

Roddy, sated with fresh air, flushed by wine and good food, and relentlessly prompted by his nephew John, was in his element, carried along on an unstoppable flood of anecdotes that reached far back into the past.

Around the polished, candle-lit table, old retainers, eccentric relations, domineering dowagers, most of them long since defunct, came back to life. There was the story of the Christmas house party when the tree caught fire; the grouse-shoot at which a universally disliked young cousin peppered the guest of honour with shot and was sent home in disgrace; the long-forgotten winter when the blizzards cut the house off for a month or more, and its occupants were reduced to boiling snow to make the porridge and playing endless charades to keep themselves amused.

There were the sagas of the overturned boat, the sheriff's Bentley, which, inadvertently left with its hand brake off, had finished up in the bottom of the loch; and the gentlewoman of reduced circumstances, who had come to stay for a week-end, and remained firmly installed in the best guest room two years later.

It took a long time to run out of stories, and even when he did, Roddy remained inexhaustible. Just as Victoria was about to suggest that perhaps it was time to retire to bed (it was now past midnight) he pushed back his chair, and led them all purposefully away from the table and across the hall to the deserted, dust-sheeted drawing room. There stood the grand piano, draped in an old sheet. Roddy turned this back, pulled up a stool to the keyboard, and started to play.

The room was piercingly cold. The curtains had long since been taken down, and the windows shuttered, and the old melodies echoed like cymbals against the empty walls. High above, descendant from the centre of the lavishly decorated ceiling, a crystal chandelier of immense proportions sparkled like a cluster of icicles, and scattered facets of coloured light that were reflected in the bars of the brass fender that stood before the white marble fireplace.

Roddy sang songs from before the war. Noel Coward at his most sentimental, and Cole Porter.

> I get no kick from champagne,
> Mere alcohol doesn't thrill me at all,
> So tell me, why should it be true . . .

The rest of the party grouped themselves about him. Oliver, his dramatic senses stirred by the turn that the evening had so unexpectedly taken, leaned against the piano and smoked a cigar, watching Roddy as though he could not bear to miss a single nuance of the other man's expression.

John had crossed to the fireplace, and stood before it, with his hands in his pockets and his shoulders propped against the mantelpiece. Victoria had found a chair in the middle of the room draped in faded blue gingham, and had perched herself on one of its arms. From where she sat, Roddy had his back to her, but above him, flanking a centrally hung mirror, were two tall portraits, which she knew, without being told, were of Jock Dunbeath and his wife Lucy.

With her ears full of the nostalgic tinkling music, she looked from one to the other. Jock had been painted in the full dress kilt of his regiment, but Lucy wore a tartan skirt and a bracken-brown sweater. She had brown eyes and laughter on her mouth, and Victoria wondered if it was she who had decorated this room, and chosen the pale carpet with its swags of roses, or whether she had inherited it from her mother-in-law, and liked it just the way it was. And then she found herself wondering if Jock and Lucy knew that Benchoile was going to be sold. Whether they were sad about it, or angry, or understood John's dilemma. Looking at Lucy, Victoria decided that she probably understood. But Jock . . . Jock's face above the high collar, the golden epaulettes, was carved into an expression of suitable blankness. The eyes were deep-set and very pale. They would reveal nothing.

She realised that she was slowly freezing. She had put on, that evening, for some reason, a most unsuitable dress, sleeveless and far too light for a winter evening in Scotland. It was the sort of dress meant to be worn with suntanned arms and bare sandals, and in it she knew that she looked thin and colourless and cold.

> You're the cream in my coffee,
> You're the milk in my tea . . .

Victoria shivered, and rubbed her arms with her hands, trying to warm herself. From across the room, John Dunbeath's voice came quietly, 'Are you cold?' and she realised that he had been watching her, and this made her self-conscious. She put her hands back in her lap and nodded, but made a secret face to let him know that she did not want to disturb Roddy.

He took his hands out of his pockets and left the fireplace and came over to her side, on the way gathering up a dustsheet, revealing the French rosewood chair that it had been protecting. He folded the dustsheet like a shawl, and bundled it around her shoulders, so that she was swathed in folds of soft, old cotton, very comforting to the touch.

He did not go back to the fireplace, but settled himself on the other arm of her chair, with his arm lying along its back. His nearness was somehow as comforting as the dustsheet that he had wrapped around her, and after a little she did not feel cold anymore.

Roddy stopped at last for breath, and to refresh himself from the glass that stood on top of the piano. 'I think that's probably enough,' he told them all. But John said, 'You can't stop yet. You haven't played "Will Ye Go, Lassie, Go".'

Over his shoulder Roddy frowned at his nephew. 'When did you ever hear me play that old song?'

'I suppose when I was about five years old. But my father used to sing it, too.'

Roddy smiled. 'What a sentimental guy you are, to be sure,' he told him, but he turned back to the piano, and the old Scottish tune, in the three-four time of a slow waltz, filled the empty, haunted room.

> O the summer time is coming
> And the trees are sweetly blooming
> And the wild mountain thyme
> Grows around the blooming heather.
> Will ye go, lassie, go?

I will build my love a tower
Near yon pure crystal fountain
And on it I will pile
All the flowers of the mountain.
Will ye go, lassie, go?

If my true love, she were gone,
I would surely find another
Where wild mountain thyme
Grows around the blooming heather.
Will ye go, lassie, go?

## CHAPTER 12

## SUNDAY

It was ten o'clock on the morning of the Sabbath. Once more the wind had come round to the north-east, swirling in from the sea, clean and bitterly cold. The sky, overcast with high, sailing clouds, glimpsed through, blue as a robin's egg, only occasionally, and it was hard to believe that only yesterday they had been picnicking at the waterfall, sitting in the sunshine with pleasant anticipatory thoughts of the approaching spring.

John Dunbeath sat by the fire in the Guthrie's kitchen and drank a cup of tea. The kitchen was snug as a nest. A fire burned redly in the stove, and thick walls and tightly closed windows defied the blustering wind. The air was filled with the smell of burning peat, overlaid by the fragrance of simmering broth, and the table in the centre of the room was already laid for the Guthrie's midday dinner.

Jess was going to church. At the sideboard, she took up her hat, and, sagging slightly at the knees, in order to see her reflection in the mirror, put it on. Watching her, and then looking back at Davey, John decided that of all the Benchoile people, the Guthries had changed the least. Jess was still slim, still pretty, with only a trace of grey in her springy fair hair, and Davey looked, if anything, even younger than John remembered him, with his bright blue eyes and tufty, sandy eyebrows.

'Now,' Jess picked up her gloves and pulled them on. 'I must get away. You'll have to excuse me, but I promised I'd pick up Ellen Tarbat and give her a lift to the kirk.' She glanced at the portentous clock in the middle of the mantelpiece. 'And if you two are going to be up the hill and home again in time for your dinner, you'd better not be sitting here all day, drinking your tea.'

She departed. A moment later there came a great crashing of gears and the revving of a hard-worked engine, and Davey's small grey van bounced down the bumpy path in front of the house and disappeared in the direction of Benchoile.

'She's a terrible driver,' Davey observed mildly. He finished his mug of tea, set it down on the table and stood up. 'But she's right. We should go.' He went through to the little lobby and took down his waterproof jacket from the peg by the door, collected his deerstalker, his crook, his spyglass. The two golden Labradors, who had been lying, apparently asleep, by the fireside, now sprang into feverish action, scenting walks. They barged to and fro, nuzzling Davey's knees, tails going like pistons. They were, Jess had told John, Jock Dunbeath's dogs.

'Poor creatures, they were with him when he died. And afterwards they wandered about Benchoile like a pair of lost spirits. There was some talk of putting the old one down. She's nearly nine years old now. But we couldn't abide the idea. The colonel had been so fond of her, and she's a great lass to the gun. So they both came to live with us. Mind, we've never had a dog in the house. Davey would never have a dog in the house. But these two had never been in a kennel in their lives, and so he had to relent. They could have stayed at Benchoile, I suppose, but Mr Roddy has his own dog, and Ellen has enough to do without caring for a couple of great babies like these two.'

Now Davey opened the farmhouse door, and the two Labradors escaped into the windswept, scrubby garden, racing like puppies around the blowing grass beneath the washing line. At their appearance, Davey's sheepdogs, shut up in their pen, began dementedly to bark, racing to and fro in the netted run. 'Shut your mouths, you silly bitches,' Davey told them goodnaturedly, but they went on barking, and could still be heard long after the two men and the two dogs had gone through the gate in the wall at the back of the house, and started the long walk up through the heather.

It took them over an hour to reach the march fence that separated the northern boundary of Benchoile from the desolate Glen Feosaig which lay beyond. A long, steady climb, taken at Davey Guthrie's unhurried pace, pausing only to point out some landmark, to scan the hill for deer, to watch the

soaring, hovering flight of a kestrel. The dogs were kept well
to heel, but even so, every now and then a pair of grouse
would explode from the heather at their feet, and go wheeling
away, their flight lying close to the slope of the hill; 'go-back,
go-back', they called.

It was immense country. Slowly, Benchoile sank below them,
the loch a long ribbon of pewter grey, the house and trees concealed by the swelling contours of the land. To the north the
summits were still snowclad, and snow lay in deep corries as
yet untouched by the low winter sun. As they climbed, Creagan
itself came into view, reduced by distance to a cluster of grey
houses, a strip of green that was the golf course, the tiny
spire of the church. Beyond was the sea, the horizon blanketed
in cloud.

'Yes, yes,' observed Davey, 'it is a dreich sort of a day.'

At the crest of the hill there was not even heather underfoot; only pits of peat starred with strange mosses and lichens.
The ground was boggy. Black water oozed up around their
feet as they trod upwards, and the hoofprints and droppings of
deer were everywhere. When they came at last to the straggling
dike, the wind pounced on them from the north. It filled ears,
nostrils, lungs; whistled through stormproof clothing and
brought tears to John's eyes. He leaned against the wall and
looked down into Feosaig. The loch at its foot lay black and
deep, and there was no evidence of human habitation. Only
the sheep and the kestrels, and showing white against the distant hill, a pair of gulls, working their way inland.

'Are those our sheep?' John asked, raising his voice against
the wind.

'Yes, yes,' Davey nodded, and then turned and sat himself
down, out of the wind, with his back to the wall. After a little
John joined him. 'But that's not Benchoile land.'

'And this is not Feosaig land, either, but we have many
Feosaig sheep grazing with ours.'

'What happens, do you have a roundup?'

'We start to gather them in, around the end of this month.
We bring them down to the sheep folds in the fields by the
farmhouse.'

'When do the ewes start lambing?'

'About the sixteenth of April.'

'Will it still be as cold as this?'

'It may well be colder. Some big storms can blow in April,
and they can leave the hills as white as midwinter.'

'That can't make your job any easier.'

'Indeed, it does not. I have seen myself digging ewes, heavy with lamb, out of the ditches and drifts. Sometimes a mother will desert her lamb, and then there's nothing for it but to take it back to the farmhouse and hand rear it with a bottle. Jess is a great one with the sickly lambs.'

'Yes, I'm sure she is, but that doesn't solve the problem of how you're going to cope with all this on your own. Roddy's told me how much my uncle did at the lambing. You're going to need another man, probably two, to help you during the next six weeks.'

'Yes, that is indeed a problem,' Davey agreed, not looking in the least perturbed. He felt in his pocket and came out with a paper bag. From this he extracted two large bread-and-butter sandwiches. He gave one to John and began to eat the other himself, munching at each mouthful like a ruminating cow. 'But I have spoken to Archie Tulloch and he says that this year he will give me a hand.'

'Who's he?'

'Archie is a crofter. He farms a few acres down the road to Creagan. But he is an old man – seventy years or more – and he won't be able to carry on with the crofting much longer. He has no son. A month or so before your uncle died, he spoke to me about Archie's croft. He had the idea that he would buy the place from Archie, and take it in with Benchoile. We can always use more land for the arable, and he has a fine cattle pasture down by the river.'

'Would Archie be agreeable?'

'Yes, yes. He has a sister in Creagan. He has talked for some time of going to live with her.'

'So we'd have more land and another house.'

'Your uncle thought we would maybe take on another man, and put him to live in the croft. Your uncle was a fine man, but after that first heart attack he had begun to realise that, like the rest of us, he was not immortal.'

He took another mouthful of bread and munched some more. A movement on the side of the hill caught the attention of his blue eyes. He laid down his half-eaten sandwich, drove his crook into the ground, and took out his spyglass. Using his crook and the thumb of his left hand as a steadier, he put the glass to his eye. There was a long silence, broken only by the buffet of the wind.

'A hare,' said Davey. 'Just a wee hare.' He put the spyglass back in his pocket, and reached for the crust of the sandwich. But the old Labrador had already wolfed it. 'You are indeed a greedy bitch,' he told her.

John leaned back against the wall. Awkward stones dug into his back. His body was warm from the hard exercise, and his face cold. Ahead of them a gap had appeared between the racing clouds. A gleam of sunshine broke across the gloom, and lay like a shaft of gold across the dark waters of Loch Muie. The bracken on the hill turned russet. It was very beautiful, and he realised in that instant, with some shock, that the land, for almost as far as he could see, belonged to him. This was Benchoile. And this . . . he took up a handful of black peaty soil, crumbling it between his fingers.

He was assailed by a sensation of timelessness. This was the way things had stayed for decades; tomorrow they would be no different, nor the weeks, nor the months that lay in the future. Action, of any kind, had all at once become distasteful, and this took him unawares, because apathy was a mood he had never suffered from. He had made his reputation, achieved a considerable personal success in his job, simply by means of swift and shrewd decision, immediate action, and a confidence in his own convictions that left no room for moral shilly-shallying.

He had arranged this morning's expedition with the sole intention of getting Davey on his own, and letting fall the information, as tactfully as possible, that by the middle of next week Benchoile would officially be up for sale. And yet now he found himself discussing its future policies with Davey, as though he had every intention of digging himself in for the rest of his life.

He was procrastinating. But did that matter so much? Was today, this morning, this moment, the right time to bring to an end everything that Davey Guthrie had worked for? Perhaps, he told himself, knowing that he was ducking the issue, it would be better to hold a sort of board meeting in the dining room at Benchoile, thus protecting himself from the human element of the problem by erecting a shield of business-like formality. He would get Ellen Tarbat around the table, and Jess as well, and Roddy, to lend a little moral support. Better still, he would ask Robert McKenzie, the lawyer, to come from Inverness and take the chair at this meeting. Then he could be given the job of breaking the bad news to them all at one fell swoop.

The sun went in. It was cold and dark again, but the silence between the two men remained companionable and totally unstrained. It occurred to John that the true Highlander like Davey Guthrie had much in common with the ranch hands who worked for his father in Colorado. Proud, independent, knowing that they were as good as any man – and probably better – they found no need to assert themselves, and so were the most straightforward of beings to deal with.

He knew that he must be straightforward with Davey. He said, breaking the silence, 'How long have you been at Benchoile, Davey?'

'Nearly twenty years.'

'How old are you?'

'Forty-four.'

'You don't look it.'

'It's the clean living that keeps a man healthy,' Davey told him, without a smile. 'And the good air. Do you not find working in London and New York and such big cities, that the air is very oppressive? Even if Jess and I have a day's shopping in Inverness, I cannot wait to get home and breathe the clean air of Benchoile.'

'I suppose if you have a job in a place, you don't think too much about what you're breathing.' He added, 'Anyway, if I get to feel too stifled, I usually head back to Colorado. There, the air is so rarified that the first gasp is as intoxicating as a jigger of Scotch.'

'Yes, yes, that ranch must be a fine place. And a great size, too.'

'In fact, not as big as Benchoile. About 6,000 acres, but of course we carry more stock. Six hundred acres of that is irrigated hay meadow, the rest is known as open range grazing.'

'And what breed of cattle do you rear?'

'No particular breed. They vary from fine Hereford and Black Angus, all the way down to what's known in the West as Running Gear. If the snows have been heavy, and the high meadows are well irrigated and we don't have a killing frost in the late spring, we can graze a thousand head.'

Davey ruminated on this, chewing on a blade of grass, and gazing peacefully ahead of him. After a little, he said, 'There was a farmer from Rosshire, and he went to the bull-sales in Perth, and there he met one of those big cattlemen from Texas. And they got talking. And the Texan asked the farmer how much land he owned. And the farmer told him, "2,000 acres".'

At this point John realised that Davey was not continuing their dissertation on farming, but telling a joke. Anxious not to miss the punch line, or worse, to laugh at the wrong moment, he listened with sharpened attention.

'And then the farmer asked the Texan how much land he owned. And the Texan said to the farmer, "You would not understand. You could not comprehend, if I told you how much of Texas I own. But I'll tell you this. If I got into my car and drove all day around my boundary fence, I still should not have circled my property." And the farmer thought a little while, and then he said to the Texan, "I had a car like that, once upon a time. I got rid of it." '

There came a long pause. Davey continued to gaze ahead. John stayed straight-faced as long as he could, and then the grin, unstoppable, crept up his face. Davey turned his head and looked at him. His blue eyes held a certain gleam, but otherwise he was as dour as ever.

'Yes, yes,' he said, in his gentle Sutherland voice. 'I thought that you would enchoy that. It is a very good choke.'

Ellen Tarbat, dressed in her good Sunday black, pulled her hat down over her ears and pierced it to her bun with a formidable hat pin. It was a decent hat, only two years old, and trimmed with a buckle. There was nothing like a buckle for lending a bit of dignity to a hat.

She looked at the kitchen clock. It was a quarter past ten, and Ellen was going to church. She was giving them a cold lunch today instead of the usual roast. She had peeled the potatoes, and made a jam tart, and the dining room table was ready and laid. Now, she was ready for Jess to pick her up. Davey was not coming to church with them, because he and John Dunbeath had gone up the hill to look at the sheep. Ellen did not approve of such goings-on on the Sabbath and had said as much to John, but he had pointed out that he had not all the time in the world, and would soon have to go back to London. Ellen could not imagine why he should want to get back to London. She herself had never been to London, but her niece Anne had taken a trip a couple of years ago, and what she had told Ellen about it had left Ellen in no great hurry to follow her example.

Her hat settled, she picked up her coat. She had brought all her things downstairs earlier in the morning so as to save a trip up all those flights of stairs to her attic bedroom. Climbing stairs was one of the things that tired her. She hated being tired. She hated the way her heart thumped when she was tired. Sometimes she hated being old.

She put on her coat and buttoned it up, and adjusted the lapel where she had pinned her best Cairngorm brooch. She took up her bulging handbag, her black gloves. From the front of the house, the telephone rang.

She stood still, waiting, trying to remember who was in the house and who out of it. Mrs Dobbs had taken the little boy out for a walk. John was with Davey. The telephone continued to ring, and Ellen sighed and laid down her bag and gloves and went to answer it. Out of the kitchen, across the hall, into the library. The telephone stood on the colonel's desk. Ellen picked up the receiver.

'Yes?'

There came a series of clickings and buzzings, distasteful to her ear. The telephone was another thing she hated. 'Yes?' she said again, beginning to sound testy.

A final click, and a man's voice. 'Is that Benchoile?'

'This is Benchoile.'

'I want to speak to Oliver Dobbs.'

'He's not here,' said Ellen, instantly. Jess Guthrie would be at the door at any moment, and she did not want to keep her waiting.

But the caller was not so easily put off.

'Is there no way you can get hold of him? It's very important indeed.'

The word *important* caught her attention.

It was splendid when important people came to stay and important things happened. It gave a body something to talk about that wasn't simply the price of lambs or the weather.

'He . . . he'll maybe be over at the Stable House.'

'Could you go and get him?'

'It may take a moment or two.'

'I'll hold on.'

'The telephone is very expensive,' Ellen reminded him sharply. Important or not, it was a sinful thing to waste good money.

'What?' He sounded taken aback, as indeed he might. 'Oh. Well, never mind about that. I'd be grateful if you could get him. Tell him it's his agent.'

Ellen sighed, and resigned herself to missing out on the first hymn. 'Very well.'

She laid down the receiver, and made the long journey down through the back of the house to the stableyard. When she opened the back door the wind swirled and gusted and nearly pulled the doorknob out of her grasp. Bent against this, holding on her good hat, she crossed the cobbles and opened Roddy's front door.

'Roddy! ' Her voice, raised, cracked a little.

There was a pause, and then footsteps crossed the floor above her, and Mr Dobbs himself appeared at the head of the stairs, as tall, thought Ellen, as a lamppost.

'He's not here, Ellen. He's gone to Creagan to get the Sunday papers.'

'There's a telephone call for you, Mr Dobbs. The man says he is your agent, and it is very important.'

His face lit up. 'Oh. Right.' And he came helter-skelter down the stairs, so fast that Ellen was obliged to step sideways to avoid being knocked flat. 'Thanks, Ellen,' he said, as he shot past her.

'He's waiting at the other end of the telephone . . .' she raised her voice to his retreating back '. . . and the Lord himself knows what it's costing him.'

But Mr Dobbs was already out of earshot of her grumblings. Ellen made a face. Some people. She pulled her hat down, and followed him at her own pace. In the kitchen, she saw, through the window, the Guthrie's van, waiting for her, with Jess Guthrie at the wheel. She was flustered and halfway through the door before she realised that she had forgotten her gloves.

Oliver's telephone call from London lasted for more than half an hour, and by the time he got back to the Stable House, Roddy had returned from Creagan with all the Sunday papers, was ensconsed in his deepest leather armchair in front of a furnace of a fire, and was already looking forward to the first gin-and-tonic of the day.

He laid down the *Observer,* and looked up over his spectacles as Oliver came bounding up the stairs two at a time.

'Hello,' he said. 'I thought I'd been deserted.'

'I had a phone call.' Oliver came to sit in the chair opposite to Roddy, with his hands hanging loose between his bony **knees.**

Roddy sent him a keen look. He sensed the suppressed, secret excitement. 'Good news, I hope.'

'Yes. Good. It was my agent. It's all fixed. The new play's moving to London when it's finished the run at Bristol. Same cast, same producer, everything.'

'Fantastic.' Roddy dropped the paper to the floor, reached up a hand to pull off his spectacles. 'My dear boy, that really is the most splendid news.'

'There are other goodies in the pipeline as well, but those can wait till later. I mean, they're not actually signed and sealed yet.'

'I couldn't be more pleased.' Roddy glanced at his watch. 'The sun's not over the yardarm yet, but I think this calls—'

But Oliver interrupted him. 'There's just one thing. Would you mind if I left Victoria and Thomas with you for a couple of days? I have to go to London. I have to go tomorrow. Just for one night. There's a plane from Inverness about five o'clock in the evening. I wondered, too, if someone would be able to drive me over to catch it.'

'But of course. You can leave them here as long as you like. And I'll take you over in the MG.'

'It's only for two days. I'll be coming back the next day. And after that I'll pack the others up and we'll make our way back south in the car.'

The very idea of them all leaving made Roddy feel miserable. He dreaded being on his own again, not simply because he loved to have young company about the place, but because with Oliver and Victoria and little Thomas gone, he knew that there would no longer be an excuse not to face up to facts. And the facts were cold. Jock was dead. John was going to sell Benchoile. Ties and traditions would be broken forever. It was the end of a way of life. This was the last house party.

He said, with the vague notion of putting off the evil moment. 'You don't have to go. You know you don't have to go.'

'You know that we have to. As it is, you've been more than kind and marvellously hospitable, but we can't stay forever. Anyway, fish and guests stink after three days, and we've been here three already, so tomorrow we're going to start stinking.'

'I'll miss you. We all will. Ellen has lost her heart to Thomas. It won't seem the same without you all around.'

'You'll still have John.'

'John won't stay longer than he has to. He can't. He's got to get back to London.'

'Victoria tells me that he's going to sell Benchoile.'

Roddy was surprised. 'I didn't realise he'd discussed it with Victoria.'

'She told me last night.'

'Yes. He's going to sell up. He really has no alternative. To be truthful, it's what I expected.'

'What will happen to you?'

'It depends who buys the place. If it's a rich American with sporting instincts, perhaps I could get a job as ghillie. I rather see myself touching my cap and collecting massive tips.'

'You should get married,' said Oliver.

Roddy sent him another sharp look. 'You're a fine one to be talking.'

Oliver grinned. 'I'm different,' he said smugly. 'I'm a different generation. I'm allowed to have a different set of morals and values.'

'You certainly have those.'

'Don't you approve?'

'It would make no difference whether I approved or not. I'm too idle a man to take up attitudes about matters which really don't concern me. Perhaps I was too idle to get married. Or perhaps I didn't get married, because getting married was expected of me. I never really did anything that was expected of me. Not getting married was just part of the pattern. Like writing books and watching birds and drinking too much. My brother Jock despaired of me.'

'I think it's a good way to be,' said Oliver. 'I suppose I've followed pretty much the same pattern myself.'

'Yes,' said Roddy, 'but in my case I had a golden rule. I never got involved with anybody, because I knew that once I did I was in danger of hurting them.'

Oliver looked at him, surprised 'You're talking about Victoria, aren't you?'

'She is very vulnerable.'

'She is also intelligent.'

'The heart and the head are two separate entities.'

'Reason and emotion?'

'If you like.'

Oliver said, 'I can't be tied.'

'You already are,' Roddy pointed out. 'You have the child.'

Oliver reached for his cigarettes. He took one and lit it with a spill kindled from the fire. When it was alight, he tossed the spill on to the flames. He said, 'In that case, isn't it a little late to start talking to me like a father?'

'It's never too late to rectify matters.'

Across the hearthrug their eyes clashed, and Roddy recognised the coldness in Oliver's pale gaze. When he spoke, it was to change the subject. 'Do you know where Victoria is?'

It was a sort of dismissal. Roddy sighed. 'I think she took Thomas for a walk.'

Oliver stood up. 'In that case, I'd better go and find her. Tell her what's happening.'

He went, running down the wooden staircase, and slamming the front door shut behind him. His footsteps rang across the cobbles of the stableyard. Roddy was left no wiser as to Oliver's intentions, suspecting that he had done more harm than good, and wishing that he had kept his mouth shut. After a little, he sighed again, hauled himself out of his chair and went to pour himself that longed-for gin-and-tonic.


Victoria, making her way back through the birch wood, saw Oliver emerge from beneath the stableyard archway, and walk out on to the gravel in front of the house. He was smoking a cigarette. She was about to call out to him, when he caught sight of her and Thomas, and came across the grass to meet them.

Thomas, whose legs had given out on him halfway home, was riding pickaback on Victoria's shoulders. When she saw Oliver coming towards them, Victoria bent down and let Thomas slip to the ground. He ran ahead of her and reached Oliver before she did, butting his father in the legs with his head and hobbling Oliver's knees with his arms.

Oliver did not pick him up, but stood there, penned, waiting until Victoria was within earshot.

'Where have you been?' he asked her.

'Just for a walk. We found another stream, but not as pretty as the waterfall.' She reached his side. 'What have you been doing?'

'Telephoning,' he told her. The walk, the cold air, had brought colour to her cheeks. Her pale hair was blowing and tousled. She had found, somewhere, a clump of yellow aconites, and had picked one or two and put them in the buttonhole of her jacket. Oliver pulled her into his arms and kissed her. She smelled cool and fresh, of apples and the outdoors. Her lips were sweet and clean, her kiss tasted as innocent as clear water.

'Telephoning who?'

'I wasn't telephoning anybody. I was being telephoned.'

'Who by?'

'My agent.' He let her go, and stooped to disentangle Thomas from his legs. They began to walk towards the house, but Thomas protested, so Victoria went back to lift him up in her arms. When she was alongside Oliver once more, she asked, 'What did he say?'

'Good things. *Bent Penny's* going to London.'

She stopped dead. '*Oliver!* But that's *marvellous*.'

'And I'm going to London too, tomorrow.' Her face dropped. 'I'm leaving you and Thomas behind.'

'You can't mean it.'

He laughed. 'Don't look so tragic, you ninny. I'm coming back the next day.'

'But why can't we come with you?'

'What's the point of coming to London for one day? Anyway, I can't talk business with you and Thomas under my feet all the time.'

'But we can't stay here without you!'

'Why not?'

'I don't want to be left behind.'

In a flash, Oliver became irritated. He stopped his good-natured teasing, and said, in some exasperation, 'I'm *not* leaving you behind. I'm simply going to London for a night. I'm flying down and I'm flying back. And when I get back, we're packing up and we're getting into the car and we're all going south again. Together. Now, does that make you happy?'

'But what am I going to do without you?'

'Exist, I imagine. It shouldn't be too difficult.'

'I just feel it's so awful for Roddy. We dumped ourselves on him in the first place, and now . . .'

'He's fine. He's delighted at the idea of having you and Thomas to himself for a day or two. And as for dumping ourselves on him, he doesn't want us to go. Once we've gone, he'll have to face reality, and he doesn't relish that in the very least.'

'That's a horrible thing to say about Roddy.'

'OK, it's horrible, but it's true. OK, he's charming and amusing, a character straight from the pages of some old nineteen-thirties comedy. Rattigan, perhaps, at his most fresh-faced. But I doubt if he's ever faced an issue in his life.'

'He was in the war. Anybody who went through the war was bound to face issues. That was what it was all about.'

'I'm talking about personal issues. Not National Emergencies. You can't hide from a National Emergency by climbing behind a brandy and soda.'

'Oh, *Oliver*. I hate it when you're like this. And I still don't want you to go and leave Thomas and me behind.'

'Well, I'm going.' She did not reply, and he put his arm around her, and bent and kissed the top of her head. 'And you are not to sulk about it. And on Tuesday, when I fly back, you can jump into the Volvo and come and meet me. And if you're particularly charming, I shall take you out to dinner in Inverness. And we'll eat haggis and chips and join in the folk dancing. Can you think of anything more riveting?'

'I'd rather you didn't go.' But she was beginning to smile.

'I have to. Duty calls. I'm a successful man. Leaving you behind is one of the prices I have to pay for being successful.'

'Sometimes I wish you weren't.'

He kissed her again. 'You know what's wrong with you? You're never happy.'

'That's not true.'

He relented. 'I know it isn't.'

'I've been happy here,' she told him, and she was suddenly shy. She hoped that Oliver would tell her that he had been happy too. But he did not say anything, and she heaved Thomas's weight from one arm to the other, and together, they walked back to the house.

## CHAPTER 13

## MONDAY

Roddy stood at the top of his staircase and called, 'Victoria!'

Victoria, who had spent the morning ironing shirts and hand-kerchiefs for Oliver, sorting out socks and sweaters, and finally packing a suitcase, straightened up from her task, pushed a lock of hair from her face, and went to open the bedroom door.

'I'm here!'

'John's here, and Oliver. Come and join us. We're having a drink.'

It was nearly half past twelve, a bright, cold day and the sun was shining. Roddy and Oliver were leaving for the airport after lunch. A quarter of an hour previously, Ellen had appeared to take charge of Thomas and to get him ready for lunch, for lunch today was to be a substantial affair, cooked by Ellen and Jess Guthrie and eaten in the big dining room at Benchoile. This was Ellen's decision. She had always been of the opinion that no person should set out on a journey, however short, without a good meal inside him, and Oliver was, apparently, no exception. Accordingly, she and Jess had been busy all morning. Appetising smells had wafted through from the big house, and there was a certain sense of occasion in the air, as though something important was happening, like a birthday, or the last day of the holidays.

Above her, in Roddy's sitting room, Victoria could hear the murmured conversation of the others. She closed the suitcase and snapped shut the locks. She went to the mirror and combed her hair, and gave a final glance about the room to make sure that nothing had been forgotten, and then went upstairs to join the rest of the party.

Because of the sunshine and the brightness of the day, she found them gathered, not about the fireside, but at the huge window. Oliver and Roddy sat on the window seat with their backs to the view, and John Dunbeath on a chair that he had pulled back from the desk. When Victoria appeared, Roddy said, 'Here she is, come along, we've been waiting for you,' and John stood up and moved his chair to one side in order to make space for her. 'What'll you have to drink?'

She considered this. 'I don't think I really want a drink.'

'Oh, come on,' said Oliver. He held out a long arm, and drew Victoria to his side. 'Don't be prissy. You've been beavering around all morning, being domestic. You deserve a drink.'

'Oh, all right.'

John said, 'What would you like? I'll get it for you.'

Still caught in the circle of Oliver's arm, she looked across at him. 'A lager, perhaps?' And he smiled, and went through to Roddy's kitchen to collect her a can out of the fridge.

But there was scarcely time to open the can and pour the lager before they were interrupted by the sound of the front door opening, and Ellen's voice from the foot of the stairs, raised to tell them all that lunch was ready, it was on the table, it would spoil if they didn't come immediately.

Roddy said, sotto voce, 'Drat the woman', but there was obviously nothing to be done about it, and so, carrying their various glasses, they all got to their feet and made their way downstairs and across the yard to the big house.

They found the dining room full of sunshine, the big table laid with a white cloth. A roast of beef steamed on the sideboard, dishes of hot vegetables stood on the hot plate, and Thomas was already installed, hungry and feedered, in an ancient wooden high chair that Jess Guthrie had brought down from the old nursery.

Ellen pottered to and fro on her unsteady legs, telling everybody where they were to sit, complaining that the roast was getting cold, and what was the point of cooking good meat if folks couldn't be on time for their meals?

John said, good-naturedly, 'Now come on, Ellen, that's not true. We were off our backsides the moment you hollered up the stairs. Who's going to carve?'

'You,' said Roddy instantly, and went to sit down with his back to the window, as far from the sideboard as possible. He had never been any good at carving. Jock had always done the carving.

John sharpened the horn-handled knife with all the élan of a master butcher, and got to work. Ellen took the first plate for Thomas, and herself dealt with it, cutting up the meat and squashing the vegetables and gravy into a mess like brown porridge.

'There he is, the wee man. You eat that up now, pet, and you'll turn into a great big boy.'

'Not that we have too many problems,' Roddy murmured when Ellen had departed and closed the door behind her, and everybody laughed because this morning Thomas's cheeks appeared to be fatter and rounder than ever.

They had finished their first course and were just starting in on Ellen's apple pie and baked custard, when the telephone started to ring. They all waited, as seemed to be the custom at Benchoile, for somebody else to go and answer it. Finally Roddy said, 'Oh, damn.'

Victoria took pity on him. 'Shall I go?'

'No, don't bother.' He took another leisurely mouthful of apple pie, and pushed back his chair and ambled from the room, still grumbling. 'What a bloody stupid time to ring up.' He had left the dining room door open, and they could hear his voice from the library. 'Benchoile. Roddy Dunbeath here.' Then a pause. 'Who? What? Yes, of course. Hold on a moment and I'll go and get him.' A moment later he reappeared, still holding the table napkin, which he had taken with him.

'Oliver, dear boy, it's for you.'

Oliver looked up from his plate. 'Me? Who is it?'

'No idea. Some man or other.'

He returned to his apple pie, and Oliver pushed back his chair and went to take the call. 'I can't think,' said Roddy, 'why they can't invent some device so that when you sit down to a meal, you can stop the telephone ringing.'

'You could always take it off the hook,' John suggested mildly.

'Yes, but then I'd forget to put it back again.'

Thomas was beginning to be bored with his pudding. Victoria picked up his spoon and began to help him. She said, 'You could always just let it ring.'

'I'm not strong-minded enough. I can let it ring for just so long, and then I can't bear it for another moment. I always imagine that someone is waiting to tell me something tremendously exciting, and I go cantering off to grab the receiver from the hook, only to find myself voice-to-voice as it were with the Inland Revenue. Or else it's a wrong number.'

John said, 'If you're a wrong number, then why did you answer the phone?' which was somehow all the funnier, because he didn't often make jokes.

By the time Oliver returned, their meal was over. Roddy had lit a cigar, and John brought the tray of coffee through from the kitchen. Victoria was peeling an orange for Thomas, because however much he ate, he always liked oranges more than anything. The orange was juicy and the task absorbed her, so that she did not look up when Oliver came back into the room.

'Good news, I hope,' she heard Roddy say. The last of the peel fell away, and she broke the orange into sections and handed the first one to Thomas. Oliver did not reply. 'Nothing serious?' Roddy now sounded concerned.

Still Oliver said nothing. The silence suddenly caught Victoria's attention. It grew longer, more strained. Even Thomas was stilled by it. He sat, with a piece of orange in his hand, and stared across the table at his father. Victoria's cheeks began to prickle. She realised that they were all looking at her. She looked at Roddy, and then up at Oliver. She saw his face, intensely pale, and his cold, unblinking eyes. She felt the blood drain from her own cheeks, and a reasonless sense of doom, like a sickness, knot her stomach.

She swallowed. 'What is it?' Her voice sounded thin and insubstantial.

'Do you know who that was on the telephone?' Oliver asked her.

'I've no idea,' but she could not keep her voice from trembling.

'It was Mr Bloody Archer. Ringing up from Hampshire.' *But I told her not to ring up. I said I'd write again. I explained about Oliver.* 'You wrote to them.'

'I . . .' Her mouth was dry, and she swallowed again. 'I didn't write to him. I wrote to her.'

Oliver advanced to the table, he laid the palms of his hands flat upon its surface, and leaned towards her.

'I told you not to write to her.' Each word came out like a hammer blow. 'I told you you were not to write to her, nor telephone her, nor to get in touch with her in any way at all.'

'Oliver, I had to . . .'

'How did you know where to write, anyway?'

'I . . . I looked it up in the telephone directory?'

'When did you write?'

'On Thursday . . . Friday . . .' She was beginning to be flustered. 'I can't remember.'

'What was I doing?'

'I . . . I think you were still asleep.' It was beginning to sound so underhand, so secretive, that she was impelled to stand up for herself. 'I *told* you I wanted to write to her. I couldn't bear her not knowing about Thomas . . . not knowing where he was.' Oliver's expression softened not one whit. Victoria realised, with horror, that she was going to cry. She could feel her mouth shaking, the lump grow in her throat, her eyes began to swim with terrible, shaming tears. In front of them all, she was going to start crying.

'She *knew* where he bloody was.'

'No, she *didn't*.'

'She knew he was with me. And that's all that bloody matters. He was with me and I am his father. What I do with him, and where I take him, is no concern of anyone else. Least of all, you.'

Tears were now running down her face. 'Well, I think—' she managed before he interrupted her.

'I never asked you to think. I simply told you to keep your stupid little mouth *shut*.'

This was accompanied by Oliver's fist coming down in a massive blow on the dining room table. Everything on it shivered and bounced. Thomas, who had been stunned into silence by the unfamiliar violence of words that he did not know, but understood only too well, chose this moment to emulate Victoria, and burst into tears. His eyes screwed up, his mouth fell open, the remains of his half-chewed orange dribbled from his mouth down on to his feeder.

'Oh, for God's sake . . .'

'Oh, Oliver, *don't*.' She sprang to her feet, her knees trembling, and tried to lift Thomas out of his chair, to comfort him. Thomas clung to her, burying his sticky face into her neck, trying to hide from the shouting. 'Don't, in front of Thomas. *Stop!* '

But her anguished appeal was ignored. By now Oliver was past stopping. 'You knew why I didn't want you to get in touch with the Archers. Because I guessed that as soon as they knew where we were, I'd be bombarded with maudlin appeals, and when they failed, threats. Which is precisely what has happened. The next thing we know, there'll be some black-coated little bastard on the doorstep delivering a letter from some lawyer or other . . .'

'But you said . . .' She couldn't remember what he had said. Her nose had started to run, and she could scarcely speak for crying. 'I . . . I . . .' She scarcely knew what she was trying to say. *I'm sorry,* perhaps, but it was just as well that this final abasement was never uttered, because Oliver was in no mood to be placated by anything. Not his weeping son, nor his weeping mistress, nor all the apologies in the world.

'You know what you are? You're a deceitful little bitch.'

And with this final broadside, Oliver straightened up from the table, and turned and stalked out of the room. Victoria was left, trapped by her own tears, with the weeping hysterical child in her arms, with the appalled silence of the other two men, with the shambles of the ruined meal. Worst of all, with humiliation and shame.

Roddy said, 'My dear,' and got up from the table and came around to her side, and Victoria knew that she must stop crying, but she couldn't stop, or wipe away her tears, or even start looking for a handkerchief, while still burdened with the howling Thomas.

John Dunbeath said, 'Here.' He was beside her, lifting Thomas out of her arms and up against his broad shoulder. 'Here, come along now, we'll go and find Ellen. She'll maybe have some candy for you to eat.' Bearing Thomas with him, he made for the door. 'Or a chocolate biscuit. Do you like chocolate biscuits?'

When they had gone, 'My dear,' said Roddy again.

'I . . . I can't help it . . .' Victoria gasped.

He could bear it no longer. Streaming face, running nose, sobs and all, he pulled her into his arms and held her against him, cradling the back of her head with his gentle hand. After a little, he reached up and took the red and white handkerchief from the breast pocket of his aged tweed jacket, and gave it to her, and Victoria was able to blow her nose and wipe her eyes.

After that, things got a little better, and the nightmare scene started to be over.

She went in search of Oliver. There was nothing else to be

done. She found him down by the edge of the loch, standing at the end of the jetty, smoking a cigarette. If he heard her coming across the grass, he gave no sign of it, for he never turned round.

She reached the jetty. She said his name. He hesitated for a moment, and then threw his half-smoked cigarette into the sun-dappled water, and turned to face her.

Victoria remembered him saying, *If you so much as pick up a telephone, I'll batter you black and blue.* But she hadn't really believed the threat, because in all the time that she had known him, she had never seen the true violence of Oliver's uncontrolled rage. Now, she knew, she had seen it. She wondered if his wife, Jeanette, had seen it. If that, perhaps, was one of the reasons why his marriage had lasted only for a few months.

'Oliver.'

His eyes rested on her face. She knew she looked hideous, still swollen from weeping, but even that didn't matter any longer. Nothing mattered except that the dreadful quarrel, for Thomas's sake, had to be patched up.

She said, 'I really am sorry.'

He still said nothing. After a while, he gave a long sigh, and then shrugged.

She went on, painfully. 'It's difficult for you to understand. I know that. And I don't suppose I understood, either, because I'd never had a child of my own. But after I'd been with Thomas for a bit, I began to realise what it was like. I mean, having a little boy, and loving him.' She wasn't doing it right at all. She was making it sound sentimental, and that wasn't what she was trying to be at all. 'You get bound up with a child. Involved. As though it were part of you. You begin to feel that if anybody hurt it, or even threatened it, you could kill them.'

'Do you imagine,' said Oliver, 'That Mrs Archer was going to kill me?'

'No. But I did know that she was probably out of her mind with anxiety.'

'She always hated me. They both did.'

'Perhaps you didn't give them much reason to do anything else?'

'I married their daughter.'

'And fathered their grandchild.'

'He's my son.'

'That's the whole point. Thomas is your son. You've told me over and over that the Archers have no legal claim on him. So how can it hurt you to be a little generous to them? He's all they have left of their daughter. Oh, Oliver, you must try to understand. You're perceptive and clever, you write plays that wring people's hearts. Why can't you come to terms with a situation that should be so close to your own heart?'

'Perhaps I haven't got a heart.'

'You've got a heart.' She began, tentatively, to smile. 'I've heard it beating. Thump thump thump, all through the night.'

It worked. His grim expression softened a little, as though the situation had, in its way, a wry humour. It wasn't much, but, emboldened by this, Victoria went down the jetty to his side, she put her arms around his waist, beneath his jacket, and pressed her cheek against the front of his rough, thick sweater.

She said, 'They don't matter anyway, the Archers. What they do can't make any difference.'

His hands rubbed up and down her back, as though he were absently fondling a dog. 'Any difference to what?'

'My loving you.' It was said. Pride, self-esteem no longer mattered. Loving Oliver was their only talisman, all she had to hold on to. It was the key of the lock that held the two of them, and Thomas, together.

He said, 'You must be mad.'

He did not apologise for any of the searing remarks and accusations he had thrown at her down the length of the lunch table. She wondered if he would apologise to Roddy and John, and knew that he would not. Simply because he was Oliver Dobbs. But that didn't matter. Victoria had bridged the breach between them. The wound of the hideous scene was still open, and agonising, but perhaps, in time, it would heal. She realised that it was always possible to pick yourself up and start again, however many times you fall.

She said, 'Would you mind very much if I was?'

He did not reply. Presently he laid his hands on her shoulders and put her away from him. 'I must go,' he told her. 'It's time I was going, or I'll miss my plane.'

They went back to the Stable House and collected his suitcase, a couple of books. When they came out again, they saw Jock's old Daimler parked in front of the house, and Roddy and John standing beside it, waiting.

It seemed that everybody had decided to behave as though nothing had happened. 'I thought it would be better to take the big car,' Roddy explained. 'There's not much room for luggage in the MG.'

His tone was quite matter-of-fact, and Victoria felt grateful to him.

'That's great,' Oliver opened the back door and heaved his case in, and the books on top of it. 'Well,' he grinned, quite unrepentant, even perhaps a little amused by the lack of expression on John Dunbeath's face, 'I'll say goodbye, John.'

'I'll see you again,' John told him. He did not hold out a hand. 'I'm not leaving till Wednesday.'

'That's great. Bye, Victoria,' he stooped to kiss her cheek.

'Tomorrow,' she said. 'What time does your plane get in?'

'About seven-thirty.'

'I'll be there to meet you.'

'See you then.'

They got into the car. Roddy started the engine. The Daimler moved away, ponderous and dignified, tyres crunching on the gravel. Down through the rhododendrons, over the cattle grid, through the gate.

They had gone.


He was terribly afraid that now it was all over, now he was alone with her, she would start to cry again. It was not that he was afraid of tears, or would even be embarrassed by them. In fact, he would have almost welcomed them. But he knew, too, that this was not the right time to take her in his arms, to comfort her as Roddy had done.

She was standing with her back to him. She was done with waving goodbye. To John, her erect and slender back seemed immensely courageous. He saw the firm set of her shoulders under the thick sweater, the long silky tail of fair hair, and was reminded of a colt his father had reared, long ago, on the ranch back in Colorado. Once frightened by a clumsy hand, only the most patient and perceptive of handling had finally brought it back to anything approaching trust. But little by little, letting the colt take his own time, John himself had achieved this.

He knew that he had to be very careful. He waited. After a bit, perhaps realising that he was not going to simply melt away and tactfully disappear, Victoria pushed her hair out of her face, and turned to face him. She was not crying. She was smiling. The sort of smile that lights up a face, but does not reach the eyes.

She said briskly, 'Well, that's that.'

He said, 'They've got a good day for a drive. It'll be very beautiful, going over Struie.'

'Yes.'

'Don't you think we ought to go for a drive, too?' Victoria's smile froze and became agonised, and he knew that this was what she had been dreading; he was sorry for her and so he was going to be kind to her. He went on, quickly, 'I have to go to Creagan, anyway. I have to go to the chemist. I've run out of shaving soap. And I thought the newsagent might have a *Financial Times*. I haven't seen the market prices for three days.' This was not true, but it was a face-saver, and as good an excuse as any.

Victoria said, 'What about Thomas?'

'We'll leave Thomas here. He's happy with Ellen.'

'I haven't taken Thomas to the beach yet. I've always meant to take him.'

'You can take him another time. If you don't tell him where you're going, he won't want to come.'

She considered this. She said at last, 'Well . . . all right. But I must go and tell Ellen that we're going out.'

That was good enough. 'You'll find them out at the back, on the drying-green. I'll get the car and meet you here in a moment or two.'

When he returned, at the wheel of the hired Ford, she was back on the steps by the front door, waiting for him. He knew that in Creagan it would be windswept and cold, and she was wearing no sort of coat, but there was a spare sweater of his own lying on the back seat of the car, and he did not want to put off any time. He drew up beside her, leaned across to open the passenger door, and let Victoria get in beside him. Then, with no more discussion, they were on their way.

He took it slowly. There was no hurry. The more leisurely their passage, the more relaxed he hoped she would become. He said, casually, 'How was Thomas?'

'You were right. He and Ellen are perfectly happy. Ellen's taken a chair out into the sun, and she's doing her knitting, and Thomas and Piglet are playing with her clothes pegs.' She added, a little wistfully, 'They looked very peaceful.'

He said, 'Thomas isn't your child, is he?'

Victoria, beside him, was very still. She stared ahead at the convolutions of the narrow road. Her hands lay clasped in her lap. She said, 'No.'

'I don't know why, but I always imagined that he was. I suppose Roddy thought he was, too. At least, he never gave me any reason to suspect that he wasn't. And he looks like you. That's the extraordinary thing. A bit fatter, perhaps, but he really looks like you.'

'He isn't my child. But he's Oliver's. Thomas's mother was called Jeanette Archer. Oliver married her, but then the marriage broke up and she was killed in an aircrash soon after.'

'How do you come into it?'

'I've been in it for years . . .' Her voice began to shake. 'I'm terribly sorry, but I think I'm going to start crying again.'

'It doesn't matter.'

'Don't you mind?' She sounded surprised.

'Why should I mind?' He leaned forward and opened the cubbyhole on the dashboard, and revealed an enormous box of Kleenex. 'See? I'm even prepared.'

'Americans always have paper handkerchiefs.' She took one out and blew her nose. 'Crying's horrible, isn't it? Once you start, it's like a terrible addiction. However many times you stop, you always start again. I don't usually ever cry.'

But this brave assertion dissolved, even as she made it, into tears. John waited peacefully, taking no notice, saying nothing. After a little, when the sobs had reduced themselves to chokes and then to sniffs and she had blown her nose, determinedly, once more, he observed, 'If a person wants to cry, I never see any reason why they shouldn't. I always cried when I was a kid and being sent back to Fessenden. And my father never tried to stop me nor to tell me that it wasn't manly. In fact, he sometimes looked as though he were about to burst into tears himself.'

Victoria smiled wanly, but made no comment on this, and John decided to leave it, and nothing more was said until they reached Creagan. The little town lay bathed in cold afternoon sunshine, its streets swept and empty of the modest throngs who would fill it later on in the year as the summer season swelled.

He drew up in front of the chemist. 'Do you want to do any shopping?' he asked Victoria.

'No. I'm all right, thank you.'

He left her and went into the shop and bought the shaving soap and some razor blades. Next to the chemist was a newsagent, so he went in there and asked for the *Financial Times*, but they didn't have one, so he bought a bag of peppermints instead, and bore these back to the car.

'Here.' He tossed them into Victoria's lap. 'If you don't like them, we'll give them to Thomas.'

'Perhaps Ellen would like them. Old people always like peppermints.'

'These are toffees. Ellen can't eat toffees on account of her false teeth. Now, what shall we do?'

'We could go back to Benchoile.'

'Is that what you want to do? Don't you want to go for a walk or something? Don't you want to go to the beach?'

'Do you know the way?'

'Sure I know the way, I used to come here when I was knee-high to a bee.'

'Haven't you anything else you'd rather do?'

'Not a mortal thing.'

The beach at Creagan was divided from the town by the golf links, and there was no access by road to the sands, so John parked the car by the clubhouse. When he switched off the engine, they could hear the whine of the wind. The long pale grasses that flanked the fairways lay flat beneath its blast, and the brightly coloured waterproof jackets of a couple of hardy golfers were filled with it, so that they resembled balloons. John pulled up the zipper of his old suede jacket, and reached back for the sweater that lay on the back seat. He gave it to Victoria. 'Put this on.'

It was blue and very thick with a tall polo neck. She pulled it over her head and the tight, ribbed collar dragged her hair. She flipped it free and shook it loose. The cuffs of the sweater covered her hands, the hem reached below her narrow hips.

They got out of the car, and the wind pounced on the open doors and it was a struggle to get them shut. A path, a right-of-way, led down towards the sea across the fairways. Wild thyme grew underfoot, and there were hazards of whin and gorse. Beyond the links lay dunes of coarse grass, 'bents' they were called in this part of the world, and there was a little caravan site, and small, ramshackle edifices, which in summer would open their shutters and sell chocolate and fizzy drinks and ice creams. The dunes ended abruptly in a sloping cliff of sand. The tide was out. Now there was nothing but white beach and the distant sea. Far away, the rollers creamed in, crested with spray. There was not another soul about, not a dog, not a scampering child. Only the wheeling gulls hung overhead, screaming their disdain at the world in general.

After the soft, dry, sand of the dunes, the beach seemed very flat and firm underfoot. They ran, trying to get warm. As they approached the sea, shallow pools, fed from some mysterious source, reflected the brightness of the sky, and there were immense quantities of shells. Victoria's attention was caught by these. She picked up one and then another, marvelling at their size and unbroken state.

'They're so beautiful. I've never seen shells before that weren't all broken to bits. Why aren't these broken?'

'I suppose because this is a shallow, sandy shore' He joined in her ploy, grateful for any diversion that would take her mind off her woes. He found the skeleton of a starfish, the delicate fossilised claw of a miniature crab.

'What's this?' she asked him.

He inspected it. 'A sand gaper. And the blue one is a common mussel.'

'And this? It looks exactly like a very small baby's toe-nail.'

'That's called a banded wedge.'

'How do you know their names?'

'I used to come and collect shells when I was a boy, and Roddy gave me a book so that I'd learn to identify them.'

They walked on in silence, and came at last to the sea. They stood, facing the wind, and watched the breakers pouring in. The waves rose and curled and broke and hissed in over the sand, and the water was clear and clean and the colour of aquamarine.

The shell lay, just out of reach of the ebbing tide. John stooped and picked it up, and placed it, wet and shining, in the palm of Victoria's hand. It was the colour of coral, with a sunburst of raised ribs, semispherical in shape, so that if it had still been attached to its twin they would have formed a whole roughly the size of a tennis ball.

'Now there's a prize,' he said.

She was open mouthed. 'Whatever is it?'

'That's a queen scallop, and what a size of one.'

'I thought you only found shells like that in the West Indies.'

'Well, now you know you can find them in Scotland.'

She held it away from her, taking enormous pleasure in its shape, the very feel of the shell. She said, 'I shall keep it for always. Just for an ornament.'

'And a keepsake, perhaps.'

Victoria looked at him, and he saw the beginnings of her first smile. 'Yes. Perhaps as a keepsake too.'

They turned their backs on the sea, and started on the long return journey. The sands stretched forever, and the dunes seemed very far away. By the time they had reached the steep cliff of sand down which they had tumbled so easily, Victoria was beginning to flag, and John had to take her hand, and pull her, floundering and slipping, to the top. Halfway up, she began to laugh, and when they finally reached the summit, they were both breathless. In wordless agreement, they collapsed, exhausted, into a sheltered hollow, where the sand gave way to a thick, coarse grass, and the tussocks of bents protected them from the worst of the wind.

Here, there even seemed to be a little heat in the sun. John lay back on his elbows, and let its warmth generate through the thick, dark suede of his jacket. Victoria sat forward, her chin on her knees, still gloating over her shell. Her hair had parted at the back of her neck, and his enormous sweater made her look even thinner and frailer than she actually was.

After a bit, she said, 'Perhaps I shouldn't keep it. Perhaps I should give it to Thomas.'

'Thomas wouldn't appreciate it.'

'He would, when he's older.'

'You're very fond of Thomas, aren't you? Even though he isn't your child.'

Victoria said, 'Yes.'

'Do you want to talk about it?'

'It's difficult to know where to begin. And you probably wouldn't understand anyway.'

'You could try me.'

'Well . . .' She took a deep breath. 'The Archers are Thomas's grandparents.'

'I gathered that.'

'And they live in Hampshire. And Oliver was driving back from Bristol, and he passed near Woodbridge – that's where the Archers live . . .'

Slowly, hesitantly, the story unfolded. All the time she was speaking, Victoria kept her back turned to John, and he was forced to listen to the entire saga while staring at the back of her neck. He found this intensely frustrating.

'. . . that night you brought me back from the Fairburn's

party, and Thomas was crying – that was the evening they turned up.'

He remembered that night, the evening before he had flown to Bahrein. The dark windy skies and the little house in the mews; Victoria with her chin buried in the fur collar of her coat, and her eyes filled with apprehension and anxiety.

'. . . and all come away for a little holiday. So we came to Benchoile on account of Oliver knowing Roddy. I told you about that.'

'I take it you don't have a job to keep you in London?'

'Oh, yes I do. But I work in a dress shop in Beauchamp Place, and Sally, the girl I work for, wanted me to take a holiday anyway. So she said I could have a month off, and she's got a temporary girl in to help out till I get back again.'

'And are you going back?'

'I don't know.'

'Why don't you know?'

'I may just stay with Oliver.'

This silenced John. He could not comprehend how any girl could want to stay with that raving egotist. Despite all his original and laudable intentions of keeping a fair and open mind, he found himself becoming more and more incensed.

She was talking again. '. . . I knew how worried Mrs Archer must be, so I said to Oliver that I thought I should write to her, and Oliver was furious because he didn't want them to know where we were. But I did write, although I explained to her about Oliver being so difficult, and I asked her not to get in touch, but I suppose Mr Archer got hold of my letter.'

Now that the telling was safely over, Victoria appeared to decide that the time had come to look John in the eye. She turned to face him, her attitude confiding, her weight resting on one hand, her long legs curled up beneath her.

'And it was he who rang up Oliver at lunchtime. So now you see why Oliver was so angry.'

'Yes, I suppose I do see. But I still think it was a fairly gruesome scene.'

'But you do understand?'

It was obviously important to her that he did. But, for John, understanding made things no better. In fact, if anything, a good deal worse, for his most pessimistic suspicions had proved themselves well-founded. It was all in place now, the pieces of the jigsaw slotted together and the pattern clear. A person was selfish. Another person was greedy. Pride came into it, and resentment and even a sort of spite. Nobody came out of it well, and only the innocent suffered. The innocent. A noxious word, but how else to describe Victoria and Thomas?

He thought of Oliver. From the first encounter, there had been an antipathy between the two men. Like dogs, they had circled each other, hackles bristling. John had told himself that this antipathy was reasonless, instinctive, and with the inbred good manners of a man staying in another man's house, had fallen over backwards in his efforts not to let it show. But the antipathy was obviously mutual and before long John found himself resenting Oliver's casual treatment of Victoria, his offhand attitude to Roddy, his lack of interest in his child. After a couple of days in Oliver's company he had to admit that he actively disliked him. Now, after the appalling scene over the lunch table, he knew that he detested him.

He said, 'If you stay with Oliver, will you marry him?'

'I don't know.'

'Do you mean you don't know if you'll marry him, or if he'll marry you?'

'I don't know.' A flush crept up into her pale cheeks. 'I don't know if he'll marry me. He's funny. He . . .'

All at once, John was filled with a boiling, unaccustomed rage. Brutally, he interrupted her. 'Victoria, don't be a fool.' She stared at him, her eyes enormous. 'I mean that. Don't be a fool. You have a whole, wonderful life in front of you, and you talk about getting married to a guy, and you don't even know if he loves you enough to marry you. Marriage isn't a love affair. It isn't even a honeymoon. It's a job. A long hard job, at which both partners have to work, harder than they've worked at anything in their lives before. If it's a good marriage, it changes, it evolves, but it goes on getting better. I've seen it with my own mother and father. But a bad marriage can dissolve in a welter of resentment and acrimony. I've seen that, too, in my own miserable and disastrous attempt at making another person happy. And it's never one person's fault. It's the sum total of a thousand little irritations, disagreements, idiotic details that in a sound alliance would simply be disregarded, or forgotten in the healing act of making love. Divorce isn't a cure, it's a surgical operation, even if there are no children to consider. And you and Oliver already have a child. You have Thomas.'

She said, 'I can't go back.'

'Sure you can.'

'It's all very well for you to talk. Your marriage may have broken up, but you still have your parents, your job. You have Benchoile, too, whatever you decide to do with it. If I don't have Oliver and Thomas, then I don't have anything. Not anything really precious. Not anyone to belong to, not anyone to need me.'

'You have yourself.'

'Perhaps I'm not enough.'

'In that case, you dismally underestimate yourself.'

Victoria turned swiftly away from him, and John was presented once more with the back of her head. He realised that he had been shouting at her, and this astonished him, because it was the first time in many months that he had felt sufficiently involved or aroused to shout at anyone. He said, gruffly, 'I'm sorry,' and when she did not move nor speak, he went on, more gently, 'It's just that I hate to see someone like you make such a goddamn mess of her life.'

She said, sounding sullen as a child, 'You forget. It's still my life.'

'It's Thomas's too,' he reminded her. 'And Oliver's.' Still she did not move. He put his hand on her arm and pulled her around to face him. With an immense effort she met his eyes. He said, 'You have to love Oliver very much. Much more than he loves you. To make it work, I mean.'

'I know.'

'In that case you're going into it with your eyes open.'

'I know,' she said again. Gently, she eased herself free of his grasp. 'But you see, there was never anyone else. There was never anyone but Oliver.'

# CHAPTER 14

## TUESDAY

The wind, he thought, was the same wind that blew in Scotland, but in London it took on a different shape. It sneaked from around corners, it tore the first buds from the trees in the park, and littered the streets with torn scraps of paper. It was not a friend. People pressed against it, their faces agonised, their coats wrapped tight against them. The wind was an enemy, invading the city.

The rain came as the taxi, which had brought him out from Fulham, turned at last into the complexities of Heathrow Airport. It came through tunnels and circled rotaries, a tiny entity in an endless stream of traffic. Lights flashed, reflected in the wet roadways; overhead a jet droned, waiting to land. There was the heavy smell of petrol.

This taxi, in a long queue of taxis, drew in at last under the terminal building. Oliver got out, pulled his suitcase after him, and stood at the pavement's edge feeling in his pocket for the fare. The driver, waiting, let his eyes move over his passenger, his passenger's luggage.

'Here,' Oliver handed the notes over.

'Sure I've brought you to the right place, mate? This is domestic flights here. Terminal one.'

'Yes, that's right.'

'Just saw the label on your case. You ought to be over in international flights, terminal three.'

'No. This is the one I want.' He grinned. 'Keep the change.'

'Well, it's you who's travelling. You ought to know.'

He picked up his case and went in through the glass doors,

across the polished expanse of the great building, up the escalator, following the signs that led to domestic departures.

The departure hall was crowded as usual, every seat taken with travellers waiting for their various flights to be called. There was the smell of coffee, and cigarette smoke and humanity. Oliver moved slowly down the room, looking about him, like a man with a rendezvous. He saw the woman with her five exhausting children; a pair of nuns. He saw the man in the tweed overcoat and bowler hat, immersed in his newspaper. His briefcase stood on the floor between his legs. Oliver stopped before him.

'Excuse me.'

Startled, the man looked up from his paper. He had a long pale face, a neat collar, a dark tie. He wore spectacles. A lawyer, thought Oliver. A businessman. He said, 'I *am* sorry, but I saw the label on your briefcase. Are you flying to Inverness?'

'Yes,' said the man, sounding as though he did not think it was any of Oliver's business.

'On the five-thirty plane?'

'Yes.'

'I wonder if you'd be very kind and deliver a letter for me.' He reached into his pocket and took out the envelope. 'The thing is, I'd arranged to catch this flight, but I'm not going to be able to make it after all, and there's someone meeting me at Inverness.'

The man in spectacles continued to look unenthusiastic. He probably thought the envelope contained some sort of an explosive device, and that he and the rest of his fellow passengers were going to be blown to kingdom come whilst in transit over the Pennines.

'This has just all cropped up in the last couple of hours, and I can't telephone her – the girl who's meeting me, I mean – because she's driving to Inverness from Sutherland, and she'll have left by now.'

The man in spectacles looked at the envelope and then back at Oliver. Oliver put on his sincere and open expression. The man laid down his newspaper.

'If I do take your letter, how shall I know the young lady?'

'Well, she's young, and she's got long fair hair, and she'll probably be wearing trousers. She's called Victoria Bradshaw.' He added, as though it were a little lure, 'She's very pretty.'

But the other was not to be so easily seduced. 'What shall I do if she isn't there?'

'She will be there. I promise you. She'll be there.'

The man took the envelope at last, gingerly. 'Wouldn't it be better to hand this over to the air hostess?'

'I suppose we could, but you know what they're like, always so busy giving people cups of tea. And anyway, I haven't got time to wait till she turns up, because I've got to get over to the international terminal and catch another plane.'

'Very well,' said the man at last. Having made the decision, he allowed a small smile to cross his chilly features. 'You can leave it with me.'

'Thank you,' said Oliver. 'Thank you very much. I'm really sorry to have bothered you. And I hope you have a good flight.'

'The same to you,' said the man in spectacles, and went back to his paper.

Oliver picked up his suitcase and turned away. He would go down the stairs and out of this building, and he would walk through the rain, over to terminal three, and check in on the New York flight, and after that he was on his own once more. He was on his way.

He was free. It was over. An interlude, a brief encounter finished. The actors had departed, and the stage lay empty. Like an untouched canvas, it waited for Oliver to inhabit it with his own people, his own private and absorbing world.

*You're back then.*

*That's right.*

*She's gone, then.*

*Yes, she's gone.*

*You can tell. A house has got a funny feeling when the last child goes. You think they're there forever but they go. And there's nothing much left, really. Except the telly. There's always the telly.*

'Oh, excuse me.'

He had reached the top of the stairs. He turned and found himself face to face with the man in the bowler hat. It took an instant's mental reorganisation before Oliver even recognised him. He carried his briefcase in one hand, and Oliver's letter in the other.

'I'm sorry, but the young lady I have to give this to, I can't remember what you said she was called. You've written it on the envelope, but your writing's not all that clear. Is it Miss

Veronica Bradshaw?'
  'No,' said Oliver. 'It's . . .' he hesitated, having to remember. 'It's Victoria.'

He supposed there came a time for starting to feel old. Not
just mature, or experienced, or any of the other euphemisms.
Just old. He was sixty. Jock had died at sixty-nine. If he,
Roddy, were to die at sixty-nine, that meant that he had only
nine years left to enjoy. Or did it mean that he had nine years
to fill in before he was finally released? And if so, then how
was he to fill them? He would not have Benchoile to cushion
him against the cold winds of the outside world, and he knew –
had known for some years – that to all intents and purposes he
had outwritten himself. There was no longer a readable book
inside his head, and scarcely the most banal of articles. His
friends, his social life, which had once so satisfyingly filled
his time, were fading. His contemporaries had started to die;
the delightful women who had once charmed him were becoming grandmothers, unable to cope – as inflation swallowed
everything and old servants went into retirement – with house
parties and dinner parties and all the endless, pleasant diversions of former days.
  Pouring his second drink of the evening, trying to cheer himself up, Roddy Dunbeath told himself that in many ways he
was fortunate. He would become old and he would probably
be lonely, but at least he would not be penniless. All right, so
Benchoile was to be sold, but Roddy Dunbeath was in a financial position that would allow him to buy, outright, some
modest house in which to spend the rest of his days. Where
this house was to be, he had not yet decided, but Ellen was
another problem which loomed like a shadow at the back of
his mind. There could be no question of abandoning Ellen.
If none of her many relations could be persuaded to have the
cantankerous old thing to live with them, then Roddy would
have to take her on himself. The very prospect of living in a
small house with no one but Ellen Tarbat for company gave him
the shivers. He prayed, fervently, that it would never have to
happen.
  It was eight o'clock in the evening, and he was alone in his
house, and it was this very solitude that had brought on his
gloomy mood. Oliver was in London, by now – Roddy glanced
at his watch – by now probably on his way back to Scotland.

Victoria had departed in that immense Volvo to meet him at the airport. Thomas was in his bedroom downstairs, asleep, having been bathed and put to bed by Ellen. John was over in the big house, doing God knew what. The whole business of Benchoile seemed to have got the boy down, for he had been going around all day with a face like a wet weekend and with scarcely a word for anybody. To put the final lid on things, the weather had degenerated dismally with sleet showers and a force eight gale, and the summits of the hills were once more blanketed in snow.

Where, Roddy asked himself, was the spring? On such an evening, in such a mood, it was possible to believe that it would never come again. There would be some freak in the cosmos, the stars would start clashing, earthquakes erupt and the planet Earth be trapped forever in the grip of eternal winter.

Enough. That was as far as a man's depression could be allowed to go. Supine in his chair, his slippered feet sharing the hearthrug with his old dog, Roddy decided that the time had come to take some positive step to raise his spirits. He looked once more at his watch. He would go over to the big house and take a drink with John. They would then eat dinner together, and later, when Oliver and Victoria returned from Inverness, would all sit around the fire and listen to Oliver's news.

This pleasant prospect stimulated him sufficiently to make the effort of pulling himself up out of his chair. The newspaper that he had been reading sometime before slipped from his knees. Outside, the wind howled, and an icy draught came up the stairs and stirred the rugs on the polished floor. The Stable House was usually cosy, but no door or window built by man's hands could keep that north-west wind from penetrating. The room felt chilly. The fire was dying. He took logs from the basket, tossed them on to the dying embers, building up a good blaze that would still be alight when he returned later on in the evening.

He turned off the lamp and said, 'Come along, Barney,' and the old dog heaved himself up, obviously feeling, as Roddy was, his age. 'You're not the only one,' he told him, and he turned off the centre light, and together, slowly, they started down the stairs.

Without occupants, the darkened room was still and quiet. The fire flickered. A log cracked and kindled into flame. There came a crack of splitting wood, and a shower of sparks erupted like fireworks, out on to the hearthrug. Unattended, they smouldered. Then a draught snaked in up the stairs, a spark flared for a second, and caught the corner of the abandoned newspaper. Tiny flames began to lick and then grew larger. They played up the leg of Roddy's chairside table, where he kept his books and his cigars and a pile of old magazines. They reached the tindery withies of the old basket where he kept his logs. Soon, the hem of the curtain had started to smoulder.

John Dunbeath sat at the desk in the library, where he had spent most of the afternoon going through his uncle's papers, sorting out farm accounts from personal accounts, arranging neat piles for the attention of Robert McKenzie, for Jock's stockbroker in Edinburgh, for his accountant.

The old man had kept a neat and efficient tally of his affairs, and this task had not been complicated, but tedious and inevitably sad. For there were as well old diaries, dance cards, and faded photographs of people whom John had never known. Regimental groups taken in the Red Fort at Delhi; a snapshot of a party of guns in jungly surroundings, gathered for what looked like a tiger shoot; a wedding. Some of the photographs were Benchoile. He recognised his father as a small boy, and Roddy, a slender stripling, wearing white flannels and looking as though he were about to burst into song, the juvenile lead in some prewar musical comedy.

The door opened and the present-day Roddy ambled in. John was pleased to see him and to have the excuse to stop working. He pushed his chair back from the desk and held up the photograph.

'Look what I've just found.'

Roddy came to inspect it over John's shoulder. 'Good God. Inside every fat man there's a thin man struggling to get out. Where did you find that?'

'Oh, put away with some other old papers. What time is it?' He looked at his watch. 'A quarter past eight already? I didn't realise it was as late as that.'

'Quarter past eight on a vile cold winter's evening.' He shivered. 'I was nearly blown away just coming across the yard.'

'Let's have a drink.'

'Spendid idea,' said Roddy as though he had not thought

of it himself. He headed over to the table where the bottles
and glasses had already been set out by Ellen, and John wondered how many private Scotches his uncle had already consumed, and then told himself that it didn't matter anyway,
and it was none of his business. He only knew that he felt
tired, and the prospect of a restoring drink was all at once very
welcome.

He got up and went to build up the fire, and to draw a chair
close to the blaze, for Roddy. Roddy brought the drinks over,
and handed John his, and then sank into the chair with what
sounded like a sigh of relief. John remained standing, and the
warmth of the flames crept up his back, and he realised that
he was stiff and cold from sitting in the bay of the window.

'Slainthe,' said Roddy, and they both drank. 'When are the
others getting back, do you know?'

'No idea,' John's dark face was impassive. 'Around ten, I
guess. Depends on whether the plane's on time or not. This
gale might delay them.'

'Are you really going back to London tomorrow?'

'Yes, I should. I'll probably be back again, next week or the
week after, but we've got this big thing going just now, and I
should be around.'

'It was good that you were able to come.'

'I've liked it. I'm just sorry that it had to end this way. I'd
have liked Benchoile to go on.'

'Dear boy, nothing can go on forever, and we've had a
good run for our money.'

They started talking about the old days, and as they both
relaxed in the warmth, and each other's companionship, the
time slipped pleasantly by. They were on to their second
drink (or John's second drink and Roddy's fourth) when there
came a scuffling sound from outside the door, the door opened,
and Ellen advanced into the room. Neither of the men were
surprised by this sudden appearance, for Ellen had long since
given up knocking on doors. She was looking tired and particularly old. The wind and the bitter cold were bad for her
bones, and she had been on her feet most of the day. Her
expression showed this. Her mouth was buttoned up. She
seemed determined to be put upon.

'I don't know when you two are wanting your dinner, but
you can have it anytime you like.'

'Thank you, Ellen,' said Roddy, with a mild sarcasm that
was wasted upon her.

'And when the others are getting back from Inverness I do not know, but they'll just have to make do with a bowl of broth.'

'That'll be all they'll want,' John assured her, and added, with some idea of placating her. 'We'll be in the dining room in a moment. We're just having a drink.'

'So I can see for myself.' She hovered for a moment, trying to think of some other fault to find. 'Did you check on the little boy before you came across, Roddy?'

'Um?' Roddy frowned. 'No, I didn't. Was I meant to?'

'It seems it might have been a sensible thing to do instead of just leaving the mite there, abandoned for the evening.'

Roddy became exasperated. 'Ellen, I've only just got over here. Anyway, we leave him happily every evening.'

'Oh, well, never you mind. I'll go and look for myself.'

She began to shuffle off, but seemed in truth, so tired, so old, with her sticklike black legs and her trodden shoes that John couldn't bear it. He laid down his drink. 'Here, Ellen, don't you worry. I'll go.'

'It's no trouble.'

'It's no trouble for me either. It'll take me one minute. And when I get back, we'll come and eat dinner, and then you can take ourself off to bed.'

'Who said anything about bed?'

'I did. You're looking tired, and it's the best place for you.'

'Well, I don't know . . .' Shaking her head, she made for the kitchen, and John started down the long flagged passages that led to the stableyard. Tonight they were as cold as dungeons, eerily lighted by naked bulbs which swung in the draughts. He seemed to be surrounded by looming shadows.

He opened the back door to the outside. The wind snatched at it and nearly blew it out of his hand, and for a second, that seemed like forever, he stood there in the doorway.

For ahead of him, across the cobbles of the yard, every upstairs window of Roddy's house was filled with dancing orange light. Smoke and flames gushed from the roof, and above the wind's fury, he could hear the terrifying sounds of the fire, a roar like a furnace, the splinter and crack of wood, sharp as rifle fire. Even as he stood there, a window exploded into a shatter of glass as its frame disintegrated in the heat. Instantly, flames leaped from the empty void, and John felt the heat of them sear his face.

Thomas.

He was across the yard and had opened the door before he considered the consequences. The stairs were already alight, and the wind caught the flames and the whole edifice turned into a sort of blast furnace from which he reeled. The smoke was suffocating. He turned from it, and holding his arm up to his face, made his way down the narrow passage and threw open the door of the first bedroom.

'Thomas!' He had no idea where Thomas was sleeping. *'Thomas!'*

This room was empty. The second room. *'Thomas!'*

Now, he was directly under Roddy's sitting room, and the smoke was blinding; his eyes began to stream and sting, he started to cough.

*'Thomas!'* His voice was a croak. He plunged on through the smoke and found the other door, the other bedroom.

Here, mercifully, the air was a little clearer.

*'Thomas!'*

A wail answered him. There was no time to be relieved, to give thanks that the child had not already died from asphyxiation, for it was clear that the charred ceiling of the room was about to give way at any moment. As John scooped Thomas up in his arms, there came a great load of plaster and charred lathe, spilling down from above and making a sound like falling rocks. He looked up, and saw the ragged crater of the hole, the inferno beyond. Thomas let out a scream, and John pressed the child's face against his shoulder and stumbled from the room.

He was scarcely through the door before the remainder of the ceiling collapsed, and the floor, the carpet, Thomas's bed, everything was obliterated beneath an avalanche of burning debris.


The London plane, fifteen minutes late on account of head winds, could be heard long before it was seen. The dark evening was stormy, the cloud ceiling very low, and when the aircraft did appear, it was with great suddenness, breaking through the murk at the end of the runway as it came in to land on the black, puddled tarmac.

Soon after this, the usual small activities began to take place. Trucks and tankers converged on the stationary plane. Steps were wheeled up to its side by two men in black oilskins. Doors opened. An air hostess appeared at the head of the steps.

Slowly the passengers began to alight, to walk across the windswept apron towards the terminal building. They struggled with cases and baskets and awkwardly shaped parcels. The wind caught their clothes, they ducked their heads against the rain. One woman's hat blew off.

Victoria, with her hands in the pockets of her coat, stood just inside the plate glass doors and waited. One by one the other people, who had waited with her, claimed their various friends and relations. 'There you are, pet. And did you have a good flight?' Affectionate kisses. There were two nuns met by a priest in a black biretta. 'I've got a car waiting,' he told them matter-of-factly. A woman with far too many children and no husband to help her, a few businessmen with briefcases.

The straggle of passengers thinned. There was still no sign of Oliver. She imagined him still sitting in the aircraft, taking his time, waiting until the first ugly rush was over. Then he would unfold his long legs, reach for his coat, make his own leisurely way down the aisle. He would probably stop to chat with the air hostess. Victoria found herself smiling wryly, because she knew him so well.

'Excuse me.' The voice spoke from just behind her. Startled, she turned. She saw one of the businessmen, with his bowler hat and his stiff collar and his briefcase. 'Are you by any chance Miss Victoria Bradshaw?' He held an envelope in his hand.

'Yes, I am.'

'I thought you must be. This letter's for you. Your friend asked me to give it to you.'

She did not take the letter. 'My friend?'

'A young man with a beard. I'm afraid I never caught his name. He asked me to give you this.'

'But isn't he on the plane?'

'No, he couldn't come. But I'm sure this will explain everything.'

Victoria took her hand from her pocket and took the envelope. She saw Oliver's tightly formed black writing. Miss Victoria Bradshaw.

'But where is he?'

'He just said he couldn't make the flight, and he told me what you looked like and asked me to give you the letter.'

'I see. Well, thank you. I . . . . I'm sorry you were bothered with it.'

'No bother. It was no bother at all,' he assured her. 'Well,

I must be off. My wife's waiting in the car, and she'll wonder what's happened to me.' He began to back away, eager to be off. He tipped his bowler hat. 'I'll say goodbye.'

'Goodbye.'

She was alone. Everybody had gone. Only a few official-looking people moved briskly about. A man in overalls wheeled a trolley of luggage. Shocked, confused, Victoria stood there, with Oliver's letter in her hand. She could not think what she was meant to do with it.

On the other side of the arrivals hall, she saw a small refreshment booth. She went across the polished floor and sat on one of the tall stools and asked for a cup of black coffee. A homely woman poured it for her from an urn.

'Do you take sugar?'

'No. No sugar, thank you.'

She slit the envelope and took out the letter.

'It's a terrible night, isn't it?'

'Yes it is.' She opened her bag and found her purse and paid for the coffee.

'Have you far to go?'

'Yes. I have to drive to Sutherland.'

'Oh, my, what a way. Rather you than me.'

She unfolded the letter. He had typed it, on his battered old typewriter. She was filled with cold apprehension. With her hand closed around the mug of hot coffee, she began to read.

> Fulham
> Tuesday
> 24 February

Victoria,

If I were any other sort of a man I should start this letter by telling you that it is a difficult one to write. But I'm not going to say that, because writing is the one thing I have never found difficult, even when it has to be a letter like this one.

I am not coming back to Scotland. I have spent most of the day with my agent, and he is very anxious that I should go to New York where a director called Sol Bernstein is already waiting to sign on the dotted line and to launch *A Man In the Dark* – with, I hope a tremendous fanfare of trumpets – on Broadway.

So I am going, catching a plane out of Heathrow this evening.

But he can't do this to me.
*Oh, yes he can. He has.*

I don't know when I shall return. This year, next year, sometime, never. Certainly not in the foreseeable future. There is too much at stake for plans to be made. Too much to think about. To much buzzing around in my head.

I haven't made this decision without thought of you. In fact, I thought about you most of last night. The night is a good time to get things sorted out. It's dark and quiet and the truth comes more clearly. It's easier to see.

And the truth is that I could never stay with you, because I could never stay with any woman. A long time ago, when I left you for the first time, I told you that I'd never loved anybody, and it's still the same way. I suppose what I feel for you is something rather special, but still the only thing that really turns me on is what goes on inside my head and somehow putting all that down on paper.

This decision had nothing to do with what happened when we were at Benchoile. It has nothing to do with the letter that you wrote the Archers, it really has nothing to do with you. The few days we spent together were unforgettable, and you gave me the closest thing to delight that I have ever known. But they were days stolen out of time and now I have to get back to reality.

There are things that you will have to do. You'll have to get Thomas back to the Archers for one, and hand him over once more to their loving care. I still resent their hold over him. I still curl up at the sort of conventional life they will undoubtedly map out for him, but it is obvious that this is just one of those things that I am going to have to accept.

The Volvo is another problem. You probably won't feel like driving it south by yourself. If this is the case, then ask Roddy if he will take it off your hands and perhaps find a buyer for it in Creagan. Tell him I shall be writing to him.

There is also the vexing problem of cash, but I have spoken to my agent and I will put his name and address at the bottom of this letter, so that if you get in touch with him when you get back to London, he will reimburse you and cover any expenses that you may have to incur.

So that's it. I did not mean to finish on such a mundane and mercenary note. I did not mean anything to finish quite this way. But happy endings are things that don't seem to be part of my life. I've never expected them, and in a funny way, I don't suppose I've ever wanted them.

She was crying. Now the words swam and shimmered before her eyes, and she could scarcely read them. Tears fell on the paper and blurred the handwritten signature.

Take care of yourself. I wish I could end by telling you that I loved you. Perhaps I do a little. But it could never begin to be enough, either for you or for me.

*Oliver*

Victoria folded the letter and put it back into the envelope. She fumbled in her bag and found a handkerchief. It wasn't any good crying. With a two-hour drive ahead of her through the stormy night, she had to stop crying. Otherwise she would drive into a ditch, or a river, or another car, and have to be dragged, mangled, from the wreckage of the Volvo, and then what would happen to Thomas?

After a little the kindly woman behind the bar, unable to ignore the obvious distress of her lonely customer, said, 'Are you all right, dear?'

'Yes,' lied Victoria.

'Was it bad news?'

'No, not really.' She blew her nose again. She tried to smile, 'I have to go.' She got off the stool.

'Have another cup of coffee. Have a bite to eat.'

'No, I'm all right. I'm really all right.'

The Volvo stood lonely in the deserted car park. She found the key and got in behind the wheel. She fastened the seat belt. High above, a hidden plane droned, perhaps coming in to land. She thought of being in an aeroplane, going somewhere, anywhere. She thought of landing on some sunbaked airstrip surrounded by palm trees, in a place where nobody knew her, where she could lick her wounds and start again. Like a criminal searching for a new life, a new identity.

Which was, of course, exactly what Oliver had done, settling his few affairs with a single letter, shedding his responsibilities like an old coat. By now he would be in the transatlantic plane, high over the ocean. Victoria and Thomas already fading into the past, into forgetfulness. Unimportant. Important was what lay ahead. She imagined him, drinking a highball, filled with anticipation for the excitement ahead. A new production. Probably a new play. New York.

Oliver Dobbs.

*The only thing that really turns me on is what goes on inside my head.*

This was the key to Oliver, his own personal, private key. And Victoria had never come near to understanding the private obsessions of his innermost mind. Perhaps if she had been his intellectual equal, a brilliant bluestocking with a university degree, it might have been different. Perhaps if she had known him longer, or closer; if she had been a stronger personality, able to stand up to his moods. Perhaps if she had not always been so dependent upon him, and been able to give him something in return.

But I gave him myself.

*That wasn't enough.*

I loved him.

*But he never loved you.*

I wanted to make a life for him. I wanted to make a life for Thomas.

She was back to Thomas. At the thought of Thomas, the old, ridiculous, protective tenderness took possession of her. For the time being Thomas still needed Victoria. For his sake, she would be efficient, calm, practical. Thomas must be delivered back to his grandparents with as little upheaval as possible. She saw herself calmly packing, buying train tickets. Hiring a taxi, taking him to Woodbridge, finding the Archers' house, ringing the bell. She saw the door opening. . . .

But beyond that her imagination shied. Because once Thomas was gone from her life, then it really was the end. It would be all over. Not simply the reality, but the dream as well.

She started the car, switched on the headlights and the windscreen wipers and moved forward, away from the little airport and out on to the main road.

Two hours later she had reached Creagan, but it was not until she had turned into the single track road that led to Benchoile that she began to realise that something was wrong. The weather conditions, unpredictable as always, had begun to improve. The wind had dropped slightly, the clouds thinned, and as these were blown to rags across the night sky, the stars were revealed, and a pale new moon rose out of the east.

But it was not starlight that warmed the darkness ahead of her, and stained the sky like the glow from a whole city full of street lamps. It was not starlight that flickered and billowed and sent great storms of smoke up into the wind. She rolled down the window and smelled the reek of bonfires. Bonfires? More likely burning heather. Someone had started to burn heather, and it had got out of control and started a hill fire. But did one burn heather in February? And even if one did, surely the fire would have been extinguished by now?

Suddenly, she was afraid. She put her foot down on the accelerator, and the Volvo surged forward, swinging around the bends of the narrow road. The brightness of the fire seemed to grow no less. She had passed the Guthrie's house, she was coming at last to the final bend of the road. Then the house lay ahead of her, the gate and the pine trees, and she knew then that it was neither heather nor bonfires that burned, but Benchoile itself.

With a roar of its powerful engine, the Volvo racketed over the cattle grid and up the slope to the sweep in front of the house. The light of the flames made all as bright as day. She saw the cars lined up at random, the fire engine, the huge snaking hosepipes. There seemed to be people everywhere, all grimed and red-eyed. A man ran across the beam of her headlights, shouting instructions to a colleague, and she saw, with a shock, that it was Davey Guthrie.

The big house was untouched, although lights blazed from every window. But the Stable House . . . She brought the Volvo to a screeching halt, struggled with her seat belt, the door handle, remembered the hand brake. Panic, like the worst sort of sickness, threatened to choke her.

Thomas.

The arch to the stableyard was there, but Roddy's house was almost gone. Only the stone gable end had withstood the onslaught of the flames; it loomed, stark as a ruin, the void where the window had been bright as an eye, with the glow of the conflagration that still raged beyond.

Thomas, in his room, on the ground floor, in his bed. She had to know, but there was not time to ask, no time to wait for answers. She began to walk towards the fire, to run. The smoke was acrid in her nostrils, and the heat was blown towards her on great gusts of wind.

'*Thomas!*'

'Look out there . . .' a man shouted.

She had nearly reached the archway.

'Victoria! '

She heard the footsteps coming up behind her. Arms came around her, caught her, held her. She struggled to be free.

'Victoria.'

It was John Dunbeath. Because she could not hit him with her hands, she kicked backwards at his shins with the heels of her boots. He swung her round to face him.

'Don't you understand?' she shouted into the blur that was John Dunbeath. 'It's Thomas.'

'Listen, stop . . .' She kicked him again, and he took her by the shoulders and shook her. 'Thomas is all *right*. He's all *right*. He's *safe*.'

She was still at last. She could hear her own breathing, laboured, like a person on the point of death. When she felt strong enough, she looked up into his face. In the glow of the fire, she saw his dark eyes, red-rimmed and bloodshot, and there was dirt all over his face and down the front of his shirt.

She said, faintly, 'He's not in there?'

'No. We got him out. He's fine. He's all right.'

Relief made her weak as a kitten. She closed her eyes, afraid that she was either going to be sick or faint. She tried to tell John that her legs had started to feel like cooked spaghetti, but somehow could find neither the words nor the energy to speak them. By then it didn't matter anyway. Because by then John had already picked her up in his arms and was carrying her across the gravel and in through the front door of the big house of Benchoile.

By midnight it was more or less over. The fire was out, the ruin of the Stable House a still-smoking confusion of charred stone and fallen timber. The cars John had managed to rescue, backing them out of the garage on to the grass by the loch while Roddy telephoned the fire brigade. With them disposed of, and the cans of petrol that stood about, fuel for the motor mowers and the chain saws, he had felt a little easier in his mind for the safety of the big house. But even so, the garage roof had been swallowed and destroyed in the conflagration, and all that remained within it had gone as well.

And yet, the main house stood, miraculously unharmed. Within it, in various rooms, the survivors of the household were now bedded down. Thomas had wept, heartbreakingly, not from fear, but because he had lost Piglet. There was no way to tell him that Piglet was no more. Ellen had found him some other toy, a teddy bear that had once belonged to John's father, but at the very sight of this harmless, threadbare creature, Thomas had screamed more loudly than ever, and had finally gone to sleep with his arms wrapped around a wooden engine, the paint scarred and scratched and one of the wheels long since missing.

Ellen had come through it like the tough old thing she was. Only at the very end had she given way and started to tremble, and John had sat her down and given her a brandy, and Jess Guthrie had helped the old woman to bed. For Jess and Davey had been on the scene almost before Roddy had made his telephone call, and it was Davey who organised the team of fire fighters, and helped the men from Creagan – torn so abruptly from their own firesides – to set up the pumps and go about extinguishing the flames.

As for Victoria . . . As though he were controlling, reining-in a bolting horse, John's thoughts came to an abrupt halt. But one indisputable fact stood out. She had returned from Inverness alone, and nobody had had the time nor the inclination to ask her what had happened to Oliver. As far as John was concerned, her sudden reappearance in the midst of chaos, her mindless dash towards the holocaust which was all that remained of Roddy's house, had simply been the unthinkable climax of what had so nearly been a ghastly tragedy, and then he had had no thought in his head but to grab her back from the edge of the fire and carry her to safety.

He had taken her, for want of anywhere better, to his own bedroom, placed her on his own bed. She had opened her eyes and said once more, 'Thomas is really safe, isn't he?' and he had time to do no more than reassure her before Jess Guthrie came bustling in to take over with soothing words and hot drinks. Now, presumably, Victoria was sleeping. With luck, she would sleep till the morning. In the morning there would be all the time in the world to talk.

So, it was midnight, and it was over. He stood at the edge of the loch, with his back to the water, staring up at the house. He realised that he was exhausted, drained of emotion and energy, and yet beneath this aching lassitude lay a calmness and a peace that he had not known for years.

Why he felt thus was a mystery. He only knew that Thomas was alive, and Victoria was safe, and Benchoile still stood, and Oliver Dobbs had not come back from London. He sighed with an enormous content as though, single-handed, he had successfully achieved some impossible task.

Around him, the stormy evening was slipping into a peaceful night. The wind had dropped, the clouds thinned to a few sailing shreds, like billows of mist. Above, a sliver of moon hung in the sky, and the dark waters of the loch were touched with the silver of its reflection. A pair of ducks flew over. Mallards, he guessed. For an instant he glimpsed them, silhouetted against the sky, and then they were swallowed into the darkness and their cry faded to an immense silence.

But there came other sounds. The wind in the topmost branches of the pines, the whisper of water nudging against the wooden piles of the old jetty. He looked at the house and saw the comfort of lights in windows. He saw the dark swell of the hills that rose behind it.

His hills. Benchoile hills.

He stood there for a long time, his hands in his pockets, until a fit of the shivers made him realise that he was growing cold. He turned back for a final look at the loch, and then, slowly, made his way up the slope of the lawn and so indoors.


Roddy had not gone to bed. Roddy waited still in the library, slumped in Jock's old armchair by the dying fire. John's heart bled for his uncle. Of all of them, Roddy was the one to suffer most. Not simply because he had lost his house, his clothes, his books and papers, all the personal and cherished possessions of a lifetime, but because he blamed himself for what had happened.

'I should have *thought*,' he had already said, over and over again, his usual loquacity overwhelmed by the potential tragedy, by the ghastly realisation of what could have happened to Thomas. 'I simply never thought.'

But he had always piled logs on to his open fireplace, carelessly trodden out his random sparks on his old hearth-rug, never bothered about a fireguard. 'One of the last things Jock ever said to me was that I should have a fireguard. But I never did. Put it off. Lazy, procrastinating bastard that I am. Simply put it off.'

And then, again, 'Supposing Ellen hadn't had the wit to think about the child. Supposing, John, you hadn't gone along then to check . . .' His voice trembled.

'Don't think about it,' John had interrupted quickly, because it didn't bear contemplating. 'She did have the sense, and I did go. Come to that, it should have occurred to me to go without Ellen's prompting. I'm just as much to blame as you are.'

'No, I'm totally to blame. I should have thought . . .'

Now, John stood in the chilling room, looking down at his father's brother and filled with a sympathy and affection that were, for the time being, of little use to Roddy. He was inconsolable.

A log crumbled into the dying fire. The clock showed a quarter past twelve. John said, 'Why don't you go to bed? Jess has made beds up for all of us. There's no point in staying down here.'

Roddy rubbed a hand over his eyes. 'No,' he said at last. 'I suppose there isn't. But I don't think I could sleep.'

'In that case . . .' He did not finish the sentence. He stirred the ashes of the fire, and put on more wood. In a moment the flames began to lick up around the dry bark. Roddy stared at them morosely.

'It's over,' John told him firmly. 'Don't think about it anymore. It's over. And if it helps to lessen your guilt, just remember that you've lost everything you possess.'

'That's of small account. Possessions have never mattered.'

'Why don't you have a drink?'

'No. I don't want a drink.'

John managed not to look surprised. 'Do you mind if I do?'

'Help yourself.'

He poured himself a small brandy and filled the glass up with soda. He sat, facing his uncle. He raised his glass. 'Slainthe.'

A spark of wry amusement glimmered in Roddy's eye. 'What an old Scotsman you're becoming.'

'I've always been one. Or half one, at any rate.'

Roddy heaved himself up in the chair. He said, 'Oliver didn't come back from London.'

'Apparently not.'

'Why not, I wonder?'

'I have no idea.'

'Do you suppose he's coming?'

'Again, I have no idea. I simply dumped Victoria on my bed, and after that Jess took over. No doubt we'll hear about it tomorrow.'

'He's a strange man,' mused Roddy. 'Clever, of course. Perhaps a little bit too clever.' Across the fireside, their eyes met. 'Too clever for that little girl.'

'Yes, I guess you're right.'

'Still, she has the child.'

'I have news for you. Thomas is not her child.'

Roddy raised his eyebrows. 'Really? Now you do surprise me.' He shook his head. 'The world is full of surprises.'

'I have more surprises up my sleeve.'

'You do?'

'Do you want to hear about them?'

'What, now?'

'You've already told me you don't want to go to bed. If we're going to sit here for the rest of the night, we might as well talk.'

'All right,' said Roddy, and composed himself to listen. 'Talk.'

## CHAPTER 15

## WEDNESDAY

John Dunbeath, bearing a tray laid for breakfast, cautiously opened the kitchen door with the seat of his pants, and made his way across the hall and up the stairs. Outside a breeze, baby sister of last night's gale, stirred the pine trees and disturbed the surface of the loch, but already a cold and brazen sun, rising in a sky of frosty blue, was beginning to penetrate the house. Roddy's old Labrador had already found a bright lozenge of sunshine by the fireplace, and lay there, supine, basking in its frail warmth.

John crossed the landing and, carefully balancing the tray on one hand, knocked at the door of his own room. From within, Victoria's voice called, 'Who is it?' and he said, 'The floor waiter,' and opened the door. 'I've brought you your breakfast.'

She was still in bed, but sitting up and looking quite alert, as though she had been awake for some time. The curtains had been drawn back, and the first oblique rays of sunshine touched a corner of the chest of drawers and lay like gold on the carpet. He said, 'It's going to be a beautiful day,' and set the tray, with something of a flourish, on her knees.

She said, 'But I don't need breakfast in bed.'

'You've got it. How did you sleep?'

'As though I'd been drugged. I was just going to come down. The thing is, I must have forgotten to wind my watch, and it's stopped, and I've no idea of the time.'

'Nearly half past nine.'

'You should have woken me before.'

'I decided to let you sleep.'

She wore a nightdress lent to her by Ellen. It was peach-pink crêpe-de-chine, much hemstitched and embroidered and had, in fact, once belonged to Lucy Dunbeath. Over this, in lieu of a dressing-gown, was wrapped a white Shetland shawl. Her hair, tangled from sleep, lay forward across one shoulder, and there were dark shadows, like bruises, beneath her eyes. She seemed to John, in that moment, intensely frail. As though, if he were to take her into his arms, she would break into pieces, as fragile as china. She looked about her. 'This is your room, isn't it? When I woke up I couldn't think where I was. Is it your room?'

'It is. It was the only bed that happened to be made up at the time.'

'Where did you sleep?'

'In Uncle Jock's dressing room.'

'And Roddy?'

'In Jock's bedroom. He's still there. We sat up talking till four o'clock in the morning, and he's catching up on his beauty sleep.'

'And . . . Thomas?' She sounded as though she could scarcely bring herself to say his name.

John pulled up a chair and settled himself, facing her, with his long legs stretched out in front of him, and his arms folded.

'Thomas is downstairs in the kitchen, being given breakfast by Ellen and Jess. So now, why don't you start eating *your* breakfast before it gets cold?'

Victoria unenthusiastically eyed the boiled egg and the toast and the coffeepot. She said, 'I don't actually feel very hungry.'

'Just eat it, anyway.'

She began, half-heartedly, to take the top off the egg. Then she laid down the spoon again. 'John, I don't even know how it happened. I mean, how the fire started.'

'None of us does, for sure. We were having a drink in the library before dinner. But Roddy says he made up his fire before he came over. I suppose, as usual, the logs sparked all over the hearthrug, and there wasn't anybody there to put them out. Added to which, there was the hell of a wind blowing. Once it started, the whole room went up like a tinder box.'

'But when did you first realise the house was on fire?'

'Ellen came to tell us supper was ready, and then she started fussing about Thomas being on his own. So I went along to check on him, and found the place blazing away like a bonfire.'

She said, faintly, 'I can't bear it. What *did* you do?'

He proceeded to tell her, playing down the circumstances as much as possible. He felt that Victoria had enough trouble on her mind as it was, without adding to it by graphic descriptions of the nightmare of Thomas's smoke-filled bedroom, the collapsing ceiling, the flaming crater, and the inferno overhead. He knew that the memory of that moment would return to haunt him, like some ghastly dream, for the rest of his life.

'Was he frightened?'

'Of course he was frightened. It was enough to frighten any man. But we got out all right, through one of the bedroom windows, and then we came back here, and Ellen took Thomas over, and Roddy rang the fire brigade in Creagan, and I went back to get the cars out of the garage before the petrol exploded and we were all blown to kingdom come.'

'Did you manage to salvage anything from Roddy's house?'

'Not a thing. It all went. Everything in the world that he owned.'

'Poor Roddy.'

'Losing his possessions doesn't seem to bother him much. What bugs him is that he feels the fire was his fault. He says he should have been more careful, he should have had a fireguard, he should never have left Thomas alone in the house.'

'I can't bear it for him.'

'He's all right now, but that's why we sat up talking till four in the morning. And Thomas is all right too, except that he's lost Piglet. He spent last night with an old wooden engine in his arms. And, of course, he's lost all his clothes as well. He's wearing his pyjamas, but this morning sometime Jess is going to take him into Creagan and buy him a new outfit.'

Victoria said, 'I thought he was still there. I mean, when I got back from the airport, and saw the fire. At first I thought it was a bonfire, and then I thought it was someone burning heather, and then I saw it was Roddy's house. And all I could think of was that Thomas was in the middle of it somewhere...'

Her voice had begun to shake. 'But he wasn't,' John said quietly. 'He was safe.'

Victoria took a deep breath. 'I'd been thinking of him,' she said and her voice was quite steady again. 'All the way back from Inverness. The road seemed to go on forever, and I was thinking of Thomas all the way.'

'Oliver didn't come back from London.' He made it, not a question, but a statement of fact.

'No. He... he wasn't on the plane.'

'Did he call you?'

'No. He sent a letter.' With some determination, as if the time had come to put fancies aside, Victoria took up her spoon again and ate a mouthful or two of the boiled egg.

'How did he do that?'

'He gave a letter to one of the passengers. I suppose he told him what I looked like, or something. Anyway, the man delivered it to me. I was still waiting. I still thought Oliver was going to get off the plane.'

'What did the letter say?'

She gave up the impossible task of eating breakfast and pushed the tray away from her. She leaned back on her pillows and closed her eyes. 'He isn't coming back.' She sounded exhausted. 'He's going to New York. He's in New York now. He flew out yesterday evening. Some producer's going to put on his play, *A Man In The Dark,* and he's gone out to see about it.'

Dreading the answer, it took a certain courage to ask the question. 'Is he coming back?'

'I suppose he will one day. This year, next year, sometime, never.' She opened her eyes. 'That's what he said. Anyway, not in the foreseeable future.' He waited and she finished, 'He's left me, John,' as though there could be any doubt still in his mind.

He did not say anything.

She went on, her voice inconsequent, trying to make what she was saying of small importance. 'That makes it twice he's left me. It's almost becoming a habit.' She tried to smile. 'I know you said I was being a fool about Oliver, but this time I really, truly thought it would be different. I thought he would want the things he'd never wanted before. Like maybe buying a house and making a home for Thomas . . . and getting married, too. I thought he wanted the three of us to be together. To be a family.'

John watched her face. Perhaps the abrupt disappearance of Oliver Dobbs, the paralysing shock of the fire, had acted as a sort of catharsis. He only knew that the barriers between them, her frigid reserve, were tumbling at last. She was being, at the end of the day, honest with herself, and so had nothing left to shut away from him. He was filled with a marvellous sort of triumph, and recognised this as a carry-over from his private elation of the previous night.

She said, 'Yesterday, on the beach at Creagan, I wouldn't listen to you. But you were right, weren't you? You were right about Oliver.'

'I wish I could say "I wish I weren't". But truthfully I can't.'

'You're not going to say "I told you so".'

'I'd never say that in a thousand years.'

'You see, the real trouble was that Oliver doesn't need anybody. That's what's wrong with him. He admitted as much in his letter. He told me that the only thing that turns him on is his writing.' She managed a wry smile. 'And that was a smack in the face. I'd been telling myself it was me.'

'So what will you do now?'

Victoria shrugged. 'I don't know. I don't know where to start. But Oliver says I have to take Thomas back to the Archers, and I've been trying to think how I'm going to do it. I certainly don't know what I'm going to say to them when I get there. And I don't want to lose Thomas, either. I don't want to have to say goodbye to him. It's going to be like being torn apart. And there's the business of the car. Oliver said that if I left the Volvo here, perhaps Roddy could sell it. He said that I could drive it south if I wanted to, but I really don't want to, not with Thomas. I suppose I could get a plane or a train from Inverness, but that means. . . .'

John found that he could not stand it for another instant. Loudly he interrupted her, 'Victoria, I don't want to hear another word.'

Halted in mid-sentence, astonished at the roughness of his voice, Victoria stared open-mouthed. 'But I have to talk about it. I have to do things . . .'

'No, you don't. You don't have to do anything. I shall see to it all. I shall arrange to get Thomas back to his grandparents . . .'

'. . . but you have enough to think about . . .'

'. . . I shall even placate them . . .'

'. . . with the fire, and Roddy, and Benchoile . . .'

'. . . though from the sound of things they're going to require some placating. I shall take care of Thomas, and I shall take care of you, but as for Oliver's car, it can rot on a rubbish heap for all I care. And Oliver Dobbs, for all his genius and his sexual prowess and whatever it is that turns him on – can rot as well. And I never want to hear that self-centred son of a bitch's name again. Is that totally understood?'

Victoria considered this. Her face was serious. 'You never really liked him did you?'

'It wasn't meant to show.'

'It did, a little. Every now and again.'

John grinned. 'He was lucky not to get his nose punched

in.' He looked at his watch, stretched like a cat, and then pulled himself to his feet.

'Where are you going?' she asked him.

'Downstairs to the telephone. I have a million calls to make. So why don't you eat that breakfast now. There's nothing more to worry about.'

'Yes, there is. I just thought of it.'

'What's that?'

'My shell. My queen cockle. It was on the window ledge in my bedroom. In Roddy's house.'

'We'll find another.'

'I liked that one.'

He went to open the door. He said, 'The sea is full of gifts.'


In the kitchen he found Jess Guthrie, peeling potatoes at the sink.

'Jess, where's Davey?'

'He's away up the hill this morning.'

'Will you be seeing him?'

'Yes, he'll be down for his dinner at twelve.'

'Ask him to come down and have a word with me, would you? This afternoon sometime. Say about half past two.'

'I'll give him the message,' she promised.

> If my true love, she were gone
> I would surely find another,
> Where wild mountain thyme,
> Grows around the blooming heather,
> Will ye go, lassie, go?

He went into the library, shut the door firmly behind him, built up the fire, sat at his uncle's desk, and settled down to a positive orgy of telephoning.

He rang the office in London. He spoke to his vice-president, a couple of colleagues, and his secretary, Miss Ridgeway.

He rang directory inquiries and was told the Archers' address and telephone number in Woodbridge. He made the call and spoke, at some length, to them.

With this safely behind him, he called the station in Inverness, and booked three seats on the Clansman for the following day.

He rang the lawyers, McKenzie, Leith and Dudgeon. He spoke to Robert McKenzie, and then, later, to the insurance company about the fire damage.

By now it was nearly midday. John did a few swift time-lag calculations, put a call through to his father in Colorado, dragged that good man from his early morning sleep and talked to him for an hour or more.

Finally, at the very end, he rang up Tania Mansell, dialling her London telephone number from memory. But the line was engaged, and after waiting for a little, he rang off. He did not try the number again.

CHAPTER 16

THURSDAY

It did not take very long to pack for the simple reason that they had nothing to pack. Everything that Victoria and Thomas had brought to Benchoile with them had been lost in the fire. And so they left bearing only a paper carrier containing Thomas's pyjamas and the old wooden engine, which Ellen said that he could keep.

Goodbyes were brief and brisk, for the true Highlander is neither demonstrative nor sentimental. As well, there was little opportunity for prolonged farewells. No sooner had breakfast been eaten in the kitchen at Benchoile than it was time to be off. Before Thomas had finished munching his toast, John Dunbeath was behaving like a family man with a punctuality complex, rounding them up and insisting that it was time to leave.

For this Victoria was deeply grateful. She even suspected that he was overplaying his role a little. His car was parked and waiting in front of the door, already loaded with his own suitcase, and John himself appeared to have deliberately taken on a new image, for he had abandoned the casual and com-fortable clothes in which they were used to seeing him, and appeared at breakfast in the formality of a dark suit and a tie. The different clothes changed him. Not just the way he looked, but his entire manner. He was no longer the amiable, easy-going houseguest of the last few days, but a man used to responsibility and authority. A man to be reckoned with. He was in charge, not aggressively, but comfortingly, so that Victoria was left with the good feeling that nothing would go wrong. They would not have a puncture, they would not lose their tickets, there would be porters and reserved seats, and they would not miss the train.

'It's time to go.'

Ellen put the last finger of toast into Thomas's mouth, wiped it clean and lifted him from his high chair. He wore tartan dungarees and a blue sweater, chosen for him by Jess Guthrie in the small shop in Creagan that was owned by her sister-in-law, so Jess had got discount. His new shoes were brown lace-ups, and there was a small blue anorak with red stripes to go on top. Ellen had brushed his red-gold hair flat to his head. She was wanting to kiss him goodbye, but decided not to with everybody watching. Her eyes had a way, these days, of filling with tears at the most inconvenient moments. Running, Ellen called it. 'My eyes are starting to run,' she would say, blaming the wind or the hay fever. She never cried. At times of great emotion, like anniversaries or weddings or funerals, she would shake a body's hand, but nothing more. So now, 'There he is,' she said, setting Thomas firmly down on to his feet. 'Put your coat on.' She picked up the new jacket, and stooped over him to help him with the zipper.

They were all on their feet. Victoria gulping the last mouthful of coffee. Roddy standing, scratching the back of his head, but not looking as disconsolate as she had feared he might. He seemed to have recovered with amazing rapidity from the shock of the fire and losing everything he owned. Indeed he was really being quite organised; had spent most of yesterday with the man from the insurance company, and had already started to make a little nest for himself in the big house, sleeping in his brother's old bedroom and tossing logs as carelessly as ever on to the fire in the library. The library fire was surrounded by a hearth of stone flags and a huge club fender, but still, said Roddy, he would get a proper fireguard. One of those chain curtains. He had seen one advertised. Just as soon as he could find the advertisement, he would order one for Benchoile.

'We must go *now*,' said John, so they all left the kitchen and the remains of breakfast and trooped out, across the hall and through the front door. Outside, it was cold again and frosty, but it was going to be fine. It was goodbye. To the garden, the loch, the hills beyond, sparkling in the crystal clear morning air. It was goodbye to the friendly, peaceful house, goodbye to the sad charred remains of what had once been Roddy's domain. It was goodbye, Victoria knew, to a dream.

Or perhaps a nightmare. Only time would give the answer to that one.

'Oh, Roddy.' He opened his arms and she went to him, and they hugged. 'Come back again,' he said. 'Come back again and see us all.' He kissed her on both cheeks and let her go. Thomas, with the cheerful prospect of a car ride in front of him, had already climbed, independent of anyone, on to the back seat, had taken his wooden engine out of the paper bag, and had started to play with it.

'Goodbye, Ellen.'

'It's been nice to know you,' said Ellen briskly and stuck out her gnarled, red hand to be shaken.

'You've been so endlessly kind. You and Jess. I can't thank you enough.'

'Away with you,' said Ellen, brisk and much embarrassed. 'Into the car, and don't keep John waiting.'

Only John was allowed to kiss her. She had to stand tiptoe in her flat old shoes to receive his kiss, and then she had to fumble up the sleeve of her dress for her handkerchief. 'Oh, my, what an edge to that wind,' she remarked to no one person in particular. 'It fairly makes your eyes run.'

'Roddy.'

'Goodbye, John.' They shook hands, smiling into each other's faces, two men who had come together through a bad time.

'I'll be back sometime, but I'll call you and let you know when.'

'Anytime,' said Roddy.

That was all. They got into the car, fastened the safety belts, John started up the engine and they were away. There was scarcely time for Victoria to turn in her seat and wave a last farewell – scarcely time for a final glimpse of the two of them, Roddy and Ellen, standing there on the gravel sweep in front of the house. Roddy was waving, and Ellen was waving too, her white handkerchief a tiny flag. And then they were hidden, gone, lost behind the curving bank of the rhododendrons.

'I hate saying goodbye,' said Victoria.

John's eyes were on the road ahead. 'Me too,' he said. He was driving very fast.

Behind them Thomas rolled his three-wheeled engine up and down the seat. 'Meh meh, meh,' he intoned to himself.

He played with the engine for most of the day, taking time
off to sleep, to look out of the window, to be taken down the
corridor at decent, regular intervals, to be given lunch, to be
given tea. As the train thundered south, the weather, dis-
obligingly, degenerated. They were no sooner across the
border than thick clouds rolled up, obliterating the sky, and
soon the rain started to fall. The hills were left behind them,
the countryside became flat and incredibly dull, and watching
acres of flat, wet plough wheel past the window, Victoria's own
spirits sank accordingly.

She discovered that it was all very well being brisk and
sensible about your future when you happened to be eight
hundred miles from it, but now, with every moment and every
turn of the wheel, it was drawing closer. She felt lamentably
unprepared.

It was not just the distant prospect of the remainder of her
own life, which would, presumably, fall into some pattern of its
own. As for Oliver . . . she was not thinking about Oliver just
now. Later, she told herself, she would find the necessary moral
courage. When she was back in her own flat, with her own
familiar possessions around her. Possessions helped, whatever
anybody said. And friends. She thought of Sally. She would
be able to talk to Sally about Oliver. Sally's robust attitudes,
her impatience with the vagaries of the opposite sex in general,
would swiftly cut the whole disastrous episode down to size.

No, worse was the immediate and dreaded ordeal of having
to hand Thomas back to the Archers; of having to say goodbye
to him forever. Victoria could not imagine what she was going
to say to his grandparents. Unfortunately, without much
difficulty, she could imagine what they might be going to say
to Victoria in her role of Oliver's accomplice.

There were other hideous possibilities as well. Suppose
Thomas did not want to return to them? Suppose he took one
look at the Archers, and burst into tears and had hysterics
and clung to Victoria?

He had adjusted so easily to her in two weeks, had been so
happy and become so affectionate. She found that she was torn
in two opposite directions where Thomas was concerned;
one half of her wanting him to need her as much as she
needed him, the other shying like a frightened horse at the
idea of any sort of a scene.

She looked at Thomas. He was sitting on the opposite side
of the first-class carriage, his legs sticking straight out in front

of him, his head, tousled by now, leaning against John Dunbeath's arm. John was entertaining him by drawing pictures with a felt pen on the pink pages of the *Financial Times*. He had drawn a horse, a cow, a house, and now he was drawing a pig.

'He's got a big nose that sticks out in front. That's for snuffling with and finding stuff to eat. And he has a tail with a curl in it.' He drew the tail. Thomas's face broke into a smile. He settled down more cosily. 'More,' he ordered, and plugged his mouth with his thumb.

Victoria closed her eyes and leaned her head against the rain-streaked window of the train. It was sometimes easier not to cry if you didn't keep your eyes open.

It was dark long before they reached Euston, and Thomas had gone to sleep again. When the train stopped, Victoria picked him up in her arms. His head lolled on her shoulder. John carried his suitcase, and the little party stepped out on to the dark platform, into the usual confusion of barging passengers, trolleys, porters, luggage and mail vans. Victoria, weighed down by Thomas's considerable weight, felt overwhelmed. She supposed they must now trudge the length of the platform, wait in a queue for a taxi . . .

But she supposed wrong, and realised that in this supposition she had totally underestimated John Dunbeath. For from the confusion emerged a figure, grey-suited, with a grey uniform cap.

'Good evening, Mr Dunbeath.'

'George, you're a wonder. How did you know where we'd be?'

'Had a word with the ticket collector, he said you'd probably be down this end.' With no more fuss, he relieved John of his suitcase. John duly relieved Victoria of Thomas. They followed the neat, uniformed figure down the length of the platform.

'Who is he?' asked Victoria, having to run every now and then to keep up with John's long legs.

'He's the office driver. I told my secretary to send him to meet us.'

'Has he brought a car?'

'I hope he's brought my car.'

He had. Outside the station, they were left waiting for a

moment or two while George disappeared into the rainy darkness. In no time he was back, at the wheel of John's Alfa-Romeo. He got out and they got in. Victoria with Thomas still sleeping on her shoulder.

'Thanks a lot George, that was very good of you. Now, how are you going to get back?'

'I'll pop into the tube, Mr Dunbeath. Very handy.'

'Well, thanks again, anyway.'

'A pleasure Mr Dunbeath.'

'How nice,' said Victoria.

'Nice of him?'

'Yes, nice of him, but nice to be met. Not to have to wait for a taxi, or wait for a bus, or fight your way down the underground. Just nice to have a friendly face on a station platform.'

'It makes all the difference between travelling hopefully and arriving,' said John.

She knew what he meant.

The car sped west down the rain-drenched motorway. Three-quarters of an hour later, they had turned off it, and down the side road that led to Woodbridge. Now, there were little fields and hedgerows, and water meadows fringed with willows. Lights shone, here and there, from the windows of small, red-brick houses. They came over a bridge, and a train screamed past beneath them.

John said, 'That's lucky.'

'What is?'

'Going over a bridge the same time that the train's going under it.'

'What else is lucky?' She needed luck.

'Letters crossing. If you write someone a letter, and he writes to you and the letters cross, that's enormously lucky.'

'I don't think it's ever happened to me.'

'And black cats and picking up pins and new moons.'

'There was a new moon the night of the fire.'

'Disregard new moons, then.'

At last, the lights of the village twinkled ahead of them. They passed the sign, WOODBRIDGE. The road swung around into a curve, and the long, wide main street sloped away before them. The car idled down to a gentle crawl. There were shops and a pub with a lighted sign. A church, set back behind a stone wall.

'We don't know where they live.'

'Yes, we do. It's on the right hand side, and it's red brick, and it has a yellow front door, and it's the only one in the street that is three storeys high. There it is.'

He drew up at the pavement's edge. Victoria saw the flight of steps that led up to the door from the pavement, the pretty fanlight, the tall lighted windows. She said, 'How do you know this is the house?'

He switched off the engine. 'Because I rang Mrs Archer, and she told me.'

'Did she sound furious?'

'No.' He opened his door. 'She sounded very nice.'

Thomas, disturbed by the sudden cessation of movement, chose this moment to wake up. He yawned, bleary with sleep, rubbed his eyes, gazed about him with the confused expression of a person on whom some terrible trick has been played. He still held the wooden engine.

'You're home,' Victoria told him gently. She smoothed down his hair with her hand, with some vague idea of tidying him up.

Thomas blinked. The word 'home' apparently meant little to him. He gazed out at the darkness. Then John opened the door and lifted Thomas and his engine up and off Victoria's knee. She reached around into the back of the car, retrieved Thomas's paper carrier luggage, and followed them.

They stood in front of the yellow front door, and John rang the bell. Almost immediately, as though the person inside had been waiting for them, there was a footstep and the door was flung open. From the bright, warm hallway, light poured out upon the three of them, so that they were caught in its beam, like actors spotlighted upon a stage.

'Good evening,' said John, 'I'm John Dunbeath.'

'Yes, of course.' He looked nice. Sixtyish, grey-haired, not tall, not particularly impressive, but nice. He did not try to snatch Thomas from John's arms. He simply looked at Thomas and said, 'Hello, old boy', and then stepped back, and went on, 'I think you should all come in.'

They did so, and he closed the door behind them. John stooped and set Thomas on his feet.

'I'll just call my wife. I don't think she can have heard the bell . . .'

But she had heard it. From a door at the far end of the narrow hall, she appeared. She had curly white hair and the sort of complexion that would go on being young, even when she was in her eighties. She wore a blue skirt with a cardigan to match and a rose-pink shirt with a bow at the neck. In her hand she carried her spectacles. Victoria imagined her, sitting in some chair, trying to read, or to do a crossword, anything to fill in the time while she waited for them to bring Thomas back to her.

There was a long silence. She and Thomas eyed each other down the length of the hall. Then she began to smile. She leaned forward, her hands on her knees. 'And who is this,' she asked him, 'that Thomas has come home to?'

Victoria was frigid with anxiety, but she need not have had any worries. For Thomas, after an astonished silence, suddenly realised what was happening. Slowly, his rosy face became suffused by an expression of total, incredulous delight. He took a single enormous breath, and let it all come out in the first proper sentence that anyone had ever heard him utter.

'It my *Ganny*!'

He flung himself towards her, and was instantly swept up, lost in her embrace.

It was all very emotional. Mrs Archer laughed, and cried, and then laughed again, and hugged her grandson. Mr Archer took out his handkerchief and blew his nose. From upstairs, alerted by the noise, came running helter-skelter a young girl, round and plump and pretty as a milkmaid, and when Mrs Archer could be persuaded to relinquish Thomas, he was engulfed in yet another pair of loving arms. Finally, he was set down and allowed to go to his grandfather, who had stopped blowing his nose, and who, in his turn, picked him up and jigged him up and down, in a manly sort of way, which Thomas seemed to find wholly satisfactory.

While all this was happening, Victoria and John could do nothing but stand and watch. Victoria wanted to go, to get away while everyone was still happy and before any possible recriminations could set in, but it was hard to know how to achieve this without appearing rude.

It was Thomas who finally put an end to the great reunion scene. He wriggled himself down from his grandfather's arms, and with deadly determination made for the stairs that led to his nursery, where he remembered leaving a number of delightful toys. His grandparents sensibly let him go, and the little au pair girl went with him. As they disappeared around the bend in the staircase, Victoria took hold of John's sleeve and gave it a tug, but if Mrs Archer noticed this, she showed no sign of it.

'I am sorry, keeping you standing there like that. But it's all just so . . .' She wiped away the last of her happy tears, and blew her nose on a lacy handkerchief. 'You must come in and have a drink.'

'We really ought to go . . .' Victoria began, but Mrs Archer would have none of it.

'Of course you must stay, for just a moment. Come along in by the fire. Edward, I am sure Mr Dunbeath would like a drink . . .'

There was nothing for it but to follow her, through a door that led into a pleasant, chintz-upholstered sitting room. A fire flickered pleasantly from an old-fashioned grate, there was a grand piano arrayed with family photographs, there were flowers, beautifully arranged, and the sort of cushions that looked as though nobody ever sat on them.

But it was warm and welcoming and under the influence of Mrs Archer's obvious good intentions, her obvious gratitude, Victoria began to relax a little. The men had gone, presumably, to fetch the drinks, so she and Mrs Archer were to be left alone together for a moment or two. Cautiously Victoria let herself down on to the sofa, and Mrs Archer did not look disappointed about the cushions being squashed.

'Have a cigarette? You don't smoke. You must be tired. You've been travelling all day. And with a little boy, too. And I know how active Thomas can be.'

Victoria realised that Mrs Archer was just about as nervous as she was, and her manner was so different from the antagonistic reception that Victoria had anticipated that she felt totally confused.

She said, 'He was good. He's always good. He's been good all the time we were away.'

'It was you who wrote that kind letter, wasn't it? You're Victoria?'

'Yes.'

'It was sweet of you. Very thoughtful'.

'Oliver was furious.'

'I wanted to apologise about that. I would never have tried to ring you or get in touch, but my husband read the letter, and he was so incensed by the whole business, that I could do nothing to stop him telephoning Benchoile and having it out with Oliver. Nothing. It isn't very often,' she added, her sweet face concerned, 'that I don't get my own way, but there was nothing I could do to stop Edward making that call.'

'It didn't matter.'

'I hope not. You see, Edward never liked Oliver, even when he was married to Jeanette. But he was very fond of Thomas. And when Oliver just walked into our house, out of the blue, and stole Thomas, you can imagine the scenes. I had Helga in hysterics, poor girl, as though it could possibly have been her fault. And Edward saying he was going to put the police on to Oliver, and all the time I had no idea where the little boy was. It was a nightmare.'

'I do understand.'

'Yes. I believe you do.' Mrs Archer cleared her throat. 'Your . . . your friend, Mr Dunbeath. He rang me up yesterday to say you were bringing Thomas back. He told me, too, that Oliver has gone to America.'

'Yes.'

'Something about a play?'

Victoria said, 'Yes,' again.

'Do you suppose he'll come back to this country?'

'Yes, I suppose he will. Sometime or other. But I don't think he'll ever bother with Thomas again. I don't mean that he wasn't fond of him, and very good to him, but being a father isn't exactly Oliver's scene.'

Their eyes met. Victoria smiled. Mrs Archer said, very gently, 'Nor being a husband, my dear.'

'No, I suppose not. I really wouldn't know.'

'He's a destroyer,' said Mrs Archer.

Perhaps no other person could have told her. She knew it was true. She knew something else as well. 'He hasn't destroyed me,' she told Mrs Archer.

The men returned, Mr Archer bearing a tray with glasses and bottles, and John following with a soda syphon. The conversation turned to day-to-day matters. The weather in Scotland, the weather in Hampshire, the state of the stock market, the variable fluctuation of both dollar and pound. John, without waiting for her to ask for one, quietly handed Victoria a whisky and water. This small service filled her with gratitude. She seemed to spend her time being grateful to him for one reason or other. It occurred to her then that his perception was remarkable, all the more so because he seemed to achieve it with so little fuss. He was, perhaps, the kindest person she had ever known. She had never even heard him

say an unkind thing about any person, except to call Oliver
Dobbs a son of a bitch, and he hadn't done that until Oliver
had taken himself off to America, and there was no point in
prevaricating any longer.

Now, she watched him, deep in conversation with the
Archers. She saw his heavy, serious face, which could light
up so unexpectedly in a smile. The dark, close-cut hair, the
intensely dark eyes. He had been travelling all day with a small
child, and yet he gave no sign of the sort of exhaustion that
Victoria felt. He appeared as fresh and alert as the moment
they had set out from Benchoile, and it was this resilience
that she so envied and admired, because she knew that it was
lacking in herself.

She thought, nothing defeats him. His disastrous marriage
had left behind no apparent trace of bitterness. Things will
always go right for him, because he likes people, but mostly
because people like him.

Even over the telephone, it seemed, this genuine benevolence came through, for how else had he contrived, in the
short space of the trunk call he had put through to Mrs Archer
yesterday morning, to make everything all right for Victoria,
to somehow condone the circumstances of Thomas's abduction,
and to pave the way for Mrs Archer's reunion with Thomas.

One thing, she thought, I haven't had time to start taking
him for granted. Before she knew what was happening, they
would be saying goodbye. He would drive her to London, and
leave her at the door of Pendleton Mews. There wouldn't even
be the excuse of carrying luggage to invite him in and up the
stairs, because she had no luggage to carry. They would just
say goodbye. Perhaps he would kiss her. He would say, 'Take
care now.'

That would be the end. John Dunbeath would walk away
from her, and be instantly absorbed back into that busy, important life about which Victoria knew nothing. She remembered
the anonymous girlfriend who had not been able to come to
the Fairburns' party with him. Probably the first thing John
would do when he returned to the peaceful familiarity of his
own flat would be to dial her number and tell her he was safely
back in London. 'How about dinner tomorrow night?' he
would say, 'And I'll give you all my news then.' And her voice
would float back at him over the line, 'Darling, how heavenly.'
Victoria imagined her a little like Imogen Fairburn, beautiful,
sophisticated, and knowing everybody.

'We really mustn't keep you.' John's drink was finished. He stood up. 'You'll be wanting to go and talk to Thomas before he goes to bed.'

The Archers, too, rose to their feet. Victoria jerked back to reality, began to struggle up out of the deep sofa, but John took her empty glass from her, gave her his hand, and helped her.

'I feel,' said Mrs Archer, 'that we should offer you something to eat.'

'No, we really must get back to London. It's been a long day.'

They all went out into the hall. Mrs Archer said to Victoria, 'Do you want to say goodbye to Thomas before you go?' But she said, 'No.' And then, because this sounded a little abrupt, she explained. 'I mean, it wouldn't do any good, upsetting him again. Not that I think he would be upset, he's obviously so glad to be home, but . . . well, I'd rather just go, I think.'

'I believe,' said Mrs Archer, 'that you've become quite fond of Thomas.'

'Yes.' They were all looking at her. She wondered if she was going to start blushing. 'Yes, I suppose . . .'

'Come along,' said John, putting an end to all this by opening the front door. Victoria said goodbye, and was surprised when Mrs Archer leaned forward to kiss her.

'You've looked after him so beautifully. I can't thank you enough. He looks rosy and well, and I'm sure the little experience has done him no harm at all.'

'I hope not.'

'Perhaps one weekend, when the weather is better, you'd like to come down one Sunday and see him. We could have lunch. You could take him for a walk.' She looked at John, including him in this invitation. 'You too, Mr Dunbeath.'

'That's very kind,' said John.


'You're very quiet.'

'I'm trying not to cry again.'

'You know I don't mind if you do cry.'

'In that case, I probably won't. Isn't it extraordinary, if you know you can cry, and nobody is going to become upset or embarrassed about it, then you stop wanting to.'

'Did you want to cry about anything in particular?'

'Thomas, I suppose. Thomas in particular.'

'Thomas is fine. Thomas is nothing to cry about, except that you're going to miss him. Thomas has got a great home, and he's surrounded by people who love him. And what did you think of that welcome he gave his grandmother?'

'I nearly cried *then*.'

'I have to admit to a lump in my throat myself. But you can see him anytime you want. Mrs Archer liked you. It isn't good-bye to Thomas. You've got a standing invitation to go and see him.'

'They were nice, weren't they?'

'Did you think they wouldn't be?'

'I don't know what I thought.' She remembered something. 'I didn't say anything to Mrs Archer about the fire.'

'I told Mr Archer while we were in the dining room getting the glasses out of a cupboard. At least, I told him what had happened. I didn't enlarge too much on the possibility of Thomas being frizzled to a cinder.'

'Oh, *don't*.'

'I have to say things like that every now and then to lay my own private spectre of what might have happened.'

'But it didn't happen.'

'No. It didn't happen.'

They fell silent. The car nosed its way back along the narrow country road. A soft persistent rain blurred everything like mist. The windscreen wipers swung to and fro.

Victoria broke the silence at last. 'I suppose,' she said, 'I could cry for Benchoile.'

'What a girl you are for thinking of things to cry about.'

'It's just that I so hated leaving it.'

John made no comment on this. The car travelled on, swiftly, down the winding road, but they passed the sign of an approaching lay-by, and he began to slow down. Moments later they came to the lay-by itself, and here John drew off the road, pulled on the handbrake and turned off the engine.

The windscreen wipers ceased their demented dance. There was only the whisper of the rain, the ticking of the dashboard clock.

Victoria looked at him. 'What are we stopping for?'

He switched on the interior light and turned towards her 'It's all right,' he reassured her. 'I am not about to ravish you. It's just that I want to talk to you. Ask you some questions. And I want to see your face when you answer them. You see, before we go a step further, I have to be totally and absolutely certain about Oliver Dobbs.'

'I thought you never wanted his name mentioned again.'

'I didn't. This is the last time.'

'Mrs Archer was talking about him. She was very wise. I didn't realise that she would be such a wise person. She said that Oliver was a destroyer.'

'What did you say to that?'

'I said that he hadn't destroyed me.'

'Is that the truth?'

She hesitated for an instant before replying. Then 'Yes,' she said. She looked at John and smiled, and it felt as though his heart was turning over. 'It is the truth. Perhaps I've always known it was the truth, but I wouldn't admit it, even to myself. I suppose everybody has to have one great traumatic love affair in his life, and Oliver was mine.'

'What about when he comes back from America?'

'Somehow, I don't think he'll ever come back . . .' She thought about this, and then went on, in tones of the greatest conviction, 'And even if he did, I wouldn't want to see him.'

'Because he hurt you, or because you've stopped loving him?'

'I think I stopped loving him when we were at Benchoile. I can't tell you the exact moment. It just happened gradually. Now . . .' she made a vague gesture with her hands. 'I don't think I even like him any more.'

'That makes two of us,' said John. 'And with Oliver Dobbs disposed of, we can now go on to talk of other things. Just before I stopped the car, you said that you supposed that if you needed something to cry about, you could cry about Benchoile. And I think that this is as good a time as any to tell you that you don't have to. You'll be able to go back there, any time, and see them all, because I'm not going to sell it. At least not just yet.'

'But . . . you said . . .'

'I've changed my mind.'

'Oh . . .' She looked as though she were going to burst into tears, but she didn't do this. She said 'Oh, *John*' and then she began to laugh, and finally she flung her arms around his neck and kissed him.

He was immensely gratified, but as well taken totally unawares by her spontaneous delight. He had known that she would be pleased, but scarcely expected this throttling embrace.

'Hey, you'll strangle me! ' But she took no heed.

'You're not going to sell it! Oh, you marvellous man! You're going to keep Benchoile.'

He put his arms around her and pulled her close. She felt small-boned and fragile, and her fair hair was soft against his cheek, and she rattled on, excited as a child. 'You said it wasn't viable, it wasn't practical.' She drew away from him but he still kept his arms about her. 'Without your Uncle Jock to run the place, you said that Benchoile would fall to pieces.'

'Like I said, I changed my mind. I'm going to hang on to it, anyway for a year, till we see how things work out.'

'What made you change your mind?'

'I don't know.' He shook his head, a man still confused by the reasons for his sudden volte-face. 'Perhaps it was the fire. Perhaps a man doesn't realise how much something means to him until he's in danger of losing it. That night, I had visions of the whole place going up. You weren't there, but it was only by the grace of God that the big house wasn't burnt to the ground with everything else. Late that night, I went out into the garden, and just stood there, and looked at it. And it was still standing, with the hills behind it, and I don't think I've ever been so grateful for anything in all my life.'

'But who's going to run it?'

'Roddy and Davey Guthrie between them, and we're going to get another man in to help.'

*'Roddy?'*

'Yes, Roddy. It was you who pointed out that Roddy is more informed and more interested in the land than any of us. He knows more about Benchoile than I could learn in a hundred years. The only reason that he's never become more actively involved before is because he's idle, and because there was always Jock there to do the thinking for him. I have a feeling that without Jock, and with a real job to do, Roddy has a good chance of laying off the booze and astonishing us all.'

'Where will he live?'

'In the big house with Ellen. You see, all my problems have been solved by one inspired decision. They'll squabble like crazy, as they always have. But the big house is large enough to contain the two of them, without one murdering the other.' He thought about this. 'At least,' he added, 'I devoutly hope so.'

'You really think it will work?'

'I told you, I'm going to give it a year. But, yes, I think it will work. And what is more, my father thinks so too.'

'How do you know what your father thinks? He's in Colorado.'

'I called him yesterday morning, we had a long talk about it all.'

Victoria could only marvel. 'What a morning you had on the telephone!'

'I'm used to it. In my office I'm on the phone most of the day.'

'Even so,' said Victoria, 'I'd never think of calling someone up in Colorado.'

'You should try it sometime.'

So, at least, for a little longer, Benchoile would go on. And perhaps John was right, and Roddy would take on a new lease of life. He was, after all, only sixty. Perhaps he would turn into a tremendously keen outdoorsman, felling trees and climbing hills, losing weight and generally becoming tanned and fit. The image was not particularly convincing, but there was no denying that it had distinct possibilities. And, living in the big house, perhaps he would be persuaded to enliven his social life a little. Throw small dinner parties, and have people to stay. Ellen would take the dust covers off the furniture in the drawing room, and rehang the curtains. Someone would light a fire in the fireplace, and people in evening dress would dispose themselves about the room while Roddy played the piano to them, and sang his old songs.

She said 'I know it will work. It has to work.'

'So. With Benchoile and Oliver Dobbs safely out of the way, we can now get on to much more important things.'

'Like what?'

'Like you and me.' Victoria's expression became wary, and before she could start protesting, he went firmly on. 'I thought it might be an idea for us to start over, from the beginning. It seems to me that from the moment we first met, we set out on the wrong foot, and it's only now, after all this time, and so much happening, that we've finally fallen into step. And the first thing to be rectified is that I've never gotten around to taking you out for dinner. So I thought that when we get back to London, we might go out some place. If you want we can go straight there, and eat. Or you'd maybe want to wash up first and change your clothes, so I could take you to your flat, and then come around and pick you up later. Or we can both go straight to my flat and have a drink, and then go out to dinner

from there. The permutations, as you will realise, are endless. The only constant is that I want to be with you. I don't
want to say goodbye. Does that make sense?'

'John, I don't want you to be sorry for me. And you don't
have to go on being kind.'

'In fact,' he told her, 'I'm not being kind. I'm being utterly
selfish, because it's what I want more than anything else
in the world. I always knew I'd fall in love again one day. I
didn't think that it would happen just this way. I didn't even
think that it would happen so soon. But what I don't want is
for you to get tangled up in a new relationship until you've
had time to take a deep breath and look around and generally
get used to the idea.'

*I don't want to say goodbye.*

She thought, if this were a movie, it's where they'd start playing the really soupy theme music. Or there'd be an explosion
of stars, or shots of sun shining down through branches laden
with apple blossom. None of these things was happening.
There was just the car, and the darkness beyond, and the man,
with whom already she seemed to have come so far.

She said, thoughtfully, 'You know, I don't think I ever met
any person as nice as you.'

'Well, that'll do for a start,' he told her. They watched each
other, and she began to smile, and he took her face between
his hands, and bent his dark head and kissed her smiling
mouth. When he had finished kissing her, he put her gently
from him, turned back to the driving wheel, switched on the
ignition, started up the powerful engine. The car moved forward. Soon they came to the junction that marked the end
of the quiet country road and the beginning of the motorway.
The car came through a tunnel and then swept up the curved
ramp. They waited to filter into the three-lane stream of cars
which poured east.

Victoria said, 'When we were with the Archers, I suddenly
realised that I didn't want to say goodbye to you. But I never
imagined that you wouldn't want to say goodbye to me.'

A gap appeared in the traffic. Smoothly John slipped the
Alfa-Romeo into gear; the engine changed tune, and the car
swept forward.

He said, 'Perhaps not wanting to say goodbye is just another
word for loving.'

The wide, fast road curved ahead of them, leading to
London.

# THE DAY OF THE STORM

# Chapter One

It all started on a Monday at the end of January. A dull day at a dull time of the year. Christmas and the New Year were over and forgotten and yet the new season had not started to show its face. London was cold and raw, the shops filled with empty hope and clothes "for cruising". The trees in the park stood lacy and bare against low skies, the trodden grass beneath them dull and dead, so that it was impossible to believe that it could ever again be carpeted with drifts of purple and yellow crocus.

It was a day like any other day. The alarm woke me to darkness, but a darkness made paler by the wide expanse of the uncurtained windows, and through them I could see the top of the plane tree, illuminated by the orange glow of distant street lights.

My room was unfurnished, except for the sofa bed on which I lay, and a kitchen table which I was going to strip of paint when I had the time, and polish with a coat of beeswax. Even the floor was bare, boards stretching to the wainscotting. An orange box did duty as a bedside table, and a second one filled in for a chair.

I put out a hand and turned on the light and surveyed the desolate scene with the utmost satisfaction. It was mine. My first home. I had moved in only three weeks ago but it belonged entirely to me. With it, I could do as I pleased. Cover the white walls with posters or paint them orange. Sand the bare floor or stripe it in colour. Already I had started to acquire a

1

proprietary interest in junk and antique shops, and could not pass one without scanning the window for some treasure that I might be able to afford. This was how the table had come into my possession, and I already had my eye on an antique gilt mirror, but had not yet plucked up the courage to go into the shop and find out how much it was going to cost. Perhaps I would hang it in the centre of the chimney breast, or on the wall opposite the window, so that the reflections of the sky and the tree would be caught, like a picture, within its ornate frame.

These pleasant imaginings took some time. I looked again at the clock, saw that it was growing late, and climbed out of bed to pad, barefooted, across the floor and into the tiny kitchen, where I lit the gas and put the kettle on to boil. The day had begun.

The flat was in Fulham, the top floor of a small terrace house which belonged to Maggie and John Trent. I had met them only at Christmas, which I had spent with Stephen Forbes and his wife Mary and their large family of untidy children, in their large and untidy house in Putney. Stephen Forbes was my boss, the owner of the Walton Street bookshop where I had been working for the past year. He had always been enormously kind and helpful towards me and when he found out, from one of the other girls, that I would be on my own for Christmas, he and Mary had immediately issued a firm invitation – more an order, really – that I should spend the three days with them. There was plenty of space, he insisted vaguely, a room in the attic, a bed in Samantha's room, somewhere, but I wouldn't mind, would I? And I could always help Mary baste the turkey and pick all those torn bits of tissue paper off the floor.

Considering it from this angle, I finally accepted, and had a wonderful time. There's nothing like a family Christmas when there are children everywhere and noise and paper and presents, and a pine-smelling Christmas tree, glittering with baubles and crooked home-made decorations.

On Boxing Night, with the children safely in bed, the Forbeses threw a grown-up party, although we still seemed to continue playing childish games, and Maggie and John Trent came to this. The Trents were young marrieds, she the daughter of an Oxford don, whom Stephen had known well in his undergraduate days. She was one of those laughing, cheerful, out-going people, and after she had arrived the party went with a swing. We were introduced but we didn't manage to talk until a game of charades, when we found ourselves side by side on a sofa, trying to guess, from the most incoherent gestures, that Mary was trying to act to us, in dumb show, the title of a film. *"Rose Marie!"* somebody yelled, for no apparent reason.

*"Clockwork Orange!"*

Maggie lit a cigarette and sank back on the sofa, defeated. "It's beyond me," she said. She turned her dark head to look at me. "You work in Stephen's shop, don't you?"

"Yes."

"I'll come in next week and spend all my Christmas book tokens. I've been given dozens."

"Lucky girl."

"We've just moved into our first house, so I want lots of coffee table stuff so that all our friends think I'm wildly intelligent . . ." Then somebody shouted, "Maggie, it's your turn," and she said "Cripes," and shot to her feet, and went stalking off to find out what she was going to have to act. I can't remember what it was, but watching her make a cheerful fool of herself, my heart warmed to her, and I hoped that I would see her again.

I did, of course. True to her word, she came into the shop a couple of days after the holiday wearing a sheepskin coat and a long purple skirt, and carrying a bulging handbag stuffed with book tokens. I wasn't serving anybody at that particular moment and I came out from behind a neat stack of shiny-jacketed novels and said, "Hello."

"Oh, good, there you are. I was hoping I'd find you. Can you help me?"

"Yes, of course."

Together, we chose a cookery book, a new autobiography which everybody was talking about, and a marvellously expensive volume of Impressionist paintings for the legendary coffee table. All this came to a little more than the book tokens did, so she groped around in that handbag and took out a cheque book in order to pay for the balance of the amount.

"John'll be furious," she told me happily, writing out the amount with a red felt pen. The cheque was yellow and the effect quite gay. "He says we're spending far too much money as it is. There." She turned it over to write her address. "Fourteen Bracken Road, SW6." She said it aloud in case I couldn't read her writing. "I haven't got used to writing it yet. We've only just moved in. Terribly exciting, we've bought it freehold, believe it or not. At least our parents chipped in with the deposit and John managed to con some building society or other into giving us a loan for the rest. But of course because of this, we've got to let the top floor to help pay the mortgage, but still, I suppose it'll all work out." She smiled. "You'll have to come and see it."

"I'd like to." I was wrapping her parcel, being meticulous about matching the paper and folding the corners.

She watched me. "You know, it's terribly rude, but I don't know your name. I know it's Rebecca, but Rebecca what?"

"Rebecca Bayliss."

"I suppose you don't know of a nice peaceful individual who wants an unfurnished flat?"

4

I looked at her. Our thoughts were so close I scarcely had to speak. I tied the knot on the parcel and snapped the string. I said, "How about me?"

"You? But are you looking for somewhere to live?"

"I wasn't until a moment ago. But I am now."

"It's only a room and a kitchen. And we have to share the bath."

"I don't mind if you don't. And if I can afford the rent. I don't know what you're asking."

Maggie told me. I swallowed and did a few mental calculations and said, "I could manage that."

"Have you got any furniture?"

"No. I've been living in a furnished flat with a couple of other girls. But I can get some."

"You sound as though you're desperate to get out."

"No, I'm not desperate, but I'd like to be on my own."

"Well, before you decide you'd better come and see it. Some evening, because John and I both work."

"*This* evening?" It was impossible to keep my impatience and excitement out of my voice and Maggie laughed.

"All right," she said. "This evening," and she picked up the beautifully wrapped parcel of books and prepared to depart.

I suddenly panicked. "I . . . I don't know the address . . ."

"Yes you do, silly, it's on the back of the cheque. Get a twenty-two bus. I'll expect you about seven."

"I'll be there," I promised.

Jolting slowly down the Kings Road in the bus I had to consciously damp down my enthusiasm. I was out to buy a pig in a poke. The flat might be totally impossible, too big, too small or inconvenient in some unimagined way. Anything was better than being disappointed. And indeed, from the outside, the little house was entirely unremarkable, one of a row of red brick villas, with fancy pointing around the doors and a depressing tendency towards stained glass. But inside Number 14 was bright with fresh paint and new carpets and Maggie herself in old jeans and a blue sweater.

"Sorry I look such a mess but I've got to do all the housework, so I usually change when I get back from the office. Come on, let's go up and see it . . . put your coat on the banisters, John's not home yet, but I told him you were coming and he thought it was a frightfully good idea . . ."

Talking all the time, she led the way upstairs and into the empty room which stood at the back of the house. She turned on the light. "It faces south, out over a little park. The people who had the house before us built an extension on underneath, so you've got a sort of balcony on its roof." She opened a glass door and we stepped together out into the cold dark night, and I smelt the leaf-smell of the park, and damp earth, and saw, ringed by lamplight from the streets all around, the stretch of empty darkness. A cold wind blew suddenly, gustily, and the black shape of the plane tree rustled and then the sound was lost in the jet roar of an aeroplane going overhead.

I said, "It's like being in the country."

"Well, next best thing perhaps." She shivered. "Let's go in before we freeze." We stepped back through the glass door, and Maggie showed me the tiny kitchen which had been fashioned out of a deep cupboard, and then, halfway down the stairs, the bathroom, which we would all share. Finally, we ended up downstairs again in Maggie's warm, untidy sitting-room, and she found a bottle of sherry and some potato crisps which she swore were stale, but tasted all right to me. "Do you still want to come?" she asked.

"More than ever."

"When do you want to move in?"

"As soon as possible. Next week if I could."

"What about the girls you're sharing with just now?"

"They'll find someone else. One of them has a sister

who's coming to London. I expect she'll move into my room."

"And what about furniture?"

"Oh . . . I'll manage."

"I expect," said Maggie comfortably, "your parents will come up trumps, they usually do. When I first came to London, my mother produced the most wonderful treasures out of the attic and the linen cupboard and so . . ." Her voice died away. I watched her in rueful silence, and she finally laughed at herself. "There I go again, opening my mouth and putting my foot in it. I'm sorry. I've obviously said something idiotically tactless."

"I haven't got a father, and my mother's abroad. She's living in Ibiza. That's really why I want somewhere of my own."

"I am sorry. I should have known, you spending Christmas with the Forbeses . . . I mean, I should have guessed."

"There's no reason why you should guess."

"Is your father dead?"

She was obviously curious, but in such an open and friendly way that all at once it seemed ridiculous to close up and shut up the way I usually did when people began asking me questions about my family.

"I don't think so," I said, trying to sound as though it didn't matter. "I think he lives in Los Angeles. He was an actor. My mother eloped with him when she was eighteen. But he soon got bored with domesticity, or perhaps he decided that his career was more important than raising a family. Anyway, the marriage lasted only a few months before he upped and left her, and then my mother had me."

"What a terrible thing to do."

"I suppose it was. I've never thought very much about it. My mother never talked about him. Not because she was particularly bitter or anything, just that when something was over and in the past, she usually forgot it. She's always been

7

like that. She only looks forward, and always with the utmost optimism."

"But what happened after you were born? Did she go back to her parents?"

"No. Never."

"You mean, nobody sent a telegram saying 'Come back all is forgiven'?"

"I don't know. I honestly don't know."

"There must have been the most resounding row when your mother ran off, but even so . . ." Her voice trailed away. She was obviously unable to understand a situation which I had accepted with equanimity all my life. ". . . what sort of people would do a thing like that to their daughter?"

"I don't know."

"You must be joking!"

"No. I honestly don't know."

"You mean you don't know your own grandparents?"

"I don't even know who they are. Or perhaps who they were. I don't even know if they're still alive."

"Don't you know anything? Didn't your mother ever say anything?"

"Oh, of course . . . little scraps of the past used to come into her conversation but none of it added up to anything. You know how mothers talk to their children, remembering things that happened and things they used to do when they were little."

"But – Bayliss." She frowned. "That's not a very usual name. And it rings a bell somehow but I can't think why. Haven't you got a single clue?"

I laughed at her intensity. "You talk as though I really wanted to know. But you see, I don't. If you've never known grandparents, then you don't miss them."

"But don't you wonder . . ." she groped for words ". . . where they *lived*?"

"I know where they lived. They lived in Cornwall. In a stone house with fields that sloped down to the sea. And my mother had a brother called Roger but he was killed during the war."

"But what did she do after you were born? I suppose she had to go out and get a job."

"No, she had a little money of her own. A legacy from some old aunt or other. Of course, we never had a car or anything, but we seemed to manage all right. She had a flat in Kensington, in the basement of a house that belonged to some friends. And we stayed there till I was about eight, and then I went to boarding school, and after that we sort of . . . moved around . . ."

"Boarding schools cost money . . ."

"It wasn't a very grand boarding school."

"Did your mother marry again?"

I looked at Maggie. Her expression was lively and avidly curious, but she was kind. I decided that, having gone so far, I may as well tell her the rest.

"She . . . wasn't exactly the marrying type . . . But she was always very, very attractive, and I don't remember a time when there wasn't some adoring male in attendance . . . And once I was away at school, I suppose there wasn't much reason to go on being circumspect. I never knew where I was going to spend the next set of holidays. Once it was in France, in Provence. Sometimes in this country. Another time it was Christmas in New York."

Maggie took this in, and made a face. "Not much fun for you."

"But educational." I had long ago learned to make a joke of it. "And just think of all the places I've seen, and all the extraordinary places I've lived in. The Ritz in Paris once, and another time a gruesomely cold house in Denbighshire. That was a poet who thought he'd try sheep farming. I've never been so glad in my life when that association came to an end."

"She must be very beautiful."

"No, but men think she is. And she's very gay and

improvident and vague, and I suppose you'd say utterly amoral. Maddening. Everything is 'jokey'. It's her big word. Unpaid bills are 'jokey' and lost handbags and unanswered letters, they're all 'jokey'. She has no idea of money and no sense of obligation. An embarrassing sort of person to live with."

"What's she doing in Ibiza?"

"She's living with some Swedish man she met out there. She went out to stay with a couple she knew, and she met this guy and the next thing I knew I had a letter saying that she was going to move in with him. She said he was terribly Nordic and dour but he had a beautiful house."

"How long is it since you've seen her?"

"About two years. I eased out of her life when I was seventeen. I did a secretarial course and took temporary jobs, and finally I ended up working for Stephen Forbes."

"Do you like it?"

"Yes. I do."

"How old are you?"

"Twenty-one."

Maggie smiled again, shaking her long hair in wonderment. "What a lot you've done," she said, and she did not sound in the least bit sorry for me but even slightly envious. "At twenty-one I was a blushing bride in a beastly busty white wedding dress and an old veil that smelt of mothballs. I'm not really a trad. person, but I've got a mother who is, and I'm very fond of her so I usually used to do what she wanted."

I could imagine Maggie's mother. I said, resorting to the comfort of clichés, because I couldn't think of anything else to say, "Oh, well, it takes all sorts," and at that moment we heard John's key in the lock and after that we did not bring up the subject of mothers and families again.

It was a day like any other day, but it had a bonus attached to it. Last Thursday I had worked late with Stephen, trying to complete the last of the January stocktaking, and in return he had given me this morning off so that I had until lunchtime to my own devices. I filled it in cleaning the flat (which took, at most, no more than half an hour), doing some shopping and taking a bundle of clothes to the launderette. By eleven thirty all this domesticity was completed so I put on my coat and set off, in a leisurely way, for work, intending to walk some of the way, and maybe stand myself an early lunch before getting to the shop.

It was one of those cold, dark, damp days when it never really gets light. I walked, through this gloom, up into the New Kings Road, and headed west. Here, every other shop seems to sell either antiques or second-hand beds or picture frames, and I thought I knew them all, but all at once I found myself outside a shop which I had not noticed before. The outside was painted white, the windows framed in black, and there was a red and white awning pulled out as protection against the imminent drizzle.

I looked up to see what the shop was called and read the name TRISTRAM NOLAN picked out in neat black Roman capitals over the door. This door was flanked by windows filled with delectable odds and ends and I paused to inspect their contents, standing on the pavement bathed in brightness from the many lights which burned within. Most of the furniture was Victorian, re-upholstered and restored and polished. A buttoned sofa with a wide lap and curly legs, a sewing box, a small picture of lap dogs on a velvet cushion.

I looked beyond the windows and into the shop itself, and it was then that I saw the cherrywood chairs. They were a pair, balloon backed, with curved legs and seats embroidered with roses.

I craved them. Just like that. I could picture them in my flat, and I wanted them desperately. For a moment I hesitated. This

11

was no junk shop and the price might well be more than I could afford. But after all, no harm could be done by asking. Before I could lose my nerve, I opened the door and went in.

The shop was empty, but the door opening and closing had rung a bell, and presently there was the sound of someone coming down the stairs, the woollen curtain that hung over the door at the back of the shop was drawn aside and a man came into view.

I suppose I had expected someone elderly and formally attired, in keeping with the ambience of the shop and its contents, but this man's appearance rocked all my vague, preconceived notions. For he was young, tall and long-legged, dressed in jeans – faded to a soft blue and clinging like a second skin – and a blue denim jacket, equally old and faded, with the sleeves turned back in a businesslike way to reveal the checked cuffs of the shirt he wore beneath it. A cotton handkerchief was knotted at his neck and on his feet he wore soft moccasins, much decorated and fringed.

That winter the most unlikely people were drifting around London dressed as cowboys, but somehow this one looked real, and his worn clothes appeared as genuine as he was. We stood and looked at each other, and then he smiled and for some reason this took me unawares. I don't like being taken unawares, and I said "Good morning" with a certain coolness.

He dropped the curtain behind him and came forward, soft footed. "Can I help you?"

He may have looked like a genuine, dyed-in-the-wool American, but the moment he opened his mouth it was clear that he was no such thing. For some reason this annoyed me. The life I had led with my mother had left me with a thick streak of cynicism about men in general, and phoneys in particular, and this young man, I decided then and there, was a phoney.

"I . . . I was going to ask about these little chairs. The balloon-back ones."

12

"Oh, yes." He came forward to lay his hand on the back of one. The hand was long and shapely, with spade-tipped fingers, the skin very brown. "There's just the pair of them."

I stared at the chairs, trying to ignore his presence.

"I wondered how much they were."

He squatted beside me to search for a price ticket and I saw his hair fell thick and straight to his collar, very dark and lustrous.

"You're in luck," he told me. "They're going very cheap because the leg of one has been broken and then not very professionally repaired." He straightened up suddenly, surprising me by his height. His eyes were slightly tip-tilted, and a very dark brown, with an expression in them that I found disconcerting. He made me uncomfortable and my antipathy for him began to turn to dislike. "Fifteen pounds for the pair," he said. "But if you'd like to wait and pay a little more, I can get the leg reinforced, and perhaps a small veneer put over the joint. That would make it stronger and it would look better too."

"Isn't it all right now?"

"It would be all right for you," said the young man, ". . . but if you had a large fat man for dinner, he'd probably end up on his backside."

There was a pause while I regarded him – I hoped coldly. His eyes were brimming, with a malicious amusement which I had no intention of sharing. I did not appreciate the suggestion that the only men who would ever come and have dinner with me would necessarily be large and fat.

I said at last, "How much would it cost me to have the leg repaired?"

"Say five pounds. That means you get the chairs for a tenner each."

I worked this out, and decided that I could just afford them. "I'll take them."

"Good," said the young man and put his fists on his hips and smiled amiably, as though this were the end of the transaction.

I decided he was utterly inefficient. "Do you want me to pay for them now, or to leave a deposit . . .?"

"No, that doesn't matter. You can pay for them when you collect them."

"Well, when will they be ready?"

"In about a week."

"Don't you want my name?"

"Not unless you want to give it to me."

"What happens if I never come back?"

"Then I expect they'll be sold to someone else."

"I don't want to lose them."

"You won't," said the young man.

I frowned, angry with him, but he only smiled and went to the door to open it for me. Cold air poured in, and outside the drizzle had started and the street looked dark as night.

He said, "Goodbye," and I managed a frosty smile of thanks and went past him, out into the gloom, and as I did so I heard the bell ring as he shut the door behind me.

The day was, all at once, unspeakable. My pleasure in buying the chairs had been wrecked by the irritation which the young man had generated. I did not usually take instant dislikes to people and I was annoyed not only with him, but with myself, for being so vulnerable. I was still brooding on this when I walked down Walton Street and let myself into Stephen Forbes's bookshop. Even the comfort of being indoors and the pleasant smell of new paper and printers' ink did nothing to dispel my wretched mood.

The shop was on three levels, with new books on the ground floor, second-hand books and old prints upstairs, and Stephen's office in the basement. I saw that Jennifer, the second girl, was busy with a customer, and the only other person visible was an old lady in a tweed cape engrossed in the Gardening section, so I headed for the little cloakroom, unbuttoning my coat as I went, but then I heard Stephen's heavy, unmistakable footsteps coming up from downstairs, and for some reason I stopped to wait for him. The next moment he appeared, tall, stooping and spectacled, with his usual expression of vague benevolence. He wore dark suits that always managed to appear as though in need of a good press, and already, at this early hour, the knot of his tie had begun to slip down, revealing the top button of his shirt.

"Rebecca," he said.

"Yes, I'm here . . ."

"I'm glad I've caught you." He came to my side speaking low-voiced, so as not to disturb the customers. "There's a letter for you downstairs; it's been forwarded on from your old flat. You'd better nip down and collect it."

I frowned. "A letter?"

"Yes. Airmail. Lots of foreign stamps. It has, for some reason, an air of urgency about it."

My irritation, along with all thoughts of new chairs, was lost in a sudden apprehension.

"Is it from my mother?"

"I don't know. Why don't you go and find out?"

So I went down the steep, uncarpeted stairs to the basement, lit, on this dark day, by long strip-lights let into the ceiling. The office was marvellously untidy – as usual – littered with letters and parcels and files, piles of old books, and cardboard boxes and ashtrays which nobody ever remembered to empty. But the letter was on the middle of Stephen's blotter and instantly visible.

I picked it up. An airmail envelope, Spanish stamps, an Ibizan postmark. But the writing was unfamiliar, pointed and spiky, as though a very fine pen had been used. It had been sent to the old flat, but this address had been crossed out and the address of the bookshop substituted in large, girlish, handwriting. I wondered how long the letter had lain on the table by the front door, before one of the girls realised that it was there and had taken the trouble to forward it on to me.

I sat down in Stephen's chair and slit the envelope. Inside,

15

two pages of fine airmail paper, and the date at the head was the third of January. Very nearly a month ago. My mind sounded a note of alarm and, suddenly frightened, I began to read.

Dear Rebecca,

I hope you do not mind me calling you by your Christian name, but your mother has spoken to me of you a great deal. I am writing because your mother is very ill. She has been unwell for some time and I wished to write to you before but she would not let me.

Now, however, I am taking matters into my own hands, and with the doctor's approval I am letting you know that I think you should come out to see her.

If you can do this, perhaps you will cable me the number of your aeroplane flight so that I can be at the airport to meet you.

I know that you are working and it may not be easy to make this trip, but I would advise you to waste no time. I am afraid that you will find your mother very changed, but her spirit is still high.

With good wishes.
Sincerely,
Otto Pedersen.

I sat in unbelief, and stared at the letter. The formal words told me nothing and everything. My mother was very ill, perhaps dying. A month ago I had been asked to waste no time but to go to her. Now it was a month later, and I had only just got the letter and perhaps she was already dead – and I had never gone. What would he think of me, this Otto Pedersen whom I had never seen, whose name, even, I had not known until this moment?

16

# Chapter Two

I read the letter again, and then again, the flimsy pages rustling in my hands. I was still there, sitting at his desk, when Stephen finally came downstairs to find me.

I turned to look up at him over my shoulder. He saw my face and said, "What is it?"

I tried to tell him, but could not. Instead I thrust the letter at him, and while he took it, and read it, I sat with my elbows on his desk, biting my thumbnails, bitter and angry, and fighting a terrible anxiety.

He was soon finished reading. He tossed the letter down on the desk between us, and said, "Did you know she was ill?"

I shook my head.

"When did you last hear from her?"

"Four, five months ago. She never wrote letters." I looked up at him and said, furiously, choked by the great lump in my throat, "That was nearly a *month* ago. That letter's been lying in the flat, and nobody bothered to send it to me. She may be dead by now and I never went, and she'll think I simply didn't care!"

"If she had died," said Stephen, "then we'd have surely heard. Now, don't cry, there isn't time for that. What we have to do is get you out to Ibiza with all convenient speed, and let . . ." he glanced down at the letter again ". . . Mr Pedersen know you're arriving. Nothing else matters."

I said, "I can't go," and my mouth began to grow square

and my lower lip tremble as though I were a ten-year-old.

"Why can't you go?"

"Because I haven't got enough money for the fare."

"Oh, my dear child, let me worry about that . . ."

"But I can't let you . . ."

"Yes, you can, and if you get all stiff-necked about it then you can pay me back over the next five years and I'll charge you interest, if it'll make you feel happier, and now for God's sake don't let's mention it again . . ." He was already reaching for the directory, behaving in an altogether efficient and un-Stephen-like fashion. "Have you got a passport? And nobody's going to clamp down on you for smallpox injections or anything tiresome like that. Hello? British Airways? I want to make a reservation on the first plane to Ibiza." He smiled down at me, still fighting tears and temper, but already feeling a little better. There is nothing like having a large and kindly man to take over in times of emotional stress. He picked up a pencil and drew a sheet of paper towards him and began to make notes. "Yes. When? Fine. Can we have a reservation, please? Miss Rebecca Bayliss. And what time does it get to Ibiza? And the flight number? Thank you so much. Thank you. Yes, I'll get her to the airport myself."

He put down the receiver and surveyed, with some satisfaction, the illegible squiggles his pencil had made.

"That's it, then. You fly tomorrow morning, change planes at Palma, get to Ibiza about half past seven. I'll drive you to the airport. No, don't start arguing again, I wouldn't feel happy unless I saw you actually walk on to the aeroplane. And now we'll cable Mr Otto Pedersen . . ." he picked up the letter again ". . . at the Villa Margareta, Santa Catarina, and let him know that you're coming." He smiled down at me with such cheerful reassurance that I was suddenly filled with hope.

I said, "I can't ever thank you . . ."

"I don't ever want you to," said Stephen. "It's the least I can do."

I flew the next day, in a plane half-filled with hopeful winter holiday tourists. They even carried straw hats against an improbably blazing sun, and their faces, as we stepped out into a steady drizzle at Palma, were disappointed but resolutely cheerful, as though, for certain, tomorrow would be better.

The rain never ceased, all the four hours I waited in the transit lounge, and the flight out of Palma was bumpy with thick, wet clouds. But as we rose above them and headed out across the sea, the weather brightened. The clouds thinned and broke, disclosing an evening sky of robin's egg blue, and far below the crumpled sea was streaked with the pink light of the setting sun.

It was dark when we landed. Dark and damp. Coming down the gangway beneath a sky full of bright southern stars, there was only the smell of petrol, but as I walked across the puddled tarmac towards the lights of the terminal building I felt the soft wind in my face. It was warm and smelt of pines, and was evocative of every summer holiday I had ever spent abroad.

At this quiet time of the year the plane had not been full. It did not take long to get through Customs and Immigration, and – my passport stamped – I picked up my suitcase and walked into the Arrivals Lounge.

There were the usual small groups of waiting people standing about or sitting hunched apathetically on the long plastic banquettes. I stopped and looked about me, waiting to be identified, but could see nobody who looked in the least like a Swedish writer come to meet me. And then a man turned from buying a newspaper at the bookstall. Across the room our eyes met, and he folded the newspaper and began to walk towards me, pushing his paper into his jacket pocket as though it were no longer of any use to him. He was tall and thin, with hair that was either blond or white – it was impossible to tell in the bright, impersonal electric light. Before he was halfway across the polished floor I smiled tentatively, and as he approached he said my name, "Rebecca?" with a question mark at the end of it, still not entirely certain that it was I.

"Yes."

"I'm Otto Pedersen." We shook hands and he gave a formal little bow as he did so. His hair, I saw then, was pale blond, turning grey, and his face was deeply tanned, thin and bony, the skin dry and finely wrinkled from long exposure to the sun. His eyes were very pale, and more grey than blue. He wore a black polo-necked sweater and a light oatmeal-coloured suit with pleated pockets, like a safari shirt, and a belt which hung loose, the buckle swinging. He smelt of aftershave and looked as clean as if he had been bleached.

Having found each other, it was suddenly difficult to find anything to say. All at once we were both overwhelmed by the circumstances of our meeting and I realised that he was as unsure of himself as I. But he was also urbane and polite, and dealt with this by taking my suitcase from me and asking if this was all my luggage.

"Yes, that's all."

"Then let us go to the car. If you like to wait at the door, I will fetch it and save you the walk . . ."

"I'll come with you."

"It's only across the road, in the car park."

So we went out together, into the darkness again. He led me to the half empty car park. Here, he stopped by a big black Mercedes, unlocked it, and tossed my case on to the back seat. Then he held the door open so that I could get in before coming around to the front of the car to settle himself beside me.

"I hope you had a good journey," he said, politely, as we left the terminal behind us and headed out into the road.

"It was a little bumpy in Palma. I had to wait four hours."

"Yes. There are no direct flights at this time of the year."

I swallowed. "I must explain about not answering your letter. I've moved flats, and I didn't get it till yesterday morning. It wasn't forwarded to me, you see. It was so good of you to write, and you must have wondered why I never replied."

"I thought something like that must have happened."

His English was perfect, only the precise Swedish vowel sounds betraying his origins, and a certain formality in the manner in which he expressed himself.

"When I got your letter I was so frightened . . . that it would be too late."

"No," said Otto. "It is not too late."

Something in his voice made me look at him. His profile was knife sharp against the yellow glow of passing street lights, his expression unsmiling and grave.

I said, "Is she dying?"

"Yes," said Otto. "Yes, she is dying."

"What is wrong with her?"

"Cancer of the blood. You call it leukaemia."

"How long has she been ill?"

"About a year. But it was only just before Christmas time that she became so ill. The doctor thought that we should try blood transfusions, and I took her to the hospital for this. But it was no good, because as soon as I got her home again, she started this very bad nose bleed, and so the ambulance had to come and take her back to hospital again. She was there over Christmas and only then allowed home again. It was after that I wrote to you."

"I wish I'd got the letter in time. Does she know I'm coming?"

"No, I didn't tell her. You well know how she loves surprises, and equally how she hates to be disappointed. I thought there was a chance that something would go wrong and you wouldn't be on the plane." He smiled frostily, "But of course you were."

21

We stopped at a crossroads to wait for a country cart to pass in front of us, the feet of the mule making a pleasant sound on the dusty road, and a lantern swinging from the back of the cart. Otto took advantage of the pause to take a cheroot from the breast pocket of his jacket and light it from the lighter on the dashboard. The cart passed, we moved on.

"How long is it since you have seen your mother?"

"Two years."

"You must expect a great change. I am afraid you will be shocked, but you must try not to let her see. She is still very vain."

"You know her so well."

"But of course."

I longed to ask him if he loved her. The question was on the tip of my tongue, but I realised that at this stage of our acquaintance it would be nothing but impertinence to ask such an intimate and personal thing. Besides, what difference did it make? He had met her and wanted to be with her, had given her a home, and now, when she was so ill, was cherishing her in his own apparently unemotional manner. If that wasn't love, then what was?

After a little, we began to talk of other things. I asked him how long he had lived on the island, and he said five years. He had come first in a yacht and had liked the place so well that he had returned the next year to buy his house and settle here.

"You're a writer . . ."

"Yes, but I am also a Professor of History."

"Do you write books on history?"

"I have done so. At the moment I am working on a thesis concerned with the Moorish occupation of these islands and southern Spain."

I was impressed. As far as I could remember, none of my mother's previous lovers had been even remotely intellectual.

"How far away is your house?"

"About five miles now. The village of Santa Catarina was

quite unspoiled when I first came here. Now, however, large hotel developments are planned and I fear it will become spoiled like the rest of the island. No, that is wrong. Like some parts of the island. It is still possible to be entirely remote if you know where to go and have a car or perhaps a motor boat."

It was warm in the car and I rolled down the window. The soft night air blew in on my face and I saw that we were in country now, passing through groves of olives, with every now and then the glimmering light of a farmhouse window shining beyond the bulbous, spiked shapes of prickly pear.

I said, "I'm glad she was here. I mean, if she has to be ill and die, I'm glad it's somewhere like this, in the south, with the sun warm and the smell of pines."

"Yes," said Otto. And then, precisely as ever, "I think that she has been very happy."

We drove on in silence, the road empty, telegraph poles rushing to meet the headlights of the car. I saw that now we were running parallel to the sea, which spread to an invisible, dark horizon and was dotted here and there with the lights of fishing boats. Presently there appeared ahead of us the neon-lighted shape of a village. We passed a sign reading SANTA CATARINA and then were driving down the main street; the air was filled with the smell of onions and oil and grilling meat. Flamenco music flung itself at us from open doorways, and dark faces, filled with absent curiosity, turned to watch us pass. In a moment we had left the village behind us, and had plunged forward into the darkness which lay beyond, only to slow down almost immediately to negotiate a steep corner which led up a narrow lane between orchards of almond trees. The headlights bored into the darkness, and ahead I saw the villa, white and square, pierced by small, secretive windows and with a lighted lantern swinging over the great, nailed front door.

Otto braked the car and switched off the engine. We got out, Otto taking my suitcase from the back seat and leading the way

23

across the gravel. He opened the door and stood aside and I walked in ahead of him.

We were in a hallway, lit by a wrought-iron chandelier and furnished with a long couch covered in a bright blanket. A tall blue and white jar stood by the door containing a selection of ivory-handled walking sticks and sun umbrellas. As Otto closed the front door, another opened ahead of us and a small, dark-haired woman appeared, wearing a pink overall and flat, worn slippers.

"Señor."

"Maria."

She smiled, showing a number of gold teeth. He spoke to her in Spanish, asking a question to which she replied and then, turning, introduced me to her.

"This is Maria, who takes care of us. I have told her who you are . . ."

I held out my hand and Maria took it: we made friends by smiling and nodding. Then she turned back to Otto and spoke some more. Presently he handed her my suitcase, and she withdrew.

Otto said, "Your mother has been asleep but she is awake now. Let me take your coat."

I unbuttoned it, and he helped me off with it and laid it across the end of the couch. Then he went across the floor towards yet another door, motioning me to follow. I did, and was suddenly nervous, afraid of what I was going to find.

It was the salon of the house into which he led me. A long low-ceilinged room, whitewashed like the rest of the house, and furnished with a pleasing mixture of modern Scandinavian and antique Spanish. The tile floor was scattered with rugs, there were a great many books and pictures, and in the centre of the room a round table was laid out, seductively, with neatly ordered magazines and newspapers.

A wood fire burned in a great stone fireplace, and in front of this was a bed, with a low table alongside, holding a glass of water and a jug, a few pink geraniums in a mug, some books and a lighted lamp.

This lamp and the flicker of flames provided the only light in the room, but from the door I could see the narrow shape which humped the pink blankets and the attenuated hand and arm which was extended as Otto came forward to stand on the hearth-rug.

"Darling," she said.

"Lisa." He took the hand and kissed it.

"You haven't been long after all."

"Maria says you have slept. Do you feel ready for a visitor?"

"A visitor?" Her voice was a thread. "Who?"

Otto glanced up at me, and I moved forward to stand beside him. I said, "It's me. Rebecca."

"Rebecca. Darling child. Oh, how blissfully jokey." She held out both arms to me, and I knelt down beside the bed to kiss her; her body gave me no resistance or support at all, so thin was she, and when I touched her cheek it felt papery beneath my lips. It was like kissing a leaf that has long since been wrenched by the wind from its parent tree.

"But what are you doing *here*?" She looked over my shoulder at Otto, and then back at me again. She put on the pretence of a frown. "You didn't *tell* her to come?"

"I thought you would like to see her," said Otto. "I thought it would cheer you up."

"But darling, why didn't you tell me?"

I smiled. "We wanted it to be a surprise."

"But I wish I'd known, then I could have looked forward to seeing you. That's what we always used to think, before Christmas. Half the fun was anticipation." She let me go and I sat back on my heels. "Are you going to stay?"

"For a day or so."

"Oh, how utterly perfect. We can have the most gorgeous gossips. Otto, does Maria know she's staying?"

25

"Of course."

"And what about dinner tonight?"

"It's all arranged . . . we'll have it together, in here, just the three of us."

"Well, let's have something now. A little drinkey. Is there any champagne?"

Otto smiled. "I think I can find a bottle. In fact, I think I remembered to put one on ice for just such an occasion."

"Oh, you clever man."

"Shall I get it now?"

"Please, darling."

She slid her hand in mine and it was like holding chicken bones. "And we'll drink to being together."

He went away to fetch the champagne and we were alone. I found a little stool and pulled it up so that I could sit close to her. We looked at each other, and she could not stop smiling. The dazzling smile and the bright dark eyes were still the same, so was the dark hair that spread like a stain over the snowy pillowcase. Otherwise her appearance was horrifying. I had never known anyone could be so thin and still be alive. And to make it more unreal, she was not pale and colourless but quite brown, as though she still spent most of the day lying in the sun. But she was excited. It seemed she could not stop talking.

"So sweet of the darling man to know how much I would love to see you. The only thing is, I'm so boring just now, I don't feel like doing anything, he should have waited until I'm better and then we could have had some fun together, and gone swimming and out in the boat and had picnics and things."

I said, "I can come again."

"Yes, of course you can." She touched my face with her hand as though needing this contact to reassure her that I was really there. "You're looking gorgeous, do you know that? You've got your father's colouring, with those big grey eyes, and that corn-coloured hair. Is it corn, or is it gold? And I love

26

the way you're doing it." Her hand travelled to the single plait which fell forward, like a rope over my right shoulder. "It makes you look like something out of a fairy story; you know, those old-fashioned books with the magical pictures. You're very pretty."

I shook my head. "No. I'm not."

"Well, you look it, and that's the next best thing. Darling, what are you doing with yourself? It's such ages since I wrote or heard from you. Whose fault was that? Mine, I suppose, I'm hopeless at writing letters."

I told her about the bookshop and the new flat. She was amused by this. "What a funny person you are, building a little nest for yourself without anybody to share it with. Haven't you met anybody yet you want to marry?"

"No. Nor anyone who wants to marry me."

She looked malicious. "What about the man you work for?"

"He's married, he's got a charming wife and a brood of children."

She giggled. "That never bothered me. Oh, darling, what a dreadful mother I was to you, trailing you round in that reprehensible fashion. It's a wonder you haven't collected the most ghastly selection of neuroses or hang-ups or whatever they call them these days! But you don't look as though you have, so perhaps it was all right after all."

"Of course it was all right. I just grew up with my eyes open and that was no bad thing." I added, "I like Otto."

"Isn't he divine? So correct and punctilious and *northern*. And so blazingly intelligent . . . So lucky he doesn't want me to be intelligent too! He just likes having me make him laugh."

Somewhere, in the middle of the house, a clock struck seven, and as the last note chimed Otto came back into the room carrying a tray with the champagne bottle in a bucket of ice, and three wine glasses. We watched as he expertly loosened the cork and the golden foaming wine spilled into the three glasses,

27

and we each took one and raised them, all of us smiling because it was suddenly a party. My mother said, "Here's to the three of us and happy times. Oh, so divinely jokey."

Later, I was shown to my bedroom, which was either simply luxurious or luxuriously simple, I couldn't decide which. A fitted bathroom led off it, so I showered, and changed into trousers and a silk shirt, and brushed my hair and replaited it, and returned to the salon. I found Otto and my mother waiting for me, Otto also changed for the evening, and Mother wearing a fresh bedjacket of powder blue with a silk shawl embroidered with pink roses flung across her knees, its long fringe brushing the floor. We had another drink and then Maria served dinner on a low table by the fire. My mother never stopped talking — it was all about the old days when I was growing up, and I kept thinking that Otto would be shocked, but he wasn't shocked at all, he was curious and much amused and kept asking questions and prompting my mother to tell us more.

". . . and that dreadful farm in Denbighshire . . . Rebecca, do you remember that terrible house? We nearly died of cold and the fire smoked whenever we lit it. That was Sebastian," she explained for Otto's benefit. "We all thought he was going to be a famous poet, but he wasn't any better at writing poetry than he was at sheep farming. In fact, if anything, worse. And I couldn't think how on earth I could leave him without hurting his feelings and then luckily Rebecca got bronchitis so I had the most perfect excuse."

"Not so lucky for Rebecca," suggested Otto.

"It certainly was. She hated it just as much as I did; anyway he had a horrible dog that was always threatening to bite her. Darling, is there any more champagne?"

She ate hardly anything, but sipped glass after glass of the icy wine while Otto and I worked our way steadily through Maria's delicious, four-course dinner. When it was finished, and the dishes cleared away, my mother asked for some music, and Otto put a Brahms concerto on the record-player, turned very low. Mother just went on talking, like a toy that has been overwound and will only stop whirring senselessly around the floor when it finally breaks.

Presently, saying that he had work to do, Otto excused himself and left us, first building up the fire with fresh logs and making sure that we had everything we needed.

"Does he work every evening?" I asked, when he had gone.

"Nearly always. And in the mornings. He's very punctilious. I think that's why we've got on so well because we're so different."

I said, "He adores you."

"Yes," said my mother, accepting this. "And the best bit is that he never tried to turn me into someone else; he just accepted me, with my wicked ways and my lurid past." She touched my plait again. "You're growing more like your father . . . I always thought you looked like me, but you don't, you look like him now. He was very handsome."

"You know, I don't even know what his name was."

"Sam Bellamy. But Bayliss is a much better name, don't you think? Besides, having you all on my own like that, I always felt you were my child and nobody else's."

"I wish you'd tell me about him. You never have."

"There's so little to tell. He was an actor, and too good-looking for words."

"But where did you meet him?"

"He came down to Cornwall with a Summer Stock company doing open-air Shakespeare. It was all terribly romantic, dark blue summer nights and the damp, dewy smell of the grass, and that divine Mendelssohn music and Sam being Oberon.

> Through the house give glimmering light
>     By the dead and drowsy fire;
> Every elf and fairy sprite
>     Hop as light as bird from brier.

It was magical. And falling in love with him was part of the magic."

"Was he in love with you?"

"We both thought he was."

"But you ran away with him, and married him . . ."

"Yes. But only because my parents left me with no alternative."

"I don't understand."

"They disliked him. They disapproved. They said I was too young. My mother said why didn't I marry some nice young man who lived locally, why didn't I settle down and stop making an exhibition of myself? And if I married an actor, what would people say? I sometimes thought that was all she cared about, what people would say. As if it could possibly matter what anybody said."

It was, unbelievably, the first time I had ever heard her mention her mother. I said, cautiously prompting, "Didn't you like her?"

"Oh, darling, it's so long ago. It's so difficult to remember. But she stifled and repressed me. I sometimes felt she was trying to choke me with conventions. And Roger had been killed and I missed him so dreadfully. Everything would have been different if Roger had been there." She smiled. "He was so nice. Almost too nice. A real BV right from the very start."

"What's a BV?"

"Bitches' Victim. He always fell in love with the most impossible girls. And finally he married one. A little blonde doll, with dolly hair and dolly china blue eyes. My mother thought she was sweet. I couldn't stand her."

"What was she called?"

"Mollie." She made a face as though the very word tasted bad.

I laughed. "She can't have been as bad as all that."

"I thought she was. So maddeningly tidy. Always cleaning

out her handbag or putting trees into her shoes, or sterilising the baby's toys."

"She had a baby then?"

"Yes, a little boy. Poor child, she insisted on calling him Eliot."

"I think that's a nice name."

"Oh, Rebecca, it's sickening." It was obvious that nothing Mollie had done could find favour in my mother's eyes. "I always felt sorry for the child, being saddled with such a dreadful name. And somehow he lived up to it, you know how people do, and after Roger was killed the poor scrap was worse than ever, always hanging round his mother's neck and having to have a light on in his room at night."

"I think you're being very unkind."

She laughed. "Yes, I know, and it wasn't his fault. He probably would have turned into quite a personable young man if his mother gave him half a chance."

"I wonder what happened to Mollie?"

"I don't know. I don't particularly care, either." My mother could always be cruelly off-hand. "It's like a dream. Like remembering dream people. Or perhaps . . ." her voice trailed away ". . . perhaps they were real and I was the dream."

I felt uncomfortable, because this was too near the truth that I was trying to keep at bay. I said quickly, "Are your parents still alive?"

"My mother died that Christmas we spent in New York. Do you remember that Christmas? The cold and the snow and all the shops full of the sound of 'Jingle Bells'? By the end of that Christmas I felt I never wanted to hear that damned tune again. My father wrote to me, but of course the letter didn't reach me until months later by which time it had followed me half round the world. And then it was really too late to write and say anything. Besides, I'm so useless about writing letters. He probably thought I simply didn't care."

"Didn't you ever write?"

"No."

"Didn't you like him either?" It seemed a sorry state of affairs.

"Oh, I adored him. He was wonderful. Terribly good-looking, attractive to women, frightfully fierce and frightening. He was a painter. Did I ever tell you that?"

A painter. I had imagined everything, but never a painter. "No, you never said."

"Well, if you'd had any sort of education at all you'd probably have guessed. Grenville Bayliss. Doesn't that mean anything to you at all?"

I shook my head sadly. It was terrible never to have heard of a famous grandfather.

"Well, why should it? I was never any good at trailing you round art galleries or museums. Come to think of it, I was never much good at anything. It's a wonder you've turned out so well on a solid diet of maternal neglect."

"What did he look like?"

"Who?"

"Your father."

"How do you imagine him?"

I considered the question and came up with Augustus John. "Bohemian, and bearded and rather leonine . . ."

"Wrong," said my mother. "He wasn't like that at all. He started off his life in the Navy, and the Navy left an indelible stamp on him. You see, he didn't decide to be a painter until he was nearly thirty, when he threw up a promising career and enrolled at the Slade. It nearly broke my mother's heart. And moving to Cornwall and setting up house at Porthkerris simply added insult to injury. I don't think she ever forgave him for being so selfish. She'd adored queening it in Malta, and probably fancied herself as wife to the Commander-in-Chief. I must say, he was tailor-made for the part, very blue-eyed and imposing and terrifying. He never lost what was known in those days as a quarter-deck manner."

32

"But you weren't terrified of him?"

"No. I loved him."

"Then why didn't you go home?"

Her face closed up. "I couldn't. I wouldn't. Terrible things had been said, by all of us. Old resentments and old truths had all come boiling up, and threats were made and ultimatums handed out. And the more they opposed me, the more determined I became, and the more impossible it was, when the time came, to admit that they'd been right, and I'd been wrong, and I'd made a hideous mistake. And if I had gone home, I would never have got away again. I knew that. And you wouldn't have belonged to me any more, you'd have belonged to your grandmother. I couldn't have borne that. You were such a precious little thing." She smiled and added rather wistfully, "And we did have fun, didn't we?"

"Yes, of course we did."

"I would have liked to go back. Sometimes I very nearly did. It was such a lovely house. Boscarva it was called, and it was rather like this villa, standing square on a hill above the sea. When Otto first brought me here, it reminded me of Boscarva. But here it's warm and the winds are gentle; there, it was wild and stormy, and the garden was honeycombed with tall hedges to shelter the flower beds from the sea winds. I think the wind was the thing that my mother most hated. She used to seal all the windows and shut herself indoors, playing bridge with her friends or doing needlepoint."

"Didn't she ever do things with you?"

"Not really."

"But who looked after you?"

"Pettifer. And Mrs Pettifer."

"Who were they?"

"Pettifer had been in the Navy, too; he looked after my father and cleaned the silver and sometimes drove the car. And Mrs Pettifer did the cooking. I can't tell you how cosy they were. Sitting by the kitchen fire with them making toast and listening to the wind battering at the windows, knowing that it couldn't get in . . . it made you feel so safe. And we used to read fortunes from the teacups . . ." Her voice trailed off, memories uncertain now. And then, "No, that was Sophia."

"Who was Sophia?"

She did not reply. She was staring at the fire, her expression far away. Perhaps she had not heard me. She said at last, "After my mother died I should have gone back. It was naughty of me to stay away, but I was never over-endowed with what is known as moral fibre. But, you know, there are things at Boscarva that belong to me."

"What sort of things?"

"A desk, I remember. A little one, with drawers down the side, and a lid that opened up. I think it's called a davenport. And some jade that my father brought home from China and a Venetian looking-glass. They were all mine. On the other hand, I moved around so much that they would just have been a nuisance." She looked at me, frowning a little. "But perhaps you don't think they are a nuisance. Have you got any furniture in this flat of yours?"

"No. Practically none."

"Then perhaps I'll see if I can get hold of them for you. They must still be at Boscarva, provided the house hasn't been sold or burned down or something. Would you like me to try and get hold of them?"

"More than anything. Not just because I need furniture, but because they belonged to you."

"Oh, darling, how sweet, too jokey the way you long for roots, and I could never bear to have any. I always felt they would just tie me down in one place."

"And I always feel that they would make me belong."

She said, "You belong to me."

We stayed talking until the early hours of the morning. About midnight, she asked me to refill her water-jug, and I found my way into the deserted kitchen and did this for her, and realised then that Otto, with gentle tact, had probably taken himself quietly off to bed, so that we could be together. And when at last her voice grew tired and her words began to trail off in a blur of exhaustion, I said that I was sleepy too, which I was, and I stood up, cramped from sitting, stretched, and put more logs on the fire. Then I took away her second pillow so that she lay, ready for sleep. The silken shawl had slipped to the floor, so I picked this up and folded it and laid it on a chair. It remained only to stoop and kiss her, turn off the lamp, and leave her there in the firelight. As I went through the door, she said, as she always used to say when I was a little girl, "Good night, my love. Goodbye until tomorrow."

The next morning I was awake early, aware of sunshine streaming through the gaps in the shutters. I got up and went to open them, and saw the brilliant Mediterranean morning. I stepped out through the open windows on to the stone terrace which ran the length of the house and saw the hill sloping down to the sea, maybe a mile distant. The sand-coloured land was veiled in pink, the first tender blossoms of the almond trees. I went back into my room, dressed, and went out again – across the terrace, down a flight of steps, and through the ordered, formal garden. I vaulted a low stone wall, and walked on in the direction of the sea. Presently, I found myself in an orchard, surrounded by almond trees. I stopped and looked up at a froth of pink blossom and beyond it a pale and cloudless blue sky.

I knew that each flower would bear a precious fruit which, when the time came, would be frugally cropped, but even so I could not resist picking a single spray, and I was still carrying this when an hour or so later, having walked to the sea and back, I retraced my steps up the hill towards the villa.

It was steeper than I had realised. Pausing for breath, I looked up at the house, and saw Otto Pedersen standing on the terrace watching my progress. For an instant we both stood still; then he moved and started down the steps, and came down the garden to meet me.

I went on more slowly, still holding the spray of blossom. I knew then. I knew before he came close enough for me to see the expression on his face, but I went on, up through the orchard, and we met at last by the little dry-stone wall.

He said my name. That was all.

I said, "I know. You don't have to tell me."

"She died during the night. When Maria went in this morning to wake her . . . it was all over. It was so peaceful."

It occurred to me that we were not doing much to comfort each other. Or maybe there was no need. He put out a hand to help me over the wall, and kept my hand in his as we walked together up through the garden to the house.

She was buried, according to Spanish law, that very day, and in the little churchyard in the village. There was only the priest present, and Otto and Maria and myself. When it was all over, I put the spray of almond blossom on to her grave.

I flew back to London the next morning, and Otto drove me to the airport in his car. For most of the time we travelled in silence, but as we approached the terminal he suddenly said, "Rebecca, I don't know whether this has any significance, but I would have married Lisa. I would have married her, but I already have a wife in Sweden. We do not live together, and have not done so for a number of years, but she will not divorce me because her religion will not allow it."

"You didn't need to tell me, Otto."

"I wanted you to know."

"You made her so happy. You took such care of her."

"I am glad that you came. I am glad that you saw her."

"Yes." There was, all at once, a terrible lump in my throat,

36

and my eyes filled and brimmed with painful tears. "Yes, I am glad too."

In the terminal, my ticket and my luggage checked, we stood and faced each other.

"Don't wait," I said. "Go now. I hate goodbyes."

"All right . . . but first . . ." He felt in his jacket pocket and took out three fine, worn silver bracelets. My mother had worn them always. She had been wearing them that last night. "You must have these." He took my hand and slipped them on to my wrist. "And this." Out of another pocket came a folded wad of British notes. He pressed it into my palm and closed my fingers over it. "They were in her handbag . . . so you must have them."

I knew they hadn't been in her handbag. She never had any money in her handbag except a few coppers for the next telephone call, and some dog-eared bills, long overdue. But there was something in Otto's face that I couldn't refuse, so I took the money and kissed him, and he turned on his heel, without a word.

I flew back to London in a state of miserable indecision. Emotionally I was empty, drained even of grief. Physically I found that I was exhausted but I could neither sleep nor face the meal that the stewardess offered me. She brought me tea and I tried to drink that, but it tasted bitter and I left it to grow cold.

It was as though a long-locked door had been opened, but only a crack, and it was up to me to open it wide, although what lay behind it was dark and fraught with uncertainty.

Perhaps I should go to Cornwall and seek out my mother's family, but the glimpses I had been given of the set-up at Porthkerris were not encouraging. My grandfather would be very old, lonely and probably bitter. I realised that I had made no arrangement with Otto Pedersen about letting him know that my mother was dead, and so there was the hideous possibility that if I went to see him, I should be the one who would have to break the news. As well, I blamed him a little for having let his daughter make such a mess of her life. I knew that she was impulsive and thoughtless, and stubborn too, but surely he could have been a little more positive in his dealings with her. He could have sought her out, offered to help, inspected me, his grandchild. But he had done none of these things, and surely this would always stand like a high wall between us.

And yet, I longed for roots. I did not necessarily want to live with them, but I wanted them to be there. There were things at Boscarva that had belonged to my mother, and so now belonged to me. She had wanted me to have them, had said as much, so perhaps I was under an obligation to go to Cornwall and claim them as my own, but to go only for this reason seemed both soulless and greedy.

I leaned back and dozed and heard again my mother's voice. *I was never frightened of him. I loved him. I should have gone back.*

And she had said a name – Sophia – but I had never found out who Sophia was.

I slept at last and dreamed that I was there. But the house in my dream had no shape or form and the only real thing about it was the sound of the wind, battering its way inland, fresh and cold from the open sea.

I was in London by the early afternoon, but the dark day had lost its shape and meaning, and I could not think what I was meant to do with what remained of it. In the end I got a taxi and went to Walton Street to seek out Stephen Forbes.

I found him upstairs, going through a box of books out of an old house which had just been sold up. There was no one else with him, and as I appeared at the top of the stairs he stood up and came towards me, thinking that I was a potential customer. When he saw that I was not, his manner changed.

38

"Rebecca! You're back."

I stood there, with my hands in my coat pockets.

"Yes. I got in about two." He watched me, his face a question. I said, "My mother died, early yesterday morning. I was just in time. I had an evening with her, and we talked and talked."

"I see," said Stephen. "I'm glad you saw her." He cleared some books from the edge of a table, and leaned against it, folding his arms and eyeing me through his spectacles. He said, "What are you going to do now?"

"I don't know."

"You look exhausted. Why not take a few days off?"

I said again, "I don't know."

He frowned. "What don't you know?"

"I don't know what to do."

"What's the problem?"

"Stephen, have you ever heard of an artist called Grenville Bayliss?"

"Heavens, yes. Why?"

"He's my grandfather."

Stephen's face was a study. "Good Lord. When did you find that out?"

"My mother told me. I'd never heard of him," I had to admit.

"You should have."

"Is he well known?"

"He was, twenty years ago when I was a boy. There was a Grenville Bayliss over the dining-room fireplace in my father's old house in Oxford. Part of my growing up, one might say. A grey stormy sea and a fishing boat with a brown sail. Used to make me feel seasick to look at it. He specialised in seascapes."

"He was a sailor. I mean, he'd been in the Royal Navy."

"That follows."

I waited for him to go on, but he was silent. I said at last, "What am I to do, Stephen?"

"What do you want to do, Rebecca?"

"I never had a family."

"Is it so important?"

"Suddenly it is."

"Then go and see him. Is there any reason not to?"

"I'm frightened."

"Of what?"

"I don't know. Of being snubbed, I suppose. Or ignored."

"Were there dreadful family rows?"

"Yes. And cuttings-off. And never darken my door again. You know the sort of thing."

"Did your mother suggest that you went?"

"No. Not in so many words. But she said there were some things that belonged to her. She thought I should have them."

"What sort of things?"

I told him. "I know it's nothing very much. Perhaps not even worth making the journey for. But I'd like to have something that belonged to her. Besides . . ." I tried to turn it into a joke ". . . they might help to fill up some of the blank spaces in the new flat."

"I think collecting your possessions should be a secondary reason for going to Cornwall. Your first should be making friends with Grenville Bayliss."

"Supposing he doesn't want to make friends?"

"Then no harm has been done. Except possibly a little bruising to your pride, but that won't kill you."

"You're rail-roading me into this," I told him.

"If you didn't want my advice, then why did you come to see me?"

He had a point. "I don't know," I admitted.

He laughed. "You don't know much, do you?" and when at last I smiled back, he said, "Look. Today's Thursday. Go home and get some sleep. And if tomorrow's too soon, then go down to Cornwall at the weekend. Just go. See how the land lies, see how the old boy is. It may take a few days, but that doesn't matter. Don't come back to London until you've done all you can. And if you can get hold of your own bits and pieces, well and good, but remember that they're of secondary importance."

"Yes. I'll remember."

He stood up. "Then push off," he said. "I've got enough to do without wasting my time running a private Tell Auntie column on your account."

"Can I come back to work when all this is over?"

"You better had. I can't manage without you."

"Goodbye then," I said.

"Au revoir," said Stephen, and as if on an afterthought, leaned forward to give me a clumsy kiss.

"And Good Luck!"

I had already spent enough money on taxis, so, still carrying my case, I walked up to the bus stop and waited until one came, and lurched my way back to Fulham. Gazing, unseeing, out of the window at the grey, crowded streets, I tried to make some plans. I would go to Cornwall, as Stephen suggested, on Monday. At this time of year it shouldn't be difficult to get a seat on the train or find somewhere to stay when I finally got to Porthkerris. And Maggie would keep an eye on my flat.

Thinking of the flat made me remember the chairs I had bought before I had gone to Ibiza. That day seemed a lifetime ago. But if I did not claim them then they would be sold as the disagreeable young man had threatened. With this in mind, I got off the bus a few stops before my own so that I could call into the shop and pay for the chairs and thus be certain that they would be waiting for me when I returned.

I had steeled myself to do business once more with the young man in the blue denims, but as I let myself in and the bell rang with the opening and the closing of the door, I saw with some relief that it was not he who stood up from behind the desk at the back of the shop, but another man, older, with grey hair and a dark beard.

He came forward, taking off a pair of horn-rimmed spectacles, as I thankfully put down my suitcase.

"Good afternoon."

"Oh, good afternoon. I came about some chairs I bought last Monday. Cherrywood, balloon-back ones."

"Oh, yes, I know."

"One of them had to be repaired."

"It's been done. Do you want to take them with you?"

"No. I've got a suitcase. I can't carry them. And I'm going away for a few days. But I thought if I paid for them now, perhaps you'd keep them until I got back."

"Yes, of course." He had a charming, deep voice, and when he smiled his rather saturnine face lit up.

I began to open my bag. "Will it be all right if I write you a cheque? I've got a Banker's Card."

"That's all right . . . would you like to use my desk? And here's a pen."

I began to write. "Who shall I make it out to?"

"To me. Tristram Nolan."

I was gratified to know that it was he who owned this pleasant shop and not my mannerless, cowboy friend. I wrote the cheque and crossed it, and handed it to him. He stood, head down, reading it, and took so long that I thought I must have forgotten something.

"Have I put the date?"

"Yes, that's perfect." He looked up. "It's just your name. Bayliss. It's not very common."

"No. No it's not."

"Are you any relation to Grenville Bayliss?"

Having his name flung at me, just now, was extraordinary and yet not extraordinary at all, in the same way that a name, or a relevant item of news, will spring at you, unbidden, from a page of close print.

I said, "Yes, I am." And then because there was no reason why he shouldn't know, "He's my grandfather."

"Extraordinary," he said.

I was puzzled. "Why?"

"I'll show you." He laid my cheque down on his desk and went to pull out from behind a drop-leafed sofa table a large, sturdy oil painting in a gilt frame. He held it up, balancing one corner on his desk, and I saw that it was by my grandfather. His signature was in the corner, and the date below it, 1932.

"I've only just bought it. It needs cleaning, of course, but I think it's very charming."

I stepped closer to inspect it, and saw sand dunes in an evening light, and two young boys, naked, bent over a collection of shells. The work was perhaps old-fashioned, but the composition charming – the colouring delicate and yet somehow robust – as though the boys, vulnerable in their nakedness, were still tough, and creatures to be reckoned with.

"He was good, wasn't he?" I said, and could not hide the note of pride in my voice.

"Yes. A marvellous colourist." He put the picture back. "Do you know him well?"

"I don't know him at all. I've never met him."

He said nothing, simply stood, waiting for me to enlarge on this odd statement. To fill the silence I went on. "But I've decided that perhaps it's time I did. In fact, I'm going to Cornwall on Monday."

"But that's splendid. The roads will be empty at this time of the year, and it's a lovely drive."

"I'm going by train. I haven't got a car."

"It will still be a pleasant journey. I hope the sun shines for you."

"Thank you very much."

We moved back to the door. He opened it, I picked up my suitcase. "You'll look after my chairs for me?"

"Of course. Goodbye. And have a good time in Cornwall."

# Chapter Three

But the sun did not shine for me. Monday dawned grey and depressing as ever and my faint hopes that the weather would improve as the train rocketed westwards soon died, for the sky darkened with every mile and the wind got up and the day finally dissolved into pouring rain. There was nothing to be seen from the streaming windows; only the blurred shapes of hills and farmsteads, and every now and then the clustered roofs of a village flashed by, or we raced through the half-empty station of some small anonymous town.

By Plymouth, I comforted myself, it would be different. We would cross the Saltash Bridge and find ourselves in another country, another climate, where there would be pink-washed cottages and palm trees and thin winter sunshine. But of course all that happened was that the rain fell even more relentlessly; as I stared out at flooded fields and leafless wind-torn trees, my hopes finally died and I began to be discouraged.

It was nearly a quarter to five by the time we reached the junction which was the end of my journey, and the dark afternoon had sunk, already, into twilight. As the train slowed down alongside the platform, I saw an incongruous palm tree, silhouetted like a broken umbrella against the streaming sky, and the falling rain shimmered and danced in front of the lighted sign which said "St Abbotts, change for Porthkerris." The train finally stopped. I shouldered my rucksack and opened the heavy door which was instantly torn out of my grasp by the wind. The sudden impact of strong cold air, driven inland over the dark sea, made me gasp, and with some idea of making haste I picked up my bag and jumped out on to the platform. I followed the general exodus of travellers up and over the wooden bridge to the station building on the far side. Most of the other passengers seemed to have friends to meet them, or else walked through the ticket office in a purposeful fashion, as though knowing that a car was waiting for them on the far side. Blindly, I followed them, feeling very new and strange but hoping that they would lead me to a taxi. But when I came out into the station yard, there were no taxis. I stood about, hopeful of being offered a lift, but too shy to ask for one, until the tail light of the last car, inevitably, disappeared up the hill in the direction of the main road and I was forced to return to the ticket office for help and advice.

I found a porter, stacking hen coops in a smelly parcels office.

"I'm sorry, but I have to get to Porthkerris. Would there be a taxi?"

He shook his head slowly, without hope, and then said, brightening slightly, "There's a bus. Runs every hour." He glanced up at the slow-ticking clock high on the wall. "But you've just missed one, so you'll 'ave to wait some time."

"Can't I ring up for a taxi?"

"Isn't much call for taxis at this time of the year."

I let my heavy rucksack slip to the floor and we gazed at each other, both defeated by the enormity of the problem. My wet feet were slowly congealing. As we stood there, there came, above the noise of the storm, the sound of a car, driven very fast down the hill from the road.

I said, raising my voice slightly in order to make my point, "I must get a taxi. Where could I telephone?"

"There's a box just out there . . ."

I turned to go in search of it, trailing my rucksack behind me, and as I did so I heard the car stop outside in the yard; a door

45

slammed, footsteps ran, and the next moment a man appeared, banging the door open and shut against the icy wind. He shook himself like a dog before crossing the floor and disappearing through the open door of the Parcels Office.

I heard him say, "Hello, Ernie. I think there's a parcel here for me. From London."

"'Ullo, Mr Gardner. That's a dirty night."

"Filthy. The road's awash. That looks like it . . . that one over there. Yes, that's it. Want me to sign for it?"

"Oh, yes, you'll 'ave to sign. 'Ere we are . . ."

I imagined the slip of paper, smoothed on a table top, the stub of a pencil taken from behind Ernie's ear. And for the life of me I could not remember where I had heard that voice before, nor why I knew it so well.

"That's great. Thanks very much."

"You're welcome."

The telephone, the taxi, forgotten for the moment, I watched the door, waiting for him to reappear. When he did, carrying a large box stuck with red GLASS labels, I saw the long legs, the blue denims drenched in mud to the knee, and a black oilskin, beaded and running with rivulets of water. He was bare-headed, his black hair plastered to his skull, and he saw me for the first time and stopped dead, holding the parcel in front of him like an offering. In his dark eyes was first a flicker of puzzlement, and then recognition. He began to smile. He said, "Good God!"

It was the young man who had sold me the two little cherrywood chairs.

I stood open-mouthed, feeling obscurely that someone had played me a mean and unfair trick. If ever I was in need of a friend it was at this moment, and yet fate had chosen to send me possibly the last person on earth I ever wanted to see again. And that he should see me thus, drenched and desperate, was somehow the last straw.

His smile widened. "What a fantastic coincidence. What are you doing here?"

"I've just got off the train."

"Where are you going?"

I had to tell him. "To Porthkerris."

"Is someone coming for you?"

I very nearly lied and told him "yes." Anything to get rid of him. But I was always a useless fibber, and he would be bound to guess the truth. I said, "No," and then I went on, trying to sound competent, as though I could take good care of myself, "I'm just going to phone for a taxi."

"It'll take hours. I'm going to Porthkerris, I'll give you a ride."

"Oh, you don't need to bother . . ."

"No bother, I'm going anyway. Is that all your luggage?"

"Yes, but . . ."

"Come on then."

I still hesitated, but he seemed to consider the matter already settled, going over to the door to open it, and holding it open with his shoulder, waiting for me to follow. So eventually I did, edging past him, and out into the fury of the dark evening.

In the dim light I saw the Mini pick-up, parked, with the sidelights burning. Letting the door slam behind him, he crossed over to this, and gently loaded his parcel into the back, and then took my rucksack from me, and heaved this in too, covering the two bundles in a cursory fashion with an old piece of tarpaulin. I stood watching him, but he said, "Go on, get in, there's no point us both getting wet through," so I did as I was told, settling myself in the passenger seat with my bag jammed between my legs. Almost at once he had joined me, shutting his door with an almighty slam, and switching on the engine as though there were not a moment to be lost. We roared up the hill away from the station, and the next moment had turned on to the main road and were heading for Porthkerris.

47

He said, "Tell me more, now. I thought you lived in London."

"Yes, I do."

"Have you come down for a holiday?"

"Sort of."

"That sounds good and vague. Are you staying with friends?"

"Yes. No. I don't know."

"What does that mean?"

"Just that. It means I don't know." This sounded rude but it couldn't be helped. I felt as though I had no control over what I was saying.

"Well, you'd better make up your mind before you get to Porthkerris, otherwise you'll be spending the night on the beach."

"I . . . I'm going to stay in a hotel. Just for tonight."

"Well, that's great. Which one?"

I sent him an exasperated look and he said, reasonably enough, "Well, if I don't know which one, I can't take you there, can I?"

He seemed to have me cornered. I said, "I haven't booked in to any hotel. I mean, I thought I could do that when I arrived. There *are* hotels, aren't there?"

"Porthkerris is running with them. Every other house is a hotel. But at this time of the year most of them are closed."

"Do you know some that are open?"

"Yes. But it depends what you want to pay."

He glanced at me sideways, taking in my patched jeans, scuffed shoes, and an old fur-lined leather coat that I had worn for warmth and comfort. At the moment this garment looked and smelt like a wet dog.

"We go from one extreme to the other. The Castle, up on

the hill, where you change for dinner, and dance the foxtrot to
a three-piece orchestra, right down to Mrs Kernow who does
Bed and Breakfast at Number Two, Fish Lane. Mrs Kernow
I can recommend. She looked after me for three months or
more before I got into my own place, and her prices are very
reasonable."

I was diverted. "Your own place? You mean you live here?"

"I do now. Have done for the last six months."

"But . . . the shop in the New Kings Road . . . where I bought
the chairs?"

"I was just helping out for a day or so."

We came to a crossroads, and, slowing down, he turned to
look at me. "Have you got the chairs yet?"

"No. But I've paid for them. They'll still be there when I
get back."

"Good," said the young man.

We drove for a little in silence. Through a village, and up
over a wild bit of country high above the sea; then the road
leaned down again, and there were trees on either side of us.
Through these, through twisted trunks and branches tortured
by the wind, there presently appeared, far below us, the
twinkling lights of a little town.

"Is that Porthkerris?"

"It is. And in a moment you're going to have to tell me if it's
to be The Castle or Fish Lane."

I swallowed. The Castle was out of the question, obviously,
but if I went to Fish Lane I would necessarily place myself
under an obligation to this managing person. I had not come to
Porthkerris for any other reason than to see Grenville Bayliss,
and I had an uncomfortable feeling that if I once got involved
with this man he would stick like a burr.

I said, "No, not The Castle . . ." meaning to suggest some
other, more modest establishment, but he cut me short.

"That's great," he said, with a grin. "Mrs Kernow of Fish
Lane it is, and you won't regret it."

My first impression of Porthkerris, in the dark and the gusty rain, was confused to say the least of it. The town was, on this unsalubrious evening, nearly empty of people; the deserted streets gleamed wetly with reflected light, and the gutters ran with water.

At a great speed, we plunged down into a warren of baffling lanes and alleys, at one time emerging out on to the road which circled the harbour, only to turn back once more into the maze of cobbled roads and uneven, haphazard houses.

We turned at last into a narrow street of grey terrace houses, with front doors opening flush on to the pavement.

All was seemly and respectable. Lace curtains veiled windows, and there could be glimpsed statuettes of girls with dogs, or large green pots containing aspidistras.

The car slowed at last and stopped.

"We're here." He switched off the engine, and I could hear the wind and, above its whine, the nearby sound of the sea. Great breakers thundered up on to the sand, and there was the long hiss of the retreating waves.

He said, "You know, I don't know your name."

"It's Rebecca Bayliss. And I don't know yours."

"Joss Gardner . . . it's short for Jocelyn, not Joseph." With this useful bit of information he got out of the car and rang a bell in a door and, while waiting for an answer, went to retrieve my rucksack from underneath the tarpaulin. As he heaved it out, the door opened and he turned and was illuminated in a shaft of warm light which streamed from inside the house.

"Joss!"

"Hello, Mrs Kernow."

"What are you doing here?"

"I've brought you a visitor. I said you were the best hotel in Porthkerris."

"Oh, my soul, I don't belong to take visitors at this time of the year. But come along in now, out of the rain, what weather isn't it? Tom's down at the Coastguard lodge, been some sort of a warning up from the Trevose way, but I don't know, I haven't heard no rockets . . ."

Somehow we were all inside and the door shut and there was scarcely room for the three of us to stand in the narrow hall.

"Come along in by the fire . . . it's nice and warm, I'll get you a cup of tea if you like . . ." We followed her into a tiny, cluttered, cosy parlour. She knelt to poke the fire to life and add more coal, and for the first time I was able to take a good look at her. I saw a small, bespectacled lady, quite elderly, wearing bedroom slippers and a pinafore over her good brown dress.

"We don't really want tea," he told her. "We just want to know if you can give Rebecca a bed – for a night or so."

She stood up from the fireplace. "Well, I don't know . . ." She looked at me doubtfully, and what with my appearance and the dog-smelling coat I didn't blame her for being doubtful.

I started to open my mouth, but Joss sailed in before I could say a word. "She's highly respectable and she won't run away with the spoons. I'll vouch for her."

"Well . . ." Mrs Kernow smiled. Her eyes were pretty, a very pale blue. "The room's empty, so she may as well have it. But I can't give her supper tonight, not expecting anybody, I haven't anything in the house but a couple of little pasties."

"That's all right," said Joss. "I'll feed her."

I started to protest, but once again I was overborne. "I'll leave her here to get settled in and unpacked, and then I'll be back about . . ." he glanced at his watch ". . . seven thirty, to pick her up. That all right?" he flung casually in my direction. "You're an angel, Mrs Kernow, and I love you like a mother." He put an arm around her and kissed her. She looked delighted; then he gave me a final, cheerful grin, said, "See you," and so departed. We heard his car roaring away down the street.

"He's a lovely boy," Mrs Kernow informed me. "I had him living here three months or more . . . now come along, pick up your little bag and I'll show you your room. 'Course it'll be

51

cold, but I've got an electric fire you can have, and the water in the tank's nice and hot if you want a bath . . . I always say you feel so mucky coming off those dirty trains . . ."

The room was as tiny as all the other rooms in this little house, furnished with an enormous double bed which took up nearly all the space. But it was clean and, presently, warm, and after Mrs Kernow had shown me where to find the bathroom she went back downstairs and left me to myself.

I went to kneel by the low window and draw back the curtains. The old frames had been jammed tight shut against the wind by rubber wedges, and the dark glass streamed with rain. There was nothing to be seen, but I stayed there anyway, wondering what I was doing in this little house, and trying to work out why Joss Gardner's sudden reappearance in my life had left me with this unexplained feeling of unease.

# Chapter Four

I needed defences. I needed to build up my confidence and my self-esteem, disliking the role of rescued waif in which I had suddenly found myself. A hot bath and a change of clothes went a long way towards restoring my composure. I did my hair, made up my eyes, splashed on the last of a bottle of expensive scent and was halfway towards being in charge again. I had already unpacked a dress from the ubiquitous rucksack and hung it hopefully to shed its wrinkles; now I put it on, a dark cotton with long sleeves, and dark stockings, very fine, and shoes with heels and old-fashioned buckles which I had found, long back, on a stall in the Portobello Road . . . As I fastened my pearl ear-rings I heard, over the rattle and bang of the gusty wind, the sound of Joss Gardner's little van, tyres drumming on the cobbles, coming up the street. It screeched to a noisy halt outside the door, and the next moment I heard his voice downstairs, calling first for Mrs Kernow and then for me.

I continued, slowly, to screw the fastening of the last ear-ring. I picked up my bag, and then my leather coat. This I had draped near the electric fire in the hope that it would dry off, but it hadn't. The heat had merely emphasised the smell of a spaniel come in from a wet walk, and it still weighed heavy as lead. Lugging it over my arm, I went down the stairs.

"Hallo, there." Joss, in the hall, looked up at me. "Well, what a transformation. Feel better now?"

"Yes."

"Give me your coat . . ."

He took it from me intending to help me on with it, and instantly became a comic weightlifter, sagging at the knees with the sheer bulk of it.

"You can't wear this, it'll drive you into the ground. Anyway it's still wet."

"I haven't got another." Still toting the coat, he started to laugh. My self-esteem began to drain away and some of this must have showed on my face, because he suddenly stopped laughing and shouted for Mrs Kernow. When she appeared, with an expression both exasperated and loving on her face, he bundled my coat into her arms, told her to dry it for me, unbuttoned and removed his own black oilskin and laid it, with a certain grace, around my shoulders.

Beneath it he wore a soft grey sweater, a cotton scarf knotted at the neck. "Now," he said, "we are ready to go." He opened the door, on to a curtain of rain.

I protested, "But you'll get wet," but he only said "Scuttle" so I scuttled, and he scuttled too, and the next instant we were back in the van, scarcely wet at all, with the doors banged tight and shut against the storm, although small puddles of rain on my seat and at my feet gave rise to the suspicion that this staunch vehicle was no longer as watertight as it had once been. But he started the noisy engine and we were away, and with the volume of water both outside and inside the car it was a little like being taken for a fast ride in a leaky motor boat.

I said, "Where are we going?"

"The Anchor. It's just round the corner. Not very smart. Do you mind?"

"Why should I mind?"

"You might mind. You might have wanted to be taken to The Castle."

"You mean to foxtrot to a three-piece orchestra?"

He grinned. He said, "I can't foxtrot. Nobody ever learned me."

We flashed down Fish Lane, around a right-angled corner or two, beneath a stone archway and so out into a small square. One side of this was formed by the low, uneven shape of an old inn. Warm light shone from behind small windows spilled from a crooked doorway and the Inn sign over the door swung and creaked in the wind. There were four or five cars already parked outside, and Joss inserted the van neatly into a tidy space between two of them, turned off the engine, said, "One, two, three, run," and we both got out and sprinted the short distance between the car and the shelter of the porch.

There Joss shook himself slightly, brushed the rain from the soft surface of his sweater, took the oilskin off my shoulders and opened the door for me to go ahead of him.

It was warm inside, and low-ceilinged and smelt the way old pubs have always smelt. Of beer and pipe smoke and musty wood. There was a bar, with high stools, and tables around the edge of the room. Two old men were playing darts in a corner.

The barman looked up and said, "Hi, Joss." Joss put the oilskin up on a coat hook, and led me across the room to be introduced.

"Tommy, this is Rebecca. Rebecca, this is Tommy Williams. He's been here man and boy; anything you want to know about Porthkerris, or the people who live here, you come and ask Tommy."

We said, "How do you do." Tommy had grey hair and a lot of wrinkles. He looked as though he might be a fisherman in his spare time. We sat ourselves on two stools, and Joss ordered a Scotch and soda for me and a Scotch and water for himself, and while Tommy fixed these the two men began to talk, falling comfortably into conversation the way men in pubs always seem to.

"How are things going with you?" That was Tommy.

"Not too bad."

"When are you opening up?"

"Easter, maybe, with a bit of luck."

"Place finished is it?"

"More or less."

"Who's doing the carpentry?"

"Doing it myself."

"That'll save you something."

My attention wandered. I lit a cigarette and looked around me, liking what I saw. The two old men playing darts; a young couple, jeaned and long-haired, crouched over a table and a couple of pints of bitter, discussing, with avid and intense concentration – existentialism? Concrete painting? How they were going to pay the rent? Something. But it mattered, intensely, to both of them.

And then a party of four, older, expensively dressed, the men self-consciously casual, the women unwittingly formal. I guessed they were staying at The Castle, and out of boredom with the weather, perhaps, had come down the town for a spot of slumming. They seemed uncomfortable, as though they knew they looked out of place, and could scarcely wait to get back to the padded velvet comfort of the big hotel on the hill.

My eyes moved on around the room, and it was then that I caught sight of the dog. He was a beautiful dog, a great red setter, his coat handsome and shining, his tail a silken plume of copper fur against the grey flags of the floor. He sat very still, close to his master, and every now and then the tail would move slightly in a thump of approval, a private applause.

Intrigued, I inspected the man who appeared to own this enviable creature, and found him almost as interesting as the dog. Sitting, with an elbow on the table top, and his chin resting on his fist, he presented to me a clear and unblurred profile, almost as though he were posing for my inspection. His head was well shaped, and his hair had that thick silver-fox

56

look of a person who has started to go grey early in life. The single eye which his profile allowed me was deep-set, and darkly shadowed, the nose was long and aquiline, the mouth pleasant, the chin strongly formed. And, from the length of his wrist, emerging from a checked shirt cuff and the sleeve of a grey tweed jacket, and the way he disposed of his legs beneath the little table, I guessed that he was tall, probably over six feet.

As I watched him, he laughed suddenly at something his companion had said. This drew my attention to the other man, and I felt a shock of surprise, because, for some reason, they did not match. Where the one was slender and elegant, the other was short, fat, red of face, and dressed in a tight-fitting navy blue blazer and a shirt collar that looked as though it were about to strangle him. It was not overly warm in the pub, but there was a shine of sweat on the ruddy brow, and I saw that the dark hair had been barbered with some ingenuity, so that a long oiled lock was combed up and over, concealing what would otherwise have been a totally bald head.

The man with the dog was not smoking, but the fat man suddenly crushed out his own cigarette in the brimming ash-tray on the table, as though emphasising some point that he was making, and almost instantly reached into his pocket for a silver case and another cigarette.

But the man with the dog had decided that it was time to go. He took his hand from his chin, pushed back his shirt cuff to consult his watch, and then finished his drink. The fat man, apparently anxious to comply with the other's arrangements, hastily lit the cigarette and then tossed back his whisky. They began to get up, pushing back their chairs with a hideous scraping sound. The dog stood up, his tail swooping in exultant circles.

Standing, one so short and fat and the other so tall and slim, the two men looked more ill-assorted than ever. The thin one reached for a raincoat which had been lying across the back of his chair and slung it over his shoulders like a cloak, and then turned towards us, heading for the door. For an instant I was disappointed, because full face, his finely drawn good looks did not live up to the promise of that intriguing profile. And then I forgot about being disappointed, because he suddenly saw Joss. And Joss, perhaps sensing his presence, stopped talking to Tommy Williams and turned to see who was standing behind him. For an instant they both looked disconcerted, and then the tall man smiled, and the smile etched lines down his thin brown cheeks and creased up his eyes, and it was impossible not to be warmed by such charm.

He said, "Joss. Long time no see." His voice was pleasant and friendly.

"Hi," said Joss, not getting off his stool.

"I thought you were in London."

"No. Back again."

The creaking swing of the door caught my attention. The other man, the fat man, had quietly left. I decided that he had an urgent appointment and thought no more about it.

"I'll tell the old boy I've seen you."

"Yes. Do that."

The deep-set eyes moved in my direction, and then away again. I waited to be introduced, but nothing happened. For some reason this lack of manners on Joss's part was like a slap in the face.

At last, "Well, see you around," said the tall man, and moved off.

"Sure," said Joss.

"Night, Tommy," he called to the barman as he pushed the door open and let the dog out ahead of him.

"Good night, Mr Bayliss," said the barman.

I felt my head jerk around as though someone had pulled a string. He had already disappeared, leaving the door swinging behind him. Without thinking, I slipped off the stool to go after him, but a hand caught my arm and restrained me, and I turned to find Joss holding me back. For a surprising second our eyes clashed, and then I shook myself free. Outside I heard a car start up. Now it was too late.

I said, "Who is he?"

"Eliot Bayliss."

Eliot. Roger's boy. Mollie's child. Grenville Bayliss's grandson. My cousin. My family.

"He's my cousin."

"I didn't know that."

"You know my name. Why didn't you tell him? Why did you stop me going after him?"

"You'll meet him soon enough. Tonight it's too late and too wet and too dark for family reunions."

"Grenville Bayliss is my grandfather, too."

"I thought there was probably some connection," said Joss coolly. "Have another drink."

By now I was really angry. "I don't want another drink."

"In that case, let's go and eat."

"I don't want to eat either."

I thought that I truly didn't want to. I didn't want to spend another moment with this boorish and overbearing young man. I watched him finish his drink and get down off his stool, and for an instant I thought that he was actually going to take me at my word; was going to drive me back to Fish Lane and there dump me, un-nourished. But, luckily, he did not call my bluff, simply paid for the drinks, and without a word led the way through a door at the far end of the bar, which gave on to a flight of stairs and a small restaurant. I followed him because there didn't seem to be anything else to do. Besides, I was hungry.

Most of the tables were already occupied, but a waitress saw Joss and recognised him and came over to say good evening, and led us to what was obviously the best table in the room, set in the narrow alcove of a jutting bay window. Beyond the window could be seen the shapes of rain-washed roofs, and beyond them again the liquid darkness of the harbour, a-shimmer with reflections from the street lamps on the quay and the riding lights of fishing boats.

We faced each other. I was still deeply angry and would not look at him. I sat, drawing patterns with my finger on the table mat, and listened to him ordering what I was to eat. Apparently I was not even to be allowed the right of making my own choice. I heard the waitress say, "For the young lady, too?" as though even she were surprised by his cursory behaviour, and Joss said, "Yes, for the young lady, too," and the waitress went off, and we were alone.

After a little I looked up. His dark gaze met mine, unblinking. The silence grew, and I had the ridiculous feeling that he was waiting for me to apologise to him.

I heard myself say, "If you won't let me talk to Eliot Bayliss, perhaps you'll talk about him."

"What do you want to know?"

"Is he married?" It was the first question that came into my head.

"No."

"He's attractive." Joss acknowledged this. "Does he live alone?"

"No, with his mother. They have a house up at High Cross, six miles or so from here, but about a year ago they moved into Boscarva, to be with the old man."

"Is my grandfather ill?"

"You don't know very much about your family, do you?"

"No." I sounded defiant.

"About ten years ago Grenville Bayliss had a heart attack. That's when he stopped painting. But he always appears to have had the constitution of an ox, and he made a miraculous recovery. He didn't want to leave Boscarva, and he had this couple to take care of him . . ."

"The Pettifers?"

Joss frowned. "How do you know about the Pettifers?"

"My mother told me." I thought of the long-ago tea parties by the kitchen fire. "I never imagined they'd still be there."

"Mrs Pettifer died last year, so Pettifer and your grandfather were left on their own. Grenville Bayliss is eighty now, and Pettifer can't be far behind him. Mollie Bayliss wanted them to move up to High Cross and sell Boscarva, but the old man was adamant, so in the end she and Eliot moved in with him. Without noticeable enthusiasm, I may add." He leaned back in his chair, his long clever hands resting on the edge of the table. "Your mother . . . was she called Lisa?" I nodded.

"I knew Grenville had a daughter who'd had a daughter, but the fact that you call yourself Bayliss threw me slightly."

"My father left my mother before I was born. She never used his name."

"Where's your mother now?"

"She died – just a few days ago. In Ibiza." I repeated, "Just a few days ago," because all at once it seemed like a lifetime.

"I'm sorry." I made some sort of vague gesture, because there weren't any words. "Does your grandfather know?"

"I don't know."

"Have you come to tell him?"

"I suppose I may have to." The idea of doing so was daunting.

"Does he know you're here? In Porthkerris?"

I shook my head. "He doesn't even know me. I mean we've never met. I've never been here before." I made the final admission. "I don't even know how to find his house."

"One way and another," said Joss, "you're going to give him something of a shock."

I felt anxious. "Is he very frail?"

"No, he's not frail. He's fantastically tough. But he's getting old."

"My mother said he was frightening. Is he still frightening?"

Joss made a gruesome face, doing nothing to comfort me. "Terrifying," he said.

The waitress brought our soup. It was oxtail, thick and brown and very hot. I was so hungry that I ate it right down to the bottom of the bowl without saying another word. As I finally laid down my spoon, I looked up and saw that Joss was laughing at me.

"For a girl who didn't want to eat, you haven't done so badly."

But this time I did not rise. I pushed the empty bowl away, and leaned my elbows on the table.

"How is it that you know so much about the Bayliss family?" I asked him.

Joss had not bolted his soup as I had. Now, he was taking his time, buttering a roll, being maddeningly slow.

"It's easy," he said. "I do a certain amount of work up at Boscarva."

"What sort of work?"

"Well, I restore antique furniture. And don't gape in that unattractive fashion, it does nothing for you."

"*Restore antique furniture?* You must be joking."

"I'm not. And Grenville Bayliss has a houseful of old and very valuable stuff. In his day he made a lot of money, and he invested most of it in antiques. Now, some of the things are in a shocking state of repair, not that they haven't been polished to within an inch of their lives, but then years ago he put in central heating and that wrecks old furniture. Drawers shrink and veneers curl and crack, and legs fall off chairs. Incidentally . . ." he added, diverted by the memory ". . . it was I who mended your cherrywood chair."

"But how long have you been doing this?"

"Let's see, I left school when I was seventeen, and I'm twenty-four now, so that makes it about seven years."

"But you had to *learn* . . ."

"Oh, sure. I did joinery and carpentry first, four years of it at a trade school in London, and then when I'd got that under my belt, I apprenticed myself for another couple of years to an old cabinet-maker down in Sussex. I lived with him and his wife, did all the dirty jobs in the workshop, learned everything I know."

I did a few sums. "That's only six years. You said seven."

He laughed. "I took a year off in the middle to travel. My parents said I was becoming parochial. My father has a cousin who runs a cattle ranch up in the Rockies, south-west Colorado. I worked as a ranch hand nine months or more." He frowned. "What are you grinning about?"

I told him. "That first time I saw you, in the shop . . . you looked like a ranch hand . . . you looked real. And somehow it annoyed me that you weren't."

He smiled. "And you know what you looked like?"

I cooled off. "No."

"The head girl of a nicely run orphanage. And that annoyed *me*."

A small clash of swords, and once more we were on opposite sides of the fence.

I eyed him with dislike as he cheerfully finished his soup; the waitress came to take away the empty plates, and to set down a carafe of red wine. I had not heard Joss ordering the wine, but now I watched him pour two full glasses and I saw the long spade-tipped fingers; I liked the idea of them working with wood and old and beautiful things, turning and measuring and oiling and coaxing into shape. I picked up the glass of wine and against the light it glowed red as a ruby. I said, "Is that all you're doing in Porthkerris? Restoring Grenville Bayliss's furniture?"

"Good God, no. I'm opening a shop. I managed to rent these premises down on the harbour six months or so ago. I've been here, off and on, ever since. Now, I'm trying to get it into some sort of order before Easter, or Whitsun, or whenever the summer business really starts."

"Is it an antique shop?"

"No, modern, furniture, glass, textiles. But antique restoring goes on in the background. I mean I have a workroom. I also have a small pad on the top floor which is where I now live, which is why you were able to take over my room at Mrs Kernow's. One day when you've decided that I'm trustworthy you can climb the rickety stairs and I'll show it to you."

I ignored this fresh little sally.

"If you work down here, what were you doing in that shop in London?"

"Tristram's? I told you, he's a friend; I drop in and see him whenever I'm up in town."

I frowned. There were so many coincidences. Our lives seemed to be tied up in them, like a parcel well-knotted with ends of string. I watched him finish his wine and once more was visited with the unease which I had known earlier in the evening. I knew I should ask him a thousand questions, but before I could think of one the waitress arrived at our table once more, bearing steaks and vegetables and fried potatoes and dishes of salad. I drank some wine and watched Joss, and when the waitress had gone I said, "What does Eliot Bayliss do?"

"Eliot? He runs a garage up at High Cross, specialises in highly-powered second-hand cars, Mercedes, Alfa Romeos. If you've got the right sort of cheque book he can supply you with practically anything."

"You don't like him, do you?"

"I never said I didn't like him."

"But you don't."

"Perhaps it would be nearer the mark to say he doesn't like me."

"Why?" He looked up, his eyes dancing with amusement. "I haven't any idea. Now why don't you eat up your steak before it gets cold."

He drove me home. It was still raining and I was, all at once, deathly tired. Outside Mrs Kernow's door Joss stopped the car, but left the engine running. I thanked him and said good night and began to open the door, but before I could do so he had reached across and stopped me. I turned to look at him.

He said, "Tomorrow. Are you going to Boscarva?"

"Yes."

"I'll take you."

"I can go alone."

"You don't know where the house is, and it's a long climb up the hill. I'll pick you up in the car. About eleven?"

Arguing with him was like arguing with a steamroller. And I was exhausted. I said, "All right."

He opened the door for me and pushed it open.

"Good night, Rebecca."

"Good night."

"I'll see you in the morning."

# Chapter Five

The wind did not drop during that night. But when I woke, the little window of my room at Mrs Kernow's gave me sight of a square of pale blue traversed by ballooning white clouds travelling at some speed. It was very cold, but bravely I got up and dressed and went downstairs in search of Mrs Kernow. I found her outside in the little yard at the back of the house, pegging out her washing on a line. At first, battling with flailing sheets and towels, she didn't see me, but when I appeared between a shirt and a modest lock-knit petticoat she gave a great start of surprise. Her own astonishment amused her, and she shook with shrill laughter, as though the two of us were a double act on the halls.

"You gave me some shock. I thought you were still asleep! Comfortable were you? That dratted wind's still around the place, but the rain's stopped, thank heaven. Want your breakfast do you?"

"A cup of tea, perhaps."

I helped her peg out the rest of the washing and then she picked up her empty basket and led the way back indoors. I sat at the kitchen table and she boiled a kettle and began to fry bacon.

"Have a good supper last night did you? Go to The Anchor? Tommy Williams keeps a good place there, always packed, winter and summer. I heard Joss bring you home. He's a lovely boy. I missed him when he moved out. Still, I go down sometimes to his new place, clean it up a bit for him, bring his washing home and do it here. Sad, a young man like that on his own. All wrong somehow, not having someone to take care of him."

"I should think Joss could take care of himself."

"It's not right a man doing woman's work." Mrs Kernow obviously did not believe in Women's Lib. "Besides, he's busy enough working for Mr Bayliss."

"Do you know Mr Bayliss?"

"Everyone knows he. Lived here nearly fifty years now. One of the old ones, he is. And some lovely painter he was before he took ill. Used to have an exhibition every year, and all sorts used to come down from London, famous people, everybody. 'Course, lately we don't see so much of him. He can't walk up and down the hill like he used to, and it's a bit of a business Pettifer getting that great car down these narrow lanes. Besides, in the summer, you can't move for traffic and visitors. The place is teeming with them. Sometimes you'd think half the population of the country is jammed into this little town."

She flipped the bacon on to a warm plate and set it in front of me. "There now, eat that up before it gets cold."

I said, "Mrs Kernow, Mr Bayliss is my grandfather."

She stared at me, frowning. "Your grandfather?" Then, "Whose child are you?"

"Lisa's."

"Lisa's child." She reached for a chair and slowly sat down upon it. I saw that I had shocked her. "Does Joss know?"

It seemed irrelevant. "Yes, I told him last night."

"She was a lovely little girl." She stared into my face. "I can see her in you . . . except that she was so dark and you're fair. We missed her when she went, and never came back. Where is she now?"

I told her. When I had finished she said, "And Mr Bayliss doesn't know you're here?"

"No."

"You must go now. Right away. Oh, I wish I could be there to see the old man's face. He worshipped your mother . . ."

A tear gleamed. Quickly, before we were both awash with sentiment, I said, "I don't know how to get there."

Trying to tell me, she confused the two of us so much that finally she found an old envelope and the stub of a pencil and drew a rough map. Watching her I remembered Joss's promise to come at eleven o'clock and take me to Boscarva in his ramshackle van, but suddenly it seemed a much better idea to go at once, on my own. Besides, last night I had been altogether too meek and compliant. It would do Joss's boundless ego no harm to arrive here and find me already gone. The thought of this happening cheered me considerably and I went upstairs to fetch my coat.

Outside I was instantly buffeted by the wind which tunnelled down the narrow street like the draught in a chimney. It was a cold wind, smelling of the sea, but when the sun burst out from behind the racing clouds the brightness was dazzling, full of glare, and overhead gulls screamed and floated, their wings white sails against the blue of the sky.

I walked and soon I was climbing. Up narrow, cobbled streets, between haphazard lines of houses. Up flights of steps, and leaning alleys. The higher I went the stronger became the wind. As I climbed the town dropped below me, and the ocean revealed itself, dark blue, streaked with jade and purple and flecked with white horses. It spread to the horizon where the sky took over, and below me the town and the harbour shrank to toy-size, to insignificance.

I stood looking at it, catching my breath, and all at once a funny thing happened. For this new place was not new to me at all, but totally familiar. I felt at home, as though I had returned to somewhere I had known all my life. And though I had scarcely thought of my mother since making the decision to come to Porthkerris, she was suddenly beside me, climbing the steep streets, long-legged, breathless, and warm with exertion as I was.

I was comforted by this sense of *déjà-vu*. It made me feel less lonely and much more brave. I went on and was glad I had not waited for Joss. His presence was disturbing, but I could not for the life of me decide why. He had, after all, been quite open with me, answering questions, giving perfectly believable reasons for his every action.

It was obvious that there was no love lost between himself and Eliot Bayliss, but I could easily understand this. The two young men would have nothing in common. Eliot, albeit unwillingly, was living at Boscarva. He was a Bayliss and the house was, for the time being, his home. On the other hand Joss's occupation in the house would give him the freedom to come and go in his own time. Be found, unexpectedly, at odd hours of the day, perhaps when his presence was neither convenient nor welcome. I imagined him on easy terms with everybody, sometimes getting in the way, and worst of all, blithely unaware of the trouble he was causing. A man like Eliot would resent this and Joss, in return, would react to his resentment.

Busy with these thoughts and the exertion of climbing, I did not observe my surroundings, but now the road levelled off beneath my feet, and I stopped to look around and take my bearings. I was on top of the hill, that was for sure. Behind and below me lay the town; ahead stretched the rugged coastline, curving away into the distance. It bordered a green country, patchworked with small farms and miniature fields, traversed by deep valleys, thick with hawthorn and stunted elm, where narrow streams channelled their way down to the sea.

I looked about me. This too was country. Or a year ago it had been. But since then a farm, perhaps, had been bought out, the bulldozers brought in, old hedges demolished, the rich earth torn up and flattened, and a new housing estate was in the process of being erected. All was raw, stark and hideous. Cement mixers churned, a lorry ground through a sea of mud, there were piles of brick and concrete, and in front of it all, like a proud banner, a hoarding which announced the man responsible for this carnage.

ERNEST PADLOW
DESIRABLE DETACHED HOUSES
FOR SALE
Apply Sea Lane, Porthkerris
*Telephone Porthkerris 873*

The houses were certainly detached, but only just. Scarcely three feet lay between them, and one window stared straight into another.

My heart mourned for the lost fields and the lost opportunities. As I stood there, mentally redesigning the entire project, a car came up the hill behind me, and drew to a halt in front of the hoarding. It was an old Jaguar, navy blue, and the man who stepped out of it, shutting the door behind him with a resounding thump, wore a workman's donkey jacket and carried a clip board and a lot of papers which fluttered in the wind. He turned and saw me, hesitated for only a second and then walked towards me, trying to flatten his hair down over his bald head.

"Morning." His smile was familiar as though we were old friends.

"Good morning."

I had seen him before. Last night. At The Anchor. Talking to Eliot Bayliss.

He glanced up at the hoarding.

"Thinking of buying a house for yourself?"

"No."

"You should. Get a good view up here."

I frowned. "I don't want a house."

"Be a good investment."

"Are you the foreman?"

"No." He glanced, with some pride, up at the hoarding which reared above us. "I'm Ernest Padlow."

"I see."

"Lovely site this . . ." He looked around at the devastation with some satisfaction. "Lot of people after this site, but the old girl who owned the land was a widow, and I managed to charm her into letting me have it."

I was surprised. As he spoke he reached for and lit himself a cigarette; he did not offer me one, his fingers were stained with nicotine and he seemed to me the most uncharming man I had ever met.

He turned his attention back to me. "Haven't seen you around, have I?"

"No."

"Visiting?"

"Yes, perhaps."

"It's better out of season. Not so crowded."

I said, "I'm looking for Boscarva."

Caught unawares, the bonhomie slid from his manner. His eyes were sharp as pebbles in his florid face. "Boscarva? You mean old Bayliss's place?"

"Yes."

His expression became wily. "Looking for Eliot?"

"No."

He waited for me to enlarge on this. When I didn't he tried to make a joke of it. "Well, I always say, least said, soonest mended. You want Boscarva, you go down that little lane. About half a mile. You'll see the house down towards the sea. It's got a slate roof, a big garden round it. You can't miss it."

"Thank you." I smiled politely. "Goodbye."

I turned and began to walk, feeling his eyes on my back. Then he spoke once more and I turned back. He was smiling, all friends again.

71

"You want a house, make up your mind quickly. They're selling like hot cakes."

"Yes, I'm sure. But I don't want one. Thank you."

The lane led downhill towards the great blue bowl of the sea, and now I was truly in the country, in a farmland of fields grazed by sweet-faced Guernseys. Wild violets and primroses grew in the grassy hedges, and the sun came out and turned the rich grass to emerald. Presently, I came around a corner and saw the white gates, set between low dry-stone walls; a driveway curved down, out of sight, and there were high hedges of escallonia and elm trees, tortured to unnatural shapes by the relentless winds.

I could not see the house. I stood at the open gates and looked down the drive, my courage seeping away like bathwater after the plug has been pulled out. I could not think what I was meant to do, nor what I was going to say once I had done it.

My mind was, unexpectedly and mercifully, made up for me. Down by the house, out of sight, I heard a car start up and come at some speed up the drive towards me. As it approached, a low-slung open sports car of some age and style, I stood aside to let it flash past between the gate posts and up the hill in the direction from which I had come, but still there was time to see the driver and the great red setter sitting up on the back seat, with the deliriously joyful expression of any dog being taken for a ride in an open car.

I thought that I had not been noticed but I was wrong. A moment later the car stopped with a screech of brakes and a shower of small stones flung from the back wheels. Then it went into reverse, and returned, with scarcely less speed back to the spot where I stood. It stopped, the engine was killed, and Eliot Bayliss, leaning an arm on the driving wheel, surveyed me across the empty passenger seat. He was bare-headed and wore a sheepskin car coat, and his expression was one of amusement, perhaps intrigue.

"Hello," he said.

"Good morning." I felt a fool, bundled in my old coat, with the wind blowing stray strands of hair over my face. I tried to push them away.

"You look lost."

"No. I'm not."

He continued to regard me, frowning slightly. "I saw you last night, didn't I? At The Anchor? With Joss."

"Yes."

"Are you looking for Joss? As far as I know he's not arrived yet. That is, if he's decided to come today."

"No. I mean I'm not looking for him."

"Then who – " asked Eliot Bayliss gently, "are you looking for?"

"I . . . I wanted to see old Mr Bayliss."

"It's a little early for that. He doesn't usually appear till mid-day."

"Oh." I had not thought of this. Some of my disappointment must have shown in my face, for he went on, in the same gentle and friendly voice, "Perhaps I could help. I'm Eliot Bayliss."

"I know. I mean . . . Joss told me last night."

A small frown appeared between his eyebrows. He was obviously and naturally puzzled by my relationship with Joss.

"Why did you want to see my grandfather?" And when I did not reply, he suddenly leaned across to open the door of the car and said, with cool authority, "Get in."

I got in, closing the door behind me. I could feel his eyes on me, the shapeless coat, the patched jeans. The dog leaned forward to nuzzle my ear; his nose was cold and I reached over my shoulder to stroke the long, silky ear.

I said, "What's he called?"

"Rufus. Rufus the Red. But that doesn't answer my question, does it?"

I was saved by another interruption. Another car. But this time it was the Post Office van, rattling scarlet and cheerful, down the lane towards us. It stopped, and the postman rolled down the window to say to Eliot, good naturedly, "How can I get down the drive and deliver the letters if you park your car in the gateway?"

"Sorry," said Eliot, unperturbed, and he got out from behind the driving wheel and went to take a handful of mail and a newspaper from the postman. "I'll take it — it'll save you the trip."

"Lovely," said the postman. "Be nice if everyone did my job for me," and with a grin and a wave he went on his way, presumably to some outlying farmstead.

Eliot got back into the car.

"Well," he said, smiling at me. "What am I going to do with you?"

But I scarcely heard him. The pile of mail lay loosely in his lap, and on the top was an airmail envelope, postmarked Ibiza, and addressed to Mr Grenville Bayliss. The spiky handwriting was unmistakable.

A car is a good place for confidences. There is no telephone and you can't be unexpectedly interrupted. I said, "That letter. The one on the top. It's from a man called Otto Pedersen. He lives in Ibiza."

Eliot, frowning, took up the envelope. He turned it over and read Otto's name on the back. He looked at me. "How did you know?"

"I know his writing. I know him. He's writing to . . . to your grandfather to tell him that Lisa is dead. She died about a week ago. She was living with Otto in Ibiza."

"Lisa. You mean Lisa Bayliss?"

"Yes. Roger's sister. Your aunt. My mother."

"You're Lisa's child?"

"Yes." I turned to look directly at him. "I'm your cousin. Grenville Bayliss is my grandfather, too."

His eyes were a strange colour, greyish-green, like pebbles washed by some fast-moving stream. They showed neither shock nor pleasure, simply regarded me levelly without expression. He said at last, "Well I'll be damned."

It was hardly what I expected. We sat in silence because I could think of nothing to say, and then, as though coming to a sudden decision, he tossed the pile of mail into my lap, started the car up once more, and swung the wheel around so that once more we were facing the drive.

"What are you doing?" I asked.

"What do you think? Taking you home of course."

Home. Boscarva. We came around the curve of the drive and it was there, waiting for me. Not small, but not large either. Grey stone, smothered in creeper, grey slate roof, a semicircular stone porch with the door open to the sunshine, and inside a glimpse of red tiles, a clutter of flowerpots, the pinks and scarlets of geranium and fuchsia. A curtain fluttered at an open upstairs window and smoke plumed from a chimney. As we got out of the car the sun came out from behind a cloud and, caught in the spread arms of the house, sheltered from the north wind, it was suddenly very warm.

"Come along," said Eliot and led the way, the dog at his heels. We went through the porch and into a dark, panelled hallway illuminated by the big window on the turn of the stairs. I had imagined Boscarva as being a house of the past, sad and nostalgic, filled with the chill of old memories. But it wasn't like that at all. It was vital, humming with a sense of activity. There were papers lying on the table, a pair of gardening gloves, a dog's lead. From beyond a doorway came the kitchen sounds of voices and the clatter of crockery. From upstairs a vacuum-cleaner hummed. And there was a smell compounded of scrubbed stone and old polished floors, and years of woodfires.

Eliot stood at the foot of the staircase and called, "Mamma." But when there was no answer, only the continued hum of the vacuum-cleaner, he said, "You'd better come this way." We went down the hall and through a door which led into a long, low drawing-room, palely panelled and sensuous with the brightness and scent of spring flowers. At one end, in a fireplace of carved pine and Dutch tiles, a newly lit fire flickered cheerfully, and three tall windows, curtained in faded yellow silk, faced out over a flagged terrace, and beyond the balustrade of this I could see the blue line of the sea.

I stood in the middle of this charming room as Eliot Bayliss closed the door and said, "Well, you're here. Why don't you take your coat off?"

I did so. It was very warm. I laid it over a chair where it looked like some great, dead creature.

He said, "When did you get here?"

"Last night. I caught the train from London."

"You live in London?"

"Yes."

"And you've never been here before?"

"No. I didn't know about Boscarva. I didn't know about Grenville Bayliss being my grandfather. My mother never told me till the night before she died."

"How does Joss come into it?"

"I . . ." It was too complicated to explain. "I'd met him in London. He happened to be at the junction when my train got in. It was a coincidence."

"Where are you staying?"

"With Mrs Kernow in Fish Lane."

"Grenville's an old man. He's ill. You know that, don't you?"

"Yes."

"I think . . . this letter from Otto Pedersen . . . we'd better be careful. Perhaps my mother would be the best person . . ."

"Yes, of course."

"It was lucky you saw the letter."

"Yes. I thought he would probably write. But I was afraid that I would have to break the news to you all."

"And now it's been done for you." He smiled, and all at once he looked much younger . . . belying those strange-coloured eyes and the thick silver-fox hair. "Why don't you wait here and I'll go and find my mother and try to put her in the picture. Would you like a cup of coffee or something?"

"Only if it's not a nuisance."

"No nuisance. I'll tell Pettifer." He opened the door behind him. "Make yourself at home."

The door closed softly, and he was gone. Pettifer. *Pettifer had been in the Navy too, he looked after my father and sometimes drove the car and Mrs Pettifer did the cooking.* So my mother had told me. And Joss had told me that Mrs Pettifer had died. But in the old days she had taken Lisa and her brother into the kitchen and made hot buttered toast. She had drawn the curtains against the dark and the rain, and made the children feel safe and loved.

Alone, I inspected the room where I had been left to wait. I saw a glass-doored cabinet filled with Oriental treasures, including some small pieces of jade, and wondered if these were the ones that my mother had mentioned to me. I glanced around, thinking that perhaps I might find the Venetian mirror and the davenport desk as well, but then my attention was caught by the picture over the mantelpiece, and I went to look at it, all else forgotten.

It was a portrait of a girl, dressed in the fashion of the early 1930s, slender, flat-chested, her white dress hanging straight to her hips, her dark, bobbed hair revealing with enchanting innocence the long, slender neck. She sat, in the picture, on a tall stool, holding a single long-stemmed rose, but you could not see her face, for she was looking away from the artist, out of some unseen window, into the sunshine. The effect was all pink and gold, with sunlight filtering through the thin stuff of her white dress. It was enchanting.

Behind me the door opened suddenly and I turned, startled, as an old man came into the room, stately, bald-headed, a little stooped, perhaps; treading cautiously. He wore rimless spectacles and a striped shirt with an old-fashioned hard collar, and over it all a blue and white butcher's apron.

"Are you the young lady wanting a cup of coffee?" He had a

deep, lugubrious voice, and this, with his sombre appearance, made me think of a reliable undertaker.

"Yes, if it's not too much trouble."

"Milk and sugar?"

"No sugar. Just a little milk. I was looking at the portrait."

"Yes. It's very pleasing. It's called 'Lady Holding a Rose'."

"You can't see her face."

"No."

"Did my . . . Did Mr Bayliss paint it?"

"Oh yes. That was hung in the Academy, could have been sold a hundred times over, but the Commander would never part with it." As he said this, he carefully took off his spectacles, and was now staring at me intently. His old eyes were pale. He said, "For a moment, when you spoke, you reminded me of someone else. But you're young and she'd be middle-aged by now. And her hair was dark as a blackbird. That's what Mrs Pettifer used to say. Dark as a blackbird's wing."

I said, "Eliot didn't tell you?"

"What didn't Mr Eliot tell me?"

"You're talking about Lisa, aren't you? I'm Rebecca. I'm her daughter."

"Well." Fumbling a little he put his spectacles back on again. A faint gleam of pleasure showed on his gloomy features. "I was right then. I'm not often wrong about things like that." And he came forward, holding out a horny hand. "It's a real pleasure to meet you . . . A pleasure that I never thought I should have. I thought you'd never come. Is your mother with you?"

I wished that Eliot had made it a little easier for me.

"My mother's dead. She died last week. In Ibiza. That's why I'm here."

"She died." His eyes clouded. "I'm sorry. I'm really sorry. She should have come back. She should have come home. We all wanted to see her again." He took out a copious handkerchief and blew his nose. "And who . . ." he asked ". . . is going to tell the Commander?"

"I think . . . Eliot's gone to fetch his mother. You see, there's a letter for my grandfather in the post, it came this morning. It's from Ibiza, from the man who was . . . taking care of my mother. But if you think that wouldn't be a very good idea . . ."

"What I think won't make no difference," said Pettifer. "And whoever tells the Commander, it's not going to lessen his sorrow. But I'll tell you one thing. You being here will help a lot."

"Thank you."

He blew his nose again and put away his handkerchief.

"Mr Eliot and his mother . . . well, this isn't their home. But it was either the old Commander and me moving up to High Cross or them coming here. And they wouldn't be here if the doctor hadn't insisted. I told them we could manage all right, the Commander and me. We've been together all these years . . . but there, we're neither of us as young as we used to be, and the Commander, he had this heart attack . . ."

"Yes, I know . . ."

"And after Mrs Pettifer passed on, there wasn't anyone to do the cooking. Mind, I can cook all right, but it takes me a good part of my time taking care of the Commander, and I wouldn't want to see him going about the place looking shabby."

"No, of course not . . ."

I was interrupted by the slam of a door.

A hearty male voice called, "Pettifer!" and Pettifer said, "Excuse me a moment, Miss," and went out to investigate, leaving the door open behind him.

"Pettifer!"

I heard Pettifer say, with what sounded like the greatest satisfaction, "Hello, Joss."

"Is she there?"

"Who, here?"

"Rebecca."

"Yes, she's right here, in the sitting-room . . . I was just going to get her a cup of coffee."

"Make it two would you, there's a good chap. And black and strong for me."

His footsteps came down the hall, and the next moment he was there, framed in the doorway, long-legged, black-haired, and it was obvious – angry.

"What the hell do you think you're doing?" he demanded.

I could feel my hackles rising, like a suspicious dog. Home, Eliot had said. This was Boscarva, my home, and whether I was here or not was nothing to do with Joss.

"I don't know what you're talking about."

"I went to pick you up and Mrs Kernow told me you'd already left."

"So?"

"I told you to wait for me."

"I decided not to wait."

He was silent, fuming, but finally appeared to accept this inescapable fact.

"Does anyone know you've arrived?"

"I met Eliot at the gate. He brought me here."

"Where's he gone?"

"To find his mother."

"Have you seen anyone else? Have you seen Grenville?"

"No."

"Has anyone told Grenville about your mother?"

"A letter came by this morning's post, from Otto Pedersen. But I don't think he's seen it yet."

"Pettifer must take it to him. Pettifer must be there when he reads it."

"Pettifer didn't seem to think that."

"I think it," said Joss.

His apparently outrageous interference left me without words, but as we stood glaring at each other across the pretty patterned carpet and a great bowl of scented narcissus, there came the sound of voices and footsteps down the uncarpeted staircase and along the hall towards us.

I heard a woman's voice say, "In the sitting-room, Eliot?"

Joss muttered something that sounded unprintable, and marched over to the fireplace where he stood with his back to me, staring down into the flames. The next instant, Mollie appeared in the doorway, hesitated for a moment and then came towards me, hands outstretched.

"Rebecca." (So it was to be a warm welcome.) Eliot, following behind her, closed the door. Joss did not even turn round.

I worked it out that by now Mollie must be over fifty, but this was hard to believe. She was plump and pretty, her fading blonde hair charmingly coiffed, her eyes blue, her skin fresh and lightly scattered with freckles which helped to create this astonishing illusion of youth. She wore a blue skirt and cardigan and a creamy silk blouse; her legs were slim and shapely and her hands beautifully manicured, decorated with pale pink fingernails, and many rings and fine gold bracelets. Scented, immaculately preserved, she made me think of a charming little tabby cat, curled precisely in the centre of her own satin cushion.

I said, "I'm afraid this is something of a shock."

"No, not a shock, but a surprise. And your mother . . . I'm so dreadfully sorry. Eliot's told me about the letter . . ."

At this Joss swung around from the fireplace.

"Where is the letter?"

Mollie turned her gaze upon him, and it was impossible to guess whether this was the first time she had realised he was there, or whether she had seen him and simply decided to ignore him.

"Joss. I didn't think you were coming this morning."

"Yes. I just got here."

"You know Rebecca, I believe."

"Yes, we've met." He hesitated, seeming to be making an effort to pull himself together. Then he smiled, ruefully, turned to lean his broad shoulders against the mantelpiece and apologised. "I'm sorry. And I know it's none of my business, but that letter that came this morning . . . where is it?"

"In my pocket," said Eliot, speaking for the first time. "Why?"

"It's just that I think Pettifer should be the one to break the news to the old man. I think Pettifer is the only person to do it."

This was greeted by silence. Then Mollie let go of my hands and turned to her son.

"He's right," she said. "Grenville's closest to Pettifer." "That's all right by me," said Eliot but his eyes, on Joss, were cold with antagonism. I did not blame him. I felt the same way myself – I was on Eliot's side.

Joss said again, "I'm sorry."

Mollie was polite. "Not at all. It's very thoughtful of you to be so concerned."

"None of my business, really," said Joss. Eliot and his mother waited with pointed patience. At last he took the hint, heaved his shoulders away from the mantelpiece, and said, "Well, if you'll excuse me, I'll go and get on with some work."

"Will you be here for lunch?"

"No, I can only stay a couple of hours. I'll have to get back to the shop. I'll pick up a sandwich at the pub." He smiled benignly at us all, not a trace of his former temper showing. "Thanks all the same."

And so he left us, modest, apologetic, apparently cut down to size. Once more the young workman, an employee, with a job to do.

# Chapter Six

Mollie said, "You must forgive him. He's not always the most tactful of men."

Eliot laughed shortly. "That's the understatement of the year."

She turned to me, explaining, "He's restoring some of the furniture for us. It's old and it had got into bad repair. He's a marvellous craftsman, but we never know when he's going to arrive or when he's going to go!"

"One day," said her son, "I shall lose my temper with him and punch his nose into the back of his neck." He smiled at me charmingly, his eyes crinkling, belying the ferocity of his words. "And I'm going to have to go too. I was late as it was, now I'm bloody late. Rebecca, will you excuse me?"

"Of course. I'm sorry, I'm afraid it was my fault. And thank you for being so kind . . ."

"I'm glad I stopped. I must have known how important it was. I'll see you . . ."

"Yes, of course you will," said Mollie quickly. "She can't go away now that she's found us."

"Well I'll leave the two of you to fix everything up . . ." He made for the door, but his mother interrupted gently.

"Eliot." He turned. "The letter."

"Oh yes, of course." He took it from his pocket, the fateful letter, a little crumpled now, and handed it to Mollie. "Don't let Pettifer make too big a meal of it. He's a sentimental old chap."

"I won't."

He smiled again, saying goodbye to both of us. "See you at dinner."

And he was gone, whistling up his dog as he went down the hall. We heard the front door open and shut, his car start up. Mollie turned to me.

"Now," she said, "come and sit by the fire and tell me all about it."

I did so, as I had already told Joss and Mrs Kernow, only this time I found myself stumbling a little when I got to the bit about Otto and Lisa living together, as though I were ashamed of it, which was a thing which I had never been. As I talked and Mollie listened, I tried to work this out, and to understand why my mother had disliked her so much. Perhaps it was simply a natural antipathy. It was obvious that they would never have had anything in common. And my mother had never had much tolerance for women who bored her. Men, now, were different. Men were always amusing. But women had to be very special for my mother to be able to tolerate their company. No, it could not all have been Mollie's fault. Sitting across the fireside from her, I resolved that I would be friends with her, and perhaps compensate, in a small way, for the short shrift she had received from Lisa.

"And how long are you going to be able to stay in Porthkerris? Your job . . . do you have to get back?"

"No. I seem to have been given a sort of indefinite leave."

"You'll stay here, with us?"

"Well, I've got this room with Mrs Kernow."

"Yes, but you'd be much better here. There's not a lot of space, that's the only thing; you'll have to sleep up in the attic, but it's a dear little room if you don't mind the sloping ceilings and you manage not to bump your head. You see, Eliot and I seem to have filled up the guest rooms, and as well I've got my niece staying for a few days. Perhaps you'll make friends with her. It'll be nice for her to have someone young about the place."

I wondered where the niece was. "How old is she?"

"Only seventeen. It's a difficult age, and I think that her mother felt it would be a good thing if she was out of London for a little. They live there, you see, and of course she has so many friends, and there is so much going on . . ." She was obviously finding it difficult to find the right words ". . . Anyway, Andrea's down here for a week or two to have a little change, but I'm afraid she's rather bored."

I imagined myself at seventeen, in the unseen Andrea's shoes, staying in this warm and charming house, cared for by Mollie and Pettifer, with the sea and the cliffs on my doorstep, the countryside inviting long walks, and all the secret crooked streets of Porthkerris waiting to be explored. To me it would have been heaven, and impossible to be bored. I wondered if I would have very much in common with Mollie's niece.

"Of course," she went on, "as you've probably gathered, Eliot and I are only here because Mrs Pettifer died and really the two old men couldn't manage on their own. We've got Mrs Thomas, she comes in each morning to help do the housework, but I do all the cooking, and keep the place as bright and pretty as I can."

"The flowers are so lovely."

"I can't bear a house without flowers."

"What about your own house?"

"My dear, it's empty. I shall have to take you up to High Cross one day to show it to you. I bought a pair of old cottages just after the war and converted them. Even though I shouldn't say so, it is very charming. And, of course, it's so handy for Eliot's garage; as it is, living here, he seems to be perpetually on the road."

"Yes, I suppose so."

I could hear footsteps coming down the hall again; in a moment the door opened, and Pettifer edged around it, cautiously, carrying a tray laden with all the accoutrements of mid-morning coffee, including a large silver pot with steam drifting from its spout.

"Oh, Pettifer, thank you . . ."

He came forward, stooped with the weight of the tray, and Mollie got up to fetch a stool and place it swiftly beneath the tray so that the old man could put it down before it tilted so sharply that everything on it went hurtling to the floor.

"That's splendid, Pettifer."

"One of the cups was for Joss."

"He's upstairs working. He must have forgotten about the coffee. Never mind, I'll drink it for him. And, Pettifer . . ." He straightened, slowly, as though all his old joints were aching. Mollie took the letter from Ibiza off the mantelpiece where she had placed it for safety. "We thought, all of us, that perhaps it would be the best if you told the Commander about his daughter and then gave him this letter. It would be best, we thought, coming from you. Would you mind?"

Pettifer took the thin blue envelope.

"No, Madam. I'll do it. I'm just on my way up now to get the Commander up and dressed."

"It would be a kindness, Pettifer."

"That's all right, Madam."

"And tell him that Rebecca is here. And that she's staying. We'll have to make up the bed in the attic but I think she'll be quite comfortable."

Again a gleam came into Pettifer's face. I wondered if he ever really smiled, or whether his face had dropped permanently into those lugubrious lines and a cheerful expression had become physically impossible.

"I'm glad you're staying," he said "The Commander will like that."

When he'd gone, I said, "You'll have a lot to do. Shouldn't I go, and get out from under your feet?"

"You'll have to collect your things from Mrs Kernow

anyway. I wonder how we could manage that? Pettifer could take you, but now he'll be occupied with Grenville and I must speak to Mrs Thomas about your room and then start thinking about lunch. Now what are we going to do?" I could not imagine. I was certainly not going to be able to carry all my belongings up the hill from the town. But luckily Mollie answered her own question. "I know. Joss. He can take you and bring you back up the hill in his van."

"But isn't Joss working?"

"Oh, for once we'll interrupt him. It's not often he's asked to put himself out – I'm sure he won't mind. Come along, we'll go and find him."

I had thought that she would take me to some forgotten outhouse or shed where we would find Joss, surrounded by wood shavings and the smell of hot glue, but to my surprise, she led me upstairs, and I forgot about Joss, because these were my first impressions of Boscarva, where my mother had been brought up, and I didn't want to miss a thing. The stairs were uncarpeted, the walls half panelled and then darkly papered above and hung with heavy oil paintings. All was at variance with the pretty, feminine sitting-room which we had left downstairs. On the first-floor landing passages led to left and right, there was a tallboy of polished walnut, and bookcases heavy with books, and then we went on again, up the stairs. Here was red drugget, white paint, again the passages led away to either side, and Mollie took the right-hand one. At the end of this passage was an open door, and from behind it the sound of voices, a man's and a girl's.

She seemed to hesitate and then her footsteps quickened, determined. Her back view became, all at once, formidable. With me following she went down the passage and through the door, and we were in an attic which had been converted, by means of a skylight, to a studio, or perhaps a billiard room, for against one wall was a massive, leather-seated sofa with oaken arms and legs. Now, however, this cold and airy room was being used as a workshop, with Joss in the middle of it, surrounded by chairs, broken picture frames, a table with a crooked leg, some scraps of leather, tools and nails, and a gimcrack gas ring on which reposed an unsavoury-looking glue pot. Wrapped in a worn blue apron, he was carefully fitting beautiful scarlet hide over the seat of one of the chairs, and as he did this, was being entertained by a young and female companion, who turned, disinterested, to see who had come into the room, and was so breaking up this cosy *tête-à-tête*.

Mollie said, "Andrea!" And then, less sharply, "Andrea, I didn't realise you were up."

"Oh, I've been up for hours."

"Did you have any breakfast?"

"I didn't want any."

"Andrea, this is Rebecca. Rebecca Bayliss."

"Oh, yes," she turned her eyes on to me. "Joss has been telling me all about you."

I said, "How do you do." She was very young and very thin, with long seaweedy hair that hung on either side of her face, which was pretty, except for her eyes which were pale and slightly protuberant, and not improved by a great deal of clumsy mascara. She wore, inevitably, jeans, and a cotton tee-shirt which did not look entirely clean and which revealed, with no shadow of a doubt, the fact that she wore nothing beneath it. On her feet were sandals which looked like surgical boots that had been striped in green and purple. There was a leather bootlace around her neck upon which hung a heavy silver cross of vaguely Celtic design. Andrea, I thought. So bored with Boscarva. And it made me uncomfortable to think that she and Joss had been discussing me. I wondered what he had said.

Now, she did not move, but stayed where she was, legs straddled, leaning against a heavy old mahogany table.

"Hi," she said.

"Rebecca's going to stay here," Mollie told them. Joss looked up, his mouth full of tacks, his eyes bright with interest, a lock of black hair falling over his forehead.

"Where's she going to sleep?" asked Andrea. "I thought we were a full house."

"In the bedroom along the passage," her aunt told her crisply. "Joss, would you do a favour for me?" He spat the tacks neatly into his palm and stood up, pushing his hair back with his wrist. "Would you take her, now, down to Mrs Kernow, and tell Mrs Kernow that she's coming here, and then help her with her suitcases and bring her back up to Boscarva again? Would that be very inconvenient?"

"Not at all," said Joss, but Andrea's face assumed an expression of bored resignation.

"It's a nuisance, I know, when you're busy, but it would be such a help . . ."

"It's no trouble." He laid down his little hammer and began to untie the knot of his apron. He gazed at me. "I'm getting quite used to carting Rebecca about."

And Andrea gave a snort, whether of disgust or impatience it was impossible to tell, sprang to her feet and marched out of the room, leaving the impression that we had been lucky to escape without a monumentally slammed door.

And so I was back where I started, with Joss, crammed into the ramshackle little van. We drove in silence away from Boscarva, through Mr Padlow's building estate, and on to the slope of the hill that led down to the town.

It was Joss who broke the silence.

"So, it all worked out."

"Yes."

"How do you like your family?"

"I haven't met them all yet. I haven't met Grenville."

He said, "You'll like him," but the way he said it, he made it sound, "You'll like *him*."

"I like them all."

"That's good."

I looked at him. He wore his blue denim jacket, a navy polo-necked sweater. His profile was impassive. I felt it would be easy to be maddened by him.

"Tell me about Andrea," I said.

"What do you want to know about Andrea?"

"I don't know. I just want you to tell me."

"She's seventeen, and she thinks she's in love with some guy she met at Art School, and her parents don't approve so she's been rusticated with Auntie Mollie. And she's bored stiff."

"She seems to have taken you into her confidence."

"There's no one else to talk to."

"Why doesn't she go back to London?"

"Because she's only seventeen. She hasn't got the money. And I think she hasn't quite got the courage to stand up to her parents."

"What does she do with herself all day?"

"I don't know. I'm not there all day. She doesn't seem to get up until lunch-time, and then she sits around watching television. Boscarva's a house of old people. You can't blame her for being bored."

I said, without thinking, "Only the boring are bored." This had once been drummed into me by a wise and well-meaning headmistress.

"That," said Joss, "sounds uncomfortably sanctimonious."

"I didn't mean it to."

He smiled. "Were you never bored?"

"Nobody who lived with my mother was ever bored."

He sang, "You may have been a headache, but you never were a bore."

"Exactly."

"She sounds great. Exactly my sort of female."

"That's what most men thought about her."

When we got to Fish Lane Mrs Kernow was out, but Joss seemed to have a key. We let ourselves in and I went upstairs to pack my rucksack while Joss wrote Mrs Kernow a note to explain the new arrangements.

"How about paying her?" I asked as I came downstairs, bumping the rucksack behind me.

"I'll fix that when I next see her. I've told her so in the note."

"But I can pay for myself."

"Of course you can, but let me do it for you." He took my rucksack and went to open the door, and there did not seem to be opportunity for further argument.

Once more my belongings were heaved into the back of the little truck, once more we headed for Boscarva, only this time Joss took me round by the harbour road.

"I want to show you my shop . . . I mean, I just want to show you where it is. Then if you want to get hold of me for any reason, you'll know where to find me."

"Why should I want to get hold of you?"

"I don't know. You might need wise counselling; or money; or just a good laugh. There it is, you can't miss it."

It was a tall narrow house, boxed in between two short fat houses. Three storeys high with a window on each floor, and the ground floor still in a state of reconstruction, with new wood unpainted and great circles of whitewash splashed over the plate glass of the shop window.

As we flashed past it, tyres rattling on the cobbles, I said, "That's a good position, you'll get all the visitors coming in to spend their money."

"That's what I hope."

"When can I see it?"

"Come next week. We'll be more or less straight then."

"All right. Next week."

"It's a date," said Joss, and turned the corner by the church. He put the little truck into second gear and we roared up the hill with a noise like a badly tuned motor bicycle.

Back at Boscarva, it was Pettifer who, hearing our arrival, emerged from the front door as Joss lifted my rucksack from the back of the truck.

"Joss, the Commander's downstairs and in his study. He said to bring Rebecca in to see him just as soon as you arrived."

Joss looked at him. "How is he?"

Pettifer ducked his head. "Not too bad."

"Was he very upset?"

"He's all right . . . now you leave that rucksack, and I'll carry it upstairs."

"You'll do no such thing," said Joss, and for once I was glad that he was being his usual bossy self. "I'll take it up. Where's she sleeping?"

"In the attic . . . the other end from the billiard room, but the Commander did say, right away."

"I know," Joss grinned, "and naval time is five minutes beforehand. But there's still time to take the girl up to her room, so stop fussing, there's a good man."

Leaving Pettifer still mildly protesting, I followed him up the two flights of stairs that I had already climbed this morning. The sound of the vacuum had stopped, but there was the smell of roasting lamb. I realised then that I was very hungry and my mouth watered. Joss's long legs sped ahead of me, and by the time I reached the slope-ceilinged bedroom which was to be mine, he had set down the rucksack and gone to fling wide the dormer window, so that I was met by a blast of cold, salty air.

"Come and look at the view."

I went to stand beside him. I saw the sea, the cliffs, the gold of bracken and the first yellow candles of gorse. And below was the Boscarva garden which, because of the stone balustrade of the terrace, I had not been able to see from the drawing-room window. It had been built in a series of terraces, dropping down the slope of the hill, and at the bottom, tucked into a corner of the garden wall, was a stone cottage with a slate roof. No, not a cottage, perhaps a stable, with a commodious loft above it.

I said, "What's that building?"

"That's the studio," Joss told me. "That's where your grandfather used to paint."

"It doesn't look like a studio."

"From the other side it does. The entire north wall is made of glass. He designed it himself, had it built by a local stonemason."

"It looks shut up."

"It is. Locked and shuttered. It hasn't been opened since he had his heart attack and stopped painting."

I shivered suddenly.

"Cold?" asked Joss.

"I don't know." I moved away from the window, undoing my coat, dropping it over the end of the bed. The room was white, the carpet dark red. There was a built-in wardrobe, shelves full of books, a washbasin. I went over to wash my hands, turning the soap beneath the warm water. Over the basin was a mirror which gave me back a reflection both dishevelled and anxious. I realised then how nervous I was of meeting Grenville for the first time, and how important it was that he should get a good impression of me.

I dried my hands, went to unbuckle my rucksack, and found a brush and comb. "Was he a good painter, Joss? Do you think he was a good artist?"

"Yes. The old school, of course, but magnificent. And a marvellous colourist."

I pulled the rubber band from the end of my plait, shook the coils free, and went back to the mirror to start brushing. Over my reflected shoulder I could see Joss watching me. He did not speak while I brushed and combed and finally re-plaited my hair. As I fastened the ends, he said, "It's a wonderful colour. Like corn."

I laid down the brush and comb. "Joss, we mustn't keep him waiting."

"Do you want me to come with you?"

"Please."

I realised then that this was the first time I had ever had to ask him to help me.

I followed him downstairs, down the hall and past the sitting-room, to a door which stood at the end of the passage. Joss opened it and put his head around.

He said, "Good morning."

"Who's that? Joss? Come along in . . ." The voice was higher pitched than I had imagined, more like the voice of a much younger man.

"I've brought someone to see you . . ."

He opened the door wide, and put his arms behind me to propel me gently forward into the room. It was a small room, with french windows leading out on to a paved terrace and a secret garden, warm with trapped sunshine, and enclosed by dense hedges and escallonia.

I saw the fire flickering in the grate; the panelled walls covered either with pictures or books; the model, on the mantelpiece, of an old-fashioned naval cruiser. There were photographs in silver frames, a table littered with papers and magazines, and a blue and white Chinese bowl filled with daffodils.

As I entered, he was already heaving himself – with the aid of a stick – out of a red leather armchair, which stood half turned towards the warmth of the fire. I was amazed that Joss did nothing to help him, and I began to say, "Oh, please don't bother . . ." but by then he was on his feet and erect, and a pair of blue eyes surveyed me calmly from beneath jutting brows and bristling white eyebrows.

I realised then that I had steeled myself to finding him pathetic in some way, old, infirm, perhaps a little shaky. But Grenville Bayliss, at eighty, was formidable. Very tall, very upright, starched and barbered, smelling faintly of Bay Rum, he was a credit to his servant Pettifer. He wore a dark blue blazer, of naval cut, neatly creased grey flannels, and velvet slippers with his initials embroidered in gold. He was also very tanned, his bald head brown as a chestnut beneath the thinning strands of white hair, and I imagined him spending much time in that little sunny secret garden, reading his morning paper, enjoying a pipe, watching the gulls and the white clouds scudding across the sky.

We looked at each other. I wished that he would say something but he simply looked. I hoped that he liked what he saw, and was glad I had taken the time to brush my hair. And then he said, "I've never been in this situation before. I'm not quite sure how we're meant to greet each other."

I said, "I could give you a kiss."

"Why don't you do that?"

So I did, stepping forward and raising my face, and he stooped slightly and my lips touched the smooth clean skin of his cheek.

"Now," he said, "why don't we sit down? Joss, come and sit down."

But Joss excused himself, said that if he didn't start work soon then he would have done nothing all day. But he stayed long enough to help the old man back into his chair, and pour us both a glass of sherry from the decanter on the side table, and then he said, "I'll leave you. You'll have a lot to talk about,"

95

and with a cheerful wave of his hand, slipped away. The door closed quietly behind him.

Grenville said, "I believe you know him quite well."

I pulled up a stool so that I could sit and face him. "Not really. But he's been very kind, and . . ." I tried to think of the right word. "Convenient. I mean, he always seems to be there when people need him."

"And never when they don't?" I was not sure if I could entirely agree with this. "He's a clever boy, too. Doing up all my furniture."

"Yes I know."

"Good craftsman. Lovely hands." He laid down his sherry glass, and once more I was subjected to that piercing blue stare. "Your mother died."

"Yes."

"Had a letter from this Pedersen fellow. He said it was leukaemia."

"Yes."

"Did you meet him?"

I told him about going to Ibiza and the night I had spent with Otto and my mother.

"He was a decent chap, then? Good to her?"

"Yes. He was immensely kind. And he adored her."

"Glad she ended up with somebody decent. Most of the chaps she picked on were just a lot of bounders."

I smiled at the old-fashioned word. I thought of the sheep-farmer, and the American in his Brooks Brothers shirts, and wondered how they would have liked being called bounders. They probably wouldn't even have known what it meant.

I said, "I think she sometimes got a little carried away."

A gleam of humour showed in his eyes. "You seem to have adopted a fairly worldly attitude?"

"Yes. I did. Long ago."

"She was a maddening woman. But she'd been the most enchanting little girl it was possible to imagine. I painted her often. I've still got one or two canvases of Lisa as a child. I'll have to get Pettifer to look them out, show them to you. And then she grew up and everything changed. Roger, my son, was killed in the war, and Lisa was always at loggerheads with her mother, rushing off in her little car, never coming home at night. Finally she fell in love with this actor fellow, and that was it."

"She really *was* in love with him."

"In love." He sounded disgusted. "That's an overrated expression. There's a lot more to life than just being in love."

"Yes, but you have to find that out for yourself."

He looked amused. "Have you found it out?"

"No."

"How old are you?"

"Twenty-one."

"You're mature for twenty-one. And I like your hair. You don't look like Lisa. You don't look like your father either. You look like yourself." He reached for his sherry glass, raised it carefully to his mouth, took a sip, and then replaced the glass on the table by his chair. In such cautious actions did he betray his age and his infirmity.

He said, "She should have come back to Boscarva. At any time we would have welcomed her. Come to that, why didn't *you* come?"

"I didn't know about Boscarva. I didn't know about you until the night before she died."

"It was as though she'd put the past out of her life. And when her mother died and I wrote to tell her, she never even replied."

"We were in New York that Christmas. She didn't get your letter till months later. And then it seemed too late to write. And she was so bad at writing letters."

"You're standing up for her. You don't resent the fact that she kept you from this place? You could have been brought up here. This could have been your home."

"She was my mother. That was the important thing."

"You seem to be arguing with me. Nobody argues with me nowadays. Not even Pettifer. It gets very dull."

Once more I was fixed with that blue stare. "Have you met Pettifer? He and I were in the Navy together about a century ago. And Mollie and Eliot? Have you met them?"

"Yes."

"They shouldn't be living here at all, of course, but the doctor insisted. Doesn't make that much difference to me, but it's hard luck on poor Pettifer. And Mollie's got a niece here as well, dreadful child with sagging breasts. Have you seen her?"

I managed not to giggle. "Yes, for a moment."

"A moment would be too long. And Boscarva. What do you think of Boscarva?"

"I love it. What I've seen of it, I love."

"The town's creeping out over the hill. There was a farm at the top, belonged to an old lady called Mrs Gregory. But this builder fellow talked her into selling up to him and now they've bulldozed the fields flat as a pancake and they're putting up houses nineteen to the dozen."

"I know. I saw them."

"Well, they can't come any further, because the farm at the back of this place and the fields on either side of the lane belong to me. Bought them when I bought Boscarva, back in 1922. Wouldn't like to tell you how little it cost me. But a bit of land around you gives you a feeling of security. Remember that."

"I will."

He frowned. "What's your name again? I've forgotten it already."

"Rebecca."

"Rebecca. And what are you going to call me?"

"I don't know. What do you want me to call you?"

"Eliot calls me Grenville. You call me Grenville too. It sounds more friendly."

"All right."

We drank our sherry, smiling, content with each other. Then, from the back of the house, came the sound of a gong being struck. Grenville put down his glass and got painfully to his feet, and I went to open the door for him. Together, we went down the passage towards the dining-room and family lunch.

# Chapter Seven

Exhaustion hit me at the end of that long, eventful day, and unfortunately in the middle of dinner. Luncheon had been a sustaining, homely meal, eaten at a round table set in the bay window of the big dining-room. This had been laid with a simple checked cloth, and everyday china and glass, but dinner was a different affair altogether.

The long, polished table in the middle of the room was set for the five of us, with fine linen mats, and old silver and glass sparkling in the candlelight.

Everybody, it seemed, was expected to change in honour of this apparently nightly ritual. Mollie came downstairs in a brocade housecoat the colour of sapphires, which emphasised the brightness of her eyes. Grenville wore a faded velvet dinner jacket and Eliot a pale flannel suit in which he looked as elegant as a greyhound. Even Andrea, probably under much protest, had put on a different pair of trousers and a blouse of broderie anglaise which looked as though it could have done with a press, or a wash, or maybe both. Her lank hair was tied back with a scrap of velvet ribbon, the expression on her face continued to be one of resentful boredom.

Not in the habit of attending formal dinner parties, I had nevertheless packed a garment which would obviously have to appear every evening as long I stayed in this house, for I had no other. It was a caftan of soft brown jersey wool, with silver embroidery at the neck and the wrists of the flowing sleeves. With it, I wore my silver bracelets and a pair of hoop ear-rings which my mother had given me for my twenty-first birthday. Their weight, on this occasion, gave me odd comfort and confidence, two things which I badly needed.

I did not want to have dinner with my newly acquired family. I did not want to have to make conversation, to listen, to be intelligent and charming. I wanted to go to bed and be brought something undemanding, like Bovril or a boiled egg. I wanted to be alone.

But there was soup and duckling, and red wine, dispensed by Eliot. The duckling was rich and the room very warm. As the meal slowly progressed I felt more and more strange, disembodied, light-headed. I tried to concentrate on the flames of the candles in front of me, but as I stared at them they separated and repeated themselves, and the voices around me became blurred and unintelligible, like the hum of conversation heard from a distant room. Instinctively, I pushed my plate away from me, knocked over the wineglass, and watched, in hopeless horror, as the red wine spread amongst the shattered splinters of glass.

In a way the accident was a blessing, for they all stopped talking and looked at me. I must have gone quite pale, for Eliot was on his feet in an instant and at my side . . .

"Are you all right?"

I said, "No, I don't think I am. I'm sorry . . ."

"Oh, my dear." Mollie flung aside her napkin and pushed back her chair. From across the table Andrea eyed me with chill interest.

"The glass . . . I'm so sorry . . ."

From the head of the table Grenville spoke. "It doesn't matter about the glass. Leave the glass. The girl's exhausted. Mollie, take her up and put her to bed."

I tried to protest, but not very hard. Eliot drew back my chair and helped me to my feet, his hands firm beneath my elbows. Mollie had gone to open the door, and cooler air moved in from the hall – already I felt better, as though, perhaps, after all, I was not going to faint.

As I passed Grenville, I said, "I'm sorry," for the third time. "Forgive me. Good night." I bent and kissed him, and left them all. Mollie closed the door behind us and came upstairs with me. She helped me undress and get into bed, and I was asleep before she had even turned off the light.

I slept for fourteen hours, waking at ten o'clock. I had not slept so late for years, and beyond my window the sky was blue and the cold bright northern light reflected from the sloping white-painted walls of my room. I got up, pulled on a dressing-gown and went and had a bath. Dressed, I felt wonderful, apart from the sinking sensation of shame at my behaviour the night before. I hoped they had not all thought that I was drunk.

Downstairs, I finally ran Mollie to earth in a little pantry, arranging a great mass of purple and pink polyanthus in a flowered bowl.

"How did you sleep?" she asked at once.

"Like the dead. I'm sorry about last night . . ."

"My dear, you were tired out. I'm sorry I didn't realise before. You'll want some breakfast."

"Just coffee."

She took me into the kitchen and heated coffee while I made some toast. "Where is everybody?" I asked.

"Eliot's at the garage, of course, and Pettifer's taken the car to Fourbourne to do some shopping for Grenville."

"What can I do? There must be something I can do to help."

"Well . . ." she debated. I looked at her. This morning she wore a cashmere sweater the colour of caramel and a slender tweed skirt. Immaculately made up, with every strand of hair in place, she seemed almost inhumanly neat. "You could go and fetch the fish for me in Porthkerris. The fishmonger rang up to say he'd got some halibut and I thought we'd have it for dinner. I could lend you my little car. Do you drive?"

"Yes, but couldn't I walk down? I like walking and it's such a lovely morning."

"Of course, if you want to. You could take the short cut over the fields and along the cliff. I know . . ." she appeared to be suddenly struck by inspiration ". . . take Andrea with you, and then she can show you the way, and show you where the fish shop is. Besides, she never takes any exercise if she can possibly help it and a walk would do her good." She made Andrea sound like a lazy dog. I did not particularly relish the idea of Andrea's company for the entire morning but I was sympathetic to Mollie, being encumbered by this unengaging girl, so I said that I would do as she suggested, and when I had finished my breakfast went in search of Andrea whom Mollie had last seen out on the terrace.

I found her bundled in a rug, lying on a long cane chair in a patch of sunshine, and peevishly regarding the view, like a seasick passenger on a liner.

"Will you walk down to Porthkerris with me?" I asked her.

She fixed me with her protuberant stare. "Why?"

"Because Mollie's asked me to go and pick up some fish and I don't know where the shop is. Besides, it's a lovely morning, and she thought we might go down to the cliffs."

She considered my suggestion, said, "All right," uncoiled herself from the rug and stood up. She wore the same dirty jeans as yesterday and a vast black and white sweater which reached below her narrow hips. We went back to the kitchen to fetch a basket and then set out, by way of the terrace and the sloping garden, down in the direction of the sea.

At the bottom of the garden, stone steps led up and over the wall, and Andrea went ahead of me, but paused because I wanted to inspect the studio from this new angle. It was, as Joss had said, locked and shuttered, and somehow desolate, and the great window on the north wall had been closed off by tightly-drawn curtains so that not a chink presented itself to any inquisitive passer-by.

Andrea stood on the top of the wall, her gaze following mine.

"He never paints now," she told me.

"I know."

"I can't think why. There's nothing wrong with him." She jumped, hair flying, down off the wall, and totally disappeared. I took a last look at the studio and then followed her and we took a trodden path that led down through small, irregular fields, and came out at last, through the hazard of some waist-high gorse bushes, to a stile, and so on to the cliff path.

This was obviously a favourite walk with visitors to Porthkerris, for there were seats set in sheltered view points, and litter bins for rubbish, and notices warning people not to go too near the edge of the cliff which was likely to collapse.

Andrea instantly went to the very edge and peered over. Gulls wheeled and screamed all around her, the wind tore at her hair and the baggy sweater, and from far below came the distant thunder of surf on rocks. She flung her arms wide and teetered slightly as though about to fall over the edge, but when she saw that I didn't care whether she committed suicide or not, she returned to the path, and in single file we walked on, Andrea in front.

The cliff curved and the town came into view in front of us, the low grey houses nestled around the sweep of the bay and climbing the steep hill to the moor behind. We went through a gate, and were now on to a proper road, and so able to walk side by side.

Andrea became conversational.

"Your mother's just died, hasn't she?"

"Yes."

"Aunt Mollie was telling me about her. She said she was a tart."

Painfully, I remained serene. It would have been instant victory for Andrea if I had been anything else.

"She didn't really know her. They hadn't seen each other for years."

"Was she a tart?"

"No."

"Mollie said she lived with men."

I realised then that Andrea was not merely trying to needle me, she was genuinely curious, and there was envy there as well.

I said, "She was very gay and very loving and very beautiful."

She accepted this. "Where do you live?"

"In London. I've got a little flat."

"Do you live alone, or with somebody?"

"No, I live alone."

"Do you go to parties and things?"

"Yes, if someone asks me and I want to go."

"Do you work? Do you have a job?"

"Yes. In a bookshop."

"God, how grim."

"I like it."

"Where did you meet Joss?"

Now, I thought, we're getting down to business, but her face was empty of expression.

"I met him in London . . . he mended a chair for me."

"Do you like him?"

"I don't know him well enough to dislike him."

"Eliot hates him. So does Aunt Mollie."

"Why?"

"Because they don't like having him around the place all the time. And they treat him as though he should call them Sir and Madam, and of course he doesn't. And he talks to Grenville and makes him laugh. I've heard them talking."

I imagined her creeping up to closed doors, listening at keyholes.

"That's nice, if he makes the old man laugh."

"He and Eliot had a terrible row once. It was about some car that Eliot had sold to a friend of Joss's and Joss said it wasn't roadworthy and Eliot called him an insolent, interfering bastard."

"Did you listen in to that one as well?"

"I couldn't help hearing. I was in the loo and the window was open and they were out on the gravel by the front door."

"How long have you been staying at Boscarva?" I asked, curious to know how long it had taken her to dig all these skeletons out of the family cupboards.

"Two weeks. It seems like six months."

"I should have thought you'd have loved coming down."

"For heaven's sake, I'm not a child. What am I meant to do with myself. Go bucket and spading on the beach?"

"What do you do in London?"

She kicked a pebble, viciously, hating Cornwall. "I was at an art school, but my parents *didn't approve* . . ." she put on a mealy voice ". . . of my friends. So they took me away and sent me here."

"But you can't stay here for ever. What are you going to do when you go back?"

"That's up to them, isn't it?"

I felt a twinge of pity for her parents, even parents who had somehow raised such an obnoxious child.

"I mean, isn't there anything you *want* to do?"

"Yes, just get away, be on my own, do my own thing. Danus, this fabulous chap I went around with, he had a friend who was running a pottery on the Isle of Skye, and he wanted me to go and help . . . It sounded super, you know, living in a sort of commune, and right away from

106

everybody . . . but my grotty mother shoved her great oar in and spoiled it all."

"Where's Danus now?"

"Oh, he went to Skye."

"Has he written to tell you about it?"

She tossed her head, fiddled with her hair, would not meet my eye. "Yes, actually, long letters. Reams of them. He still wants me to go there, and I'm going to, just as soon as I'm eighteen and they can't stop me any more."

"Why don't you just go back to art school first, and get some sort of a qualification . . . that'd give you time . . ."

She turned on me. "You know something? You talk like all the rest of them. How old are you anyway? You sound like someone with one foot in the grave."

"It's crazy to wreck your life before it's even started."

"It's my life. Not yours."

"No, it's not my life."

Having thus stupendously quarrelled, we continued our walk into the town in silence, and when Andrea did speak again, it was to say, "That's the fish shop," and wave a hand in its direction.

"Thank you." I went in to collect the halibut but she stayed, pointedly, outside on the cobbled pavement. When I emerged again, she had gone, only to appear the next moment from a paper-shop next door, where she had been buying a lurid magazine called *True Sex*.

"Shall we go back now?" I asked her. "Or do you want to do more shopping?"

"I can't shop, I haven't any money. Only a few pence."

I was suddenly, irrationally, sorry for her. "I'll stand you a cup of coffee if you'd like one."

She looked at me with sudden delight and I thought she was

going to gleefully accept my modest offer, but instead she said, "Let's go and see Joss."

I was taken unawares. "Why do you want to go and see Joss?"

"I just do. I often go and see him when I come down to the town. He's always pleased to see me. He made me promise always to go and see him if I'm down here."

"How do you know he'll be there?"

"Well, he's not at Boscarva today, so he must be at the shop. Have you been there? It's super, he's got a sort of pad on the top floor, just like something out of a magazine, with a bed that's a sort of sofa and masses of cushions and things, and a log fire. And at night . . ." her voice became dreamy ". . . it's all closed-in and secret, and there's nothing but firelight."

I tried not to gape. "You mean . . . you and Joss . . ."

She shrugged, tossing her hair. "Once or twice, but nobody knows. I don't know why I told you. You won't tell the others, will you?"

"But don't they . . . doesn't Mollie . . . ask questions?"

"Oh, I tell her I'm going to the cinema. She doesn't seem to mind me going to the cinema. Come on, let's go and see Joss . . ."

But after this revelation, nothing would have induced me to go near Joss's shop. I said, "Joss will be working, he won't want to be interrupted. And anyway there isn't time. And I don't want to go."

"You said there was time for coffee, why isn't there time for Joss?"

"Andrea, I told you, I don't want to go."

She began to smile. "I thought you liked Joss."

"That's not the point. He doesn't want us under his feet every time he turns round."

"Do you mean me?"

"I mean *us*." I was beginning to be desperate.

"He always wants to see me. I know he does."

"Yes, I'm sure," I said gently. "But let's go back to Boscarva."

I reminded myself that from the very start I had not liked Joss. Despite his concern and apparent friendliness he had always left me with that strange sensation of disquiet, as though someone were creeping up behind my back. Yesterday I had begun to forget this initial antipathy, even to like him, but after Andrea's confidences it was not hard to whip back to life my first distrust of the man. He was too good-looking, too charming. Andrea could be a liar, but she was no fool; she had pigeon-holed the rest of the family with disconcerting accuracy, and even if there was only a grain of truth in what she said about Joss, I wanted to have no part of it.

If I had known him and liked him better, I would have taken him aside and taxed him with what she had said. As it was, he held no importance for me. Besides, I had other things to think about.

Grenville did not come down for lunch that day.

"He's tired," Mollie told us. "He's having a day in bed. Perhaps he'll join us for dinner. Pettifer's going to take him up a tray."

So the three of us ate lunch together. Mollie had changed into a neat woollen dress and a double string of pearls. She was going, she said, to play bridge with friends in Fourbourne. She hoped that I would be able to occupy myself.

I said that of course I would be perfectly all right. Across the table, we smiled at each other and I wondered if she had really told Andrea that my mother was a tart, or if this was simply Andrea's interpretation of some vague euphemistic explanation that Mollie had given her. I hoped it was the latter, but still I wished that Mollie had not found it necessary to discuss Lisa with Andrea. She was dead now, but once she had been funny and enchanting and full of laughter. Why couldn't she be remembered that way?

As we sat around the table, the day outside changed its face. A wind got up from the west, and with great speed a bank of grey cloud sped over the blue sky, obliterating the sunshine, and presently it started to rain. It was in this rain that Mollie set off for her bridge party, driving her little car, and saying that she would be home about six. Andrea, perhaps exhausted by her morning's exercise, but more likely bored to death with my company, disappeared up to her bedroom with her new magazine. Alone, I stood at the foot of the stairs, wondering how to amuse myself. The silence of the gloomy afternoon was broken only by the ticking of the grandfather clock and small, occupied sounds which came from the direction of the kitchens, and which, investigated, proved to be Pettifer, seated at a wooden table in his pantry and cleaning silver.

He looked up as I put my head around the door.

"Hello. I didn't hear you."

"How's my grandfather?"

"Oh, he's all right. Just a bit weary after all the excitement of yesterday. We thought it would be better if he had a day with his toes up. Has Mrs Roger gone?"

"Yes." I pulled up a chair and sat opposite him.

"Thought I heard the car."

"Do you want me to help you?"

"That'd be very kind . . . those spoons there need a good rub up with the shammy. Don't know how they get so marked and stained. But, there, I do know. It's this damp sea air. One thing silver really hates it's damp sea air." I began to rub at the thin worn bowl of the spoon. Pettifer looked at me over the top of his glasses. "Funny to have you sitting there after all these years. Your mother used to spend half her life in the kitchen . . . When Roger went off to boarding school there wasn't anyone else for her to talk to. So she used to come and spend her time with Mrs Pettifer and me. Taught her to make fairy cakes, Mrs

110

Pettifer did, and how to play two-handed whist. We had great times. And on a day like this, she used to make toast at the old range . . . mind, that's gone now, we've got a new one and good thing too . . . but that old range was cosy, with the fire burning behind the bars, and all the brass knobs polished up lovely."

"How long have you been at Boscarva, Pettifer?"

"Ever since the Commander bought it, back in 1922. That was the year he left the Navy, decided to be a painter. Old Mrs Bayliss didn't like that. For three months or more she wouldn't even talk to him."

"Why did she mind so much?"

"She'd been with the Navy all her life. Her father was the Captain of the *Imperious* when the Commander was First Lieutenant. That was how they met. They were married in Malta. A lovely wedding with an arch of swords and all. Being with the Navy meant a lot to Mrs Bayliss. When the Commander said he was going to leave they parted brass rags good and proper, but she couldn't make him change his mind. So we left Malta, for good and all, and the Commander found this house, and then we all moved down here."

"And you've been here ever since?"

"More or less. The Commander enrolled at the Slade, and that meant working in London, so he had this little *pied-à-terre*, just off St James's it was, and when he went up to London I went too, to keep an eye on him, and Mrs Pettifer stayed here with Mrs Bayliss and Roger. Your mother wasn't born then."

"But, when he'd finished at the Slade . . .?"

"Well, then he came back for good. And built the studio. That was when he was painting at his best. Lovely stuff he did then, great seascapes, so cold and bright you could smell the wind, feel the salt on your lips."

"Are there many of his pictures in this house?"

"No, not many. There's the fishing boat over the dining-room fireplace, and one or two little black and white drawings along the upstairs passage. He's got three or four in his study,

111

and then there's a couple in the room where Mrs Roger sleeps."

"And the one in the drawing-room . . ."

"Oh, yes, that one of course. 'Lady Holding a Rose.'"

"Who was she?"

He did not reply; was, perhaps, preoccupied with his silver, rubbing away at a fork as though determined to flatten the pattern.

"Who was she? The girl in the picture?"

"Oh," said Pettifer. "That was Sophia."

Sophia. Ever since my mother had fleetingly mentioned her I had wanted to know about Sophia and now here was Pettifer bringing up her name as though it were the most natural thing in the world.

"She was a girl who used to model for the Commander. I think she first worked for him in London when he was a student, and then she used to come down here sometimes during the summer months, take lodgings in Porthkerris and work for any artist who was ready and able to pay her."

"Was she very beautiful?"

"Not my idea of a beauty. But lively, and what a talker! She was Irish, she'd come from County Cork."

"What did my grandmother think of Sophia?"

"Their paths never crossed, any more than your grandmother would have had social dealings with the butcher or the girl who did her hair."

"So Sophia never came to Boscarva?"

"Oh, yes, she used to come and go. She'd be down at the studio with the Commander, and then he'd get tired, or lose his patience with her, and call it a day, and she'd come up the garden and through the back door calling out, 'Any chance of a cup of tea?' and because it was Sophia, Mrs Pettifer always had the kettle on."

"She used to tell fortunes from teacups."

"Who told you that?"

"My mother."

"That's right, she did. And wonderful things she told us were going to happen to us all. 'Course, they didn't, but it was fun listening to her, just the same. She and your mother were great friends. Sophia used to take her down to the beach and Mrs Pettifer would pack a picnic. And if it was stormy weather they'd go for long walks up on the moor."

"But what was my grandmother doing all this time?"

"Oh, playing bridge or mah-jong most afternoons. She had a very select circle of friends. She was a nice enough lady, but not really interested in children. Perhaps if she'd been more interested in Lisa when she was a child, they'd have had more in common when Lisa grew up, and maybe your mother wouldn't have run off like that, breaking all our hearts."

"What happened to Sophia?"

"Oh, she went back to London, she got married and she had a baby, I think. Then, in 1942, she was killed in the Blitz. The baby was down in the country and her husband was overseas, but Sophia stayed in London because she was working in a hospital there. We didn't hear about it for a long time, till long after it happened. Mrs Pettifer and I felt as though a light had gone out of our lives."

"And my grandfather?"

"He was sorry, of course. But he hadn't seen her for years. She was just a girl who'd once worked for him."

"Are there any more pictures of her?"

"There's pictures of Sophia in provincial art galleries up and down the country. There's one in the gallery in Porthkerris if you want to go and look at that. And there's a couple upstairs in Mrs Roger's bedroom."

"Could we go and look at them now?" I sounded eager and Pettifer looked surprised, as though I were suggesting something faintly indecent. "I mean Mrs Bayliss wouldn't mind, would she?"

"Oh, she wouldn't mind. I don't see why not . . . come on."

113

He got laboriously to his feet, and I followed him upstairs and along the first-floor passage to the bedroom over the drawing-room, which was large and furnished in a very feminine fashion with old-fashioned Victorian furniture and a faded pink and cream carpet. Mollie had left it painfully neat. The two little oil paintings hung side by side between the windows, one of a chestnut tree with a girl lying in its shade, the other of the same girl hanging out a line of washing on a breezy day. They were scarcely more than sketches, and I was disappointed.

"I still don't know what Sophia looks like."

Pettifer was about to reply when, from the depths of the house, came the ringing of a bell. He cocked his head, like a dog listening. "That's the Commander, he's heard us talking through the wall. Excuse me a moment."

I followed him out of Mollie's room and closed the door behind me. He went on down the passage a little way and opened a door, and I heard Grenville's voice.

"What are you two muttering about in there?"

"I was just showing Rebecca the two pictures in Mrs Roger's room . . ."

"Is Rebecca there? Tell her to come in . . ."

I went in, past Pettifer. Grenville was not in bed, but sitting in a deep armchair with his feet propped up on a stool. He was dressed, but there was a rug over his knees and the room was cheered by the flicker of a fire. Everything was very neat and ship-shape and smelt of the Bay Rum he put on his hair.

I said, "I thought you were in bed."

"Pettifer got me up after lunch. I get bored stiff lying in bed all day. What have you been talking about?"

"Pettifer was showing me some of your pictures."

"I expect you think they're very old-fashioned. They're going back to realism now, you know, these young artists. I knew it would come. You'll have to have one of my pictures. There are racks of them in the studio that have never been

114

sorted out. I closed the place up ten years ago, and I haven't been there since. Pettifer, where's the key?"

"Put safely away, sir."

"You'll have to get the key off Pettifer, go down and nose around, see if there's anything you'd like. Got anywhere to hang it?"

"I've got a flat in London. It needs a picture."

"I thought of something else sitting here. That jade in the cabinet downstairs. I brought it back from China years ago, gave it to Lisa. Now, it belongs to you. And a mirror that her grandmother left her – where's that, Pettifer?"

"That's in the morning-room, sir."

"Well, we'll have to get it down, give it a clean. You'd like that, wouldn't you?"

"Yes, I would." I felt greatly relieved. I had been wondering how to bring up the subject of my mother's possessions, and now, without any prompting, Grenville had done it for me. I hesitated and then, striking while the iron was hot, mentioned the third thing. ". . . and there was a davenport desk."

"Hm?" He fixed me with his ferocious stare. "How do you know?"

"My mother told me about the jade and the mirror, and she said there was a davenport desk." He continued to glare at me. I wished all at once that I had said nothing. "I mean, it doesn't matter, it's just that if nobody did want it . . . if it wasn't being used . . ."

"Pettifer, do you remember that desk?"

"Yes, I do, sir, now you come to mention it. It was up in the other attic bedroom, but I can't remember having seen it lately."

"Well, look for it some time, there's a good fellow. And put another bit of wood on the fire . . ." Pettifer did so. Grenville, watching him, said suddenly, "Where is everybody? The house is quiet. Only the sound of the rain."

"Mrs Roger's out to a bridge party. I think Miss Andrea's in her room . . ."

"How about a cup of tea?" Grenville cocked an eye at me. "You'd like a cup of tea, wouldn't you? We haven't had the chance of getting to know each other. Either you're keeling over in the middle of dinner, or I'm too old and infirm to get out of bed. We make a fine pair, don't we?"

"I'd like to have tea with you."

"Pettifer will bring up a tray."

"No," I said. "I will. Pettifer's legs have been up and down these stairs all day. Let's give him a rest."

Grenville looked amused. "All right. You bring it up, and let's have a good big plateful of hot buttered toast."

I was to wish, many times over, that I had never brought up the subject of the davenport desk. Because it could not be found. While Grenville and I ate our tea, Pettifer began to look for it. By the time he came to take the tray away, he had combed the house from top to bottom, and the desk was nowhere.

Grenville scarcely believed him. "You've just missed it. Your eyes are getting as old as mine."

"I could scarcely miss seeing a desk." Pettifer sounded aggrieved.

"Perhaps," I said, trying to be helpful, "it was sent away to be mended or something . . ." They both looked at me as though I were a fool, and I hastily shut up.

"Would it be in the studio?" Pettifer ventured.

"What would I do with a desk in the studio? I painted there, I didn't write letters. Didn't want a desk cluttering the place up . . ." Grenville was getting quite agitated. I stood up, "Oh, it'll turn up," I said in my best, soothing voice, and picked up the tea-tray to carry it downstairs. In the kitchen I was joined by Pettifer, upset by what had happened.

"It's not good for the Commander to get worked up about anything . . . and he's going to go after this like a terrier after a rat. I can tell."

"It's all my fault. I don't know why I ever mentioned it."

"But I remember it. I just can't remember having seen it lately." I began to wash the cups and saucers and Pettifer picked up a tea towel in order to dry them. "And there's another thing. There was a Chippendale chair that used to go with it . . . mind, they didn't match, but the chair always sat in front of that desk. It had a tapestry seat, rather worn, birds and flowers and things. Well, that's gone, too . . . but I'm not going to tell the Commander that and neither are you."

I promised that I wouldn't. "Anyway," I said, "it doesn't matter to me one way or the other."

"No, but it matters to the Commander. Artistic he may have been, but he had a memory like an elephant and that's one thing he hasn't lost." He added gloomily, "I sometimes wish he had."

That evening when I went downstairs, changed once more into the brown and silver caftan, I found Eliot in the drawing-room, alone except for that inevitable companion, his dog. Eliot sat by the fire with a drink and the evening paper, and Rufus was stretched, like some glorious fur, on the hearth-rug. They looked companionable, caught in the light of the lamp, but my appearance disturbed the peaceful scene, and Eliot stood up, dropping the paper behind him on the seat of the chair.

"Rebecca. How are you?"

"I'm all right."

"I was afraid last night that you were going to be ill."

"No. I was just tired. I slept till ten o'clock."

"My mother told me. Would you like a drink?"

I said that I would and he poured me some sherry and I went to crouch by the fire and fondle the dog's silky ears.

As Eliot brought me my drink I asked, "Does he go every-where with you?"

"Yes, everywhere. To the garage, to the office, out to lunch, into the pubs, anywhere I happen to be going. He's a very well-known dog in this part of the world."

I sat on the hearth-rug, and Eliot subsided once more into his chair and picked up his drink. He said, "Tomorrow I have to go over to Falmouth, see a man about a car. I wondered if you'd like to come with me, see a bit of the country. Does that appeal to you?"

I was surprised by my own pleasure at this invitation. "I'd love it."

"It won't be very exciting. But perhaps you can amuse yourself for an hour or two while I'm doing business, and then we'll stop at a little pub I know on the way home. They serve delicious sea food. Do you like oysters?"

"Yes."

"Good. So do I. And then we'll come home by High Cross, and you can see where we normally live, my mother and I."

"Your mother told me about it. It sounds charming."

"Better than this mausoleum . . ."

"Oh, Eliot, it's not a mausoleum . . ."

"I was never much of a one for Victorian relics . . ."

Before I could protest further, we were joined by Grenville. At least, we heard him coming, step by step downstairs; heard him talking to Pettifer, the high-pitched voice and the low growl; heard them coming down the hall, the tap of Grenville's stick on the polished wood.

Eliot made a small face at me and went to open the door, and Grenville moved in, like the prow of some great, indestructible ship . . .

"That's all right, Pettifer, I can manage now." I had got up from the hearth-rug, wanting to help push forward the chair which he had used the night before, but this seemed to madden him. He was obviously not in a good mood.

"For God's sake, girl, stop fussing around. Do you think I want to sit *in* the fire, I'll burn to death sitting there . . ."

I edged the chair back to its original position and finally Grenville reached it and sank into it.

"How about a drink?" Eliot asked him.

118

"I'll have a whisky . . ."

Eliot looked surprised ". . . Whisky?"

"Yes, a whisky. I know what that fool of a doctor said but tonight I'm having a whisky."

Eliot said nothing, just nodded his head in patient acquiescence and went to pour the drink. As he did so Grenville leaned round the edge of the chair and said, "Eliot, have you seen that davenport desk around the place?" and my heart sank into my shoes.

"Oh, Grenville, don't start that again . . ."

"What do you mean, start that again? We've got to find the damned thing. I told Pettifer just now, got to go on looking till we've found it."

Eliot came back with the glass of whisky. He drew up a table and set the glass within Grenville's reach.

"What davenport desk?" he asked patiently.

"Little davenport desk, used to be in one of the bedrooms. Belonged to Lisa and now it belongs to Rebecca. She wants it. She's got a flat in London, wants to put it there. And Pettifer can't find it, says he's been through the house with a toothcomb, can't find it. You haven't seen it, have you?"

"I've never set eyes on it. I don't even know what a davenport desk is."

"It's a little desk. Got drawers down the side. Bit of tooled leather on the top. They're rare now, I believe. Worth a lot of money."

"Pettifer's probably put it somewhere and forgotten."

"Pettifer doesn't forget things."

"Well, perhaps Mrs Pettifer did something with it and forgot to tell him."

"I've already *said*; he doesn't forget things."

We were joined at this moment by Mollie, who appeared, smiling determinedly, as though she had heard the angry voice raised beyond the closed door, and was about to spread oil on troubled waters.

"Hello, everybody, I'm afraid I'm a little late. I had to go and do some very exciting things to that delicious piece of halibut Rebecca bought for me this morning. Eliot, dear . . ." she kissed him, apparently seeing him for the first time that evening. "And Grenville . . ." she stooped to kiss him too ". . . you're looking more rested." Then, before he could contradict her, she smiled across the top of his head at me. "Did you have a good afternoon?"

"Yes, thank you. How was the bridge?"

"Not too bad. I won twenty pence. Eliot darling, I'd love a drink. Andrea's just coming. She won't be a moment . . ." But she finally ran out of defensive small talk, and Grenville instantly opened fire. "We've lost something," he told her.

"What have you lost? Your cuff-links again?"

"We have lost a davenport desk."

It was becoming ludicrous.

"You've *lost* a davenport desk?"

For her benefit, Grenville went through the whole rigmarole. On being told that it was I who had precipitated this crisis, Mollie looked at me with some reproach, as though she thought this a poor way to return her hospitality and kindness. I was inclined to agree with her.

"But it must be somewhere." She took her glass from Eliot, drew up a stool and sat, all ready to work the whole thing out. "It must have been put somewhere for safety."

"Pettifer has looked for it."

"Perhaps he hasn't seen it. I'm sure he should get his glasses changed. Perhaps it's been put somewhere and he's forgotten."

Grenville thumped the arm of his chair with a balled fist. "Pettifer does not forget things."

"In fact . . ." said Eliot coolly ". . . he forgets things all the time."

Grenville glared at him. "And what does that mean?"

"Nothing personal. Just that he's getting older."

"I suppose you're blaming Pettifer . . ."

"I'm not blaming anybody . . ."

"You just said he's too old to know what he's doing. If he's too old what the hell do you think I am?"

"I never said that . . ."

"You blamed *him* . . ."

Eliot lost his patience. "If I was going to blame anybody," he said, raising his voice almost to the pitch of Grenville's, "I'd ask a few questions of your Joss Gardner." There was a pause after he'd come out with this. And then, in a more controlled, reasonable voice, he went on. "All right, so nobody wants to accuse another man of stealing. But Joss is in and out of this house all the time, in and out of all the rooms. He knows what's in this place better than anybody. And he's an expert, he knows what it's worth."

"But why should Joss take a desk?" asked Mollie.

"A valuable desk. Don't forget that. It's rare and it's valuable, Grenville just said so. Perhaps he needed the money. To look at him he could do with a bit of extra cash. And he's an expert. He's up and down to London all the time. He'd know where to sell it."

He stopped, abruptly, as though realising that already he had said too much. He finished his whisky, and went, without speaking, to pour himself a second glass.

The silence became uncomfortable. To break it, Mollie said, briefly, "I don't think that Joss . . ."

"Just a lot of poppycock," Grenville interrupted her savagely.

Eliot set down the whisky bottle with a thump.

"How do you know? How do you know anything about Joss Gardner? He turns up, like a hippy, out of nowhere, says he's going to open a shop, and the next thing you've opened up the house to him and given him the job of patching up all the furniture. What do you know about Joss? What do any of us know about him?"

121

"I know that I can trust him. I was trained to judge a man's character . . ."

"You could be wrong . . ."

Grenville raised his voice and rode over Eliot's, ". . . and it would be no bad thing if you were to take a few lessons in choosing your companions."

Eliot's eyes narrowed. "What does that mean?"

"It means that if you want to be made a fool of, try doing business with that little shyster Ernest Padlow."

If I could have escaped at that moment, I would. But I was caught, jammed into the corner behind Grenville's chair.

"What do you know about Ernest Padlow?"

"I know you've been seen around with him . . . drinking in bars . . ."

Eliot shot a glance at me, and then said, under his breath, "That bastard Joss Gardner."

"It wasn't Joss who told me, it was Hargreaves, at the bank. He came up for a glass of sherry the other day. And Mrs Thomas came in to do my fire this morning, she'd seen you with Padlow, up at that gimcrack nightmare he calls a housing estate."

"Back-stairs gossip."

"You hear the truth from truthful people. It doesn't matter in which direction they live. And if you think I'm selling up my land to that jumped-up little beachsweeper, you're wrong . . ."

"It won't always be your land."

"And if you're so sure it will be yours, all I can say is, don't count your chickens before they're hatched. Because you, dear boy, are not my only grandchild."

And at this dramatic moment, like a nicely stage-managed play, the door opened and Andrea appeared to tell us that Pettifer had told her to tell us that dinner was ready.

# Chapter Eight

It was hard to sleep that night. I tossed and turned, fetched a glass of water, paced the floor, looked out of the window, climbed back into bed and tried once more to compose myself, but always, when I closed my eyes, the evening came back to me like a film played over and over, voices drummed in my ears, and would not be stilled.

*All right, so nobody wants to accuse another man of stealing. What do any of us know about Joss?*

*If you want to be made a fool of, try doing business with that little shyster Ernest Padlow. And if you think I'm selling my land to that jumped-up little beachsweeper, you're wrong . . .*

*It won't always be your land . . .*

*. . . you, dear boy, are not my only grandchild.*

Dinner had been a gruesome meal. Eliot and Grenville had scarcely spoken a word from beginning to end. Mollie, to make up for their silence, had kept up a patter of meaningless conversation to which I had tried to respond. And Andrea had watched us all, a gleam of triumph in her round, seeking eyes, while Pettifer trod heavily to and fro, removing dishes, handing round a lemon soufflé rich with whipped cream, which nobody seemed to want.

When at last it was over, they had all dispersed. Grenville to his bedroom, Andrea to the morning-room from whence we presently heard the blare of the television set. Eliot, with no explanations, put on a coat, whistled up his dog and banged

123

out of the front door. I guessed he had gone to get drunk and didn't entirely blame him. Mollie and I ended up in the drawing-room, one on either side of the fire. She had some tapestry and seemed quite prepared to sit and sew in silence, but this would have been unbearable. I said, plunging straight in with the apology which I felt I owed her, "I am sorry about this evening. I wish I'd never mentioned that desk."

She did not look at me. "Oh, it can't be helped."

"It was just that my mother had mentioned it to me, and when Grenville spoke about the jade and the mirror, well, it never occurred to me that I'd start such a storm in a teacup."

"Grenville's a strange old man. He's always been stubborn about people, he'll never see that there can be two sides to every situation."

"You mean about Joss . . ."

"I don't know why he's so taken with Joss. It's frightening. It's as though Joss were able to exert some hold over him. Eliot and I never wanted him in and out of the house this way. If Grenville's furniture needed to be repaired, surely he could have come and fetched it in his van and taken it down to his workshop, like any other tradesman would do. We tried to talk Grenville out of it, but he was adamant, and, after all, this is his house. It isn't ours."

"But it will be Eliot's one day."

She sent me a cold look.

"After this evening, one wonders."

"Oh, Mollie, I don't want Boscarva, Grenville would never leave a place like this to me. He just said that to win a point; perhaps it was the first thing that came into his head. He didn't mean it."

"He hurt Eliot."

"Eliot will understand. You have to make allowances for old people."

"I'm tired of making allowances for Grenville," said Mollie, viciously snapping at a strand of wool with her silver scissors.

"My life has been disrupted by Grenville. He and Pettifer could have come and lived at High Cross; that's what we wanted. The house is smaller and more convenient and it would have been better for everybody. And Boscarva should have been made over to Eliot years ago. As it is, death duties are going to be exorbitant. Eliot is never going to be able to afford to keep it going. The whole situation is *so* unrealistic."

"I suppose it's hard to be realistic when you're eighty and you've lived in a place most of your life."

She ignored this. "And all that land, and the farm. Eliot is simply trying to make the best of it all, but Grenville won't see that. He's never shown any interest, never encouraged Eliot in any way. Even the garage at High Cross, Eliot got that going entirely on his own. At the beginning, he asked his grandfather to help, but Grenville said he wasn't going to have anything to do with second-hand cars, and there was a row, and finally Eliot borrowed the money from someone else, and he's never asked his grandfather for a shilling since that day. You'd think he'd deserve some credit for that."

She was pale with anger on Eliot's account – a little tigress, I thought, fighting for her cub, and I remembered my mother's low opinion of the way in which she had possessed and molly-coddled the young Eliot. Perhaps neither of them had ever grown out of the habit.

To change the subject I told her about Eliot's invitation for the next day. "He said he'd take me into High Cross on the way home."

But Mollie was only momentarily diverted. "You must go in and see the house, Eliot's got the key. I go up most weeks to make sure everything's all right, but really I get so depressed having to leave my darling little house and come back to this gloomy place . . ." and then she laughed at herself wryly. "It's getting me down, isn't it? I must try to pull myself together. But really I'll be glad when it's all over."

When it's all over. That meant when Grenville finally died. I didn't want to think about him dying any more than I wanted to think about Joss coupled with the unsavoury Andrea; any more than I wanted to think about Joss helping himself to a davenport desk and a Chippendale chair, heaving them into the back of his little truck, and selling them to the first dealer who made him a good offer.

*What do you know about Joss? What do any of us know about him?*

For my part I wished I knew nothing. I turned in bed, thumped at the pillows, and waited, without much hope, for sleep.

It rained in the night, but the next morning it was still and clear, the sky a pale, washed blue, everything wet and shining, translucent in the cool spring light. I leaned out of the window and smelt the dampness, mossy and sweet. The sea was flat and blue as a sheet of silk, gulls drifted lazily over the rim of the cliff, a boat moved out from the harbour, heading for distant fishing-grounds, and so still was the air that I could hear the distant chug of its engine.

My spirits rose. Yesterday was over, today would be better. I was glad to be getting out of the house, away from Mollie's reproach and Andrea's unsettling presence. I bathed and dressed and went downstairs and found Eliot in the dining-room, eating bacon and eggs, and looking – I was thankful to see – cheerful.

He looked up from the morning paper. "I wondered," he said, "if I was going to have to come and wake you up. I thought perhaps you'd forgotten."

"No, I didn't forget."

"We're the first down. With any luck we'll be out of the house before anyone else appears." He grinned, ruefully, like a repentant boy. "The last thing I want on a beautiful morning like this is recriminations."

"It was all my fault, mentioning that stupid desk. I said I was sorry last night to your mother."

"It'll all blow over," said Eliot. "These little differences of opinion always do." I poured myself a cup of coffee. "I'm just sorry that you were involved."

We left straight after breakfast, and there was a marvellous feeling of relief to be in his car, with Rufus perched on the back seat, and to be escaping. The car roared up the hill away from Boscarva; the wet road was blue with reflected sky, and the air smelt of primroses. As we climbed up and over the moor, the view spread and dipped before us – there were hills topped by ancient cairns and standing stones, and tiny forgotten villages, tucked into the folds of unexpected valleys where little rivers ran, and ancient clumps of oak and elm stood clustered by narrow, hump-backed bridges.

But I knew that we could not enjoy our day together, that we could not be entirely at ease, until I had made my peace with him.

I said, "I know that it'll blow over, and that perhaps it *wasn't* important, but we have to talk about last night."

He smiled at me, glancing sideways. "What do we have to say?"

"Just that, what Grenville said about having another grandchild. He didn't mean it. I know he didn't mean it."

"No, perhaps he didn't. Perhaps he was just trying to set us against each other, like a pair of dogs."

"He'd never leave me Boscarva. Never in a thousand years. He doesn't even know me, I've only just come into his life."

"Rebecca, don't give it another thought. I'm not going to."

"And, after all, if it is going to be yours one day, I don't see why you shouldn't start thinking about what you're going to do with it."

"You mean Ernest Padlow? What a lot of gossips those old people are, carrying tales and making mischief. If it isn't the bank manager it's Mrs Thomas, and if it isn't Mrs Thomas it's Pettifer."

I made myself sound casual. "Would you sell the land?"

"If I did I could probably afford to live at Boscarva. It's time I set up on my own."

"But . . ." I chose my words tactfully ". . . but wouldn't it be rather . . . spoiled . . . I mean, living there with rows of Mr Padlow's little houses all round you?"

Eliot laughed. "You've got entirely the wrong end of the stick. This wouldn't be a building estate like the one at the top of the hill. This would be high-class stuff, two-acre lots, very high specifications as to the style and the price of the houses built on them. No cutting down of trees, no despoiling of the amenities. They'd be expensive houses for expensive people, and there wouldn't be a lot of them. How does that sound to you?"

"Have you told Grenville this?"

"He won't let me. He won't listen. He's not interested and that's it."

"But surely if you explained . . ."

"I've been trying to explain things to him all my life and I've never got anywhere. And now, is there anything else you want to discuss?"

I considered. I certainly didn't want to discuss Joss. I said, "No."

"In that case shall we forget about last night and enjoy ourselves?"

It seemed a good idea. We smiled at each other. "All right," I said at last. We crossed a bridge and came to a steep hill, and Eliot changed down, expertly, with the old-fashioned gear stick. The car purred up the savage slope, its long, elegant bonnet seeming to point straight to the sky.

We got to Falmouth about ten o'clock. While Eliot attended to his business I was turned loose to explore the little town. Facing south, sheltered from the north wind, with gardens already filled with camellias and scented daphne bushes, it made me think of some Mediterranean port, and this illusion was strengthened by the blue of the sea on that first warm spring day, and the tall masts of the yachts which lay at anchor in the basin.

I felt, for some reason, impelled to shop. I bought freesias for Mollie, tightly in bud with their stalks wrapped in damp moss so that they would not wither before I got home, a box of cigars for Grenville, a bottle of fruity sherry for Pettifer, a record for Andrea. The sleeve portrayed a transvestite group with sequined eyelids. It seemed to me to be right up her street. And for Eliot . . . I had noticed that his watch strap was wearing thin. I found a narrow strap in dark crocodile, very expensive, exactly right for Eliot. Then I bought a tube of toothpaste for myself, because I needed one. And for Joss . . .? Nothing for Joss.

Eliot picked me up, as we had arranged, in the lounge of the big hotel in the middle of town. We drove very fast out of the town and through Truro, and down into the little maze of lanes and wooded creeks that lay beyond until we came to a village called St Endon, where there were white cottages, palm trees and gardens full of flowers. The road wound down towards the creek, and at the very bottom was a little pub, right on the water's edge, with the high tide lapping at the wall below the terrace. Kittiwakes perched along the top of it, their eyes bright and friendly, unlike the greedy, wild gulls of Boscarva.

We sat out in the sunshine, drinking sherry, and I gave Eliot his present, then and there; he seemed inordinately delighted, ripping off the old watch strap right away and fitting on the new, shining leather one, adjusting the little clips with the blade of his penknife.

"What made you think of giving me that?"

"I noticed your old one was worn. I thought perhaps that you might lose your watch."

He leaned back in his chair, watching me across the table. It was so warm that I had pulled off my sweater and rolled up the sleeves of my cotton shirt. He said, "Did you buy presents for everybody?"

129

I was embarrassed. "Yes."

"I thought you had a lot of parcels. Do you always buy presents for people?"

"It's nice to have people to buy presents for."

"Isn't there anyone in London?"

"Not really."

"No one special?"

"There's never been anyone special."

"I can't believe it."

"It's true." I could not think why I was confiding in him this way. Perhaps it had something to do with the warmth of the day, surprising me by its beneficence, lowering all my guards. Perhaps it was the sherry. Perhaps it was simply the intimacy of two people who had weathered such a storm as the row that had taken place last night. Whatever the reason, it was easy that day to talk to Eliot.

"Why is that?" he asked.

"I don't know. It may have something to do with the way I was brought up . . . my mother lived with one man after another, so I lived with them too. And there's nothing like living at close quarters with people to destroy that marvellous illusion of romance."

We laughed. "That could be a good thing," said Eliot. "But it could be a bad thing, too. You mustn't close up altogether. Otherwise nobody's ever going to get near you."

"I'm all right."

"Are you going back to London?"

"Yes."

"Soon?"

"Probably."

"Why not stay for a bit?"

"I don't want to wear out my welcome."

"You won't do that. And I've hardly spoken to you. Anyway, how can you go back to London and leave all this behind you . . .?" His gesture included the sky, the

130

sun, the quiet, the lap of water, the promise of the coming spring.

"I can, because I have to. I've a job to get back to and a flat that needs painting, and a life to pick up and start all over again."

"Can't that wait?"

"Not indefinitely."

"There's no reason to go." I did not reply. "Unless," he went on, "you were put off by what happened last night." I smiled and shook my head, because we had promised not to mention that again. He leaned on the table, his chin on his fist. "If you really wanted a job you could get one here. If you wanted a flat of your own you could rent that too."

"Why should I stay?" But I was flattered at being so persuaded.

"Because it would be good for Grenville, and for Mollie, and for me. Because I think we all want you to stay. Particularly me."

"Oh, Eliot . . ."

"It's true. There's something very serene about you. Did you know that? I noticed it that first evening I saw you before I even knew who you were. And I like the shape of your nose, and the sound of your laugh, and the way you can look marvellously ragamuffin one minute, in jeans and with your hair coming all unravelled, and then, the next minute, like a princess in a fairy story, with your plait over your shoulder and that stately gown you wear in the evenings. I feel as though I'm finding out new things about you every day. And this is why I don't want you to go. Not just yet."

I found that I could think of no rejoinder to this long speech. I was touched by it, and embarrassed too. But still, it was gratifying to be liked and admired, and even more gratifying to be told so.

Across the table, he began to laugh at me. "Your face is a picture. You don't know where to look and you're blushing.

131

Come along, finish your drink and we'll go and eat oysters. I promise I'll not pay you any more compliments!"

We lingered over lunch in the small, low-ceilinged dining-room, eating at a table which wobbled so much on the uneven floor that Eliot was forced to prop up one of the legs with a scrap of folded paper. We ate oysters and steak and a fresh green salad and drank our way through a bottle of wine. We took our coffee back into the sunshine, and sat on the edge of the terrace wall, watching two boys, sunburned and barelegged, rig up a dinghy and take her sailing out on to the blue waters of the creek. We saw the striped sail fill with some mysterious, unfelt breeze, as the dinghy heeled and went away from us, around the tip of a wooded promontory. And Eliot said that if I stayed in Cornwall, he would borrow a boat and teach me to sail; we would go mackerel fishing from Porthkerris – in the summer he would show me all the tiny coves and secret places which the tourists never found.

At last it was time to go, and the afternoon wound itself in like a long, shining ribbon. I was sleepy and replete when he drove me slowly back to High Cross, taking the long road that led through forgotten villages and the heart of the country.

When we got to High Cross, I realised that it stood at the very summit of the peninsula, so that the village had two aspects, one north to the Atlantic, the other south to the Channel; it was like being on an island, swept with clean winds and ringed by the sea. Eliot's garage stood in the middle of the village street, a little back from the road, with a cobbled forecourt set about with tubs of flowers, and inside the glass-fronted showroom stood the gleaming, racy cars. Everything was very new and expensive-looking and immaculately kept. I wondered, as we crossed the forecourt towards the showrooms, how much Eliot had had to sink into such a venture, and why he had decided that it was a viable proposition to open such a specialised garage in this out-of-the-way spot.

He pulled one of the sliding glass doors aside and I

went in, my feet making no sound on the highly polished rubber floors.

"Why did you decide to start your garage here, Eliot? Wouldn't it have been better in Fourbourne or Falmouth or Penzance?"

"Psychological selling, my dear. Get a good name for yourself and people will come from the ends of the earth to buy what you've got to sell." And he added with disarming candour, "Besides, I already owned the land, or at least my mother did, which was an excellent incentive to build the garage here."

"Are all these cars for sale?"

"Yes. As you can see we concentrate on continental and sports cars. We had a Ferrari in last week, but that was sold a couple of days ago. It had been crashed, but I've got this young mechanic working for me, and by the time he'd finished with it it was as good as new . . ."

I laid my hand on the gleaming yellow bonnet. "What's this?"

"A Lancia Zagato. And this is an Alfa Romeo Spyder, only two years old. Beautiful car."

"And a Jensen Interceptor . . ." That was one that I recognised.

"Come and see the workshop." I followed him through another sliding door at the back of the showroom and decided that this was more like my idea of a garage. Here was the usual clutter of dismantled engines, oil cans, long flexes trailing from the ceiling, naked bulbs, tool benches, old tyres and trolleys.

In the middle of all this a figure was stooped over the stripped-down engine of a skeletal car. He wore a welding mask which made him appear monstrous, and worked with the roaring blue flame of a welding gun. The noise of the gun was overlaid by non-stop blaring music from a surprisingly small transistor radio perched on a beam above him.

Whether or not he saw us coming was anybody's guess, but

it was only when Eliot switched off the radio that he shut off
his gun and straightened up, pushing the welding mask up and
back off his face. I saw a thin, dark young man, oil-stained and
in need of a shave, his hair long, his eyes sharp and bright.

"Hello, Morris," said Eliot.

"Hello."

"This is Rebecca Bayliss, she's staying at Boscarva."

Reaching for a cigarette, Morris looked my way and gave me
a nod. I said, "Hello," just to be friendly, but got no more
response. He lit his cigarette, then slipped the fancy lighter
back into the pocket of his oily overalls.

"Thought you'd be coming in this morning," he told Eliot.

"I told you I was going over to Falmouth."

"Any luck?"

"A 1933 Bentley."

"What sort of condition?"

"Looked OK. A bit of rust."

"Get the old paint spray out. There was a chap in the other
day, wanting one of them."

"I know, that's why I bought it. Thought we'd take the
transporter over, tomorrow or the next day, pick her up."

They fell silent. Morris went to his transistor and turned it
on again, if anything louder than before. I looked down at the
confusion of engineering on which he had been working and
finally asked Eliot what sort of a car it had originally been.

"A 1971 Jaguar XJ6 4.2 litre, if you really want to know.
And it will be again when Morris has finished with it. This is
another that was in a crash."

Morris came back to stand between us.

"What exactly are you doing to it?" I asked him.

"Straightening out the chassis, fixing the wheel alignment."

"What about the brake shoes?" said Eliot.

"It could have done with new brake shoes, but I fixed the old
ones to cover us for the guarantee . . . and Mr Kemback rang
up from Birmingham . . ."

They began to talk shop. I drifted away, deafened by the sound of rock, went back through the showroom and out into the forecourt where Rufus waited, with dignity and patience, behind the driving wheel of Eliot's car. Together we sat there until we were rejoined by Eliot. "Sorry about that, Rebecca; I wanted to check on another job. Morris is a good mechanic, but he gets shirty if he's expected to answer the telephone as well."

"Who's Mr Kemback? Another customer?"

"No, not exactly. He was down here last summer on holiday. He runs a motel, a garage, just off the M6. He's got quite a selection of old cars. Wants to start a museum, you know, a sort of sideline to the bacon-and-egg trade. He seems to want me to run it for him."

"You mean go and live in Birmingham?"

"Doesn't sound very tempting, does it? Anyway, that's it. Let's go and look at my mother's house."

We walked there, just a little way down the street, then up a short lane and through a double white gate, and the path sloped up to a long, low white house, which had been converted from two ancient thick-walled stone cottages. Eliot took a key out of his pocket and opened the door and inside it was cold, but not musty or damp. It was furnished like an expensive London flat, with pale, thick, fitted carpets and pale walls and sofas upholstered in mushroom-coloured brocade. There were a great many mirrors and little crystal bag chandeliers hanging from the low-beamed ceilings.

It was all charming, and just what I had imagined, and some-how wrong. A kitchen like an advertisement, a dining-room furnished with gleaming mahogany, upstairs there were four bedrooms and three bathrooms, a sewing-room and a linen cupboard of mammoth proportions, richly smelling of soap.

At the back of the house was a little patio, and then a long garden sloped up to a distant hedge. I looked at the patio and could see Mollie out there, entertaining her friends, with cane furniture set out on the flagstones, and martinis to drink, served from an expensive glass trolley.

I said, "It's a perfect house," and meant it. But I did not love it as I loved Boscarva. Perhaps because it was too perfect.

We stood in the elegant out-of-place drawing-room and eyed each other. Our day together seemed to have come to an end. Perhaps Eliot felt this too and wanted to postpone it, for he said, "I could put on a kettle and make you a cup of tea, only I know that there's no milk in the fridge."

"I think we should go home." I was surprised by an enormous yawn, and Eliot laughed at me. He took my shoulders between his hands. "You're sleepy."

"Too much fresh air," I answered. "Too much wine."

I tipped my head back to look up into his face, and we were very close. I could feel his fingers tighten over my shoulders. He wasn't laughing any more, but his deep-set eyes held an expression as gentle as anything I had ever seen.

I said, "It's been a wonderful day . . ." but that was as far as I got, because he kissed me then, and for some time I was not able to say anything at all. When at last he drew away I was so shaken that all I could do was lean limply against him, wanting to cry, feeling a fool, knowing that the situation was fast slipping out of my control. My cheek was against his coat, and his arms around me held me so close that I could feel, like the throb of a drum, the solid beating of his heart.

Over the top of my head, I heard him say, "You mustn't go back to London. You mustn't ever go away again."

# Chapter Nine

The shopping which I had done in Falmouth proved to be an unexpected blessing. I must have been inspired, for, without thinking, I provided exactly the small talking point we all needed to smooth over the embarrassment of the previous uncomfortable evening. Mollie was charmed with her freesias; she couldn't grow them at Boscarva, she explained, the winds were too cold, the garden too exposed. She paid me the compliment of arranging them with more artistry than one would have thought possible, and finally giving them the place of honour in the middle of the mantelpiece in the drawing-room. They filled the room with their rich romantic scent, and the cream and the violet and the deep pink drew one's eye, quite naturally, up to the portrait of Sophia. The flowers seemed to complement the glowing skin tones and the fragile shimmer of the white dress.

"Beautiful," said Mollie, standing back, but I could not be sure whether she was referring to the flowers or the portrait. "It was sweet of you to bring them. And did Eliot take you to see my house? So now you can understand how I feel about having to live in this great place." She regarded me thoughtfully, her eyes narrowed. "You know, I believe the day has done you good. I could even imagine you've caught the sun. You've got quite a good colour. The air must agree with you."

Pettifer accepted his sherry with dignity, but I could tell that he was pleased. And Grenville was wickedly delighted with his cigars, for the doctor had warned him against smoking and Pettifer had hidden his usual supply. I understood that he was parsimonious about doling them out. Grenville took and lit one instantly, puffing away with immense satisfaction and leaning back in his big chair like a man without a care in the world. Even with Andrea I had for once done the right thing. "*The Creepers!* How did you know they're my favourite group? Oh, I wish there was a record-player here, but there isn't and I left mine in London. Gosh, aren't they fabulous, groovy . . .?" And then she came down to earth again, searching for the price tag. "That must have cost you something."

It was as though, with peace offerings, we had all formed an unspoken pact. Last night was never discussed. There was no mention of the davenport desk, of Ernest Padlow, of the possible sale of Boscarva Farm. There was no mention of Joss. After dinner Eliot set up a table, and Mollie got out the rosewood box containing the mah-jong set, and we played until bed-time, Andrea sitting with Mollie in order to learn the rules.

I caught myself thinking that, if a stranger were to come, unexpectedly, upon us, how he would be charmed by the picture we made, caught, like flies in amber, in the pool of light from the standard lamp, absorbed by our timeless occupation. The distinguished painter, mellow in the twilight of his years, surrounded by his family; the pretty daughter-in-law and the handsome grandson – and even Andrea, for once alert and interested, absorbed by the intricacies of the game.

I had played as a child with my mother, sometimes making up a foursome with two of her friends, and found myself comforted by the remembered touch of the ivory and bamboo tiles, by their beauty, and the satisfying sound they made, like sea pebbles disturbed by the tide, as we stirred them around in the middle of the table.

At the start of each round we built the four walls, two tiles high, and closed them together into a tight square, "to keep the evil spirits out," we were told by Grenville, who had learned to play as a young sub-lieutenant in Hong Kong and knew all the traditional superstitions of the ancient game. I thought how easy it would be, how safe, if ghosts and doubts and skeletons-in-the-cupboard could be thus shut out and kept at bay.

The travel brochures and holiday posters of Porthkerris inevitably portrayed a place where the sea and the sky were always a bright and unsullied blue, the houses white with sunshine, the odd palm tree in the foreground lending that suggestion of Mediterranean glamour. The imagination was led, naturally, to visions of fresh lobster, eaten out of doors; artists with beards and paint-stained smocks; and weather-beaten fishermen, picturesque as pirates, sitting on bollards, smoking their pipes and discussing last week's catch.

But Porthkerris, in February, in a north-east gale, had no shred of connection with this nebulous paradise.

The sea, the sky, the very town were grey, the maze of baffling, narrow streets subjected to onslaughts of bitter wind. The tide was high; the waves broke against the sea-wall and splashed across the road, misting the windows of the houses opposite with salt, and filling the gutters with yellow foam, like dirty soapsuds.

It was as though the place were under some sort of a siege. Shoppers were wrapped, buttoned, scarved in every sort of protective clothing, their faces half hidden by hoods or deep coat collars, their bodies bundled into ambiguity, so that men and women all looked alike, gumbooted and shapeless.

The sky was the colour of the wind, the air filled with flying flotsam, old leaves, twigs, scraps of paper, even tiles torn from roofs. In the shops, people forgot what they had come to buy, the talk was all of the weather, the wind, the damage the storm was going to do.

I had come, once more, to shop for Mollie, fighting my way down the hill in borrowed raincoat and rubber boots, because I felt safer on my feet than I would have driving Mollie's insubstantial car. Now that I was more familiar with the town I no longer needed Andrea to show me the way . . . anyway Andrea was still in bed when I left Boscarva, and for once I did not blame her. The day was not inviting and it was hard to believe that only yesterday I had been sitting out, in my shirtsleeves, basking in a sun as warm as May.

The last of the shopping completed, I emerged from the baker's as the clock in the tower of the Norman church struck eleven. Normally, under such conditions, I would have headed straight back up the hill to Boscarva, but I had other plans. With my head down, the heavy basket over one arm, I made for the harbour.

The Art Gallery, I knew, was housed in an old Baptist Chapel, somewhere in the maze of streets which lay to the north of the town. I had thought that I would simply go and look for it, but as I braved the harbour road, battling with alternate assaults of wind and spray, I saw the old fisherman's lodge which had been converted to a Tourist Information Bureau and decided that I would save myself both time and effort if I made a few enquiries.

Inside, I found an unenthusiastic girl huddled over a paraffin stove; booted and shivering, she looked like the sole survivor of some Arctic expedition. When I appeared she did not move from her chair but said, "Yes?" and stared at me through a pair of unbecoming spectacles.

I tried to feel sorry for her. "I'm looking for the Art Gallery."

"Which one did you want?"

"I didn't know there was more than one."

Behind me the door opened and shut and we were joined by a third person. The girl looked over my shoulder and a faint interest gleamed behind her pebble glasses.

140

"There's the Town Gallery and the New Painters," she said, much more lively.

"I don't know which I want."

"Perhaps," said a voice behind me, "I can help."

I swung around and Joss stood there, in rubber boots and a streaming black oilskin, a fisherman's cap jammed down on to his head. His face was wet with rain, his hands rammed into the deep pockets of the coat, his dark eyes glinting with amusement. One half of me could see exactly why the sluggish girl behind the counter had suddenly come to life. The other half was maddened by his extraordinary ability to turn up just when I was least expecting him.

I remembered Andrea. I remembered the desk and the chair. I said, coolly, "Hello, Joss."

"I saw you come in. What are you wanting to do?"

The girl chipped in. "She wants the Art Gallery."

Joss waited for me to enlarge on this and, thus cornered, I did so.

"I thought perhaps there might be some pictures of Grenville's there . . ."

"You're quite right, there are three. I'll take you . . ."

"I don't need to be taken, I just want to be told how to get there."

"I'd like to take you . . . here . . ." he removed my heavy basket from my arm, smiled at the girl and went to open the door. A howl of wind and a blast of spume-laden air poured in from the outside and a pile of leaflets flew and scattered from the counter all over the floor. Before we could do any more damage, I hurried out, and the door swung shut behind us. As though it were the most natural thing in the world, Joss took my arm and we made our way down the middle of the cobbled road, Joss carrying on a cheerful conversation despite the fact that the wind tore the words from his mouth, and that, even with his arm in mine, it was taking all my efforts to progress at all.

"What on earth brings you down to the town on a day like this?"

"You're carrying it. Mollie's shopping."

"Couldn't you have brought the car?"

"I thought I might get blown off the road."

"I love it," he told me. "I love a day like this." He looked as though he loved it too, wind-whipped and wet and bursting with vitality. "Did you have a good day yesterday?"

"What do you know about yesterday?"

"I was up at Boscarva and Andrea told me you'd gone to Falmouth with Eliot. Don't imagine you can keep any secrets in this place. If Andrea hadn't told me, Pettifer would, or Mrs Thomas, or Mrs Kernow, or Miss Bright-Eyes in the Information Bureau. It's part of the fun of living in Porthkerris, everybody knows exactly what everybody else is up to."

"I'm beginning to realise that."

We turned away from the harbour and began to climb a steep cobbled hill. Houses closed in on either side of us, a cat flashed across the street and disappeared through a crack in a window. A woman in a pot-hat and a blue apron was scrubbing her steps. She looked up and saw us, and said, "'Ullo, my lover," to Joss; her fingers were like a bunch of pink sausages, made so by the hot water and the cold wind.

At the end of the street, we found ourselves in a little square which I had not seen before. One side of this was taken up by a large barn-like structure, with arched windows set high along the wall. By the door was a sign, PORTHKERRIS ART GALLERY, and Joss let go of my arm, pushed open the door with his shoulder and stood aside to let me go ahead of him. Inside it was bitterly cold, draughty, totally empty. The white walls were hung with paintings, of all sorts and shapes and sizes, and two great abstract sculptures were marooned in the middle of the floor, like rocks exposed by an ebb tide. There was a table by the door, with neat stacks of catalogues and folders and copies of *The Studio*, but despite this window-dressing

142

the gallery stayed thick with the atmosphere of joyless bygone Sundays.

"Now," Joss put down my basket and took off his cap, shaking it free of rain as a dog shakes its coat, "what do you want to see?"

"I want to see Sophia."

He glanced at me sharply with a sudden turn of his head, but in the same instant smiled and put his hat on his head again, pulling the peak down over his eyes, like a guardsman.

"Who told you about Sophia?"

I smiled sweetly. "Perhaps it was Mrs Thomas. Perhaps it was Mrs Kernow. Perhaps it was Miss Bright-Eyes in the Information Bureau."

"Insolence will get you nowhere."

"There *is* a portrait of Sophia here. Pettifer told me."

"Yes. It's over this way."

I followed him down the length of the floor, our rubber-booted footsteps sounding loud in the emptiness.

"There," he said. I stopped beside him and looked up, and she was there, sitting in a beam of lamplight with some sewing in her hands.

I stared at it for a long time and finally let out a long sigh of disappointment. Joss looked down at me from under the ridiculous peak of his cap.

"What's that sigh for?"

"You still can't see her face. I still don't know what she looks like. Why didn't he ever paint her face?"

"He did. Often."

"Well, I still haven't seen it. It's always the back of her head or her hands or else she's so small a part of the picture she doesn't have a face at all, just a blob."

"Does it matter what she looked like?"

"No, it doesn't matter. It's just that I want to know."

"How did you know about Sophia in the first place?"

"My mother told me about her. And then Pettifer, and the

picture of her – the one at Boscarva in the drawing-room –
is so charming and feminine, one feels she must have been
beautiful. But Pettifer says that she wasn't beautiful at all. Just
very charming and attractive." We looked again at the picture.
I saw the hands, and the shine of lamplight on her dark hair.
"Pettifer says that art galleries up and down the country have
portraits of Sophia hanging on their walls. I shall just have
to go on from Manchester to Birmingham, to Nottingham, to
Glasgow, until I find one that isn't of the back of her head."

"What will you do then?"

"Nothing. Just know what she looks like."

I turned from my disappointment and began to walk back to
the door where my laden basket waited for me, but Joss was
there first, stooping to swing it up and out of my reach.

I said, "I must go back."

"It's only . . ." he consulted his watch ". . . half past eleven.
And you've never seen my shop. Come back with me and let
me show it off, and I'll make you a cup of coffee and drive you
home. You can't possibly walk up the hill with this great weight
on your arm."

"Of course I can."

"I won't let you." He opened the door. "Come along."

I couldn't go without the basket and he obviously wasn't going
to give it up, so, resigned and reluctant, I went with him,
pushing my hands into my pockets so that he could not take
my arm. He seemed in no way put out by my ungraciousness,
which in itself was disconcerting, but when we got back to the
harbour and were once more in the teeth of the wind, I nearly
lost my balance with the unexpectedness of it, and he laughed
and pulled my hand out of my pocket, taking it in his own. It
was hard not to be disarmed by this protective and forgiving
gesture.

As soon as the shop came in view, the tall narrow house shouldering up between the two short fat ones, I saw that indeed changes had taken place. The window frames were now painted, the plate glass had been cleared, and a sign put up over the door. JOSS GARDNER.

"How does that look?" He was full of pride.

"Impressive," I had to admit.

He took a key out of his pocket and unlocked the door and we went into the shop. Packing cases stood about on the flagged floor, and around the walls, shelving was being erected in varying widths, up to the ceiling. In the centre of the room was another structure, rather like a child's climbing frame, and this had already been set out with modern Danish glass and china, cooking pots in bright colours, and brightly striped Indian rugs. The walls were white, the woodwork had been left in its natural state, and this and the grey floor provided a simple and effective background to the bright wares which he had to sell. At the back of the shop an open staircase rose to the upper floors, and beneath this was another door, ajar, leading down into what appeared to be a dark cellar. "Come upstairs . . ." He led the way.

I followed him. "What's that door there?"

"That's my workshop. It's in a dreadful mess, I'll show you that another time. Now this . . ." we emerged on to the first floor, and could scarcely move for baskets and wickerwork ". . . I haven't exactly got this straight but, as you can see, this is where you buy baskets for logs, clothes pegs, shopping, babies, laundry, anything you care to put in them."

None of it was very spacious. The narrow house was just a glorified staircase with a landing on each floor.

"Up again. How are your legs? Now we come to the *pièce de résistance*, the owner's palatial living quarters." I passed a tiny bathroom squeezed into the turn of the stairs. And lagging behind Joss's long legs found myself remembering Andrea's yearning descriptions of his flat, and hoping it would not be the way she had described it to me, but entirely different, so that I would know that her imagination had taken control, and that she had made the whole thing up. *Just like something out of a magazine. With a bed that's a sort of sofa and masses of cushions and things and a log fire.*

But it was just the way she had said. As I came up the last stairs, my fleeting hope swiftly died. And there *was* something closed-in and secret about it, with the ceiling sloping down to the floor and a dormer window set into the gable with a seat below it. I saw the little galley, enclosed behind a counter, like a bar, and the old Turkish carpet on the floor, and the divan, red-blanketed, pushed against the wall. As she had said, it was scattered with cushions.

Joss had put down my basket and was already divesting himself of his wet clothes and hanging them on an old-fashioned cane hat-stand.

"Take your things off before you die of cold," he told me. "I'll light a fire . . ."

"I can't stay, Joss . . ."

"No reason not to light the fire. And please, take off that coat."

I did, unbuttoning it with frozen fingers, pulling off my damp woollen hat and shaking my plait down over my shoulder. While I hung these up beside Joss's things, he was busy at the fireplace, snapping twigs, balling paper, scraping together the ashes from some previous fire, lighting it all with a long taper. When it was crackling he took some pieces of driftwood, tar-soaked, from a basket by the fireplace, and stacked them round the flames. They spat, and spluttered, and swiftly caught. And the room, by firelight, sprang to life. He stood up and turned to face me.

"Now, what do you want? Coffee? Tea? Chocolate? Brandy and soda?"

"Coffee?"

"Two coffees coming up." He retired behind his counter,

filled a kettle and lit the gas. As he collected a tray and cups,
I went over to the window, knelt on the seat and looked down
through the fury of the storm to the street below, washed by
spray as the waves broke over the sea wall. The boats in the
harbour bobbed about like demented corks, and huge herring
gulls floated over their swinging mastheads, screaming at the
wind. Absorbed in the task of making our coffee, Joss moved
with economy from one side of the galley to the other, neat-
fingered and self-sufficient as a single-minded yachtsman. So
occupied, he appeared harmless enough, but the disconcerting
point about Andrea's revelations was that they all seemed to
contain an element of truth.

I had known Joss for only a few days, but already I had
seen him in every sort of mood. I knew he could be charming,
stubborn, angry, and downright rude. It was not difficult to
imagine him as a ruthless and passionate lover, but it was
distasteful to imagine him with Andrea.

He looked up suddenly and caught my eye. I was embarrassed, caught with my thoughts. I said, quickly, to divert us
both, "In good weather you must have a lovely view."

"Clear out to the lighthouse."

"In the summer it must be like being abroad."

"In the summer it's like Piccadilly Underground at rush
hour. But that only lasts for two months." He came out from
behind his counter, carrying a tray with the steaming cups, the
sugar bowl and the milk jug. The coffee smelt delicious. He
pulled forward a long stool with his foot, set the tray at one
end of it and himself at the other. Thus, we faced each other.

"I want to hear more about yesterday," said Joss. "Where
did you go besides Falmouth?"

I told him about St Endon and the little pub by the
water's edge.

"Yes, I've heard about it, but I've never been there. Did you
get a good lunch?"

"Yes. And it was so warm that we sat out in the sunshine."

147

"That's the south coast for you. And what happened then?"

"Nothing happened then. We came home."

He handed me my cup and saucer. "Did Eliot take you to High Cross?"

"Yes."

"Did you see the garage?"

"Yes. And Mollie's house."

"What did you think of all those elegant, sexy cars?"

"I thought just that. That they were elegant and sexy."

"Did you meet any of the guys who work for him?"

His voice was so casual that I became wary.

"Who, for instance?"

"Morris Tatcombe?"

"Joss, you didn't ask me here for coffee at all, did you? You're pumping me."

"I'm not. I promise I'm not. It's just that I wondered if Morris was working for Eliot."

"What do you know about Morris?"

"Just that he's rotten."

"He's a good mechanic."

"Yes, he is. Everybody knows that, and it's the only good thing about him. But he's also totally dishonest and vicious to boot."

"If he's totally dishonest, why isn't he in jail?"

"He's already been. He's just come out."

This took the wind out of my sails, but I soldiered bravely on, sounding more sure of myself than I felt.

"And how do you know he's vicious . . .?"

"Because he picked a quarrel with me one night in a pub. We went outside and I punched him in the nose, and it was lucky for me I hit him first, because he was carrying a knife."

"Why are you telling me this?"

"Because you asked. If you don't want to be told things, you shouldn't ask questions."

"And what am I meant to do about it?"

"Nothing. Absolutely nothing. I'm sorry I brought it up. It was just that I'd heard Eliot had given him a job and I hoped it wasn't true."

"You don't like Eliot, do you?"

"I don't like him, I don't dislike him. He's nothing to do with me. But I'll tell you something. He picks bad friends."

"You mean Ernest Padlow?"

Joss sent me a glance that was full of reluctant admiration.

"You don't waste much time, I'll say that for you. You seem to know it all."

"I know about Ernest Padlow because I saw him with Eliot that first night when you gave me dinner at The Anchor."

"So you did. That's another rotten egg. If Ernest had his way the whole of Porthkerris would be bulldozed into car parks. There wouldn't be a house left standing. And we would all have to go up the hill and live in his fancy little semis which in ten years' time will be leaking, leaning, cracking up and generally bagging at the knees."

I did not reply to this outburst. I drank my coffee and thought how pleasant it would be to have a conversation without being instantly drawn into longstanding vendettas which had nothing to do with me. I was tired of listening to everybody I wanted to like running down the reputations of everybody else.

I finished my coffee, set down the cup and said, "I must get back."

Joss, with an obvious effort, apologised. "I'm sorry."

"Why?"

"For losing my temper."

"Eliot's my cousin, Joss."

"I know." He looked down, turning his cup in his hands. "But, without meaning to, I've become involved with Boscarva, too."

"Just don't take your prejudices out on me."

His eyes met mine. "I wasn't angry with you."

149

"I know." I stood up. "I must go," I said again.

"I'll drive you back."

"You don't have to . . ." But he paid no attention to my protest, just took my coat from its hook and helped me on with it. I pulled the wet woollen hat over my ears and picked up the heavy basket.

The telephone rang.

Joss, in his oilskin, went to answer it, and I started downstairs. I heard him call, just before he took the receiver off the hook, "Rebecca, wait for me. I won't be a moment . . ." and then, into the telephone, "Yes? Yes, Joss Gardner here . . ."

I went down to the ground floor and the shop. It was still raining. Upstairs I could hear Joss deep in conversation.

Bored with waiting for him, perhaps a little curious, I pushed open the door of the workshop, turned on the light, and went down four stone steps. There was the usual confusion, benches, woodshavings, scraps, tools, vices; over all hung the smell of glue, of new wood, of polish. There was also a clutter of old furniture, so dusty and ramshackle it was impossible to tell whether it was of any value or not. A chest of drawers missing all its handles, a bedside cupboard without a leg.

And then, at the very back of the room, in the shadows, I saw them. A davenport desk, in apparently perfect repair, and alongside it a chair in the Chinese Chippendale style, with a tapestry seat, embroidered in flowers.

I felt sick, as though I had been kicked in the stomach. I turned and went up the steps, turning off the light and closing the door, going through the shop and out into the bitter windblast of that wicked February day.

*My workshop's in a dreadful mess, I'll show you that another time.*

I walked and then found that I was running up towards the church, into a warren of little lanes where he would never find me. I was running, always uphill, encumbered by the shopping basket, heavy as lead, and my heart pounded in my chest and there was the taste of blood in my mouth.

Eliot had been right. It was too easy for Joss and he had simply taken his chance. It was my desk; it was *my* desk that he had taken, but he had taken it from Grenville's house, flinging the old man's trust and kindness back in his face.

I could imagine killing Joss, and it was easy. I told myself that I could never speak to him, could never bear to be near him again. I had never been so angry in my life. With him; but worse with myself, for having been taken in by his empty charm, for having been proved so totally wrong. I had never been so angry.

I stumbled on up the hill.

But if I was so angry, then why was I crying?

# Chapter Ten

It was a long and exhausting climb back to Boscarva, and I have never found it possible to sustain extreme emotion for more than ten minutes. Gradually, fighting my way up the hill against the weather, I calmed down, wiped my tears away with my gloved hand, pulled myself together. In an apparently intolerable situation, there is nearly always something one can do, and long before I reached Boscarva I had decided what it was. I would go back to London.

I left the shopping basket on the kitchen table and went upstairs to my room, took off all my drenched clothes, changed my shoes, washed my hands, carefully re-plaited my hair; thus calmed I went in search of Grenville and found him in his study, sitting by the fire and reading the morning paper.

He lowered this and looked over the top of it as I came in.

"Rebecca."

"Hello. How are you this wild morning?" I sounded determinedly cheerful, like a maddening nurse.

"Full of aches and pains. The wind's a killer even if you never go out in it. Where've you been?"

"Down in Porthkerris. I had to do some shopping for Mollie."

"What time is it?"

"Half past twelve."

"Then let's have a glass of sherry."

"Is that allowed?"

"I don't give a damn if it's allowed or not. You know where the decanter is."

I poured two glasses, carried his over and set it carefully down on the table by his chair. I pulled up a stool and sat facing him. I said, "Grenville, I have to go back to London."

"What?"

"I have to go back to London." The blue eyes narrowed, the great jaw thrust out; I hastily made Stephen Forbes my scapegoat. "I can't stay away for ever. I've already been away from work nearly two weeks, and Stephen Forbes, the man I work for, he's been so good about it, I can't just go on taking advantage of his kindness and generosity. I've just realised that it's Friday already. I must go back to London this weekend. I must be back at work on Monday morning."

"But you've only just come." He was obviously thoroughly disgusted with me.

"I've been here three days. After three days fish and guests stink."

"You're not a guest. You're Lisa's child."

"But I still have commitments. And I like my job and I don't want to stop working." I smiled, trying to divert him. "And now I've found the way to Boscarva, perhaps I can come again, when I've got more time to spare, to spend with you."

He did not reply but sat, looking old and grumpy, staring into the fire.

He said dismally, "I may not be here then."

"Oh, of course you will be."

He sighed, took a slow, shaky mouthful of sherry, set down his glass, and turned to me, apparently resigned.

"When do you want to go?"

I was surprised, but relieved, that he had given in so easily.

"Perhaps tomorrow night. I'll get a sleeper. And then I can have Sunday to get myself settled into my flat."

"You shouldn't be living in a flat in London on your own. You weren't made for living alone. You were made for a man,

153

and a home, and children. If I were twenty years younger and could still paint, that's how I'd show you to the world, in a field or a garden, knee-deep in buttercups and children."

"Perhaps it'll happen one day. And then I shall send for you."

His face was suddenly full of pain. He turned away from me and said, "I wish you'd stay."

I longed to say that I would, but there were a thousand reasons why I couldn't. "I'll come back," I promised.

He made a great and touching effort to pull himself together, clearing his throat, re-settling himself in his chair. "That jade of yours. We'll have to get Pettifer to pack it in a box, then you can take it with you. And the mirror . . . could you manage that on the train, or is it too big? You ought to have a car, then there would be no problems. Have you got a car?"

"No, but it doesn't matter . . ."

"And I suppose that desk hasn't . . ."

"It doesn't matter about the desk!" I interrupted, so loudly and so suddenly that Grenville looked at me in some surprise, as though he had not expected such bad manners.

"I'm sorry," I said quickly. "It's just that it really doesn't matter. I couldn't bear everybody to start quarrelling about it again. Please, for my sake, don't talk about it, don't think about it any more."

He regarded me thoughtfully, a long unblinking stare that made me drop my eyes.

He said, "You think I'm unfair to Eliot?"

"I just think that perhaps you never talk to each other, you never tell each other anything."

"He'd have been different if Roger hadn't been killed. He was a boy who needed a father."

"Couldn't you have done as a father?"

"Could never get near him for Mollie. He was never made to stick to anything. Always chopping and changing jobs and then he started that garage up three years ago."

"That seems to be a success."

"Second-hand cars!" His voice was full of unjustified contempt. "He should have gone into the Navy."

"Suppose he didn't want to go into the Navy?"

"He might have, if his mother hadn't talked him out of it. She wanted to keep him at home, tied to her apron strings."

"Oh, Grenville, I think you're being thoroughly old-fashioned and very unfair."

"Did I ask you for your opinion?" But already he was cheering up. A good argument was, to Grenville, like a shot in the arm.

"I don't care whether you asked for it or not, you've got it."

He laughed then, and reached forward to gently pinch my cheek. He said, "How I wish I could still paint. Do you still want one of my pictures to take back to London with you?"

I was afraid that he had forgotten. "More than anything."

"You can get the key of the studio from Pettifer. Tell him I said you could have it. Go and nose around, see what you can find."

"You won't come with me?"

Again the pain came into his face. "No," he said gruffly, and turned away to take up his sherry. He sat, looking down at the amber wine, turning the glass in his hand. "No, I won't come with you."

At lunch he broke the news to the others. Andrea, livid that I was going back to London while she had to stay in horrible, boring Cornwall, went into a sullen sulk. But the others were gratifyingly dismayed.

"But do you have to go?" That was Mollie.

"Yes, I really must. I've got a job to do and I can't stay away for ever."

"We really love having you here." She could be charming

when she wasn't aggressive and possessive about Eliot, resentful of Grenville and Boscarva. I saw her again as a pretty little cat, but now I was aware of long claws hidden in the soft velvet paws, and I knew that she had no compunction about using them.

"I've loved it too . . ."

Pettifer was more outspoken. After lunch I went out to the kitchen to help him with the dishes, and he minced no words.

"What you want to go away for now, just when you're settling down and the Commander's getting to know you – well, it's beyond me. I didn't think you were that sort of a person . . ."

"I'll come back. I've said I'll come back."

"He's eighty now. He's not going to last for ever. How are you going to feel, coming back and him not here, but six feet under the ground and pushing up the daisies?"

"Oh, Pettifer, *don't*."

"It's all very well saying 'Oh, Pettifer, *don't*.' There's nothing I can do about it."

"I've got a job. I must go back."

"Sounds like selfishness to me."

"That's not fair."

"All these years he's not seen his daughter, and then you turn up and stay three days. What sort of a grandchild are you?"

I didn't reply because there was nothing to say. And I hated feeling guilty and being put in the wrong. We finished the dishes in silence, but when they were done and he was wiping down the draining board with a damp cloth, I tried to make my peace with him.

"I'm sorry. I really am. It's bad enough having to go without you making me feel a brute. And I will come back. I've said I will. Perhaps in the summer . . . he'll still be here in the summer, and the weather will be warm and we can do things together. Perhaps you could take us out in the car . . ."

My voice trailed away. Pettifer hung his cloth neatly over

the edge of the sink. He said, gruffly, "The Commander said you were to have the key of the studio. Don't know what you'll find down there. A lot of dust and spiders, I should think."

"He said I could have a picture. He said I could go and choose one."

He slowly dried his worn, gnarled hands. "I'll have to find the key. It's put away for safe keeping. Didn't want it lying around where anyone could get their hands on it. There's a lot of good stuff down in the studio."

"Any time will do." I could not bear his disapproval. "Oh, Pettifer, don't be angry with me."

He melted then. "Oh, I'm not angry. Perhaps it's me who's being selfish. Perhaps it's me who doesn't want you to go."

I saw him suddenly, not as the ubiquitous Pettifer around whom this household revolved, but as an old man, nearly as old as my grandfather and probably as lonely. A stupid lump came into my throat and for a terrible moment I thought I was going to burst into tears, which would have made it the second time that day, but then Pettifer said, "And don't go choosing one of them nudes, they wouldn't be suitable," and the dangerous moment was behind me and we were smiling, friends again.

That afternoon Mollie lent me her car, and I drove the five miles to the railway junction and there bought myself a ticket back to London and reserved a sleeper for the night train on Saturday. The violence of the wind had dropped a little, but it was still wild and stormy, with trees down and devastation everywhere, smashed greenhouses, broken branches, and fields of early spring bulbs flattened by the gales.

I got home to find Mollie in the garden at Boscarva, bundled up against the weather (even Mollie could not look elegant on such a day) and trying to tie up and rescue some of the more fragile shrubs that grew around the house. When she saw the car, she decided to call it a day, for as I put it away and walked back towards the house I met her coming towards me, stripping off her gloves and tucking a strand of hair into her head-scarf.

"I can't bear it a moment longer," she told me. "I hate wind, it exhausts me. But that darling little daphne was being snapped to ribbons, and all the camellias have been burnt by this wind. It turns them quite brown. Let's go in and have a cup of tea."

While she changed I put the kettle on, and set out cups on a tray. "Where is everybody?" I asked her when she reappeared, miraculously neat once more, down to her pearls and her matching ear-rings.

"Grenville's having a nap and Andrea's up in her room . . ." she sighed. ". . . I must say, she really isn't the easiest of girls. If only she'd do something to amuse herself instead of skulking around in this tiresome manner. I'm afraid it's not doing her any good being down here, I didn't think it would, to be quite honest, but my poor sister was quite desperate." She looked around the comfortable kitchen. "This is cosy. Let's have our tea in here. The drawing-room's so draughty when the wind's from the sea, and we can scarcely draw the curtains at half past four in the afternoon . . ."

She was right, it was cosy in the kitchen. She found a cloth and laid the tea, setting out cakes and biscuits, sugar bowl and silver milk jug. Even for kitchen tea, it appeared, her standards were meticulous. She pulled up two wheel-back chairs, and was in the act of reaching for the teapot when the door opened and Andrea appeared.

"Oh, Andrea, dear, just in time. We're having kitchen tea today. Do you want a cup?"

"I'm sorry, I haven't got time."

This unexpectedly mannerly reply made Mollie look up sharply. "Are you going out?"

"Yes," said Andrea, "I'm going to the cinema."

We both stared at her like fools. For the impossible had happened – Andrea had suddenly decided to take much trouble with her appearance. She had washed her hair and tied it back off her face, found a clean polo-necked tee-shirt, and even, I

was delighted to see, a bra to wear beneath it. Her Celtic cross
hung around her neck on its thread of leather, her black jeans
were neatly pressed, her clumpy shoes polished. Over her arm
was a raincoat and a fringed leather handbag. I had never seen
her look so presentable. And, best of all, the expression on her
face was neither sulky nor malevolent, but . . . demure? Could
one possibly describe Andrea as looking demure?

"I mean," she went on, "if that's all right by you, Auntie
Mollie."

"Well, of course. What are you going to see?"

"*Mary of Scotland*. It's on at the Plaza."

"Are you going by yourself?"

"No, I'm going with Joss. He rang me while you were out
gardening. He's going to give me supper afterwards."

"Oh," said Mollie, faintly. And then, feeling that further
comment was expected of her, ". . . how are you going to get
down there?"

"I'll walk down, and I expect Joss will drive me home . . ."

"Have you got some money?"

"I've got 50p. I'll be all right."

"Well . . ." But Mollie was defeated. "Have a good time."

"I will," she flashed us both a smile. "Goodbye."

The door swung to behind her.

"Goodbye," said Mollie. She looked at me. "Extraordinary,"
she said.

I was concentrating on my cup of tea. "Why so extraordinary?" I said casually.

"Andrea and . . . Joss. I mean he's always been quite polite
to her, but . . . to ask her out . . .?"

"You shouldn't sound so surprised. She's attractive when she
cleans herself up and bothers to smile. Probably she smiles at
Joss all the time."

"You think it's all right, letting her go? I mean I do have
responsibilities . . .?"

"Honestly, I don't see how you could have stopped her

159

going. Anyway she's seventeen, she's not a child. She can surely look after herself by now . . ."

"That's just the trouble," said Mollie ". . . That's always been the trouble with Andrea."

"She'll be all right."

She would not be all right, and I knew this, but I could not disillusion Mollie. Besides, what did it matter? It was no business of mine if Joss chose to spend his evenings making firelit love to an adolescent nymphomaniac. They were two of a kind. They deserved each other. They were welcome to each other.

When we had finished tea, Mollie tied a neat apron around her waist and started preparing dinner. I cleared away the cups and saucers and washed them up. As I was drying the last plate, and putting it away, Pettifer appeared, bearing in his hand a large key which looked as though it might unlock a dungeon.

"I knew I'd put it somewhere safely, found it in the back of a drawer in the Commander's bureau . . ."

"What's that, Pettifer?" Mollie asked.

"The key to the studio, Madam . . ."

"Heavens, who wants that?"

"I do," I said. "Grenville said I could go down and choose a picture to take back to London."

"My dear child, what a task you'll have. The place must be in the most terrible mess, it hasn't seen the light of day for ten years."

"I don't mind." I took the key which weighed heavy as lead in my hand.

"Are you going now? It's getting dark."

"Aren't there any lights?"

"Oh, yes, of course, but it's very cheerless. Wait till tomorrow morning."

But I wanted to go now. "I'll be all right. I'll put on a coat."

"There's a torch on the hall table, you'd better take that as well, the path down the garden is quite steep and slippery."

160

And so, buttoned into my leather coat, and armed with the torch and the key, I set off, letting myself out of the house by the garden door. The wind from the sea was still violent, carrying with it squalls of thin, cold rain, and I had to struggle to get the door closed behind me. The dismal afternoon was turning early to darkness, but still there was enough light to pick my way cautiously down the sloping garden, and I did not turn on the torch until I reached the studio when I needed its beam to find the keyhole.

I fitted the key and it turned reluctantly, needing oil; the door swung inwards, creakingly. There was a damp and musty smell, a suggestion of cobwebs and mould, and I quickly put my hand inside and felt for the light switch. At once a single naked bulb, high in the roof, sprang to a chill and insubstantial life, and I was surrounded by leaping shadows, for the draught caused the long flex to swing to and fro like the pendulum of a clock.

I went in and shut the door behind me and the shadows, slowly, were stilled. Around me, dust-covered shapes loomed in the half-light, but across the room was a standard lamp, with a crooked, broken shade. I picked my way over to this, found the switch and turned that on, and at once everything looked a little less forlorn.

I saw that the studio had been designed on two levels with a sleeping gallery at the south end, reached by a stair like a ship's ladder.

I went halfway up the ladder and saw the divan and the striped blanket. Over the bed was a window tightly shuttered, and a pillow had shed feathers, perhaps the work of some marauding mouse. The remains of a small dead bird lay, twig-like and dehydrated, in the corner of the floor. I shuddered slightly at the desolation, and descended again to the studio.

The wind banged and rattled at the huge north window. A complicated contraption of strings and pulleys worked the long curtains, and I struggled with these for a moment, but was finally defeated by their mechanics and left the curtains closed.

In the middle of the floor was a model's throne, with a sheeted shape in the middle which proved to be an ornate gilt chair. The mice had been at the seat of this, too – scraps of red velvet and horsehair were scattered about, along with mouse-droppings and a great deal of dust.

Under another sheet I found Grenville's workbench; his brushes, his trays of paint-tubes, palettes, knives, bottles of linseed oil, piles of unused canvases, grimy with age. There was also a little collection of *objets trouvés*, small things which, perhaps, had taken his fancy. A sea-polished stone, half a dozen shells, a bunch of gulls' feathers, probably collected for the practical purpose of cleaning his pipe. There were curling, faded snapshots, of nobody I recognised, a blue and white Chinese ginger jar filled with pencils, some bottles of fossilised Indian ink, a scrap of sealing wax.

It was like prying, as though I were reading another person's diary. I put back the sheet and went on to the true purpose of my visit, which was the stack of unframed canvases standing around the wall, each with its face turned inwards. These had been dust-covered too, but the sheets had slipped, draping themselves about the floor, and as I dislodged the first pile my fingers touched cobwebs, and a huge, disgusting spider went scuttling across the floor and lost itself in the shadows.

It was a slow business. Five or six at a time, I lifted out the pictures, dusted them off, leaned them in rows against the model's throne, shifting the rickety standard lamp so that the light should shine on them. Some were dated, but they were stacked away in no sort of chronological order, and for the most part I could tell neither when nor where they had been painted. I only knew that they encompassed the whole of Grenville's professional life and all his interests.

There were landscapes, seascapes – the ocean in all its

162

moods, charming interiors, some sketches of Paris, some that looked like Italy. There were boats and fishermen, street scenes of Porthkerris, a number of rough charcoal sketches of two children, whom I knew were Roger and Lisa. There were no portraits.

I began to make my selection, setting aside the pictures which I found particularly engaging. By the time I had reached the final pile, there were half a dozen of them propped against the seat of a sagging couch, and I was dirty and cold, with grimy hands and cobwebs clinging to my clothes. With the good feeling of a task nearly completed I went to sort out the last pile of canvases. There were three pen and ink drawings, and a view of a harbour with yachts at anchor. And then . . .

It was the last canvas and the biggest of all. It needed two hands and all my efforts to lift it out of its dark corner and turn it around to face the light. I held it upright with one hand and stood back, and the face of the girl leapt out to meet me, the dark, tip-tilted eyes smiling with a vitality undimmed by the dust of the years that passed. I saw the dark hair and the bumpy cheek-bones and the sensuous mouth, not smiling, but seeming to tremble on the brink of laughter. And she wore the same fragile white dress, the dress that she had worn for the portrait that hung over the fireplace in the drawing-room at Boscarva.

Sophia.

Ever since my mother had mentioned her name I had been fascinated by her. The frustrations of never knowing what she looked like had only increased my obsession. But now that I had found her and we were face to face at last, I felt like Pandora. I had opened the box and the secrets were out, and there was no way in the world of packing them back and locking the lid once more.

I knew that face. I had talked to it, argued with it; seen it scowl and smile; seen the dark eyes narrowed in anger and glint with amusement.

It was Joss Gardner.

# Chapter Eleven

All at once I was bitterly cold. It was dark now and the studio was icy, but as well I could feel the blood drain from my face like water out of a basin; I could hear the laboured thumping of my own heart, and I started, violently, to shiver. My first instinct was to put the portrait back where I had found it, pile some other canvases on top of it and hide it, like a criminal trying to conceal a body, or something worse.

But in the end I reached for a chair and arranged it carefully, so that it supported Sophia's portrait like an easel, and then I backed away on shaking legs and carefully lowered myself on to the sagging seat of the aged sofa.

Sophia and Joss.

Sophia the enchanting, and the baffling Joss, who I had finally learned was not to be trusted.

*She went to London, she got married, she had a baby, I think*, Pettifer had told me. Then in 1942 she was killed in the Blitz.

But he had not mentioned Joss. And yet Joss and Sophia were so obviously, inextricably linked.

And I thought of my desk, my mother's desk that she meant me to have, hidden away at the back of Joss's workshop.

And I heard Mollie's voice. *I don't know why Grenville's so taken with Joss. It's frightening. It's as though Joss were able to exert some hold over him.*

Sophia and Joss.

It was dark now. I had no watch and I had lost all track of time. The wind drowned all other sound, so that I did not hear Eliot coming down the garden from the house, picking his way through the darkness because I had taken the torch. I did not hear anything until the door burst open, as though on a gust of wind, causing the light to start up its demented swinging, and frightening me nearly out of my wits. The next instant Rufus bounded in and flung himself up on the sofa beside me, and I realised that I had company.

My cousin Eliot stood in the open doorway framed in darkness. He wore a suede jacket and a pale blue polo-necked sweater and he had slung a raincoat around his shoulders like a cloak. The cruel light drained all the colour from his thin face, and turned his deep-set eyes into two black holes.

"My mother told me you were down here. I came to . . ."

He stopped, and I knew that he had seen the portrait. I couldn't move, I was too petrified with cold, and anyway, now it was too late to do anything about it.

He came into the studio and closed the door. The leaping shadows, once more, were slowly stilled.

We neither of us said anything. I held Rufus's head, instinctively seeking comfort in his soft, warm fur, and watched while Eliot shrugged off his raincoat, dropped it across a chair, and came slowly to sit beside me. His eyes never left the portrait.

At last he spoke. "Good God," he said.

I said nothing.

"Where did you find that?"

"In a corner . . ." My voice came out as a croak. I cleared my throat and tried again. "In a corner, behind a lot of other canvases."

"It's Sophia."

"Yes."

"It's Joss Gardner."

There was no denying it. "Yes."

"Sophia's grandson, do you suppose?"

165

"Yes. I think he must be."

"Well, I'll be damned." He leaned back, and crossed his long, elegant legs, suddenly relaxed, like a knowledgeable art critic at a private view.

His obvious satisfaction puzzled me, and I did not want him to think that I shared it.

I said, "I wasn't looking for it. I've been wanting to know what Sophia looked like, but I had no idea there was a portrait of her down here. I just came to look for a picture because Grenville said I could have one to take back to London."

"I know. My mother told me."

"Eliot, we mustn't say anything."

He ignored this. "You know, there was always something funny about Joss, something unexplained. The way he turned up in Porthkerris, out of the blue. And the way Grenville knew that he was there; the way he gave him a job, and the run of Boscarva. I never trusted Joss farther than I could see him. And the desk disappearing – the desk that should have come to you. It was all fishy beyond words."

I knew that I should tell Eliot then that I had found the desk. I opened my mouth with the intention of doing just this thing, and closed it again because somehow the words would not be spoken. Besides, Eliot was still talking and had not noticed my incipient interruption.

"My mother swore he had some sort of a hold over Grenville."

"You make it sound like blackmail."

"Perhaps, in a modified form, it was. You know, 'Here I am, Sophia's grandson, what are you going to do for me?' And Pettifer must have known as well. Pettifer and Grenville have no secrets from each other."

"Eliot, we mustn't say that we found the picture."

He turned his head to look at me.

"You sound anxious, Rebecca. On Joss Gardner's behalf?"

"No. On Grenville's."

166

"But you like Joss."

"No."

He pretended to be amazed. "But everybody likes Joss! Everybody, it seems, has fallen under his spell of boyish charm. Grenville and Pettifer; Andrea is besotted by him, she never leaves him alone, but I think there may be something just a little physical in that attraction. I thought that you were bound to have joined the club." He frowned. "You *did* like Joss."

"Not now, Eliot."

He began to be intrigued. He shifted his position slightly, so that we half-faced each other on the sofa, his arm along its carved back, behind my shoulder.

"What happened?" he asked.

What had happened? Nothing. But I had never felt quite easy about Joss, and all the coincidences that seemed to tie our lives together. And he had stolen my mother's desk. And he was now, at this moment carrying on his clandestine affair with the unsavoury Andrea. At the very idea of this, my imagination was apt to turn and run.

Eliot was waiting for my reply. But I only shrugged and shook my head hopelessly and said, "I changed my mind."

"Could yesterday have had anything to do with it?"

"Yesterday?" I thought of sitting with Eliot on the sunbaked terrace of the little pub; of the two boys sailing their dinghy down the blue waters of the creek; and finally Eliot's arms, encircling and holding me, the feel of his kisses, and the sensation of losing control, of sliding over a cliff.

I shivered again. My hands, cold and grimy, lay in my lap. Eliot put his own over them and said, in some surprise, "You're freezing."

"I know, I've been here for hours."

"My mother told me you want to go back to London." We seemed to have dropped the subject of Joss and I was thankful for this.

"Yes, I have to go."

"When?"

"Tomorrow night."

"You never told me."

"I didn't decide until this morning."

"You seem to have changed your mind and made a lot of decisions all in one day."

"I hadn't realised how the time had flown. I've been away from work for nearly two weeks."

"Yesterday I asked you to stay."

"I have to go."

"What would make you stay?"

"Nothing. I mean . . . I can't . . ." I was stammering like a fool, but I was too cold, too dirty and too tired for such a conversation. Later, perhaps, I would be able to cope . . .

"Would you stay if I asked you to marry me?"

My head shot up. Something like horror must have shown on my face, for he put back his head and laughed.

"Don't look so shocked. There's nothing shocking about getting married."

"But we're cousins."

"That doesn't matter."

"But we don't . . . I mean . . . You don't love me."

It was an appalling thing to say, but Eliot took it in his stride.

"Rebecca, you are stammering and stuttering like a shy schoolgirl. Perhaps I do love you. Perhaps I would have loved you for a long time before asking you to marry me, but you've precipitated this situation by suddenly announcing out of the blue that you're going to go back to London. So if I'm going to say it at all, I'd better say it now. I want you to marry me. I think it would work very well."

Despite myself, I was touched. No one had ever asked me to marry them before, and I found it flattering. But even as I listened to Eliot with one part of my mind, the other part ran round in circles like a squirrel in a cage.

Because there was still Boscarva, and the land that Eliot needed to sell to Ernest Padlow.

*You are not my only grandchild.*

". . . it seems ridiculous to say goodbye and walk out of each other's lives when we've only just met each other, and there are so many good things going for us."

I said quietly, "Like Boscarva."

His smile froze slightly around the edges. He raised an eyebrow. "Boscarva?"

"Let's be honest and truthful, Eliot. For some reason you need Boscarva. And you think that Grenville might leave it to me."

He took a deep breath as though to deny this, hesitated, and then let it all out in a long sigh. His smile was rueful. He ran a hand over the top of his head.

"How cool you are. The Ice Princess all of a sudden."

"You need Boscarva so that you can sell the farm to Ernest Padlow to build his houses."

He said, carefully, "Yes." I waited. "I needed money to build the garage. Grenville wasn't interested so I approached Padlow. He agreed and the security was the Boscarva farm. Gentleman's agreement."

"But it wasn't yours."

"I was sure it would be. There was no reason why it shouldn't be. And Grenville was old and ill. The end could have come any day." He spread his hands. "Who would have imagined that three years later he'd still be with us?"

"You sound as though you want him dead."

"Old age is a terrible thing. Lonely and sad. He's had a good life. What is there for him to cling on for?"

I knew that I could not agree with Eliot. Old age, in Grenville's case, meant dignity and purpose. I had only just got to know him, but already I loved him and he was part of me; I could not bear to think of him dying.

I said, trying to stay practical, "Isn't there some other way you could pay off Mr Padlow?"

"I could sell the garage. The way things are going I might have to do that anyway."

"I thought you were doing so well."

"That's what everybody's meant to think."

"But if you sold the garage, what would you do then?"

"What do you suggest I should do?" He sounded amused as though I were a child with whims to be indulged. I said, "How about Mr Kemback, and the car museum in Birmingham?"

"What an uncomfortably good memory you've got."

"Would working for Mr Kemback be such a bad thing?"

"And leave Cornwall?"

"I think that's what you should do. Make a new start. Get away from Boscarva and . . ." I stopped, and then thought, *in for a penny, in for a pound*, ". . . and your mother." I finished in a rush.

"My mother?" Still that amusement, as though I were a beguiling fool.

"You know what I mean, Eliot."

There was a long pause. Then, "I think," said Eliot, "you have been talking to Grenville."

"I'm sorry."

"One thing's for certain, either Joss or I will have to go. As they say in Westerns, 'This town ain't big enough for the two of us.' But I'd rather Joss went."

"Joss is unimportant. He's not worth taking a stand over."

"If I sold the garage and went to work in Birmingham, would you come with me?"

"Oh, Eliot . . ."

I turned away from him and came face to face once more with Sophia's portrait. Her eyes met mine and it was as though Joss sat there, listening to every word we were saying, laughing at us. Then Eliot put his hand beneath my chin and jerked my head around so that once more I was forced to meet his eye.

"Listen to what I'm saying!"

"I am listening."

"We don't have to be in love with each other. You know that, don't you?"

"I always imagined it was important."

"It doesn't happen to everyone. Perhaps it won't ever happen to you."

It was a chill prospect. "Perhaps not."

"In that case," his voice was very gentle and reasonable, "would a compromise be such a bad thing? Wouldn't a compromise be better than a nine to five job for the rest of your life and an empty flat in London?"

He had touched me on the raw. I had been alone for too long, and the prospect of staying alone for the rest of my life was frightening. Grenville had said, *You were made for a man and a home and children*. And now they were all there, waiting for me. I had only to reach out my hand, to accept what Eliot was offering me.

I said his name, and he put his arms around me, and drew me very close, kissing my eyes, my cheeks, my mouth. Sophia watched us and I did not care. I told myself that she was dead, and Joss I had already put out of my life. Why should I care what either of them thought of me?

Eliot said at last, "We must go." He held me away from him. "You must have a bath and wash all those dirty marks off your face, and I must get the ice out of the fridge, and be all ready and dutiful to pour drinks for Grenville and my mother."

"Yes." I drew away from his arms, and pushed a lock of hair out of my face. I felt deathly tired. "What time is it?"

He looked at his watch, the strap that I had given him still shining and new. "Nearly half past seven. We could stay here all night, but unfortunately life has to go on."

I got wearily to my feet. Without looking at the portrait I took it up and put it back in its hidden, dusty corner, along with the cobwebs and the spiders, its face to the wall. Then I picked up other pictures, at random, and piled them around and against it. Everything, I told myself, was just as it had been before. We tidied up in a cursory fashion and covered the canvases with the fallen dust-sheet. Eliot switched off the standard lamp, and I picked up the torch. We went out of the studio, turning off the light and closing and locking the door. Eliot took the torch from me, and together, following the bobbing circle of light, we went up the garden, stumbling a little over hidden verges and tussocks of grass, mounting the shining wet steps of the terrace. Above us the house loomed, lighted rooms glowing behind drawn curtains, and all around us was the wind and the silhouettes of leafless, tormented trees.

"I've never known a storm to last so long," said Eliot, as he opened the side door and we went inside. The hall felt warm and safe, and there was the good smell of the chicken casserole that we were to have for dinner.

We parted, Eliot heading for the kitchen, and I upstairs to shed my filthy clothes, draw a bath and wallow in warm, scented steam. Relaxed at last I thought about nothing. I was too tired to think. I would fall asleep, I decided, and probably drown. For some reason the idea of this did not alarm me.

But I did not fall asleep, because as I lay there, I heard, above the noise of the wind, the sound of an approaching car. The bathroom faced over the back of the house, the drive and the front door. I had not bothered to draw the curtains and the headlights of the car flashed for a second against the dark glass. A door banged, there were voices. Thus disturbed, I climbed out of the bath, dried myself and started across the passage to my room, but stopped dead

172

when I heard the raised voices carrying up the stairwell from the hall.

". . . found her halfway up the hill . . ." a man's voice, unrecognised.

And then Mollie, ". . . but my dear child . . ." This was interrupted by a wild cacophony of sobbing. I heard Eliot say, "For heaven's sake, girl . . ." And then Mollie again. "Come in by the fire . . . come along now, you're all right. You're safe now . . ."

I went into my room, pulled on my clothes, buttoned the neck of the brown caftan, brushed and plaited my hair, all in the space of moments. I painted on a layer of lipstick – there was no time for more – thrust my bare feet into sandals and ran downstairs, screwing on my ear-rings as I did so.

As I reached the bottom of the stairs Pettifer appeared through the kitchen door with a face like a thundercloud and bearing in his hand a glass of brandy. It was indicative of the gravity of the situation that he had omitted to put it on a silver salver.

"Pettifer, what's happened?"

"I don't know what's happened, exactly, but it sounds as though that girl's having hysterics."

"I heard a car coming. Who brought her home?"

"Morris Tatcombe. Says he was driving home from Porthkerris when he found her on the road."

I was horrified. "You mean *lying* on the road? Had she been hit by a car, or something?"

"I don't know. Probably just had a tumble."

At the far end of the hall the drawing-room door burst open and Mollie came towards us, half running.

"Oh, Pettifer, don't stand talking, hurry with the brandy." She saw me standing, quite at a loss. "Oh, my dear Rebecca, what a terrible thing, quite terrible. I'm going to ring the doctor." She was at the telephone, thumbing through the book, unable to see because she had somewhere mislaid her

glasses. "Look it up for me, there's a dear. It's Doctor Trevaskis
. . . we ought to have it written down somewhere, but I can't
find . . ."

Pettifer had gone. I took the telephone book and started to
look for the number. "What's happened to Andrea?" I asked.

"It's the most ghastly story. I can hardly believe it's true.
What a mercy Morris found her. She could have been there all
night. She could have died . . ."

"Here it is. Lionel Trevaskis. Porthkerris 873."

She put a hand to her cheek. "Oh, of course, I should know
it off by heart." She lifted the receiver and dialled. While she
waited she spoke to me, swiftly. "Go and sit by her, the men
are so useless, they never know what to do."

Mystified and oddly reluctant to know the details of
Andrea's unhappy experience, I nevertheless did as she asked
me. I found the drawing-room in something approaching a
shambles. Grenville, apparently nonplussed, stood in front of
the fireplace with his hands behind his back and said nothing.
The rest of them were grouped around the sofa; Eliot had
given Morris a drink, and they watched while Pettifer, with
commendable patience, was trying to trickle some brandy
down Andrea's throat.

And Andrea . . . despite myself I was shocked and frightened
by her appearance. The neat sweater and the pressed jeans in
which she had set out so gaily were soaking wet and smeared
with mud. Through the tear in the jeans I could see her knee,
cut and bleeding, vulnerably childlike. She had lost, it seemed,
a shoe. Her hair clung, like seaweed, to her skull, her face was
blotched with crying, and when I said her name she turned her
head to look at me from pathetic, streaming eyes; I saw with
horror the great bruise on her temple, as though she had been
savagely struck. The Celtic cross on its leather thong was also
lost; torn off, perhaps, in some unthinkable struggle.

"Andrea!"

She gave a great wail and heaved herself over to press her

face into the back of the sofa, spilling the brandy as she did so, and knocking the tumbler clean out of Pettifer's hand.

"I don't want to talk about it. I don't want to talk about it . . .!"

"But you must!"

Pettifer, exasperated, collected the glass and went from the room. I told myself that he had never liked the girl. I took his place beside her, sitting on the edge of the sofa, trying to turn her shoulders towards me.

"Did somebody do this to you?"

Andrea flung herself back at me, her body convulsed. "Yes!" She screamed at my face as though I were deaf. "Joss!" And with that she dissolved once more in a welter of sobs.

I looked up at Grenville and was subjected to a stony, unblinking glare. His features might have been carved from wood. I decided there was no help to be expected from that quarter. I turned to Morris Tatcombe.

"Where did you find her?"

He shifted, one foot to another. I saw that he was dressed as though for a night on the town. A leather jacket, decorated with a rash of embroidered emblems, and spotted with rain, skin-tight jeans and boots with high heels. Even with high heels the top of his head scarcely reached to Eliot's shoulder, and his long hair hung damp and lank.

He tossed this back, a gesture both aggressive and self-conscious.

"Half-way up Porthkerris Hill. You know, where the road narrows and there isn't a pavement. She was half-way up the bank, half in the ditch. Lucky I saw her, really. Thought she'd been hit by a car, but it wasn't that. Seems she had this row with Joss Gardner."

I said, "He asked her to go to the cinema with him."

"I don't know how it all started," said Morris.

"But this, it seems . . ." said Eliot gravely ". . . is how it ends."

"But . . ." There had to be some other explanation. I was about to tell them this when Andrea let out another wail, like some aged sibyl keening at a wake, and I lost my temper.

"Oh, for goodness sake, girl, shut up!" I took her by her shoulders and gave her a little shake so that her head bobbed on the silk cushion like a badly stuffed rag-doll. "Stop making that dementing noise and tell us what happened."

Words began to spill out of her mouth, made ugly with weeping. (I thought briskly, *at least she isn't missing any teeth*, and hated myself for my own hard heart.)

"I . . . we . . . went to the cinema . . . and wh . . . when we came out, we went to a pub, and . . ."

"Which pub?"

"I don't know . . ."

"You must know which pub . . ."

My voice rose in impatience. Behind me, Mollie, whom I had not heard come into the room, said, "Oh, don't shout at her. Don't be unkind."

I made an effort and tried again, more gently.

"Can't you remember where you went?"

"No. It was d . . . dark . . . and I . . . couldn't see. And then . . . and then . . ."

I held her firmly, trying to calm her. "Yes. And then?"

"And Joss had a lot of whisky to drink. And he wouldn't bring me home. He wanted me to g . . . go back to his flat with him . . . and . . ."

Her mouth went square, her features dissolved into uncontrollable weeping. I let her go and stood up, backing away from her. At once Mollie took my place.

"There," she said. "There, there." She was more gentle than I, her voice as soothing as a mother's. "Now there's nothing more to worry about. The doctor's on his way, and Pettifer's putting a nice hot bottle in your bed. You don't need to tell us any more. You don't need to talk about it any more."

But, perhaps calmed by Mollie's manner, Andrea seemed

anxious to make a clean breast of it, and, through interminable sobs and gasps, we were to hear the rest of the story.

"And I didn't want to go. I . . . I wanted to come home. And I . . . left him. And he came after me. And . . . I tried to run, and I tripped on the p . . . pavement, and my shoe . . . c . . . came off. And then he c . . . caught me, and he be . . . began shouting at me . . . and I screamed and he *hit* me . . ."

I looked at the faces around me, and the same horror and consternation, in varying degrees, was mirrored upon them. Only Grenville appeared coldly, deeply angry, but still he did not move, he did not say a word.

"It's all right," Mollie said again, her voice shaking only a little. "Now, everything's all right. Come along, upstairs."

Somehow Andrea, wilted and bedraggled, was eased off the sofa, but her legs would not hold her weight, and she started to collapse. It was Morris who, standing nearest to her, stepped forward and caught her before she fell, swinging her up, with surprising strength, into his puny arms.

"There," said Mollie, "Morris will carry you upstairs. You'll be all right . . ." She moved towards the door. "If you'll come this way, Morris."

"OK," said Morris, who did not appear to have much option in the matter.

I watched Andrea's face. As Morris moved, her eyes opened and looked straight into mine, and our glances clashed and held. And I knew that she was lying. And she knew that I knew she was lying.

Leaning her head against Morris's chest, she began to cry again. Swiftly, she was borne from the room.

We listened as Morris's burdened footsteps went down the hall, started up the staircase. Then Eliot said, with masterly understatement, "An unsavoury business." He glanced at Grenville. "Shall I ring the police now or later?"

Grenville spoke at last. "Who said anything about ringing the police?"

"You surely don't intend to let him get away with it?"
I said. "She was lying."

Both men looked at me in some surprise. Grenville's eyes narrowed and he was at his most formidable. Eliot frowned. "What did you say?"

"Some of her story may be true. Most of it probably is. But still, she was lying."

"How was she lying?"

"Because as you said yourself, she was besotted with Joss. She wouldn't leave him alone. She told me that she'd been often to his flat, and she must have been, because she described it to me and every detail was right. I don't know what happened this evening. But I do know that if Joss wanted her to go back with him, she'd have gone like a shot. No arguments."

"Then how," asked Eliot smoothly, "do you account for the bruise on her face?"

"I don't know. I said I don't know about the rest of her story. But that bit, for sure, she made up."

Grenville moved. He had been standing for a long time. Slowly, he went to his chair and lowered himself carefully into it.

"We can find out what really happened," he said at last.

"How?" Eliot's question came out like the shot of a gun.

Grenville swung his head around and fixed his gaze on Eliot. "We can ask Joss."

Eliot let out a sound, which in old-fashioned novels would have been written as "Pshaw."

"We shall ask him. And we will be given the truth."

"He doesn't know what the truth means."

"You have no justification for making such a statement."

Eliot lost his temper. "Oh, for God's sake, does the truth have to be thrown in your face before you recognise it?"

"Don't raise your voice to me."

Eliot was silent, staring in disbelief and disgust at the old man. When at last he spoke, it was in scarcely more than a

178

whisper. "I've had enough of Joss Gardner. I've never trusted him nor liked him. I believe he's a phoney, a thief and a liar, and I know that I'm right. And one day you too will know that I'm right. This is your house. I accept that. But what I will not accept is his right to take it over, and us with it, just because he happens to be . . ."

I had to stop him. "Eliot!" He turned to look at me. It was as though he had forgotten I was there. "Eliot, please. Don't say any more."

He looked down at his glass, finished the drink in a single mouthful. "All right," he said at last. "For the moment, I won't say any more."

And he went to pour himself another whisky. As he did this, with Grenville and I watching him in silence, Morris Tatcombe came back into the room.

"I'll be off then," he said to the back of Eliot's head.

Eliot turned and saw him. "Is she all right?"

"Well, she's upstairs. Your mother's with her."

"Have another drink before you go."

"No, I'd better be off."

"We really can't thank you enough. What would have happened if you hadn't seen her . . ." He stopped, the unfinished sentence conjuring up visions of Andrea dying of exposure, exhaustion, loss of blood.

"Just lucky I did." He backed away, obviously anxious to be off, but not quite sure how to get there. Eliot put the stopper into the decanter, left his freshly filled glass on the table and came to his rescue.

"I'll see you to the door."

Morris ducked his head in the general direction of Grenville and myself.

"Night, all."

But Grenville had hauled himself to his feet with massive dignity. "You've handled things very sensibly, Mr Tatcombe. We're grateful to you. And we would be grateful, too, if you would keep the girl's version of what happened to yourself. At least until it has been authenticated."

Morris looked sceptical. "These things get around."

"But not, I am sure, through you."

Morris shrugged. "It's your affair."

"Exactly. Our affair. Good night, Mr Tatcombe."

Eliot led him away.

Grenville laboriously settled himself once more in his chair. He passed a hand over his eyes, and it occurred to me that such scenes could not be good for him.

"Are you all right?"

"Yes. I'm all right."

I wished that I could confide in him, tell him that I knew about Sophia, and Joss being her grandson. But I knew that if there were any telling to be done, it had to come from him.

"Would you like a drink?"

"No."

So I left him alone, busying myself in tidying the cushions on the flattened sofa.

It was some time before Eliot reappeared, but when he did he seemed quite cheerful again, the sudden row which had flared between him and Grenville now quite forgotten. He went to pick up his drink. "Good health," he said, raising his glass to his grandfather.

"I suppose we're in debt to that young man," said Grenville. "I hope one day we'll be able to settle it."

"I shouldn't worry too much about Morris," Eliot replied lightly. "I should think he's quite capable of settling it for himself. And Pettifer has asked me to tell you both that dinner is ready."

We ate alone, the three of us. Mollie stayed with Andrea, and in the middle of dinner the doctor arrived and was taken upstairs by Pettifer. Later, we heard him talking to Mollie in the hall, then she showed him out and came into the dining-room to tell us what he had said.

"Shock, of course. He's given her a sedative, and she has to stay in bed for a day or two."

Eliot had gone to pull out a chair for her, and she sank into this looking exhausted and shaken. "Imagine such a thing happening. How I'm going to tell her mother, I can't think."

"Don't think about it," said Eliot, "till tomorrow."

"But it was such an appalling story. She's only a child. She's only seventeen. What could Joss have been thinking of? He must have gone out of his mind."

"He was probably drunk," said Eliot.

"Yes, perhaps he was. Drunk and violent."

Neither Grenville nor I said anything. It was as though we had entered into some sort of an unspoken conspiracy, but this did not mean that I had forgiven Joss, nor condoned anything that he had done. Later, probably, when he had been interrogated by Grenville, the whole truth would come out. By then I would probably be back in London.

And if I was still here . . . Slowly, I ate a little bunch of grapes. This could be my last dinner at Boscarva, but I truly did not know whether I wanted it to be or not. I had reached a crossroads, and had no idea which was the way I should take. But soon I was going to have to make up my mind.

A compromise, Eliot had said, and it had sounded tepid. But after the histrionics of this evening, the very words had a solid ring to them, sensible and matter-of-fact, with their feet planted squarely on the ground.

*You were made for a man and a home and children.*

I reached for my wineglass and, glancing up, saw that Eliot watched me across the polished table. He smiled, as though we were conspirators. The expression on his face was both confident and triumphant. Perhaps, while I was thinking that I would probably end up by marrying him, he already knew that I would.

We were back in the drawing-room, sitting around the fire and finishing our coffee, when the telephone started to ring. I thought that Eliot would go to answer it, but he was deep in a chair with the paper and a drink, and managed to linger so long that it was Pettifer who finally took the call. We heard the kitchen door open and his old feet go so slowly across the hall. The ringing stopped. For some reason I glanced up at the clock on the mantelpiece. It was nearly a quarter to ten.

We waited. Presently the door opened and Pettifer's head came around the edge of it, his spectacles glinting in the lamplight.

"Who is it, Pettifer?" asked Mollie.

"It's for Rebecca," said Pettifer.

I was surprised. "For me?"

Eliot said, "Who's ringing you at this hour of the day?"

"I've no idea."

I got up and went out of the room. Perhaps it was Maggie, wanting to tell me something about the flat. Perhaps it was Stephen Forbes, wondering when I was going to return to work. I felt guilty, because I should have been in touch with him, letting him know what I was doing and when I planned to go back to London.

I sat on the hall chest and picked up the receiver.

"Hello?"

A small, mouse-like voice began speaking, sounding very far away.

"Oh, Miss Bayliss, we were passing, and he was lying there . . . my husband said . . . so we got him up the stairs and into the flat . . . don't know what happened. Covered in blood and he could hardly talk. Wanted to call the doctor . . . but he wouldn't let us . . . frightened leaving him there on his own . . . there ought to be somebody there . . . said he'd be all right . . ."

I must have been exceptionally slow and stupid, but it took me a little time to realise that this was Mrs Kernow, calling me from the phone box at the end of Fish Lane, to tell me that something had happened to Joss.

# Chapter Twelve

I was amazed and gratified to find myself in a state of almost total calm. It was as though I had already been prepared for this crisis, been given my orders and told what to do. There were no doubts and so no indecision. I must go to Joss. It was as simple as that.

I went up to my bedroom and got my coat, put it on, did up the buttons, came downstairs again. The key of Mollie's car lay where I had left it, on the brass tray in the middle of the table in the hall.

I picked it up, and as I did so the drawing-room door opened and Eliot came up the passage towards me. It never occurred to me that he would try to stop me going. It never occurred to me that anyone or anything could stop me going.

He saw me, bundled into my old leather coat. "Where are you off to?"

"Out."

"Who was that on the telephone?"

"Mrs Kernow."

"What does she want?"

"Joss has been hurt. She and Mr Kernow were walking home along the harbour road, they'd been visiting her sister. They found him."

"So?" His voice was cold and very quiet. I expected to be intimidated, but I was not.

"I'm going to borrow your mother's car. I'm going to him."

183

His thin face hardened, the skin drawn tight over the jutting bones.

"Have you gone out of your mind?"

"I don't think so."

He said nothing. I slipped the key into my pocket and made for the door, but Eliot was faster than I, and in two strides was in front of me, standing with his back to the door and with his hand on the latch.

"You're not going," he said pleasantly. "You don't really think I'd let you go?"

"He's been hurt, Eliot."

"So what? You saw what he did to Andrea. He's rotten, Rebecca. You know he's rotten. His grandmother was an Irish whore, God knows who his father was, and he's a womanising bastard."

The ugly words, which were meant to shock me, slid off my back like water from a duck. Eliot saw this and my unconcern infuriated him.

"Why do you want to go to him? What good could you do? He won't thank you for interfering, if it's thanks you're looking for. Leave him alone, he has no part of your life, he's none of your concern."

I stood watching him, hearing him, without making sense of anything he said. But I knew, all at once, that it was over, the uncertainty and the indecision, and I felt light with relief, as though a great weight had been lifted from my shoulders. I still stood at the crossroads. My life was still a confusion. But one thing had made itself abundantly clear. I could never marry Eliot.

A compromise, he had said. But, for me, it would have been a poor bargain. All right, he was weak, and probably not the most successful of businessmen. I had recognised these flaws in his character and had been prepared to accept them. But the welcome he had shown me, the hospitality, and the charm which he could turn on and off like a tap, had blinded me to his vindictiveness and the frightening strength of his jealousy.

I said, "Let me go, Eliot."

"Supposing I say that I won't let you go? Supposing I keep you here?" He put his hands on either side of my head, pressing so tightly that it felt as though my skull would crack open, like a nut. "Supposing, now, that I said I loved you?"

I was sickened by him. "You don't love anyone. Only Eliot Bayliss. There's no room for anyone else in your life."

"I thought we decided that it was you who didn't know how to love."

His grip tightened. My head began to pound and I closed my eyes, enduring the pain.

"When I do . . ." I told him through clenched teeth ". . . it won't be you."

"All right then, go . . ." He let me loose so suddenly that I nearly lost my balance. Savagely he turned the handle and flung the door open, and instantly the wind poured in, like some monstrous creature that had been waiting all evening to invade the house. Outside was the dark and the rain. Without another word, not stopping to look at Eliot, I ran past him and out into it, as though to some sanctuary.

I had still to get to the garage, to struggle with doors in the darkness, to find Mollie's little car. I was convinced that Eliot was just behind me, as frightening as an imagined bogey man, waiting to jump, to catch me, to stop me from getting away. I slammed the car door shut, and my hand shook so much I could scarcely get the ignition key fitted. The first time I turned it, the engine did not start. I heard myself whimpering as I pulled out the choke and tried again. This time the engine caught. I put the car into gear and shot forward, through the darkness and the rain, up the puddled driveway with a great spattering of gravel, and so at last out and on to the road.

Driving, I regained some of my previous calm. I had eluded Eliot, I was going to Joss. I must drive with care and good sense, not allow myself to panic, not risk a skid or a possible collision. I slowed down to a cautious thirty miles per hour. I deliberately loosened my death-like clutch on the driving wheel. The road ran downhill, black and wet with rain. The lights of Porthkerris came up towards me. I was going to Joss.

Now, the tide was at full ebb. As I came out on to the harbour road, I saw the lights reflected in wet sand, the boats drawn up out of the reach of the storm. Overhead tattered scraps of cloud still poured across the sky. There were people about, but not very many.

The shop was in darkness. Only a single light glowed from the top window. I parked the car by the pavement and got out and went to the door and it opened. I smelt the new wood, my feet brushed through the shavings which still lay about the place. From the light of the street lamp outside I could see the staircase. I went up it, cautiously, to the first floor.

I called up, "Joss!"

There was no reply. I went on, up into the soft light. There was no fire and it was very cold. A squall of rain swept the roof above me.

"Joss."

He was lying on his bed, roughly covered by a blanket. His forearm lay across his eyes, as though to shut out some unbearable light. When I spoke he lowered this, and raised his head slightly to see who it was. Then he dropped back on to the pillow.

"Good God," I heard him say. "Rebecca."

I went to his side. "Yes, it's me."

"I thought I heard your voice. I thought I was dreaming."

"I called up, but you didn't reply."

His face was in a terrible mess, the left side bruised and swollen, the eye half-closed. Blood had trickled and dried from a cut in his lip, and there did not seem to be any skin on the knuckles of his right hand.

"What are you doing here?" He spoke muzzily, perhaps because of the lip.

"Mrs Kernow rang me."

"I told her not to say anything."

"She was worried about you. Joss, what happened?"

"I fell amongst thieves."

"Are you hurt anywhere else?"

"Yes, everywhere else."

"Let me see . . ."

"The Kernows bandaged me up."

But I stooped over him, gently drawing back the blanket. As far as his rib-cage he was naked and below this tenderly swathed in what looked like strips torn from an old sheet. But the ugly bruising had spread up and on to his chest, and on his right side the red stain of blood had started to seep through the white cotton.

"Joss, who did this?"

But Joss did not answer me. Instead, with a strength surprising in one so hurt, he put up an arm and pulled me down so that I was sitting on the edge of his bed. My long, blonde plait of hair hung forward over my shoulder, and while he held me with his right arm, his left hand was occupied in slipping off the rubber band which held the ends together, and then, using his fingers like a comb, he loosened the strands, unravelling them, so that my hair hung like a silken tassel, brushing on to his naked chest.

He said, "I always wanted to do that. Ever since I first saw you looking like the head girl of . . . what was it I said?"

"The head girl of a nicely run orphanage."

"That's it. Fancy you remembering."

"What can I do? There must be something I can do?"

"Just stay. Just stay, my darling girl."

The tenderness in his voice . . . Joss, who had always been so tough . . . dissolved me. Tears sprang into my eyes and he saw these and pulled me down, so that I lay against him, and I felt his hand slip up beneath my hair and close around the back of my neck.

"Joss, I'll hurt you . . ."

"Don't talk," he said, as his seeking mouth found mine. And then, "I've always wanted to do this, too."

It was evident that none of his infirmities, his bruises, his bleeding, his cut lip, were to deter him in any way from getting exactly what he wanted.

And I, who had always imagined that loving was something to do with fireworks and explosions of emotion, discovered that it was not like that at all. It was warm, like sudden sunshine. It had nothing to do with my mother and the endless procession of men who had invaded her life. It was cynicism and preconceived ideas flying out of an open window. It was the last of my defences gone. It was Joss.

He said my name and he made it sound beautiful.

Much later, I lit a fire, piling on the driftwood so that the room was bright with flickering firelight. I would not let Joss move, so that he lay with his dark head propped on his arms, and I felt his eyes following every move I made.

I stood up, away from the fire. My hair fell loose on either side of my face, and my cheeks were warm from the fire. I felt soft with content.

Joss said, "We have to talk, don't we?"

"Yes."

"Get me a drink."

"What do you want?"

"Some whisky. It's in the galley, in the cupboard over the sink."

I went to find it, and two glasses. "Soda or water?"

"Soda. There's a bottle-opener hanging on a hook."

I found the opener and took the cap off the bottle. I did

this clumsily and it fell to the floor, rolling in the maddening manner of such things into a dark corner. I went to retrieve it and my eye was caught by another small and shining object, lying half under the kickboard beneath the sink. I picked it up and it was Andrea's Celtic cross, the one that she had worn on a leather thong around her neck.

I kept it in my hand. I poured the drinks and took them back to Joss. I handed him one, and knelt on the floor beside him.

I said, "This was under the sink," and showed him the cross.

His swollen eye made it difficult for him to focus. He squinted at it painfully.

"What the hell's that?"

"It's Andrea's."

He said, "Oh, to hell." And then, "Get me some more pillows, there's a good girl. I could never drink whisky lying down."

I gathered up a couple of cushions off the floor, and propped him against them. The action of sitting up was agony for him and he let out an involuntary groan.

"Are you all right?"

"Yes, of course I'm all right. Where did you find that thing?"

"I told you. On the floor."

"She came here this evening. She said she'd been to the cinema. I was working downstairs, trying to get the shelving finished. I told her I was busy, but she just came up here, as though I'd never said a word. I followed her up and told her to go home. But she wouldn't go. She said she wanted a drink, she wanted to talk . . . you know the sort of drivel."

"She's been here before."

"Yes, once. One morning. I was sorry for her and I gave her a cup of coffee. But this evening I was busy; I had no time for her and I wasn't sorry for her. I said I didn't want a drink. I told her to go home. And then she said that she didn't want

189

to go home, everybody hated her, nobody would talk to her, I was the only person she could talk to, I was the only person who understood."

"Perhaps you were."

"OK, so I was sorry for her. I used to let her come and get in my way when I was working at Boscarva, because there wasn't much else I could do about it, short of bodily throwing her out of the room."

"Did you do that this evening? Throw her out?"

"Not in so many words. But finally I'd had enough of her batty conversation and her totally unfounded belief that I was ready, willing and eager to jump into bed with her, and I lost my temper and told her so."

"What happened then?"

"What didn't happen? Screams, tears, accusations, routine hysteria. I was subjected to every sort of vilification. Face slapping, the lot. That was when I finally resorted to force, and I bundled her down the stairs and threw her raincoat and her beastly handbag after her."

"You didn't hurt her?"

"No, I didn't hurt her. But I think I frightened her, because she went then, like the hammers of hell. I heard her clattering down the stairs on those ghastly clogs she wears, and then I think she must have slipped because there was the most frightful thumping and bumping as she went down the last few stairs. I shouted down to make sure she was all right, but then I heard her running out of the shop and slamming the door behind her, so that I imagined she was."

"Could she have hit herself on anything? Bruised her face when she fell?"

"Yes, I suppose she could. There was a packing case full of china standing at the bottom of the stairs. She could have collided with that . . . Why do you ask anyway?"

I told him. When I had finished he let out a long, incredulous whistle. But he was angry too.

190

"The little bitch. I think she's a nymphomaniac, do you know that?"

"I've always thought so."

"She was always talking about some guy called Danus, going into the most gruesome of intimate details. And the bloody cheek of telling everyone that I had asked her to go to the cinema with me. I wouldn't ask her to empty a dustbin with me . . . What's happened to her now?"

"She's been put to bed. Mollie got the doctor."

"If he's worth his salt he'll have diagnosed self-induced hysteria. And he'll prescribe a good walloping and send her back to London. And that'll get her out of everybody's way."

"Poor Andrea. She's very unhappy."

As though he could not keep his hands off it, he reached out to touch my hair. I turned my head and kissed the back of his hand, the lacerated knuckles.

He said, "You didn't believe her, did you?"

"Not really."

"Did anyone else?"

"Mollie and Eliot did. Eliot wanted to call the police but Grenville wouldn't let him."

"That's interesting."

"Why?"

"Who was it who brought Andrea home?"

"I thought I'd told you. Morris Tatcombe . . . you know, the boy who works for Eliot . . ."

"Morris? Well I'll be . . ." He stopped in mid-sentence, and then said again, "Morris Tatcombe."

"What about him?"

"Oh, Rebecca, come along. Pull yourself together. Use your wits. Who do you think gave me this beating?"

"Not Morris." I did not want to believe it.

"Morris and three others. I went along to The Anchor for a glass of beer and a pie for my supper, and when I was walking home, they jumped me."

"You knew it was Morris?"

"Who else would it be? He's always had this grudge going for me ever since we last crossed swords and he ended up on his backside in the gutter. I thought his putting the boot in this time was just a continuation of our running feud. But it seems that it wasn't."

Without thinking I began to say, "Eliot . . ." and then stopped, but it was too late. Joss said quietly, "What about Eliot?"

"I don't want to talk about Eliot."

"Did he tell Morris to come after me?"

"I don't know."

"He could, you know. He hates my guts. It fits."

"I . . . I think he's jealous of you. He doesn't like your being so close to Grenville. He doesn't like Grenville being so fond of you. And . . ." I looked down at my drink, turning the glass in my hand, feeling suddenly nervous. "There's something else."

"From your expression one would think you'd murdered somebody. What is it?"

"It's . . . the desk. The desk downstairs in your workroom. I saw it this morning, when you were telephoning."

"I wondered why you'd suddenly gone cantering out into the rain. What about it?"

"The desk and the Chippendale chair. They came from Boscarva."

"Yes, I know."

His calmness shocked me. "You didn't *take* them, Joss?"

"*Take them?* No, I didn't take them. I bought them."

"Who from?"

"A man who runs an antique shop up beyond Fourbourne. I'd been to a sale about a month ago, and I dropped in to see him on the way back, and I saw the chair and the desk in his shop. By then I knew all Grenville's furniture and I knew they'd come from Boscarva."

"But who took them?"

"I regret to have to shatter your innocence, but it was your cousin Eliot."

"But Eliot knew nothing about them."

"Eliot most certainly did. They were in one of the attics, as far as I remember, and he probably imagined they'd never be missed."

"But why . . .?"

"This is like playing the truth game. Because Eliot, my love, my darling child, is head over heels in debt. That garage was financed by Ernest Padlow in the first place, it cost a bomb and it's been losing money steadily for the past twelve months. God knows what use fifty pounds would have been to Eliot, a mere drop in the ocean one would have thought, but perhaps he needed a little ready cash to pay a bill or put on a horse or something . . . I don't know. Between you and me, I don't think he should be running his own business. He'd be better working for some other guy, being paid a regular salary. Perhaps, one evening, when you're sitting over drinks at Boscarva, you could try and persuade him."

"Sarcasm doesn't suit you."

"I know, but Eliot makes me edgy. Always has done."

I felt, obscurely, that I must stand up for Eliot, make excuses for him.

"In a way, he thinks that Boscarva and everything in it already belong to him. Perhaps he didn't feel it was . . . stealing . . .?"

"When did they realise the things were missing?"

"A couple of days ago. You see, the desk belonged to my mother. Now it belongs to me. That's why we started to look for it."

"Unfortunate for Eliot."

"Yes."

"I suppose Eliot said I'd taken them."

"Yes," I admitted miserably.

"What did Grenville say?"

"He said that you'd never do a thing like that."

"And so there was another monumental row."

"Yes."

Joss sighed deeply. We fell silent. The room was growing cold again, the fire beginning to die down. I got up and went to put another log on it, but Joss stopped me.

"Leave it," he said.

I looked at him, surprised. He finished his drink and put the empty glass down on the floor beside him, and then pushed back the blanket and began, carefully, to get out of bed.

"Joss, you mustn't . . ."

I flew to his side, but he pushed me away, and slowly, with infinite caution, got to his feet. Once there, he grinned triumphantly down at me, a bizarre sight, bruised and battered, and dressed in bandages and a crumpled pair of jeans.

"Into battle," he said.

"Joss, what are you going to do?"

"If you'll find me a shirt and a pair of shoes, I'll get dressed. And then we're going to go downstairs, and get into the truck and drive back to Boscarva."

"But you can't drive like that."

"I can do anything I want," he told me, and I believed him. "Now find my clothes and stop arguing."

He would not even let me take Mollie's car. "We'll leave it there, it'll be all right. Someone can fetch it in the morning." His own little truck was parked around the corner, up a narrow alley. We got in, and he started the engine and backed out on to the road, with me giving directions because he was too stiff to turn around in the seat. We headed up through the town, along streets that had become familiar to me, over the crossroads and up the hill.

I sat, staring ahead, with my hands clasped tightly in my lap. I knew that there was still something else we had to talk about. And it had to be now, before we reached Boscarva.

For some reason, as though he were immensely pleased with life in general, Joss had started to sing.

> The first time ever I saw your face
> I thought the sun rose in your eyes
> And the moon and stars . . .

"Joss."

"What is it now?"

"There's something else."

He sounded shocked. "Not another skeleton in the cupboard?"

"Don't joke."

"I'm sorry. What is it?"

I swallowed a strange obstruction in the back of my throat. "It's Sophia."

"What about Sophia?"

"Grenville gave me the key of the studio so that I could go and choose a picture to take back to London. I found a portrait of Sophia. A proper one, with a face. And Eliot came to find me, and he saw it too."

There was a long silence. I looked at Joss but his profile was stony, intent on the road ahead. "I see," he said at last.

"She looks just like you; or you look just like her."

"Naturally enough. She was my grandmother."

"Yes, I thought that was probably it."

"So the portrait was in the studio?"

"Is . . . is that why you came to live in Porthkerris?"

"Yes. Grenville and my father fixed it between them. Grenville put up half the capital for my shop."

"Your father . . .?"

"You've met him. Tristram Nolan Gardner. He runs an antique shop, in the New Kings Road. You bought a pair of balloon-back chairs from him. Do you remember?"

"And he found from my cheque that I was called Rebecca Bayliss."

"Right. And he found out, by cunning question and answer, that you were Grenville Bayliss's granddaughter. Right. And he found out that you were catching the train to Cornwall last Monday. Right."

"So he rang you up and told you to meet the train."

"Right."

"But why?"

"Because he felt involved. Because he thought you seemed lost and vulnerable. Because he wanted me to keep an eye on you."

"I still don't understand."

"You know something?" said Joss. "I love you very much."

"Because I'm being stupid?"

"No, because you're being marvellously innocent. Sophia wasn't only Grenville's model, she was his mistress as well. My father was born at the beginning of their relationship, long before your mother arrived. Sophia married, eventually, an old friend she'd known from childhood days, but she never had any more children."

"So Tristram . . .?"

"Tristram is Grenville's son. And Grenville is my grandfather. And I am going to marry my half-cousin."

"Pettifer told me that Sophia meant nothing to Grenville. That she was just a girl who'd worked for him."

"If it meant protecting Grenville, Pettifer would swear that black is white."

"Yes, I suppose he would." But Grenville, in anger, had been less discreet. " 'You are not my only grandchild!' "

"Did Grenville say that?"

"Yes, to Eliot. And Eliot thought he meant me."

We had reached the top of the hill. The lights of the town were far behind us. Ahead, beyond the huddled shapes of Ernest Padlow's housing estate, lay the dark coastline, pricked with the tiny lights of random farms, and beyond it the black immensity of the sea.

I said, "I don't seem to remember you asking me to marry you."

The little van bumped and lurched down the lane towards Boscarva. "I'm not very good at asking things," said Joss. He took his hand off the wheel and put it over mine. "I usually just tell people."

As once before, it was Pettifer who came out to meet us. As soon as Joss switched off the engine of the van, the light in the hall went on, and Pettifer opened the door, as though he had known instinctively we were on our way.

He saw Joss open the car door and ease himself out, in obvious discomfort and pain. He saw Joss's face . . .

"For heaven's sake, what happened to you?"

"I had a difference of opinion with our old friend Morris Tatcombe. I probably wouldn't look like this except that he had three of his chums with him."

"Are you all right?"

"Yes, I'm fine. No bones broken. Come on, let's go in."

We went indoors and Pettifer closed the door.

"I'm glad to see you, Joss, and that's the truth. We've had a proper how-do-you-do here and no mistake."

"Is Grenville all right?"

"Yes, he's all right. He's still up, in the drawing-room, waiting for Rebecca to come home."

"And Eliot?"

Pettifer looked from Joss's face to mine.

"He's gone."

Joss said, "You'd better tell us about it."

We ended up in the kitchen, around the table.

"After Rebecca had gone, Eliot went down to the studio and

came back with that portrait of Sophia. The one we looked for, Joss. The one we never found."

I said, "I don't understand."

Joss explained. "Pettifer knew Sophia was my grandmother, but no one else did. No one else remembered her. It was all too long ago. Grenville wanted it to stay that way."

"But why was there only one picture of Sophia with a face? There must have been dozens Grenville painted of her. What happened to all of them?"

There was a pause while Joss and Pettifer looked at each other. Then it was Pettifer's turn to explain, which he did with much tact.

"It was old Mrs Bayliss. She was jealous of Sophia . . . not because she had any notion of the truth . . . but because Sophia was part of the Commander's other life, the life Mrs Bayliss didn't have no time for."

"You mean his painting."

"She would never have anything to do with Sophia, more than a frosty 'good morning' if she happened to meet her in the town. And the Commander knew this, and he didn't want to upset her, so he let all the pictures of Sophia go . . . all except for the one you found. We knew it was somewhere around. Joss and I spent a day looking for it, but we never turned it up."

"What were you going to do with it if you found it?"

"Nothing. We just didn't want anyone else to find it."

"I don't see why it was so important."

Joss said, "Grenville didn't want anyone to know about what happened between him and Sophia. It wasn't that he was ashamed of it, because he'd loved her very much. And after he's dead, it won't matter any longer, he doesn't give a damn who knows then. But he's proud, and he's lived his life according to a certain set of standards. We probably think they're old-fashioned, but they're still his own. Does that make sense to you?"

"I suppose so."

"Young people now," said Pettifer heavily, "talk about a permissive society as though it were something they'd invented. But it's not new. It's been going on since the beginning of time, only in the Commander's day it was handled with a little more discretion."

We accepted this meekly. Then Joss said, "We seem to have gone off at a tangent. Pettifer was telling us about Eliot."

Pettifer collected himself. "Yes, well. So down to the drawing-room Eliot went, and stormed in, with me behind him, went straight to the mantelpiece, and dumped it up there, alongside the other picture. The Commander never said a word, just watched him. And Eliot said, 'What's that got to do with Joss Gardner?' Then the Commander told him. Told him everything. Very quiet and very dignified. And Mrs Roger was there too, and she just about threw a fit. She said all these years the Commander had deceived them, letting Eliot believe that he was his only grandson, and he'd get Boscarva when the Commander died. The Commander said he'd never said anything of the sort, that it was all surmise, that they'd simply been counting their chickens before they were hatched. Then Eliot said, very cold, 'Perhaps now we can know what your plans are?' but the Commander said that his plans were his own business, and *quite right* he was too."

This little bit of championship was accompanied by Pettifer's fist coming down with a thump on the kitchen table.

"So what did Eliot do?"

"Eliot said in that case he was going to wash his hands of the whole lot of us . . . meaning the family, of course . . . and that he had plans of his own and he was thankful to be shed of us. And with that he collected a few papers and a brief-case and put on his coat and whistled up his dog and walked out of the house. Heard his car go up the lane and that was the end of him."

"Where's he gone?"

"To High Cross, I suppose."

"And Mollie?"

"She was in tears . . . trying to stop him doing anything stupid, she said. Begging him to stay. Turning on the Commander, saying it was all his fault. But of course, there wasn't anything she could do to stop Eliot. There's nothing you can do to stop a grown man walking out of the house, not even if you do happen to be his mother."

I was torn with sorrow and sympathy for Mollie.

"Where is she now?"

"Up in her room." He added gruffly, "I made her a little tea-tray, took it up to her, found her sitting at her dressing-table like something carved out of stone."

I was glad I had not been here. It all sounded very dramatic. I stood up. Poor Mollie. "I'll go up and talk to her."

"And I . . ." said Joss ". . . will go and see Grenville."

"Tell him I'll be there in a moment or two."

Joss smiled. "We'll wait," he promised.

I found Mollie, white-faced and tear-stained, still sitting in front of her frilled dressing-table. (This was in character. Even the deepest excesses of grief would not cause Mollie to fling herself across any bed. It might crease the covers.) As I came into the room, she looked up, and her reflection was caught three times over in her triple mirror; for the first time ever, I thought that she looked her age.

I said, "Are you all right?"

She looked down, balling a sodden handkerchief in her fingers. I went to her side. "Pettifer told me. I'm so very sorry."

"It's all so desperately unfair. Grenville's always disliked Eliot, resented him in some extraordinary way. And of course, now we know why. He was always trying to run Eliot's life, come between Eliot and me. Whatever I did for Eliot was always wrong."

I knelt beside her, and put my arm around her, "I really believe he meant it for the best. Can't you try to believe that too?"

"I don't even know where he's gone. He wouldn't tell me. He never said goodbye."

I realised that she was a great deal more worried about Eliot's abrupt departure than she was about the evening's revelations concerning Joss. This was just as well. I could comfort her about Eliot. There was not a mortal thing I could do about Joss.

"I think," I said, "that Eliot may have gone to Birmingham."

She looked at me in horror. "*Birmingham?*"

"There was a man there who wanted to give him a job. Eliot told me. It was to do with second-hand cars. He seemed to think that it might be quite interesting."

"But I can't go and live in *Birmingham.*"

"Oh, Mollie, you don't have to. Eliot can live on his own. Let him go. Give him the chance of making something of his life."

"But we've always been together."

"Then perhaps it's time to start living apart. You've got your house at High Cross, your garden up there, your friends . . ."

"I can't leave Boscarva. I can't leave Andrea. I can't leave Grenville."

"Yes, you can. And I think Andrea should go back to London, to her own parents. You've done all you can for her, and she's miserable here. That's why all this happened, because she was unhappy and lonely. And as for Grenville, I'll stay with him."

I came downstairs at last carrying the tea-tray. I took it into the kitchen and put it on the table. Pettifer, sitting there, looked up at me over the edge of his evening paper.

"How is she?" he asked.

"All right now. She's agreed that Andrea should go home, back to London. And then she's going back to High Cross."

"That's what she's always wanted. And you?"

"I'm staying here. If that's all right with you."

A chill gleam of satisfaction crossed Pettifer's face, the nearest he could get to a look of delight. There was no need for me to say more. We understood each other.

Pettifer turned his paper. "They're in the drawing-room . . ." he told me ". . . waiting for you," and he settled down to the racing page.

I went and found them, backed by the two portraits of Sophia in her white dress, Joss standing by the fire, and Grenville deep in his chair. They both looked up as I came in, the long-legged young man with his villainous black eye, and the old one, too tired to pull himself to his feet. I went towards them, the two people I loved most.